“BROTHERS, SISTERS..

JONAS CLEARY

WITH FOREWORDS BY

INGRID GROTCHALCKX
ERVIN LASZLO
ULRICH HERZOG
JAMES BROOKES
ROBERT MARBLE
JANA VALENCIC

MAMMAS PRESS

"Brothers, sisters..
First published in Great Britain in 2006 by
Mammas Press
41 Brownswood Road
LONDON N4 2HP
www.mammaspress.com

All the characters in this book are wholly fictitious; the use of identifiable names and/or characterisations of anyone alive or dead is purely inadvertent/coincidental and for which, where relevant, the author apologises in so doing. Places and events are also the product of the author's imagination or they are used entirely fictitiously.

A catalogue record of this book is available from the British Library.

ISBN-10: 0-9551700-0-1
ISBN-13: 978-0-9551700-0-3

Main text typeset in FF Scala 11/13 pt
Printed and bound by Arsis

TO CALLIOPE

CONTENTS

FOREWORD

I first met Jonas Cleary on a bus travelling to Canindé in Brazil. Few outsiders travel this far into the country's Nordeste and so it was not surprising that we fell into conversation. During our discussions not only did I discover that Jonas had travelled far deeper into the backlands of the region than I but of the shocking social conditions he had witnessed.

As Jonas related yet more of the litany of the terribleness he had seen I was struck how the bus we were in had been travelling for several tens of kilometres alongside the same white painted fencing posts of the extensive plantation of an obviously rich landowner. At the same time, however, I was not only also assailed by the smell of unwashed clothing of the weary, ragged plantation workers on the bus but at their wretchedly poor and malnourished state of health. To me this was a graphic depiction that this truly is a land of a few very wealthy 'haves' and very many desperately poor 'have-nots'.

In *"Brothers, sisters..* Jonas narrates the pitiless reality between rich and poor that lies hidden below the surface of samba and eternal carnival which is often thought of as being Brazil. He details that behind the façade of idyllic white beaches featured in its holiday brochures, there is a land where many tens of millions of people are condemned to a life of medieval oppressiveness.

The book further depicts, however, a world where the present unjust order is replaced by one in which not only are the poor, wretched people of Brazil freed from their oppression but so too are all of the 'Wretched of the Earth'.

However, as our bus journey continued I also discovered that we had more in common than our fascination for 'beleza' Brazil. Uncommonly for a man, Jonas was most sympathetically interested in my [then] professional involvement in the pursuit of equality of opportunity for women. This I found to be most unusual. One of the hardest aspects of this job is getting men to be genuinely understanding in this matter at all. I also found Jonas to be fascinated by the relationship between men and women and how this would, over time, evolve.

The issues of women's financial independence and enhanced career opportunities (*read:* better paid) and the entwinement of recent discoveries and possibilities on fertility and reproduction were also part of Jonas's awareness. What is more, he had the perception to grasp that the evolution of biological sciences are destined to inevitably reduce men's paramouncy within society. Included in his awareness was that parents can now decide the gender of their unborn child. Working on the premise that every mother wants nothing but the best for her child, Jonas asks: "Will the fact that girls live longer, their chances of prematurely dying as a result of violence or a stress related disease significantly less than boys increasingly affect a prospective mother's gender decision?"

For those who have considered these particular matters in depth as well as those of inter-relationships between genders and also pondered the inevitable question: "What would happen if the roles were reversed?" *"Brothers, sisters..* is indeed an extraordinary study. What it enfolds goes way beyond any rose-tinted, woolly conclusion that everything will be so much better were there to be such a role reversal. However, and as this book further explores, what would happen if women then decided to implement yet bigger changes and would the world be a better place as a consequence? Perhaps it is for the reader to find out and to discover that one should be careful what [s]he wishes for!

"Brothers, sisters.. is not only giftedly narrated but Jonas manages to catch new slants on political topics, socio-economic and technical developments, social issues in a most captivating non-fictional fictional piece of writing. And as a good story should - must! - our individual emotions are brought to a higher level. The result is a book which, while at times extremely coarse and shockingly violent, nevertheless offers unexpected optimistic outcomes for the angst facing many human beings in our contemporary society.

In conclusion, would the world Jonas Cleary portrays really be so out of the question? While I am writing these words, the newsreader on my radio tells me that presently here in Belgium in primary, secondary and college schools there are hardly any male teachers remaining.. they are all simply just fading away.

Ingrid Goetschalckx
Antwerp
September 2005

Ingrid Goetschalckx, is at the forefront in the advance and empowerment of women in Belgium. In 2002 Ms Goetschalckx was appointed by the Ministry of Flanders HR director of Loodswezen Pilotage, Antwerp, the world's second largest port.

FOREWORD

Ever since Jonas Cleary shared with me his manuscript, I have been fascinated with the Susem. I have never come across extraterrestrials who would not be only advanced and superior to us earthlings, but also so extraordinarily friendly as to share their wisdom with us. The Susem do just that, and their wisdom extends not just to complex and for us quasi-miraculous gadgetry - expected of people who master the art of space-travel - but to new and revolutionary insights about the most fundamental nature of matter, mind, life, and the universe.

It is these insights that intrigue and fascinate me. They are beyond the received wisdom of the mainstream of the contemporary sciences, but not entirely beyond the insights that currently emerge at science's leading edge. Is the Susem insight fiction or foresight? The reader will have to decide for herself and himself.

Recognizing the wisdom of Susem-insight doesn't necessarily mean, of course, admiring and agreeing with all that the Susem maintain and all they do - some of their thinking and doing seem, to put it mildly, somewhat singular and at times unnecessarily violent. But, as a scientist, what they maintain about the fundamental nature of reality I find highly interesting - and rather familiar. For I have come to insights that resemble those of the Susem in some basic respects - for example, the wave nature of matter and the understanding of observed phenomena as the interaction of waves and wave-structures. Perhaps Jonas Cleary's reading of one of my earlier books (*The Creative Cosmos, 1993*) may have something to do with it. But, even if so, it is remarkable that his Susem come up with concepts that foreshadow those I have developed in recent years - which had not even been published when *"Brothers, sisters.."* was committed to paper.

These are the "coincidences" that impelled me to accept Jonas Cleary's invitation to write this brief foreword to his book. Rather than belabouring these coincidences and commenting on other features of his surprising (and at times quite shocking) book, I put forward my own modest attempt at depicting the emerging insights in an imaginative, but not entirely imaginary, form - my "poetic vision of the cosmos." It is written entirely independently from the book that follows: I had not known of this work until well after I had completed the book to which this "vision" is a poetic complement, and, before he came to see me in Tuscany in the summer of 2004, Cleary had no way of knowing that I was even contemplating doing anything along these lines.

In my book I give an image of an interconnected wave-interaction based cosmos, coming not from a visitor from outer space but from a mere Earth-bound scientist.*

Ervin Laszlo
Montescudaio
August 2005

Ervin Laszlo, Visiting Professor at Yale, is author of 69 books on physics and philosophy. Dr Laszlo headed the UN's Council of Interregional Cooperation, he is a member of the Club of Rome and of Budapest. Dr Laszlo is a recipient of many awards including the Goi Peace Prize of Japan.

* *Science and the Akashic Field: An Integral Theory of Everything* Ervin Laszlo, (Rochester, VT, Inner Traditions International, November 2004)

FOREWORD

When Jonas Cleary asked me if I would be available for certain feedback on socio-economic sections of a book he was completing I became very intrigued. During the time I had known Cleary I knew him to be a person of very wide knowledge and deep intellectual curiosity for all aspects of our socio-economic environment. Upon receipt of his completed manuscript, however, I soon found myself reading more that the sections he had indicated for my critique. All of it proved to be fascinating reading. Not only is Cleary's book a continuous sequence of beautifully crafted pictures but also a profound analysis of our present day political, economical and social environment (agreeably not a nice picture): it deals as much with the problems of today as it deals with war, violence and sex. A challenge indeed - and an interesting mix!

It is evident however, that one of Cleary's main concerns is the instability of the world's economic and financial systems. And rightfully so! The handwriting of a collapse has been 'on the wall' for quite some time even though governments and banks try to assure us that all their systems are intact. This is not so.

Many Britons will forever remember Wednesday, September 16th 1992. By the evening of that black day, such was the loss of confidence in the British currency that Britons had to hand over 20 per cent more of their money (paper with a promise to pay the sum on the face by an establishment that does not have it) for imported goods and services than they did in the morning. Though the knock-on socio-economical consequences of such a dramatic devaluation, were, for the ordinary British people, calamitous, 'Black Wednesday' was little more than a repairable puncture compared to the big bang blow-out looming.

Since 1992 international finance's balloon has become ever more pumped up with [nothing but] 'confidence'. And though the panels of this balloon's skin have now become integrated and 'sophisticatedly interwoven' as never before, they have become stretched all the thinner as a result. A rip in one part of this balloon will now instantly rent the rest asunder.

Another cause for concern is that international finance's balloon is increasingly inflated with the 'low grade confidence' of unsecured 'IOU' debt, US dollar debt in particular. Though the dollar is the world's de-facto currency (historically that of last resort) much of this dollar debt is owed by Americans to non-Americans; the latest figures show that this US external debt is the equivalent of more than $40,000 for every American man, woman and child. Should external lenders withdraw a mere two per cent of these dollar funds (call in their 'IOUs') confidence in the US currency will instantly evaporate. And when America sneezes..

The impending collapse of General Motors and the House of Saud are but two hatpins poised to puncture the world's financial system's big balloon. The more than $4,000bn OECD-wide pensions deficit is another. The implosion of the completely unregulated financial derivative markets is yet a further cause for deep concern. The consequential global repercussions the moment just one of these pins plunges will be such as to not only make the collapses of Enron, Parmalat and their like, appear as "little local difficulties" but hundreds of millions of people worldwide will see their livelihoods disappear before their eyes.

Throughout the 1930s following the then world financial crash, the US dollar retained its value (though then it was backed by gold) and was an even keel of sorts for the world to weather the decade's economic turbulence. Today with it being backed only by 'confidence' it won't, it can't.

Within three years from 1930 world trade contracted by a third. This time the contraction will be greater and will take place much faster. In the fragmented financial world of the 1920s, and three months on from the collapse of world markets, millions of people were reduced to scavenging for food. In today's integrated financial world, with faith in all currencies instantly expired, it will take just weeks before people are forced to scavenge.

During the days prior to Britain's withdrawal from the ERM, and as the 'ordinary British people' who lived through those times will tell, they were stunned by the suddenness with which this 'financial Dunkirk' befell them. They will also tell of how on the evening before 'Black Wednesday' and on the day itself and as the actual dénouement played out, they were filled with a sense of utter powerlessness to do anything to safeguard their own personal futures from the financial turmoil unleashed upon them by their inept ministers and currency speculators.

The British, despite the hardships they subsequently endured, were able to recover from their government's ERM debacle. However, when the international financial system's balloon bursts it will not be a 'Dunkirk' which visits us but a 'Dresden'. This time though not only will we all be as utterly powerless as Britons were in 1992 but there will not be any prospect of any foreseeable recovery.

But does our financial future have to be as precarious as this? Do we 'the ordinary people' really have to live in a world of such vacuous fragility? Are there not viable alternatives to the unstable helter-skelter world of dubious high finance? Is there not an alternative to our labours and endeavours being remunerated with something other than [potentially] worthless pieces of paper? Do the savings accrued from our toil need to wagered by others - often to their [considerable] financial benefit but at our risk - in the casinos that are the world's financial markets, markets which can only exist with the continuous injection of us ordinary people's savings?

"Brothers, sisters.. shows that there is a sounder, attainable alternative to all of this danger and dubiousness. This book outlines how it is perfectly possible to achieve a sure, transparent financial system with a copper-bottomed currency. One, in which, step by step, the wages, savings and livelihoods of everyone from the highest to the lowliest are safe and protected. However, if what *"Brothers, sisters..* outlines is feasible or not is another matter. For what it advocates entails removing the fruits of our endeavours out of the maws of bankers, financiers and politicians and back into the safe hands of us 'ordinary people'.

Though this may not be the sole solution to safeguarding our financial futures, carrying on as at present is not now an option long open to us.

Ulrich Herzog
Geneva
September 2005

Ulrich Herzog is economic and financial advisor to many international corporations and governments. Dr Herzog is past president of UN Third World Sustainable Development Projects.

FOREWORD

The science of computing is my lifelong discipline and is, compared with other sciences such as astronomy, a comparatively young one, its birth occurring even after mine. Perhaps because of its youthfulness, it is also a science whose facets really are determined by logic and verifiable data. If, however, this regimen of logic and verification is applied to other, longer established areas of science, particle and astrophysics in particular, contradictions within them start to arise.

For instance, the following is a verifiable fact, albeit one which is little known: the four elements of helium, beryllium, carbon and oxygen need to combine in a specific collective ratio before galaxies can fully form. That this is so is spectrographically confirmable across the entire observable universe. Moreover, if the ratios between these four elements were any less precise heavier ones couldn't be formed. It is an exact and consistent ratio of one to nearly 300,000 trillion (287,659,408,505,240,000 to be precise), the equivalent of the combined odds of many consecutive lottery 'rollovers'. It is known as the 'Anthropic Constant'.

Yet a theory, one so widely espoused that it is often given as being 'factual', especially by particle and astrophysicists, claims that fifteen or so billion years ago the universe exploded from a singularity (a point) and has continued to expand ever outwards ever since. It is universally referred to as the 'Big Bang'.

In terms of logic, however, it is most unlikely that a constant - more so one as precise and as extensive as the Anthropic - will exist within an expansion. One of the dictums of the late great Richard Feynman, a blunt speaking physicist of world renown was: "If the facts don't fit the theory, then it's the theory which is wrong."

Many 'facts' are in fact not facts at all but empiricisms: that the (seemingly) obvious is indeed so. The Sun circles the Earth because it can be seen to do so is an example of an 'empirical fact'.

Moreover it was this particular assumption, that not only did the Sun circle the Earth but it **had** to because, according to Aristotelian and Christian concepts the Earth was the centre of the universe. Not unnaturally perhaps, it was this notion which led the Vatican, despite its astrolabes, other Aristotelian paraphernalia and laws failing to reliably predict future dates of religious festivals. By the early 16th century the situation became so hopelessly awry that in 1514 the Vatican commissioned the mathematician Copernicus to resolve the problem of accurately determining these dates. Copernicus did indeed accomplish this task but only after basing his calculations on the concept of a *hypothetical* heliocentric universe first advanced by the Greek astronomer Aristarchus 1,800 years earlier. Nonetheless established beliefs die hard for 86 years later and having been accused of 'heresy' by the Vatican for publicly proposing the deletion of [the word] *'hypothetical'*, the philosopher Bruno was burned at the stake.

Four centuries later, another philosopher, Bertrand Russell opined: "The trouble with Christianity is that it has too much religion (dogma) in it."

These five centuries later other luminaries of science - particle physicists in particular - are in a similar dilemma to their pre-Copernican forebears in their quest for a 'General Unified Theory' (GUT) of matter. GUT is indeed their Holy Grail for it will - theoretically - unify the four forces unleashed by the - theoretical -

'Big Bang', one of which is 'gravity'. These four forces will - theoretically - also unify particles and matter. This is particle physicists' 'Standard Model'. To date they claim to have discovered more than 256 different particles (though this number is continually increasing). However, after many decades, the expenditure of billions of [taxpayers'] money and clutches of Nobel Prizes, the unifying particle of these physicists' pursuit: the 'Higgs Boson', which - again theoretically - **has** to give all the other particles 'mass' remains as unfound as the Ark of the Covenant. Particle physicists are as yet also unable to integrate the force of 'gravity' into either their Standard Model or GUT.

In the light of these physicists' fruitless pursuit for their Standard Model and GUT, two questions are raised. Are their searches also based on empiricisms? Where is the verifiable evidence for the actual existence of 'matter' and 'particles'?

Particle physicists, however, are not the only ones in a pre-Copernican quandary, astrophysicists are as well. As elusive as the mass cohering Higgs Boson is for the former, so too, for the latter, is the - theoretically - missing 'Dark Matter' of the - theoretical - ever expanding universe. For astrophysicists' (and particle ones' as well) calculations of the universe's composition to be correct there **has** to be 20 times more 'matter' than has been currently found. As confounding to astrophysicists' - theoretical - 'Big Bang' exploded expanding universe is its unevenness. What 'matter' there is, is not dispersed uniformly but is grouped in isolated groves of galaxies with starless deserts between them. What is more, instead of expanding, every one of the galaxies in every one of these groves is, and as observations confirm, coming ever closer to one another.

Again, questions over these physicists' quest for the 'Missing Dark Matter' of their 'Big Bang' expanding universe arise. Is their as yet fruitless search also based on further empiricisms? Where is the truly verifiable evidence that our universe is actually expanding?

As *"Brothers, sisters..* makes most clear, there is no more verifiable evidence for the existence of the 'certainties' of particle and astrophysicists' theories on matter and space than there is for an Earth-circling Sun. Perhaps Russell's opine should have 'particle and astrophysics' added alongside 'Christianity'?

While this sometimes amusing, sometimes shockingly rude yet most readable book is more than about mere matters astral and particle, it could be said that Jonas Cleary provides a convincingly logical and verifiable explanation for the phenomena currently perceived of as 'matter' and 'space'.

James Brookes
Marshfield, England
September 2005

Having studied mathematics at Corpus Christi, Oxford, Professor Brookes worked with Alan Turing's research team on the advancement of computing sciences and later MIT's. Before returning to Britain and establishing Bath University's computing facilities, Professor Brookes worked with NASA developing its deep space missions programs. Professor Brookes is former CEO of the British Computer Society and Visiting Professor at Strathclyde and Portsmouth Universities and has also lectured on computing sciences across the world. Professor Brookes has received many British and international awards for his contributions to computer sciences.

FOREWORD

Go and study a newly hatched spider weaving a web. Look for this young spider's head. You may just be able to see it.

Then consider the size of this spider's brain and more relevantly, that no more than a fraction of it will be concerned with constructing the web. Next contemplate the size and complexity of the computing program and memory needed for the web's formation: site selection, those of materials, methodology of construction, stresses and flexibility in its assembly. If in doubt as to the extent of this complexity consult a builder of suspension bridges. Also note that included into this program are the further instructions informing the spider why it should make a web in the first place as well as determining that the formation of the web itself be species specific. Then consider how this newly hatched spider came to be in possession of all this data and computing facility.

Put simply, this facility is either within the spider at birth or comes in part or in whole from outside of it. *"Brothers, sisters..* maintains that the necessary data originates from without. If this is a creditable hypothesis or not is open to debate but, and as this book details, it has greater creditability than the standard explanations of it originating wholly from within the spider either by way of its genes as advanced by such authorities as Richard Dawkins, or holistically as proposed by Scott Turner and others.

For the data necessary for web building - and much else - to originate solely from within and be determined by the spider's genes it will have to have originated from its mother and hers from hers and so on back to who knows how many generations ago. It is not merely the possibility of miniaturisation of data, even down to molecular levels but that of reproducible fidelity which further makes the notion of such generational genetic data transference implausible: it has to be perfect every time. A single distorted coordinate could well mean no web. Even the most advanced printing systems of computer chip wafer fabrication cannot maintain such copy of copy fidelity. Spiders, as with all other beings, have by comparison and for current explanations to be creditable, to make do with the relative imprecise method of reproductive data transference by electro-nitrogenous synaptic transmission.

The holistic hypothesis: that the spider's web is an extension of the spider, as fingernails are to us humans; that it is, in a sense 'alive' also does not survive scrutiny. The silk of the spider's web, like the keratin of nails is not sentient. The web may relay data but it is the spider which is its receptor. Though the coordinates of the web during its construction may well serve as information terminals they will not have been emplaced by the web itself.

"Brothers, sisters.. further maintains that it is not just the program for webs which is 'written' from outside of the spider but everything else and for every other being from viruses to whales as well; from individual cells to entire individuals and rainforests alike. Again, if this is creditable or not is perhaps open to debate but as Cleary makes most clear, the current explanations of how life forms and functions do not withstand analysis. All omit consideration of the volume, complexity and fidelity of information transference required and the means necessary to achieve it.

If, however, Cleary's 'without' hypothesis proves plausible then it implies that many of the established concepts of biology are most misplaced and is likely to have significant ramifications throughout the fields of medicine and science including what is presently thought of as 'genetics'.

While the writing of *"Brothers, sisters..* was in progress I became interested in and indeed consulted by Cleary on many of the possible outcomes of his 'without' hypothesis. However, within my own particular discipline I am now already aware of possible first glimmerings of at least one of his premises of 'without' perhaps coming to pass: that of the resonances of cellular structures, both internally and externally determine how beings form and function.

Recent advances in the field of Ultra-weak Bioluminescence - the aura-like phenomenon which surrounds living cells from seeds to entire beings (a human's approximate to about 20 watts) - show that it is not a constant luminosity but is constantly oscillating in response to cellular activity. Also within the past year researchers at UCLA have detected aural resonances between cells (healthy human ones are in C sharp).

In *"Brothers, sisters..,* Cleary goes further and advances that it is the control and orchestration of these resonances - including those within genes - where the future wellbeing of human health lies. He also shows that this could indeed be a creditable explanation as to how a spider gets to weave its web.

Perhaps the most intriguing and entertaining aspect of the book, however, is that of the Susem. For generations it was believed that the male of our species was the dominant sex. *"Brothers, sisters..* raises the question that maybe males are, evolutionarily, actually weaker than females. The Susem are a fascinating group (even though we might agree that their amorous activities are taken to extreme in this work) who hint at the prospect that human females really are the dominant sex.

Due to the scientific advances made in medicine over recent years the notion of women being able to overtake men is not now as far-fetched as was once thought. It is, for instance, certainly possible to manipulate fertilization to ensure the desired gender of offspring. One of the questions Cleary raises is why, given a male's shorter lifespan and increased disposition towards ill health should any prospective parent want to give birth to a boy?

The Susem and their exploits are definitely entertaining and through their discussion with humans allow us to question the future roles of men and women in our societies. However, it is ultimately left up to the reader to form his or her own conclusions concerning the future role of the sexes in our society.

Robert Marble MD
Jackson, Mississippi
November 2005

Doctor Robert Marble, presently at Vanderbilt University, is viewed by many as one of the most gifted upcoming geneticists of his generation. Already the results of many of his findings are challenging the established orthodoxy on genetic research.

FOREWORD

As a Slovenian I grew up in Yugoslavia where pupils - 'Tito's pioneers' - as well as the population at large were endlessly exposed to Marshall Tito's mantra: *"Bratstvo i jedinstvo"* ("Brotherhood and unity"). This was the cornerstone of the post-WW2 federation of seven republics and two autonomous provinces, a mosaic of creeds, nations, minorities and myths.

This ideal of brotherhood and unity was, to some degree - at least immediately following the slaughter of WW2 - maintained by the army, the Communist party and the police. *'Shovinism'* (the ugly face of nationalism) was denounced as the most deplorable offence - sometimes brutally suppressed - as the SFRJ (the Socialist Federal Republic of Yugoslavia) forged its home grown brand of multiculturalism.

And indeed, for my generation nationalism was no longer an issue. We felt at ease with our multiple identities in an inclusive society, a patchwork of histories, culinary traditions, musical heritages, aspirations: a veritable haven of diversity. From the 1960s onwards Yugoslavia was also a relatively prosperous country which attracted foreign loans and other inward investment. Everybody could obtain a passport and freely travel and work abroad (and hopefully send home money from their savings). Yugoslavia also became a popular destination for mass tourism.

In the early seventies, during the pioneering era of these mass holidays I had a summer job as a tourist guide on a bus with 45 foreigners. I took them on fortnight-long tours which included travelling throughout Bosnia and Herzegovina, the very territory of much of Jonas Cleary's present book.

The land he describes does not correspond to my distant memories of warm, hospitable people, open in their diversity - but neither do the facts of today's Bosnia and Herzegovina, a land savaged by years of war and inter-communal hatred. After this inexplicable Bosnian tragedy nothing would surprise me any longer - not even the surreal landscape of Cleary's epic *"Brothers, sisters..*

I have learned the value of extreme results of daydreaming in conjunction with academic research. During my time in the Netherlands, I was concerned with a project postulating the distant future of that country, and which sprung from the premise that while it is impossible to predict events in the longterm, it is however, useful to define the extreme scenarios - the more extreme the better. The course of future developments is thus likely to fall somewhere within the field defined by those extreme parameters. This method reduces complete randomness to a matrix.

Similarly, *"Brothers, sisters..* could be interpreted as an essay in gloom futurology, a smorgasbord of all and sundry, spiced with some truly bizarre propositions. Nevertheless, it has an intrinsic value as the "What if" dimension. However implausible, it is a warning that past horrors might again return to Bosnia, or for that matter, to any other country with peace imposed as a thin veneer of tranquillity by well-meaning foreign powers; a peace which will last only for as long as foreigners care to sustain their interest in it.

Wounded countries though, need time to heal themselves. They also need ongoing support to rebuild their sense of self. This process of healing and rebuilding will be greatly helped by sustained attention on the part of the international community - even if fuelled by fiction.

I sincerely hope that with this book Jonas Cleary has overstepped the limits of decency and that he has vastly exaggerated the human zest for inflicting pain on another human being. The book prophesies chaos. The future, however, may well be worse.

Jana Valencic
Ljubljana
September 2005

Jana Valencic is foreign and London correspondent to many Slovenian newspapers and periodicals. Ms Valencic is also a regular broadcaster on the BBC World Service.

1: KEN

"Brothers, sisters, I have news of great importance."

The moment I heard that voice I said to myself "That's that Danny Collins," and then, "what's he up to now...what's he got himself into this time?"

There I was, I had a good position up at the bar. I'd gone in the Greenwood early to make sure I actually got a seat. I knew they were going to be busy so I got a four pint jug in. I could have watched the match at home but they have this new big screen in the Greenwood and anyway a game's always best when you watch in company. Sometimes I go to see them play, when they're at home that is, well Highbury's only 15 minutes away. They have been their best ever this season. Of course no one could actually see the match what with it being played behind closed doors over at Upton Park. So that night everyone had to watch it on television.

I was really looking forward to the Arsenal Spurs replay, especially after what happened when they first played at Highbury, Tuesday last. It was the last match of the season and Spurs were staring at sure relegation if they lost. Arsenal though had to win if they were going to finish top of the Premier ahead of Man United.

The referee stopped the match after 20 minutes because of fighting. Tensions were that high that after the first clash they had all pitched in. There weren't just punch-ups on the pitch either but afterwards outside. With all the extra police on duty the situation was all set for a riot. Not just between Arsenal and Spurs' fans but between police and anybody who got in their way. The Law did a lot of smacking that night.

All the newspapers made a big thing about it, as did the politicians and Lord knows who else about how "shameful and shocking" it had been. There was even talk of the FA penalising both of them with a points deduction. All this did though was to talk up the replay. SLI-TV stepped in offering extra money for the exclusive rights, the League settled on fining both of them a hundred grand apiece and the replay on neutral ground with no spectators.

That night the atmosphere in the Greenwood, with everyone watching the warm-up, was intense to say the least. The off was for eight but by 7.30 the pub was packed with hundreds chanting "Come on you Reds" and "Arsenal... Arsenal," and clap, clapping all the time. By quarter to eight Harry, the landlord had to close the doors, they couldn't get any more in and that's never happened in all the years I've been drinking in the Greenwood. The chanting grew louder and louder. Every time they showed a replay clip of Arsenal scoring the noise got so deafening you could hardly hear yourself think.

Of course they were bunging in commercials like anything. Every five minutes there would be another load of them. Then it got to just before eight, the cameras were showing the officials, linesmen round the pitch. Everyone in the pub was shouting "Arsenal...Arsenal." The clapping got louder and louder, faster, faster. People were waving scarves, stamping the floor. The cameras switched to the players' tunnel. The chanting and clapping got even louder. Then the screen went all blank.

Not dark switched-off blank but fuzzy white, interrupted transmission blank. An even louder roar went up. The blankness couldn't have lasted more than a couple of seconds though. And there up on the screen was the face of Danny Collins.

Most people, me included, thought it was another commercial. But we soon saw it wasn't. Those first few seconds when Danny's face came on I didn't recognise it as being him. Well, I'd not clapped eyes on him for months and it wasn't as though I was expecting to see him, not on TV that is, especially then.

But as soon as he gave that half shrug of the shoulders I'd half a feeling it was him. When he spoke though I knew it was him all right. I've met a lot of Irish in my time, there's a good few round here, but none have that thin quivering paddy brogue Danny Collins has.

"Brothers, sisters, I have news of great importance. No longer are we alone."

I wasn't the only one in the Greenwood who knew Danny Collins but I knew him more than most. He lived in the flat below mine. In the three years I lived above him I got to know him well. "A rogue, likeable, but a rogue all the same," would best sum Danny up. "Take a little from a lot and they'll never notice," he always said. And all the time he did just that he did all right. It was when he took a lot off a little that he got into trouble. Big trouble.

When I first knew him he was into water purifiers. He was running adverts all over the place telling of the horrible things in tap water and how his device, it was a jug sort of thing with crystals that got rid of them. When he sold them at "only £19.952 he did all right but it was when he started advertising them as "Buy two for £39.95 and get one Free!" sales really took off. He shifted thousands and thousands of them. "No one can resist a bargain even though it does cost them money," he'd said at the time.

In many ways Danny was too successful. His adverts got bigger and bigger. Then the water companies got together and ran a campaign against him. They effectively had him closed down. He lost a lot of money because of them. He even had to give up his place in Wales. He was right down over that. I wasn't exactly pleased either, I used to like going down there myself. Danny was a bit low for a while but before long he was into something else, this time to do with computers and data, that sort of thing.

For a while I didn't see much of Danny, he was hardly ever home and I never saw him in the Greenwood. Then last August I bumped into him one evening on the way out of the house. It was also the first time in a long while since I'd seen him back to his old chirpy self. We ended up having a good drink that night, during which he told me he was on the verge of selling his new business, "And for more than a few bob," he had said. He was all for buying a place back in Cilgerren down in Wales.

A month later though, it was a different story entirely. I was just going to bed and there was all this banging on the door. I opened it and there was Danny. He was in a terrible state. He was as white as a sheet, his eyes were all wet and his hands covered in blood. He was blubbing "Ken, Ken...look what they've done...look what they've done...they've got in...They've killed Henrietta ...they've cut her head off." I was down those stairs like a shot.

Henrietta wasn't a human. She was a snake, eleven foot of African python. Danny had her a few years before I moved in. He had bought her after he had been broken into. At first I thought it was over the top, just as I had over the live wires across his windows, the giant hogweed in the front garden and thistles in all the window boxes. I thought he was a nutter but as he said later, "Burglars only break into the expected. They leave the unexpected alone." And he was right, nigh on everyone where we live in Dare Crescent has been done the past three years but us, never.

Although I was dead apprehensive at first I really got to like that Henrietta. But Danny was really attached to her. So was Chloe. She's my daughter. She took a shine to that snake. Every time she would stay over she would always be having Henrietta coil round her. Pleased me, that did (though I think that young student Jim, who Danny had lodging with him might also have had something to do with her interest).

So when I went down with Danny into his flat and saw that poor snake lying in the hallway all slashed and cut about, not only was I turned over but I was mad angry. I said to him "Whoever did it were worse than animals."

Then I saw into his sitting room. It was in a right mess. Books, papers were everywhere. I asked how they had got in and what had been taken, "video, DVD, money?"

But even before he had said "Nothing, nothing like that," it dawned on me it was no ordinary break-in. The only way they could have got in was by doing the locks. They must have been professionals. And they wouldn't have been after videos. When he said not to call the police, I grasped he was into something he shouldn't. I had it out of him eventually. He had sold his business for more than it was worth and the buyers not only wanted their money back but were looking for "compensation". But as it turned out that was only half the story.

That night was the last I saw of Danny. The next morning there was some freshly dug earth in the back garden where he had buried Henrietta but by then he had gone. It wasn't long though before people, including the Law started coming round looking for him. At the time I got annoyed. Living in the same house some of them caused me a right amount of aggravation. Things quietened down though when his flat got boarded up after the building society repossessed it.

So that evening when I gathered it was him, my first thought was that I was glad he was still alive. The second, what had he got himself into? What was he up to? And knowing Danny it would be more than likely something iffy. But I was soon changing my mind about that, well just a bit.

After the first roar, the noise quickly went back to chatter and chanting but attention was still on the screen. And on Danny.

“Brothers, sisters, I have news of great importance. No longer are we alone. We have visitors.”

He went on, “They have asked...” but that was as far as he got. He was soon groaning “Oh no, oh no..." and then shouting, yelling "Don't shoot! don't shoot!, please don't...” With that there was the sound of gunfire.

That had the pub go quiet. As did what happened next. Danny's face promptly disappeared off the screen and this pair of legs took its place. At the same time there was this really loud piercing scream of “Danniee!” And then sounds of even more shooting and bullets pinging off something.

By then the whole pub was in silence. I saw Harry aiming the channel changer and muttering “It’s on all of them.”

Then a voice on the screen was yelling “Hanja! hanja!” or something. Then there was more firing. Then a ‘whooshing whishing’ sound, like arrows being shot. All the while there was all this gurgling and coughing, like some-one throwing up. Then the legs on the screen started jerking and writhing like anything, then shuddering. Then they stopped.

Firing was still going on but it was further off. Then there was all this screaming and yelling. That was further away as well, then a voice calling out something I didn't catch.

During all this Danny could be heard, fainter, as though half muttering to himself, but whimpering might be more exact, “Terrible trouble now...I told her...I told them not to...they'd not listen...they've shot him, the bastards have killed him....we're all done for...” The firing stopped. Then all this blood started coming down the legs.

There were a few gasps round the pub but even more with what happened next. Either side of the legs, coming down from the top of the screen were these lines like little metal claws. Then there was a whizzing sound and with that, the legs just seemed to float off the ground. Then the legs and claws disappeared up off the screen. All that was left was blood on the grass.

Oh, and Danny's continued muttering. Though a bit different this time, “We're alright now...thank God...everything's ruined...they've ruined everything ...oh shit, it’s still switched on.” With this the screen went blank. Then the match came on.

2: THE TWO-TWENTY TWO

From Fortaleza to travel west, Route Two-Twenty Two is the highway that's the best.

Because Route 2-22 is all inland the roads out along the coast may at first appear the more appealing. They do indeed offer some most spectacular scenery, mile after mile of sand dunes and palm fringed beaches. Big Atlantic rollers afford some of the finest, yet undiscovered surfing in the world. Being just a few degrees from the Equator, the climate along the coast, cooled as it is by continual soft sea breezes, is never anything but warm, comfortably warm, night and day, every day. For those who have the time it will be time well spent. In the sea or on the beaches by day, of an evening in one of the many simple yet exquisite sea-front cafés dining on lobster or fish freshly caught and accompanied by Antárctica or caipirinha. And by night, sleep in a hammock strung under the stars.

But beyond Pecém the roads are unmetalled. Past Paracuru they turn to tracks and by Mundaú even these begin to disappear.

Route 2-22 is the only highway to the west.

3: JAMES

I arrived home around 10.30, poured some coffee and switched on Channel Two for the late news. I had been half expecting something on the General Motors takeover but there was nothing. I continued to half watch while making notes of the evening's meeting. It really is quite amazing. I have been in my job at Morgan's for little more than a year and here I am being courted by people twice my age, veritable 'Captains of Industry' and all because they want to raise money. Our meal at the Savoy must have set the pair of them back a couple of hundred to say nothing of the drinks.

As the taxi home drew up on to the Strand I just had to cast my eye in the direction of the Aldwych and gave a smiling thought to my economics tutor and the marking he awarded me. Everyone one else I knew in my year finished with at least a 2-1 but all I merited apparently, because of him, was a 2-2. Eighteen months later, however, not only am I the only one from my year with a job but I am probably earning more than he ever will.

The news went on, the Bosnian refugees, the Liverpool corruption scandal, the Queen's illness. Then something which immediately drew my attention, "Was it a hacker's hoax or was it for real? Earlier this evening viewers of satellite television were treated to a programme depicting horror which was on nobody's schedules..."

At first I watched more out of curiosity than anything but as soon as I heard the voice I was watching intently. I realised it was none other than that of Danny Collins. As I listened to what he said, I was inwardly remembering one of what I came to call 'Dannisms', "If you don't hook 'em with the first line you'll never net them with the rest." "Brothers, sisters, I have news of great importance," that was vintage Danny Collins.

As I watched there were also thoughts of "Where is he?" and "What on earth is he up to now?" It wasn't as though we had lost touch with one another, it was more a case of he was here one moment and gone the next. Although to be truthful, I wasn't really surprised. I did warn him he was getting out of his league. If he had waited just a little while longer his business would have provided him with a more than adequate income.

I was taken aback by the sound of gunfire, the torso and the blood, thinking that if it was all a hoax it was, to say the least, pretty realistic. The newscaster, it was Old Wired, snapped on, "...At 8 o' clock, just as SLI viewers were about to see the Arsenal-Spurs replay, an unscheduled programme filled their screens."

What next intrigued me, apart from a frightened sounding Danny, were the two silver lines snaking down either side of the body. I was trying to think what they could be, how they seemed to lift the body up off of the ground, when the screen then switched back to Wired's "Well what is to be made of that? SLI TV have issued a statement denying it was anything to do with them...they go on to point out that not only did what they are terming "a rogue transmission" appear simultaneously on all of their channels but as far as they are aware, on other satellite channels as well...they go on to say that a full and immediate investigation is already under way...as SLI says, they were not the only sufferers. Satellite transmission from as far afield as Kuwait and Vancouver were also briefly affected...statements are still awaited from EuTel-Sat and SES in Luxembourg..."

As I sat half watching the rest of the news my mind was filled with Danny Collins and the last of his 'bright' ideas. Although I have to say it was a brilliant one and he did market it very cleverly. It was a pity he blew it.

I first met Danny because of 'Bomber' Harris, or rather his statue. And funnily enough, the last I saw of Danny was because of it as well. "Dowding that's all who should be up there, he should be by himself. It's an insult to the man having Harris stood next to him," were Danny's first words to me. It was in the October of my final year. A group of us were in the George just off Lincolns Inn Fields round from College. We were thirsty and freshly grazed from a skirmish with the police over a demo for the removal of the 'Bomber' Harris statue.

At first I brushed him aside as someone intruding into our circle. I had cockily replied "Who?" and "What's it to do with you, you're Irish?"

"Irish I might be but British I am. Dowding saved this country and he didn't kill anyone. Harris not only killed hundreds of thousands but he was a traitor," was Danny's reply.

Before I had managed an answer, someone was saying "Tell us more?" At the same time the two men at the bar who Danny had been drinking with said they were going. Later I learnt one was his solicitor.

During the next hour not only did Danny relate to us the deeds of Dowding and Harris and much else besides but I ended up agreeing to have a look at the spare room in his flat with a view to renting it. By the following weekend, as I was still looking for a new place I had indeed done just that. I spent the rest of my last year with him, and his snake.

During those months I got to know Danny well. Even though he was much older than me I came to like him and found him amusing. Not just because he was funny or witty but for all the things he was involved in. I also found his snake, Henrietta, a great attention-getter with women, especially Frankie. Though Danny was Irish he was in many ways more English than the English themselves, especially over his passion for history and cricket.

Though I moved on and took up a flat with Frankie, I still kept in touch with Danny. By the time I began with Morgans, Danny was setting up his next business. It was a media analysis service. He developed a faster method of evaluating a company's press coverage than his competitors.

Until he came along even the fastest computer media analysis programs took several days. Danny gave a same day service. And he had it delivered by

5am. Because he provided it before most people had their newspapers delivered, let alone read them, he attracted interest. He generated business by offering the first month free as well as undercutting everyone else. Where he really scored was providing within the price an analysis of a customer's competitors. What really attracted the business was telling companies that their rivals were already being provided with evaluations on them. And of course, they then wanted to know just what it was that their competitors were finding out about them.

Danny didn't stop there, his letterhead boasted a WC1 address and he had a secretary, the steadfast Iris, who kept him organised. He also wined and dined the customers. They thought he had the most sophisticated software. So did his competitors. Danny didn't disabuse any of them. If anything he heightened their convictions by refusing to let anyone see anything of his operations. 'Client security' and 'confidentiality' prevented him, he would say. The reality, of course, was rather different.

A WC1 address it might have been but a crumbling Dickensian warehouse off Theobald's Road was what it really was. As for sophisticated computer software, Danny had none. What he did have though, working throughout the night were two dozen impoverished students desperate to augment their finances. At midnight one of them would collect the first editions of newspapers from the newsvendor outside Kings Cross station. On their return other students would pore though the papers looking for mentions of the relevant companies and awarding scores for size and content. Others tabulated the results and then e-mailed them to the customers.

Some nights Danny would oversee progress (picking up the sobriquet "O'Gradgrind"), while on others a slave-driver of a manager called Nail would be in charge (he was the students' "Quilp"). I became involved initially because of Frankie. She had been in the first year reading philosophy when I was in my third. Through her Danny recruited the students, two at first then more as business grew. In six months Danny built the business up to analysing hundreds of companies, 50 of them customers. Each paid him £1,000 a month.

Danny then considered it was time for expansion. He decided the stock-broking fraternity would be interested. Several promptly took his services. Soon they wanted to provide him with backers so he could expand yet further.

However, one of the stockbrokers he canvassed had an interest in another media evaluation company, MISS (Media Information System Services). They had recently gone public and Danny, as this stockbroker saw it, was a threat to MISS's prospects and share price.

MISS tried all manner of tactics to thwart Danny but all to no avail. They continued losing business to his faster and cheaper service. MISS then tried another tactic. Their stockbroker acting as intermediary offered to buy his company for £200,000. Because others were also offering him money for an interest, Danny declined MISS's offer saying it was worth more. Danny thought that was the end of the matter. He was also aware he wasn't in a position to sell anything.

Should anyone have wanted to invest in, let alone buy, they would of course investigate the company and its finances. While Danny through his accountants was able to keep the Inland Revenue at bay he wouldn't be able to hide what really went on. Because all of the students had to be paid in cash, otherwise half of them would have to pay higher tuition fees and the other half weren't supposed to be working at all, Danny resorted to all sorts of ruses to take the cash out of the company. One was the creation of fictitious invoices for non-existent computer equipment.

MISS returned with a higher offer and then, after Danny turned it down, another. On it went throughout August. At the end of the month Danny telephoned me.

"They've offered me half a million quid," were his first words, followed by "You're in merchant banking, what should I do?" One of his 'Dannisms' was "Nobody ever takes advice unless it coincides with what they have already planned to do." It was a pity Danny didn't heed his own observations. I did my best to point out the impossibility of him accepting the offer but to no avail. The argument he justified to himself was, MISS flush with funds from their recent share offering weren't really interested in buying, only having him out of the market and taking over his customers.

Another of Danny's weaknesses was his partiality for large sums of instant money. It clouded his judgement. I told him to seek the advice of his solicitor thinking as I hadn't succeeded in making him see sense he would. Alas though, he was away on holiday. Doubly unfortunately Iris was also away. Danny then thought he could do everything himself. I don't know the full details of the deal but MISS would pay half the money immediately and once his business had been merged with theirs, they would settle the balance.

MISS duly paid over the £250,000 but when they discovered what really lay behind his company's facade they had wanted out and their money back. Danny said MISS had bought what they asked for and owed the balance. There was a falling out. Solicitors became involved. Danny took the view he wasn't returning MISS's money. MISS had other ideas.

What Danny hadn't taken into account was the pressure put on MISS's managing director, Gerald Dawson. Nor was Danny in a position to make a check of the big holders of MISS's shares. It was only after it was too late did he discover the biggest of them was a Bermuda based investment company, managed or rather fronted by Alfredo Falconi and Angelo Calzone. Although they are no longer in business, having fallen foul of the US's RICO legislation, they did not take kindly to what those they represented, considered to be a misapplication of "their funds". They put pressure on Dawson to recover the money.

Danny, believing he had a watertight case and it was just a matter of time before the balance was paid over to him, decided to treat his erstwhile student employees by (apart from giving them several hundred pounds each) taking them out to a farewell supper. He took them to the Shah in Covent Garden. I was invited. After drinking a considerable quantity we proceeded en-masse to the White Horse in Portugal Street for yet more.

It may have been because the White Horse had a 'Half Price All Day' which made the place more attractive, or that many of their fellows from college would also be there (the prices being lower than in the Union). Whatever the reason, we met up with other philosophy students, recently returned from an exchange study tour of Saxony and Dresden. It may have been that philosophy students are, by their very nature, rebellious and anarchist, it may have been the thoughts of Dresden still looming large in their minds. But it was most probably drink which led, at closing time, to most of us trooping to the Strand and the statue of 'Bomber' Harris. Some of the others had plastic bags filled with red paint.

Danny also went down to the Strand to catch a taxi home. When he saw the students assembled around the statue he stopped to see what they were doing. It wasn't long, however, before he was calling out "No, no, not like that, overarm, over your arm..." It was soon followed though by "Like this, see, like this" But as the bag of paint left his outstretched arm there was a change of tone in his voice to "You murdering, treacherous bastard."

No sooner had the paint begun to flow down 'Bomber' Harris's face than there was a screeching of brakes as police cars appeared from behind St. Clement Danes. A chase ensued. Some of us managed to get away including Danny. Those the police arrested were soon persuaded to give the names of everyone else who was there including mine. For me, being a 'mere bystander', matters did not amount to much but I gathered Danny was being sought. I telephoned him several times but to no avail. I telephoned everyone I knew who knew him including his trusted Iris but with the same result.

That night was the last I saw of Danny until his television appearance, that is. It was as if he had disappeared off the face of the earth.

4: FORTALEZA

Route 2-22 winds from Fortaleza the main port on the north coast to Acailãndia and nowadays, with a change of numbers, to Callao on the Pacific more than 5,000 kilometres away.

Unlike the roads along the coast Route 2-22, as it snakes across the north of the state of Ceará, is metalled all the way to the border with Piauí. It is a well maintained, two-lane, all-weather highway and at any one time has only a moderate level of traffic. However, for the unwary it is unsafe.

Although Ayrton Senna is long dead, he lives on within the soul of every Brazilian motorist (though absolutely none have inherited his patience, calm and caution). Yet motorists from outside of Ceará are loathe to drive in that state. In their view Cearenese drivers are dangerous. In this they are justified.

The only safe way to travel Route 2-22 and for that matter every other highway in the Nordeste (the Cearenese not being alone in their dire driving) is by long-distance coach. These, in the Nordeste, are usually powerful Mercedes or Scanias. They are especially sturdily built to withstand not only travelling long distances but for also driving on the region's many un-metalled roads. They are designed so that their chassis are raised higher from the ground than is the case with coaches elsewhere. Apart from also having higher interior floors, these coaches have comfortable if basic seating and extraordinary large windows from which passengers have an unparalleled view of the passing scenery.

Fortaleza like all major towns in the Nordeste has a rodoviária (central bus station) from where long-distance coaches depart. In Fortaleza the rodoviária is six kilometres from the centre in the southern bairro (district) of Fátima. It is possible to buy tickets prior to a coach's departure but to guarantee a seat it is advisable to book at least a day in advance. The seats at the front of the coach, opposite the driver afford the best view. If they are already booked, those on the driver's side offer the next best view if travelling west.

While waiting for the coach's departure it is worth seeing Fortaleza. Not for any historical reasons, as all of the original pre-20th century buildings have been long demolished. Nor is it worth seeing for its current architecture, consisting as it does of a grid of streets lined with two and three storey nondescript buildings with high rise blocks dotted here and there, all of which are bland or ugly. The city's once beautiful seashore is not worth visiting either. It is unsafe for swimming due to the city's sewers emptying into the sea and the view from the beach is also disfigured by oil and gas rigs operating a few kilometres offshore.

But Fortaleza has two especial attractions. It is the hammock centre of the world. It also has the liveliest nightlife in the entire Nordeste, especially for followers of the lambada, the whiplash dance and that of the forró, the wild music of the vaqueiros (cowboys) of the Sertão.

There is something else to be seen in Fortaleza. Something, the significance of which, is not often grasped by those who pass through that city. Between the city's cathedral in the bairro of Meireles and the yacht club at Muicuripe, five kilometres to the east, there are, along Avenida Presidente Kennedy, the corniche which goes between them, numerous high rise, luxury apartment blocks and hotels. Several are more than 30 storeys high. Some are uncompleted and have been so for years. All are unoccupied.

These properties are owned directly or indirectly by people who, during the Rule of the Generals (which began in Fortaleza) were either in the military or closely associated with it. The owners were lured into investing their acquired wealth in beachfront property. Unfortunately for them more apartments and hotel rooms for the rich were built in Fortaleza than there were wealthy people willing to reside in them. These developments took place in the late 1980s and '90s. By then, as informed property developers already knew, the beaches of Fortaleza had been ruined and the wealthy were flocking to the newly fashionable resorts in Rio Grande do Sul and Uruguay.

Although no one resides in these properties there are those who dwell beside them. On the waste ground and abandoned construction sites by these buildings live people from the old to children, even babies. They do not do so during the day but by night they can be seen there. There are many of them.

They possess sheets of cardboard, a few utensils, the clothes they are wearing but usually nothing else. They have no food except what can be scavenged or stolen, nor work for there is none to be had, no education for none have money to pay. And no expectations of a long life either. Most of them will be dead before they are 40. For those who survive beyond infancy, childhood is an especially dangerous time. In Fortaleza for the five years past, 256 children have been shot dead by the police or security guards (who are usually off-duty policemen). Unofficially the toll is higher, much higher.

The abandoned people of the abandoned buildings on Avenida Presidente Kennedy are not alone. There are many in Fortaleza, unnoticed by day, unseen by night. Most are not natives of the city but from elsewhere in Ceará. In good times they would have been part of the state's biggest export commodity, migrants. But nowadays this export is depressed. Without the wherewithal to travel let alone any marketable skills, they are unable to go to anywhere but to Fortaleza. And only the gatos (bosses of labour gangs) will hire them. Take them into virtual slavery.

At the rodoviária in Fátima, apart from the office for tickets there is another for travellers from out of town. It is adjacent to the platforms for coaches arriving from the west and the south of Ceará and bears the sign '*Posto de Apoio ao Migrante*', the welfare office for migrants. Within an hour of travelling from Fortaleza on Route 2-22, or any of the other roads of Ceará for that matter, it is possible to understand why there is a need for such an office and why there are in Fortaleza so many abandoned, desperate people.

5: IRIS

"Go out and buy a copy of the Mail, turn to page five and see if you recognise someone," was all that the message Stewart left on the answerphone said. So on my way to work I did just that. It was only when I looked at the photograph at arm's length could I make out who it was. It had been taken from the television and was fuzzy. The people on the tube probably thought me as most odd as I kept moving the paper back and forth.

I must have read the article half a dozen times before I arrived at Victoria. So many emotions were passing through my head. They went from being so glad Danny was still alive that I was a little tearful, to feeling I could still cheerfully throttle him! It was just all so unnecessary.

Throughout the day, and although I was busy, my thoughts kept turning to Covent Garden and Danny. Of how it had all been such fun working with all the other girls in the shop he had, then later over in Cilman Street. And of how everything ended so dreadfully. I had just two week's work at Warwick Rep (the first acting I'd managed in a year) and I came back to learn that he had sold the business!

Not only was I upset with him but I was hurt. I had worked so hard to make a go of it, we all had. Then just as things were beginning to take off, he goes and does a silly thing like that. I still feel if only he had just talked it over with me he never would have ended up in all the trouble he did. Even though at the time I understood his reasons, not wanting to lose everything as he had with the water filters, and of course I was grateful for the money he gave me. More than grateful actually. My bonus paid for the redecoration of my flat. The next business Danny was planning, an umbrella gallery, sounded a good idea and I knew I could have worked there if I had wanted to but all the same he still should have consulted me.

My thoughts also went back to the shop in Nell Street and all the good times we had there. At one point there were a dozen of us, all actors, actual, aspiring and resting. Mainly resting! I had known Danny from when I worked behind the bar at the Keys. He was a regular there. When I said I was leaving because of the new landlord, Danny offered me a job. I worked for the Safe Water Company for nearly two years. Although Danny would show his face at the beginning of the day, more often than not we wouldn't see him for the remainder of it. "Us girls" were usually left to run the shop ourselves. The first 18 months were really bubbling and busy. Every time sales would reach another high Danny would throw a party. As the sales grew and grew so did the size of the parties and their sumptuousness. Then one day it all ended. The water companies started spreading stories that his filters didn't work and the newspapers stopped taking his ads. Sales slowed to a trickle then finally dried up altogether. And we were all out of work.

Three months later though, Danny was in business once more and I was working for him again. It wasn't as though there was 'anything' between us, we just seemed to get along, to the point where I could tell him when he was in the wrong. And I had to do that more than once, sometimes in no uncertain terms! Although I always ensured he saw it was for his own good.

When I returned from Warwick and discovered what he had done, I was furious with him. I just knew it was wrong and I told him so, of just how short-sighted he had been. And of course as it turned out I was right.

My thoughts also went back to the last time I saw him, the day he called at the house. It was 7 o'clock in the morning when the doorbell woke my mum who then woke me. And there down in the hallway was Danny. The moment I saw his expression and the way he hunched his shoulders I just knew something horrid had happened. Before I had a chance to ask what was wrong he said "Have this," and thrust an envelope into my hand adding "I owe it you."

Instantly, I saw it contained money, a lot of money.

I finally had it out of him what actually happened, or at least some of it. I told him to report the break-in of his flat to the police but he wittered on of how he couldn't do that because of what had taken place with the students. I then noticed the paint on his hands.

Again I felt like saying "I told you so" and a lot else besides, but what I actually said was "If you're going on the run you'd better remove the evidence," pulled him into the bathroom and handed him the nail brush.

As I stood over him and he scrubbed away what paint he could, he told more of what had happened. But I could see from his reflection in the mirror he was feeling very sorry for himself. When he told me Henrietta had been killed I saw there was a tear in his eye and I remember how I wanted to give him a hug. Instead I asked what he planned to do next. Typically, he mumbled and wittered on about how it was all over for him in London, that maybe he would go back to Kinsale where he still had relatives, or perhaps to Australia. I told him to make a clean breast and go to the police. But he said being Irish he wouldn't be safe with them.

As he left he looked at me with the most pleading of eyes and said "Tell no one you've seen me, or know anything of me. Will you promise me that?" After I said I would, he said "I'll call you soon."

He never did. But I kept my promise, I told nobody.

6: PONDS

Westbound coaches leaving Fortaleza first travel through the sprawl of favelas and factories that is Fátima but within half an hour they are passing through open farmland.

When Caucaia, 15 kilometres west of Fortaleza, is reached, fields have given way to grassland. Though green during the occasional rains, it is, for most of the time a parched brown. Thirty kilometres later and after crossing the Rio Curu, the 2-22 skirts along the lower slopes of the Serra do Machado. Here grass is replaced by black-brown caatinga scrub interspersed with tall green cacti. This is the Sertão. It stretches across the Nordeste and for 3,000 kilometres to the south.

Rain is rare in the Sertão. A decade can pass before any falls but when it does it is usually torrential and there will always be flooding. Yet there is no shortage of water in northern Ceará.

Every few kilometres or so by the side of the 2-22 there are large ponds and lakes filled with water pumped from artesian wells. Most of these were sunk when Ciro Gomes was the state governor. He oversaw their creation so that farmers could irrigate their land. In northern Ceará the earth is red with the abundance of iron and other ores, minerals which make the soil ideal for growing many crops. It is possible to also see either side of the 2-22 orchards of cashew trees, groves of oranges, lemons, babaçu (oil palm) and plantations of sugar cane, cotton and coffee, all stretching kilometre after kilometre. They give ample testimony to the richness of the land once it is watered.

It is also possible to see that many of these ponds are well maintained. Willows and reeds planted around their banks reduce the effects of evaporation and seepage. Fencing protects against unwanted animals fouling and drinking from them. Pipes leading to the irrigation systems can sometimes be seen but usually they are buried safely underground. These ponds have been made for the farms which form part of the latifúndios (landed estates). These belong to one or other of the Ceará's grandees, usually a member of either the Sampaio - Saraiva or the Alancar families. However, not all the ponds are as these.

Many more of these ponds are no more than water filled holes with bare muddy earth banks. Scrawny zebu cattle stand in their midsts drinking and defecating. Children swim in and women wash clothing by them. They are also the source of water for drinking. About these ponds there are no orchards or fields filled with lush crops. Instead there is no more than barely tended, dry, dusty earth as lifeless as anywhere in the Sertão.

Not long after the wells were sunk, Gomes was superseded as governor of Ceará by Tasso Jereissati. Although Gomes' handpicked successor, Jereissati did not possess Gomes' political agility to combat the power of the grandees. And it is they who own nearly all of the land in Ceará. They are also the state's real controllers. Further plans made by Gomes to provide the necessary irrigation systems and agricultural assistance to the camponês (peasantry) were blocked by the grandees. Funds originally provided for their implementation 'disappeared' into the waiting pockets of Ceará's Marajás (its high living, corrupt officials).

Thwarted by the grandees in his attempts to continue Gomes' agrarian reforms, Jereissati turned his back on the needs of the camponês. Instead he set about attracting investment for industrial development. During his two terms of office he secured several textile and plastic factories, nearly all of which were sited in Fortaleza or in Sobral, the second city of the Ceará. But this investment provided little benefit to the camponês of the Sertão. Jereissati's successors have fared no better in breaking the grip on power of Ceará's grandee's.

In the years since Jereissati's governorship there have been further schemes to bring Brazil's abundant water resources to its parched northeast. All, however, have also floundered including one imbued with the Presidential power and patronage of the leftward leaning 'Lula' da Silva. In fulfilment of pledges made while campaigning for re-election, da Silva inaugurated a project to irrigate the entire Nordeste with water diverted from the Rio São Francisco (which skirts the southern border of his home state of Pernambuco) north-wards into the Sertão. Though the digging of two canals to take water from the river began, they advanced no further than Carbarobó, a few kilometres into Pernambuco before the entire project collapsed under the wave of corruption scandals which bedevilled the final years of Da Silva's second term in office. With his governing coalition replaced by one dominated by rightwing politicians, funds set aside for the project were reallocated to urban areas in the south instead. Meanwhile the impoverished people of the parched Sertão still remain bereft of adequate sources of water with which to farm.

The consequences of failure to institute any agrarian reforms in the Sertão are to be seen all along the 2-22. Most of the artesian wells were sunk close by the villages and hamlets. Their dwellings ('houses' would be too grand a description) consist of windowless mud hovels. The land on which they stand belongs not to the occupants but to a latifúndio. What land these people do have to cultivate crops is barely enough to feed a person let alone a family.

Being Catholics as well as poor, birth control is not part of the camponês' considerations. Their birthrate is high but so is infant mortality. More than one in ten children dies within their first year. Illiteracy is also high. Less than 40 per cent of all Cearenese children receive any formal education. In ignorance as well as poverty the only choice open to the camponês is employment on the latifúndios of the grandees or emigration.

7: SIÂN

"He was a lousy lover," Anne said, putting the newspaper down.

I almost replied "How come you went out with him for the best part of two years, he couldn't have been that lousy," but I kept my mouth closed. I didn't want to have another argument with her. Anne might be the younger of us but she has dominated me more than I have her. Instead, I said "You know Danny was in Cilgerran last September?"

"Oh was he?" she said trying to sound disinterested, but I just knew she wasn't really.

"Yes, Daffyd saw him in the Pendre, he was staying there, but it was just the night." She still affected not to be interested but I could see she couldn't stop from picking up the newspaper again and looking at the photograph once more.

"It's amazing what they can do with computer enhancement," she continued, "It makes him look better than he was, if it really is him that is." Anne can be such a caustic little madam when she chooses.

"It was Danny alright," I said, "Daffyd recognised his voice and the way he hunched his shoulders when he spoke, he said it was typical Danny and someone shouted out his name as well."

"Brothers and sisters', what nonsense, it's pathetic," she said oh so contemptuously, but continued, "and as for pleading and whimpering, now that is typical Danny Collins, though knowing him it would have been put on..."

I just had to stop her there. "You're being rotten to him," I said, "Daffyd and the boys saw it all last night when they were watching the football. They said there was firing and screaming, of people being hurt. You would be pleading and whimpering if someone was firing at you. And anyway it says in the paper, all the other satellite transmissions were affected as well. It must be something significant."

"If he was involved, and knowing him, he's probably in with those hackers, the ones all the governments are trying to stop," she snorted back.

I saw no point in continuing talking to her about him but then Anne is always so scathing about her ex-boyfriends or 'companions' as she calls them. The pity is she's still not settled down with anyone. It's a pity too she didn't settle with Danny. I really liked Danny. He had the white house up on the hill just above Llanynis.

We first met Danny in the Pendre, me and Daffyd that is. It was about the first day he came to Cilgerran and when we asked him where he was living he said, "By the valley of the flowers beyond the water meadows." Of course it reverted back to 'Pantyblodau' after he had had to sell it but I found its name in English really romantic.

Daffyd found him very interesting, well, what with him working up in Aberystwyth, he doesn't get much in the way of stimulating conversation in

Cilgerran. Though every time I joined the pair of them they seemed to be forever discussing Glamorgan cricket club and how they never won anything. With Danny coming from London, Daffyd always sought him out whenever he was in the village. Sometimes Danny would come for a week or more. On other occasions it would be just for a day or so on his way to Ireland but barely a month would pass without us seeing him.

Of course, being Regional Secretary, I used to go up to London once a month myself on Association business and with Danny's shop being only just down from Store Street, I would always make a point of popping in to see him. I wouldn't ever say Danny was a charmer but the second time I met him, instead of calling me by my name, he called me "Gracious Gift", saying that's what it means in the original Hebrew. I liked the thought of being 'Gracious Gift', I found it very romantic.

If Danny was in his office when I called he would always insist on taking me out for something to drink and a snack. He took me to all sorts of places I would never have found on my own. But when he first asked me out to supper, when I was once staying overnight, I wasn't quite sure if it would be proper, so I asked if I could come with my sister. I always stay with her at her flat up in Islington when I have to be in London overnight.

"Of course," he said, and that's how Danny met Anne.

Well, they hit it off straight away. It wasn't long before we were seeing her in Cilgerren along with Danny. Before then the only times we ever met one another was either up in London or at our parents' in Cwmpennar. Anne always said we were too far "out West" for her.

After a couple of months though, it wasn't always what I'd call harmonious. When it was good it was really good but when it was bad, oh was it bad! I didn't exactly become Anne's 'agony aunt' but for six months after she began going out with Danny she was forever on the phone all upset and asking what she should do. But I always seemed to be saying the same thing to her though, because it was usually the same reason why she would be in such a state. "Don't keep arguing and rowing," I'd say and always end up telling her, "Work out other ways of getting him to do what you want him to do". Well, there's no need to ever have an argument. I never have any with Daffyd. I would never let him.

Eventually this seemed to sink in and I was really beginning to think she might have at last found someone to settle down with. Then one day, right out of the blue she told me she'd finished with him. Anne never did go into all the details but she said Danny had been going with one of the girls in his shop. Well, I didn't really believe her, that's just not like Danny, the same as I didn't take seriously about her saying he wasn't any good in bed. Of course I didn't say anything, well you can't really, not over those sorts of things.

We still saw Danny, then his business got into a spot of bother and he had to sell his house. At first, after he and Anne had split up he was a bit down in the dumps and he would ask after her. After a couple of months though he seemed to have got over it all and he never mentioned her any more. But deep inside I just knew he still missed her. I went to see him in Covent Garden a couple of times after the house was sold but then one day when I went to his shop it was all shut up. I often wondered what happened to Danny. I missed my little outings with him.

When I saw his picture in the Standard I just couldn't wait to show it to Anne. There I was thinking she would be all interested and sympathetic.

So when she was so disparaging about him I was disappointed and a little bit hurt as well.

In the past emigration was invariably the first choice for the young, the poor and the landless of Ceará. Like others in the Nordeste, many Cearenese fled from the Sertão seeking work in the newly industrialising regions of the south. In less than 40 years, despite their high birthrate, the population of Ceará as a result of emigration, halved. Today it is little more than 4 million.

Others, who didn't want to migrate to Rio de Janeiro or São Paulo and the misery of their falavas, were persuaded to travel westwards to clear and farm land in Amazonia. No sooner was Route 2-34, the Trans-Amazonia Highway begun, than politicians were, with the slogan "A land without people for people without land", cajoling Nordestinos with promises of title to an estrada (small farm) along the highway. Hundreds of thousands of Cearenese took up the offer and trekked westwards. All were cheated.

The promise of a title to an estrada often never materialised. For the fortunate few for whom it did, many were soon tricked or forced into surrendering it. Those who managed to remain on their land found that after a few seasons the soil was too poor for the sustained growing of crops. In their impoverishment and desperation many sold out for a pittance to one of the Fazenderios (ranchers).

Although large tracts of the rainforest have been cleared (from the Amazon at Manaus, for example, there is not a single strand of remaining forest on either side of the river, from horizon to horizon) the soil of these clearances sustains nothing but grass, suitable only for ranching and then at less than a single head of cattle for every dozen hectares of the land.

Many of these emigrants died of disease. Others were murdered in land disputes. In the state of Amazonas itself, there have been more than 5,000 reported murders of settlers from the Nordeste (with not one prosecution of a single perpetrator). The survivors either drifted to the gold fields of the Amazon and Serra Pelada or returned to the Sertão. By the end of the 1990s, westward emigration from the Nordeste ceased. By then, the outlet of the south had also begun to narrow.

As the south's need for unskilled labour declines, the uneducated of the Sertão are increasingly superfluous. They also have to compete with the growing numbers of impoverished people already in the cities of the south, many of whom are descendants of those who came from the Nordeste. For those in the Sertão of Ceará there is nowadays, apart from crime, only one other choice of a living, to work on a latifúndio.

Although Brazil abolished slavery in 1888, the conditions and living standards of those who are obliged to work on these estates has not improved. The difference between then and now is that in the days of slavery the owner was duty bound and had a vested interest in the wellbeing of his workforce. Today he has no such interest or sense of duty.

In the past he had obligations to feed and clothe his workers, now he needs only to pay them for the days they are hired. And pay no more than he needs. Because there is a bigger workforce available than there is work for them to do, many in the Sertão often go workless. And for the few days they do work they are paid a pittance. Sometimes they are even cheated out of this.

Once, a grandee would reside on his estate. Now more often than not he is absent, usually living far away in the south, sometimes even in Europe or the United States. The running of his estate is left to a gerante (manager). To keep his job and because he is always under pressure to maximise profits, a gerante will do all in his power to reduce costs. One of which is the wages of workers. To this end he frequently enters in a contract with a gato.

Gatos are notorious throughout the Nordeste and other parts of Brazil for their labour practises. A gato's usual ploy is to give unemployed camponês contracts of work in places far from their homes. The camponês are then trucked to a latifúndio hundreds, sometimes thousands, of kilometres away. There the camponês are set to work, only to discover at the end of their contracts that they have been charged by the gato for everything they have consumed or used, including the cost of their tools and, often, even the transport taking them to the latifúndio in the first place. At best, at the end of their contracts the camponês will be paid next to nothing. Often they receive less than this. Sometimes they end up in debt to the gato, a debt which is always enforced. Usually the gato obliges the luckless camponê to work on a further contract until his debt is paid off. Frequently the gato ensures that it never is.

Should any camponê be caught attempting to flee from a gato's grip, be it trying to evade a debt, or just simply trying to leave before their contract has ended, they will dealt with by a man whom no gato ever operates without, his pistoleriro (a gunman in his hire). Every year throughout the Nordeste there are reports of scores of workers murdered by pistoleriros. But like their counterparts in the Amazon, there has not been a single prosecution of their killers. Gatos are not the only hirers of pistoleriros. Grandees and their gerantes are also users of their services.

Anyone trying to organise the workforce, in pursuit of better conditions (they don't even have to be a union official), in fact anyone who is seen as a troublemaker or a threat to the grandees or gerantes, the pistoleriros are despatched to silence them. This is usually done by first the delivery of an 'annunciado' (a message of impending assassination). Such is the power of an annunciado it invokes in the recipient fatalism akin to a rabbit mesmerised by a stoat before being bitten through the neck. Every year throughout Brazil there are many such murders, not just of labour and community organisers but of ordinary workers. Such murders are so commonplace that seldom any of them rate even a newspaper mention.

Within the communities of Sertão so deep is the fear of an annunciado it induces a sense of fatalism towards the wretched conditions in which they are condemned to exist, to the indignities, to their exploitation. For them, no authority exists to whom they might seek help in righting the wrongs committed against them. Even priests are not immune from an annunciado. Either they are cowered into accepting the power of the grandees, or face the enactment of a pistoleriro's contract. Neither can the camponês seek redress through the forces of the law. For the people of the Sertão, law has no real force. There is only the force of order, the Polícia Militar.

The Polícia Militar with their military uniforms and helmets not only look like soldiers but actually are soldiers. Only the blue colour of their uniforms sets them apart from the regular ones. In Brazil even the Polícia de Turismo (the tourist police) are members of the armed forces. The command of the Polícia Militar is directly subordinate to the hierarchy of the Army. In turn, this hierarchy is influenced by, and also influences, the elite and landed classes. (Most of the senior ranks of the Army are filled by the sons of the ruling classes). In this, Brazil of course is no different from the Military in many other countries. Neither are they any different in that they exist not to protect the People but to protect the State (those in power) from the People.

In Ceará the exercise of this power is all too evident. Not only in the huge barracks situated on Rue Senador Pompeu in the centre of Fortaleza or other, smaller ones in every town in Ceará but even on the 2-22 itself. Every hundred kilometres or so along the 2-22 as well as other roads in the Nordeste there is a checkpoint manned by the army. Trucks, cars and coaches are obliged to stop at them. Sometimes soldiers will even board coaches and check the passengers. The first checkpoint on the 2-22 is 75 kilometres west of Fortaleza, at Itapagé.

9: MONIB

"Just have a look at this!" called Ahmed as he came up the stairs. "One of our old clients is in the papers. Look, here!" he said, thrusting his paper at me. At first I was having to squint at the photograph before I could make out that it was Danny Collins. All the time Ahmed was chuckling "Did you see what he did! He'll be getting a big roasting for it! It won't just be VAT who will be wanting to have talks with him now!"

Ahmed kept going on and on in this manner till I was saying "Shut up Ahmed, go and make tea." By the time he was coming back with tea I had completed the reading of the article down the side of the photograph and I was having a jolly big chuckle also. I started saying, "I am not understanding about the TV," when Ahmed still laughing regaled the last VAT inspection we had for Danny. We were still laughing when the telephone began ringing. Ahmed took it. Afterwards he was not laughing so.

"It was Westminster VAT, they are saying they are coming to inspect Shine Windows' returns," and sighing, added, "on 29th."

At this I was unhappy also. "Oh no," I said to Ahmed, "Stratford VAT are coming on 28th. Are you realising what this will be doing to us. You must say to them they cannot be coming on this day." I almost was pleading with him.

"No, they were very, very insisting. We are unable to put them off for any longer time. We had better tell Shah to be cooking for us also on 28th as well as 27th."

As he was saying this I was wincing with the thoughts of having to be consuming so many dishes of chana dahl with the garlic and the extra onions, as well as bandhgobi two evenings on the running. I was filling up with forebodings.

"Still at least we are making one of our clients richer with all the business we are giving to them," Ahmed said.

"Having to," I was lamenting. "Why do we not get out of doing these inspections, why cannot we be like other accountants and do things by the books," I asked of him.

"Lose all our clients?" Ahmed replied. "Goodness me no," and adding, after a pause, "Not all of our clients can be like Danny was, remember?"

And soon I was remembering alright. Although Ahmed and myself also, have learned English at Hassan Abdul School Peshawar, we would always be speaking with Punjabi accent to inspectors from Tax and VAT so we had them thinking we were not understanding them so well. But this is only part of why we have been so successful minimising inspections of Tax and VAT.

On morning Tax or VAT person is coming to see us for inspection of client's books we are closing all office windows then smoke like the troopers. We are also able to effect much breaking of the wind caused by build-up of gas from dahl and bandhgobi we have been consuming on evening before.

Further, when we speak to Tax or VAT person we are also breathing over them the garlic, which of course is no longer so fresh.

People from Tax and VAT are always wanting to go away, so are not looking too much at the books, especially when their eyes begin the watering. They are also not so keen in wanting to come back. Because of this Tax and VAT are always sending only rookies to us.

We became involved with Danny four years ago. He heard us talking in Shah over tamperings of balls going on in the cricket. After conversation on this subject and terrible state of English cricket also, he was saying, after we had informed him what we were and how we did it, that we were the accountants he had always been dreaming of. Of course, that is what all our clients are saying to us always. So we took over keeping Danny's books as well.

We conducted Tax and VAT returns for Danny without hitch during this time. However, Holborn VAT last May tried a flanking. They sent a lady inspector onto us who did not have a sense of smelling. She was rookie also, and was very, very keen. When she was wanting to inspect books of Danny's business and we began noticing she was not affected by air of the office, we were worrying. She was also most bossy and questioning and when she was telling us she was wanting to see Danny at his premises we were worrying in the extreme.

We told Danny what was going to be happening, he told us not to be worrying. When VAT lady came to visit Danny's I was there also. He was dressed in knee-length high heeled boots, white leggings and long silk scarves. He was wearing lipstick also and shadowing round the eyes. Danny like this was appearing to be surprising to VAT lady also. After he had been shaking her by the hand he kept coughing and his nose was running with always wiping it. The lady from VAT became most filled with apprehensions. When Danny started saying things which were suggesting he was going down with the HIVs she was backing off and not wanting to touch anything, not even handles of doors. She had not even begun looking at books when she was saying she had headache and must go away.

All the time VAT lady was there I had to keep turning my face away so I did not begin the giggles. After she had gone away I could not withhold from laughing. All the boys up the stairs who were hiding were laughing also. At this time we were thinking it was the last we would be hearing from VAT but after one month they came back with a new flanking.

In the June VAT sent a man, Ranjit Singh to take another look at Danny's books. Immediately Mr Singh came up stairs to our office we saw he was Sikh. When we saw also he was carrying a copy of Adi Granth, the Sikh holy book we were knowing also this was spelling big trouble. Sikhs who carry Adi Granth are not only most religious but are very, very strict also. Our speaking with the Punjabi was no good, because Mr Singh being Sikh came from

"Dad, dad, look there's something weird on the video," shouted Raymond. He is my eldest. When I went into the Den and saw what was on the screen I was flabbergasted. Seeing that writhing body in obvious distress I was somewhat annoyed. At the time I was thinking of lodging a most stern protest to the Television Authority. I do my utmost to keep my boys from seeing violence on television. In my view there is just too much of it. The football was scheduled for a whole hour before the 9 o' clock threshold. I asked Raymond if he had set the video correctly. Of course he immediately assured me he had. I was none too keen on them seeing the match myself but it was what Raymond and Kevin, he is my youngest, had wanted. So as a special treat for them participating in our athletic club's evening's events I agreed they could stay up late to watch the Arsenal versus Tottenham replay knowing that all their friends would have been bound to have watched it as well.

I was about to tell Raymond to switch the video off when I heard a sound of someone half muttering to himself. "What is that?" I asked.

"It's the man who was on at the start," replied Raymond. And before I had a chance to say anything further Raymond was saying, "Look," and with that he was rewinding the tape back to the beginning.

It was not long after it began replaying when I was half wishing Raymond had not rewound. As I watched I was inwardly saying to myself "Collins, Daniel Michael, account number 09666976..."

Oh how that name and number are engrained in my memory. He took the Bank for more than £97,000, plus accruing interest.

All the same, after the boys had gone to bed I simply had to have another look at the beginning of the video. In fact I viewed it several times to see if I could ascertain any clues to Collins' whereabouts. But I became none the wiser for looking. Of course I took in everything else which appeared on the screen. I was trying to make some sense of it all when June, my wife, called down for me to come to bed.

Before I went to sleep and also the next morning on the journey to work Collins was still on my mind. There was a small piece in the Telegraph making mention of the interruption of transmission to and from a number of communication satellites as well as on much television reception. The article also went on to comment on the growing nuisance of data hacking despite all the international surveillance. It was not until the start of the morning conference however, that I was occasioned to take the matter further. No sooner had I taken my place in the conference room than Jenkins in Securities, slid a copy of the Daily Mail across the table to me, adding a touch gleefully I thought, "Is this your man Gordon?"

At first I was not sure how to react. I did not know whether to affect an air of surprise or alternatively retort "That is the man who cost me my promotion," instead I merely replied, after I had looked at the photograph of Collins, "How interesting, thank you Howard."

Unfortunately this was not the end of the matter. After we had dealt with the last item on the agenda, Mr Gibbons, he is our group manager, asked if there was any other business. Jenkins would have to go and pipe up with "I say Sir, have you seen the article on page five of today's Mail?"

Soon all eyes were on me. I had a most uncomfortable few moments handling Mr Gibbons' questions. What I really wanted to say was "It wasn't my fault, I just inherited the Safe Water Company's account when I was promoted to manager, it wasn't me who lent Collins all that money on an unsecured basis, it was my predecessor, Peter Harrison, now retired, who sanctioned the loan. It was me who had tried extremely hard for two years, to get it back by having him reduce his overdraft. It was you, all of you who hampered my attempts." But instead I said "No Mr Gibbons I do not have anything further to report on resolving the realisation of the Safe Water Company's assets. Yes, Mr Gibbons I will contact Kendal Court & Co at once to see if they are able to ascertain if their enquiry agent has anything further on Collins' whereabouts."

However, before we rose from the table, Mr Gibbons being the professional that he is, did say and with a wry smile I noticed, "How many of us are still using one of Mr Collins' water jugs?" To which nearly all of those present but not Jenkins I noted, said that they were indeed still doing so. One in the eye for Jenkins I thought as we left the room.

Back in my office I did indeed telephone Kendal Court and spoke to their Mr Endersby but of course it was as I had anticipated in him having nothing more to add on the Collins' case. In my view these solicitors seem to have a greater enthusiasm in running up large bills than in achieving any successful outcome for the Bank. All we have ever had back from them was although Collins may have signed a consent to the Bank having a floating charge on all of his assets we were unable to effect any recovery action because he had further signed two other such consents with other banks. So while three sets of solicitors argued over whose clients had a premier claim over Collins' assets he was walking about unaffected by any of us. When they had finally deigned to resolve their differences it was too late, not only had Collins vanished but his Building Society had stepped in and repossessed his property.

If anything it was I who came nearest to getting anything done, though I must admit it was purely by chance. Last September I was attending a Bank seminar on small business accounts when I fell into conversation with Terry Ashcroft of our Holborn branch. He made mention of a very successful little business just around the corner from him which he had been trying for some time to acquire the account away from the Royal. On hearing his description not only did I exclaim "Terry, don't touch it, he's mine!" but I was immediately taking a taxi to Cilman Street. "Collins is in business again" I was saying to myself but alas when I arrived at the said premises he was no longer there.

It was all rather unfortunate really. Collins' Safe Water Company was not the type of account I would have accepted myself but having inherited it I set out upon my appointment to have its overdraft reduced. To be an effective manager I am of the view it is good practice to know as much as possible of a customer's business. I also find it so much more beneficial to discuss banking matters with them away from the confines of the Bank. To this end I make regular visits to all my commercial customers. Normally this is a straight forward affair but in Collins' case alas, this could never be said.

Every time I was to pay a visit to him I would receive requests from other members of our staff to bring back Water Jug Kits. Apparently Collins had arranged with Peter Harrison to supply them to all of the Bank's staff at a third off the price. Sometimes I felt more of a delivery boy than a bank manager. Often I had difficulty getting all of the boxes of jugs into the taxi taking me back to the Bank.

At first I did not resent this, fulfilling these requests made me quite popular not just with the staff but with Mr Gibbons. He said his wife, who was having chemotherapy found the purified water most beneficial. At the time I considered it would do my promotion prospects no harm at all. June was also pleased, she even had me buy one of the Water Jugs.

While the ladies in the Safe Water shop would be packing up the orders I had brought (and I must say Collins did have some most vivacious young ladies in his employ, they could most certainly never be described as mere "shop girls"), he would always invite me to lunch in one of the nearby restaurants. At first I used to think that we could discuss ways of trimming his overdraft but somehow I never seemed to be able to find the appropriate moment. Before I could ever get anywhere with him, Collins would have me engaged in discussion of the state of the world, or the even worse state of English cricket and before long it would be "You'd be having another drink now will you Gordon?" and he would have my glass refilled.

Looking back, I am sure Collins purposefully had his ladies pack up my orders as slowly as possible. For on every occasion when one of them would pop her head around the door of the restaurant where we were dining to say, "Your orders are now packed and ready Mr Moore," Collins would have us well into a second bottle of wine. After my first visit to his shop I learnt never to make afternoon appointments with other customers. On one occasion, on my journey home, I was feeling so much the worse for wear I felt obliged to alight from the train at Harlow and walk the two miles to Bishopsbury in order to clear my head. June, I remember was most upset at my being so late.

After the second occasion this occurred I decided instead to have a discussion with Collins in my office regarding the reduction of his overdraft. This alas was also in vain. By then orders for Collins' water jugs were coming into my office so thick and fast, not only from our branch which is one of the biggest but from many other branches of the Bank as well. For unbeknown to me Sharon, she is my personal managerial assistant, had taken it upon herself to make mention of the availability of Collins' jugs at half price in the Bank's monthly staff magazine, with a further 10 per cent discount to pregnant and nursing mothers. So when I did not provide the regular monthly delivery of jugs I had to suffer Sharon's admonishments. She was not the only one in whose bad books I fell. Mr Gibbons' wife on behalf of members of her bridge club had placed a bulk order as well.

The best I ever managed was an agreement from Collins that moneys received in the Bank for his jugs would be set aside directly to reduce his overdraft. Not that this did any good, he just overspent all the same. As I saw it I couldn't foreclose on Collins' overdraft. That it was not really secured was bad enough but it would mean if I was seen to be responsible for Collins' business closing and thus the supply of jugs ceasing I would be admonished not just by Sharon but probably by Mr Gibbons as well.

However, at one time I was all geared up to be remonstrate with Collins when, in my judgement, he was being just too profligate with what amounted, when all is said and done, to the Bank's money. This was over the size of the celebrations he had arranged for the sale of his 250,000th jug. Alas, this was also in vain. Not only was I invited to attend but the size of his invitation cards was so big that mine became the talk of the post room. If that didn't make things difficult enough for me, before I had time to contact Collins, Sharon said she had been told by Carlotta Bertocini, she was Mr Gibbons' new personal assistant, to ask Collins if it would be possible if both she and Mr Gibbons could also attend his celebration. Sharon said this was because not only was her name in English the same as the street where the restaurant was which Collins had hired, but her surname was almost the same as the restaurant itself. With a directive like this, what could I do but ask? If only I had but known the consequences.

As a rule I would have declined such an invitation as I do not really consider it to be appropriate for a bank manager to go to such gatherings. June was most reticent about my attending. But because both Mr Gibbons and Miss Bertocini were going to do so, I did not really have any alternative than to put in an appearance. Although Mr Gibbons and Miss Bertocini evidently enjoyed themselves at Collins' celebration, for me it was a most frustrating evening. I tried to make polite conversation and I have to admit the ladies in Collins' employ did afford me a not inconsiderable amount of attention. However, I constantly noted and with increasing concern just how much wine and food was being consumed and what it would be costing, costing the Bank. I also noted Mr Gibbons was in frequent and friendly conversation with Collins, though I further noted that later on Mr Gibbons appeared to be in serious conversation with Miss Bertocini. On the train home I remember thinking how unusual it was that after only one month working at the Bank, Mr

Gibbons was allowing her to address him as "William".

When, six months later, Collins announced to me by way of a yet bigger invitation card, even more grandiose celebrations for the sale of his 333,333rd jug I gave up any attempt to remonstrate with him over his overdraft for he had also sent an invitation card to Mr Gibbons directly. For this next function Collins booked a restaurant in Bloomsbury. Again, because Mr Gibbons said he and Miss Bertocini were attending, I felt obliged to do likewise.

Although the square in front of the restaurant was small and secluded, it was also paved. So when what amounted to a small orchestra which Collins had hired began to play and because it was also a warm summer's evening, the square soon became filled with hundreds of people dancing. As waiters weaved between tables, serving those sitting there with bottle after bottle, canapé after canapé I again kept thinking how much the event would cost, cost the Bank.

I do not know how many among those present were people Collins had actually invited or merely happened to be passing by, but I did notice a man who I had seen earlier selling copies of the 'Big Issue' heartily tucking in. When a troupe of fire eaters and jugglers on monocycles made their appearance I could have put my head in my hands. To make matters more complex Mr Gibbons really enjoyed the evening. He and Ms Bertocini were dancing together all of the time even when most of the other people had stopped to look at the performers. I do remember recalling Sharon telling me there was talk in the tea room over Ms Bertocini's addressing Mr Gibbons as "Villie". To cap it all, I later noticed Mr Gibbons vigorously shaking Collins by the hand after he had had the orchestra play some Italian tune for Miss Bertocini.

Three weeks later matters could not have been more different. At a morning conference, several of those present, including Jenkins I remember, made mention of a series of press articles critical of Collins' water jugs. But Mr Gibbons said he did not consider it be anything of consequence. But a week later on his return from Italy Mr Gibbons, when he saw all the further adverse press articles on the water jugs, adopted a different attitude altogether. Then it was all "I didn't realise you had let this account get so out of hand. Get it back into balance without delay. Halve the facility immediately." For the next fortnight Mrs Wallis, she was then Mr Gibbons' new assistant, was forever requesting information on the state of Collins' account. Even I have to admit I considered Mr Gibbons' requirements too strict. Within no time Collins' shop had closed and the Bank was left holding a debt which I knew we were going to have difficulty in getting repaid. The thing was, not only did I receive admonishments from Sharon but from Mr Gibbons as well. And June became most upset with my promotion prospects.

12: THE TABAJARA

From Sobral the 2-22 travels due west rising gently upwards over a series of small hills. It then passes over a flint covered plain stretching to the horizon. Here it is so dry that even caatinga scrub cannot survive. During the day the sun bakes everything to a crisp. At night, so great and rapid is the fall in temperature that rocks fracture and split. The prevailing westerly winds sometimes manage to blow clouds from the Amazon but they are usually too small to bring rain. In the early winter occasional rain-bearing clouds do roll in from the Atlantic. But unlike other arid places, where, after rain the ground becomes briefly covered in flowering plants, here nothing results. It is bereft of all apparent life, even vultures.

As the 2-22 crosses this lifeless plain it is possible to see, faraway on the western horizon a thin pale blue line of hills. This line appears little bigger, when, 20 kilometres later the plain breaks up into a series of small scattered hills and mesas. As the highway undulates and winds through and around them but climbing all the while, the pale blue hills momentarily disappear from view. After a further ten kilometres and 15 before Tianguá, the highway finally reaches the crest of the last of these small hills. As it does, there, suddenly, stretching in an unbroken line as far as the eye can see, rising cliff-face sheer a thousand metres high are those once far away blue hills. They are the Serra da Ibiapaba.

Because the escarpment of the Ibiapaba is so steep the 2-22 has to veer sharply northward, skirting round its base before continuing westward once more. At the northern tip of the Ibiapaba, nestling in its foothills is the small sleepy town of Tianguá. Most travellers never stop here any longer than their coach does and after half an hour or so it is on its way into Piauí. Few travellers passing through Tianguá know what lies to the south atop the Ibiapaba. Even fewer travel up onto it.

While no roads traverse the Ibiapaba there is one, starting at Tianguá, which travels part of the way along its length. It is a memorable journey.

Taxis ply the road but there is also a solitary bus from Tianguá which travels along it. Although the bus is old, scruffy and slow, it is preferable to the taxis, and is safer. For the first few kilometres the road twists and winds upwards, precariously hugging the western rock face. It then passes through a series of gorges choked with dense, lush vegetation. Within twenty minutes of the bus leaving Tianguá, however, the dry broiling heat of the plain is left behind. By the time the bus has climbed to the top of the Ibiapaba it is on a plateau stretching southwards for a 100 kilometres. Here the air is fresh, comfortably warm and often moist.

Apart from the early winter months rainfall is scarce on the Ibiapaba, but when clouds blown from the west brush against it they are promptly relieved of their moisture. It is also the reason why the plain below is so parched.

Sometimes of an evening or early morning the Ibiapaba is swathed in mist but a few hours after sunrise it has evaporated.

Blessed with such ideal growing conditions the plateau is covered in luxuriant forest. Because the soil is so fertile there is also intensive farming. That the land isn't owned by Ceará's grandees but by camponês, owes much to the Ibiapaba's position, geographical, historical and political.

Apart from the coastal region, European settlement of Ceará and neighbouring Piauí did not take place until the late 18th century and then by no more than bands of vaqueiros moving up from the south in the search of fresh grazing for their cattle. However, as far as the vaqueiros were concerned neither the Ibiapaba nor the land either side of it (there is a similar plain and as arid for the same reasons, to its west) were of interest.

Unlike the eastern coast of Brazil, the northern one does not possess a zona da mata (a [once] forested coastal plain) and was, in the eyes of the first settlers in Brazil, unappealing for farming. It was a century after they had first arrived in Brazil before there was sufficient demand to develop land away from the east. Being so far to the west Ceará was not permanently settled by the Portuguese until late in the 17th century.

The first attempt to settle in 1603, at the site of present day Fortaleza, was beaten off by ferocious Indians, the Tabajara. The Tabajara not only captured the first settlers' bishop but for good measure they ate him. The arrival of the Dutch (who actually built the first fort at Fortaleza) in 1637 delayed further Portuguese settlement until 1654 when, this time in league with the Tabajara, the Portuguese drove out the Dutch. However, the alliance soon broke down and as a result of continuous attacks by the Tabajara, Portuguese settlement was confined to a small area around Fortaleza.

Brazil had become independent by the time the Tabajara were finally overwhelmed by a combination of settlers and vaqueiros. But the importance of agriculture to Brazil's economy was by then in decline. With the flow of capital and resources focused on the new source of wealth, gold and diamonds to the south in the state of Minas Gerais (literally 'General Mines'), the pressure of the grandees of Ceará for further plantations, especially in the west of the state ceased.

Although the Tabajara were subdued they were by no means eliminated. They merely withdrew to their last and at that time, impregnable fastness, the Ibiapaba. Its name is in fact a Portuguese derivation of 'Tabajara'.

During their long contact with the Portuguese the Tabajara acquired many European mores including farming, trading and love of the forró. They also accepted numerous outsiders into their midst, traders, farmers, fugitives. The inevitable miscegenation resulting from their mixing can be seen along the length of the Ibiapaba in the high cheek bones and flat, almond shaped faces of many of the inhabitants.

At the time of the original settlement of the Nordeste the Portuguese king,

Jão III, fearing the ambitions of other European powers, divided the coast into twelve parallel captaincies. Each captaincy was 50 leagues (about 300 km) of coastline and unlimited territory inland. But it wasn't long before those whom the king appointed to govern regarded themselves as barons and the captaincies as their 'fiefs'. This view still persists among many governors (and their families) in the states of the Nordeste.

With Brazil's independence from Portugal in 1822 and its capital moved from Salvador to Rio de Janeiro, the borders of its states were marked out by the new government. There were, however, areas where borders were left ill-defined but being in remote regions they were not seen as a matter of importance to the states concerned. At the end of the 19th century, when precise borders came to be demarcated and the resulting disputed territorial claims made, the Federal government decided, so as to avoid conflict, to classify the regions in contention as 'Litigated Areas', matters for a future generation to resolve. Between Ceará and Piauí there are two such disputed areas, one of which is the Ibiapaba.

Although the disputes between the two states were held in abeyance they were by no means ended. Throughout the 20th century both of them, or rather the ruling governors and their respective followers vied with each other for control of their Litigated Areas. They also blocked each others' moves towards them, the outcome of which was that both sides stopped each other from the acquisition of land in the Ibiapaba. The only thing they could agree on, and again so as to thwart the aspirations of the other, was the creation of 'National' parks throughout the Ibiapaba. (However, this static state of affairs was about to end).

Just such a park, the Parque Nacional de Ubajaba is a few kilometres southeast of Ubajaba, a small town on the road from Tianguá. Another, the Parque Nacional de Tabajara and also named after the village next to it, is a further 15 kilometres along the road to the south.

The bus, after it has left Ubajara climbs up through two steep sided ravines, then arrives in Tabajara. For the bus Tabajara is the end of the line. The road goes no further.

13: AILEEN

Football bores the pants off of me. But if I didn't let Ryan, he's my husband, watch a match no matter what I wanted to see, he would sulk. I used to go and do something else whenever it was on but now my parents have bought me a little television all of my own, I can watch what I want. Mind, it's only when Becky and Patrick are away or asleep.

So on the Tuesday night when Ryan wanted to watch the Arsenal, Spurs match and invited a few of the boys round to watch it as well, I left them to it. I took them their pizzas just as, from the racket they were making, the match was starting.

The moment I walked in the room the picture went on the blink. For a moment I thought I'd be having them rushing out to see the match somewhere else. Eamon was getting up to give the TV bit of a tap when the picture came back on again. But when it wasn't the football Sean was effing and blinding, until Ryan told him to wash his mouth.

I wasn't really minding that, you hear it all working in the Salutation. My eyes were on the screen. I nearly said "I know him, I know that man," but I was putting my hand to my mouth with what I was seeing next. The sight of that poor fellow writhing in pain had the boys go quiet as well. And they were all gasping at the sight of him floating up in the air. I didn't know if they took in what was being said but hearing that voice on the screen, fretting on the way it was, told me I'd not been mistaken, it was him alright. It was Danny.

The screen then went fizzy white and the football came on. Brendan began saying "Well what do you make of..." but the others were telling him to shut up. They're Arsenal mad, all of them. After I'd told them to keep the noise down I went up to Becky and Patrick to see if they were okay. Then I was back down in the kitchen. I put the kettle on and turned on my TV to see if there was anything worth watching but my mind wasn't really on what I was seeing, it was filled more with what I'd already seen.

"Danny my boy," I used to think of him and I'd a little smile when I thought of what he used call me. The week after I told him my name was Aileen he was ever after calling me "Gracious Light", saying that's what it meant in the original Greek. And there had been my own parents thinking they were giving me a good Irish name! I liked the thought of being "Gracious Light".

The kettle boiled, I made some tea and almost without thinking was rooting in one of the drawers for the photos, ones I took the last time I was home. No sooner than I had, than I was laying them out on the table. And as I did I had another little smile when I thought, if anything, I took them especially to show Danny. Thing is though since I'd been back I've not set eyes on him.

It would be a Thursday or Friday night Danny would come in the Sallie. He'd not talk to anyone, just sit and read his paper. When I come to think of it he was always reading, I've never seen anyone who read so much. If it wasn't a paper it would be a magazine and if it wasn't a magazine it'd be a book. No one else knew him in the Sallie, he had the air that he'd just slipped in for a quiet couple of pints. One evening he came to the bar for a refill and carried the dead glasses from his table. "You're a good man," I said.

And when I was actually serving him he said "Will you be caring for one yourself?" I don't usually but on that evening I said to him I would.

Then he was asking where I was from, and when I said "Wexford" he came back with "I thought you might be, it's in your voice," and then we fell into having a bit of a chat about the old place. In the time we've been over, Ryan and me that is, Danny was the only person I've met who wasn't from Wexford but knew something of it.

Being just up the road from Rosslare, Wexford as Danny said, has armies of people going by on the N25 travelling west or whizzing up and down from Dublin, but hardly any bother to set foot in the place. Others when I've mentioned Wexford to them have said things like "It's got a lovely big harbour hasn't it?" Or they would go on about the opera, or Cromwell and 1649 and all that. Not Danny though. He would be saying "Did you ever go to the Centenary? And The Goal, did you used to go in there?" He seemed to know the places I knew. All the places I'd a craic or two. They were good days, me and the other girls from the Regional when I was there. I first met Ryan in The Goal, funny that.

From that evening on every time Danny came in the Sallie it would be the same, had I been here, did I know about there. Thing was, sometimes I'd be coming back to the flat feeling homesick.

Looking back on those evenings when Danny came in, and it was only for about five or six months he came, I never really found out anything about him. His people came from Kinsale, he went over see them every now and then and he was into computers. I had that much from him but that's about all, except of course he wasn't married, or so he said. But he got to know everything about me. Not that I'd tell, he would just ask and it'd just sort of tumble out. And if it didn't tumble he would somehow end up tickling it from me.

After a month we weren't talking about the bars and pubs but all sorts of other things. Things I've never really talked of with anyone else, not even with Ryan. One evening I ended up telling Danny about when I was at the Presentation, the school I went to. In no time at all he'd me telling him all about the history project I did on Aoife.

I had just gone thirteen when I did it. I really loved doing that project but I had never spoken to anyone about it since. At the time no one seemed to be interested, not even m'mam or my dad. And there was Danny, a dozen years later talking with me all about Aoife or Eva, as he said she used to be known. And Strongbow who she married, and about her father, Diarmuid, who was a terrible cruel man, and how Dervorgille (who was a queen) and was still married to another man, had run off with him and he was past sixty at the time! Though all the same, Dervorgille was no spring chicken herself.

I remember as well how I couldn't wait to see Danny the next time he would come in so I could talk about it some more. When I did I was telling him how we all went on a school trip to Tintern Abbey (not the one over here, but the one over there) and on to Bannow Bay, where Strongbow and his army had come ashore to fight the Vikings. I remember Danny telling me how it was really led by Raymond le Gros and me laughing when he was calling him "Big Fat Ray" and again when he crooked his finger, saying "By Hook..." and I was joining him with "and by Crook!"

Last September I went back home I was dead disappointed when I couldn't find my schoolbooks and then to discover m'mam had chucked them out years ago. I remember how next I left Patrick and Becky with her while I had dad drive me all the way to Bannow Bay just so I could take photos of the place. And not being content with that I'd him take me all the way down the Hook to Baginun Head, so I could photograph the exact spot where Strongbow and "Big Fat Ray" had come ashore.

And the next day, I'd really the bit between my teeth that weekend, I left Patrick and Becky with m'mum and made dad drive me to the beach again. This time though in the other direction, to Curracloe. I didn't want to go there with anyone but him. When we got there he was smiling and going on about how on his days off he used to take me there when I was little. If only he knew it was one of the reasons why I wanted to go back, go back, just me and him! But somehow I couldn't tell him that I especially wanted to go there so that I would have some more photos for Danny, show him where I knew.

It was such a lovely day I had a Curracloe. And on the way back dad was filled with again telling me how he used to take me there. We had not been back in the house for more than a minute when he was saying "Remember this?" and he had fetched out a photo of me at Curracloe when I was little.

No sooner had I looked than I was saying "I'll have that, it's mine, it's mine, it's me!" I had it from his hand faster than he could blink.

Suddenly, there was crying upstairs. The boys had woken Patrick. After telling them, and in no uncertain terms, what they had done I was trying to quieten him. I rocked and hushed the little fellow for a while but he was for having none of it. I walked back and forth, still rocking him and while I did I looked into Becky's room to see if she was okay. She was fast asleep and before I knew it I was thinking I must have been the same age as her when dad took that photo of me.

Patrick went to sleep. I laid him in his cot. When I was back down again I was looking at that photo and as I looked I had another little smile. There I was with my bucket and spade, standing there in my little green swimsuit, a big red sun hat hanging down my back. And ice cream and a big grand grin all over my face. Then I was having a sigh as I remembered that I so wanted

Danny to see that photo. Every day for weeks I took it with me along with all the others to the Sallie to show him. I've not shown it to anyone else, not even Ryan.

Then I thought of Danny, the way he had been on the TV and was half forgiving him when Patrick started crying again. And in the darkness of that room as I rocked him once more, I'd a little wish hoping Danny would be alright. Silly really, I couldn't have spoken to him more a couple of dozen times. Anyway, he's years older than me.

14: TABAJARA

The village of Tabajara is at the foot of Monte Macambirá, a hill rising 200 metres high, its eastern face falls almost sheer for 1,200 metres to the plain below. It is the highest point of the Ibiapaba. The entrance to the Parque Nacional is halfway up the hill and a kilometre from the village. A further kilometre inside the park and just below the peak of Monte Macambirá is a flat rock shelf which juts out from the cliff face. From here there is an uninterrupted view sweeping from north to south. It is like being in the cockpit of an aeroplane. From here the 2-22 appears as a silver vein as it crosses the plain below. For those with good eyesight, so clear is the air, it is possible to see vehicles on the highway up to 30 kilometres away and the western peaks of the Serra do Machado 150 kilometres to the east.

In times past the Tabajara used this platform as a lookout for approaching enemies. More recently many people stood on the platform and marvelled at the vista before them. Nowadays almost no one goes there.

Until two years ago people primarily visited the park not for the view but to see the Groto de Tabajara, the huge labyrinth of caves which lie within the cliff face 500 metres below the platform. They also came to experience the ride in the almost all-glass cable car which plunged down to the caves. But in the winter rains of that year a resulting landslip sent boulders crashing against the lower cable station, hurtling it along with its telephone mast 400 metres onto the plain below. It has yet to be rebuilt and the mast replaced.

The park wardens, operators of the cable car, the guides in the caves, the owner of the kiosk which sold postcards and maps, along with the family running the small café were not the only ones affected by the absence of visitors. The five hundred or so villagers of Tabajara suffered too.

Although the villagers grow sufficient crops, not just for themselves but produce a surplus to sell in the markets at Tianguá, they too had come to depend on the income generated by visitors to the park. Over the years a lively industry making and selling native Tabajara ornaments and jewellery had developed among many families of the village. Now they have more ornaments and jewellery than they know what to with, but little money. There are others who have suffered.

A dozen men made a good living hiring out themselves and their mules. They took people southwards from the park along mountain tracks through the uninhabited forest in the centre of the Ibiapaba and on to the waterfall, the 'Bico do Ipu' above Ipu. They also guided visitors to the stone stairway built by the Tabajara indians, then on to Oiticara by the Rio Poti 50 kilometres away. The youth of the village earned money acting as guides to the more adventurous showing them the cliff-face pathways which lead not only down to the caves but onto the plain as well. The children acquired money by begging from visitors. So did a demented cripple, known only as Lucia, who would squat outside the park gates. Her wails for alms and the smack of her stick upon the ground can still be heard from afar.

With the park bereft of visitors the muleteers eke out a small living carrying goods along the Ibiapaba. The youth and children of the village are obliged to work keeping the village clean and help tend their families' crops. Lucia has become dependent on the charity of the village.

There is also a hotel, the Pousada Elana. It once attracted custom from visitors to the park staying overnight. It also has a café and bar which catered for them. Now the villagers are the only patrons of the bar and no guests stay at the Pousada. Almost none, that is.

The villagers along with the wardens and other employees of the park petitioned the state authorities of Ceará and Piauí for a new cable station. In the past the people of the Ibiapaba were used to both states falling over themselves in outbidding each other to provide them with their requests. Over the years they had developed to a fine art the playing-off of the two states against one another in wheedling from them benefit after benefit.

The reason for Ceará and Piauí's past largesse was their awareness that one day a decision would be made on the Litigated Areas between them. As such a decision would likely depend on the voting sympathies of the people who lived in these affected areas, it was in the interests of both states to curry the favour of their inhabitants.

A year before the cable station's destruction, a ruling in the Federal Court had handed down a judgment decreeing that there was indeed to be such a decision made and for it to be decided by such a vote. The court had also fixed the day for the voting to take place.

VIGORA - the hard truths

Scientists 'knew the risks' Profits before safety

Fizer facing huge claims as victims sue

Sarah Finn New York

FRESH FEARS WERE raised today over the long-term effects of Vigora the once wonder cure for male impotence.

Latest figures show that more than 20,000 women worldwide are at risk of permanent blindness from their partner's use of the drug. This figure far outstrips the handful of men who have become blind from using the love drug.

More than 2,000 British women are now thought to also be at risk of blindness resulting from the effects of the partners taking Vigora.

In America, new research by the Federal Drug Enforcement Agency (FDEA) shows than the risk of side effects

Should there be further side - effects from the female partners of Vigora users then the

the costs to Fizer could rise to several billions. There are, as a consequence, market

Echelon Trial: 'Warwick 4' -

'These cyber-terrorists could have killed' – says He

'They threatened National Security' – says Mini

By Wendy Jones
Legal correspondent

THE FOUR WARWICK University students facing charges of sabotaging vital security communications jeopardised the lives of 1000s of innocent people a Court was told yesterday.

Jack Heywood, the ex-

the ninth day of the trial of four students accused of compromising the security of GCHQ, Cheltenham. He said: "These students, by their malicious actions threatened large numbers of under-cover security agents with exposure."

Mr Heywood refuted suggestions by Justin Fore

during his government he through dracon ion outlawing m which were a on the civil ordinary law citizens.

Mr Heyw dismissed claim legislation was

Of empires and colonie colons and natives

by Ted Lear

IN THE DAYS OF Empire rulers imperiously distrusted their subject peoples. Perennially fearful of the natives becoming restless rulers established networks of informers to abet the elimination of dissenters disputing through disruption the regime of their imperial authoritarian rule.

It was a regime which in part, was the facilitation of systematic exploitation by colons - settlers - of the subject territory's resources. Another was the subsuming of the indigenous economy by the 'mother' country's.

Economically captive and politically powerless native peoples were at the mercies of colons. Free from the scrutiny and supervisions of their mother country, colons could carpet bag and buccaneer the colonies' resources and potential without need or care including making good the damage and ravage they wrought. It was left to the indigenous peoples be they the then current generation or future ones to live with, pay for the consequences of colonial despoliation.

Having repatriated their privateered fortunes to faraway places of safely, colons moved on to exploit imperial territories new. They did so assured that its authorities provided protection and indemnity against the indignation of the indigent peoples who, should they protest at their plunder and subsuming, would be branded subversive and suppressed in the name of the imperial power.

Empires, imperialism and the ruthless exploitation of powerless natives by

colons all came to an end in the last century didn't it? Think again.

Imagine you are a man in late middle age. A decade ago in an endeavour to perk up your flagging libido you took Vigora. With the drug only available through your GP could you be blamed for believing it was anything other than absolutely safe?

But what now of the consequences of your yearnings for continued virility? What of your remorse as you view the prospect of your partner's probable blindness, as you see her stumbling in a blue hued twilight of declining sight?

What of your conscience as you realise that her increasing blindness is caused solely by your desire to make love to her or perhaps merely the base motive of just making love?

What if there was more than one woman you have had an intimate liaison with this decade past? What, if being consumed by remorse for the consequences of your past 'extra-affair' you telephoned or e-mailed your sorrow, your shame to her?

Or conversely you called your lawyer in a bid to minimise the size of her claims for damages and also the harm to your current relationship?

Again being this man, how would you feel in also knowing that as you phoned, or e-mailed her or your solicitors, every word you said was not 'confidential'? What would this man's reactions be in knowing - as we all do now - his calls, their confiden ces, like everyone else' were listened into and

(continued overleaf)

Vigora: Fizer's defence fails to stand

Damages claims could outstrip drug giant's market value FDEA investigation looming

By Barry Taylor
In New York

FIZER, the makers of Vigora suffered a major defeat in its attempts to avoid paying out billions of dollars in compensation to the victims of the anti-impotence drug.

The one-time pharmaceutical giant's latest offer was derided by the victims' representatives as "insultingly inadequate".

'Insulting offer'

Solicitors acting for the victim's support group V-VAG (Vigora-Victims' Action Group) said: "Fizer has ruined the lives of more than 10,000 women yet what they are offering is less than $10,000 per victim. Travel insurance companies pay out

using Vigora, they are refusing to countenance a similar amount to women.

'5,000 women blinded'

"We are faced with 5,000 women who have been completely blinded and a similar number facing the same fate all as a direct result of this drug. Fizer must realize that unless a settlement is arrived quickly they will face a class action not just for compensation but punitive damages as well."

Fizer's spokesman, speaking after the break-up of a meeting where he reiterated the company's claim of innocence added further fuel to the controversy. Saying there was "no way" Fizer could be held responsible for

impaired vision are the wives or long-term partners of Vigora users. The spokesman also said many of the cases were the result of activity indulged in so long ago that Fizer could not be expected to be held responsible of even a minor causative factor.

'Felt sorry for them'

Fizer's spokesman reaffirmed that company had only entered into discussion with the victims out of a sense of benevolent concern for their plight. "Thus the company is saddened their generous and genuine offer of assistance has been so brusquely rebuffed," he said.

It is the maintaining of such intransigence on Fizer's part towards the effects of Vigora which is raising City

Phone fea spread

'There are no sa limits to mobile phones' - experts w

EVEN AS little as minute a day of m phone use could harm brain. Even using phone with earphones i defence against a pho microwaves experts are warning.

Researchers at Shep University now have futable proof that longe exposure to low levels microwave radiation har brains. Professor Andr Jarvies, head of University's Department Neurology and who hea the latest research sa "On one level the dange of long-term exposure low level microwave radia ion is with the deteriorati of neuron inter-transmissi function.

"At Sheppey we hav established that the chem icals facilitating this tran mission over time becom degraded. This synaptic inte change degradation affec all areas of the brai However, our research ha identified that the areas o the brain most affected ar the dulallium and its ability

DULLALIUM DAMAGE DANGER: mobile phone firms on defensive

Massive damage claims could soon loom

By John Williams

VAM'S CEO, SIR CHRIS Bloke hit back at the latest massive wave against mobile phone use swept across the country. "People must not get carried away by all this anti-phone phobia," Sir Ron said yesterday.

Speaking at the opening of the Birmingham Telecoms Exhibition, Sir Chris said, "People just do not realise the damage certain sections of the media are causing by whipping up this tide of hysteria against the telecoms

Brushing aside the latest scientific revelations that mobile phones cause permanent damage to the dullalium, Sir Chris said: "These reports claiming that autopsies on motorists killed while illegally using their mobiles whilse driving their cars and all of whom had damage to their dullaliums could have been brought about by a whole number of different causes.

"As of yet, he said, there is absolutely no proof whatsoever that their mobiles caused the damage."

turn, Sir Chris thinks that he expected it to be no more than temporary. "These scare stories come and go," Sir Ron said, "It's just that this latest crop are bigger. But they will pass, just you wait and see."

Markus Esser, head of Citronic and one of VAM's chief rivals was less bullish that his opposite number. He said, "We could be on the edge of a self fulfilling abyss if we fail to address the fears of consumers.

"It is vital," he said, "tha urgent research is carrie

Mobile phones cause 'thick kid

Attention deficit disorder caused by phones, experts clai

Rosie Williams reports

DO YOUR CHILDREN lack the power to concentrate? If they do then mobile phones could be the cause.

Research just published now shows that every time your child uses their mobile phone its harming their brain.

In a massive joint US-Mongolian research programme, groups of Californian children who had continuous use of mobile phones compared with those of Mongolian children who had never used them.

The differences in attention span between the two groups were "very pronounced and gives cause for

deep concern," say the researchers.

Dr Louise Bakewell of UCLA coordinating the research said: "For some considerable time attention span decline among American children had been observed. But this the first time we have been able to quantitatively and qualitatively compare on a like for like basis.

"In the US it is virtually impossible to find any groups of children who have not used or been exposed to cell phones. Even children of the Amish now regularly use cell phones. In the US, children are under peer pressures to

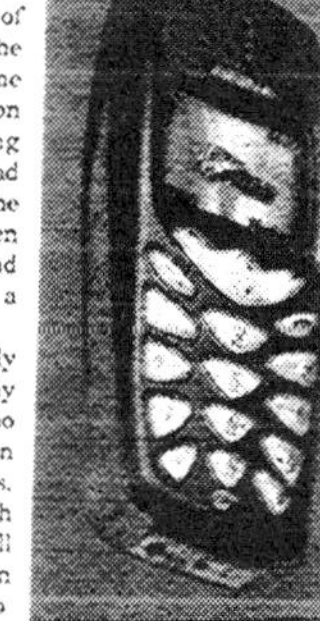

Fizer shares plunge to new low

By Barry Taylor
City Editor

Nearly £800m was wiped off the stock market value of Fizer yesterday. City analysts warned that in the wake of the latest revelations the price could fall further.

Fizer's share price tumbled nearly 20 per cent to a record low of 94p leaving the drug giant valued at only $26bn. Little more than a year ago share were changing hands for 470p and the company valued at $130 billion.

Market fears are based on

Having recently weathered similar class action brought by a number of elderly male

Women's class action could cripple drug behemoth

users of the drug and which cost Fizer $500m to settle, it appears that the company has misjudged the fervour of this latest

for less than 100 male victims of Vigora who succumbed to blindness from using the drug to now dispute liability of upward of 20,000 women who are suffering from loss of vision is seen by many as commercial suicide

For Fizer to refuse to agree terms with female Vigora victims it runs the risk of losing shareholder confidence among institutional investors with a strong female employment base such as the teaching and medical professions.

There are also fears that

15: SARA

I didn't think much of it at the time. Only crossing the bridge on the way home and hearing it as news items on the radio did I connect the two. I had been on a site visit to Berkeley and went to call Pete Gilmore in Washington only to hear a disconnected tone. The recent flooding must have affected the phone cables I'd thought. Back in my office I called Washington again, it was 1.45. This time I got through and half joked with Pete about being cut off, that I knew we had had our budget cut but didn't think the Fed had stopped paying our bills. But he said transmissions to ours as well as the Los Angeles office had been disrupted. "Around 3 o'clock our time, lasted 10, 15 minutes," he said.

"Cyberhackers strike again and this time it's the big one," the newscaster blared, "at precisely 3pm Eastern Standard, all non-terrestrial transmissions were interrupted...millions of television viewers across continental United States were shown a scene of purported violence."

"So that's why I couldn't get through," I thought to myself. But it wasn't until I'd arrived home in Sausalito and saw the 7 o'clock CNN did it take on a real, personal significance.

I wasn't sure but I had the feeling it was him they showed. With no newscasts on any channel till nine I waited for Newsnight and with the record button poised. This time the clip was briefer but the playback confirmed it was him alright. I knew Danny was in a heap of trouble when he was over but I didn't realise there was that sort of number out on him!

Danny came over in the fall. After college in England we had always kept in touch. He would call once in a while asking how I was doing and we would promise to meet up "one of these days". Then last September, straight out of the blue, there was his message in my voice mail saying he was at the airport.

He called again and I had him take the Transporter. Driving over to Larkspur to collect him I still had the image of that one helluva crazy guy I'd known. In London he would always call me "Princess", but when he stepped off the bus it was just plain Sara and I was saying "What's wrong Danny?"

His replies were all "Oh nothing, just tired, needed a break, thought I'd pop over to see you." It took a little while but I had him give in the end. A business deal had soured, some guys were looking for him. He had heeled out of London "Until things cool down," he said.

After a few days he had relaxed, became more the Danny I knew and began calling me "Princess" again. I hadn't moved into his house in London more than a couple of days and he was calling me "Princess", saying it was what my name meant in the original in Hebrew.

Then that was Danny all over. Not long after I moved into his place I told him I was looking for an evening job. He said there was one going in "the other Office." And that is what I thought he meant, working in another office he had.

'Warwick 4' given long sentences

Students given total of 44 years gaol

'Deterrent sentences necessary'

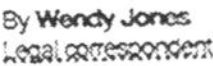

By Wendy Jones
Legal correspondent

FOUR UNIVERSITY students were given prison sentences ranging from 15 to seven years imprisonment after being found guilty of sabotaging government surveillance communications.

In an evident show of satisfaction of the outcome of the trial, senior Home Office officials were saying the way is now open for further for further prosecutions against other 'cyber-terrorists'.

Meanwhile the four stud-ents were beginning the prison sentences. Sim[...] Branbridge (23) the head [...] the four to 15 years, Ja[...] Humbert (24) and Gil[...] Daw-son (23) both to [...] years and Carolyn Charl[...] (25) and girlfriend [...] Branbridge to five years.

Solicitors for all four sai[...] they will be appealin[...] against the sentences whic[...] he] said were savage an[...] vindictive. Humbert's solic-itor John Wright said: "My client was engaged i[...] nothing more than activit-ies which are considered[...]

Phone fears 'unfounded'

Webster derides mobile worries as 'groundless'

By John Wilkens
Telecoms Correspondent

"MOBILE PHONES are perfectly safe" was the government line yesterday as concern over their safety grew and shares in telecoms companies collapsed.

In a bid to allay growing public anxieties over the dangers of mobile phones, William Webster, junior Home Office minister, in joint statement from the Departments of Trade and Health, said that all the Departments had carried out research into mobile phones and had found nothing wrong with them.

The same was true[...] said, of microwave [...]iation. There was n[...] single shred of tan[...] evidence that micro[...] radiation could pos[...] harm people in either long or short term.

Mr Webster said: "M[...] wave radiation techn[...] has been with us for s[...] decades and no k[...] harmful effects of it have been recorded.

"Thus it is saf[...] conclude that all [...] stories that they are more than fanciful tattle," Webster sa[...] and department had [...]

VIGORA MAKES YOU BLIND - OFFICIAL

Did your partner wear a paper bag when you made love? You could be danger if he didn't. MAUREEN CLEEVE reports on the latest shock revelations on Vigora the banned love drug

IF YOU'RE SEEING BLUE, you could soon be seeing red. You could soon be seeing nothing at all!

Vigora, the one-time wonder love-pill for the over 40s males is now known to be responsible for the ruined sight and total blindness of more than 100,000 women worldwide. What is more, the pill's makers knew of the sight killing threat to women even before the pill was launched!

Top government officials in Britain and the US are expected to take a strong line against Fizer, the rogue drug firm which pushed the demon drug on unsuspecting oldies.

The faces of love partners of Vigora users were subjected to a fine sweat spray as they huffed and puffed to the climax of their lovemaking. In the droplets of this spray were tiny particles of pills' sight threatening chemical cocktail[...]

Vigora compen[...] offer slammed

'Fizer's $5bn insulting' say V-VAG

By Joanne Withers
In Chicago

LEADERS OF VIGORA sufferer's threw out Fizer's latest and 'final' offer of compensation claiming as inadequate and insulting.

After a meeting with Fizer lawyers in Chicago a spokeswoman for V-Vag, Ira Lebonvitz said: "There is no chance whatsoever of a settlement on these terms.

"Unless there is a substantial increase of Fizer's offer immediately forthcoming we shall be lobbying for a full FDA investigation into the testing and evaluation protocols employed in this drug's authorization."

V-VAG's hardline against Fizer comes just days after further damaging revelations made against the company by one of its former senior researchers of a cover-up by the drug giant of the potential dangers of Vigora.

Dr Howard Klein, former assistant head of research at Fizer stated in deposition[...] made public yesterday, that the dangers of possible absorption through ocular fluid of Vigora expiate was voiced by fellow researchers long before the anti-impotence drug was submitted to the FDEA for evaluation.

Use a paper bag

Dr Klein revealed that the potential danger of absorption of sidnafil citrate - Vigora's active ingredient - was so widely known by his co-worker's that plans were made for the takers of the drug to wear paper bags over their heads when making love to their partners.

This, he said was overruled by Vigora's marketing directors. Also, according to Dr Klein's deposition, designs for the paper hoods, complete with holes for the eyes, mouth and nostrils were made as well as they coming in a range of 'appropriate colors'.

The deposition also states that instructions and user guidelines were also drawn[...]

Have hac[k...] had their [...]

New law means hackers can be t[...]

Howard Biggs reports from Brus[...]

ONE OF THE PROVISIONS OF THE EU's new Internet regulation means that hackers can no longer operate with impunity. They can now be traced.

Hidden away in section 12a sub paragraph 12.a.3 (ii) is the following arcane text: "It shall be incumbent on all Service Providers, their agents and all other associated parties to liaise with Law Enforcement Agencies listed in Appendix II". And who is on this list? Under 'E' is Echelon'.

Echelon, a branch of the US's Department of Homeland Security, ceaselessly declines to confirm that it continuously monitors all of the world's telecommunications traffic. However, these assertions are widely disbelieved in many circles.

The US administration is not alone in its wish for an international crackdown on hackers persistently penetrating supposedly secure systems. Apart from [...]

[...]iduals with CCTV surveillance

Of empires and colonies, colons and natives

recorded by a super fast computer's data bank?

How would he/you feel in knowing that should you make the call on your mobile telephone you were literary taking your life in your hands? That as you spoke, the radiation from your mobile was slowly microwaving your brain to premature senility!

All of this may well cause a sincerity of sadness, a rage of righteousness but what of your anger if you also knew that the manufacturers of the impotence drug your doctor prescribed were aware of its potential dangers even before the drug was on the market?

And further, that these manufacturers, in pursuit of profits and a puffed-up share price purposely withheld this data from the regulatory agencies of governments around the world?

What also of your rage when you are told that not one of these supposedly august agencies ever considered the risk such drugs posed to women's eyesight? (Is this perhaps due to the fact that the senior staff of these drug companies were mostly men as were those on Britain's SMC as well as the US's FDA?)

And furthermore, would such ire increase in the knowledge that three of the current directors of Fizer were once employed by the FDA?

But armed with this knowledge will there also be anger at the cognisance of your impotence on another level? That there is absolutely nothing you or any other of us 'little people' can do against the world's titanic multinational companies.

(continued overleaf)

FIZER DENIES 'PAPER BAG' CLAIM

Compensation claims could cripple medical multinational

By Jennie Roberts
Legal Correspondent

THE makers of Vigora, the anti-impotence drug, denied claims staff considered it essential for takers of the now banned drug to wear a paper bag over their heads when making love.

In a statement issued yesterday, Fizer, the makers of Vigora also denied allegations that they knew of the potential dangers women faced by their partners using the drug.

Meanwhile Fizer whistle-blower Dr Howard Klein and former senior employee with the company were standing by their revelations. He said: "Plans were once made for paper bags, complete with eye holes to be issued with every sachet of the drug. But, senior management, were more concerned with the detrimental effects on marketing Vigora overruled scientist's warnings."

Dr. Klein also revealed that so great was the concern of some of his fellow researchers even went so far as to recommend that users of the anti-impotence [...] 'doggy position'.

Dr Klein said: "This again was ruled out by senior management on the grounds that making love in this position would damage the marketing of Vigora as well as such a coupling was illegal in a number of states across the US including Florida and California."

Dr Klien also said that he was warned by the company's legal and compliance departments not to reveal details of his work nor of his and his fellow researchers' reservations about the drug to outsiders.

The full impact of Howard [...]

Vigora - vital tests suppressed

Revelations show drug researchers dismissed adverse effects on women

By Nancy Keeps
Health Correspondent

VITAL TESTS WHICH would have shown the dangerous side effects of Vigora were purposely suppressed by the all-male management of the manufacturers, Fizer.

Documents made public yesterday show the danger of saturated perspiration plumes of sidnafil citate - the active component of Vigora - permeated tear ducts and ocular neural pathways were dismissed by 'irrelevant' by marketing directors.

Although a number of men have succumbed to blindness using the drug it is women, the principal sufferers. They have been exposed to levels of the drug which reduced [...] are demanding a full enquiry into what one said was a blatant case of "arrogant male chauvinism."

Papers released show that the 'so-called' 'Last Straw Effect' (LSE) of nitrate was known, its effects on third parties were not investigated by Fizer's researchers.

LSE is where small amounts of a substance are absorbed into the body without any noticeable effect. However, once a critical level is reached the consequences of past absorption has rapid deleterious and irreversible effects on the body.

The documents also show that while Fizer was aware of impaired colour vision - loss of red/yellow recognition - resulting from the absorption of elevated levels of sidenafil citate into the nervous system through bodily fluids especially those of the mucus membranes of the eye.

Fizer had conducted an investigation into the loss of vision in males using Vigora several years ago, no such investigation was made into the potential outcome of impaired vision on third parties. [ie. women]

The earlier investigation' however, concerned the cases of no more than a handful - all elderly - of male victims of Vigora who had become blinded by it.

But rather than publish results of their then research, [...]

But instead he wheeled me into the Keys pub and I realized he had fixed me a job behind the bar! I reminded him of that and all the other crazy things going on in his place when I was there.

I had some vacation due so I took the Thursday and Friday to show Danny the sights. In those two days I saw more of San Francisco than I'd seen in the entire two years since moving here. We went everywhere, Chinatown, Fisherman's Walk, Cannery Row, cable cars, Alcatratz, everywhere! Oh, and a wild night with the HPP over in Haight Ashbury. That weekend we drove down to Santa Cruz and Monterey. He wanted to see Big Sur and San Simeon but Highway One was washed away again, so I drove him up across the Pacheco Pass instead.

Danny stayed through the next week and most days he would catch the ferry across the Bay, sightsee in the city then stop by at my office on Fremont and we would drive back to Sausalito. It was great, every night he would insist we dined out and he'd always pick up the tab. It's a long time since I'd that kind of treatment! Things went really well but on the second Friday on the way home things changed.

We had just turned off of Highway 101 when Danny said "We're being followed". He noticed that a red Sentra a few vehicles behind had been with us since we had left the Embarcadero. I told him he was being paranoid. No one was going to follow him here, not 8,000 miles away. People just do not do those kind of things. That night he was nervous, kept looking the restaurant over I took him to in Tiburon. I told him to stop being silly and threatened a return trip to the HPP. That quietened him!

On Sunday we went to see the redwoods over at Muir and he seemed to have the Sentra out his mind. Or so I thought. As I sat replaying the video clip I wondered all over again what could have happened to Danny? What was he really into? I had the same thoughts on Monday after we had seen the redwoods.

I had waited until 6.30 for Danny to show then drove home. Turning in the driveway I noticed footprints on the door. And when I put my key in the lock it didn't turn too well. After I had finally unlocked the door I found the patio windows wide open. I called the police thinking there had been a break-in. But by the time they arrived not only had I found I hadn't been robbed but Danny's bag was gone. I waited up late that night for him to come home but he never did. He never showed again.

World telecoms agree US terms

Communication majors submit to US backed GloCoSP. **Brian Jacks** reports

ALL SEVEN LEADING world leading world telecommunications companies agreed to abide by the US Government's Global Communications Security Protocol (Glocosp), laying out conditions for the future use of satellite transmission facilities into and out of the United own satellites come within the terms of the agreement.

Glocosp means that the US led Echelon Council, a department of America's Homeland Security has the power to eavesdrop on every transmission, be it encrypted or not. Because of the telecom majors' agreement, all other to follow suit.

Although the protocol negotiations have taken more than seven months, the eventual outcome - agreement on US Government's terms - was never been in serious doubt.

Telecoms insiders predicted as long ago as last Federal Government the cooperation of satel launch companies, telec companies would be next in line for an embracing supervision their transmissions. those who operate inte company networks will be subject to US over

'Fizer dumping Vigora stocks with florists'

BY DAN WAGONER

FIZER, the rogue drug firm has denied allegations that they had ordered stocks of Vigora - the blindness causing anti-impotence drug - to be 'dumped' on Third World markets.

But sources within the pharmaceutical industry been paid "significant sums" by Fizer to dispose of the now banned drug.

One wholesaler who did not wish to be named said "Fizer are so desperate to get rid of it [Vigora] that they are even supply crushed up tablets to florists to keep their stems stiff for longer"

Microwave mobile phone fears slated

Fanning phone phobia thoughtless' says Sir Chris

By Rosemary Willis
Telecoms Correspondent

"MOBILE PHONES are absolutely safe. And that's an absolute fact," says Sir Chris Bloke head of VAM, the world leader in mobile telecoms.

Sir Chris was replying to the latest research which claims that using mobile phones is bad for us and can harm our brains. "We have all heard these scare stories many times before and all of them have been baseless," he said.

"VAM like other responsible operators," Sir Chris said, "has carried out a lot of unbiased and independent research into this matter. Not one of them has found a using our phones.

"All this talk about microwave radiation causing people to go doolally is a load of tosh. We have spent more then £10m on this unnecessary research, money which could have been spent slashing prices.

"What people forget about all the research we have to do counteracting these scare stories," Sir Chris said, "is that you, our customers have to pay more for our services.

"Another thing which must be remembered is that if the public are scared off of using our phones many of our loyal employees will lose their jobs.

"It's about time," he added, "that these ivory tower academics realised that by spreading these groundless scare stories is that people livelihoods are being put jeopardy," he said.

Hakka Latkarrensen, he of Nokkie, the worl biggest mobile phone mak said: "In Finland we ta great concern with eve thing we do and these inclu the making of our mol phones.

"We have also tested longterm exposure and we Nokkie can only concl that any fears as to their are without any foundatio he said. "It is a great sha that these people who saying these things a mobile phones had not and spoken with us first.

Meanwhile, further search published yeste in *Bug Worries Monthl*

Why we have to be harsh with hackers

'Those who threaten out security must be prepared to pay the price,' says ex-Home Secretary Jack Heywood He speaks exclusively to **Sandie Wilson.**

ON HIS APPOINTMENT to Government Jack Heywood was thought by many of his then erstwhile supporters to herald a more relaxed regime than his predecessors.

Instead his term in power at the Home Office was used to pass into law a raft of legislation strengthening the administration's powers in the battle against terrorism, that of 'cyber terrorism' in particular.

As such Heywood sees the recent Old Bailey trial of the four Warwick university students and their subsequent conviction as justification of his time in office.

He said: "The 'Offences Against Media and Communication Interference' Bill provided a much

"If society is to be protected from these terrorists and international terrorism in general it is inevitable that all of us must be subjected to a certain degree of surveillance and monitoring. If a person is innocent then they will have nothing to fear from the law."

Asked if the sentence handed down by Mr Justice Jefferies [the judge taking the 'Warwick Four' trial] were unduly severe, drew Hey-wood's immediate support for the judge's decision.

Heywood said: "The actions of these four young misguided but never-the-less dangerous men and women in 'hacking' into the Government's mobile tele phone monitoring arrange

down the lengthy sentences he has. An example has to be made in order to deter other would-be selfish opport unists from compromising

Of empires and colonies, colons and natives

And will there be this same sense of powerless rage on the news that the perils of microwave radiation emitted by mobile phones and transmission masts have, these many years past been known to their manufacturers and telecommunications companies alike?

Will this rage rise now it has been revealed than any such pronouncements of the danger was suppressed in the same pursuit of increasing corporate profits?

Will there be the same outrage towards government backed 'Technology Watchdogs' who were swayed to silence in the names of 'National prestige'; 'inward investment', 'thousands of jobs at stake'; 'new technology'? (It is again interesting to note that no member of any culpable Quango has so far acknowledged their culpability in ruining so many people's lives).

Will there be similar anger towards governments themselves - our supposedly elected representatives - now that some have tacitly acknowledged they had quietly harnessed 'new technology' to covertly pry into the intimacies of our lives? Coupled with his impotent rage could this man be forgiven for concluding that he, along with the rest of us are imperiously distrusted by our rulers? Would this man (or any of us) be considered paranoid if he thinks he is being suppressed/exploited by 'them'?

For the directors and managers of these mega drug and communications companies their impending corporate collapses and prospects of Chapter 11 or worse will be of little matter-

(continued overleaf)

Mobile phones – cancer fears grow

Latest research shows increased risk

By Sue Ward
in New York

SCIENTISTS IN THE US discovered disturbing new evidence which suggests that the use of mobile phones is more dangerous than previously though.

In a forthcoming article in the prestigious magazine, *Neural Monthly* researcers at Hopkins Burns Institute demonstrated that rats exposed up to as little as one hour a day over two year time period developed a range of neurological disorders ranging from disorientation to aggressiveness towards their fellow rats.

Head of the research team Dr John Vencill said: "Although the outcome of our research is still at a preliminary stage it is consistent similar findings elsewhere.

It can now be said fairly convincingly that continuous exposure to low level microwave radiation over the long-term has detrimental effects on cerebral synaptic function within the dulallium.

"Presently we're unable to quantify what extent our findings can be extrapo- should be limited to an absolute minimum. The advice we now give to al our research personnel i not to use these phones a all."

Dr Vencill's finding follow a raft of research or longterm mobile phone use The area of most concern t scientists is the dulallium an area deep within the lef frontal cortex. Little known to scientists until recently

State snooper's 'Big Brother'

The EU's IPA gives the State even more power, writes Ma

BY CLAMING TO BE 'protecting the public' from international terrorism and other assorted 'evil doers' governments the world over have passed laws giving them yet further powers over the workings of the Internet.

The EU's 'Internet Protocol Agreement' is yet the latest of such legislation.

Governments and their officials proclaim they have the noblest of reasons for their actions: the elimination of pornography, tracking down terrorists, promoters of racial hate and religious intolerance, drug traffickers, money launderers.

Yet none of these officials have been prepared - at least publicly - to acknowledge that they have any intention of taking away from us yet more of our personal freedom, our individual liberty.

But this loss, be it intentional or not, is precisely what this year-long and worldwide flurry of legislation against the Internet has brought about.

By enforcing on Internet Service Providers the near impossible task of verifying the address of every user who logs onto their site exposes them to horrific risks which very few will have the resources to effectively

Schools heads ban mobiles

Phone use set to plummet

By Harriet Hounds
Education Correspondent

HUNDREDS OF SCHOOLS across Britain have banned the use of mobile phones. Some have gone so far as to issue warnings to parents about the potential harm these phones can cause to their pupils.

Broomfield School in Enfield, is one of the schools banning mobile phones. Headmistress, Joan Salisbury, said: "In the light of all the research being published we would be irresponsible if we did not take steps with regard to our pupils safety.

"In the same way as we tell the children of the need for road safety and the dangers of smoking too much, we now also warn of the harm mobile phones and microwave radiation can cause to growing children, especially their brains and minds."

The Department of Education (DoE) mean while has adopted a more cautious approach. A DoE spokesperson said: "The Department has no view on this matter.

"However, should individual schools and LEA decide to do so then there i very little we can do to stop them. As is the case o insurance claims brough about injuries caused on school premises."

Mobile phone companies meanwhile, have been thrown on the defensive a the actions of schools banning. VAM, one of th biggest operators is reporte to have sent scores of it sales force into schools in bid to reassure hea teachers of mobiles' safety.

However it is open t doubt if their endeavour will succeed. With parent of many of the children i the schools affected by th

16: TIRADENTES DAY

The Federal Court's ruling arose because of a dispute over another Litigated Area, the Ilha das Cotias. This sparsely inhabited swamp of an Amazonian island lies between the states of Pará and Amazonas. When substantial gas reserves were discovered beneath it both states campaigned bitterly against one another for its ownership. To resolve the dispute the Federal Government pressured Pará and Amazonas to submit their rival claims to the Court for a decision. After much deliberation the Court ruled that it was for the islanders to decide by way of a vote as to which state they wanted to be part of. It also ruled that the time had come for the jurisdiction of all other such areas to be resolved once and for all in this way. The Court decreed that elections were to be held in two years time on the May Day public holiday and with no electioneering after Tiradentes Day, the 21st of April, also a public holiday.

The rulers of both Ceará and Piauí quickly realised there was little benefit for them continuing to dispense largesse to the people of their Litigated Areas if there was a chance they would vote to be part of the other state. Both states also concluded, perhaps cynically, that promises of future favours could be used as levers to persuade the people to vote for them. And this was all the inhabitants received, promises. As a consequence the Parque Nacional de Tabajara did not receive a new cable station.

The people of the Ibiapaba, however, were unimpressed with either state's electioneering promises. Their enthusiasm for any change to their present status was also muted, for no matter the outcome of the election they would have to pay state as well as federal taxes. But this wasn't the only change which would assail them.

Regardless of which state won, the outcome would mean the land of the Ibiapaba's parks would pass into the control of one or more of the grandees. These would log and clear the forests and turn them in latifúndios, on which the people of the Ibiapaba would in all probability be obliged to labour. Sadly, perhaps, the people of the Ibiapaba had not given this matter much consideration.

Piauí put up most of the running. Their grandees considered they had the most at stake. The governor's son, Fernando Burity, saw winning the election in terms of his own personal prestige. He had already managed to become head of Sudene, the Federal Government's development agency for the Nordeste. Success in winning the vote would boost his political career. It would also help dispel the cloud of corruption hanging over him, which, even by Brazilian standards was considered excessive. His father saw his son's success as vindication of his own actions three years before when he had shot his chief political rival, Tarciso Cuhna in the face for publicly casting aspersions on his son's honesty (which, with a governor's legal immunity no charges were ever made).

Echelon supremo 'pleased' with Warwick 4's sentences

GENERAL HOWARD SCHUTZ, Secretary-General of Echelon, a department of the US's Homeland Security, expressed satisfaction yesterday at the sentences passed in London on the latest cyber terrorists

He said: "I am glad that last you Brits have bitten the bullet and come down hard on your cyber-terrorists. The Courts in your country have set an example for those of other freedom loving nations elsewhere to follow

"It is vitally important that in our international struggle against international terrorists and fellow travellers, that governments across the world stand united

"Should the forces of darkness ever gain a foothold in the democratic freedom loving nations of the world and are allowed to unleash their evil upon us we

EU Internet protocol agreement

Pornography and subversion now outlawed Internet service providers face harsh terms

By Hilary Jardine
Media correspondent

FROM TOMORROW all Internet service providers (ISPs) must know every individual user who logs onto its site. This is just one of the stringent measures contained within the Internet Protocol Agreement (IPA). Should an ISP fail to do they could face a lengthy ban from using telecom networks as well an

The European Internet Service Providers Forum, which had fought against the speed of the Protocol's imposition claim that they need more time to implement the necessary programs.

The Association's spokesman, Stuart Williams said: "We do not understand why Brussels has felt the need to rush this half-baked legislation onto the statute books. It is obvious that this law has nothing to do with stopping pornography and so-called 'hate sites' but all about politics.

"The Association has its own voluntary code of practice which has effectively stamped out child porn and hate from the Web. We are talking about free speech issues here."

Many people share Williams' concerns over the matter of free speech. Liberty,

Internet Protocol Agreemen the next small stab?

John Jones in Brussels

HOW OFTEN HAVE WE heard: "The innocent have nothing to fear. If giving up a little of our freedoms means we will all be protected from those who would harm us, it is a price worth paying. The Government is our government therefore if it is going to work on our behalf it also needs protection. If our Government is going to work for us it also needs to protect all those it appoints to help it govern and administer all its tasks we want it to do?"

How rarely do we hear: "Freedom is slain not by the single slash of a sword but by a thousand pinprick stabs?" The latest restrict- wrote '1984', a depiction of a nightmare world ruled and administered by the paranoid, where 'Big Brother' was always 'watching you'.

Following the latest moves of EU Governments to control the Internet have we not moved a step further into Orwell's world?

Ever since the fall of Soviet Communism - the supposedly ultimate watching 'Big Brother' - we are being snooped upon ever more by governments – supposedly 'our' governments' - and their appointed agents

'Our' governments tirelessly inform us that their surveillance of our actions are solely in the interest of the greater good. But who is to define was not the 'greater g

terrorism, internationa organised crime, dru cartels, money launderin and a whole list more o threats actual and suppose every communication system needs to b continuously monitored an scrutinized. But we ar never told how man 'baddies' have bee brought to book as a resu of ever increasing survei lance. By all account however, there appears t be precious few terrorist and gangsters apprehende as a result and mo certainly none of their 'M Bigs'.

Is this State snooping our personal lives a cov for something else? Is

Telecoms shares slu

Minister's: 'Mobiles are perfectly s speech prompts mass sell off

John Welcome
City Editor

TELECOMS SHARES suffered their biggest one day fall across world stock markets yesterday. The sharp collapse in confidence follows government assurances that mobile phones were safe.

VAM led the rout plummeting from 461p to 287p at the close, this compares with a price of 874p the week before. Citronic was another big loser falling 43p to 387p. Citi analyst Kathy Sontag said: "Investors were going by the age old rule regarding technology stocks: do the opposite of what the government says."

Telecoms were not the only

Of empires and colonies, colons and natives

ial concern. All will have secreted their years of fat salaries and realised stock options securely away.

To date not one of these fellows have offered a single word of atonement or apology for their actions let alone a cent or penny from their wealth for the victims.

Instead they are, to a man, paying sizable sums to well heeled cabals of corporate lawyers to protect them and their personal fortunes from would-be litigants whose lives they have ruined.

For the patronage appointed governmental Watchdog Quangos of 'techo-experts' what acknowledgment of their parts in this calamitous farrago of misfeasance? What of their joint and several accountabilities? Sadly but perhaps predictably, these experts like their corporate counterparts, have as yet, declined to proffer a single word of contrition for their culpability, nor have any resigned their 'public' office.

Instead, and displaying they are as serially skilled as their political masters in the slippery arts of obfuscation, explanations of their laxity, ineptitude have come ready wreathed in dissimulated excuse. Most of these experts however, have already progressed to patronages new and remunerations richer.

Meanwhile it is we the people who are left to bear the social costs of this carpet bagging corporate greed.

It is us who will pay through yet higher taxes the care of 10,000 and more women in Britain alone whose eyesight will have been damaged by Vigora.

It is we who must now finance the health and societal care costs of the many thousands of our fellow citizens plunged into mental illness, premature senility solely brought about by the radiation of mobile telephones and their transmission masts.

It is us taxpayers who – unasked – funded and still continue to fund, the lucrative fees of government Quango appointees. It is us hapless taxpayers who must now also pay the consequences of their ineptitude and sloth.

It is not just in higher taxes that us 'little people' will pay for these corporate rogues' and satraps' shenanigans but in higher insurance premiums as well.

If and when any of the claims for damages and compensation against these culpable companies succeed it will be their insurers who will foot the bill. And they in turn will recoup their payments though charging higher premiums to us all.

We will also pay for these debacles in reduced pensions. More than half of Fizer's equity was held by institutional investors. So were those of all the telecoms companies.

And what are our politicians doing to right these wrongs? Rather a lot - for themselves that is - but not much for us.

The opposition is united in blaming the government for the current situation. Its members are also as one in their hypocritical amnesia.

It was they after all, who, when in office facilitated the 'market friendly climate' which enabled these companies to exploit and deluge us with their now suspect wares. It was this coterie of 'concerned' politicians who were responsible for appointing the 'experts' to safeguard our wellbeing, oversee our safety!

What of the rest? There are those on the government's own benches whose raised voices of protest are perhaps sincere in their outbursts of outrage at these current calamities

(continued overleaf)

Jodrell Bank demand m phone tower move

Leaking microwaves distorting telescop

JODRELL BANK, Britain's world famous radio telescope, is up in arms over a nearby mobile phone mast. According to the observatory's star gazers their radio dishes are delivering distorted measurements as a result of microwaves leading from a nearby transmission tower.

Bill Herschal, Jodrell Bank's chief technician said: "Every since VAM switched on their transmitting tower over at Peover Heath our reading have gone haywire

"Our radio telescopes work in the same radio wave frequencies as do these mobile telephone microwave transmissions. It has to be shut down or moved or Jodrell will have to shut down."

VAM's microwave transmission tower on Peover Heath is three kilometres from Jodrell Bank, stand 150 metres high and is visible for miles. The tower has been a continual source of annoyance to many local residents. The tower is unmanned and yesterday no one at VAM's Canary Wharf HQ was prepared to discuss Jodrell Bank's complaints

Earnest Caldwell, landlord of the Three Bells at Peover,

concern as to wha happening to those who live in the mast's sh What is happening to children, our brains as a of these death rays beamed at us."

Vigora victims - Government to a

Fizer facing huge claims for treating vi

John Roberts in New York

FIZER THE BELEAGUERED pharmaceutical company and manufacturers of the Vigora anti-impotence drug is facing huge claims from US Federal agencies for the cost of treating the victims of passive absorption of the drug.

Some legal commentators expect the claims to be in excess of $10 billion. Fizer also faces the prospect of EU and oth

similar sums in compens treating their countries victi

On Wall Street yesterda saw Fizer's share price fa another all time low at $0 97 company's share price is se lower if the reported clas mounted on the behalf of also lodged with Fizer

EU mandarins threat to your page 3 girls

Chron's website faces ban

YOU CAN ADMIRE THE charms of today's page 3 stunner - petite Tamsin Stubbs - but you can't see this bouncy beauty from Balham if Brussels bigwigs get their way.

These ivory tower spoil-sports have just passed another of their daft laws barring you from seeing our

Barely a week would pass in the months before polling day without the young Burity touring the villages and hamlets of the Ibiapaba in his helicopter (which was acquired with funds taken from the Sudene). The villagers of Tabajara became resigned to their cattle running away as it landed on the flat stretch of open ground 200 metres away on the park-side of the Pousada. They grew bored seeing his podgy form clamber from it then stride towards the village in jodhpurs, riding boots, an invariable white shirt and his black hair permanently greased back. They became blasé over his promises as well as by the way he addressed them as “Meu povo” (“My people”). They also became ever frustrated at the cable station remaining unbuilt.

As the last remaining days of the campaign passed and the fate of the Ibiapaba's national parks hung precariously in the balance, they were left in all but undisturbed silence. With the cable station not working there were few visitors who came to marvel at the uniqueness of a forest which has grown and evolved in the clouds. And there were none who saw it at evening time or by night. Almost no one, that is.

There was almost no one to see the forest in the cool of an evening. See it as the light begins to fade, watch fingers of cloud sliding, swirling silently between the trees, forming into white blankets around the base of their trunks, then with the slightest breeze languidly rise again in slow moving snake-like plumes up into the leaves and branches. These mists deaden almost all sound. At night the forest is often completely silent. It is small wonder that the Tabajara indians believed their ancestor's spirits dwelt here.

But at this time there was someone who saw the forest by night and marvelled at its haunting beauty. Someone who also saw from the viewing platform what very few had ever seen from there, the stars.

Because the air is so clear, the elevation so high and the Equator close by, stars appear from the platform in abundance and with a brightness seldom seen elsewhere. Though this spectacle is impressive to the naked eye, viewed through a telescope the intensity of the stars increases in number, size and brilliance by many, many times.

Hour after hour, night after night, sitting on the viewing platform peering at the stars through his telescope would be Danny Collins.

Danny bought the telescope secondhand from a man who had a photographic shop and who he had met in a bar on one of his monthly trips to Fortaleza. The telescope was not particularly powerful giving only a magnification of a 100 but he derived infinite pleasure from it. During April he was pointing his telescope to the north, studying Arturus, Spica and the curve of the Milky Way. Then he would swing his telescope southwards, along the Milky Way to the host of bright stars shining there, Antares, Rigal, Hadar and fresh on the horizon, Canopus.

After two or three hours of stargazing Danny would collapse his telescope, walk back through the silence of the park and down to the Pousada Elana.

Mobile microwaves: the unseen menace

Seven vital steps in protecting you and your loved ones fro

By Holly Blackwell, Health Editor

STEP ONE, say experts is to 'think' cigarettes and passive smoking. If you have difficulty in kicking the habit of mobile telephoning try cutting back to no more than 20 calls a day.

STEP TWO: NEVER use a mobile phone in front of children. Remember, even passive microwave radiation can KILL.

STEP THREE: Place a lead shield between you and your mobile. As an alternative use silver...

DANGER! - Your mobile will make you doolally - OFFICIAL

M.waves in mobiles brings on madness experts claim
Urgent government moves to curb phone use

Douglas Jones reports

ANYONE WITHIN two feet of an active mobile phone is in danger of their minds being microwaved, scientists have found. For heavy phone users it might already be too late to save their brains from

can, over 20 years can cause HSE, the incurable 'Mad Human Disease', it was claimed yesterday.

This latest shock news came ... Dhaka ... now hi...

those given out by millions of mobiles has 'cooked' the brains of their lab rats. Research chief, Dr Bandringan said: "The results of our findings are ... the

Florists stiffen up stems with Vigora

BRITTA RUFF reports

IF BLOOMS FROM your florists are firmer and they are lasting for longer, don't sniff them – you could go blind.

The Chron can reveal that scores of Britain's florists have resorted to using Vigora – the banned impotence drug – to stiffen up their wilting blooms.

This one-time wonder ... over 40's ...ng libidos is ...icitly used by ...er sellers to ...r rose stems ...ard.

...uquet of red ...ight by your ...ld well have ...e ridged by the

PAI will not stop us' say h

Defiant group see themselves as 'secrets liber

By Valerie Swift Security correspondent

EVERY LOCK can be picked, every bastion can be penetrated, every encryption decoded", is the defiant motto of Pete' (not his real name) who is known in the cyber world of hackers as 'C de la C'.

In this select world of hackers or 'Secrecy Retrievalists' as many call themselves Pete's exploits are legendary.

Until recently he and friends even boasted their own website detailing their latest successes. As recently as last week Pete and pals' site detailed some of the claimed innermost secrets of Mokelumne Hill a supposedly innocent agricultural research station but in reality an undercover operation of Los Alamos. "If Governments did keep secrets they would have nothing to hide," said Pete.

To Pete and apparently those like him ... EU Internet legislation poses

Although infiltrating secure syste... has many of the aspects of a comp... game, there is, so he maintain... serious side to their activities.

Pete said: "We are living in an ... when governments, transnat... companies and organisations ... gaining increasing control of our ... All this talk about getting at ... merchants and drug dealers is ... cover to try and stop people like u... uncovering what they are hidin... their own citizens."

Pete refutes utterly the ... that hackers are 'cyb... Instead he sees what he ... hackers are doing as ... public good. "When you ... 'dirty little secrets' that ... have to hide and which ... have uncovered who are ... who are the gainers," he ...

"The general public h... and may indeed stand ... we uncover. The loser...

Our children protected at last from Net filth

New Internet law will bring abusers to book

Penny Howard, Ethics Editor

PEDDLERS OF NET porn and hate will be nailed at last. No longer will these perverts and sick racists be free to poison our children's screens and minds with their wicked wares. And all thanks to the British Government helping to knock lawmakers' heads together in Brussels.

In an eleventh hour intervention late last year a delegation led by Cheltenham's MP Sir Hugh Russet Brown persuaded some the

change their minds and press for a rapid introduction of this vital law.

Last night a... Hugh said: "I ... that at long la... proper restricti... media of the In... its operators wil... to the same re... of other media ... Press and Televi... well including the...

"For too long t... and 'E-mail have ... of international l...

MOBILE meltdown!

Phone network implodes

By Roger Heath City Editor

WITH THE PUBLIC throwing away their mobile phones by the skipful, those still brave - or foolish - enough to keep them are finding it nigh impossible to send or receive calls.

With Lemon the latest

the entire transmission network is fast collapsing.

Users in many parts of the country were unable to get transmission signals throughout much of Britain during yesterday.

Florist peddled banned love drug

Arnold Johnson Court Correspondent

'SAY IT WITH FLOWERS' used to be the florists' slogan to the lovelorn plighting their troth.

But one flower seller provided something more than mere blooms to bolster the bashfuls' ardour: Vigora, the banned anti-impotence love drug.

At Horseferry Road magistrates court, yesterday, Brixton florist, Julian Spriggs (36) pleaded guilty to 15 specimen charges of unlawfully supplying reconstituted Vigora pills to elderly male customers for the purpose of securing erections.

Justice Margaret Smith sentencing Spriggs to six month imprisonment said: "As a result of your greed you have jeopardised the wellbeing of the partners of these pathetic, stupid men. It is therefore necessary to make an example of people like you."

Defence barrister, John Hughes said: "My client was continuously pestered by his customers for the drug. He was often threatened by them and

Mobile market carnage

VAM, Lemon, 5, all file for Chapter 11

By John Harkness, City Editor

TELECOMS COMPANIES worldwide collapsed under waves of panic selling yesterday.

With next to no one buying, share in all the companies fell to zero

In the US a string of cell phone companies filed for Chapter 11. British based VAM called in the receivers at 11am yesterday. A spokesman for the French Lemon said that

With financial institutions left nursing huge losses following the phone companies' collapse, there were fears that many of Britain's pension providers will have to announce ...

Doolally victims' plight

Mobile phone collapse threatens compensation claims

By Sally Brown
Health Correspondent

WITH THE COLLAPSE OF telecoms companies worldwide, mobile phone victims are facing a bleak future. With their chances of compensation from the companies all but vanished the possibility of any government payout was also dashed yesterday.

A Department of Health spokesman said that claimants who are suffering from doolallitus will have

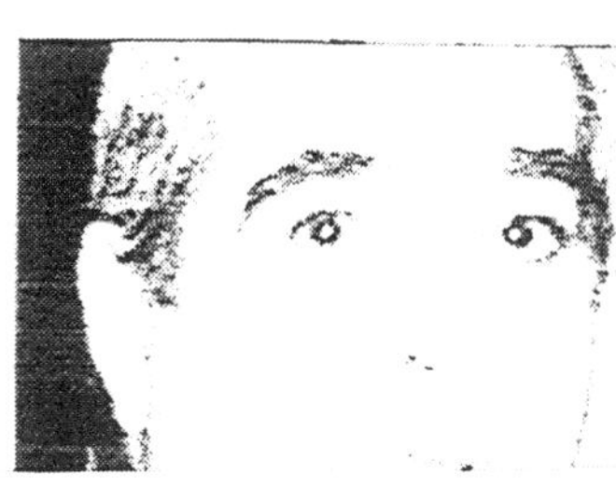

Of empires and colonies, colons and natives

but all are past their prime. And any prospects of office.

Those who still do have such prospects are doubtless, by their continuing silence abiding the whips' strictures for solidarity in safeguarding the government's slender majority and that the current furore will blow over or at least abate. So not much hope of action on our behalf from this quarter either.

The 19th century economist Ricardo wryly remarked that when more than two businessmen gather together they usually do so to conspire against the common good. Nowadays Ricardo's words could be reworked to: "whenever executives of big business, top politicians and their teams of experts so gather, they similarly to conspire."

In the lifetime of our middle aged man this frightful triumvirate has perpetuated one confidence trick upon a hapless public after another, that of nationalisation then a few decades later 'privatisation'. In between and subsequently, this trio has unloaded onto a misinformed public their overpriced and unnecessary nuclear power, comprehensive urban redevelopment, thalidomide, growth enhancers, BSE, GM crops and a long list of more, all the way to Vigora and mobile telephones. All have enriched their multinational promoters, all have benefited their political and professional proponents. And all have cost us, we the people dear.

What of the organisations protesting so vocally, voraciously against these latest violations to our wellbeing? What recompense can they wring in righting these latest wrongs? What are their chances of success? The late Des Wilson, veteran campaigner of causes numerous, once, in a candid moment, acknowledged that in terms of substance the sum total of he and his colleagues' lifetime of protest was absolutely zero. That was then, what hope now?

The combined resources of all the current campaigners compared to those a single, large multinational company can marshal to protect itself, are puny. Supplementing any such company's arsenal - as veteran campaigners will verify - are those of the State.

From a panoply of judicial gagging and restraining orders, those curtailing assembly, all backed by the power of police forces, their armoury of public order enforcement, the security services' surveillance and spying, their operatives' reputed extra-legal proclivity for burglary and agent provocateuring to the ubiquity of CCTV, the might of its power ensures a State enforces whatever it deems is right. Which translates into: protecting the privileged positions of the powerful; suppressing those who challenge them or it.

Should protest win through against such gauntlets, states have always possessed further, darker deterrents, deadlier weapons within their arsenals to bludgeon down dissent. Apart from old fashioned physical elimination, states have now added 'new fangled' information technology to their armouries.

Today, "we the people" are as those oppressed natives of the empires of old. It is "we, the ordinary people" who are denied the right of self-determination and freedom from our colonial rulers and their exploitation of us.

However, the only ones who can ever liberate us from those who oppress and exploit us are ourselves: "We, the little people".

© Ted Lear

At the Pousada he would eat the meal Elana, the proprietor's wife would always prepare for him. Afterwards he would perhaps watch television, attempt to read what newspapers were available or engage in halting conversation with people at the bar. He would, however, always drink several cervejas (beers) accompanied with cachaça (fermented sugar cane). Then he would retire to his room, his hammock and to sleep.

But not every evening for Danny Collins was as this. Sometimes the cachaça would get to him first and he would not see the stars.

One such cachaça-filled occasion was Tiradentes Day. Every Tiradentes Day is a thinly veiled excuse, as is every other public holiday in Brazil, for the population to celebrate whatever event it is in honour of by consuming food and drink the day through.

For the villagers of Tabajara this Tiradentes Day was celebrated with extra zest. They considered that they had cause to. They had, hopefully, waved off for the last time the rotund figure of Fernando Burity. The blustering of electioneering had ended. In ten days time no matter which state won, there would be the new cable station both states had promised and hordes of visitors to buy their craftwork. They were also cheered by the news that the then rainy weather all along the Atlantic seaboard of Brazil had devastated the coffee growing areas in the south (it meant the price for their coffee crop would rise). It was also the silver wedding of Elana and her husband Rico.

Danny participated in the celebrations with numerous glasses of cachaça. Needless to say, by 5 o'clock Rico and a few others momentarily broke away from celebrating in order to carry a very drowsy Danny down the corridor from the bar to his hammock.

The Susem went round once but it was far away. Then they came in. It was about 10 o'clock in the morning in Tabajara when they straightened out of their steep parabolic dive 25 kilometres above the sea and a 1,000 west of Cape Flattery. There it was just 4 o'clock and still in darkness. They sped southwest and within the hour were crossing over the island of Waigo in the Halmahera Sea 8,000 kilometres away. Someone on that island might have seen them but as they were still 17 kilometres up and it was 10 o' clock at night, it is doubtful. In another hour not only had they passed over the islands and seas of Sulawesi and Java but were above the eastern Indian Ocean and the approaching daylight.

As the Susem sped westwards continually slowing their speed and reducing height they saw nothing but water. It was noon when they passed by Cape Agulhas but they were 300 kilometres to its south, and as they had by then descended to 5,000 metres it was beyond their horizon.

By the time the Susem had crossed the Atlantic it was 4.30 in the afternoon. They crossed the coast above Jacumá, 80 kilometres north of Recefe. By then they had descended to 2,000 metres but they still didn't see any land, nor did anyone see them.

Between the Susem and the ground, blown in from the Atlantic was a thick blanket of dark clouds. With these busily dispensing their rain there were few people outside let alone looking upwards. Onward the Susem flew, their speed still slowing, their height dropping. On they went, above the rain clouds, still flying in the same straight line.

The clouds, stretching inland for hundreds of kilometres, continued to mask the land from the Susem but the now setting sun began to bathe the tops of the clouds in a pale pink hue. Then, with the sun slipping below the Susem's horizon they saw, rising up above the clouds, almost black in the gathering darkness, the Serra da Ibiapaba, its tabletop wreathed in evening mists. Monte Macambirá, its peak rising clear of the clouds, lay directly in their path. For Susem it was their first sight of land.

The Susem slowed, circled the peak and in doing so saw between the swirls of mist, the lights of Tabajara. It was their first sign of life. The Susem circled again, slowed yet more and hovered above the village for five minutes or so. Then they came in to land.

The villagers still busily engaged in their Tiradentes Day's celebrations did not at first notice the Susem's impending arrival. It was only when children rushed into the bar shouting and screaming to what was happening outside did they go out to see. As the villagers did so they saw the lights of the Susem circling as they sought a place to land. Then, in the mellowness of their inebriated day and further filled with fear and belief of ancestral spirits, they gathered up their children and fled.

By the time the Susem landed, on the same stretch of open ground Fernando Burity's helicopter had always done, the entire village was speeding away in pick-up trucks, cars, on bicycles, mules, even in the commandeered Tianguá bus down the road through the mists and on to Ubajara.

In their haste to depart, however, the villagers neglected to take Lucia with them and it was only as they approached the first ravine did Elana remember Danny. But Rico, unable to turn his truck around even if he had wanted to, pressed on with the others down the road.

"Cachaça is a terrible drink. I'll be glad when I've had enough before I've had more than enough."

That was my first thought of the day. The next, on managing to open both eyes together, was "Where's my coffee Elana's daughter always brings me in?" Then, "Why is it so quiet, not everyone could be feeling as I do?" Then I'd stirrings from within. The floor was like a ship in a storm, I nearly fell back again. Instead, I put a towel around and groped across the hall to the bathroom and sat down in there. My head was thumping. I felt terrible. I took a shower hoping it might do some good. It didn't.

Worse, I dropped the towel in the water. Though all wet I wrapped it round and nipped back to my room for a dry one. No sooner was I there than the door, which I'd not fully shut, began to open. Thinking it was Elana's daughter bringing coffee, I was about to make some comment about every one being late but when I turned around, there "it" was.

I gave a swipe with the towel thinking it was a hornet. In the Ibiapaba they can get to a terrible size and give nasty stings. But it didn't buzz off. I gave it another flit of the towel. It still didn't fly away. Instead it came into the room. It had yellow and black hornet's stripes alright and little wings going up and down as well, and a shiny black bit at the front. But it wasn't a hornet. It was nearly a foot long. It hovered a couple of feet away looking at me. I yelled "Buzz off," but it came closer as though for a sting. I threw the towel at it so as to knock it to the floor. The towel flew back. I took a swipe at it with my hand. I'd another shock. As I brought my arm forward it was suddenly swept back as though someone was pushing on it. I nearly toppled over. I was still shouting for it to buzz off as I fled out of the room.

I ran down the corridor towards the parlour shouting for help. No one appeared. I looked over my shoulder. The 'hornet' was following. I banged my head on the shelf outside the kitchen as I grabbed a couple of brushes and threw them at it. They came whizzing back. I was still yelling for help when I ran out of the back doorway. It was only later that I realised just how much I'd knocked my head. And that I'd not a stitch on. But as I rushed out of the door they were the last things on my mind. For there, a couple of hundred yards away on the far side of Elana's vegetable patch, was this "thing".

I tried to go to the side but the hornet shot round in front of me, hovering, blocking my path. I felt a stab of pain to my hip. I turned to run in the other direction, but it was in front of me and I'd a stab to my other hip. The hornet zoomed to the back of me. With that I was running full tilt across the vegetable patch with it chasing right behind.

With all its angles the "thing" looked like one of those American stealth plane things but it wasn't like any in pictures I'd seen. I was chased by the hornet so fast I'd not time to shout, yell, except when I got to the far side of the vegetable patch and the hedge of prickly pears. I couldn't go through them. And I wasn't just yelling, I was blubbing and pleading with it to let me go. Then another strange thing happened.

The hornet zoomed to the path a few feet away leading to the gate in the hedge. It stopped there a moment as though directing. I'd not even time to go in the opposite direction before it had whizzed back behind me. Catching my breath I began walking but soon felt a jab to my bum and I was running once more, and blubbing "Okay, okay, I can take the hint," then realising how stupid I was to shout out. But at the gate I was shouting at it again for time to let me undo the latch. And again it did. Though the moment I had it was having me run again. Run in the direction of the plane and a ramp coming from its side. I was run straight up this ramp. I'd not even time to stop at the bright blue light flashing all over me as I ran through the doorway.

The hornet then circled me as though hinting to stop, so I did. I was gasping and panting so that I could hardly stand. Apart from thinking "This is no way to start the day," there were other thoughts, "There's no need to have gone to this length, I would have given it all back, they had only to ask! What were they going to do to me?" I worried I'd not a stitch on, half relieved for having gone to the lavatory. My head was still thumping. My feet were bleeding. The left foot began hurting. I eased onto the right, this hurt as well. Being naked, how you feel so utterly helpless when you are. What was this place, this thing I was in? What was going to happen next? Then, a few feet away I noticed Lucia lying half slumped on the floor.

I shouted "Lucia," only to wish I'd not. It started her off. Her banshee wailing is a pain to be hearing at the best of times. But then, it was the last thing I needed. She'd also next to nothing on. Her scrawny, withered body as she tried to move towards me was not something I wanted to behold either.

Then, over her wailing I heard a sliding sound, like a door going back. I looked to where the sound came from and saw it was. In the doorway a shape appeared. The space we were in wasn't really a room, neither was it like a plane. It had inwardly curving walls, more like a boat's. There wasn't much in the way of illumination either. Apart from the light by the outside doorway it was on the dark side. I couldn't make out more than the figure's outline. The doorway was 30 feet away. The figure stood, then came towards us.

When it was ten feet away, I was clasping my hands in front of me for I wasn't sure if it was a woman. I couldn't tell from the tunic but when the light from outside caught more of her face I saw it was a she's. And thoughts were tumbling all over again.

She was on the tall side, perhaps a little full of figure as well but the tunic she was wearing (full length overall with sleeves) was loose fitting. I blurted to her "What's going on, oh please, oh please, what's going on..." and was at once aware how pathetic I sounded. She gave me a blank look, like women who you call out to when you think you've recognised them and then realise you've made a mistake do. Then she gave me that cold up and down look they give as well. Her face had a full tan. Was she Brazilian? Their air force spend heaps of money but I'd not realised they were buying these sorts of planes. But she couldn't be one of them because they don't have women pilots in their air force. Perhaps 'she' wasn't a she but a transvestite, they have lots of those in Brazil.

Having looked at me, she had stepped across to Lucia, who by then had slumped back down onto the floor and was looking up at 'she' in the plaintive way she does when she crawls round the village begging. Once 'she' had given Lucia the once over she was back looking at me, or my body rather. I stood, still clasping myself and trembling. She rubbed her hand over my nipples and the hair on my chest. She pulled at them. And that really hurt. I yelled for her to stop. I went to brush her hand away. I felt a stab to my shoulder. The hornet was still hovering. Before I'd time to protest more, she darted over to Lucia and gave her a closer look. Then she was back in front of me and brushing my hands away. Because of the hornet I dared not do anything but let her look. I know I'm not very big but by then because of the state I was in, the little fellow had almost gone back in on himself, like a tortoise does. Then I felt her fingers on him.

I whined "Please don't squeeze me...oh please don't...go and find someone else to play with...I'm 39, past my best...I don't feel like it...I've got a headache..." I wasn't just blurting but blubbing. She took no notice. She straightened herself and strode back to the doorway. I was still snivelling when the whole area suddenly became brightly lit and the door opened again. This time it wasn't just 'she' coming through the doorway, there was a whole bunch of them.

I trembled as they approached. Then I trembled even more when they stood around looking at me. Some started peering underneath and touching my private parts, pulling my cheeks apart. I was shaking and snivelling. I felt like a small boy who'd been caught by the women in the street for doing something like knocking on all their doors, who stand around with their arms folded, looking down and making comments while they wait for mum and you know as soon as she gets you home you're in for a whacking.

Despite the dread, I tried to make out who they were. They were all about the same height and size though not as tall or full as the first one, but were all about the same age, twenty, thirtyish, although one appeared older. The original one did all the talking and pointing but soon they were all talking. I tried to make out their language (Japanese? No, not rasping enough, Chinese? No, too melodic. Not anything European. They didn't look Asiatic or European, something in between, Indian perhaps). When another slid her hand under my testicles and giggled and I saw what I took as smirks from the others, I was blubbing "Leave me alone...let me go...it's not fair."

The older one, sounding reproving, said "Lathia."

Upon which 'Lathia', the one who'd been touching me stood upright. The older one then clapped her hands. At this the others, including those looking at Lucia, stopped talking and looked towards this older one. She held up her left forearm with her palm towards me, gave a bit of a smile and said "Susem."

Seeing I didn't respond, she swept her hand around, indicating the others and again said "Susem." The others then smiled at me, the smiles you get from people when you're introduced to them.

I blurted out "Daniel Michael Collins," but sounded like a squeaky ten year-old.

She pointed to herself and said "Paceillo." She pointed to the others, giving their names. As she did they each raised their palm to me. I couldn't take in all, though I took in "Tearo," the one I'd seen first. There were nine of them. I began to relax, just a little.

'Paceillo' next raised the index finger on her right hand and said "Hax din," she then pointed to her right eye and said "Hax arn."

I cottoned on. I pointed to mine "Right eye," and soon I was pointing and saying "Nose...mouth...teeth..." She looked upwards, beyond me, gave a sweep of her hand to the hornet. "Knee...leg...foot..." and as I did, I was so conscious there were nine pairs of eyes on me. I felt stupid pointing to the various bits and calling them out but I was so relieved all appeared friendly. Some repeated the words I said, as though they were at language class (like the kids in the village when I taught them). As they repeated the words I was thinking, either they were taking the mickey, for they must have been educated and at least one of them have some knowledge of English, or if they were genuine, something very odd was going on.

Lucia started wailing again so I pointed to her saying "Lucia," then tapping the side of my head, "insane, mentally ill." From their expressions they appeared to understand. But I'd another shock with what happened next. Paceillo turned towards the doorway and called out "Terbal." Through it came, at shoulder height, a white misty, head-sized ball with tangled fronds hanging down, it looked like a jellyfish. It whizzed through the air to Paceillo. She cast her head in Lucia's direction. It went and hovered over her for a couple of moments then whizzed back through the doorway. I was still in a state of surprise when it reappeared but I was putting my hand to my mouth. Behind it, also floating in the air but at knee height, were two silver coloured snakes, though when I looked again I saw they were separate little shoe-like things. They formed in an oval around Lucia, they then dropped to the floor. Making a whirling sound, both they and Lucia then floated up into the air and just as fast as they had come, they and Lucia, her wails and all, disappeared back through the doorway.

I was worried. What were they going to do to her? What were they going to do to me? Part of me was thinking "I'm going to stop drinking cachaça, I'm having a dream, a bad one." I pinched myself, like I've read people are supposed to do on such occasions. There was no need. Another part was thinking "I've got to get away before anything does happen to me." And at once I was working on a getaway plan.

As the Susem turned back to me, I bent over and touched the floor and said "Floor." After they had mouthed this I made to the outside doorway and said "Doorway." Then "Village," next "Home" pointing to the Pousada, then at myself and then back at the Pousada, followed by a cupping movement with my hand and a sweep of my arm gesturing them to follow me. I stepped outside (the first part of my scheme) and started down the ramp. By the time I was at the bottom, four of them including Paceillo, were walking down. She was the last out but as she left she called "Terbal."

I wasn't too worried about 'Terbal' coming along with us, the important thing was getting outside. All I had to do was to get them across to the Pousada (they wouldn't know their way in there but I did). So on I led, "Grass ...stones...prickly pears," everything I could point to, "gate...path...trees... door." I took them in the front (this stopped them seeing the side entrances). Taking them to the Pousada and noticing no one around, I thought something nasty had happened. But when I took them through the bar, saw the rarity of unconsumed drink, it was evident everyone must had left in a heck of a hurry. The TV was still switched on but with the sound down. "Television," they stopped to gape, it was showing the end of Globo's ColOsso (a terrible introduction to Brazilian television for anyone). On the bar was a jug. "Jug...glass...guava juice ...drinking," (it was the first liquid I'd had all morning). The wall clock said nearly nine. I needed to get them to my room as quickly as I could. I took them down the corridor, still naming every-thing. Once in my room I was able to implement the second part of my plan.

"Pants" (such a relief, I'd bit of dignity back), "shirt," then "trousers...sock... socks...shoes...watch." They were looking at everything else in the room (all was going perfectly). The next part was to really divert their attention. The clock on the radio showed almost nine. "Radio..." I switched it on, "..especificamente conforme as necessidades do cliente Copore Marcelo," (the local Radio Casablanca). They turned to look. I switched to the World Band and to 118, back a little and there it was, "This is London." First there was the music, the pips, announcer and then the news itself. I turned up the volume, "The fall of Sarajevo, further Serb outrages...Fishery talks break up...England collapses, 57 for 8 against Namibia..." (no changes there). With them looking, listening intently, I was ready for the next, last part of my plan.

I went to the dressing table and pulled open the bottom drawer. I took out my little Dell laptop computer. I flipped it open (that had their fresh attention). I switched it on, gave it time to come to life, then as quickly as I could had the illustrated OED program up on the screen. They saw me operate the scroll bar. They (just as I hoped) crowded round it. I stepped back. As casually as I could and without turning away from them, I slid my hand into the top drawer of the dressing table. I fingered, felt, found, extracted my passport and bankcard and slowly slid them into my back pocket. They were still engrossed in the computer to the point where one of them was scrolling up and down. With all their backs still turned (my plan had worked perfectly) I quietly tip-toed out of the room.

With the difficult part accomplished all I had to do was make it down the corridor. From there it would be easy. I'd have the cover of the line of trees leading from the Pousada to the road. Then I'd just leg it up to the park, the viewing platform, down the cliff-face paths and I'd be away (I'd never actually been down them but I was sure I would be able to manage them). London, Wexford, San Francisco and now Tabajara, I'd got away from them all.

So much for plans. I made it down the corridor alright but stepping outside I came face to face with a hornet hovering.

I turned around to retreat to the other end of the corridor. The Susem were looking at me. They were standing in silence, hands on their hips. I trudged back to them. I felt again as though I was that small errant boy.

I'd expected scowls but they gave me smiles, though I wasn't sure if they were out of friendliness or forbearance. They intimated they wanted to go back with me into my room. Inside, they indicated they wanted to take some of the things.

"Take anything, take everything you like," I said, not really being in much of a position do to anything else. Of course, no sooner had I spoken than I knew they would not have understood a word. They took the radio, computer and a couple of other things. Then they indicated they wanted to take me as well.

What could I do but go? There were more of them than me. And anyway, it is never wise to argue with women. Better to let them think I was going with them willingly and so give me more room to manoeuvre until I could come up with something else. All the same I was more than a little apprehensive.

We walked back through the bar. They wanted to take the TV. I didn't want to appear to refuse. Not being in a position to explain the TV didn't belong to me, I pointed to the wall bracket and waved my hands, shrugged my shoulders indicating it couldn't be removed. We went down the path and towards the plane. Paceillo walked in front with Terbal bobbing alongside her head, the other three walked with me. They called out the names of the objects I'd pointed out on the way to the Pousada. I was impressed. They had picked things up much faster than the village kids ever did. They kept tugging at my sleeve calling "Danielmichaelcollins", pointing to the things I'd not mentioned, asking me their names. After a couple of times I had them settle for "Danny". Paceillo and Terbal were in conversation. I was surprised to hear sound coming from that misty ball. But as we walked, that wasn't the only inanimate voice I heard.

There were several more of the hornet things flitting about. I gestured to one of the Susem, who I'd learned was "Anuria", what were the hornets called? She said "Hen-ger". She called to one of them. It came over and flew around us like an amiable bumble bee. Anuria began talking to this Hen-ger, including saying my name. It gave out with a gabble of high pitched sounds, like some-one speaking on a record played at too fast a speed. It next gently touched the side of my cheek. As it brushed by it made a little purring sound like a cat being friendly.

On the walk to the plane I finally concluded the Susem couldn't have come from Earth. I did think they might be from America. But then they couldn't be. None knew English and Americans wouldn't be stopping at such an out of the way place as Tabajara. But if they weren't from here then where did they come from? And why were they here?

I went up the ramp. As I did I was greeted by the spectacle of not only the two lines of tiny shoes speeding out the doorway, but between them was Terbal and an assortment of little shiny creatures whizzing out with them. They sped out of the doorway as if on an invisible flying carpet.

But when I saw them heading in the direction of the Pousada unease came over me. This turned to worry when I saw them coming back. I knew there was going to be trouble. Not only were they bringing back the TV but a large chunk of the wall it was fixed to. That was bad enough but they'd nicked the video as well. Just as bad or even worse, I noticed as they whizzed back by they had also brought the dirty videos Rico kept stuffed down the back of the TV, the ones he puts on when his missus is not around. No sooner had Terbal and assorted wizardry returned from their thieving than I was in for another surprise, as big as any of the others.

As they flew through the inner doorway, out from it came Lucia. At first, I didn't recognise her. Not only was she clad in a long white hospital type gown but she was walking. She was walking unaided. And she was as silent as could be. There was something else. As she drew by, I saw her face no longer had the look of torment, fear, suffering that had always been upon her. Now her countenance had the softness of a nun at prayers. It's silly to say but as she passed me and I took in the touch of a smile she gave, I became a little moist round the eyes. I was seeing a miracle.

And I saw something else. I was not alone in watching Lucia walk across the floor. Through the doorway several Susem were watching her as well. Their faces were filled with smiles, warm smiles. In that moment fears of the Susem and everything about them left me.

A few minutes later with the rest of the Susem gathered about her, Paceillo said to me, and sweeping her hand round them all as she did, "Home?" What could I do but go?

I went with them through the inner doorway. I hadn't an earthly idea where "Home" might be, what it was, what it had in store.

It had been one heck of a day and I'd only been up an hour.

Curiosity also overcame apprehension. The Susem took me to the front of the craft (which they called a 'Veda' and this one, 'Kubber', I later learnt it is also a 'he'). Apart from a curve of seats at the back and a curved window around the front, the cockpit was empty.

A voice intoned as though counting. The Susem began counting along with it. The counting ended and this Kubber began to rise. Slowly at first then he shot off at a terrible fast speed. There was no difference in air pressure and when the Earth changed from brown to blue, there wasn't a sense of weightlessness either. Surrounding us cocoon-like were hundreds of hen-gers continuously switching on and off little lights at the ends of them.

After an hour and noting the position of the Earth as it appeared in the windows, we veered away from the sun. Shortly afterwards a cigar shaped craft came into view. Kubber, slowing all the while, headed towards it. By the time we were alongside, he was no bigger than a tug to a liner. It was surrounded by many other vedas. As Kubber approached the first of them a wall of thousands and thousands of tiny twinkling lights appeared.

As Kubber neared this bigger craft they switched off their lights and the vedas in front moved away. We passed between them and then flew to go alongside this craft which Anuria said was a 'Tocan'. I learnt later from Paceillo that this one's name was 'Sieba' and that it's a 'he' as well. When Kubber was a short distance away from it a thin band of yellow light lit along its middle. As Kubber came near, I saw it was an opening. He then flew into it.

We passed a short distance into this Sieba and in doing so were momentarily bathed in brilliant blue light. This was replaced by white light. We came to a halt. The Susem departed taking me with them. They took me to a travolator, then a lift. Lines of other parked vedas stretched away either side of us.

From the lift we passed through a spacious area filled with palms and ferns. It all reminded me of Kew. We walked to the far end, up a slope, through a doorway and into a big, dimly lit half domed space. The walls and ceiling were illuminated with star-like lights. I thought it was a planetarium but when I saw immediately in front several Vedas, I realised the lights actually were stars.

Three of the Susem took me to the wall of the dome. The others went away through a door. Apart from the wonderfulness of the stars, I was able, by looking along the side of the wall, to see the Earth. Anuria, one of the three with me pointed out a star which I thought was Sirius. That I gave it a name pleased her. She could only have distracted my attention for a minute for when I looked back to the Earth I had a shock. It was barely visible. Not only were we now moving but doing so at one heck of a speed.

Minutes later Paceillo reappeared. She and the others took me to a room thirty or so feet along and the same wide. It was well lit. In the centre was a table. Hovering above it was Terbal. On the table was my laptop. On its screen was still the OED program. Paceillo indicated for me to read from the screen. After I'd done this from "Why" to "Wicket," she waved for me to stop. Terbal to my amazement began repeating everything I had said. Although he did so with a thick teutonic accent and spoke slowly, I immediately grasped he had deciphered the language, and done so within a couple of hours.

At the end of the OED program is a section titled "How to write and speak English." I clicked to it. I started to read. After two paragraphs I stopped. Terbal repeated what I had said. I let him continue to read, which he did, again falteringly and with me speaking out the words he was unable to. By the time we came to the end of the first page he had grasped the lot. All the while, nine faces were on us, intently and in silence.

It was broken by Paceillo clapping her hands. Leaving Terbal, we went into another room. This was not as brightly lit. There were further tables laid out with plates, mugs and bowls and stools round them. It was meal time. The food was vegetables, fruit and water. There were even fork-like implements. After the meal I wanted to go to the lavatory (embarrassing but pressing). The only way I could raise the subject was pointing. Lathia, though giggling, led me down a corridor and pointed to a doorway. Inside was a squat down loo. I wondered what they did for paper. I was greeted with sprays of warm water then jets of even warmer air.

Returning, the three I had been with took me back to the observation dome. Paceillo and the others looked up and nodded as I passed. However, I wasn't in this space for more than a few minutes before I was taken back through the plants, down in the lift and into another one. The floor area was smaller but it had the same curved, transparent wall as the first, except it went the other way, as though the bottom half of the dome. In the front were a row of stools. Anuria motioned to me to sit on one.

No sooner had I, than a strip of the window in front changed from clear to black, then to a picture screen. Images of the outside of a tocan appeared. Anuria said "Sieba."

It was as though a camera was travelling along the side of it, close to its surface one moment, moving away the next. It went up over the top, down the other side and round again. Though the sides of Sieba were smooth the camera, as it passed along the bottom, showed it was flat instead of curved with a groove along its centre and circular indents either side. It was as though the camera was mounted on some free-flying thing. Because the screen was curved, the images so clear, the effect, as I looked was as if I was the camera zooming round.

It next went inside Sieba, past where we had first been, along the line of vedas, round the other side, where there were many more, down a sloping chute and into a level below. It sped the length of this which was huge, dimly lit and empty. At the end was another chute. The camera sped down and into yet another space. This was well lit but it was far from empty.

There were rows and rows of huge egg-like objects. I had no way of gauging their size, except by the vedas I'd been shown. So I could only guess that they were about 20 feet high. Anuria said "Soufin." When more rows of much smaller ones appeared, she said "Scule soufin," (I took 'scule' meant small). As she pointed at these the camera slowed, but when she stopped pointing it sped on past rows of other objects, some large, others even bigger. At the end the camera went upwards into another chute, a steeper one.

It emerged into another big, loftier space. This was brightly lit and looked like a workshop. At first, the camera looked down on groups of white, translucent domed tents. Glows of pulsing light came from them. Anuria said "Carlomone." Some were joined by tubes made of the same material. The camera flew past them and as it did I saw the first signs of activity. Anuria said "Sherpals." As she pointed the camera slowed, then circled a pile of rocks. Clambering over them were hundreds, thousands, of little silver robot machines. I could tell they were tiny because the hen-gers hovering above them were much bigger. The sherpals were hewing, drilling, cutting and carrying chips of rock to a series of little conveyor belts. They were working in teams, with different shaped ones doing different things. I could have happily looked for longer but the camera moved on.

It passed dozens and dozens of other teams of sherpals all busily working away. Some were in circular groups assembling hosts of different objects. More were carrying things and even more were stacking them onto lines and lines of shelves. Several times the camera veered to one side as if to miss fleets of laden flying carpets, just like the one Terbal had used. The whole place was a veritable hive of activity.

The camera left this level and went up to another. This one was as a huge garden. Again the camera at Anuria's pointing slowed and hovered here and there amid clumps of plants each laid out in a patchwork of little plots. Here and there were hedgerows of different bushes. I became really intrigued.

"Hay-lo, Darn-neigh." I didn't turn, I spun round. There, with a smile to her face was Paceillo. "Hello Danny," she said again, followed by "How are you?" and "I am pleased to meet with you." Standard phrase-book to be sure and imperfectly pronounced but you could have knocked me down with a feather.

Terbal had only read what was put in front of him. Here was Paceillo an hour later not only speaking in English, she had an understanding of it. Lathia then appeared. She greeted me in English as well. Seeing I understood, they spoke on. I tried hard not to become carried away by the significance but I was bursting with questions.

"We welcome you to our friendship...I hope you pleased with us...soon we will be arriving at our home."

I responded with "Hellos," "Thank yous" and "Will we?" And we were.

The screen went away and Paceillo, pointing her finger, said "See," followed by "Sieba slowing."

Except for the stars and vedas I saw nothing.

"See," Lathia added.

Then I saw what they were pointing to, a speck of grey.

The 'speck' grew bigger. And bigger again. Anuria said "La-ra Ling," and afterwards just "La-ra." Soon it more than filled the entire window, but I could see we were still a distance away for the vedas flitting over its surface were as mayflies on a whale.

Paceillo began talking again, at first I thought to herself. But almost at once Sieba started to rise up above this 'La-ra'. As he did I could see it had a flat top but not smooth as such, like a pitta bread before it's baked. It was the same shape as well. After Sieba had risen above La-ra, he flew slowly forward over its surface. There wasn't much change in its terrain but apart from the vedas, there were continuous flicks of light over its entire surface. But what struck me most was La-ra's size. It was just so big! I learnt later it was twenty five miles long and ten wide, bigger than the Isle of Wight.

When he came to the end of La-ra, Sieba turned and glided downwards then slowly along its side. As he did I could see, apart from yet more vedas, four other tocans lying alongside La-ra. There were others lying further out as well. I was reminded of American aircraft carriers and their task forces, except this one was on a rather grander scale. There must have been a dozen craft and all just suspended, seemingly motionless.

Halfway along La-ra, Sieba turned and flew towards it. Once again a wall of twinkling lights greeted us and after passing them, vedas glided from our path. An illuminated strip appeared and Sieba flew into it. This time there was further to travel before we were inside but the leaving and what followed, travolators and a lift, was much the same. But that was all.

I could sense from the looks on their faces that the Susem wanted to surprise me. Not that I'd not enough surprises already. But the moment the lift doors opened I could hardly believe my eyes. Paceillo exclaimed, almost jubilantly "Home! home!" as did the others. And what a "Home" it was.

19: ROBERTO

My name is Roberto Carvalho, I am 22 years of age. My family home is at Federação in the western environs of the city of Sobral.

My father is employed as the senior cashier with Banco do Nordeste in Sobral. My mother is a dressmaker. Nowadays she works from our home. My sister, Isobella, is two years older than me and resides with her husband Fabio in Fortaleza in the district of Vicente Pinzon. They manage his father's guest house, the Pousada Vida da Praia. My brother Paulo is five years my junior and is in the final year of his studies at Colégio da São Joao in Sobral.

Currently I am a student at the Universidade Federal do Ceará, the University of the State of Ceará, which is situated in Fortaleza. I am at the beginning of the third year of my course which is of four years' duration. On this course I study Journalism and Social Communication Skills. Along with me, also presently studying is a group of fifteen fellow students. At the conclusions of both our first and second years I have been awarded, out of all my colleagues, the highest assessments given to us by our professors.

On graduation from the University my intention is to seek assignation as a reporter for the newspapers of either Folha de São Paulo or Jornal do Brasil in Rio de Janeiro. I am also interested in working for the television News Services of O Globo TV or SBT.

Although I am still a student I have already been successful in having the Fortaleza edition of O Povo publish five of the articles I submitted to them. The first was the reporting of an omnibus crash by the canal on Avenida Eduardo Girão in November of the year before last. The latest was published one month ago and concerned the political campaigning for the forthcoming elections in the Serra da Ibiapaba. Though I have received only modest sums for my contributions from this publication, I consider this to be of secondary importance relative to the advancement of my future career. I am the only one among my colleagues at the University to have had any article published.

With the money I have received from O Povo, plus also some further monies I have accumulated working in the guest house of my brother-in-law, I have been able to buy, via my father when he recently visited Manaus, a Sony 30E camcorder. I am sure this will assist me in improving the skills required in television news and documentary reporting.

In weekdays during University term-time, I live with my sister and her husband at their guest house. At the weekends and during the university holidays I frequently return to my parents' home in Sobral. This was the case during the last weekend in April. I undertook this journey to collect the camcorder my father had purchased for me. I arrived at the rodoviária in Sobral off of the Teresina bound coach. The coach was scheduled to arrive in Sobral at 10 o'clock on the Saturday morning. Because of the inclement weather in all of Ceará it was late in arriving in Sobral. The fulsome rain, which had continued unabated for several days, had permeated the road. This presented difficulties for the driver of the coach to travel at the usual speed. Fortunately, my father, who came to collect me from the coach, was still in his old VW Fusca waiting to convey me to Federação.

Within a short time of arrival at our home, my mother informed me she had not heard for several days past from my Uncle Jorge, her younger brother. This was not normal. For many years, Uncle Jorge since he became Assistant Warden of Parque Nacional de Tabajara na Ibiapaba was in the position to telephone from the Park at no expense. However, as my mother further related, both she and my uncle have their birthdays on the same day, April the 22nd. This year it was Friday and she viewed he would have telephoned on that day. I suggested to her the probability that the functioning of the telephone cables was disrupted by the storms.

While I took heed of my mother's concerns, my paramount interest was inspecting the camcorder my father had obtained for me. Soon I was practising at becoming versed in its usage. Both my father and brother participated in my videoing. Afterwards, when I replayed the tape through the television both my parents and brother were enthralled with my recording endeavours.

After luncheon I visited, with my father and brother, the homes of several family friends. My mother did not accompany us stating she wished to remain at home in case my Uncle Jorge should telephone her. During our visiting I took my camcorder and videoed further those acquaintances whom we met.

On our return shortly after 9 o'clock, it was evident from the countenance of my mother that she still had not received a communication from my uncle. To calm her, both my father and I suggested that she should instead place a telephone call to Uncle Jorge. This she agreed to do if she had not heard from him by time we left for Church on Sunday morning.

During the morning of Sunday, before we departed for our worshipping, there were two telephonic calls. On both occasions my mother hurried to the telephone in anticipation they would be from my uncle, but neither of them was from him. One was from a friend of my brother inviting him, as the rain had then abated, to a game of tennis during the afternoon. The other was from my sister in Fortaleza who consistently telephones to my parents at this time.

Returning from Church my mother immediately placed a telephone call to my uncle. Within a few minutes of my mother placing this call, the operator in Sobral telephoned saying that the lines to the Tianguá exchange were continuously giving an engaged signal. My mother said that the operator had further informed her that the lines to Tianguá had been registering such a signal for a considerable time. She added that the operator had concluded the rainstorms may have dislodged some cable poles and were being responsible for the difficulty in obtaining a connection. However, my mother further said that the operator would try again at a later time for a connection to my uncle.

At 3 o'clock the operator telephoned saying she was connecting my mother to my uncle's telephone. As my mother held the handset to her ear I observed the expression on her face evolve from anticipation to agitation as she continued to wait for a response. Finally the operator interjected onto the line informing my mother that as there had not been a reply to the call, the line must then be made available to another telephone user. As my mother replaced the handset I observed she was unhappy. Both my father as well as I tried to console her but we were both unsuccessful in this endeavour.

Later, while my mother was in the kitchen cooking our supper and my father and I were viewing again the video images I had recorded, he told me of his discomfiture caused by my mother's unhappiness. He then proposed I accompany him on his journey to the bank on the morrow, and after we had arrived there, that I take the Fusca and travel to my uncle in Tabajara in order to ascertain his condition. And also as to why he had neglected to telephone my mother. Although I should have returned to Fortaleza and further my studies, because of both my parents' unease I agreed to my father's request.

My mother, when she was informed of my father's proposal and also of my acceptance, brightened. She then requested that I carry to my uncle her birthday present to him. This was a waistcoat which she had tailored.

In the morning my mother handed to me my uncle's present to give to him. She also provided a considerable quantity of food for me to eat on my journey. My mother further insisted on stowing many articles such as rainwear and galoshes in the front boot of the Fusia. After I had delivered my father to his place of work, I proceeded to drive to the Ibiapaba and Tabajara.

I was well acquainted with the route having travelled there on many occasions during the past years. When I was attending school in Sobral and resided at our home, I was accustomed to spending part of my vacations with Uncle Jorge in his residence at the Gate House of the Parque Nacional. The last time I had visited him was four weeks previously. This was for my article on the political campaigns being waged in the Ibiapaba.

I had not long departed the environs of Sobral when I was assailed by a fresh outburst of rain. Due to its ferocity I was obliged to proceed along the highway with caution. Because the Fusca is eight years old, its windscreen wipers were unable to remove fast enough the water which came upon the windscreen. Driving conditions were made further hazardous by spray generated from the vehicles travelling in the opposite direction. It was not until some minutes past 11 o'clock that I arrived in Tianguá. This was more than one hour later than I had originally anticipated.

Because the gas station in Ubajara does not possess álcool (sugar cane fuel) facilities, I refuelled at the station in Tianguá. The rain was still continuing as I wound down the window of the car and gave my request to the pump attendant. Engaging him in conversation, he asked where I had travelled from. When I had answered, he further enquired as to my destination. When I replied "Tabajara," he promptly crossed his arms and then swept them out across his body. At the same time he began shaking his head, saying as he did so, that the road up onto the Ibiapaba was closed. He then said "Bad things on the Ibiapaba, do not travel there, see." Upon which he pointed his finger in the direction of the rodoviária.

On turning my head in that direction I observed a large number of people crowded under the nearby boardwalk sheltering from the rain.

I was expecting more of what I had already seen, but the 'Home' over which the Susem so effusively proclaimed wasn't like that at all. As the lift doors opened, there before me was a grove of trees and a vista of rolling countryside.

A hay meadow sloped down to a hedgerow with more trees a quarter mile distant. Beyond them were further fields stretching away to woodland hazing into the horizon. I could have been back in Ireland or the west of Wales. But this was just the beginning.

I would have looked for longer but with a tug to my arm I was taken up the dry earth lane by which we had been stood, through the grove of trees, at the end of which there was another sight to astound. Not of fields or trees but terraces with steps and buildings beyond. For half a mile they curved away in a gentle arc, some in stepped storeys, others rising sheer. And beyond them was a surround of steeply rising hills.

With the Susem I climbed the terrace steps and when we reached the top of them, I was stood upon a most grand boulevard. It was wide and paved with smooth flagstones. A balustrade stretched all along the terrace edge and on the other side were houses and halls. With their arches, doors and windows, graceful decoration here and there, they had an enchantment which pleased my eye. But as I stood and looked I saw something else. Other Susem were there.

They were not close by but I could see them sat at tables as though outside of some café. But again I was tugged on, across the flagstones, through an archway and into a small courtyard. We crossed this then went through a doorway and along a long corridor at the end of which was a huge hallway. Not only was it huge but grand also. Fluted columns reached up to a white moulded ceiling high above. Something, marble perhaps, glistened from panelled walls and more, in large chequered squares of white and grey, composed a polished floor. Grand though this was, it was little more than an anti-chamber to the splendour that was to come.

At a brisk pace across and then along this hall the Susem took me, past columns, through archways. All nine were now in a circle around me, their pace propelling me on. From them I heard not a sound, my footsteps was all there was. At the end of the hallway was a pale gold light. On we went, and as we did I saw this gold light was shimmering.

Even before the last columns were past I heard the sound of water tumbling and sensed a moistness in the air. Falling water it was indeed, and as we reached the hallway's end the tumbling sound became a roar.

From the hall we stepped upon another terrace of flagstone and balustrade beyond which a mere few feet away there was a waterfall. It was fifty feet perhaps more wide and as I looked up I could see it fell from far above.

However, this falling water was but a veil to the wonder which lay beyond.

I would have stood and looked but again I was tugged on. I was taken along the terrace and from under the waterfall. I looked down to see where the water poured and saw that it fell a hundred feet and more. And from where it fell there rose fountains of mist and spray with arcs of rainbows all around. Along the terrace we still went, it now curving out beyond the falls. As their roar and spray began to fade I saw what lay below.

There were many terraces cut from steep hillsides. Beside them were buildings carved in and from the rock itself. They reminded me of those in Petra, such was their colour, size and style. On the terraces were many other Susem, strolling, standing, others sitting.

Looking back to the falls and fountains, I saw the water from them flow into a large maelstrom pool from which, in turn, it tumbled down a cataract, whose sides then widened, slowing the water into a river. Across this river lower down were three bridges, all with identical slender single spans. I wanted again to stop and look but still the Susem urged me on. And as they did there were so many other things which caught my eye but alas, again I was tugged on. There were plants, flowers, and as I was hurried by I caught their scents, honeysuckle, rosemary. Creatures like birds, butterflies flew about them. Stone slabs, ornately carved, made the terrace walls and pathway. Both had me recall Gaudi in Barcelona.

The sky was the colour made by a setting sun through the haze of an autumnal day. All was bathed in its lustre of golden light. The path changed to a flight of steps which went upwards then around onto a headland and I stumbled breathless to the top. Here the Susem stopped and thankfully, so could I. Though they were silent I was gasping. But when my breath returned and I saw what lay beyond I became silent too.

The river flowed into a lake, oval in shape, which stretched some distance, its far shore disappearing into the haze. There was silence. It was broken, momentarily, by the sound of a flock of swimming, swan-size birds taking to the air, then flying away low over the water. Silhouetted against the light off of the lake were a number of masted barge-like boats. Their sails were furled and all, seemingly, drifting languidly, noiselessly off of the near shore. As we stood there, still in silence, I saw the light, the centre of which appeared to be beyond the lake's far end, begin to dim. Strings of lights appeared along the terraces below. Others shone from windows and doorways. The light in the sky dimmed yet more, its glow catching upon small streaks of cloud, colouring them a redder gold. I sensed the cool of a light breeze and heard faint sounds of voices now carried up from the terraces below. All reminded me of Turner's paintings, his sunsets of Italy especially. I've rarely seen such a splendid end of a day.

And I began to grasp again the magnitude, the splendour of the Susem achievements. Somewhere in space was this perfect, idyllic domain. I recalled too, from my schooldays, lines from Keats, his Chapman's Homer and "Stout Cortez silent upon a peak in Darian." (Except of course I wasn't master as Cortez, not even noble enough for a savage). I looked at the Susem. They were grouped together, silent, their faces as they looked towards the setting light were in profile. The last rays lit upon their cheeks and brows, the breeze gently blew back their hair. They had an aura of serenity, majesty. It was they who were noble.

The air began to cool and the light fade. In that gloaming the Susem, now with smiles, turned to me as though seeking acknowledgement for the wonder of their achievement. Which of course I was so wanting to give. Lathia, finally breaking the silence said "Good 'ere innit?" (and I swear I heard her sniff).

Paceillo clapped her hands, upon which we trooped down further steps which lay the other side of the headland and onto the first of the terraces. Apart from having a sense of humour the Susem had taken me to where we were headed by way of the 'Pretty Route'. Terbal, had taken the direct one.

We went inside one of the first buildings we came to, then through several rooms in the last of which was Terbal. Other Susem were there as were other Terbals (later, I learnt they're called 'Sinteens'') There was also a strong lemony aroma in the air.

I was a little surprised inasmuch as both Susem and Sinteens didn't make much ceremony of my presence. "Laid back," "unfazed," were words which came to mind. I was disappointed. The Susem were sat around a large table, the Sinteens hovering above. On the table were the television and video Terbal and his helpers had 'lifted' from the Pousada. The power leads from them were connected to one of the egg-shaped scule soufins. Also on the table, apart from some of Terbal's little helpers, were the videos which had been behind the television.

"Ah Dommy, power ve haf, picture not, you vil show us, ya?" said Terbal, as he eventually acknowledged my presence (he may have managed the language, but he was still terribly teutonic, including calling me "Dommy"). Despite being an advanced civilization they were unable to operate the video. However, I knew something they didn't. I knew what was on those videos, well some of them. And if I got the video to work they would inevitably insist on playing them. I was in a dilemma.

There I was surrounded by two dozen and more women, their eyes were on me, the video and doubtless the tapes as well. If I made the video work and they saw what was on them, what conclusions would they draw about me, and the rest of humanity? If I pretended I didn't know how the video worked and they did manage later to fathom it out, they were going to see what was on the videos anyway. And what would they think of me then? Either way I was going to be in for it.

I tried to explain to Paceillo and others who had been with her earlier learning English, as well as to Terbal, that the videos weren't mine, that they were 'bad' videos. What I said had no effect on them. Paceillo just said, and in a tone almost commanding, "Picture."

The first one, "A Day in the Life of a Travelling Dildo Salesman," was bad enough but after that it was downhill all the way. I was so embarrassed. They watched it in near silence. But when the Susem saw the next video, "Cirkus", they started laughing, especially over the bit where the big fat women with almost nothing on are riding round on white horses and all the dwarfs dressed as clowns complete with painted smiles and pointed hats, run out of little doors in the ring, drag all the women off of the horses and then have them away in the sawdust. On it went one after another. The thing about such videos in Brazil, it professing to be a deeply devout and religious country, is they don't make any there. Also they are usually all from Europe rather than America. I remember Rico telling me that the American ones were "too timid" for the likes of Brazilians. A few were dubbed but most were just sub-titled. In some of them the dialogue could be heard, including one in English, "Hamlet, To Do or Not To Do," and there's an awful lot 'doing' it, everyone is, including Hamlet's mother (to my mind it's no way to introduce strangers to the work of Shakespeare).

I expected the Susem to be disgusted with what they were seeing for the videos are truly shocking. But apart from when they laughed, they showed no signs of disapproval. Not even over the one about the Borgias, including the scene where the women are doing naughty things to the Pope on the banqueting table and all his robes get stained with fruit and goodness knows what else. The Susem appeared to be more interested in the decor and were more quizzical over the action than anything. But when they came to view the last part of the last video their reactions changed somewhat.

This one, "The Autobiography of a Flea", I was dreading. All of it is bad enough but the last scenes are utterly depraved (it's no wonder it is still banned just about everywhere). The scene where the bishops with big willies are debauching the novice nuns is bad enough but that's nothing compared to what they and the Mother Superior then get up to in the belfry (I can never hear church bells ringing without remembering that particular bit). When those scenes came on I could have hung my head in shame. However, what I heard from the Susem weren't sounds of disgust, not even disdain, but inward gasps and more than a few at that. Some of them, Tearo especially, were most attentive to the bishops' doings.

At 8 o'clock the videos ended. Apart from being shamefaced and sheepish I was feeling peckish (and I could've done with a drink as well) but Paceillo said it was time for sleep. I wasn't going to argue with her even though I was hungry. One of the others, Milophenia led me out to the terrace, into another building and then to a room inside.

"You rest," she said.

In I went, the door closed. But rest was the last thing on my mind. I was buzzing. There was a bed, pillows, cover and a bathroom off to one side. I was wide awake with the awareness that I had lived through the most momentous day of my entire life. My head was filled with questions fighting to get out. I stopped pacing up and down and sat on the bed. There was a strong chocolaty smell. I don't remember a thing after that.

It was mint in the morning. Not only did it wake me but I was as fresh as a daisy. Milophenia then reappeared. "You eat?" she asked.

Having said "Yes," she took me to the front of the building and the other Susem. They served me a plate of bacon. At least it looked, smelt and tasted like bacon but it was kangaroo. That's what the creatures the Susem showed me later and which they said it came from looked like. I also smelt the same lemony aroma of the evening before.

During the night the Susem had made major strides in English. While their pronunciation and intonation were sometimes odd to my ears, I couldn't but be impressed that they had gained such fluency and in such a short time. But as a result we were able to engage in conversation. Some of the things they told me I understood, but many I didn't.

They have been travelling for eight years from Sirius (that meant they had been travelling nearly as fast as light). I gathered this from the maps they showed. And impressive maps they are, when one edge is pressed the image moves, a press on another edge actually enlarges it. On one I noticed their writing and how similar it is to Japanese. However, the Susem aren't from Sirius. Anuria said that close by Sirius was the end of what she called a "Time Tunnel" through which they had travelled. The 'Tunnel's other end, from what I could gather, is near a star we call Epsilon. From the little astronomy I know, Epsilon is in Canis Major and that is hundreds of light years away.

Everything we discussed involving measurement and time had to be forever recalculated. The Susem count in units of eight rather than ten. A thumb counts as 'four' or a half. Their day, a little longer than Earth's, is split into 32 'hours', 'minutes' and 'seconds' (which, in turn, are divided into 32 smaller units, and funnily enough they are called 'Points').

The planet the Susem come from, they called Sin-cu-ra and has seasons like Earth. Their 'year' is a few days longer than ours. Sin-cu-ra orbits another star in Canis Major which they call Saldees and isn't much different in size than our sun.

The Susem's basic unit of length, 'sayer', is about five feet and is divided or multiplied by 32 and so on. Their unit of weight, 'soun', is near enough a kilo. Once we had those things sorted out it was easier to converse.

After the Susem had explained Sirius and Epsilon I asked about the hundreds of years they must have taken travelling between the two. Did they go in hibernation, did they just sleep? They just looked at me as though I was stupid. Anuria attempted to explain that in this 'Time Tunnel' between the two stars, 'time' doesn't exist but I still couldn't comprehend.

I asked where we were. More maps. We were near the Asteroid Belt. In the four hours we had taken to reach La-ra we must have been travelling at more than 30 million miles an hour. I asked when they would be bringing me back to Earth. Paceillo said "Today."

After breakfast Paceillo said she and some of the others had things to do but three of them would show me more of La-ra. I felt as though I was being treated like a pupil starting at a new school, where the first lesson had finished and the teacher was telling some of the others to show me around.

Off we set, Anuria, Tearo, Menpemelo and me. On leaving, I noticed the light in the sky was centred in the direction of the waterfall. I also saw a stream of Susem making towards the building we had first been in the evening before. The three took me down the terraces, across one of the bridges, up some of the terraces on the other side, then into an open countryside sort of area. As we walked they pointed to objects and creatures giving their names, most of which I promptly forgot. In turn I tried asking about them.

It's funny how so often that a question asked in all innocence degenerates a conversation into talking about sex. Sadly this is what happened. I asked, simply because I'd not seen any, "Where are all the men?" At first they didn't understand. I went on about male (pointing to myself) and female (pointing to them) but again they didn't understand. Tearo then grasped what I meant and explained why. It's not just the Susem but all the different forms of life they know of, and not just from Sin-cu-ra but all the other places they had been to or had knowledge of as well. There is a genetic difference between all the life they know and that of Earth. Apart from stunning me, it fascinated them, immensely.

All the life forms known to the Susem begin as male and then mature to female. When I said that on Earth there were two separate sexes, Tearo retorted this was wasteful. "What is the point," she said, "apart from procreation and providing pleasure to females, what sense is there in remaining male?"

We had begun walking alongside a field of grass. In it were kangaroo-like creatures. Some were grouped in circles of a dozen or so with other, lone ones in the centres of them. These, Tearo said were called "Apoodas" and were what we'd had for breakfast. Tearo then said "In the centre is a juvenile, or male, and those surrounding it are mature, female apoodas guarding it."

I asked what from, she said "The others."

When I asked why, I noted forbearance to her reply. "This group here," she said, pointing to one of the nearest circles, "as you can see (which of course I couldn't) is composed of the strongest females. These have selected the male they consider will be the best to breed with. The other groups are composed of other females who have been unable to compete with the stronger ones. They are obliged to pick the next best male and so on."

I then asked "What happens when the male actually comes into season, and the other males as well, what happens to them?"

Tearo said "The female with the best sense of smell will make the first mating approach, but if she is not the strongest or speediest she will be pushed aside by the one who is. There is sometimes initial fighting within the group but it is usually, after such a skirmish, quite orderly."

"After they've mated, what happens then?" I asked.

"The females just keep going until the male is spent."

"How long is that?" I asked.

"The actual procreation is completed within minutes but the mating goes on for days and days," Tearo said, then added that Menpemelo knew more about the habits of apoodas than she did.

Menpemelo who is less strident than Tearo continued to relate the mating habits of the apoodas. "When the females have finished with their chosen male," she said, "they continue to mate with any of the remaining males until they are also finished."

"What do you mean by 'finished'?"

"When the males cannot perform any more," and adding, "this is usually because they are exhausted by the continual mating to be of any further use to the females."

I asked about the 'season', how long did it last? Menpemelo said about twenty days. I asked what happened if a male wanted to stop mating.

"Males have no choice," she said, "females, after the initial mating give off a scent which causes the male organ to be permanently erect."

"What if males, through exhaustion or soreness do not want to mate?"

"Again, they have no choice," she replied, "that is another reason why the females are in groups. Should a male attempt to refuse to mate the females kick him with their hind legs until he does respond to their wishes."

As I cast my eyes over the apooda males I had half a feeling of pity for them. There they were nonchalantly munching away unknowing that they were in for days and days of non-stop gang-banging by avidly amorous females.

Menpemelo described the different ways other creatures from Sin-cu-ra behave during their mating seasons. All have a common thread. All are born male. They then procreate after which they change into females and progress to maturity. Tearo commented that the moment when a male is able to procreate it is at its most vigorous and thus provides not only better quality sperm but as she graphically put it, "Give a capable and sustained thrusting."

The conversation inevitably moved on to the Susem themselves. Though their mating is less forceful than the apoodas, from what they told, it's still rather vigorous. Tearo said that the Susem are in a "mateworthy" male state for about five years. They too have a 'mating season'. It lasts for about a month annually during their Springtime.

I then said, and I do wish I'd kept my mouth shut, "That means you only have the chance for sexual encounters during that single period of the year?"

After Tearo had said "Yes, this is correct," I stupidly blurted out "Human males are able to perform the whole year round."

It wasn't just the tone in which she said "Can they!" but the way she looked at the others as she did, which had me wish I'd not said anything. From the looks on their faces I could see the way the conversation could develop, I tried hard to change the subject. I wasn't entirely successful.

I asked about La-ra. What was the reason for the large area of parkland, lake and the waterfall. Menpemelo said they preferred travelling in conducive conditions. She said La-ra was typical of the places they live in. Anuria said on Sin-cu-ra all the Susem lived in such places. I said, half in jest, "What caverns like this?"

"Yes," she said and in all seriousness.

I was given a brief history of how the Susem had originally lived in caves, then terraces of caves carved into the walls of canyons. The canyons became covered and as their populations grew, they took to burrowing directly into hillsides and underground. Some of their 'cities' have populations of half a million and more. Transportation between cities is also underground. When I told them on Earth nearly all the habitation was on the surface they were surprised. Their responses were of how inefficient it was and wasteful too. The Susem do have some settlements above the ground. These, from what they described, are 'holiday villages' in nature reserves. In fact from what they said, the whole of the surface of Sin-cu-ra is one big nature reserve.

Anuria said there were small villages outside the surface entrances to their cities. She also said everyone from everywhere else they knew also lived below the ground. She then said that at first this was what they took Tabajara to be and had spent some time trying to find the entrance to the city they thought must be there.

I said they must have seen the lights of cities when they came to the Earth and other signs of human activity, such as farming. But Anuria said they had seen only water and clouds. Tabajara was the first habitation they saw. That is why they landed there, she said.

They did also say that at one stage in their past, some of the surface of Sin-cu-ra was used for agriculture but nowadays this too is also all underground, as is everything else they do. I said while that was all very well for them, on Earth we had not developed so far, we were unable to build underground chambers, let alone anyone actually wanting to live in such places. They however, didn't appear to understand why anyone wouldn't want to live beneath the ground. By then we had walked back to the first of the terraces.

The three of them stopped to talk with other Susem we met. There was the friendliness of greeting but on each occasion, after acknowledging my presence by a polite raise of their hand, those they met carried on talking as though I wasn't there. It was like when I was a child out shopping with my mum. She would forever stop to talk with the neighbours and I'd to hang around until she had finished. After the fifth time this happened I asked Anuria "As I'm not a Susem, why aren't those we meet noticing me?"

She paused for a moment then said "Why should they?" And after a further pause she added "If we did, others who are not from Sin-cu-ra but who are travelling with us, would consider it impolite to do so."

"Others?..." but before I could say more Tearo butted in saying the physical differences between myself and everyone else on La-ra were such that I would be looked on as a freak. Again I wished I'd kept my mouth shut.

Tearo continued, harrying me with "When I first looked at you and your companion (I took this to be Lucia) I responded in the manner I did because you appeared to be half male and half female."

"What do you mean?" I retorted.

"You have a penis as well as nipples and you have hair round them as well." Before I had even time to say that I'd known girls who had hair there too, she continued with her onslaught. "If you were a properly formed male you would not have developed nipples. To have them as a male is wasteful is it not?" She harried on and oh so assertively. I tried to get a word in but to no avail. But thankfully Anuria stopped her in mid-flow, saying it was she who was now being impolite.

I quickly changed the subject. "Others," I gasped, "you mean there are other beings from other planets?"

"Yes," said Anuria and in a tone as casual as could be.

"But they all look just like you," I said, though again I was soon wishing I'd not continued.

"Yes," said Anuria, and in the same casual tone adding "why should they not be so?"

I jabbered about the probability of humans and Susem looking alike was, in terms of in the randomness of evolution, rare enough but the chances of other beings from elsewhere looking the same was just too great to be. I got no further. All three stared at me as though I was spouting gibberish.

Menpemelo, with the air of grown-up sister talking to a younger brother, explained their facts of life. She said when a particular lifeform evolves to its highest level of achievement it transmits the mantle of its aura to the next lifeform best suited to develop it further. Evolution, as the Susem see it, is like passing the baton. "Life everywhere is, with certain exceptions, always alike," she said. For me this raised even more questions.

By then we were walking down the last steps before re-crossing the bridge. I was about to ask Menpemelo what did she mean by "mantle" and "aura" when my foot slid off of one of the steps and I tumbled down the rest. Before I had time to pick myself up, Tearo was jeering "Can you not even walk properly?" I'd no chance to say it was because the steps were so smooth that I had slipped, than she was saying "Like this."

And with that she was floating a couple of inches in the air. The other two were soon doing the same. All three then glided across the bridge, zig-zagging from side to side and calling out "Like this!...like this!" They were as children skating on the ice. In the space of a couple of minutes not only had the law of evolution gone out of the window but the one on gravity as well.

As they waited for me to walk across the bridge, I saw as I drew near that they were catching their breath as though they had been running. "Is it special shoes you have?" I asked.

"No," they all replied. And as they did, Anuria took hers off and floated up in the air again. As I looked, I'd another surprise, she only had two toes.

Not two toes exactly, there was a big toe but the other four were joined together and both parts were separate almost up to her ankle, her feet looked like lobster claws. Menpemelo seeing me looking at them, said "With certain exceptions, remember?"

She tried to explain how they levitated. It's something to do with concentrating, the more they did the higher they rose. But the higher they did the more exertion it was for them. While she was telling me this I saw Anuria pick up a pebble with her two toes then skim it across the water. Menpemelo also said levitation was something they learned in infancy. The Susem don't walk as we do, they glide over the ground. And that's why they don't fall over.

Climbing the terraces all three kept egging me on with "Concentrate, concentrate, think of rising." Although I did, I couldn't, rise up that this. They were still egging me on and I still trying, when we branched off along one of the terraces. After a few yards we stopped by a building with tables and chairs outside. As we sat down another Susem came from inside, spoke to them, disappeared then returned with a flask and glasses on a tray.

The contents of the flask could have passed as a rather decent Meursault, lightly dry with just the hint of nuttiness. But that wasn't the only similarity. I went inside the building to where the Susem who had served us pointed to where the loo was. I also smelt something familiar. Groups of Susem were sat in circles around large egg shaped containers with the tips of connecting tubes in their mouths or hands.

Outside again, I asked what those within were smoking and what we were drinking. From what Menpemelo said, if they weren't grass and grapes, the plants from which they came, they were as near enough as to make no difference. And I recalled her words, "All life everywhere will always be the same."

As we drank, I looked at the park and fields beyond the terraces. I asked who looked after the land. Menpemelo said they all did, taking it in turns, but from what she said it is more of a pastime than a chore. She also said what I saw wasn't really where their productive agriculture was. Anuria added it wasn't just the farm work they shared but everything else. They also said that there were about 10,000 of them on La-ra all grouped in units of nine, which in turn were also grouped together in nines and then nines again.

After the wine we returned to where we had set out. There was a big queue crowding outside the building we had been in first of all. As we passed the queue Paceillo pushed through it saying as she did, that she needed my help. Something had gone wrong with the video. It wasn't really anything much, someone had been fiddling with the screen's vertical hold. I said surely she could have worked it out but she said Terbal was away and it was 'olden technology' which she didn't understand. I was also aware that the Susem sitting in the room were smiling at me.

Outside again, the four of us returned to the house and to the room we had breakfasted in, and for another meal. My watch showed nine o'clock but I was hungry. We were joined by the others, Paceillo being the last to arrive. I had asked Menpemelo how La-ra was run, who governed it, how was it policed. She was in the process of telling me that she didn't understand me, when I became aware that her attention wasn't really on me but Paceillo. Or rather her and Tearo who were talking in hushed tones and then glancing at me. The others stopped talking and were listening to what Tearo was saying as well. Then they were all looking at me. And they were grinning.

There were more hushed voices, this time from the others to Paceillo. This was followed by silence. Then Paceillo, after a pause said "We have been travelling for ten of your years. We have a further ten before we reach our destination. None of us of La-ra have had contact with males since we departed from Sin-cu-ra. You have said your males are continually in season."

As she spoke I was aware of the continuing silence from the others, that they were all still looking at me, the grins on their faces unchanged. Paceillo continued, "We ask that you assist us..."

Images of those encircled apooda males and thoughts of which one of the Susem was going to make the first move? Was this the purpose for the lemony aroma? Was it the reason they had brought me to La-ra in the first place? Would they knock me about? I blurted out "Not all of you, not in an afternoon, not at my age."

Needless to say I had the wrong end of the stick for Tearo immediately, said (and disdainfully I might add) "No not you, proper ones, like those in the images you have shown to us."

Though in a way relieved I felt more than little humiliated. Paceillo though continued, "...in meeting your males."

At that moment I didn't grasp the significance of what she had said. However, in my mind there was a vague notion that the Susem were intent on something ulterior. Something they had purposely not let on about. With this thread winding round in my mind, I did my best to explain and endeavoured to do so as light-heartedly as I could. "What you have seen on the videos is not typical of human males," I said. In the same jocular manner, I asked why didn't they bring some of own their males along with them?

They replied they had but all were now matured. Lathia promptly piped up with "I was male when we left," only to be followed by Pheterisco, half singing "So was I, so was I."

"Don't you have appliances providing sexual pleasure and fulfilment?" I asked. Tearo said they did but nothing in her view could match actual natural experience. As she spoke I saw, apart from Lathia and Pheterisco, all were earnestly nodding their heads. Trying to keep things light-hearted, I joked that they would be disappointed, human males in Susem terms tired easily.

But before I could say more Paceillo said, and in such a matter-of-fact tone, "As we will be on the Earth for a time we will be able to discover for ourselves, will we not?"

I was taken aback. I asked why, for how long, what were they going to do, what did they want? In my mind that thread began to tighten. At first, Paceillo just said "Patu Ling."

Noting no doubt my incomprehension, Paceillo added "Pa-tu, a companion of La-ra came to the Earth, we will collect him." Before I had time to ask more she, then Milophenia said it was time to rest.

It was so frustrating. Each time I wanted to know something, the Susem seemed to end the discussion. With my unanswered questions buzzing about in my head I sat on the bed. It was 12 o'clock when I was woken by the mint.

No sooner had I returned to the front room than all nine were gathered there as well. Before I could ask Paceillo about this Pa-tu, Milophinia handed all of us baskets and had us walking to the river. Two other Susem in boats rowed up. A few minutes later we were going to the lake. Not long after we were on board a barge.

The sails were raised and the barge set off across the lake. Within minutes of casting-off, most of the Susem were casting off as well. Like young otters they were, jumping and diving and swimming around the barge, then clambering back up ladders only to jump and dive again. All of them, with the exception of Tearo perhaps (she being on the fuller, muscular side), were a perfection of beauty and radiant health.

The barge came by a flock of swans (the Susem called them 'San-ga-vans') and as it did I observed a most enchanting scene. Several Susem were soon swimming amid them. Both birds and they appeared to enjoy each others' company. Not long after the san-ga-vans were around the barge than Pheterisco and Paceillo (they and me being the only ones on board) were throwing the san-ga-vans tidbits of food. The other Susem caught what the birds missed and fed it to them from their hands.

While this was happening, opportunity presented itself inasmuch as I had Paceillo's attention. I asked again about this Pa-tu. She told me not only about him but much else besides. Part of the usual Susem route is between Sirius and another star which I think is Procyon, near where there is another 'Time Tunnel'. La-ra had been diverted from this course in order to locate this missing Pa-tu.

Given that his size was similar to La-ra, my first reaction was that the Susem were mistaken. Paceillo said Pa-tu had gone missing sometime between 80 and 100 years ago. When I told her an object of this size hadn't come to Earth she appeared unconvinced. I added that even if it was out of control, because of its size it wouldn't have burnt up in the atmosphere but crashed. In doing so it would have caused a large crater, to say nothing of a noise, and no such crater had ever been recorded. Even if it had crashed in the sea, the explosion would have caused huge waves and flooding and no such things had been recorded either. Her conviction was still unshaken.

I asked her how the Susem could be so sure Pa-tu had come to Earth. Paceillo said that from the end of the 'Time Tunnel' they had been able to track Pa-tu's trajectory to our solar system. I asked her how were they able to do this. She said "By its wave signature."

Because I didn't understand, Paceillo explained what "wave signature" meant. Although Menpemelo had said that the Susem understand life everywhere was the same, they apparently perceive things very differently from us humans.

Paceillo began her explanation by picking from a basket some food and drop-ping it overboard. No sooner had it plopped on the water than a san-ga-van had nabbed it. She said "Observe the ripples." She dropped another morsel, which landed close by the first. As it did, she again said "Observe the ripples," then, "notice how the ripples of the second interact with the first." A san-ga-van swam by and gobbled up both bits of food. As it paddled away, Paceillo said yet again "Observe the ripples the san-ga-van is making and notice how they have affected the ripples made by the food."

I said the ripples caused by the san-ga-van had obliterated those made by the food. But Paceillo said "They may appear to have disappeared but the ripples caused by the food will have affected the form of the ripples made by the san-ga-van," She then went on to say that every ripple made on the water will affect the form of all ripples made later. At first I could just about comprehend her but what she said next I had difficulty with.

I said "Evaporation and rain will cancel out the effects of the ripples."

But Paceillo said this wasn't the case. Once ripples had been made, not just in water but in everything for that matter, air, solids, space, she said, they remained all the while there was time. No time, no ripples but everywhere else there were ripples caused by everything which had ever occurred. She said every ripple is caused by other ripples or a combination of them. Even if all the water in the lake was removed the record of the ripples would still remain (Paceillo had by then begun referring to them as waves).

I followed what Paceillo was saying up to then, though puzzled by her mention of time as either existing and not existing, but it is what she said next that I've not really been able to grasp. At first I said "Recorded in what, how can they be read, deciphered?"

"It is possible," she continued, "to read the wave patterns in terms of time. On some occasions it is as though they are layers one upon another. In other incidences it is possible to reconstruct where a pattern of waves emanated from by following them to their source of creation." This was easier to do, she continued, in some instances than in others. In deep space, she said, it is a much simpler task to do than elsewhere.

When Paceillo said they had been able to locate the waves made by Pa-tu, I exclaimed "What after 80 years?" She explained (and in all seriousness) that for the Susem this wasn't a particularly difficult thing to do, though she said it was laborious. She told me that the other tocans I had seen on our arrival were part of the fleet which had located Pa-tu's path.

Suddenly Pheterisco called out and, on turning round, I saw she was carrying a tube of buckets. As she called I noticed not only had we passed by the san-ga-vans but a number of fish were leaping from the water and heading in our direction. Soon I saw why. Following closely behind were a school of dolphins, at least they looked like dolphins (the Susem called them 'delosins'). In no time at all not only were they catching the fish but proceeded to present them to the Susem. Those in the water promptly took the fish from their mouths and threw them up onto the deck. And just as promptly, Paceillo, Pheterisco and me were popping them into the buckets.

Though this was amazing, what followed was more so. No sooner had the delosins finished fishing than the Susem were clambering onto their backs. Amid shrieks of delight and clicking sounds from both delosins and Susem, the pairs of them were dashing away then zooming back to the barge again.

And while this happened I was able again to talk with Paceillo about Pa-tu. Could it have crashed on the Moon I asked. She said they had checked, as they had the moons of Mars and the planet itself. They also knew, she said, from other tocans which had returned to La-ra after us, Pa-tu had travelled no further than the Earth. I said if they had been able to track its path to the Earth why hadn't they been able to locate the specific site where it had landed. Paceillo said this was something they would normally have been able to do, but in the Earth's case there is occurring what she termed a "phenomena", distorting their readings to meaninglessness and why, she added, they had to search by other means.

I was about to ask what she meant by "phenomena" as well as "other means" but our attentions were distracted by the barge nearing the far side of the lake. Soon it drew up to a small pier. The delosins leapt into the air then sped away. No sooner had we disembarked than Lathia, seeing me noticing the barge sailing away, said "It has a mind of its own."

From the pier, with Milophinia leading, we walked between tall, reed-like plants. With me wondering how we were going to get back, Milophinia gave a loud whistle. Soon there was a thundering sound, like horses galloping. No sooner were we through the reeds than I saw, waiting for us, white animals which were indeed identical to horses (the Susem called them 'saquinas'). There were dozen and more of them.

After exchanging nuzzles the Susem were soon astride these saquinas. Seeing I lacked their agility I was unceremoniously assisted onto Menpemelo's mount. With my arms clasped around her waist we set off at a gentle trot but in no time at all it was at a gallop. While I hung on for dear life, the Susem looked like part of the saquinas themselves. It was a fine sight, the saquinas galloping along together, just the sound of their hooves.

We raced for some miles across a plain then up onto a slope, but slowed as it became covered in bushes. When these changed to trees, the unmounted saquinas returned down the slope. The ones we were on took us along a pathway between the trees. The slope then became a steep hill and the path narrowed. We dismounted and walked with the saquinas alongside us. We then came to a glade.

By the glade was a small lake with a cataract of a waterfall flowing into it and another flowing out of the other side. The saquinas munched the grass then waded into the lake. Pheterisco opened the baskets. The others set off along a path up by the side of the cataract. Paceillo beckoned me to join them. Minutes later we stopped on a ridge overlooking the falling water. Here the Susem, except Paceillo, took off their tunics and climbed soundlessly to a ledge a few feet below. Still in silence, with Paceillo tapping my lips, they stood in a line with their backs to us. They then clapped their hands. As the echo faded the wall of rock on the far side of the cataract took to the air. However, it wasn't a wall as such but creatures which looked like butterflies, thousands upon thousands of bright orange ones. In a cloud they flew to the Susem and in no time at all the seven of them were covered from head to toe in a fluttering of orange. Paceillo whispered "Salts from the lake."

The Susem stood there laughing and giggling as the butterflies licked the salt away. When all the salt was gone the butterflies flew back to where they had been and became, as they folded their wings, a wall of grey again. With the butterflies gone, the Susem next clambered down the cataract, bathing in the pools, showering under the falling waters. Paceillo handed me some of their tunics to carry and we went back down the path.

The tunics had the texture and lightness of silk. However, when I squeezed a handful of the material it didn't become creased as silk does. It was the same when I pulled at it. Although the material stretched it immediately reverted to its original size. I also noticed, on the insides at the fronts, lines of little pockets.

Back in the glade I was in time to see a saquina, with Anuria astride it, stepping from the water. Both their bodies were glistening and shimmering in late afternoon light. Behind them stepped Lathia with another saquina by her side. As they and then the others flicked away the water from their hair and took their tunics from me, they seemed not to have the slightest care of inhibition. And in a way neither did I. To me (with the exception of Tearo) they were beauty and perfection.

Pheterisco had prepared the fish and had them roasting atop some hot flat rocks. As I delighted in the smell of their cooking, I saw a line of little black creatures each a fingernail long. Paceillo said “Morfs,” (though they looked like ants to me). They were travelling from the fishes’ remains to the far side of the glade. Evidently they were having fish for tea as well.

The fish tasted like tuna and the wine was good as well, like a young vihno verde. An hour later, baskets packed, Milophinia whistled to the saquinas. Not long after we were galloping again across the plain and to the pier. With a neigh or two the saquinas bade us goodbye and we boarded another barge.

This time we weren't alone. Not alone in terms of passengers, the barge was full. Or alone in terms of barges either, there was a flotilla of them. The light began to fade and clouds took on hues of reds and gold. There were more of them than the evening before. Mentioning this to Menpemelo she said it was one of the advantages of living enclosed. They decided how their sunsets would be. “That was why” she continued, “we were in a hurry last evening, it was the Searcher's turn, which includes us.”

“Whose turn now?” I asked

“Musicians,” she said, sweeping her arm around the barges and pointing to where we were headed, “and many more of them over there as well.”

As the daylight faded the barges became festooned with lights. The air cooled as a breeze came off the lake. While charming enough it became even better when the refreshment came round. As clarets go it wasn’t bad at all. However, the further events of the evening were, in some respects, an anti-climax to the day.

Not long after the wine began being served, those Susem at the front of the barges took up their instruments. They made a most terrible commotion, Chinese plinkity-plonk crossed with Greek caff. The moment they ceased, a similar racket started up from the far shore. On they went, one side playing after another, without harmony, rhythm or a single tune between them. When the barges reached the river and both groups came together the noise became nigh intolerable.

In the circumstances, continuing to partake of the claret was the only sensible thing to do, especially after the singing started. The moment the barges moored in the river the Susem started up, on the barges, bridges and along the terraces as well. They were terrible, Tibetan dirges are more melodic.

Not being in a position to do anything and not wanting to upset anyone, I endeavoured to bear the evening with my best behaviour. Though for me it was like being at one of those boring family festivities I used to be dragged to when I was a boy, where if I wasn't on my best behaviour I would get a telling-off and sometimes a smack. The only thing of interest was sampling the aunts' sherry when no one was looking. Even worse, because sometimes nobody did look, I'd keep drinking and fall asleep. Alas, this now happened to the claret and me.

And just as bad, I was woken with the same suddenness and remonstration. The tone of Tearo's voice was so like my mum's "Come on, wake up," a pause, then menacingly, "you've been sleeping," that I half expected the smack to be coming as well. However, it wasn't this I received but another surprise. We weren't on the barge, we were back on Sieba.

I only knew where I was when Menpemelo and Tearo took me into the upper observation dome. As they led me there and seeing it was 7.30 I was staggered that I could have been asleep for so long. Amid the further suffering from Tearo's tongue over my resting, I tried to figure how it was possible to move from one place to the other without waking. But before I had time to ask, the pair of them went away leaving me on my own. As La-ra filled most of the dome's window I took it we could have only recently left. I also noticed there weren't any craft lying alongside. There were, however, many more flicks of light about La-ra's surface than when we arrived. I was looking at these lights as I continued to wake myself up, when to my surprise both they and La-ra suddenly disappeared, the dark and stars of space replacing them.

No sooner had I risen from my seat to see where La-ra was, than I heard "Hello Danny." And once again, I was in for yet another surprise. The voice wasn't Susem, nor was it Terbal's. It was a deep, male, almost booming, echoic voice, though soft sounding all the same. I turned to see who was there, but there was no one. As I did the voice again said "Hello Danny." This time though, there was a bit of a chuckle in his tone. I was still looking to see where he was, when and in the same jovial tone, he continued, "I am Sieba. Now that I have been programmed I can talk to you and you can talk to me."

"Oh," I said. By then, having had so many surprises I was fast becoming, after the initial reaction, almost nonchalant. I was suffering from 'surprise exposure' (or maybe it was just the drink). I replied to Sieba as though I had known him from before. "You can, can you?" I said.

"Yes," said Sieba, "Terbal has programmed all of us. Now we can all speak to you and all your friends."

"We? Friends?" I said.

"Yes, all your friends of your planet. Terbal says you can help us find Pa-tu Ling," then after a pause, "if you let me be your new friend I will be your special friend."

"Oh, you will, will you?" (and unease crept through my mind).

"Yes," said Sieba, this time sounding as if breathless, then after another pause, "I have to go now, Terbal is asking me to finish preparing the dispatch bay ready for Kubber." He had another pause, then said, "Until we meet again, goodbye Danny." With that, I was left alone again.

From the dome I saw between the surrounding lines of vedas, the Earth. That I could see it surprised me, that it was the size of my thumbnail was worrying. It was not yet 8 o'clock but unease began creeping back. La-ra had travelled much closer to the Earth and this meant alas, that the Susem were serious in what they had said. With the appearance of Tearo and Milophenia a few minutes later my unease grew the more. “Come, Danny, we are departing,” Tearo said. A few minutes later I was boarding Kubber.

Just as Sieba had said, others were indeed programmed for English. The moment I stepped inside Kubber I was greeted in laconic Californian with, “I'm Kubber. Launch time minus 10,000 points, and counting.”

It wasn't just Kubber who had been programmed but the hen-gers too. Their greeting was a massed high pitched “Hadodani.”

There were many more hen-gers than before. They were clustered around the walls and ceiling. But the hen-gers weren't the only objects on board. As I looked around and saw the menagerie of machines, nodded and waved acknowledgement to their “Hadodani”s, I asked Milophinia what they were and what were they for. “To trace Pa-tu,” she replied.

With Kubber's “Minus 7,000 points and counting,” Terbal wafted by, a carpet laden with further objects flying behind him. As he drifted across the area he too was greeted by the objects.

By “4,000 points” the rest of the Susem arrived and received the same multi-toned reception. At 2,000 points and with the outer door closing, Sieba boomed “Goodbye Kubber, take care of Danny, he is my new friend,” and just as they closed, Kubber's, “Shall do.”

At 1,000 points I was sat with the Susem in the front of Kubber. At 800 they were calling out his countdown with him and finally his “Away!” The side of Sieba slid open and the area became bathed in blue light. The lines of other vedas immediately in front of us moved away. Beyond them the wall of lights switched momentarily off then on again and clearing a path as they did so. However, Kubber didn't appear to move.

I asked Anuria, why was he still stationary. But Kubber replied “Secondary wave orientation,” then, “wait.” Once again, I wished I had kept my mouth shut. No sooner had Kubber spoken than he began sliding out from Sieba. He wobbled back and forth a few times as though trying to find his balance, paused for a moment, then shot away so fast that within seconds Sieba was little more than a speck. Also within those seconds Kubber became surrounded by a cocoon of hen-gers. I asked why they were surrounding us. “Field protection,” said Kubber curtly.

Anuria added "They generate an area of energy around them. This neutralises, counters Tertiary waves in Kubber's path."

“Yup,” confirmed Kubber.

“What happens if the hen-gers are hit?” I asked.

“Replaced,2 replied Kubber.

Half an hour after leaving Sieba the Earth was filling the windows. In that half hour not only was I in wonder at the Earth as it increased in size but at seeing the brilliance of the stars as well. However, as we sat there in silence my uneasiness continued to grow. The Susem appeared to have given not a thought to the reception they will receive on Earth. This will, in all probability, be hostile to them. All nine seemed to be under the almost naive belief that they could just arrive on Earth, ask and poke about for their lost craft. That everyone is going to be, apart from a little backwardness, just like them, kind, civilised and trusting.

Yet at the same time here was a civilization which by comparison made the Earth, not just backward but little more than the Bate's Motel of the Universe. Apart from having amorous requirements, the Susem had so much knowledge and technology which would benefit all on Earth. There was also another important consideration. For the first time in my life I was onto something really big. I was in a unique position. Not only did I have the Susem's confidence, I had unrivalled access to everything they had developed. The money I stood to make made what I had stowed in Miami appear peanuts. How could I possibly pass up such opportunities?

My thoughts were disrupted by the sight of the hen-gers in front suddenly darting away forward from us, then veering slightly to our right. All told there must have been several hundred of them. At the time, the Earth was in shadow and because of the sun's glare, Kubber's windows had become darkened. Despite this darkness, the lights of these hen-gers, even through the lines of others which had replaced them, were visible for some distance ahead of us. Within seconds from where they appeared to be there was a brilliant flash as though there had been an explosion.

No sooner had I shouted "What is that?" than Terbal's excited voice could be heard. I didn't know what he said but it caused a response from Kubber. Despite his speed he slowed, stopped then turned around.

Not long after, Terbal was in the cockpit asking me "Vat ist dat?"

As it happened I knew. I also knew that at that moment not only were we 25,000 miles from Earth but above the equator and someone was minus a communications satellite.

As Kubber edged closer and I saw the blackened husks of hen-gers covering its remains, I explained what it was or tried to, and what it did. I also told Terbal and the Susem that satellites cost a lot of money. I asked why it was necessary to attack it.

"Because it was a threat," said Kubber.

"How could it have been a threat, it wasn't even in your path?" I said.

"It was making waves. They confused me," though this time Kubber sounded defensive, then after a pause added "sorry."

In the circumstances what could I do but say "Don't do it again."

Kubber turned around and continued on his way. After the Susem apologised for the satellite, and my reply it was nothing to do with me, I was left with my thoughts again. What would happen when we landed? Would everyone in Tabajara run away? What about Friday when they did? They would have been bound to have told someone, the police, the army. Would there be trouble? And what would happen to me? Some of the police don't like foreigners? Besides the worries, though, there was also awareness of the opportunities. All those vedas doing trips round the Earth at $1,000 a head, even on as little as ten per cent commission there was a fortune just waiting. The material of the Susem's tunics, there would be a huge demand for that, and I was in a position to have the patent,

Twenty minutes later my thoughts were again disrupted as I witnessed once more what Kubber meant by "replaced." One after another of the foremost hen-gers' tail lights ceased blinking. Next they became blackened, glowed red then they disintegrated. "Atmosphere friction," said Anuria. The hen-gers behind them moved forward taking their positions. As these hen-gers burnt they too were replaced.

Five minutes and many hen-gers later the "friction" ended. Though still descending I could see, with the sun glowing from behind the curve of the Earth, also that Kubber was travelling south-westwards. I had thought that as we descended, lights of cities would be visible but I saw none. As Kubber came lower the sun's glow and the horizon both disappeared, leaving a near darkness. But I could just see we were travelling towards a blanket of cloud. I asked were we on course for Tabajara. After a pause Kubber said "Yup."

He began skimming along the top of the clouds. Then he called "Minus 10,000 points and counting." At 6,000 points, lights above cloud height appeared. As Kubber intoned "4,000" he was flying to the left of them. Although I had not seen it from the air, I could see we weren't above Tabajara but somewhere else, somewhere larger. By "3,000" Kubber also appeared to realise this. He did, however, switch on most powerful lights and then swept around the edges of those below. As he called, "2,000," I realised we were over Ubajara. On yelling this, Kubber replied "Aborted," followed by, as he flew back away from the lights "Adjusted." He then switched off his lights and we were in near darkness again.

Paceillo's "Kubber, how could you?" had a tinge of reprobation.

But he replied "Those waves," then after pause, "I'll go the way I came."

With this he flew alongside the Ibiapaba and even closer to the clouds. Monte Macambirá came into view and Kubber flew by the side of it. No sooner had the lights of Tabajara appeared than he switched on his. He also began his countdown again but this time from "3,000." However, before his, "2,000," Kubber was calling "Hazard...animate...dissuading." He repeated this several times. As he did, I could see we were again above the field opposite the Pousada. I could also see the lights of cars and trucks beetling away along the Ubajara road. Kubber had counted to "Plus 2,000," before he had called "Arrived."

I observed the people sheltering from the rain. But at that time I did not regard them further or the utterances of the gas station attendant. Instead, after he had returned with my change I drove onto the Ibiapaba road.

I had not ventured more than a kilometre up onto this road, when I was confronted by a group of soldiers blocking my path. They requested of me to halt. Seeing these soldiers in their waterproof capes puzzled me. The Military at the checkpoint at the intersection of Routes 2-22 and 0-71 had not ventured from their posts because of the intensity of the rain and had allowed traffic to pass unimpeded. But on this minor route I was being obliged to stop, even though the rain was pouring as resolutely!

One of the soldiers asked me where I was travelling. I replied "Tabajara." He then informed me I must not proceed along the road. Having travelled the distance I had and in the conditions I had experienced, as well as the purpose of my journey, I was not readily disposed to accept his command. I said that he must allow me to pass to ascertain the well-being of my uncle.

Upon hearing my exclamations several of his comrades came towards my car, one of whom I took be their officer. I again repeated my request to travel to Tabajara. He repeated what the first soldier had said. I asked of him the reason why I was being prohibited from travelling onwards. He informed me that the only traffic allowed on the road was down from the Ibiapaba. I stated that if vehicles could proceed down from the Ibiapaba it intimated I could travel upwards onto it. He shrugged his shoulders saying he was obeying orders. He then stated that there had been an incident in Ibiapaba and further added that most of people had already departed from there. He suggested, in the same placatory tone, that perhaps I would find my uncle in Tianguá itself. With this guidance I reversed the Fusca and returned to Tianguá.

Within half an hour of returning to the town and after enquiring from the proprietor of a café, I was successful in locating the whereabouts of my uncle. He was at the premises of a trader friend of his. Also with my uncle were his colleagues from the parks of both Tabajara and Ubajara. He was surprised at my presence but I was relieved to see him. Returning to Tianguá I had concerns that something untoward had befallen him.

I asked of my uncle what was happening. Why also had so many people descended from the Ibiapaba. The expressions upon his face and of those of his colleagues were of unease. He told what had occurred during the recent days. His colleagues also related their observations and experiences. I then noticed that my uncle appeared to be weary. I learnt that neither he nor his colleagues had slept properly for two nights. I suggested he returned with me to Federação and convalesce with my family. This he readily agreed to do.

Driving to Federação I managed to persuade my uncle to retell again his recent fearful experiences. I also tried to place into his narration the information his colleagues had also voiced. This was not an easy task for my uncle fell into sleep for most of the journey.

Listening to his disclosures, I became aware of the possibility of a strong news article. I was also filled with the notion that with my camcorder I could possibly produce footage for a television news station to broadcast.

By the time of our arrival at my parents' home I had resolved to return to the Ibiapaba. My mother was elated to see her brother and made effusive ceremony over his presence. Amid this exhilaration I informed her that I was departing again, that I must hurry to catch the Fortaleza-bound coach which departed at half past four. I speedily packed my belongings including my camcorder. After my mother had bade her farewell I drove to my father's Bank, parked the VW there, removed my waterproofed jacket from the boot of the car, deposited its keys with the receptionist and hurried to the rodvíaria. I arrived at 4 o'clock just in time to board the coach bound to Teresina. Fortunately I was able to take a seat for my journey to Tianguá.

Gazing from the coach window at the passing scene I noticed that the weather had become showery. Also I thought over the events experienced by my uncle and his colleagues. In my mind I further constructed how I would ascend the Ibiapaba.

My uncle told me that in the early evening of Thursday, he and the villagers of Tabajara had witnessed a series of beams of light emanating from the forest. They appeared to be above the trees then disappeared among them. The lights reappeared but much brighter than before. The electric lighting of the village, my uncle then said, began to flicker. At which moment the entire area of the village was suddenly bathed in strong light, "As bright as day," he had said. This brightness continued for some moments. It next swept across the village in the form of several beams. These proceeded to circle Tabajara. I had asked him if there was any sound accompanying these lights. He replied there had not been any. He also added that at the time there was an amount of mist floating about the village.

This and the silence accompanying the lights, he said, caused them to appear unworldly. When an imbiber from the Pousada Elana, where he and most of the villagers had been congregated celebrating Tiradentes Day, shouted "Espírito, espírito," others soon were also soon making the same cry. They exclaimed that they were being visited by ghosts and spirits of ill omen. These cries, as well as the beams of light continuing to circle the village, produced, so my uncle had said, a sense of strong apprehension within many of those present with him. Immediately, all of the villagers decided upon fleeing. In minutes, he further said, they were in flight along the Ubajara road and did not stop until they had arrived there.

I have learnt from my University studies how groups of people, when exposed to unfamiliar phenomena, are hostile and frequently consumed with apprehension towards it. I have also been taught that panic arising from a small group of people can be contagious upon others becoming alike to animals and stampeding. Also from my visits to the Ibiapaba I am aware of the extent to which its people are still ardently superstitious. Though nowadays they are Christians, their bygone beliefs have not departed from them.

I had further asked of my uncle why did not Padre Alves come to the aid of the villagers. To this my uncle laughingly retorted "He was getting drunk along with the rest of us and he fled as the rest of us as well. He was the one who drove the coach and crashed it, knocking the cable pole down!" This was the first part of my uncle's narrative. The second concerned the events of the Friday when the villagers of Tabajara returned to their homes.

On their arrival in Ubajara the villagers were mocked by its inhabitants who accused them of drinking more than excessively. But when the children, who of course had not been imbibing, testified to also seeing the illuminating beams, the people of Ubajara maintained it must have been the lights of Fernando Burity's helicopter. The villagers remained during the night in Ubajara. Some found shelter organised by Padre Alves in the school of São Miguel, others congregated in the square in front of the church itself.

The next morning, the appearance in Ubajara of the villagers came to the attention of the Prefect, José Neto who resides on the outskirts of the town. He ordered the local Polícia Militar to drive to Tabajara in both of their two vehicles. Upon their return, the police reported that they had not discovered anything to be amiss in Tabajara. They did state, however, so my uncle had said, that they would be preparing a report and laying charges against Padre Alves for traffic and vehicle misdemeanours. The villagers returned to Tabajara but were subjected, as they departed from Ubajara, to scorn from the townspeople for causing the coach accident which was delaying their travelling to the markets in Tianguá. They also chided the villagers for being backward, stupid and unable to manage their drinking.

On their return, my uncle along with others of the village assisted in pulling the Tianguá coach back up onto the road. Apart from a few indentations and scratches, the coach was in a condition good enough to travel the route to Tianguá. Its rightful driver was very concerned that the incident would be reported to his superiors. The telephone cable to the village was dislodged and only partly repaired by the afternoon of the next day. Upon his return, my uncle, like many of the villagers, took to his hammock.

In the evening my uncle again visited the bar of the Pousada. Engaging in conversation with other patrons he was soon aware there actually had been incidents occurring in Tabajara contingent to the Thursday night. The television set in the Pousada had been stolen. At the time this had been ascribed to the Polícia Militar. The 'Inglês', as my uncle called him, had also vanished. He had been residing at the Pousada and was asleep at the time of the villagers' departure. Although his possessions were still in his room, the proprietor's wife claimed some were missing. She had told my uncle their disappearance was also linked with the Polícia Militar.

Of greater puzzlement was what my uncle told of Lucia. To me Lucia, from the times I had visited Tabajara was a frightening demented hag. In my boyhood her howls filled me with dread. And when I suffered the misfortune of her espying me, a deep sense of unease would pass over my body. The villagers, when they realised Lucia was neither with them or anywhere to be found, concluded she too must have gone into hiding but was still within the village. By the evening when she did not reappear by the church as she usually did for food Padre Alves and others would leave out for her, people began inquiring as to her whereabouts. Some of the children asserted they had seen the ghost of Lucia. Although most people, my uncle said, disbelieved them, her 'ghost' was very much the topic of conversation in the bar that Friday evening as was the discovery on the pasture to the rear of the Pousada of Lucia's walking stick, of which, no one had an explanation.

The next day life in the village had been normal. People went about their routines as though nothing had occurred. The Tianguá coach resumed its usual service, although the driver was rebuked by his superiors for allowing its misuse. But there was still no sign of the Inglês or Lucia. My uncle, having not much work to do, ascertained these items when he visited the Pousada at noontime. He also added that a pair of fellows in the bar asserted they too had seen the 'ghost' the children had mentioned. But others with them in the bar retorted they had also imagined what they said they had seen.

The third part of my uncle's testimony regarded the events which occurred on Saturday evening. At nine o'clock as he had walked to the village on his way to visit the Pousada, he saw in the sky to the north, a brightness. By the time he had arrived at the Pousada this brightness had increased its intensity. He drew the patrons of the Pousada outside so that they could also observe the light in the sky. Although it was still to the north of them, they then noticed it appeared to begin travelling eastward. This light, so my uncle said, then disappeared. Some of those present with him, he said, concluded it was the lights of Fernando Burity's helicopter.

They were about to return to the bar when there suddenly appeared, rising up above the tree line from the direction of Monte Macambirá, beams of strong bright lights.

These lights began moving swiftly, so my uncle recounted, in the direction of the village. Upon which once again people began shouting “Espírito, espírito,” and ran to their houses to collect their children. I had asked my uncle if there was any sound of an aircraft approaching. And again he had said there had been none. He also said there was only a little mistiness in the air. My uncle then became partially unclear of the events which then ensued.

But from what he told, it enabled me to construct the scenes of the occasion. The beams of light were either brighter or more plentiful than those witnessed on the Thursday evening. They did not circle the village as had those ones. Instead they travelled directly towards it and then hung stationary over the grazing land to the rear of the Pousada. During this time there was much commotion. Villagers scrambled into or onto their modes of travel and began proceeding briskly along the Ubajara road.

My uncle, being without his truck, departed along with some of the others in the back of the proprietor of the Pousada's. However, as they began alighting on to it, one of his fellow passengers gustily drew their attention to the area of illumination. Looking in that direction they saw a figure in a swirling shroud of white with its arms cast upwards. I had asked my uncle if it was a he or a she. "A 'she', it was Lucia, it was the ghost of Lucia," he had averred.

I had always considered my uncle, as he does not hail from the Ibiapaba, to be above the superstitions of its people. But when he related this part of his narrative I detected unease within him. No sooner had the fellow exclaimed, than the 'ghost' began waving her arms towards them. It was as if my uncle had said that she was inviting them to join with her. Again I had asked him if there was any sound but he replied there was none. The attentions of the 'ghost' caused those in the back of the truck to become agitated. "We struck the back of the cab for Rico to hurry and get us from there, we were that frightened," my uncle said.

I had asked how he knew it was the ghost of Lucia. His response was it must have been Lucia's because in real life she had been a cripple and she could not have danced as the ghost had done. To my view, here was yet another example of the powerful effect of hysteria on the thinking of people. I was able to establish this point further from him when I asked how could it be possible to make out her features from such a distance. To this question he was unable to provide a satisfactory response. All he had to say was, "I just knew it was Lucia, we all did." However, this was not the last of the events my uncle experienced on that evening.

He travelled with the others down the Ubajara road. When they arrived in the town it was empty of the inhabitants. The villagers did not know then that the people of Ubajara had also received a visitation of circling beams of light. Nor that all of its inhabitants, including José Neto and the Polícia Militar had then fled away down to Tianguá. When the villagers were confronted with the sight of the lighted buildings, opened doorways, unconsumed food and drinks, many televisions and radios operating but a complete absence of people, they became apprehensive once again. "It was as though the people of Ubajara had disappeared into the air," my uncle had said. Of course he had forgotten that Tabajara had been left in the same situation!

The villagers travelled onto Tianguá where they met with the people from Ubajara. By this time the Church school in Tianguá was already filled with people. The villagers had to spend the night in the covered market.

On the morning of Sunday detachments of the Polícia Militar, as well as others from the Military itself, arrived in Tianguá. They promptly blocked the road to the Ibiapaba. At this time, so my uncle said, there were many rumours circulating among the people gathered in Tianguá that the Inglês, like Lucia, must also have been turned into a ghost and if anyone returned to the Ibiapaba they also would be turned into one. These stories, to me, were further evidence of how hysteria can instil unreasoned notions into people.

Later on Sunday, so my uncle and his colleagues said, members of the Polícia Federal had also arrived in Tianguá and summoned people for questioning. Though they had added, they had not been personally approached by them. My uncle said this was something to be expected from the Polícia.

22: LUCIA

The moment I saw those cars and trucks heading away I feared for the worst. If only Lucia hadn't made such a to-do there might have been a chance of stopping them. Instead, Tabajara was as on Thursday, empty.

The Susem made a fuss over Lucia and she behaved like a lost child finding her parents. I left them to it. Then was not the time to tell them of the troubles looming. However, in every adversity there is always an advantage to be had. In this one it was an untended bar.

Except for a haze and smell of smoke it was like Thursday. Though supping an unpaid for cerveja did give me a feeling of unease it soon passed. I'd not more than a sip, however, when Terbal, flying carpet in tow zoomed through the door. It was laden with his helpers, the TV and the video.

"Return der equipment, ve haff come, ya?" he said.

The little objects lifted the TV, video and plaster, heaved them through the air as though all were flying. Others, with the appearance of shiny cockroaches ran up and down the wall. In no time at all they whizzed back to the carpet, job completed. And they did a good job, I couldn't even see the joins. The entire operation was done, the TV working before I'd finished my glass.

The screen came to life. Terbal said "Vat ist dat?"

I felt like saying "Rubbish," but instead said "Game Show." Next he asked where the pictures came from. I told him how television worked, cameras, transmission, the dish on the roof, satellites. And I just had to add "Like the one Kubber blew-up." In turn, I said I didn't understand why he and the Susem didn't understand. They must surely have similar means of transmission. But Terbal said they didn't. I asked how they communicated, transmitted, received? At the time he was hovering in front of the screen almost blocking the view.

"Free" he said.

"What?" I asked, thinking he was replying to me.

"Free der next number ist."

As he spoke, the woman on the screen picked the top off of a box numbered 'five'. With the presenter revealing 'three' to be the correct one, I asked "And how did you know that?"

Before he had time to reply Milophinia and Paceillo with "We thought you might be here," came into the bar. I nearly said "I've heard that before," but they launched into a length of questions.

"Where are the people of Tabajara?"

"Fled to the next habitation probably, everyone."

"Why?" asked Paceillo.

"Frightened, you've scared them all away."

"Why would they be scared of us? There was Lucia to show we are beneficial," she said.

"Beneficial you might be but they've gone all the same. And that means trouble."

"Why?" she asked again

"Because when the villagers come back they'll not come alone. They'll probably have half an army with them. I suggest you push off now before they do."

"Army? What is that?" she asked

"Organised body of persons, armed vor battle..." said Terbal butting in, and continuing, "...standing army, professional body of soldiers permanently in existence, the military service, vast host, organised body of people. Salvation Army, Church..."

"Thank you Terbal," interrupted Paceillo in a pained tone.

"Why?" she asked again, "would anyone want to harm us. We wish only to recover Pa-tu?"

I told them that humans are forever afraid of the unknown and they would view the Susem as a threat. I also told her that as it was Saturday night nothing would happen until the morning, and it being Sunday, probably nothing then.

Terbal said "Seven." All eyes were then on the screen.

"If we'd entered you, we would've won a few bob," I joked.

"Bob?" asked Milophinia.

"Shilling, disused coinage, slang, plural same, source dubious, quoted vrom 1912..."

"Terbal!" snapped Paceillo upon which he became quiet again.

No sooner had she snapped than she said it was time for them to rest. The weather forecast came on the screen. It showed rain continuing in the eastern half of Brazil. They stopped to look. Following was details for Ceará. This showed rain as well. After the weather came the News. I did my best to translate the Brazilian but even after half a year I have difficulties. Nearly all the news concerned dubious deeds of politicians but the overseas section showed a clip of the final collapse of Bosnia and the last fighting there. It had been networked and the commentary was in English.

"This is what an army looks like and that is what it does" I said, adding almost unconsciously, "the bastards."

"Bastards?" queried Milophinia. Terbal stayed silent.

"People who are nasty, bad and evil," I said. I went on to tell them that the army in Brazil isn't as vile as the Serb's but it was merely a matter of degree. The News ended, Milophinia was about to ask something but Paceillo said it was time to leave. They left, taking Terbal with them. I had another cachaça then took to my hammock.

Tired I might have been but sleep wasn't forthcoming. Even when it did it wasn't lasting. I was wide awake before the dawn. Although it had been a long and eventful day, and I should have slept soundly, my mind just kept buzzing. Buzzing with all the things I'd seen, experienced and become aware of. There was a big book of the tales to tell. And probably a few bob from them as well. But it was also the troubles I saw looming which stopped me sleeping soundly. Worrying with what could come and keeping half an ear open in case any did.

The dark was undisturbed and with the dawn only nature made a noise. I had showered, shaved and was sipping coffee in the kitchen when the first light came (and that's something I'd never seen in all the time I'd been in Tabajara). From the window I saw, as the light strengthened, Kubber change from being a shape to a craft. Not long after, from his side floated Terbal and followed by objects brought from La-ra. Out of curiosity I walked to where they were and asked what they were doing.

"Ve are going to do experiments," replied Terbal, stressing the last word and waggling his fronds.

"And what might they be?" I asked.

Though before I'd an answer, Paceillo appeared at the doorway and called Terbal to her. As she spoke she sounded agitated. Terbal returned, his fronds hanging lank. He hovered over his objects for a moment, then, with what sounded like a sigh, they and he trooped back to Kubber. They went up the ramp dejected but Paceillo walked down with a smile and I'd the caution of suspicion.

It has been my experience that whenever a woman smiles at a man she is after something. And Paceillo proved no exception.

"We do not wish to cause alarm to anyone," she said. "We have decided before we begin our search for Pa-tu, that we will do so in accord with your representatives. Please will you approach them on our behalf."

(I did think this was a variation on "Take me to your leader" but none the less said) "Representatives?"

"Yes, your representatives," she said.

I thought for a moment then I said "There aren't any."

"What do you mean there are not representatives? You must have representatives. How can your population organise themselves unless they have representatives?" she asked with her voice now possessing a touch of incredulity and her smile beginning to go.

Again I thought, then I said "Humans don't organise, they're organised."

"Why would people want to be organised? There must be representatives surely?" she said with her incredulity increasing.

"People aren't given a choice," I said and adding "but there are individuals and organisations who promote themselves to be representatives of people. If that is what you can call representatives, then there are them indeed."

"Will you then approach these on our behalf?" she said, with bafflement displacing disbelief and her smile quite gone.

"The two people who say they represent the local population are the

Governors of the States of Ceará and Piauí," I said. "Both are from families who own all the land and have all the power. These families select one of their members to represent not just the population in the Congress in Brasilia but the territory itself. As they don't usually meet with ordinary people it will be difficult to contact them. Also, it will take a long time. Should I be able to meet with one of them they will more than likely use what you have to their own personal advantage. Do you really want me to contact them?"

"No," said Paceillo quietly, then adding "the Congress, can you not approach them?"

"Not only is today a day of rest," I said, "but the members of the Congress are probably still recovering from Tiradentes Day. Everyone is away from their place of work and can't be contacted. Just as with the Governors, it will take a long time to contact anyone in Brasilia. And it's time you do not have. The army will have arrived long before then. If it wasn't Sunday and it wasn't still raining below, they would have been here by now."

As we spoke the sun began to rise and the air to warm. Two of the others, Milophinia and Lico came and joined us. "How will we know when it has stopped raining?" asked Milophinia.

"When the clouds disappear," I said.

"How will we know that?" she asked.

"Come with me," I said (I'd had a thought) "I'll show you the clouds." I took them up the road to the park and the viewing platform. We were joined by some of the others and several hen-gers. During the twenty minutes it took to walk (or rather for them to glide), and apart from it being nature ramble for the Susem and an answering session for me, Paceillo pressed me yet more regarding 'representatives'.

"The map we saw last night, that was of Brazil was it not?" she asked.

"Yes," I replied

"That is not all of the Earth, is it?"

"No. Brazil is part of a land mass called South America. There are several other land masses. Brazil is a country in South America, there are others..."

"Country?"

"Territory of a nation with distinct existence ast to name, language, customs, government und der..." said Terbal as he breezed alongside and restored with the confidence of his interrupting self. He then bobbed away ahead of us, his fronds flowing giving him the appearance of a swimming squid.

Paceillo gave a pained sigh as she passed and half muttered "I wish he had not come."

"Is there," she continued, "a Congress of the countries of South America we could travel to and speak with the representatives there?"

"There isn't one," I said. "Though there is the OAS, the Organisation of American States."

"Could we speak with those representatives?"

“The OAS is based in the United States, which is in North America. The United States not only dominates the OAS, it is the most powerful country on the planet. If you flew anywhere near it, their army would probably blast not only you to pieces but Sieba and La-ra too. In fact, if they knew you were here they would be firing missiles at you right now. You should have seen what they did in Iraq, Cuba, Chiapas.”

We came to the viewing platform. A blanket of clouds stretched to the horizon. Though the clouds were several hundred feet below us, as they blew against the Ibiapaba they sent plumes billowing high above. The Susem were evidently impressed but Terbal, who had arrived ahead of them, had become quite carried away. He was bobbing along the edge of the platform his fronds waggling with excitement. He then started frenziedly shaking them.

At this, some of the Susem making cries similar to “Oh no!” raced towards him, arms outstretched, calling “Terbal, Terbal,” as they ran. They tried to take hold of him but with a “Whee-eh!” of delight, he promptly whizzed away and into the rising swirls. His form quickly merged into the grey and white of the clouds. Only the sounds of his pleasure signified his presence.

The sternness of Paceillo's expression and folded arms showed her annoyance at Terbal's aeronautics. Within minutes though, she too had joined with the others in shouting his name. Hen-gers were despatched. Eventually, accompanied by two of them he was escorted from the clouds. Susem and hen-gers immediately gathered around him.

With all the demeanour of a deflating balloon Terbal began sinking slowly towards the ground. While some of the Susem kept calling his name to him, Milophina spoke to one of the hen-gers. It immediately flew away over the trees in the direction of Kubber.

I asked her what was happening. “We should never have let him know where we were going,” she said testily. “As he gets older he gets worse. He was just the same on Sin-cu-ra. Let him anywhere near a cloud and he’s off, there is no holding him. He is a cloudholic, that is what he is. The other Sinteens are not like this. Sometimes I wonder why we should ever have had him assigned to us.”

The flying carpet, replete with helpers appeared from over the trees. After what seemed an infusion of sustenance Terbal regained his shape though not his hovering. The claws of the carpet swept around him and whisked him away to Kubber. But before he left Terbal whispered to Paceillo.

“At least,” she said, as the carpet flew away, “he gathered something useful. The clouds will be here throughout today and tomorrow. On the following day they will begin to disappear.” Though I didn’t ask, I did wonder how he had been able to find out such a thing.

Having looked at the clouds and delighted in the sun shining on them as they rolled and swirled away, we went back to the Tabajara. As we did, Paceillo again returned to the subject of ‘representatives’.

"These land masses, do they have a Congress?" she asked.

"No," I said and added, "But there is the United Nations, it's a congress of all countries."

"Could we speak with their representatives?" she asked.

"You could, but they have no authority," I said.

"No authority? Why do they not?" she asked.

"Each representative is appointed to further the interests of their own country's government. As the countries have conflicting interests the United Nations is reduced to impotence. And anyway, it's situated in the United States. In brief," I finally said and hoping it was the end of the matter, "everywhere on Earth, there are only representatives of interests and areas, not of people."

After Paceillo had quietly said "Oh," we went on in silence. It was eight o'clock when we arrived back in the village.

At 10 o' clock Paceillo was once again harking on about 'representatives'. I had allowed myself to be talked into giving a tour of the village. When I had explained the purpose of Father Alves' little church, Catholicism and then religion (all of which bemused them), Paceillo asked "As it is such a powerful and influential worldwide movement, could they be approached?"

"You would be seen as a threat to everything they stood for and their authority," I told her and adding, "and like every other authority they would probably have you killed as soon as look at you." Once again she fell into silence.

And once again I pressed on her how it was unsafe for them to stay at Tabajara. That the moment the clouds cleared the army would fly into the Ibiapaba, probably kill them and just as probably me as well. But all she said was, "If the army is so powerful could we speak with them?"

"Because," I said, "the Brazilian army would also see you as a threat, especially to their authority."

"Why?" she asked again

I was just beginning to tire of her "whys". Every time I answered one it only prompted another. And all they were doing was pursuing the pointless. But I bore with it as best I could. "The Brazilian army is The Authority," I said. "The army, although it doesn't say so, runs the country. And it isn't just in Brazil but most other places as well. If you are seen by them to be above their authority they will attack you. Even if you do nothing they will still attack you, justifying it as a "pre-emptive defensive strike" just in case you were going to do something."

As we walked back to the Pousada I noticed a child's bicycle. It put an idea in my head. "The only way there can be any possible protection is if the people of Tabajara can meet you and see that you are friendly, that you intend them no harm. If they are in Ubajara I will visit them there and try to persuade them to return. I will travel on this," I said, pointing to the bike.

After lunch I did just that. It has been a long time since I have ridden a bicycle. Cycling to Ubajara I was struck by how utterly bizarre the whole situation was. Here was an advanced civilization, on a wild goose chase, despatching me on a kid's pushbike in order that they could seek safety in having a village of backland people around them. It was ridiculous. But all the same, what was the alternative?

Though it took an hour to Ubajara it took two to return. It wasn't just the hills on the way back, or that I'm out of condition which slowed me so but the consequences of what I found in Ubajara. Nobody was there. And like Tabajara, the place bore all the signs of the instant flight by frightened people. There were even unfinished drinks on the bar at the Urcezino. The Scala was the same. This just never happens in Ubajara, even the dying drink up before they go. Only cattle and chickens were on the streets.

Although the return was tiring I had time to think. There was only one way everyone could have travelled and that was north to Tianguá. Tianguá may be sleepy but it has a police post. That meant the military not only now knew of events but would already be taking action, controlling the crowds if nothing else. It may still be raining in Tianguá but there was nothing to stop the army driving up on to the Ibiapaba, and of them doing so at any time.

There was only one course of action. The Susem, for their own sakes as well as mine, must leave. As I'd not succeeded in convincing them their pursuit of Pa-tu was pointless, all I could do was to persuade them the Earth was a nasty place filled with diseases which would be deadly to them, and with humans who would be even deadlier. If I couldn't persuade them to go, then I would leave anyway. "You're a long time dead," I thought to myself. I did also think that perhaps the Susem could go and base themselves somewhere else but then the outcome would be the same. There would still be governments and their armies intent on annihilating them no matter where they went. I wouldn't even put it past the Americans or the Russians firing missiles at Sieba once they had located him.

It was five o'clock by the time I returned to Tabajara. Kubber's door was shut and the Susem were resting. I did the same. At seven however, I was sat with some of them outside the Pousada relating the emptiness of Ubajara and the consequences. I was most intent in impressing on them that they depart without delay and by the morning at the latest. But Paceillo, however, appeared to take no notice of my advice whatsoever.

Instead she held up an old copy of 'O Povo' and asked me what it was. After I had explained about newspapers she said, "Can they be approached so they can tell of our mission?"

We were back in the "why" mode again. "All newspapers are restricted in what they are allowed to publish," I said. "Publishing news against the interests of people in power results in the newspaper being punished. And newspapers avoid being punished by censoring themselves."

"What about your television?" she asked.

"It is self-censoring too."

"Radio?"

"The same. The only chance might have been Internet, but not here."

"Internet?"

I did my best to explain though it took some time. Of how everybody used to be able to send anything to anyone, but now just about every country has it regulated. "The only positive thing about the Internet," I said, "is that it is still possible to enter information before the sender is traced."

"How can we inform and ask on the Internet?" Milophinia asked.

"From here you can't," I said. "The landline telephone system in this part of Brazil is so old, it still uses human operators. It can only transmit speech. There was a telephone system which used radiowaves but it ceased to function when the transmission mast collapsed. There are satellite telephones which can be used but there isn't one of those in Tabajara either. In Brazil these are not allowed for ordinary use."

"Well," said Paceillo with finality in her voice, "we will just have to search for Pa-tu without the accord of your people."

Although aghast I tried again to tell her and the others they were mistaken over the whereabouts of Pa-tu. I also told them Earth was a lousy place and they wouldn't like it at all. This also backfired.

It was nearly eight o'clock. I fetched my radio and tuned to the World Service in time for the News. Knowing there would be reports on events in Bosnia I hoped they would give the Susem an idea of how horrible soldiers and armies could be. The reports were indeed terrible but instead of them causing the Susem alarm they aroused their curiosity.

On their asking I told them about Bosnia, of how both Serbia and Croatia had waited for NATO and others' forces to leave following the Dayton peace settlement, how after a decent interval, they had swiftly carved the country up between them slaughtering the poor Bosnians as they went. When I told them of the thousands of rapes and other atrocities they were taken aback but Tearo asked a question which changed the tenor of the conversation.

"Does this mean that males are engaged in the fighting as well?"

I was about to reply "Of course it's men, it's all men, who else do you think?" when it dawned on me the significance of what she had said. After this much of what I said met with their incredulity that men should be in charge, in charge of anything.

They all made mention of it, though Tearo was the bluntest. "How is it," she said, "that the immature form of your species is in all the positions of power?"

Apart from my discomfort I tried my best to give explanations. The course of history, man the hunter, Gods, greater strength, bigger build, ability to procreate, male dominance, female submissiveness, but they were quite unimpressed and utterly unconvinced.

"The chemicals causing males their virility..." said Tearo, (I ventured, "Testosterone") "...produce as a side effect certain behavioural characteristics which we have always found necessary to curb." As she spoke there was an earnest unison of nodding heads. "While we are male," she continued, "we have our testosterone levels continually checked. If the level is too high it is lowered. It would appear the same is needed for some of your males."

There followed an interesting though academic discussion almost among themselves, regarding testosterone levels. Higher in Susem males during their mating season, human males being continually 'in season' was probably reason for their aggression.

Milophinia returned the conversation to Bosnia with "Why do not the rest of the people of Earth stop this terribleness?"

I replied there were many who were protesting but as they had no power they could do nothing. "Those who have the power, rulers, armies and the like, seeing little benefit for them in becoming involved again, aren't really bothered." But I added that Bosnia wasn't the only place where fighting and atrocities were happening.

And again, after the sardonic "It appears your males in power need their testosterone levels raised not lowered," I received the same response, "It's always men isn't it?" and "why has not such brutality been stopped?"

"While there are weapons there will always be wars," I shrugged.

"And where do the weapons come from," asked Tearo assertively and adding before I could reply, "from other men I suppose?"

Not knowing of an arms company run by women, I had to reply "Yes."

Paceillo then said "But it is the users of weapons who cause the brutality. Remove their willingness to use them and the brutality will cease, will it not?" Then, and somewhat to my surprise, she added "Such brutality can best be countered by disciplined, organised, overwhelming terror against these apparently undisciplined perpetrators."

Almost without thinking and only half seriously, I said "Send in the Gurkhas." They asked me who they were. I explained, "Disciplined, fearless, feared fighters from Nepal who have a habit of creeping up quietly, their kukris, super sharp small swords, unsheathed and slaying their adversaries silently by swiftly slitting their throats with a single slash."

Amid my telling more of their exploits, Menpemelo appeared out of the darkness, Lucia at her side. Though I could see it was Lucia, she was a very different Lucia than even just the day before. Her face, apart from the smiles, was fuller and as she moved against her gown, I could see her figure was as well. While the others greeted her, I turned to Menpemelo and said "She's put on a bit of weight in a day, what have you been doing to her?" She explained, some I grasped most I didn't, but she mentioned "aura" again.

"While Lucia's prime disorder was diagnosed as chronic aura-cerebral dysfunction, her resultant secondary and tertiary disabilities, lower limb paraplegia and resultant tissue imbalances, could only be addressed afterwards," said Menpemelo matter-of-factly, taking a breath and then continuing in the same casual tone. "Though Lucia responded positively to operative photonic correction and new, sustainable auralate-falx cerebri pathways were successfully established, it was necessary to correct the prior pelvic and left posterior thigh physio-neurological imbalances before tissue restitution could be initiated. Once the secondary disorder remedial therapy, an assured, self-administered protocol of psycho-postplegic somatic convalescence had been completed, we were able to institute an extended hyper tissue-cell infusion regime, which, as you can now observe, has had a positive outcome."

"Oh," I said.

Noting, no doubt I was a little confused over this, Menpemelo then said "Expressed simply, malfunctions to Lucia's head and legs were corrected on the first day of our arrival. She was subsequently left to walk on her own volition for a day in order to her becoming used to doing so and today she has been fattened up."

"And very nicely so," I said, at last grasping what she had said (and giving Lucia another glance). But what Menpemelo said next had me really confounded.

"Lucia's suffering has led to an almost total absence of auralate development. Although cerebrally and neurally she is now functioning perfectly, her aura is of a very young being. During tomorrow we will provide therapy which will begin to reduce the extent of this under-development. As this will take some time before Lucia perceives any benefit, we will, as we have calculated her age to be about 35 of your years, begin a course of selective cellular regression. Over time, this will reverse her physiological age by an equivalent of between ten and fifteen years which should match the maturity development of her aura."

Apart from her nonchalant tone, the consequences, repercussions of what she said quite took my breath away. If the Susem could do this for Lucia, it could be done for everyone. People could become younger, no one need grow old. (A feeling of money, lots of it, came creeping over me).

But the second breath, the cold hard realistic one, had me saying "When you go tomorrow morning, take Lucia back to La-ra with you, there's no future for her here."

"So we are leaving tomorrow morning, are we?" said Paceillo in a wry tone and smile to match (and her English apparently advancing to irony).

"Yes, and as early as possible, go before the army comes."

"Leave? We are unable to," she said, with her smile unchanged.

"And why not?" I asked.

"Terbal. Until he recovers, Kubber cannot move," she matter-of-factly replied.

"And how long might that be?" I asked with alarm.

"It is difficult to know. Perhaps this time tomorrow, perhaps sooner, perhaps later, we are not sure," she said, with her voice now as nonchalant as Menpemelo's had been. Then after a pause and smile unchanged, she added, with a touch of finality, "We have come to Earth to find Pa-tu. We will not leave until Pa-tu is located, we must know what has happened to him."

I then continued where I had left off. That Earth was a terrible place, it would be the death of them. But everything I mentioned, the poverty, injustice, inequality, over-population, pollution, deforestation, over-fishing and so on received the same retort, "It is caused by your males, is it not?"

By then I felt I was at a feminist revivalist meeting. Tearo, as sardonic as ever, even added "If the Earth is so bad then why do you not go somewhere else?" When I said there was no where else to go, I received her demonstrative "Why do you not do something about it then?"

I was cheesed off with them. I didn't even bother to mention germs and diseases. Males may well, in their minds, be inferior but the ones coming in the morning would be armed. The Susem had nothing with which to respond. With Kubber stuck there they were sitting ducks. They just didn't grasp the danger they were in. And the danger they were putting me in as well.

After they had returned to Kubber, I concluded there was only one course open to me, I had to go. And do so not just quickly but quietly.

I had everything packed before I took to my hammock. I had even crept out in the darkness and collected the bike again (I didn't fancy walking the 30 miles to Tianguá). From there I could catch a coach to Fortaleza and plan where to go next. Apart from removing myself from the coming conflagration, I had another reason why I needed to travel to Fortaleza, Henri Benedini.

Henri, apart from owning a photographic shop, had connections with the Polícia Federal at Pinto Martins, Fortaleza's airport. Brazil has a stupid system of entry visa extensions. The only way for a foreigner to legally stay more than six months is to marry a Brazilian. Those who don't have to depart for another country then come back in again. However, for $100 Senhor Benedini can 'arrange' with the Polícia Federal for a brand new visa. The only inconvenience being that a new visa can only be had in exchange for the old one. It also had to be handed over two days before expiry. Because mine expires on the 29th I needed to visit Fortaleza for Wednesday.

It wasn't that I wanted to leave the Susem to their fate, I just daren't stay. Pity though. But then reality always rules.

23: ROBERTO

The coach arrived in Tianguá at half past six. By this time daylight had begun to fade. However, the rain had also ceased. My intention was to first travel along the narrow road which led southward from Tianguá, alongside the base of the Serra Ibiapaba to Ipu. Thirty kilometres along this road just before the trackway to the hamlet of Pacuja and close by where the fallen pylon from the cable station lies, there are pathways ascending to the top of the serra and to village of Tabajara. I have climbed upon these pathways on several occasions during my boyhood.

My journey from the rodoviária to the edge of the town was without incident. There were several military vehicles on the road but I was not confronted by any roadblocks. By the time I was into the open country night-time had fallen and I walked along the road in darkness.

I estimated that by hiking it would take me five or six hours to cover the distance to the fallen pylon. It was my intention when I reached this point to find shelter among the rocks and rest until dawn. Then I would climb up the face of the serra. This climb I considered would take me two or three hours.

Although I was prepared to walk the distance, I also planned to signal to passing vehicles in the hope of gaining a lift to my destination. This I proceeded to do but I was not initially anticipating much success, for vehicles were sparse along this road. After walking for some five kilometres, however, I saw lights of a truck travelling in my same direction. No sooner had I held out my hand to it, than I saw it belonged to the military. Overtaking me, the truck braked to a halt. Because I was alone I was at first apprehensive over its stopping. But when the driver in a friendly manner called from the cab offering me a lift, my apprehension eased. Of course I did not tell him of my true destination. Instead I said to him that I was travelling to Pacuja. He invited me to climb into the rear of the truck. With the aid of other soldiers sitting there, I clambered aboard.

As the truck travelled along the road I engaged the soldiers in conversation. Talking to them I gathered they were returning to their barracks at Ipu. I asked of them, as innocently as I could manage, from where they had travelled. As I had anticipated, they replied "Tianguá."

I was aware that by conversing with these soldiers they could provide possible further information in the formulating of my news article. With this intention I endeavoured to elicit as many facts from them regarding their duties in Tianguá as I could. But I obtained little new information from them. All that the soldiers told me was that the weather had been uncomfortable for them but it was preferable to the boredom of idling in their barracks. Even should they return to Tianguá and it was still raining it would again be preferable to being at Ipu. I asked of their purpose for being in Tianguá but to my alacrity one of the soldiers asked of me why I was asking so many questions of them. I replied I was simply making conversation. After this query I ceased making such enquiries.

But to my unease this soldier began to interrogate me as to why I was travelling to Pacuja. I hastily replied that I was visiting some friends I had known there since my boyhood. This appeared to satisfy him and his comrades' curiosity. The remainder of my journey was continued in almost silence. I confined myself to responding jovially to the soldier's exclamations as to the bumpiness of the road.

After an hour had passed, the truck arrived at the place of the fallen pylon. Shortly afterwards it stopped for me to disembark. As I bid the soldiers farewell I was relieved to see their truck continue on its journey. Although the ride in the truck had saved me the exertion of walking, the soldier's questioning had caused me to become ill at ease.

To assure my safety I walked for ten minutes along the trackway to Pacuja in case the soldiers should return. I then retraced my steps to the Ipu road and walked back to where the fallen pylon lay. I took further precaution against being seen by travelling away from the road and walking amid the rocks which lay to the Ibiapaba side of it.

I arrived where the pylon lay a few minutes before 10 o'clock. For 20 minutes I scrambled over the rock strewn terrain making my way towards the base of the serra. The clouds had kept the air warm and by the time I reached the serra I was perspiring. I rested and ate some of the food given to me by my mother. While doing so I observed the locality. Because of the sky's cloudiness there was little light to see by. Also, the rain of the past days had made the rock surfaces damp and slippery. I concluded it to be unwise to venture at this time up onto the cliff face itself.

Because of the likelihood of further rain, I also considered it to be expedient to seek shelter. After a short while I had located such a refuge between two large boulders which had become leant against one another. I spent the remainder of the night-time there. Although I had been awake since the early hours of the day I was still unable to sleep for more than short periods. Before the dawn had arrived I was prepared for the ascent of the cliff face.

Having climbed the serra from the same location in earlier times and knowing the exertion involved, I emptied from my satchel as many items as I could. I stowed them between the two rocks I had slept under with the intention of collecting them on my return. At half past five and with the first light approaching, I embarked on my ascent.

The sky was filled with many clouds. Some of them obscured the crest of the serra from my view. My ascent would cause me to become heated but I still donned my waterproofed jacket in case of rain. Although it was red in colour I concluded that the clouds would obscure me from anyone looking downwards from the serra's crest. I was also grateful for the clouds because of the heat intensity radiated by the sun. I had experienced from my previous times on the Ibiapaba that its eastern face is unsafe for climbing upon until the afternoon. For this climb the clouds would provide protection from the sun for at least part of my ascent.

The dampness and slipperiness of the pathways slowed my progress. There were many loose stones which had also tumbled onto the paths, washed away doubtlessly by the recent rains. Such was their profusion that they slowed the progress of my ascent. Frequently, because of the excessive number of stones lying on the pathways, especially when these narrowed, it became necessary to push the stones over their edges. I was reluctant to do this. As they fell they caused further stones in their wake to dislodge and fall with them. Although this created a noise I was usually presented with no alternative than to remove them or I would have fallen over the edges instead. In an hour I managed to ascend no more than 200 metres.

By this time the full light of the day was about me. There were still many clouds but I sensed that the temperature of the air was beginning to rise also. At a widening of the pathway and because of my exertions, I rested for a short while. This I was to regret.

Not all the pathways necessary for the ascent to the top of the serra led upwards. Some went horizontally along the side of the cliff face. Such a stretch, 300 metres in distance, was the next assignment. This pathway was narrow and even before I had stepped upon the path I could see many stones lay upon it. I was thankful that the full heat of the sun would not be on me as I progressed along this ledge. However, my progress was still at a slow pace. Some stretches of this path were so narrow that it was necessary not only to remove the stones as I went but also to grasp the rocky surface of the cliff face with both of my hands.

I had almost traversed this stretch of pathway when I heard and then saw below me, a military truck travelling along the road towards Tianguá. I had both of my arms outstretched against the cliff face. I was unable to hide from the eyes of those in the truck. Also to my regret there was the sound of the many dislodged stones tumbling downwards. The truck appeared to decelerate. I could only remain motionless and hope the occupants did not espy me.

I could have cried. The numerals looked like '29' but they weren't, they were '24'. Even though the visa clerk's stamp was faint and his handwriting barely legible, I should have checked the wording. I should have seen it was 'vigésimo quarto' and not 'vigésimo nono'. Now I am too late, I'm an illegal. I daren't go to Tianguá or anywhere else, not even Ipu. The police and army are bound to be checking everyone's papers. I'd be arrested. Though should I still be in Tabajara when the army arrived they would arrest me instead, that is if I didn't become shot.

No matter who did the arresting, should I survive I would experience a Brazilian jail. Should I survive this I would be deported back to London and face the Police, the Inland Revenue, the VAT, Dawson's mob, my mum, her nagging.

Departing with the Susem, even though it meant spending the rest of my days drifting round the stars, was the only hope for survival. I could say goodbye to my money in Miami. No matter what, I was done for.

All day I asked after Terbal's health hoping his recovery would enable the Susem to leave and take me with them before the army arrived. But every attempt to persuade them, especially Paceillo, to return to Sieba failed. Instead the Susem have embarked on the opposite, that of staying.

Although at first light I saw from the viewing platform only clouds, I kept expecting soldiers. I went to the platform again at 10 o'clock, noon, then at three but I saw no more than clouds. I went to the Ubajara side of the village and the narrow valley the road passes through, with thoughts of blocking it but there aren't loose boulders big enough. I took my telescope to Mont Macambirá for a better view of the road but saw that beyond the edge of the village the road dips from sight. I watched the television News one after another but there were no mentions of the Ibiapaba. I listened to Radio Casablanca but there were no mentions of anything out of the usual either. Although the Pousada's telephone is working I didn't know anybody to ring. And anyway, if I used it, the exchange down in Tianguá would know someone was here and only accelerate the army's arrival.

All day I listened for sounds of people and vehicles but there was none. By evening I was quite worn out with it all.

Meanwhile, the Susem carried on regardless as though there was nothing to worry over. By eight o'clock an assortment of objects were arrayed around Kubber. This time though, instead of Terbal they were superintended by Anuria and Pheterisco. One object, a circular drum about knee-height, made, every minute or so, letter-box 'zump' snapping sounds and emitted a shiny paper-like sheet a foot square from a slot in its top. Each of the sheets momentarily hovered in the air then scrunched themselves up into tiny balls and shot skyward at great speed. Throughout the afternoon they returned and after flattening themselves back into sheets, whizzed back inside the drum.

Other drum-like things wandered the area. Some of them were also knee-high but had little legs and ran at a fast speed, momentarily stopped then ran on again. They reminded me of the way spiders move. Yet more of them hovered in the air at head height. These would momentarily fly fast, also stop then dart to another spot. It was if they were hunting something. Each time any of them came near me they would give a "Hadodani". Also, the hen-gers, as they whizzed to and fro, kept calling my name as well.

Between my own toing and froing I asked Anuria what they were for, what were they doing. "This first drum is called 'Sava-ve' and he is projecting monitoring units," she said.

"Monitoring what?" I asked.

"Ooh just scalar wave profiles," she said and adding "Each cell of the unit records a base register prior to departure and then, as you can see, they compact and ascend to a pre-determined height in the atmosphere."

I ventured a "What for?"

"Well," she said with sigh, "as we were unable to monitor from outside your planet's atmosphere we have to go through the task of taking it from the inside," then added "This part is rather boring."

"And him," I said pointing to one of those running along the ground, "what's he doing?"

"That is Sacu, he's a cito. He and the others are transmitting soliton wave probes. You will see them come back in a short while to collect the results."

"And those ones hovering in the air?" I asked.

"They are cisons, I am afraid, as they have only recently been made, I have not remembered all their names yet." With this Anuria called a passing one over. He hovered by her head for a moment then flew off. "He says he is Mobo," she said.

Anuria began explaining Mobo's tasks, it's something to do with measuring more waves, when Paceillo emerged from Kubber with Milophinia and Menpemelo either side of her. I didn't have a chance to mention the pointlessness of their experiments and the need to depart without delay, before she said "We have decided after all, to still conduct our search for Pa-tu in accord with the people of Earth. We cannot conclude," she continued, "as you appear to have done, that all of the people of Earth wish to harm us. We have, however, taken consideration of the matters you mentioned to us yesterday. We are able to offer assistance in resolving some of those problems and will willingly do so in return for assistance in recovering Pa-tu."

"Such as?" I asked.

"We can provide assistance in increasing the production of food so that none of your fellow humans need be hungry," she said.

"There is no shortage of food," I told her and added "If anything there's a glut of the stuff. The poor are hungry because they haven't any land on which to grow crops and thus no wealth to afford anything. Even if by some wondrous way you could supply the poor with food, you will upset the interests of the big landowners and food producers. And because they are powerful they will have the army on you." As the smile on her face disappeared, I added "Just forget it, the best thing you can do is depart."

She gave a small "Oh," and all three walked back to Kubber. However, this wasn't the end of the matter either.

Two hours later Paceillo approached me with a further proposal, or rather another daft idea. "We can provide assistance in the production of minerals, so that the land need not be ruined and the waters poisoned," she said.

"Not only are the organisations, they're called companies who mine minerals, without interest or care for the land, they are powerful," I said. "Even the army has its own mining company, Grande Carajás. It's the biggest in Brazil. Apart from ruining everything for miles around, they run it as their own private territory. Another, called 'Consolidated'," I continued (and remembering what my friend David, a geologist, had once told me), "controls half the coast of Namibia, a place where the people are also poor. The coast is white with diamonds but they are guarded by armed soldiers. The diamonds are just left there so Consolidated can become richer, rather than be given to Namibia's poor people. Upset the interests of any of these and they will also attack you."

After again telling her not to bother and just depart, she gave another "Oh," and once more returned to Kubber. However, she persisted throughout the day, fish, forests, water, pollution, disease. Paceillo doubtless meant well, but of course she has no understanding of the complexities and complications arising from upsetting the powerful.

Trying to be as diplomatic as I could but also to have her see sense, I said "Yes, there are all the terrible things I and you have mentioned, but just as countries are powerful interests on Earth there are yet other powerful interests, such as companies. Some companies are even more powerful than many countries. But like countries, companies use their power to protect their interests. Individual people and communities have no real power." That, I thought, was the end of the matter. Again I was wrong.

However, at the time of telling her, I heard sounds of a problem which was evidently beginning to press. The villagers' cows hadn't been milked for two days. Their mooing and hobbling made it obvious they were in agony. While I can turn my hand to a thing or two, milking cows is not one of them, though I know what happens if they're not milked.

I was worrying what to do, when Pheterisco came by. When I told her what the problem was, she said "Oh," and went away. But two minutes later she was back, this time with a carpetful of little helpers, the shiny cockroach ones. In no time at all they were running down the cows' sides and attending their udders. A sad waste of milk to be sure but I don't think any of the cows minded. These cockroaches, it seems, can turn their feet to anything. They are called 'Sherpels', so Pheterisco said (and similar to 'Sherpas', I thought).

With the Susem set on staying, the arrival of the army imminent, and me resigned to being shot or deported, I saw the evening as the last I was ever going to have as a free man.

Whenever a situation is hopeless there's only one salvation, the drink.

But alas, even the sanctuary of this last haven was denied me. After only the second cachaça, bursting into the bar, wobbly Terbal in tow, came Anuria and Paceillo effusing "Look at this!" and holding a roll of panels.

"We have defined why our earlier readings were distorted," said Anuria still effusive.

"Oh you have, have you, that's very good," said I with a past-caring tone.

"It is good for us perhaps but certainly bad for you," said Anuria still all demonstrative.

"And why might that be?" I asked.

"Unnatural waves," both Paceillo and Anuria exclaimed.

And naturally I'd not the faintest idea what they were on about, though for them to rush through the doorway in such a tizzy it had to be significant. So out of politeness and forbearance I let them continue.

"Look," said Anuria, laying out some of the panels, "this is what we would normally expect to find," and pointing to what appeared to me a jumble of coloured squiggly lines. "But there," she said, pointing to a concentrated squiggle, "and there, and there," pointing to others.

I mumbled a "Yes, so?"

"There are more on these, look," she continued, pressing the panel's side and another set of squiggles appearing, "and here, and here," and she pressing up image after image, "they are appearing in every sampling frame we have taken from the higher levels of the atmosphere."

"And in some of the lower ones too," said Paceillo and adding "they were not evident either when we first measured, before we came that is, beyond the ionosphere."

"So?" I said, "I don't understand a thing you're talking about."

"They are rising up from the surface of the Earth," exclaimed Anuria, her effusiveness now turned to earnestness. "They cannot be coming from within the planet. Our strata sample soliton wave analysis has shown us this. Therefore, they must be being created on the surface."

"If they have not yet reached beyond the ionosphere it also means they must be of recent creation," added Paceillo with her effusiveness also gone.

"So?" I said

"Do you not see what this means?" said Anuria, her earnestness increased.

I shook my head but said "Venezuela versus Uruguay, second leg, first half, the score's one all," in reply to Terbal's "Vat ist dis?" as he hovered by the TV.

"This means the protective atmospheric layers of the Earth are able to be weakened and thus penetrated not just by soliton cosmic waves as at present, see here on this panel, but also scalar cosmic waves as well," continued Anuria in her earnestness.

As the inside of my glass was becoming dried, I gave it a fresh moistening. Being courteous I offered the pair of them some, only to see their eyes do contortions as they caught the cachaça on the back of their throats.

Anuria, seeing I still didn't understand, continued, "Although our analysis is of only a small part of the Earth's atmosphere, the even distribution of these particular abnormalities, combined with the distortion of our readings we experienced before we came here, suggests they are occurring throughout the Earth's atmosphere. Also, their incidence appears to be increasing. They may not have reached up far enough yet, but soon they will enable cosmic scalar waves to penetrate not just through the Earth's atmosphere but well inside the Earth itself, all organic activity will cease."

Just about comprehending the last, I said "So life on Earth is going to be wiped out, is it?"

"Yes, and within the next hundred years," exclaimed Anuria.

"A hundred years!" I said with incredulity. "Do you seriously expect me to be worried about the next hundred years? By this time tomorrow I, you, all of us, are likely to be dead. Don't you realise what is going to happen? Soldiers are going to come, and if you are still here you will end up, along with me, being seriously shot. And you are worried about the next hundred years! By the way, your glass is empty, is that another you'll be having?" I took a refill myself. Sensing a silence and seeing hands covering glasses, I felt perhaps I had caused offence.

"If we are a danger to you why do not you depart," said Paceillo in a cold quiet tone and adding as a barb, "and leave us here, all alone?"

It has always been my experience that women have a unique ability of getting at you in such a way, that regardless of how much trouble they have heaped upon themselves, that if you don't stand by them you know you will be filled with guilt for all eternity. And what is more, they can do it with just a phrase, a movement of the eyes, even a slight shrug of the shoulders. Paceillo was no different.

They had me backtracking and apologising in no time at all. They then softened and had another drink. It was also half-time.

"All of der analysis I haff been analysing," said Terbal as he floated over, "haff caused mine conclusions to be indicating emanations vrom vormations in existence vor 70 years or less only are dese unnatural vafes coming from." Then after a pause, "Tell me Dommy of dese young vormations are you knowing?"

I said I didn't know about such things.

"Dese vormations of strong concentrations vill be," continued Terbal, "if correct I am, und I am correct I conclude, generating radiation of vafes of high strengths."

I was still lost but "radiation" rang a bell. It wasn't long before I was telling about atom and hydrogen bombs, nuclear power stations. Again I said I didn't know of any nearby, adding that they are mainly in North America but I did add "There's one down Rio way where there's been some trouble of late and perhaps there's another in Montevideo."

"Montevideo? Vere der vootball ist coming vrom, ya?" exclaimed Terbal.

"It's a repeat," I said. As I spoke, Anuria strode in haste out the door. With her gone and Terbal back watching the match I had a most uncomfortable experience, Paceillo asked a question.

No matter what you do or say, women will always twist it around in such a way so as to engender either a feeling of guilt in you, or that you have slighted them. Generally speaking, I've found it to be both. Ask a man where he bought the meat from he will reply "The butchers," but ask a woman the same question and she will say "Why, what is wrong with it?" Give a woman a present as a surprise and she may thank you, but inside she will be thinking "What is this for, what has he a conscience (and it's inevitably "guilty") over, what terribleness is about to unfold?" And this, of course, is but the beginning of the twisting.

Another of my experiences has been that women are only happy when they have something to brood over. And the best are slights and insults received, actual or imagined, with the wrongdoing of those males close to them coming a good second. If, however, women can combine the two they go into raptures of delight.

I have observed that while men go for the quick stab in the back, women only stick the knife in a little way. Then they twist it. And later they twist it again and again, and again, for years and years if needs be. They never stop until they've extracted the maximum retribution possible.

I have also found women do not usually strike in the melee of a conflict but wait until they are alone with their victim and especially when he is relaxed, when he's at his most vulnerable. It is then when they strike. The initial attack, so I have also experienced, usually comes in the form of a short, mildly accusative question.

And so it was with Paceillo. "Why have you not left us?" she said quietly, yet oh so menacingly.

I have learnt that the best form of defence against a woman's accusations, no matter what the consequences might be, is to make an immediate and full confession and ask for mitigating circumstances to be taken into account. Should this fail it is then best to throw oneself on their mercies and beg for forgiveness. However, I have also learnt to hear out the whole accusation first, because that is what actually has to be 'confessed' to, truth is only an incidental to the equation. It is what a woman considers to be one's wrong-doing which has to be addressed. The consequences of making the 'wrong' confession are as bad as not making one at all, the knife goes in and is immediately twisted. I have lost count of the number of 'confessions' I've made to things I've not even done, and all just to stop those knives from going in.

So I listened to the rest of what Paceillo had to say. "Do you also have reasons for remaining here?" she said.

I was all prepared to listen on but she said nothing more. However, the pressure of her silence was as onerous as receiving a barrage of chastisement. I 'confessed' and thought up mitigating circumstances as fast as I could.

"Am I to understand," she said, breaking her silence and cutting me short, "you have been here with us, not to help us but only because you cannot leave?" And continuing just as coolly, "Am I to also understand that if you could have left us, you would have done so?" Then came the killer question, the one where the knife is poised to go in, "What benefit are you to us?"

I continued pleading the mitigation. They were lucky to have met me, anyone else would have been hostile. It was me who gave them all the information they have, as well as the use of English, the world language. I was their lucky one in a million find.

All the while Paceillo was looking forward from me, slowly rocking her body back and forth and nodding her head while at the same time making closed mouthed “Umm...umm..” sounds. She was still “umming” when I finally ran out of mitigation.

She stopped rocking, stood up, looked down at me and with eyes unsmiling, summarily said “It appears we are stuck with one another, does it not?” With this she turned on her heel and, with Terbal following, went out into the night.

Watching them return to Kubber I felt as squalid as a schoolboy caught mis-demeaning, suffering the contempt of the teacher's disdain. I found myself mumbling “Oh me of little faith,” and felt Paceillo's knife had already gone in ready to turn should I, in her eyes, ever fail her again.

I also heard the “zump” snapping of Sava-ve and saw, reflecting in the light from Kubber, the shine of sheets before being sent aloft into the darkness.

I drank no more.

The truck did not stop. As it was at least a kilometre distant, I became assured that its occupants had not noticed me. However, I continued to remain stationary for some minutes more, regretting as I did the folly of my earlier relaxation. With feelings of relief I then resumed my ascent.

By eight o'clock I had climbed to the height of the clouds. For half an hour I had to contend with their fogginess reducing the visibility of my view. Because of my earlier climbing upon the serra I was better versed in the conjunctions of the higher pathways than those on the lower slopes. I was able without too great a difficulty to make my way to the base of the lower cable station where the pylon, which lay below, had once stood. By nine o'clock I had reached the entrance to the Grota de Tabajara. Here I rested again and then prepared myself for the final part of the ascent. At the elevation of the Grota, the density of clouds was much reduced. As the heat of the sun had become more apparent I discarded my jacket with the intent of collecting it on my descent.

At 100 metres above the Grota I passed through the last of the clouds. I was now exposed to the full vigour of the sun. The surfaces of the upper pathways were dry but my progress became as slow as it had been on the lower slopes. The rays of the sun were powerful. I was obliged to frequently rest in the shadowed sides of the larger rocks. The crest of the serra came into view. I was also aware I would be viewed by anyone standing there. Climbing for a further 100 metres I was able to take advantage of some shade and cover provided by slight growths of shrubs. Eventually the steepness of the cliff face began to abate. My progress quickened and shortly I was amid small trees which grow at the forest's edge. Here the temperature was lower and my cover fuller. Soon I was amid the fulsome shade of the forest. By 10 o'clock I had finally reached the top of the serra.

For ten and more minutes I rested there. I had climbed for four and a half hours. This was a considerably longer time than I had anticipated. Also I was exhausted from my exertion and needed a period to recoup my strength and regain my breath.

Remembering the lessons taught to me in my boyhood by the older boys of the village, I remained silent and stationary. While resting I looked about me. I was able to take in the fullness of the silence of the forest. I continuously observed in every direction. I did not detect any movement, not even an insect's. The forest atmosphere was the same as I experienced in my boyhood. Many memories of the games I and other children had conducted there returned to me.

26: NIOBES

Sava-ve was still "zump2 snapping and sending sheets when I awoke. Although I was up and about before the dawn and there were still swirls of mist, Anuria and Pheterisco were already attending to Sava-ve and a dozen and more different other objects arrayed in a wide circle to the rear of Kubber as well. They were upright tubes about waist high and like Sava-ve they were stationary.

"He is a niobe and he is Shepo," said Pheterisco seeing me looking at one of them and me hearing his "Hadodani." When I asked what he did, Pheterisco said "He and the others are about to send a series of soliton pulse waves between the strato and ionosphere. From these readings we should be able to form our first reference vectorial plane."

As she spoke, I heard a rumbling sound coming from within Shepo's tube and Anuria shouted "Stand back!"

The rumbling became a roar and out shot a series of bright blue rings (as though from a giant cigar). They slowly rose and as I looked, the other niobes were puffing out the same. All the rings grew quickly in size and as they did I saw they were comprised of expanding bubbles. These then merged into a single cloud of light so bright it lit the dark as day. The cloud rose a few feet above us and then hovered. Anuria, who was on the opposite side of the circle of the niobes, raised her arm. Phetorisco did likewise, and looked down into a dial in her other hand, as did Anuria. They then both brought down their arms in unison. A hissing sound came from above the bubbles and I saw a disc which was brighter. I stepped back from under the cloud and saw that it had grown even bigger. Then with a "whumph" the disc shot away skyward.

"There it goes," called Pheterisco, but all I could see was a twinkle no bigger than a star. But all around was a sea of luminescent blue bubbles tumbling over the grass and then bursting into oblivion. Anuria and Pheterisco then walked around and adjusted the niobes then left them to it. Every half hour there would be another "whumph," a billowing of brightness diminishing away to a shooting star and a carpet of bubbling shining blue.

After the second display I left them and walked to the platform. The clouds were now lighter. The sun, I reasoned would soon burn the rest away.

During my return I resolved not on fleeing but fighting for the Susem. Though weighing up the options for defence I concluded that despite their wizardry the Susem had nothing which I had seen in the way of weaponry. I made a mental note to check what they had which could be of use.

Events deflected this endeavour. The first was Lucia flitting and scampering in her fresh white gown, her face full of smiles. From the ones on Menpe-melo's face, it was evident that she too was pleased with the outcome of Lucia's therapy. "Progressed faster than predicted," she beamed. ("And now her hair's been washed, cut and combed, even better looking as well," I thought).

I wasn't given time to look and talk more before Anuria appeared. There was something which needed to be seen she said. Grabbing my hand she rushed me up into Kubber with Menpemelo following on behind.

27: ROBERTO

After I had rested and regained my strength I made my way through the forest to my uncle's Lodge House. As I did so I remembered the further lessons the older boys had taught to me of moving from tree to tree stealthily and noiselessly.

I arrived at my uncle's home without incident. His truck was still parked by the Lodge. The front door was unlocked. I went inside and spent some minutes looking into each room. After seeing there was no disturbance I departed from the Lodge.

I travelled towards the village walking along the road vigilantly and keeping to its verge, my eyes and ears peeled. After walking for a kilometre the edge of the forest came into view. During this time I had not seen or heard anything except the forest's trees and their movements caused by breezes.

I now considered it prudent to travel no further upon the road but to make the remaining 200 metres to the village from amid the fuller cover of the forest. I travelled from tree to tree and again moving silently. I continued looking and listening for any movement but I was aware of none.

I approached closer to the pasture lying between the edge of the forest and the village. The shining of sunlight between the trees became more apparent. I came to within a few metres of the last groups of trees. From gaps between these I surmised I would be able to gain a full view of the village. I edged closer. The green of the pasture came into view. I moved forward. As I did so I saw that there was a something dark situated upon the pasture. I came to the last of the trees. I stood close behind one of them. I peered from around its edge.

On the pasture, dark against the sunlight, I saw a plane 30-40 metres in length. I knelt down on one knee. I slid my satchel from my shoulder. I took from it my camcorder. I removed the lens cap. My hands were trembling. I rose to my feet. Suddenly, I heard an explosion and saw beyond the plane a light of extreme brilliance.

I became disconcerted. I raised the camera. My hands became unsteady. I considered I would record a better image from a kneeling position. I rested down on both knees. I lifted the camcorder to my face. But as I did so I heard another, though faint noise.

I looked about me. I became aware of the panting of my breathing. I heard a further slight sound as if something was treading on fallen leaves. I was aware of the thumping of my heart. I glanced upwards. From around the tree to my side an arm appeared. Then I saw a face. I lost my balance. I was filled with fear. I was looking up at, just as my uncle had foretold, the ghost of Lucia.

28: TERBAL

Inside of Kubber I saw parts of him I had not seen before including the area Anuria tugged me into. Within were walls of screens, the other Susem, Terbal, and floating at head height, a large misty grey bubble. No sooner was I there than Paceillo said "It has now been possible to adjust our earlier readings." As she spoke the bubble transformed to a globe of the Earth.

At first it was blue and white but, with her "Subsequent findings of the later monitoring sequences have enabled a reinterpretation of our prior readings..." the white turned to browns and greens of land, "...resulting in identification..." she continued and in the same schoolteacherly tone, "...of the possible sources, of what we have now termed 'letum' waves."

As hundreds of lights, some bigger than others, appeared over the globe Terbal asked "Dese are you knowing Dommy?"

I turned to where I knew and spoke them out, "Dungeness, Sizewell, Sharpness, Sellafield (a big light there), Dounreay." As neither the Susem nor Terbal spoke, I continued making stabs at some of the others, "Three Mile Island (another big light) Chernobyl (an even bigger one, though it still wasn't the brightest) Lop Nor, Mururoa, Bikini, North Korea..."

I could have gone on but Paceillo interrupted with "What are they Danny?" Though she spoke quietly, the tone of her voice had an air of seriousness. With the silence of everyone else the atmosphere felt the same.

"Nuclear power stations, sites of nuclear tests, explosions..." As I spoke I continued looking at the globe, "...probably missile silos, nuclear accidents, possibly dumping sites of spent fuel (the really bright lights)."

"Yes, but what are they, what are they for, what do they do?" asked Paceillo still sounding earnest.

"Produce power, protect countries, provide prestige," I said.

"Produce power, how ist dis?" asked Terbal. And as he did so the room was still in silence.

I said I didn't really know but mentioned uranium and splitting of atoms generating electricity and explosions.

After Terbal's "Ah! Fission, dis ist explaining..." there were inward gasps coming from all nine of the Susem.

And as they gasped out again there was almost a unison of whispered "Oh no, not that." Then there was silence again. Utter silence.

But in that silence I saw them all giving wide eyed, open mouthed glances to one another. As they did, the globe began to reduce in size and little plumes spouted from where the lights had been. The plumes billowed then merged into one another covering the globe in a haze. Through the haze I could see the globe becoming smaller and smaller.

Paceillo broke the silence. "Not only must they cease functioning but be removed. Removed immediately," (and emphatically so, if the tone of her voice was anything to go by).

Before I had chance to ask "Why, what for?" Paceillo, unsmilingly continued, “The consequences of this letum wave creation, if unchecked is not only a threat to Earth but if this rate of generation continues, much of elsewhere will also be affected, including even the structure of our routes of travel. This we will not have.”

Though the last of what she said sounded ominous and I did try to take on the tenor of the moment, I still had no idea of what she was talking about. “What do you propose?” was all I could, dare to say.

“They must be stopped. And stopped now,” she said even more emphatically.

I said, and as quickly as I could and before I was interrupted, “How? If it’s nuclear power stations you want so see the back of, you can’t. They provide energy for a large amount of the world. Remove them and the world’s economy will collapse. Nuclear waste, they've been trying to get rid of it for years but without success. Nuclear weapons keep a peace of sorts. The countries and companies who control things nuclear are the most powerful in the world. How in goodness do you, sitting here in the middle of nowhere, expect to be able to change any of this when you don't even have enough to repel the army that's going to be coming here anytime soon?”

Before any of them had time to reply there was another “whumph” as the niobes went into action again.

“Two free eight, two free nine, two vor one,” said Terbal as he hovered in front of one of the screens, “are probably letum vafes generating,” then after some “umming,” “as 235 is freshold, I conclude also, der virst ist not so causing but others?...dey are der guilty.” He then called out more numbers, all the way to “...and perhaps also two sixty...perhaps higher,” then added “239 is appearing der main letum progenitor.”

By now, Paceillo having gravitated to a state of ire, growled “If they cannot, or will not be removed, then we will remove them.”

But before I’d even time to finish thinking, let alone to say, "Don’t be daft,” Kubber’s “Uh..huh, we have a visitor,” took the tension away.

If there was a monitor I didn’t see it, neither did the Susem. We all piled out and into the cockpit. Coming from the parkside trees was a young man, his hand being tugged by Lucia. “Go out and talk to him, go on,” said Paceillo with a jab to my ribs. So (partly because of last night) I did.

By his appearance, including the ragged fluff of beard and matching hair, I took him to be a student. By the look on his face when he saw me, I could also see there was surprise. But all the same, as I strode towards him I said “Oi. Como está?” When I saw he still had a look of surprise, I added “Meu nome é Danny, como é seu nome?”

He still had a puzzled expression but eventually exclaimed “Aah, English?”

(I didn’t think my pronunciation was that bad and I would have preferred “British” but) when I said I was, he said he was Roberto. We shook hands. This I'm sure helped him relax for he was still in a state of anxiety and awe, to say nothing of apprehension. I said he was among friends. And as I spoke, one by one the Susem stepped down from Kubber. Roberto seemed to take them in his stride but when he saw Terbal I had to repeat “Friends, all friends," before he had calmed down again.

Thankfully Roberto's English was fairly fluent and when he said he was Jorge's nephew, I not only saw he had his lean features and figure but also felt a sense of kinship. The Susem were soon around him and looking him up and down (with Tearo doing the most, I noted). Questions and answers flowed between us though Roberto gave a start when the niobes billowed and boomed again. And though I also noticed that he kept glancing at Terbal, such is the assuredness of the young, that he was soon taking everything in his stride including Terbal.

I was relieved when Roberto described the army were behaving in their traditional manner, ineptitude steeped in indolence. When he also confirmed that the people of the Ibiapaba were sheltering in Tianguá, I saw an opportunity of him persuading them to return and so provide a shield of protection. When he mentioned Jorge's truck was still outside his house I was all set for having him go to Tianguá without delay. Then a thought struck me. There was no guarantee Roberto would be successful, and no guarantee either he would not have the army arriving instead.

Not unnaturally Roberto was in a most excited state. With him mentioning that he was studying journalism, he was writing things down as fast as could be. However, when he took a camcorder from his satchel and Terbal said "Vat ist dat?" things changed.

During the next few hours I was able to appreciate yet again just how advanced is Susem technology. Not in the sense of massive resources but what can be achieved in using what is to hand, plus a little wizardry here and there.

Not only did the wish of the Susem to communicate to the wider world come to be, but it would provide defence and protection, the likes of which I could have only dreamt of. I felt a weight of worrying lift away.

Terbal was most enthusiastic and confounded any scepticism I might have had. I said there was no way the images from the camcorder could be transmitted but within minutes he had sherpals convert the Pousada's satellite dish from a receiver to a transmitter. When I said there wasn't sufficient power to boost the signal he had several soufins arrayed to do the job. And when I said because of scrambling there was no chance of the satellites' transponders accepting signals from the dish, he had that soon solved as well including the really tricky one of re-scrambling the onward signals.

Paceillo was also taken with the turn of events. It wasn't long after Terbal was embarked than she was once again concerning herself with the eradication of letum waves. "We have decided," she said, "to provide a replacement source of electricity from that being produced presently by your nuclear power generation."

At first, when she held up a soufin, I laughed, scoffed even. However, I did so out of ignorance. It wasn't long before Terbal was demonstrating their wonders. "Oxide of hydrogen here ist put," he said pointing to a thimble sized hole on the top (Roberto said "Water"). "Dis vor pressure (Roberto said "Volts") dis vor quantity ("Watts," said Roberto) here vor der vafes ("Hertz cycles"). For Tabajara, dese der settings are." As Paceillo did as Terbal instructed I saw that all the little dials weren't even halfway. "Und here der connections are."

"And how long will it last?" I asked.

"Ven fuel here ist, power ist dere. Nein oxide, nein power."

"But how long will it last?"

"Vith oxide it vill always last."

"For ever?"

"Ya."

While Roberto set about seeing if what Terbal said was true (in no time at all he had the Pousada fully connected, bypassing the mains and all the lights shining) I continued with my caution. "How on earth can you seriously expect these soufins to take the place of nuclear power stations?" I said to Paceillo. "These power stations supply hundreds of millions of people and industries. How can you ever expect to supply the world? You'll need millions and millions of them."

Paceillo went over to Terbal. At the time he was with Roberto, who had attached the soufin to a metal plate on which he had placed twigs and grass. As Paceillo walked back I saw a plume of smoke rising from the plate.

"The total production of soufins by the combined tocans which are with La-ra, is more than twenty million each day but this amount can be rapidly increased," she said.

"And just how do you think it possible to distribute such a number, and every day?" As I spoke I saw Roberto, holding the soufin under his arm, walking towards Jorge's place with Terbal and helpers flying alongside.

"The tocans should be able to do this," Paceillo said.

"So you're proposing to provide free power for everyone on Earth affected by the loss of nuclear power?"

"Yes," she said.

Lucia appeared wanting Paceillo's attention. I didn't really know why but it was something about not being able to find anyone else.

It was nearly two o'clock. I decided to walk to the viewing platform to see the state of the clouds. I still had the soufins on my mind. They were handy to have, but as for replacing electricity supply they couldn't be taken seriously. Even if they could do as Paceillo and Terbal said, there would not be a chance of closing anything down, especially nuclear things, power stations and weapon-making places.

For me, however, it was more a case of going through the motions. Keeping Paceillo happy was achievement enough. I didn't want to upset her again, especially after last night. But I was intent in getting the televising to take place. It wouldn't really matter what was said just as long as enough people saw it. It would stop anything nasty happening, for the while at least.

All the same though, I had still to shake my head at the moment of it all. Here in the middle of nowhere there were all these amazing events taking place. Yet at the same time there was an air of utter normality. Even when the niobes let off another “whumph” and billow of brightness, or Sava-ve still sending sheets, they didn't seem to be anything out of the ordinary.

I got as far as the forest’s edge when I heard a truck. Round the corner came Roberto driving as fast as could be. I had to jump to one side as he screeched to a halt. There were big black marks all down the road.

He alighted from the truck holding up both his thumbs and yelling “Bom! bom!” He was still raving over the truck’s acceleration now that it was powered by a soufin when Terbal with his carpet of helpers whizzed round the corner.

They too screeched to a sudden halt. “Power you like, ya?” said Terbal waggling his fronds. After Roberto said he did, Terbal carried on flying back to Kubber. But as he did I noticed there was a pair of hen-gers hovering above as if keeping an eye on him.

I never got to see the clouds. At Roberto’s insistence I climbed into the truck. He wanted to show me just how much power a soufin could provide. But it was little different from ordinary everyday Cearánese driving. Back in the village I baled out shaking and needing to lie down.

At three o’clock Terbal said, “Now ve test, ya?” With a wild wagging of fronds he was soon proclaiming “Ven der button vor ‘on’ ist on, everything vill be on.”

“Everything?” I asked.

“Everything ya. Everything everywhere der transmissions vill be having.”

“Everywhere?”

“Time to analyse transmissions von satellites’ transponders dere hast not been. Sherpals und solvers’ von Sieba sole success hast achieved sending our transmission on all transponders at 45,000 kilometres altitude only.”

“All? You mean not just television but telephone, surveillance, navigation, the others, all of them?”

“All.”

What could I do but shrug my shoulders?

When Terbal announced the link-up was operative it came time to attend to a few considerations of a practical nature. The first being who was going to say what was going to be said. With reluctance, the reticence of others and Tearo's bullying look I agreed that I would do it. The niobes would be blasting till four thirty. Roberto said it was best to do it on the hour, adding the light at 5 o’clock would be just right for my face (the young can sometimes be so blithely cruel) but all the same I had another shave and put on some of Elana's make-up (I've still not forgiven the TV News crew who came round one afternoon when the water filters were faltering and later broadcast showing me looking like Nixon along with their announcing “Would you risk purification from this man?”)

The second consideration was what to say. Presentation being always the essence of substance, a short, strong, though measured introduction was needed. As I was tapping it into my laptop Paceillo appeared with a soufin in her hand and said what she wanted to be said.

To which I replied “Is that all?”

"Just about Pa-tu, the stopping of letum waves and soufins," she said.

"I have a list here of all the things you mentioned yesterday," I said.

"We have no wish to be involved in the affairs of Earth any more than is necessary to obtain what we seek," she said.

With that she turned on her heels and went back to Kubber leaving me the soufin.

It was four thirty. There was a final "whumph" from the niobes. Anuria and Pheterisco walked them and Sava-ve back up into Kubber. Roberto set up his camera on some empty cerveja crates. As I sat and stood for him while he attempted to be a camera man, I was struck by how bizarre it all was. If I had not drunk more than I should have last Thursday I would not even have been in Tabajara. I read through what I was going to say as though learning lines for a play, speaking them silently over and over. Here I was in one of the remotest places I could, at the time, six months ago, find, only to land up in the middle of the most almighty event to occur for years. Roberto said the time was a quarter to five and my nose was shining. I rubbed the cream off of it. I looked at the camera in his hands. I still had difficulty taking in that such a tiny thing was connected to a system which was going to beam down to every satellite dish over half the world. I took his point about the sunlight, it was softening into a golden-ness and the shadows in the parkside trees behind him had hues of blue. I remembered how you always look your best when the main light is behind you. Lucia appeared with Menpemelo and they sat on their haunches up by the door of Kubber. The other Susem appeared and stood in a group behind them. The time was ten to five. Roberto said it was best if I stood after all, adding he had to hold the camera so as to swing round and show the Susem. I turned to them and said to them "You said you weren't going to be in it?" But Paceillo, smiling, silently pointed at Lucia. Being unaware of this alteration had me confused. Roberto said it was five to five and began counting down the time. He must have been on a TV course. I told him to stop it. We compromised with him stage whispering. I still half believed it wasn't going to work but was hoping like heck it would. I could have done with a drink but I had been forbidden. Even Roberto joined in with this. He stopped stage whispering and said "20," then "15, 10...8...6.5.4.3.2.1...Açáo!"

29: MAHADEVI

Terrible it was, terrible. There was no need, quite uncalled for. They ruined everything. No "Stick 'em up," no "I say, I say, what's going on here?" It was just as I said they would, fire first, question survivors later.

I had barely begun. They came out from the trees over on the park-side. First a few, then more. Then they raised their rifles. Shouting did no good. Roberto swung around to look and took a bullet to the side of him.

I was on the ground before they fired again. It was their last, in an offensive capacity that is. A swarm of hen-gers were soon upon them. Roberto was in a terrible state, he began hurting and bleeding. The poor lad did cry out so, but a carpet had him swiftly whisked up into Kubber.

Kubber's door then clump closed but even before it had I heard the soldiers firing fending off the hen-gers. Though I knew they had not a chance, I stuck my head up to see. To my embarrassment the camcorder's little red light was on. I clicked it off.

As sheep dogs do, the hen-gers hounded the soldiers, twelve of them, towards us (though when I looked, there was only me, and Kubber). As the soldiers were run, some stumbling, they pleaded back at the hen-gers.

With a flurried chorus of "Hadodanis" the hen-gers delivered the soldiers in front of me. I was annoyed, scared. I didn't know what to do but instead shouted "On the ground, flat" (there wasn't time for the Portuguese), and motioned the same with my hand. And I only said and did it because I had seen it in the movies. One soldier instantly did as I told them, the others quickly followed suit.

The one who went down first turned his face up to me and asked "Americano?"

"No," I snapped but instinctively added "você fala inglês?"

"A little," he said.

Fearful the soldiers could yet be dangerous, as well as still remembering the movies, I yelled "Tell them to take off their boots and uniforms, you as well." All knelt up to do so. But the hen-gers began hovering lower. I thought they might be going in for a stinging. So did the soldiers. Without thinking, I raised my hands and said "Up." The hen-gers did so. The soldiers gasped relief (they must have believed I had control over the hen-gers).

I next yelled "Tell them to sit in two rows, knees up, hands behind their heads" (I took that from the movies as well). This they did, again as soon as they were told. There didn't seem to be any fight in them.

With the soldiers in their underwear any knives and the like away from them, I began to ease a little, have (with hen-gers still hovering) a sense of authority. Emboldened, I snapped "Who is in charge?"

The one who spoke English said he was.

Still recalling the movies, "Name, rank, serial number?"

"Lucina, Pedro Lucina, Tenente, Z76 36 50," he said.

Noting how readily he replied I became bolder, "Others...where are they?"

He said there were none. From the pained look on his face I half believed him but dared not give that impression. I barked it again, harder.

With the raising of my voice the hen-gers came lower again. This scared the soldiers. The speaking one, Pedro, implored that there were no 'others'. I began to believe him.

But amid his further "Please sir, I swear it is the truth," and "I beg, do not let the vespãos sting," I heard faint hissing, babbling sounds of a radio.

I became unnerved. It came from over by the park-side. I shouted "You lie," and pointing to where the radio was coming from, "where are they?" The hen-gers hovered even lower.

"It is ours," he said, gulping, crying then pointing to the soldier behind him adding "telefonista." This soldier nodded vigorously. Relaxing, I raised my flattened hands. The hen-gers rose, but only a little.

There was then silence, including from the radio. With their heads bowed and hands behind their necks the soldiers continued sitting in two lines facing Kubber. I still worried over other soldiers appearing, what the radio had said and the fact that, apart from Kubber and the hen-gers, I was all on my own.

Twenty, long, minutes passed.

To every question I asked this Pedro he readily replied. He said they had come from Tianguá but were based at Crateús. They were members of the Forças Armadas Especiais (the US trained ones with tough repute). But when I asked why they hadn't come by the road from Ubajara, he shrugged his shoulders. He was about to speak again when Kubber's door opened.

The soldiers momentarily glanced up. I turned and saw Tearo at the top of the ramp. She stood looking down at us. The image of Churchill in his Siren Suit passed through my mind. She came down the ramp. And then, fortunately (as well as unfortunately), over to us.

Fortunate in that she was able to talk to the hen-gers. I said I wanted two soldiers to collect the radio and rifles but I needed hen-gers to escort them. This she did. Still keeping the facade of sternness I told Pedro what I wanted.

Unfortunate, because as the two soldiers he selected rose to their feet Tearo's eyes were upon them. As they trotted away to collect, she said "Tell the others to stand up." This was when the trouble started.

It was a quarter after six, daylight was beginning to go. The remaining soldiers rose to their feet. They stood, heads bowed and still in two lines. Ten young males in the peak of physical condition in just their white, close fitting army issue vests and pants. First she inspected the front row, then the second. As she looked at these I couldn't help notice the soldier in the middle of the front row. Apart from the moustache, there was a lot of him. I remember thinking "You won't get many of them to the pound, or kilo, as the case might be."

Tearo had also noticed, for when she came back to the front row she tapped him on the shoulder. Then she beckoned him to come with her. Like a tamed bear (he was about that size), he padded off behind her. They disappeared round the far side of Kubber. Within minutes I knew what she was doing with him (and I'm still sure it's against the Geneva Convention).

Meanwhile, the two soldiers returned with the rifles and radio. I told all of them to sit down again. With these soldiers silent it was impossible for them not to hear the twelfth one and Tearo. It was embarrassing and worrying, knowing that there would nothing but trouble. There's so much VD and AIDS in Brazil, and should go down with a dose of clap, all hell would break out. I feared for the worst.

It came to quarter before seven. The light was fading but in what little remained, I couldn't help notice the soldiers were taking an increasingly keen interest in the sounds from behind Kubber. Half an hour passed before the pair of them reappeared. The soldier silently padded back and took his place with the others. Tearo came and stood by me. She had a smirk on her face.

"Orrh...that is better," she sighed, panting as though she'd been running, "All tension from my body is now gone." She followed this with more deep contented 'umming' purrs and a languid flexing of her body.

"You want to be careful," I said, "get yourself checked out, you might have got something off of him. They've got an awful lot of disease in Brazil."

In the same sated tone she said "I had an urge, he was there, I just could not resist a brief congress." ("Half an hour," I thought, "and that's a 'quickie'?") After a pause and an air of self-assuredness, she said "Should I be infected with anything that my body cannot manage I will know here." Brushing back her hair she pointed to a small raised line to the side of her ear. But in a purring lower tone and casting eyes over the soldiers, added "Ooh, I still have urges."

I changed the subject. "Roberto, how is he? Are they operating on him, will he be alright?"

"I do not know."

The radio came to life again, "Tenente Lucina...abaixo...Tenente. abaixo..."

I was in a quandary. The soldiers' base was obviously trying to contact them. Was it to know what they were doing, send a message to them? It was important to discover what it was. But I couldn't risk any of the soldiers answering, my Portuguese was too limited. The only person who could help was Roberto. I explained this to Tearo. But having seen his condition I wasn't hopeful. She went back up into Kubber to see. The door closed behind her.

No sooner had Tearo left than the soldiers started making darting, grinning glances and murmuring "Você transou com ela?" between themselves but mainly to the one who had been with her. I could just about catch his voice, it was gravelly deep. I tried to make out what he was saying for it was evidently of great interest to them all. I asked Pedro "What did the "Eta te agarrou," the soldier kept saying, mean?"

From the tone of his reply I sensed Pedro was ill at ease, "Luiz's fellows are enquiring of him details of the assignation with your colleague...Luiz is replying, saying your colleague...is a very nice lady...they have had a very pleasant meeting...and he is looking forward to...an opportunity of...meeting with her...again..." But I'm sure Luiz was saying something else. Especially when I saw him opening and closing his hand as he kept repeating the words "Seu pulso." And I know "Pernas" means legs but I don't know what the "Pernas de quebra-noze castanha," he kept mentioning meant and why the eyes of the others seemed to widen each time he said it. Also, what "Trovoada", which I'm pretty sure means thunderstorm, had to do with it.

The light had almost gone and mist was now forming. The soldiers, apart from Luiz, were becoming restless, and some I could see wanted to relieve themselves. It was becoming necessary to move them to somewhere secure or at least do something with them. Pedro had already asked what was going to happen and I, still affecting to be authoritarian, said "Awaiting orders."

To deflect his questions I asked more of him. Why had they fired on us? Why hadn't they just approached us, they must have seen we weren't threatening them? As he replied I could see he was becoming nervous again. He said they had waited in the forest for some time watching us, heard and seen the flash of the niobes going off and became convinced we were armed. They were scheduled to contact Tianguá on each hour. Just as his operator was about to radio a message, a terrible noise came over his earphones. Pedro thought we were jamming them and therefore that we were about to attack. What he said was all rather flimsy but at least it proved that Terbal's grand system worked, or leastways something came from it.

Pedro also said that Roberto had been spotted climbing the Ibiapaba, they had followed his trail. I was questioning Pedro about the radio messages when the whole tenor of events changed in a way I could never ever imagined.

Kubber's door opened with a greater suddenness than usual. The brilliance of light from within him glowed beacon-like into the mistiness of the night. Partly silhouetted by the glow were the Susem. I don't know if they did it for dramatic effect but all nine were levitating.

Paceillo was in the centre. Immediately behind her were Menpemelo and Milophinia, both supporting Roberto upright in their arms. Like Lucia had been, he was clad in a long white gown.

From the top of the ramp, Paceillo roared "Who did this?"

"Now look what you've done," I muttered to Pedro, "you've upset her," but I don't think he and the others heard. They were staring ahead transfixed, mouths agape.

Paceillo pulled open the top of Roberto's gown and slid it from his shoulders, revealing a scar to one side of his body and a smaller one on the other.

With Menpemelo and Milophinia still supporting him the Susem floated down towards the soldiers and me. Roberto, his eyes wide, glazed and staring, along with his drawn features was obviously still in a state of shock. However, combined with the inherent scragginess of his body, raggedness of his beard and hair, he had the soldiers crossing themselves and falling on their knees. With hands clasped as in prayer they were crying and whimpering, begging for forgiveness. With Paceillo still leading, the Susem came ever closer. With the only light being from Kubber, they and Roberto did indeed have a heavenly countenance.

"Who did this?" Paceillo thundered again.

Pedro, tears streaming down his face, cried out "As officer in charge, I must take personal responsibility for this wicked crime. I beg your forgiveness oh Lord," and threw himself in front of them.

But Pedro had not finished his pleading when from behind him another of the soldiers leapt up, rushed forward crying "Eu, Pardel," and made personal claim for the shooting. And like Pedro he too beseeched for forgiveness. But within no time all the soldiers were claiming personal responsibility and seeking salvation and redemption. Despite being tough hardened soldiers, so loud were the sounds of their blubbing and beseeching they could have been heard from afar.

Terbal, no doubt curious over the commotion, next appeared on the scene. With the light from Kubber shimmering off of him the soldiers were genuflecting all over again and crying "Espírito santo, Espírito santo." All that was missing was a crown of thorns.

Paceillo and the others, taken aback by the soldiers' contrition, stood looking at them in confusion. But seeing an opportunity arising I nipped smartly over to her.

As quickly as I could I whispered "Remember the Catholicism yesterday? They think he's him. Keep it up and we'll be all right. Give them forgiveness and they'll do anything, they'll be all yours."

"You do it," she swiftly whispered back.

"I'll need the help of one of you," I said.

"Pheterisco?"

"Done."

Blasphemous, but needs must. While Pheterisco patted their heads I intoned with as much sanctity as I could muster, "If you will promise to be on the side of the Lord he will forgive you your sins." And with their promises promptly and contritely received, "You are forgiven, for you knew not what you have done." And finally, when I had them following Pedro in their tear-filled "Amens," so as to heighten the moment, I intoned "Pax verbriscus."

With atoning accomplished, Roberto along with the Susem departing to Kubber, and half thinking that everything was getting utterly out of hand, I got down to the nitty gritty.

I asked Pedro "What was the radio saying? Who else was coming? What were they armed with, what was their backup?" He promptly provided the answers.

They hadn't come by road because there was half a company of other soldiers who were. These had been laying up in Ubajara but could already be on their way. Both groups had planned for a coordinated assault at 8 o'clock. The time then was 7.30. Defence was needed without delay. And the best form of which is always surprise, then attack.

It was all over in minutes. Their trucks and jeeps went into the narrow valley before Tabajara. The niobes, both behind and before them, went off. The hen-gers zoomed in. Pedro shouting "Cercaho...cercaho...entrega-te!" ("You are surrounded, surrender") was more perfunctory than anything. In no time the fifty soldiers, with hen-gers hovering above, were being run up into the village, hands above their heads.

As with the first contingent, the second were in a state of shock and amazement. While some of Pedro's men collected the trucks and jeeps, I told the new arrivals, through Pedro, to take off their uniforms and boots. None spoke any English, but from Pedro I learnt no other soldiers were expected.

Tearo appeared and from the way she looked the new arrivals over, it was evident her urges were still very much with her. But before she could indulge, Paceillo also appeared and it was evident her ire hadn't abated either. Her arrival coincided with those of the trucks and jeeps.

As Pedro's men carried cases of ammunition from the trucks, Paceillo asked "What are these?" Then, in a quieter tone, as more ammunition and arms were unloaded, "these...and these?" Sensing wrath constrained in her voice I swiftly passed over to Pedro to provide her answers.

In a voice so cool and measured it dripped with menace, she asked him "And what were these going to be used for?"

She rammed his unthinking "Pre-emptive defensive response" reply back down his throat with such force, that from the look on his face I thought he was going to choke.

But rather than expire upon her wrath he adroitly demoted himself to "mere interpreter" to his superior, Capitão Carlos Reis, commander of the second contingent. Unfortunately for the Capitão there was no one further to deflect to, and doubly unfortunately he attempted to stand by his actions. For him this was a strategic error. He should have known never to argue with a woman, especially when she's in a position of power.

Although a mismatch, it was nevertheless an interesting bout, a boxer of bantam weight forced to go ten rounds against a heavyweight all-in wrestler. For his own sake the Capitão, although a man of strapping countenance, should really have thrown in the towel before he began.

Paceillo's opening forearm smash of accusation surprised him. Her subsequent ones had him reeling. At the beginning the Capitão did try some jabs of justification but alas for him not only were these ineffectual, Paceillo immediately grabbed each one he made and slammed him onto the ropes of creditability with them.

Realising he was routed the Capitão tried to run out of the ring by refusing to respond to Paceillo's further questioning blows. But by taunting him in front of his men for being a coward in not replying, and with his no doubt induced belief to maintain machismo in their eyes, she forced him to vainly soldier on.

Seeing she had the upper hand Paceillo soon had the Capitão entangled in the ropes. Then she went at him. Two fast flying dropkick questions, "Why had he driven at the rear of the column?" and as he had, "How much did he care for the fate of his men?" She had him confessing to being an uncaring coward. His confession alienated him from his troops.

Realising his error that he was now not only defenceless but also without support, the Capitão voluntarily offered his submission by crying. But Paceillo had barely begun. She laid rabbit punch after Cuban kick of accusation into him, of how he would not have stopped his men assaulting Lucia, her and the others, the cattle and goodness knows what other heinous crimes and atrocities. She delivered each kick and punch of her haranguing in a cold, deliberate manner. But should the Capitão, on Pedro's interpreting, fail to give an instant admission of guilt, he would receive her butting bashings of wrath until he did.

Even when the Capitão knelt on his knees offering himself up for a further submission, Paceillo still wouldn't let go of him. Again and again he suffered the full body slamming effects of her disdain, each one delivered pile-driver fashion. And in turn, she followed up each one with sadistic butterflies and full-nelsons of insinuations as to his inadequacy. He was all but screeching out his readiness to renounce the army, all forms of aggression and much else besides. As the Capitão slumped, sobbing before her, the spine of his spirit broken along with his standing among his men (who all seemed to be inwardly continually counting to ten), Paceillo finally kneed him into proclaiming unending peace and love to all, insects included.

By the end Paceillo had him eating out her hand even though she had never laid so much as a finger on him. To my mind that's skill. It's also a salutary lesson of what can happen should anyone be unwise enough to upset her.

The Capitão was not the only one who had decided on the Damascus road. When, via Pedro, Paceillo asked the watching soldiers, did they also forsake aggression, she was met with their chorus of "Viva Miguella! Viva Miguella!"

Pedro explained the meaning and consequences of their cheers. During the Capitão's conversion, Pedro's men, especially Pardel had told the soldiers what they had experienced, that they were in the company of angels, and so Paceillo must be the archangel (though I did wonder which angel they thought Tearo might be). Pedro said that the soldiers, just as he and his men had been, were converted to following the Susem and more especially Roberto, though they added "Afilhado de Deus" to his name. (I'm dreading the consequences when they find he's not).

If at 7.30 I had thought matters were getting out of hand, by 10.30 they were totally and utterly out of my control. Between then and then the sixty two soldiers had drunk the Pousada's bar dry, Paceillo had completely changed her mind, and I was dreading the consequences. However, the worry of who was going to pay Elana for all the drink was as nothing compared to Paceillo's intentions.

I did say "You can't do that," and "it won't work," but after the first couple of times I gave up. In part it was my not wanting to upset her and partly because it's been my experience that once a woman has made up her mind, there's no changing it, until she decides to do so. All I could do was explain the difficulties and hope she might change her mind yet again. Though seeing her zest I wasn't hopeful.

In another hour two further vedas, Konnet and Kershaw were lying alongside Kubber. Thirty minutes later the soldiers, dutiful and mellow and still in nothing but their underwear, were boarding all three. The ones I saw on Kubber were each handed, by Lathia, a small silver white container the size of a matchbox and told to put it on. Following her instructions they tapped one end of the boxes and as they did they stretched out into tunics with boots attached. Apart from wondering why I wasn't given one I was curious as to how they appeared to fit each soldier perfectly.

Two hours later I said "This looks like it" and I'd never been there in my life. We arrived as the dawn did. It was just as my friend David the prospector had said, shrouded in fog. However, we arrived with the dawn so there would be the fog. The only other thing he had mentioned when he told me of the Sperrgebeit was that it's halfway between the islands of Roastbeef and Plumpudding.

I sat in the cockpit of Kubber observing events unfold. Paceillo, beside me, tongue in cheek, sardonically said, "Pre-emptive defensive response?" Then, "Where are the soldiers you said would be here?"

I did try to envisage events from their perspective, the Namibian soldiers' that is. What it must have been like with the dawn breaking to have seen, walking noiselessly from the sea, looming through the swirls of mist, lines, groups of silent figures clad in white cowl tunics.

And also what it must have been like for soldiers stationed further inland and above the level of the mists as they saw the first light reflecting off of the vedas hovering above the foreshore? What would their reactions have been, I wondered, as they saw, then heard, black swarming clouds of hen-gers, the rising sun glinting off of them and flying fast above them and then beyond? And as soon as these had passed, what would their reactions have been on seeing the further swarms of hen-gers slowly approaching them? What would it have been like for those soldiers as they saw the seaward sky fill with them and then the first flights of hen-gers, now dark against the sun, zooming back for attack?

What would all of these soldiers' reactions have been as, suddenly, the whole sky erupted with countless screeching squadrons of hen-gers stuka diving down, fast flying in all directions, seeking, nullifying any movement of any being or thing, with curtains and pulses of energy so powerful that bullets and all other projectiles bounced back to where they had been fired and the firers themselves receiving zapping paralysing stings? Or those soldiers seeking to fight from behind protection, finding the surfaces of their shelters swiftly covered in seething, entwining vines of hen-gers who unitedly detonated themselves creating holes through which further hen-gers swarmed, stinging any remaining occupants into an agonising then stupefying numbness. And of those soldiers attempting to radio for assistance finding transmission as well as reception jammed?

Although there were no signs of soldiers there was thankfully an abundance of diamonds. And just as David had said the whole beach from horizon to horizon was covered with them. Within minutes the soldiers had filled the pockets at the fronts of their tunics with diamonds. Other soldiers with sacks collected the diamonds and in turn, tipped them into larger ones. In an hour there was a dozen and more sacks stacked in a line waiting to be carried on board Kubber and the other vedas. I shudder to think what those diamonds are worth but they must have come to millions. I did try thinking that the taking of them was all in a noble cause, but a voice within kept saying "They've been lifted."

Before the sun had burned the sea mist away the diamonds and everyone was on board and the vedas were rising up above the shore flying eastward once more.

Looking into the rear bay I caught the smell of chocolate and saw the soldiers falling asleep on the floor. I also saw hen-gers tightly packed, noses upward, covering all the ceilings. "Taking in energy," said Lathia. As Kubber climbed higher, I saw, through the surrounding curtain of yet more hen-gers, Konnet and Kershaw, the sunlight shining off of their wings and below them the beige brown of Africa. Within an hour and a half, and with the sun now high above, we were passing over the northern tip of Madagascar.

Five hours later the smell of mint awoke me. The sun was low on the horizon and I had a deep sense of foreboding. Until then Paceillo's ploys had paid off, but her next one I felt was nigh impossible. I just hoped I had the facts right or rather the laptop's 'Atlas-Gazetteer' program had. From Terbal's room I could hear his monotone teutonic voice intoning yet again, "5,700 square kilometres, population 298,000, oil, gas main exports are...Lapangan Terbang, main airport ist..."

But as I walked to where he was and saw Paceillo, Lathia and Lico there as well, he began giving information which wasn't on the program, "...concentrations identified, free...vun at Jerudong, adjacent to structures larger dan odders surrounding...two, 12 kilometres further suid-vest, insular coastal habitation it ist naar...free, 40 kilometres furver suidvest also to der ost of area identified as Seria, locations second und fird close to der vater...der virst open land to der nord...dis der best option ist presenting..."

They looked round as I asked "And where did you get all that from?"

"Fenserfs," replied Terbal matter-of-factly. With this he gave a frond half a waggle towards one of the screens. Up on it appeared the same sort of images I had seen shown on Sieba, except these were of barracks.

"At least you are correct about soldiers, this time," said Paceillo dryly.

"Why didn't you use these fenserfs at Tabajara?" I exclaimed. "There wouldn't have been all the trouble we have had."

"They only arrived with Konnet," and without a change of tone, Paceillo added "how do you think we located the diamonds?" Then, just as dryly, she asked "Which one do you consider to be the most appropriate?"

I almost said "How should I know?" and "None of them, it won't work, just get out of here, there is no way they would ever come with you, even though you have the hen-gers they will still chop your heads off," but instead, and with my eyes on another of the screens, I said "The biggest one I suppose." On this other screen I saw lines of yet more vedas, dozens and dozens of them.

Events and Paceillo's plans had now passed the point of no return. It was just a question of what sort of dust-up was going take place. I saw nothing but trouble looming. Then a thought about avoiding confrontation sprang into my mind, of applying charm.

"Mahadevi," I said.

The three of them, and I suppose Terbal too, turned and looked at me.

It has been my experience that, given in the context of conversation, women can never fail to warm to a compliment regarding their disposition and appearance. So I said to them "Use the strengths of your opposition against itself, did you not say to me regarding overcoming the soldiers from Ubajara?"

As they were now attentive I continued, "The Brazilian soldiers are Catholics and they think you are angels. These are Hindus. Mahadevi is not only their Great Goddess of Creation and Destruction, but she is believed to have many different forms from fearsome to placid."

Having now their interest and addressing myself to Paceillo in particular I added "If you present yourself in the right way they may well think you are Mahadevi, for like you, she is revered for being both dynamic and possessing great beauty."

"Do you think they will?" she said, giving a hint of a grin.

"Apart from knocking the life out of them, and you will have to knock it out of every last one, what alternative is there? And a little levitating probably wouldn't go amiss either."

But with the grin quickly gone, Paceillo retorted "You said the diamonds would make them come, why did you not make mention of this Mahadevi before?"

Scoring a point back I said "I'd not thought of her then."

A few minutes later Paceillo spoke to Terbal and he, folding in his fronds, become a ball and I was ushered back into the cockpit along with Lathia and Lico. As we went I asked "What is happening now?"

"You will soon see," said Lico. And I did.

Kubber dropped down at such a speed that when I saw the sea appearing, I thought we were going into it. We came that close I could see tops of waves but at the last moment he straightened out. I could also see Konnet and Kershaw either side of us, a little to the rear. Land appeared and as it did, the hen-gers surrounding Kubber and the other two shot away from us. As soon as they were gone their replacements shot away too. This happened many times. We crossed the coast. There was a beach, lines of trees, open parkland, a road, a golf course. The entire experience was like looking out a plane's window when it comes to land, except this was many times the speed. Then we stopped.

From the edge of the park the land rose at a slight slope. Even before we landed I could see the gold dome of the Istana Nurul palace. The Gazetteer said it was bigger than the Vatican but now here it was, sticking up above the crest of the hill and, in the fading light, one side gleamed with the last of the sun. I also saw the soldiers, still clad in their white tunics, leaving Kubber, Konnet and Kershaw. Then I saw figures, dark against the light, coming to the brow of the hill.

Paceillo and Pedro formed the soldiers into a curved line and with her at the front of them. The soldiers began walking slowly up the slope with a halo of hen-gers hovering above them. Some of the soldiers were carrying the sacks of diamonds. I had not long watched them walk away, when I felt a tug to my sleeve. As Lathia and Lico led me down the ramp I could see more figures appearing on the top of the hill. The other Susem joined us and we went up behind the soldiers.

The Susem, soldiers and me (though I wasn't particularly willing) continued walking up the hill with no one saying a word. More figures appeared but still none moved towards us (though I kept looking round to see if any were creeping up on us). We came within a 100 yards of them but still they didn't move (to me this was worrying, they just had to be planning something). A few yards more and I could see over the brow of the hill. Before us was the palace in all its now floodlit splendour (or "no expense spared gaudiness"). Also arrayed down the other side of the hill and others hurrying up it, were yet more men, hundreds of them. In the fading light it wasn't possible to see exactly who they were (but fearing for my throat, was all for legging back to Kubber).

We stepped a few yards more. One of the men who had been hurrying up the hill, and with an entourage behind, shouted but I didn't understand what he said (though from the tone of his voice I was all ready for the outbreak of gunfire). Paceillo motioned to Pedro, who in turn told the soldiers to halt.

The man with the entourage shouted again. Paceillo turned to me but I shook my head and hands intimating I didn't understand (though part of the shaking was from apprehension). She faced him again, raised the flat of her hand and took a couple of steps forward (and with me thinking that all hell was going to break out, we might have hen-gers but these men were so tough they'd probably eat them). The man shouted again, this time in English, "Stop, you are in a forbid..." but this was as far as he got.

A light, like a laser beam immediately shone down from far above. It shone down on Paceillo, and just on Paceillo. A murmur of gasps rippled away down the slope. As the light fell upon her Paceillo called out "Peace."

Then another murmur of gasps from these men was rippling away. For as she called out, all the hen-gers about us switched on their little lights. There was then another murmur of gasps as the thousands of other hen-gers hovering above the slopes switched on their lights as well. And another as all the palace lights and elsewhere suddenly went out.

In the darkness the hen-gers sparkled like diamonds. Murmured gasps, one after another, rippled away as the hen-gers swooped, swept, cascaded through the sky as though in some grand ballet. And Paceillo, waving her arms like a conductor, was their choreographer. For several minutes and more she had them dance about the dark, building them up to marvellous formations of flying monsters at one moment then scattering them like stardust the next. As a finale she had hen-gers form into a long lolloping serpent with a ferocious grand grin. After Paceillo had it gambol above us all, she, with an upward clasp of her arms had it slide snake-like backwards slowly down the beam of light still shining on her.

As the hen-gers wound around and down the beam of light on Paceillo, they came and hovered over us forming layer upon layer of glittering lights above our heads. When only the serpent's smile remained, Paceillo had the hen-gers then shoot, all as one, forward from us. They zoomed away fast down the slope then, parting into dozens of separate rippling banners of light, the hen-gers rose steeply upwards. Then, in an instant, they were gone and all that remained was the darkness.

However, even before the resulting applause had ended, a surround of pillars of cold white light suddenly beamed down from above. It was as though we all were in a huge high oval hall, one which stretched from the palace up to the vedas. Then from between these columns, the hen-gers first like moths then fire-flies, fluttered back down again.

After this there wasn't much in the way of contest. Paceillo, beckoning to Milophinia and Menpemelo, went over to the man who had shouted and who was by then cowering face down. The three of them lifted him up and carried him down the slope. I couldn't see if they were levitating or not, but whatever it was they were doing, they received, as they went, hurrah! after hurrah! And as the men bravoed their admiration, the hen-gers flew about them alighting on their shoulders, caressing their hair and cheeks with their wings.

When Paceillo first told me of her intentions I never believed she could possibly pull it off. I also had the impression she had brushed aside my remarks regarding their toughness, fearlessness and steadfast sense of allegiance, but she had indeed taken note of all I'd said. Within the hour she had everything wrapped, packed and making ready to leave.

There was the theatrical spectacle of Paceillo taking the sword of the man in charge, a Colonel Tambassing, and had Terbal, who had by then also appeared on the scene, pass his fronds between it and two hen-gers. When this was done she took the sword, had one of the colonel's men hold up his one, then with a swipe sliced this man's in two. A roar went up of course and after she had pricked her finger with the Colonel's sword before handing it back to him, another hurrah (she really had taken in everything I'd told her including that once unsheathed a sword had to draw blood).

Immediately all the men were queuing to have their swords made extra sharp and strong. And as they did, Paceillo outlined to the Colonel what she had in mind. He readily agreed chuckling as he did so, adding that he and some of his men were there in '96 and knew a bit of the lingo. After he had outlined what was wanted and causing even more chuckles, he called for 500 volunteers. But this didn't go down too well. So Paceillo and the Colonel came to a compromise with his men, which was to take all the volunteers. This turned out be every last one of them. We didn't really need diamonds.

The Colonel said it was their first chance in years to do any real soldiering and they couldn't wait for a bit of cut and thrust (especially the cutting). The Paduka, so the Colonel also said, was away visiting his cattle station in Australia, but he didn't think he would really mind as he had another regiment of them which was also doing nothing particular either. The Colonel did leave a message, but it was almost as if he'd pinned a note on the palace door, saying they would be away for a week or two doing a bit of actual soldiering.

I suggested hanging on to the diamonds but Paceillo insisted they were all given out, a handful to each volunteer. More than a thousand handfuls and Paceillo ensured that not a single stone remained. Pity that, I had hoped there might have been a few going spare.

As we went back to Kubber I asked Paceillo why she had been so insistent I was there, when I had done nothing?

"Just in case you were needed," she said.

She made me feel like I was a small boy now being told to "run along."

Before Kubber took to the air the columns of lights were disappearing as, one after another, the vedas from Sieba landed. As we flew away I asked Lathia where Lico was.

"She, Anuria and Tearo are travelling to Sieba to oversee our guests."

"Tearo, with all those soldiers?"

"Yes."

I feared for the worst.

I'd had a busy day and not a wink of proper sleep either, but any hopes of a rest were soon dashed. Even before we were back in Tabajara, Paceillo had outlined her 'orders', or "proposals" as she kept calling them. She had me labour the day through. My task wasn't made easier either by continual distractions, including those from her ever-changing mind.

I would work on what she said she wanted, there would be an interruption of her "What is this?" I would traipse up to Kubber, look at Terbal's screens and more often than not I would say "I don't know, ask Pedro" (though I did recognise the Serra Pelada which, being 500 miles away, surprised me). I would then go back to my laptop, tap in a few more lines. Paceillo would appear again and say "We have decided..." I would then say "Oh no, not that as well" (there were variations, "You can't have that, it won't work, they will never do it, that's impossible, you can't be serious, do you realise the consequences"). She would give me a cold stare, and I would sense the scraping of her knife on my back. I would then say "Alright I'll put it in," and then start re-writing. I did make a comment about kitchen sinks, but after I'd explained it I realised it hadn't gone down at all well.

As I tapped in everything that Paceillo wanted, part of me was thinking "This is absolute madness, it will never work, it will be scoffed at." The rest was thinking "It's for real, she means it, it's going to happen." But in between, there was a nagging thought, that there is something else behind her 'proposals', some hidden agenda. What also nagged at me was, with all the resources and organisation the Susem had displayed, why were they playing around with the likes of us here at Tabajara? With what they had shown in the past dozen hours, let alone what is planned for tomorrow, they could have demonstrated themselves anywhere in the world, and with impunity. When they brought all those machines with them from Sieba, why didn't they bring fenserfs with them as well? There is no way they could have 'forgotten' them. What are the Susem really after?

While Paceillo played with the fenserfs (they look like binoculars with umpteen bits on) the soldiers played with their trucks. We hadn't been long back before Terbal told them how to fit soufins. I wish he hadn't, for no sooner were they fitted than the soldiers were taking turns to drive their trucks as fast as could be. It's a wonder no one has been killed. When the soldiers weren't driving, Pheterisco and Pedro had them tending the villagers' livestock and cleaning up the Pousada. And when they weren't driving or working,

Menpemelo and Milophinia or the other Susem would also conduct them in classes, though I still have no idea what they are about. They also had Pedro darting everywhere, interpreting for them and identifying for Paceillo.

Terbal was also a distraction. He was attracted to the soldiers' radios. After the two operators had shown him how they worked, that they use satellites, he realised they could be used as telephones as well. Within a couple of hours he had us connected (and via my Citicard) to the Internet. Apart from it fascinating him he kept bagging my laptop.

Roberto was another distraction. His wellbeing restored and his gown exchanged for a tunic, he was promptly apprised of his new status. At first, though, the soldiers would go down on their knees each time he passed but he wisely told them to stop doing it and instead concentrate on their rehearsals. A student he might be but he takes his television seriously. So seriously that, like Paceillo, he too was forever wanting to change what I was writing.

Most of what Paceillo wanted I didn't agree with. It was either naïve or just plain stupid but usually it was both. I did endeavour to explain that people don't like being told what to do, even if it is for their 'own good'. They resent others trying to 'save' them, but she took no notice. And no notice either that I have spent my entire life avoiding 'do gooders' wanting to 'save me' and now here I am being made to look like one of them. It was so humiliating. Even worse was what they wanted me to say lacked punch, it read more like a manifesto than a script. I did my best to put some life into it but at one point I became so exasperated with their meddling I all but exclaimed "Do it yourself," but not daring to upset Paceillo I carried on to the bitter end.

The soldiers aren't the only members of Roberto's cast. Lucia is as well. And what a distraction she's become. She becomes lovelier every time I look at her.

Four o'clock came. I said "That is it, no more changes," and went away to shave. At five o'clock precisely Roberto called "Açáo!"

NEWS IN BRIEF

Bandits seize police

BRASILIA: Brazilian Interior Ministry statement claimed suspected Columbian nacro-criminals were holding 60 members of regional police force hostage in remote region of Ceara State, north-east Brazil. Ministry claims bandits have taken control of local airstrip for suspected onward trans-shipment of cocaine to Europe and forcing thousands of villagers to flee their homes. Army reinforcements are being rushed to affected areas to regain control, the Ministry said.

Glamorgan slump

Glamorgan v Namibia, One day match: Namibia 372 for 3 (declared), Glamorgan 57 all out. Namibia win by 7 wickets.

TV hacker

30: KEN

I'd not been home long when he was on again. I was getting a bit of supper before I went out when I heard a fizzing coming from the tele. I turned round and there he was, Danny Collins as bold as brass.

Naturally I dropped everything and looked. He was calmer this time, didn't even shrug his shoulders. I listened but the thing about Danny you never know if what he's saying is the truth or whether it's a front for something else. While I watched I kept thinking "Where's the catch?" And with Danny there always has to be one.

He went on about aliens. I was highly sceptical. What he said about Bosnia, about them all living in their own countries was a fair enough. But when he said he was giving them all half an hour to agree I fell about. Especially as everyone has been trying to sort them all out for years and have got nowhere. When he said later, the Serbs and Croats only having a week to get out and he read out all the things that would happen to them if they didn't I was agreeing with him but he's no chance of it ever happening. I did have a flick through the other channels but he was on all the satellite ones. One of the things that got me though was all those other people.

Having seen him yesterday I have to say that without a shadow of a doubt he had been genuinely scared. So when this bloke comes on saying he was in charge of the shooting and he was sorry, I began thinking there might be something about what Danny was going on about. Then when he showed all those others, there was a whole crowd of them calling out "Alfred de Dewis2 and shouting "Viva Harmonica" I started thinking he might actually be serious. On top of that there was, as the camera went from one group to the other, in the background all these planes.

So this morning when I read in the Express that they were all calling it all a hoax I wasn't convinced. Danny is up to something alright. And there is no justification for them slagging him off him like that. What he said about closing down all those nuclear power stations I agree with. And all this harm he's supposed to have done about disrupting television and the like is a load of tosh. Nobody missed anything. Everyone knows there's nothing worth watching on the TV of a Wednesday night.

Now we know - they're desperately seeking Susan!

By Stephen Solomans

THE TELE-PRANKSTERS who interrupted the Arsenal Spurs telecast were back on our screens last night - this time telling us we've been invaded from outer space!

We're having this close encounter of the absurd kind because the invaders - they're the Susem, from a galaxy that's 600 light years away from Earth - are seeking their spaceship that's been lost in space, said the batty broadcasters.

"They come in peace... They have come to locate one of their spaceships which has fallen to Earth. It is their intention to recover it. They request our assistance in their search," said the broadcast.

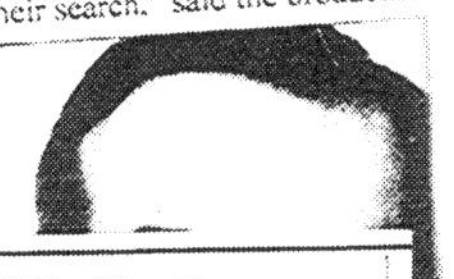

However UFO experts last night were more down to earth. Said Prof. Hartley Makepiece of Sheppey University: "We are continually monitoring space and there is no evidence whatsoever that we have had an interplanetary visitation of any sort. It is quite obvious this is a prank of some kind."

This view was endorsed by the government. A Home Office spokesman said: "Any talk of UFOs, space invasions, little green men from Mars is, of course ludicrous. We believe this to be no more than a sophisticated practical joke.

"We are, however, taking this matter seriously, because these broadcasts could upset vulnerable people."

Last night's broadcast was considerably longer than the one on Tuesday night, when a man, believed to be named Danny, was seen to blasted by gunfire.

It claimed that the invaders will, in return for help, rid the world of its woes, including:

- the war in Bosnia
- nuclear danger
- pollution

In the meantime red-faced TV chiefs will continue with their investigation into how our airwaves are being invaded.

CYBER-LOONY PUTS HUNDREDS OF LIVES AT RISK

V'S MADCAP cyber hacker struck again last night – putting the lives of hundreds of air passengers at risk

By NICOLA KAY

N HOUR-LONG INTERRUPTION SLI TV's Beavis and Butthead so caused chaos in the skies. his is because the autopilot atellite communication links were disrupted by the gue broadcast.

Pilots and air traffic controllers ere forced to use radar and voice ommands.

A spokesman at the Southampton TCC said: "This man's prank could ve cost the lives of hundreds. It as highly irresponsible and potently dangerous. The sooner this ot is bro...

On Tuesday the cyber-maverick interrupted the Spurs-Arsenal match with ten minute burst of barmy broadcastin that ended with gunfire. Last night h drew up a Green wishlist: Save the tree fish, stray dogs.

Sounding drunk he called for a ban c all things nuclear - and promised us a free electricity if we did! He finished l promising peace in the Balkans.

Meanwhile SLI chiefs were fumi over the interruption of their pr grammes. "We will be pressing the Hor office for immediate action to block a repeat of this brazen act of Netwo piracy," said SLI boss Derek Igg. A

TV Joker is conman wanted for drug deals

By RICHARD SPARROW

THE PRIME-TIME PRANKSTE who invaded our TV screen with scare stories about clos encounters with extra-terrestrial looking for a crashed flyin saucer, is exposed today as Daniel Collins, a failed north London businessman. He is suspected by both British and Brazilian police of being behind an international drug smuggling ring.

Police sources say that Collins, 44, is suspected of operating a number of bogus businesses which were little more than fronts for money laundering. Collins has reportedly been behind several such 'scams'. One – bogus water filters – duped thousands of unsuspecting members of the public out of ten of thousands of pounds.

Collins is also being sought over a numerous Tax and VAT fiddles. A Metropolitan Police spokesman said: "We have known about Collins' Latin American connection for some time and his frequent trips to Columbian drug cartels."

UN Bosnian stalemate

By Tom Fletcher
In New York

CROATIAN and Serbian foreign ministers, apparently acting in unison with one another, as well as with their respective German and Russian patrons, stymied moves to impose UN sanctions against the both counties.

Kresimir Prije, Croatia's foreign minister, said after Germany's UN Security Council "No" vote: "We are pleased that commonsense has prevailed. We continue to refute utterly, the false and malicious allegations made against us by those who have a Hidden Agenda to ferment discord between Croats and the Bogomils minority in our country."

Asked about reports of atrocities committed by the Croatians forces against Bosnian civilians, Prlic stated: "It has been necessary to conduct a pacification campaign against a small number of terrorists and criminals. This campaign is now drawing to a close, but unfortunately a small number of the civilian population have been caught in the crossfire so to speak, but this happens in all such cases, look at Chiapas."

• A spokesman for the Croatian embassy in London, scoffed at comments made in this evening's rogue telecast, referring to the former Bosnia. The spokesman, said: "You sort out your troublemakers and we will sort out ours."

TV Chiefs fuming

TOP SLI-TV EXECUTIVES were seething last night over the further interruption to their schedules.

Derek Igg, SLI's CEO said, "This wanton criminal must be tracked down without any delay and brought to justice."

SLI's concern stems from the cyber-hacker's effects on advertising revenues.

Earlier, *so Ian Maxwell writes*, Scotland Yard sources named the man behind the TV blitz as failed businessman Daniel Michael Collins, 43, who is wanted for a string of suspected crimes ranging from false accounting to Tax and VAT fraud. He is also being sought in connection with defacing the Bomber Harris Memorial statue

IN BRIEF

Spanish riot over quota comment

By Our Foreign Staff

FOR THE second day, riots brought the Spanish port of Bilbao to a standstill over reduced EU fishing quotas.

New Fisheries Commissioner, Herman Rohm's remarks, on recent tour of the Spanish port, have further enraged local trawlermen. Rohm is reported as saying: "If they [the Spanish seamen] will not obey directives, we have ways of making them." EU Commission spokeswoman Claretta Petacci, denied allegations that Rohm was being dictatorial, saying he had been misinterpreted.

Sperm down in sperm whales

By Emma Lawrence, Environmental Correspondent

SEA MAMMAL experts from Aberdeen University's Marine Research Laboratory revealed yesterday results of post mortems on six sperm whales washed ashore off of Thuro in February. Lab director Doctor Campbell Maclean, announced details at a meeting of marine conservationists, yesterday.

"Although the three males were juveniles, their sperm count was so low that it is doubtful they would have ever been able to reproduce." Dr. Maclean said.

His views were echoed by other delegates. "All recent marine mammal autopsies show a dramatic decline in sperm counts," said Prof. Praid of UCLA's Pacific Center.

Other speakers told of the worldwide spread of the decline. Several blamed widespread pollution of the oceans and the reduction of food sources.

Selectors' threats

By A Staff Reporter

POLICE are investigating a series of threatening calls and letters received by England's Test Selectors. These follow the broadcast of addresses and telephone numbers by London radio station ABH.

"It was totally irresponsible thing to do, broadcasting my address," said chief selector Alan Barraclough. Asked if he was resigning he said, "Under no circumstances. We may have got off to a weak start, but we should not be judged from one result."

Thai fire raging

By Our Foreign Staff

Fires caused by indiscrimate logging, continued blazing out of control yesterday. Fanned by strong winds, area of 2,000 kilometres of forest, north east of Three Padgodas Pass in Taunggyi mountains is on fire.

Flights to Bangkok are subject to delay as winds blow smoke southward. Pilots report spoke plumes above 30,000 feet.

31: JAMES

I didn't see it myself. It was only when I glanced at Penny's copy of the Mail did I first connect Danny's television 'appearance' with the disruption of our NYSE monitors. There was nothing in the FT but a sizable piece in the Times, though nowhere as acerbic as the Mail's.

While the Times concentrated on the disruption and the Mail on what they considered to be the outrageousness of Danny's actions, both scoffed over what he was supposed to have said. Neither though appeared to link last night's interruption with Tuesday's. Both, in dismissing Danny as little more than a "cyber-hacking prankster", failed to grasp the significance of what has occurred.

The resources required to produce and install a system to take control of just one communications satellite is formidable, to take over dozens of them must be massive. And with resources as extensive as this, why should anyone want to do so? Adding to this is the poor picture production quality, "amateur video" the Times called it. With the resources required to hack into satellites, it is more than likely some would have been invested in not just decent camera equipment but professional camera operators as well.

As for Danny being involved in drug running, that is laughable. As for false accounting? Yes. Danny is probably guilty but then who in business isn't? (The Fraud Squad only charge someone with this when they have insufficient evidence for anything else). Defacing a national monument? Guilty of that I suppose as well but he at least he hasn't hurt anybody. 'Bomber' Harris is personally responsible for the slaughtering of more than half a million innocent, defenceless people.

As for what he is supposed to have said regarding the Serbs and Croats I agree with him. They need to be given a bloody nose, though I don't think anyone can stop them, especially the Serbs, not with the Russians behind them. As I read the Times article, I had a bemused thought to suggest the market-makers put Utilities on 'sell'.

However, Danny's portents have had no effects on the markets whatsoever. Yesterday's Dow closed, despite his interruption, on a 52 week high. At midday I looked at a Reuters screen but there was nothing out of the ordinary. The money markets were all unchanged. Gold, always the first hedge against uncertainty, was, if anything, drifting lower.

But all the same, what on earth can Danny be up to?

Mystery broadcaster: drug smuggler or just trickster?

By Tony Perry
General Affairs Editor

A CONTRADICTORY picture was emerging of the mystery broadcaster who interrupted satellite television broadcasts of the Spurs-Arsenal soccer match.

On air for nearly an hour last night, he claimed that the Earth has been visited by aliens from outer space.

He was named as failed Irish businessman Daniel Collins, 45 who runs a number of companies that are currently under investigation by both the Inland Revenue and Customs and Excise.

A Metropolitan Police spokesman last night confirmed that Collins' also faces charges of false accounting and criminal damage.

The spokesman said, that Collins will now be facing further charges of contravening the Broadcasting and Telecommunications Act as well as the Internat-ional Telecommunications Protocol.

The spokesman also confirmed that the Drug Squad are cooperating with Brazilian Federal Police regarding possible narcotics [illegible] that Colombian cocaine cartels are behind the illegal broadcasts.

However, people in Covent Garden, where Collins was well known, ridiculed suggestions of his drug involvement. 'Danny didn't do drugs," says Brian Brody (39), landlord of The Keys public house. "He was always in here," he added.

A former Collins employee, now working in the Keys, backed up these claims: "He was into a lot of things but never drugs." Lynne, who declined to give her full name but admitted she was an out-of-work actress, said he was always up to all sorts of pranks: "Interrupting a TV broadcast would be just the sort of thing he would do."

"Always good for a laugh," said regular Roy Bellamy (37).

"He was mad but he wasn't bad, always stood his round, you can't say fairer than that," said fellow regular Jim Callaghan (83).

But the Met spokesman confirmed they want to interview Collins' regarding Brazilian allegations should he ever set foot [illegible]

Stiffer penalties for cyber-hackers called fo[r]

Latest transmission disruption causes communications cha[os]

By Joy Combo
Political Correspondent

FOLLOWING the second disruption of global communication networks in as many days, stiffer penalties against 'Cyber-hacking' were demanded last night.

Sir Hugh Russet-Brown (C.Lib Cheltenham), chairman of the Commons Communications Security Committee, called for firmer international action on the prosecution crime of cyber-hacking.

"Once again, we have experienced the menace unregulated and unauthorised broadcasters can have on the integrity of even the most secure of transmission," Sir Hugh said. "Through a thorough system of licensing and vetting of transmission terminals we have virtually wiped out these pirates in this country.

"It is essential," he said, "that all countries use the same successful methods which are applied in the UK and in many other EU states. I shall be pressing at next month's Pan Intergovernmental Communications Integrity Conference (PIG-CIC) in Mauritius, for the outlawing of member states that decline to adopt our rigorous high standards.

A spokesman for GCHQ, the government's communications centre, was unable to confirm if its satellite communications had been disrupted as a result of the unauthorised transmissions.

However, Michael Andrews, a security consultant with FIA, said: "There is bound to have been a total blackout both at Cheltenham and at Langley (the U.S. distance listening facility). Both are more than likely to react robustly to eliminate any [communication] disruption source."

Bosnian stalemate in UN

By Our FOREIGN STAFF

SERBIAN and Croatian Foreign Ministers, apparently acting in unison with one another, as well as with their respective Russian and German patrons, stymied moves to impose UN sanctions against both countries.

An aide to Jovica Seselj, Serbia's foreign minister, reading from a prepared statement, said, following Russia's UN Security Council "No" vote: "We are pleased that commonsense has prevailed. We continue to refute utterly, the false and malicious allegations made against us by foreign Moslem extremists in an attempt to sow discord during this difficult period of Serbo-Croatian realignment."

Asked about reports of atrocities committed by Serb forces against Bosnian civilians, the aide said: "Serb military forces are assisting the civilian administration in limited police actions against bandits who, supported by external Moslem extremists, have committed untold evil crimes against the Serbian people, bayoneting babies, raping young girls, throwing old people alive into cauldrons of boiling fat.

"We have no territorial ambitions in the former Yugoslavia other than to unite the historic Serb lands. If criminals and crazed terrorists should oppose us in our sacred mission, then we have no alternative but to exercise our legitimate right to punish them for their crimes."

A spokesman for the Serbian embassy in London and asked to comment on mention of Bosnia in this evening's rogue telecast, said he was unwilling to respond [to "lunatics"].

Could 'They' have landed?

Lisa Williams
Science Correspondent

FOR an hour last night, satellite viewers were served a different fare from Beavis and Butthead.

Instead viewers were treated to a heady brew of aliens, a nuclear-free world, free electricity, an agenda of prescriptions any Green would go envious for, and oh, by the way, universal peace in our time.

But could we really have been visited by aliens? Is it possible to physically travel the distances needed in time enough to be meaningful?

Winston Norwood, Dean of Astronomy at the University of Sheppey, like many in his profession, is skeptical: "There have been untold reports of UFOs and goodness knows what, yet there has not been one single creditable, independently authenticated sighting" he says, "not just in recent times but throughout the historical record."

Professor Norwood, whose forthcoming book, 'Its All in the Mind' (HarperCollins), deals with the phenomena of UFO sightings, said there are just two creditable pieces of evidence suggesting possible past visits by extraterrestrials. 'These are," says Norwood, "the Dogon-Sirius connection and the Piri Rei's cartographic compilations.

"However, these are based on events thousands of years ago. Today and for several decades, a number of observatories continuously scan a range of wavebands right across the entire spectrum from the visible to X-rays, including radio waves.

"After three decades, covering an area of 15 light years distant, precisely nothing that cannot be readily explained has been reported.

"Even if by some fluke, an alien visitor or evidence of their existence should have remained unlocated, they would have, in their approach to the Earth, been detected by the U.S. distance radar arrays.

"Although satellites are able to ascertain data approaching the earth, their ability to do so is limited when compared to these radar arrays.

"Based in Alaska, Hawaii and Morocco, and built to detect incoming missiles during the Cold War, they span the entire globe. These arrays are so precise they are capable of detecting a pencil at 100 kilometres. Nothing untoward has been reported over these many years past," said Professor Norwood.

News in Brief

Outrage over pensio[n] rise thwarted

SMALL shareholders of Central Utilities were dismayed at proxy votes cast in favour of Central's CEO, David Hardwick's 65 per cent pension rise to Li 5m.

At yesterday's EGM, shareholders overwhelmingly voted for the motion sacking Hardwick There were angry shouts when shareholders were told of the proxy votes in favour o[f] Hardwick staying.

Major's memoirs withdrawn

JOHN MAJOR'S literary agent Theo Tenpersentus withdre[w] the manuscript, "It Wasn't My Fault" detailing the merging of the Conservative and Liberal Democrat Parties, from yesterday's Publisher Auction.

The withdrawal had been widely forecast *James Carvel*

Leader's 'warlordism'

BEIJING Politburo spokesman accused Guandong leader, Lui Chao Clii of 'Warlordism' in the latest war of words between the factions.

Lui's office countered with accusations of Beijings Wan Chin being no more than Running Dog Stalinist Fascist Pig of Militarist Gangsters' in describing Politburo chairman.

Comments made in prelude to 'Fraternal Brotherhood Conference' Monday in effort to mend differences between central and south China's differences which have led to recent skirmishes

Both sides are reported to be marshalling forces in prospect of conference breakdown.

Human rights Senators

MOSCOW Friday: Team of US Senators arrived in the Russian capital today to investigate fresh outbreaks of human rights abuses in Chechna and Dagestan. Leading the delegation is Senator Al 'Packer' Packard. Senator Packard said: "In the light of reports we have received, [President] Sheybal has some serious explaining to do. His record is appalling. If we don't get some straight answers to the massacres committed by his forces, we will be recommending to both Congress and President Warren to cancel all US military arms credits to Russia immediately."

32: IRIS

I was so annoyed when Chrissie, who I work with, showed me the piece about Danny in the Sun. They printed nothing but horrid things about him, including saying he was dealing in drugs. Just about anything else I wouldn't put past him, but drugs, not Danny. Smoke, perhaps, but then who hasn't? But deal, smuggle? Never, no, not Danny.

As fate would have it, I saw his television appearance last night, or rather part of it. I missed the end because of Peter starting another argument. I had sent him out at half seven to get the pizzas. We were all set to watch 'Manhattan'. The film started at eight but he was late getting back. Of course, by then, Danny was on instead. The first thing he said as he came through the door was, and so derisively, "That's not Woody Allen." Being glued to the screen and without thinking, I 'sshed' him.

When later, he said "Your pizza is getting cold," I could tell he was sulking. What made things worse I suppose, was that I hadn't stopped talking about Danny, or so Peter kept reminding me, from the moment he had met me from work. But at that moment, I was so absorbed with what was on the screen, not just Danny but the others as well, that I wasn't really caring about pizza. When a man with a moustache appeared dancing with a girl, Danny said her name was Lucia and he then looked towards the camera as it zoomed in on him, and he gave wink as he smiled. I lightheartedly burst out with "Wow, break me off a bit of that!"

Before I had finished, Peter snorted "That's it, I've had enough, I'm off."

By the time I finished telling him not to be so childish, I missed the last of Danny. The remainder of Manhattan came on, so I watched it, on my own.

I was cross with Peter last night. There was no need for him to say the horrid things about me and Danny, though I suppose he will be ringing saying "Sorry" before long. Sometimes, men can be so childish.

And I was angry this morning with the Sun. Danny may not be a paragon of virtue but neither is he the shocker they have made him out to be. It wasn't his fault he couldn't refund all those people their money they had paid for the water jugs. As for calling him a "Woolly Green Nerd" and saying he was on the run from the police, that was really rotten.

Although it's past noon, Peter still hasn't phoned to say sorry. That's unusual for him, he always says sorry by lunchtime.

33: SIÂN

"At least there will be a chance of getting rid of those," joked Daffyd as we passed through Crymych.

As I looked up to the top of Frenni Fawr and the dozens of white turbines whirling round, I had to agree. They are such an eyesore.

"And end all their noise as well, just listen," Daffyd said. He stopped the car, turned off the music and wound down the window. "What a racket, they're at least a mile away, you can't hear a bird sing," he said.

"It's not the money the farmers receive for the electricity, it's the grants they get for having them in the first place," I told him. "Come on," I added, "I'll be late for the boys' tea."

"Did you read what else he was supposed to have said?" Daffyd said as he re-started the car.

Although I hadn't a chance until after this morning's meeting to read the paper, on the train back from London I had read what they had printed about Danny, more than once. "If only it could be so," I sighed.

"What's that bit about stopping the fishing and tree felling?" Daffyd asked.

"Yes and the mining," I said, though I then added "What on earth is he playing at?"

"Beats me," said Daffyd, "but knowing Danny he could be into goodness knows what. Though I think he must be certainly mixed up in something. What was it they said on the news, about all the satellites from Kuwait to Vancouver being affected?"

I fished the paper out of my bag and read it to him, "Planes had to use real pilots and radio to land, phone users waiting for their calls and viewers of SLI missed Beavis and Butthead..."

"The Telegraph said he has contravened the International Telecommunications Protocol, or something," Daffyd said and added "If they catch him he will go down for that."

"That's what Anne said."

"Oh, how is she? What did she have to say about Danny?"

"Don't ask. She can be so scathing when she wants."

As we drove into Cilgarren I asked Daffyd what time it was.

"Just after six, why?" he replied.

"It's very quiet," I said, "where is everyone?" When, a few minutes later, we stepped in the house, I immediately knew why.

"But fair," retorted Paceillo to my "Cruel," then after a pause, she adding "They knew what was happening was wrong yet they chose to do nothing to stop it. Therefore they are accomplices are they not?"

"None of them are blameless," I lamely replied.

"That is beside the point," she added, then with added assertiveness, "Problems of conflict are resolved by assisting the victim against the aggressor," followed by she demonstrating that her English has advanced to the idiomatic "First things first, resolving the victim's own shortcomings is secondary. This has always been our experience."

"Experience?" she had me thinking, "What experience might this be?"

Then with a further flourish of self-assuredness, she said "No one need be physically harmed and such actions will act as a deterrent to others."

Even my "Couldn't you have just told them to go?" was met by her "You did, remember..." and putting emphasis on the 'you' (though conveniently forgetting it was she who had me announce it) "...and did they depart?"

With me reduced to "No I suppose not," in reply, she just as assertively and assuredly said "It is needless to say more" and added as she departed, "Events are already in progress."

As she walked up to Kubber, he still shrouded in morning mist, I became ever more aware that I now have no influence on events. Though at the same time I also know that I dare not leave Tabajara, the risks of falling into the Brazilian army's hands are too terrible to contemplate. But all at the same, by staying I have no choice than to accept what the Susem or Paceillo rather, wants of me. On Monday she was seeking my assistance, now here she is running the show. Not only am I snared into staying but I've been marginalised.

I had the same feeling when I tried to talk to Menpemelo about an appliance, it's like an instant-photo booth, which Terbal and his helpers have made. While the other Susem were giving tuition to the soldiers, all of whom were in rapt attention with Pedro and Roberto busily interpreting, Menpemelo was supervising this booth. The soldiers, one after another, took off their clothes then sat inside of it. After a minute of flashing lights the soldiers would step out with a smile. But when I asked her what it was, she said she was "busy."

I went up into Kubber to ask Terbal what the booth was for but he said he was busy too. He had hundreds of sherpals scampering about the place building yet more things. I asked him what it was they were making.

"Screens, more screens ve are fabricating," he said.

When I asked him what they were for, he said "Invormation, more invormation I must haff." Then, as if an afterthought, he added "More area I am needing also. You are knowing auf some Dommy?" Though when I said I didn't he whizzed away.

I went into Kubber's cockpit and spoke to him.

"I am busy right now helping co-ordinate La-ra's flight-path, as soon as I'm free I will come right back to you..." was all he said, again and again.

I went back outside. But as I did I saw the soldiers driving away in their trucks and jeeps, shouting, cheering "Viva Harmonia!"

"Where are they going?" I asked Menpemelo.

"To bring back the villagers," she said.

"But they have left without their guns," I said, noticing them still piled by the Pousada and adding with alacrity, "They will be up against other soldiers in Tianguá who are armed."

"Oh do not concern yourself, they will be most safe," she said, "Roberto has gone with them."

"He's already been shot the once," I replied with alacrity growing, "isn't that enough?"

"They have hen-gers with them," she added.

"Oh, that's alright then," I replied with relief.

Seeing that Menpemelo was no longer busy I asked her about the booth.

"Oh, the mormic creener?" she said, "What a mormic does is identify imbalances in cellular structures then corrects them."

"Imbalances?" I asked.

With her eyes fixed on my face she said "I noticed it yesterday in the soldiers with us aboard Kershaw. As all of them exhibited physiognomic cellular-balance dysfunction, I had Terbal organise a mormic for us."

"Oh," I said, "What does it do?"

"Try it for yourself," she replied, then after a pause, remonstratively adding, "Take off your clothes first."

Though bashful, I did as she said, then stepped inside. In an instant I was bathed in bright blue then purple pulsing lights. They came from all directions but after a minute or so they stopped and I'd a tingling pins and needles sensation from head to toe. Then in no time at all the bright blue came back on again and Menpemelo was saying "You can come out now."

As I dressed, she matter-of-factly read from a small sheet of paper reeling out from the side of the booth, "Hmm, you had a potentially weak respiratory tract ...bile duct-liver damage...motor neural susceptibility...urinary tract-prostate dysfunction," she said.

"How do you mean had?" I asked.

"As I said, had," she replied and adding "but not any more. Imbalances within you will soon be corrected."

"I won't suffer illness, infection? Clear up this rash as well? (Two days of close shaving and Elana's make-up were taking their toll).

"Generally, yes."

Casually (though with thoughts of opportunity) I asked "How does this mormic work?"

"Nothing complicated," she said. "We already had data on Lucia's cellular resonances. Their bases are, as we suspected, virtually identical to ours and so there was no difficulty while attending to Roberto in adjusting the mormic to accommodate the male genome as well. The outcome of course will be testosterone reduction but this should not be of consequence..."

"You mean," I said (and with thoughts of opportunity waning), "I have just surrendered part of my maleness so as to have a healthier body?"

"Yes, but only a little," she said in the same nonchalant tone.

(With thoughts of opportunity waxing back) I asked "By how much?"

"At the stage of your maturity," she said, looking me up and down, "it will probably not be noticeable. But with younger males, it will be."

"By how much?" I asked.

"Hmm, difficult to say, reduced libido probably, perhaps a more placid disposition, but it is..."

"You mean," I said cutting in again, "those soldiers who have just gone off to Tianguá are now all peace-loving individuals?"

"Something as such," she said with a smile, and me with images of placid soldiers meeting war-like ones.

"You, like them," she continued, "with a balanced cellular structure should never suffer disability from external agonists."

"External agonists? What, germs, viruses?"

Pausing for a moment she said "Oh and the rest."

"The rest? There are other things besides infection?"

"Anything destabilising the body's cellular and inter-cellular resonances will bring about imbalances and thus weaken what you term your immune system," she said, "however, harmonise resonances and any imbalances will be corrected."

"But how does this mormic do all this?"

Menpemelo did start to describe how the mormic works, what it does, but because I didn't really understand what she was saying I kept asking questions. Then as if tiring of my "whys" she gave the same 'pin back your ears, be quiet and listen' look Paceillo gives me and said "I will begin at the beginning."

What Menpemelo told me amounted to a physics lesson, but one oh so very different from the ones I had had at school. Those always bored the pants off me but Menpemelo's had my rapt attention from beginning to end. More to the point though, she overturned much of what I remember being taught. Needless to say, like any good teacher, she had me bursting with questions.

According to the Susem there are no such things as solids, matter, particles, bits of things. Everything, so Menpemelo said, is waves, Primary, Secondary and Tertiary ones. What is more, Tertiaries evolve out of Secondaries and they from Primaries, so, in a way, there's only the one kind of wave.

Menpemelo said that Secondary waves are to a Primary wave what ocean waves are to an ocean itself. Stressing this point she said that just as it isn't possible to have ocean waves without an ocean, so too with Secondary waves, they being no more than surfaces of a Primary one.

What is more, Menpemelo said, that just as ocean waves come out of the ocean and then sink back into being part of it again, it's the same with Secondaries to Primaries. Also, just as an ocean's force, momentum, currents generate its waves, it's the same for Secondary waves to Primary ones. She also said that just as the life of an ocean wave before it goes back to being pure ocean again can be long to short-lived, it's the same for Secondary waves as well. Menpemelo then said that Secondary waves can be further thought of as being what we call 'energy'. Though she did stress that this was a simplification as to what these waves actually are.

With me musing "If they are 'energy' then what are 'Primaries'?" Menpemelo moved on to Tertiary waves. These, she said, are generated from cresting Secondary waves just as the froth and spume of sea waves are. She also said that the Susem often refer to Tertiary waves as 'frothicles' and 'wavicles'.

Just as froth and foam formed from cresting sea waves still continue to exist after the breaking wave which made them rolls on leaving them to float about all by themselves, she said, it's the same with frothicles. Menpemelo then said that frothicles can also be thought of as what we call 'matter'. Though, once again, she stressed that this is a simplification as well.

Grasping what she was saying meant that 'matter' and 'energy' aren't separate as we think of them as being, but that matter comes out of energy. I had thoughts of a glass of Guinness. Though the head comes out of a liquid, is it a 'solid'? And if it's still a liquid then are foam mattresses liquid too?

Menpemelo said that although the Secondary wave which made a frothicle may well have moved on, there was still some of its energy inside, 'held within' the frothicle, the vibration (Menpemelo called it 'oscillation') of which caused it to 'resonate'. The Susem are able to manipulate the wavicle resonance and this is what lies behind the workings of the mormic.

As Menpemelo mentioned this, she all but had me saying "Oh come on, there's more to it than this?" However, I was glad I stayed silent for she promptly told that there is 'more', much more. There are Secondary waves and Secondary waves, she said, big ones, small ones, slack rolling ones and ones which not only move at fast pace but sometimes become steeper, concentrated, concertinaed, compacted almost. The forthicles on the backs of these Secondary waves come closer together with one another as well. Sometimes they come so close that they fuse into one another. In doing so, she said, these frothicles combine their energies or they fuse to become a bigger frothicide and sometimes a combination of the two.

With me thinking that these frothicles appear to be rather robust for 'mere' oscillations, Menpemelo then said that as far as some frothicides are concerned their compacting and enlarging can go on again and again. Obviously I could see that what she was saying was really the same difference of what we understand in the supernovae fusion creation of one heavier element after another heavier one.

All the same I said nothing and listened on to what she had next to say.

This dealt with clusters of frothicles, some of the same kind, others of differing densities. Not only do the oscillations of the individual frothicles in these clusters affect those of the others, but that these clusters in turn have their own, collective oscillation.

It doesn't end there either. According to what Menpemelo said next, frothicle clusters joining up with other clusters have their collective oscillations as well. Clusters of clusters have their oscillations too, and so on all the way up to bigger things including us humans. Everything has its own particular 'oscillation signature'.

What the Susem have done, so Menpemelo then said, is develop the technology to identify each and every one of these different levels of signatures. More to the point though, the Susem can also manipulate them all and in turn change bad vibrations into good ones.

By then I was bursting with questions though before I could get one out, Paceillo appeared from Kubber. Punching the air with her fist she shouted, "Pan! Pan! La-ra has transversed the ionosphere and is making his final descent." Upon which she went back inside again.

"She seems happy," I said.

"Well, it is a difficult, not to say risky manoeuvre," Menpemelo said and adding, "especially after what happened to Pa-tu."

Seizing the opportunity of the diversion, I managed to get a question in. "How do all these frothicles, their clusters stay kept together?" I asked. However, and alas maybe, Menpemelo's reply confounded me the more.

Pulling then tugging at a fold in the sleeve of her tunic, she said "Secondary and Tertiary wave interaction acting upon the surface of a sea," she said, "the movement of one is affected by those of the rest. The movement of one also has an effect on the others, there is a 'collective dynamic' to them."

Menpemelo then went on to explain that Secondary waves behave in a similar way to one another as sea waves do. She then stretched at her sleeve again, tugged it out taut and said "This is a plane," then letting go of her sleeve, it reverted back to folds, she added, "and this is still that same plane."

Menpemelo, still holding her sleeve, then said to think of, call the 'plane' a 'field' instead. All the entities in a field, she said, are connected by the movement, 'dynamic' of this field.

"It is perhaps pertinent to be aware," Menpemelo continued, "that although frothicles evolve into clusters, individual frothicles are distant from one another. If a frothicle of one of the most concentrated clusters, that of osmium, a platinum element was this size." At this she clenched her fist and added, "it would be no nearer to the next than those trees over there (the park-side ones half a kilometre away), the frothicles of your atmospheric nitrogen will be further from one another than your planet is to its moon."

By now Menpemelo had me concentrating hard and I'd questions dying to come out, but still facing the park-side I noticed Petruee, Pheterisco and Lucia strolling out from between the trees. As they came closer I could see from their wet hair, especially Lucia's because hers is longer, that they must have been bathing in one of the mountain pools. Lucia, like the other two was also in a white Susem tunic. As they walked toward us, all three chatting away as though lifelong pals, I noticed from the way Lucia walked, not a swagger as such but that she had an air of assuredness about her.

With me thinking that just yesterday she had been as timid as a mouse, and what a difference a day makes, I had my attention back to Menpemelo.

"Though sea wave movement only exists on the surface of the sea," Menpemelo next said, "Secondary wave field function exists in a multitude of layers throughout that of a Primary wave."

I was all set to get in, "How thick, deep is this Primary wave then? What actually is it?" when Pheterisco called out in a greeting to us. As she did so, Lucia was taking hold of the length of her hair, running both her hands down it and squeezing out water. As she casually flicked her hair back over her shoulder she laughed with the other two as they tried to squeeze water from their shorter hair.

As the three of them stood by us and from Lucia's smiling face I could see she truly did have an air of confidence about her. And when she gave a laugh, she also had me inwardly saying "They've fixed her teeth as well." But from the way she stood there, weight on one foot, back of hand rested on hip, I was further silently saying "What a difference a few days can make."

All three of them then stepped up into Kubber and Menpemelo continued detailing fields and planes, and I bursting with questions about Primary waves. Eventually I managed to get in "How thick, deep is a Primary wave?" Menpemelo's reply confused me yet more.

"It varies," she said. "Many conclude that Primary waves are of a uniform depth of some 100 million of our light years. However, our recent findings indicate that there are variations of between one and 200 of your light years in Primary waves' depths. Indeed one of the reasons for our current journey is to present these findings at the Congress."

With me thinking "Congress? what Congress might this be?" Menpemelo continued telling about fields. But I still had Primary waves on my mind. But she had not been talking for more than a minute when we both became aware of the sound of arriving trucks and another wave then swept over me, that of apprehension.

It subsided though when I also heard the shouts of "Viva!" then saw a convoy of trucks and jeeps sweep up over the hill leading into the village. That there were more than had departed took me aback but so did the sight of the new arrivals waving their shirts aloft as though triumphant banners.

In the leading jeep was Pedro. They drove straight to the front of the Pousada. The soldiers with him jumped out and began marshalling the trucks into a line. The new arrivals alighted, their "Vivas!" fading as they stared at the vedas. Then when they saw us, or rather Menpemelo, followed by Petruee appearing from Kubber, they put their shirts back on. Menpemelo waited for Petruee to join her. They then went over to the soldiers.

I don't know if they did it for theatrical affect or just felt it coming on but they levitated a little. Everyone fell to their knees and crossed themselves.

Pedro hurriedly explained what had happened in Tianguá. There was confusion among the soldiers manning the roadblock. Pardel, who was in the truck behind Pedro, jumped out proclaiming that the Son of God was with them. Some of these soldiers at a roadblock recognised Roberto. Pardel, still impassioned, told what had happened and had a reluctant Roberto show his scars. Because of his scraggy appearance the soldiers readily believed what they were told and fell in with Pedro's men. Events then snowballed. Filled with tales of the wonders they had seen, angels, chariots of the Lord, that they had flown to mystic lands, diamonds on the beaches, more in the sky, how they were all cured of their illnesses, a new world and paradise was dawning. Pedro's men had the newcomers even more fervent in joining them.

In the centre of Tianguá they were confronted with a detachment of other soldiers. Their officer accused Pedro's men of being high on drugs and ordered his soldiers to arrest them. He also had them raise their rifles at Pedro's men but the hen-gers then zoomed in and stung all their hands and they ran back behind this officer.

Pedro then said, and he was quite nonchalant about it, the officer called on the men to fire again and also reached for his pistol. Captitão Ries then threw himself forwards shouting not to shoot anyone or if they must, then shoot him first. The officer called Capitão Ries a traitor and a turncoat, drew his pistol and fired. Several hen-gers immediately ricocheted the bullets to around this officer's feet and for good measure some stung him. Pedro pointed him out to me and to my surprise I saw that he and Capitão Ries were laughing and talking with one another. Pedro tartly remarked it was just the Capitão's attempt to regain his standing in the eyes of his men. Most of the remaining soldiers then came over to Pedro's. Though he did mention some others, including the majority of officers and Polícia Militar, had sped away.

After this, so Pedro said, events took on a momentum all of their own. Filled with the success, Pardel and some of the others, including now Roberto, became quite carried away. They were aided by the willingness of the crowds in the market, all of whom had seen what had happened with the soldiers. Many believed what they were being told. Pedro, however, concentrated on what he had been asked to do, to tell the people of Tabajara to come home. He left Pardel and some of the others, proclaiming that there had been a "Second Coming." Roberto, he said, was last seen conducting mass conversions in the market square. I feared for the worst.

Half an hour after the soldiers, the first villagers arrived. Like them, they gaped and gasped in amazement at the vedas but went down on their knees and crossed themselves when they saw the Susem. Their genuflecting however turned to tears when they saw Lucia. At first they didn't grasp that it was her but when the children and then the women came to look more closely they started crying again. At first Lucia smiled at the attention but when the women went down on their knees again and began a chorus of "Milagre, milagre..." she froze, her eyes wide staring at them. When the women attempted to kiss her feet she had her clenched fingers to her mouth and, still staring, began shaking. In no time she too was in tears. But hers were scared ones. She ran to Petruee and with a loud howl flung her arms around her. In an instant she had lost all her young woman assuredness and was as a child again. Even I had become a bit wet eyed by then.

Concerns of a practical nature, however, were soon pressing. Pedro broached the first, what to do with the soldiers, there were now nearly 300 of them. How were they going to be fed, where were they going to be billeted, what about their pay now that they had deserted? Their euphoria was bound to wear off, it always does if they don't get paid. How were the villagers to react with hundreds of deserting soldiers in their midst?

What about the villagers, and the others who would be bound to come and gawp if nothing else? There was a security problem looming and not just controlling the crowds. The soldiers and police who had sped away from Tianguá would be bound to tell their superiors now that the cat was out the bag. I did so remember telling Paceillo not to put in that bit in the telecast about them having to leave. I know in a way we are safe, but in another we were more exposed ever. Then I thought "What am I saying "We" for?"

I went over to Milophinia who was surrounded by children (I was glad to see some of my English teaching was coming in useful). I tried telling her the problems looming but she gave a shrug. It was the same with Petruee and Pheterisco. Only Lathia had anything constructive to say though even this didn't amount to much. "Go and see Paceillo," she said.

I had no sooner stepped into Kubber when I all but bumped into Paceillo coming the other way. She was most ecstatic. "La-ra is now at 80,000 metres altitude and on course!" she exclaimed, and just as elated, "He is exactly on time!

"Oh, that's good," I said, "but there are problems, we need your help..."

But it was though Paceillo had not heard me for she next exclaimed "La- ra is 2,500 kilometres to the west crossing the central meridian, and in little more than one hour he will have crossed the northern temperate meridian, 3,000 kilometres to the northeast!" And with her exuberance unabated, exclaimed "Everything is going to work exactly as planned!"

I did get a word in but all she said was, "Later," and went back inside.

35: SONIA

The first recorded sighting was made mid-day Thursday by Doctor John Baker. It filled his windscreen. He braked so hard that he stalled. At first he thought it was a blimp, similar to ones he had seen above London. But when it reappeared through another gap in the clouds, he instinctively knew that it was travelling too fast for a blimp. And that it was too big. Much too big.

Doctor Baker was already part way up the Las Cañadas ridge road, returning to the Izaña Solar Observatory. Driving as fast as he could he was soon above the clouds. Though when he was, all he saw, speeding away north-eastward, was a speck.

He watched it, then raced to the observatory. He telephoned Tenerife Air Traffic Control. Nothing unusual on their screens, including microlights, they informed him, let alone anything big, powered and flying at the 20,000 metres he had estimated. Not content, Doctor Baker contacted the NSA listening facility south of Rabat, due north-east of Tenerifie, telling them what he had seen. "Nothing. Not even an airborne pencil 1,000 miles away," they intoned, was appearing on their screens. Jovially ridiculed by his colleagues, Doctor Baker went to his computer programming.

Although he had not then been believed, Doctor Baker was at least able to communicate to the outside world. The people of the Atlas Mountains who also saw what he had seen were unable to do so.

On the coast it was different. At 3 o'clock, Melillia, the Spanish enclave in eastern Morocco, was still in siesta. But those who were not asleep saw, in the stillness, a shadow sweep over them. It took four minutes to pass by. Among those awake was Phillipo Gomes, local representative of *El Pais*. As he raced outside with the others, he took his camera.

By 4 o'clock in London, the blurred images of Phillipo Gomes' photographs of what had been 10,000 metres above, along with a digest of his telephone call to his newspaper's Madrid office, were on news agencies' screens worldwide. His was the first report. Soon, from boats, planes east of the Balearics, there were others. Then reports came from further to the north-east. These told not of shadows but of darkness.

La-ra's ovoid shape, black against the sky in every one of Gomes' prints had, he estimated, passed over at 800 kilometres an hour. Now, so these later reports said, La-ra was travelling at barely 500 and at 5000 metres altitude. As La-ra sped over the 40 kilometre length of the Straits of Bonifacio, he covered them from end to end. The darkness he brought caused many along the strait's Sardinian and Corsican coasts to panic. Church bells from Porto Tòrres to Bonifacio itself rang in his wake. Forty minutes later, on the other side of the Tyrrhenian Sea, more than bells rang.

People along the straits had experienced darkness at the edge. For those on the mainland it was different.

Orbetello was first. It was straight in La-ra's path. What had been a shadow in Melillia was now blackness from horizon to horizon. Although La-ra was still 4,000 metres above and now travelling at no more than 400kph, the speed of his arrival left little time for people to take refuge. Most were left to gawp and stare upwards. Many were motorists. Numerous accidents occurred.

After Orbetello it was southern Tuscany's turn. The pattern was the same. Trepidation upon La-ra's arrival, total blackness as he passed, people gazing upwards in awe, church bells still ringing as the late afternoon sunshine returned and roads jammed with crashed cars. Orbetello's darkness lasted for ten minutes. Further northeast as La-ra continued to slow the darkness lasted for longer. And because he continued to descend the darkness deepened as well.

Of course, those at La-ra's edges saw his shape. But even they, however, were unable to see that he was shrouded in a cloak of many millions of hengers. Their continually adjusting cloak protectively deflected away anything airborne, from particles to induced vibrations and waves, including those of radars. They also deflected inwards the vibrations caused by La-ra as he moved though the air. All that observers, who were away from the cacophony of cars, churches, people, heard as he progressed on his way, was silence.

While civil air traffic controllers across central Italy puzzled as to why nothing appeared on their radar screens, military ones further afield did likewise over theirs. However, reports continued to fill news agencies' screens.

Most of these related to events overhead, but others now told of those below, of chaos and rage on the roads. At Albinia, the main west coast highway became blocked. Stampeding cattle on the north-south Autostrada, south of Chiusi, caused an oil tanker to career up an embankment. Although the driver escaped unscathed, the resulting explosion, after the tanker had rolled back downwards, caused, in the pitch darkness, vehicles in their hundreds to crash into one another. In no time a tailback stretched half-way to Rome. Soon all roads north from there, as well as from Florence and Bologna, became blocked with wrecked trucks and cars.

After La-ra had passed over the hills of Tuscany, the mountains of Umbria were next. Perùgia was in utter darkness for a quarter of an hour, Fabriano, 50 kilometres away in the eastern Appennines, for longer.

Police forces, Interior and Defence ministries, ever uncoordinated stifled into inaction. In contrast, the moment reports from Spain were received by NATO's Southern European Command, it requested launching a "Defensive Reconnaissance in Force." By the time authorisation from Brussels arrived, La-ra was east of the Appennines. Nonetheless, twenty F16s from an airbase near Naples duly took to the air.

Meanwhile, media people recalled the previous day's "rogue" telecast, along with its mention of the northern Adriatic. Plotting La-ra's path, they saw it pointing directly to one place, Ancona.

However, anyone plotting with a topographical map would have also seen that La-ra's course pointed to the shallowest part of the Adriatic. But those with even bigger maps would have also seen that it led directly to somewhere else mentioned in the telecast as well.

After Umbria, La-ra passed over the plains of Marche. Though he continued to descend and decelerate, for those beyond his edges La-ra still appeared to be travelling at speed as he swept over the entire length of Route 76. With the darkness he brought lasting for longer, there was more time for more accidents. The A14, the east coast Autostrada, also became blocked with crashed cars.

Two hours after passing over Sardinia La-ra arrived above Ancona. He took twenty minutes to pass over the port. Half a kilometre beyond the shore and 1,000 metres above the sea, La-ra stopped. In the half hour of daylight remaining Ancona's citizens began nervously peering from windows and doors.

With flights throughout Italy being grounded, newspaper, radio and television crews struggled along chaos strewn roads. (Ancona possesses neither radio nor television stations). Though there were transmitters of the police and harbour authorities, ships and radio hams, it being Italy all broadcast only in Italian (apart from those in the Bosnian refugee camps, few in the south speak anything other than Italian). However, radio transmissions from Ancona, including those from mobile telephones, as for those elsewhere beforehand, were suffering from intermittent disruption. Continuously consistent communication came only from landline telephones.

Italian television and radio stations had been deluged with callers observing, experiencing events. Calls now came from Ancona. Italian stations were not the only ones relating events but because every observer's call was in Italian, foreign stations had to translate them. This took time.

Signora Carassalini unintentionally altered this.

Signora Sonia Carassalini and her husband Tosca, own La Terrazzo restaurant, close by Ancona's Duomo, its Byzantine cathedral. The Duomo is on top of Monte Guasco, an 80 metre high bluff on the seaward side of the old town. La Terrazzo, such as its name suggests, consists of terraces built into the side of the bluff. A piazza surrounding the Duomo affords a panoramic view of the city and the sea. Many people from the old town rushed up to it (others took to the cliffs which run south from the bluff to Numona). Sonia Carassalini, however, viewed events from her terraces below. Although resident in Ancona for a decade, Sonia was forever telephoning her mother. On that Thursday evening, as she looked out to sea, she was again calling home.

Sonia's family live in Great Barford, a village near Bedford in Britain. Sonia's sister, Serina, still lives at home. Serina works in sports promotion at Woburn. She quickly grasped the significance of her sister's call. Twenty minutes later it was being broadcast live on Radio Bedford, then the BBC itself. Then around the world, not just on radio but television too.

Listeners missed Sonia's descriptions of La-ra hovering above the water (she was to his right-hand side), of him stretching "many kilometres," was "at least a mile high," had curved "cliff-like" sides, was absolutely silent and was "just hanging there doing nothing." They also missed her descriptions, in between, of the cloudless evening, the fading light, of how the last of the sunlight still shone on "the spaceship's top," and the ever growing crowds arriving to look, including those climbing the cranes of the Fincantieri ship repair yard which lay to her left below her.

Although in shortened re-broadcasts technicians took away "umms" and "errs" and engineers improved the sound quality, none removed the fact that her commentary came from a telephone. Nor did they diminish the effect of Sonia having lived those ten years among Italians. During the minutes missed by listeners, and due to this Italian influence, Sonia had been building up an emotive head of steam. Listeners, fortunately, first heard her just as La-ra was about to do "something."

> *"I can see a glow...its glowing, it's getting brighter. No, no...it's lights, they're lights...mille migliaia di lucí.. Its covered, absolutely covered in lights...they're getting brighter, brighter.. They're sparkling ...diamente...millions of diamonds.. Reflections in the water...bello!... bellissimo!. The water as far as I can see...shining, glistening, bella, bellisima...beautiful...they're rippling.. The lights are rippling...down the side...la lucce, lights...pushing outwards...oh!...some...are leaving... shooting into the air.. There's another...more...they're streaming out... balls of fire.. Four...five...streaming away, with tails.. Now there's more, twenty...thirty.. They're zooming up in a line...ooh, there's another line ...and another.. Heading together...towards Numona...up now...they're going up...up..*
>
> *"..Oh...I can see white streaks in the sky...trails, straight lines of trails...like planes. They are planes!. Coming...they're coming straight at the spaceship! Balls of light...the balls of light are going up to them.. The planes are coming towards.. Balls turning to sheets...joining together...like a shield.. It, they're...brighter...brighter...now gone!. Disappea...no they haven't...the lights are...back again...brighter... they've gone.. The planes...no!. No...oh no!...oh no!...they're going down...some are...others all over the place.. There's one flying into...* (her scream, following by a booming sound*)...they're falling into the sea.. They're dead...*(sobbing*)...killed, they've killed our...no, no...I can see a parachute...another...others.. They're coming...into the sea.. The lights are going for them!...they're attackin...*(scream*)...no they're not... they're pushing them through the air.. I can't believe it!.. They're actually pushing them through the air!.. They're...lights...*(crying*)...pushing them through the air to the cliffs...they've saved them...they're safe...marvellous...meuo male...*(crying again)*...ooh they're good.. Listen to everybody...can you hear them cheering?...can you hear the people over at Fincanteri?..*

"Ooh the lights are flying back to the...no they're not...the lights, the lights on the spaceship are moving...they're all moving out, outwards from the sides...underneath as well!...all sweeping away, all together... oh, é bellissimo...so beautiful...the whole sky is filled...millioni, millions of stars...I can see...I'm right underneath them...a cupola... enorme duoma stella...stars, they fill the sky...all of it...as far as I can... semra paradiso é stupedo...(crying again)*...oh they are so beautiful... beautiful.. They're coming brighter...oh fading...brighter again... brightness pulsing back and forth...back and forth...back and forth... ooh bello, lovely...back and forth...bello, bello...presto, presto...molto chiaro...piú veloce...brighter, brighter, faster, faster...sky filled with brilliance...ooh, ooh...bello, bello...ooh so lovely, lovely..*

"..The spaceship's side is moving in...no, it's a line...a dark line along the side...getting bigger...bigger...light...I can see a light...a blue light...brilliant blue light.. It's fading...no something's coming out... coming out of the side.. Shining, black, sembra un 'unova...no not an egg...piú grande...bigger...it's out of the side now.. Enome...enome!... another coming...another...more...all coming out of the side.. They're gigantic...bigger than ships, liners...it's darker, night-time now...I can only make out their shapes...like sigari gigantici é neri...a line of them ...twenty, no, more...more on the other side as well...I can just see them all.. They're moving away...100 metres...200 now..

"..It's moving...the spaceship's moving...sinking...coming, going down...down.. It's stopped.. There's a sound...purring sound...it's...no it's water...it's taking away the water!. Now louder...can you hear?... louder...un rumore forte...roaring, rushing...like ships propellers.. All the water...ooh look!...(shriek)*...the boats in the harbour si stanno... capsizing...the Greek, the Superfast ferry is rolling right over on its side, all going over.. Look, there's lights!..*

"..Lights...beam of lights...the spaceship's, the ones either side have switched on beams...shafts of light.. Azure, brilliant blue...now purple ...blue again...purple.. Bello, bello...blue and purple...blue and purple, beautiful...pulsing, pulsing...ripple after ripple.. The spaceship's blowing the water away!. From 300 metres!. The power...ooh what power ...beams of light now blue, purple, blue.. They're going faster, faster.. Ooh Momma...sembra paradise, lovely, lovely.. It's all going...all the water's going!. The shafts of light have joined...both sides have joined each other...huge flat Vee under the spaceship. They are lighting its underneath...there's grooves, holes...the noise has stopped...can you hear?. It's stopped blowing down.. Ooh, ooh!...l'aqua é soffo piena di luci...underneath the lights!.. They're holding the water bac...they're moving...the waves of light are moving...moving apart...taking the water with them!.. Back...back...they're still going back...the other side

as well, I can see it.. They're almost straight now... They've parted the waters!.. They've parted Mare Adriático!.. Walls of blue...hundreds of metres high, parting the waters as far as I can see.. Oh Momma it is like the Read Sea...meraviglioso...(crying)*...so moving..*

"..Spaceship's rising...started to move...forwards between walls of light...now rising up...up above.. Still going up...the stars...starlights closing in around it...they've joined together...it, they're rising higher... higher...they're smaller now...smaller...esiguo...I can't see them...they have gone...gone...but the walls of light are still here..

".. They're clearer now...see them more...they go on...as far as I can see...so far apart...the other side, line is...beyond Falconara...I can just make out the lights of Falconara and...the line is beyond them...they must be fifteen kilometres away.. What power!...light holding back water... é miracolo!...é um miracolo!...miracle..

"..Beams...the beams are pulsing.. They're going to do it again!... (joyous shriek)*...they're all doing it again!.. Lentemente...blue...now purple, such strength...blue...and purple...blue...now purple.. People at Fincantieri, can you hear them calling?...azzurro...marone?. Ooh, people are holding one another, so enchanting...delizioso, dolce... d'azzurro...marone...azzurro...marone...light beams have a rhythm now...azzurro é marone, blue and purple...ooh Momma so lovely...they keep going on and on...blue and purple...azzurro...marone...ooh it's good, it's good...such strength, power...so bright, strong...now faster, faster...brighter, brighter...and faster and faster...ooh! ooh!...brilliance of purple bursting...ooh and again and again...ooh magnifico...magnifico...fantastico!.*

"..Oh, the nearest ones are curving away from us...sweeping towards Falconara...far ones are coming to join, join them...they've joined...now they're sweeping inwards, shallower.. Like the bow of a boat... huge boat of light.. Now they're moving...all moving, going away from us, leaving across Mare Adriático.. The water's coming back!.. Waves rushing in...can you hear? Such a sight...waves rising right up into the air!.. Spumes of white foam and spray.. More waves as water fills the harbour..

"..The lights...spaceships are leaving us now...oh, going away so soon...a boat of light sailing into the night...so beautiful...like an ark... mervigliso...mervigliso...so wonderful.. Ooh what are the people over at Fincantieri doing?. Ooh.."

Sonia's telephone conversation continued for several minutes more but at this point, when listeners heard her drawing heavily on a cigarette, then remonstrating with Tosca for looking at the people over at the Fincantieri boatyard through his binoculars, most broadcasters ended it there. Other facets of the evening's events pressed upon them.

36: TOCANS

The people of the northern Illyrian islands saw the walls of light from many kilometres distant. But workers on the off-shore oil rigs by the northern tip of the island of Molat, on seeing the tocans' lights then speeding straight towards them, fled. Some distance from the islands, however, the lights disappeared.

What watchers on either side of the Adriatic were not to know was that the spectacle they witnessed was incidental to the main purpose of the event. This was the in-situ testing of all the fleet's component parts for the tasks lying ahead of them. Also, that the northern Adriatic was the only stretch of shallow water on the fleet's journey in which to test their effectiveness in Earthly conditions.

After crossing over to Croatia, 79 of the 81 tocans continued on the same straight north-easterly course and to their next appointment 1,500 kilometres away. They all banked uniformly up from the coast and over the Dinaric Alps, and an hour later they were at 10,000 metres altitude above the Carpathian Mountains of the western Ukraine.

One of the other tocans, Sardon, still keeping to the same straight course, ascending yet higher, flew faster and within two hours had taken up station on the Equator many kilometres above the island of Marajó. The other, Sieba, once the western Dinaric Alps were crossed, veered sharply to the south and within minutes had taken up position there.

37: JAMES

I was glued to the television. I think everyone must have been, if not television then radio. I saw the first news on the Reuters screens and everyone gathered round them. I did hear some cries of "Sell, sell," but as trading was closing I don't think there was time enough then to do much. Nonetheless it's a one-way bet that the markets will take big hits in tomorrow's trading. As I read the screen texts Danny was foremost in my mind. What he had said yesterday hadn't been a hoax.

After work I had arranged to meet Frankie in Quagalianos on Wood Lane. I had tried all day phoning her but without success. I went to the wine bar anyway, on the off-chance she might be there. The moment I opened the door I immediately noted the absence of conversation and a wall of backs. More than "massive unidentified object" was the "news" on the bar's television screen. At first I was surprised that a mere postcard photograph could command so much attention but on hearing the commentary I understood why. As the air battle took place I wasn't the only one with an open mouth. When the woman giving the commentary started crying, one of the barmaids, I think she's Italian, was quite beside herself. However, the atmosphere eased as the woman then described the pilots and their parachutes being flown through the air.

Fifteen minutes later, Frankie arrived. For the first time ever I told her to be quiet. It was also the first time I didn't agitate about not being served. We stayed until the commentary ended then went home. Fortunately we're only walking distance away. The traffic at Shepherds Bush had jammed to a halt.

On the way back I told Frankie what I had heard. I also mentioned Danny. She retorted she knew about his telecast but then said, "You haven't asked about me, asked about the wretched week I've had up in Manchester?"

I could sense something was upsetting her. I did my best to deflect by saying, "Sorry," but it didn't suffice. By the time we arrived home she was in a sulk and it was left to me to get supper. The meal didn't placate her either.

Because of events I naturally turned on the television. It was still tuned to Channel Two on which was a "Newsnight Special." As on Tuesday, it was anchored by Wired. This time though with maps and a panel of 'Rent-a-Prof' pundits. My knowing Danny gave added interest and having listened to the woman from Ancona's commentary I was aware the object was big. However, when clips from Italian television were shown I was staggered by its size. Not that the pictures showed much detail and were taken from a distance, but all conveyed its immensity. One of the panel, a Professor Eden of Portsmouth, described its size best, as long as the Isle of Wight is wide. But no sooner had he spoken than an inane computer graphic appeared showing what it would have been like over London. Wired snapped "From Heathrow to Ilford long, from Wandsworth to Finchley wide."

Following that mind boggling revelation the commentary from Ancona was broadcast again, during which I took the food from the microwave and we sat down to eat. My attention was split between the commentary and Frankie. I did ask about her father's illness and her mother's health, but in turn received a non-stop recitation of how she hated railways, Manchester and her mother. I listened as attentively as I could but all I received after she had finished was, “You're not really listening to a thing I say, are you?”

And to be truthful, I wasn't, I'd heard it all before, many times. Listening to the Ancona commentary was much more absorbing, even though the last part had been edited. I did think of saying “We're being visited by beings from another planet and all you talk about is your bloody mother,” but instead I tried to impress on Frankie the importance of what had happened.

Unfortunately the commentary ended at that point and was replaced, after Wired's snapped “Well, what is to be made of that?” by, “We now go over to David Morrell, our Washington correspondent and Senator Monk of the Senate Armed Services Committee.” But before he could say “Senator,” Frankie started noisily clearing the dishes. My “I'll do all that, just wait a moment,” only made matters worse. Not only did she dump everything in the sink but promptly stormed off into the bathroom, and I realised it was indeed left to me to “do all that.”

While she was there I did at least manage to catch the rest of the interview with the senator. Most was waffle, even the matter of the air attack only elicited We are carefully watching events." However, the last part was ominous, “With my fellow committee members we will be meeting with President Warren within the hour to discuss the threat to our national security.” The mention of 'threat' and 'security' in the same sentence worries me when I hear them from the lips of American military. They are the words they always use as a prelude to their invading somewhere.

After the interview with the senator there was a telecast from an intrepid American reporter and her team. She and her crew had managed to make it to Ancona on the backs of a pack of motorbikes. Frankie appeared from the bathroom and without saying a word swept into the bedroom. As before, I was torn between attending to her sulk and watching the television. Because of the importance of the news I just had to watch.

One of the things which struck me were the people who the reporter and her interpreter interviewed and had witnessed events. They all appeared to be quite relaxed, exuberant even. Numerous couples were holding each other's hands and many of them were smoking cigarettes. All the same, she kept asking “Were you scared?” The most she elicited was “At first.” It was only after several interviews did she realise there had been an air battle. But all she received in reply was that it was pilots' own fault. One even said “We were not attacked, so why should the war planes want to harm something so beautiful?” Apart from a chorus of consensus from the others, this nonplussed her. She became more so when another added "And they saved the pilots." But no sooner had she exclaimed "Saved them?" than she was holding her hand to her ear. She next said "This is Marie Clare Stockwell for APTV, Ancona, Italy" and was replaced on the screen by Wired.

Upon which he fired at one of the pundits with "Where do you think they are now, where have they gone, what do you think professor?" Fifteen minutes of waffle ensued during which I washed the dishes and cleared away. The pundits were stopped mid-waffle by Wired announcing "We are now going live to Washington and David Morrell at Martin Druz, the US Secretary of Defense's press conference at the Pentagon."

"I have met with President Warren...he has authorized me to issue the following statement, "Consequent to the unprovoked attack, earlier today, against US forces off the coast of Italy by as yet unidentified craft, the government of the United States has instructed all US forces to Watch Com Two. We are conducting urgent consultations with our NATO allies with regard to coordinating..." My attention was diverted from Druz by the sound of Frankie sobbing. When I asked her why she was so upset, she cried "You humiliated me in front of all those people," I was taken aback.

When I said that she often put her finger to my lips, her "That's different", had me stuck for a reply. When I said I was sorry and promised never to do it again, she stopped crying, creased a smile and cooed "Come to bed, I've missed you," then, "azzurro, maroni, azzurro..." I took the hint and said I'd just go and turn everything off.

I was about to switch off the television when Wired, cutting off Secretary Druz mid-sentence, said "We're receiving reports from the Russian news agency Interfax, of disturbances in Ukrainian capital Kiev, we now go over immediately to Vitaly Lutkino in Kiev..." I just had to watch.

Or rather, listen. The reception was poor and although there was nothing but a stock photo stating it was Kiev, I was riveted. "A little more than one hour ago, lines of immense aerial craft flew over Kiev. Soon after, a series of huge bright blue lighted raft-like objects began floating down onto open spaces in the city's environs. More have been reported from other centres, Vinnitsa, Khmel' Nitskiy, Zhitomir, many others. At about this same time reports were received from Chernobyl, 100 kilometres north of Kiev, of similar aerial craft circling the nuclear facility there, then powerfully illuminating the locality from many hundreds of metres altitude. Shortly afterwards, Kiev was struck by widespread loss of electrical power. Only those entities with private generators currently have electricity supply. There have been reported incidents of public order disturbances in the city and further reports, as yet unconfirmed, of huge numbers of people arriving at the central station in Kiev from Slavutich and Cernigov. Meanwhile, unofficial Government sources..."

My concentration was broken by Frankie yanking the bedroom door open and her tearful outburst of "Are you coming to bed or not?"

What could I do but do as she said, turn off the television and go to bed.

At first I feared for the worst. The Susem retreated to Kubber and Paceillo was engrossed with La-ra. None showed a care for the problems presented by the soldiers and villagers. The villagers were disheartening as well. Their surprise and wonder was gone within the hour. All they then thought about was the benefits the Susem might bring and the trouble the soldiers could cause. And when Elana returned I received nothing but an earful over her emptied bar and empty till.

Being an outsider and having some connection with the Susem, villagers and soldiers alike looked to me to answer their questions, resolve their anxieties. But I kept thinking, "Why me?" and wishing Rainbow was here. She would have sorted everything. But pragmatism eventually overcame panic and by the end of the day events were turned to everyone's advantage, including mine.

In an hour not only had I, with Pedro, organised a checkpoint of soldiers on the Ubajara road, but more of them patrolling to the north of the village. A further platoon was despatched in a truck to Tianguá laden with soufins. They went with orders to sell them, buy supplies with the money, and rein in Roberto and disciples (he would have done enough evangelising for one day). The children were set guarding the forest paths to the south (they knew them better than the soldiers, saved on manpower and kept them quiet).

The soldiers sent to Tianguá left amid cries of "Viva harmonia!" but returned three hours later to "Viva acoolica!" They had also bought some other items, cigarettes, as well as Roberto, his disciples and more than 1,000 Reals (Brazilian dollars) to spare. These soldiers said soufin sales had been slow until Roberto was collared. One of the sellers, a natural born marketing man if ever there was, had the inspiration of Roberto autographing each one. With his signature on the soufins business became brisk. Prices doubled, tripled. Within the hour every last one had gone.

Outsiders arriving to see the vedas were also a source of income. Because security was a concern, visitors were told to leave cameras at the checkpoint. However, the Park's defunct cable car tickets, issued at first as stand-in receipts, soon changed the checkpoint into a box office. At two Reals (or whatever these sightseers had on them) for admission, another 2,000 was in the coffers before the day was done.

Security was actually solved by the soldiers Pedro had kept as a strategic reserve, doubling up as guides conducting parties of a dozen or so on half hour tours. The villagers, whose sense of opportunity soon overcame that of apprehension, added further attractions by setting up stalls selling snacks and their store of jewellery and handicrafts.

Because their incomes were being boosted, the villagers readily agreed, in exchange for a soufin and Roberto's endorsing their wares (which lifted their sales and prices no end), to house and feed five soldiers for a week. After completing his endorsing, Roberto, who had by then, even by Brazilian standards, had become thoroughly over-excited with his busy day, was made, with Elana's blessing to lie down in the shade of the Pousada. Elana (who is back on talking terms, now her stock is replenished) was also the catalyst resolving another problem.

The soufins were acquired from Terbal in exchange for promising him his "More space for screens I am needing, you get for me, ya?" (The Susem were, he had said and to my irritation, resting). At the time, I'd no idea where I could find him such space and when I asked around there was none to be had. But Elana's light-hearted suggestion of "Groto de Tabajara?" sparked the solution.

Knowing on board Kubber there would be excavating equipment for the search of Pa-tu and also the Susem liking for the subterranean, I suggested to Terbal he dug the space. I didn't expect him to be quite as overjoyed as he was, his fronds began wagging frantically, but neither did I anticipate the consequences.

The sight of Mobo and other cisons flying from Kubber, criss-crossing the area, calling "Hadodani" as they passed, then congregating over by the park-side attracted onlookers' attentions. But after the cisons' return, the brigade of machines and other objects which ran out from Kubber and Konnet's doors then rushing across to the park-side, caused quite a stir. It was as though they were racing one another (I was reminded of nursery rhyme illustrations of plates and spoons, the only difference being there weren't faces for grins).

No sooner had the frontrunners arrived by the trees than they were burrowing like moles in a thunderstorm. As they disappeared the rest followed down the hole. Booms and whirrs ensued but an hour later and after the noise had abated, there was more than surprise when Terbal and a carpet of his helpers in tow, floated into view. Several people sank to their knees wailing "Esprito Santo" but a few fainted as well. Terbal hovered for a moment, as though taking a bow, then whizzed away down the hole.

With Pedro, a few emboldened others, and the element of curiosity, we followed. We were in for a big surprise.

Fifty feet down was an illuminated cavern with studded shiny walls, floors, and a 10 foot high ribbed ceiling stretching all the way to the side of the Ibiapaba, where there are windows. Terbal, as he flew to and fro, explained, when I asked, that the rock had been compacted by fusing it to glass. He also said "Strong, plastic, no moving anything."

I'd not the chance though to ask where the amazing power needed to do such fusing had come from or provide the lighting, a uniform white-green glow, before he, whizzing past again said "Occupied I am now, you go, return later, ya?" So we did as he said but not before we heard yet more 'booms' and 'whirrs' from further below. As we left the cavern we were passed by a stream of more machines from both Kubber and the other two vedas. They were like a factory shift on their way to work. As they passed us many of them called out "Hadodani" (and again boosting my standing no end).

By five o'clock the last visitors had left and the villagers were clearing their stalls away. I was sipping a cerveja and counting the day's takings. And all was well. The soldiers were soldiering, the villagers had been selling, the children were quiet, Elana had her bar restocked, Roberto was resting, as were the Susem, and Terbal was happy down his hole. As I looked across to the setting sun, I thought of him (the sun) as being happy in his heaven as well. Things were like they were in London, everyone engaged in tasks I had them do while I sat in the centre managing the money, and the prospects.

As I saw it, both money and prospects were rosy. If Roberto, I reasoned, could continue to enhance prices by endorsement, there would be no end to the cash coming in. Send him and the disciples into a town of a morning, have them do a spot of evangelising, then arrive in the afternoon with a lorry-load of merchandise, he would put his mark on them and we would clean up. All I needed now was stock. The only difficulty I saw, knowing only too well how quickly I tire of day to day tasks, was securing a good manager.

Thoughts inevitably drifted to the best manager I have ever known and she was Rainbow. Everyone, everything was kept in line, nothing went wrong when Rainbow was in charge and she would do it all without fluster. Senior management was her obvious metier but like all the others in my employ, acting was all she really lived for. Her actual name was Iris but I think she liked me calling her by what it meant. It was fitting for another reason. Her mother came from Livingston, 15 miles west of Edinburgh. Her father also came from Livingston, the one just east of Baton Rouge, Louisiana. That's why, I suppose, her surname wasn't Lewis but Louis. Besides being the best basher I have known (she's that skilful I would often never know she was doing it until long after), she also took no lip. Sometimes I'd call her "the Rainbow Warrior" ('warrior' being what Louis means).

Her father had been in the air force and while stationed in Germany met her mother who was a dancer. Thus, though Rainbow was American, her mother's influence had her attending RADA and as an outcome she spoke with beautifully rounded vowels. But like it is for actors everywhere, thespian work is hard to find and Rainbow not being white found it harder than most. While other actors I employed came and after a while went, Rainbow stayed (and I never ever wanted her to leave).

Though she was loyal as could be and by nature modest, Rainbow possesses a quality the others hadn't, presence. When she walked into a room heads turned. It is the way she moves. Rainbow has grace (she had said it was because her mum made her walk with books on her head, but I'm sure there is some-thing more to it than that).

Alas my rest and reflection came to an abrupt and dismal end with the appearance of Paceillo. She gave no gratitude or appreciation of my endeavours and enterprise, only criticism. I should not have taken the soufins, I had exploited people, made a spectacle of the Susem and I had failed to obtain the

ALIENS ATTAC[K] EARTH

WORLD LEADERS CALL FOR CALM

WORLD LEADERS were calling for calm following yesterday's invasion of Earth by giant space craft.

The craft 30 kilometres in length, 20 wide and a kilometre high; bigger than anything made by mankind settled off of the Italian Adriatic port city of Ancona.

First sightings of the craft came from Melilla, Spain at 2pm BST. It flew in a straight line across the Mediterranean, over Sardinia, Corsica then central Italy stopping off the Adriatic coast at Ancona.

As the craft passed ovehead, its shadow left many areas in darkness for up to 15 minutes. Sonia Gierek-Carassalini, a UK resident

President Warren's speech in full: page 4

who has lived in Ancona for ten years, said the craft attacked NATO airplanes, then conducted a series of

(Full details of Mrs Gierek-Carassalini's account, page 3).

On its two hour journey across Italy, the craft was responsible for causing extensive chaos to the entire road and rail system throughout the centre of the country. Italian police sources were predicting many casualties and deaths.

US President, Howard Warren, said: "During this period of grave uncertainty, may 'calmness' be our watch word. Calmness in response. Calmness in assessment of the situation the entire world has been confronted with today.

"The position we are in is without precedent. That we must now stand back, stay

THE DAY THE WORLD CHANGED - FOR EVER

THE WORLD HAS BEEN INVADED BY ALIENS FROM OUTER SPACE.

At 3pm yesterday the people of Earth knew that they were not alone in our Universe.

Leaders from around the world untied in pledging their security forces to protect all the people of the Earth against the Alien invaders.

The prime minister Edward Campbell in a communiqué for Downing Street told the nation: "Stay calm."

Thousands of people f[...] fear as the Alien's m[...] spacecraft slammed t[...] the Earth's atmospher[...] the Mediterranean ye[...] afternoon.

The spacecraft, esti[...] be more than 40 kilo[...] length - the size of t[...] Wight - was first spo[...] the Spanish enclav[...] and flew north[...] towards the Itali[...] Sardinia then [...] mainland proper.

Entire cities [...] into total darkn[...] flew overhead. Italians are t[...] perished or [...] mass panic s[...] the land.

On the na[...] (motorways[...] crazed wit[...] one anoth[...]

Among [...] Alien's cr[...] Italy was [...] Gierek, [...] residen[...] countr[...]

Soni[...] Alien[...] NATO [...] dest[...] And [...] wa[...]

THE Chron

INVASION FROM OUTER SPAC[E]

See pages,4,5, PM speaks 7, Protect your home 9

DAILY glass

ALIENS INVADE EARTH!

Full story pages 2,3,4,6&7

[N]ATO Jets Downe[d]

[So]uthern Command [co]nfirmed yesterday, [...]s had been shot [...] Adriatic by the [...] planes were on [...] mission and two [...] seen to eject. [...] fate is unknown.

[C]ouncil chiefs in [...]e meeting later [...]cuss the crisis. [...]mander, Herman "The situation is [...]TO is already on [...]vasion. However, [...]s out of sector we [...]e unless we are requested, and have consent from NATO member states."

villagers' consent for Terbal's cavern. It was like it was being with my mum when she would march me home for doing something wrong, bewailing I had brought shame on her and what would the neighbours think.

I was upset and hurt by Paceillo's attitude, then annoyed, for as she berated, she insisted I went with her to the cavern. "If it's so wrong," I inwardly said, "why are you using it?"

But before I had time to say anything, Paceillo had changed the subject. "Why were the new arrivals waving their clothing when they first came to Tabajara?" she asked.

Apart from being surprised she had noticed such a small thing, I explained how some people like waving banners, and if they didn't have flags they would wave whatever came to hand. It helped give a sense of emboldened unity to a congregation. I would have continued, relieved her haranguing had eased, but she started "Hmm hmming" again, so I didn't. We walked the rest of the way in silence.

In the space of two hours the cavern had been transformed. Though the machines were still busy they had already installed dozens of circles of screens. Terbal, the other five Susem and yet more machines, moved from circle to circle. I was there an hour. I saw the first events unfold. They began for me with Paceillo saying "What are these?"

She ushered me to one of the circles and a four foot wide screen. Though the image was pinpoint sharp I didn't immediately know what it was. From the shadows not only could I see it was being lit from above but viewed from there as well. Before I had time to speak Paceillo, pointing to circles to the left of the screen, asked "These here, what are they?"

I recognised the little black speeding specks first. They were shadows of people running. The circles were tops of towers. I had barely a chance to say as such before I was taken to another screen.

This was easier to identify. There were also many more black specks. But despite my "Water, ships, quays, submarines..." Paceillo said "No, these here?"

After I had told her that they were beached and dry-docked submarines, she whisked me to yet another screen. This wasn't so clear. A hill, several ponds, trees and a runway but that was all. When I said I couldn't identify more she left me and joined Terbal.

I went back to the second screen. The black specks had disappeared. I was mesmerised. But when I returned to the first screen I was staggered. In the centre, hovering above the buildings, was now a glowing red disc. Two curved inwardly sloping lines of intense blue light had also appeared. Both had begun from a point to the left of the towers and were progressing slowly, each in an arc across the screen and either side of the disc. It was as if I was looking down from just inside one of the arcs. These lights were so powerful that I couldn't see through the far arc, the top of which disappeared off of the screen. I could also see whatever was making the arc directly below was also the

NEWSPAPER OF THE YEAR

We must keep calm says PM

THE Prime Minister's Office, last night issued a Release to the Press on the Alien invasion. The release calls for calm. Government action, says the release, "will be determined by the outcome of events now occurring."

The release, signed by Edward Campbell, said government agencies were in urgent contact with all their EU and NATO counterparts.

Unofficial MoD sources, last night were saying, contingency plans already exist for just such an event - invasion from space - and able to be put into effect immediately.

These would involve evacuating government departments to designated locations, and the cabinet itself to disused mines believed to be in either Yorkshire or Wales. It is not known what such plans contain for the general population. According to MoD this is beyond their remit.

Miracle or menace in Ancona?

Was the parting of the Adriatic Sea by the Aliens a demonstration of their devastating power? Or have we seen the Second Coming? writes **Adrian Warley**

Will the Aliens attack us? Do we need to fear for our lives? Or are we witnessing the arrival of a force which will, for once unite us all? Unite us against a common foe? Or instead will the Aliens unite us all in a force for the good of mankind?

Of these and other questions only time will tell. But asked to a citizen of Ancona and their replies will be of the wonder they have just experienced. While all will tell no harm happened upon them, many are indeed convinced they were witness to a miracle.

Alien invasion bad for business confidence

By Andrew Jones New York

The alien invasion of Earth yesterday has unsettled business confidence. Investment will be badly shaken and will have a detrimental effect on future profits; job prospects are also likely to suffer.

While there be undoubtable beneficaries in defence and related industrial sectors others are sure to suffer in the short term at least.

Yesterday's 150 point fall of the Dow Jones is sign of the unsettling effect the invasion is going to have when markets open today.

US Business leaders were said to be pressing for immediate clarification of Gover-

Until US Government response is clarified both bond and stock markets worldwide are likely to plummet. Turmoil can be expected in other markets especially metals and many nfas (non-food agriculturals). Although the Lond Metal Exchange will be closed today, Nick Budgen at LME traders Redwood Cash said, "There is likely to be frantic trading as users attempt to consolidate their reserve positions whether the LME is open or closed."

Meanwhile, because of the Europen holidays, UK and EU business leaders are exp

Alien's arrival foretold

Saul Boot

We were told two days ago that Aliens had landed, but chose to ignore it. On Wednesday we were told in detail of their arrival yet we chose to ridicule the message.

We were told exactly when and where to expect the Aliens to appear. And they did! With precision such as that, it would be timely to examine what else was said in their Wednesday telecast.

We were told they came in peace. They have retali-

They said nuclear weapons, waste and power stations were dangerous and had to go. "Your're welcome to the lot", would no doubt be the joyous cry from many quarters. Sell those nuclear shares - now.

Nuclear shares are not the only ones to be rid of if what the Aliens - or Susem as we should now call them - say is so. Deep sea fishermen and lumberjacks should decide a career change - immediately.

Also it might not be a good time to own a mine or prospect for diamonds and gold.

it ... ke ... the ... into ... it by ... aker ... oved. ... e-end, ... e. The ... that is ... lock- ... epend- ... ocking ... rop or ... locks. ... e are ... st be ... ghtly ... d up ... rifle ... his- ... kes ... act

IN BR

e eng... n shad...

H Morocc... of Melilla ... d in Alien ... shadow for 20 minutes ye... proximately 3pm ... cecraft's speed ... d be at more tha... h and estimated ... ore than 40 kilor... o reports of pan... most of the popu... were in siesta.

Aliens cause Corsican chao...

AJACCIC: Southern ... sican city of Boni... suffered serious chao... wake of Alien space... yesterday. Inhabitants ... in fear as sky darkene... craft flew overhead at 4... Many traffic accid... reported. Churches pac... with worried worshipp... *AFP*

Sardinians' shadow shock

CAGLIARI: Thousands ... inhabitants along Sar... inia's northern coast fl... in fear as Alien spacecra... flew over the Gulf of Asi... ara plunging it into dar... ness late yesterday afte... noon. The town of Sassar... 10 kilometres inland wa... also in the wake of th... shadow made by Alien's... craft for more than 10 min... utes. Numerous motorists ... injured as they looked up

Emergency NATO ... to counter Alien th...

by Roger Liddle in Brussels

NATO chiefs were reported to be in emergency session last night in attempt to draw up a plan to counter the worldwide threat poised by the arrival of Aliens.

Reports from defence circles here in Brussels say that the Alliance does not have any prepared plans to counter such an emergency in drawing up any effective strategy to combat the threat posed by the Aliens.

At present it is unclear if the reasons for the Alien's arrival on Earth are benign or malign. The only evidence of the Alien's awesome technological superiority is the patchy reports coming from Italy

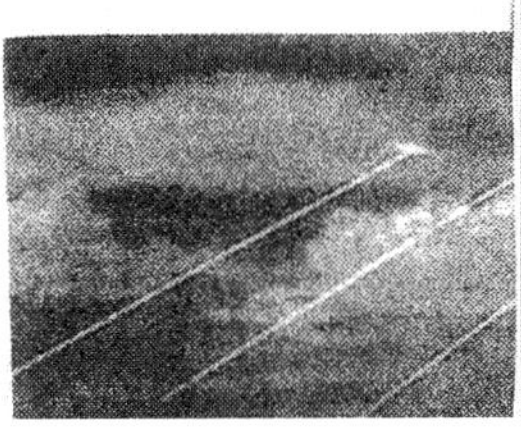

European flights affecte...

Many cancellations, delays **Italy off-limi...**

By Helen Wears

HUNDREDS OF flights across Europe were cancelled yesterday in the wake of the Alien's.

More than 80,000 passengers at all UK's major airports were faced with either cancellations or long delays.

Passengers attempting to fly to Italy, southern France and Switzerland suffered the most. Every single flight to destinations in these countries most affected, said: "More than 30,000 of our company's passengers have been affected by the arrival of these Alien's. We are currently waiting on air traffic control as to when we have clearance. Until we have received it we are advising everyone to stay at home until we have the all-clear to resume flights."

Both Heathrow and Gatwick were witness to

same thing that the 'camera' was positioned on, for as the arcs lengthened, the image on the screen appeared to move with it.

Using the towers as a guide, I estimate that when the two arcs finally interlocked, the distance from one end to the other must have been a mile and perhaps half a mile across. The moment the arcs met their blue light changed to purple. It was like looking along a huge bloodshot eye.

It was only when I heard cries of "Pan! pan!" did I realise anyone else was looking. I turned and saw all six Susem and Terbal. They said nothing more but Petruee pointed back to the screen. The arcs of light gave a rippling pulse, then my hand was on my mouth. The ground inside the arcs began to rise.

And it kept on rising. (It was like the TV pictures taken from a space launch gantry, where the rocket's nose cone slowly rises up towards the camera and then there's just the sight of the speeding rocket itself going up and up). As it rose I saw that the disc was actually a sphere, then what looked like part of a power station, its towers. I momentarily saw trucks, other buildings, roadways. Then no more than the bare ground beneath the power station. I'd not time to even dwell on the immense power I was witnessing before Petruee had tugged me to a screen opposite. With yet more Susem shouts of "Pan! pan!" my hand was on my mouth again (and the Ride of the Valkeries pounding in my head).

This screen had a red cast and the images appearing were black. They were uniform triangular shapes and all but touching one another. There were lines and lines of them, hundreds and hundreds. And they were travelling at great speed. The 'camera' viewing them was positioned just above and to their rear. I grasped it was from there, for on the screen appearing above them was a bright, downward pointing triangle of light and they were racing towards it. I then realised what they were. They were vedas but they were flying upside down, and the light was that of the arcs.

Lathia tapped my arm and motioned me to the screen next to it. At first I thought I was seeing a mirror of the same thing, then I realised they were other vedas flying towards the first ones. I next saw both fleets manoeuvring into flattened curves, as if they were giant manta rays. And as they did they slowed, until by the time they had met they were momentarily stationary. On meeting, both fleets began beaming lights from their tops (or, strictly speaking, their bottoms). Within seconds the lights became so bright they merged into a single intense blue, obliterating even the light of the arcs. But this lasted only for an instant. It then changed to purple. As soon as it had there was a huge sudden jolt from the vedas (and Siegfried's Funeral March in my head). They were like a battery of artillery guns recoiling. This happened again, then again, four times in all. After the last there was laughter from behind me.

"Each time," said Lathia still laughing, "your head jolted backwards."

Almost without acknowledging her mirth I asked "What am I seeing? The power station, where has it gone?" As I asked I saw the vedas, in unison, parting backwards and righting themselves.

She said nothing more than "Look," and pointed to yet another screen.

In the reflected light of their downward beams I realised I was looking along a line of tocans, each in pairs, staggered half a length to the left of one another. The front pair went forward from the line. Within moments, the paths of their lights parted, turned to blue, converged, changed to purple and another triangle of light rose up into the air to be followed by a carpet of blue then pulses of purple (and more Wagner). No sooner had these ended than another pair of tocans flew forwards.

I watched another sequence then again asked Lathia "What am I seeing, what's happening? Where is it all going?"

"Your star," was all she said.

The others were grouped within another circle of screens. Lathia went to them, I followed.

They were speaking agitatedly, as though to one another, but they stopped when they saw me and started talking in English as though they were purposely changing the conversation (not that I would have understood them).

"Everything going up," I asked Lathia again, "is going to the Sun?"

"Yes."

"Where it belongs," added Paceillo quietly, but sounding almost as if it were a growl.

"How does it do that? What makes it keep going up, what stops any of it coming back down?"

"Focused and accelerated inter-wave retro-resonance," replied Lathia matter-of-factly.

Menpemelo's "Contra-Secondary wave, but extremely concentrated," explanation left me none the wiser either.

I received no answer to my "Contra-Secondary wave?" for her attention was with the others on the screen in front. Soon, so was mine. There was another power station but much bigger. Like the first, there were black specks but this time there was also speech coming from the screen, as though it or someone was speaking to the Susem. This was followed by Paceillo speaking back. She sounded agitated again.

This time almost in a whisper I asked again "What's going on?"

"We want this tocan group to wait until all your fellows have departed," whispered back Pheterisco. "The tocans," she continued, "are concerned with the delay to their schedule and want to proceed with disposal. Their vedas have already despatched hen-gers in an attempt to speed evacuation, but some are still reporting incidents of reticence. Paceillo is suggesting they be more insistent." She paused for a moment, as though listening to the commentary, then said "Oh good, the area is now vacated," then after another pause, "there goes the first rameek."

"Rameek?" I asked as another red sphere flew, then hovered into position.

"The guidance module, it ensures course direction and positioning,"

Pheterisco replied, her eyes fixed on the screen.

"Oh," I said, and as I did, I saw the others joining Milophinia amid another circle of screens. I arrived to see the figure of Tearo half turned away from the camera. But as she turned to face to it I saw Colonel Tambassing striding towards and then standing beside her. His head barely came to her shoulder. When he addressed Paceillo with "Good evening Missus" and a salute, he appeared awkward and ill at ease. But when Paceillo asked them both about the progress of their campaign, he became relaxed and began stroking his upper lip as he told her what they expected to achieve during the next 24 hours.

Paceillo, evidently pleased, was soon complimenting him (the word 'favouritism' passed through my mind). However, one of the things which struck me was the way Tearo stood there, saying nothing and looking down at him with what can only described as a beatific smile.

Everyone bid each other goodbye and the screen went blank. Paceillo, with a smile for the first time in a long while, clapped her hands and said "Time to depart." So along with the six of them, I did. But I was left to just tag along, for the Susem talked among themselves, ignoring me as I wasn't party to them. Menpemelo was the only one to speak to me and that was because she saw me rubbing a sore spot behind my ear.

"Your mormic bump," she said, "it is evolving, soon it will cease to irritate."

Matters weren't any more convivial when we reached the surface. The Susem went up to Kubber still talking to one another, with Paceillo nodding me goodbye but as though saying "Don't follow."

If ever I am unhappy I either drink or sit on my own. But only Rico was in the bar and the soldiers were with the villagers, he said. Because he bemoaned the loss of his television I didn't drink. Elana was fawning over Roberto still believing him divine and as I had missed the World Service news I saw no sense of even sitting in my room. Instead I picked up my telescope and went to the viewing platform. But as I walked my ire welled within.

It continued welling as I set up the telescope. By the time I was looking to the north and focused on Arcturus it had become anger. Neither the Susem nor the villagers appeared to appreciate the benefits I had brought them. I tried concentrating on the star but still my sense of unfairness wouldn't go away. If it hadn't been for me, the Susem would have been in deep trouble. From Arcturus I swung down to Bootes. And just why were the Susem bothering with such a two bit place as Tabajara? The Susem had the power to do anything. Why were they going about things the way they were? It could only make sense if they were up to something. I next swung down to Hercules. Although it was a moonless night, perfect for seeing stars, my mind wasn't concentrating on them, I was peering, not looking. I rubbed behind my ear, the lump was still itching. Had my body really been given protection from infection? But what if my immune system became over-infective and started

Neapolitans panic

John Freeman
in Rome

Both Italian Interior Ministry Poliza and Defence Ministry Carabiniere forces were thrown into confusion last night in the wake of the Alien spacecraft.

Both Ministries were closed and no one was available for comment. Meanwhile Traffic Police reported complete blockage of all major roads, including Autostradas between Rome and Florence. However, they were unable to give details of fatalities, although many expected. Rail travel north from here is also disrupted.

Italian TV and radio stations were the only source of hard information on events and this was supplied by telephone callers. Terrestrial communications are said to be blocked by Aliens.

Rome resident Ceare Rossi, returning from Grosseto and who saw the spacecraft, said, "It was a lovely sunny day one moment, the next there was this darkness. It was very scary, I was okay, but I saw very many crashes all about me."

"I don't think anyone could have known what was happening. I thought the end of the world had come. It took three hours to get home, the traffic was bad."

"The spacecraft was so quiet, I never heard it, then suddenly everything went dark and there it

PARIS: Residents along southern Corsican coast gave vivid eye witness accounts of the Alien spacecraft.

"It was so sudden," says Pierre Moufon, fisherman from Bonifacio, "I was about to set sail, when suddenly there was a big shadow. I looked up and there it was. So huge, travelling so fast, I thought the end of the world had come". *Paul Bates*

LAS PALMAS: British astronomer, Dr. John Baker may go on record as having made the first recording sighting of the Alien craft. Dr. Baker, currently seconded to the Izana Solar Observatory on the Canary Islands.

Dr. Baker first saw the craft shortly after midday. Although he reported his sighting to Tenerife Air Traffic Control, they were unable to spot it on their radars. *Reuters*

MADRID: Mellilia, normally a sleepy place at the busiest of times was awash with it newfound attention. Phillipo Gomes the first man to send details to the Aliens' told was he saw. "It took four minutes to cross", he said "it was so dark, I thought the end of the world had come". *Philipe Horedez*

No 5,220 www.independent.co.uk

PM calls for urgent contact with Aliens

By JOANNA REDWOOD
Chief Political Columnist

EDWARD CAMPBELL, the Prime Minister, last night instructed the BBC's World Service to transmit his call for Aliens to make immediate contact with BBC, his office or "any other acknowledged World

The PM's office said Mr Campbell had full acceptance of his proposal with the exception of Pierr Foch, the French President.

However, EU Commission chiefs were annoyed a the PM's initiative.

EU Secretary General Konrad Potzners office said Campbell had overstepped authority.

"Foreign policy i

Aliens send Itali flocking to chur

Pope prays for deliverance from "the forces o

By Donald Mintoff in Rome

CHURCHES across Italy were packed yesterday as worried worshippers prayed for deliverance from the Alien threat.

In the Vatican, St Peters Square was overflowing with worshippers as the Pope delivered prayers for deliverance from the Aliens.

His Holiness, addressing the estimated 100,000 worshippers, said of the Aliens: "We do not know what forces of darkness have befallen us. We must pray for protection from them. We must also see their arrival as a challenge to the true spirit of mankind. All the peoples of the world must unite in their love of God to stand against this unworldly evil which is upon us."

Meanwhile, across the whole

Many cities across Italy also recorded record church attendances of people fearful of the Alien's arrival, seeking salvation from God.

In Milan, the Duomo, the fourth largest cathedral in the world, had so many people attending its evening service that worshippers overflowed into the Piazza Castello surrounding the Duomo.

Churches in Bologna were also filled to overflowing with people praying for deliverance from the Aliens. It was same story across the length and breadth of Italy from Turin to Otranto: churches filled with the newly found faithful fearful for their futures in the wake of the Aliens

SONIA AND SERINA -SUPER SISTERS

JUST who are the two amazing *sisters* who between them, relayed to the World full details of the Alien invasion?

In an exclusive interview, Serina Gierek 25, told how, the moment she listened to her sister Sonia's telephone call, she grasped its world shattering importance.

"I rang Radio Bedford on my mobile immediately," says Serina, a petite blond, events coordinator with Woborn based Tavistock.

"They were here in minutes," added Serina, speaking from her home in Great Barford, Beds.

Serina also told of the close bonds between her and her sister. "Although we are almost a thousand miles apart, Sofia is ever in my thoughts," says Serina. "She was always my grown up sister. Although I'm grown up now, she still is always there with big sisterly advice."

Asked if she was scared for her sister's safety in the face of the Aliens, Serina said: "No not really."

Sonia and husband Tosca have lived in Italy for years," says Serina "The Aliens were probably a lost less scary than some of the men you meet out there. And Serina has been able to handle them," Serina adds.

"Some Italian men are horrible. Last year when I was out there I was introduced to this man, he was my grandfather's age, and do you know, within five minutes his hands were all over me."

President pledges assistance

BY TOM SAWYER

WASHINGTON: President Warren today pledged US assistance to any country threatened or attacked by the Aliens.

He said: "Any nation anywhere, no matter how different their values may be from our own, who is attacked or threatened by these Alien invaders will be offered support from the United States."

In nationwide telecast, the President called on Congress and Senate to pass a Bill rushed before both Houses allowing immediate increase in military procurement.

The President said it was essential that entire nation "stands united" against Aliens. The President also said he was prepared to enter into immediate and unconditional dialogue with "these visitors to our home" and urged the Aliens to

WHERE DO THE ALIENS COME FROM

Simon Williams reports

Where do the Aliens come from? This is the number one question astronomers around the world are now seeking answers too.

The rogue television programme purporting to me from the Aliens' base here in Earth claims that they are from a planet 350 light years away. Yet, until confirmable proof that this claim is indeed true is made available, the world's experts are keeping their minds and options open.

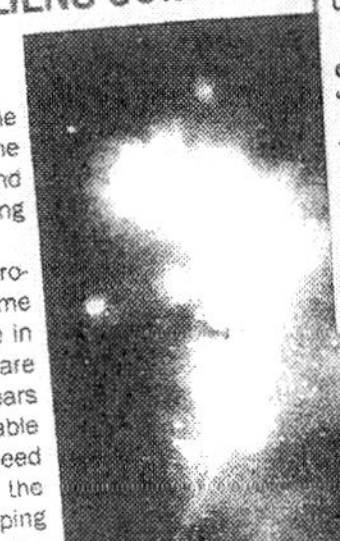

attacking me, I could get arthritis, MS? As I looked at the stars I smiled that I was actually observing concentrations of Secondary and Tertiary waves being made ever concentrated. My leaving Tabajara was out of the question, at least for the time being. All I could do was to continue to demonstrate how useful I was to both villagers and Susem. From Hercules I swung all the way up to Antares then down to the Milky Way. What I had to do was take control of the situation and ask, no, insist that the Susem say precisely what they wanted of me.

Then on the other hand, it wouldn't really be wise to upset anyone. Roberto might be out as far as a source of income is concerned but there would bound to be other opportunities. I rubbed behind my ear again, at an itch on my leg, then the money in my pocket. I stroked my pocket again. It hadn't really been such a bad day. What were a few slings of indifference, arrows of ingratitude, so long as I could turn in that much at the end of a day?

From Antares I swung west to Rigil, Hadar then to the Southern Cross. Making money in such a way is all right but it's of the dart, dip and dash variety, a couple of stages up from picking pockets and could only occur in the chaos of uncertainty such as Tianguá today. Sustained commerce needs stability, but stability only comes if there's security and just how much of that is there going to be? Not just here in the Ibiapaba, not just in the area Paceillo says she wants cleared either, and that's not small, it's bigger than France, but the rest of the big wide world beyond? What is happening right now is momentous enough but with everything else Paceillo has planned more than a few individuals are going to be upset, especially the Americans. If ever there are people who are paranoid over perceived threats it's the American government. What they did in Chiapas, Cuba, Iraq was sheer delusion of dread. But that apart, they have punch and are unlikely to lie back and do nothing.

I swept along the Milky Way, looking at the string of little stars down from Vela. By then I had calmed down, telling myself not to be so sensitive. That I should be grateful for the experiences, more in a week than most people in a lifetime, to say nothing of all the surprises. I smiled over how there had been so many that I couldn't be surprised anymore. Then to my surprise I was.

After Vela I swept down to Canopus. There it was all on its own, shining bright. Next I swung down almost to the horizon and looked for the faint blur which is the Large Magellanic Cloud, one of my favourites. I saw it alright but I also saw a big star shining beside it. I was confused. There's not supposed be a star there. Switching eyes, ensuring I'd not made a mistake, I saw that it wasn't a new star but thousands of them. They were in every direction, like a dome they were. Then they gave a synchronised twinkle and I realised they weren't stars but hengers.

"Well that's the Susem air defence system set up," I said (and by now I was talking out loud). No sooner had I spoken than the ones right in front of me parted. Through the parting and despite the darkness, I saw the bat-like silhouette of an approaching veda. Expecting it to pass overhead I worried when it flew downwards. I thought it was going to crash into the cliff-face. Because it had slowed I had time to nip to the edge of the platform. Looking down I saw a blink of blue then the veda disappearing. "So that's what all the noise below was about," I said out loud again.

"That is so."

I nearly popped out of my skin. It was Paceillo. I was about to lay into her. The way she had behaved and treated me the day through was bad enough. Now here she was creeping up trying finish me off with fright. It was the last straw. But even before I had finished holding my thumping heart she was confounding me all over again.

"We have concluded," she continued, and coming closer, "that we have not afforded the appreciation due to you..."

Although my heart was still thumping, in an instant she had me on my guard. It has always been my experience that whenever a woman offers an unextracted apology, it's always an opening gambit for something else. Or if not, it's being stored up as a bargaining chip for later.

"...for the resolution of the difficulties presented by the people who have arrived here today..."

She continued effusing apology but all the while I was inwardly saying "Wait for it, wait for it, it's coming any moment now," and sure enough it did.

"However, we wonder if you would care to assist us in..."

Of course I said "Yes." Not that I'd much alternative but I did have room for negotiation. And I used it to the full. First the ploys of "I don't know, I don't think I'm capable, I wouldn't want to let you down," then the "I'll have to think about it," followed by a temporary change of subject (and seeing the third veda arriving), "how many more, what are they for, who is in them?"

"Biologists," she said, then after a pause and another veda arriving, "Botanists," followed by, "We wish most strongly you undertake the assign-ment, not just on our behalf but that of everyone."

Although aware of the opportunities I egged it a little bit more with "If I'm going to do it, it has to be done properly," followed by and after her "Pisci-culturists," "I can't do it all on my own, I'll need assistance."

"What form of assistance?"

"People I can rely on."

"Get them. Aqueourists."

"I'll need a free hand and do what I think necessary when the needs arise."

"Providing you keep us informed," she said. "Aborealists…"

"Alright, I'll do it."

"Good. Minero-horticulturalists...Crystographers...Aurologists..."

39: IRIS

It had gone midnight, I was almost asleep. I cursed forgetting to switch on the answering machine. The phone kept ringing. I half expected it to be Peter but only one person calls me “Rainbow.”

When Danny said “Do you want to appear on television, have your own programme?” I didn't take him seriously. Instead I asked what on earth did he think he was doing? He said he had missed the news. I told him what I had seen on television. He said events had moved on from there. He described what he had just seen, and how the people in the village where he was thought the visitors were angels. He rushed out many other things he had experienced and were happening "As I speak," he said.

He asked again, did I want to appear on television? This time I could tell he was actually being serious. I said it was impossible to leave my job.

He replied with "Four thousand...” then after a pause, almost instinctively, “...cash.”

I still said no.

But he didn't stop. “Six thousand...there's a Virgin flight to Miami early Saturday morning and an inter-connecting Varig Air to Fortaleza two hours afterwards...my debit card number is Citicard...”

Again I said no.

But still he didn't stop, “Seven thousand in advance...” followed by a plaintive “please...if only just for a month.”

I said I would think about it, that I’d phone him back.

To which he said “You can’t, I'll phone you in an hour.”

In that hour I thought over what to do, stay in my safe job in London or risk it for a month of mayhem in South America with Danny? I phoned my bank. The April salary cheque had cleared and Danny's credit was good.

The job in Victoria is safe but its humdrum, I can do it standing on my head. As for acting, I was getting nowhere except older. And as for Peter, I’m just beginning to tire of his tantrums. A month away might give him cause to reflect, bring his ego down to earth, that I wasn’t around just for his beck and call. It might also stir him into getting a proper job.

When Danny called again I said “Yes.”

The man with the moustache who appeared in the telecast, the one who had smiled and winked as he danced by did also pass through my mind.

40: BOSNIA

Even before tocans were observed over the Ukraine, two brigades of Gurkhas, unseen as well as unreported, had already arrived and were slashing into action. One, in sixteen groups of sixteen men, flew down in sixteen vedas, accompanied by swarms of hen-gers. Each group landed outside a circle of villages, small towns and military encampments centred on Vitovlje 50 kilometres southeast of Banja Luka. By 9.30 that same evening the second brigade landed around Kupres 40 kilometres further south.

Within hours of their arrival streams of women, children and old men, filled with tales of what had happened to them and to the younger men, were pouring into the larger towns. As news of the arrivals and their tales spread, more than alarm filled people's minds, men's especially.

Each tale told was similar. Of the village or neighbourhood being suddenly brightly lit from a veda hovering above. With the lights came hen-gers. The occupants were driven by them into the centre or outside of the village. Anyone resisting received stings till they stopped. People who hid were blasted and stung from their refuge. Those who threw missiles saw them rebound back at them, those who shot suffered the ricochets of their bullets' return. Within minutes everyone would be herded to the waiting Gurkhas.

Women, children and old men had their hands sprayed with green luminous dye and were told "Idi za Hrvatsku, idi za Srbiju," (return to Croatia, go to Serbia). Each man, once a Gurkha had sprayed his face and head with red luminous dye, was held by a further two, while a fourth, with a single swipe of his kukri castrated him. Any resisting were stung into stupefying numbness and then castrated. All of the men were instructed "Idi Korčula."

As hen-gers encouraged the women, children and the old on their way to Hevatska or Srbija, the freshly bereft men slowly, painfully made their's west to Korčula. Meanwhile vedas, hen-gers and Gurkhas continued clearing and castrating in ever widening circles throughout the night. At 4 o'clock the next morning groups from both brigades met up outside the village of Prusac, midway between Donji Vakuf and Bugojno. By dawn an area 100 kilometres by 60 stretching from Maslovare in the north to Duvno in the south had been cleared of its occupants. Only those in the now isolated towns remained. By 7 o'clock the women and children of Donji Vakuf were fleeing north to Jajce and the men hobbling west. By 8 o'clock those of Bugojno were travelling in the same directions and through deserted villages, past lines of severed scrotums stuck on sticks.

A kilometre to the northwest of Bugojno the Gurkhas came across a prison camp. Although the freed Bosnian prisoners cheered when the guards received the swish of the Gurkhas' kukris, many then set upon their former captors. While most guards managed to stagger away, Gurkhas had to protect a number from being beaten to death by the starved and tortured inmates.

At 9 o'clock the vedas, hen-gers and Gurkhas returned to Sieba but only to be replaced by another 32 vedas and another two brigades of Gurkhas. This time to northwest Bosnia, centred on the villages of Gornja and Prisika to the east of Bihać. By the end of the day they had cleared and castrated an area stretching from Čadavica west to the Croatian border itself. In the morning some vehicles leaving Bihać for the east quickly returned, their drivers telling tales of penises and scrotums littering empty villages. These men were the fortunate. Others were caught by the hen-gers and Gurkhas. Soon they too had red heads, hands clasped between their loins and were heading to Korčula. By evening the whole road was cleared right up to the outskirts of Bihać itself.

Croatian soldiers, rushed into this new 'Bihać pocket', met the fate of those who had resided there. Some endeavoured to resist and others even attack, including with heavy weaponry, firing increasingly desperately to the end. But none could withstand their ammunition's ricocheting return, the hen-gers' stings and finally, the swish of a Gurkha's kukri. Others in armoured vehicles and even tanks sought to flee. None succeeded. Armour proved no protection against the vaporising detonations of writhing vines of hen-gers. In the afternoon a flight of F15s flew over from Croatia, but only to meet a fate similar to the Americans the day before. Three of them crashed. Their parachuting pilots found further hen-gers and Gurkhas waiting for them.

Castratees attempting to evade going to Korčula soon discovered the red on their heads contained a substance acting as a tracking beacon. Out of nowhere it would seem, hen-gers appeared and stung strayers back towards the coast.

Authorities in both Croatia and Serbia, while noting with alarm reports received from their territories in Bosnia, had more pressing problems. At 11 o'clock Thursday evening two shafts of brilliant blue light appeared across the Zagreb to Maribor motorway, just north of the frontier town of Donji Maceij. Seconds later, a hundred metre section momentarily rose into the air then dropped onto its side. Minutes later the border bridge over the Drava, south of Ormož was lying on the river's bank. By daybreak Sieba had severed all Croatia's northern road and rail links. During the morning, Serbia's links with the outside world were also severed.

Afternoon brought, from vedas flying offshore, swarms of hen-gers sweeping aboard boats along the Dalmatian coast, buzzing and stinging their passengers and crews. Before day's end the eastern Adriatic was cleared of shipping. Quays from Punta in the north to Ulcinj in the south were deserted. By 4 o'clock, the roads at Vas and Bregana, Croatia's last links with the outside world, also had hundred metre stretches lying on their sides.

Throughout Friday both countries appealed for outside assistance. But governments across Europe, now with concerns of their own, did not feel particularly disposed to assist what many had termed 'pariah states'. Even their respective patrons, the German and Russian governments, were busy with events occurring in their own countries.

Aliens attack Russia

David Borger

BOTH Russia and Ukraine have reported thousands of deaths after wides-pread attacks by fleets of Alien spaceships. Nuclear power stations throughout the two countries, including Chernobyl, reported as being obliterated and reports from Norway say Alien fleets are preparing to attack Russian nuclear submarine bases.

Itar News Agency Victor Cliurbin reports: 'Panic broke out in Kiev today as thousands people from outlying municipalities flocked to the city Rail and road transport has ground to a halt. Refugees from Chernlgov, have told of massive explosions at nearby Chernobyl nuclear power facility. Others report seeing massive shining objects rising above power station as explosions occurred.

"Most of Kiev is without electrical power. Streetcars no longer operating and widespread disruption to industrial production is expected. At a special government press conference on Friday, a spokesman for President Boris Nokitov said leave for the military authorities also reported enlisting reservists. Ukraine 5th Military District, which encompasses Kiev, said to be rushing forces north to Chernlgov area.

"Nokitov also instructed Kiev's population not to touch many thousands of egg shaped modules arriving from Alien spacecraft on huge carpets of blue foam. They are probably bombs', he said. It is also unofficially reported that Nokitov is ready to declare formal state of war.

Carolyn Brown, Moscow reports: Russian President Vladimir Sheybel today announced, emergency measures to repel Alien invaders from territories of CIS by all means the country's dispos Sheybel is said to be set declare a formal 'State War' against Aliens.

Some military analyst here are asking why Russ tans are being attacked and not the West. Ivan Purastin defence spokesman for extreme rightwing nationalist party Ogosnw [Russia is Ours] claims the Aliens are in league with US to attack Russia, "All Westerners should be immediately called from Russia".

CHERNOBYL GONE!

Ukrainian, Russian nuclear power stations attacked
President Sheybel vows retaliation against Aliens
Aliens' 'Blue clouds' rain down over Ukraine

By Jon Midgley, Foreign Staff

REPORTS FROM RUSSIA CLAIM THAT Chernobyl, the troubled Ukrainian nuclear power station has been obliterated.

In the early hours of Friday, according to Itar-TASS, Alien craft appeared over the nuclear station. An hour later massive explosions were heard and sections of what was claimed to be parts of the station, were seen rocketing skyward.

Reports also claim that further nuclear stations have suffered attacks from Alien fleets, including those in eastern Ukraine, at Zaporozhe, Europe's biggest nuclear complex. Also in Russia there are reports of Akien attacks at Kursk, Obnisk, Balakovo and Smolensk.

Itar-TASS also reports that Alien fleets have been seen above nuclear plants further east, at Beloyarsky, Tatarskaya and even in Siberia at Tomsk and Krasnyarsk.

The same sources also report numerous luminous blue clouds being emitted by the Alien craft over cities adjacent to power plants.

Meanwhile, Russian military commanders are said to be coordinating an immediate and vigorous attack against Aliens. Russian President Sheybel, is reported mobilising the country's entire military forces to combat the Aliens.

Norwegian wireless operator, Sven Nansen, claims to have monitored Russian reports of Aliens' presence over Kola Peninsula. Kola has numerous bases of nuclear submarines and extensive nuclear waste dumps dating from the Soviet era.

"Why weren't we told" - says MP

"Why were we left in the dark", demanded an angry MP last night

By Joy Combe

"It's an absolute disgrace," fumed Cheltenhams MP, Sir Hugh Russet Brown. "The moment I return I shall be tabling for an immediate debate as to why this country, and European NATO partners for that matter, were not kept better informed over the invasion."

"What is the point of having all these air defence systems if they can't spot something the size of this Alien spacecraft. If that can get through then what else can, that is what I want to

"The Americans are supposed to have all manner sensitive radars and satellites, why didn't they spot it? And all these telescopes, what earthly reason is there for spending the vast amounts of money we do on them if they can't spot it either?"

Last night Sir Hugh was demanding a full scale investigation into what he called "a glaringly large gap of the international community's security." Adding weight to Sir Hugh's demands are though of fellow LibCon MP, Andrew Marsden.

He said: "When one considers the

'The Lord has spoken' says Bishop

By Jo Gummer
Religious Correspondent

CHURCH LEADERS said yesterday that the Alien invasion is a sign of God.

The Right Rev. Joanna Hapgood, Bishop of Colchester, told the World Ecumenical Conference, Westminster Cathedral yesterday: "On Wednesday we were told the Lord was in our midst. On the next day we saw the wonder of his works with the parting of the waters.

Did we not also hear on our screens the cry, the Son of God? Did we not see Peter - for is that not our name for Pedro - with all his worldly contrition, confess his wrongdoing and of how he had turned to the path

Did we not see the men of war who have laid down their arms? Did we not see the miracle of Lucy - is that not our name for Lucia - and her tears of happiness now she has been reborn whole?

"I say unto to you, we are witnesses to the coming of the Lord - rejoice!"

The Rev. Euan Presley, said at yesterday's Ulster Free Church Assembly: "The Lord has come and he has shown he has taken the path of reason.

"Yesterday he [the Lord] cast his shadow over the papists in their heartland, today he is punishing

Energy shares turm

Alien station attacks sends power down bu

By Mary Phillips in New York

WALL STREET was in turmoil yesterday as news of Alien attacks on nuclear power plants grew.

Shares in energy corporations with a strong nuclear capacity fell sharply with Edison falling $1.92 and Cal Power a massive $2.24 on the day. According to Citi's Kathy Sontag: "With the Aliens ripping out Russian and with nuclear generation elsewhere in the world are seen as a reason to sell."

Another sector hit by the threat to nuclear power is insurance market. Underwriters in both London and Bermuda were reported to be demanding a doubling of premiums from power companies with nuclear generating capacity. Shares in McLennon fell at one point by more than

rises on the day with both Exxon and Shell gaining more that $1.00. Market watchers believe that with the downgrading of nuclear generation there will be a surge in demand for natural gas.

Also coming in for market scrutiny is the detail of statements made in the Alien's rogue television broadcast. While claims were made during the programme that the ... with peaceful

the Alien ... everythi... face of t... One ... likely t... defence... aircraft... nuclear... warhea... focus i... toward... Whi... appea... Alien

At 9 o'clock on Friday evening and as the second group of Gurkhas flew back up to the Sieba, the first, rested and recharged, returned. This time they landed in the south, centring on Glavatičevo and Berkovići. By Saturday morning they had cleared an area stretching from the eastern outskirts of Mostar to the River Trebišnjica, 20 kilometres north of Dubrovnik. They also discovered three more prison camps. Prisoners from the camp near Vrapčići showed the Gurkhas areas containing mass burials of many of their fellow Bosnians.

On Saturday morning, as the Gurkhas flew back to Sieba, the first castratees were arriving on the coast. During the morning further detachments of Gurkhas descended on the island Korčula.

Having the previous day experienced the hen-gers actions, as well as hearing of events on the mainland and elsewhere, most islanders had decided to unite with the people of Dubrovnik, as did most others of the province. From Dubrovnik had come first rumours that their entire 45 kilometre long island was about to be filled with hundreds of thousands, if not millions of men. Next came other rumours that Croatians were to be expelled from Ragusa, of which Korčula was part. By Friday afternoon many in Dubrovnik had decided they were not Croatian but once again Ragusan.

On arrival at the island's villages, the Gurkhas were greeted with white flags waving from every window and doorway. Everywhere were hand printed signs proclaiming "Nez Avisua Republika Ragusa" and Dubrovnik's four red banded coat of arms. Seeing the signs and flags, and being unsure of what to do, the Gurkhas contacted Colonel Tambassing.

With the aid of fenserfs he and Tearo decided on compromise. Half of which was that only male Croatians had to leave. In no time, relieved villagers were giving the whereabouts of those who were Croatian. These it transpired were mostly soldiers, police and government officials. The other half of the compromise was that all men who had served in the Croatian military had to go to the island. Korčula city's English speaking mayor, attempting to telephone this arrangement to his counterpart in Dubrovnik, discovered he had been arrested by a contingent of Croatia's Special Forces who, with the police had taken control of the city.

Half of one Gurkha brigade positioned itself along Ragusa's borders (there being only the coastal highway and a few mountain tracks). The rest, complete with maps and information given by the now over-enthusiastic Korčulians, went to Dubrovnik. Some went to Hotel Lapad, two kilometres west of the old town, the commandeered headquarters of the Special Forces. Others descended on the main police station at Brsaije by the old city's Pila Gate. Within an hour the now red-headed once former occupants of both buildings were hobbling north along the coast to Korčula.

News of the Gurkhas' impending arrival quickly spread throughout Dubrovnik. All of the population there quickly assisted the Gurkhas in locating other deployments of the Special Forces. Some soldiers tried to evade the hen-gers and Gurkhas but, of course, none succeeded.

In the afternoon when all 50,000 men of Ragusa, headed by the mayor of Dubrovnik, arrived off of the coast road at the Ston isthmus, the Gurkhas were taken aback. But another compromise was soon made that the men interrogated themselves as to their involvement in Bosnia and that they were all deemed to be guilty until they could prove themselves innocent.

Those who had no involvement, the old, the disabled and schoolboys, separated others who could also prove their innocence from the remainder. These, and there were not many, left with their hands dyed blue. Those who could not prove but proclaimed innocence, departed with their hands dyed purple and a day to return with evidence. Those who confessed left with red and were told to return on Sunday for work. All were continually reminded, as other men with red heads shuffled past them, of the consequences of dishonesty.

During Saturday morning the Serb authorities, whose territories in Bosnia had been spared the main thrust of the clearances, contacted the BBC World Service saying they wanted immediate talks on the implementation of the "Requests made to us." They also said they had already halted their attacks on the "...remaining Moslem enclaves." Their message was duly broadcast on the 11765 Radio Band. This was not the first such request that the Serbs had made but it was the first to evoke a response from the Susem.

41: SATURDAY

All the money made on Thursday is gone. It's gone on a television and dish for Rico and the villagers, not that any of them have watched it much. And just as bad I've had to fork out from reserves for Rainbow. Goodness knows how I'll make up the loss. While this is bad enough, events have interrupted progress on the project. As fast as something is planned it's thrown into disarray. I don't know if I'm coming or going. Everything is getting utterly out of hand.

Yesterday, each time I visited the Susem seeking assistance, I was met with busyness bordering on the manic. Terbal has fixed up a dozen and more appliances to the Internet connection, all absorbing data non-stop. I dread the damage it will do to my Citicard when the billing begins.

The Ibiapaba has been hollowed out for hundreds of feet and umpteen levels. Yesterday the machines were putting in lifts. They have also carved a second landing bay for vedas. This morning Konnet, Kubber and Kershaw flew down to it and parked themselves inside as well.

Although at first glance there's not now apparent sign of Susem in the village, dozens more of them have now arrived. Yet more of them flew in last night and bringing goodness knows what with them. They have not stopped to rest or saunter either. From the moment they landed, excepting for sleep, they have worked non-stop. Yesterday after orientation, these new arrivals with Pheterisco and Lathia at the head, were criss-crossing the area with machines and hen-gers, gathering and sampling. Though I have no idea what they are doing they have also emplaced tiny monitors everywhere.

The soldiers have been busy as well. Last night all of them were so weary that they didn't even stop to drink but took to their hammocks and slept. The villagers haven't really rested either. I have never seen them work so hard, though it must be said, that they, like the soldiers have embarked on everything filled with an enthusiasm I've not seen in any of them before.

Outsiders arriving at the checkpoint yesterday were told by the soldiers manning it that the village was closed for the day. They said the same this morning. Sightseers though did go to the viewing platform to see the remains of the plane and the helicopters lying at the foot of the Ibiapaba.

These came over yesterday afternoon. Silly of them really, fenserfs spotted them miles away and the hen-gers had them down in minutes. The crew of the plane were able to eject before it crashed but the helicopters, being slower and lower, were able to land. Pedro with some soldiers flew down in Kennet and picked the crews up. At first they were afraid and apprehensive but within the hour they had decided to stay as well.

Their arrival, however, was fortuitous. One of the helicopters was equipped with a camera rather better than Roberto's. And, of course, the helicopters are handy for Fortaleza. Their crews told of reactions and preparations against us. Route 2-22 is closed either side of Tianguá, but with Sunday being May Day and a public holiday following, that is about all.

N calls for urgen alogue with Alien

IAN SHEPHERD in NEW YORK

nited Nations Secretary General, Gonzales has called for an iate Security Council Resolution e authorizing him to make contact nd enter into immediate talks with ens.

ing an emergency session of the full UN, the General stressed the importance of all nations orld presenting a united stance in the face of n invasion and that it speaks with one voice. United Nations is the only global forum that t with our Alien visitors, it is the only vehicle nankind to establish formal contact with Sr Gonzales said.

Secretary General of this forum [the UN] it ust fall to me to take on this responsibility on of all the nations of the world," he said.

essing the Security Council later this evening, zales called on the 15 member council to give authorization to enter into a dialogue with the so as to discover why they have arrived on the nd what their intentions are.

members of the Security Council's five nent members are to meet on Tuesday to decide

NATO on 'Full Aler

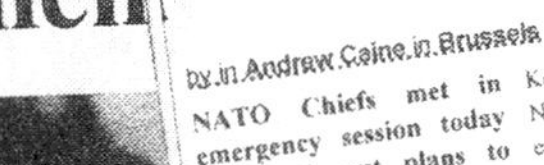

by in Andrew Caine in Brussels

NATO Chiefs met in emergency session today to thrash out plans to combat the Alien invasion of Russia and Ukraine.

NATO spokesman Galeazzo Ciano said Supreme Commander Herman Rheinfeldi had ordered NATO liaison officers in Moscow and Kiev to offer immediate military assistance to both states, as 'well as for assessments of current situation in both countries.

Ciano also said that all of the Alliance's forces are already on Full Alert, with all leave for NATO assigned forces cancelled.

Senior Ciano was unable to provide any information for "security reasons" on reported Kola Peninsula but said that NATO is watching reported events in Northern Cape region with "heightened scrutiny," he said.

Ciano also said he was unaware of reports Alien spacecraft being sighted over eastern Germany.

On the question of Allied fatalities following the clash of NATO warplanes with the Aliens over the Adriatic, the spokesman admitted that earlier claims of fatalities were inaccurate.

There had in fact not been any fatalities. The planes had crashed because of "pilot error" and not Alien attack. "All pilots were rescued from the sea unharmed," he said.

Nuclear shares crash

by Kevin Clarke, Business Desk

SHARES in the nuclear industry collapsed yesterday as investors around the world rushed to dump them.

Britain's Nuclear Energy Corporation (NEC) saw its price plummet from 705p to 256p on the day. Extensive after hours dealing is expected to have reduced the price yet further. Trading in the company's shares on indicated that the price dip below the £1 markets open again on

US nuclear stocks far Central & Southwest $1.68. Duke Power whose stock suffered investors' hands.

Citi analyst, Kat calculates that Duke's does not even cover liabilities. "At this ra be seeking Chapt Monday," she opined.

Lord Cedric, chairm said that he wa company's share slide simple market over events in Russia and

"Russian nuclear plants, their RBMK and Graphite reactors date from the Soviet era and were acknowledged as being leaking sieves as far as radiation was concerned. They were all inherently dangerous," Lord Cedric said.

"UK nuclear reactors," he added, "have an impeccable safety record.

Radiation levels for our [nuc power stations are even lower those emitted by coal fired such as Drax B. There would b sensible reason for any of nuclear power stations needin close.

"Just you watch," Lord C said, "investors will be buying our shares again Monday

Who are they?

by Roger Dobcombe

THE SUSEM come from an Earth-like environment, said experts last night at a hastily arranged conference on extra-terrestrial intelligence

Dr Bob Nixon, former head of the now disbanded SETI Observatory, Ohio, said: "If reports from Bosnia are correct, it would appear the Susem are beings from an nitrogen-oxygen atmospheric environment similar to our own

"That these beings are able to move with comparative ease and without especial protective shielding, suggests that the gravity in their environment is also similar to our own.

"This leaves me to conclude that the planet they come from would have many similarities to our own But of course this can only be highly speculative," he added

However, Doctor John Chang, Professor of Robotics, ULCA Los Angeles has come to very different conclusions He said: "From the shapes of their craft - ovoid - they give every indication that the beings inside must exist under different atmospheric pressures than our own.

"It follows, that these so-called beings seen in Bosnia, are inanimate, advanced forms of robotics. We should be very careful."

Professor Robert Gill from the Open University's Astronomy Faculty said: "The rogue telecast claimed that these beings are from a planet more than 300 light years distant from Earth. If this is indeed the case, then it needs to be establi

Sheybel rallies Russians

Military masses to repel Alien attacks on bases

By Felicity KENT in Moscow

RUSSIA IS TO END all of its military campaigns against rebels in Chechna, Dagestan and elsewhere in the Caucasus region. All Russian forces are to withdrawn immediately.

The move is seen as a direct response to the threat posed by Alien attacks against Russia's nuclear and military installations. Alex Saratov, Russia's Defence Minister said: "Today, our motherland is facing its deepest crisis since 1941.

"Then we were subjected to an unprovoked attack by the dark forces of the Fascist invaders. So it is today. We are facing an equally unprovoked attack by yet another force of evil and darkness.

"But just as in the Great Patriotic beat back the forces of fasci darkness, so too will the people our great country beat back the evil Alien invaders."

The Russian president, Vladim Sheybel, speaking after conference with visiting a delegation of Senators, led Senator Al Packard, said: Duri this period of national crisis it vital that all the forces of freed unite in fighting this Alien men which is threatening all dem cratic peace loving nations such Russia and our great ally United States."

It is rumoured that Sheybel agreed to US demands fo peaceful end to the conflicts in Caucasus in return for mili assistance in combating Aliens. As yet what form

Blue sheets in Kiev

A BRITISH exchange student today gave the first eye witness account of the Aliens 'blue sheets 'and their egg shaped cargos.

Hilary Mendal, 23, said: 'They are like big ostrich eggs, about a foot long."

In a telephone call to her parents Dr. Gregory Mendal, a consultant in the horticultural industry and his wife Ruth, of New Southgate, she said: "During Wednesday evening in Kiev there had been massive power cuts. Then a huge bright blue cloud billowed down over a nearby park. It was like an enormous carpet of bright blue bubbles," she told her parents.

By STEVEN THOMPSON

"The bubbles were rolling and popping all over the place. Among them we saw these 'eggs'. There were thousands and thousands of them. Some of my friends said they might be dangerous, but they looked so lovely, they were all shiny and

Then I saw it had a little flap at one end a lever on a dial at on one side and two leads at the other end."

Dr Mendal said that Hilary and her

the one shown on Wednesday's television broadcast," said Dr "So I told Hilary to put some wate hole below the flap and connect her house's electricity see

The airmen were aware of events abroad they said, but knew little of them. The O Globo newscasts and those on the other channels have been similarly scant and none made mention of the Ibiapaba or Tianguá. However, Roberto has been persuaded to sit with his ear to my radio listening to the World Service writing down details of its news bulletins.

Yesterday, Roberto, when he awoke, appeared to have come down to Earth and given up all idea of divinity. Nobody, except Elana perhaps, seems over-worried about this. By the time he was up and about everyone else was either in awe again over events, or too busy participating in them.

The awe, in part, came from what the villagers saw occur with their seeds. They were each asked to bring a handful of them and accompany Milophinia down to the cavern. This they duly did. I went with them, as did some of the soldiers. We went past the screens to a dimly lit level several below them. This one is laid out in gardens set at table height and identical to those I had seen on Sieba. The difference being that these ones contained nothing but little globules of dark rubbery looking jelly.

The villagers, one after another, had their seeds put into a drawer at the top of an object which looks like a tiny filing cabinet. Seconds later its bottom drawer, in which the seeds now were, slid open. Some of the new Susem arrivals took each villager and their seeds to a garden and where they were planted. Within fifteen minutes all the seeds were sown. I asked Milophinia what was happening.

"The seeds," she said, "are being subjected to resonance analysis in order to assess their programme of growth and growing requirements. This information is relayed to the field areas and the resulting plants cultivated."

I soon saw what "cultivated" meant. As soon as the last seeds were sown, the space above the gardens began to brighten. A few seconds later it was, as Milophinia described, "Sunlight bright." It was also sun warm. The brightness lasted for no more than a few minutes then faded away. A fine mist of spray then blanketed the area. This lasted for a further few minutes. The villagers looked on in rapt silence.

The light returned and the mist disappeared. No sooner had Milophinia said "One day has now passed," than a child peering at one of the gardens called out "Olhar!"

Everyone rushed to look. Sprouting from the jelly were shoots. For half an hour one "Olhar!" followed another as villagers raced from garden to garden. My friend George's hydro-culture speeding his marijuana was nothing compared to this, it was like time-lapse photography. The seeds were sown just after eight o clock and by four in the afternoon the villagers were gathering the harvest. A hundred days were compressed into a third of just one.

On the plants' 'third day', Milophinia, when I asked, said that the efficiency of their growing and growing conditions had merely been accelerated. To my "By hundreds of times!" she said "Ordinarily, plants are subjected to many variables, most of which are not conducive to them. Plants survive on the surface not so much because of their environment but

NATO swings into action

FROM ADAM SAGE IN BRUSSELS

NATO DEFENCE chiefs lost no time in gearing the alliance's forces into immediate action to combat the threat posed by the Alien invaders.

In continuous session since the first sightings of the Aliens were confirmed, NATO's Grand Council have agreed to set up a high powered sub-committee to coordinate proposals for attack.

It is expected to have the sub-committee composition agreed upon as soon as tomorrow, a sign - if any were needed - of the seriousness NATO attaches to the crisis.

"Because of the many uncertainties in the current we consider all the options open to the alliance," said NATO spokesman Galeazzo Ciano.

"This can best be done if we obtain the full agreement from all the alliance's members. As you know, the US's current relationship is very ambivalent towards NATO's back-up relationship with the EU's Rapid Defence Force and we must have their cooperation before it is safe for us to proceed," he said

Meanwhile, the Aliens are reported to have wiped out most of Russia's nuclear missile capability along with its nuclear power plants.

May Day parades cancelled

by Joanna Phillips in Moscow

RUSSIA'S TRADITIONAL Red Square May Day Parade on Sunday is to be cancelled because of "the current uncertainty," Russia's Defence and Interior Ministries in a joint statement. They also implied that a 'State of Emergency' may be declared.

The cancellation of this symbolically important event in the Russian calendar at 48 hours notice is an indication of the growing alarm in top Russian political and military ... the Aliens' attacks.

Other reports speak of extensive troop movements on Moscow's outer ring road wit traffic heading to both south an north from the city.

Androv Grenadriv Pravd defence correspondent sai "Short of nuclear rocketry, C forces . 92 per cent Russiar have nothing with which combat Alien forces.

"Our country desperately ne NATO and especially assistance and quickly," he There are other reports sug ing that the Aliens are bus

Aliens Target Nuclear Power Stations

By WILLIAM FROST AND AGENCIES

NUCLEAR power stations, including Chernobyl, which has been obliterated are being targeted by Space Aliens who landed on Earth earlier this week.

Alien craft appeared over Chernobyl in the early hours of Friday. An hour later a series of massive explosions were heard, say official sources.

The explosions were believed to have been parts of the station which has been blown skywards.

Alien fleets have also ...

plants further east, at Bele varsky, Tatarskaya and even i Siberia at Tomsk and Krasyarsk Numerous blue clouds hav been emitted by Alien craft ove cities close to the plants.

Russian military commande are said to be coordinati immediate and vigorous attac against Aliens. Russian Presi ent Vladimir Sheybel is report to be mobilising entire arm forces to combat Aliens.

Norwegian wireless operat Sevn Nansen, claims to ha monitored Russians commu cating Aliens presence ov Kola Peninsula. Kola has nu erous military bases and nucle ...

Big share falls expected

by Time Slave

HUGE FALLS are expected when markets open tomorrow. Friday's close saw a record 437 point fall taking the FTSE to 20 month low of 4253.

Citi analyst Kathy Sontag expects similar falls on Monday. "It will be another Black Day.

With the Aliens continuing to blast the world's nuclear power facilities to the Sun with apparent impunity it seems a one way bet that share in anything nuclear are going to tank to nothing.

However, there are likely to be many third parties which are also ... adversely affected by the

Greens praise Aliens' nuclear send-off

"It's what we've been wanting for years," says FoE

WITH THE ALIENS blasting one nuclear power station and missile battery after another into the Sun, Green groups around the world are cock-a-hoop.

Friends of the Earth ...

most of our nuclear radioactive mess the Aliens can remove the happier we are. Our only concern at present is that the Aliens won't go far enough, that they will only remove the nuclear power stations ...

'Sovereignty is inviolate' says Warren

US President throws down gauntlet to Alie

by Tom Sawyer in Washington

IN MOVES SHOWING AN increasing hardening of US attitude towards Alien actions, President Warren announced yesterday, an upgrading of military readiness to 'Watch Com One'. This is just one stage below seeking Congressional consent for opening of hostilities.

In a third unprecedented national TV broadcast in as many days, the President, said: "Without equivocation, the sovereignty of the United States is inviolate. We will defend our right as a democratic peace-loving nation against all who seek to rob us, the American people, of our freedoms."

President Warren said that all members of the National Guard were to report for duty with immediate effect. The President also said that US forces worldwide were now in a similar state of 'battle readiness'

The President also said that ...

With the US girdin up to combating the there is surprise amon members of NATO. W alliance is preparing t at the Aliens there is that any unilateral m the part of Americ plunge any NATO into disarray and play into the Aliens' hands.

One unnamed observer in Bruss "The trouble with being a hyper-power still thinks that it can sees fit, with the rest following its dictat. Aliens here on ear days are over."

(President Warren's ... full page 7; see David ...)

precisely 1.49am, *Sweet FA*, a ... sound and no script". It lived up to its ... grow as

Aliens attack Adri

ROME, Friday: Cross-Adriatic shipping was attacked on Friday by Alien missiles.

All ferry services between Italy and Croatia suspended and most vessels reported to have made for safety of Italian ports.

Crews and passengers of being "buzzed" and "stung" by 30 centimetre long free flying "darts". There was some damage to boats' superstructures but no reports of casualties among crews and passengers.

Italian naval vessels are now said to be on standby to repel further Alien attacks.

Sailings to G iterranean from central Italian p suspended. How from Bari an Greece still op already fully b May Day holida

Dubrovnik declares UDI

ROME, Friday: Dubrovnik has seceded from Croatia said a statement faxed last nig news agency ANSA from Dubrovnik's mayor.

The statement headed, Nez Avisna Republika Ragusa" (Independent Republic of of an edict expelling all Croatian nationals and 'Croatian atrocities in sovereign st Herzogovina".

The original name of Dubrovnik is Ragusa, which was an independent city state before being incorporated in French then Austrian Illyian Provinces and form following First World War. Dubrovnik is UNESCO World heritage city.

despite it. Here, any such hindrances are removed."

As she spoke the 'daylight' transformed to a kaleidoscope of different coloured pencil-thin beams. Seeing me noticing them, she said "To maximise the efficiency of each plant's growth, variable yet specific inputs of sustenance and energies are required. Blue light to shoots, for example, accelerates leaf formation. On the surface of your planet, as on ours and those of others, such things are provided haphazardly. Here they are delivered as and when the plant requests."

My "Requests?" met with her "Resonances." When she saw I didn't understand she added "A plant responds to its environment. Yet a plant is also part of that environment. In natural conditions both evolve harmoniously. Harmony is achieved by each responding to the other's requirements. Response is communicated by resonances, be they cellular, crystal-line, protein, Tertiary and Secondary waves."

Seeing that I still didn't comprehend, and I must say she's the patience of Job, she said "Put simply, a plant through its roots and leaves communicates its needs, and its surroundings do their best to provide. Here they are delivered on demand, and not just to each plant singularly but also as part of a whole."

As Milophinia spoke I felt a breeze begin to blow. "Strengthens stems," she added nonchalantly. What she said next, though first intriguing me, explained much. "Though a plant's growth is cellular," she said, "ordinarily, out of every thousand cells it initiates, no more than one progresses to full formation and to instigate further growth. A further few partially formed cells are recycled into the plant's continuing growth. The remainder of its initiations are dissipated, lost as indeed are the majority of the fully completed cells, into the immediate environment. By programming the seed, then plant, to retain more of its cellular manufacture, as well as providing a conducive environment in which to do so, growth will be further strengthened and thus accelerated by many times."

Throughout the day I saw villagers going back and forth down to the gardens. It wasn't long before they had agreed to Susem terms for the gardens' use. They took not just seeds but cuttings, fruit and flowers. I even saw a posse of boys and hen-gers, accompanied by Menpemelo, triumphantly carrying down a nest of bumble bees.

With lunchtime approaching villagers and soldiers alike were sat in front of the screens and studying from them. By then as well, Roberto had handed me his transcripts of news bulletins he had been listening to.

I had a smile over how little notice has been taken of what Paceillo had me say on Wednesday, and of how much of actual events weren't being broadcast. Meanwhile, I was seeing events unfold on the screens below. By the end of Friday the tocans had sent a string of nuclear power stations in both the Ukraine and western Russia to the Sun. And from what I also saw, a few more things nuclear went that way as well. Since then the tocans have begun moving north and eastwards.

Brazil vows tough action against the Alien invaders

By Polly Portillo in Brasilia

BRAZILIAN DEFENCE Chiefs were planning today to airlift 'substantial' forces to the country's troubled north-eastern states of Ceará and Pauli.

It is thought that the Brazilian armed forces should be able to deliver a powerful, if not devastating punch against the Aliens.

General Jorge Ramos said: As soon as the May Day holiday is over we will send all available forces to the north."

Brazil has extensive Air and Land forces, including:

- An estimated 400,000 men under arms.
- An Air Force equipped with some of the latest American, French and Israeli weaponry.
- 200 recently delivered Mirage 3050s
- Many American F15s and more than 100 Blackhawk multi-rocket attack helicopters.
- 'Many hundreds' of operational Cobra helicopter 'gun-ships'

Besides air attack craft, the Brazilian Army is thought to have more than 3,000 operational tanks of various categories as well as APC's (armed personnel-carriers).

Both the Brazilian Army and Air Force have, in recent years, made extensive purchases of ground-to-air and surface-to-surface missiles including Red Star missiles form China and which have a range of 1,500 kilometres.

Both forces have received extensive training from the many suppliers of weaponry. It is thought that several thousand instructors and technicians from the supplier countries still operate alongside the Brazilian armed forces.

Defence Ministry offices were closed Friday because of the May Day holiday.

A Brazilian soldier

Gold soars to record high

Paul Miles

GOLD soared $258, a near 60% rise ...

The ITC said tha although its members buffer stocks had help ed counter ...

NATO: the tied giant

David Weatherall
Defence Correspondent

Dutch NATO troops embarking at Skipol for Poland in readiness to combat the Alien

NATO might be the most powerful military alliance in history but it is nevertheless, ill-suited to face the Aliens.

Created half a century ago to defend the West against the then Soviet treat, NATO has, in recent years been mired in stifling bureaucratic red tape and infighting.

In this age of globalization and need for instant action, NATO still cannot operate outside of the territory of its alliance members unless it has permission from the outside state concerned.

Though even when NATO does have such an agreement from a third party to operate 'out of area', the alliance's organizational shortcomings are only all too evident. NATO's recent ill-fated foray into Bosnia is a typical example of the alliance's weakness.

No sooner had NATO sent its forces into Bosnia, and at the request of the beleaguered Bosnian government it should be remembered, than the alliance was beset by political infighting. Every single military operation NATO undertook in Bosnia had to be first cleared by all of its members.

With the Germans and Italians openly siding with the Croatians, the British, French and Greeks supporting the Serbs, the alliance's ... capability was initially to actually take a lead in combating the Serbian and Croatian rebels was nullified by the French demanding that the EU's Rapid Reaction Force had an equal say in determining strategy. It is little wonder that the US walked away from the situation.

With the American's taking no further part, the rest of NATO showed its true mettle by withdrawing the remainder of its forces in quick succession, country ... At the time of ... of the alliance's Out Sector leaning curve'.

That may have been t... then but it is also t... today. In the interven... time NATO has d... nothing to put its hous... order. It is still as enmes... in political infigh... between its members ... was before it went ... Bosnia.

If NATO is incapab... tackling bands of a... thugs in the Balkans, how on Earth is it goi... defend us, let alone ...

Aliens over Germa...

Will German nuclear power stations be next on the Alie...

Julian Horricks in Berlin

UNCONFIRMED reports say Aliens were observed above Mecklenburg's disused Soviet era nuclear station complex. Eva Goethe of German Power Inspectorate IED, said operation of Germany's 25 nuclear power stations was under review.

Nuclear power provides 30 per cent of Germany's electricity supply. Although the number of nuclear power stations is two-thirds of Britain's, they supply more than half of the country's energy.

Ms Goethe declined to comment on the threat to German energy shortfall should its nuclear power stations suffer the same fate as the Russian and Ukrainian nuclear facilities ...

Aliens isolate Serbs and Croa...

John Borger in Ljubljana

ALIEN destruction of the of the Rijeka-Ljubljana highway effectively isolated Croat ia and Serbia today. The two countries no longer have any land, sea or air links.

Slovenian Interior Minister Igor Bavcar's office said a 200 metre section near Croatian border town of Vas was lifted into the air and laid to one side. Alien craft were not observed, but a violet-blue light appeared across the highway and many vehicles were trapped on the section.

Traffic leaving Croatia jammed the highway and travellers from Croatia reported a mass influx of refugees into the south of country from Croatian areas of former Bosnia. ...

Dusan Mitevic, SRNA, Serbian News Agency, writes: "Without reason or just cause, the Serbian nation was savagely bombarded and attacked by unworldly forces. Although valiantly resisting this unprovoked and criminal assault on our country, we appeal to the world for assistance in repelling these evildoers from our territory.

"Many thousands of people from the country's western provinces have been forced to flee their homes and seek refuge in Serbia proper. Refugees report tales of unspeakable atrocities against innocent people, including bayoneting pregnant mothers and throwing old people into cauldrons of boiling fat. Thousands of young girls have been repeatedly raped by the pagan and Muslim ...

Minutes after three, Roberto rushed from the radio saying the World Service was calling for the Susem to contact them. But with the Brazilian air-crews arriving at the time there a bit of a bustle was going on. It was nearly four before I was able to mention it to Paceillo. However, she said "Wait."

Beginning yesterday afternoon and continuing throughout today the soldiers, who had been formed into groups of nines, took turns to visit the caverns. On their return they would sit together talking with one of the Susem supervising them. Then they would spend some time soldiering, manning the checkpoint, patrolling, after which they went back down below. I asked Milophinia what the soldiers were doing. It was then that I grasped the extent of Susem and, more particularly, Paceillo's organising ability.

"Effecting our assistance productively requires efficient implementation," Milophinia said. "We became aware of your fellows' potential for so doing, thus they are embarked on a programme of enhancing their abilities. While thoroughgoing and continuous, the programme will enable them to soon proceed with preliminary implementation of that assistance."

I soon understood what "thoroughgoing" entailed, including the carrots and sticks. It has little to do with what the soldiers, or the villagers for that matter (for they are now embarked on the same), have seen of the Susem below. It has little to do with intelligence and knowledge either, but all to do with endeavour. It wasn't long before I became involved.

The screens and what's behind them (not that there is much, they are the size and thickness of an A4 notepad) are teaching machines, but oh what amazing machines they are. Two plus two and writing four with my finger on to the screen to begin, but minutes later my mental arithmetic was challenged with 37 times 28. My hesitation reduced the question to 30 times 25, followed by 37 times 30. After I had answered, the screen cleared and out from underneath it slid a sheet of paper with a list of sums to be answered.

No sooner had I looked down the list than the screen was printing the alphabet with gaps for missing letters. Within minutes I was struggling with spelling and, not long after, I'd another sheet of homework. Geometry followed, then topography. We were all at school again and up against our shortcomings. But it is overcoming them which earn rewards.

However, the soldiers and villagers alike aren't left to struggle alone. After each session group members confer and swap awareness. Though there's cordiality, there is not a chance of cheating, there is no point in it anyway. The next session won't start unless the sheets are slid back. The replies reflect the next questions. No advancement in endeavour means no reward either.

Cordiality is fostered in no small part by the other half of the tuition. This is taken on a group basis. Not only is the group participating collectively but progress is determined by individual abilities. Members of each group have incentive to push the advancement of their fellows.

Tuition is an hour on, with another off. And the 'off' isn't resting either. Thirty minute seminars or study tours, accompanied with instruction, some

Croatia cowers from Aliens

Tens of thousands of Bosnian Croatians flee in the face of the Aliens' onslaught

by **Jon Stalwart** in **Ljubljana**

TENS OF THOUSANDS Bosnian Croatians have fled the Alien and have sought refuge in Croatia.

During Friday and yesterday a reported 50,000 refugees streamed over the former border between the two countries at Bihac and Bosanski Novi. Such was speed of the refugees' departure that most of them fled with no more than they could carry.

These refugees also brought with them frightening stories of horrendous onslaughts by the Aliens against the civilian population and military alike.

While no firm details have emerged of the nature of Alien attacks have been given by the Croatian government, there are growing reports of a large scale engagement by the Croatians against the Aliens on the outskirts of Bihac on Friday.

According to these reports the Croatians mounted a major combined air and tank attack against the Aliens. But not only were they quickly routed by the Aliens but the entire Croatian force fell into the hands of the Aliens.

Many refugees spoke of teams of small dark, human-like creatures clad in white, descending from the Aliens' spacecraft and surrounding villages then ordering the occupants to leave for Croatia itself.

According to refugees from the village of Gudavac, 15km to the east of Bihac, all the men were first separated from the rest of the villagers and then summarily castrated. They were then forced to march to the town of Korcula 200km away. The rest of the villagers were them ordered to immed-

These refugees also claimed that the Aliens were accompanied by flying wasp-like creatures which gave out stinging rays which paralyzed anyone who refused the Alien's orders to leave their homes and go to Croatia.

Because of the reports of summarily castrations are so widespread it thought that this is the principal reason for the sudden massed flight of so many men northward in Croatia proper.

Meanwhile in the capital, Zagreb, the population is in a state of near panic, especially among men. There are also reports, as yet unconfirmed, of increasing numbers of men dressing up in women's clothes so as to protect themselves from being castrated by the Aliens.

However, with the Aliens' also severing all road and rail links to the outside world as well as the cancellation of all air flights out of the country, most Croatians feel that they are trapped and at the mercy of the Aliens..

Also, many Croatians are openly blaming the government and its policy of annexing much of Bosnia for the Aliens' attacks against them.

Although the HDZ led government may be facing rising criticism, it is also widely rumoured that with the security situation rapidly deteriorating, it will declare a countrywide State of Emergency within the next 48 hours.

Leaving Croatia itself is extremely difficult. With the Aliens severing all road and rail links out of country I had to trek more than 50 kilometres over rough mountain tracks at

US rushes battle fleet to Adriatic

By **Paul Sweetenham** in **Naples**

IN A BID TO COUNTER Alien attacks against NATO's eastern flank the US aircraft carrier Franklin Roosevelt and much of the US 5th Fleet were dispatched to Straits of Otranto at southern end of Adriatic, NATO Southern Command announced today.

The USS Roosevelt currently at Tel Aviv on goodwill mission to Israel and the rest of the 5th Fleet expected off Albanian coast Monday.

Other NATO seaborne forces are expected to arrive Straits in near future.

'Nuke 'em' says top US General

FROM TOM SAWYER IN PHOENIX ARIZONA

Former US General Walter 'Hell' Klunz at the ReGIDI conference yest

RETIRED US General Walter 'Hell' Klunz is urging the Pentagon to destroy the Aliens' HQ.

He told thousands of delegates at the ReGIDI Congress, "We know the location of their command and control centre. Before they have a chance to attack US defence interests, it is vital for us to strike first and take these Aliens out.

"It is important," he said, "that we nip this vipers' nest in the bud. And to do that we need to hit them with everything we have."

Cigar smoking General Klunz, who served in the US Army during the Cold War, says that attacking the Aliens would not be tantamount to attacking a friendly country.

"Hell, these Aliens have invaded, they're already moving out from their lair, we do not have time for niceties. The military down there in Brazil are unlikely to get themselves organized in time. Anyway they've nothing to hit them with. It just has to be nuclear," he said.

Asked about the effect of a nuclear blast at a press conference held at the close of the Congress, General Klunz said: "Hell, there's nothing down there except a few peons. It's the threat to the Developed World that's important."

The General went on to claim the people currently in charge of US defence policy were incapable of making fast enough decisions

"Druz (US Defense Secre is not up to the job," Klunz "Hell, Druz does not grasp the simple fact if the A invade the US they will auto ically take control of our defense industries."

"If the Pentagon won't act, hell, just one call to [Presic Warren should get some acti said the General.

A spokesperson for Pentagon said they had contacts with ReGIDI (Reti Generals in Defense Industries

'Ils ne passeron

Weygand throws down France's *'They shall not pass'*

y **John Fairhall in Paris**

RANCE'S Defence Minister, Maurice Weygand, outlining his country's response to he Aliens did not mince his words. With clenched fists and n a voice trembling with emotion, he declared: 'Ils ne passeront pas' ('They shall not pass').

After quoting the phase stemming from the battle of Verdun in 1916 and which is inscribed on countless War Memorials across France, M. Weygand said that that his country's armed forces are ready to confront the Aliens and to repel them.

Weygand said: "Any attack on France's nuclear power interests will be seen as constituting an attack on France itself. Our Defence Forces will retaliate with all necessary force to any attack. If this requires the launching my country's nuclear missiles then so it will be."

The Defence Minister also said that each of France's 67 nuclear power stations will be ringed with the recently developed *Mêmeviril* surface to air nuclear missiles.

In response to German and Belgium concerns at French policy, M Weygand said that while he acknowledged that there could be a possibility of France's nuclear weapons being detonated over its neighbours' territory, it was very remote.

M. Weygand said: "With all of our nation's nuclear power stations situated along our borders and coasts, France does not any alternative than to accept this theoretical possibility." He also undertook to pay full reparations to any country should it be so affected by French missiles exploding on their territory.

He added: "With nuclear energy providing more than 70 per cent of France's electricity supply we have no alternative than to defend our power plants. Without electricity France will be finished as a world power. This we can never allow."

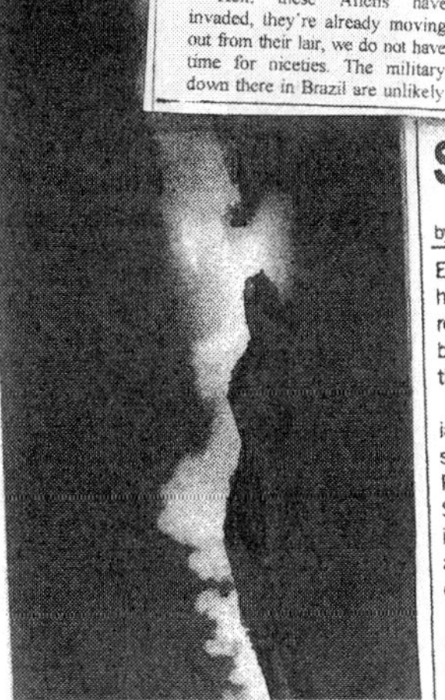

Sovereign debt plummet

by **Cynthia Ramone, City Desk**

EASTERN European took a hammering on Friday in response to the Aliens blasting everything nuclear to the sun.

Both Russian and Ukrainian shorts and mediums suffered dramatic falls. Russian 5 year bonds from $57.65 to $42.70. Ukrainian shorts fell even further, averaging 32% fall on the day.

Slovakian shorts fell back almost as their Ukrainian counterparts. Czech shorts and mediums the worst of worldwide wavered in the wake of the Aliens' attacks.

UK Gilts all experienced historically steep falls. Treasury shorts and mediums were showing losses between £5 and £10 on the day.

Simon Bateson of gilt traders Smithers Davis said: "Today has been the worst I have experienced in all of my 35 years in the market. But I fear that there is worst to come.

"We were flooded with sell orders from 7am in the morning until the close.

from the Susem, others by soldiers and the villagers themselves. After which there is practical participation in the subject of the lecture.

Though everyone began just before noon yesterday by this morning all were studying before sunrise. In part, I think it's because of what they stand to gain by way of benefits, but I'm also convinced they actually like doing it.

Whatever the reason though, by this afternoon, everyone enjoyed the fruits of their labours. The children advanced the most, especially in English, my past lessons not falling on as fallow ground as I thought. Each now has a hen-ger hovering about them, much as one has a faithful hound. Both children and hen-gers have had a fine old time scampering and flitting through the forest playing with one another.

With Pheterisco as a guide, the children also had another treat. Kershaw took them on a tour. Tomorrow, so I'm told, if they work hard they are going to the seaside for the day (none has seen the sea). The children aren't alone in their English endeavours. I'm constantly called on for coaching and perfecting phrases. Everyone has also now earned enough points for a session in the mormic, and in due course I expect there to be some rubbing behind the ears.

Although it is the children and men who have taken to this education with the greatest enthusiasm, it is the women who have been the most diligent in ensuring that studying doesn't slacken. They are intent on owning gardens, and as quickly as possible.

I have also noticed, despite the difficulties of language, that the women have established their own special rapport with the Susem. Yesterday evening a large group of them were sat for several hours by the Pousada conversing most amicably. Some even brought their children and pointed to bits of their anatomies which were worrying them. In turn the Susem were quite taken by the novelty, for them, of the girls having never seen such before.

Despite her still limited English, this gathering also brought Lucia into her own. Acting as an interpreter cum go-between has helped her overcome the shyness she had shown the day before. And of course she serves as a shining example of what the Susem can bring.

Although on Thursday morning Lucia appeared to the villagers as a miracle, by the evening she was seen, by adults and children alike, as a long lost loved daughter and sister returned. As Elana expressed it, it is as though Lucia has been woken from the sleep of an unending nightmare. I'm also reminded of the ugly duckling and the swan. She's become quite attractive.

At nine o'clock last night Roberto reported another request from the World Service for contact. He heard yet another at six this morning. But on being told each time, Paceillo again said "Wait."

During the morning, however, I managed to see Menpemelo. I wanted answers to questions her Thursday 'tuition' had raised especially about Primary waves. Where do they come from?

"Primary waves do not come from anywhere specific," she said, "they evolve." But no sooner had I asked "Out of what?" and she replying with

"From nothing perceptible," she added "All, from evolvement to inevitable entropy is interconnected, never static but dynamic." Noting I didn't understand her, she glibly said "Ripening matures into rotting," then with "For example," promptly launched into explaining were planets come from.

When a cloud of gas and dust swirls around a freshly formed star, some it, Menpemelo said, sometimes, just as candyfloss does, whirls into fast spinning circling spheres. Most of these though, she added, eventually end up either being burnt by the star or whizzing away back out into space. But every now and then, she said, some stick around and circle a star. Jupiter, Saturn and probably Uranus, she said, are our solar system's.

The moons currently circling these planets, she said, are the agglomerations of interstellar dust to rocks arriving later and why moons are all of differing compositions. Similarly, it is why, she said, that they have different orbits and axis as well.

But before I could say "Very interesting, but I still want to know about where Primary waves come from," what Menpemelo said next had me most intrigued. "Not only are the larger planets, and their moons, the major attractant of interstellar debris," she said, "but its arrival will eventually cause disruption to the orbits of their moons. In this dynamic yet unstable environment, some of these moons will eventually be dislodged from orbiting their planet and establish one of their own around the star. They change from being moons to planets." Then as if to emphasise this, she added "The rocky planets circling your sun began life as moons in the nurseries around the larger planets. When they had grown large enough and the appropriate circumstances occurred, they departed to lead their own independent solar existences.

"With each new planet orbiting a star," Menpemelo next said, "it will affect the orbits of the others. Usually this is a gradual process but it can also be very rapid indeed. From the data we have of your planetary system, your second planet (Venus?) is one which has moved suddenly, quickly and recently as well."

With me musing over this, Menpemelo then said, "Eventually the star, your sun, maturing into entropy, expands and in doing so consumes all of the planets orbiting it. As I said, planets are an example of seemingly nothing evolving into existence then further evolving out of existence."

Then she said "In a like manner the evolving of Primary waves." But no sooner pinned back for Menpemelo's detail of the answer to my question then sadly, we were interrupted by Roberto running from the radio with news of the latest request from the World Service.

Because this 'request' was so differed from the earlier ones I had no alternative than to rush its contents to Paceillo. Having read it she immediately talked to Tearo. After they had spoken, Paccillo then said "When is your colleague arriving?"

I was impressed when Danny, despite his remoteness, said he was online and had at short notice, managed to book me the flight. It was only later did I discover there had been many cancellations.

Danny said to expect excitement, adventure and challenge, but not from the moment my plane touched down. He said there would be people at the airport to greet me. But not burly men in white tunics surrounding, then boarding the bus from the runway and chanting "Viva harmonia!" I was worried for a while. Only when the men's leader, who said he was Pedro, called out "Rainbow?" did I relax.

Danny said there would be transport to whisk me away, but I didn't imagine it would be a fleet of army helicopters and, once airborne, a massed escort of what I learnt were hen-gers flying alongside.

He said I would receive a warm welcome, but not, as my helicopter swept in, hundreds of men, also in white, waving. Nor as I alighted, their cheers of "Viva harmonia!" changing to "Viva Rainbow!" I would have acted like a celebrity if I'd not been so tired.

I had expected to spend the weekend resting and recovering from the flight and the airline's inoculations, not to be told on arrival, and after Danny's welcoming kiss, "You're on in 30 minutes."

I had no chance to ask questions or finish my first drink when he had handed me my script. I barely had time for a shower and a change of clothes before a tap on my door and a "Five minutes."

But I then did have time to say "Is that it? Is this all you have? Are you serious, that?"

There was nothing. No lighting, no autocue, let alone a studio. Nothing but a camcorder rested on a pile of beer crates operated by some nervous young man. This wasn't television, it was experimental theatre and improvised at that. But as ever, the show must go on, so I did my best, my very best. Though I was on air for less than twenty minutes, at the time it felt much longer. This was because I didn't really understand half of what I had been given to read, and the other I could hardly believe.

My arm was aching from the inoculations. I had been awake since three, travelled through five time zones, back through another two, risked life and limb and goodness what else, given up a good job. And for what? A flyblown madhouse in the middle of nowhere, that's what!

I have made a terrible mistake. I was livid. I want to go back to London. Immediately.

After the "Pax verbriscus" (which I considered silly) and Danny's "Very good, very good," I went for him.

43: KEN

I will definitely say that about her, she is much better looking than Danny, very fetching. And she was class as well. I have always said that that is the best combination, a good looker with a bit of class. I have lost count of the times I have tried telling my Chloe that, but she won't listen. But then kids they never do.

Danny was on earlier, I didn't see him myself, but the girls in the flat upstairs said he had come on the tele just before one o'clock and saying there would be a full broadcast at nine. The Greenwood was nigh empty until half past. Harry, the landlord was dead choked. His bar staff were stood about doing nothing, then when the custom did come in, he was short-handed.

I told him to put a sign up saying that he was cutting his prices Tuesday for when she comes on again, and also that he had his new big screen they all could all watch her on. But I don't suppose he will take any notice, he never does. Harry is not very enterprising, that is why he is still only a manager I suppose.

Of course all the talk was about the broadcast. My mate John, who is with London Electricity, says that if all the nuclear power stations are going, electricity prices will go through the roof to pay for the cost of the loss. He says it's because they still haven't finished paying for them. As I said to him, that is a con by my book.

But the thing I want to know and from what I have read in the papers this morning, they want to know as well, and that is, why weren't we told about what is going on? Why weren't we told about the fish being radioactive? Why weren't we told about this Neptunian, I've never heard of it before, why have they been keeping so quiet about it? Why weren't we told about what the Russians have really been up to, making all that mess and why hasn't it been stopped? As far as I'm concerned the sooner all those nuclear things are gone the better. And if those Russians suffer, then tough on them, serves them right for what they have done.

And if them Serbs and the other lot are getting a drubbing, serves them right as well. They have been asking for it. Though when she said none of them have actually copped it, I was dead disappointed. By my book a good few of them need a topping for what they have done.

Another thing which struck me is what I kept hearing along the bar. It's amazing, twenty minutes of Earth shattering news and all that half of them could talk about was the cut of her blouse. If they get worked up about a bit of cleavage in this day and age then things have definitely come to a pretty pass.

44: JAMES

Though the picture resolution was a little better, it was still amateur quality but nonetheless I was taken aback. I recognised her immediately. So did Frankie. Though all that Frankie did was to make catty remarks at Iris's appearance. I was about to comment that it was only envy over Iris making it into television news, whereas Frankie, despite all her efforts and courses, has so far failed, but I thought better of it.

When Iris announced herself as "Rainbow," I sensed the influence of Danny. But when Frankie 'hrumphed', I was compelled to remind her that she never objected to Danny calling her "Freedom."

To this though, she snorted "That's different."

I didn't say anything and instead tried concentrating on the screen. But almost immediately I was saying "For God's sake will you be quiet...Iris is probably doing the best she can. And anyway her voice is a darn sight better than Danny's."

There was another snorted 'hrumph' from Frankie, upon which she got up from the settee and stormed off into the bathroom. By then I was in no mood to mollify her, instead I turned once more to the screen.

I kept puzzling. How did Iris get there? And for that matter, where was "there"? It couldn't be that remote. Or had Iris been with Danny from the outset? But then she couldn't have been, because if she had then she would have appeared on Wednesday and not him.

Apart from puzzling over Iris, I also most attentive to what she had to say. Though she read everything in an almost matter-of-fact manner, it didn't disguise in the least the import of what she said. Monday is going to be one heck of a day, one which is sure to make Friday seem quiet. Nuclear shares will be bombed out, so will defence stocks but RECs should rise and commodities too, especially gold, which is bound to go though the roof. I also made a mental note to check through Morgan's East European's loan stock derivatives, Friday's hammering was bad enough.

I made another note to check the nfa index. But I had watched no further before the bathroom door was flung open and I was greeted by the sight of Frankie storming to the bedroom. I knew I had better make my peace, but inwardly I was sighing "Oh God, here we go again."

This time it wasn't just tears but "Don't touch me...I've had enough... you're being really shitty to me...I can't take it any more," upon which she threw herself on the bed and wrapped the duvet around her.

After this tantrum, and with Rainbow saying "Pax verbriscus," I concluded it was time to go for a drink.

When I had returned from the wine bar, Frankie had locked the bedroom door. I spent the night on the couch.

Aliens tell the world: 'We come in peace. You have nothing to fear from us, but...

The Nuclear Age has ended

- Nuclear bombs, missiles, subs to go
- N. power stations to be eradicated
- Clean energy supplies promised
- Aliens in Bosnian peace talks

by David Lumley and Paul Spicer

THE ALIENS SPELT OUT THEIR INTENTIONS here on Earth in a worldwide television broadcast yesterday. Billions of anxious viewers around the world were given reassurances by the Aliens that have come to the Earth in peace.

The Aliens also said that they do not have any desire or intention to cause any harm to the Earth or to mankind.

It was further stated that the Aliens, who call themselves 'Susem', have come to Earth to search for one of their space-craft which they claim has crashed on to our planet. As soon as they have located the remains of this lost spacecraft, it was said, they will depart from the Earth.

The programme further stated that shortly after the Susem's arrival on Earth, they had registered what they termed 'Letium Waves'. These, so they claimed, are being emitted by the element neptunium. This element and what they further termed as its transmuted derivatives' posed a threat not only to the safety of the Earth but also to the rest of the galaxy.

Because of the existence of these lethal substances, it was said, that the Susem have been given no alternative than to remove them from the Earth and send them to the safety of the Sun. The Susem further said that the removal of these elements was for the Earth's own good as well as for the rest of the galaxy.

Last night, nuclear expert, Dr Iain Stewart said: "Apart from neptunium, what the Aliens were alluding to are, in all probability, the other man-made elements such as plutonium and the uranium isotopes as well as those other radioactive ones."

Adding a yet further twist to the enigma of the Alien's presence on Earth, was that the half hour long programme was given by a being who had the appearance of young woman.

What is more, she spoke with an impeccable English accent

'Ms Lewis' also gave details of the Aliens' removal of a string of nuclear power stations across Russia and the Ukraine. She said all the nuclear power stations in the area north of the Crimea to Smolensk, and between the Carpathian and Ural mountains - an area bigger than Western Europe - no longer exists. If true this represents the loss of more than 20 plants.

Rainbow Lewis then went on to say that all remaining nuclear stations in the rest of Europe would be wiped out by the Aliens during the coming week. If what she said is indeed true, then it is a variance with Russian claims.

'The Susem will give the Serbs terms for ending the Bosnian war at a meeting in Pale today'

According to Moscow, only those stations in the extreme south of the country and northern Ukraine, such as the Chernobyl complex have been affected by Susem actions. If the Susem claims of the Russians' losses then it indicates that Russia is facing grave energy supply difficulties.

The broadcast mentioned other 'related nuclear facilities' have also been removed. According to Dr Iain Stewart this is likely to mean missile silos, nuclear weapons assemblies and nuclear waste storage disposal sites.

No mention was made in the broadcast of the effects of the

Sizewell to go

by JAMIE PRIOR

LAST night's eagerly watched Alien telecast spelt the end of nuclear power.

While world leaders drew up plans for combating Alien's attacks, their English sounding telecaster coolly announced one Earth shattering ultimatum after another.

Its goodbye to nuclear power and weapons - for ever. Power chiefs must be anxiously waiting the fate of their nuclear plants.

The attractive telecaster, who said she was Rainbow Lewis, reading from a script announced:

- All nuclear power stations are to go, Britain's as soon as next week.
- A new replacement energy source to be supplied by the Aliens.
- All nuclear arms to be sent to assembly centres for disposal.
- Arms sales to end as well as fighting everywhere
- Fish from the North Sea and other seas are dangerous to eat.
- A ban on all fishing, forestry and blood sports.
- A breakthrough in the Bosnian war, with peace talks today.

A British Nuclear Energy spokesman said: "The details of the telecast are currently being studied, therefore it would be inappropriate to comment further, although BNE maintains nuclear energy can be the nation's only long term energy supply source."

Greens rejoiced. Said FoE's Jonquil Taylor, "Anything or anyone who rids the world of the nightmare of the nuclear legacy which scientists and politicians have bequeathed, they'll have the support of all sensible people."

A Ministry of Defenc[e] source says the contin[gency] measures are likel[y] to be announced o[n] Monday, regarding th[e] security of Britain['s] nuclear plants.

In the light of the re[ve]lations of the extent [of] Russian losses a quest[ion] mark must hang over s[uch] measures. Meanwh[ile] reports from Russia [say] Alien energy caps[ules are] already in use in affected areas.

Soufins: the new energy sou[rce]

Bridget Kendwick reports from Moscow: Muscovites returning from the southern provinces of Kursk, Smolensk and Tula have brought the first Alien 'Soufin' power capsules into the capital.

Pravada journalist, Oleg Bukharin has a soufin in his dacha. It is egg-shaped, about 25cm long and 12cm wide. It has a flattened base, water inlet at the top, connecting rods at one end and a levered dial at the other end.

The installed soufin bypasses the mains electricity supply and provides enough power for all Oleg's electrical appliances. Obviously pleased with the result he said: "This is the very first time I have been able to have everything switched on at the same time. And what is more, it's free!"

All that remains of the Chernobyl nuclear com[plex]

UK NUCLEAR POWE[R] STATIONS COULD B[E] ALIENS NEXT TARGE[T]

by Neil Stugis

BRITAIN'S nuclear power stations could be next on the Aliens' list. All of the UK's N stations could be wiped out as early as next week. This shock news was delivered in the Aliens' worldwide TV broadcast last night.

A British Nuclear Energy spokesman, in response to the Aliens' plans said: "Although the details of the broadcast are currently being studied by BNE board, the company strongly maintains that nuclear energy is the nation's only longterm environmentally friendly energy source."

Last night's TV broadcast was watched by as many as 3 billion people around the world. It was given by a human-like being who said that it was called 'Railsowlus'. Speaking in top quality English, it also announced a further list of the Aliens' demands. These included:

The Dead Seas

by WILLIAM HASKINS
Environmental Editor

RADIOACTIVE waste has contaminated sea and oceans throughout the world, the Susem revealed last night.

They dramatically confirmed the worst predictions of Prof. Per Strand who, has campaigned for the end of fishing in northern European waters.

Russian authorities have always maintain[ed] Western Arctic wate[r] flowed eastward in[to] Arctic ice-shelf. But Pr[of] Strand said prevailin[g] winds blew westward an[d] "sailed" icebergs and flo[es] into Norwegian wate[rs] before flowing into th[e] North Sea and Atlantic.

The Susem now confir[m] Strand's claims. Satu[r]day's telecast stated wi[de] areas of Russian coastli[ne] to be removed. Affect[ed] areas stretch from Novay[a] Zemlya to Murmansk.

Will they want our waste?

by LILLIAN WALDERGRAVE

ON WEDNESDAY we were told that the Aliens were going to remove our nuclear power stations. But will they take our nuclear waste as well?

"It's all a question of what they want it for?" says Cambridge University's Professor John Burgess. "And secondly can understand why they might what the uranium and plutonium and other nuclear fuels as an energy source But the spent fuel and things like luminous meter dials - which is what most nuclear waste is - would be no use to them whatsoever."

Other experts however, are more circumspect. Dr Bill Jones

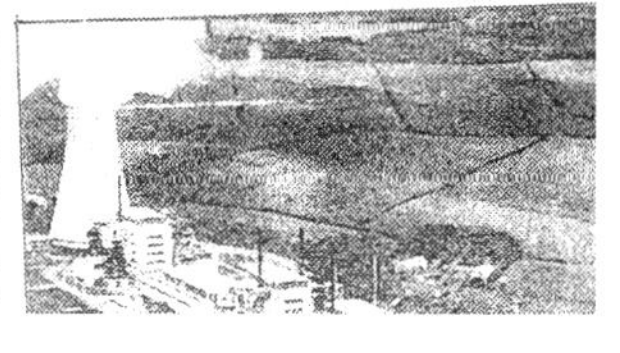

45: SIÂN

We all watched it. Daffyd, the boys, my parents who were here for the weekend, and myself of course. Nobody said a thing, well not until it was all over. Then everyone was talking at once.

It was dad saying "What is their harm and what is their good?" which focused everyone's minds.

"They are getting rid of the nuclear power stations," he next said, "and all the nuclear weapons and waste. Something we have all wanted."

But Daffyd countered with "They haven't gone yet, the weapons, the Americans could still use theirs, and NATO and Russia, China, even this country, and the French of course."

"But if they use them, they will kill ordinary people as well," dad said.

"Do you seriously think that will stop them?" Daffyd said, countering him again.

Dad didn't say anything to this. Sometimes he and Daffyd don't see eye to eye. But I didn't want any upsets, not with us all set for a day at St David's tomorrow, so I packed the pair of them off to the Pendre. Their differences never get serious when they are drinking together. I told them that mum and me would clear the dishes and join them later. But there was another reason why I wanted them out of the house.

With the boys out of the way repairing Glyn's motorbike, I told mum that I thought I knew who the girl in the television was. That she was the one Anne said Danny was having an involvement with.

"Very pretty," mum said, piling the plates, "gorgeous hair...lovely eyes," then, as she put away the glasses, "but I don't think she would be Danny's type." And after another pause and almost as an afterthought, "I shouldn't think he will be hers either." I was going to jibe how she could possibly know that, but she said "Come on, let's join the men."

The first question I asked Daffyd was, "Will those Susem power units be able to power motorbikes, and if they can will they stop them making such a racket?"

I was grateful when he said "Probably," and "yes." The noise of that bike gets on my nerves. I have lost count the number of times I have told Glyn to stop revving the blessed thing the way he does.

My next question was, "If Trawfynhydd nuclear power station is going to be going, are we in the area which will have these power units?"

Daffyd wasn't sure, though he thought so but said that some people from Cilgerren would be out of a job if the station went. He joked about getting a supply of candles in, but he also said that if the power units did arrive, there would be no need for wind farms, including Frenni Fawr's.

Aliens tell Serbia and Croatia: 'Hand over the guilty'

by Michelle Howard

THE ALIENS have told Croatia and Serbia to hand over their past and present leaders to face war crimes charges in Bosnia. If they fail to do so, the Aliens warned, both countries must be expected to face the consequences.

In the Aliens' television broadcast yesterday, the Aliens called for every person who has served either the Croatian or Serbian regimes during the previous 20 years to hand themselves over to the Aliens. During the programme demands were also made for Serbs and Croats throughout the world to also be rounded up and handed over to the Aliens for questioning about their parts in the Bosnian War.

Later, Professor Josip Zorb head of Croatian studies at Graz University said: "Croat and Serb communities are spread throughout the world though mainly in Germany, the US, Australia and Argentina. It is ... in the extreme that any of ... to anywhere in the former Yugoslavia, especially as, according to the Aliens' spokeswoman, they are all deemed guilty unless they can prove their innocence.

"In a similar manner," he said, "I do not know how any of the governments concerned could send them back there even if they wanted to do so."

In London both the Croatian and Serbian embassies refused to officially comment on the Alien's demands on their fellow countrymen. However, one senior Croatian diplomat who on the condition o...

Power to the people

Julia Bale investigates the truth behind the Aliens' claims of a new energy sou...

DO THE ALIENS' 'energy eggs' really work? Are the reports of these eggs lighting the power-stricken homes of Ukrainians to be believed? How long will these eggs last? Are they safe? These are some of the questions being asked by many of us.

The Aliens' energy eggs also raise another question: if they provide their power for free, why should any of us continue to pay for existing non-nuclear electrical supply? Experts, however, are cautious as to these energy eggs' effectiveness, especially over the longterm.

One 'egg sceptic' is Professor Gareth Rees, head of the Central University, Newcastle-on-Tyne's School of Physics. Prof Rees said: "Obviously, these Alien energy units will be some form of electrical storage batteries. Therefore, these so-called energy eggs will only be ... where will the energy to do this come from? From a yet further, external, source of electricity generation, that is where! No matter how much power these eggs give out it will have had to come from somewhere else, it is as simple and obvious as that."

As to the use of water as a power source for the eggs, and as shown on one of the Aliens' last Wednesday's telecast, Prof Rees is equally dismissive. He said: "Water is oxidized hydrogen and as such most of the energy latent in both of the component elements - hydrogen and oxygen - has already been depleted in their initial reaction with one another.

"If there were significant amounts of energy in water," he said, "then the Earth would be a very dangerous place. It must never be forgotten that all living things, including us humans are composed of more than 90 per cent water.

"While I have a completely open mind as to ... energy eggs' effect-

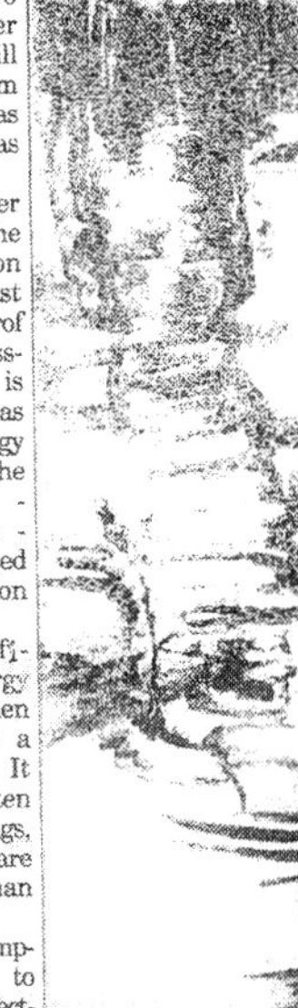

LORD JOHN STEPHENS

Why we should rejoice

'That' telecast examined

WE were forewarned on Wednesday that we were to experience Alien action. Yet we all stupidly chose to ignore it! But should we fear it?

Taken at face value, neither the statements made in that first rogue telecast, coupled with the one last night do not contain anything over which we need be overly concerned.

Nowhere in either telecast was there any mention of the Aliens - the telecaster called them 'Susem' - announcing anything which could be construed as threatening to life on Earth. On the contrary, if anything the Susem are set to make this planet of ours a darn sight safer than some of us humans have made it.

Nuclear power is to go. But then it has never been popular to except to the barons of the nuclear-industrial complex. We are told the Susem will replace what power capacity they remove with something which is clean, safe and doesn't pollute our environment. Couldn't have come soon enough is what I say.

Nuclear waste has been another of our manmade nightmares. If the Susem awaken us from this one by sending the wretched stuff to the sun then we should all be eternally grateful to them.

The Croatian and Serbians are to be punished for their unspeakable barbaric crimes against the helpless Bosnians, which our leaders have disgracefully chosen to ignore. May these Balkan ogres be forced to answer for their actions and if necessary suffer for them.

The patrons of these Yugopariahs, the so-called 'democratic' states of Germany, Austria and Greece along with crypto-murderous thugs in the Kremlin are to 'fined' for their connivance. May they indeed be penalised.

The forests are to be protected. Good I say. I have always thought too much of it has been felled. And who is so suffer from this protection of our heritage? Why, rapacious Japanese industry and greedy third world tin-pot dictators that is who. May these despots' Swiss bank accounts suffer as a result.

Animal sports are to cease. Good I say. It is about time the likes of the Spanish and other Latins ceased their unspeakably cruel pastime in the name of 'sport'. May they find something better to do, like wash.

Mining is to cease. Good I say. Why only the other day, with my wife, Lady Rosemary, when visiting in Staffordshire we drove past one of those opencast mines. Ghastly sight, there was mess everywhere. The sooner these blots on the landscape are gone, the better I say. May their greedy owners get their comeuppance for their wanton vandalism.

There are several further matters the man on the first telecast mentioned, as indeed did the young woman in the second but none of which should give us ordinary mortals undue cause for alarm. Indeed, the Susem appear to be most humane.

Greens jubilant with the Alien...

...ut fishermen, foresters and min... ...eel threatened writes Julia Porr...

THE ALIENS' call for a halt to fishing ...orestry has been warmly welcomed ...Greens the world over.

"It's everything we and environmental... everywhere could have hoped for," ... Jonquil Taylor of the FoE. "At long last," ... added, "trans-national and other big co...anies have been brought up sharp by ... Aliens. These companies can no lo... freeboot around the world pillaging ... resources of our planet for the sake of ... own corporate enrichment."

Other environmentalists have expressed their wholehearted support t... Aliens' edicts on conservation of the w... resources. Vincent Day of the World Fo... Trust said: "Although it has taken b... from another planet to use their pow... bring a halt to the ravishing of this pla... forests, it is indeed a heaven sent blessi...

"At the WFT not only are we lo... forward to the safeguarding of E... remaining forests but to the chanc... replacing those which have been previ... chopped down."

While Greens see the Aliens as bles... others view their presence as little sh... disaster. John Trelawny, General Secreta... the National Union of Trawlerpersons ... that the Aliens' fishing ban will spell dis... for his union's members.

"We always fished in a respon... manner," he said, "it is the Spanish ... other Continentals who have caused ... depletion of the UK's fishing stocks.

"For years we have complained about ... foreigners' rampant overfishing and ... they had ruined our members' liveli... And now with this Aliens' threat to s... fishing our members are once again ... hardship brought about by the gre...

What is Neptunium

by Jennie Green
Environment Reporter

JUST WHAT is the substance Neptunium so frequently mentioned in the recent Susem telecast? Why hasn't the general public been told of its existence before?

And why is it claimed to be so dangerous? These are the questions that many millions of people around the world are anxiously asking.

Dr Iain Stewart a world authority on nuclear physics says: "Neptunium is the first trans-uranium element to be created.

"Or put another way, it has never existed naturally until it was created by scientists at Berkley part of California University in 1941. Today it is usually produced as a result of the processes in nuclear reactors converting uranium into plutonium.

"Although all radioactive materials are poisonous, most lethally so, neptunium is the deadliest killer of them all.

"Neptunium has a half-life of more than 2,000,000 years. This means that after this time only half of it converts back to uranium. By comparison, plutonium has an incredibly short half-life ... a 'mere' 14 years.

"However, the bad new... about plutonium is that ... decays into neptunium. No matter how 'pure' plutonium may be it wil... from the moment of it... creation it will alway... contain amounts ... neptunium."

Dr Iain Stewart

So why haven't we the public been told about neptunium? "The answer," Dr Stewart say, "is simple, it's never been in the interests of the nuclear industries and government authorities to do so."

But for all intents and purposes, neptunium means radioactivity. The general public are now, with the help of the Susem, about to be well rid of this Frankenstein creation of scientists.

46: AILEEN

It was the first really warm day we have had this year. Des, the landlord spent all afternoon cleaning up the garden, laying out the tables. Very proud of his garden is Des. And it did look nice, lots of the flowers were out and he had his new outside lights dotted here and there. Thing was, nobody came in until half nine. By then it was getting cold outside.

At eight, we were that empty that Des went down the Kings Head, then to the Crown. He came back saying they were the same as we were. And the Blackstock Road was as empty as a Christmas morning in Wexford. Having next to nobody in upset him, so did the takings.

We all knew why, of course, because we had time to watch the broadcast ourselves. And when people did come in, it was all they talked about as well. Though some of the men disgust me, like overgrown children they are. Whatever would their wives and daughters think if they knew.

Before we became busy and after the broadcast had ended, I'd time for a little walk in the garden and a bit of a think. Should we go back to Wexford? Would it be safer there? It's an out of the way place I thought, and there's no real work there, but if there is trouble here in England, work would disappear as well. Or was I just being silly?

It was on my mind all evening. Mitchell, a photographer on the newspapers, who always sits at the end of the bar, was giving forth. He is a bit of a know-all bore, always trying to buy me drinks, but he's harmless enough. He said the papers had a load of stuff on the Aliens and pictures too, but couldn't print it. When I asked why, he said "D Notices."

After he had explained what they are (I had never heard of them before), he told some of the things he knew. He said a lot of military and security stuff was being kept out of the papers. And about things in Russia, how their army is falling to pieces and was retreating. Of course with people like him you never know whether to believe them or not.

When I came home the kids were asleep. So was Ryan, in front of the TV. I woke him but he had been drinking. He was plastered. I let him fall asleep again. The place was a tip. He had cleared nothing away. I was left to pick up all the kids' things. It was nearly one before I got to bed. I was cheesed off. Ryan's drinking is getting me down. In a way I almost wouldn't mind if he drank as much as he does if it were in company, but he is doing it ever more on his own.

As I lay there trying to get to sleep, I had another think. Becky's term ends in July, and if Ryan hasn't bucked his ideas up by then, then maybe, regardless of the Aliens, we will go back to Wexford. But without him.

The '3B' Column

memory of Sir Bryne Searle, we print his final weekly column unabridged)

The Susem Venus

HEN the Susem telecast ain, what a difference from at tired worn old face we w Wednesday, what a dream surprise - Ms Rainbow wis.

Last night, for twenty captivating nutes, we were given the heart opping beauty of Rainbow. This nus, more beautiful than tticelli's, with beguiling raven ir in caressable sheens of dark, ll luxurious waves tumbling to her ft, suntanned, almost bared, slen- r shoulders, filled our screens th "please, oh never let it end" light.

As Rainbow read the Susem's ommunicate, her perfect enuncia- d rounded, rose filled English oice gave the word "diction" a new, eeper, fresher meaning, that of sensuousness". A sensuousness hich, with every sentence, flowed nd flowed, from a dancing lyrical tream of enchanting melody to the ascade of a symphony in full flood, whose music will fill and resonate my memories for all my days to ome.

Not only was it heaven to hear her voice but to actually see her speak. When Rainbow told us of the removal of Russian reactors, I could not help but notice the seemingly challenging pout of her soft red rouged lips.

When she turned to the camera after turning the page of her script, and just before she spoke anew, I noticed in the way she raked the tip of her tongue along her teeth with assertiveness. The assertive-ness of a feline, hungrily poised, ready to pounce upon her prey

When Rainbow announced the end of nuclear power and weaponry, I was quite taken by the way she, almost without note, gracefully, brushed back with fingers so beautifully slender, a ringlet of her hair. With unaffected nonchalance, her hand giving emphasis, if any were needed, to her perfectly formed face and soft smooth, sun lustred skin, she caused I'm sure, many a heart to skip a beat, I know mine did.

As Rainbow looked up from her script after announcing the end of forestry and fishing, I sensed within her large, alluringly dark, restrained smiling eyes, a deep smouldering welling of unbridled passionate intensity. The like of which I have not seen in the eyes of a woman since the days on my travels, long ago in the foothills of the Sierra Guadarrama, where I visited on the wild gypsy girls of Aragon and Castile.

When Rainbow told us the Susem had halted the Bosnian war, and looked again to the camera, imperceptibly moving her head to one side then tossing back the tresses of her deep jet hair, I glimpsed anew, in her dark, lash flickering eyes those of long ago. The eyes of those untamed bared-footed contessas of the high Sierras. For a moment I relived seeing their looks of sensually haughty contemptuousness entwined with the wells of wanton desire lying within their cold, coal dark, simmering lynx-like eyes.

And at the end, when sadly Rainbow bid us farewell, calling Pax Verbriscus - go in peace - as she went, I was filled not with the calm such should bring, but with wild tumult.

As I screened the video recording to notate what she had said to us, for my Neo-Right Review column, those last moments of her presence filled me yet again with that same continuing tumult. Tumult over her beauty, tumult as she took that last breath for that last sentence, the way her firm, full, lithe figure, pulsating with the vibrancy of youth, was straining taut against the thin crisp white cotton and the small tiny delicate pearl buttons of her vee-necked bodice.

Rainbow said she will be with us again on Tuesday. I strongly recommend you should watch, I know I most certainly shall.

Sir Bryne rushed to hospital with heart attack p.12
The life and times of 'Big Boy' Bryne: the politician who never quite made it p.14; Obituary p.2

Serbs and Croat face conscriptio

Aliens demand repatriations for Bosnia dam

by Fiona Hathersage

THE ALIENS have made yet further tough, no-nonsense demands on both Croatia and Serbia: send 50,000 men each immediately for work in Bosnia.

The men are required, the Aliens say, to work on reconstruction projects in the war ravaged country. Each man will be required, the Susem telecaster, Rainbow Lewis said, to work for up to six months in rebuilding damaged property and the restoration of services. Ms Lewis also said that more men from both countries may be required at a later date.

The men, she said, are to present themselves for work at the former border crossing points between their respective countries. She also said that, providing the men have not committed any crimes in Bosnia during the recent war there, their safety will be guaranteed by the Aliens.

In the same telecast Rainbow Lewis repeated the Aliens' earlier demands that the leaders of both Croatia and Serbia and those involved in the recent war in Bosnia must present themselves in Bosnia itself to face trial for their alleged roles in committing War Crimes and other acts of war there.

Their refusal to come forward, she said, would be viewed by many as indication that they are indeed guilty of committing such crimes.

The Aliens are also demanding that those countries sheltering fugitive Serbs and Croats must also hand them over for trial in Bosnia.

The exact whereabouts of both Croatia and Serbia's rulers and many of the high ranking members of their regimes are unknown. However, it is suspected that they are still trapped in their own countries. Reports from both Hungry and Austria say that road and rail links between their countries and Croatia are still remain closed as a result of the Aliens' actions.

The Croatian ambassador in London, Ante Kvarner, said: "At this present time the situation in my country is unclear. All communications with Zagreb are blocked."

Mr Kvarner said, howe far as the Aliens' charg Croatia are concerned, without any foundation w

The Croatian ambassador: A

"My country, the ambass "has a historical duty to p fellow Croatians and this includes those living in t Yugoslavian province o Because so many of the communities in Bosnia w attacked Croatia has had ative than to protect th unfortunately has let to out

ALIENS' TERROR SQUADS STRIKE FEAR IN BOSNIA

BY MARTIN SHOEBRIDGE

ALIEN beings are striking dread and terror into the hearts of tens of thousands of fleeing Croats and Serbs.

Across the entire Serb and Croatian regions of Bosnia these invaders from another world have forced many millions of people to be driven from their homes. Serbs and Croats alike have fled in fear of their lives in the face of unspeakable acts of the Aliens' savagery.

Refugees who have come face to face with the Aliens describe them as small, dark-skinned, almost human-like beings clad in white space suits. Armed with swarms of flying, hornet-like miniature attack craft, these Aliens swoop down on unsuspecting villages.

Armed with murderous sword-like weapons, the Alien beings, so these refugees say, next separate the men from the woman and children. Once separated, the men are then held down by the Aliens, who proceed to cut off the men's private parts.

If any of the villagers attempt to resist the Aliens they are immediately blasted with invisible, body-stopping, stinging rays which momentarily, though painfully paralyzes their victims.

Other refugees tell of the harrowing ordeal of being forced to make their way along empty roads and deserted villages and towns strewn with hundreds of severed penises and scrotums.

According to other refugees even seeking to hide from the Aliens is to no effect. The Aliens' killer 'hornets' seek out those in hiding no matter where they are and sting them into submission.

"We thought they were ghosts," says Olga Djovnik, a grandmother from Jajace and still quaking with fear from her ordeal. "Then they started their slashings," she says. "There is no escape from these from these vespas."

The Aliens then drove the town's women and children from their homes and into Croatia proper. Their men-folk, she says were then led away by Aliens. "We do not know what will become of them," said Olga, "the last I saw of them, were their willies stuck on poles."

"Susem's Screen Stunner" picture p.11

Refugees fleeing Jajce in the face of the Aliens' cas

Serbs smug at bei first to greet Alie

by **William Hawkings** in **Belgrade**

HUNNED BY MANY as ariahs, the Serbian regime rejoicing at being the rst country to receive the lien's offer to meet with em rather than other of e world's leaders.

According to the Serb uthorities, the meeting ith the Aliens is to be eld this morning at Pale, the former Bosnia. In an bvious bid to further olster their new found atus, the normally sec- tive authorities in Belgrade ave allowed outside urnalists to attend the eeting in Pale. This is the st time that Serbia has rmitted journalists to ter Bosnia war-zone nce the outbreak of ghting began began.

The leader of the Bosn- n Serbs, Bran Kostkei d who is to head the legation which is to et the Aliens, said: Although I have been chosen to represent the people of Serbia in meeting with our visitors from another world, I am, in reality, also acting on the behalf of all of the people of the Earth. To this I am deeply honoured.

"I shall fulfil," Kostkei said, "what I regard as my scared duty to the Earth. I will do my utmost to assure our visitors that it is not only are Serbians peace-loving people but so are many of those of the rest of the world."

Bran Kostkei, the Serb leader

Despite Kostkei's self assuredness, th indication that are meeting wi as the resul dictates and on

Reports fro Serbia's erstw in the Bosnia indicate that have been att counties' arme putting them t

The ques remains howev the Aliens hav make meeting their contact world. Perhaps ance in Pale may well cas on this enigma

There is a worrying as Aliens meetin Kostkei as v senior Serb Zacoven A Ilkmar Dlati cited for nu

Terrible she was, terrible. No Rainbow, all Warrior. Her bashing was merciless. If rage left marks I would be black and blue.

I did my best to explain but having learnt, and I've the scars to prove it, never to argue with a woman, I let her storm on until she was all done. Trouble was her accumulated cumulus from yesteryear teemed down on me as well, so it took some time to pass. It ended in a bit of blubbing and a few thumps from her fists (I can handle those, it's her silences I have the difficulty with).

So I said sorry for dropping her in at the deep end, I would do all the things she said to do and get her everything she said she wanted. The first of which was a bed, she was dead set against hammocks. The second was a fully equipped television studio. Both were in short supply.

Locating a bed was the first worry though. Everyone in Tabajara has hammocks. Only the Susem sleep on beds and even they are taking to them.

I had intended introducing Rainbow to the Susem gently, after she'd had a bit of a rest, I didn't want to tire her with too much surprise all in one go. But because she said she was so weary and looked so dejected, and because of her bashing, I took her to see the Susem in the hope they had a bed to spare.

Pheterisco said providing a bed was no trouble, including one with a room attached. After the introductions and Rainbow's initial surprises, Pheterisco also offered her refreshment. Two hours later when I left them, Rainbow, her tiredness now apparently long gone, and the Susem were still going strong.

I don't know if the Susem have Saturday nights where they come from but they most certainly were having one down here.

I had noticed earlier in the day the machines carving out rooms with a flat bit out the front. At the time, Lathia had said they were just making somewhere to stay and putting in a few home comforts. When I arrived with Pheterisco and Rainbow, I was reminded of an Italian hill town. There is now carved from and into the cliff face itself, terraces of houses complete with details, mouldings and ageing. Plants complete with flowers were everywhere. Lathia's "flat bit out the front" is now a grand balustraded terrace with tables. Susem were sat drinking and chatting and I also caught whiffs of marijuana drifting across. The place was a cross between somewhere in Umbria and a university refectory. There were differences though. Trolleys with legs ran around taking and delivering orders, and I was the only bloke.

Rainbow and the Susem hit it off from the start, my chaperoning quite unnecessary. Besides food and drink they plied her with attention and questions. But even before my first glass was downed, diction was top of their list. The Susem were most taken with Rainbow's. Until then they had had only mine and the World Service's to go by.

I stayed for a second glass, the wine was too good not to (alike to Reserva Chianti, full and fruity with just he right hint of astringency), but seeing I was

'SUSEM STOLE MY GAL' SOBS TAXI DRIVER PETE

another Chron EXCLUSIVE!

By LINDA HARTLEY and STEVE MANN

THE broken-hearted boyfriend of TV's latest sensation - the Susem's small screen star, said last night: "Aliens stole my gal!"

Peter Albright, a taxi driver, said the small-screen-stunner was Iris Louis, a 29 year old actress from Tuffnell Park, North London, who temped as an office worker with Mayal Kitts, a firm of top Westminster surveyors.

Mr Albright said: 'She's just disappeared, it is definitely not like Iris to go off like that."

"I blame her disappearance on that man Collins, her old boss. He always had a Svengali-like hold over her. I just wish I could be with Iris so I could protect her from the clutches of those Alien fiends"

Only a lovers' tiff

Mr Albright admitted he and Iris had argued when he last saw her Wednesday night.

"But it was only a little tiff we had, the way lovers sometimes do. I was all ready to kiss and make up on the weekend, but she was taken from me," he said.

Peter, a qualified arts administrator and synchronised swimming invigilator, but currently working between appointments as a mini-cab driver, is now waiting "for the day my beloved Iris returns to my arms," he said.

Nights of passion

"Our years together were filled with the bliss of unending romance and the continuous passion of my making love to her During times abroad, often on remote islands, such as in the Seychelles, we would

SERBS IN BOSNIA PEAC TALKS WITH THE ALIEN

Joanna Pilger

ALIENS have stopped the fighting in Bosnia, it was announced in their broadcast last night.

They also announced an offer of immediate talks with the Serbian faction at Pale.

The BBC World Service had already issued a statement Saturday, saying Serbs had requested talks. The swift response suggests settlement will be offered.

Serb delegation expected

military commander.

It is not known why how the Aliens have m aged to bring about su rapid change in the tary balance. However known that no Alien ence was reported Bosnia before Friday.

Communications wi former Yugoslavian have suffered from

Greens war 'safe' energ

by Jean Porett

GREENS everywhere are giving the Aliens' 'energy eggs' their full backing. "Anything which reduces pollution and slows the depletion of the world's resources just has be a 'good thing'," said Jonquil Taylor of FoE.

Overjoyed at the news of the energy eggs' arrival in the Ukraine and Russia, Ms Taylor said: "If as the Aliens said, Britain's nuclear power stations are to meet the same fate as the Russian's I cannot wait for the arrival of the Aliens' energy eggs raining down over this country as well."

'They're safer than nuclear'

Asked if she thought the eggs' effectiveness in replacing the energy lost by the removal of nuclear power stations would really be safe, she said: "Why shouldn't we believe what the Aliens said about the effectiveness and safety of these eggs? And for that matter, why shouldn't we believe what people in the Ukraine and Russia have been saying about these eggs effectiveness. This same energy apparently powers the Aliens' spaceships and everything else they have, so why shouldn't they work just as effectivel for us here on Earth?"

As to the eggs safety, M Taylor said she did not thin the eggs are in any wa dangerous. "Nothing coul be more dangerous," sh said, "than nuclear fuel ca it?"

Steve Hawkins of E (Earth in Peril) is als looking forward to t Aliens' energy eggs arrivi over Britain. He said: " their removing of nucle power stations and weapon the Aliens are doing all of a great big favour. By th giving us ordinary peop clean, safe energy it c only bring benefits for t entire Earth. And what is more, it's free!

Losers are energy baron

"The only losers from Aliens' energy eggs," said, "are the energy bar who have held us all capt with their state endor monopolies while at same time messing up planet. I do not think th will be many tears for likes of them," he said.

In France, however, th is a very different atti among the Greens at prospect of their nuc power stations going same the same way as the

Leading nuclear expert warms of

Aliens' 'Energy Eggs' 'danger

by Jamie Prior: Science Editor

THE ALIENS' so-called 'Energy Eggs' are a potential hazard and could possibly be lethal a world expert warned yesterday.

Dr Rob Hambring, a senior professor at the world famous Rutherford Centre and one of the world's leading authorities on the safety of nuclear power, said: "If these 'eggs' really do provide continuous electrical power then it stands to reason that they must be powered by nuclear material of one form or the other.

Therefore it follows," Dr Hambring said, "that they are more than likely to represent a potential hazard, especially in the hands of the ordinary layman or woman."

Dr Hambring was speaking after returning from San Francisco, where he gave one of the keynote lectures at the international conference on the future of nuclear power.

> *'It is far better that these 'energy eggs' are handled by experts, in a layman's hands they could prove dangerous'*
>
> **Dr Rob Hambring**

"It is far better," he said, speaking of the Aliens' 'energy eggs', "especially from the general public's standpoint, that these Aliens' energy capsules are first examined by those who are experts in the matter.

Just as importantly is that these Alien capsules are examined in a place of utmost safety such as here at the Rutherford Centre.

"Just as important as safety regarding these energy capsules is expertise as well, Dr Hambring said.

Rutherford's Dr Rob Hambring

"Of course, the Rutherford," he said, "is not the only centre of excellence in matters of nuclear safety and where these capsules can be brought to for assessment but it is one o world's leading ones.

"At Rutherford not onl do we have the necessar facilities on hand but team of world class exper as well. It is only whe centres such as ours hav conducted exhaustive tes on these capsules an declared on their safe should they be allow into the hands of th ordinary public."

Dr Hambring, who shortly to deliver t Skipper Memorial Lectu in Georgetown, Washingt on his work on ozo regeneration, also said t he was doubtful of the uni

Aliens warn Braz 'CLEAR OFF -

by Paul Killan
in Rio de Janerio

THE BRAZILIAN Government is reported to have reacted angrily to the Aliens' demand that its armed forces immediately vacated a large swathe of the country's Nordeste region or face the consequences.

The head of Brazil's armed forces, General Ramos is reported as saying that the country's armed forces will mount a major offensive against the Aliens within the 'very near future' and oust them from Brazilin territory once and for all.

However, General Ramos may have some difficulty in mounting such an attack, for if the Aliens' telecasts are true, a substantial number of his forces have already deserted and gone over to fight for them.

not needed I went away. I had work to do, part of which was worrying how I could get television equipment, and quickly.

I was no nearer a solution this morning when Rainbow, back above ground, was also back to her assertive self. "Television studio," she'd demanded and firmer, "when will you have it?"

I said it was Sunday, and Monday being a public holiday, everywhere would be closed. I would work on it, I would do the best I could but it might take a time to have everything she'd wanted.

"By Tuesday," she said with her tone unchanged and rubbing behind her ear, "or I'll go."

"Oh dear," I said, "please don't do that."

"Tuesday."

With such an ultimatum there was no alternative but to consider radical action. A raid upon an existing studio seemed the only way to get what was required. I was in a tizzy, so seeking assistance I went to see Paceillo. I picked a fortunate moment.

I arrived just as Colonel Tambassing was taking a terrible ticking-off and he, sounding contrite, half muttering, "I didn't mean to but he got lippy missus, so I had it off."

And Paceillo's gruff, "Let it pass this time but do not do it again."

"Yes Missus."

"The other end next time."

"Yes Missus."

Not wanting to interrupt with the thought that had suddenly come to mind, I couldn't help but listen on. And as I listened I winced. Colonel Tambassing said his men were more than eager to continue their activities and they didn't mind doing a spot of garrisoning as well. So popular was their sojourn the Colonel thought that thousands of his fellows in Nepal would be queuing up for a bit of the cut and thrust as well. But, he said, none was experienced enough to oversee what she and Tearo had said she wanted next. However, he said, he knew some people in Bat Dâm Bâng who did, and with his contacts he could arrange for some to come across. He also added, apart from being extremely experienced, they liked doing that sort of thing.

It was when Paceillo said "Well, get them then," that I winced.

Seeing Colonel Tambassing looking beyond her, Paceillo turned her head and seeing me, she brusquely said "Yes?"

The tone of her voice elicited timidity from mine. "I wondered,2 I began (though I nearly started off with "Please Miss2), "as the Serbs won't be needing their television studio in Pale, could we have it over here?" Though I refrained the "Please" at the end I involuntarily blurted "Rainbow says she'll go if I don't get her one."

Her "Hmm" was followed after a pause, and turning to Colonel Tambassing, by "Can you?"

The Colonel, no doubt eager still to please, beamed a smile and said "No sweat Missus."

Paceillo next called over Tearo and Anuria, who had been hovering behind the Colonel. "Will you handle the details?" and after they said they would, "Arrangements for trials and punishments, how are they progressing?" At which point she turned to me and gave a "You can go now" nod. So I did.

Up in the sunlight again and buoyed with success, I announced triumphantly to Rainbow "I've done it! I've pulled it off! I've got you proper cameras, lights, monitors, everything."

"Oh good," she said in a distracted tone and not looking up and, in the same breath, "What is 87 times 43?" Before I'd time to work it out she added, "Don't bother..." then more to herself, "...three seven four one." She then looked up and said in a cold hard voice, "Equipment is useless without technicians. Camera operators, no, not Roberto, lighting engineers and all the rest, will they be here for Tuesday? And a studio as well? You can't expect me to present properly without a studio."

No doubt relishing that she had me over a barrel, Rainbow continued her needling. "You promised me television, so television it will be," she said. "I'm not going to appear again unless everything is done properly. I'm a professional, goodness only knows what I must have looked like. I have certain standards. Therefore, as I said, everything will be done professionally or not at all." Turning to her teaching screen once more, she added "Tuesday."

With my buoy well and truly sunk I sloped off. Past the groups of soldiers and villagers stuck in their studies. Past Pheterisco and Lucia taking a crocodile of white tunicked children on their way to Kershaw and the seaside (in Father Alves' absence, church attendance appears optional) and past teams of other Susem and accompanying hen-gers en route to the forest. And all the while I worried what on earth what was I going to do. Eventually I sought Terbal.

"Ah, so spaces you are needing now also?" he said with more than a hint of schadenfreude (and still pronouncing me as 'Dommy'). He flitted over a screen or two, returned, and asked "How much are you vanting of space?"

I told him how much, that I needed it in a hurry, and how worried I was should there not be anything available.

He drifted over the screens again, returned and said "For you Danny, the worry is over..." I was grateful for what he said (but the way he said it grated, "Vor you Dommy, the var..ist over"). "Space you like can be here...or dere ...possibly here also..."

The screens showed sections of the Ibiapaba illuminating. After I had told him dimensions, pointed to an area nearest the surface, he asked for requirements, "Sound proofing, absorbent?..non-absorbent?..lighting, high...low... variable?..."

I tried remembering what a TV studio looked like, what it needed, hoping I hadn't too much wrong. He read out so many options, and so fast, I half expected to hear, "aisle, vindow, smoking, non-smoking?"

Up above ground once more, I announced to Rainbow (and keeping the triumphing muted) "I have a studio, it will be ready this afternoon."

"Oh good," she said in the same distracted tone as before and walking past me carrying a towel and bathing hat. Then, and still showing no appreciation of my endeavours, she asked, and with such a cold riposte, "Technicians?" and seeing I'd not an answer, "Tuesday."

She walked to where Lathia and Petruee were waiting and all three sauntered over to the park-side together. And as they walked and chatted they had the appearance of knowing one another for ages.

In the afternoon when the veda arrived with the equipment, the terror of Tuesday still loomed large. The little sherpels over there are just as capable and thorough as those over here. They had brought everything including tables and chairs, even bits of floor and walls. They had also brought a pile of documents and books, including the 'How to do it' sort.

Not knowing much about television studios I started reading as fast as I could. I had not long begun when Terbal appeared. With "Vat ist dis...und dis...und vat ist dat?" he flitted over the equipment.

I did my best to explain and that I didn't really know how everything fitted together or how many technicians were needed to run it all. And that as there weren't any technicians around I was doing the best I could. That I had to have everything ready and working by Tuesday or else. And I didn't really know where to turn.

"Vat ist dat?" he asked.

"An instruction manual," I said.

"You show me, ya?"

Three hours later when Terbal said "Vor you Dommy, der var..ist over," I didn't mind how much it grated, and I wasn't just grateful, I was astounded.

With my buoy bobbing high I rushed up above to exclaim to Rainbow my resounding success and accomplishment. She now had the most automated, advanced television studio ever. She could have anything, every effect, lighting, sound, editing, everything. But she wasn't there.

"Oh good," she said after I had at last tracked her down, and briefly breaking away from the elocution class she was giving. "Now I can stay," she said before turning back to the group of Susem and saying "Once more, repeat after me, 'Peter Piper picked a peck of..." followed by, and Rainbow can be so wickedly withering when she wants, "Pressure, proficiently applied propels progress perfectly."

48: KEN

I know it's wrong but I had to laugh. He had it coming to him, all his lot did.

I watched the tele from 10 o'clock when they first started right through to the end. I wanted to see the Aliens. See what they looked like.

The commentator went on for ever about how everyone was waiting to see them. The programme kept going back to the studio and a load of boring old experts giving their five minutes worths. Then back to outside this hotel in Pale and another few minutes about how the place was packed with hundreds of journalists and TV crews.

There was also all these soldiers strutting up and down. One of them looked as if he was really enjoying himself ordering everyone about. The Serb side turns up, and the commentator interviews a couple of them. They were going on about their importance and everything. Then back to the studio again. A couple of the experts started saying that perhaps the Aliens weren't coming. Then back to the commentator. He said it was three minutes to twelve their time. Then there was some Serb crowing "We are here, we have showed good faith, where are they?"

He had no sooner finished when, whoosh, down they came. From the shaking of the picture you could tell that the cameraman was running, but the picture also showed dozens of others running as well. They were all running towards this plane thing. It didn't land actually but you could half see it hovering above the roof of the hotel, then it went out of sight.

The television picture was next from inside the hotel. By the background noise I could tell there were a lot of people there. The commentator said it was the press-conference room. He said the Aliens and the Serbs were in a room just down a corridor leading off the pressroom. Some Serb got up on the stage and said that the talks had just begun. The picture switched back to London and they were asking the commentator "What did you see...did you see them...what were they like?"

He had barely time to say that he had seen nothing, when, all gasping, he said "The doors are opening...they're coming out..."

And as soon as he had spoken, this man in a white tunic appeared. He walked down the bit of clear floor alongside the stage. He didn't get up on it or anything but stood in front of it. He then said, and because everyone was looking at him, there was only the sound of the cameras clicking and whirring, "Ladies and gentlemen, the head of the Serb delegation."

And with that, he rolls it across the floor!

Oh I did laugh. And at what happened next, when all those other Serbs came out.

49: JAMES

Spending the night on the settee ensures one thing, an early waking. I had washed and breakfasted by eight. As Frankie rarely rises before noon on Sundays, I was able to read the papers and watch television in peace.

From 10 o'clock it was "rent-a-prof hour" anchored by Son of Wired. Because the papers were particularly newsworthy my attention wasn't really on the screen. I glanced up each time they went over to Pale. And each time they did, I had the same sense of frustration that there was nothing except interviews with those ogres who would be facing charges of genocide if the Hague international court had still existed.

The commentator's "They're here!...they've arrived!" had me put my paper down but even so his excitement proved little more than a damp squib. For all that was shown it could have been a helicopter on the roof of the building rather than his "Their spacecraft...look there it is...there it is!" The papers soon had my attention again. But a few minutes later they had fallen to the floor.

The figure striding through the doorway may have been an "Alien" but he looked pretty human to me (I automatically took 'him' to be male). He spoke like one as well. Apart from him being fluent in English, he also appeared confident in addressing a mass of people. I must have concluded all this in a matter of seconds, for as soon as he had said "The head of the Serb delegation," he took his hand from behind his back and tossed a severed head onto the floor.

He also had a keen sense of the dramatic. For no sooner had the head landed than there was a commotion from behind him, and a huddled, shuffled crocodile of men were herded through the doorway by more men also in white tunics. Though there was the continued whirr of cameras, flashlights, and a massed gasped intake of breath, not one word was said.

Not only was the crocodile bent double, hands clasped in front but all of them sported bright red heads. The silence was broken by another collective inward gasp, when a bevy of what I took to be "the darts" appeared.

But even so, this lasted no more than seconds before there were yelps and pleas. The camera shot to where they came from and showed the Serb who had been on the rostrum, now to be on the floor with his legs kicking between those of several of the other men in white. His yelping stopped but was immediately followed by a high pitched screech, whereupon one of the men in white threw what were obviously this Serb's genitals in the direction of the severed head.

Again all this took place in a matter of seconds. As this Serb was also hustled away, the man who had spoken, added "All Serbs and Croats must leave Bosnia. This conference is now concluded. Good day." With this, he and the others turned on their heels and strode back through the doorway.

HEAD SERB BEHEADED

by HAROLD EPPANS in Pale

TOP YUGO THUG Bran Koskscl had his head cut off by the Aliens yesterday. The rest of the Serbs with him were luckier, they were only parted from their penises by the Aliens.

This shock event occurred within minutes of the hastily arranged ceasefire talks between the Aliens and the Serbs taking place. The Serb side, led by Koskscl were all cockahoop with confidence as they swaggered into the conference room to meet the Aliens to discuss the terms of peace talks and who were waiting for them.

Within ten minutes of the talks taking place however, and while the Serb press officer was addressing the international press in lobby of the conference centre on the Serb's position, than one of the Aliens marched into the lobby.

First sighting of Aliens

This sudden and low key, first ever sighting of one of the Aliens took all those present by surprise. Although the Alien being had a human-like male appearance it was obvious that 'he' was not a human.

Severed head rolled

Surprise grew, when amid the flashes and clicks of hundreds of cameras, the Alien spoke in good quality English.

Apparently appearing completely relaxed at being in front of so many human beings, the Serbs had to leave Bosnia forthwith or else.

No sooner had the Alien said this than through the doors of lobby came the rest of the Serb delegation herded by more Aliens and who, in their white tunics were of similar human-like appearance to the first Alien.

Serbs castrated and dyed

From the way the Serbs had their hands clasped between their legs it was immediately obvious that all they were in immense discomfort.

All those present soon saw why. Every one of these men had just been castrated. What is more they all had their heads sprayed bright red.

Not unnaturally there were more than sharp intakes of breathe from everyone but this soon turned to even greater shock when another

Peace Talks Shock: Serb leader beheaded

By JOHN DEANS IN PALE

BRAN KOSTKCI, head of the Bosnian Serb delegation to the Pale Peace Talks was executed by the Susem representatives.

The Susem delegates are thought to be humans.

Within minutes of the talks commencing the leader of the Susem delegation threw down Kostkci's decapitated head in front of members of the international media.

The surviving members of the Serb delegation are believed to have been castrated and sent into captivity.

In front of reporters, the Serbian press spokesman was also castrated by other Susem representatives.

Before stunned members of the international media, the leader of the Susem delegation at the Pale Peace Talks threw down the decapitated head of his Serb opposite number.

Immediately, the rest of the Serbian delegation, including self-styled 'prime minister' Zacovan Ardradik and Ilkmar Dlatco, the military leader - both of whom have international arrest warrants against them - were marched past shocked journalists by other Susem delegates who were armed. The Serbs were bent double in pain, also their heads sprayed with dye.

The leader of the Susem delegation then issued an ultimatum for all Serbs to leave Bosnia immediately. With that he declared the talks to be at an end, whereupon he and colleagues

SERB LEADER EXECUTED

By MICHELLE FOOT in Pale

THE head of the Susem's delegation appeared before the press with the severed head of Bran Kostkci, leader of the Serb delegation, in his hand.

Moments later the remainder of the Serb delegation were herded before the press by armed members of the Susem delegation. They had been castrated. And as the Serb ... he was

The Susem leader then announced that all Serbs must leave Bosnia ... the conference closed. Announcing the conference closed, he and those with him immediately departed back to the conference room.

I chased after the Susem and while ... I heard only the sound of a departing lift. I saw the mayhem of the conference room. There was Kostkci's ... a bloody pile of severed

ALIENS EXEC... SERBIAN LEA...

by JON SHARECROSS in Pale

BRAN KOSKSCI, THE LEADER OF THE SERB delegation at the Bosnian ceasefire talks with the Aliens was summarily beheaded by them within minutes of the talks beginning.

The rest of the 20 man strong Serb negotiating team were then apparently castrated by the Aliens. They were also subsequently taken into captivity by the Aliens.

Bran Koskscl, head of the Serbs in the former Bosnia led his negotiating team into the ceasefire talks with the Aliens at the Holiday Inn, Pale. The talks, held in the hotel's conference suite began at 12 o'clock this morning.

The Aliens, unseen by anybody since their arrival minutes earlier, were apparently, already in the suite.

Within ten minutes of the talks beginning, the head of the Susem delegation strode into the hotel's lobby where a Serb press officer was addressing journalists.

> 'All Serbs must leave Bosnia. This conference is now concluded. Good day.'
>
> *Head of the Aliens' delegation*

Speaking in perfect

No sooner had the Alien thrown the Serb's head onto the floor than there was a further shocked commotion as the remainder of the Serb delegation were pushed from the conference suite by yet further Aliens and towards the hotel's main doorway.

In part much of the surprise at seeing these Serbs was caused by their heads being sprayed a bright red colour. However, alarm grew among those present by the way all of the Serbs were holding their hands between their legs and appeared to be in considerable pain.

With the Alien's marching the shuffling Serbs to the exit, those present were witness to a further attack by the Aliens on the Serb's press officer and who had been cowering behind the lectern.

With most of those present now also cowering behind the seats in front of them and to screams from the press officer, the Aliens proceeded to castrate him.

Shock outcome of Sarajevo conference

Serb leader executed Serb delegation assaulted

BY PAUL REEVES IN SARAJEVO

SUNDAY'S Pale Peace Conference came to an abrupt and dramatic end within minutes of beginning.

The talks began at 12 noon precisely. At 12:07, the leader of the Susem delegation walked into the press briefing room flourishing the severed head of the leader of the Serb delegation, Bran Kostkci.

'Peace talks' were an outright 'farce'

The Susem leader was immediately followed by another Susem. They herded the remaining members of the Serb delegation, including Zacovan Ardradik, Ilkmar Dlatic and Dragon Bokaslav - all wanted internationally, along with Kostkci, for Crimes Against Humanity - before the press cameras.

All appeared to have been castrated, and were bent double in pain.

Each one's head was also dyed a bright red. The Serb press spokesman, despite his attempts to escape and to everyone's alarm, then suffered the same fate.

The Serb delegation were then pushed from the room by the Susem's flying darts. Yet before they were outside, the leader of the Susem delegation, announcing the end of the conference, said: "All Serbs must leave Bosnia immediately."

World leaders condemn Alien 'atrocities'

BELGRADE: A spokesman for the Serbian leader, Milo Gadan, called the Pale Talks an "evil betrayal by heinous unworldly murderers." He added: "After this farce [of the ... valiantly resist to their last breath rather than be cowed."

Serbian towns all along the River Drina border with Serbia proper, were witness to an unending exodus of refugees streaming from Bosnia. At Zvornikand Visegrad, on the main routes from Sarajevo, there was near panic as their river crossings caused long tailbacks for those trying to cross.

Aliens thought to be using humans

Many world leaders expressed their alarm at the Kostkci's death. The Russian President, Vladimir Sheybel's office issued a statement condemning the killing as a brutal and senseless act. German President, Friedrich Ebert, speaking at the Schleicher Centre, said: "Because you do not agree does not mean you have to kill. This [Serb] slaying achieves nothing."

Dad was lucky mum didn't catch him. I told the pair of them to stop it immediately and behave themselves. Grown men sniggering and chortling like that was so childish.

And Daffyd's "Serves them right," cut no ice with me either. It is not right doing that to people, no matter how terrible they may have been. There is no justification in cutting someone's head off, or their private parts. There should be proper trials like they used to have in the Hague. And repeat showing it on the six o'clock news, and on a Sunday, was in bad taste.

The news also showed columns of Serbs hurrying away back to Serbia. Then it showed Bosnian people in Sarajevo telling what it had been like cut off without food or medicines. There was also a clip from a Bosnian refugee camp somewhere in Italy, showing people saying that they could not wait to go home. The news then went to France and showed soldiers with their equipment on their way to protect a power station in Normandy, La Hague I think. At this Daffyd said "I told you that the French would make trouble. If they fire anything, and the wind is in the right direction, we will cop it as well."

But dad said what with the winds always coming from the southwest, Wales wouldn't be affected but London would. They both started giggling at this until I reminded them Anne lives in London. That shut them up quickly enough. Grown men can sometimes be so childish. By then I had become irritated, so I left them to it and started on the supper.

By the time we were ready to eat, the pair of them had pulled themselves together, though it was still left to the boys to pose the more sensible questions. Glyn asked "People who have these power units will have free electricity, but the people who don't, won't. Is that fair?"

Before there was an answer, Rowan piped up with "Will the people who haven't got any units try to get them from the people who have, and will there be fighting for them?"

Dad said that only the people supplied by nuclear power stations would get the units, which might include Cilgerran. But Daffyd said this wouldn't be the case. Because all the power from the stations went into the National Grid, it meant that everyone would be affected. Then Rowan piped in again with "Then everyone will get one, and will they work in cars?"

At first Daffyd said they were bound to, but then he added it would put the petrol companies out of business and so he didn't think they would be allowed. Dad added that the government wouldn't allow them either, not unless they could put a tax on them.

At this I started clearing the table. I was becoming confused.

Alien enigma

By LILLIAN WALDERGRAVE

THE WORLD caught their first sight of the Aliens on Sunday. But are they really so Alien?

Although events of recent days more than confirm the presence of extra-terrestrials here on Earth, but are they the 'beings' we saw on our screens yesterday?

Or are they indeed as we saw -

The men seen yesterday tally with the descriptions given by many Croatian refugees. The 'flying darts' accompanying them yesterday, and the flying craft they travelled in to Pale, are also the same as refugees have reported. And it goes without saying their actions in castrating the hapless Serbs leaders, is the same as has occurred throughout Bosnia since Thursday.

But if the Susem are such an advanced society, why would they feel ... to resort to such a primitive

NATO prepared

By Wendy Cash, in Brussels

HERMAN RHEINFELDT, NATO's Supreme Commander, has appointed General Walther Nehring to be in charge of NATO's Eastern Forward XIX Planning Group.

General Nehring's forces are to go immediately to Poland. General Falkenhorst has been appointed to command NATO's operations on its northern flank and will be based at Narvik. Generals Liguarian and Weichs will liaise NATO operations in Italy.

Aliens are 'human'

By STEPHEN SOLOMANS

"THERE'S no doubt about it, these Aliens are as human as you and me," says a leading authority on anatomy.

Dr. Grace Toby, Dean of Anatomy at Sheppey University, in collaboration with colleagues from the University's Faculty of Aerobic Studies, has made a careful, frame by frame study of the Aliens. "We ha...

respiration and eye movement. And they are identical in every detail to human males," Dr. Toby claims.

By superimposing video stills of the Aliens over those of human males, Dr. Toby convincingly illustrates her theory. Dr. Toby says with her experience of anatomy, she is able to tell exactly what a person's physic is like no matter what clothes they are wearing. "All I can't tell with 100 per cent accuracy, is how hairy they are."

Russian 'successes' questioned

Roisin Devlin
In Washington

MILITARY experts are doubting Russian claims to have fended off Susem attacks on their civil and military nuclear installations.

General Valdimir Bessonov, Russia's Minister of Defence claims that Susem attacks at missile sites at Zlatoust have been beaten off. But Pentagon sources say that both installations no longer exist.

What concerns Washington is that the Russian army and air force might, in desperation might actually use their remaining nuclear weapons against the Susem.

"The consequences if they (the Russian) should fire their nuclear weapons at the Aliens is just too horrible to contemplate," said the US's National Security Authority spokesman, Nathan Weitz.

"The resulting likelihood of massive contamination over many parts of the world including North America will render the affected regions uninhabitable for decades. Just look at what happened at Chenobyl," he said.

Norwegian sources also report that a string of Russian naval facilities in the north of the Kola Peninsula have been evacuated in the face of wide ... Alien attacks.

Susem strike south

By Ardrian Warley

SUSEM craft, operating for the first time outside Russia and Ukraine have removed a string of nuclear installations throughout Eastern Europe and the Middle East.

Before dawn Romania's nuclear station at Cernovoda was sent skyward. An hour later the two reactors at Kozloduy, Bulgaria were also seen heading in the same direction.

Yanko Yanev, head of Bulgaria's Nuclear Safety Authority said, "I don't have a job any more. While I'm glad to see the back of the [Russian] VVER, the other a pressurised water reactor, generating 2,000 megawatts was installed by the Canadians and was almost new. We hadn't even made the first payments on it yet." As has been reported from Russia, the arrival of the Susem was preceded by thousands of their blue blankets falling on the areas around the nuclear plants and delivering more of 'Energy Eggs'.

Israeli Nuclear bombs go

By Harriat Levy
In Tel Aviv

ISRAEL'S entire nuclear arsenal no longer exists. Israel's much vaunted nuclear capacity proved no match for the Susem. Within in an hour everything nuclear was gone. The experimental HCR reactor at Qaffin, north of Tel Aviv was the first to go. Twenty minutes later the Susem were over Dimona in the Negev and suspected site of Israel's nuclear weapons store.

Nathan Rotblat an employee at the nearby nuclear plant said: "When they (the Susem) came over, we all knew it was time to go. A voice boomed down saying we'd ten minutes to leave. But Manny Cohen, the station director, called back on the plant's tannoy system that we couldn't possibly leave in less than 20. They replied that 12 was their absolute limit. But Mr Cohen said that if we hurried the quickest we could possibly be out in 18. In the end a deal was done on 15."

51: AILEEN

It was cleavage and busts last night. Lunchtime it was beheading and gelding. It was all they could talk about. Some things really bring out the worst in men.

Not that I have shed any tears for those Serbian men either. But what I hardly heard mentioned the whole lunchtime, were the other men, the ones in white. Leastways I took them as being men, for they looked just like men. Indian men, a little on the short side, and the one who spoke sounded like one as well.

I make no claim to know much about anything, but I do know that what is happening is more serious than handing out a bit of ready justice. Hardly any of them in the Salutation seemed to have a care about this.

Ryan was the same. I tried telling him that there is more going on than is appearing on the television, but all he could say was that I was being stupid, worrying unnecessarily. Everything would sort itself out. And when I said how could he be so sure, all he could say was "Because it always does."

I tried telling him that if trouble started over here, there wouldn't be any work for steel erectors like him in London either. He said nothing to this except, "Where there is trouble there will always be work."

With Patrick and Becky away for the day at my friend Margaret's, I had only to make lunch for Ryan. With him eating it in silence I could tell he had another of his moods coming on. After he had finished he said that he was going over to his mate Gary to watch the car racing. And when I said why couldn't he watch it in the flat, he said he was going because he wanted to. From the tone of his voice I said no more, I wasn't wanting another argument with him.

With Margaret bringing Becky and Patrick back at five, it gave me an hour or so to myself. During this time I had another little think. Although I left the Regional before the end of my second year, I was doing quite well in both Sociology and Business Studies. Maybe, I thought, as I still qualified for the rest of my grant, I could go back and finish the course and get my degree. M'mam and dad would be more than willing to look after Patrick and Becky. Also Ryan would still have to contribute to their upkeep. But if I was going to go back I had to get my application in during the next week. I made a note to phone m'mam tomorrow to get the application forms sent to her, or maybe I could have them sent to the Sallie. The last thing I wanted at this stage is for Ryan to know.

Electricity "may be rationed"

By Julian Gray

BRITAIN could face a country-wide switch-off if its nuclear stations are removed.

'The lights over Britain may well go out,' warned Lord Brown, chairman of the Council of Energy Suppliers (CES).

Britain's 38 nuclear power stations currently provide 20 per cent of the nation's electricity. A further five per cent is also supplied from French stations. As a percentage of total energy supply, nuclear power represents approximately ten per cent.

Britain could survive unscathed until the Autumn. But then it is an open question what the likelihood of power cuts would be.

Should CES's predictions prove accurate there will be steep rises in the unit cost of electricity rather than in rationing. This will mean a further rise of profitability

Aliens 'thought to be Gurkhas'

By William Frost

EXPERTS examining film and photographs of the Aliens at Pale are convinced that they are in fact humans.

"They are definitely of northern Indian origin," said Prof. Stephen Ward of Hull University's Department of Comparative Anthropology. "Their slight build, stature and locomotion are those of mountain people. The flatness of facial features are alike to those of the peoples found all along the central southern Himalayan foothills," con- ... Prof. Ward.

However, Colonel Leo Messenger, curator of Sandhurst museum is more specific. "You can take it from me, I know a gurkha when I see one, served in the 6th Queen's Own with them long enough, steadfast chaps. Also know a kukri when I see one, cuts through a throat in a flash. And take it from me, if a gurkha is 'agin' you, then watch out. There's no messing with those chaps. Damn fearless fighters," said Colonel Messenger.

If the men reputed to be Aliens are in fact Gurkhas, then how - and also why - did ... known to anyone, ...

Indian, Pakistani Nuclear bombs go

By Fatima Brutto in Karachi

...KISTAN'S Kahuta nuc... research laboratory and ...pected site of it nuclear ...apons has been elimina... It was the last in a list of ...clear installations ranging ...om Romania to India, to be ...moved by the Susem during Sunday.

Turkeys nuclear plants at ...ankaya and Bursa were first ... be blasted skyward. A ...econd Susem fleet, having ...rst swept through Romania ...nd Bulgaria and eliminating ...heir nuclear power stations, ...were seen over El Dabaa, Egypt's Red Sea nuclear plant. After this was removed the Susem flew on to Kenya and removed their nuclear station at Kilifi.

After eliminating Turkey... remaining nuclear plants ... Konya and Adana, the fi... Susem fleet flew south ... Israel and removed its Neg... nuclear facilities. It then fle... to Iraq.

Three hours later, ... INNA the Iranian ne... agency reported, this fl... was seen over Ishafan a... later Babol where th... "devastated" the countr... civilian nuclear research fa...ilities (Both centres, how...ever, were suspected to ... involved in extensive wea...ons research).

On arrival in India t... southern Susem fleet remo...ed the nuclear plant ... Mecara,

"Purely defensive" says France

By Adrian Warley in Lyon

LYON: The missile batteries surrounding the country's power stations will act as a deterrent against attack, said a Defence Ministry spokesman today.

Speaking outside the nearby Creys-Malville French military base, he endeavoured to convince a sceptical audience the safeness of French action in placing missiles around his country's nuclear installations.

"France is acting in full consultation with all its NATO, WEU and EU partners", he said, in a response to questions of German and Belgian unease.

"France has a right to ...fend ... its sovereignty...

What he did not mentio... was the matter of Frenc... prestige and its 'Force d... Frappe'. Should France lo... its status as a nuclear powe... it will lose, in French perce...tions, its standing in the ey... of the world as a First Ra... power.

There are also financial co...siderations. During its ma...moth nuclear building p...gramme, the French gove...ments of the day borro... heavily to finance their c...struction.

Revenue from electri... sales was used as collat... for the loans. Deprived of... revenue, the French gov...ment will have difficult... servicing its debts.

This will lead, so fina... markets feel, to a weak... of the Franc and French...

IAEA awa... its fate

By Isabella Fontaine in Vien...

WITH the air of condemned prisoners awaiting their executions, officials at the IAEA (International Atomic Energy Agency) appear resigned to their jobs disappearing.

IAEA's palatial offices on Vienna's prestigious Wagramerstrasse were rife with rumour as officials speculated the fate of each other's prospects.

The news that nuclear plants outside Russia and the Ukraine were now being targeted by the Susem, only served to ...

Pierre Ro... representat... inspectorat... the sentim... "No more ... expense a... accommoda... sions.

Going Home

By QUENILLA DAVIES
In MANFREDONIA, ITALY

Apulia: As Sancia Kreco helped her mother Slavisa, and older sister Jasmin, pack their few modest belongings, she was looking forward to going home.

Like others in the Polvera refugee camp, little Sancia, although facing an uncertain future, cannot wait to return to her village of Lokvine, near Zenica.

Neither she nor Jasmin have seen their father since the Red Cross airlifted them to safety last year but, like their mother, they are confident he is still alive.

Although Sancia is a typically happy seven year old, 11 year old Jasmin's big dark eyes still bear the scars of her and her mother's ordeal at the hands of their Croatian neighbours.

"How can we ever forgive them", says Salvia, a former

Rainbow wasn't alone in proficiently applying pressure. The teaching machines did so as well. Whereas earlier they had tested and advanced ability, on Sunday afternoon the machines began 'programming'. Within seconds of a session starting and their pupils' competence pushed to his or her limit, the machine's screen for two minutes or so began rapidly flashing questions with the answers included. It then returned to its usual slower speed but posed questions more difficult than before. After the sheets of homework had appeared, it proceeded with the next subject. After a few seconds it would again be flashing and programming anew.

At the same time as the screen began programming images, the machine itself exuded a faint lemony smell, the same as I had smelt in the Susem houses on La-ra. This lemony smell is now present every time I switch my machine on.

Though the programming is tiring to the eyes, the results are spectacular. Not only, for example, is my numeracy much improved (I can do sums in my head I once needed a calculator for) but so is the speed at which I am able to calculate.

Although my advancement, for me is impressive, it is as nothing compared to the others. On Thursday many of the villagers were illiterate and at best barely numerate. Now, not only have they all advanced to fractions and decimals but many have progressed to algebra, trigonometry and writing words in English, sentences even. The villagers' oral advancement is also impressive. In the evening I heard many conversing in English, and they weren't just doing it for show either.

Not long after sunset and accompanied by Menpemelo and Milophinia, Paceillo made an appearance. Both villagers and soldiers had been told she was coming to meet with them and so they had gathered outside of the Pousada to hear her. Although all of them by know of Paceillo's existence, until this evening few had actually seen her and so all were aware of the meeting's significance.

With Pedro and Roberto interpreting for those who were less advanced, Paceillo told them that now that their English and mathematics had progressed to a level where they and the Susem could freely converse, they would have a teacher sent through their screens that would tutor and talk with them. Paceillo then said, and with such a beguiling (and to me suspicious) smile, the teacher had to have a name. She asked them to choose one, a person who inspired them the most she added.

All bar one called back "Lucia!"

After those trying to kiss and hug Lucia had finished, Paceillo smiled, nodded, then she proceeded with the rest of the meeting. Her every request met with further unison (but I became convinced that she is definitely up to something).

She said she wanted everyone to talk with the Susem whenever they wished. "But also be as are we," she said, "form into groups of three, have one be the representative of the other two. Let these representatives also form into groups of three and again select one to represent the other two." As everyone was already happily learning in teams of nines, such a suggestion was obvious enough. But what Paceillo said next confirms (to my mind) that she really is up to something.

"In turn," she said, "let these representatives form into groups of nine, then also select a representative. And may these also select a representative. Do this," she added, "and we will know, as will you and quickly, what are your concerns, wishes and needs."

It might work for the Susem but humans are different. And apart from being 'representative sodden', it smacked of 'do goodism'. And like all 'do gooding' everywhere, it is naive. There would be consensus among the soldiers and villagers to do as the Susem wished but only for so long as it was in their interests. The moment it wasn't, they wouldn't.

I can see a possibility of the soldiers operating in such a way, simply because armies organise soldiers into platoons and no matter whom their officers are, they have to carry the confidence of their men, as Capitão Ries found to his cost. But as for the villagers, there is little chance. The women might gather together, as they are now doing over the gardens, but this is only because they have this in common, and the piles of amazing quality produce ready to sell in Tianguá. I suppose families and their neighbours might also have things in common as well and perhaps at a stretch the households in each of the lanes. There might be other groups, such as those who have children (then all families have children). Or old people, but then most of these have families as well and the ones who haven't are looked after by others. The people who work in the Park (should it ever re-open) might also have something in common, similarly the traders who used to sell to the tourists, but this is about all. There is a sort of camaraderie among the regulars of the Pousada, I suppose, and with those who have cattle. I can see some purpose in the children being together, it will help keep them quiet and out of trouble. As for the rest of the villagers, I don't see any of them having any reason for wanting to get together at all.

But it has always been my experience that the only beneficiaries of 'do gooding' are the 'do gooders' themselves. And what further raises my suspicions is that every organisation that has ever been formed from the bottom up always evolves into one being manipulated from the top down. For the Susem not to have grasped this is simply not credible. Therefore they must be intending to control the villagers and soldiers, and Rainbow and me for that matter. But for what? This is the question I do not yet have a handle on. All the same, I am going to be on my guard from now on.

Everyone else though came to a quite different conclusion. When the meeting was over there were groups of them milling throughout the village in avid and animated discussion, the like of which I had not seen since I've been here. But gathering together in nines was not the only matter under debate, it was everything else Paceillo said as well.

While Paceillo did not dispel any of my suspicions, I have to admit that she is a skilful manipulator. And she's not a bad orator either. Her rhetoric had the villagers responding in a way they had certainly not shown to Fernando Burity when he had helicoptered in with his dodgy promises. She delivered everything she said in the form of questions. Each framed in such a way that not only did villagers and soldiers alike yell back "Yes!" but with each one their fervour grew and grew.

With Pedro and Roberto now interpreting like mad and she stressing "you" and "your," Paceillo began. "Are you pleased with the gardens and the crops you have grown in them? Are your crops of better quality than before and will they bring you greater wealth? Are you pleased with the education and instruction you and your children have received?" She went on with a few more "Are yous", all of which had the enthusiasm of those assembled nicely whetted, then she moved on to the "Do yous", and they really had them going.

"Do you and your children wish to have freedom from illness? (and she giving a glance in Lucia's direction as she did so, and after the approving roar), Then it can be yours!" On Paceillo went, promising them everything just short of paradise, then she moved over the political edge with, "Do you wish to have freedom and command of your destiny?"

Having become so fired-up yelling "Yeses," the villagers automatically, and without stopping for thought, shouted another.

After pressing home the point with "Then it can be yours!" Paceillo took a pause. Then she hit them with "These freedoms you now have can only be truly safeguarded if others have them too." She then followed it up with "Do you wish others to gain this freedom, e liberade?"

The villagers promptly gave another loud "Yes!" (Though perhaps a cynic might conclude they had been manoeuvred into a position where they couldn't really say "No").

Her "Then so you shall," was quickly followed by, "Many of the soldiers are leaving tomorrow to tell and give others the skills, abilities and advances they have made. Do you wish to assist them?" But before any of the villagers had a chance to offer themselves as volunteers, Paceillo promptly added "One representing each group of nine is all that is required."

The assembled had no time to even mull among themselves as to who was going and who wasn't, before she called out "And who among you will assist in showing others what you have achieved so that they may, like you, dwell in health, happiness and harmony?"

Pride is a beguiling quality, especially that of accomplishment. A quality very few of the villagers are currently lacking. And Paceillo played upon it to the full (and blatantly so, a cynic might conclude).

Before the roar of offers had finally faded away, Paceillo told those volunteering to be by the Pousada at dawn. She then, and with the smile on her face now turning to earnestness, drew from her tunic a sheet of white cloth. Waving it aloft, she shouted "Viva harmony! Viva harmonica!" Then, after a split second pause, tightening her cloth-holding hand into a fist, and with a deeper yet louder, growlingly emotive voice, shouted "Viva liberade!"

She had barely finished this last 'Viva' before everyone at the top of their voices were shouting back "Viva liberade! Viva Paceillo!" again and again. And as they did so, they waved whatever they had to hand, hats, hankies, shirts and all.

With the cheering and waving at full tumult, Paceillo promptly turned and left them. But such was the villagers' euphoria, that if there had been an election taking place (as there was supposed to have been today) Paceillo would have had all the votes of every last one of them.

53: BOSNIA

The Gurkhas, following their meeting with the Serbs at Pale, continued their operations throughout the remainder of Bosnia. By Tuesday, May 3rd, all the villages and small towns of eastern and northern Bosnia as well as Sarajevo were devoid of Serbs and Croats. These had either fled to the larger towns of Banja Luka, Brčko, Mostar and which they still occupied, or to Serbia and Croatia proper. The armed forces of both countries, fearful of the castrational and other consequences of being captured, were in full flight.

Bosnians who had survived imprisonment began returning to their homes. Those who had fled to hills and mountains did likewise. Bosnians in the few pockets of surviving resistance in Sarajevo and other towns saw shelling stop and encirclement fade away.

The mass influx of refugees from Bosnia into Serbia and Croatia caused chaos in both countries. In Bosnia, in the Croat and Serb held towns conditions were far worse with any semblance of order collapsing. Many irregular Serb and Croat soldiers, in their bids to evade Gurkhas and hen-gers, fled to hills and forests. However, be it in town or hillside all sought refuge in vain.

The latter were easy targets. Swarms of hen-gers soon located these hapless men, and with stings drove them forward (much as beaters do grouse) onto waiting lines of Gurkhas. During Monday and Tuesday alone tens of thousands of hectares were cleared of Croat and Serbs.

On the coast at Korčula and Pelješac, the numbers of castratees with red heads and clasped hands continued to grow. Though there was no food for them, there was at least water. Ragusan schoolchildren as well as increasing numbers of women interrogated new arrivals as to their involvement in the Bosnian conflict.

Meanwhile up above in Sieba, Anuria and Lico along with some of Colonel Tambassing's aides finalised procedures for the trials and sentencing. There were by Tuesday evening, however, no signs of any soldiers or other men arriving in Korčula from either Croatia or Serbia. But this state of affairs was set to change, as was the fate of those in the larger Croat and Serb held Bosnian towns.

In the late afternoon a flotilla of vedas returned from their flight to Bat Dâm Bâng. Aboard them were Tearo, Colonel Tambassing, several companies of Gurkhas and an intake of new arrivals. Both Tearo and the Colonel stopped momentarily to view these men cowering, gawping in disbelief as Gurkhas shepherded them to their billets below.

"Four hundred and fifty two, not a bad day's bag," said the Colonel to Tearo as they turned to walk away. But the Colonel's arithmetic was wrong, there were in fact 454 ex-Khmer Rouges.

54: SERRA PELADA

I didn't want to go. I had seen the pictures and they were grim enough. And it seemed such a long way for so little. But I was given no choice. Paceillo was insistent we went, as was Rainbow.

I went in Kubber, and regardless of Rainbow's reservations, as well as there being nobody else, I took Roberto with me. After the brown of the Sertão and miles of forest, the Serra Pelada suddenly appeared amid the green.

It was a terrible sight, a red raw scarred blemish stretching in all directions for miles and miles. In its centre and surrounded by smaller ones, was a brown-grey, festering, ulcerated sore two miles wide and a 1,000 feet deep. Encircling it was a congealed rind of rain-hardened puss yellow slurry. Crawling, slithering about its sides like a carpet of pulsating black headed muck-caked maggots were miners, the fabled 'formigas'. Besides being truly the depths of despair, it is the biggest, deepest man-dug pit in the world (100,000 men have been digging for gold for decades).

Kubber flew over it a couple of times. I held Roberto as he filmed. Those below us skeltered in all directions. When Roberto had filmed and we had also seen enough, Kubber flew 60 miles west to Grande Carajás.

Here the devastation was as bad if not worse. Entire mountains had been hacked open for iron-ore and bauxite. The difference being that here it was being done by machines. There were mammoth excavators and house-sized trucks in two mile long train-loads continuously trundling the 500 miles to the coast and the smelter at Sáo Luis. Again there were people scurrying away at our presence. This time though I was worried. The place is controlled by the Military. They might have started shooting.

On the journey home we circled the dams across the Araguaia and Tocantins rivers and filmed them as well. It was evening by the time we arrived back in Tabajara.

Though the afternoon was depressing, Rainbow and Paceillo depressed me more. They had changed their minds.

Everything we had agreed to last night they no longer considered relevant. If what I (and Roberto) had done wasn't good enough, I would be man enough to acknowledge. But just changing their minds is so hard to take. I was up at dawn, as was Roberto. I had had him film the departing soldiers and village volunteers (including the ones Pedro couldn't accommodate and who will have to wait for another day). After their departure, he had filmed the children in their white tunics reciting, in English, their arithmetic. From the children, Roberto had next filmed the women amid their bumper piles of produce ready for market tomorrow. Roberto recorded the ones who spoke English well enough, to relate the wonders happening to them and their families, including the boon of free electricity. Then to the men who had remained, showing soufins powering trucks and tell, as well as show, just how amazing is the acceleration and the 'fuel', just half a cup of water. And as soon as Roberto had finished filming Lucia, we had been up and away to the Serra Pelada.

With Terbal hovering behind and Rainbow to her side, Paceillo said what with the studio being fully automated, it is possible to transmit transcriptions of Susem "visual archive" as Terbal termed it. At once I wondered why they had not mentioned its existence earlier, let alone shown me any of it. But before I could say anything, Rainbow added "It's very good, spellbinding."

What irked me most was that I was supposed to be in charge! We had barely begun and already I was being usurped. Though before I had chance to say as such, Paceillo asked to see the afternoon's filming. She then showed it to Tearo and the others on Sieba. They all agreed that both the Sierra Pelada and Grande Carajás would do wonderfully.

Mollified, I asked to see some of this Susem "visual archive." I sat in silence for an hour and would have watched for longer if there had been time. "Which ones do you think should be shown?" was all I could say.

But by then Rainbow and Paceillo had changed their minds yet again! Both said that there should be some of this, a little of that, including a showing of Sardon (he is the tocan which now hovers above us). I mentioned that there was only a day remaining to do what had to be done including the voiceover. Rainbow said she saw no problem with this.

With no assurances they wouldn't change their minds yet again, I left them and sought Menpemelo. What I had seen raised more questions.

"Before I can answer, it is best that I explain some other related topics," Menpemelo said. And once again I was rapt with attention. "You may recall," she began, "how all is waves, vibrations and resonance."

I said I did, but didn't dare add that I had forgotten a fair amount.

"Once the pitch of a wave is known, it is possible to neutralise it with another one."

White noise came to mind.

"Counter, neutralise, Secondary inter-Tertiary wave resonance and their, what you call 'gravitational' effect, will cease. While it is a faculty we Susem have developed, it also appears to be possessed by some humans."

"What? Levitation by humans!" I exclaimed.

Upon which she took me to Terbal.

"Secondary inter-Tertiary resonance nullification by humans you vant?" Terbal said, appearing eager to please, and me realising that five days of ten screen non-stop Internet accessing had been as much to do with searching as surfing.

"By occurrence dates you vant?"

"Yes," said Menpemelo.

"All?"

"Just the most recent."

"Vitnessed?"

"Yes."
"Independent verification?"
"Yes."
"Daniel Home, Hartford, years 1852 to '92, Henry Gordon, New York, 1858, James Cathcart, Indiana, same year, William Eglington, Calcutta, 1862, Father Luiz, Santa Cruz, 1911, Nikoli Damascolluf, Warsaw, 1933, Sabbyar Pullavar, Shivapur, 1936, Nana Owuku, Togo, 1975..."
"That is sufficient Terbal, thank you," said Menpemelo.
"You're velcome," said Terbal as he whizzed back to his screens.
Menpemelo then said "Sweep your hand across this screen."
It was Rico's old TV. As I did as she asked I sensed a tingling sensation and heard cracking. "Static," I said
But Menpemelo said "Channelled Secondary wave concentration reacting to your like channelled concentrations." And seeing I didn't understand, she said "Like charges repel, do they not? The screen gives out a positive charge and so do you. Positive charges are continuously emitted by all lifeforms. In a like way, so is the ability to levitate. However, to have any effect, just as electricity has to, it requires enhancing and concentrating."
As she spoke, I recalled schooldays, rubbing feet on nylon carpets, fingertips on zip fasteners of girls' dresses (and they then hitting me).
Half convinced of the plausibility of levitation by humans, I listened on. "Just as electricity can be generated in quantity, concentrated into intensity and thus powerfulness," Menpemelo said, "so too can levitation. Not just to neutralise the effects of what you term gravity but to generate an opposing force. It is the harnessing of this which enables hen-gers, vedas, tocans and other to rise and hover. It is also the intensity concentrated emission of this power which enables objects to be raised from the surface of the Earth for example."
While still having difficulty grasping what she said, focused light, lasers, slicing through steel did pass across my mind, of how a century ago such a notion would have been scoffed at. But being a trite cocky, I asked "How do they fly, what propels them?"
"I was about to come to this," she said and giving me an "oh do be quiet" look. "As you know," she continued, "water is the consequence of oxygen and hydrogen combining.
"The two frothicles of hydrogen in the water molecule, though 'entrapped' by a single yet bigger frothicle of oxygen, still exist unchanged. And as I mentioned earlier, the combining or 'moleculing' of frothicles creates a resonance."
An image of the imprisoned "Hydrogen Two" rattling the bars of their "Oxygen Cell" passed through my thoughts.
"However, if water is passed over the surfaces of certain other frothicles," Menpemelo continued, "these will enhance the hydrogen-oxygen resonance. In turn, this new, resulting resonance can be further increased by passing it

over yet different frothicles. Providing that all of these are in specific concentrations and combinations, and are positioned in a particular way relative to one another, it is possible to increase the original hydrogen-oxygen resonance an indefinite number of times."

The heightened sound of the "Hydrogen Two" rattling their bars and rebounding throughout the prison now filled my mind.

"Inside such 'architecture'," continued Menpemelo sounding technical, and I just about following her, "not only will many Tertiary deflected Secondary waves enter and be accommodated, they will also be detained."

"Where does such a concentration of Secondary waves..." I attempted to ask but got no further before she, and without pause, gave the answer or rather, answers.

"Secondary waves, as I mentioned before," Menpemelo continued, "continuously pass by Tertiary ones. As I also mentioned, some Tertiary waves cause Secondary ones to defect more than others and thus concentrating them. Although Secondary waves enter into such a structure, it is possible to so construct it so they will have difficulty in leaving until such times as they are enabled or "allowed" to. They are, if you like, compressed, concertinaed. When the structure is filled to its capacity with Secondary waves, others unable to enter, pass it by."

The image of the prison's hall jam-packed with listless visitors of the "Hydrogen Two" eagerly awaiting their chance to leave, and a "No Vacancies" sign stuck on the prison gates, also passed through my thoughts.

"The moment they are allowed to do so," she added, "the Secondary wave concentration departs the structure as one. It is this sudden burst of force which provides propulsion."

With the vision in my mind of the visitors charging out of the prison gates in unison, I continued listening to Menpemelo.

"Though at first it appears implausible that such energy can be obtained from the thinness of air for example, it is no more than a simple matter of concentration. By employing a number of these structures collectively, it is possible to provide energy for continuous propulsion. As one discharges others are recharging. Discharging Secondary waves from several structures simultaneously produces accelerated propulsion.

"Hydrogen is used because its wave formation is the most basic and it is easier to manage its resonance. Also it is universally available. The water molecule is used because it is a convenient form of bounded hydrogen. The resonance of other elements can and are also used as initiators of energy but we have found them to be only useful in exceptional circumstances."

With almost a sigh, she added "If you on Earth had devoted the effort and resources you have on the development of nuclear power, to this form of energy instead, there would not be all the damage fission has caused."

I though it inappropriate to mention that nuclear power had little to do with providing electricity but all to do with Big Power military machismo (threatening people with water weapons doesn't have the same panache as nuclear ones) for I knew what her reply would be.

Instead I asked "How long will such structures last?"

"It varies," she said matter-of-factly, "from an instant to infinity."

"Indefinitely, for ever?" I asked.

"Some of the scule soufins on Kubber are..." she said with her tone unchanged, "...older than me, and I am..." and pausing again, "...in Earth years 120, 125...something such as that."

"One hundred and twenty five?" I exclaimed.

"Hmn uhm, I have not really given it much thought but when one is travelling, keeping a record of the passing of time loses relevance."

"But you only look twenty five?"

"Cellular resonance therapy," she said with a casually assured tone.

HRT had nothing on this. The acronym "CRT" immediately sprang into my mind. Thoughts of money nipped in there as well. Those of levitation and propulsion promptly went up the back.

"How is this regression therapy done?" I casually asked.

"Although advanced lifeforms are composed of cells, it is cells combining which form advanced life," replied Menpemelo enigmatically. "If the composition of a cell at the optimum point of its development is known, it is possible, once the initial record of its resonances has been made, to ensure that this resonance is maintained. Keep it unchanged and the cells' constituents and their interactions will also remain unchanged."

I was about to say "That is all very well for cells but what about the rest?" but she promptly said "This is the beginning, the simple part."

So I said "Oh," instead.

"The resonances of the optimum interactions between cells and groups of cells can also be similarly kept unchanged, in turn, the same applies to those between the constituent parts of a lifeform, such as me," she said with a smile and adding, "also the interactions between them all."

"But this must come to billions?"

"Billions of billions," she said giving another smile.

"How long does it take to do?"

"About two hours to set up the initial templates, then ten minutes once every 250 days thereafter for a check-up."

"But when does it happen, how do you know when it is the right time for it to be done?"

"As soon as we have matured from male to female we are monitored. If there is need for any regression or corrective treatment, this is done first. When it is completed the templates are made."

"You mean you live for ever?"

"Of course not, there would be little sense!" she said with her smile turning to laughter, then adding, "My aura would become tired if I did."

"For how long then? Aura? What is this aura?"

"Ooh, I will probably exist in this form for a while longer yet?" she said sounding like a knowing older sister talking to her younger brother.

I looked at her, then thought of my wrinkles, the differences in our ages and then said "Can I have it done?"

"No. It would not work for males."

"Oh," I said (and thoughts of half the customer base disappearing).

"For us, being male is a state we mature from, there has been no need to develop templates for the male form. Except for mating, being male is something we cannot wait to mature out of."

"But couldn't you just adjust for males, as you did the mormic?"

"No."

"Why not?"

"The cells of your males are the same as when we are male. When we repaired Roberto we analysed and compared his cells with Lucia's."

"And?"

"Congenitally constricted chromosomal development."

"Oh. What's that?"

"Males are a part short of a full genome."

"Oh Ys and Xs?" I said knowingly.

"And the consequential resonationial differences," she said.

"It's only a little bit of difference."

At this she laughed loudly and retorted "Look at the resulting physical differences! Who forms offspring!" And before I had time to reply, "But these are almost as nothing compared to the neurological changes."

I wished I had not questioned, for Menpemelo flowed on, "Sensory neural responses increased by a factor of at least twenty, the brain compresses and progresses into functioning increasingly bi-hemispherically. The consequent auralate-falx cerebri pathways only really begin to develop when they do. And also," she said stroking her hand, "our skin improves."

I was about to ask, because she had mentioned it yet again, what did she mean by "aura" when Paceillo appeared and said "Come, look."

So we did, and after I had overcome my initial terror, I realised, as I watched the event unfold, we were all having to change our minds over what was going to be shown on Rainbow's next telecast.

55: KEN

Serves them right. Let them squirm, that's what I say. But then I always knew there was something fishy about the French. A nation of cowards and bullies, they've never won anything in a fair fight and they're always causing trouble.

That Rainbow came on the tele Monday saying there would be a long programme Tuesday night at eight about the Susem. Harry was happy, gave him time to put a sign up saying he had the big screen and was putting his prices down for the evening.

Eight o'clock comes, there's a fair crowd in the Greenwood and Rainbow duly appears. But without further ado she said there had been a change of programme. It wouldn't be about the Susem but something more urgent.

Dead clever how she started off. First she said "These are the ladies of Tabajara preparing to take their crops to market." And as she spoke there's scenes of women carrying baskets filled with different things. Rainbow then interviewed them. They tell her how everything is wonderful and things like that. Other women are shown loading baskets onto an old bus.

Then, "These are the children reciting their times tables," and the camera switched to a dozen and more knee-high kids in little white uniforms. They follow up their tables with smiles and waves then they all start singing "Frere a Jacque." They are still singing when the middle ones step back to show this pair of legs in dark trousers. The camera pans up the legs and as it does, and all the kids still singing "donnez vous...sonnez..." Rainbow is saying "And this is Captain Jac Forissier."

As it does it is obvious from the man's uniform that he is in the navy. By then the camera showed his face. Rainbow went on, "and these are his crew." With that the camera showed this crowd of matelots all sat together.

I was trying to make out what was going on when she said "And this is their submarine the Tonner, which they all sailed in." The camera then switches to a desert scene and right in the middle of it is this submarine but it's in two bits.

I'm still trying make out what is going on when Rainbow said "And this is the nuclear missile Captain Forissier ordered his men to fire from their submarine at the ladies, the children and everyone else in Tabajara." With that, this big long missile came on the screen.

And as it did, there were a good few gasps round the pub. But they hadn't died down before Rainbow said "And now Captain Forissier is going to tell why he and his crew fired it."

Harry might have put his prices down but at that moment no one was drinking, let alone buying. All eyes including the bar staff's were on the screen, but this French captain hadn't been talking for long before there were shouts from round the bar of "Bastards" and a good few other things as well.

He went on about how he had been ordered to fire the missile. As Rainbow interviewed him you could see from the questions she asked him, that he was not a happy man. She went through with him bit by bit of how they had been in the Atlantic, were given orders on Saturday to go south just off the coast of French Guinea. He said he had been ordered to wait till Monday evening when the European Space place they have down there were due to launch a rocket. At the same time as they sent theirs up he had been ordered to fire one of his at the Susem.

He told how his submarine was hundreds of fathoms below the sea when they had been suddenly plucked out of it. There was a good bit of laughing round the pub when he said the submarine was landed on the shore somewhere, but they couldn't get out because there was all this water pouring down on them. And the moment it had stopped the submarine was picked up again and carried through the air. There was even more laughter when he told how all he could see through his periscope were stars and clouds.

Rainbow asked him what would have happened if the missile had gone off. He said it was programmed to explode above the ground and would have killed everything for hundreds of miles. With that Rainbow picked up one of the kids and said "Like Emilia?"

He muttered all shamefaced, "Oui."

With that she picked up another, "And Guido?"

With both kids smiling and waving at the camera, he muttered "Oui" again.

Rainbow asked him more questions but from the way she asked them you could see she was enjoying making him squirm. And from the remarks going round the pub everyone else was as well.

Every question she asked she kept repeating it till he had answered her properly. And when she had put the kids down, ooh did she ask them. But as she was going at him I remembered, as from their remarks, so did a good few others round pub, that her name's the same as that boat they blew up down in New Zealand or somewhere. Everyone round the bar was soon shouting "Go on Rain, give it him," and things like that.

"Do you know why you were ordered to fire your missile at the same time as the Ariane launch? Why couldn't you have fired from the Atlantic and not at some other time?"

"We were doing as instructed," he said all shamefaced.

"Who told you?"

"Brest, département de la Guerre, Ministry de l'Défense nationale."

"Who in the Ministry of Defence would have authorised such a mission?"

"Le Ministre...Maurice Weygand."

"And he would not have approved such an action alone would he?"

"Non."

"And you said earlier did you not, Captain, you could not have launched your missile without the use of American navigation satellite coordination codes?"

"It is so."

With that there was more than a gasp round the pub. But more with what she had him say next.

"And it is also your understanding is it not, captain, that your missiles could not have been fired without the consent of the American government?"

"It is so."

"Why do you think they and your government would have wanted to do such a thing as exploding a nuclear missile, killing many people and contaminating the land?"

"It was not for me to question...to erase the Alien invaders I think...to protect la France...er, I do not know."

"And to kill so many people...such as these?"

With that the camera panned away to hundreds of people all dressed in white. And as it swept over them, Rainbow went on questioning, "Do they look as though they have been invaded, that they are in fear?"

And as he said "Non" the people started shouting "Viva Harmony! Viva Susem! Viva Freedom!" and few more Vivas! on top of that.

"Do you think the people of France would have approved of you and your government's intentions to kill all these people?"

"Non."

"Are you sorry for your actions?"

"Oui...yes."

"Could you ask your crew if they are also sorry?"

With that he turned to them and shouted "Avez-vous 'onteu de ce que vous avez fait?"

And they all shouted back "Oui."

"Do you think your government should also say that it is sorry as well?"

"Yes."

"And what do you think your government should do now, to show how sorry it is?"

"I do not know, I cannot say."

"Ten billion US dollars paid over in seven days perhaps?"

"Er...yes, yes."

Rainbow turned to the screen and with a well pleased look said "As was said here on Saturday, all nuclear power stations including those of France will be removed during the coming days. However, until the apology to the people of Tabajara and the compensation mentioned by Captain Forissier have been received, it will be inappropriate to provide soufin energy modules to the territory of France."

That caused a good few roars and cheers round the pub.

"The nuclear reactor of the submarine," she continued, "has been removed as have the warheads of its missiles but not the other explosives and ammunition on board. As there is no wish in Tabajara for the rest of the submarine to remain where it is, it will be sent back to France on Thursday and unless otherwise informed, returned, give or take a kilometre, to the Ministry of Defence in Paris, from a height of 10,000 metres."

The roars and cheers in the pub got even louder.

"Captain Forissier and those of his crew wishing to return to France will be flown back on that day. Also on Thursday the programme scheduled for today will be shown at this same hour."

Looking across the bar I saw Harry rubbing out 'Tuesday' on his board and chalking in 'Thursday'.

56: BOSNIA

In east Mostar, the once Bosnian part of that city, there is a railway tunnel. It is a kilometre and a half long and stretches between the northern suburb of Brankovac and the southern one of Bjelousine. In the early hours of Wednesday it became crammed with many thousands of people from both suburbs seeking refuge. But their sanctuary was short lived.

Just as many people had fled to the central district of Stara Caršija. Their stay there was also brief. More had streamed in a panicked, jumbled throng over the sole remaining bridge spanning the River Neretva into west Mostar. Amid the turmoil dozens of people fell into the Neretva and were swept away by its fast flowing snowmelt waters.

With increasing trepidation people on the west bank watched events in the east. Most already knew that there was no escape from their side of the city either. Every road, pathway, even tracks were blocked by swarms of hen-gers who stung those who had not yet been sprayed with dye.

Single vedas had been seen before but now hundreds encircled the city. As they hovered above, their downward beams created a continuous wall of light. Yet more vedas lit the entire east bank. And this time there were not single platoons of Gurkhas but half a brigade. With them were the Khmer Rouge equipped with wooden poles, ropes and large foamed lined clogs.

Women and children were corralled, sprayed and sent on their way to Croatia. But the men, although their heads were sprayed red, were not castrated. Instead they were harnessed together by necks and wrists yoked to the poles into teams four abreast and ten deep. With a circling escort of hen-gers and a whip wielding Khmer Rouge behind them they were driven, shod in clogs to the countryside and mine clearance.

Some people tried to resist and hide from the Gurkhas and hen-gers. None succeeded. Those hiding in the railway tunnel, once their presence was detected, were driven from one end by a swarm of hen-gers and onto waiting Gurkhas at the other. Within an hour of the vedas' arrival east Mostar was empty of people.

West Mostar took longer. Not only is it bigger with many more blocks of high rise flats, but once the rubble remains of Kujundžjluk, the old Turkish quarter had been cleared as well as the nearby pristine Hotel Ero, the luxurious billet of the former EU administration, the emptying of the first suburbs began in earnest. Zahum to the south was first.

Along Markovica Gupca, Zahum's principal thoroughfare, the flats are ten and twelve storeys high. All were crammed with people, their windows and entrances barricaded. Many occupants were armed and sought to defend themselves by firing at the approaching Gurkhas. They did so in vain. The bullets' ricocheting back at the firers' from the hen-gers' protective screen soon brought shooting to a halt. Swarms of more hen-gers blasted through the rooftops of the first flats. Their occupants, waving white flags of surrender, soon streamed onto the streets. People in the other blocks watching events and seeing the pointlessness of resistance began following suit.

For many, as they stepped gingerly into the pre-dawn darkness it was an ironic re-enactment of events of 1992. Then, it was their once Bosnian neighbours with white flags who had emerged to baying Croatian mobs. But this time unlike then, the surrendering men were not butchered nor the women raped. Now there was only the sound of crying.

Groups of women and children traipsed by the Tudjman Centre and along Bulevar Parovića, joining those from the east. Word of their fate, and of those who resisted, swept through the nearby suburbs of Bakšim and Zgoni. Block after block emptied onto the streets in mute acceptance of their fate. The only difference being that the occupants had time to change into their best clothes.

By six o'clock only cats and dogs remained in Mostar. As the women and children began their 40 kilometre journey to Croatia they heard the sounds of the first mines detonating.

At the same time and 170 kilometres to the north, another column was making the much longer trek eastward from Banja Luka to Serbia. By noon all the remaining towns and cities had been emptied of their Serb and Croatian populations. And teams totalling 20,000 men began clearing the countryside of mines located by the accompanying hen-gers. Others had been despatched to their own former prison camps at Batković, Omarska and Previja to await their turn at mine clearing but none were subjected to the brutalities inflicted on the former Bosnian inmates.

By nightfall many Bosnians who had fled from Croats and Serbs to forests and mountains began the return to their former homes. Those whose homes no longer stood soon found another.

By the end of Wednesday a further 500 Khmer Rouge had arrived at Neum, Bosnia's port city. During the day, further to the south at Ragusa, Colonel Tambassing's aides, under Tearo's guidance, began organising the school-children and students who had volunteered as interpreters to work with his men in Bosnia.

Others, who had worked non-stop for four days, completed preparations for the first trials. The men sent to Korčula and still nursing the soreness between their loins anxiously awaited their fates. More continued to arrive. Despite the thousands now gathered, both the Susem and Colonel Tambassing were aware that none from either of the Croatian or Serbian administrations and military had presented themselves at Pelješac. Similarly, there were no signs of Serb and Croatian men gathering at the Bosnian border crossings.

Although not unduly concerned at this lack of willingness on the part of Serbs and Croatians to give themselves up, both the Susem and the Colonel were irked at the prospect of having to spend so much effort unnecessarily. But by Thursday, in Croatia at least, events changed this unwillingness.

57: CAPTAIN FORISSIER

After the terror there was irritation but after that, cordiality. It took an hour before the submarine was dunked down in front of the Ibiapaba. I was all for meting out a bashing to the crew for attempting such a terrible thing. So were the villagers and soldiers. But Paceillo said "Use your adversary's strength against themselves and to your advantage. Shame them," then added, "use charm." So we did.

The crew wouldn't come out, so the hen-gers exploded in and started stinging. The conning tower promptly popped open and crew were zipping out in no time at all. Like the pilots on Saturday, the sailors were apprehensive when soldiers and vedas whisked them up to the green by the Pousada. They had expected, so they said later, a lynching party not a welcoming one. Some, including the captain understood English so the villagers engaged them in friendly conversation as to why they did it.

The Pousada's takings were up for a Monday night. This was due not just to Elana, on asking me the EuroFranc-Real exchange rate and doubling her prices for the occasion, but such was their anxiety the French were only too willing to do all the buying. (Free drink does wonders for international relations).

But the drinking had barely begun when the sky was lit blue and purple as Sardon and his vedas removed the submarine's reactor and missile warheads. At the time no one, me as well, knew precisely what Sardon was doing and probably none of the others, sailors included, had ever seen anything so big, let alone hovering above. The villagers did look up from time to time at Sardon but they didn't really let the sight of him interfere with their drinking.

Rainbow appeared not long after the sailors. Soon she had charmed everything out of them from the captain to crew. Though I think their disorientation from the moment they had fired their missile had something to do with them spilling the beans. After another hour, with any money on them long gone, their watches and rings in hock to Elana, Rainbow outlined her revised programme. The captain was only too ready to agree. Though I think the cachaça had more than got to him by then.

On Tuesday morning and after the sailors had spent the night sleeping outside the Pousada (they being in no state to go further) Rainbow swung into action. Not only did she marshal the entire village and sailors but the firmness of her instruction improved Roberto's abilities no end. By nine o'clock she was overseeing the editing. The end result looked as though all was recorded in one go and not the umpteen rehearsals and retakes it actually took. I was surprised, and impressed, that Rainbow knew so much.

Paceillo meanwhile was scheming. She had already asked a string of questions about the submarine and the sailors. Once again I grasped she had taken in more of what I had mentioned before, this time the reactions of the people in power to being usurped. Though when I told her about the captain telling about the Americans, I just had to add the French were small fry and I'd not be surprised if the Americans hadn't actually put them up to it.

Through Tuesday and right up to when they went away today, the sailors had not a moment to themselves. The women, with Elana leading, had the entire village organised. In no time at all each little group adopted a trio of sailors and had them busy the days through. On Tuesday they were helping round the smallholdings and elsewhere. Though this was not before Elana had children conduct some sailors down the cliff face pathways to the submarine, or what was left of it, and take the money from the captain's safe.

Apart from their tasks, which all the sailors appeared to enjoy, there were the distractions of the children and their hen-gers and of course the teaching machines. Now there is the voice of Lucia being beamed from each screen, everyone's attention and enjoyment is much increased. Although also attentive, the sailors were fascinated with them. Those who spoke English were soon participating with talks on life in France and the sea. By the end of the afternoon it was hard to credit that the day before they had been set on annihilating us all. And at five o'clock, along with everyone else, they were watching themselves on the TV.

The sailors asked me and everyone else about the Susem and were asking to see them. The villagers, children included, didn't really need the word from Paceillo about keeping mum. As far as they are concerned they look upon the Susem as their own special secret.

Pedro, the soldiers and villagers who went with him returned to Tabajara Tuesday evening. There was coolness when they and the sailors first met but being flush with Francs, the atmosphere soon warmed with the drink. By evening's end international relations were not just cemented but set in stone. It wasn't just the flow of free drinks (so many did, that on Wednesday Elana had to send out for fresh supplies) which fuelled friendships further, it was Pedro and the others telling of events on their two days away.

It was also the main reason for their return. The towns of Ubajara, Tianguá and the hamlets in between, were soon seeing advantages in accepting the proposals Pedro proffered. Of course, there had been some softening among these people by their last Wednesday's experiences, the sightseers from Ubajara, Roberto's evangelism in Tianguá and the soufin sales there too. The village's women, their stalls in Tianguá's markets on Tuesday piled high with the best produce, swayed waverers as well to the wonders awaiting. Pedro and the others, he said persuaded no end of people to form in threes and nines and groups of nine times nine. He had returned to tell Paceillo and the villagers the expected numbers arriving today to see the wonders brought and wrought by the Susem.

Pedro hadn't stopped at the Ibiapaba. By Monday evening he and the others had fanned out across the countryside to the east, though the roadblocks

World condemns French nuclear attack on S...

France erupts in fury

Jullian Haricks in Paris

THE FRENCH Government was on the defensive yesterday.

Hundreds of thousands of people throughout France took to the streets in an unprecedented display of protest against their government's actions.

A number of protests became violent as huge crowds attempted to storm government buildings. Security forces were unable to contain many of the protests which often turned into full scale riots as people turned the anger against the government on to the police.

The area outside the Defence Ministry saw some of the most violent confrontations between rioters and the paramilitary police, the CRS.

Extensive damage was reported to have...

The Foreign Ministry and the National Assembly were also attacked by rioters The Interior Ministry has so far declined to issue any comment to the disturbances and their scale.

However, there are reports of many casualties, some serious, from all the hospitals through-out the capital. The Central Paris fire brigade is said to have attended more than a hundred blazes caused by rioters.

Disturbances were reported from cities across the country Those with military bases nearby were the worse affected. Both Toulon and Brest saw rioting and frequent battles between protesters and the police. In Lyon and the nearby military base of Creys-Malville experienced many thousands of protesters demanding the clo-

Riots sweep France

by Allen Morley in Paris

RIOTING SPREAD throughout France yesterday in protest against the country's naval undercover action against the Susem.

Many government buildings were ransacked. The main Ministry of Defence office complex on the Pal de Fontency was stormed and set ablaze by rioters.

Security forces were taken aback by the scale and ferociousness of popular protest. There are many reported incidences of the police being forced to flee from the rioters.

Paris' Boulevard St Germain was litter stones and broken glass and signifying the rout of the city's gendarmerie and its tougher CRS

An estimated 500,000 people of all ages and classes took to Paris' streets in protest at the government's attack against the Susem base in Brazil in a spontaneous show of indigonation of what had been ...tedly in the coun... greater

HE TELEGRAPH

Space Agency outraged at French

By Polly Portillo in Kourou

THE French were branded "absolutey bloody fools" by Dr. Hans Nies, Operations Director of the European Space Agency, for their the abortive firing of a nuclear missile

Dr. Nies said the French missile launch jeopardises the Space Agency's credibility. He said: "The French, by their actions, the good name and international standing of the Agency has become besmirched.

"They have undermined the many years of advancement in launch vehicles not only for satellites but for the Alpha Space Station. The French military are worse than fools, what if their missile's warhead had exploded, as they patently planned it to do, we also could have been contami-

"Everyone at the Agency, including my French colleagues, are signing a declaration dissassociating the Agency from the French Government and demanding that in the future we report directly to the EU", he said.

Dr. Nies also said that he and his senior staff were of the view that there was more to gained from cooperating with the Aliens. "They are an advanced civilisation and should be given considerat

Paris burns

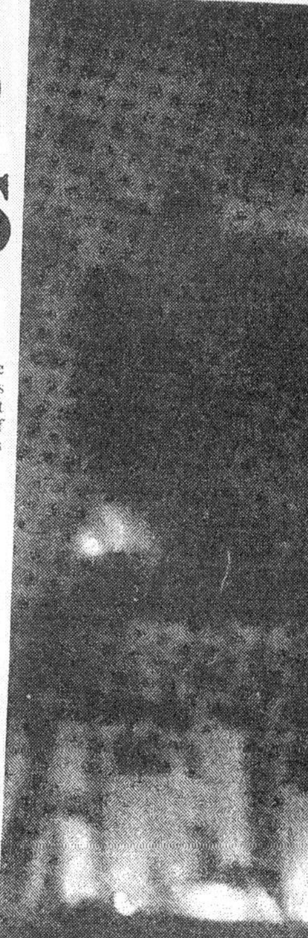

BY JOHN DEAN IN PARIS

GOVERNMENT buildings across France were under siege yesterday as angry protestors against the French government's attempted attack against the Susem in Brazil.

Many of the country's police and security forces were unable to contain the protestors' onslaughts. Police in a number of cities were themselves forced to flee from the wrath of enraged protestors.

Scores of deliberate attacks by the rioters sent many government buildings up in flames and with the firs services unable to break though the angry mobs.

CGT, the French TUC, and its sister, though communist dominated trade union movement, the RDF held a series hastily organised protest rallies in Paris and other major cities throughout France including Lyon, Bordeaux, Marseille and Nantes

"These fools have besmirched the nation's honour The government must resign immediately if France is ever to regain its dignity."

The Defence Ministry's main department offices in the Pal de Fontency was reported to have been seriously damaged by fires set alight by angry protestors. The nearby Ecole Militare and the adjacent Ministry of Communications were also centres of fierce and ugly confrontations between rioters and CRS security forces.

The Foreign Ministry on the Quai d' Orsay and the nearby General Assembly, saw further fierce confrontations between police and protestors. Only repeated baton charges and water cannon eventually succeeded in driving the rioters back from both buildings.

However, when the police pursued the protestors into

around Tianguá stopped them going further along the main roads. Instead they had concentrated on backland villages. Pedro and the others related the wretchedness they had found. In some places, he said, there had initially been apprehension at their arrival. But the telling by villagers from Tabajara accompanying him of wonders awaiting assured away any anxieties. He also said that in some of the villages they had come across what he called "pequeno pistoleiros", petty gun toting thugs.

These he said, often held such sway over the inhabitants that they were in fear of even talking to Pedro let alone accepting his proposals. However, he said, a flurry of hen-gers soon routed these hoodlums. He also added, and he was quite nonchalant about it, he had Big Luiz (Tearo's acquaintance) bang pairs of these thugs' heads together, whereupon the others stripped them of their clothes, tied them on their horses and sent them packing. There was much laughter when he told of how in one instance they had piled half a dozen naked hoodlums into their truck, which, such was their keenness to speed away that they promptly skidded the truck down a ditch and were all pitched out again.

Whenever these confrontations occurred they were soon followed, so Pedro said, by the villagers giving the whereabouts of other local pequeno pistoleiros. In turn these too were sent stripped on their way. He said he was willing to do this because it aided acceptance and saved on time. Though he did add he had drawn the line at a hamlet near Granja where the locals wanted him to take-on a nearby latifundia which was diverting away their water supply.

Pedro had also brought back for Milophinia, who now represents the minero-horticulturists, the soil samples she had asked him to take.

By Wednesday morning Captain Forissier had become Pedro's bosom pal. And he had arranged for the captain and other sailors to accompany his men and fresh village volunteers on their next foray, this time to the west.

They were away all the day. And while they were, everyone in the village, between study and work, began preparing for today's guests. In between my studies I was busy down below abetting Paceillo's next plan, as well as working with Rainbow for her telecast tonight. But there was time too to talk to Menpemelo and Milophinia. I asked her about the soil samples.

"The significance of these," she said, "is that they reinforce the observations made during our preliminary assays on Mont Macambirá."

Before I had time to say "Oh," she had gushed on. "There is hereabout an abundance of the minerals required, not only for most of the horticultural growth needs of the fields, but for aqueourist, especially nekteric biomass planktonic enhancement as well as for fabrication smelting applications. The ground, see here in this assay sample analysis," she gushed and furling out her chart screen, "suggests in some instances the terrain is capable of yielding more than one part in eight of iron."

Again, and even before I had time to conjure images of strip mines and

Features Page 15

mbassies sacked French trade banned

France faces World backlas

by Polly Portillio in Rio de Janerio and Foreign Staff

FRANCE faced international condemnation around the world launching nuclear siles against the em base in northern zil.

ithin minutes of zil announcing the ering of diplomatic ations with France, French embassy in asilia was ransacked d set ablaze by angry owds. French conlates in Rio de neiro and Sao Paulo re also attacked.

Brazilian President, olivar Rocha told a acked joint session of ne Congress and enate: "The Brazilian ation has been stabbed the back in an act of nprovoked aggression y a country we had his-

President Rocha announced a list of sanctions and other measures against France and asked for immediate ratification by both chambers of parliament. These included the unilateral cancellation of sovereign and other debt due to France, the expelling of all French military personnel, the breaking of all trade and cultural ties between the two countries.

The President brushed aside calls for the annexation of French Guiana as "inappropriate". He also refused calls for the arrest of French nationals in Brazil. "Our quarrel is not with the French people but with their Government", he said.

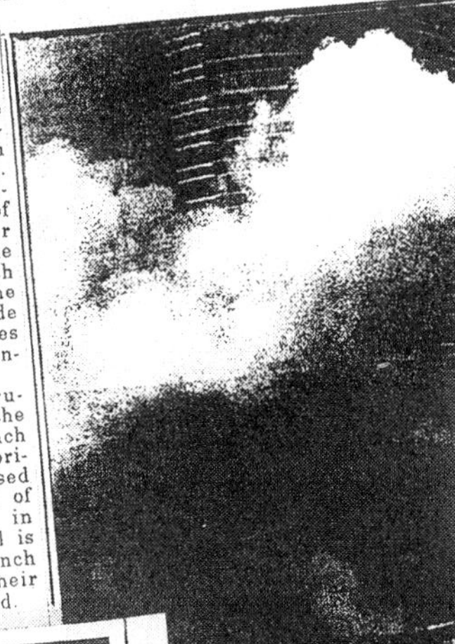

Page 2

Latin attac Frenc

by JOHN SHAWCROSS IN BUENOS AIRES

FRENCH commercial and cultural interests across Argentina came under attack as angry Argentineans protested against France's attempted nuclear strike against neighbouring Brazil.

The French embassy in Buenos Aires was the scene of ugly scuffles between police and demonstrators attempting to set fire to the building. The nearby French cultural centre was not so fortunate. Angry mobs burnt the building to the ground.

Many car showrooms selling French cars suffered similar fates. Both Renault and Citroen dealerships in Buenos Aires and Argentina's second city of Córdoba reported that every single one of their distributors had suffered at the hands of protestors.

Eduardo Duhalde, director of Argentina's biggest Renault distributors suffered at the hands of angry mobs. Standing in front of his burnt out, boarded up showroom, said: Our business is ruined. We have lost everything."

Elsewhere in South America the protests have been no less than

BAC

Latins oust French

By JULIAN SHEPHERD in Panama City

CENTRAL and South America have severed diplomatic relations with France, in an unprecedented show of unanimity.

An emergency meeting of the Organisation of American States (OAS), issued a joint declaration stating its members were severing diplomatic relations with France immediately. Only Canada and the US abstained.

The Brazilian representative, Henri Cardoso, received a standing ovation as he called for further tough measures against France in retaliation for the attempted nuclear attack on his country

one American nation is an attack against us all. South America is covered by the Tlarelolco Treaty making our continent a nuclear free zone. All the big five nuclear powers, including France, are signatories agreeing to abide by the Treaty".

Other South American countries are now expected to follow the Brazilian lead in making tough trade sanctions against France.

When asked of the Alien presence in South America, OAS general Secretary Carlo Salinas said: It is an internal matter for Brazil. The OAS has not been asked by Brazil for assistance, therefore we cannot do anything until they do".

France mu pay 'fine immediat

by Arian Morley in Paris

OPPOSITION Parties throughout France have demanded an immediate settlement of Susem demands for a billion dollars for attempting to attack them with nuclear missiles.

Socialist leader, Gespard Dumas told at a party conference in Lille: "Unless the Government of France acknowledges the folly of this criminal act, all France will suffer. Reynaud must realize the peril he has plunged the country"

The conference later unanimously passed an emergency resolution stating: "The PSF on behalf of the French Nation dis-associate [ourselves] from the action of the ruling Gaulists. We call upon the Govern-

accede to the penalty incurred by its illegal activities"

Similar demands were made by France's Greens, the so called Coalition Verde. Their spokesperson, Michelle Bercer said: "The Government must pay the Susem or else we will all suffer. Reynaud and his cronies are fools, they must now see they have caused a calamity. If they do not pay by Thursday Paris will be finished".

Paul Lavel, leader of the National Front, whose votes the Government coalition are dependant upon, issued a sharply critical statement: "People of France, in this period of darkness, brought about by

Similar demands were made by France's Greens, the so called Coalition Verde. Their spokesperson, Michelle Bercer said: "The Government must pay the Susem or else we will all suffer. Reynaud and his cronies are fools, they must now see they have caused a calamity. If they do not pay by Thursday Paris will be finished".

Paul Lavel, leader of the National Front, whose votes the Government coalition are dependant upon, issued a sharply critical statement: "People of France, in this period of darkness brought about by the perfidy of wrongdoing by those in power

Gran Carajás, Milophinia, unabated, flowed on, "As we have already succeeded in adapting, by accelerated genome and cellular advancement, several of the plants already existent on the upper elevations of Mont Macambirá to extract iron, the next procedure is to establish suitable preliminary in-situ growing areas. This will begin as soon as there are among your fellows those capable of so doing."

I did actually manage an "Oh" at this point but still utterly unabated she flowed on, "Potassium is also abundant and these marcasasite pyrite fragments are indicative of sulphur also." With that she showed me some slivers of pale yellow rock. I had no sooner glanced at them than she was flowing again, "However, there appears an overall nitrite-nitrate deficiency in all the samples. While ameliorative replenishment by way of atmospheric nitrogen does not present difficulties as such, it is always preferentially efficient, because of the extensive areas required for minero-horticulture, for the plants to receive the relevant nitrogenous frothicules, molecules directly into their roots systems." By then my mind was beginning to glaze but she continued and out of politeness I carried on listening.

She and the others have bred plants, they look like marigolds, which absorb iron into their roots and then leaves. The crop is mown, the reaping burnt and amid the resulting ash is iron. They are in the process of perfecting other varieties for other ores and minerals. She also said they are planning, as an interim, to intersperse them with another plant they are working on. It looks like a sweet pea, which with a strain of soil bacteria they have mutated acting as go-betweens will act as stop-gap nitrogen fixers.

While all this was impressive enough, I felt it incumbent at the time to mention they had forgotten one small thing, water. There isn't any. The Ibiapaba has plenty but out on the Sertão there's not a drop, only a deluge a decade which drowns things like cattle and people and then it's all gone. But even before I had time to finish saying "The green you see is because of recent rains. It will be gone within the week," Milophinia, way ahead of me, flowed on, "Although Sardon oversees for us, he and his sherpals were scheduled to burrow conduits from the Parnaiba and Tocantins rivers. But because of the disruption to Tuesday's planned announcements, they have had to be delayed."

Though the delay was due to the submarine and sailors arriving and their missile almost, I then understood why Paceillo had been insistent on announcing that non-residents depart forthwith, or face dire consequences.

I mentioned artesian wells and water tables. But Milophinia said it was undesirable upsetting underground water levels and wasteful too. Such, she said, provided buoyancy to the strata above. Remove it and not only in time will the land sink but the water itself would salinate the soil. I did mention irrigation also increased soil's salinity, but after she had described what the Susem mean by irrigation I realised it wouldn't. She also said river water was rich in nutrients beneficial to plants.

Franc falls

By Julian Gray

THE Franc fell to an all-time low of Ff3.56 against the Euromark, following world reaction to the nuclear attack on Brazil.

Although major currencies have exhibited wide swings through the past week they have stayed unchanged relative to one another (the US dollar being the one showing any comparative appreciation).

The Franc has slipped from

There is a widespread view in all the financial markets, that French exports will be adversely affected by worldwide consumer sentiment against their products and services. This is likely to be sustained unless there is a radical reversal of French policies.

Meanwhile, French Government stock rose sharply in all the world's bond markets in anticipation of a hike in French interest rates, with

French missile attack crisis

America fingered

BY JOHN DEAN IN PARIS AND TOM FLETCHER IN WASHINGTON

UNOFFICIAL French defence sources are suggesting that France's attack on the Aliens' base in South America had the backing of the US.

These sources claim that representatives from the US National Security Agency (NSA) arranged with the French Defence Minister, Pierre Weygand's top officials as early as last Thursday to make a series of covert actions against the Aliens. One of which involved the firing of a submarine launched nuclear missile at the Susem's base in northern Brazil with the intention of eliminating them..

These sources are also alleging that an agreement was made be...

French and Americans where France would launch a surprise attack against the Aliens in the west. In return, the US would deploy all of its forces against the Susem in Europe including also using air and ground based nuclear missiles against the Aliens while they were still over the Ukraine and western Russia.

While there has not yet been and official US response to the rumours, unofficially they are dismissed by American defence analysts as 'unrealistic'.

Peter Hunt of the IoS defence think-tank said: "Chiapas and Cuba are one thing but be party to firing at nuclear missile over Brazil at the Alie...

US denies missile involvement

Roisin Devlin
in Washington

PENTAGON officials have vehemently denied claims of US involvement in the abortive French missile attack on the Aliens in Brazil.

The Pentagon said in a terse statement: "The action by French naval forces off the coast of Guiana came as a complete surprise to the United States Government. We rebut in total, all claims implicit and otherwise of providing any assistance in this ill-considered exercise.

"While any aggressive and unilateral action against any of our neighbours and allies, such as ... is condemned utter-

However, defence experts in both the US and Europe question the Pentagon's assertions. "There is no way the French could have launched [their missile] without US assistance," said Daniel Ichan of Georgetown University's Faculty of International Studies.

"What the French submarine captain said is basically true. The French do not have one military satellite capable of providing the detailed data necessary for precision target location. They could not have launched without alerting US hemispheric radars. But most implausible of all in my view, is that the warhead launch controls are provided by our Government and can only be activated with its per-mission" he said.

France isolated in Europe

Julian Horicks in Strasbourg and
David Walle in London

FRANCE was condemned and isolated by all of its European allies yesterday.

An emergency sitting of the European parliament saw speaker after speaker condemn France's covert and failed abortive attack by one of its submarine launching a nuclear missile aimed at northern Brazil and the Susem.

French MEPs were among their country's fiercest critics. French Socialist MEP, Yves Piquet pleaded to his fellow MEPs that France and the French people should not be blamed for the unilateral actions of their government.

Piquet said: "Today, just as yesterday and so it will be tomorrow, the people of France have filled the streets of every city, town and hamlet across my country in protest against the government of Reynauld's criminal actions. I am sure that nobody in France will rest until these criminals are banished from office."

Other European governments' reactions towards have been muted in making any official critical comment to the French actions. Unofficial governmental response has, however, has been less reserved with reactions ranging from regret to outright anger and exasperation.

Sven Järpen, a prominent member of Sweden's Christian Democrats is among those highly critical of France's actions. He thinks that France would have been wiser if it come to terms with the arrival of the Susem and their systematic removal of nuclear power stations, missiles and warheads. He said: "Here in Sweden we are already preparing to say goodbye to our nuclear power stations.

"The Swedish people, hearing so many favourable reports from Russia of the Susem energy eggs, that almost everyone in the country is looking forward to receiving them as well. Perhaps the French actions are the result of their being a little backward toward nuclear power. They have become obsessed in hanging on to it."

Otto Kemp, a member of Austria's rightwing nationalist party, Österreich Ein said: "The French are crazy criminal pigs, they could have us all killed. Their entire government must be put on trial and imprisoned immediately.

In Britain, the government is endeavouring to have a more even-handed approach to France's difficulties. One Foreign Office official, who wishes to be nameless, said: "It's a bit of a bad show all round really. Perhaps the French did respond a trifle hastily towards these Alien chappies. Their letting off one of their missiles at the same time as European Space Agency fellows were sending up one as well was a tad underhand but then one has to see things from the French point of view as well you know.

"After all they wouldn't feel happy without their nuclear power stations, would they?" he said.

Brazil takes it case to the UN

FROM TOM FLETCHER IN NEW YORK

Brazil's foreign minister, Joao Goulart pressed the General Assembly of the United Nations to condemn France's firing of a nuclear missile against his country.

An overwhelming majority of the UN agree with the Brazilian's motion. It is unlikely, however, to be put before the Security Council for several days. The motion is also likely to meet with stiff behind the scenes negotiations before it actually comes before the Security Council.

Following the General Assembly's overwhelming support for Brazil and its strong condemnation of France, UN Secretary, Felipe Gonzales said: The purported French actions while lamentable, need to be seen in the context of the current world situation.

"It is vital," he said, "that during this period of uncertainty and until we know the Alien invaders true purposes here on Earth, that all member states of the UN act in unison towards them.

"To this end it is essential that the UN, being the only truly world forum, be the sole conduit through which all member states to coordinate their policies of response towards the Aliens and that they do not act unilaterally."

Susem irrigation, as outlined by Milophinia, comprises not of dams and wide lined waterways but a myriad of tiny tubes which can be removed from a river at will. At a tube's river end there is a little lump for a pump and a filter, after which it travels up and down, hugging just underground. In turn it's linked with other pipes coming from other parts of the river and other rivers as well. The entire system is alike to arteries, except it has hundreds of little beating hearts. And when they arrive where the water is wanted, just as arteries branch out and become capillaries, so do the pipes. While this is wonder enough, it's what happens to the water when it arrives which is the really amazing part. It doesn't go into the soil but up in the air.

Not all but most. Milophinia said the caatinga (the high, impenetrable, black thorny scrub which grows all over the Serão and never has leaves except when it rains) was an ideal aid for irrigation. When I asked why, she explained. By cutting rings of half acre circles in the caatinga and intermittently pumping a fine spray across each circle, a micro climate, complete with little low lying clouds, is formed in every one. The system the Susem are setting up, she said, comes complete with abilities to add and adjust the composition of the spray including nutrients and temperature. Evaporation, Milophinia added, was caused by heat and that is best stopped by a cooling cover of clouds. And the walls of caatinga acting as windbreaks would stop them from blowing away too soon.

I told her how the Israelis, Americans and others cultivate crops in dry climates by drip feeding each plant. She said that while this was interesting it appeared not to take account of the understanding the Susem have of plants existing not just singularly but as collective entities. The wellbeing of one related to all the others. Plants, she said, communicate to one another. Noting, no doubt, my scepticism she described how the leaves of some plants they had come across on Mont Macambirá exude, when bitten, chemicals into the air which in turn are sensed by their companions. These then prime their prickles and pump poison out of their leaves to keep the biters at bay. She also said there were plants just like that on Sincula and all the other places she had been.

And just as Menepemelo had mentioned, she said that growing food crops above ground was wasteful, inefficient and backward. "Unadvanced," was the word she used.

Meanwhile, above the ground and among the sailors who didn't go with Pedro was Andre LeBlond, the chef and his galley staff. Being French and surrounded by a surfeit of the finest fresh food, they were by Wednesday unable to constrain their cravings for cooking any longer. Word soon went round the village that they were, and with Elana's encouragement, embarked upon exhibiting their culinary capabilities on a farewell feast. And oh what remarkable skills they are. With all the tools of the submarine's kitchens and contents too, fulsome contributions from many of the villagers and willing

ALIENS ATTAC
GREAT BRITA

by SALLY O'SHEA
Defence Reporter

ALIEN reconnaissance craft have been spotted over the east and south coasts of Britain.

The Ministry of Defence media liaison officer, Colonel Giles Sackville in a bid reassure a troubled nation said: Britain's armed forces are on full alert to defend the country's nuclear facilities."

However, the ease with which the Aliens' pathfinder craft arrived over Britain raises questions as to the effectiveness of Britain's defence forces' effectiveness in repelling the expected Alien armada.

Among the many people who reported seeing the Aliens' craft was George Abrams, 67 of Saxmundham in Suffolk.

"I was out on my allotment," Mr Abrams said, "I heard this whirring sound and I stood up to see where it was coming from and there, lo and behold there it was peering down at me.

"Funny looking thing it was," said George, "it was like a huge pair of binoculars and hovering about ten feet up in the air. It was there for a moment, as though it was looking at me and then it buzzed off," he said.

Coldingham, Lothian to Weymouth in Dorset.

Margo MacDee, 35 of Rye, East Sussex, who also saw one of the Aliens' craft said: "I was just coming out of the Ship [public house] and this black crow-size object was hovering above the car park. At first, when I ran back inside no one believed what I had seen.

"But when I persuaded the other to come out and see for themselves," Margo said, "they soon saw that I was telling was the truth and that I hadn't had too much to drink after all.

"It hovered about the car park for some time and as though it was looking at us," Margo said. "It had two circles at the front which I estimate were about 40 centimetres in diameter. There were also a number of other, smaller circles around its edges and was about 20 centimetres thick.

"At this point it started to rain at which it buzzed off and went back in the Ship," she said

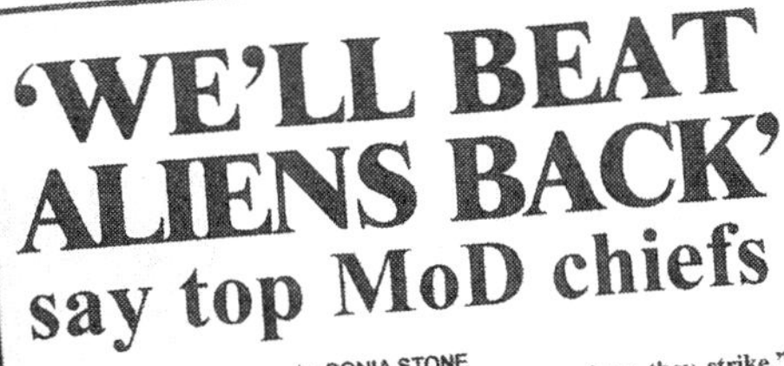

'WE'LL BEAT ALIENS BACK' say top MoD chiefs

by SONIA STONE

"WE ARE READY for the Aliens no matter where they strike," Britain's top brass declared yesterday. The Ministry of Defence press officer, seconded Royal Hussars' Colonel James Sackville said, "The entire British armed forces are trigger poised to repel any of the Aliens the moment they cross our shores."

Colonel Sackville, who has extensive battlefront experience both in Cyprus and Bosnia, outlined yesterday, the full magnitude of Britain's military readiness to combat the Alien's threat to the country's nuclear power station and other nuclear facilities such as the Windscale reprocessing plant and the weapons centre at Aldermaston.

Colonel Sackville said that because 'considerable elements' of Britain's armed forces were fighting in Europe with our NATO partners against the Alien's, they had considerably slowed the Alien's westward advance across the continent.

The Colonel also said that one of the reasons for NATO's current lack of success in slowing the Aliens' ... been because of the ... and

PM's: 'We will fight them on the beaches' speech, p9

"However," Colonel Sackville said, "here in the UK our armed forces do not suffer from that sort of thing. Make no mistake," the Colonel said, "should these Alien chappies dare to show their faces over here we will soon see them off and with a bloody nose to boot."

NATO retrencl

By Max Baldslow in Brussels and Defence Staff

NATO forces have withdrawn to the west bank of the River Elbe and are establishing a new defensive line along the River Weser and the Thuringer Wald Mountains.

NATO spokesman, Galeazzo Ciano, said: "Presently the situation in the East is very fluid. General Nehring's forces have had a ... slowing the rate of the

In private, military experts are voicing reservations at NATO's bullish statements.

"Retreat after retreat," said one who wished not to named, "every time we form for attack, we have been sure-footed The Susem know our every move We've tried hitting them with everything missiles, artillery, you name it and they've thrown it all back at us. The situation is hopeless."

According to some observers, all Allied casualties have been caused by the ricocheting of their own ordinance There are also reports circulating in Brussels that many ... the battlefront in

'Even defence is pointless' says top US General

BY ROSS WALKER IN WEISABADEN

"EVERYTHING we hit them with boomerangs right back," said US General Howard Ruff yesterday.

General Ruff, Commander of the US XII Army Group assigned to NATO's Central Command, has recently returned from the alliance Eastern Theatre.

The General said: "Our Airborne has nothing to hit the Aliens with that will have any effect on them. These Aliens have some kind of rays, energy shields that kind of stops our missiles getting anywhere near them.

"Their space craft just cruise our barrages brushing everything form of ordinance we fire at them as though it's nothing more than cloud

General Ruff was equally pessimistic over the chances of NATO being able to protect any of Europe's nuclear power stations. He said, "These Alien space craft turn up at one power station after another. They send down swarms of those hornet looking things which sting everyone in sight to get the hell out of wherever they are and then hey presto, within the hour yet another power station is rocketing to the sun."

Germany now non-nuclear

All German N. stations removed Chancellor in crisis meeting

FROM TOM WALKMAN IN FRANKFURT

GERMANY'S 25 nuclear power stations were blasted from the face of the earth yesterday. The stations represented one third of the country's electricity supply which means there will now be critical energy shortages to both industry and domestic consumers.

The nuclear power station at Griesfeldt, in the east of the country was the first to go. Susem craft arrived above the station shortly after 4 o'clock in the morning. By 5 o'clock nothing remained but a vast hole, hundreds of metres deep.

The surrounding towns and countryside were showered with falling brilliant blue clouds of foam containing Susem energy units. Crowds of people gathered around each cloud as it landed snatching up as many of the egg shaped units as they could.

The nuclear stations at Buchen and Munich soon fell victim to Susem action. Huge crowds, despite torrential rain, gathered on the hills above Kahl in northern Bavaria to watch sections of the station there propelled skyward. Thousands watched in near silence as section after glowing section disappeared ...

At Wackerdorf, further to the south, the gathered crowds actually cheered as the Susem arrived. Pieter Keluh, a leader of the German Greens said, "For a long time now we have been campaigning for the removal of this nuclear reprocessing plant.

"In one hour only, the Susem have this danger taken away from us. We are very pleased. We are hoping also that all the other nuclear poisons are taken from us as thoroughly."

By early afternoon the last nuclear stations at Kalker and Lingen on the Dutch border disappeared through the clouds.

Although the energy units, which have arrived in their millions, will perhaps alleviate any immediate energy shortfalls concern over the longer term power supply is being expressed by Germany's leaders.

Eva Goethe, director of IED, the German Power Inspectorate, said, "For now Germany will probably be okay, it is the summertime, but when the winter comes some shortages we will be experiencing."

cooperation from every one, chef LeBlond, with hair to match and galley staff enthusiastic, prepared a most magnificent meal. The staff with village helpers, all under Andre's emotive instruction, beavered in the Pousada's kitchen and numerous others' too. During the afternoon and early evening they laboured over stoves frying, baking, boiling as well as simmering wonderful sauces.

Other villagers, already amid preparations for today, soon adjusted their endeavours to those for the evening instead. Their efficiency and extent of cooperation was impressive to behold. With Elana and the other representatives of all the groups (who all bar one are women), requests for help and helpers were rapidly relayed. Lines of tables in a half circle of radiating spokes were soon set upon the green in front of the Pousada. Plates, cutlery, candles and chairs for everyone swiftly followed.

At seven o'clock and within minutes of Pedro and the others' return, a thousand people and more sat down to a most splendid supper. With only the little lines of candles illuminating the night, the banqueting began. With soldiers, some sailors and villagers intermingled and Andre with the rest of the crew waitering, dish after dish and course after course of the most succu-lent food was served. Each mouthful was consumed to the accompaniment of a continuous chorus of appreciation and a similar supply of good wines from Bordeaux.

Amid the meal there were many toasts, and some speeches too, were made. Captain Forissier's apologising more than effusively for his, his men's and his country's misdeeds was met with friendly cries of “Perdão, você perdão,” and from those who knew, “pardoned, you are forgiven,” upon which he became quite carried away. Though his eyes were still wet he concluded with toasts to peace, happiness and harmony but above all, his abiding affection and friendship for all the people of Tabajara. Each toast he made elicited raised glasses and choruses of “Viva!” and “Vive le” from the French. All the others' toasts received the same response.

Even before the feasting was finished music from the Pousada's sound system had begun to play. Dancing soon followed. The women, all in their best white frocks, or skirts with embroidered matching tops, were soon partnered by sailors in their white uniforms and soldiers and others in their tunics. With only the Pousada's lights and those of the remaining candles illuminating, there was the most delighting sight of myriad couples elegantly gliding by. There being such a surfeit of males meant every lady of every age had a willing partner and some more than a few. But after half an hour and a change of tape, the graceful gliding gave way to the lambada.

With its whiplash rhythm producing as it does wild shrieking rushes and pouting swirls, the near darkness was instantly filled with circles of rising white skirts. And as the dancers rushed, jumped and swung, filled with enthusiasm and bereft of inhibition, it was noticeable that all the ladies

Paris panics

BY STEPHEN THOMSON
IN PARIS

RIOTERS besieged Pierre Reynauld's embattled the government in Paris yesterday.

Fearful, for their safety and well-being, many French MPs joined outside the National Assembly, and the Qua d' Orsey in solidarity with the protestors.

Many of the defecting MPs then joined with protesters in jeering with apparent impunity at the riot police and security guards. With taunts that they should not be attempting to crush the protestors for trying to avert the catastrophe of the submarine Tonnant falling on their heads but in preparing for the city's evacuation in case it did.

Many organizations...

French defenc[e] minister sacke[d]

By Adrian Moreley in Paris

FRENCH premier, Pierre Reynauld, bowing to public outrage over France's firing a nuclear missile at the Susem, has sacked his defence minister, Maurice Weygand. He has been replaced by Maxime Gamelin.

Though Reynauld's government must be desperately hoping that Weygand's dismissal will take the heat out of the current volatile situation, his going is unlikely to sufficient to calm the anger of the French people and the wider international community.

"Weygand has been made a scapegoat for Reynauld," said leading political commentator of *Le Monde*, Kevin Chercher. "All of Reynauld's cabinet are implicated in this affair," Chercher said, "including Reynauld himself."

"If France is going escape from the dangerous situation we are placed in," he said, "then [President] Lebrun must now ...

ation of the entire cabinet including Reynauld."

With street anti-government demonstrations throughout France showing no signs of abating, Chercher's comments appear to be in tune with the protestors. As each day passes an increasing number of the protests are turning into full scale riots.

From Lille in the north of the country to Toulon in the south, as well as in Paris itself many dozens of government building have been attacked by rioters, with many completely burned to the ground. Both the regular police as well as those of the CRS security forces have been stretched to breaking point in their attempts to quell the rioters.

There are also increasing fears throughout France that unless the situation is resolved very soon, the entire country could collapse...

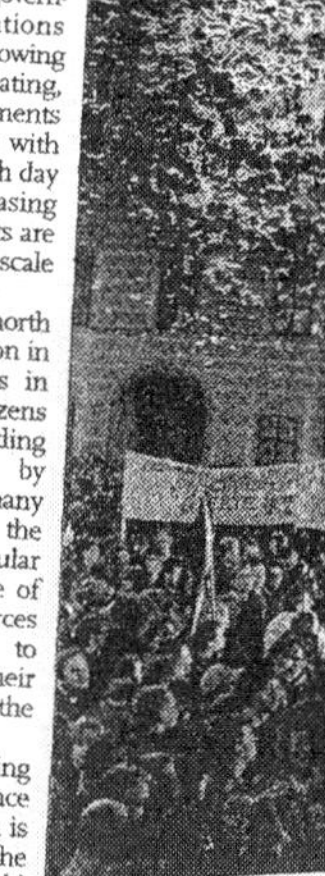

[Ri]val bankers unite in rush to raise $1bn Susem f[...]

Bankers gambl[e] on saving Pari[s]

[B]y Julian Gray in Paris

[F]RANCE'S major banks and other financial institutions are reported to be devising an emergency plan to save Paris from devastation.

In the face of government inaction, leading banks are planning to divert the sales of government stock to pay the US$1bn compensation demanded by the Susem. In doing this they hope to avert the French nuclear submarine being dropped on the centre of Pa[ris]...

over... Jaco... Suc... cash...

for various government departments. "If they wish to sue us then let them. But if they take their future business elsewhere we will sue them instead," he said.

Argent's opposite number at Banc Voleur, Charles D'lev, was more forthright, saying: "Either Reynaud pays or we do. And if it is us, Reynaud is finished. Already we have many radio and television stations prepared to broad...

French de...

News in brief

Croatian coup rumoured

FIGHTING is reported to have broken out between factions of the Croatian military. The disturbances are said to centred around the coastal town of Sibenik.

Radio broadcasts monitored in Slovenia, suggest Croatian 110 Brigade commander Darko Praljak's forces have taken control of an area bounded by the coast and the border of the former Bosnia.

If reports are substantiated, it would indicate Dalmatian provinces are isolated from Croatia proper.

John Borger in Ljubljana

AND WILDLIFE S...

Gunman seizes children

WORLD IN BRIEF

Was French PM pushed or did he jump?

Disgraced Reynauld bolts

FROM JOHN DEAN IN PARIS

SACKED French premier, Pierre Reynauld was keeping a low profile yesterday. Calls to his private residence on the Ile St Louis went unanswered. Maurice Weygand, his former Defence Minister, however, was giving interviews to all who asked.

In the absence of firm news, let alone official government announcement, Paris is awash with rumours as to what really took place which led to the government's denouement. That they volunteered or were forced to resign is also a matter of heated debate.

The "they were pushed" school argues that President Lebrun's statement was broadly accurate. That the government of Pierre Reynauld allowed themselves to ruled by delusions of the grandeur of 'la France', that the attack on the Aliens was an attempt to protect French interests. "If Reynauld and his cabinet had succeeded [in annihilating the Susem] they would have been feted as national heros," said, Claude Auteur, a political columnist with the *Le Monde*, "but as their little adventure in Brazil failed they are seen as scoundrels and had to hounded from office."

Protagonists of "they jumped" camp advance that there has been a massive cover-up at the very highest levels of France's establishment. "There must have been some deeper reason why Reynauld and his cronies could have done something so utterly stupid," says Henri Shave, of the satirical magazine *Canard*.

"They must have known what would happen," Shave said, "As for Lebrun stating that he did not know, I do not believe him, no one does. There must be another, deeper reason for Reynauld and his cabinet's wholesale departure.

"It is my experience that Reynauld is a wilily old fox," he said, "The missile our submarine fired at the Aliens could not have been have been launched without the Americans knowing. That Reynauld was doing the US's dirty work for them is very evident. But the question still remains as to why did Reynauld do it."

Aliens attack Cambodia

Bangkok: Alien craft have been sighted attacking western Cambodia.

Thai military forces stationed at Ban Laam on the Thai-Cambodian border, have reported seeing "substantial numbers" of Alien craft. They have been sighted flying over the Kravanh Mountain range which forms the border between the two countries. The craft are said to be smaller in size than seen previously elsewhere.

Kravanh is used as supply base area by Khmer Rouge guerillas.

AF PRESS

Chinese factions agree truce

swishing against the Pousada's lights had come to the party with their knickers on.

While waiting with other wallflowers I continued keeping company with the claret. I also spoke with soldiers who had spent the day to the west. There, in Piauí they said, were sights more wretched than before. Whereas Tuesday they had seen few cases of chagas' disease (the one which doomed Darwin to a decades slow painful death), in the western villages it abounded. When their representatives arrive Friday, they said, be prepared for some shockingly sad sights of malnourishment and ill health. Some sailors who had travelled with them became most moved when they too told their observations. Again and again they asked, rhetorically perhaps, why in a land burgeoning with plenty should there be such terrible poverty?

I tried as best I could to tell, as did others, the reasons why. But the difficulties of language, the loudness of the music and the distractions of so many skirts swirling high as the ladies' enthusiastic lambadaring rose to new heights, made discussion difficult.

Other sailors recuperating from dancing remarked on the ladies' lambadaring zest. But I had to tell them that it was nothing and how lucky they were the ladies hadn't them dancing to the forró. Not knowing it, and unknowing of its dangers, some sailors asked me to explain. I said the forró, the music of the vanquerios of the Seatão, was so wild it made the lambada seem sedate, restrained. I told how the forró is performed by partners first dancing away from one another, the lady twirling for all her worth, the man pacing like a cavorting colt, then with a cry of "Olhar!" backs straight, shoulders, hips swinging they stride in a rush to one another, whereupon they dance with the movements, limbic closeness and intensity of the tango but at many, many times the speed. And this is only at the beginning. As each dance comes to its climax another is commencing with the music faster, more ferocious than before. And it keeps on going faster, wilder. So does the dancing. Dancers of the forró have been known to collapse from exhaustion, some have even died.

The tempo and duration of dancing the forró is determined more often than not by the stamina of the man. In the Nordeste as there is usually an imbalance of more women than men the music does not last too long before the dancers rest. But, I told them, as there were now so many soldiers and sailors in Tabajara the balance was now the other way and that was where the danger lay. I told them what happened when a Uruguayan Navy frigate arrived in Fortaleza on a goodwill tour and the crew went out dancing on their last night. With such a sudden surplus of men the ladies had danced on. And on. Because there had not been a break, each new tune had become faster than the last. The sailors were so spent and shattered by the time the ladies had finished with them their ship was a day late in putting to sea. Roberto's tap on my shoulder drew my attention away.

Despite the dancing, Roberto had continued meticulously monitoring

France surrenders

Lebrun says he was tricked
France to pay Susem 'fine'

Government dismissed
Paul Lavel new premier

By Julia Horicks in Paris

IN A SHOCK revelation the French president, Albert Lebrun claimed that he had been tricked by the former prime minister, Pierre Reynauld, into allowing the use of nuclear missiles against the Susem in Brazil.

President Lebrun also announced the immediate payment of $1 billion to the Susem.

The President, who is recovering from prostate surgery, said in a nationwide telecast, that both Pierre Reynauld and defence minister, Maurice Weygand had connived in bypassing his (Lebrun's) control of the nuclear launch keys for the attempted attack on the Susem.

The President claimed that when he was told what had happened, he had demanded the immediate resignation of Reynauld's government. He also announced that due to what he called "the period of uncertainty and destabilisation" which had engulfed the country he had asked Paul Lavel, leader of Front National, the junior member of the outgoing government, to form a new administration.

Until Lavel has formed a new government, the President said, he had requested the National Assembly to give powers to rule by decree. This and the appointment of Lavel are likely to prove highly unpopular among many factions within France's political parties especially the Socialists.

President Lebrun also announced, and as though already ruling by decree will be gain automatic consent from the National Assembly, the immediate payment of the $1billion to the Susem.

Lebrun's announcement of the payment, however, is sure to come as a great relief to most Parisians fearful for the property and livelihoods.

The deployment of France's defence forces in the protection of the country's nuclear power stations and other nuclear facilities was also called into doubt by the President's speech. He said that they would now only be defended if "appropriate". This is seen as an indication that the French may now be ready to abandon their status as one of the world's nuclear powers.

See: **The Unanswered Questions, p9**

The unanswered questions

By Paul Reeves Defence correspondent

THE FRENCH President Albert Lebrun's apologised to the Susem yesterday for the attempted missile attack on them. He also announced that France would bow to Susem demands and pay the $1bn compensation they are seeking.

In his speech, broadcast yesterday, President Lebrun laid the blame for France's actions against the Susem fair and squarely at his former government's door and on Pierre Reynauld as well as Maurice Weygand, the former defence minister, in particular. The President in his telecast, however, failed to shed light on a number of still puzzling aspects of France's 'Force de Folie' as the debacle has come to be known.

Did the former French prime and defence ministers really purloin the President's nuclear launch keys to order the launch of the missile? Did they really need to?

"No not necessarily," says SIPRI's Fred Barnes. "Presidential control over the submarine launched ballistic [nuclear] missiles (SLBMs) is a myth," says Barnes. "Submarines have never been constrained by PALs (Permissive Action Links).

"A submarine commander - be he French, American, Russian, British - can launch his boat's missiles without any reference to his superiors any time he wants," Barnes said. "Reynauld or any one for that matter could have told Captain Forissier - the commander of submarine Tonnant - to launch the missiles."

Was President Lebrun's speech a fig-leaf concealing something much more Machiavellian?

"Very likely," says Jacques Mordal, one of France's foremost historians. "Everything points to not only the French government's continuing illusion of holding on to its belief in its 'Big Power' status but also of outside forces helping to maintain this pointless belief," he said.

As France concedes Susem demands its Big Power status is over

France capitulates

by Arian Warley in Paris

PRESIDENT Albert Lebrun, agreed yesterday to Susem demands for admission and apology in attempting to attack them with nuclear weapons.

He also undertook to pay the Susem US$1bn compensation for French actions. The President also announced resignation of Pierre Reynaud's Government.

In a rare national telecast address from his home near Poitiers, where he is convalescing after a recent prostrate operation, President Lebrun said Pierre Reynaud and his Government had 'cruelly deceived" not only the French nation but also him.

The President claimed that Reynaud and Defence Minister, Mauric Weygand, had overstepped their authority in using nuclear weapons. "They [Reynaud and Weygand] operated without my knowledge and sanction. By deception they took advantage of my temporary indisposition and operated the security keys to authorise the use of [France's] nuclear weapons.

"Their actions have caused deep pain to our nation and damaged our standing in the eyes of France's allies and friends throughout the world."

The President, still looking tired from his recent operation, announced a series of measures including naming a new Prime Minister, Paul Lavel Until Lavel has formed a new cabinet, the President said he had put before the National Assembly, ratification to rule by decree.

Apparently assuming such decree would automatically be granted, President Lebrun said, that the compensation demanded by the Susem would be paid immediately to them. "We await only to know to whom and where," he said.

He also said France would still defend its nuclear facilities including power staions, but added: "Should this be the appropriate thing to do."

(Lebrun's speech in full, p5)

News in brief

Croatian 'coup' speads

AMID reports of continuing fighting between Croatian goverment forces and rebel factions in Dalmatia, there are reports of a fresh military uprising in the east of the country.

Dissident elements of Croatian National Guard in the eastern province of Slavonia, had rallied to Mile Dedakovic at Vinkovci. Dedakovci best known from the Serbo-Croat conflict of 1992 as the defender of Vukovar, issued a proclamation bitterly attacking the government in Zargreb.

Dedakovici is reported to have said, according to radio transmissions monitored in Lubjljana, that his forces had not played a part in the "Bosnian atrocities" and should not continue to pay for Zargreb's "evil adventure," Dedakovici is said to have called for seperation of Slavonia from Croatia.

by John Borger in Lubjljana

Gunman seizes children

FRIDAY MAY 6, 20

WORLD IN BRIEF

Alien attacks on Cambodia continuing

Bangkok: Alien craft are widening their invasion of western Cambodia. Thai military forces stationed at Ban Laam in the east of the country have reported seeing further flights of Susem craft. Other army border posts at Nong Ian and Ban Paa have also reported seeing substantial numbers of Susem Craft flying low over the Kravanh Mountains. *AF PRESS*

Buff Bondi bathers in barefaced cheek slap

Sydney: Police are threatening huge fines on bathers at Australia's premier gay nudist beach following further outbreaks of what Sydney's Superintendent of Police, Bruce O'Rourke described as "disgusting lewd behaviour in cavorting with another in a flagrant suggestive manner"

As a riot torn nation licks its wounds

Paris counts the cost

By Adrian Morely in Paris

AS THE ANTI-GOVERNMENT protests across France subside, the ruins of countless official buildings burnt-out by rioters cease to smoulder, the costs to the nation are

World Service newscasts. The nine o'clock (London, midnight) news announced the French Government's contrition and capitulation. They wanted only, Roberto said, a promise not to bomb the submarine's remains down on Paris, the release of all prisoners and hostages, or so he said they had called them, and to whom and where the money was to be paid. As I looked across at the sailors dancing, drinking with abandon, the words "prisoners" and "hostages" had me smile. But looking into that gloaming I saw, glowing neon bright in my mind, the sequential numbers of my bank account, sort code and all. It soon passed and looking again, I picked out Rainbow lambadaring like mad with Big Luiz.

Despite the noise I told her the news, I told Pedro and Elana too. And she told Rico to turn down the sound. Though the lambadaring ceased it was at once replaced by hundreds of lustily cheered "Viva!"s as Elana announced the news. With Roberto then called to relate verbatim what he had heard and Captain Forissier tell how happy he and his men now were, I with Pedro and Rainbow slipped off to see Paceillo.

On being told the news she had a wry smile. Paceillo then said it was time to see the sailors before they went away, adding she would see them at ten.

With Pedro I walked back to the party but we had not gone far before I heard the music. Now it wasn't taped but live and I was crying "Oh no, not the forró." By the time we had returned events were utterly out of hand.

As the minutes ticked on to ten, the music too loud for conversation or announcements and still (thankfully now) a wallflower in the shadows, I continued keeping quiet company with the claret. But the dancing was speeding on. Soon I was surrounded by men gasping, slumped like husks, their sustenance sucked from them. The music grew faster, louder, the ladies' "Olhar!"s too, and their dancing demonstrative. With white forms in the near darkness flashing and dashing, the ladies like the musicians, became oblivious to this world. The surplus of spare men fast declined but the ladies', their "Olhar!"s became ever assertive. Spent men were coerced into replacement partners, though instead of young colts they now moved like lame hacks. Not the ladies though. The kaleidoscope of their white dresses swirled faster and faster. And the music was played faster too. The time ticked on to nearly ten. The supply of willing men dwindled but still the ladies danced on. Within minutes there were those without partners. But such was their passion and the music's frenzied rhythm that with each cry of their "Olhar!"s and demonic with grins and glints in their eyes they dragged soldiers, sailors and other young men from the tables avid on having every last drop of their vibrancy. But before they got to me, the music thankfully, suddenly died.

All eyes were soon on the park-side. Over by the cavern there now came a rolling glowing green-white cloud. Slowly, soundlessly it billowed and blew towards us, its luminescence lighting the ground around. No one said anything. All were spellbound. Apart from people catching their breath there was silence. All eyes gazed transfixed upon the cloud. It tumbled up and down the rises and falls, plumes of lighted swirling wisps rose and fell and enveloped around its billowing edges. Still no one made a sound.

Thirty, twenty feet from us, with wisps still swirling, the cloud slowed then stopped. We were still staring and all still in silence.

Then, in an instant the cloud's uppermost billows blew back as though an opening oyster of luminous gossamer. Inside were not pearls but Paceillo and two dozen Susem, perhaps more. The Susem were clad not in their regular tunics but ones which had a sheen as they reflected the glow of the gossamer, and they were so thin that their folds fluttered with the breeze. The Susem stood there, as though by Botticelli, looking at us, expressionless, saying nothing, luminescence still glowing on their clothes and hair as well as swirling about their feet.

Many heads bowed. Those about me were soon on their knees. Even I knelt. Paceillo called out Captain Forissier's christian name. With her hand she beckoned him to her, then and in such a quiet gentle voice "Your comrades too."

As though dumbstruck the captain, using his arms, signalled to his men to join with him. At first they knelt but with her hands Paceillo signed for them to stand. She further signalled we should all do the same. Still in silence she and the other Susem continued looking at them. It seemed they did so for such a long time. Still not saying a word Paceillo then handed him a paper tube. Then turning on their heels the Susem glidingly strode into the night.

As all of us stood watching them walk away, wisps of luminescence still lighting them and where they had stood, more blowing and swirling, some alighting the table tops, there still was silence. And there was silence too as everyone made for their homes and their hammocks.

During the night Captain Forissier and many of his crew became quite changed. When the vedas arrived to fly the sailors home he had eschewed all vestiges of uniform including his hat. Others had done the same. That apart, the entire village turned out to see the sailors off. With exchanges of addresses, hugs, kisses and tears, the sailors bid adieu. To cries of "Bon Voyage" they boarded Konnet, Kubber and Kerhaw and flew away to France.

An hour later the first people from the Ibiapaba and the villages to the east arrived. It was easy to identify who was from the Ibiapaba and who wasn't. All, as people often do on such occasions, wore their best clothes. But for many, theirs were their only clothes. So little was their wealth some had started trekking to Tabajara as soon as Pedro had left them.

A week ago Menpemelo made mention of the poor state, by Susem standards, of many people's physiques (including mine) but as she said later, she was shocked by those from the Seatão. But of course, those she saw today are among the healthier ones.

The villagers of Tabajara proudly showed what a week had achieved, how their lives were quite changed. Visitors were toured without stop to home after home, each piled with perfect produce, past seminars and study groups sat at teaching machines, then down to the gardens and crops rapidly rising, past the mormic and next up to the platform to see the remains of the plane and submarine. Then, on their returning to Tabajara, a demon-stration of the soufins' powerful vehicle propulsion and limitless electrical power. And all the while as they went there were "Oohs" and "Aahs" of awe.

Apart from the visitors' amazement and wonder there were their apprehensions of the Susem. But these were soon smoothed and soothed by the village guides' forever expressed affections and admiration of them. The Susem meanwhile, although keeping a keen eye on everything, kept away from any outsider's gaze.

Each tour ended with food, drink and discussion. Though others of Tabajara joined in, Elana led in outlining Paceillo's last Sunday's tenets. At the beginning there was disbelief among visitors that everything shown could also be theirs for so little in exchange. Overcoming this took up much of the talking. For most it was difficult to grasp the notion that advancing educationally provided empowerment. Power for them for all of their lives had come only from force, money and privileged birth.

In the end everyone accepted Elana's assurances as well as the assistance of an advisor, be it a villager or one of Pedro's men. As time passed the more enthusiastic they each and all became. In part the prospects of material improvement weighed and swayed but I also observed something else, hope. Though in a way this is wonderful, it is also worrying.

For most of them for most their lives the people from the Seatão who came to Tabajara today have been little more than serfs, hirelings, knowing only privation and fruitless longing. They had lived with little to hope for and for some there had probably been none at all. While what the Susem are giving is of course marvellous they will not always be here. To be without hope is sadness, but to be given hope and then have it snatched for ever away is tragedy. When the Susem are gone, what then? What protection will these people have from those in power?

And those who have power never really let it slip their grip. All the histories of ordinary people, alas, can be writ upon and from the piled corpses of their dashed hopes. Dashed and died upon the vested interests of the powerful.

58: KEN

In a way I was dead disappointed. But Harry was well pleased. He had a fair crowd in for a Thursday night. I saw him smile, he doesn't often do that.

At eight, on the dot, the screen goes fizzy, there's a "Dum-dum dum dum" tapping drum sound and Rainbow appears. "Hello," she says. She gives the time, a list of news items and last, the bit I'm waiting for "...and an introduction to the Susem."

Everything else was sort of interesting, the French matelots being sent home but we already knew about that and how some of them have turned strange, but then that's your French. Rainbow mentions the Serb and Croats not turning up for work and how they better had or they would be in for it, which is fair, neither lot deserve mercy for what they have done. She next shows this whopping big hole in the ground, it's enormous. She says it's an utter disgrace and needs to be filled in, which is only reasonable. She says those they catch up to no good are going to doing the filling and that includes anyone who shouldn't be round where they are. That sounded fair as well, for a lot of villains it will be the only thing they understand. Rainbow goes on with a few more things, power stations, energy units and the like but of course I'm still waiting for the main bit, about the Susem themselves.

I'm not saying what she said wasn't important but there's been so much about the Susem and their doings that I can't take any more in. Then at last she says "And now an introduction to some of our guests."

A bit of music comes on and then there she is dancing with this big wasp thing flying and buzzing about her. It flies around for a bit to the music then it lands on her shoulder. "This is Sol..." she says, "...and he's a Henga." With that she gives it a stoke and it purrs back. Then she says "Sol can do some really clever things." Whereupon she throws an orange in the air. Quick as a flash this Sol zooms up and heads it straight back at her. She, all laughing, catches it and throws it back at him. The orange goes way to the side, he makes a dive, he is still nowhere near but it comes straight back at her. She throws it again and again. Each time he's nowhere and still he knocks it back to her.

Nigel, next to me remarks "Arsenal could do with him, in goal."

But he had no sooner spoke than Rainbow says "And these are some of Sol's companions." The camera goes back a bit and there's hundreds of them flying about, like a swarm they are. Rainbow's cupping her hand and they are in a circle, they look just like a tyre. Then they're going round and round at the rate of knots.

All very entertaining but I'm starting to think "Where's the beef, this is a kid's show," and I see others round the bar thinking the same.

Rainbow, waggling her hands then says, "And these are some of their friends." The hengas go into a straight line, do a couple of loop the loops, then, with the camera following, they zoom over to this crowd of kids. They buzz all round them and the kids start running about chasing them. By now I'm definitely becoming bored and get another pint in.

The picture changes to something dark with lots of little black holes in it. Rainbow then says "Sometimes Sol and his companions live in here." As she does, she's brushing her fingers round one of the holes. “Come out Sol,” she says, “I know you're in there.” There's a gurgling sound coming from the hole. “Come on,” she says again. With that this Sol, making a “Whee!” sound, zips straight out of his hole, flies around her and she's trying to catch it.

By now I am definitely bored but I still haven't got a pint in. The barmaids have gone all soppy, “Oohing” and “Aahing” and “Isn't he loverlee.” I can't say anything of course, because if I do they make a point of never serving me.

Rainbow is running about trying to catch this Sol. As she does she's getting further and further away from the dark behind her. The screen now shows what the dark is, it's flat with an edge. She's still getting further away, the camera from her as well. All of her is now on the screen and it's showing the flat thing is the wing of a plane looking thing. From the size of Rainbow, the plane is big, a good hundred feet long and it's dark.

Sol lets Rainbow catch him, she holds him in her arms and the camera closes back to them. Sol's still wriggling and chirping, she half turning, said, “This is Kershaw and he's a Veda.”

The camera goes all round this veda and at last I'm getting interested, the barmaid's “Usual?” gets only a nod. This veda is like a long thin triangle, thicker along its middle. It has two, what I take to be windows near the front. It's obviously the same as I saw when Danny was on, but of course then, there was only the brief glimpse. As I'm looking at this veda, Rainbow says, “He can do some really clever things, can't you Kershaw?”

“What do you want me to do then?” comes this voice. At first I don't catch on it's the veda's. “Oh, I tell you what,” he next says, “I'll do a little hover,” and I'm spluttering in my beer. Seeing an Aliens' spaceship is big enough, hearing it talk and in English another but then to find out on top of all that its gay, I just don't know what to make of it, I really don't.

In no time he's ten feet up in the air and hovering. I'm impressed, there's no sound, no grass blowing back. “Now what do you want me to do next?” he says “shall I do a twirl? I can do a nice twirl, look.” And he's doing just that, going round and round. “Shall I do a slow one now? There.” It is impressive, I have to say, fantastic control. “Shall I waggle my wings as well?” Not only does he, but he is just brushing the ground with either wing tip. Then, as he does he says “I'd give a flash of my lights if it was darker.” As the wings go up, the camera shows his underside, it has rows of little bumps. “Well, I can't hover here all day,” he says, “I've things to do.”

He lands back down, a door flips open on his side up the back. When I looked first I didn't make one out. A ramp comes out of the door. No sooner is it down than there are all these yelling kids running up it.

The camera is next inside of him and there are the kids milling about. “Right boys and girls, where are we going to today?” he says. The camera is going along a corridor with what look like doors. The kids are yelling, “The seaside...waterfall...the Moon.” The camera goes into what must be the cockpit. “Will you be quiet, I can’t hear myself think,” he says. The camera swings round, there are windows with kids looking out, seats with more kids clambering over them. “Stop standing on my seats and sit properly...we don't want a mess like the other day,” he says. I'm looking for things like dials and instruments but don't see any. “Oh good, here is Lucia,” he says. The camera leaves the cockpit and is pointing down the corridor. A woman, girl really, walks along it and past the camera. “They just will not make up their minds.,” he says. The camera leaves the corridor and passes into a big unlit area. “You as well?” he says, “Oh we are all waiting for Feterisco?” The camera swings round the area. “We could be here all day...all the ages I’ve known her, she's been always late,” he says. I make out what look like ribs curving along the sides. “Will you be quiet,” he says. The camera turns to the outside door. “Oh here she comes... at last,” he says. Kids are running down to the doorway shouting, “Feterisco, Feterisco come on.” The light by the door darkens as if someone’s coming in. I’m all eyes, is this going to be the first sight of a Susem? Then the picture suddenly switches back to Rainbow.

“Goodbye,” she says, “there will be a further programme at this hour on Saturday, with some more coverage of our guests.” With that the screen goes blank and I'm in definite need of another drink.

59: JAMES

Frankie's departure, while somewhat sudden, was not altogether unexpected. Saturday's upset rumbled through to Tuesday evening. Iris's television appearance was the last straw as far as she was concerned, or rather my comments on Iris's professionalism. Yesterday, here to greet me, was her leaving note saying she had gone to her mother's. At least I've been able to sleep in the bed and watch television uninterrupted.

If Tuesday's programme (or what little I saw of it) made attempts at professionalism this evening's was more so. A good firm, rapid delivery of news items, though each one had its mystifying elements. The crowds bidding the French sailors farewell gave the appearance of being filled with genuine bonhomie and lends credence to other news reports of the sailors' forswearing fighting. Iris's announcement that the submarine's remains, providing the ten billion dollars were delivered on time, would not be dropped on Paris was a relief. Not just for Parisians but the markets as well, they are nervous enough as it is. But from what she also said both the Serbs and Croats are the ones who must actually have cause for nervousness. With most news-teams departing from Bosnia, hard facts as to what is happening there are scant to say the least. Although I have seen magazine articles of the Serra Pelada, the tele-clip of it showed it to be more horrific than I had realised. Though I think it's going to take a lot of people a long time to fill it in. The news of the nuclear power stations, however, and the Susem energy units naturally drew most of my attention.

Not the loss of the power stations as such but the impact of energy power units. If the pattern of eastern Europe occurs here, the generation of electricity is going to be adversely affected. In turn this is bound to have a downward pressure on the share prices of the generators. As Morgans is a major dealer in utilities' shares we stand to be big losers.

The antics of the Susem's machines, though 'toys' might be more appropriate, had me curious. On one hand how are these hengers able to manoeuvre with such agility? Yet on the other they appear to be so friendly, cuddly almost. Quite the opposite, if news reports are anything to go by, of the "killer wasps" and "Alien swarms" terrorising the Balkans and nuclear power stations. The veda was much the same. It is difficult to square something so benign with the reported fleets of them marauding and obliterating power plants and goodness knows what else. It was disappointing in not actually seeing any of the Susem but whatever it is they look like, from the children's reactions they can't be that unusual. Perhaps they are indeed alike to the "Angels" the Frenchmen described.

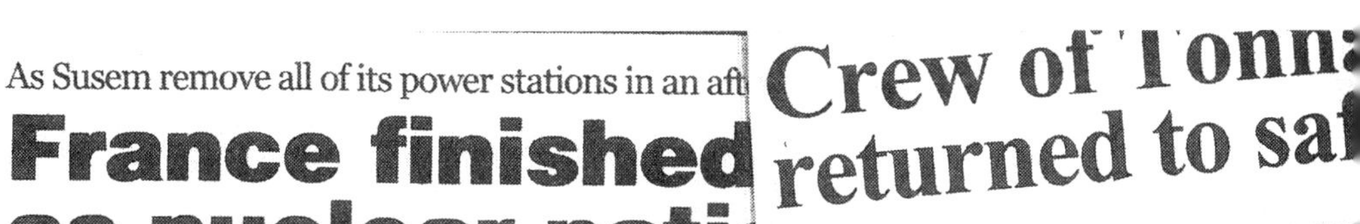

As Susem remove all of its power stations in an aft

France finished as nuclear natio

David Webster in Paris

THE FRENCH nuclear industry suffered a series of devastating losses yesterday afternoon when all attempts at halting Susem attacks on the country's nuclear power stations failed ignominiously.

All of France's nuclear weaponry from missiles to bombs suffered the same fate at the hands of the Aliens.

The Susem obliterated a chain of nuclear power stations stretching from Liege in the north of the country to Creys-Malville, near Lyon on the south in a matter of hours. Simultaneously a further flotilla of Susem Station Busters' removed a string of further nuclear power stations along the Channel and Atlantic coasts.

Before today more than two thirds of France's electricity supply came from nuclear power stations. After today and the depredations of the Susem, none does. "What will we do now it has gone," lamented Remy Carle, head of Electricite de France. "Because of Reynauld's folly, we French do not even have the succour of Susem] energy units," he said.

France's few remaining coal reserves and oil and gas powered stations, and although now operating at full capacity, can only provide a fraction of the nations power needs. Hydro-electric power and renewable energy sources, such as wind farms are comparatively under-developed in France.

While the comparative warm weather of the approaching summer and low user demand may just keep the nation functioning on an standby level, the economic prospects for French industry is little short of catastrophic. With Germany also losing its nuclear power stations and those of Spain expected to soon follow suit, the chances of either country being able to supply with any surplus power is also remote.

There is however, hope in some quarters that as soon French government has out the $1bn to the Susem receive a supply of their e units. If this hope borne desperation remains to be s

Meanwhile the price of liqu propane gas has rocketed more the EF5.00 a litre. Hea oil has rocketed by a sim amount to EF4.50 a litre.

Crew of Tonna returned to saf

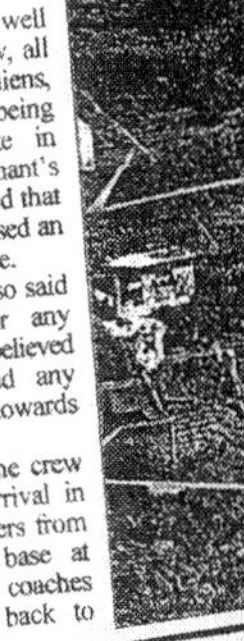

THE ENTIRE crew of the Tonnant, the ill-fated French nuclear submarine have returned safely to France. The submariners, all of whom were taken prisoner by the Aliens after their submarine had launched a nuclear missile at base in northern Brazil, walked into the tiny Brittany seaside resort of Auray, this morning.

Lead by their captain, Jacques Forissier, the entire crew appeared none the worse for their ordeal, so Kevin Delon of *l' Express Nantes* reports, nor for their experience among the Aliens in Brazil.

Captain Forissier told how he and his crew had been well treated by their captors and had not been imprisoned or ill-treated by them in any way.

In fact, so Captain Forissier claimed, both he and his men ...

who had joined in with the Susem. The Captain also added that they had complete freedom of movement throughout the locality during the period of their stay.

Captain Forissier as well as members of his crew, all of who had met the Aliens, described them as being completely human-like in form. Many of Tonnant's crew however, also said that the Susem also possessed an ethereal godly presence.

Captain Forissier also said that neither he nor any member of his crew believed that the Aliens had any harmful attentions towards mankind.

Two hours after the crew of the Tonnant's arrival in Auray, liaison officers from the nearby naval base at Brest arrived with coaches and ferried them back to their quarters

'Aliens Angels' Captain claims

By Former PA reporter PETER ANDERSON

BEFORE FRENCH naval redcaps had chance to muzzle the commander of the nuclear submarine, Tonnant, Captain Jacques Forisstier and the rest of his crew, he gave me details of the bungled French attack on the Aliens in South America.

Captain Forisstier was also able to reveal that both he and his men were now completely allied to the Aliens' cause.

N Sub crew spoke freely

I was able to witness the French sailors' arrival in the tiny Brittany fishing port of Auray as well as the Aliens' spacecraft which had flown them from northern Brazil. I was also able to hear at first hand from Captain Forisstier and his crew members of their dramatic experiences while in the hands of the Susem.

On talking with both captain and crew I immediately realised the wider significance of my chance meeting with them. ... outsiders who had had direct contact with the Aliens.

All men 'deeply moved'

Before the French redcaps arrived I was able to talk with Tonnant's crew without restrictions of any kind. In turn all of the men freely replied to all of the questions I put to them. As result of my talking with them it also became abundantly clear that all of them had been deeply moved by their experiences.

All ashamed of their actions

All of the men also expressed their deep shame in carrying out their, thankfully abortive, attack on the Susem and the people who are in close company with the Aliens. All of the men loudly castigated, the French Naval Authorities, the Department of Defence and the French government for ordering them to attack the Aliens.

Susem are 'Angels'

From other details that it appears that Susem a in form and stature. So further said that the Al were not only fema "women of overpoweri

Entire crew leavi

As a result of thei meeting the Susem Tonnant's crew sai now forsaken involvement in any any kind. Many sai immediate intentio at the earliest oppo

Captain to w

Captain Forissti he too is inten command and re as soon as possi himself to aid Bosnia.

During my Tonnant's cre many of the had encounter

Weygand clai US in on Frenc missile launch

David Webster in Paris

FRANCE'S aborted attack on the Susem was initiated by the US, ousted French defence minister, Maurice Weygand claimed yesterday. Accusing the Americans of hiding behind French actions, M Weygand said that he considers it to be unfair that his country should be the one to shoulder the blame for the abortive missile launch.

"The Americans were with us all the way and from the very start, from the planning to the execution of the adventure," Weygand said yesterday.

If the former defence minister's claims against the US administration are confirmed it will place the American authorities in an embarrassingly difficult position not only with the rest of the world but with their own public.

According to Weygand, US and French defence chiefs had agreed a united plan of attack against the Aliens as early as last Friday, the day after their arrival over Europe.

The French agreed to do the US's 'dirty work' as Weygand termed it in return for America's full commitment and assistance in attacking the Alien's space craft with nuclear missiles while they were over eastern Europe and Asia.

"The Americans did their side of the bargain lamented Weygand. "A France is the nation suffers. I am the one wh too. We are without s electricity to fuel our e without a nuclear force to ourselves and we ar without friends," he said.

Weygand also claimed t French president, Albert despite his being in hospi well aware of the planned "If we had succeeded," W said, "we would have had friends, but failure, Quasimodo is always sh nobody admits to knowing

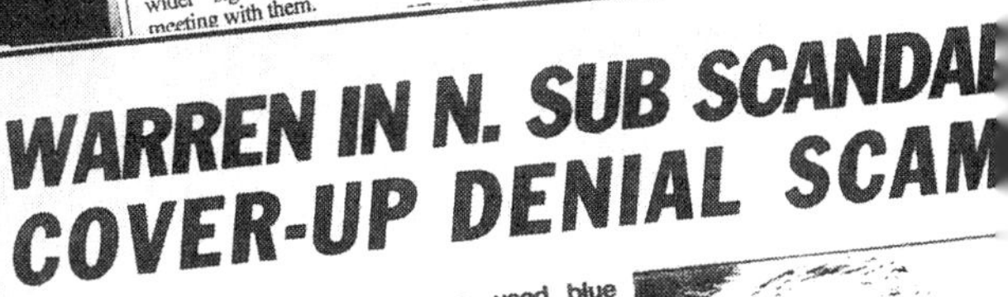

WARREN IN N. SUB SCANDAL COVER-UP DENIAL SCAM

WHITE HOUSE aides, red with rage, used blue language in blackening ex-French Defense Minister Maurice Weygand, likening him to a 'yellow rat' and a greenhorn in military matters.

However, despite being browned off with the French, they used purple prose to depict President Warren and the Pentagon's innocence in the bungled Brazilian missile bombardment.

White House Press Secretary, David Shutz, said: "The President of the United States rejects utterly and totally, any suggestion his administration would jeopardize the peace and ...

60: SIÂN

The hengars were lovely. The one the girl played with was really cute, like a little flying puppy. But the boys, including Daffyd thought otherwise. They were bored within a couple of minutes. The plane, a vedar the girl called it had their attentions but again not for long. I had to tell them to be quiet. Where they learn those words from I shall never know. They could have only picked them up from school. I am going to raise it at the next parents' evening. In this day and age it is important more than ever to teach tolerance of others.

Although at the time nobody mentioned it, there was another thing which puzzled me, the children. Apart from obviously enjoying themselves, it was their English which impressed me. I looked up where they're supposed to be, it is poor, backward and the language is Portuguese. They spoke and understood as though they were English, or leastways British.

There were other things as well. The sailors were supposed to have been prisoners and hostages, the people outraged at their attempting to kill them. The papers have been filled with reports of riots and protests in Brazil and everywhere else. But those people and sailors saying goodbye to one another appeared the best of friends. Another thing which doesn't seem to add up is everyone else seems to be so friendly, including their machines, the children showed no sense of inhibition.

Yet there was that girl, as cool as a cucumber, announcing all manner of veiled threats to trespassers. As for the people in Croatia and Serbia, well put it this way, if they don't do as she told them to I wouldn't want to be in their shoes.

Something else, which the more I think on it, worries me and this is electricity. I am glad of course to see the back of nuclear power stations and all those stupid weapons but what happens to existing supplies? As important, will we get one of these Aliens' power units? Just how good are they really? There have been so many conflicting reports, experts saying they are no good, dangerous even, then there are others from Russia and elsewhere singing their praises. I mentioned this to Daffyd but all he could say was he didn't know. It's been the same with everyone at work. Although they asked the same question, no one had an answer. If there are going to be shortages, will there be power cuts, or rationing, will prices go up? Hyder Power, when I telephoned, gave me nothing but blather. And I am surprised, upset really, that the Government hasn't announced anything either. All there has been from them in the papers is more blather about how all of the power stations are defended against attack and that there is no cause for alarm.

Spain's nuclear power stations sent skyward

BY PABLO FERRAN IN BARCELONA

SUSEM craft wiped out Spain's 11 nuclear power stations within the space of two hours. The stations produced a quarter of the country's electricity and Prime Minister Mendico Gonzalez has called for a rapid increase in solar power generation and energy conservation.

Isobella Mocco who witnessed the arrival of the Susem in Catalonia writes: Huge crowds gathered in brilliant sunshine in the hills around Vandellos nuclear power station, 20 km west of here. They witnessed a display of power unsurpassed in the experiences of all who watched.

Notification of the Susem's imminent arrival at Vandellos was given by countless luminescent blue clouds descending onto the parks and open spaces of Barcelona and nearby towns and villages.

Then we saw the Susem craft descend through the clouds They were huge, larger than in the photographs I had seen. They were bigger than the American aircraft carriers or supertankers.

It was as though with their arrival they had brought the sunshine, for the clouds soon disappeared.

As we raced westwards from Barcelona to Vandellos I was distinguished more clearly their shapes. I could see they had flattened bottoms and grooves along their sides. At first, there were four of them, but when we neared Sabadell, I was greeted with cries of "Look!, look!", and them we saw the rest of them flying in from the north. I counted at least 20, their huge shapes darkened the sky.

On the hills above Vandellos the station was clearly visible in the valley below as well the Susem craft circling above it. I arrived just in time to see two of the Susem craft flying parallel with one another, leaving what appeared to be brightly flashing trails behind them.

Suddenly, rising from the ground there came a section of the power station. It appeared to rise slowly at first but then gathered speed. As it rose up the air above us, it glistened like a huge dagger blade reflecting the sun

Those about me watched this soaring "dagger" rise in almost silence. But soon there were cries of "Look!, look!", and as I turned to where arms were pointing, I saw what at first appeared to be swarms of specks, black against the sky speeding towards the dagger. Then to more cries, I saw other specks speeding towards it from the other direction.

These specks were flying at such tremendous speed that within seconds they had transformed into delta shaped craft. Within a few seconds more both groups had formed into formations so close they each appeared to have joined. They both sped towards one another beneath the dagger's tip So fast were the craft flying that I thought they must collide with each other. But the did not.

As the two groups of craft met they both came to an abrupt halt. Just before they did both groups arched upwards as though they gigantic bats catching moths. Within seconds of their conjoining I could see a blue glow emitting from within their cowls

The light from within them grew in intensity, then suddenly it changed to a purple of such brilliance that many watching had to turn their heads away Suddenly all the craft gave a huge jolt, as though they were a cannon firing. The purple changed to a dull blue again, and as it did I saw segment of the station rocket away. But within seconds the blue light had changed to purple, and again to be followed by another recoil from the craft. The craft did this four times before the parted.

Minutes later, a further segment of the power station began to rise into the air. For the next hour the process is repeated again and again. Within two hours a nuclear power station which took many years to construct has been completely removed from the face of the earth.

As we watch spellbound by the event we can only marvel at the power of our Susem visitors.

Stinging 'wasps' rout nuclear defender

French army flees Aliens' onslaught

By JOHN HENDRY
In STRASBOURG

THE FRENCH High Command announced this afternoon that all of its frontline forward forces had made a 'tactical withdrawal' from the east of the country.

Reeling in the face of the relentless Susem assault French forces are in reality in headlong retreat.

General Flavigny's 21st corps of armoured ground to air missile launchers stationed at Caltenom were one of the first units to come under Susem attack in the early hours of this morning. According to unofficial reports Flavigny's forces were eliminated before they had a chance to fire a single salvo and within seconds their entire launch vehicles vapourised into a mass of melted metal by the Aliens' attack craft.

Other ground to air units who did manage to launch some of their missiles at the Susem experienced an even more devastating fate when their missiles were batted straight back to the Susem. A number of French casualties have been reported.

In face of such overwhelming Susem firepower many French units stationed in the north west of the country are reported to fled from their positions. Metz is reported to be in a state of confusion as several thousands of troops have

boils over PAGE 3 ... PAGE 7

As the French army flees in the face of Su

ALIENS' SP OVER BRIT

LESLIE ALLEN, DEFENCE CORRESPONDENT

THE ALIENS spy ships flew over England yesterday and not one single RAF reconnaissance aircraft let alone fighter jets did anything to stop them.

This shocking act of negligence was admitted by junior defence minister, Andrew Wordsmith in the House of Commons this afternoon. Before a shocked and angry House the minister admitted that not only had the Aliens' spy craft been snooping Britain's nuclear defence facilities since early yesterday morning but that they had able to criss-cross the country completely unopposed by both the RAF and the army let alone repulsed by them.

Aliens intruding into UK airspace. Wordsworth said: These Aliens have definitely not given Britain's defence forces the run around.

'We know where they are'

"We know where they [the Aliens] are. We have a good idea when their main force will arrive in this country and all the armed services are ready to repel them."

There was further uproar in the Commons when MPs learnt the extent and ease of the Alien's penetration of Britain's airspace. Claiming that he had briefed by 'confidential sources' LibCon MP Hartley Shawcross said: "It would appear that the main reason why the RAF did not send any of their airplanes to intercept these Aliens' craft was that they did not want to lose any of them."

In mini clair as a agai RAF caut with W forc Ali def be suc W be the of fo the w

61: AILEEN

Normally Becky would have been in bed, but we had been out for the day with Margaret and her kids. I let her watch television while I put Patrick to bed and when I came down the programme was already on. And I hadn't the heart to turn it off. They were lovely. Both Becky and myself knelt in front of the TV barely saying a word. It was lovely the way that little fellow buzzed about the woman, Rainbow. And when he was playing hide and seek in that little hole and she found him and he was giggling in there, Becky's eyes were almost on the screen looking for him. And when all of a sudden he popped out I had such a laugh the way she shrieked and fell back on me.

And the other fellow, the plane, he was lovely as well. He reminded me of Uncle Fergel, he was forever moaning about us kids but he would do anything for us and we all loved him. As those children clambered about the plane and he was telling them to behave, memories of him came back.

After I had taken Becky up and put her to bed, I made a cup of tea and with peace and quiet at last, I had a little think. Those machines and the children all seemed so happy with one another. Rainbow appeared to be at ease with all of them as well. Perhaps they are not as terrible as people make them out to be? And if they are friendly, then what about all those big things which they are removing the nuclear power stations and bombs and things, what about them? Are they friendly as well? What about the Susem? Those French sailors, the ones from the submarine I saw on the six o'clock news round Margaret's, saying they had seen Angels and how they were loved by the people, and were they giving up the navy? They couldn't all have been making it up.

Before I started cleaning up the flat I had another cup of tea and another little think. Maybe there isn't going to be the trouble I thought there was going to be? Perhaps staying London will be alright after all?

Then I thought about Ryan. Shall I still leave him? I had another cup of tea and before I had drunk it, he came home and made my mind up for me. Not only was he the worse for wear but he had brought his friend Gary and he was just as bad. As I cleared up and looked at the pair of them slumped in front of the TV watching some video of car racing, both half asleep, I decided there and then to have m'mam to get me an application form for the Regional.

ALIENS ATTA[C]
GREAT BRITA[IN]

by SALLY O'SHEA
Defence Reporter

ALIEN reconnaissance craft have been spotted over the east and south coasts of Britain.

The Ministry of Defence media liaison officer, Colonel Giles Sackville in a bid reassure a troubled nation said: Britain's armed forces are on full alert to defend the country's nuclear facilities."

However, the ease with which the Aliens' pathfinder craft arrived over Britain raises questions as to the effectiveness of Britain's defence forces' effectiveness in repelling the expected Alien armada.

Among the many people who reported seeing the Aliens' craft was George Abrams, 67 of Saxmundham in Suffolk.

"I was out on my allotment," Mr Abrams said, "I heard this whirring sound and I stood up to see where it was coming from and there, lo and behold there it was peering down at me.

"Funny looking thing it was," said George, "it was like a huge pair of binoculars and hovering about ten feet up in the air. It was there for a moment, as though it was looking at me and then it buzzed off," he said.

Coldingham, Lothian to Weymouth in Dorset.

Margo MacDee, 35 of Rye, East Sussex, who also saw one of the Aliens' craft said: "I was just coming out of the Ship [public house] and this black crow-size object was hovering above the car park. At first, when I ran back inside no one believed what I had seen.

"But when I persuaded the other to come out and see for themselves," Margo said, "they soon saw that I was telling was the truth and that I hadn't had too much to drink after all.

"It hovered about the car park for some time and as though it was looking at us," Margo said. "It had two circles at the front which I estimate were about 40 centimetres in diameter. There were also a number of other, smaller circles around its edges and was about 20 centimetres thick.

"At this point it started to rain at which it buzzed off and went back in the Ship," she said

'WE'LL BEAT ALIENS BACK'
say top MoD chief[s]

by SONIA STONE

"WE ARE READY for the Aliens no matter where they strik[e] Britain's top brass declared yesterday. The Ministry of Def[ence] press officer, seconded Royal Hussars' Colonel James Sackville s[aid] "The entire British armed forces are trigger poised to repel an[y] the Aliens the moment they cross our shores."

Colonel Sackville, who has extensive battlefront experience both in Cyprus and Bosnia, outlined yesterday, the full magnitude of Britain's military readiness to combat the Alien's threat to the country's nuclear power station and other nuclear facilities such as the Windscale reprocessing plant and the weapons centre at Aldermaston.

Colonel Sackville said that because 'considerable elements' of Britain's armed forces were fighting in Europe with our NATO partners against the Alien's, they had considerably slowed the Alien's westward advance across the continent.

The Colonel also said that one of the reasons for NATO's current lack of success in slowing the Aliens' ... been because of the ... and

PM's: 'We will fig[ht] them on the beach[es]' speech, p9

"However," Colonel Sac[kville] said, "here in the UK our ... forces do not suffer from that ... thing. Make no mistake," the C[olonel] said, "should these Alien ch[iefs] dare to show their faces over h[ere] will soon see them off and ... bloody nose to boot."

Page 2

NATO retrenc[h]

By Max Baldslow in Brussels and Defence Staff

NATO forces have withdrawn to the west bank of the River Elbe and are establishing a new defensive line along the River Weser and the Thuringer Wald Mountains.

NATO spokesman, Galeazzo Ciano, said: "Presently the situation in the East is very fluid. General Nehring's forces have had a ... slowing the rate of the

In private, military experts are voicing reservations at NATO's bullish statements.

"Retreat after retreat," said one who wished not to named, "every time we form for attack, we have been sure-footed The Susem know our every move. We've tried hitting them with everything missiles, artillery, you name it and they've thrown it all back at us. The situation is hopeless."

According to some observers, all Allied casualties have been caused by the ricochet-ing of their own ordinance. There are also reports circulating in Brussels that many ... fled the battlefront in

Germany now non-nuclear
All German N. stations removed Chancellor in crisis meeting

FROM TOM WALKMAN IN FRANKFURT

GERMANY'S 25 nuclear power stations were blasted from the face of the earth yesterday. The stations represented one third of the country's electricity supply which means there will now be critical energy shortages to both industry and domestic consumers.

The nuclear power station at Griesfeldt, in the east of the country was the first to go. Susem craft arrived above the station shortly after 4 o'clock in the morning. By 5 o'clock nothing remained but a vast hole, hundreds of metres deep.

The surrounding towns and countryside were showered with falling brilliant blue clouds of foam containing Susem energy units. Crowds of people gathered around each cloud as it landed snatching up as many of the egg shaped units as they could.

The nuclear stations at Buchen and Munich soon fell victim to Susem action. Huge crowds, despite torrential rain, gathered on the hills above Kahl in northern Bavaria to watch sections of the station there propelled skyward. Thousands watched in near silence as section after glowing section disappeared ...

At Wackerdorf, further to the south, the gathered crowds actually cheered as the Susem arrived. Pieter Keluh, a leader of the German Greens said, "For a long time now we have been campaigning for the removal of this nuclear reprocessing plant.

"In one hour only, the Susem have this danger taken away from us. We are very pleased. We are hoping also that all the other nuclear poisons are taken from us as thoroughly."

By early afternoon the last nuclear stations at Kalker and Lingen on the Dutch border disappeared through the clouds.

Although the energy units, which have arrived in their millions, will perhaps alleviate any immediate energy shortfalls concern over the longer term power supply is being expressed by Germany's leaders.

Eva Goethe, director of IED, the German Power Inspectorate, said, "For now Germany will probably be okay, it is the summertime, but when the winter comes some shortages we will be experiencing."

'Even defence is pointless' says top US General

BY ROSS WALKER IN WEISABADEN

"EVERYTHING we hit them with boomerangs right back," said US General Howard Ruff yesterday.

General Ruff, Commander of the US XII Army Group assigned to NATO's Central Command, has recently returned from the alliance Eastern Theatre.

The General said: "Our Airborne has nothing to hit the Aliens with that will have any effect on them. These Aliens have some kind of rays, energy shields that kind of stops our missiles getting anywhere near them.

"Their space craft just cruise our barrages brushing everything form of ordinance we fire at them as though it's nothing more than cloud ...

General Ruff was equally pessimistic over the chances of NATO being able to protect any of Europe's nuclear power stations. He said, "These Alien space craft turn up at one power station after another. They send down swarms of those hornet looking things which sting everyone in sight to get the hell out of wherever they are and then hey presto, within the hour yet another power station is rocketing to the sun."

In the east and west of Croatia many men, sick of the internecine fighting, eagerly sought comparative sanctuary by enlisting for reconstruction in Bosnia. By Saturday such were the numbers at the border crossings at Slavonski Brod in Eastern Slavonia and Strmica in northern Dalmatia, many were still queuing as night fell. Some came with their families but despite their pleas only men were allowed into Bosnia.

Once past the border post and with Gurkhas and hen-gers ensuring security, each Croatian was required to undress to his underclothes. Still so dressed they were then processed. First they reported to a line of desks, each staffed by two women and a computer literate student. A third woman or a teenager sat to the side of them.

The three at the table were Tearo's and Colonel Tambassing's trained volunteers up from Ragusa. The fourth, a Bosnian, was learning from the others. This trainee also searched each Croatian's clothes. The computer literatee recorded who the man was, what he had done and where he had been. What he told was also cross-referenced against a continuously updated 'Wanted' list. The other two's task was to disbelieve everything he said.

It was for the man to prove his innocence of any activity, be it in Bosnia or service in the Croatian army and administration. Though many men failed this hurdle, those who succeeded were passed on to another line of desks.

Though similarly staffed, these recorded the men's abilities and skills. Each man was next directed to one of another line of like-staffed desks. The people at these desks appraised the man's skills and directed him to gathering groups of those similarly skilled. And while each man awaited his induction he was first sent to a fifth line of desks. Here he was questioned for information of violations and the names and whereabouts of any transgressors he knew. The staff at these desks, as at the others, reminded him of the castrational consequences of untruthfulness. Such was the trauma experienced by their induction that men willingly divulged all they knew. It was only after satisfying these interviewers was he allowed to put his clothes back on.

When three of a like skill had gathered they were assigned together. Each trio was teamed with a further two. The nine appointed one as their representative. In turn he was answerable for them. Each nine were assigned to tasks of repair or renewal, rebuilding, restoration of services. The list was long.

For those who failed to convince staff at the first desks the treatment was different. The line of desks they were next passed to, although similarly staffed as the others, had a Gurkha stood by re-enforcing repercussions of untruthfulness. Their presence also helped each man relate fully their involvement in the Croatian regime. Those innocent of misdemeanour against Bosnians were passed on to lines of other desks whose staffs consigned these men, regardless of their abilities, to trios and teams assigned to tasks of labour, road repair,

Ready for the Aliens!

By **MORRIS AUSTIN**
DEFENCE CORRESPONDENT

"BRITAIN will not be conquered by these Aliens," the MoD and Army Top Brass said yesterday.

"We know where the Aliens are, we know when they willl arrive and we re ready for them," said defiant Col. Sackville.

In an upbeat public briefing the Colonel, seconded from the battle hardened 5th Hussars, cooly outlined the extent of Britain's military preparedness to counter the Alien threat.

"Though the entire country is defended, the CoGS does not underestimate the Alien's cunning," Colonel Sackville said.

"They are likely to strike in a pincer movement from the south and the north. The armed might of the UK forces will be there to confront them," he said.

"Every nuclear power station, every nuclear defence establishment is protected by layered rings of multiple surface to air missiles," the Colonel said.

In reply to concerns of the dangers of nuclear fallout resulting from firing nuclear missiles at the Aliens, Colonel Sackville gave the assurance that nuclear weapons would only be used as weapons of last resort.

"However," he said, "the MoD does not anticipate for one moment that such weapons need be used to counter the

With Germany facing power shortages

Kinkel calls energy crisis committee

By Simon Moore in Berlin

GERMAN Chancellor Klaus Kinkel and top government ministers were in emergency session yesterday over the nation's energy crisis. At the same time, top industry bosses were calling for restrictions on the domestic supply of electricity.

With serious energy shortages looming across the whole of the EU resulting from Alien actions in the removal of nuclear power stations, the government met to decide a crash plan for conserving the nation's energy resources.

Likely cuts are said to include a ban on outdoor illuminations, voltage [...]ductions and rota cuts [...] domestic supply. Mo[...] balled coal fired static[...] will have to be brought [...]

E.Zone anger rises

Harold Jones Defence correspondent

THE ANNOUNCEMENT of exclusion zones around Britain's nuclear power stations met with wide-spread anger yesterday. It was claimed that the five mile wide zone around the power stations and other nuclear facilities with disrupt many small business and the everyday lives of countless ordinary people.

'There is no alternative'

Colonel Sackville: MoD spokesman

The Ministry of Defence (MoD) however, is adamant that the exclusion zones (EZs) will be strictly enforced. Colonel Sackville, the MoD's spokesman said: "While we naturally regret any inconvenience the EZs may cause, there is absolutely no alternative to them being implemented, and with immediate effect. In the face of the means of course the firing of all kinds of ordinance including missiles. The very last thing the MoD wants is to cause are unnecessary civilian casualties as a result of any of these forthcoming engagements."

In many of the areas affected by the EZs opinion is strongly against the MoD decision. In Suffolk where both Sizewell and Thorpeness nuclear power stations are situated, the view in towns such as Saxmundham and Aldeburgh was that no matter what Britain's defence forces attempt there is nothing to stop the Aliens from removing the power stations.

Charles Landbrigh, the landlord of the Maltings pub at nearby Snape, said: "The full force of NATO's armies right across Europe have been inc[...] Susem fr[...]

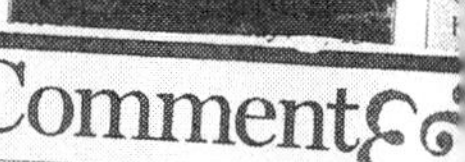

This week

SOUNDING more like a spokesman for a Dads Army than an elite fighting force equipped to the teeth with lethal technology, Colonel Sackville tried his upmost to convince a sceptical audience that Britain's is able to defend its nuclear facilities.

Replying to questions of the ease to which Alien craft were

Pardoned Parisians pleased

By **PAULINE MOU**

PARISIANS breathed a sigh of relief yesterday when they learned their city will not now be blasted by their errant submarine falling on them.

Cafe proprietor Maxine Jeune said: "We may be without electricity and friends but we have Paris. It is springtime and now the sunshine is with us again," she said.

Smiling,, Maxine pointed up to the sky outside her café overlooking the Quai St Michel and the Notre Dame. Madame Jeune's wistful attitude is shared by many in the world's City of Romance, even though it may be accompanied by a Gallic shrug.

Paul Maison, owner of several apartment blocks in 7th Arrondissment, an area which had been directly threatened by the submarine, summed up the feeling of many of the nation's property owners: "We have difficulties, but they will pass.

"The important thing is that the buildings of Paris are still here," he said. "The follies and machinations of politicians will always bring [...]

All French nuclear power stations gone

David Webster in Cherbourg

LA HAGUE, the last of France's 67 nuclear power stations was blasted skywards early yesterday morning by the Aliens.

Crowds gathered in the pouring rain as the huge, two kilometre long Susem space craft propelled section of the doomed power station upwards through the cloud filled skies and to the sun.

Though there was an extensive police presence around the power station, people watched its departure in glum silence.

Although the sky was heavily overcast with rain clouds it was possible to see bright pulses of light emitted by other Susem craft blasting segment after segment of the power station out of Earth orbit and to the sun.

The eradication of France's much vaunted nuclear industry and its near monopoly of the nation's electricity supply poses grave problems to industry and consumers alike. Many experts are already predicting that France's role as a leading industrial power has come to an end.

Adding to the French people's woes is that whereas countries affected by the Susem removing their nuclear facilities have been supplied with the Aliens' energy units, France, because of its actions will not receive any.

France's new energy minister, Mimi la Flousie said: "The actions of the Aliens in removing our

rubble removal, demolition.

During the first days there was little busyness at a further set of desks. These were staffed to deal with miscreants, soldiers who had served in Bosnia and others who had actively abetted Croatia's activities there. Men who found themselves at these desks were made even more aware of the disadvantages of dishonesty. There were many confessions and more than a little contrition proffered. Those who so did and satisfied the women staffing these desks, were passed on to the next lines and to tasks more onerous, supervised disinterring the bodies of Bosnian victims of murder and massacre as well as the compare-ative lighter task of rounding up the many thousands of stray, now savage dogs.

Beyond these frontline desks there was another set. During the first days these desks went unmanned. They were set up to deal with the real wrong-doers. But none had yet shown at the border posts.

Those interviewing did so for two hours then were replaced by another team. After resting they returned to a desk assigned to different stages of the processing.

With the information gleaned from the inductees the list of the wanted guilty grew. Names on it began cross-referencing with those with red heads at Korčula and others engaged in mine removal. The legal teams in Ragusa began interviewing anew. They came away with further confessions and yet more names.

With much of the world's attention elsewhere and news reporters absent, little notice was made of the fleet of military transport planes flying from France and landing during Sunday at the newly cleared and repaired runways at Tuzla. In the lead plane was Jacques Forissier.

He was overseeing the delivery of the first cargo of a billion dollars of emergency supplies. The French government had eagerly agreed the Susem offer he had brought back from Tabajara, of the supplies of Aid in exchange for soufins. The terms for their delivery of the units over France added extra urgency to the aircrafts' departures.

With the arrival at Neum of the second contingent of Khmer Rouge, the Serbian and Croatian inmates incarcerated inside their own prisons were now harnessed into teams for more mine clearance. Though there were no direct deaths due to the clearances (the shock absorbing cushioning of the foamed filled clogs prevented them) there were a number of heart attacks among the clearers. The clogs while preventing direct fatalities could not, of course, protect against strains and dislocated joints. Sufferers of such were uncoupled and left by the wayside for the conscripted Croatians to collect and return them to their prisons.

Although there was sometimes reluctance from the mine clearers at the front to proceed, the involuntary pace of those at the back propelled them on. The lash of the Khmer's driver's whip drove away any desire to slacken. However, there was succour awaiting those at the front. On every hour the team was rested for a few minutes, after which it was their turn to go up the back (and a whipping should they too slacken from a satisfactory speed). At the end of each dawn to dusk day, the remains of the team were watered, fed and rested for the night. And ready to begin another day in another freshly formed forty manned gang. By Sunday tens of thousands of mines had been detonated. But there were still millions more awaiting the tramp of their feet.

Colonel Tambassing, despite the many Croatians queuing at the two border posts, was aware there was still an absence of senior members from the Croatian regime presenting themselves at Pelješac. Neither had there been any from Serbia. Even ordinary Serbian men were staying away. The bridges over the Drina, the Serbian border with Bosnia, were still deserted. These absences now irked both the Colonel and Tearo. But again, events were soon to change this state of affairs.

Meanwhile, in Ragusa the final preparations for the trials and sentencing of those Serbians and Croatians already in custody on Korčula, and who stood accused of crimes in Bosnia, were put in place. The panels of volunteering judges were also selected, many of whom were of school and student age, as were most of those of the prosecution.

63: SHERPALS

Things are moving faster. And there are more of them. The physical condition of the first people from Piauí arriving last Friday took Menpemelo aback. So much so that she insisted that every singe one of them took a session in the mormic before they were let leave. Other arrivals from the west have received the same attention. I dread the deluge, once word of a cure for chagas spreads. Pedro, his men, evermore the villagers, including women and younger ones are ranging even further west, east and with the Brazilian soldiers now gone, northward as well. Tabajara would be half empty were it not for steady streams of outsiders taking educational inspections and inductions. So many, that Elana and the others now arrange guides in rota.

Rainbow's Thursday telecast has had its effect on outsiders within the territory Paceillo wants cleared. Seen from the viewing platform the 2-22 where once was the occasional vehicle is now nose-to-tail eastward day and night with the military, miners from Serra Pelada and many others. Roads to the west and south are said to be the same. The American's resolve cracking has brought home to many that there is now no one of significance to oppose the Susem.

The sight of Sardon, as he and his sherpals laid irrigation infrastructure, I'm sure also helped outsiders to move. The irrigation pipeways from the Tocantins and Paraiba rivers, so Milophinia's maps show, stretch for hundreds of miles not just eastward but to the south as well. The first clearings of caatinga have been made between Pacuja and Carire. Sowing of the iron ore plants begins tomorrow.

The children who flew with Milophinia and other Susem overseeing the clearings described the machines making the circles. They said they are a cross between large sherpals and hover mowers. Each team cleared rings of circles, cut one, left the next and so on all the way round. Following them were thousands of regular sherpals descending on carpets, racing over each cleared area making millions of minute holes. Holing completed they carpeted to the next. More sherpals clicked the irrigation lines in place and within minutes, so the children said, clouds were forming. Two continuous days of nutrient rain, Milophinia mentioned, moistens the ground ready for sowing.

Minero-agriculture has not been the children's only interest, the teaching machines have moved them on. As they have me and everyone else. Lucia's voice beaming from our screens, disorientating at first, has progressed for most students from straightforward tuition to discussion. It is still strange though to hear several Lucia's conversing differently to different people. Every time a machine is switched on, apart from the scent of lemon there is Lucia's "Hello, how are you?" I don't know about others' Lucia but I'm becoming quite attached to mine.

I think Rainbow is attached to hers as well. She is definitely attached to the sherpals. She made a marvellous half hour programme with them and the

Aliens' UK N power wipe-out!

Dramatic pics of Susem stations sun-ward send-off

CHRONICLE NEWS STAFF

ALIEN station buster spaceships made short work of Britain's nuclear power stations yesterday.

The Aliens arrived at dawn, they were gone by noon and so had Britain's entire nuclear industry.

While the Aliens were last seen flying west, countless nuclear power stations, reprocessing plants, missiles and bomb factories were speeding towards the sun.

At the same time millions of British households were the grateful owners of the Alien's cost-free energy units.

As the Aliens blasted one power station skywards Britain's much vaunted armed forces were nowhere to be seen.

The Aliens' fleets of two kilometre spacecraft were spotted at first light over the North Sea off Lowestoft. From there flotillas of them made the way across Britain destroying every nuclear

ALIENS OBLITERATE ALL UK NUCLEAR POWER STATIONS

By MAX BALDSLOW, and Defence Staff

IN LESS THAN four hours, all of Britain's nuclear power stations were wiped out by Alien action. Attempts at defensive action were swept aside as the Alien invasion conquered the country from east to west, blasting the country's nuclear facilities to the Sun.

Britain's Defence forces proved no match to the superior Alien technology. The first Alien sorties were detected at dawn along the entire length of the East coast. Countless illuminated blue sheets plummeted through an overcast sky from as far afield as Edinburgh and Brighton.

At 6am and before people power units, the nuclear power stations at Torness and Hartlepool were under attack from Alien battlefleets.

An hour later, while Hunterston and Chapelcross suffered a similar fate, a third battlefleet was attacking Sizewell, the jewel in BEC's crown.

Despite a thunderstom and torrential rain many local residents gathered to watch Sizewell's destruction. Other crowds gathered to see nearby Bradwell meet a similar fate. Said Edith Sidcome, from nearby Burnham-on-Crouch, "Its sad in a way to see it go, many local people worked at Bradwell. With it gone nobody

Harwell has had it

by JOANNA REDWOOD

HARWELL, founding home of the nation's nuclear research, and the nearby Rutherford Centre were gone within the hour. Hundreds of staff fled from their laboratories and there was traffic chaos on the A34 and surrounding roads in Oxen as commuters stopped their cars to grab the thousands of energy units floating down on bright blue sheets of foam.

But even before the last of the units had been snapped up, people were gazing upwards in wonder at two huge Susem craft descending from the clouds and flying towards Harwell.

Distraught laboratory and other staff watched

Sellafield sent skyw

By DAVID SEWARD

THE THORPE nuclear plant at Sellafield was destroyed within minutes of Alien craft arriving. British Nuclear Fuels, owners of the plant, declined to comment on the loss of their central facility.

Thorpe, Britain's controversial plutonium reprocessing plant, was blasted to the Sun in ten sections the plant and adjacent facilities were blasted from the Cumbria ... Each glowed as though ... newly a... Nippon ... tonium ... tion.

ALDERMASTON DESTROYED!

By JOHN HARWOOD

BRITAIN's nuclear bomb factory was snatched by the Susem and sent skyward to the Sun in the time it takes to drink a cup of tea. Thousands of anti-nuclear demonstrators cheered as their favourite hate establishment was propelled to the heavens in double quick time.

Elaine Dodds, a veteran campaigner from nearby Newbury, who was outside the plant as it went to the Sun, said: "Ever since the Susem started removing nuclear plants in Russia we have prayed for this moment. It is an evil abomination, we are thankful to the Susem for doing this for us."

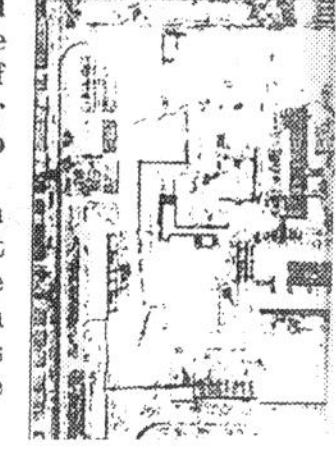

FAREWELL FASLANE

EXPRESS REPORTER

BRITAIN'S nuclear submarine base at Faslane on the Clyde was removed within the space of 90 minutes after a squadron of Susem craft appeared over the base from the east shortly before 8 o'clock this morning.

Their arrival was preceded by immense sheets of blue foam carrying countless energy units floating down over the surrounding towns and villages including as far afield as Glasgow and East Kilbride.

Within 30 minutes of the Susem arriving a section of the base including water was observed rising up into the clouds. Nearby residents said it glowed red

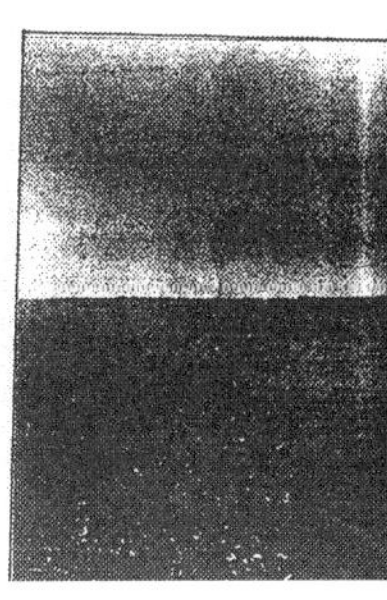

children. The couple of minutes she had them dancing on a table top was a delight. All the same though, it took hours of rehearsal to get them performance perfect. Most of which was teaching the sherpals to dance in the first place. The Susem, possessing no sense of musical rhythm, were the first difficulty to be overcome. But once Rainbow explained to Terbal what was wanted, he and she overcame everything and the sherpals soon had the hang of it.

It is not as if the Susem haven't heard the music of down here, I just don't think that they had ever really listened to any. The sherpals' dancing was the last part of their routine. The first part showed the sherpals mending a punctured children's bicycle tyre. Four of them undid the wheel, twenty more carried it away, removed the tyre, fixed the hole, ran back and all of the sherpals put the wheel back on again. All this was accomplished against a background of sitting, silently watching children.

From the bike the sherpals moved on to climbing a breadfruit tree. By linking their legs together they swung in chains from branch to branch and up to a fruit. They then broke it off from the tree, rolled themselves round it and brought it back down.

There was a nice little turn of dozens of the sherpals creeping aboard a lazing dog. After a couple of them had given the dog's tail a tug, and it running off, the sherpals did acrobatics on its back including climbing up on one another as acrobats do on motorbikes. (The sherpals got off when the dog became bored and laid down again).

It was after the dog show that there were the shots of sherpals dancing to Martha and the Vandellas' "Dancing in the Street". Fifty of them in moving curving lines and all in unison kept turning back to front in time to the music. And when the bit about "people swaying" came on, the camera panned to another fifty of them linked in a necklace around Rainbow, doing just that. With the music ending and a beaming Rainbow waving goodbye till next time, she had the sherpals gathered in two long lines as though bowing a goodbye as well.

Sadly though, there are sometimes downsides to the new. Word of Rainbow's dance routine has spread among the Susem. Many of them came to the rehearsals. All went away addicted. The music came from Rainbow's iPod. She, like many, is into the revival of the revival of American '60s music. Rainbow's tuition with the Susem is now as much to do with singing as it is speech therapy. They train with her disks and I shudder to think what sense they make of the words. But they have undertaken tuition seriously, including sharing turns at leading and backing. The outcome of which, alas, and despite they being an advanced civilisation, is non-stop karaoke. It's just so common. I fear for standards.

Greens jubilant

Daniella Lyon
Environment Editor

BRITAIN'S environmentalists and Anti-nuclear campaigners have welcomed the Alien destruction and removal of the country's nuclear power stations and weapons.

Said Jonquil Taylor of FoE: "In 4 hours the Susem removed what we and others have campaigned for 40 years and more. Britain is rid at last of its nuclear nightmare."

Steve Jones of the Anti-nuclear Alliance said: "The mad scientists, mad politicians and the even madder men of the military-industrial complex have had their come uppance. What the Susem have done to these people serves as a wa-

Energy Units gl

by Daniella Lyon
Environmental Editor

SO MANY Susem "Soufin" energy units have fallen in the areas around the former sites of nuclear power stations that there is now a "glut" of them. Many have been reported as being sold for "substantial" sums.

John Watson 52, of Bolton Road, Ipswich said: "One of the Susem blue blankets came down in Christchurch Park, just across the road. Within minutes there was a mad scramble for the units. Whole families were carrying off armfuls of them. By my last trip every last unit was gone."

Mr Watson said he found the units easy to instal. He showed how he and his neighbour had connected one of his soufins to the wiring of his flat. "It took seconds to do. You just turn off the mains supply, clip off the ... cables to the

BEC

By Robert Burns

BRITISH Energy Corporation was floored in four hours by the Susem Its Mayfair offices BECs chairman, Lord Cedric was in crisis conference over the company's future.

In less than four hours the Susem wiped all the company's assets off the map and blasted them to the Sun. The company's bankers and markets will now be wanting to know BEC's proposals as to how they are going to repay the estimated £3 billion plus loans.

Lord Cedric, and other directors, whose recent 40 per cent salary hikes outraged citizens and City alike, is unlikely to receive a sympathetic hearing from institutional lenders as well as banks. Immediate winding up is the only way

The seizure of Sizewell

Sizewell nuclear power station was attacked by Susem craf and completely destroyed within two hours. John Rosewel who was at the perimeter of the Sizewell Exclusion Zone

The Susem came before the dawn. Luminescent sheets of blue bubbles, lighting the darkness, drifted down their cargos of alien energy units. They came to earth in cities and towns as far afield as Ipswich, Norwich, Ely and Hertford. People in their thousands, despite the early hour and torrential rain, rose from their slumbers and rushed to gather this manna from the heavens.

The rain, as though in prophetic omen, shrouded the coming morning in another tempestuous squall. But as the dawning day illuminated the huge spheres and cooling towers of Sizewell, reflected off the surrounding wettened green fields of growing grain, the next Susem came.

Four of their spacecraft slipped silently through the clouds, their black triangular shapes at first barely visible against the overcast above. They swooped low over the power station, briefly disappearing from view behind the reactor buildings. With the last vestiges of night remaining, and the rain still unrelenting, bursts, flashes of blue and purple light were soon coming from within the power station's confines.

Within minutes, an assortment of army and station vehicles sped through Sizewell's gates. And running, their arms waving about them, came soldiers and others. All fled as though in fear and were being pursued. Soon it became apparent that indeed they were.

Behind vehicles and men were small flying hornet shaped objects, harrying them on their way. Amid this mayhem of shrieks, shouts, accelerating trucks and cars, other Susem now came.

From the east across the North Sea, descending from the clouds, black against the gathering brightness, there appeared a line of ten cigar shaped craft. Even though they were some distance from Sizewell, it was obvious

they were huge. Two kilometres or so from the shore, they stopped and hovered motionless, as though aerial aircraft carriers at anchor. Minutes later the small delta shaped craft flew up from the power station, and as they did, two of the larger craft moved towards it together.

They flew first to the north of Sizewell then slowly over it to the south, dropping a line of red glowing spheres as they went. As the last floated down, both craft arced apart. Immediately, beams of brilliant blue light shone down from them. But as each craft moved slowly forwards, the beams of light did not. They stayed where they were as though suspended in mid-air.

The Susem craft continued to send down more beams of the same blue brilliance. Soon there were two curving walls of light behind them.

As the craft came closer the magnitude of their size became apparent, they were at least a kilometre in length, nearly half as wide and more than two hundred metres high. Save for their dulled grey colour and flattened undersides, from which the beams emitted, they had no noticeable features. And they made no discernable sound.

After travelling more than a kilometre, the two craft started arcing inwards. The nearest wall of light began obscuring the other. They were as curtains being slowly, yet relentlessly drawn around a bed in a terminal ward. After a further kilometre both craft met. From tip to tip they took ten minutes. Ten minutes to suspend two walls of brilliant blue light each three kilometres long and hundreds of metres high.

As the two walls of light met, their blue colour changed to purple. They then began to pulse and glow brighter. The pulsing became ever faster, the brilliance even stronger. Then from within the walls, the land and buildings they'd enclosed rose up. Slowly at first as though unsure, but then gathered speed.

As this hapless eye shaped section of the station, three kilometres lor though less wide, soar into the sky, and away fr the walls of light, its sid radiated a white yell brilliance. Up and up still rose, glistening in t sky like a huge downwa pointing diamond dagg blade. Its brilliance sho like a beacon against t dark storm clouds.

Up and up it still ro and then disappeare through them. With t speed of a switch, the wa of light disappeared too.

No sooner had the ea day darkened down aga than the heavens, althou hidden by the clou erupted in a rage of bl and purple. Not once t many times. It was though Thor and all t other gods of thunder a storm had unleashed the ire as one.

Even though the clou were heavy, darkened, w rain, such was the enorm ty of power unleash above them, that the la all about and all those a everything which sto upon it, from horizon horizon became, in tur flashed blue then purp Again and again. The was no other colour.

But with the last pulse purple rage there ca two more Susem cr above Sizewell. And on more with walls of lig they were soon sendi another section of the s tion shining and soaring and through the cloud and the awaiting hamme and anvils of angry gods.

Section after doome section relentlessly f lowed skyward. Within 100 minutes of the Susem arrival, Sizewell nucle power station, the jewel British Energy Corp ration's crown was gon gouged from the face of t earth. The Susem cra their task completed a without apparent pau then flew westwards.

Where once stood nuclear power statio which cost £2 billion build and once suppli five percent of t Britain's electricity, the is now a very large ho Ideal for a fish farm?

Round here, they have all got them in their motors. I don't drive myself but I got one for the flat. Cost me £30, well worth it, works a treat, the LEB can cut me off anytime they like for all I care. I got mine off Jerry at work. He lives up Chelmsford way. He says people round where he is were picking them up by the armful. We didn't get any round here, well not directly, but they were soon about. Harry said at the end of last week he saw a couple of blokes round the back of Finsbury Park with a transit full of them. Knocking them out for £90 a time he said, and they had a queue.

Of course there have been the moans from petrol stations and the electricity people but who cares, serves them right, all those fat salaries. A week ago they were saying we were going have power cuts and rationing. Let them sweat that's what I say.

Though it's nearly the summer, I reckon this winter there's going to be a big run on heaters, electric ones, so I'm getting mine in now before the prices go up. I have gas for the central heating but why use it when there's free electricity?

And it's not just homes and motors either. Dave, my boss at work also had some off Jerry and he's running everything off of them. As he says, apart from cutting costs no end, well, those processors do eat up a lot of power, the competition is bound sooner or later to have them and he's just getting in first. It will be interesting to see if anyone puts their prices down though.

I mentioned this to Harry now he has the Greenwood running on them. But he shook his head, saying his prices were already low.

There has been talk, as the government stands to lose billions because of people not buying petrol or using electricity, mains that is, they are going to be putting up VAT and income tax. But with the size of their majority just let them try, and then see what happens to them. Though I suppose it wouldn't be unreasonable if they put the Road Fund Licence up. All the same though, because it's costing no extra to drive anywhere the roads are jammed, so no one is actually doing any more miles than they were before. And that is another reason for not having a car.

But no matter what the government tries to do, I reckon that when everything is said and done, that little soufin sat in my meter cupboard will save me a good £700 a year. And that is the equivalent to me earning £25 a week, before stoppages that is, which is not bad at all especially when it's only cost me thirty quid.

UCLEAR POWER STATIONS LOSS AFTERMATH

'There was nothing we could do'

BY SALLY O'SHEA
Defence Reporter

SOMBRE assessment of ritain's defence debacle was iven by Ministry of Defence pokesman, Colonel James ackville yesterday. In a downeat statement, Colonel Sackville aid: "There was nothing we ould do. The Aliens hit up with reaponry against which Britain's rmed forces had no defence.

"We had pea shooters to the hallenger tanks," the Colonel said. Defence personnel in every DEZ Designated Enforcement Zone) were argeted arrays of paralysing darts red from their delta-winged attack raft. Our radars were unable to egister their arrival until it was too ite. Every missile battery was nmobilised before their crews had pportunity to identify suitable argets.

Col. Sackville also said those RAF ornado fighter jets which were irborne, their crews were either orced to passively observe the enemy's ctions or if they attempt to attack heir plane were immobilised by the liens and their crews forced to eject rom their craft. Even microwave ommunications with [Command and

PM calls for calm

"WE MUST ALL STAY CALM," the prime minister, Edward Campbell said yesterday. The prime minister was speaking in the wake of the Aliens attack on Britain's nuclear power stations and strategic defence installations. Stressing that is important for the nation to keep a cool head while the losses caused by the Alien's to Britain's vital resources are assessed.

The prime minister, addressing a sombre House of Commons, said that the longterm consequences of the Aliens' attacks might not be as devastating as was first thought.

By WALLY BAGSHOTT

He said: "Although Britain has forgone an important part of its electrical generating capacity, by careful husbanding of our remaining resources, the nation's energy needs can still be met."

Mr Campbell said that he had already ordered the Department of Energy to present to him within the next few days the contingency plans he had asked for more than a week ago.

He also said that the major power companies had informed him that a national electricity supply

defence capability now that the Aliens have removed all of the country's nuclear facilities, the prime minister said: "While it is too soon for me to give the House a full and accurate forecast of the United Kingdom's defence position, precise figure are not yet available the country security situation has not been significantly compromised by the Aliens' attacks.

When asked as to the number of causalities suffered by the armed services as a direct result of the Aliens' attacks, the

Alien energy units proving a boon

by Joanna Whitestone
Environment Editor

THERE were cheers all round yesterday for the arrival of the Alien energy units. People across East A...

But it is not only homes these units power. They can also be used to drive cars and other ...and again all for ... lon't have to ...ything off now

do we," said Tom Watkins, 25, of Ipswich. "We don't have pay to run the car either," he said, "what our local garage is going to do now we don't need petrol I shudder to think."

With the arrival of free power in many parts of the country it also means that many businesses will be placed at distinct commercial advantage. It means that many of them

'BIG POWER CUTS COMING' WAR

By EDWARD STRONG
Industrial Editor

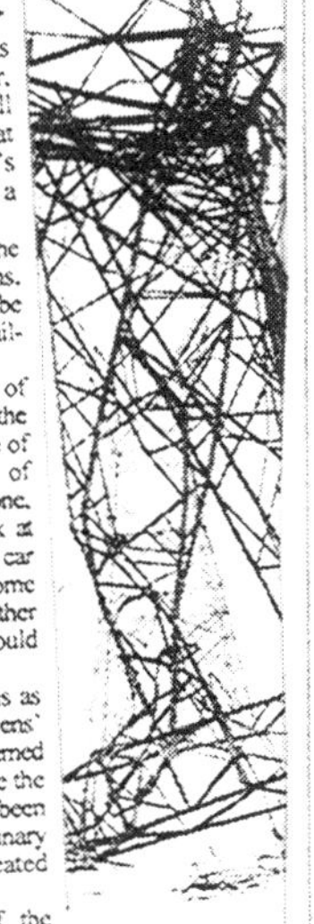

"EXPECT POWER CUTS and rationing this winter," says the chairman of National Power, Lord Curzon. "With the Susem removing all of the UK's nuclear power station it means that more than 20 per cent of the country's electricity generating supply is gone at a stroke," he said.

Lord Curzon is equally pessimistic over the introduction of new gas fired power stations. "There is no chance that enough of them could be built let alone commissioned in time there is available before the cold weather sets in," he said.

He is also just as dismissive over the impact of the Aliens energy units being able to plug the energy gap. "There is not a cat in hell's chance of their noddy units making the slightest bit of difference," he said. "When all is said and done, what are they? No matter what way you look at them they can little more than glorified car batteries. And where's the power going to come to charge them up? That is what I and many other people in the power generation industry would very much like to know."

Lord Curzon's deputy, William Sherman, is as equally dismissive of the efficiency of the Aliens' power units. However, Sherman is also concerned about the units' safety. He said: "Not only are the Alien units untested, it has not yet even been ascertained if they are compatible to ordinary household appliances, let alone sophisticated industrial requirements."

Mr Sherman added: "These reports of the ... Russians, Ukrainians and other eastern

Where were they?

By LORD JOHN STEPHENS

WHERE was Britain's much vaunted defence? Where were our so-called 'Triggers-at-the-ready-Tommies'? Where was the military might of leading edge technology on which we taxpayers have spent so lavishly? There was no sign of any of them yesterday. Only 'Defeat' put in an appearance.

Or is the right word: 'Rout'? The British armed forces' performance yesterday was as lamentable as our footballers and cricketers.

The Susem walked right over us without even pausing for breath. Their 'station buster' spacecraft arrived with the dawn and they were gone by noon without so much so much as a single British bullet being fired in defence let alone in anger.

Meanwhile this country was being raped of all its nuclear power stations power stations which have cost us consumers dear. Also whisked away in same short space of time is, or rather was, country's nuclear deterrence, a deterrence which has cost us taxpayers even more. If all this was not injury and humiliation enough our government now insults us by claiming that we can live without these power stations and bombs.

If indeed this is the case then the question needs to be asked why it was so 'essential' to the nation's security to spend so much of our money on them in the first place let alone on defending them?

65: JAMES

Troubles for me never seem to come singly but in threes. This time there has been the break-up with Frankie of course. The second has been that the newly installed washing machine in the flat on the floor above mine sprang a leak during my weekend away which has meant a ruined home and most of my possessions therein. And the third? I don't have a job any more.

I arrived in the office on the following Monday and was greeted by the contents of my desk in a black plastic bag and security guards escorting me off the premises. Being big promoters of utilities' equities not just in Europe but worldwide, the impact of the Susem energy units has hit Morgans badly. They were also specialists in raising finance for utilities too, more so to the East Europeans. Although further income from that source is gone, there is also little prospect of business from elsewhere making good the shortfall. The outcome of which is that Morgans have slashed Corporate Banking in half and 200 unfortunates including me have been 'let go'.

I had an inkling that something was afoot and Morgans have not been alone in cutting staff, or "repositioning their presence in the corporate utilities sector," as the redundancy letter put it, but they have certainly been the most ruthless. All the same I am annoyed with them. There was no consultation, the only consolation being the cheque enclosed with the letter, although it is almost a year's salary it is minus any bonus I may well have been due.

But thankfully it, along with my savings, eases away any immediate financial worries. Giving some thought on what to do next, I am still torn between seeking another job in banking or taking a sabbatical and travel.

Regardless of what I decide, times ahead are going to be bumpy. The advent of free power, pollution-free and portable as well, will mean the economies of many countries are going to experience some rather radical changes. How many sheikhs can stay in power with the oil price plummeting the way it is, it's already down to $10.90? How are the banks, Western governments who have lent to them, going to get their money back?

With free electricity, the remaining conventional power stations, once assets are now liabilities. How is the energy sector going to service its debts? How secure will banks be now many of their loans to these companies are unsecured and soon to be non-performing? Perhaps it is no real surprise Morgans are hurriedly "repositioning" themselves. But the knock-on effects are going to reach far beyond the energy sector. How secure will currencies be, including the dollar and the Euros?

Although I am still thinking on what to do, I have decided to invest my redundancy money in what I can be sure of, gold and Swiss francs.

President orders National alert

FROM TOM FLETCHER IN WASHINGTON

[A]LL UNITED STATES forces [h]ave been put on armed alert to [c]ombat any possible Alien [i]nvasion. This step has been taken [b]y President Warren because of [t]he gravity of public unease [o]ver the Aliens plans.

News of the Aliens' progressive destruction of European and Asian nuclear power stations and weapons is being reported almost hourly.

The loss of nuclear power generation - which is considerably smaller than many other countries - is not as great a concern (apart to the owners of the nuclear plants). But the loss of the US's nuclear arsenal would leave the country exposed and vulnerable, large sections of the public believe.

"It's a nice time for the US to divorce itself from the nuclear option," said Daniel Ichan of

However, other voices give [a]n opposite view. Although not [as] powerful as the pro-nucle[ar] lobby, the "antis" are a growi[ng] force. Apart from the young a[nd] veteran anti-nuclear campaigne[rs] several respected defence analy[sts] are suggesting that the remov[al] of the US nuclear stockpil[e] might actually be more of a bles[s]ing than a disaster.

"If the Susem rid us of the he[ad]aches of Savannah River and Han[ford] Reservation (troubled nuclear w[eapons] sites) then it's a fair price to pa[y] parting with our nuclear ars[enal] and power plants," he said. Professor Ichan's view, Ame[rica] without nuclear weaponry wo[uld] lead to a more open government.

"Because nuclear weapons are wrapped up secrecy," he said, inevitably leads, as the past sh[ows] to all manner of shenani[gans] wouldn't be at all surprised Pentagon really did have thing going with the French

Weygand survive[s] assassination atte[mpt]

BY OLIVER MOSLEY IN PARIS

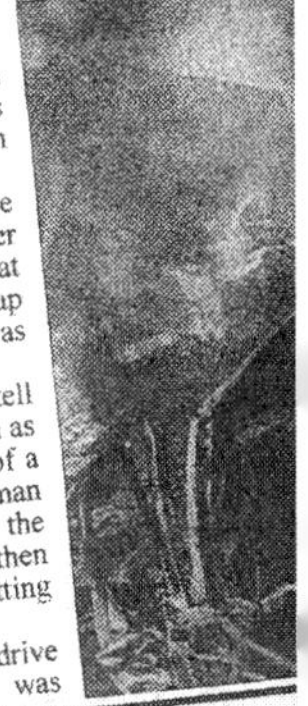

DISGRACED former French defence minister, Maurice Weygand has been seriously injured in an attempted assassination yesterday evening. His chauffeur was also seriously injured in the attack.

The attack took place outside the village of Ponthiery as the ex-minister was being driven to his home at Fontainbleau. A motorcyclist drew up alongside Weygand's car as he was being driven along the motorway.

Weygand's chauffeur was able to tell police that the motorcyclist's uniform as well as his motorcycle, were those of a traffic policeman. The bogus policeman signalled for them to stop. When the chauffeur did so, the 'policeman' then fired into Weygand's citroen hitting both him and the minister.

The chauffeur then managed to drive the car at the gunman before he was

ALIENS ATTACK US AIRCRAFT CARRIER

by Jose Servem in Rome

[A]MERICA'S ONCE [p]owerful 5th fleet [h]as been dealt a [m]ajor knock-out [b]low by the Aliens.

In the early hours of [y]esterday morning two Susem [n]ation-buster spaceships [s]wooped down on the aircraft [c]arrier US Franklin Roosevelt [w]hile it was sailing off of [It]aly's Adriatic coast. Within [se]conds the two kilometre [lo]ng spaceships had lifted the [8]5,000 tons aircraft carrier [th]ousands of feet up into the [ai]r.

The Aliens then 'flew' the [st]ricken carrier along with the [w]ater surrounding it across [s]outhern Italy and dumped it [d]own in the Gulf of Taranto.

Eye witness, Enrico Tellini, [a] port manager at Brindisi [an]d who saw the carrier [be]ing flown through the air, [sa]id: "It was like an icicle [gl]istening in the sun. The two [A]liens spaceships carried the [A]merican's ship though the [ai]r as if it were a kite, that it [w]as their plaything."

No sooner had the Aliens [sp]aceships dropped the [ai]rcraft carrier down in the [w]ater again, than they were [zi]pping down powerful rays [w]hich cut massive gashes in [th]e Roosevelt's sides.

According to those who [sa]w the Susem in action, they [to]ok only a matter of minutes [to] gouge out the aircraft [ca]rrier's nuclear reactors and [bl]ast them up into space and [to]wards the sun.

[L]ater reports say that many [of] the US sailors still trapped

In the wake of the attempted assassination of Ma[urice Weygand] questions are being asked as to the extent of [the US' knowledge] and involvement in the French missile attac[k]

Denial doubts

WITH FRANCE still reeling from the latest casualty in their leaders' murky affair of their submarine *Tonnant's* nuclear missile attack on the Susem, a number of unanswered questions still remain.

According to Weygand a senior delegation of the French navy met with US State Department representatives on the island of Miquelon, a French possession off the Canadian coast the day after the Aliens' presence was first confirmed.

Weygand further claims that the US delegation arrived with

Alien invaders already p[...] "It was though they ha[d] them down from a s[...] dusted them down," We[ygand is] on record as saying.

Was the attempt on W[eygand's] life a bid to stop h[im] revealing further deta[ils of the] *Tonnant* debacle th[at ...] would prefer were kept [...]

Both the French [...] administrations have [...] others' ill-tempered [...] for decades. So why [...] Weygand has any s[...] would US involve th[...] such an operation a[...] Susem and in

US proves powerless against Alien attack

Edward Trelawny
in Naples

TWO Alien battleships effortlessly plucked the mighty US 88,000 tons 5th fleet aircraft carrier, Franklin Roosevelt from one sea and flew it to another.

At first light the Aliens swooped on the unsuspecting ship, stationed off the Italian coast, lifted it 1,000 feet into the air and 30 minutes later plopped it down without so much as a splash in the Ionian Sea 80 miles away.

With the crew then abandoning the Roosevelt the Aliens set about carving out the ship's nuclear reactors and missiles. By 8 o'clock the once mighty

Once again the Alien's have shown that no matter what the military might of the world may throw at them, they are unstoppable. What is the US military going to do, as now looks likely, when the Susem cross the Atlantic?

Marin Friedland in Washington reports: The prospects for the military appear bleak indeed. The moment the Susem arrive over the North American continent the use of nuclear missiles becomes impossible for fear of the consequent blast and radiation on the American public.

With threats of legal action against the US military from numerous civil interest groups compounding President [illegible]'s current political woes, it is

"If you don't want it in the house, I will use it for the car," Daffyd said, "I've not forked out fifty quid for nothing."

"Fifty pounds!" I said. Well that was it. I wasn't having him putting it in the car, he spends too much money on it as it is. "In the house," I said. At first when he brought the soufin home I was worried about safety. And it looked uncanny. Not the shape or the size but the colour, dull silver and smooth and it was cold as winter.

But since then though, I have become quite attached to our soufin. I even call it "Sam," after one of my teachers, Samuel Prior, who was a bundle of energy. Although he took us for English in his spare time he taught every one of us to swim. He was also always taking us up to London and Stratford to see Shakespeare. In the sixth form he had all of us signed up to CND and Plydd Cymru. In his spare time he wrote poetry, he even had some published. We all bought his 'Rebel Pilgrim' and it wasn't just to boost sales either, I still have mine. I got into Manchester University because of his extra tutorials. I often wonder where Mr Prior went after the scandal of him running off with a CND woman from London, she half his age and everyone calling him "Sam the Ram."

But my "Sam the Soufin" sits quietly in the cupboard under the stairs by the old meter. I stroke him every time I go for the vacuum or the iron and say "Thank you Sam for the electricity." He's still very cold though.

It is funny how we have all got used him. Glyn says he likes him because I don't go round nagging to keep turning things off when they are not being used. Boys can be so unthinking the way they say things but I understand what he means. It's something I don't have to worry about any more.

We aren't the only ones in Cilgerren with a soufin but up in Gwynedd and Clwyd they were covered in those blue bubble sheets of them, all the way down to Machynlieth. Well they have, or did have nuclear power stations at Trawsfynydd and Anglesey, as well at Llandudno. The Susem took all the railway trucks and the lines from there as well. At first I didn't realise why they had to do that, then Daffyd explained it was a marshalling yard for the spent fuel up to Sellafield, of course that has gone as well now.

Daffyd also said that the day after the Susem had gone there were hundreds of soufins on sale in Aberystwyth, but by the time he went out at lunchtime they had all been snapped up. Sam came from someone Daffyd works with. I still think £50 is a bit of a cheek, especially as he came for nothing in the first place.

'Tonnac Water takes its toll

Martin Friedland in Washington and David Webster in Paris

THE US administration's denials of involvement in the attempted nuclear missile attack by the French submarine Tonnant against the Aliens are unravelling following further revelations from France and the testimony of a Department of the Navy employee.

Ex-French defence minister, Maurice Weygand initial claims of Pentagon and National Security involvement in the French attack on the Aliens were brusquely dismissed by US officials. But Weygand, speaking from his hospital bed following an attempted assassination attack on him has revealed further details of US involvement in the 'Tonnac Water' affair.

According to Weygand, senior US navy and NSA (National Security Agency) officials met with their French counterparts on the French island of St Pierre on the Friday morning following the Aliens' attack on NATO warplanes over Italy.

Weygand said that the meeting...

Americans' request and that they arrived with several alternative plans for combating the Aliens. "It was if the Americans had formulated them a long time ago and had merely dusted them down from their shelves," he said.

Weygand's claims of US involvement have been given a further twist by the attempted suicide of Nathan Leventhal.

Leventhal, reported to be a senior military planner at the US's Department of the Navy, and is one of the officials named by Weygand. Although Leventhal's suicide attempt was unsuccessful - his wife found him in time - his suicide note has come into the possession of the *Washington Morning Post.*

According to the Post, Leventhal's note was filled with remorse for being part to such a 'dastardly act'.

Leventhal, a father of two young sons was, according to his wife, visibly shaken by the scenes of children shown in the Susem telecast following the thwarted French attack.

Croat govt. facing rebellion as fierce fighting flares

THE EFFECTS of the tightening Susem blockade of Croatia is placing severe strains upon the Zagreb government's hold of country *AFP reports from Ljubljana.*

Fierce fighting between government forces and separatist groups who are attempting to break away from Croatia proper is reported to be continuing.

In both Dalmatia and Eastern Slavonia, forces formerly loyal to Zagreb are said to have sided with the main rebel factions. In both regions government forces are also reported to be engaged in heavy fighting in a bid to queil these dissident groups but have met with stiff opposition from the rebels. It is further reported that they have lost ground to the rebels especially in Dalmatia.

In the north and central regions of Dalmatia, former army general, Darko Pralak, commander of the 110 Brigade based at Sibenik is reported to be putting up ferocious resistance against government forces repeated attempts to regain control Drnis, a key town which straddles both road and rail links between the Adriatic ports of Split and Makarska.

In Eastern Slavonia, units under the control of another top general, Antic Dedakovic, are reported as extending their control across the entire south of the province with exception of its main town of Oajiek. Although still remainin under government control, Oajie is coming under sustained reb attempts to take the town and not expected to hold out for mo than a further two days unless th arm receives immediate r enforcements.

There are further reports th within Zagreb itself, there growing dissent between the choosing to remain loyal to government and those who was have the entire leadership hand over to the Susem in Bosnia face war crimes charges.

To what extent Croatian r have also responded to Su demands to report for work reconstruction in Bosnia unknown. But there are indicat that as fighting spreads in Cro and with the country's econ life ground to a halt there is likelihood that many ordi Croatians have fled from fighting the...

Czech's quiet cars

E: So many cars and trucks talled Susem soufins energy the sound of traffic in the streets has almost ceased. ally powered cars are now so nplace that petrol stations are ining over their loss of trade. nova, one of Prague's busiest hfares is now resounding to the of birdsong. Many of the residents are not only pleased ounded by the suddenness of the s the new energy units have

y Krumlov, who runs a rest- ...ilkonova, said: "The ... noise

...s those implicated in the Tonic Water scandal ...videns, US President Warren claims: 'I DID NOT KNOW'

BY SONIA FACE IN WASHINGTON

...A WHITE HOUSE statement issued yesterday concerning the growing 'Tonic Water' scandal, President Warren claimed that he had no knowledge of the affair. A White House press spokesman said that the senior Pentagon officials had acted without the President's authority in their dealing with the French government.

With yet further revelations of US involvement in France's attempted nuclear attack on the Alien's base in northern Brazil coming into the open, public protests across America against the government are growing.

More than two dozen major cities were brought to a standstill yesterday as protesters staged marches and processions US involvement in the 'Tonic Water Affair' as it has become known.

Most the protests passed of without violence and had widespread support not only from the ordinary public but from major corporations and other businesses doubtlessly concerned at the effects of anti-American sentiment outside of the US especially in Latin America.

Aliens carry US aircraft carrier through the air

From 'Shining sea to shining sea' in less than half an hour

BY MANLIO MORGAGNI
Reporting from the Gulf of Taranto

TWO SUSEM spacecraft plucked the US aircraft carrier Franklin Roosevelt from the Adriatic Sea early yesterday morning. The two spacecraft carried the stricken carrier through the air for 120 kilometres over Salentine Peninsula and dropped it down into the Ionian Sea.

Rear Admiral Dayton-Smith, Commander of the US 5th Fleet who was on board the 82,000 tonne carrier, is reported to have suffered a heart attack.

Navy's pride notwithstanding, seven airborne F-15s from the carrier at the time of the attack were forced to make emergency landings on the Italian mainland.

There was, so US Naval sources say, no direct material damage to the carrier during the attack. However, the Susem craft, described as the 'Station busters' later cut large sections from the hull of the aircraft carrier and removed the ship's nuclear reactors.

67: AILEEN

I had let Becky stay up to watch the little Susem objects on the TV. Her eyes were fair popping with glee as they played and tap danced. And when they ran along Rainbow's arms she was rocking with laughter.

Ryan came in just as Rainbow and the creatures were waving goodbye. Becky dashed up to him yelling to come quickly and see the last of them. Instead he told her to shut up and get to bed. This made her cry. I could see he was in one of his moods. I took Becky upstairs. She cried a long time and I got angrier and angrier with him. He had no cause to treat her like that. Though Becky quietened I was still seething.

When I went back down he was slumped on the settee. I could see he had had a fair bit of drink, even though it wasn't yet nine. Part of me wanted to have it out with him there and then but the other had me going in the kitchen to finish the ironing. I had not been there long though when he lurched in with, "Where's my dinner?"

"Get it yourself," I said and threw him the oven gloves. I was that angry still.

Then it was his "Why you...don't you ever dare...you..." and coming at me with his arm raised. I shouted to keep away but he would not. I could hear Becky start crying again. I was up against the cupboards, I couldn't get out of his way. His eyes were dark they were that filled with his temper. I still had the iron in my hand. He made a swipe at me. He knocked the iron away but not before the hot water had gone down his arm. He let out such a holler. I tried to get out of the kitchen, the flat if wasn't for Becky and Patrick, I was that frightened. He was shouting something terrible what he would do to me. Then he thumped me across my back and shoulders.

I shouted "Don't you dare touch me," but he gave me another whack. It caught my head. I slipped to the floor. The ironing board came with me. He fell over it. I fled upstairs, grabbed Patrick and ran into Becky's room. I spent the night with them there. But I'd not sleep, I was trembling so.

In the morning it was his "Sorrys" but it was too late for them.

Margaret, when I saw her, said I should have booted him out ages ago, though it's always easier to say than do. But by then I'd had the night to make up my mind. She took me to Christofides, the solicitors up on the Seven Sisters. The woman lawyer, when she saw the lump on my head and bruise to my face had an Ouster Order made up within in the hour. In another two me and Margaret had the locks changed and the Order stuck on the door. She had her brother Cian take the copy of it to Ryan where he's working down in Docklands.

'Tonicwater'- the sins of omission

By **John Hisman**
in Washington

PRESIDENT WARREN has about changed his administrations stance on the "Tonic-Water Affair'. For the first time Press Secretary Shuter has acknowledged that: Unauthorised liaison with non-US parties had been initiated by Department of Defense personnel, which may have compromised the integrity of the United States."

This has been interpreted in most quarters as a guarded admission of US-French collaboration in the abortive attack on Alien nerve centre in northern Brazil. Coming in the wake of the Washington Morning Post's revelations, the White House admission is expected to cause widespread uproar both

NY in UN US KO

By Tom Fletcher in New York

THE United States has not suffered the international the criticism as France over the "TonicWater" affair. But it is a different matter altogether for its administration. Even New York, the UN's fiercest detractor, is siding with the sentiments of its delegates against their own Government.

Seasoned observers of politics of New York politics and the even more arcane variety of the UN are bemused at the turn of events. "Who would have thought the day would come when the mayor of this city would appear alongside a bunch of guys from the UN," said the veteran columnist Will Bradlee of the New York Post.

"For years [Mayor] De Pescalo has branded them as a pit of no good leeches and snakes. Now here he is sharing the same platform and signing joint declarations criticising his own government! Who would have thought, that in a matter of days, public opinion in this country could swung so dramatically" he said.

The mayor's stance is widely, and enthusiastically shared by many New Yorkers. When asked to give reasons why, Bradlee's answers range from concern over US overseas interests; "We saw what happened to the French," he said. "There was also a sense of outrage that our government could go and do something so stupid - and bad, immoral.

"It was those kids who did it though. In the [Susem] telecast those kids singing and waving at the camera. It was the thought that our government could be party to the wholesale killing of kids that's really turned people against it. Killing Aliens maybe, but kids, never. That's no way to focus popular attention to the cause of maki

Embattled Warren pleads for calm

Martin Fiedland
In Washington

President Warren made a desperate call for calm over the 'Tonic-Water' scandal yesterday

Still trying to distance himself from those he called loose cannons in Department of Defense, the President said he has called for immediate Congressional and Senate Committees to be inaugurated to investigate US involvement.

"The current uproar is 'blinding' the real problem faced by the United States, that of the threatened Alien invasion," the President said.

Despite the President Warren's claims of innocence, public opinion has turned against him.

Many people throughout the US now as feel as threatened by dissention at home, as they do by any impending Alien invasion.

The President's calls for investigative committees are likely to fall on indifferent ears. The relevance of such gatherings may have already

Employees in thousands of government offices across the US, in an effort to protect themselves from being the focus of hostile protest, have signed petitions disassociating them from their employer. The noticeable exceptions being, predictably, the Department of Defense.

The General Accounting Office has gone as far as ordering its regional offices to display huge signs voicing protest at government action.

In San Francisco GAO

'Soufins illegal' top energy chie

by ALEX ANDREWS

THE USE of the Aliens' 'Soufin' energy units could be illegal says Sir Michael Edwards, the boss of Northern Utilities.

But no matter if Sir Michael is right or wrong, many hundreds of thousands of his customers are taking no notice of his strictures. The markets appeared to take the same view as Northern's customers and marked the energy company's share price down a whacking 52p, a new two year low.

According to Sir Michael, use of the soufin energy units by Northern's customers is against the terms of supply. Sir Michael said: "It is illegal for any customer to tamper with Northern Utilities' property and this includes the company's cabling."

"What is more," Sir Michael said, "Tampering with anything to do with electricity is always dangerous and potentially lethal.

Others, however, see things differently from Sir Michael. North London electrician, Tony Glynn said: "Like crossing the road, electricity is perfectly safe providing you take the right precautions." Tony says that he has fitted up scores of households with soufins.

"Who is going to turn down the chance of free

But is using a soufin in the home safe? Or are there any risks? "No," says environmental expert on renewable energy, Caroline Edwards (29). "Perhaps," says head of Energy Generation at Sheppey University, Professor Roland Smithers (45).

According to Caroline that if the Susem have and are using soufins then this proof that they have to be safe.

Professor Smithers takes a more cautious approach. "We are playing with a whole series of imponderables here," he said.

"For example, we do not as yet know that what might be perfectly safe exposures to the Susem may not be safe for humans, " he said.

While the professor admitted that he has still to see a soufin, Caroline has. She has several she says, so have all of her friends and neighbours..

Caroline Brown

In the interests of research we, at the Express have taken up Caroline's invitation to try one of her soufins in our offices at Canary Wharf.

'We must act on defence' says Russet-Brown

By Joy Combe

BRITIAN has a unique opportunity to increase it exports of defence equipment it was claimed yesterday.

Sir Hugh Russet-Brown, LibCon MP said that the government must act immediately in helping Britain's defence industry to boost its exports.

Speaking from his Tuscany vineyard estate, Sir Hugh said: "Now that these Susem have removed every country's nuclear weapons that the British defence industries seize upon the opportunity of the worldwide 'Defence Vacuum' their removal has caused.

The British defence industry is one of the country's successful exporting sectors. It is also a the forefront of technology. Thus it is also vital that these skills are not allowed to go by the

Although Sir Hugh admits that he acts for several of Britain's defence manufacturers. He claims however, that he is as a result in also directly responsible for maintaining many thousands of jobs across Britain.

"In my capacity of representing my clients around the world I consider that I have my finger on the pulse of defence needs of many countries. And I can most assuredly tell you that the demand for lower level defence equipment is now higher tan in time in many years.

"However, the UK defence industry is up against severe competition for other countries. Moreover most of these overseas rivals receive support from their own governments. Therefore it is vital that our defence industries receive no less

The fighting and unrest in Croatia continued to propel steady streams of men to the Bosnian border. The disturbances in Serbia also persuaded a trickle of volunteers from there to cross the Drina. But none of the senior members from either country's regime had yet presented themselves at Peljesac.

With the training of increasing numbers of Bosnian women and students as interviewers, pressure on those from Ragusa eased. It also enabled these to prepare for their next eagerly volunteered assignations.

After a week the first formed teams of craftsmen and labourers were split into trios, which in turn were all enlarged by fresh recruits into new groups of nines. The self-management with which each team was encouraged to operate meant none needed overseeing or compulsion to do what was asked of them. For most, after initial disorientation there was the pleasure of being able to apply their abilities in peace and be provided with the certainty of food, keep and some Euromarks (the Balkan hard currency and, along with tobacco and beer, part of the aid provision specified by Jacques Forissier).

The dog catchers were given the further tasks of digging deep steep-sided pits in which to house their charges, and collect abandoned or dead domestic and farm animals with which to feed them. Once a district's feral dogs were impounded the teams moved on to catch and en-pit other districts.

In the mine-clearing gangs those still able to run were now offered the opportunity to take over the Khmer Rouges' jobs. All enthusiastically accepted. But as ex-smokers are to those who still do, each took to their new status of whip wielding drivers with even greater zealotry than did ever the men from Bat Dâm Bâng. And they in turn were able to be prepared for their next and for them, avidly awaited assignment.

During the week supplies of aid continuously arrived from France to Tuzla, and at Sarajevo and Mostar airports now their runways had been cleared. The supplies were distributed by Gurkhas to Bosnian women formed in groups of nines, or "Nonettes" as they quickly became known. All were representatives of further trioed Nonettes.

While sensible Bosnian men were busy rebuilding their lives and homes, others complained at being excluded from the management of Aid deliveries. But the women were either too busy distributing what they had been delegated to collect, or in expanding their own trios to Nonettes to trifle with these men's belittling gripes. And anyway, most had memories of the profiteering and corruption in which such men had previously been involved. But in their disgruntlement some of these men attempted acquiring supplies of Aid by theft. However, in their ignorance and inexperience they found not only was security at airports assisted by hen-gers, it was overseen by yet more Nonettes. With news of the summary castrational and mine-clearing consequences of these men's inept intrusions spreading, attempts at theft did not re-occur.

US Inc. lines up with Latins

BY POLLY PORTILLO IN RIO DE JANEIRO

FROM Bogotá to Buenos Aires a string of major US corporations have loudly proclaimed their condemnation of the US administration's actions in colluding with the French in the attempted launching of a nuclear missile at the Aliens' base in northern Brazil.

From soft drinks makers to automobile manufacturers, US companies large and small have filled newspapers, television networks and other media with a flood of advertisements voicing their disapproval of US President Warren's policies as well proclaiming their undying support for all South American nations.

In Rio de Janeiro and other major Brazilian cities, the sides every Coca Cola delivery truck is emblazoned with hastily plastered signs denouncing the US government's actions and expressing solidarity with the Brazilian people.

To date such pre-emptive action appears to be paying off. There are no reports of US firms suffering any loss of trade let alone coming under physical attack as did French commercial interests.

There have not been any offensive actions against US citizens either.

There is, however, one area where the US is likely to suffer: narcotics eradication. In Columbia and Peru as well as Bolivia, government agencies assisting the US military in the spraying of defoliants of suspected areas, has all but ceased.

What the longer term consequences of this non-cooperation between the US and the affected countries is likely to see a fresh surge of both cocaine and heroin northwards to American cities as well as to Europe.

As far as the diplomatic relationships between South and Central America are concerned, it would appear that the same approach has been adopted as with businesses: President Warren is being denounced.

Officials at the US embas[sy in] the Uruguayan capital Montevideo have gone so f[ar as] announcing that Presi[dent] Warren's portrait has [been] removed from throughout [the] embassy and consulates.

Meanwhile, the presence [of] the Aliens in northern Brazi[l as] well as taking large swathe[s]

Druz's dismissal seen as sacrifica[l]

by Martin Friedland
in Washington

US SECRETARY of Defence, Martin Druz has resigned today, saying he and his Department must shoulder the blame for clandestine US involvement with France of the attempted missile firing of the Aliens in Brazil and the subsequent cover up.

Secretary Druz's resignation is widely seen as an attempt by the White House to stabilize the US. Following 48 hours during which the President's position has plummeted seemingly out of control someone's head had to roll. This time it was Druz's.

However, the Secretary of Defense's departure is unlikely to assuage the current mood of public opinion. Even ...

there were calls for more administration heads to be delivered before the American public's appetite is sated.

The President's standing has probably been irreparably damaged by the "TonicWater" fiasco. If he was ignorant of the machinations of those in his administration - as he continually claims - then, so the argument goes, he was at fault for appointing them in the first place. The opposite argument is that President Warren knew about everything, and Druz has been made little more than scapegoat.

There is third, though little discussed argument, that may be the true reason - rogue elements. Those within the bowels of the US defence establishment are unscathed ...

Fleeing Serbs in clashes with avenging Albanian[s]

Fierce fighting in Kosovo

FROM ZDRAVO PRIJATINO IN SKOPJE

ARMED CLASHES between elements of the Serbian army and Albanian irregulars have broken out across east and central Kosovo. Many casualties and deaths are thought to have resulted such been the ferocity of the fighting.

Following its rout at the hands of the Aliens' forces in Bosnia and demands that they face war crimes charges, many members of the Serbian armed services as well as militias are attempting to flee the country to Macedonia. Their only remaining escape route however, is through the semi-autonomous province of Kosovo.

With the recent hurried evacuation of the remaining EU Rapid Reaction Force ... Kosovo the security situation there has rapidly deteriorated.

Freed of any restraint previously imposed by the RRF, many of Kosovo's majority Albanian population have lost little time in settling old scores against the remaining Serbian minority.

Mitrovica, to the north of the province and which has a majority Serb population, has been the scene of some of the most serious of the earlier clashes between the two sides.

However, with increasing numbers of Serbs fleeing from Serbia proper and all heavily armed, retaliatory actions by them against Albanians have taken place with a vengeance.

With a combination of desperation and long standing ethic hatred towards Albanians, Serb soldiers have, in many ...

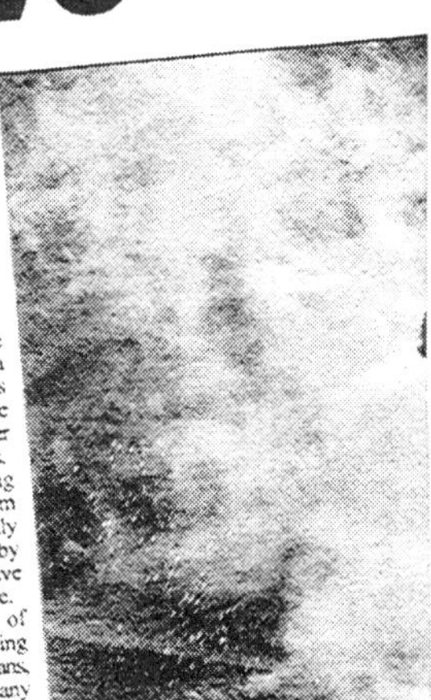

As the 'Tonic Water' scandal grows

Embassies oust Warren

By John McVicar
Diplomatic Correspondent

US EMBASSIES around the world are displaying notices condemning President Warren's policies.

Doubtlessly mindful, of the fate faced by French embassies, many US embassies have been quick to head off anti-American protests in their host countries.

This worldwide move, (there were more than 80 at the last count, including Paris) is a double blow to the embattled US President. America's ambassadorial appointments are made by the incoming President and are usually bestowed in return for past political favours including campaign finance for his election.

To lose so much support among these patrons and their circles of powerful friends does not auger well for President Warren.

The second humiliation, though perhaps more galling for the US Department of Defence, is that every American embassy is guarded by an armed detachment of US Marines. These are, technically employees of the very Department causing the cur-

As use of the Aliens' fuel cells increases

Big Oil in troubled water[s]

FROM DICK WESTEDGE, DEPUTY BUSINESS EDITOR

THE WORLD'S major oil producers are suffering, or so they claim.

The rapid spread of Susern fuel cells and the free energy they provide to industry, homes and motor vehicles are causing growing holes in oil industry's once deep pockets. So deep and so sudden is their plight that they are seeking 'special case' status from governments. Their cries of penury, however, are unlikely to receive a sympathetic ear from anyone.

With the price of oil down to below ...

In Ragusa during this second week of May the first trials took place. These were for offenders of minor misdemeanours, such as theft and profiteering. As Prosecutors had ensured that all who appeared for trial were unable to establish their innocence, panels of judges found passing judgement and sentences easy. However, after the first day Tearo and Colonel Tambassing's aides considered it necessary to council the Prosecutors to press for less severe sentences. They met with some success, in that 'Or' sometimes replaced 'And' between "Castration" and "Mine-clearing."

Colonel Tambassing meanwhile still took flotillas of vedas on recruitment trips to the east. But during that week he travelled not to Bat Dâm Bâng but to the airfield at Pokhara. By Friday not only had he visited his home village of Sangu and the house where his wife had died but, through the Panchayat communities along the nearby Himalayan foothills, he had enlisted sufficient eager recruits from amid the British army's demobbed Gurkhas for a further two regiments.

In the Susem's Saturday, May 14th's telecast, Rainbow once again advised offenders within both the Serbian and Croatian regimes and their respective armies to go to Pelješac without delay. While she also said that ordinary people from both countries could only benefit by the guilty among them surrendering by Sunday evening, none had appeared.

But her appeal, coupled with the two countries' continuing unrest, persuaded even greater numbers of ordinary Croatian men, and now also many Serbian ones as well, to go during the Sunday to Bosnia to enlist for reconstruction. And as darkness fell there were still queues awaiting induction at the crossing points along both of Bosnia's borders

Also during Sunday and because of the high altitude at which they flew they were unseen from the ground, fenserfs criss-crossed the skies above Serbia and Croatia. The sites the fenserfs were sent to see added accuracy to Tearo and Colonel Tambassing's next, though still most reluctant, campaign.

Soon after sunset and with queues at the border crossing points still stretching into the night, another queue quietly formed. Out over and high above the Adriatic, tocans, their neptunium removal duties for the most part completed, lined up ready for Monday and their next task.

Pentagon heads roll

Martin Friedland
in Washington

PRESIDENT Warren has sacked a number of senior defence staff. However, their abrupt departure is already being viewed as a desperate attempt on the part of the President to head-off threatened impeachment proceedings by both the Senate and House of Representatives over the Tonic Water affair

Even before President Warren's new secretary of defence, George McKinley has been confirmed in office by Congress, he has lost no time in cleansing the Pentagon's Augean Stables.

McKinley, the President's surprise replacement after Martin Druz's forced resignation, was at one time CEO of General Motors. There he gained the reputation as a no nonsense reorganiser of corporate structure.

Among the seven departmental heads to be replaced, is Rear Admiral Harvey Schister who is seen as one of the

Susem blast US nuclear missile silos to the sun

Martin Friedland
in Washington

FROM MONTANA, the Dakotas and all the way south to New Mexico are now thousands of now very empty holes. Holes which once housed the nuclear tipped missiles which were once the backbone of the United States' strategic defence.

Within the space of just 24 hours, a fleet of Susem spacecraft blasted the contents of each silo towards the sun. Meanwhile other Alien craft were turning their attentions to removing the US's nuclear warhead recycling and assembly plant in Amarillo, New Mexico, the Lawrence Radiation Laboratory, Berkley, California and many other nuclear sites across the country.

At many of the affected sites huge crowds gathered to watch the spectacle of the huge Susem 'station buster' craft propelling the doomed nuclear facilities up into the sky. Crowds of onlookers then

Oil price meltdown sets sheikhs shivering

By David Barnes
in Vienna

THE COLD realities of debt, doom and despair cast dark cold clouds over the meeting of OPEC ministers yesterday.

With closing price down to $10.35 a barrel for WTI, Saudi Oil Minister, Ued Bin Haaq demanded an immediate 50 per cent cut in output. He also complained of the discounts being made by some of the oil cartel's members as well as non-OPEC producers alike.

Despite Ued Bin Haaq's tough demands, the future for oil producers worldwide is bleak. Many of OPEC members are caught in the double bind of needing oil revenues to service external debts while at the same time satisfy their peoples' demands.

Should any of the OPEC producers fail to service their debts the sources of any new loans is likely to dry up. However, if they fail to provide for their subjects' increasingly vocal demands, they face the prospect of growing civil unrest. For the more autocratic Gulf States and perhaps

Susem wipe out all US nuke sites

FROM LYNNE POLLOCK IN SAN FRANCISCO

NORTH AMERICA no longer has nuclear weapons, power stations and waste dumps. Only the nuclear plants in Washington State and its huge Hanford Reservation waste site remain.

The removal of the nuclear installations which have been replaced with energy units, by the Susem has passed off without significant protest.

However, yesterday there was one exception - at the Lawrence Livermore Laboratories.

Lawrence Livermore, birthplace of the hydrogen bomb and SDI, was the scene of protest as the Susem spacecraft showered the nearby towns and cities with energy units.

The scientists and others draped huge signs over the buildings pleading for the Institution to be spared. Professors in the Edward Teller Memorial Wing ...

Albanians rebuff Serbs

By Valenk Kocani in Skopje

FLEEING Serb military factions have been forced to retreat from by Kosovo's Albanians.

In a desperate bid to escape Serbia to Macedonia in the face of Susem demands that they face war into fighting superior armed Albanians bent on revenge for past atrocities.

According to those Serbian soldiers managing to cross over into Macedonia, there have been many casualties meted out by Albanian militias with no quarter ... wounded in the clashes. The area just north of the border with Macedonia is said to littered with burnt out Serb vehicles and many bodies on the sides of roads. The stretch of road between Urosevac and Kacanik is reported to have been the ... of many of the ambushes which have waylaid Serbs.

There are also fears that Macedonia's only substantial Albanian minority is also involved in fighting those military units fleeing Serbia. In Macedonia itself, the country's predominantly Serbian population are concerned

69: TAMLA MOTOWN

I knew no good would come from Rainbow's iPod and her CDs. The karaoke-ing in the refectory is bad enough but now the Susem play them everywhere and all the time. They're like children with new toys. The Supremes, Ronettes, Temptations, even the Four Tops, and last night Pheterisco and Petruee, and to much applause, were belting out River Deep, Mountain High.

But it's not stopped with Rainbow's disks. With Susem resources and Terbal's abilities, there has been non-stop scouring the airways and the Internet for more music. And of course the inevitable has happened, it has spread to the machines.

That Terbal is into Bach and Burt Bacharach's easy listening is just bearable, but yesterday morning when Roberto and I flew in Kubber to film the iron ore fields, I discovered all the big sized sherpals are into heavy metal. The noise was terrible, even the vultures had flown off.

Kubber isn't much better. It was MJQ all the way on the flight to the Serra Pelada, and Thelonious Monk and Sonny Rollins all the way back to Tabajara. As I stood on the edge of the Pelada, looking down into that vast vacated hole and with Roberto filming the emptiness, the bass solo from Blue Monk was beating and blasting from Kubber's open door. With his darkened solar windows looking like outsized sunglasses, all he needed, I thought, was a beret over his top and I would have called him "Kerouac" instead of Kubber.

The afternoon was as bad. With Rainbow and Lico we flew in Kershaw (he is into Lou Reed) up to Sardon as he cruised by floating down more soufins. "At last," I thought as we arrived and heard Peer Gynt, "decent music." But he only played Hall of The Mountain King, continuously. After the fifth time, I shouted out to him "Don't you have anything else?"

But he boomed back "I like it."

And worse, he moved up and down in time with it. Roberto, filming the views from the windows was most fraught. I shudder what will happen when he discovers Ravel's Bolero or The Flight of The Bumble Bee.

On the way back I tried impressing on Rainbow the problems her disks had caused. And I would have thought she would have been, like Roberto, impressed on seeing Sardon. But as she was sharing the headphones of her iPod with Lico, both rocking their heads in unison, I don't think what I said had much effect.

Another problem the music has caused has affected the Susem's concentration. It has started slipping. When Rainbow screened Roberto's footage to Paceillo and Milophinia they both looked at what he had done in silence and I thought perhaps they didn't like it. But no sooner was it ended than Paceillo leaned over to Rainbow and earnestly asked "What is the significance of Phil Spector and what is meant by "Wall of Sound"?"

Warren facing impeachment threat

y John Hisman
Washington

RESIDENT Warren aces the threat of mpeachment proceedings f a motion before the US Senate is passed.

Although the motion is ikely to fail, the President's "Tonic-Water" woes will not be ended In the eyes of many they are only just beginning.

Georgian Senator Sam Warner, of the powerful Senate Armed Services Committee, charges the President with knowingly entering into a compact with a foreign power without the consent of the US Senate. There are moves afoot in the House of Representatives for similar motion.

The Senate motion also charges the President with abetting a foreign power (France) to break the Monroe Doctrine. This was passed in the 19th century as a deterrent against foreign powers intervening in the territory of the Americas.

Serb leader survives cou

From Buc Fasse-Leigh
In Bucharest

EMBATTLED Serb leader, Milo Gadan, is reported to have survived a coup attempt against him. A number of dissident SNA generals attempted coup against Gadan during a troop inspection at the Paracin army base. They were, so Tanjug the Serb news agency reported, arrested before they could strike.

Tanjug said Gadan, in speech to his Serb SF5 followers in Belgrade to rally behind him during the present difficulties.

Romanian observers believe that the Serb leader's position is precarious. More moves to oust him must be expected, they say.

Reports circulating in the Hungarian capital Budapest are claiming that a disaffected faction of the Serb forces from Bosnia is massing forces in Novi Sad to the north of country. It is not yet known, however, if these forces, said to be under the command of General Milutin will mount a putsch against Belgrade.

Security along Romania's border with Serbia has been stepped up. A 'Zone of Control' 20 kilometes wide

Big Bang boffin's Big Bang

Jim Tadford
Science reporter

ONE of the world's top physicists escaped unhurt when a blast shattered his home yesterday afternoon in a leafy Oxford suburb. The blast broke windows and blew off roof tiles of Barton Road and nearby streets.

As residents fled their homes and rescue services raced to the devastated scene, the near naked, blackened figure of Dr. Hambring was seen by neighbours staggering from the wreckage of his home.

Although still dazed Dr. Hambring was otherwise unhurt. There were no other casualties reported.

As householders and council emergency services cleared up the debris strewn streets and boarded up broken windows, neighbours accused Dr. Hambring for the blast.

Next door neighbour, English don, Dr. Antony Blackburn, said: "To my mind, what Hambring has done is a diabolical liberty, he was totally out of order. He might be a Big Bang Boffin but it still gives the man no right take liberties with the lives and property of others."

Dr. Hambring's wife Margery, who was at a charity fundraising meeting at the time of the explosion said, after visiting her husband: "When I left him this afternoon he was trying to take apart one of those Susem energy units. I did tell him he needed proper laboratory facilities and not the kitchen table.

"Bob has been not been himself recently. When he returned a conference in Washington and found the Rutherford Centre, where he worked was gone, he became depressed. The prospect of not having a research department to head any more upset him, but so did the prospect of never attending all those international scientific conferences. They were a very important to Bob. He lived for those conferences, he was always going to them."

Three weeks ago many national newspapers carried Dr. Hambring's warning of the dangers laymen tampering with Alien power units.

Dr Robert Hambring

box "Th the Ste fur are fall fer of flu aid Or su op so D as se sp tr M to h u $ b m b S h S I c c a f e c r t

esperate military reels from Aliens onslaug

Power struggle in Serb

nathon Swift
Ljubjana

PUTSCH is reported to ve taken place within the rbian military.

A number of top generals io forces were heavily volved in military erations in the attacks on osnia are thought to have empted a coup against e Serbian president, Milo adan.

Milutin Kukanjac, head of rb forces in Bosnia, is ported to have led a ction of top military mmanders disenchanted ith the conduct of the rb government's response the Aliens' attacks gainst the country.

According to ASN news gency reports, Milutin was acked by the Serbian overnment for failing to ithdraw his forces in time o avoid capture by the liens. Many of who are hough to be engaged in orced mine-clearing in Bosnia.

Milutin and those forces upporting him, are said to e based at Novi Sad, the apital of troubled province f Vojvodina.

Although there are many Serb refugees who have recently fled from Bosnia there are also large numbers who, in the Serb conflicts with Croatia in the 1990s have also located in Vojvodina.

Both waves of Serbs into Vojvodina has exacerbated relations with the province's large Hungarian population.

According to reports circulating in Budapest, there has been an increasing number, albeit small scale, outbreaks of fighting

Chaos in Brazil as 500,000 flee Aliens

BY POLLY PORTILLO
IN RECEFE

MORE than 500,000 fleeing miners, foresters, ranchers, government officials and soldiers have caused widespread disruption throughout northeast Brazil.

The cities of the Northeast, Brazil's most impoverished region, have been ill prepared to handle the burden of the sudden influx of homeless, distraught refugees from Ceará and neighbouring states.

Following the Susem demand for outsiders to leave the affected area, many have flocked into region's cities with little more than the clothes they stood in.

The new arrivals in the city are said to responsible for a crime-wave including many deaths.

City authorities and Red Cross officials also blame refugees for outbreaks of cholera and dysentery. Rodrico Gomes, Recefe's mayor said: "In one week many thousands of people of disrepute have descended upon my city.

"These are the wild men, the formigas from the Serra Pelada. There are many other such bad people who have come here and causing much trouble for us," he said.

While the coastal cities of are reeling under the deluge of refugees from the interior, those to west are also suffering. Brasilia is also experiencing an upsurge of

Menpemelo was no different, “Why did Holland, Dozier and Holland leave Tamla Motown?...was their departure the reason it declined? ...and who really was Freda Payne?” As if I should have truck with such trivia? And all this before I had chance to ask her about Secondary waves, how did they evolve? But I persisted and she did explain, well a little. Though all the same, with her concentration gone it wasn’t long before the conversation was drifting.

“It is possible for order to atrophy, collapse into disorder, chaos,” she said, “but improbable that order could ever come from chaos.” (By this point she had drifted to structure). “Consider this,” she continued, “throughout the Universe four formations of Tertiary waves, frothicles, elements. Those of carbon, helium, beryllium and oxygen exist in precise ratios to one another, 73,700, 76,560, 71,187 and 71,616 respectively. It is the resonances, interactions between these four and Secondary waves of course, which are the basis of causation of all the other elements. If their collective resonance pitch was not precise to a little less than three hundred thousand trillionth parts, other, denser concentrations of Tertiary waves, more concentrated frothicles could not be created.” And seeing no doubt I had not a grasp of how big a figure it was, Menepemelo kindly added, “a little more than 28 followed by 16 noughts.”

To which I gratefully said “Oh.”

But with her “This we know as the "Anthropic Constant” she befuddled me again. And seeing so, she kindly aided with “Anthropic, from where all else is created.”

And I again thankfully said “Oh.”

She continued, “No matter what part of the Universe is observed this Constant is always present. That this is so is borne out by the unending formation of stars from within the continual evolving of galaxies. No Constant, no stars and no you nor me. But no matter how concentrated groups of Tertiary waves may become,” she next said, and again drifting slightly again, “the differing flows of Secondary waves passing them do not conflict, collide with each other.” Then, after a pause, “For instance, when Secondary waves come into close proximity of what you term magnetic substances they all are always deflected in the same direction.”

Menpemelo had lost me but no doubt seeing my blank face she became ever emphatic, “Don’t you see,” she said, “for all these to occur, Secondary waves have to exist in precise strengths, modulations of pitch.”

I still felt like saying “Oh,” but thought it best not, so instead meekly said “I don’t understand.”

Now more schoolmarmly in tone she said “The probability of any one of these factors evolving by chance from chaos is such that the Universe could not have come into being within the time it has. That all occur, and there are some other factors I have not yet mentioned, and simultaneously, as well as all harmoniously interacting with one another and all at the same time, is self

Aliens eliminate all US nuclear power station

FROM TOM FLETCHER IN PHILADELPHIA

THE SUSEM hit US nuclear power stations and other installations today.

The first go was the troubled Three Mile Island nuclear power plant at Harrisburg. Other plants in the eastern United State soon followed suit.

From West Valley, New York to Pensacola, Florida, nuclear power stations, missile silos, waste sites were sent to the Sun by Susem spaceships. And they went on their way with barely a protest.

Earlier, embattled President Warren's telecast telling the American people, that, in "this era of uncertainties and the constant threat posed by international terror organisations" it was now time to "enter into a period of calm and embrace the opportunity to have a positive relationship with our Susem friends" was met with much indifference and not a little hollow laughter by many.

More attention was focused on acquiring one of the millions of Susem energy units which had billowed down in the Susem's wake. Within hours of the first units arriving, a market for them was established with prices ranging from $20-30. However, there are indicat-

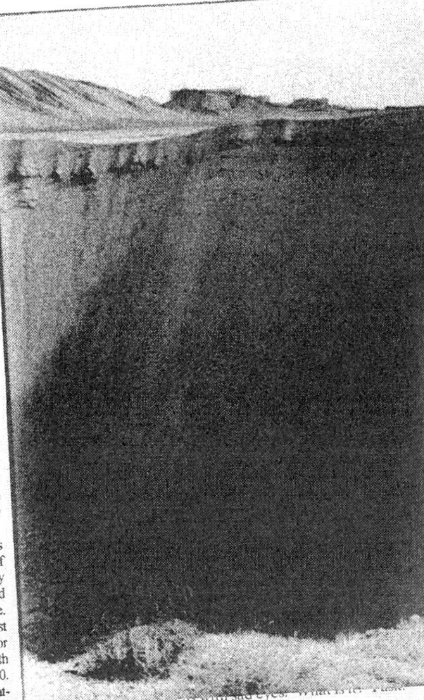

Ousting of top Serb thwarted

Mail Foreign Staff

BALKAN Butcher Milo Gadan has narrowly escaped an assassination attempt by fellow Serbs. Army generals, angered by recent rout of Serb forces in Bosnia, tried to remove him during a military parade.

Though Gadan has crushed the army chiefs' revolt, experts say it is only a matter of time before others try. "The JNA High Command must be wanting to lay the blame for Serb war crimes in Bosnia on someone other than themselves for the

Tax Soufins - says MP

By Joy Combe

SOUFINS must be taxed says a group of backbench MPs. Led by Sir Hugh Russet-Brown (LibCon), vice chairman of the influential Commons Energy Select Committee, the MPs say it is vital to collect such a tax to make good the losses suffered to Government income.

Sir Hugh said: "People using these Alien energy units must realize they are causing a considerable loss to their fellow taxpayers. It is vital the use of these units are brought into the tax net.

"Not only is the Treasury suffering from the use of these things but so are last sections of industry. The legitimate energy suppliers are subject to extensive regulation, therefore it is vital these units are brought under the same level of control."

Sir Hugh said that he did not have a soufin himself had

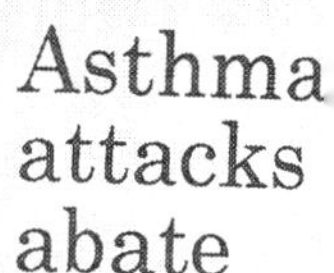

Asthma attacks abate

By Harriat Swan

DOCTORS and heal[th] professionals across th[e] country are reporting [a] significant drop in th[e] number of asthm[a] attacks. Many are con[-]vinced the sudden wide[-]spread use of Alien ene[r]gy units are responsible.

Dr. Eric Jefferies, whos[e] surgery in Ipswich ha[s] many patients who are asth[-]matic, said, "Within days o[f] the soufins arriving in thi[s] area, the number o[f] patients presenting them[-]selves or their children dropped dramatically.

Because so many cars in Ipswich, and more so in those in the residential areas where most of the children live, are now fitted with soufins, the evidence of there benefit is there for all to see," he said.

Shirley Garth, a senior teacher at nearby Christchurch Infants, said: A quarter of the pupils at this school are on [Ventolin] inhalers. Each class has a special cupboard for them. Therefore we know how many times the children use them. Since people began putting soufins in their cars the number of times those cupboards have been opened has halved."

Gillian Edwards whose daughter Amy, attends Christchurch infants said: "Since they started putting those soufins in their cars my Amy's asthma has really improved.Her wheezing has definitely got less over this past fortnight.

Serbs flee Koso

Tom Wikes in Prizren, Kosovo

THE REMAINING Serb population of Kosovo is reported to have fled the semi-autonomous province in the wake of attacks on them by armed Albanians. The mainly Serb town of Mitrovica is said to have be completely cleared of its previous Serb inhabitants.

Travel throughout Kosovo is severely hampered by roadblocks manned by the groups of Albanian National Liberation Movement (ANL) irregulars. Also, information of the state of fighting in the north and east of the province is solely from the Albanians themselves.

It is possible, however, to gauge that there has been a substantial number of clashes between Albanians and Serbs with both sides sustaining heavy losses. Such as been the severity and bitterness of the fighting that it is also evident that the deep seated historic hatred between the two population groups is as fierce as it has ever been.

With the hasty evacuation of the EU's Rapid Reaction Force from Kosovo and the arrival of elements of the

evident is it not, that their forming is not a random act?"

At this she paused for a deep breath and gave me chance to say, though perhaps a little too cockily, "So everything which occurs is pre-destined, is that what you're saying?"

"No," was the first part of her reply. The second was, "But what the consequence of this inter-factor harmony means, is that structures can only occur within the confines dictated by them. Therefore," she continued and with her expression still unsmiling, "there will be a greater likelihood of all structures being the same everywhere than they being different. This consideration includes the structures of life itself."

This time my "Oh" was reverential.

"There are differences here on Earth which we have not encountered elsewhere but in comparison with what is the same they are minor. The biggest difference we have discovered so far is the evolution of sustained separate genders." She paused again but I kept mum and she continued, "But even that is not as great as first appears."

I gave out another reverential "Oh," but added, "What do you mean?"

"Put simply, Xs and Ys. Most lifeforms on Earth appear to possess both separately. All the other life we know is born with a Y which matures and develops into an X. There is, however, no reason why life on Earth with Ys cannot be transformed into Xs. While we are here it should be possible for us to show how this can be done. I am sure it will be beneficial especially to human males."

She still had earnestness on her face but I had apprehension behind mine. And my "Oh," this time was deep and a very slow one.

"There are definite advantages. Your sensory powers will increase, you will be able to think, reason more deeply. Also you will exist for longer in your present form."

I was becoming apprehensive the way the conversation was turning. But not wanting to upset, I defensively blurted, "It wouldn't...I don't think it'll catch on...people wouldn't like it."

"Why not?" she said and adding, "When we are males we cannot wait to mature into females. There can only be benefits."

"I still don't think it would catch on," I said, "men wouldn't like it, even the thought would upset them." I had terrible images of the consequences if word got out, of how one thing could lead to another and it would become compulsory.

But almost at once there were other, calmer thoughts. In certain areas it probably could catch on. They have a lot of transvestites in Brazil paying fortunes in the hope of being turned into women.

With thoughts of money stirring, I listened on.

"It should be possible to remove cells, correct the Ys to Xs."

Calculations began whirring.

Hungary hastens troops to Serb bord

By Bela Nagy in Budapest

HUNGARIAN troops have been rushed to the border with the troubled Serb province of Vojvodina, which has a large Hungarian minority, as "a precautionary measure"

Defence Minister, János Rákosi said: "We have taken this step because of the uncertainty of the situation [in Vojvodina] it is important to protect the territory of Hungary"

No mention was made of the reactions and responses of the 100,000 or so Hungarians who have fled Vojvodina in recent years. There are indications many of these are eager to return to their former homes.

It is an open secret in the southern Hungarian provinces of Csongrad and Bacs-Kiskun that Hungarian forces will ensure their compatriots

Fighting flares in Vojvodina

Sindor Petőfi
In Budapest

Fighting flared yesterday in the Vojvodinan capital of Novi Sad. JNA (Serb) forces were engaged in street fighting with the pro-independence VFI and anti-government Serbs.

After a day of fierce fighting, the JNA withdrew across the Danube and to the Petrovaradin Citadel, from where they began indiscriminately shelling the old city

The shelling has caused widespread damage to many of the town's historic buildings dating from the Hungarian Empire.

Meanwhile, the mixed Hungarian and Serb population, have formed

Kosovo at war

MAIL FOREIGN SERVICE

THOUSANDS of ethnic Albanian refugees have fled the Serbian province of Kosovo as result of fierce out breaks of fighting between the mainl Albanian populatio and Serb militias.

The Albanian bord town of Kukes is ove flowing with people w have made the hazardo crossing from Kosov Many refugees car tales of fierce fighti between Serbs and t rebel KLA.

Areas of Pristina, t capital of Kosovo reported have be shelled by Otan's force

Montenegro breaks with Serbia

By Jose Severn in Rome

MONTENEGRAN authorities in Podgorica (Titograd) are believed to have severed links with Serbia.

The reports also states that ferry sailings from Bari to the Montegran port of Bar have still not resumed as the entire eastern Adriatic coastline is still subject to Alien blockade.

Albanian authorities still report Alien presence along their northern border with

Soufin shortage "Unfair"

Express Reporter

THE uneven distribution of soufins is producing cries of "unfairness" from many of those who lost out.

Because nuclear power stations were sited away from the main centres of population, many people in the Midlands and South East do not have the free electricity and petrol others are enjoying.

There are growing demands that power and fuel prices should be reduced in an effort to reduce the growing inequality as many see it.

"Why should we be the ones who suffer," says John Butcher, a councillor in the Arnold district of Nottingham. "Why should we and millions like us be made to pay for our electricity and petrol when others are getting it from free?" he adds.

Councillor Butcher, who has founded the fast growing FFFA (Free Fuel For All) says the only fair way to overcome the inequality is to supply electricity and petrol free. This would be paid for out of increased taxation. "It would mean the Government nationalising the means of supply and distribution.

Rocky Flats pumped up

Mail Foreign Staff
In Denver, Colorado

Rocky flats, the US's prime Plutonium processing plant, went up with a bang yesterday The 7,000 employees of 10 square mile plant no longer have a job to go to.

Denver and surrounding areas were blanketed in the early hours by myriad blue sheets bringing countless Susem energy units. An hour later, with the last of the plant's staff vacated the Susem spaceships went to work clearing the buildings and spent fuel dumps.

State and Federal police kept people away from the immediate area of the site, following orders - issued immediately after the soufin drop – by the vigilant Department of Homeland Security. Fearing terrorist's may capitalise on the excitement and confusion of events at the processing plant, measures have been installed to ensure that any breach of security is avoided

Savannah cheers for Susem

By John Hisman in Augusta

CHEERING crowds welcomed the Susem to the Savannah River nuclear waste site. The spectators were rewarded with ample supplies of energy units and the removal of nearly 300 square miles of nuclear waste.

From high ranking state officials and mayors, the local residents and ageing anti-nuclear campaigners, there were cheers as unwanted waste site was sent to the Sun. The only glum ones were employees of the US Atomic Energy Agency and those of the nearby Barnwell nuclear power station.

They've got debts and no way to pay 'em. Duke are staring at a Chapter 11," said Wayne Elko, mayor of Aiken, a town just north of the site.

England well placed for 2nd Test

From Alan Leigh

CHAIRMAN OF Selectors, Alan Barraclough, announcing England's team for the Second Test against Namibia, said he was confident he'd picked a winning side.

Brushing aside calls for his and the Board's resignation, he described criticism of the Selectors as: "Carping from a bitter and ill-informed clique, who were pursuing a personal vendetta against me."

Confirming Ian Hawes as captain for the rest of the series, Barraclough named

"Adjust what you term the immune system into an auto-immune response against Y cells."

Treat a million transvestites at say $200 each.

"Reinsert the corrected X cells. This could probably be managed in stages, probably no more than twenty."

Twenty! That would mean more. It would have to be at least $20 a session.

"At intervals of five to seven days."

Weekly attendances! Spin-off merchandising would be enormous and then there would be branding, franchising.

"Both aspects should not pose any difficulties..."

Even as low as a ten per cent net margin on turnover I'd not complain.

"However, there would have to be trials. You would be a most suitable candidate."

"I'm sure it wouldn't catch on...people would be dead against it." A shudder went over me and thoughts of money fled. I changed the subject, quickly, "Freda Payne was a one song success singer and was never heard of again...yes, Tamla Motown after Holland Dozier and Holland departed was never as good afterwards...why they went is still unknown."

"Oh," was all she said.

should be of interest to the drink cans. The top ten steel firms control 1.25% and 3.5% ...

Vojvodina in Belgrade breakaway

Following the recent uprising in Vojvodina, Sándor Petőfi, the first outside journalist to enter the troubled region, reports from the capital Subotica

THE HUNGARIAN population of the northern Serbian province of Vojvodina declared its independence yesterday.

With the surprise lifting of the Alien border patrols I was able to make the 40km journey from Zzeged to Vojvodina's capital of Subotica without hindrance.

Although I saw signs of the Serb's military's presence, there were no soldiers to be seen during my journey.

In Subotica there was also a complete absence of any Serbian armed forces. In fact the atmosphere throughout the city was calm. Many of the people were carrying rifles and other weaponry and reminding me of the uprising in Budapest more than half a century ago.

The leader of the Vojvodina Independence Movement (VFI), Torri Kadoi, when I met with him, said: "The JNA (Serbian Army) withdrew most of their forces in the area to Kosovo. We then seized the chance to liberate ourselves. At last we the people of Vojvodina can be Hungarian again!"

According to Kadoi, the JNA had been pushed back as far as the Zlatica and Cikar rivers. The VFI is also reported to be contact with the former leaders of Vojvodina who had been forced to flee by the Serbian authorities to Hungary on Belgrade's takeover of the former autonomous province in the 1990s.

Kadoi, who claims that he was elected by the VFI is

Soufins save forests

FROM RHAMSID ENGINEER IN MADRAS

THE arrival of Susem energy units is already having a dramatic impact on India's firewood crisis. Environment Minister, Narasimha Rao said, "We could do with a 100 million of soufins right away."

In the two Indian states were most of the original soufins landed, Haryana and Tamil Nadu, people who lived in the rural areas have eased the demand on the few remaining natural areas of woodland.

Jayaram Jayalaitha, director of Tamil Nadu's State forests said, "We are already noticing a reduction in the price of wood for cooking purposes but also for charcoal which is ... small local

Romania rushe[s] troops to Serb bo[rder] as unrest sprea[ds]

FROM BUC FASSE-LEIGH IN TIMOISOARA

ROMANIAN authorities have deployed thousands of Police Militia throughout the western districts of Transylvania in a desperate bid to head-off rising unrest among the region's sizable Hungarian population.

Authorities in Bucharest are concerned that Romania's Hungarian minority could follow their Vojvodinian cousins in also making a bid for independence.

The Romanian government of Ion Gheorghiu has established a strong security cordon across Timoisora Province and also stationed security forces throughout the city itself. It has also established a heavily armed police presence in the nearby town of Arad as well. Further reserve forces are reported to have to re-enforced police posts along the border with the Serbian border of Vojvodina.

While news of events taking place in the troubled province of Vojvodina is sketchy, there are several, though unconfirmed reports of Alien spacecraft being sighted along the border region. If indeed these reports are correct it could be explanation for the complete absence in western Romania of Serbs fleeing their country

Balkan ... in sink... ship...

By Antony Farra...

THE UPRISINGS in Croatia and Serbia show all the signs of desperate people acting in desperation to escape the fate awaiting them. While news from Bosnia is scant, the announcements made in the Susem telecasts indicate strong punishment is awaiting the guilty.

With the limited exception of the Hungarian Vojvodinian border the Susem patrols are still being enforced. The clashes between the factions in both Croatia and Serbia has the air of the guilty blaming one other for the crimes they have jointly and severally committed

Last of nuclear fuel removed, claim Susem

Jim Tadford

The four kilograms of plutonium jettisoned by the failed Apollo 13 mission more than 30 years ago, has been retrieved from the depths of the Tonga Trench in the Western Pacific. Its removal marks, so the Susem claimed, the last of the Earth's unnatural – man-made - nuclear material.

The announcement by the Susem comes three days after their successful recovery of the 30 kilograms of plutonium jettisoned by the aborted Mission Freedom 1997 and the two kilos in the failed Russian Martian mission off Chile.

Dr Ian Steward, an expert on nuclear material, said: "Although plutonium is lethal, it is the neptunium both the Americans and the Russians used in their nuclear fuel cells which is the really nasty substance.

Plutonium has a half-life of two to three decades, but neptunium has a half-life of at least 20,000 years.

"It is so deadly that 1/100,000th of a gram will kill. Although these fuel cells - the Russian spacecraft's apart - were dumped into deep ocean trenches (the Tonga Trench is 11,000 metres deep) there was never any guarantee that their casings could remain intact."

"As the Susem discovered, when they raised the sunken US and Soviet submarines the week before last, the casings of the reactors and warheads were severely corroded. We know very little about the dynamics of sea water and ocean currents, but we knew even less when these submarines and fuel cells were dumped. The Earth and the Oceans had a very lucky escape."

Aliens over Adriatic

BY JOSE SEVRRN IN ROME

Susem spacecraft were reported amassing along the Dalmatian coast last night.

Crews of fishing boats returning to the northern Adriatic port of Pesaro in the early hours of Monday morning, said they had seen "several dozens" of the Aliens' 'Tocan' spaceships, their so-called 'Station Busters' which have not been seen over the Adriatic since they first appeared in the region at the end of April.

To date, the Susem have made no mention of the Tocans' purpose for massing in such large numbers. It is speculated, however, that the crafts' presence is linked with Susem demands to both Croatia and Serbia to accede to their demands. That both countries hand over those of their nationals and others wanted for war crimes committed in Bosnia.

There is also speculation that the craft could also be preparing for military action against the Croatian and Serbian regimes. This follows further reports from Hungary and Romania that the borders with the former Yugoslavia have also been sealed by the Aliens.

Without outside access to both countries as well as Bosnia blocked, all communication from them is being severely disrupted. It is also not known if any of the Susem craft are already engaged in any military actions against both or either of these pariah regimes.

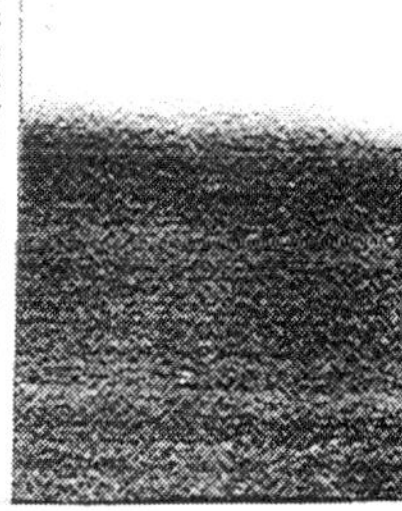

In the early darkness hours of Monday many hundreds of vedas flew over Croatia and Serbia. In their wake they played out lines of millions of hen-gers. Long before even the first rays of dawn light had shone these hovering lines criss-crossed both countries, sectoring them into ten by ten kilometres squares.

On returning to Sieba these vedas embarked their next payload, 3,000 rested, refreshed, combat-eager Gurkhas. With the dawn yet still to break the Gurkhas then fell upon the Croats and the Serbs.

Half of these Gurkhas dived down to the centres of the cities and towns. The others descended upon the villages and hamlets of the plains which lie between the rivers of the Danube and Sava. As platoons of Gurkhas charged from their vedas, hives of hen-gers swarmed out with them. No sooner had these vedas departed that there came yet more vedas and each disgorging a troop of marshalled Khmer Rouge equipped with whips, staves and ropes.

The Gurkhas first targets were government offices and military bases pin-pointed by fenserfs on Sunday. Once their occupants were cleared and all of the men within corralled, roped and yoked, the Gurkhas moved on.

With the coming light of the day, many Serbs and Croats now aware of the Gurkhas in now their midst. Filled with stories refugees from Bosnia had told, many men attempted to flee. But they did so in vain. Diving hen-gers repulsed with stings all who sought to cross their lines. Only those men at the Bosnian border crossings awaiting induction were spared their stings, those now suddenly seeking to queue were stung away.

Realising that they were corralled within each hen-ger patrolled square, men the length and breadth of both Croatia and Serbia soon grasped that no matter whom or what they may have been, it was for them all that the Gurkhas had come.

Some men attempted to resist the Gurkhas, fight them out of fear of suffering the fate of those who had failed to flee Bosnia. But just as it had been for them, all resistance to the Gurkhas soon was quelled. But this time, castrations there were none. Nor were there any killings, just their capture, corralling, roping, yoking and the spraying on of the red.

In square after 100 kilometre square all men within were marched away by Khmer Rouge whip-masters and kept in line by watchful hen-gers. Only young boys, the aged and halt were spared.

Many women sought to protect their menfolk, clinging to them, beseeching that they be spared. Others begged, pleaded that they too might go with their men. But the cries and pleas of them all were dashed aside and their men taken.

Some sought solace, safety, sanctuary in churches. But they too did so in vain for clerics, bishops and others of the cloth were also taken, their empty claims to be men of God, of peace, providing them no protection.

Going gree[...] with ENVI

Nathan O'Jacob
[T]el Aviv

[A]N ISRAELI company is [pr]oposing to turn the deserts [of] the Middle East into lands [of] green pastures. Manny [...] then head of Environmen[tal]ly and Naturally Verdant [In]dustries, said the arrival [of] soufins meant the advent [of] portable desalination [u]nits.

"With our new ENVI DeSal [u]nits we can even turn the [D]ead Sea into the Live Sea," [sa]id Manny, who was until [r]ecently was station head at [D]imona nuclear plant. "Anytime, anywhere, if you [w]ant water ENVI will bring it, [a]nd at prices you cannot refuse. [W]e have thousands of units [i]mmediately available," he [s]aid.

Questions have been asked as [t]o how ENVI has been able to [a]cquire such a large quantity of [s]oufins. And at a time when there is widespread shortage and immense demand for the units with prices reaching as high as 1,000 sheckels (£183). Mr Cohen denied suggestions that the sole reason he had Dimona's security police declare 20 km excision zone around the plant was to snaffle up the soufins which fell around it."Would I do a thing like that?" he said.

He also said, it was sheer coincidence that fellow Dimona managers were on the board of ENVI. "We were all out of a job

Gold still glittering

BUSINESS STAFF

GOLD rose to a new high o[f] $308 in London yesterday reflecting the current uncer[-]tainty.

In the past month the gol[d] price has nearly doubled an[d] only sellers have stopped th[e] price from rising even higher Edwin Cruikshank of bullion dealers Jones and Mathews said: "Although there has been some sell-ing there is still a world-wide shortage of the metal. In the medium term the price can only be expected to rise.

"There have been many new-comers into the bullion market including managed funds in a big way. Forward 30 and 90 day orders are suggesting there will only be a forth-coming shortage."

Gold futures have also seen huge rises, the LIFFE index was marking December con-tacts at $312.50 with 4048 con-tracts traded, another all-time high. Official gold

Thousands of Serbs, Croats flee Aliens' onslaught

Susem spaceships and Gurkhas swoop up male Serbs and Croats

Jonathan Swift
In Ljubjana

LARGE numbers of Susem forces, thought to be Gurkhas, are believed to have attacked both Croatia and Serbia.

Entire populations are reported to have been rounded-up and force-marched in yoked columns into the holds of waiting fleets of the giant, two kilometre long Susem spaceships. All the men are said to have then been flown them of to as yet unknown destinations.

Those men attempting to flee the Susem attackers have been tracked down and been castrated before being forced back to the marching columns.

Outside observers at the borders of both Croatia and Serbia have reported numerous of these countries' males being attacked by Susem darts patrolling the frontiers.

Only in the former Serb-ian provinces of Voyvod-ina and Kosovo have these border patrols been relaxed. However, as both provinces are still report-ed to be embroiled in fighting between Serbs and their Hungarian and Albanian minorities, it is unlikely many Serbs can escape across these borders.

The NATO Information Office in Brussels said although it was watching the situation but there is little it can do because neither Serbia nor Croatia is a member of NATO.

NATO's hands-off res-ponse was echoed in other European based organizat-ions. Hans Lubber spokesman for the Western European Union (WEU) said it was not within in the mandate of the WEU to intervene.

The spokesperson for the Organization for Security and Cooperation in Europe (OSCE) said: "Should a request be received by the OSCE to inspect claims of violations of a country's sovereignty we will meet with the parties concerned to see if we able to be of assistance to them. As of this moment in time the OSCE has not received any such request."

Dr Sarah Davies Reader of Balkan Studies, the University of Sheppey at Sheerness, said: "Things look grim for both the Serbs and Croats. But quite frankly there isn't likely to be much intern-ational sympathy for either country.

"And after the recent drubbing the Susem meted out to NATO as well as the US, there is no will to intervene on anyone's behalf again the Susem let alone pariahs such as the Serb and Croat regimes."

► Pages 4,5,6&7

Millions of Brazilia[ns] seeking Susem cures turned back

BY POLLY PORTILLO
IN RECIFE

HUNDREDS of thousands of Brazilians flocking to the ter-ritory occupied by the Aliens are being turned back by armed soldiers and police.

The Brazilian Government has sealed all road and rail links into the area. A line, stretching for 400 kilometres along the eastern border of Ceará State is blocked by a wall of steel and fighter planes constantly patrol the skies above.

The Brazilian navy is also reported to be patrolling the [n]orthern coast and westwards through Pernambuco State to the Tochins River.

Only refugees fleeing the zone are being allowed to pass. People attempting to enter are barred. How long this is situation can continue is unknown.

Among those trying to enter the zone are many of the landless poor of Brazil's impoverished North East region.

The 'Movimento dos Sem Terra' (Movement of the Landless Ones) is at the fore-front in demanding the mili-tary let them and the follow-ers cross into Ceará. Others [...] those who are suffering

The coastal citi[es of] Recefe and Natal, [...] from the lawlessn[ess...] refugees, are un[der] strain from the su[...] of an estimated [...] poor people into [...] Many are refugee[s...] Susem controlled [...] ers, loggers, ranch[...] majority of the in[...] from else-where in [...]

Rodrico Gomes, [...] mayor, speaking [...] situation through[out...] buco state said: "M[...] is the impending [...] law and order both [...] and throughout the [...]

Asthma attacks abat[e]

From Julia Bale
Health Correspondent

THE National Asthma Council has reported a sharp drop in asthma deaths. A Council spokesperson, Wendy Hotchkiss, said: "At this time of year we would normally expect to see at least 50 deaths a week due to asthma but in the past month there has been only 20."

Ms Hotchkiss also said there had been a marked drop in the number of reported asthma admissions to the Council is optimis-tic this would turn out to be the case," she said.

Much of the this reduction in asthma deaths is attributed to the reduction in motor vehicle exhaust fumes brought about by the extensive use of Sus-em energy units. A marked reduction in industrial pollution, mainly from power stations, is also thought to be a signi-ficant contributory the main traffic pollu[t]ants, especially sma[ll] particle particulate, a[re] showing a marke[d] drop compared to th[e] same period of la[st] year. We can definitel[y] say that there is [a] definite link betwee[n] not only the particulat[e] count, but nitroge[n] oxides and carbo[n] monoxide as well."

Edith Cardell of the Health Visitors Coun-cil also says her mem-bers have reported a marked reduction in

'SOUFIN TAX: UNENFORCEABL[E]'

By Tony Harwood

Moves to tax soufins were rejected by many of the[...] yesterday. "How are they going to do it?" was typical of [...] those questioned.

Les Hawkins (46) of Guildford, and who has a souf[in...] typical of those questioned, laughed aside at suggestion [...] on their use. He said: "How is any official going to know w[...] using mine or not? Are they going to have TV detector-st[yle vans] cruising the streets?"

Stan Kalms (39) of GB&H Motors of Ponders End, said: "We've been fitting hundreds of soufins into vehicles.

"How are they going to nab anyone for using them? Stand by the road side listening for silent cars going by?" he joked. "Just now," he said, "there must [...] soufins

Council admi[ts] using Soufins

By Charles Grass
Local Government Correspondent

NORWICH COUNCIL officials admitted using soufins to power the Authorities' offices. Coun-cil leader, Peter Brittan, claimed the investment was already saving the city thousands of pounds.

Councillor Brittan said: "We have a duty to the people of Norwich to manage the city as effi-ciently as possible these [soufin] units enable us to do so He defended the payment of £150 a unit as a "price worth paying" considering the "

With their guards now gone, politicians, their cronies, henchmen, even those with claims of opposition to the ruling regimes, found their hollow protestations counted for nought. And they too all were taken.

Driven from square after square the men, marshalled, yoked in columns were marched unstopping, unknowing to where and to what.

Cajoled by whip wielding Khmers and hen-gers alike, columns after fear-filled columns tramped, trudged for hour after hour along roads leading to the wider river valleys or the Adriatic coast. In the heat of the sun, cold of night many fell by the wayside. But none who were yet alive were let to linger. The lame, even the dying, were carried on the backs of the living,

By day, long before columns reached to where they were headed they saw what awaited them. Even from afar the black brooding, kilometres long ovoid shapes of the awaiting tocans appeared colossal. Cresting hundreds of metres they dwarfed all around them. And for many of the men in the approaching columns their dread deepened. But the whips of Khmers, together with the stings of hen-gers ensured none slackened the tramp trudge of their step.

As columns neared, then fell under the cast of the tocans' gigantic shadows, saw that they were rested on ground or water by huge stabilising flippers fore and aft, the men also saw further columns being driven up into the tocans, through walls of their flashed blue light then disappearing inside. They also saw that men were as shrimps are to a whale.

Inside the tocans' dark cavernous bowels the columns, hungry, thirsty, cast down, were at last let to rest. And when 100,000 were within, the tocans' flippers becoming doors, rose and with thunderous resonating booms clumped clamped closed. Three hours later their reluctant cargos were disgorged into the sweltering heat of the Serra Pelada.

For three days and three nights tocans ferried from east to west. But on the second day there came into Serbia and Croatia Colonel Tambassing's aides and the Ragusan trained volunteers. Armed with information from interviewing in Bosnia, these investigated the files and computer systems of government and other offices of the regimes. Although as yet unbroken code protected much, remarkable amounts of incriminating information were gleaned from their first day's trawl. In the days following, there came more, much more.

Throughout the third week of May, the 'Wanted List' grew. Names of people and companies who were neither Croatian nor Serbian also began to appear. So did evidence of covert dealing between both regimes against Bosnia. By Thursday morning, names and whereabouts of many of these people, companies and organisations had been sent on to Tabajara.

On the Thursday morning of that week, in Tabajara, Kershaw returned from Bosnia and Ragusa bringing the first of the Nonettes' representatives.

Meanwhile, having gained experience on minor misdemeanours, the courts in Ragusa began judging more serious cases. And handing down sterner sentences.

71: RIP THORNE

A month ago Tabajara was such an isolated, tranquil place and the villagers lived quiet, steady lives. Now it's the crossroads to goodness knows what and where. But not only have the villagers risen to the occasion they've taken to it with relish.

With Pedro and his men (and increasingly women and the young) ranging ever further, wider, the stream of their converts coming to Tabajara is now a flood. Even the children are conducting parties of visitors. Elana and the other representatives are spending more of their time schooling the first converts in establishing training centres of their own. She and others are also talking of forming a council, coordinating committees and goodness knows what else.

Gurkhas arrived on Monday en route to the Serra Pelada. They asked for volunteers to help with translation. Not that there was anyone to spare in Tabajara, but Elana, through the Ubajara representatives, found them some. More Gurkhas arrived yesterday, this time pleading for even more volunteers. Village teachers have been returning all week with qualifying results from the communities they had been assigned to. Teams of Terbal's cavern making mach-ines have flown out to make gardens and link them into the irrigation network.

Late yesterday Pedro and some others returned exhausted saying they were now operating beyond Sobral, 70 miles to the east. He said that when the police and army left the town there had been chaos. He had to work desperately hard telling the people to form into nines and groups of nine times. They had wanted him to stay but he had returned to Tabajara to tell of the consequences. Townspeople who had no contact with the land were coming. The wonders of the gardens would be meaningless to them.

Early this morning the women from Bosnia flew in. Not long after, Elana and others were in tears when they heard what Croat and Serb men had done. Though Rainbow, when she heard, went into one of her seething silences. (I keep out her way whenever she does). But I was also aghast at what the Bosnian women told, for their ordeals have been terrible indeed. Despite the tears Elana and the others insisted the Bosnian ladies ate the banquet put before them.

All week down below, with the non-stop music playing and the Susem still swaying, activity has been as hectic. Tearo or Anuria are forever on screen to Paceillo. On other screens I have observed Paceillo talking to more Susem from what must be La-ra. Though I have not understood what has been said, she's been by turn excited then agitated, not just with those on the screens but with almost everything else. Milophinia and her minero-horticulturists have now established iron ore fields stretching for miles and miles into the caatinga. They have developed zinc plants, bauxite ones, potassium, chrome, the list goes on.

Menpemelo I have barely seen. She, Terbal and his sherpels have been developing units of little plates which rebuild and replace limbs, of which of course, she has seen more than a withered and missing few these days past. My scepticism received her "Lizards do it, do they not?" I gather it is something to do with templates for bones, nerves, muscles and skin to grow upon.

In contrast, Pheterisco and Petruee have taken over where Rainbow's tuition left off in adding formation dancing to their singing. They would probably win karaoke prizes all over.

Rainbow, however, has been run off her feet. I have long resigned, in matters TV, to her being the lead, now I just help out, stop her getting in a tizzy. Though she has had more than cause enough these days past. Putting together tonight's telecast kept changing with the news coming in from Bosnia. Today's programme showing footage of the tocans arriving at the Pelada yester-day was scrapped because of this morning's news. Then it changed yet again three hours later with the arrival of Americans from SNN-TV in Ubajara.

The representatives from Ubajara phoned saying that the Americans' heli-copter had been forced to land at the cliff base below. At first I thought that they were definitely destined for the Pelada, but Rainbow commenting "Caught TV is part of them," probably saved their incarceration down the pit.

In no time at all she had outlined what had come to mind. It sounded good. Paceillo thought the same. Rainbow tested it on Elana and the others. From the way they hugged, kissed her and cried, I took it that they agreed as well.

With opportunity presenting itself I was all prepared to negotiate, the commission would be handy, but I'd not even got as far as asking Roberto to take me to Ubajara when he drove up with Rainbow sat beside him. On the way, sat in the back with the hen-gers "Hadodani"ing, I discussed with Rainbow whether half a million dollars was too much to ask as an opening bid. But to this she said nothing. I thought at the time it was because she was petrified at Roberto's driving (it's still suicidal).

We had been told that the Americans were held in the old Polícia post, but when we arrived they were across the street in the Scala bar and holding court. They had collected an admiring gathering, and with others outside cramming to peer. There were six of them but I recognised the blond bouffant head above the crowd as Rip Thorne's, the world-famed, fearless TV reporter. His court already had. And he was supping on it. Until then he would have been the first, the only TV star the locals had ever seen in the flesh, the most famous person to ever set foot in town. But before I could say anything Rainbow brushed past me, saying "As I'm American I'll best handle this."

She had difficulty pushing through the outside onlookers. Then some of them recognised her. To hushed choruses of "Rainbow!...Rainbow!" they melted a path. There were now two famous TV people in town, at the same time and in the same place (and in the same show). Rip Thorne stopped autographing, held out a hand, a smile and a "Hi, I'm Rip Thor..." but he got no further before she cut him with an icy "What are you doing here?"

He tried affability but Rainbow, colder, gave "You know the consequences." The crowd became quiet, but as in a Western stand-off, they were all eyes. He replied

it. She called him a liar. Matters then took a turn for the worse, for him.

I thought Rainbow was over brusque, her outlining proposals too blunt and her opening terms unrealistic. Rip Thorne thought so too, until she told him what would happen to him and his crew, then pointed to the hen-gers hovering outside. His sound engineer immediately contacted their Atlanta studios.

Meanwhile, Rainbow, silent, her arms folded, head down, paced back and forth. Each time Atlanta demurred, and without raising her head, the price went up, her descriptions of fates awaiting them in the Pelada more graphic. Though his smile had now gone, Rip Thorne's coolness remained, but even this evaporated when Rainbow mentioned what would happen to blue-eyed blonds in crotch tight trousers who fell into the maws of sex-craved Croats.

With her next price increase ringing in his ears he became frantic for Atlanta to agree. So did the rest of his crew. To Rainbow's mention that he would be shown on her programme weekly refilling the Pelada he was in wet eyed panic threatening Atlanta to tear up his contract and work for NBC.

Throughout the hour they took to accept her terms, the crowd listened intently to Roberto translating and watched with the intensity they would a Soap. Rainbow scripted a happy ending though. And she made Mr Thorne write it all down. After he had signed, Roberto translated to the audience. Three quarters of a million a day in advance, seven teams transmitting in real time, a two minute break every half hour and she ("or her representatives," she had him write) given full editorial control. Her final clause had an element of delighting surprise. Rainbow fished from one of her little tunic pockets, the piece of paper she had originally written my Citicard number on when I had first telephoned to her in London.

Confirming the transfer was a drag, ringing the Pousada, Elana running to the cavern, Terbal Internetting Miami, and then having it all relayed back. Meanwhile, Rainbow had the Americans huddle in Roberto's truck. While they were, she, with the grin of a cat with cream and to a chorus of "Viva Rainbow!" let the patrons of the Scala now pay court to her.

When confirmation was received, Rainbow striding from the Scala with a triumphant smile and brushing her hands as though there'd been crumbs between, said, "You may leave now." She also told the Americans that Roberto would drive them to the rodoviária down at Tianguá. Rainbow can be so mischievous when she wants. Roberto was back in half an hour. His driving probably frightened them as much as she had.

While waiting his return and amid her autographing, I remarked that she had perhaps been a tad hard with them. "I have standards," she said, "what would people have thought if I had stooped to him?" Then, with barely stopping from signing, she momentarily looked up again and with a wry grin added "As you like it, Act Five, Scene Two."

Greeks and Zippos I can understand, it's the sort of thing they do. And Krauts for that matter. As for the Russians, well that lot over there have always been iffy. But it's all the others Rainbow read out, including our own lot. They have all had their snouts in there.

It wasn't just dodgy ones either. Governments, posh companies, even those international charities, they have all been doing dealings with them. As she said, they are as guilty as the ones what pulled the triggers and killed all those poor Bosnians.

I think what she said about them getting up and saying they have done wrong is only fair. And they having to shell out half their profits is only fair as well. Also, I go along with what she said about them facing penalties if they don't cough up, in my view they deserve to suffer.

Rainbow also said what they had found was only the start. I had to chuckle when she said all those who had been dealing with the Croats and Serbs who she hadn't yet mentioned had the chance of saying sorry and telling what they are going to pay. It will be very interesting to see who comes out with their hands up. Especially after she had said it would be better for them to call out their own names before she does.

Another of the things she said was the trials of all the Croats and Serbs who were guilty are going to be shown live on TV. She said it was important for justice to be seen to be done. I go along with that any day. But in my book for what they have done none of them deserve mercy.

Rainbow was on for some time giving out all the names of the offenders, so in a way I was a bit disappointed when she only spent a few minutes showing the Susem machines and things. All the same though, I was definitely impressed with their tocan. I know they are big but I didn't realise they are that big. The picture first showed her stepping down from the plane things she had been in, vedas she said they were. Then the picture swung from her to going along a line of more of these vedas. There were hundreds and hundreds of them, all going round in a curve. Then the camera swung the other way and there were hundreds more. And as it did, there was this big booming "Welcome, I am Sardon."

After that there was this shot of Rainbow standing in this dome. I could see it was big because the camera was first pointing upwards then it panned down on her and she was tiny. And when the camera zoomed in on her as she walked forwards and said that there would be more shown later, there was all this music which really got over the effect of her being in a giant hall.

SHAME! SHAME!

GOVERNMENTS, COMPANIES, CHARITIES GUILTY OF ABETTING SERB CROAT THUGS

TOP British companies and charities were last night accused by the Susem in a TV broadcast of assisting the brutal Serb and Croat regimes.

More than half of the broadcast was devoted to exposing a list of those reportedly in league with both Serbian and Croatian rulers. Many are well known British and international companies, including Westminster Bank, H.E.R.E, British Averospace, Rascel, Camfam, Food Relief and Help the Children.

The Government are also accused of providing financial backing to many of the rogue projects by giving export guarantees to companies doing business with the regimes.

If the claims are proved, it will spell difficulties not only for the companies named, but for the DTI and the Foreign Office. Either they knew what was going on and covered up, or they are just plain incompetent.

Within hours of the telecast angry responses were being voiced from numerous quarters.

A spokesman for the influential Charity Watch, said: "Charities found guilty of dealing with the two countries will be struck from our approved list."

Losing approved status would be calamitous to any charity.

MPs from all parties were calling for immediate statement from the government. Julian Balcombe, Taunton's LibCon MP, said: "If these allegations of underhand dealing with these Balkan thugs are proved, it will be to the lasting shame of all those involved. I shall be demanding that guilty Ministers resign."

Another LibCon MP, Ian Lawrence said: "These revelations bring shame on the good name of British business. The action they stand guilty off is some-thing to be expected from foreign countries not British ones. I shall be demanding they are punished."

Even the government's own supporters

DRAMATIC BOSNIAN REVELATIONS

Top names revealed in dramatic TV disclosure
Governments, charities, companies accuse

Stuart Kettle

MORE than a hundred countries and international organisations were last night accused by the Susem of supporting the Serb and Croat regimes. The accusation was made on a TV broadcast that ended with the announcer Rainbow Louis demanded they face tough penalties.

Rainbow Louis promised there were more names and revelations yet to come.

Most of the guilty were European companies but a handful were British. Among those named were chemical giant H.E.R.E (founded in France, 1939), shipping to trading conglomerate, Harding Mathewson. A number of major British banks, oil companies were also named among those named in last night's telecast.

International British based ... including Help ... Help

Already the revelations have sent shocks waves though the City and government circles. Citi analyst, Kathy Sontag, said: "Investor sentiment can be expected to turn against those mentioned [in the telecast]. The extent of involvement of many companies' subsidiaries is, as yet un-known, but from the indications suggests it could have extensive repercussions."

As yet there has not been any official comment from any of the charities named in the telecast. All a Camfam Press Office spokesman would say was that allegations were "being looked into with utmost urgency."

The Foreign Office has so far declined to make any comment either. However indications are that a formal statement will be issued later today.

...ever, there was a ...hadow

'Just good friends' say Russians

By Joanna Phillips in Moscow

OLEG KRESTINSKI, Russian Foreign Minister, at the meeting with NATO representatives, denied abetting Serbian military actions in Bosnia.

Krestinski said, "Historically, Russia have always looked upon the Serbs as younger brothers. We have

Krestinski's assertions will be met with widespread disbelief among Balkan experts. Naser Oruc of the Prague based, Bosnian Information Centre says, "It is common knowledge that the Russians have contravened just about every International ...

Germans deny complicity

Julian Horicks in Bonn

THE German Government have denied charges of complicity in the war in Bosnia. The Federal Government also ruled out any suggestion of compensating the Bosnian people.

A tough worded statement issued by Foreign Minister, Helmut Molke, states that German foreign policy is conducted through the EU. As such it has never inter...

of the waring factions. Therefore, Molke maintains, Germany has no financial obligation to Bosnia. However, the statement does mention that the German government is prepared to offer assistance in the reconstruction of Bosnia but only in conjunction with its EU partners.

Molke's word's are likely to raise a chorus of disbelief in many circles. Critics, both inside and outside the country, of Germany's ...

frequently voiced their annoyance at Germany's one-sidedness Germany's UN Security Council vote of last Tuesday being only the latest example of partisan policy. Karl Brecht, the SPD leader, and a voracious critic of his country's pro Croatian policy said, "Molke and the rest of the CDU have backed them (Croatia) with loans, guarantees, joint ventures, and that is just on the economic front."

During the last week of May, Ragusan investigators continued to unearth evidence implicating outsiders sustaining the Serbian and Croatian regimes. Meanwhile, both countries' parlous economies collapsed into near peasantry and widespread bartering. But with men absent disorder did not occur.

At week end the first Croatian craftsmen volunteers, their places taken by subsequent inductees, began returning from Bosnia. They told of their treatment there. That it was humane and how they had worked in groups of nines. They also told of the Nonettes and the message they had given them to deliver. Within hours of arrival they were telling all who listened and were enacting it themselves. And so the notion of Nonettes began to spread through Croatia. With each group of nine formed, its members also became recipients of Jacques Forrier's Aid and possessors of soufins.

Increasing numbers of refugees in Germany, Italy and elsewhere returned to Bosnia. On arrival many met the Nonettes and saw their efficient, equitable distribution of aid and the order and orderliness they instilled. New arrivals also saw the teams of Croatian and Serbian workmen energetically engaged in reconstruction and the absence of animosity towards them. Many of the homecomers swelled the Nonettes' ranks.

As well as widening, the Nonette movement, with the return of the thirty representatives from Tabajara, also deepened. At seminar after packed seminar they related what they had seen and experienced. They also demonstrated the teaching screens they had been given. By month end twenty-five Nonette communities encompassing more than 5,000 families had been established. Many more were in formation. The absence of armies, aid agencies, police forces and politicians freed the Nonette communities to organise their affairs themselves, unhindered and in peace.

On board Sieba, Tearo, Anuria and Lathia were kept informed of these, to them, encouraging events by Colonel Tambassing's men, who in turn were kept informed by the Nonettes themselves. It was back through this conduit that the requests of the prosecutors in Ragusa were relayed. Teams, now augmented by Bosnians who had trained with them, travelled throughout the country collecting names of women who had been abused and those, if known, of their abusers. The 'Wanted List' grew. Some transgressors were already in custody and even punished for other crimes. Prosecutors also informed victims the trials of their abusers were scheduled to begin the first week of June at seven selected places, each soon known as 'Kamenito Mjesto', "The Place of Stones."

refugee children

SPECIAL REPORT: PAGE 18

SUSEM THREATEN TO NAME AND SHAME COMPANIES, CHARITIES

SERBS CROATS IN COVER-UP SHOCK

By Michael Freinson

MASSIVE undercover dealings with the brutal Serb and Croat regimes by hundreds of companies, charities, and governments were detailed last night by the Susem in a TV broadcast.

The broadcast revealed that:

- **hundreds of companies and governments were busting EU sanctions by trading with both the Croat and Serb regimes.**
- **both regimes were 'propped up' by under-cover foreign government and EU loans.**
- **many charities and other aid organizations gave bribes and 'protection money' to Serb and Croat officials.**
- **MANY OF THE GUILTY COMPANIES AND CHARITIES ARE BRITISH.**

The telecast also revealed both Serbia and Croatia governments were actively engaged in slaughtering Bosnian populations and committing other atrocities.

Announcing there were more revelations to come, the Susem telecaster demanded that:

- **guilty companies pay over half of their profits in compensation for their actions.**
- **those organizations who had not yet been named confess before they were named.**
- **charities and governments own up to their dealings with the rogue regimes and recommence the Bosnian people.**
- **all those guilty to be**

crimes in Bosnia were to be shown on television live

Shockwaves from the revelations have already reverberated through the business community both in Britain and abroad. Market analysts are forecastin major falls in many majo companies share prices.

Many in the City and elsewhere have despaired in recent weeks as what preparations should be made in order safeguard billions of pounds of investors' funds locked up in

Germany rocked by Susem revelations

Ruhe government linked to crooked Croatian deals

By Monika Landsdorf in Berlin

TOP GERMAN government officials were desperately defending their political masters today against accusations of involvement in underhand deals with the former Croatian regime.

Yesterday's Susem telecast, in giving details of the mass deportation of the male population from both Croatia and Serbia also gave details of incriminating details unearthed by their investigators. According to Susem claims many foreign companies were extensively involved in dealing with both of the former Croatian and Serbian regimes.

The Susem also claim that they have uncovered evidence that the German government gave their fulsome backing to many of the companies accused of dealing with the Croatians.

With Germany's Lander elections scheduled for just 10 days away, the Susem revelations could not have come at worse time for Walther Ruhe's CDU coalition. Already parallels are being drawn with the precipitate collapse of US President Warren's popularity in the wake of the Pentagon's covert actions in the 'Tonic Water' fiasco.

Germany's hard left party,

know this illegal activity was going on then it means that they are so incompetent that they should still resign."

According to the Susem revelations however, there are indications that focus of investigation will, in the first instance, will be on the activities of German controlled companies as well as subsidiaries in Hungary and elsewhere in eastern Europe.

Many of the names given in the Susem telecast are, according to analysts, either German owned companies or are part owned by German companies, the most notable being the IG Farben owned company of Noleyz.

According to Susem claims, their investigators the defoliant chemical 'Fűrdáért Beta' manufactured by Noleyz, was purposely sprayed on rural Bosnian populations.

Use of Fűrdáért is banned throughout the EU as well as many other countries including SE Asia because of it chloracne effects as well a birth deformities. If it the Susem claims as to the defolian spray's use are substantiated then it will lay Farben ope not just to criminal prosecutio but to massive if not cripplin

UK COMPANIES IN SER SANCTIONS BUSTING S

British firms connived in Bosnian sl governments and charities also g

FROM IAN MAXWELL

BRITISH companies, aid organizations, charities and even the government, have helped both the Croatian and Serbian regimes.

In last night's Susem telecast, the announcer Rainbow Lewis, revealed details uncovered she claimed from raids on Croatian and Serbian government offices. For more than twenty minutes she listed details of hundreds of companies and organizations from around the world.

Saying it was only the first of a whole string of names suspected involved in covert aid to the regimes, Rainbow Lewis demanded stiff penalties from those found guilty. However, she did not specify how her demands - for half of the accused company's profits were to be imposed. But the furor the revelations are likely to cause from within Britain, pressure is

Outrage over the revelations ha not been short in coming. Charity Watch, the charity watchdog organisation, in a statement issued within hours of the telecast, said: "Any charity against whom allegations made, are substantiated, will be struck from the Watch's approved list." This could spell financial disaster for many charities.

Antony Stansgate MP, one of the Government's own sternest backbench critics, said: "The matter is quite simple. Anyone one dealing with these countries has broken the law. If anyone breaks the law, no matter who they are, they have to be prosecuted, and if found guilty, punished."

Among those accused were a number of British banks, defence manufacturers, the chemical giant H.E.R.E. A spokesman for the company declined to confirm that

Fists fight Brazilia army's 'Ring of Stee

Ed Sturn reports from Natal in Brazil's impoverished 'Nordeste' re

"Deixar nós sair, deixar nós sair" "Let us pass, let us pass" pleaded the multitude to the military blocking the highway to the West and the territory occupied by the Susem aliens. But these people's pleas were in vain.

Tanks and armoured personnel carriers, a dozen deep, blocked the road. Armed soldiers, their

the air. The soldiers' officers standing atop the tanks continually shouted through loudhailers for people to return to their homes.

But for many of the tens of thousands gathered, there are no homes for them to return to. These are the among the Nordeste's poor, landless and desperate. And their hope of a home and a future lay

hundreds of kilometres away. And as such, most were unshaken by the military. Their determination to pass to the other side of the soldier's barrier of steel remains unbroken. Even the officers' claims of dangers awaiting any who should make it across the Jaguaribe River failed to dim the multitude's desire.

From early morning and

74: JAMES

Philipe, a good friend from University, lives in Rio and so, having having spoken with him, I have decided to pay him a visit on the first leg of my trip. I did go for several jobs in banking but with the City being in such turmoil I wasn't successful at getting any of them. Though to be honest I have to admit my heart wasn't really in it. Also as there isn't really anything to keep me in London and having spent the past week at home, I just can't wait to go. Mother was most worried that I had decided on going to Brazil, and father said I was a "Bloody fool and that I should get my head out of the clouds." If I had told them the real reason for going there they would in all probability have both thrown a fit!

Meanwhile, I have had time to read the papers, watch television and cruise the Internet. And a most bemusing week it has been seeing one CEO after another doing contortions of denial of any involvement with Serbia, and more so Croatia. The ones expressing their total ignorance have been among the funniest. If ever there was truth in the adage "When cock-ups occur, deputy heads will roll," the past few days have confirmed it. The papers, TV and radio have had a field day. Share prices have been tumbling all over the place. It is not just the companies named in Rainbow's telecasts either, or the ones who have volunteered admission, but those suspected of being implicated. Even denials of any 'wrongdoing' are taken as signs of covered-up guilt.

In a way, if all the double dealing was restricted to business one could shrug one's shoulders. But NGOs are another matter entirely. And I don't think excuses that they were obliged to keep quiet about the diversion of their aid to Serb and Croat militias cuts much ice with anyone. Similarly more than a few governments are going to have to do some explaining as well. So much for all those joint declarations and sanctions! Now that their undercover Croatian loans and guarantees have come into the open, I wouldn't like to be a German minister seeking re-election. Nor a Hungarian one for that matter, the protests in Budapest are getting quite out of hand.

It will also be interesting to see how many of these 'guilty' governments hand over the wanted Serbs and Croats in their countries. After the latest revelations, it will be very difficult for them to refuse Rainbow's "requests."

I have also gleaned, from what news there is, more of the state of affairs in Brazil. There has been protest and panic, Sâo Paulo stocks are down, but there has been much mañana as well. Philipe, when I called him, reinforced this. He says that most people in Rio and throughout the south of Brazil regard the north of the country as almost a foreign country and a backward one at that. One of which they know little of and care for even less. All the same though I am as determined as ever to go and see Danny, if he is still there, that is.

75: SERRA PELADA

Although all the Serbs and Croats arrived at the Serra Pelada, Gurkhas moved most of them onto Grande Carajás. They were the more fortunate ones.

The remainder were deployed filling sacks with the spoil from pits that formigas had spent decades digging. The biggest, three kilometres diameter, 300 metres deep, devoured most. Groups, 80 strong, were made to carry down and trample in 3,000 sacks before each day was done.

At first many resisted, refused, and some even instilled to rebel, but the Khmers' whips and hen-gers' stings quelled any such dissention. Others asked, as they had since they were first taken, "Why?" But there was none to give answer except among themselves. And turning inwards, they found fault for their fate in those who had served their countries' regimes. Exacerbated by heat and humidity, rain, mud, mosquitoes and leeches, blame frequently flared into fighting. There would have been more deaths, more bodies buried into the rising pit floor had Khmers and hen-gers not intervened.

At the beginning some found night-time shelter in formigas' abandoned makeshift favelas but most were obliged to sleep where they had laboured. During the first evening, in ignorance of the castrational consequences, several sought escape. Their reddened heads ensured none succeeded.

On the fourth day a regiment of further Gurkhas arrived to arrange supplies of food and water. Aboard abandoned trucks, Gurkhas, with teams taken from eager volunteers and with translators recruited in Tabajara, emptied latifúndios' barns, granaries and the fazendas of their livestock. Most of the grandees, gerantes, rancheiros had fled the region. Those who had not yet departed saw sense in first accommodating the Gurkhas' requests and then fleeing as well.

By the fifth day the Gurkhas implemented the next part of their assignment, organising the workforce into groups of 60,000. Each group was progressively subdivided by nine into groups of nines, who in turn elected one of their group to represent them. Nine representatives delegated one to speak for them, and so on, until there was one who spoke for them all. Such was this arrangement that every man could be referenced by a five digit number.

It was also an organisation through which Gurkhas issued work quotas. The first of which was filling 50 million sacks of spoil a day into the Pelada. There was soon a division of labour, fillers, carriers, tramplers, and builders of shelters. Also through this organisation, the Serbo-Croat speaking Gurkhas began interviewing each man. While the 'Wanted List' grew, so did the numbers of men sent to the island of Korčula to face trial for the crimes they had committed in Bosnia.

I have cancelled our standing order to Help the Children. I will never give money to them again, any of them. I am not just annoyed but I'm very upset. When I think what we have given could have ended up in the pockets of those criminals and murderers, I get more annoyed. And that man who came on television from the charity saying as they were an International Non-Government Organisation, or 'NGO' as he pompously kept calling it, they had to "play by the rules" and how as they worked with governments it was necessary to go along with their "practices." 'Practices' my foot, they were kowtowing to crooks. And have any of them resigned? Not one. If I met any of them I would give them more than a piece of my mind.

The government is as bad. There they were, sanctimoniously signing all those European motions and sanctions condemning them, while at the same time turning a blind eye. They must have known where all those exports to Hungary and Greece were ending up. Not that the other governments are any better. They have all been closing their eyes. With one hand they have censured, drummed them out of one European Council after another and with the other they have been lending them money, propping them up. Their "constructive engagements," "mitigating excesses," makes me sick. Weasel words is what they are. What they are really saying is that they don't know right from wrong any more, perhaps they never have.

I have told Daffyd to write to the Prudential demanding they tell us if any of our premiums are invested in any of the companies who are guilty. I have said at the library that everyone should do the same and I shall also do so at the Association when I am there next week. It is time these companies were taken to task. Some of the things they've said these days past have been pathetic. I have never seen so much spineless crawling, the people who run these big companies never seem to face up to their responsibilities.

The worst has been the European Reconstruction Bank or whatever it is called. They've lent all this money, our money, to some chemicals company in Poland, which sold what it made to a factory in Romania. The Romanian company paid for it with an EC Regional Grant, our money again, who then supposedly sold it to a company in Cyprus but it never went there, it went straight on a barge and shipped up the Danube to Belgrade.

When Rainbow says the people who are guilty will be brought to justice and face the consequences of their actions I know that I'm not the only person to agree with her.

Dutch bank admits dealing with Serbs

By Dan van der Hat
in Amsterdam

HOLLAND'S biggest bank, INBC which operates throughout the world, has admitted that its branches in several East European counties were involved in covert financing of trade deals with both Serbia and Croatia.

The bank confirmed today claims made in the Susem telecast and said seven senior managers from the region and a further two at its head office in Amsterdam had been "relieved of their duties."

Spokesman, Dan van der Vat said: "An overnight investigation of INBC's overseas transactions revealed a number of improper transactions concerning the contravening of trade sanctions concerning Croatia and Serbia

"Those who responsible for these irregularities are no longer with INBC. The Bank regrets these misdemeanours have taken place and are willing to fully cooperate with all the relevant authorities and is prepared to make recompense where necessary."

It is not known what sums INBC will be setting aside to cover its liabilities. Last year INBC declared a profit of US $2.3 billion, but only a fraction of this came from its East European operations.

INBC's prompt admission, however, is likely to increase pressure of other companies ...

MEPs demand Eurocrats' heads

By Julia Hampton
in Brussels

In a rare show unanimity the European Parliament has called for the resignations of senior officials at the European Commission in Brussels. MEPs also called for the prosecution of companies who had broken EU and international sanctions against Croatia and Serbia.

A succession of MEPs demanded to know why the EU Secretariat in Brussels had kept hidden the true purpose of much EU investment into Eastern Europe. Was it to circumvent their own trade bans?

Said Danish MEP, Sven Boordhabvn: "We want to know why Brussels have been letting so much of the EU Development Funds go to companies dodging EU regulations.

"If they know what is going on, they must resign. If they did not know, then they are no good at their jobs and must be sacked. We demand a reply to this question immediately. We must be told of the EU involvement in these terrible crimes. There ...

Mixed response by companies to accusations

By Hugo Before
Ethics Correspondent

THE response today of many bosses to revelations that their company was trading with Croatia and Serbia was a straightforward: "We did not know". Only a handful were prepared to acknowledge their guilt.

HERE's response, typical of many: "Although Magyar Chemicals is a wholly owned subsidiary of HERE, the day to day operation of the company was the responsibility of local management.

"However, a thorough review of the company's Eastern European operations is urgently underway."

The spokesman declined to comment on Magyar Chemical's claims that they were sent many of their raw materials directly from ▯'s own refinery on Humberside. "All HERE directors were busily engaged on company business and unable to speak to the press," said the spokesman.

The press office of the international trading conglomerate, Harding Mathewsons, issued a similar statement: "HM has many overseas subsidiaries and indirect investments in many other companyies. While HM condemns any contravention of EU sanctions directives imposed against Croatia and Serbia, it cannot be held responsible for actions taken by companies over which it does not have management control. Nevertheless HM is undertaking an investigation of all its overseas operations."

The HM spokesman, who declined to be named, was unable to comment on allegations that the Bermuda registered HM Financial Trust, controlled the Panamanian company Gustavo Leigh, which owned the airplanes leased to Air Hevatska, the Croatian airline, through a Hungarian based subsidiary Nem Ertem.

Kaiser Kurt's Saxon sunset

By Monkia Landoff
in Berlin

KURT Biedenkoff, for long the uncrowned CDU's "Kaiser Kurt" of Saxony, was shouted down at Lander election rally in Hanover last night.

To cries of "Lügner, lügner (liar, liar)," Herr Biedenkopf tried in vain to claim he had no knowledge of German Government involvement in supporting Croatia.

However, the crowd's cries have some justification. For the past five years Mr Biedenkopf has been Germany's Minister of Finance in Walther Ruhe's Government. That means he knew details of Germany's monetary and trade policies and had a direct hand in formulating them.

Up until a few days, ago the CDU-CSU was set to make sweeping gains in all of Germany's States in forthcoming elections. Now with the Susem revelations against the Federal ...

can be almost as hostile as Mars.

inspectors in NYC in 1911 reported that in

were announced to remove existing A...

$20bn share wipeout!

Julia Weston
Business Correspondent

Shares of companies named in yesterday's Susem telecast slumped across world exchanges and bourses. Many other companies not named in the telecast but suspected of Serbian and Croatian involvement, were also adversely affected.

Investors large and small took little notice of corporate protests of innocence or professed ignorance, major British Banks such as the ...

Although HERE, down 129p, was the only British chemical company named by the Susem, all companies in the chemical sector took a hammering. Hartington's market value was halved by close of trading to 425p. German and other Europeans suffered even bigger falls. Farben collapsed to EM 26 from an opening price of EM54 as news of its Hungarian subsidiary Nolcyz had supplied the Croatians with the banned Furdos toxic spray.

... chemical giant ...

sector saw the Union Bank of Helvetica slumping as Zurich's gnomes took their bags of gold elsewhere, fearful of the bank's profits being halved.

In Britain many of the companies named in the Susem telecast, belatedly issued statements claiming internal investigations were underway, any wrong-doing would be punished with "utmost severity." But from the falls in the companies' share prices, investors have taken little notice.

Kathy Sontang, Citi's head ...

investment trusts began the downward move, others followed, there after it became a rout. Corporate boardrooms every where, have suddenly been obliged to focus on the consequences of their activities. Even those indirectly involved, such as the Banks have suffered investor confidence as the security of many loans to customers is directly linked."

Elsewhere in the markets gloom are the orders of the day with downward pressures leaving it's mark on p...

77: GRANDE CARAJÁS

The Serbs and Croats who were marched the 100 kilometres to the Grande Carajás, while not facing the Pelada's perditional rigours, were obliged on arrival to labour as did they. And just as in the Pelada, there was initial resentment and resistance but the outcome was the same.

Also in groups of 80 they were set hewing terraces from the steep blasted mountain sides. On their fifth day, with the Gurkhas' arrival and organised into nines, teams in their tens of thousands were sent to the Itcalaiunas, the nearby Rio Tocantins' tributary, and drained its eight dams. The subsequent exposed silt was sacked, loaded onto trucks and carried to the Sao Luis-Carajás rail line and tipped into its house-sized wagons. At Carajás the silt was laid upon the terraces ready for seeding and planting.

When all of the recoverable silt had been taken, explosives from Carajás blew the dams away. By end of May, when all were gone, teams moved on to drain and demolish the dams on the Rio Araguaia and Tocantins, including the major one at Tucuruí. Three kilometres wide, 120 metres high, it held back a widening lake 150 kilometres long, and provided power to towns all the way to São Luis and Belém 300 kilometres to the north. Despite judicious draining during the days prior to silt extraction and demolition, its deluging water breached banks for many kilometres down river, flooding forest and farms alike. Lights dimmed all the way to Belém.

Daily, with work ended, more teams of Serbo-Croat speaking Gurkhas increasingly aided by English speaking interpreters from among the inmates themselves, and continuously updating 'Wanted lists', interviewed each group for suspects. By month end Korčula became overcrowded. The 'Wanted' were corralled instead, filling one of the Pelada's smaller pits.

However, not all the suspected were so incarcerated. Senior members of Croatia's HDZ, Serbia's SPRS regimes, their administrations, military and militias, Catholic and Orthodox hierarchies and other influential abetters, were offered alternative confinement gardening and road sweeping in the former management's residential compounds of VRD, the once mine owners. Though most of them accepted, knowledge of their 'cushy custody' spread, it fuelling resentment among the others. Aware of their underlings' antagonism towards them, these 'overlings', in return for the Gurkhas protection, willingly divulged yet more of crimes against Bosnians.

By mid-June further news spread down to the groups. Those adjudged innocent of involvement with their country's regimes could return home, provided it was to a Nonette community and that there were sufficient newcomers to take their places. News of the former speeded the formation of Nonettes throughout Croatia and now also Serbia. The latter had their women call for countries harbouring hunted fugitives to surrender them.

ILLION MEN IN HELL ON EARTH

SERB, CROATS' SERRA GULAG HELL SHOCKER

By JOANNA WILLIAMS

ILLIONS of enslaved Serbs nd Croats were shown on TV st night struggling to hurl ountainous piles of rock into e Serra Pelada, the world's iggest manmade mine.

Countless teams of Serbs, oked to huge carts piled high with rocks and rubble, were orced to haul then under the searing equatorial 100 degree plus heat of the Amazon jungle. Their every step of the way was overseen by savage whip wielding gang-masters..

Many thousands more captive Croats and Serbs could be seen their backs bent doubled with heavy sacks of mine waste, could be seen slithering down the pit's steep sides to its bottom, hundreds of feet below. Many thousands more were shown trampling the waste into the pit floor.

According the Aliens newscast, more than 6,000,000 Serb and Croat men are involved in either refilling the Serra Pelada or removing dams along the rivers of the Amazon.

The commentator said that the men would be forced to carry out what was termed 'Environmental Renewal' until those Serbs and Croats facing war crimes charges are brought to justice

'DYING LIKE FLIES CLAIM'

Yesterday, as experts pored over the shock Serra Pelada pictures, there were fears that many of the enslaved Serbs and Croats could fall victim to a range of tropical diseases, which, if not treated could prove fatal.

Dr. Peter Cooke (45) from the School of Hygiene and Tropical Medicine said: "Due to the speed of these men's departure from their home countries it is most unlikely that they would have been inoculated against such

---

News of suspected Serb gassing in Voyvodina cause nationwid

Budapest riot shakes governme

From Buc Fasse-Leigh in Budapest

MORE THAN A MILLION angry protestors demonstrated last night outside the Hungarian parliament after the discovery of supplies of the toxic chemical Fordószóbáért Beta in the northern Serbian province of Voyvodina, which has a large Hungarian minority.

At first the demonstrators were orderly. However, the protests turned into a riot as police reinforcements equipped with water cannons arrived.

There were reported to be hundreds of arrests and a large number of injuries. There was also extensive damage to buildings in the streets adjoining the Parliament buildings and numerous cars were set alight.

Susem investigators working in Belgrade claim to have uncovered documents detailing the sale of two tonnes of the toxic chemicals to Serbia by the Croatian Government. Half, so the Susem [...] said, had been sent [...] troubled province of K[...] the remainder to an [...] outside Novi Sa[...] Voyvodina[...]

Protestors alleged that the government was knowingly tolerating the manufacturing of poisonous chemicals on Hungarian soil that is to be used against their fellow Hungarians in neighbouring Voyvodina.

At an open air rally in Budapest's Jubilee Park, Socialist opposition leader, Janos Cegléd, said: "The Hungarian people have been betrayed. Hothy has sold out to foreign interests. Hothy has allowed Germans to make poison which are being used to massacre our brothers and sisters enslaved in Serbia. Who will they plan the next genocide of Hungarians; Romania, Slovinia?" Both countries also have Hungarian minorities.

The crowds then streamed across the nearby bridges over the Danube and, joined by others, converged on the Parliament. Security officials overwhelmed by the weight of numbers and anger of the protestors were forced back [...] turned into riot, with running battles between protestors and police.

In a television interview later, Hungary's prime minister, Miklós Hothy looking obviously shaken by the evening's events, said the organizers of the rally - the Socialists - had been intent on stirring up hatred towards foreigners, and as such had broken many laws.

Horthy said that they must be prosecuted without delay. The Hungarian premier stressed at length how important it was for foreign investment in Hungary especially from its fellow EU members.

When asked about the cause of the protestors' allegations, Hothy said: "We did not know," but added that a committee was being set up to investigate the claims. He also added the Nolcyz plant had provided employment to an otherwise depressed area of Hungary.

A spokesman for the German embassy, which, along with

Germany rocked Croatian revelatio

Government and top companies implicated

FROM MONIKA LANDOFF IN BERLIN

TOP government officials were desperately defending their political masters against accusations of involvement in Croatia., following last night's Susem telecast.

With Germany's Lander elections scheduled in ten days time, the Susem revelations could not have come at time for Ruhe's ruling CDU coalition. Already parallels are being drawn with the sudden collapse of US President Warren's popularity resulting [...] awry.

The socialist SDP, whose leader Walter Fontine, has long been critical of his country's Balkan policies made capital of the government's predicament.

Much attention is likely to be directed to the activities of German controlled businesses in Hungary and elsewhere in Eastern Europe. Many of the names given in the Susem telecast are, according to analysts, either German owned subsidiaries - or part-owned by German companies. The most notable being IG Farben owned chemical company Nolcyz.

According to [...] earthed by Su[...] gators, the defo[...] Fürdószó-báért [...] manufactured b[...] purposefully sp[...] Bosnian popula[...]

Use of Fü[...] banned throug[...] and elsewhere, [...] chlor-acne ef[...] claims are subs[...] lay Farben op[...] doubt crippli[...] damages and [...]

A string of [...] named by th[...] also been on t[...]

CDU Landar Election fortunes take a turn for the worse as voter sentiment sours

Sandwiched German - egg and tomatoed

By **Andy Williams in Frankfurt**

BAVARIA's Edmund Bietsor was forced to flee an election rally in Munich after protesters pelted him and other speakers with barrage of eggs and tomatoes.

Herr Bietsor, hit several times, was clearly shaken by the event and within minutes of the uproar police broke up the rally.

Over 50 cases of injuries were reported, but this was an underestimate, say protesters.

Until yesterday, Herr Bietsor, was looking at certain victory in the CDU sister party, the CSU.

Now they are tarred with being accomplices to their Government's Balkan polices.

In a replay of US President Warren's precipitous fall from grace, Chancellor Ruhe is likely to receive a massive thumbs down from voters.

The *Sud-Deutsch Zeitang* and other regional papers have filled many of their pages with Chancellor Ruhe's close links with the Croatians, including details of his luxurious holiday home on the Dalmatian island of Krk.

Bietsor is caught from neither disowning his Chancellor, and long time favourite of both the political

78: AILEEN

Until last week I had not known just how pathetic men can be. At first it was all banging on the door and him hollering through the letterbox. I put that down to sour grapes. Next-door came out telling him to stop making such a racket and go away. He was back a couple of hours later shouting and banging again. Because his voice was slurred I put it down to drink. And he was back the Saturday morning calling out he was sorry. Next-door told him to go away again or they would call the Police.

Margaret said she thought she had seen him when she picked Becky and hers up from the Infants. I had a worry about that. Then Tuesday he walks in the Salutation after I had just come in. He was sober but that is all that could be said. He mumbled that he was sorry for what he had done. I told him to go away but he would not.

I told him he would be hearing from the solicitor and to keep away from me and the kids but he still would not leave. There were people looking. Till then I'd told no one in the Sallie except Bridie, Des's wife, what had happened. Before I knew it, she was by me telling him to leave me alone and buzz off. With that he started crying and begging. I was shaking but there was nothing I could do than to stand there. Bridie told him to pull himself together and leave the pub. But he still would not and sobbed all the more. She said she would not tell him again. Some boys from the Arsenal Sports came over, so did Des. Though Ryan was still carrying on, he took hold of an ashtray. For a moment I thought he was going to chuck it, so did the others but he put it down and went out of the door slamming it behind him.

I was feeling terrible but Bridie had me upstairs and her arms round me as though she was m'mam. I wanted to cry but knew I'd best not. She said did I want to go home but I knew I couldn't, I needed the money. I half sobbed that to her. She gave a smile and a hug and said "Men!"

She said the same again and again when Rainbow came on the TV and named the Croats and Serbs who were wanted. But her tone changed the more Rainbow read out what they had done.

At closing time Bridie asked again if I would be okay. I said I would but she insisted Des walk me home. I'm glad he did. We had no sooner turned into the flats than there was a policeman stood at my door saying Ryan was threatening to throw himself off the Archway Bridge. It was past midnight, I was tired, the last thing I needed was him making a spectacle of himself. I nearly said "Let him jump," but thought of his pay packet and how I needed it. But when the policeman drove Des and me up to Archway they'd already talked him down and carted him off.

Pope accused of Croatian cover-up

largaret O'Connell in Rome

OPE PIOUS XIII has been ccused by the Susem lecaster of having direct nowledge of Vatican support or Croatian government iction against the Bosnian Muslims.

Documents uncovered by Susem investigators show he was personally involved in funnelling finance from Papal funds into Croatia through its Catholic ministry.

Other documents show that many Catholic priests were actively encouraging Croat militias to ethnically cleanse large areas of Bosnia of Muslims.

According to Susem claims, both Catholic and Orthodox Churches were engaged in financing the arms purchases for Croatian and Serb regimes.

The Vatican has so far declined to comment on the allegations. But with Susem promising yet more revelations to come, it is inconceivable the Vatican can maintain its silence to the allegations for long.

However, Susem claims of Papal connivance in Croatian affairs are likely to rekindle past accusations of the Vatican's support for Croatian nationalists.

Following the end of the Second World War many Croatian Catholic priests accused of war crimes by the Tito regime were give refuge in the Vatican.

Although the then Yugoslav government provided convincing evidence of their involvement in abetting the ware-time Croatian fascist regime of Anton Pavlic's ... in the slaughter

Charities diverted Bosnian Aid to Serb, Croat militas – Susem claim

CHARITY DENIES WRONGDOING

By Bridget Riley

HELP CHILDREN, the international children's charity, was accused by Susem investigators yesterday, of diverting supplies of aid meant for Bosnian children into the hands of Serb and Croat officials. The charity has, strongly defended its actions.

At first, when Help Children were presented with the Susem revelations, the charity denied the allegations.

However, Field Director Ian Goody (47) later admitted that some aid shipments sent to Bosnia had been regularly diverted to both Serbian and Croatian government officials. Goody was unable to confirm or deny that it more than half of aid shipments, as stated in the Susem telecast, were handed over to the Croats and Serbs.

Goody said: "Help Children was forced to cooperate with the former pariah regimes. He said: "In order to maintain the Charity's top-level contact with the leaders it was essential to maintain good working relations."

Asked why the Charity had not protested publicly at such practices, Mr Goody said: "It has always been Charity policy not to host government relations into the public domain."

Mr Goody would not comment on Susem claims that Help Children officials were frequent quests at Zagreb's $500 a night Hostel Esplanade and patronised its casino.

Asked how collectors for Help Children across the UK would react to the news of the Charity's diverting supplies to the Serb and Croat thugs, Mr Goody said: "As the Director of Field Operations, I do not handle such day to day matters."

No other member of the Charity was available for comment.

Long-time Help Children collector Edith Huxley of Nuneaton, said: "Quite frankly, I am disgusted. I have worked for Help Children for more than 20 years.

"During all of this time I must have collected more than £50,000 for them. But now how can I show my face in all the pubs and shops I used to regularly visit to collect," she wept.

"Everything I have I'd willed to them and I even paid out of my pension to them.

"I'll never collect for them again, and I am going to revoke them out

Business News

COMPANIES SHA BY BOSNIA PROT

Plummeting share prices force bosses into and investor worries could hurt many top c

By Maxwell Davies

MANY OF BRITAIN'S top companies, wilting under a barrage of protest were forced on the defensive against accusations of their involvement in Bosnia.

Critics against the companies involved ranged from the influential Church Commissioners to lone protesters outside company head offices.

Lord Roscommon, chairman of the Church Commissioners, said: "We have received messages of concern from many within the Church hierarchy over any possible association with those involved with underhand activities in Bosnia. Consequently we have concluded it prudent to promptly divest the Commission's investments in those thought to have been involved."

One casualty of disinvestment is the banking group Clayings, whose shares plummeted 127p to 905p

responsible for the affairs of its customers."

The statement, said Clayings, was conducting a review of its East European operations to ensure it had not been involved in covert dealings.

However, many City insiders viewed Buxstead's statement with scepticism. One bank analyst, who did not wish to be named, said: "Clayings was heavily involved with the Serbian privatizations during the late 1990s.

"It is inconceivable they would not have retained linked with the companies they advised."

Scallop directors also issued a statement denying involvement. After a day which had seen its share price fall from 957p to 782p, the oil giant said it had sold its interest in Istra Oil and Gas three years ago. "That means we cannot be held responsible for its actions," said a spokesman.

But as many industry

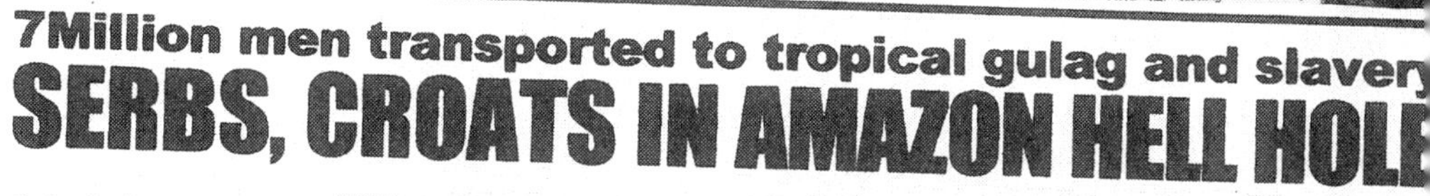

7Million men transported to tropical gulag and slavery

SERBS, CROATS IN AMAZON HELL HOLE

By Carolyn Marchant
Human Rights Correspondent

THE world's biggest manmade pit, the Serra Pelada in Amazon, was filled with countless teeming hordes of enslaved Serbs and Croats, a shock Susem TV broadcast revealed last night.

Men were shown yoked in teams, and being whipped by savage gangmasters, as they were forced to drag massive sledges of soil and rocks to the pit's edge.

More men were forced to carry sacks of soil down the steep sides of the pit to the bottom hundreds of feet below.

Thousands more, appearing as small as ants, could be seen on the pit floor trampling the soil and rocks underfoot.

The commentary accompanying the television pictures said that the Serra Pelada was to be refilled.

It added that when the pit was filled, there were others waiting.

The commentator said the Serbs and Croats had ample opportunity and warning to enlist for reconstruction work in Bosnia but had failed to do so, now they

I have failed my orals. Lucia, the teaching one, said I had too much "dee" and "der" in my "th"s. Everything else is okay but it's like matriculation, failing in one subject means re-sitting them all. Before, and at my age, it would have been something I'd have shrugged off, done nothing about. But now I have not the chance. The other eight in my group insist on egging and coaching me to passable acceptance. And it's not out of altruism either, they don't move on to visuals until we have all passed. I wouldn't really mind but a month ago none of them could speak any English, let alone enunciate it to passable perfection, and what is even more galling, apart from it being my own mother tongue, is that I'm old enough to be most of their fathers.

Thankfully for me, my teaching screen is not my only source of enlightenment. Menpemelo, and increasingly Terbal, continue acquainting me with their facts of life as well. And as I rested from practising putting more "that's" and "there's" into my "dats" and "deres", I reflected on what I have so far deduced. According to them, everything is composed of waves. The objects Earthly scientists term sub-atomic particles, electrons, photons and so on, are no more than different points, parts of those waves. Terbal, more blunt than Menpemelo, summed up the endeavours of our particle physicists with "All vrong they are haffing it." According to him all the things particle physicists say they are seeing, they aren't actually seeing anything. He says they may well be recording signs of something but that is all.

I have tried to envisage how I am composed of Tertiary waves activated by a flowing sea of Secondary waves. But Terbal says it's not quite like that. According to him the Tertiary ones are in differing directions to one another and the Secondary waves can come from different directions as well. I did say to him it didn't much smack of the harmony Menpemelo mentioned. But he said Secondary waves do move in a circular accord around the galaxy but there is local turbulence too, such as on Earth and when they flow through me.

When Terbal mentioned this I thought it an apt occasion to ask what causes Secondary waves to evolve from Primary ones. But to confuse me the more he said there were two types of them. Ones which are in galaxies and others which the galaxies are in. Though these, he said, sometimes come inside galaxies as well. He also said the Susem understood the first Secondary waves go round and round in the undulating loop of the Primary ones. However, in doing so some mutated to going round in smaller circles. These, he says are what formed galaxies.

But when I said how could Primary waves go round and round when the universe was expanding he became so agitated he began flailing his fronds. "Expansion dere ist nein! Dey haff dis all vrong as vell." In his agitation he became rhetorical too. He charged how could there be the Anthropic Constant if there is a continual expansion going on? "Nein constants nein galaxies, ya?"

'I was only obeying orders' poison factory boss claims

Jonathan Swift
in Budapest

MANFRIED WERNER, the manager of German chemical giant Farben's troubled Hungarian subsidiary caused uproar today, when he claimed "I was only obeying orders" from his masters at Farben HQ in Frankfurt. If confirmed, Werner's words will cause deep embarrassment to Farben and to its boss Max Ammann.

Farben's Hungarian subsidiary Nolcyz has admitted to making the banned toxic chemical, Fürdószóbáért Beta, known in western Europe as Furdo B.

The manager Werner, however, claimed that the ingredients, isotopes of hydrogen, carbon, nitrogen and cyanogen were delivered to Nolcyz from Farben's plants in Poland and Saxony. "We just mixed to Frankfurt's instruct-ions," Werner claimed.

When questioned over allegations Nolcyzed had broken even Hungary's lax environment laws as well as contravening the EU-wide ban on trade with Croatia and Serbia, Werner said: "We were only acting on orders from Frankfurt." He further claimed Nolcyz had no knowledge of what the Croatians were using Furdo B for.

"We were instructed by Frankfurt that all requests [for Furdo B] from Pavelic's (former Croatian Interior Minister) office were to be delivered to Barcs (on the Croatian-Hungarian border) immediately. We did not even handle the paper-work," he said.

Werner admitted his revelations contradicted statements made by Farben in Frankfurt. But after the Nolcyz plant's workforce committee had threatened to expose details of its secret activities, he said he had no choice but to reveal details.

The exposure of Nolcyz's undercover activities has caused a storm of protest in business circles in Hungary.

Edvard Pec, a director of Magyar Munitions and head of Budapest's MCB "For a long time now we have been trying to raise the ethical standing of Hungarian business. It has not been easy for us, even now we are still thought to be willing to sell our own grandmothers. Now this [Nolcyz] scandal has befallen us. It has set back our work by many years. And Hungary will continue to be known as a country of dubious standards."

Hungary's Socialis Coalition opposition part has been quick to mak capital of the Nolcy scandal to embarrass th ruling rightwing PNM.

Its leader, Janos Cegle said: "For years Hothy [Hungary's premier government has turned blind eye to the trade wit Croatia by foreign owne companies based her Whatever regulations the want to avoid, thes companies come and mak it in Hungary.

During the forthcomin election campaign thi and other scandals ar going on are going t receive much attention. will be the most talke

'Hand over your Serbs and Croats - demand Susem

BY JOY COMBE

SERB and Croat men hiding aboard must be given up, said the Susem last night.

Susem telecaster Rainbow Louis said there is evidence that many fugitive Serbs and Croats committed atrocities in Bosnia. She warned that countries shielding the fugitives will face legal action if the demands are not met.

However, the Susem demands were given a mixed response.

Amnesty International's Secretary General, Michael Howard, said: "We have a long tradition in Britain of giving refuge to those fleeing from injustices abroad, trial should they return to their home countries. We will be pressing the government to make clear it stands by these fundamentals of a free and democratic society. We hope that they will be able to make this known to the Susem."

At the Serbian Information Centre, a statement posted on its

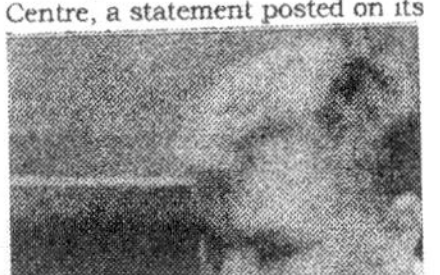

As Westminster Bank rushes to cleanse its stab has it shut its doors after the bad news has bol

Bank drops Hurd and Jone

Pauline Weston
Ethics reporter

WESTMINSTER Bank has abruptly ousted Sir Neville Hurd and Douglas Jones in a desperate attempt to rid itself of its Serbian fiasco.

In a statement issued yesterday, Westminster said: "The Bank has for some time been conducting a thorough review of its comercial relationships with some Eastern European organisations.

"In the light of present circumstances, and as a result of matters recently brought to the Bank's notice, it has decided to cease much of its activities in this region. Therefore the Bank considers it sensible practice to stand down the relevant sections of its advisory team."

Dumping Hurd and Jones, however, is unlikely to free Westminster from the Serbian swamp it has been trapped in. As more details of their dealings with the Serbs are revealed daily, Westminster is expected to pay a heavy penalty for its Balkan foray.

Its plummeting share price and faced with the prospect of surrendering half its last year's £2 billion profits is bad enough. However, its client base is haemorrhaging badly.

At the time of Hurd's appointment, Westminster heralded the recruitment of the former minister as a shrewd move. Although Jones' appointment was made with less fanfare, he was viewed as an astute ex-Foreign Office negotiator. They must now rue

Hulme, backed b Bank's CEO H Jackson, to ap his fellow members.

Yesterday's re tions of docun from the Se Central Bank's o ing their netw of launderers be causing some faces not just Westminster bu many other m national banks.

It is more likely that all major banks will accordingly by ad ing their wr doing to their sh

ENSLAVED SERBS, CROAT FORCED TO SMASH DAM

From Howard Lucan
In Rio de Janeiro

DRAMATIC PICTURES of the fate of hundreds of thousands of interned Serbs and Croats who are being forced to demolish countless Amazon dams were shown worldwide to TV audience last night.

The telecast showed multitudes of mud-stained men being made to dredge silt from drained dams.

Later, pictures showed the dams blasted away. In further 'before and after' pictures the Susem telecast showed one huge dam obviously hundreds of metres high and several kilometres long brimming with water, then of it empty and scores of men dragging the silt from where the water had been.

The telecast showed columns of men carrying sack after sack of the silt and loading them on to massive, house-sized railway trucks.

Rainbow Louis said that the silt will be used to aid in the re-forestation of the areas destroyed by the building of the dams in the first place. She also said that there more than a further twenty dams across the region presently under Susem control

As the extent of big companies involvement with the former Croat and Serb regimes grow

Riots rock Europe

From Monika Landoff
In Berlin

COMPANIES AND authorities in many European countries have been shaken by the extent of public condemnation against them, with Germany and Hungary witnessing some of the biggest outbursts of public protest.

At the Frankfurt headquarters of the chemical giant IG Farben, demonstrators broke though the company's security barriers and smashed windows before they were driven off by Police water cannons.

Farben's managing director, Max Ammann, who was caught up in the protest said: "These demonstrators know nothing. They want only to destroy the property of others. They do not care if they ruin German industry by voicing these terrible things about us."

When questioned over allegations that Farben had supplied banned toxic government to spray on Bosnians, they stormed away from reporters, shouting "Lügen, lügen (lies, lies), dat ist alle lügen."

Later Farben issued a statement saying Amman was unaware the company is conducting an urgent review of all its operations.

In Berlin, the headquarters of Mettalaglenshaft faced similar acts of protests. The glass walls of their new offices - designed by Sir Roger Richards - were daubed with red paint and slogans accusing them of genocide. There were a series of pitched battle between police and demonstrateors before order was restored.

In the Ruhr town of Dortmund, the offices of Krupp Defence Industries, also named in supplying arms to the Croatians was also under fire from protestors. Police attempted throughout the siege to restore order but with confidence between them

he said. Then before I had time to respond, "Stars und galaxies how long haff dey been? A long time, ya?" He then said Primary waves undulate round and round, back and forth, and up and down as well. Adding that from where we are in the Universe, everything carried by Primary waves, which of course is everything, may well appear to be expanding but in reality it is not. Still in an agitated mode he said "All dis Big Banging dey are haffing, it ist vrong also. How can dey say dey know ven no one vas dere? Dey are saying der vas no light vor a long time after dis Banging." He then appeared to calm down and, bending one of his fronds inwards alike to us putting our hand on hip, said "You know Dommy, der trouble mit your comrades ist dey haff not realised vafes are der rule."

What he has said has begun to make some sense, as a theory that is, but then I thought, where is the proof? Also what of the "Time Tunnel" the Susem first talked about, and Paceillo saying about reading from the wave patterns, even when there is nothing there, and what about the "auras" Menpemelo keeps mentioning? I still have confusion in my mind.

I was mulling over these when Rainbow passed by without saying "Hello," her head bowed with the obliviousness of deep thought. She had a piece of paper clenched in her hand, but after she had taken a snatched glance at it and I had called "Hi," she mentioned her failings in mental multiplication.

After agreeing to swop abilities, it was me repeating her, "Thrust the tongue's tip through the parted teeth."

And her to my "Round to the nearest whole numbers, then add or subtract the differences of the originals."

Still tongue thrusting, I walked with her to the cavern but we had not gone far before she was saying aloud to herself "Three quarters of a million at three per cent per annum...divided by 365...multiplied by eight days is..."

I had just cottoned to what she was calculating but before I had chance to explain she turned and said "..$493.16," then, "come on, hand it over."

I tried telling her that there would bound to have been bank charges and other things deducted from the daily interest rate, that I had already incurred costs, and if I hadn't a bank account she would never have been able to..

"Give it."

In my experience I have always found women forever over-focusing on detail, and as a result so often fail to see the broad sweep of an occasion. Here we were in the veritable centre of the most momentous turn of world events there has been and Rainbow was going on about a few hundred lousy dollars.

"Give."

She then gave that 'I'm brushing your back with a knife' look, so I swiftly said "Oh, alright then."

And just as swiftly she turned us around, strode me back to the Pousada, stood over me as I wrote out the cheque, checked the words and figures, gave a curt "Thank you," walked to the door, turned and adding as she left, "By the

Luxembourgers take to the streets

JULIA HAMPTON IN BRUSSELS

IN AN UNPREDEDENTED DISPLAY OF outrage, many Luxembourgers attacked their "Brass Nameplate Industry". The brass nameplate of the hundreds of thousands of overseas companies or "Etrangere" registered in Luxembourg were defaced.

Unused to public protest of any kind, Luxembourg's tiny police force was unable to contain such an outburst of popular out-rage. It took several hours before police from neighbouring Belgium restored order.

Madame de Redange commented: "For many years we have welcomed these [nameplate] companies as a source of income and employment for our solicitors and accountants but now we have been awakened to the crimes that lay behind many of them. We are enraged."

But in Brussels - which had its own share of disruptive protestors (see *EU Stormed, page 7*) - such views were met with cynical disbelief.

Accountant Wim Langendonck, of Tough Risk, said: "When Luxembourgers worry about morality, it will be the day Hell freezes over. All they are worried over is that they may lose out if the Susem do take action against them for allowing Etrangere to operate in the

"We must defend the innocent" – says MP

BY JOY COMBE

"CROATS and Serbs should be granted political asylum," said Cheltenham MP Sir Hugh Russet Brown yesterday

Sir Hugh who has just returned from the PIG-CIC conference in Mauritius, was commenting on Susem demands that both expatriate communities are sent to Bosnia for questioning.

"Asylum is the least we can do to give protection to these chaps. On no account should they be forcibly repatriated, especially the Serb and Croat embassy staff."

Sir Hugh, who was soon to join an all-party fact finding mission of Caribbean's' sugar production, said it was important that the government's

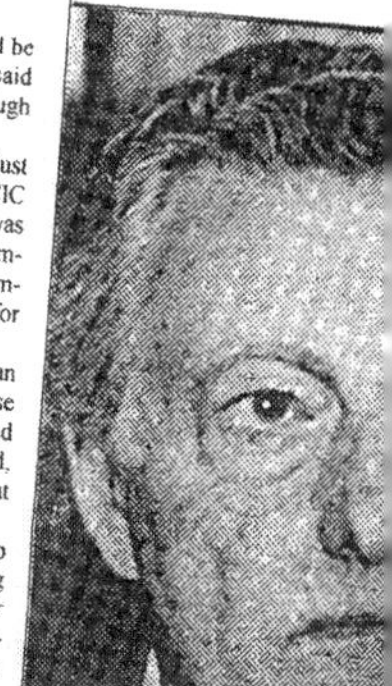

Jungle dams busted

Thousands flee as walls of water flood cit

BY POLLY PORTILLO
SOUTH AMERICAN CORRESPONDENT

ALL Amazonian dams are to go said Susem telecaster Rainbow Louis yesterday Showing dramatic images of destroyed Amazon dams, she said they were a "source of pollution, so they must be eradicated."

Viewers also saw teams of men scooping up from behind the dams accumulated silt, which would be used to fertilize the deforested areas of jungle.

The waters from the dams are reported to have caused extensive flooding to the towns downstream of them. Electrical power generated by the dams has also reported to have been diminished. The city of Belem has been without clea water for now for almost a week and

Worldwide clamour for Susem energy units

It seems we just can't get enough of Susem soufins

By Stephen Soloman

THOSE among us fortunate enough to possess Susem soufin energy units, enjoy the luxury of free electricity to power our homes and cars. The majority of us, however, still have to pay for our fuel.

Though there is envy by the 'have nots' towards the 'haves', such is the demand for these Alien marvels that prices rise by the day. Yesterday it was reported soufins were selling in California for more than $1,000.

Newspapers and the Internet are filled with an ever growing number of advertisements offering to buy the soufins. But it appears those who have soufins are reluctant to part with them.

Indeed, so great is the clamour for soufins that

professionals alike, hav seen them as a source quick cash. Police forc across Britain repo that thousands motorists have had th bonnets of their car forced open as thieve search for soufins.

Householders hav not been left unscathe either. Yesterday a Norwich couple chased a posse of schoolchildren who had broken into their home and stolen a soufin. Mrs Edwina Oaks

Government to defend rights of innocent Serbs and Croats to asylum

Serbs and Croats are safe with us - says PM

By **Sonia Stone**

BRITAIN has rebuffed Susem demands for the expulsion of Serbs and Croat. The Prime Minister said: "Anyone in Britain, no matter who he or she may be, is entitled to a fair trial in Britain.

"If it can be established there are grounds for charging an individual with committing a criminal offence, then let that evidence be presented to a British Court. Outsiders, no matter who they are, can always be assured of a fair trial in a British Court of Law."

Although the PM's words met with a warm reception in the Commons, members of Britain's Serb and Croat communities were less than heartened.

At the Serb Community Centre in Ladbroke Grove, a spokesperson commented: "We are all very worried over what will become of us. If we are transported to Bosnia we know what fate will befall us at the hands of these unearthly godless infidels, our wives and sisters will be raped, our babies bayoneted, our fathers and mothers thrown alive into cauldrons of boiling oil, and we, like our enslaved brothers will be worked to death in a tropical gulag. We also believe we would not receive a fair trial."

The Croat Centre in Clapham said they were watching the situation and

way, as my month's wages are overdue I will debit your account with a credit into mine." Rainbow can be so merciless when she chooses.

That I could write a cheque for the money is yet another of the evolvements sweeping the place. One of the first arrivals from Sobral was Jorge from the Park. He came with Roberto's parents. While Roberto's mum fussed with Elana over the detail of Roberto's behaviour, eating and underwear, his dad, so it transpired, because he worked in one, had the vision to propose to Elana the forming of a bank. However, that wasn't the only thing he and the others from Sobral suggested forming before they departed.

It began with produce. The gardens in Tabajara and elsewhere are growing so much that there are now huge surpluses. Prices locally have fallen. But nonetheless the quality is superior to anything available elsewhere, or so the two merchants from Sobral who also came, said. And yet another key ingredient for them is that the crops are free of any artificial additives. Realising the opportunity arising, they made an offer for wider distribution of the crops.

While a decision wasn't made then, by nightfall a deeper detailed one was. And it went further than the distribution of produce. The result of which has me yet again thinking Paceillo is up to something. Although the Susem aren't from this world, Paceillo already knows something of Earthly communities, their commerce and I'm sure much more besides. She has probably garnered much of this from the dozens of Internet connections Terbal now has running non-stop, but I also have the suspicion she has been listening to Rainbow and the ladies of Tabajara.

After the people from Sobral had left, I saw the ten village representatives, couriered by Rainbow, going to the cavern. They emerged two hours later as though a band of latter-day Moses down from the Mount. But when, after thirty minutes they had gathered the villagers together, their commandments were presented as "proposals." However, knowing the mandatory nature of Paceillo's 'proposals' I didn't see there would be any difference of definition.

Listening to Elana addressing the assembled, I also detected there had been some softening up of the representatives as well. And further, they had been, Elana especially, coached in how to present the 'proposals', for she said everything in the form of questions. Ones to which the villagers' replies would always be "Yes."

Were they all happy, Elana began, running the village the way they were and with everyone having a say? Did the fact more and more communities wanting to be as they, along with those who already were, give them confidence they had been wise in deciding as they had? Did they think it sensible all such communities should also gather together to manage matters which were of concern to them all? Did they think it sensible for each community to elect someone to represent them in inter-community meetings? Did they agree this person should have to seek re-election monthly, so ensuring they did what they were mandated to do and not take their responsibility for granted or

Amazing health from Susem do

Aliens bring miracle cures to hundreds: 'Inc

rom Matthew Gray
Medical
Correspondent

MANY PEOPLE suffering from fatal illnesses have been cured by the Susem.

A group of people living with the Susem last night told TV viewers they had been cured of illnesses ranging from malaria to diabetes.

One young woman, said she had been a mentally deranged cripple, but the Susem had healed her. This claim was roundly verified by people seen with her.

The villagers also showed small, barely visible bumps on the sides of their necks, which they said, protected them from all forms of infection. The women among the villagers said all their children had also been cured of a range of childhood ailments. Others said that other people had been cured and healed. Mention was made of the crippled walking and many more cured of one of the most, so the villagers said, dreaded diseases in the area called "Chagas".

The claims have impressed a number of health experts.

Dr Joanna Smithers, of the School of Tropical Medicine, said: "Chagas Disease had remained, until now that is, one of the world's major incurable diseases. To the many millions of sufferers it is known as "The Curse of the Living Death", taking many years to kill its victims. Charles Darwin was one of its victims, and condemned him to 17 years of slow and painful death.

"The reasons why so little research has been conducted on Chagas Disease, even in South America where it is found, has more to do with the disease being confined to those in the poor living conditions of adobe - mud huts - dwellings. If the claims prove to be true then it could mean that scienti-

'Susem: threat to w freedom' claims US Se

By Steven Heven
In Washington

"LITTLE BY LITTLE THE American people and those of the rest of mankind are having their freedoms stolen. I am voicing the fears of many US senior officials over the Susem's presence."

Senator Dich said he thought the Susem's claim they were seeking their lost craft was a sham. "The US and other experts have been able to prove that no unidentifiable extra-terrestrial object had landed on Earth during the recent past.

"It was vital that the US and other countries sh... be on ...

Susem had rid the world of nuclear weapons. "But the world's nations have been left more defenceless than before the Aliens' arrival," he said.

President Warren, still reeling from the "Tonic-water" fiasco, has so far, declined to make public comment on the Senators' stance. Because of the President's low standing, not just in the polls but among political heavy-weights in Washington, there is an increasing air of despondency. Nancy Williams of ...

France has 'unfai energy advantage CBI claims

By Peter Woods

FRANCE'S liberal supply of Susem energy units will undermine other counties' export competitiveness, claims CBI head, Sir Neil Trippler.

Sir Neil said yesterday: "Britain and other trading nations are already facing a distinct disadvantage over energy costs to their industries vis-a-vis the French.

"Whereas the French are currently paying nothing for their energy inputs," Sir Neil said,"we in Britain are. Therefore it is vital we are able to complete with them on a level playing field.

"To this end the CBI shall be pressing for government action in either petitioning Brussels for a levy on all French high energy products coming into the country, or alternatively calling on the government for the supply of energy for industry to attract a 100 percent subsidy.

"Of course another choice would be a call to the Susem to supply more of their energy units so as to bring us up to French levels," he said.

Other industry leaders back Sir Neil's demands. Sir Gerry Shaw, head of Sabrerattle, Britain leading war-game toy distributors, said: "It's not fair, the French are always getting away with blue murder. We should be able to play by the same rules as they do.

Shocked sheikhs face cash crisis

Oil slump could have knock-on effects

By Christine Shields

AS OIL prices slumped to below $10 a barrel for the first time in living memory, world oil producers met in an historic conference in Vienna in an attempt to agree production cuts.

Unlike Western producers, Gulf states cannot cushion the blow of falling prices with downstream operations such as plastics and fertilizers. This has led to Haaq called for an immediate production cut of 60% by all producers. It is the only way to stabilize the slide in prices, he said.

However, if such a cut was made, most oil producers would soon run out of ready cash to fuel their oil revenue dependent economies.

Shiekh ob Aharbi, ruler of the tiny Gulf state of Hutar, is caught in such a bind. Before the present downturn in prices, Hutar produced a million barrels a day. Now it is less than half of that.

He said: "How can I pay the interest on the loans which I have been given by British banks to pay for the £5bn of arms I have bought from British defence manufacturers? How can I pay the salaries of the British armed forces on secondment to operate all these planes, ships, missile batteries I have brought?

"My people are revolting against the cuts I have had to implement. Already two members of my government have had to flee the country for plotting against me.

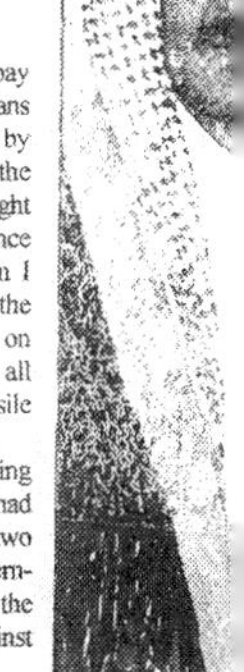

Overseas Serbs and Croats under threat

Susem telecast calls for Serbs and Croats be returned as to stand trial. Serb and Croat overseas organizations handover also demanded

Express Reporters

SUSEM telecaster Rainbow Louis has demanded all male Serbs and Croats be sent back by the countries sheltering them and to stand trial for crimes they might have committed in Bosnia.

"If they are able to establish their innocence they have nothing to fear," Louis said in a TV broadcast last night.

Overseas Serbs and Croats were given two weeks to return.

"Should they fail to do so they will be judged as being guilty of some crime in Bosnia and appropriate action would be taken to bring them to justice," added Louis.

She also demanded expatria Serb and Croat organizations sent to Serbia and Croatia tofa trial. Quoting from documen unearthed by Susem investigato in both countries, she said: "Su overseas organisations have cha nelled funds to both the paris regimes and must answer for the actions. These organisations al stand accused of shielding wante Serbs and Croats."

Singling out Croat expatia organisations in Australia, Arge tina and the US as being the ma culprits, the Susem telecaster re out a list of those wanted for crime against humanity and other human

ly me nd the een . If uss- that rgy oned ities' oved. ewart issile emb-

mis-use it? By then it was becoming a trifle tedious and predictable. But before there had been time for interest to wane, Elana changed tack.

"Do you want higher prices for your crops?" she said. After the loud approving roar, Elana continued outlining prospects of their produce's wider distribution, cooperatives, their own bank, welfare programmes and all number of other proposals. She had the villagers in unison of agreement as she continued outlining one piece of proposed paradise after another. But that is all they are of course, proposals. The villagers and others might possibly prosper while the Susem are present, but the moment they depart all these grand schemes are bound to collapse, just as others at other times always have.

However, as I listened not just to Elana but the enthusiasm of the villagers as well, I had not the heart to mention there is no such thing as a free lunch. That there must be a catch, if for no other reason than there always is one. But on Elana presented, complete with detail, proposal after proposal. The villagers had questions but generally all agreed with everything she said.

Helping the villagers to agreement were descriptions other representatives (they had been taken on a tour) gave of the Susem accommodation they had carved out from the cliff face below. Elana held out the prospect to the villagers of them all residing in such a grand place once they had achieved their next level of progress, not just in cerebral theory but, now it was on the syllabus, practical civics too. Filled no doubt, with dreams of dwelling in Soap-style palaces and an election a week away, everyone went home elated.

Needless to say Elana looks like being elected. But she didn't have to wait for the results. By the end of the next day she and the other representatives had contacted not only the communities already formed but those in the process. The day after there was a grand gathering here in Tabajara and it lasted well into evening. All told there must have been 200 sat round tables outside the Pousada discussing and debating. All agreed to everything. All went away fuelled with the same heady enthusiasm the villagers had. Before they had left agreements were signed covering marketing, financing, joint stock control, profit sharing and on and on.

While I will concede Elana and the others' organising is proceeding apace I still can't see anything which can possibly be sustained. All the things they set up are bound to fall into the hands of a few, who will then proceed to manipulate situations arising for their own ends. And just as it always has been, their fine schemes will collapse into corruption and despotism. Both of which in Brazil, of course, have been a long and engrained tradition.

And that is the main reason why I was so hesitant to hand over to this new bank the payment made by Caught TV for the television rights to the trials in Bosnia as well as the accrued $493.16 of interest. At the time I was a little upset, not only by Rainbow's insistence, but that she had said it was just in case anything happened to me and therefore she felt the money would be safer with them. Rainbow can be so cynical and untrusting when she wants.

Soufins cause crime surge

By **Joanna Redwood**
Criminal Correspondent

THE Metropolitan Police reported that 2,037 Susem energy units have been stolen in the past seven days, including from 1,748 from motor vehicles.

Chief Commissioner, Marion Link-later said: "Thieves are finding it all too easy to steal from motor vehicles. It is vital that members of the ... guard theft.

"We are advising all motorists using soufins not to leave them in their vehicles unattended," said the Commissioner.

London is not the only city suffering from soufin stealers. In Liverpool, thefts are reported to be of epidemic proportions.

A police spokes-man in Kirkby said: "There are so many cases of soufins being stolen that we are having to divert resources from other policing duties to combat this new crime wave. We are ... people to keep them under cover and do not tell anyone you have one."

But Britain's soufin crime surge pales compared to the United States. Armed gangs have been responsible for a spate of hold-ups of motorists. Both New York and Los Angeles reports dozens of shoot-ings with two fatalities.

A spokesman for NY... said: "Its primarily ... anised Latino gan... jacking to order. ... shipped to C... and Panamani... cartels for resa..."

Shiekhs shake summit

West confronted with OPEC in reverse

By Julian Gray
in Frankfurt

WESTERN BANKERS were caught off balance last night when members of the OPEC cartel issued the ultimatum: "Buy our oil or we default on our loans."

Western and other non-OPEC producers immediately threatened to take OPEC to the World Trade Organisation (WTO). Walter Keinz, Standard's CEO speaking on behalf of the fabled "Seven Sisters" oil giants said: "We will not tolerate this gun being held to our heads.

"All the majors have invested heavily over the recent time period in more efficient extraction technology. We have a fiscal duty of care to our stock and bond holders. Therefore we will continue to pump from our own field concessions," he said.

International financial institutions have not yet responded publicly to the OPEC threat. But unofficial sources say many will have little alternative than to go along with the oil producer's demands.

One senior banker said "The banks having lent the oil producers so much are unlikely to be able to ignore them.

"All financial institutions depends on cash flows, just like the rest of us. If there is more than a small percentage of their loans turning into non-performing ones their capital base will shrink.

"Governments are also heavily involved. The loans have been used to buy imports from the West. One third of world arms exports are to the Mid-East. If they are stopped factories will close and tens of thousands will be laid off. With elections due in Germany and elsewhere I do not see politicians standing back and just letting ...

Layoffs loom for defence workers

By Frank Adam
In Los Angeles

DEFENCE manufacturer Boeing Lockheed announced yesterday, the closure of eight more plants, five in the US, two in the UK and one in Germany. This comes on top of the seven already scheduled for closure.

Lockheed is the latest in a long line of US defence manufacturers announcing plant closures.

Last week Hughes say that upward of 150,000 workers in the US would be facing layoffs by year end.

Last week Scu-man Corporation's CEO Paul Nisbet was reported as saying Scuman's PX-45 Advanced Tank joint venture with Germany's Benz was "under review". This was thought be a curtailment of the project in its pre-sent form. The PX-...

Susem's charming children amaze viewers

By **Gloria Hall**
Education Editor

CHILDREN speaking in fluent English told TV viewers last night about their life with the Aliens in their midsts.

Apparently unprompted, the children told the interviewer how they spent hours each day studying from their personal teaching screens given to them by the Susem. They also spoke of their new Susem "pets" which they called "Hen-gas" who went with them everywhere they went.

In the five minutes telecast, the children spoke beyond their young years saying how a month ago none of them could speak or barely write English.

The children also to... how they studied ... groups, how they eac... helped one another wit... their lessons. All the chi... dren appeared to be prim... ary school age, treated viewers to a mental arithmetic contest following by a spelling bee.

If the children's convincing claims are to be believed they have advanced faster than once thought

MP in covert Serb arms deal cover-up scandal

Jonathan Martin

Cheltenham MP Sir Hugh Russet-Brown was among those named in yesterday's Susem telecast of involvement in major arms dealing with the former Serbian and Croatian regimes.

Documents linking the Serbian Interior Ministry and Zyclon Anti-Personnel Products plc., have been uncovered in Belgrade, it was claimed.

Sir Hugh is a signatory to a comp...x deal involving ...ovan Opacic, the ...erbian Ambassador in London, the Union Bank of Cyprus, Greek End User Certificates and a Macedonian company, Tortura, Ms Louis said.

Susem newscaster Rainbow Louis claimed that the Serbs were supplied with 2,000 shock batons, manacles and South African shamboeks (a type of whip).

At Heathrow, Sir Hugh, who was preparing to leave on a three week all-party fact finding mission to the Caribbean, denied supplying weaponry to the Serbs.

He said he had only met the Serbian Ambassador at an Embassy social func-tion, and denied any connection with ZAP plc.

Sir Hugh admitted he had been in Nicosia at the time the documents were said to have been signed with the Cypriot bank, but said it was mere coincidence. He had been holidaying at his villa near Famagusta.

Sir Hugh said: "While I have knowledge of ZAP plc and its internal security products I have absolutely no connection with them. My brother-in-law is a director of that company. I am not.

"And lest it be forgotten, and although I have no involvement in, ZAP plc is a successful company, exporting most of its production. ZAP's exporting success has in no small way guaranteed many British jobs.

"On my return from helping Britain's less fortunate dependents, I shall most vigorously contest the allegations made against me," he said. Sir Hugh refused to comment further on the

Are the Aliens really looking for their lost ship

From Tom Fletcher
In Washington

SENATOR SAM Dich, a prominent member of the Senate Arms Services Sub-Committee, yesterday accused the Susem of not looking for their lost spaceship at all but being on Earth for other, darker reasons.

The Senator told a press conference: "We do not see sign of any moves by these Aliens of substantive investigation for their claimed missing space vehicle. Evidence I have received from many sources, including that of the US Academy of Sciences, confirms there has been no known major impacts of extra-terrestrial origin onto or into the surface of this planet in recent times which would indicate the arrival of such an object. Therefore, we must draw no conclusion other than that these beings are here on Earth for other reasons."

Senator Dich's fellow Senator, Harold Lonergan said: "They (the Susem) have wiped out our nuclear defence capability, their weapons are superior to anything we possess." Senator Lonergan, a noted hawk on defence issues, called for immediate research for new forms of defence.

Both Senators are among a growing number of politicians and defence experts in the US and elsewh... have questioned the... claims.

Dr. Keller, a form... fessor at the now ... Stanford Research ... said: "There have ... number of major imp... the Earth in the past ... or so, but we know wh... were. There was the ... guska meteorite in Sibe... 1908 and another large ... corite in eastern Per... 1932, but that was all of ... size."

They are not alone in ... belief that the Susem ... planning moves against ... integrity of the US and ... "historic freedoms".

"Susem are seeking ...

The distress of Croatia and Serbia's women in losing their menfolk was eventually overcome by pragmatism. Life had to go on. Many joined the Nonettes. At first from the needs of expediency, the material benefits of Aid they ensured. Enrolling was also a requisite for their men's return. But soon, with the security and freedom that joining the movement gave, the influence of the Nonettes strengthened and deepened. With freedom for women to organise their daily lives themselves, and security through the power and unity of their combined numbers and purpose, the Nonette movement grew rapidly in both countries.

With threats of further retaliation for their past rulers' misdeeds removed, women of the Nonettes continued to amaze even sometimes themselves in increasingly managing their countries' commerce and services with so little difficulty. However, a profound change of outlook came upon many of them.

In the absence of men, violence and other crimes which once bedevilled their societies disappeared. It began to permeate the women's consciousness that acts of aggression and criminality stemmed mainly from, and had been perpetuated by, men. Also, that without the presence of men they could now travel alone without fear or harassment.

Though many of the women wanted their men to return from the Serra Pelada, it was not their only reason in demanding that those sheltering fugitives of the old regimes surrender them to Korčula. As ever more details of the previous rulers' misdeeds became public, Nonettes' attitudes and some other women (there was still a small minority who refused to join) hardened towards them. With this hardening came conviction that it was these regimes which started the wars and had committed the atrocities against the Bosnians.

By late June and the return of the first men from the Serra Pelada, the Nonette movement had spread throughout both Serbia and Croatia. Representatives of each locality were forming into larger groupings. Contacts had also been made with their counterparts across all three countries as well as those of Ragusa.

With the deporting to Korčula by most countries (with the notable exceptions of Britain, Australia and the US) of their Serbian and Croatian fugitives, half a million men arrived home from the Serra Pelada. Although a steady stream of those who had volunteered to work in Bosnia were already returning, and had adjusted to the new realities, many of those back from the Pelada had not.

Though experienced to being grouped in nines many had difficulty grasping that a male dominated society no longer existed. At best they could now only be equal to women but for many, with their shortcomings made evident, there was not even this solace. Armies, police forces no longer existed, nor political parties or the administrative jobs their patronage once gave. The exclusively male hierarchies of Orthodox and Catholic Churches, their wrongdoing exposed daily, also suffered many women's disdain.

Some men did try to return to their past ways but all found wives, mothers, daughters no longer deigned them their domestic dominance of old. Some attempted to reassert, even forcibly their authority but soon discovered that the power and influence of the Nonettes outweighed them. No longer did women need to turn blind eyes to theirs and their neighbours' domestic violence. Now there was the sisterhood strength of the Nonettes to turn to and the imposition of their instant penalty of social ostracism. Should this fail, there would be enforced exile to the mine clearing in Bosnia.

On their return from the Pelada many of the men who had had a job discovered it no longer existed, or if it did, it was now being done by a Nonette. Also there was often little they could do to get it back. Members of Nonettes no longer needed the men's earning abilities. Either they as a Nonette had a job or the Nonettes collectively provided for their needs. Sensible men joined the Nonettes.

Having been formed for longer, and men not forcibly absent from their communities, the power and influence of the Bosnian Nonettes became all pervasive. Some returning officials of the old administration attempted reasserting their previous authority but found it either bypassed, or more gallingly, ignored. The substance of their past power faded away, sensible ones also joined the Nonettes.

After each local Nonette community representative was voted into office they participated in making and acting on the decisions agreed with those of neighbouring Nonettes. The numbers of elected representatives grew until there were groups of 81 delegates representing communities totalling 60,000 people. By the end of June these groups were preparing to vote for a delegate to represent them in a further council of 81 which would potentially represent half the country's people.

By mid-June the first Susem teaching screens became available in both Bosnia and Ragusa but only in sufficient numbers of one per local Nonette. At month end with relayed transmissions from Tabajara beginning to beam down from Sieba, the machines became operative. Such was demand for access to them that terms for their use were accepted without question. With further reports of the forthcoming arrival of mormics, and the benefits they gave only available to the endeavouring studious of the teaching screens' regime, continuous queues formed in every local Nonette as people of all ages sought to demonstrate their devotion to learning.

With repair of many buildings completed, large swathes of the country cleared of mines, most highways re-opened, some agriculture in progress, and other industries and trades beginning to function once more, everyday life for most Bosnian people began to return to some normality. However, there was much talk of the forthcoming trials.

With the 'Wanted List' all but complete, the 'Wanted' nearly all in custody, and many of the minor offenders already tried and serving their sentences, the first trial dates of the major criminals were set for the last week of July. The television crews from Caught TV had arrived and were setting up their transmission terminals at the trial sites. Many journalists had also arrived to report the trials and the changes which had come to the Bosnians. Some chaffed at being escorted by Nonette guides and translators, but most acknowledged they had greater freedom of movement than the generals and politicians of old had allowed them.

The judges and prosecutors took an advised ten days respite from their sentencing so they might be refreshed and ready prepared for their tasks ahead. Some did rest but most, still imbued with the moment and thrill of their experiences, were willingly assisting the next intake of aspirants. Many also had their end of term college and school examinations to sit.

Colonel Tambassing's men, while still stationed throughout Bosnia, were no longer engaged on active duty. Even their supervision of the distribution of French aid was now managed by the Nonettes themselves. Instead some were supervising the rehabilitation of the cages at the old Sarajevo Zoo. The mechanically adept were engaged in overseeing the dismantling and reassembling of a big dipper, taken from the fairground in Split, in the Kosevo stadium nearby the zoo. Others were supervising the digging of a huge steep sided pit four metres deep. Yet more were supervising the digging of similar sized pits in the courtyards to the rear of seven almost completed Kamenito Mjesto court buildings, the hand-sized stones from the excavations being neatly piled around each courtyard.

Few knew the reason for the pits or the big dipper. Nor did the carriage repairers in Sarajevo's tramyard know why they were contracted to convert the big dipper's carriages to be split in two along the centre of their lengths. Neither did the metal workers in a forge near Tuzla know why they were asked to make what looked like outsized school classroom guillotines. Or cast and harden huge sledgehammer heads with faces the size of a man's out-stretched hand. Just as quizzical were the employees of an engineering company in Zenica, who, having been commissioned to produce what they considered to be the biggest circular saw blade they had ever seen, it was three metres in diameter, were then told its teeth were too sharp and had to blunt them.

They were just as mystified with the purpose of the three metre long stainless steel spikes they were also asked to forge, and why they were also returned several times so their tips could be made ever tougher and sharper. Carpenters at a joinery company in Travnik were also at a loss to know what the purpose was for the sets of open sided, four metres tall towers they were asked to build. Though there was a fulsome response in Sarajevo to the requests for hundreds of two metre long bamboo canes, no one knew why they were wanted. There was the same response and puzzlement from the older women over the request for unwanted hat pins.

Susem exert control over Bosnians through their women

Our gender correspondent Ian Rushmore reports from Zenica, northern Bosnia on disturbing developments of the Aliens

THE PRE-WAR political parties are shunned in Zenica.. They have been replaced by local councils and most of the city's men are denied political power. Women now govern Zenica and other of Bosnia's cities.

Under the tutelage of the Susem, this city's women are now formed into highly organized, tight knit cells. Their objective, it is widely seen, is to carry out the Aliens' bidding take over everything including all the distribution of the French Aid. Legitimate businesses are being denied the opportunity to participate in the renewal process."

Mr Kriv's fellow business colleagues confirmed his experience. Nijaz Krasti, who owned a construction company, said: "The women's groups have taken charge of all the rebuilding programmes, public transport, food distribution, everything. It's not fair."

desultorily atmosphere.

Velik Lazljiv once the local SDA party chief said: "Although the city council still technically exists, its authority has been usurped by these so called 'Nonettes.' They even have their own Alien backed security force.

"In Travnik - 30 kilometres west of Zenica and which was less affected by the war - the SDA did manage to re-establish some control but the women there were formed

Iron from plants - dramatic pictures

Jim Tadford
Environment Correspondent

IRON need never be mined again it can be grown. "And not just iron but every other mineral," said the Susem last night. A Susem telecast showed countless circular shaped fields filled with plants which take up iron or other minerals from the ground and into their leaves.

The telecast also showed the leaves of cropped plants being incinerated and droplets of iron emerging.

The telecast claimed that more iro was produced by the plants than b excavation. "There is no need t disfigure the Earth by mining. Also i was more efficient and cheaper t grow minerals than to mine them Many of the Earth's desolated places are covered in plants which extracted minerals into their leaves," said the announcer.

Dr Ian Fleming, Professor of Mineralogy, University of Lond

British AveroSpace to close Preston plan

BY BILL SCARILL

FIVE thousand people are set to lose their jobs following British Avero-Space's announcement to close factories at Fulwood, Preston, East-leigh and Totton in Southampton.

BA management said yesterday: "The delay in NATO Governments failing to confirm agreement on the second stage of the Euro-fighter meant that it was vital there was an immediate down-

that the precipitate drop in defence spending world wide, indicated there was unlikely to be significant upturn in the near-term of defence procurement in any of the company's established market sectors.

Union officials said they were unable to soften BA's factory closures. And rather than contesting BA they are now pressing for increased severance payouts.

In the wake of the Susem BA's experience - a futu with an empty order boo The cancellation of the ne stage of Eurofighter proje was the last straw as far BA was concerned.

William Friend of *Defen Equipment Monthly* sa "The knock-on effect of t BA closures among su contractors and its other su pliers will mean substantial greater numbers of skille people losing their jobs th just at BA. I estimate that

Journalists free to witness War Trials

By **Richard Sparrow**

JOURNALISTS and 'other interested parties' will be invited to witness the forthcoming trials of those indicted of crimes in Bosnia, it was announced in last night's Susem telecast.

Journalists have also invited to visit the reconstruction of Bosnia. No mention was made however of conditions in Serbia or Croatia and of visiting either country. It is thought that both countries will be opened up to outside journalists within the

SLI snatches War Trials mega deal

From Roger Phillips
Media Correspondent

A £500 MILLION TV deal to broadcast exclusively the forthcoming Bosnian War Trials has been signed by SLI Television's Richard Bear.

Bear said: "This deal [the non-US rights to transmit] is good for SLI but even better for the cause of justice."

Bear was obviously more than satisfied he had stolen a march on rival bidders.

The War Trials, scheduled to begin within the next ten days, will be transmitted live during the day with highlights shown each evening, said SLI. Asked why SLI had exchanged its diet of game shows and soaps for something so radically different trials, Mr. Bear responded: "Our negotiating team in Atlanta were appraised as to the nature and outcomes of the trials already taken place. They had no choice but to snap it up while it was still on the table."

Television industry insiders, however, questioned the commercial logic of the signing. analyst at advertising agency Garrod Olglivy & Dodwell, said: "This deal looks dodgy. Bear's viewer base is at the light end of the spectrum. These trials are at the other. I see him scorching his bankers' fingers just as he did with the US baseball deal three years ago. Just because he controls so many satellite and cable

SPORT CRICKET

England knocked for six - after six, after s

At 447 for 0, Namibia's opening bat set England a daunting task

From Judy Warring
At Edgebaston

HAVING won the toss and deciding to bat, Namibia set the first day of the 2nd Test at Edgebaston off to a cracking start. Namibia's opening batsmen, Christian Bangdala and Koos Pampoempoort had both chalked up centuries before lunch.

England's opening ball was hit for four by Bangdala. At the end of the first over the score stood at 16. By the second Pampoempoort had doubled it.

However, having sampled Hindly's bowling prowess, both batsmen then got into their strides. By the fourth over the score stood at 63. Following a brief mid-pitch conference both men set about teasing England to one humiliation after another.

Exposed to the full the home team's short-comings, the next half hour witnesses both batsmen, with evident enjoyment, playing to every one of England's fielders and allowing them to miss catch after catch.

Susem spacecraft: war machine or jovial giant?

Jim Tadford

During five soundless minutes, except for the single phrase: "This is a tocan spacecraft" - viewers were left to marvel at the great size of the Susem's cigar shaped giant spacecraft.

We were treated to a gripping fly-by along the smooth sides of its kilometre-plus length, and then an encircling of its girth, which showed this "tocan" to be more than three hundred metres high.

No sooner had the camera circled than it zoomed towards a thin lighted strip along its side. Close-to, however, the "strip" was an opening more than 20 metre high.

After passing though this opening, the silence was momentarily broken by a booming "Welcome, I am Sardon". With the resonance of the welcome fading away, the camera sped past a curving line of hundreds of the delta winged craft seen so often over the nuclear power stations.

"These are vedas" were the only further next words of commentary. The camera next swung in the opposite direction to show more hundreds of these "vedas". Though this was another example of the Susem's prowess more soon followed, plus more than a few surprises.

From the lines of vedas the next scene was a high domed hall. As the camera scanned from the ceiling to floor, its size was not at first apparent. But the diminutive speck that was the Susem commentator, Rainbow Louis, soon relayed its vastness.

The camera next zoomed in on her, and she from her smiles, was obviously enjoying her experience, called out, "Where next Sardon?"

To which she was greeted with a booming "How about my gardens?" Images of lush palms and ferns followed, as though walking through the greenhouses at Kew. These gave way to a market scene, similar to a market garden. Each small plot was filled with growing crops surrounded by shoulder high hedgerows. Ms Louis walked between these lines of bushes, picking fruits from them, and exclaiming delight as she tasted them.

She had not travelled when the sunli brightness in which the a had been bathed promp dimmed into darkness. as the darkness closed Sardon's voice boom "Time for nocturnal gro and refreshment", t "come, visit my worksh while we wait for the l to return."

Within seconds a hive of minute ro machines was shown. the next five minutes cameras dashed then h ed over one group after ther. To Ms Louis's " are these doing?" would come Sar booming replies.

More Eye witness reports page 20

But Tearo, up aboard Sieba, knew. She had planned them all. Colonel Tambassing knew why too. He had to scrutinise the feasibility of everything Tearo proposed as well as the arrangements for their sourcing and manufacture.

Although there were many differences between the Colonel and Tearo, not least in stature, there had grown over the passing weeks a harmonious working relationship which was developing, little by little into a deeper bond of attachment.

Yet despite this growing affection, Tearo, along with Anuria and Lathia, were more than absorbed with the unfolding of their programme in Bosnia. All three, however, had other thoughts beginning to stir. Though they were not alone among the Susem, now that the removal of all nuclear weaponry and power stations was completed, in having such stirrings, Tearo had taken matters further than the others. Already she had earmarked several isolated sites across southern Europe as being suitable. She was, as she expressed, "Having urges," which were growing stronger by the day.

John Bolger the first Western journalist to visit Tuzla in northern Bosnia, reports on the unique grassroots administration which runs this war-torn city

Tuzla under the control of women

This war-torn Bosnian city is now under the thumb of its women. Within weeks of returning to their homes, thousands of Tuzla's women have established complete control of every aspect of the city's administration.

Militsa Mehmed 37, a surgeon before the war, but now head of Tuzla's council, its "Nonette Savjet", said: "We have grown from small and simple beginnings to the organisation we are now. Every family has a representative, so does every street, every district. Savjets sit in constant session supervising the city and its environs."

Ms Mehmed denies the 'Nonette Savjet' system is a cumbersome structure for efficient organisation and running the city.

She said: "The decisions of the people determine the Savjet's policies and actions. I and my fellow members are only their elected delegates. We only do as the people decide.

"Because we are all agreed on policy we are able to implement all aspects of it quickly, cooperatively and thus efficiently," she said.

On a tour of Tuzla, Ms. Mehmed's claims were amply borne out. Every street, block of flats has their own smaller Savjet Nonette.

Aida Bajramovic 29, a noted Bosnian cartoonist, is the Nonette representative of the Kunosia district in the old part of the city. She showed me the rapid progress of rebuilding of the market square and described in detail the working of her Nonette council.

Aida said: "People form into groups of nine, they elect one of their group to represent them.

"The representative undertakes to carry out their decisions on their behalf. Presently they spend much of their time collecting Aid supplies from France arrive at the Kunosia distribution centre, here in this market. Also the representatives tell us of their group's future needs and the centre in turn, relays these requests on.

"Representatives form into further groups of nine. And they take on the responsibility of attending to the collective interests of their block of flats or their part of their street.

"These representatives, in turn elect one of their group to represent their immediate locality in a further a council Nonette. In turn, these oversee the interests of their area."

When asked if these groups then elect one number to represent them, Ms Bajramovica said: "No, everyone votes for their locality representative." She then said that this delegate is only elected for one month as are all the other Nonettes.

The locality representative with 80 others, forms the council which runs Tuzla. Although anyone can stand for office it appears that nearly all ar[e] women. Asked why th[is] was, Aida shrugged h[er] shoulders and said: "T[he] first Nonettes were form[ed] by women. Women a[re] more concerned with t[he] everyday, practical aspe[cts] of life. In time perha[ps] this will change and th[ere] may be more men."

In the centre of mod[ern] Tuzla, at the parti[ally] repaired Irfan Ljubijar[...] Conference Centre, mot[her] of five, Fadile Kotika[...] Savjet representative [res]ponsible for educat[ion] was supervising the d[istri]bution of Susem tea[ching] screens. She said: [...] Nonette groups t[...] these screens are oblig[...]

UK Farmers fume at crop bounty threat

By Edward Gundy
Agricultural Reporter

SURROUNDED BY baskets piled high with produce, a group of farmers told how the Susem had enabled them to grow bountiful harvests - every single day.

High speed crops

In a five minute Susem telecast item yesterday, a dozen farmers living alongside the Aliens, described how their advanced agricultural techniques had enabled the farmers to increase the productivity of their crops by many times. Some claimed it was at least a hundred times better.

The farmers showed the large variety of crops they had grown ranging from potatoes to wheat and strawberries. They also told how they also participated in daily educational sessions which had increased their farming abilities.

Completely organic

The farmers said their crops were grown with[...] than farmers elsewhere.

UK farmers threatened

Sir Graham George NFU President said: "What these farmers have said and shown are bombshells. Should the techniques they are using spread to outsiders, it will revolutionise agriculture as we know it. It will mean the end of the farming industry, not just in Britain but throughout the world. This is a threat which needs to be taken very seriously.

UK farmers' rights

"Not only would the price of ordinary farmers' crops be slashed but jobs throughout the Industry would be in jeopardy. This omen of unfair competition needs to be watched.

"We have already seen how these Aliens have obliterated the power and oil industries, now it looks as though they are about to attack out industry. My members are not going to take such threats to their

Croatians call for 'their' criminals extradition

By Toby Perry

A PLEA to "hand over the criminals who have plunged our country into this grave crisis", was issued yesterday by a group of Croatian women.

The group, calling themselves, 'Nonette Council Zupanja', claimed that the "criminals" were being shielded by Croatian expatiate communities in Argentina and Australia as well as in the US. They demanded that the governments of all countries concerned immediately repatriate them to Bosnia.

By harbouring these 'criminals', the governments of all countries were preventing their own "blameless" menfolk from returning home, said the statement. This was thought to refer to those transported by Susem to Serra Pelada in Brazil who were are awaiting their return to Croatia

PAX TO PAX

Up to a month ago - the long past - we had become accustomed to the United States of America being our security. If we needed military protection from the East, be it Russia or China, we could count upon the American spine of NATO to guard us and deter such foes. Should some tin pot despot become too big for their boots it would be US led action which cut them down to size, the most recent example being the wars in Iraq and Afghanistan as well as the War on Terror.

If the world's finances moved out of kilter, such as during the recent EMU collapse it was American stewardship which saved the day. Commerce, international law, environmental concern - there was always Pax Americana.

America may not have been a perfect Pax, just as neither was Britain's in our heyday of Empire, and its critics made have had just cause from time to time to criticize, but nonetheless it served us well. It was always there. We became used to and comfortable with it. And even took it for granted as lasting for ever.

Then in a instant, the steadfastness of this Pax of yesteryear was shattered in front of our eyes, both from within, and without. Shattered from within by the clumsiness and inept response to challenge that [...] by the arrival of a new Pax - th[at] of the Susem's.

Within weeks of the[ir] interplanetary visitors arrival o[n] Earth, they have rid our planet [of] many of its woes. The Susem ha[ve] plucked away the bogy of nucle[ar] conflagration which dogge[d] mankind for half a century. Th[e] running sore that was Bosni[a] which even Pax American[a] disdained to bandage furthe[r] the Susem have staunched. O[ur] streets and homes, to s[ay] nothing of our industries, are [...] the better for their provisio[n] pollution-free power, to sa[y] nothing of its free cost.

There are those, mainly in th[e] US, who are critical, suspiciou[s] even, of the Alien's state[d] intentions. But it ill behove[s] such carpers to question th[e] Susem's motives. For these so called doubters are the sam[e] people who, in foolhard[y] endeavour to protect thei[r] privilege, were hell-bent o[n] throwing us all, headlong an[d] unknowingly into the finality o[f] a nuclear abyss. But it was th[e] Susem, lest it be ever forgotten who and with modes[t] magnanimity, thwarted these latter day Dr Strangeloves.

Today Pax Susema strides our world, bringing daily salve to our sores and bounties of benefits to delight us all. Yet already they have fitted into all our lives, wil[l] we also come to take for granted their caring over us?

Rankin in near fatal auto crash

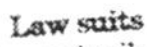

Sharon Pavolsky in Los Angles

JEANETTE RANKIN, Caught TV's foremost presenter and commentator was seriously injured in a multi-vehicle crash in Santa Barbara, CA, yesterday.

Ms Rankin, 42, known worldwide as the anchor of a raft of investigative programmes ranging from 'Capitol Crime' to 'We know where you live' was in intensive care at the Gerald Ford Memorial Hospital, Ventura.

Rankin who was due to front Caught TV's upcoming premier series covering the Bosnian War Crimes trials is expected to be hospitalized for some considerable time. Her accident comes at a [...]

Law suits

Already embroiled in a number of high profile and expensive law suits stemming from its previous investigative programmes on corruption by senior US politicians, Caught was hoping for a financial fillip the Bosnia programmes are expected to bring.

War crimes difficulties

Adding to the station's woes is that after a lengthy delay over the commencement of the Bosnian Trials, they are to start in a mere ten day's time.

The accident came as M[s] Rankin and long-time comp[anion], Gerry Hayes, wer[e] driving on Santa Barbara Carbilla Boulevard and ha[d] just departed from dinin[g] with friends at Sterns What[...] a popular entertain spot wi[th] many in the media industry

81: JAMES

"Ele locuo! ele locuo!" was Philipe's father's first, disparaging response to the sight of Danny's face appearing on the television. Mine was rather different, I was glad he was still alive and still there. Seeing it also made me all the more determined to go and see him.

Phillipe's father's next and impassioned outburst was "Onde é... (Philipe whispered, "Where's") ...Rainbow erótico?" Though wondering too, I tried listening over Philipe's translations for his parents to what Danny had to say. But this became difficult as his father's further exclamations of disbelief became ever louder.

Danny said sufficient soufins for everyone in places without Serbs and Croats would soon descend from the skies. And indeed they did. During my stay in Rio, newscast after newscast showed police forces the world over, often encouraged by eager crowds, deporting Serbs and Croats back to Bosnia one day and Susem fleets carpeting them with soufins the next.

Danny appeared on Thursday but Rainbow was back as usual for the next two telecasts. Her nonchalant voiceovers as clips showing one "corrective and remedial action" as she termed them, after another, confirmed my earlier convictions that now is not a good time to be in banking, or any other business for that matter. Forestry, land clearance and mining to be ceased were Saturday's telecast edict. Deep sea fishing and dam building were Tuesday's. Clips of those caught so doing, being unloaded from the huge Susem craft into the Serra Pelada, re-enforced the direness of Rainbow's pronouncements.

As a country and also as an economy, Brazil is affected more than most by Susem actions. People were either in a state of near panic or in happy anticipation of the imminent arrival of soufins to provide free electricity and motoring. With forest clearances halted the projected increases in Brazil's beef-stock and soya production are certain to be revised downwards. While this is bad news just now for producers it is bound to have a downward effect on the country's balance of payments. This is sure to also put a strain on its IMF loan repayments as well as weakening the exchange value of the Real.

Danny appeared on the Susem telecast the next Thursday detailing deliveries for the forthcoming week which included Rio. On the following Saturday evening as I boarded the overnight coach to Salvador, I witnessed the arrival of the first Susem craft and their countless blue phosphorescent carpets floating down.

An hour later with the coach breasting the Orgãos, a range of hills 25 kilometres north of Rio, the driver stopped so passengers could see the spectacle of thousands of blue specks drifting down in the darkness and disappearing into the lighted glow of Rio. As I watched with the rest of the passengers I had thoughts of the task ahead and Philipe's father's overheard words to him when he learnt what I was intending to do, "Ele locuo! ele locuo!"

Susem startle Spaniard's sheep

By Hilary Cardwell
In Zaragoza

SLEEPING Spanish sierra sheep are being unsettled, by small Susem spaceships.

Dozens of small Alien spacecraft have been spotted sweeping through Pyrenean valleys in the past week. Mario Conde, leader of a farmer's co-operative in Tuxent said: "We have seen them flying up and down the mountains of the Sierra de Carli for hours on end, day after day.

"They are the size of an eagle and have big eyes. They come and look at us and our sheep in the high pastures. Sometimes we say 'Shoo, shoo!' to them and they fly away.

"But it is with our animals they are causing the most problems. Our flocks like to rest and digest what they have eaten. Then suddenly these things are appearing and the sheep think they are eagles and run off.

"This is most unsettling for sheep. All this running about gives them indigestion which makes them break wind. For shepherds its terrible when they get close to their flocks. And it is not only the smell its the noise. After these spacecraft have flown away the hills are alive to the sound of farting. My members' siestas are constantly disrupted by the foul smells given off by their flocks effusive farting."

Caught picks Thorne

ATLANTA: Rip Thorne will front Caught's Bosnia War Crimes TV team, following Jeanette Rankin's near fatal car crash in Santa Barbara

Thorne, MBC's world known seasoned newsman, is report ted to have beaten off a clutch of competitors for this plum appointment.

Caught's CEO Ed Earner said: "Westing-MBC, our corporate parent were always rightfully proud of Rip's scoops, but now we at Caught can also be proud of Rip's outstanding contributions too."

On announcement of his appointment Rip Thorne said: "I am deeply honored to take on this historic assignment. I feel humbled that it should be me who has been chosen to step into Jeanette's shoes.

"Obviously my previous meetings with the Susem representatives provides me with valuable insights others do not have. And of course my negotiating the original deal for Caught has no doubt swayed their decision."

However, media insiders say Thorne's agent, Theo Tenpercentus, was largely responsible for swinging the deal his way. *Media Today's* Max Imal said:

Alpine Austrians' angst at Aliens' ar

By **Helga Aspang** in Innsbruck

WAVES OF SUSEM spacecraft are sweeping the Austrian Alps upsetting the locals, humans and cattle alike.

The tranquil summer sounds of occasional cowbells ringing has been replaced by herds of cows tolling in panicked unison stampeding away from the unwanted gaze of the Alien's craft.

Rickhard Vogel, a hotelier in the nearby mountain village of Gries who has been affected by both Aliens and cows said: "The noise of the bells is most horrible. Usually we are hearing one or two bells ringing from the cows every now and then and that is okay. But when the little flying ships from the Aliens are passing by they are zooming down on to the cows and staring at them.

"This, the cows do not like so much and they are soon running off and their bells are ringing like crazy. Once or twice maybe this would be okay but every day now the Aliens are

cows' milk become fizzy."

Stampeding cows are not Herr Vogel's only problems brought about by the Aliens.

At his hotel - the Fassbender - bookings have slumped, as have most other hotels in region. The summer months are usually the time of the year when visitors flock to walk amid the spectacular scenery of the Alpine pastures. But the appearance of the Alien craft has frightened people away.

Reports say the craft are half a metre long, have huge insect-like eyes. They fly in fast and then stop instantly to hover as though examining the terrain about. There are many theories why they are continuously sweeping through the high alpine valleys, but nobody really knows why the Austrian Alps should be subject to such extra-terrestrial visits.

The scientific world have rushed together plans to meet in the coming weeks to discuss possible causes for the strange phenomenon occurring so

Italians irritated ove Aliens in Apennines

Helena Brown
In Bologna

SCORES of small Alien spacecraft have been cruising though the Apennine mountain valleys. Many inhabitants of the remote mountain villages live in daily fear of their visits.

Most sighting, however, are from the vicinity of Lake Trasimeno, to the north of Perugia in Umbria. Roman Prodi, a fisherman on the lake claims to have seen the craft many times. He also says that these Alien craft are disturbing his catches.

"The Alien craft are coming here all of the

Many times I go out on the lake and before I know it at least one of them has come looking at me. I don't mind now that I've become used to them, but all the same they are scaring the fishes away."

Property sales have also been adversely affected by the Aliens' flying spycraft. Local estate agent, Ceseri Romati said: "This region of Umbria is very popular with people seeking isolated properties. But if people cannot feel safe, if they think that the Aliens are going to disturb their activities, then property prices are of course going

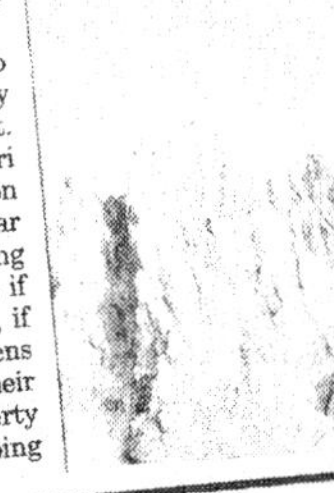

Chemicals Chief lashes governme

By Abigail Barrel
Political Analyst

THE Government must agree the Susem demands or British industry will suffer and 500,000 British jobs could be lost, claimed a major industry boss yesterday.

Sir Paul Forsyth, chairman of HERE, founded in France in 1939, said: "We are one of Britain's leading industries, exporting more than half our output. As such we are also one of the country's major users of energy.

"Unless we receive these soufin energy units, as our overseas competitors have done already, our future will be jeopardized. Why should a handful of unwanted foreigners be allowed to dictate the nation's future?"

Sir Paul, speaking to meeting of institutional investors, also urged the DTI to back his initiative of an industry-wide body to help companies fight Susem-backed demands to pay half their profits as a 'fine' for their alleged past trading with Croatia and Serbia.

Sir Paul said: "I am able to say without any question of doubt, that while we are to provide convincing evidence, we are totally innocent of these spurious claims made by the investigators against the company.

"However, it is proving extremely expensive for us to do so. Other companies though, are finding it near impossible to get sight of the documentary evidence held in the former Yugo-states for them to establish their innocence."

A spokesman for HERE added: "We consider it necessary for companies to stand together on this issue. If ever these demands were enforced, and at present we cannot see how, the share price of many companies will plummet.

"This could adversely affect long term investors as well as causing the loss of thousands of jobs and thus affect the livelihoods of countless thousands.

'Send Serbs packing' Weston deman

By **Barry Gibbon**
Political Editor

FUGITIVE Serbs and Croats should not be allowed to hold Britain ransom over the nation's energy supplies, said a senior backbench MP last night.

Gerald Weston, LibCon MP for Tunbridge Wells, is pressing the Home Office to abide by Susem and Serbo-Croat requests for their extradition to stand trial in Bosnia. He said: "Quite frankly, I'm disgusted with the government's dithering on this important issue.

"If these Serbo-Croat chaps have nothing to hide then they've nothing to fear from returning to their native countries. And if they do have something to hide then they should not be here in the first place. Meanwhile Britain is suffering because of them. If other countries can abide by the Susem wishes, which I consider perfectly reasonable, then why cannot this country?"

Gerald Weston's outburst echoes a growing chorus, from the public and industry alike for the return of Serbs and Croats in Britain to Bosnia.

To date more than 140 countries have acceded to Susem calls for the return of fugitive Serbo-Croats in return for supplies of their soufin energy units. Britain, however, is one of the few remaining nations still insisting on strict adherence to its extradition treaties of which none exist between any of the former Yugoslav states.

CBI director General George Gardiner, is among other industrialists pressing the government for a re-evaluation of energy supplies brought about by the worldwide distribution of Suse energy units. "Quite frankly," Sir George said after a meeting

"Cruel," I said.

"But fair," replied Rainbow in a 'don't disagree with me' growl, adding for good measure, "they deserve everything coming to them."

Paceillo was the same, the only difference being her matter-of-fact "It will serve as an example in dissuading others elsewhere."

Seeing no sense in suggesting caution let alone clemency I left them, now that the last absconding Serbs and Croats are gathered, discussing details of the trials. All the same I had qualms creeping over me.

The Susem actions these past months have had me in dread on more than one occasion. That they have met with general approval (the aggrieved privileged apart) has been their saving grace but this time there will not even be this. Putting it all on the TV is just asking for trouble. Showing the trials is okay but the punishings, that is not going to go down at all well.

Even just thinking what will happen when the Susem have flown off and the vested powerful start seeking scapegoats sends shudders through me. It will be alright for Rainbow. Her looks, charms and bashing abilities will overcome difficulties for her, but knowing fate I will be among the ones they will come looking for. The same can be said of what is happening hereabout.

The "Nonettes" as everybody, and that is just about everyone, has taken to calling themselves are now utterly out of hand. Commonsense alone says it is time to slow down, consolidate. But no, they are doing just the opposite. Spreading like wildfire they are, and this is without anyone crusading the cause. Villages, even entire towns are queuing to join, so many so that there is forever a shortage of trained teachers. It is now Nonette solid for hundreds of miles. The entire area Paceillo demarcated back in April will soon be Nonetted from end to end.

Though this is worrying enough was is worse is that they are deepening by the day as well. New councils, committees are springing up so fast that I have lost track of them all. There is even talk in the Pousada of football leagues. But once initial enthusiasm has worn off, Brazilian manhã will no doubt take hold and it will all collapse back into the usual inertia. And then there will be even more trouble.

However, even if I say so myself and though I still have suspicions that Paceillo's hand is behind them, everything the Nonettes have introduced is so thorough, methodical, organised, so unBrazilian.

While each village, town, suburb functions as an independent, almost sovereign territory, their monthly elections for community representation are now overseen by independent observers from the area Nonette. Apart from entitling them to a seat on the council, skulduggery doesn't arise (a great departure from Brazilian tradition). Matters beyond a community's scope or those they wish to delegate are handled by the Area Nonette. This sovereignty a la carté I have noticed when travelling around with Roberto filming, varies from place to place. I have also noticed that wherever we have gone everyone is engaged in their community's affairs. Though probably just out of novelty, it is the first time ordinary people actually have had the power of being in charge of their own lives as opposed to being under the sway of the grandees, the army, Church and all the other bigwigs.

What a community can't, or doesn't want to handle, the Area Nonette, representing about 60,000 people, does, except for the things even beyond its scope. So that they don't become distant in any way, each Area Nonette is sectioned, like the communities themselves, into nine groups of adjoining villages or suburbs. Though our Area Nonette is down in Tianguá there are always groups of people from other communities in Tabajara.

Although it has more than most, Tabajara isn't alone in this. Everybody is forever travelling to see everyone else these days, be it for a meeting on this or that, or because nearly every community is 'twinned' to another in the other 81 communities comprising our Area Nonette, or just for the sheer pleasure of it.

Most of the officials of the old regime fled Ceará causing disruption as they went, but it didn't take long for the Nonettes to have everything in order. And there is a marked improvement in most. The rate of road repairs, for example, means that now even the remotest hamlet has a paved one.

Of course the Nonettes are aided by the Susem's machines as they are in many other things. And the roads aren't really paved either, they are 'glassed'. Once the earthworks of a road are completed the machines run along its surface and fuse the soil and rock with such heat it melts into glass, not smooth but ribbed, tiny globule surfaced glass. From a distance it is as if the roads aren't there at all. And being made from the ground underneath, they expand and contract at the same rate as well.

The bridges that the machines make are also glass, and very graceful constructions they are. Though glass is the casing the insides are made from steel and bone, well it's the same as bone. And this is yet another of the things the Susem have introduced into everyone's lives, new crops.

Every Area Nonette now has its own seed resonance analyser and a little trained team of locals to operate it, and who travel from one Local Nonette to another preparing seeds for their gardens. They also introduce the new plants. There is a strain of cotton plant with the silk genes from a spider (it's the one, so Milophinia said, which weaves a web to hold in its feet and drops on passing prey). Though the crop looks and is harvested as cotton, it really is spider silk. Everyone's tunics are made from it and very good they are, tough yet light, airy, never cold or hot, wash and shake dry in an instant, fit any size and crumple back into a matchbox. I wouldn't be without one and I hate spiders.

Bone is the same. The Susem have introduced into a willow, genes from a cow which makes for the bone. The harvested crop still fresh is sliced into fingernail long slivers, kept moist and taken to where it is needed. I saw the machines using bone to build a bridge a hundred feet across. The slivers were jetted from a tube and sprayed over a mesh of thin steel wires unrolling from either side. How the arch of the bridge was determined I'm not quite sure, but I think it's something to do with other machines hovering around the spans as though blowing them into shape. As the two sides of the bridge crept towards one another more machines were spraying small rocks and sand over the completed parts. Following close behind them were other machines fusing the sand to glass. It was completed within the hour.

Bone, so Milophinia said, is many times stronger than steel but steel is more tensile. What I didn't know at the time I was watching, was that the slivers of bone are fused, or "grow" as she put it, into one. And what I also didn't know or appreciate then, but do now, is that the group I do tuition with have been studying biology the past week, and that the Susem have genetically engineered mitochondria to function in the place of, or alongside, chloroblasts in the cells of plants. That they have managed such a thing is achievement enough but the consequences are the more remarkable. Every substance the Susem require they grow, all is made from once living cells. The Susem don't use plastics or synthetics of any kind. Or pharmaceuticals, and now I come to think of it, petroleum either. Everything the Susem use are 'natural' materials. It is the sort of thing Greens would go envy green for.

Though the Susem manage wonders with natural materials it is what they do with them naturally which is even more amazing, especially of the human kind. They are growing, regrowing limbs, legs, arms, fingers, even noses, and all in a day. Menpemelo has had a clinic burrowed into the bottom of the cliff below Tabajara where the helicopters and the American spy satellites are (they're forever sending them up and Sardon is forever bringing back them down).

Early every morning there are a dozen and more patients, sent by their Nonettes, limping in, then walking away of an evening (although those for noses and fingers are usually away by noon).

While there is a big demand, legs and arms they have to be worked, or rather studied, for. Apart from the limbless learning feverishly, entire communities have donated days of study so that the limb bereft have enough achievement points to qualify. One place we filmed had a "Points means legs, study hard, give generously" sign strung across the main street. Once the limbless have enough points, they each arrive with a print-out of their mormic profile, a blood relation if they have one, and both shoes.

Menpemelo, when she explained how it was possible to do such a thing as grow a new leg, and in just a day, made it all sound so straightforward. "Lizards shed legs and tails," she said. "They do so because they are able to regrow them. All animals have ability to renew damage to their bodies. For most it is limited but it is possible to overcome this limitation and activate the body's renewal. It is also possible to accelerate the process."

I asked by how much.

She said “By several thousand times,” then added, “Though new cells are created by their division, only one in many thousands is to the exacting standard of your body’s fidelity reference, what you humans call your ‘immune system’. The rest it destroys, the remnants being recycled or excreted. In animals grown to full stature cell growth matches cell loss, but in the newly born cellular growth is faster and their bodies subsequently increase in size.

“It is possible, once the inter-cellular resonances of a fidelity reference-perfect cell are known, to ensure its divisions are maintained to this same fidelity. Providing these proliferating cells are supplied with their material requirements they will continue to multiply.”

I said legs like other bits of a body consisted of all sorts of different cells and interact with one another and the combination of all their resonances must come to billions.

But Menpemelo said “Billions of billions. Though there are 327 cell types in the human body, ours, by the way, are all but the same, they are differentiated into specialising to specific parts of the anatomy, bone cells of the upper thigh differ from those of the lower. In the bones of the leg there are more than a hundred different specialised cells. While some of the cells in the left leg are the same as the right, others are not.

“By having a close genetic relation to the recipient acting as a guide template and accelerated intravenous infusion of histocompatible sustenance, it is possible to reconstruct, stage by stage, lost or malformed limbs and digits.”

“How do you know it’s going to work, going to last?”

“How alike the regrown limb will function to the previous one and to what extent the recipient will need to re-adjust to it will always be unknown. We create to an assured histocompatible and physiological standard. There have been no complaints or rejects, only satisfied recipients. It is always my intention to give value.”

The clinic or “Limbs Unlimited” as the locals call it, and joke about going there after a night’s drinking, is one of the Susem wonders that bring outsiders to Tabajara. Another is Tabajara itself, or rather ‘New Tabajara’. Susem machines carved it from the top of the cliff face up by the old cable car station to the Grotto. With its little streets, terraces and covers of flowering vines and bougainvillaea it is very grand, very gracious, especially of a morning with the rising sun catching it. Like an Italian hill town it is, but with all mod cons.

Though impressive and carved in a couple of days New Tabajara represents a Herculean achievement by the entire village. We studied so hard on screens, seminars and projects clocking up achievement points that minds became numb with learning. There was never chance of anyone easing-off either. The collective stick propelled us all, though women were the most demonic. They took to chanting “Points means rooms,” whenever they considered their children or men were slacking. The Pousada’s takings took a terrible tumble.

New Tabajara attracts trippers from all over. Some days, so I'm told, there are more here than when the cable car was working. Of course the sightseeing has caused demand from other communities to have new villages as well. Part of the spectacle visitors also see is the demolition of the old village, another element of the deal for the new one. At the rate they are going there will only be the cowsheds, the old Pousada and Father Alves' church left.

The sheds because there is nowhere else for the cows to go, though when the new animals arrive, it means both sheds and cows will disappear. The old Pousada will go when Elana returns from the regional Nonette inauguration. She has left Rico instructions not to touch anything till she's back. (In her absence he has also been doing the cooking. Elana's might not have been the most inspired but at least her gravy had movement, and both Roberto and me look forward to her return). But the church is proving a dilemma and may remain a while. Father Alves and those who turned up with him caused no end of upset.

There had been tales circulating of clerics, all of whom, when the Susem arrived, departed to the east of Ceará, attempting a concerted comeback. The same tales told of many communities giving returning priests a hard time, with some actually being chased away. Though the Vatican's misdeeds in Bosnia are widely known, so now are those the students in Fortaleza uncovered when they occupied the bishop's palace. As soon as it was known that the Church hierarchy had been in cahoots with the Polícia and grandees, there was uproar.

With everyone benefiting from the Susem and also being aware of what they had said about intruding outsiders, and with their new education showing much of the Church's preaching to be mumbo jumbo, the returning clerics met with widespread antagonism.

So when Father Alves arrived with a bunch of other clerics in a big black Mercedes tourer, and one of them started spurting fire and brimstone proclaiming the villagers were in the grip of the anti-Christ, they received short shrift. They were gone within the hour and haven't been back. Some of the older villagers still occasionally worship in the church but that's about all.

Schools, having been completely controlled by the Church, have also closed. Some teachers attempted to keep classes going, but with the teaching screens pulling pupil's education way ahead, attendance waned away and many of the teachers have become avid students themselves. They have also found other things to do, of which there is no shortage.

The arrival of the Susem caused Ceará's wealthy, along with state officials, to decamp. With them went their money. The banks closed their doors as well. What businesses remained suffered terribly. But the establishment of the new bank by the Nonettes in collaboration with Roberto's father in Sobral has been a lifeline for many of them. So has its branch network.

Every community now has its own 'peoples' bank'. In the past most ordinary people could not qualify for loans for lack of collateral. Achievement points now count as assets, with each one valued at a dollar. These banks make loans of up to nine times the number of a borrower's assets. However, lending is carefully vetted by the community's banking committee. In turn, its decisions are overseen by the area Nonette acting as auditors. Bigger loans are also referred to it. Though more thorough than the old banks, the communities' loans are for sums smaller, most are for less than 200 dollars, than they would have ever been interested in.

The borrowers ninth of their community also collectively stands additional surety for loans and ensures no one defaults. Should a borrower's endeavour fail they have the alternative of pledging their future achievement points. These points are also becoming a quasi-currency. Though Brazilian currency still circulates, it's depreciating against both achievement points and US dollars which are increasing in circulation.

That there is US currency circulating in Ceará is due in part to the frequent flights from France delivering the 'fines' paid by erring governments and companies. All are paid in US dollars to Jacques Foressier at Villacoublay. When he has a palletful, Kennet or Kershaw on their return from Bosnia stop by and pick it up. This money will go to Bosnia when Nonettes there have established their own banking system. What happens to Ceará's economy when Bosnia does, I shudder to think. Meanwhile it's working hard and productively.

The upsurge in business activity (and employment) resulting from the loans has been quite amazing. Most communities' crops are sold through cooperatives but there are no end of enterprising people making packaging, providing transport and all sorts of other things.

With money flowing into the communities for their crops, as opposed in the past to the grandees and latifundios, there has been a surge in demand for goods from the towns. In turn these, mainly Fortaleza, have benefited. Though, at first, this didn't happen.

When the exodus of the army, police and others took place there was chaos in Fortaleza. Crowds went on the rampage with people killed and a large part of the centre looted and burnt. Vigilante groups became commonplace, thugs held sway in the favelas and thousands of people fled the city. But Pedro, his men, volunteers and a swarm of hen-gers moved in on Fortaleza and established order, though it took them a week to do so.

The population of Fortaleza were so grateful to Pedro's men that they were soon forming their own Nonette communities (the distribution of free soufins to those who joined also speeded membership) and the city's hoodlums were rounded up and carted off to the Serra Pelada.

Just as it is in all large cities, crime was always a problem in Fortaleza. But the Nonettes has eliminated most of the 'ordinary' everyday variety. What crime does occur is reported to the community office which then circulates it to the Area Nonette, which in turn notifies the other Area Nonettes, there being sixteen of these for Fortaleza. (Even suspicious behaviour is reported).

In the past there was a great gulf in Fortaleza between poor and affluent, but because most people now belong to a Nonette there has grown a fraternity between everyone. This sense of commonality has brought people together over many matters and has also helped the drop in crime. Since food is now so plentiful no one need steal because they are hungry.

Another measure Nonettes in Fortaleza have set up with volunteered locals, are watch posts at the points where several Nonette borders meet. Sobral already has these and they have proved very popular, though they have become more help and assistance points than surveillance ones.

Also in the past, Fortalezans, just as people elsewhere, regarded the Polícia with antagonism but there is none towards the communities' police forces. Theirs are representatives from each of a community's nine sub-groups. They mostly just keep an eye on their own patch but if needs be can quickly summon reinforcements. One of every little group of nine is always on standby and it doesn't take long for the entire Nonette to turn out. The other week a building collapsed on the Avenide President Kennedy trapping a number of children. Hundreds turned out marshalled for the rescue.

Another reason why crime has plummeted is that no Nonette wants to harbour anyone who has offended against another Nonettw. It would count as a stain on all the occupants' standing in the eyes of the rest and they would be ostracised. As communities do their own sentencing, victim's and accused's Nonettes' combined, a "Guilty" verdict usually means transgressors atoning in the Pelada.

Yet another reason for the drop in street crime and why so many people have taken to wearing Susem tunics, is their pockets. Being lines of little ones down both sides inside the front makes it possible to carry near everything without need of a bag. However, it didn't take long before 'fashion accessories' were added, and the tunics are often worn with a sense of style. All the same, it is quite an impressive spectacle to see so many people all dressed alike. Also the tunics convey to others that the wearer is a fellow Nonette. Some days as I have travelled, I've not seen anyone not wearing one.

The demand for them had grown so much that it outstripped the resources of the Susem to supply. This led to the spider silk plants and the tunics being produced locally. At first in Sobral's clothing factories but now in Fortaleza's too. The mills' managers making the tunics and spinners of the silk, and having all been vetted by their Nonettes, come to Tabajara for courses on how to make them. Those who pass muster have the Susem's machines go to their factories and install equipment. Though the finishing is still by ordinary sowing machines, the completed tunics are put in a tiny oven-looking appliance and shrunk to matchbox size.

Though generating jobs, tunic manufacturers have affected all the other businesses. Most have enrolled in the Nonettes. Every nine employees entitles a business to one vote in their local Nonette.

Businesses, the Nonettes concluded, being part of the community, it is logical for them to be included and make a contribution to the benefit of all. Many businesses have taken on more people so as to qualify for more votes (and free soufins). Nonettes haven't, for the most part, taken the side of employees in disputes either (not that there have been many reported). Smaller businesses such as shops have joined together so they qualify as well (though some have been in hot debate as to who gets the soufins).

Printing and publishing has also seen a surge in employment. Because of the rise in literacy their sales have soared. Every Area Nonette publishes a weekly newspaper for their 81 communities. And what is interesting is that local Nonette groups take it in turn to edit, so each week's has a fresh approach and enthusiasm doesn't wane into habitualness. They are filled with articles about events in all their communities.

From the Regional Nonettes come daily papers. Ours, the 'Nonette Times of Ceará', which is published and printed in Fortaleza, has different Area Nonettes take it in turn to be its editor for a week. But that apart, it is staffed mainly by students from the University and those of the old "O Povo" newspaper, on whose presses it is printed. (At the time of the exodus O Povo closed down its Ceará operations).

Like the weekly local ones, the Times is filled with news sent in from area Nonettes. But currently its pages are filled with proceedings of the inaugural meeting of the Regional Nonette being held in Fortaleza, representing the 81 area Nonettes. (A second is sitting in São Luis at Maranhão). Everyone is reading what representatives are saying, just as they're listening to Radio Casablanca and watching the TV stations that are broadcasting the proceedings live.

Compared with the past, it is a pleasure to view them. They are so different from the closed door chicanery of the old grandees and marajás which led to people's indifference and to all the corruption. In fact, the unanimous vote that even a hint of corruption attracts automatic interring in the Pelada of the perpetrator, has received widespread acclamation. So did the amendment adding that for males it was a mandatory castration offence as well, or 'Serbian Sever' as it's termed in these parts. Another interesting detail appearing in the papers is that all the advertisers print their Nonette numbers. That they and everyone else have such a number is another fascinating development.

Newspapers are first distributed to each area Nonette, then to their nine sub-groups and from them to their nine Local Nonettes. These then distribute them to their nine sub-groups who then deliver them to their groups of nine and then to their members. It wasn't long before a postal system (the old one having collapsed with the exodus) evolved using the newspapers' distribution network, but in reverse. As a result I'm also now known as 3A6T2,7,5, Rainbow's ends in 6. Though I haven't had a single letter she gets heaps of them, and every day. But that is how everyone, commercial advertisers included, came to have a number. Businesses feel the need to advertise theirs because other Nonettes wouldn't buy from them if they weren't also a Nonette.

It hasn't stopped there. Some people wear their numbers on the shoulders of their tunics. There have been reports of those with amorous intentions using the numbers of the intended as a means of making contact, especially on the dance floor (though lambadering, I gather, isn't what it used to be).

Another topic always filling pages of the Times (details of dubious deeds of the old regime notwithstanding) is the elucidations of the teaching screens, how most of what is imparted is at variance from that once taught at school. But top of the letter writers' topics though is "Who is Lucia?"

Lucia herself, now that her Nonette number is known, receives stacks of fanmail and her picture has appeared in the papers. But the Lucia of the Screens is still unknown. I can understand why so many people want to meet this Lucia because she has made learning a true delight. Her reputation is such that new pupils work their socks off so as to reach the stage when she will talk with them on their screens.

Lucia talks to her students as though she's always known them personally, as though a knowing older sister. Because she gives answers as well as asks for them it is as though one is having a real live conversation. Switching on my screen it is always "Hello Danny, how's your world?" And I always find myself telling her how I feel. If the world's well it's her "Good," then with a whiff of the lemon, "now let us begin the tuition." If I am down in the dumps it's "Oh I am sorry," then, "tell me about it," followed by "do this...try that," then the whiff of lemon and "now let us begin the tuition."

But there are times when Lucia can be firm, hard even, but she does so in such a way that I have never felt irked, only inadequate. Like the time I failed my English enunciation, it was her "I am so sorry but I cannot pass you... please try again...I know you can do it...I want you to pass so much." But when the entire village was on 'Structural Design Appreciation' in the run-up to the new building and I was ahead of the rest in understanding emphasising verticals, their juxtaposition of rectangles, the Golden Mean, the Fibobacci ratio (Lucia said this ratio is very important, it is the basis of harmony), spaces between shapes as vital as the shapes themselves, inter-colour correlation, she was egging on with praise from one height of achievement to another. She made me feel on top of the world. (But her "Must try harder" over my Plasmodia practical soon had me back to earth).

I had thought boys and men might make lewd suggestions to Lucia but it has not been the case. Everyone I have met regards her with reverence bordering on sacred. And she is having no small influence on men's behaviour either.

News Bulletin

Top bosses fume at free energy demand snub

The DTI's refusal to agree a 100 percent subsidy on industries' electricity supplies met with furious outburst from Britain's top business leaders yesterday.

CBI boss, George Gardiner said last night: "Unless we are able to compete on a level playing field with our foreign competitors and quickly, British industry is doomed.

"The Government's rejection of our sensible requests is little more than an act of insult and folly. The CBI is coming under enough pressure as it is from its members for a nationwide tax payment strike or non-payment of fuel bills. It is a matter of our members' survival. Also thousands of jobs could be at stake unless action is taken soon."

Gardiner's outburst was made agai backdrop of increasing frustration across in at the government's refusal to give into demands for extradition of Serbo- sheltering in Britain.

But the Cabinet itself is reportedly split ov issue. While the Home Secretary, Claire Sh against extradition others such as D

PM stands firm: 'Serbs and Croats here to stay'

Campbell's latest outburst provokes wave of moral condemnation

By Jessica Wabbitt
In Westminster

THE international standing of the UK's legal system is at sake by supporting the Serbs' and Croats' right to asylum in Britain said Edward Campbell.

He told the Worshipful Company of Ironmongers: "We are living in a world awash with turmoil brought about by the actions of our extraterrestrial visitors. But there are some principles which must not be allowed to change. One of them is the sanctity of British justice, under which a man is innocent until a Court of Law can prove he is guilty.

"If my government accedes to the calls for the extradition of people from the former Yugoslavia and who are peaceably residing in this country without the due course of Law, then the justice will be brought into disrepute. This is a principle I am duty bound to stand by and so is my Cabinet. There is no alternative."

The Prime Minister's remarks were warmly received. However, there were dissenting voices. Alfred Ramsbottom, chairman of Scunthorpe Steel, said: "The man's living in cloud cuckoo land. Up north we've no time for there

As worldwide demand for soufins energy units grows

Argentina ousts Croats

By Polly Portillo
in Buenos Aires

ARGENTINA has expelled all male Serb and Croat adults from the country. Their expulsion follows a raid on the headquarters of Comunidade Ustaste, the Croatian community association.

The raid which was led in person by Buenos Aires' chief of police, Cafa Jeste seized a list of all the names and addresses of Croats resident in Argentina.

The expulsions were announced by Argentina's president, Engano Cannanha. Addressing an estimated 250,000 strong crowd gathered in front of the Presidential Palace in the Plato de Mayo, the president claimed that Argentina was now a 'Croat-free country' and as a consequence qualified for the promised supply of Susem energy

By expelling Croats in exchange for the energy units, President Cannanha has once again exploited Argentineans' perennial desire for something for next to nothing to his political advantage by getting the credit for bringing his countrymen free energy. But Cannalha is not alone in using the expulsion of Croats from his country to gain political advantage.

From Columbia in the north of South America to Chile in the south, both Serbs and Croats have been rounded up and deported. More often than not this has been done so heavily armed police and the military and usually to applauding crowds of onlookers.

Politicians and police chief alike have seen the Serb Croat, soufins energy units as a quick fix in gaining popularity. The normally indifferent South American have been a

Susem make Serb, Croat freedom offer

By Jane Lane

THE SUSEM will release ten enslaved Serbs and Croats for every Serb Croat criminal handed over to Bosnia it was announced yesterday.

This dramatic offer was made in last night's Susem telecast. Showing a sea of countless enslaved Serbs and Croat sweltering in the tropical hell of the Serra Pelada, Susem announcer Rainbow Louis said: There is now no reason

Serbia and Croatia. Hannah Vesna, whose husband, Josef is one of those still imprisoned in the Serra Pelada said: "I call on all the countries who are harbouring these evil wrongdoers to hand them over without delay so that they can face justice for their crimes and so that our innocent menfolk can return to their homes and loved ones.

"Those who shelter these men of evil are as

While the debate of Croats and Serbs versus Susem soufins ra throughout the United States there is a deafening silence from Presid Warren. **Max Jaffa** in **Washington** reports on the growing sto

Warren silent on Serbs

US PRESIDENT, John Warren, still limping from the 'Tonic-water' scandal, appears powerless in settling the 'Serbs for soufins' issue. Proponents of both sides, Serbs Croats and industry alike, accuse him of weakness.

With reports of many Serbs and Croats in the US rushing to apply for citizenship, Jerko Janiz, head of Serbian American Association was in Washington lobbying Congress to uphold America's tradition of providing safe haven for asylum seekers.

Mr Janiz, who is based in the Serb immigrant stronghold of Madison, Wisconsin, was also appealing to Senators for assurances on the safety of Serbs in the US.

He said: "The elected representatives of the United States must realise the consequences of cowing to these Aliens' threats. If we are sent back to Bosnia we will be tortured and killed by spiteful Muslims and other infidels. These calls from people in our homeland for us to return are all tricks designed to fool the American public. They are being made by stoolpigeons and collaborators of the Aliens."

Croatians are also busy lobbying for the right to remain in the US. Gojko Tus, head of Maspok Amerika, the Croat Support Committee in Pittsburgh is also in Washington presenting their case to sympathetic Senators and Congressmen.

More organized than the Serbs in their campaign to remain in the US, the Croats have had no end of political heavyweights to trumpet their cause.

Pennsylvanian Senator Reno Trent, who is the loudest in defence of the Croatians right to remain, said: "Should ever the day pass when the administration of the United States accede to the demands of the Aliens, we will stand condemned by all true lovers of freedom throughout the entire globe. Many of those whom the Bosnian prosecutors seek are in fact American citizens.

"I and many of my fellow Senators are urging the President to maintain these people's basic human freedoms

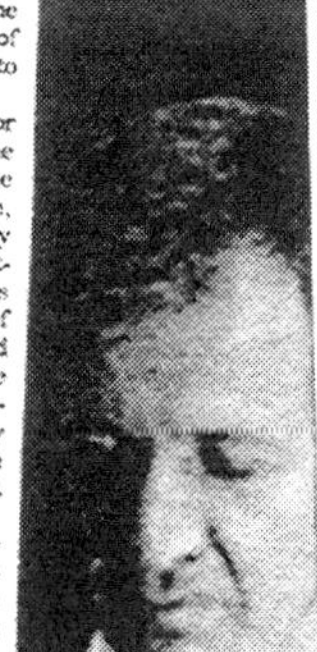

As Edward Campbell holds out against Susem demands

Gleeful frogs hop over 'rostbouefs'

by Jan Mayan in Paris

WITH plentiful supplies of free energy care of Susem supplied soufin energy units, French exporters are now outstripping Britain's it was revealed yesterday.

French businesses large and small have been able to slash prices and beat many of their former overseas competitors hands down. Latest figures suggest that overall, soufin energy units have reduced French industry's production costs by more than18 per cent.

As a result of these savings French manufacturers of bottle openers to high tech computer components have been able to out-price their UK competitors.

To many in French business understand why Briti industry is being so backwa in coming forward. And Poigne, head of Compag Énorme, said: "I cannot s why you British are being stubborn over the extradition criminals. After all you ha not seen in problem in past handing over criminals the Americans as at behest the White House even wh they were innocent.

"Just look at what you Eng are losing. Here in France have these energy units to everything including power all of our motor vehicles. can transport everything ac the country for a fraction what it cost us before."

M Poigne is but one of French companies which

If ever there is such a thing as a 'machismo society, Brazil would always top the tables. But nowadays that cannot be said of the men in this bit of Brazil. In part it's the teaching in the small mixed groups where progress depends on collective endeavour that has helped bring home to men they are not so particularly clever, especially mastering English. Another is in the teaching itself. I don't know if it is intentional or not, or merely accidental, but it's been drummed in with nigh every tuition how the female of every species is cannier and longer living than the male. The debunking during the natural history tuitions on mating started it, especially those about 'Monarch of the Glen and all the other 'monarchs', flying ones included.

I once had the image of the strong stag guarding his harem of hinds and fighting off interlopers. And when they had all loped away beaten he 'had' his hinds. But that's not the case. The reality, so I now understand, is hinds having given all the males a come-on whiff of oestrogen, stand around spectating stag after stag butting the living daylights out of one another and working themselves to a lather of testosteronic anticipation in the process. The last stag still standing, now utterly exhausted with all the thumping but also so thoroughly overexcited with arousal, is unable to resist the hinds nipping between his legs and 'having' him. If, however, any of the hinds fancies a bit of dalliance on the side while awaiting the outcome of all the heaving and thumping, they do. That they trot around in his company afterwards has nothing to do with subservience but tolerance, as if, to coin a phrase much bandied currently by women in these parts, "We love you guys but in a patronising sort of way."

These natural history tuitions also show cock-o'-the-rocks mating, where umpteen males line up to take part in solo singing contests pranced atop a rock, with the hen perched in a tree deciding who has the choicest call, and then flying off with him leaving the rest plainly wilting (this particular tuition has been very popular with ladies I gather).

Another influence changing men's attitudes has been the communities themselves. With the old dominating male hierarchies swept away, women vote for their collective and individual interests as much as their families. Most of the women are voting for other women as representatives, which has resulted in their dominating the Area and thus Regional Nonettes as well as their own local Nonettes.

As Roberto and I have travelled across the region, I have observed an assertiveness, singularly and collectively, among women which was absent before the Nonettes. When men have been uppity, a combined cold shouldering by their community's women has quickly shocked and shamed them into line. One outcome of this is the virtual elimination of prostitution (though the Times has reported increases between men as well as with transvestites).

With women acting ever communally supportive none now have need, either from penury or by pimps, to unwillingly sell themselves. (Procuring is now a mandatory Pelada offence). And no man dare use his physical superiority

Australian Government has pledged to protect Serbs & ats sheltering in the country despite their unpopularity

Keefe's Croat pledge rumpus

Barry Muldoon
In Sydney

Many are calling Premier Keefe's decision on sanctuary and protection for Croats as "Ross's last stand". However, others are saying he never had a particularly big one in the first place. This is a reference no doubt, to the Opposition Labour Party's leader, Greg Bruce's accusations to Ross Keefe's virility.

In the parliamentary debate on Croats in Australia, Bruce called Keefe "As little a pr**k as your p**rk." Keefe's "At least I stuck to the Shelias" rebuttal only infuriated Bruce who was a sheep shearer before entering politics.

The three hour debate on "Croats or soufins" then degenerated into the usual colourful exchange of insults between the two leaders including mutual accusations as to their pedigrees and carnal relationships with a wide range of Australian wildlife. However, in the closing minutes of the parliamentary session the debate actually turned to the government's motion for the Croats staying, and was passed by a majority of four votes.

Although deeply unpopular with most Australians, the coalition Liberal Government's decision was influenced by its need to cling to power. Its majority depends on the votes of two South Australian National Party MPs who represent constituencies with large numbers of Croat immigrants.

Numerous newspapers and television stations have accused the Croat community of sheltering 'Holiday Militiamen'. These are Croats normally resident in Australia, some actually with Australian citizenship, who have travelled to the former Yugoslavia, fighting with the Croatian militias in Bosnia then returning to Australia with their ill gotten gains.

One of the MPs, Kevin Kriv, boasts almost daily to having Keefe's coalition government "by the nuts" over the Croat issue. However the Australian Premier is likely to now come under increasing pressure from industry and the unions to rescind his agreement with

Croat and Serb women give thum up to Susem off

Aliens urge handover of fugitive Serb and In innocent to go free in 'Ten for one offe

By Phill Newman

GOVERNMENTS across the world came under increasing pressure last night to expel Serbs and Croats accused of war crimes to Bosnia.

This follows yesterday's Susem telecast announcement that ten innocents to go free in exchange for one wanted for war crimes.

Numerous ... tries back the Susem offer.

A spokeswoman for the communities in the Croatian capital of Zagreb said: "Those we seek are not petty crooks but those who have committed crimes against humanity."

British experts think there are a least 500 Serbs and Croat fugitives in Britain. Dr Roger Penrose, Head of Slavonic Studies at Sheppey University, Levs... down, said: "If ...

number is more tha... Add to that number must be a least a... 2-300 sheltering with... and Serb sympath... However, if the numb... first generation i... grants from these fo... countries were added number would come thousands.

"If only a fraction of th... were hand...

Sheikhs face 'doom'

By Nathan Bowles
In Hutur

SHEIKH OB Harabh, ruler of the tiny Gulf State of Hutur, predicted economic chaos following plummeting oil prices in the wake of the latest Susem offer of free soufin energy units.

The Sheikh and other Gulf oil producers have cause for alarm - not only for personal fortunes but for their positions as rulers as well.

The Sheikh's personal jet is ready for immediate take off. He has already evacuated ... family to London, follov... riots in nearby Bahrain ... student protests in Oman.

The Gulf is not the only region to be affected by the collapse of the oil usage. But it is more dependant than elsewhere for its income on oil. The prospect of the Gulf states' collapsing into anarchy has filled many outside the region with foreboding of the knock-on consequences.

It is estimated that there are upwards of ten million expatriate workers in the Gulf. It has been a major source of income for countless foreign dependents around the world. Should these remittances now dry up, ...

US business leaders decr Pres. Warren's ditherin

From Tyler Dorbin
In Washington

Business leaders across the United States are expressing increasing anger at what they see as unwarranted delays in repatriating renegade Serbs and Croats to Bosnia.

Scores of US manufacturers claim that unless they have access to the promised Susem energy ...

The big three car makers and the car workers union, the UAW, say that unless their plants receive Federal and State rebates off their energy costs, they faced closures and layoffs.

UAW president Walt Grunther said: "Unless [President] Warren agrees to send these Serbs back to where they belong and quickly, we will all suffer. It makes no sense for these un... expelled is no less voracious.

Sam Loughton CEO of the Santa Clara County Chamber of Commerce and representative of the area's computer manufacturers, is worried his members will lose out to foreign competition.

He said: "East Asia, India and all those nations have never had Serbs or Croats so it was easy for them to comply with the Susem and get their energy units.

Farbin staff in sudden Susem snatch shock

By Nicola Kay

An estimated 3,500 of IG Farbin's staff were abducted by Susem Gurkhas aided by Alien weaponry in a sudden raid on their Berlin headquarters building.

Farbin's staff were shown in last night's Susem telecast standing on the edge of Serra Pelada.

The telecaster said their abduction was in response to Farbin's refusal to pay repatriation for supplying the poisonous Furdos chemical to the former Croatian regime. She added that Farbin staff would be returned if the company paid repatriations with-from top executives to security and maintenance staff.

German police and military were powerless in the face of the Susem assault on the 30 storey Gleichschaltung Haus. Eye witnesses said a huge Susem 'station buster' craft suddenly appeared through the clouds directly above the building. As it did so, hundreds of smaller Susem craft flew from its sides. They circled the building and in turn emitted countless numbers of the Susem's feared 'stinging wasps' which chased away onlookers from the Niemoller Plein, the huge square in front of the building.

Herman Stressman, an oil broker whose office overlooks the square, witnessed at first hand the Susem attack, and to the front doors. With them are many of those wasps. They then disappeared inside the IGF and soon there are many bangings and boomings. Soon the planes are flying away but there are more of them coming with more men and wasps are racing out of them. This is happening again and again, 10, 12 times, maybe more.

"There is then some time when there are no planes but it is only a short while, then they are coming again. This time no one is going from the planes but coming to them instead, there are very many people including women. All are taken into the planes and they are flying away with them."

Later in the day, after the ... by the company's employees who had fled the sprawling complex of chemical plants throughout the Ruhr. Union representatives during the day have been pressing for urgent meetings with the Farbin board to respond to the Susem's demands for half of the chemical giant's profits.

Company sources say that Farbin's boss, Max Amman, is resisting moves to agree to the Susem demand that the company pays them half of last year's profits.

The unions are also demanding a full and independent investigation into all of Farbin's dealings with the former Yugo regimes. Similar calls have been voiced throughout the day to industries right across Germany.

against a woman any more either. A fortnight ago when a man in Baturité did, by beating his wife, the women of his community dragged him out and gave him a whipping. All of them did, including his mum, and some of the men joined in as well. Then they had him, or what was left, so the Times article said, packed off to the Pelada.

With primary educational achievement entitling enfranchisement, the electoral influence of children has also dented the power of old-time males. Because children have direct involvement in their community's affairs, it in turn has a direct interest in their children's wellbeing. Also, because children are busy the day through with learning they have no time for crime either. Despite all the other measures this has probably been the biggest positive contributor to the drop in villainy.

While everyone is filled with heady enthusiasm for the freedoms, involvements, boons and benefits the Susem have brought, it sometimes seems that the Susem themselves are forgotten. As with the Gods on Mount Olympus, the Greeks knew they were there but nonetheless lived their lives in an everyday sort of way. (Reinforcing this of course, us in Tabajara and Pedro's men apart, oh and the crew of the Tonnant, no one has actually seen the Susem). The things the Susem are up to, while fully reported in the papers and on the TV, are outside the day to day lives of most. But here in Tabajara it's very different.

Almost from the moment the Susem arrived I had said, more so to Paceillo, that they couldn't just come to Earth and start throwing their weight around. It would upset people, there would be uproar and trouble. Though there's been more than enough of all that, it is their reasoning, particularly Paceillo's, which is so confounding. I have lost count the times I have told the Susem of the difficulties and consequences involved implementing their 'proposals'. Righting some of the wrongs in Bosnia was fair enough but it's the chain of other events they have set off.

My every reply to Paceillo's 'suggestions' has met with (to paraphrase her) "It makes no sense for such things to be perpetuated, they are detrimental to humans, other creatures and the planet in general. You humans claim not to want them yet nothing happens. Just because humans are currently stewards of the Earth it does not mean they can do as they wish with it. While we Susem are here searching for Pa-tu we are also in a position, have the time and wherewithal, to right some of these matters so that humans and everything exists in harmony."

It has been in vain that I have told her countless times that history is littered with sadness wrought by 'do gooding. It's never worked, never will, and to just leave things alone. They will sort themselves out in the end, if for no other reason than they always have.

Though I am sure Paceillo listens to all I say, she possesses a particularly human-like quality, in that she takes no notice of any advice unless it coincides

Dramatic Susem offer

FREE POWER FOR ALL!

"Handover all your Serbs and Croats anc[...] we'll give you unlimited energy for free

By TOMMY JASON and POLLY EASTERN

THE world has been made an offer it cannot refuse - unlimite[...] and pollution-free energy. And it's for free. The only conditi[...] being that fugitive Serbs and Croats and their sympathisers a[...] handed over to the Bosnian authorities to face trial.

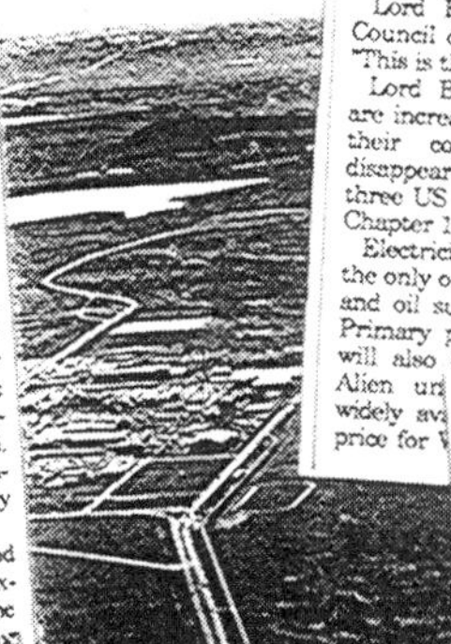

In a change from the past format, in last night's Susem telecast, announcer Rainbow Louis was replaced by Daniel Collins. Not seen since the first Susem broadcasts in April, Collins said abundant supplies of the Susem energy units - soufins - would be delivered to all those countries which sent Serbs and Croats in their midst back to Bosnia for questioning.

The Susem's offer of free energy units comes on top of their earlier one offering to exchange Serb and Croat internees in return for those also wanted for war crimes. How widely this latest offer is taken up will depend of course on the declining number of individual governments resisting the Susem's demand. But none are likely to be able to withstand popular clamour for the energy units.

The British government is now bound to end its resistance in agreeing the extradition of Serb and Croat thugs in the

GOODBY[...] FUEL BILLS

By JENNA COPELAND

[...]EE electricity for all was [...]omised last night by the [...]sem. Just handover criminal [...]rbs and Croats the Alien's [...]nouncer said and everlasting [...]sem power units will be [...]ilable to all.

[...]fficient units will be delivered for [...] office, factory and home the world

power all of our motor vehicles as well. Those who already have these units - they're actually called "soufins" - sing their phrases.

"They've saved me thousands," says factory boss Robin Coats who runs a Leicestershire hosiery company. "My only cost has been employing security guards to stop them from being nicked. But now, if the government gets its finger

will not even be that," he s[...]

The same views are ech[...] "Hand over the Serbs [...] justice and let us have ou[...] But will the government [...] demands?

FULL STORY: PAGE

Power companies i[...] energy units offer collapse shock

By George Lansdale
Energy reporter

Energy chiefs around the world were reeling from the Susem's Wednesday evening announcement of unlimited supplies of their power units.

Lord Brown, Chairman of the Council of Energy Suppliers, said: "This is the end of the end."

Lord Brown says his members are increasingly resigned to seeing their companies and industry disappearing: "Already we know of three US majors who are filing for Chapter 11 protection," he said.

Electricity generators will not be the only ones to suffer. Natural gas and oil suppliers will also be hit. Primary producers of oil and [...] will also [...] Alien u[...] widely av[...] price for [...]

down more than a staggering $4.00 on the day.

Eric Huggins, of energy industry consultants Pile and Long, said: "The energy industries, producers and suppliers alike are for all intents finished. The best any of them can hope for is that governments step in with aid. For example they could offer to pay the companies to keep their generating and distribution capacity on a care and maintenance basis.

"Alternatively they could underwrite the companies' credit liabilities. But it is my view governments would be hard put to single the power companies out for 'special treatment' [...]

Few tears for energy 'barons'

BY LIZA MCFARLAND
BUSINESS EDITOR

HOW many people will pay their gas and electricity bill once they have soufin energy units? That is the question taxing John Souter CEO of Central Utilities (CU).

When asked yesterday how many of CU's consumers with soufins could be expected to pay, he bemoaned: "On past experience there will be a high percentage of defaulters."

Souter acknowledged that even threatening CU's erstwhile consumers with legal action was not a practical option for the company. He said: "The Courts are still snarled up with actions against existing owners of soufins. Legal action is expensive and time-consuming and [...]

be bankrupt."

However, there is likely to be little sympathy among CU's customers for Mr Souter or any of the other 'fat cats' of the power industry. Vicky Sylvester, chair of CU Small Investors Association and a CU customer herself, said: "As far as I and my fellow members are concerned, Souter and all his ilk can stuff their threats right up you know where. We have all lost our investments in CU but at least we will see something of our money back by not paying our bills."

Other members of Ms Sylvester's committee said if Mr Souter and his fellow directors were concerned with CU's wellbeing, they should repay the more than £5,000,000 they have paid themselves over the past year.

power industry baron[...] there are others who wi[...] suffer from the industry[...] demise. And they are mo[...] of us. Securities broke[...] William Holliday, wi[...] investment house Conwe[...] and who specialised [...] utilities shares, said: "[...] the pension and insura[...] companies had huge p[...] folios in power compan[...] and other related inv[...] ments. Their demise [...] mean both these produ[...] pensions and insuran[...] will fall in value.

"But with an ave[...] family making a d[...] saving of at least £2,00[...] annum in fuel bills [...] personal transport co[...] will mean a pro[...] upfront net saving [...] least half that sum. [...] longer term it is not e[...] access the full impact [...] full installation of [...] across the UK. Ho[...] energy consultants [...]

Britain isolated [...] Serb-Croat issu[...]

By **Lisa Simpson**
Ethics reporter

BRITAIN stands isolated in Europe and the rest of the world in its policy towards Croats and Serbs seeking asylum from Bosnia.

With the United States set on abiding by the Bosnian Prosecutors and Susem calls for those wanted for War Crimes to be extradited, Britain and Australia are the only countries refusing to [...]

However, despite the Prime Minister Edward Campbell's proclaimed steadfast defence of the Serbs' and Croats' right to stay, there are signs the Government's policy may be softening. The Home Office said yesterday that its asylum policy was "under review in the light of changing events."

Sources close to the Home Secretary said: "Nowadays 'never' means 'shortly' as circumstances warrant it." The DTI is known to be keen in "resolving this matter quickly and pragmatically". This has been widely interpreted as meaning it wants the Serbs and Croats to go and go quickly.

In the light of the EU ruling - for each member state to make its own decision on whether or not to repatriate Serbs and Croats back to their home countries.

Meanwhile many of Britain's EU partners have [...]

with what she's already planned to do.

The Serb and Croatian men refilling the Pelada and breaking down the dams is an example of her logic and how one thing leads to another. The dam's accumulated silt fertilising reforestation of the surrounding areas led Paceillo to reiterate her 'suggestion' that it was sensible not to deforest at all. Her continual contention was that forests are being wasted by needless exploitation, the planet was being damaged and humans had no right to remove, but responsibility to conserve. Of course I pointed out to her, and at length, that land clearance is needed for farming, timber plays an important part in everyone's life, it is vital to the world economy, and logging occurs on such a wide scale it would be impossible to stop, let alone permanently. Logging and clearing has now ended, everywhere.

Those who didn't stop soon enough quickly found themselves whisked off to the Pelada for a spot of reforestation. These arrivals as with the others have enabled another matched number of Serb and Croat men to go home. Their return led to cries, from the wives of the men still in the Pelada, for countries harbouring Serb and Croats to hand them over so that their men could also go home, especially after Rainbow announced the "Send one, get ten back" special offer. This was made the more appealing when, on Tearo's suggestion, Rainbow announced the sending of abundant supplies of soufins to Serb and Croat cleared zones.

Everywhere, with the exception of Britain, America and Australia, swiftly discovered reasons why their reticent Serbs and Croats should return home, and promptly put them on planes bound non-stop for Bosnia. More of those remaining in the Pelada then went home. The cries of Croat and Serb wives still bereft grew shriller. So did those of the soufinless in the intransigent countries.

In the US President Warren, still politically bruised from Tonic-water, wavered and shuffled responsibility to the individual states, many of whom at once flew their subdued Serbs and Croats back to Bosnia. Britain also began to waver but Australia stayed steadfastly resolute. And this is how, in part, the new animals came to Ceará and soon to Tabajara.

Another reason for the new animals are the vanqueiros of the Sertão. Originally they saw no need or benefit joining the Nonettes but encountering the Brazilian military barrier bestrides the trails to their southward seasonal grazing had many change their minds.

The vanqueiros used the southern slopes of the Sertão for fattening their cattle before selling them to the stockyards along the Rio São Francisco. While near nomadic, most of them hailed from Ceará or neighbouring Paiuí and passing through the military cordon meant there would be little chance of return.

As the land to their north was then dry, the vanqueiros turned back hoping to sell their cattle in the coastal cities. At first they grazed their herds on fields of abandoned latifundios in the south but these were soon depleted. In the vanqueiro's drive north many of their animals died. Though the oasis

Warren wavers and waives responsibility for Serbs to States

Warren passes 'SerboCroat problem' to each of 50 individual states to resolve

by Bernadette Arnold
in Washington

THE US Justice Department announced yesterday that only Federal Territories, such as Porto Rico, come under the jurisdiction of the Government.

Widely seen as passing the buck on the thorny issue of Serb and Croat extradition in return for Susem energy ... US President John ... Government cannot disregard the long and established rule of 'States Rights'. Therefore each individual state legislature must decide on their own individual course of action."

For many Serbs and Croats in the US this is a body blow. Both California and Philadelphia, who have large Croat communities, are likely not just to expel these communities but insist they are deported directly to Bosnia. ... the extent Serbian and Croatian atrocities committed in Bosnia. Fuelling this anger has been a galaxy of business and power consumer lobby groups.

US business sees itself as being put at an unacceptable disadvantage to foreign competitors, especially fellow NAFTA partners Canada and Mexico, both of whom already are receiving soufins.

Domestic consumers however, see the soufins as an opportunity of making significant savings to their ... US industry than there is with the effects on the day to day maintenance of their standard

UK Serbs and Croats to go

By Lisa Simpson

IN A dramatic policy U-turn, the Home Office last night announced that all Serbs, Croats and their sympathisers named by the Bosnian Prosecutor and the Susem would be sent to Bosnia.

The Home Secretary Claire Shaw, reading from a prepared statement said: "In accordance with the Government's wish to be in accord with our EU partners, and following the European Court of Justice's advice, the following has been decided.

War crimes charges

"All nationals of the former Yugoslavian states and those associated with them, be requested to acknowledge in full the requests of the Bosnian Prosecutor's Office and present themselves to it for questioning as to their ...

Ms Shaw also said that the wanted Serbs and Croats had only be asked to go to Bosnia after receiving firm assurances from Bosnian Prosecutors that those sent from Britain received a "full hearing and if relevant, a fair trial."

Immediate extradition

She also said the Serbs and Croats would be accompanied by a team of legal experts from the Home Office to ensure that there was "fair play".

'Fair play' promised

Yesterday evening the Croat Centre in Clapham was heavily boarded, although there appeared to still be people inside the building. It was a similar picture at the Serb Community Centre in Ladbroke Grove. Police, some appearing to be armed be armed, gave no-

With Susem spacecraft sighted off its coasts, Australia's Govern... tendered its resignation yesterday Barry Muldoon in Sydney repo...

Keefe's firm stand sag...

A WEEK ago they billed the Australian prime minister's majority vote in the debate of his Yugo-immigrant policy as 'Keefe's Last Stand'.

At the time, the opposition leader, Greg Bruce's riposte that it wasn't a particularly big one was greeted with mirth. Yesterday his comments were seen as prophetic.

But now, with the Government losing the Opposition's no confidence vote and resigning, the remarks are not as to the size of Keefe's stand but as to its firmness, or rather lack of.

Other commentators however, are saying Keefe's firmness was ruptured by his wife Madge.

Frequently the butt of many jokes, the dominance of Mrs Keefe over her husband appears to actually have had a deciding influence of the prime minister's change of heart.

Two days ago when Madge Keefe attended the 'Salute to Des O'Conner Concert' at Sydney's Opera House she was greeted to a chorus of hisses and boos from the audience. This it is said infuriated her so much that it brought about Ross Keefe's decision to resign.

The announcement by the Susem to apprehend the Serbs and Croats sheltering in Australia is thought to be merely an incidental to Keefe's decision to step down ...

US Airforce in Serb-Croat airlift expulsion

By John Dexter

THE USAAF's entire fleet of Galaxy transporters is being made available to airlift Serbs and Croats, said President Warren.

Pennsylvania has already announced it will take up the Airforce's offer.

In Pittsburgh alone, police are said to taken 40,000 Croats into custody. However, complaints from civil liberties groups against the Croat round up have been muted.

There has been widespread anger in the US against both Serbs and Croats for their countries' atrocities against Bosnian Muslims. This anger has come to the fore on several recent occasions, with crowds urging the police on in their arresting of nationals from the former Yugo states. There has been mention of the similarity to the US rounding up of Japanese Americans in WWII but this has been hotly denied by authorities. Edward Phillip-Scott, ...

Farbin boss ousted

Bert Russell
in Berlin

Amman sacked

Farbin to pay EM 2.63bn fine in exchange for employees' release

Furdo B production to halt

Full investigation of company's dealings promised

FARBIN'S boss Max Amman was summarily sacked yesterday by the German chemical giant's Board of Governors. A statement from the company read: "The Board of Governors IG Farbin has received a request from Herr Amman to relinquish his post as Director. We have acceded to his wishes."

Farbin's board also announced an immediate payment of EM 2,630m - representing exactly half of the company's past year's profits - towards reconstruction in Bosnia. The board acknowledged the payment was being made in the anticipation of its staff abducted from Farbin's Berlin headquarters by the Susem, them to Germany without "undue delay".

The board also announced that an independent team of experts had been appointed to investigate Susem and Bosnian claims that Farbin's products had been used illegally in the former Yugoslavia and other parts of the world including Burma and Western New Guinea. It also said that further investigations into all the company's dealings with third parties would be urgently investigated and its findings be made public.

Farbin's response to the Susem's actions is widely seen as an attempt to cleanse its stables of any murky activities in its past and to make Amman a scapegoat for them.

The summary dismissal of its long serving boss and without any mention of compensation is indication of Farbin's acute embarrassment in leaving itself open to Susem action and in a way - the abduction of its staff, including several directors - which would cause it the maximum difficulties.

The Susem abduction of Farbin's staff has sent shudders not just though German industry but that of other countries throughout Europe and elsewhere. Similarly, Farbin's response is also seen as being a benchmark for others to follow. German industry, barely recovered from the Euro-slump, is likely to be badly affected by any reduction of its capital resulting in paying any Susem 'fines'.

Erich Schrödinger, head of the Bavarian Employers Federation, and one of the Germans most heavily affected said: "Things can only go downhill further if we continual to ignore these Susem demands.."

The longer term effects of Farbin's admission of que

pools (an outcome of the Susem irrigation network) proved irresistible to the vanqueiros' cattle, the communities' managing them as part of the region-wide programme of rehabilitation of the indigenous flora and fauna, obliged the vanqueiros to move on. More cattle died and by the time the survivors reached the coast they were near skin and bone. Worse, the markets there were glutted with a one-off influx of fattened cattle from the abandoned fazendas of eastern Amazona and no one wanted the vanqueiros' animals, not even for their hides. Facing destitution the vanqueiros readily accepted proposals put to them through the Nonettes by Milophinia.

When I once had occasion to see her, Milophinia had said cattle with their dung and hard hooves harmed the Sertão and their numbers were detrimental to the land. My mentioning they were a way of life in these and other parts, and people depended on them as source of food and materials, was met with her, "They are an alien species artificially introduced." Then she added "If animals are needed for food, have animals suitable for the land rather than foolhardily change the land to suit them."

She deluged me with data regarding "integrated reciprocity of the environment's wastes disposal." "Beetles in the Sertão, for example," she had said, "removed to eat the spherical dung pellets of the deer which once lived there. Because these beetles quickly cleared this dung new grass was able to grow. However, they are unable to remove cattle dung. Species evolved to remove their dung cannot exist in the Sertão. Because it rarely rains there, cattle waste stays. Even when dried its weight inhibits dispersal by the wind so it still stays on the land. Grass beneath it dies and new growth is stopped. Bereft of this binding protection the ground desiccates, fissures and only deep rooting scrub can grow. Bovines with their hooves further exasperate deterioration in pounding the dried soil into the degradation of dustiness."

I had said there were many mouths to feed and they are perennially partial to meat, especially the hoofed. But Milophinia said "Errors need correcting and animals suitable for the terrain of the Sertão should replace those demonstratively not. In a like way, if there is a wish for more animals for eating, it is wiser to introduce forest dwelling species than to remove the forests, for such animals will produce more food than is possible from the land once the forest has been cleared."

She then outlined the ideal animals best suited to the dryness of the Sertão and the moistness of rainforests. They were uncannily like the apoodas I had seen on La-ra. "The further they are removed genetically from their consumers the better," she had also said.

But it was Farbin's refusal to pay what Rainbow announced they should which set in train the new animals' arrival. Colonel Tambassing's men raided Farbin's headquarters in Berlin. They transported its entire staff, including several directors, to the Pelada. Farbin summarily sacked its boss, promptly paid over every pfennig due and their employees then went back to Berlin (with all the other culpable companies swiftly settling up with Jacques Foressier). This success, again with Tearo's urging, had Paceillo 'suggesting' it was repeated against the Australians.

Their government's intransigence in not handing over their Serbs and Croats was due in no small part to the voting inclinations of two MPs from Adelaide who had large numbers of Croats in their constituencies. Though these votes were vital in maintaining Premier Ross Keefe's government's majority, he made a grave strategic error in not sending back his Serbs and Croats. He should have known never to argue with a woman, especially one in a position of power. Though being an aged Australian male it was not entirely unexpected. But when he announced "Under no circumstances whatsoever will my administration be cowed by outsiders," his fate was sealed.

Paceillo, when I relayed the World Service's news item on Ross Keefe's stand, became as agitated as when she had said things nuclear were going to be going. But before the first tocans could land, Mr Keefe's Liberals were no longer in power.

But the tocans having arrived and though with no Serbs or Croats to tranship, only soufins to shower down, provided Milophinia the opportunity she had been waiting for. As so often, I winced when I learnt the lengths Colonel Tambassing's men had gone to. But Milophinia's retort was that only a mere fraction of those animals being routinely slaughtered were taken. And my "But why do the zoos?" met with her "In their natural habitat these animals are sparse, so sense dictated specimens already in captivity be taken."

And that is how the kangaroos, wallabies and wombats came to Ceará, all 10,000 of them. Most are already hopping about the Sertão (and doubtless dropping their round dry dung). The tree wallabies are undergoing accelerated breeding, and Milophinia says that the first broods will be heading for the forests before the month is out.

There have been so many other Susem escapades that for a while I had doubts if they would be searching for Pa-tu. But when I did pluck up courage to ask Paceillo, apart from her curt "Of course," I was dumbfounded when she said "ever since the last letum wave progenitors (as she still calls things nuclear) were removed." She then, off-handedly added as she went away, "Many of us here are currently engaged continuously in the quest."

Having seen no sign of them searching, be it with machines, on their screens or anything else, I was at a loss to understand. Terbal confirmed what Paceillo said but when I asked how, he added "Preliminary analysis ve now are doing." Irritatingly Chile was playing Argentina and the match had just kicked off (Terbal's become football mad) and he wanted to watch it undisturbed on one of his TVs.

But Menpemelo told me. And as she did, dawning on me yet again was just how advanced is the Susem's understanding of existence. I also began finding out about auras.

83: JAMES

Two thousand kilometres from Rio and many shaken headed "louco louco"s later, I have ended up in this backwater of a coastal hamlet called Tibiaú. Presently I am kicking my heels and half wishing I hadn't come or for having believed in the promises of Márcio Maia.

I met him in Natal 250 kilometres away and rashly accepted his offer to ferry me into Ceará. That I did so and paid him $500 for his services was, on reflection, more out of desperation than sound judgement. I had tried without success to cross the Brazilian military's southern 'front line' from Salvador. Away from the roadblocks, the Sertáo's desert terrain made any would-be attempts on foot easy to spot from the air.

Having failed there I had hoped I could find, even bribe a way through the Brazilian military's eastern barrier. But the recent Susem actions meant that the entire Northeast is under, as the tourist office staff in Natal put it, "Occupação military" and a heavily armed, officious one at that.

In a café next to the tourist office, I met up with a group of ageing American laid-backers travelling south. The army was unsettling them. Among their company was Márcio Maia. He is more Indian than European and how he came to be with them I still do not understand, except to say that he speaks English with a cockney accent claiming to have spent three years working in Stepney. At first when I said I was not travelling south but northwest the Americans shook their heads and Márcio chortled "You're mad my son." But when he gathered that not only was I intent on going north but also willing to pay, he offered to sail me along the northern coast to Ceará.

All the while he couriered me around the army checkpoints on the way to Tibiaú my confidence in him was undimmed. I was also heartened by his continual mention of the sea-going prowess of his brother Chico's jangada sailboat. But when we arrived in Tibiaú I soon had second thoughts.

Chico's jangada is no more than a narrow skiff six metres long with an outsized sail. I have grave doubts as to its seaworthiness. There is barely room for one person, a second leans on an outrigger board, and it reeks of rotting fish. I have reservations about Chico as well. He speaks no English, has staring eyes, never smiles and sports a large knife on his belt. But as the village is so isolated and being an outsider I fear for my safety should I demand the return of my money. Having come so far, however, got so close and spent so much, I am also loathe to turn back.

Chico has been waiting for, so his brother says, a moonless night and a good east wind. He also says that there are many Navy ships patrolling off the coast and they are now ramming boats rather than boarding them. He also keeps saying we will sail soon.

Susem's showering soufin units causes cheerful chaos

y George McGraph
lew energy reporter

MUCH OF Britain ground o a halt yesterday as it received tens of millions of Susem soufin energy units.

The soufins, promised two days ago by Londoner Danny Collins, were delivered right on cue beginning in the early hours of the morning.. From the Shetland Islands to Lands End the entire length and breath of Britain was showered with a bounty of a boundless supply cost-free and pollution-free energy.

For the first time since Britain's nuclear power stations were removed in May, all of the country was treated to the spectacle of countless blue luminescent foam carpets

Only those people in the extreme south west of Cornwall actually had a chance of actually see the giant Susem spacecraft delivering the energy units.

No sooner had the first carpets begun descending than people in their millions bean rushing to gather up the units. Soon wherever the carpets came to earth traffic ground to a complete halt. And it was just in the built-up urban areas either.

Police forces across the country reported not only had major trunk routes jammed but long stretches of the motorway network as well were affected. However, there have been no reports of any serious accidents as motorists stopped to gather armfuls

Solicitors, judges i[n] soufin scrum shoc[k]

John Bloom
Court Correspondent

LINCOLNS INN FIELDS was the sight of unsightly scenes as members of the legal profession fought with one another as well as passers by for possession of Susem energy units which floated down onto the Fields and neighbouring Inns of Court.

Proceedings at the Royal Courts of Justice also came to a halt as legal officials, including judges rush to gather up the units.

Within minutes of the soufin energy units landing in Lincolns Inn Fields hundreds of solicitors poured from their offices in a frenzied rush to gather them up. The Fields rapidly developed into a wild melee as solicitors fought with one another for possession of the soufins. Many ordinary passers by were caught up in the fray.

'I have never seen such grasping as I saw from these solicitors and barristers'

Carolyn Aish, 24, a technician at the ICR Institute overlooking the Fields, said: "I was on my way to work but on turning into the Fields I was nearly knocked over by all these solicitors charging from their offices to pick up soufin energy units, of which I could see there were

I saw one of these units in the forecourt of our building but no sooner had I stopped to pick it up when this solicitor barged at me crying: "It's mine, it's mine" and attempted to snatch it from me. But when I said it wasn't [his] he immediately demanded my name and address and threatened me with legal action."

Lord Chief Justice Sir Justin Fortheride arrested for fighting

Other passers by who also tried to pick up one of the units were on the receiving end of threats from other solicitors for their possession. Yet other members of the public said that they had witnessed many of the solicitors as well as barristers and judges fighting with one another for possession of the energy units.

Dave Mellor, 58, who sells the *'Big Issue'* around the Inns, said: "You should have seen them. They were like crazed animals. Some of them barristers and judges were still in their wigs and gowns. They were even fighting with one another for the units, rougher than the Wall Game at my old school.

"I've never seen such foul fighting, they were kicking and punching, and their language was downright disgusting," Mr Mellor said. "As soon as one of them had one of these units there was a crowd around trying to snatch it off of him. I have never seen such grasping in my entire life."

Last night, Desk Sergeant Masson of the nearby Snow Hill Police Station, and whose force was called in to break up the fighting, said: A number of people in the vicinity of Lincolns Inn were apprehended for Public Order Offences and committing an affray. Some of the offenders have been taken into custody and are currently helping the Police with their enquiries as to the whereabouts of those still being sought and are still a large."

Top law firm's security personnel sought by police for scaffold poles attack

Later it was revealed by police sources that that those under arrest for their part in the fighting were Chief Justice Sir Justin Fortheride and the entire staff top litigation lawyers DeLay Contest & Settle. Though DC&L's security personnel, the Moses Brothers were still being sought for attacking a rival law firm with sawn-off lengths of scaffold poles.

Sergeant Mason said that a sizeable number of soufin energy units were recovered from the scene of the fighting and are being made to members of the public in return for a suitable donation to Snow Hill Station's Benevolent Fund.

Susem zoo raid[s] puzzle Aussies

[A]lthough Australians are overjoyed, if not relieved [by] the Susem deliveries of soufins, they are also mystifie[d b]y the Aliens' thefts from many of the country's zoo[s]

[Z]O and park keepers are at a loss to [exp]lain the nature of the Susem's thefts, [ex]cept they appear to be made to order.

[...]as Whitlam, head keeper at Murdoch-[...]stbury Zoo said: "It doesn't make a lot [of] sense to me. They came here and took [...] the Bennetts Tree kangaroos but they [...] my Tasmanian Tigers alone and the [...]tail Possums which are pretty rare."

[N]ed Kelly, joint owner the Packer Zoo [Pa]rk in Coolangatta, Queensland, 3,000 [kil]ometres north of Tasmania, is just as [my]stified by the Gurkha's actions. He said: [T]hey've had all my wombats, and the [pa]rk's not a wallaby to its name, black-[...]ped, whiptails, rocks, red necks.

"Even the breeding colony of Lumholtz's [tre]e kangaroos have gone, they've had the[m]. The koalas are still here but maybe [th]at's because they've got lice, though all [th]e paederast and possums have gone and [th]ey had halitosis."

Stranger still is the hunting of thousands [of] wild kangaroos and wallabies by the [S]usem. Matilda Withy owner of the God' [...]wn cattle station at Bundooma, near [A]lice Springs, saw the Susem craft in

She said: "They rounded up all the [...] for miles. And faster than you can say [...] jumped a swagman", their little fly[ing] thingies had all the 'roos hopping up [...] their plane thingies. They even took the greys from over in the Rolf Ha[...] Memorial Park."

Further south at the G'day sheep do[...] near Wagga Wagga in New South Wa[les] sheep ranger Kerry Mckenzie also saw [...] Susem machines catching wildlife. [...] said: I was having a bit of tucker whe[n I] saw them. At first I thought it was [...] corks getting in my eyes, then that I w[as] going crook.

"But then I saw my pet dingo, B[...] running from them and for a whil[e I] thought he was a goner. But they flew [...] over him and on down to the billab[ong] where Digger Patterson has his cam[p] and, for a while I think they're going [...] them or maybe the pack of shelias Digg[...] brother Les keeps down there. There'[s a] heck of a din and I see the kookabu[rras] flying up from the gum trees, then all [of a] sudden, hopping down the paddock is [a] bunch of 'roos. But before I can [...] "Streuth" I am bowled over by this swa[...]

World fishing flee[t]s suffer Susem attack[s]

By Jason Herring

THE world's deep sea trawler fleets were attacked by Susem craft yesterday. Many of their crews were believed to have been taken prisoner. Navies proved helpless in repelling the attacks or to come to the rescue of crews from being taken captive.

A Susem telecast night, showing seamen being driven down the Serra Pelada pit claimed trawlers had ignored the warning to cease deep-sea fishing had been given in May. Many environmental and fishery scientists applauded Susem's actions.

Tens of thousands of fishery ships, worth billions were plucked from the world's oceans by giant Susem craft and dumped ashore often far inland. Virtually all of Britain's deep water fleet, consisting of 187 deepsea trawlers worth an estimated sum of US15bn were

Susem attack fores[try]

IAN BURNES
[WO]ODLAND CORRESPONDENT

[TH]E SUSEM yesterday [att]acked forestry and timber [ind]ustries. Tens of thousands [of] foresters were abducted by [the] Aliens' forces.

[S]tock and commodity [ma]rkets across the world were [thr]own into disarray as the [ext]ent of the Susem attacks [be]came known. Prices of many

environmentalists are applauding the Susem's actions.

Forestry and land clearance around the world came to an abrupt halt as scores of the huge Susem 'station busters' craft scoured the world's forests searching out for anyone felling trees or clearing woodland. With each craft were hundreds of their smaller attack planes and all-seeing surveillance aerial spy craft.

among the mos[t] affected regions. [...] State officials repor[t more] than 5,000 fore[st] lumberjacks were [...] believed abducted [...] Susem backed Gu[...] stinging hornet attac[k...]

Kent Walton, she[...] logging town of Be[...] Cascades, issued a [...] yesterday pleading [...] Susem to end their at[...]

At first Menpemelo was reluctant, saying “I do not know if you are really ready to understand.”

“Try me,” I said. And with the patience of Job, she did. And tried I was.

“Consider entities not in terms of dimensions but contexts,” she began. “My hand exists in the first context of length. Its length is within the second context of area and the third of its volume. All these, while observable, are embedded in the fourth of time, which is not (and pointing to my watch), but evidence of its presence and motion is. These four, familiar to you humans are embedded in a further one, which according to our analysis of your investigations (I took this to be Terbal’s Internetting of Earthly scientists) is not. Yet evidence of its presence, like that of time, also abounds.”

“Oh,” I said.

“Consider relativeness too. The density of an entity is consequent on the closeness, size and composition of Tertiary wave, frothicle clusters, molecules of which it is composed, and the centrifugal Secondary wave resonances effecting upon them, or ‘gravity’ as you on Earth term it. Yet, as I mentioned previously, even between the densest of clusters such as osmium or platinum there are proportionally great distances.

“Nitrogen comprises three-quarters of the Earth’s atmosphere, yet it (she flattening her hand as though to indicate it) is so sparse in clusters there is not usually consciousness of its existence. Air is denser at sea level than the elevation at Tabajara. Yet 50 kilometres higher than here the atmosphere is many times thinner still. Another 50 kilometres higher again and it is barely present at all. But there is still sufficient remaining at such height, and as you witnessed, to cause hen-gers and much else entering from outside the planetary atmosphere to burn with the friction it generates.

“As you gathered during your Plasmodia tutorial (How did she know this? I thought) the genius Utricularis (I was as surprised she should know slime mould’s proper name) being a metre in diameter is your planet’s largest single celled lifeform, yet this soft-tissued creature can penetrate, travel through and exit many metres of seemingly solid timber.”

I said nothing but nodded and knew she knew her slime moulds.

“It is not possible,” she continued, “to measure simultaneously both the precise position of an entity in motion and (and she stressing the “and”) its momentum. But it is possible to define the parameters within which it is situated and its movement occurring.”

She slid the belt from around her tunic and flicked it snake-like through the air and added “Although the ripples appear to travel they have not moved at all, I am still holding the end of the belt. The movements of Secondary and Primary waves are similar. It is the energy in them which causes their movement, their oscillation.” With a swing of her arm she gave her belt a further flick as though to demonstrate the point.

Folding the belt into where the ripples had been, she continued, “One ripple occurred in this part, another here, the third there and so on. I could put each of these waves inside a collection of boxes. So while a wave is a wave, it is also a collection of boxes, contained entities, with each one encompassing the top of the wave, its bottom and all the parts in between. Just as these oscillations (she flicked her belt open again) occur, energy affecting one wave transfers to the next because they are connected, so too are the contained entities. Energy from one automatically transfers to the next and so on."

As she spoke I had thoughts of railway wagons moving into sidings and each one banging against the next. However, as I didn't want to let on I already knew all about this, (in our physics tutorials we have just moved on to doing quantums) I said nothing.

"As you already know," Menpemelo continued, "from your introductory tuition on wave oscillation and energy transmission, the motion I induced in my belt did not end there." To demonstrate the point she had me light a cigarette (weakness induced by worry has had me take up it again). I puffed smoke into the air and she flicked her belt towards it. As the smoke rippled away she continued, "Energy in my belt is being transferred to the air beyond." She then had me stand away and hold out my hankie. She flicked her belt towards it. Though its tip was a foot away the belt had my hankie flutter.

"The energy put into the belt has transferred to the air and in turn to your handkerchief." Changing tack a little she continued. "In Tertiary wave, frothicle dense regions such as your planet, Secondary wave resonations travel slower and at steeper pitches than where Tertiary waves are sparse, such as between galaxies. Yet no matter their speed or pitch, Secondary and Primary waves themselves oscillate in wave formation. Our understanding is that there are three types of waves. The first are scalar waves, and these oscillate on a sometimes wide yet uniform front."

"How wide?" I asked.

"From a galaxy spiral to as narrow as a frothicle grouping," Menpemelo replied. With me images of countless orderly lines of linked-up matchboxes rippling up and down sea wave-wise, she continued, "The second are vector waves. These, though appearing similar in oscillation to scalar waves, emanate from a single point source and radiate outwards from it." With me now images of orderly circles of bobbing matchboxes. Menpemelo next said, "When interaction between these two forms of wave occur, uniformity of one wave's initial modulation is subsumed by the other or they are both dissipated into mutual 'dis-modulation'."

With me now images of the orderly lines and circles bobbing up and down in a melee of jumbled disarray, Menpemelo then said "The third are soliton waves. Unlike the first two, these waves, apart from usually being solitary, do not oscillate as such but propel the context in which they are situated. Soliton waves, apart from possessing the inherent energy to effect this, are powerful, have a vast pitch and travel at very fast speeds."

"How fast?" I asked.

"As fast as instantaneously," she replied. With me now images of my matchboxes speeding over the horizon, Menpemelo then said "In brief, Tertiary waves are always scalar, Secondary waves can be either scalar or vector and sometimes soliton, but Primary waves are always exclusively soliton."

"What about the waves when the tides come in?"

"The land causes the waves not the sea, nor its surface," she said, giving her "oh do be quiet and just listen" look and continuing, "The formation of waves upon the surface of the sea is affected by other waves. Their pitch, oscillation and while perhaps not immediately apparent, are influenced by those of others previously created. It is theoretically possible but difficult and complex in practise to analyse the composition and thus sources of the components and causes of a sea's waves, as well as the time of their formation."

At this point she paused, then said "Come with me." Saying nothing, not even a "Where?" or "what for?" I did.

"Ah, split beam demonstration model you vant?" said Terbal when Menpemelo asked him (it was half-time in the football). "No trouble, vor you ein moment it ist coming." He waggled his fronds, sped off but reappeared seconds later and flying behind him was a sherpal crewed carpet carrying a two foot square box. With a flurry of "Hados" the sherpals raced the box from the carpet to the table beside us. With Menpemelo's "Thank you Terbal," and his "You're velcome," the sherpals and carpet flew away and he drifted back to await the match's second half.

I looked into the open top of the box. It had matt black furry walls and two little mirrors positioned halfway along against opposite sides. A third mirror but half-silvered in vertical strips was positioned midway between them but situated near the near end of an adjoining side, its mirror-side towards the wall where there was a small hole. At the end opposite to this mirror were two small grey plaques. Menpemelo inserted a narrow tube through the hole so that one end was just inside the box. She then pressed the other end of the tube and a torch beam of light shone from it into the box.

"Half of the light," she said, "is reflected back by the half-silvered mirror into the wall, while the remainder passes through it and is shone onto the other two mirrors, each receiving half of the remaining light. They in turn each reflect this light onto the counters positioned on the back wall of the box."

As she spoke I heard little clicking sounds coming from the two plaques. "They are counting the number of wave crests reflected from each mirror," she said. "As you can see, the two reflection beams cross one another and their wave crests are each recorded by the counters on the opposite sides of the box to them. And as you will also notice (and I did) both counters are recording the same numbers. If I now placed a second half-silvered mirror (and she now holding this other mirror in her hand) where the two reflection beams cross, where will the light passing through it go?"

"The same as before, half and half, except that there will be less," I said.

Smiling, she placed the mirror where she said she would.

"Oh," I said, "why is that?"

Woodcutters felled by Susem

By Susan Bumitt and Andrew Duronamoo report from Kota Balu, Saha, Malavsia

LARGE SWATHES OF the Asian forestry industry were attacked by the Susem yesterday.

Forestry workers from Thailand to the Phillipines fled from Susem forces and many thousands are said to have been taken prisoner.

The giant Japanese conglomerate Mituslashi has completely abandoned its massive timber concessions throughout Sabah and Sarawak.

Borneo attacked

Further south, in Indonesian Borneo, or Kalimantan, Susem attacks were reported as being just as severe.

The forests on both parts of the island, which until yesterday were subject to extensive felling, were said to be emptied of all tree cutters

officials claim that more than 10,000 people trapped by the Susem have been taken prisoner.

Japan suffers

Japan, dependant on timber imports for more than 98 per cent of its requirements is likely to be badly hit by abrupt and total cessation of tree felling. Many associated industries such as construction, furniture and papermaking can also be expected to be disrupted.

However, for many of the Japanese companies who have invested heavily in forestry in Borneo and other regions throughout Southeast Asia, the ending of logging could spell disaster.

One of the biggest companies to be affected is Karveupsung, a joint ventu...

'Guilty' companies rush to pay 'Susem fines'

By Shelia Payupp
Business Editor

COMPANIES LARGE and small are rushing to pay over half of their last year's profits to the Susem representative stationed at Villacoblay airport, outside Paris.

Following the Susem's telecast instructions for payment, in US dollar notes, the demand for the greenback has been so great it has seen a rapid rise in its international value.

Fearful of Farbin's experience as well as mounting pressure from their staff's concern for their personal security, companies named by the Susem are faced with little choice than to pay up.

Clayings and Westminster were among a clutch of British banks announcing yesterday that they were making payments to Villacoublay. However, Clayings Chief Executive, Andrew Buxsted, was emphatic in his announcement that the Bank's payment was not in any way an admission of culpability of the Susem's accusations made against it.

The payment of more than a billion US dollars was being deposited with the Susem as a precautionary measure so as to assure the Bank's customers

WORLD SUSEM DIGEST

Dollar billions 'Bosnian-bound'

COMPANY bosses are falling over themselves to pay Susem 'fines' for their dodgy dealings down the Danube with the Serbs and Croats.

International chemicals giant, HELP was one of the first to pay a visit to the Alien's agent at Villcobray airport to pay over half of its last year's profits of $3.2billion. And they paid in cash!

Driven by distressed staff and customers alike Britain big five banks have also been dashing over to France to pay their dues to the Susem Bosnia Fund. However, most have had to take their place in the queue.

Companies queue to cover their wrongdoings

FOLLOWING the Susem abduction of Farbin's staff from its Berlin offices, companies worldwide have been hurriedly reassessing their responses. So far, with a few minor exceptions, all those companies affected have either already paid half of their previous year's profits to the Susem's representative at Villcobray outside Paris, or declared their intentions of imminently doing so.

This corporate volte face has been concern on the part of CEOs for the disruption to their companies' operations as well as share prices. The loss of half of their past year's profits is bound to affect the companies' investment plans to say nothing of future dividends, but market analysts say such outflows can be met by most either from resources or by increased bank borrowing

Foresters' influx will free Croats, Serbs say Susem

COLUMNS of abducted foresters from around the world were shown in last night's Susem telecast being driven into the huge Serra Pelada pit. The announcer, Rainbow Louis said an equivalent number of Serbians and Croatians, innocent of any wrongdoing in Bosnia would be returned to their own communities.

Ms Louis said that the numbers now eligible to return would likely to be more than 100,000. This figure was also taken as indication of the numbers of forestry workers captured in just one day by the Susem attacks. She said the only delaying factor for the Serbs' and Croats' was that there would be a matching Susem approved community for them to return to.

Throughout yesterday there were calls from around the world for the Susem to return the forestry abductees and pleas for their safety. But last night's scenes of the Susem to return the forestry abductees and pleas for their safety

Greens say Susem did fish and humans a favour

By Alistair Ryan
Environmental Correspondent

MANY environmentalists were openly congratulating Susem actions against all the world's deep sea trawler fleets. More that just fish will benefit from the Alien's saving the oceans' depleted fish stocks.

lor said: "While we are obviously wish to see the trawlers' crews safely returned, no one can but be cheered by the Susem decisive move in protecting what remains of the world's ocean wildlife. For many years we and others have said that mindless depletion of sea life has to stop.

"The world's governments have in the past been only to willing to cave into the lobbies of the various fish-businesses. If the huge subsidies that have been continually doled out to these vested interests were directed to those who really needed assistance, then we could

Susem in worldwide attacks on mining

By Anna Kerbang

MINING across the world came to an abrupt halt yesterday in the face of attacks by Susem backed forces.

Thousands of miners were taken captive by their forces. Shares of mining companies plummeted across the world's markets. London's International Metal Exchange saw the prices of metal rocket as news of the attacks became known.

In a Susem telecast yesterday it was announced that the attacks of mines would continue until all mining has ceased

The world was thrown into turmoil as Susem 'station buster' craft attacked countless mining operations. Across the globe mines, opencast as well as under-ground, came to halt as Susem backed Gurkhas took countless thousands of workers into captivity.

From the arctic wastes of Russia to similar ones in Chile, miners fled in terror as news of the attacks spread. But for many of them the news came too late to save them from the clutches of the Susem.

In last night's Susem telecast columns of captive miners were shown being marched into the huge disused opencast Amazonian mine of the Serra Pelada.

IN BRIEF

Nets trap Taiwanese

TAIPEI: Thousands of Taiwanese fled in fear as miles of the "walls of death" fishing nets fell out of the city's skies. Many hapless passer-bys soon became enmeshed in the 30 metre wide nets, long stretches of which contained dead fish.

The nets were those attached to an ocean trawler plucked from the China Sea by the huge Susem 'station buster' space craft. The nets fell over a wide area and were then

Following the latest Susem trawler swoo

Billingsgate gets its chips

By Oliver Crispie

Desperate fish buyers faced with the sudden shortage of supplies were met with a five fold increase in prices at Billingsgate.

Fishmongers were quick to maximise their profits from their remaining stocks. But by 8 o'clock most of the traders' slabs were bare.

Fishmonger Mike Hezza, of Ide and Sons, one of the markets's longest established traders, said: "We've never had so many big buyers in here, supermarkets, hotels even the major processors. They've been going manic and offering silly money. Well we weren't going to refuse them were we? Cleaned out we were within hours of opening, not even single red snapper left."

Fellow fishmonger, Dougie Hogg, who also saw his stocks cleared, said: "It's all very well everyone going on about the extra money we have made, but what they don't realize is that after today we will have nothing to sell. And we have overheads to keep up. All we have left is tankful of eels".

Seafood sellers, Malones were one of the few traders still left with stocks. Their chief salesperson said: "We still have cockles and mussels, and the market for them has now become very much alive, although they have a broad appeal, there is a narrow margin in

And the 'that' was a most amazing occurrence. It was as though the reflection beams coming from the wall mirrors had combined through the second half-silvered mirror and beamed all on to one counter, which was merrily clicking away while the other was quite quiet.

Menpemelo said nothing but instead moved this second half-silvered mirror and placed it a short distance from the mirror which had its beam snatched, and again it was filched and reflected onto the same counter as before. I was as mystified as ever. "Although this phenomenon," she said, has been observed and recorded here on Earth..."

Terbal without turning his attention from the match interrupted with, "Wheeler, John Archibald, Problems of Theoretical Physics, University Press, Salerno, 1984," then promptly waggled his fronds as Peru went one up.

"Its significance, however," continued Menpemelo, "appears not to have been widely grasped. It is as though the waves passing through the first half-silvered mirror know, are informed as to the path they are subsequently to take. An example of," Menpemelo then said, "vector Secondary waves..." and adding as we walked slowly back to where we had been, "...being modulated by scalar waves."

Though still confused I said nothing.

"The surface of the sea," she continued, "exists embedded as an integral part of the sea itself. In the same way so too are the first four contexts of distance, area, volume and time existent embedded within this fifth one."

"What is it called?"

She paused for a moment as though to think, then said "You do not really have a word, ours is 'Harchad'," then pausing again, "Quinth, not fifth, would be your nearest." We walked a little further, me attentive and silent but she also in silence, as though framing thoughts. "It is," she then said, "as if people on Earth perceive existence to be only on one level, the surface of the sea, whereas everyone elsewhere perceives it on two, the sea and its surface. We Susem and others also function on the two levels as though they were separate yet also as if they are one and the same. For example although we communicate to one another, distance transmission is soliton based."

(So that's why no one on Earth has ever heard from 'extra-terrestrials'?)

"Soon after our arrival, as you saw, we took specimen measurements here in Tabajara. The tocans, more so Sieba and Sardon, have conducted subsequent surveys of large sections of the Earth's surface. It is these which are now being diagnosed in the search for Pa-tu."

I'd not a chance to ask "How, what of?" before Menpemelo said "Every event imprints enduring quinth context configurations, or signatures of its existence, occurrence. No matter how transient or continuous these may be, these signatures remain, they are observable. If their imprint configuration is known they can be unravelled from those of others. It is alike to identifying a specific causer constituent of a sea wave. We seek Pa-tu's.

"Beyond your planetary system Pa-tu's configuration was easy to decipher from among those imprinted by other occurrences. This was because there

SINESS NEWS

Trawlermen petition Parliament

im Nautilus
isheries Reporter

THE National Union of Fishermen is to send a delegation to Downing Street demanding that the government negotiates with the Susem to secure the immediate release of their members imprisoned by them. But there appears little the government can do to bring about the men's return.

The NUF's General Secretary, John Tregorran, said: "What has happened to my members is diabolical. The government has a duty to press for their immediate release from that South American hellhole that is the Serra Pelada. These men were going about their perfectly legitimate and historic profession of deep sea trawlermen.

"The government has a duty for the wellbeing of all its citizens. We will be pressing them by any means possible to bring about these men's return", he said.

However, experts believe that short of it itself prohibiting Britain's fishing boats to put to sea, the government ... to do anything for

THOUSANDS FEARED ABDUCTED, HUNDREDS OF CONSTRUCTION PROJECTS HALTED AS

ALIENS ATTACK WORLD'S DAMS

By LAURA JONES

WORLDWIDE raids by Susem forces in the space of 24 hours have brought all dam construction to a halt. Sites in Asia and South America have been the most severely affected.

Last night, in a Susem telecast, many of the thousands of abducted construction workers were shown being marched into the hellhole of the disused Serra Pelada mine.

Three Gorges under threat

In western China, the massive Three Gorges dam project on the Yangtze River was one of the major casualties. The government controlled New ... the Aliens. It also said that work on the massive project had 'temporarily' stopped.

If the Three Gorges project is scrapped, as the Susem have indicated it must, it will be a major blow for China's flood control plans of the Yangtze.

Dam workers held in Serra Pelada

Though the Three Gorge's construction has been controversial it has been seen by the Chinese authorities as a symbol of the country's prowess. However, flood protection apart, the dam's prime ...

International metals markets in turmoil

By Anna Sulphur
City Editor

THE LONDON METAL Exchange saw huge upward movements in the prices of all the world's metal stocks. Three month zinc shot from $1,225 to $2 085 a tonne. Lead, nickel, aluminium all saw similar record highs. Copper rose from $2,200 to over $4,000. The Reuters index jumped 257 points to 2,383, its biggest one day rise. ... metals in the ... a tonne up $0.47.

LME traders were unable to keep up with demand for supplies. All cited the knock on effects of any shortage in any of the world's commercially used metals. Kevin Malcolm, a senior dealer at Redwood Conway said: "Steel, zinc, copper shortages are obvious but it is the other, rarer ones: palladium, cobalt, lithium which are going to hit industry badly." ...

'Fish anger overplayed' - say experts

By Wendy Healy
Socio-economics Editor

THE ENDING of deep sea fishing was welcomed yesterday by food authorities.

'Fish being the riches of the sea' is a myth and always has been: deep sea fishing has never been productive'

Prof. Sharon Whitworth

Most experts on fish stocks are agreed that not only can the world live without deep-sea fish catches but an enforced halt to trawling is good for world food production.

Hull's Dr Alan Mulford

"If the subsidies paid to the trawler fleets by the world's governments", says Dr Alan Mulford of Hull University's Ocean Resources Department, "were directed to terrestrial food production, everyone would benefit. In rich and poor countries alike, farmers, especially those who have fish ... a higher income for their produce. Or alternatively, consumers would be paying lower prices.

Sheppey's Prof Whitworth

Professor Sharon Whitworth of Sheppey University's Dept. of Nutrition Economics, says: "Fish being 'riches' from the sea' is a myth and always has been. Deep sea fishing has never been productive.

'If the subsidies paid to trawler fleets were directed to terrestrial food production everyone would benefit'

Dr Alan Mulford

"Subsidies in one form another have always been present, be it from government or underpaying the fisherm... to do a dangerous and ... shortening task," she said

In Prof. Whitworth's view, you crave for the taste of fish then try trout sprink... with grains of sodium chlor... - salt to you and me - then little difference," she said

Susem attack Britain's mines

- **Britain's mines attacked by Susem**
- **Many miners taken captive**
- **All mining ceased**
- **Stockmarkets in chaos**

Kevin Tankufin
Industrial Correspondent

BRITAIN'S mining industry ground to a halt yesterday as Susem forces backed by countless stinging 'wasp' weapons raided one operation after another.

From Aberdeen to Cornwall in scores of opencast mines thousands of miners fled from the Susem attacks. Many however, were unable to escape. The indications are that more than 10,000 men have been captured by the Susem.

The Dove Holes gritstone quarries, Derbyshire, were one of the sites attacked by the Susem. In the nearby village of Dove Holes, residents told of how a huge Susem spaceship "fell from the clouds" and hovered over the quarry. "It was awesome," said Glenda Ogden, 45, landlady of the Doves Arms, "it came over the village and then disappeared over the peak in the direction of the quarry. It was only when one of the truck drivers rushed into the village did we know they were taking the men."

Although there has been no official comment from the quarry's owners – Road Rock - as to the numbers of quarrymen taken by the Aliens, industry experts said there would have been at least 200 men working in the quarry and a similar number of ancillary staff. Villagers say nobody was seen leaving the quarry.

The numbers of men taken prisoner at the huge Pontygwaith opencast coal-mine near Aberdare, were reported to be at least ten times this number. At the same time the Susem craft was reported over Derbyshire another was attacking Pontygwaith and a string of other mine across South Wales.

Fudge Coal, the owners of Pontywaith said the mine was one of their seven opencast mines throughout the South Wales Coalfield. Although the other six mines, centred round Ebbw Vale and Rhymney, are smaller and employ smaller numb... the total of men taken w... in excess of 3,500. T... company spokesman s... that all its mining a... related activities h... ceased pending "clarificati... of the situation."

The DTI confirmed th... all mining operations ... Britain had come to ... standstill.

A ministry spokespers... said: "Although only ... small percentage of th... country's operations ha... been attacked by Alie... forces, it has been conside... ed prudent that all suc... operations should ceas... immediately until furthe... notice."

Officials at the NU... and GMUW were said to b... pressing both the Hom... and Foreign Offices t... begin negotiations for th... speedy release of th... abducted miners.

have been comparatively few of them.

"Within the confines of your planetary system, as there have been many more, it was difficult at first to unravel Pa-tu's signature, though once we had, it was no more than following the trail which of course led directly to Earth. But letum waves proliferating from your tropo-thermosphere confounded the trail. They have also increased the likelihood of radically distorting Pa-tu's signature out of recognition and so have complicated our search. As a result we are obliged to study every signature until we can establish a pattern, any pattern which might match Pa-tu's configuration co-ordinates."

Menpemelo paused into silence again. We walked on, she saying nothing and me quiet from confusion. Then returning to quinths, she said "It is like swimming. Though separate, a swimmer can swim over the surface of the sea as well as in it." Another moment of her silence (and I still staying mum), then an outburst, "You have made locating Pa-tu more onerous than it need be, not just by your letum pollution (I'd not even chance for "Don't blame me") but by your complete misdirection of assessment of phenomena."

She lost me again but I struggled a squeaked "What do you mean?"

"What is occurring all around you!" she said in a most agitated tone.

It must have been my blank face because she became the more impassioned. "All animals exist, function, can only do so because of the quinth context, even you humans, yet you chose to ignore its existence in your structures of understanding what is about you."

I was still flabbered but managed "Us? How? What do you mean?"

"Where do you think you memory is?"

"In my brain of course," I said but from the look on her face and her reply I wished I had not said anything.

"Exactly what I mean," she said almost with a snarl. Then speaking speedily not stopping for breath continued, "You can recall events of many years ago can you not? (I nodded). In detail some of them? (I nodded again). Your brain like the rest of your body is composed of protein. Yet its every cell has been replaced many times, some more than others, but all do so on a continuous basis. Amid the upheaval of this endless reconstruction and with neural transmission speeds no more than 120 metres a second, you consider you can instantly, ceaselessly, seamlessly summon a detailed recall of decades old events from within your brain?" Then slowly shaking her head and putting on a knowing smile added "I do not think so."

I was going to say "Well, where then?" but she, slowing down, continued, "Short term events are temporarily stored and processed in your brain, and memory is relayed through it but does not reside there."

"Where then?"

"In your aura about your head!" she said with her tone of exclaim still unchanged. "It exists in the quinth context (images of saintly halos promptly came to mind) and is connected with your brain through its falx cerebri (at the time I didn't know where this is but do now, its in the bit between the hemispheres, and I've discovered there's a small depression in my skull above

Malcolm Radcliff has just returned from Malaysia's biggest dam attacked by the Susem

DESERTED BORNEO DAM DOOMED

By Malcolm Radcliff

THE almost completed Busang dam lies deserted and silent.

Long billed as South East Asia's biggest construction project, the dam, in Malaysia's remote Sarawak province, was to have supplied a quarter of the country's electricity needs.

But even before the Susem attack, the dam's viability had been cast into doubt. With the widespread availability of Susem energy units throughout ... dam's hydro-electricity had vanished. Even without the energy units the environmental and social costs incurred by Busang's construction far outweighed any benefits it might have brought.

In the past access to Busang was barred to outsiders. Now, with even the dam's security staff in the hands of the Susem it is open for all to see. It is a truly horrific sight of habitat destruction. Hillsides for more than 60 kilometres have been cleared and leaving

Half a million Serbs and Croats have recently returned to their ho[mes] from the Serra Pelada. **Rosie Swain** one of the first journalists all[owed] to visit the former Croatia reports on one such reunion

The homecomin[g]

Catez is little more than a collection [of h]ouses straddling a stretch of the [m]ain highway from Zagreb and the [S]lovenian border. However, this tidy [l]ittle village is part of the strange [s]ociety that has become common[p]lace throughout Croatia - a [']Nonette Zajednicat' (community).

The new community

Three months ago Catez's 352 men [f]olk were rounded-up by Susem [b]acked Gurkhas marched from the [v]illage and shipped with millions of [o]ther men to the Serra Pelada. [T]oday many of the village's men [w]ere coming home. But the home [t]hey returned to is very different to [t]he one they left. During the men's [a]bsence the village's women have [f]ormed themselves into a tightly knit [a]nd highly organized community.

Marina Jovanic was one of a [c]luster of woman gathered at the [C]atez's one and only bus stop, [e]agerly awaiting the arrival of the [c]oach from Zagreb and the first of [t]he men to return. "The area [Z]ajednicat in Zagreb told me that [m]y husband Gorna had returned [a]nd would be arriving home today [b]ut not when," she said. The coach [d]uly arrived, and one of the first to [a]light was Gorna.

Other women were not to be as [f]ortunate as Marina. But though [t]here was sadness among those [w]hose husbands did not arrive there ... disappointment from those women still waiting.

Enthusiasm

Between the arrival of the first and second coaches the entire village it appeared was enthusiastically celebrating the men's return.

However, behind the joyfulness there lay a shadow that the men appeared to only vaguely perceive. As the village's community representative, Andrea Gavranic said: "The men will take some time to adjust to the fact that they are no longer economically required. We women are no longer dependant upon their earning capacity.

Men's depression

"In other places where men have returned they have thought they could continue their old ways. When they discover they do not have their power of old, many are unable to adjust. Most have been sensible of course, and have quickly integrated into the new society, but for those who have been unable there have been many sadnesses."

Ms Gavranic's gloomy prognosis was later reinforced by the representative of the new men's social health and wellbeing organistion, MENSAFE. The organisation has recorded a record number of men displaying symptoms of acute depression and 'IS' (inferiority syndrome) due to the newly formed ... where women have

Itaipu dam danger

SAO PAULO: The giant Itaipu dam straddling the Brazil-Paraguay border is in danger of overflowing experts say.

Overhaul of four of the dam's massive generators halted because of the attack are in danger of jamming.

Behind the Itaipu dam a 1,400 square kilometre lake built up. If this lake were to overflow it would have dire consequences for towns all along the Rio Parana river in north eastern Argentina and as far south as Buenos Aires.

Built at a cost of $18 billion and using enough concrete to pave a motorway from Moscow to Lisbon, the Itaipu dam in its hey-day was capable of generating half of Brazil's electricity. However, in recent years Itaipu has suffer-ed from serious silt accumulation.

The generators have also suffered because of silt particles dam-aging their rotor blades. As a result of these and other diffi-culties the dam was only ever able to operate

News

Brazilian miners ree[l] from Susem attacks

By Nora Smith
in Brazil

BELA Horizonte: Thousands of miners from the state of Minas Gerais were abducted by Aliens last night, causing widespread panic.

The state governor, Chica da Silva is said to be declaring a state of emergency because of the chaotic situation. Although Bela Horizonte, the state capital ... ital's is highly dependant on the mining of a whole host of different minerals.

The countryside of this mountainous and once beautiful state is disfigured by countless stretches of mining operations and their waste. Like most of Brazil, mining has continued unchecked for decades and in total disregard for any environmental consider- ... the sun.

Many of the large mining operations, such as the Siderurgica iron ore opencast mining near Curvelo has been described as an environmental disaster area, with the terrain for hundreds of kilometres made lifeless. However, the collective damage inflicted on the environment by small scale mining operations and prospectors ...

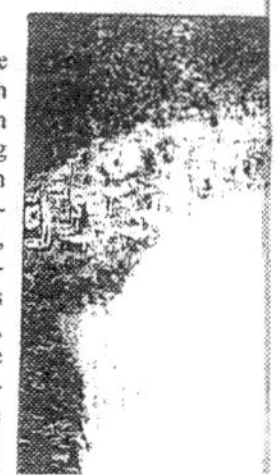

Rain saves Test for En[gland]

By John Nolty
Cricket Correspondent

THE third test against Namibia at Headingly ended in draw yesterday. With England faced a humiliating follow-on after being all out for 79 in the first innings against Namibians 652 for 3 declared. But we were rescued by two days of rain.

It had been rumoured that England captain, Mike Hedley, had been praying for rain for days. But this was a charge he strongly denies. He said: "While it is true we were faced with an uphill task in reversing Namibia's first innings lead, I remained confident that the lads could have staged an excellent comeback. It must be remembered that Namibia's first inning total was due more to luck than anything.

"As far as we are

where it is, and lots of other people have one as well). Sometimes for some," she continued, "and as you have witnessed with Lucia, though their physiological, short term memory processing may fail to co-ordinate efficiently, their aura remains intact." (As she spoke I had memories of my granddad who still recited his remembered nursery rhymes but not what he had just had for his tea).

"Short term memory acts as a two way editor. Experiences unwanted, such as particularly physiologically grievous ones are often unsent to the aura." (Again as she spoke, I had the recollection, still detailed of once waking up in hospital and the afternoon before while still at school, but not running out from behind the bus and being hit by a car in the between time).

"Conversely, the brain's short term memory is the conduit through which the aura, and thus in many aspects its being's persona, is communicated. What is actually relayed and the form of its delivery is dependant entirely on the efficiency of the brain's functioning, which at times has heightened powers of recall, at others impaired." As Menpemelo spoke, hypnotists' skills in helping people remember came to mind but before I could say so, she dryly added and with a knowing matronly nod, "As you have personally experienced no doubt following your evenings in the Pousada."

Silent still but now sheepish, I listened as we ambled on. "All beings possess an aura and are able, though to varying degrees, to directly influence and be influenced by the auras of others. For some, such is the extent of mutual auralate influence, they exist as much a collective entity as individually." As fate would have it by then we had reached the balcony of the Susem refectory and as we looked out, a flock of flamehead finches in close formation flew by. "See how they swirl," she said. And they were, hundreds of them, whizzing round and round and up and down as well.

"The birds on the outside," Menpemelo said, "are flying faster, those on the inside curve steeper, ones in between proportionally to the two. They are also collectively flying at speed (I soon saw why, there was a big hawk after them) yet none collide with another." As she spoke I had recollections of being in London under sky darkened multitudes of whirling starlings, yet never seeing collided ones knocked to the ground.

"Birds in flocks flying so swiftly do not have time to individually physically calibrate their relative positions, as doing so will slow their speed and a pursuer will catch them. By flying together only the bodily frail are vulnerable." As Menpemelo spoke a weary one fell behind and the hawk had it.

Shrugging her shoulders at the straggler's demise, she continued, "You have observed during your field study tuition on formicidae not only how they exist collectively in huge numbers but function as a cohesive entity. The leaf-cutting ant columns you studied were comprised of large ones guarding teams of middle sized ones who cut the leaves while lines of smaller ones carried the cuttings to their nest. An individual ant's brain compared to even those of the finches is very small, very rudimentary."

An automated waiter arrived, Menpemelo ordered and he trotted off. "As your tuition asked," she continued, "How did the ants know which leaves to cut and which to remain so the plant survives and grows yet more leaves? How were the numbers of ants required for each task accessed? How do the ants, each with no more than a forty day life expectancy, know their tasks so precisely? And finally, why did not the entire colony just decamp their nest and devour the leaves instead of laboriously cutting and carrying them all the way to their nest?"

Knowing the answer to the last I said "Ants can't eat leaves, so they carry them back to feed a big mould growing deep in their nest and then they feed off of that."

"And the answers to the other questions?"

"..Er, I don't know."

"Would not a collectiveness of aura be explanation?"

The waiter returned with a flask and glasses. Menpemelo, barely pausing to nod acknowledgement as he put them on the table, continued, "Remember, each event of every entity possesses a quinth context signature." The waiter trotted off, she continued. "The collective passing imprinting of many near identical signatures provide a guide for others of a like species to follow."

Gathering I was not comprehending her, she said and pouring the wine, "How big is a butterfly's brain?"

"Just a bit bigger than an ant's, I suppose," I said taking a sip.

"But not by much?"

I nodded as I took another sip, most palatable, echoes of the better Auslese vintages, zesty hints of mango, peach, perfectly served, just chilled.

Menpemelo continued, "Five thousand kilometres north-west of Tabajara and similar to a species we have on Sin-cu-ra, Danaidae Monarch butterflies with no more than an 80 millimetre wingspan and each weighing less than half a gramme, habitually hibernate in particular pine forests on the northern slopes of the Mexican Plateau. They do so in their millions. Just prior to their hemi-spherical vernal equinox, these butterflies singularly, not collectively, travel a 1,000 kilometres northwards to the edge of the Great Plains. Here they mate and lay eggs. How big is a butterfly's egg?"

"Very small. Very, very small," I said.

"Thirty days from hatching their larvae pupate. During pupation they become near liquid in form. Butterflies emerging from these chrysalises travel a further 4,000 kilometres north to the far side of the easternmost of the Great Lakes. Here this second generation mates and lays eggs. How small did you say their eggs were?"

"Extremely small," I said, and taking another sip.

"How much, by volume, of the first generation's genetic material would be conferred to the third?"

"By volume? All but nothing," I said, taking more wine (its taste becoming better with each sip).

"This third generation on maturing to butterflies, feed, fatten, then after thirty days, though never having done so before, fly southward. Again they do not do so collectively but singularly. As their autumnal equinox arrives, they are alighting on the particular pine trees their grandmothers flew from. How do they accomplish this? What do they possess to do so? Why do they fly to those particular pine trees and their prodigy to those particular lakes? Why do they not go elsewhere? Why do they bother to travel at all?"

But even before I could make a try at a reply Menpemelo added "During some of these butterflies' journeys north and southward, they are blown by strong winds east and westward. So many, that there are significant numbers of Monarch butterflies on the islands of the eastern Atlantic and central Pacific. Furthermore, though they also breed on these islands, the prodigy of these particular Monarchs do not manifest any signs of journeying in any direction let alone north or south. Why also is this?"

Still stumbling for a reply I ventured the things I'd learnt from natural history films and books, "The ones which aren't blown off course are sensitive to the Earth's magnetism."

This was met with Menpemelo's, "Your planet's magnetic poles continuously and erratically alter position. During the last decade the magnetic meridian has moved 200 kilometres eastward. Tectonic plates with differing resonances also haphazardly vary their planes relative to each other."

"They fly by the relative position of the Sun?" I next ventured.

"Due to your star's cycle of continually contracting and expanding, its position, analogous to that of its planets, constantly varies."

My proffers that smell, sight, sound and others were involved also collapsed under her argued barrage of rebuttal. In the end I tendered, "Instinct" but this was met with, "What precisely is instinct?"

I fumbled and mumbled but before I had a phrase, Menpemelo offered "An unconscious natural tendency? A stereotyped response to particular stimuli perhaps?" As I nodded she added, "A useful conceptual word in a literary milieu but nebulous for that of precise descriptive definition, would you not agree?" As I nodded I was wishing I'd stuck to sipping wine. "Would not quinth context pathways be a plausible premise?"

Nodding and still silent, I sipped some more.

"In humans, so we have had opportunity to observe, women in continually close contact with one another harmonise their monthly menstrual cycle, why do you think this is?"

"Pheromones," I said making a valiant stab of an answer.

I received her laughed, "In actual physical contact these might well be determining stimuli, but otherwise they are more than masked by the many other olfactory bodily emissions, each of which will be as variable as all other physical characteristics between one individual and another."

Before I had time for another try or receive explanation, Pheterisco with, "Ah, there you are," strode towards us, and adding, "your group dance class remember?" (this is yet another of Rainbow's innovations).

Menpemelo with "Oh yes," to Pheterisco and "We will talk on," to me, then hurried away.

Finishing the wine (it would have been blasphemy not to) I began thinking through the bag of "Whys?" Menpemelo forever leaves when I talk with her. But I had not rummaged for long (is amnesia when people lose connection with their auras, are people who have a lobotomy childlike because their aura's receptor becomes damaged, why do the menstrual cycles of women in groups harmonise, is it the same for nuns?) when I was considering something else, the circle of Susem sat on the far side of the otherwise empty refectory.

These had been animatedly chatting when suddenly they became silent and still. Then, one by one began to slowly rock their bodies back and forth. They then did so faster and faster but after a minute abruptly stopped, let out a loud satisfied "Aah!" then in unison raised clenched fists and yelled "Pan! pan!" and broke into laughter. No sooner had they done this than they noticed me and began putting their fingers to their mouths and giggling as though caught doing something they shouldn't. And with the same coyness stood up and briskly departed.

Though not the first group of Susem I have seen rocking together these past days, I don't know why they are doing it. Both Milophinia and Menpemelo claim to know nothing of them and Pheterisco's "It is of no importance," has me none the wiser either. Not that I think it is anything ominous, they usually laugh afterwards, but there must be reasons why they keep doing it and why no one will tell me. This Susem rocking and how they are alike to supping soccer fans prior to their setting off to duff up the rivals, was still in mind as I walked up to the Pousada. But no sooner was I in the bar than my thoughts were diverted once again. Rico had a most strange message for me.

He said that a man had been found wandering barely alive on the shore near Pecam. Rico said that he had claimed not only to have come all the way from England but that he knew me.

85: KEN

Up our way they came down in droves, thousands and thousands of them all over the place, Clissold Park, Aberdeen Park, on houses, gardens. There were so many on the roads all the traffic was stopped for hours. Hordes were out after them. Everyone's got at least one and not before time either, the thieving of them round here was getting seriously out of order, it was like when videos first came out. But that's all stopped now, there's so many soufins about they don't even have a resale price.

But what I want to know is why it took them, the government, so long to get their fingers out and see sense and send all those Serbs and Croats packing, every other country did and no one wanted them here, especially when we found out what they've done. The Australians I can understand, they can't be expected to know about things, not if the dozy one Harry's got working behind the bar is anything to go by. As for the Americans, well it's to be expected of them, they've always been all mouth and beliefs till they see they're losing out, then they join in with a rush, don't they?

What I also want to know is why it always seems it is Danny who comes on and says who's getting soufins and when, but it's still Rainbow who come on for everything else. Well, not having seen him for months and then there he is all of a sudden appearing every other day and just going on about these soufins and nothing else, it's a bit iffy. I can't put my finger on it but I've a feeling he's up to something, or if he isn't those Susem are. It's the same about why they're doling them out in the first place. They wouldn't be giving them away, they've no need as far as I can see unless they're angling for something back.

That's not to say Danny hasn't gone down well telling all and sundry that they're going have these soufins for free, but of course he's still not a patch on Rainbow. She's really been on form this past week. She came on, chin rested on hand, bit of a smile on her face, "I did say..." she starts off, "...long ago, no more tree felling after thirty days, but no one took any notice. So..." and with that there were these pictures of hordes of blokes being herded down that Serra Pelada and with her adding "...remember, leave the trees alone.." Tonight she was on just the same and saying "I also said no deep sea fishing..." then there's pictures of hundreds of boats lying on beaches, nets all wrapped round them, then shots of another load of blokes being whipped down the pits and she adding "...remember, leave the fish alone.."

Rainbow also said that now the last of those Serbs and Croats have been caught, the trials of all those who are guilty could now begin.

86: SIÂN

When I think what Dafydd dished out for my Sam! There's so many now they can't even be given away. Dafydd has one for the car, Glyn another for his motor bike, I'm glad to say. There's another couple in the garage going spare. I took them in for Anne but she says she can get one. But mum and dad though have also there's and with another one as a spare.

Dafydd's entire laboratory is running on them. He says they had a circular from the DoE telling them not to use soufins and stick to the mains. But his boss told them to take no notice, saying they were already suffering enough from budget cuts and every saving helped.

Mr Griffiths at work was the same, "Think of all the books we can buy with the savings?" he said. Gwyneth, who does our accounts, said we were charged more than £10,000 for electricity last year and that's without the heating. But there's fat chance of County Hall in Carmarthen paying any of it over. Though I hear they're running everything on soufins as well. Though all the same, there's just as much chance of them putting our council tax down.

I rang Anne after Danny had been on to tell her that I'd seen him but she said they'd already had. When I said, being nosy, "Who's we?" she said she was "entertaining" and couldn't speak but I think it must have been that computer fellow, Howard. She went on about him something rotten last time I was up in London. But from the dusty look she gave me when I'd said "He's married, leave him alone, it will only end in tears," I wish I had kept my mouth shut, so this time I didn't press.

When Danny came on the television last week it was quite a surprise. Well, not having seen him for ages I was beginning to wonder what had happened to him. He looked rather natty in that white tunic. And he was so relaxed, quite different from that first time in April. I was glad as well he's had his hair cut properly for once, the way I have Dafydd have his, just over the ears and neat.

The second time Danny was on saying that Australia and those places in America were having their soufins, I did wonder if we would be seeing more of him rather than Rainbow but when she came on again I realised perhaps we wouldn't. But then I've really taken a shine to Rainbow. I'd didn't at first, all glamour and no brains I thought, though I think differently now. But every time I watch her I'm forever reminded of what mum said about her and Danny and I always have to smile.

Tonight when she was on she said the trials in Bosnia were due to start. It was funny the way she just slipped it in after the bit about all those dams having to come down.

87: AILEEN

If I hadn't been so desperate I would never have done it. But now I have I'm kicking myself for not doing it ages ago, it's been a godsend. Sophie Lonikia, the solicitor I see up at Christofides put me on to it.

I was telling her that with Ryan getting himself laid off for his drinking I'd all but nothing coming in, I couldn't go on the Social in case they found my working in the Salutation and I'd not the money to pay her now separation isn't covered by the Legal Aid. But she said what with the changes I could earn something from it. Every bit of business she said I brought her way she would give me twenty per cent. As Sophie says, solicitors have not normally the habit of going out looking for business but sit hoping it will come to them.

And I've not stopped. There must be more people in the Sallie with wills than in any pub in the whole of London! And that's just been the beginning. As Sophie said, half the population has a legal problem but do nothing till it's too late, while the other half never knew they'd one in the first place. I've more money this past month than I ever had from Ryan, and that was when he would be working. And Sophie's been really decent to me. She's not always the money before she pays, but I've not gone a single week since I started without her on the telephone saying there's a cheque waiting for me.

I had not been long drumming up business in the Sal when all those soufins came down. A heap of them landed on the roof of the flats. Me and Margaret were up those stairs before you knew it. Like kids we were, laughing and chasing those blue bubbles. But we were also carrying down armfuls and armfuls of the units. We soon had a stack the height of Becky down my hallway.

The moment those blankets of blue were drifting down I had the idea the units would be an introduction to every door I knocked on. And from that night to now I've been knocking and ringing non-stop. Oh sure, most people already had one and more, but I'd always get a thank you. When I had that I would ask how they were getting on with theirs and before they knew it we would be chatting and I'd soon be arranging for Sophie to see them.

In the flats themselves I've forever people now knocking on my door asking for help on all sorts of things. In a way most are nothing to do with legal matter, instead people are wanting help with maintenance even though there's a Council Centre just around the corner. But a solicitor's letter from Sophie to the Town Hall in Upper Street has repairs done in no time at all.

As for Ryan, I'm that busy I've not the time to even regret marrying him.

Danny Boy delivers the power

By FRED BANKS

GOT your soufins yet? One for the home, one for the car, a spare in the garage?

If you have you will be just like the tens of millions of us other lucky Brits. And like them it's time for us all to give a whooping "Thanks Danny Boy."

We all owe our once-in-a lifetime bonanza to this plucky Brit. And we should all count ourselves lucky that we Brits have 'Our Man' close to the heartbeat of our ET visitors' decision-making acting on our behalf

And if it had not been for the government's daft dog-in-the-manger attitude in supporting Balkan thugs we would, just as Danny told us, have had our ...

With only television images and commentary ... of experts for their interpretations of what appears to be happening in the forbidden land under the control of the Susem and its people

What is really happening in 'Susemland'?

By Jason O'Conner
Social attitudes editor

PAUL HINES, the Senior Professor in Residence at Department of Sociology at the University of Sheppey at Queensborough said: "Obviously everything we have been shown must be taken with a certain degree of caution. As yet, it is all but impossible to know if what has been shown has been selectively edited or is a true refection ... only if the suppositions proffered can at a later time be reliably authenticated, my preliminary conclusions would suggest that there is some merit in the assertions made in these television broadcasts."

Sandra Howard of Oxford University who teache... ...olitics said: "From ... seen ... are ... time ... wea...

it was, they had that lady saying they have no police forces any more because they don't have crime any more I thought, you know, she was really like cool and when they said they've made marijuana legal I said to myself "Wow! I just want to be there." And then when they showed those little ...

EURO SUMMER SOCCER CUP FIXTURES FIXED

By ALAN SMITH

ROME: EUROFA officials gave details last night of the European Summer Cup.

The 78 teams, repre... ners was agreed after a four hour meeting between officials and the television consortium led by Dick Bear's SLI TV. ... finalists playing in Italy during September. It was this last point, agreeing match venues which had been the main stumbli...

The Briton who lighted the world

...eorgia Scott
...eneral reporter

...e have all by now ...een him on our ...creens. In little less ...f three weeks, he ...as told us night ...fter night, who are ...o be the next lucky recipients of free pollution-less energy. But who is he? Who is Danny Collins, World emissary to our Alien visitors?

We know he is British but some say Irish. He's forty-something, and lived in London. In Covent Garden he ran a once successful business selling water purifiers. Danny was also well known in many of the area's hostelries as a cheerful and outgoing.

He lived until a year ago in a flat in north London and was also well known in many of the area's hostelries as also being cheerful and outgoing.

What Collins was doing in remotest Brazil in the first place is a mystery. But some say he knew of our extra-terrestrial visitors' impending arrival.

is that a year ago he was suddenly no longer to be found in any of his usual haunts and police at the time claimed ... was a drug smugg... However, there is ... concrete evidence ... this and those w... knew him say loud... he didn't 'do' drug... he was too busy dri... ing, they add - it ... an accusation not ... be lightly dismisse...

It is known, ho...ever, that Collins ... being sought by ... police for his invol... ment in the dama... of the Bomber Ha...

...ews

Government in energy quandary

...Mark Lewis
...olitics Editor

...OVERNMENT pro...uncements to its ...n to departments ...t to use Susem ...ergy units was in ...sarray yesterday. A ...rvey has found that ...ey are being widely ...ed throughout ...vernment offices, ...en in the Department of Energy itself.

This discovery ...mes on top of the ...vernment's failure ... dissuade Councils ... stick to established ...ergy supplies. The ...vernment's policy is ...at maintaining such ...ergy sources is vital ... a form of strategic ...serve should it be ...quired. That this ...licy is being widely ...sregarded is due in no small part to the pressure of spending limits on all departmental budgets.

The government, however, is caught between a rock and a hard place. No matter how hard it may try, it is, according to one government departmental head - and talking off the record - the use of Alien energy units is now so widespread that there is not a hope of the government's policy being adhered to. He said: "As soon as one department sees another using them and with nothing happening except huge savings to their budgets, they adopt the same approach."

The DTI's policy towards the ene... units is that of ... effects on its int... national compe... tiveness. A spok... man said: "Due ... many of our overse... competitors, havi... the cost saving be... fits of these ene... units before indust... in Britain did, we ... obviously concern... that we catch up ... quickly as possib... But on the other ha... consideration must ... given to those Briti... Indus-tries which a... being adverse... affected by their (t... units) introduction."

Government poli... is also subject ... vigourous lobbying ... interests from bo... sides of the politi... spectrum. There ar... growing number ...

Pent-up anger erupts as police, army club unarmed protesto...

Brazil hit by riot...

By Andrew Pennington
in Recife

MORE THAN 1,200 people are thought to have been seriously as injured as landless peasants fought with army and police in Brazil's impoverished north east yesterday.

Following many weeks of sullen confrontation between the two sides tempers flared into open fighting with security forces clubbing and firing warning shots in a bid to hold back increasingly militant landless peasants.

In an attempt to quell the disturbance in Rio Grande do Norte State, military authorities have declared a State of Emergency.

The latest disturbances were sparked by a military vehicle careering into a crowd of women and children, killing four and injuring many more.

The crowd reportedly, dragged the four army personnel from the crashed truck and tried to lynch them but other soldiers attempted to rescue their fellows.

The situation then escalated into a full blown riot as protesters gave vent to their frustration against the security forces' past actions and they, in turn, against the many tens of thousands of peasants.

Although the rioting in Rio Grande is the most serious yet, it was, as so many commentators say, inevitable. The tension and frustration has been mounting for three months, ever since the first military barriers were erected in May.

Throughout Brazil's poor and desolate North East Region more than million poor, landless people have been gathered round military roadblocks on all routes leading to area under Alien control.

Fanning the flames of the protester's ire have been the constant stream of Alien telecasts w... watched avidly b... people in the regi...

Being so close ... area, yet denied ... the perceived ... within the atmos... heightened ...

Landless peasants were involved in running battles with security forces in atte...

One in the eye for Jenkins I thought. Of course I professed surprise when he informed me of his demotion but we all knew it was coming. When Mr Gibbons announced a week ago that a shake up in Securities was forthcoming, we all knew that meant certain individuals were for the chop. There was Jenkins drawing up a list of names of those he thought should go, and it was perhaps remiss of him however, that he had not though to append his own.

Nonetheless I mustn't be too gleeful as regards Jenkins' tribulations, for times are turbulent for us all at the bank. My customers are continuously contacting me with their tales of woe. I do not think there can be many of them who have not been adversely affected by the Alien's actions.

Today I had a customer, an importer of timber, who is suddenly faced with a threefold rise in prices, "What am I to do?" he bemoans. He has fixed price contracts and cannot thus pass on such increases, should he be able to obtain further timber that is. I did consider mentioning, as did the Alien's television girl just the other day, their warnings as to felling trees but considered it diplomatic not to do so.

Yesterday I had another customer who has investments in utilities and all of which have now plummeted in value. Again I thought it best not to mention that he too should have heeded the Alien's warnings. Though he is not alone in this, Jenkins' fall was also due to his over-reliance on bonds in the Energy sector.

But I do have some customers who are benefiting from the Alien's presence. I have noticed on my visits to my customer that many, if not all of them, are now using these energy units and are of course making significant inroads to reducing their production costs. Though, like the bank's bigger customers every single one of them are unfortunately currently unwilling to presently increase their borrowings, citing the current uncertainty as the reason. Indeed, in the bank's current quarterly bulletin there is an article commenting that even our domestic customers are reacting in a like manner. Last month it stated more was actually repaid than lent. If such a state of affairs should continue it cannot bode well for the bank's profitability, to mention nothing of our bonuses.

However, not everyone is adopting such a cautious attitude, one of whom is my wife June. I have tried to impress on her that the savings to our own fuel bills, now we have these power units, need to be saved not spent. But alas my endeavours in this direction have not been entirely successful. My athletic club has been the same. They have spent the entire year's projected savings on new floodlighting.

Although I have not said much to anybody I do have my doubts as to the durability of these energy units. This, in no small part, is because of Collins' more than effusive involvement with them.

Susem are 'Antichrist - Pope claims

Damien Trotter
Religious Correspondent

Rome: In his Papal letter, Pope Pius XII has denounced the Susem as messengers of the 'Anti-christ'. He claims in his letter that Catholic priests in Brazil have been subjected to unspeakable indignities and cruelty. He also said that the Susem are also embarked on a programme of indoctrination against Catholicism.

Speaking for the first time since Bosnian investigators six weeks ago claimed to have uncovered evidence of the Catholic Church's collaboration with the former Croatian regime. The Pope said he refuted the Bosnian claims as being "pure fabricated untruths". His letter said that such evidence could only be false and therefore must be being used to turn people against the Catholic Church.

Vatican officials said that they had reliable evidence that "millions of dollars worth" church properties in both Bosnia and the area of Brazil under Susem control had been appropriated or allowed to fall into disuse. The Vati also said that with all Catholic clergy from former Croatia being prisoned by the Su church services had unable to take place.

The Vatican has published an exte report detailing trea meted out to its Bra priests in the area Susem control. The details more thar cases which, it shows the priesth being subjected systematic campa harassment and ex The Bishop of Fo

Pentagon denies 'spying' charges

BY JAMES LIMPITT
IN WASHINGTON:

THE Pentagon strongly denied Susem assertions it had intentionally launched spy satellites to eavesdrop on them.

Pentagon spokesman Dwight Powers said: "It is a matter of regret that our Susem visitors have felt it necessary to intercept and apprehend a number of satellites owned by a number of US Government Agencies which were situated in equatorial orbits.

"However, despite claims to the contrary, the Department of Defence," he said, " on behalf of all parties concerned, I can categorically state that none of the seized craft have been engageed in any activity other than normal and routine legitimate observation which has been conducted on an ongoing basis a considerable time period."

Mr Powers' statement has been widely slated by many defence analysts. David Ichan of Georgetown University's Faculty of International Studies, said: "Once again the Pentagon is burying its head in untruths.

"The satellites shown in the Susem telecast are Hughes SInGaLo satellites," he said. "These are reputedly the latest in the range. Not only are they specifically designed for low orbit but have consequently, a short life expectancy, weeks rather than years. That the Susem should have shown six of them only goes to demonstrate just how stupid some people can be. If the launch costs are included into the price this brings the cost of each one of upwards of $150 millions apiece.

"It more to Pentagon's inanity that they have failed to notice that

Business reaps big benefits from soufins

By Steven Dunn
Economics Editor

BUSINESSES large and small are reaping massive benefits from the use of Alien energy units. The savings, so experts predict, could save industry a whooping 20 percent on

ical refineries have seen their production costs fall the most. British Steel's production boss, Ian Witherspoon said: As soon as we had units fitted to blast furnaces they were going like little demons. Going day and night they are Champion.

icularly intensive energy consumers have also been able to make big savings. Billy Hague, who runs the Westminster Sandwich Bar said: "With the savings on lighting and that we are now able to afford punters a few extr refinements like table

Brazilian soldiers shoot 2,000 landless peasants in cold blood, killing more than 8

UNARMED PROTESTERS MOWN DOWN IN COLD BLOOD

Members of Movement Sem Terra - the Landless Ones - marching against the

BY LENNY HART IN NATAL

BRAZILIAN soldiers running amuck gunned down in cold blood 2,000 unarmed peasants slaying more than 800 defenceless men, women and children.

This 'Massacre of the Innocents' took place late yesterday afternoon, on the outskirts of Rusas, a rundown hamlet straggling the main east west highway 300km west of Natal in Brazil's dirt poor northeast.

Brazil's troubled Nordeste region

As a procession, several thousand strong, of MST (Movement Sem Terra - the 'Landless Ones') who had marched for several hours in

disband. When Callado with other leaders refused to call off the march and insisted on continuing, police attempted to arrest them. As scuffles broke out between the two sides some of the marchers threw stones at the police and soldiers. At this, and without any warning, police and soldiers opened fire on the marchers, all of whom were unarmed.

MST Leader slain

Callado and those at the head of the march were among those slain with the first volleys. But as the marchers fled back towards the bridge crossing the Rio Jaguaribe, police and soldiers continued firing and cutting down many more. Soon the highway was

shooting at the dead and wounded who lay on the road as they did so. In Rusas itself the military gunned many more of the protestors as well as bystanders. Yet further peasants on the march and in a bid to escape the rampaging soldiers fled into many of the makeshift camps scattered along the highway. But soldiers again chased after them and gunned down many more as well as innocent inhabitants alike.

Military 'cleansing squads'

As darkness feel military 'cleansing squads' were reported to have thrown the bodies of the dead peasants strewn along the highway into trucks as well as hosing down the blood covered road. The

medicines and medical facilities that many of the victims are expected to die of their wounds.

'Massacara Jaguaribe'

Though far the most serious outbreak of violence by the Brazilian military against the MST and other peasant organizations, the 'Massacara Jauguaribe' as it has quickly become known, is only the latest of the many acts of violence meted out daily against the more that a million impoverished 'Nordesters' attempting to break through the army's 'Wall of Steel' and into Alien held territory.

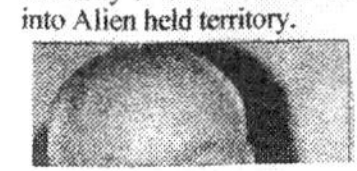

State, has become a barrier to several millions of the country's poor and impoverished in their belief of a better life under the Susem.

Wall of Steel

General George Ramos is the commander of Brazil's military forces in the Nordeste and widely held as being directly responsible for ordering the brutal crackdown and shootings of MST. Ramos has made it publicly known on many recent occasions of his frustration in having to contend with what he called "this despicable rabble" hindering, as he see it, his defence of Brazil against the Aliens and rebels, then of quashing them once the opportunity arises.

State of Siege

military are powers to deteriorating situation. It giving Ramo Costa has should there currently bei

Coup

With Ramo hand agains open to qu many mo peasants by take place them away f they are breaching th

While th protests thro the militar unarmed pe not receive

89: FROGS

Ten times I have been on the TV telling everyone they were in for a bounty of soufins. Ten times I have extolled the virtues of their free, everlasting and pollution-free energy.

"Go on, you do it," Rainbow had said, "people must be tiring of forever seeing my face and you're so much better at technical things." Being lingeringly yet silently still chafing at my demotion by Paceillo to Rainbow ever since her arrival, I had avidly grasped the offer without so much as stopping to query either's motives. There I'd been time after time alas, letting vanity get the better of me. In vainglory I had listened to the World Service for every mention of my name and basked in the universally warm reception and status of near star standing I had received.

It's no good now knowing that the minerals mined by the Susem machines from the Asteroid Belt for the soufins have a refining flaw. Neither is the explanation that they had been made in such hurry to meet the sudden surge in demand that there had not been the time to check.

It has been in vain that I've pleaded with Paceillo for help. I told her how I have repeatedly heard over the radio that because soufin use is now so wide-spread power stations are closing by the day, oil companies seizing up and shoals of sheikhs sent into exile as a result. Though this, alas, has met with nothing but her sphinx-like smile as she said "So?"

It was the same when I told her that faced with a power vacuum the entire economy of the world would collapse with catastrophic consequences for the whole of mankind. All I received from her over this was a shrug. And worse, my plea that the Susem supply those with soufins replacements of longer lasting ones met with nothing more than her "Why?"

Then rubbing in salt she said "The soufins the tocans delivered have served Tearo and the Bosnian people's purpose well in persuading those sheltering Serbs and Croats to present themselves to answer for their actions." My protestations to her that delivering longer lasting replacement soufins to the Nonettes, as the Susem are now doing, wasn't being fair either, evoked only another shrug. And even when I had said that while the powerful and privileged of the world would no doubt manage to hog what energy supplies remained, ordinary people would suffer, it met with her "Who is to say who has power and who has not?" Then rubbing in the iodine, "It is unlikely we shall be on Earth when these soufins expire, for we are now sure that we have located the whereabouts of Pa-tu."

I have also attempted to impress upon her that as it had been me who had delivered every announcement of the free soufins, it would also be me who would be blasted with the blame. My name would be worse than mud, I told her, I would be torn to pieces, strung-up should I ever leave Tabajara but again she said "So?" Even when I had said it was rotten of her and Rainbow to have led me on so, setting me up to take the blame for tricking everyone she still said "So?" And then without so much as a smidgen of mercy, she turned on her heels and left me there all alone and palely wilting.

Remonstrating with Rainbow, though she must have known from the start that the soufins were suspect, was pointless too, especially with me being in a gender minority of one. Though she was filled with fussing over the last details of the trials in Bosnia and castigating Caught TV's Rip Thorne, she confounded me further with her offhand "I'm sure everything will work out well in the end."

Then, and it's always the same with women, they forever fret and chide over the inconsequential, "your toenails need cutting...no, you've not washed your hands...now look what you have done, I spent an hour ironing that..." but important matters, their, "I've written off the car...I've spent all the money ...I'm leaving you.." they treat with as much concern as yawning. Here was a time bomb ticking to detonation and all that Rainbow could say was that something might turn up.

In the midst of all this terribleness came Milophinia with dire tidings of her findings from frogs. "The planet-wide plummeting of first order Amphibia populations is prior indication of the chronic deterioration of reproductive potential of all vertebrate lifeforms, more so the epidemically permeable, and are confirmation of our preliminary analysis of elevated vaporous absorption of abnormal carbon centric polychained frothicle groupings present in the Earth's lower troposphere being the prime facilitators," she had gushed.

"Oh," I had said. Not that I had understood a single a word.

And seeing so she had flowed on with explanation. "The Orders Salientia and Caudata, salamanders and frogs, have the thinnest epidermis of all terrestrial vertebrates and protect it with a covering of mucus excreted from their pores. External substances entering this medium can in turn pass through their skin and into the body proper. Substances to which these creatures have not evolved resistance to, or tolerance of, will deleteriously affect metabolic dis-equilibrium and eventually injurious cellular change."

"You mean they will die?"

"No," she had said darkly, "it is more insidious than that."

"Oh dear," I had said.

"Frogs and salamanders are your planet's most ancient species of air breathing, land dwelling vertebrates. These sub-aquatic creatures have survived substantially unchanged while other lifeforms have evolved through to extinction. Further, frogs exist in a wider range of habitat than most other vertebrates. That they have survived for so long and occupy so many differing environments is indication of their collectively intense tolerance to a wide range of external agonists.

"Thus the recent rapidly progressive decline of these Orders' sub-species populations in all of their ambient niches, as well as area specific malformations, is indication of a widespread yet sole quasi sub-chronic factor as a potential causent. Premature death, it has been further ascertained, is not a paramount determinant of this decline. Our own observations of these creatures as well as analysis of your studies (I again took this to be part of Terbal's Internetting) indicate that though the decline is due to falling fertility in both genders, it is more so that of males, but malformation incidence has occurrence emphasis among females.

"Fertility decline appears to have begun with a gradual reduction of viable spermatozoön with each ejaculate, followed in subsequent generations by an absolute decrease in these cells. All the time there were excess male reproductive cells for each mating, population levels of these creatures remained unchanged. However, with the proportion of fertile cells dwindling in each new generation the number of male offspring wholly sterile has increased to where their overall populations have plummeted to now near terminal levels..."

As she spoke I had thoughts of men's falling sperm counts.

""...Compared to other species," she gushed, "frogs having a short generational frequency speedily manifested the effects of a phenomenon which in due course will affect others. Our further investigations have entailed the study of other smooth moist-skinned, yet higher order Vertebrata."

I looked down at my hand and sensed the wet of my sweat.

"Because of their aquatic habitat, Sirenians and Cetaceans were our prime consideration for study. Among them we have also found evidence of corresponding deterioration in both quantity and quality of their spermatozoön (I did wonder how they had managed to get whales to give theirs, and were they happy at the time or was there a lot of threshing). Though your data (I took this again to be Terbal) does not record any recent decline in their absolute numbers, it masks the true exponential rate of their population growth potential. Given the depleted numbers at the time when extensive excessive slaughter of these creatures abated, and the period which has since elapsed, there should be many times their numbers than are current."

Endeavouring to sound clever I had stupidly, in retrospect said "But whales have thick skins and live in salt water."

"Not all of their skin," she had replied. "Whales' orifice linings are as soft as skin covering our hands. That of their bronchial alveoli is as thin and permeable as the skin of a frog. The meridian salt constituent of your planet's ocean water, is, as is ours, less than one part in a thousand. Any water ingested into these mammals' respiratory tracts will soon transform to vapour.

"Because whales and manatees," continued Milophinia returning to where she had left off, "have long generational frequencies similar to that of humans, the inexorable decline in their population potential is currently masked. Although we have yet to conduct investigation on other, fur-skinned Mammalia and Aves vertebrate, the tentative conclusions of our findings are that all air-breathing orders of Vertebrata are chronically and malignly affected. The dramatic decline in Amphibia populations can be viewed as a portent for the fates of other species."

With the word 'portent' evoking thoughts of miners and their canaries, and beginning to grasp there was seriousness in what she was saying, I had said "Well what do you think is causing this then?"

From her terse "It is not a matter of thinking, it is of establishing cause and effect beyond any speculation," I had wished that I'd phrased the question differently, so thought it best for her to flow on. "The effect is declining populations, potential and actual planet-wide, therefore the cause has also to be ubiquitous. Because these animals have not had time enough to adapt genetically to its advent, it indicated strongly to us a causant introduced widely into the troposphere and in evolutionary terms, recently. By a process of elimination we have now identified without doubt the protagonist phenomena."

"Well what?" I said with my breath now hanging.

"Polymerimic hydrocarbon intrusive frocicles, molecules," she gushed.

"What?" I had said.

"Plastics."

"Plastics?"

But she had flowed on as though I had exclaimed and questioned nothing, "By manipulating carbon frothicle grouping into non-natural occurring isotopes, the resultant effects on their plume emissions associating, interacting with, and on naturally existent forms of organic carbon, will inevitably give rise to abnormalities in structure of cells, especially the hyper-resonance susceptible reproductive cells resulting in declining male fertility and increased incidence of malformation in females...."

"You mean plastics are poisoning life?"

"Put briefly," she had said and pausing, "yes." From the then quiet tone of her voice and her face devoid of expression I saw she was being un-exaggeratingly serious, more so when she had added "Slowly, stealthily, yet assuredly."

"Plastics are part of every part of life, there is nothing which doesn't have plastic, even my mum's hip has plastic. There's no possibility plastic could ever be got rid of. The world would collapse without plastic..."

But I had been talking more to myself than to Milophinia, for she just bounced back all that I said, "The world will collapse with plastic," and then added "Human societies existed until recently without it, did they not?"

"That was then," I had said, "long ago really. Things are different now. The world has moved on and plastics have played no small part in that advancement. Even if by some miracle it is possible to stop plastic being made there is so much of it knocking about, the world would never be rid of it and people will never be persuaded to chuck what they have away either. Even if they did what could they possibly replace it with?"

"Short term gain for long-term loss and demise," Milophinia retorted, "is that progress? Is this wisdom?"

"Look," I had said, "you Susem have wiped out the world's energy production, stopped mining, forestry, fishing, construction and a whole load more. Now you are saying the entire plastics industry has to go as well? If it did, millions of people would be condemned to poverty, misery and probably premature death."

"I have only described, related what is occurring," Milophinia had said and continuing, "We Susem have progressed without need for such a damaging substance."

"It's all right for you, with your methods of growing materials to order," I'd said, "but here on Earth we don't have those sorts of things."

"Historically neither did we Susem, until we developed them," she said.

Pheteriso then appeared and took Milophinia off to her dance class (they have all become dance mad). But as Milophinia departed she left the rejoinder, "Does humankind have the right to destroy the life of others on Earth including its own heirs, or does it have a duty of care during its period of stewardship?"

A few minutes after she had left, Roberto drove up to take me to see James in the hospital at Itapipoca. It's 100 miles away and I was not looking forward to the trip. Roberto's driving has not improved and neither had, the last time I saw him, James's health.

Why James should have done such a daft thing as trying to come here I will never know. Not that I have been able to find out. He had straggled ashore, wandered about for a bit and then collapsed, and has been half ga-ga ever since. Though from all his bruises, especially those down the side of his head, he must have had one heck of a bang from something.

Though I had my eyes closed out of fear for much of the trip I had time for thought, of the soufins being dud and the uproar they will cause, what Milophinia had said about plastic, how thalidomide had produced the deformities it did by something as little as right-handed and left-handed receptors on cell surfaces becoming confused, and oranges and lemons are different for the same sole tiny reason. And I worried about James's dire state and Menpemelo's refusal to help heal him. But Roberto blithely chattered on non-stop about the Nonettes' tax plans and was forever asking my opinion.

Pedro had told the regional Nonettes that his men wanted paying. In turn the Regionals had turned to the communities through the Area Nonettes for direction. At the time I had thought it would spell the end of all the bonhomie and camaraderie, but to my surprise the opposite has occurred. Rather than there being a grumbling whip-round for Pedros men the communities, with one or two exceptions, turned the issue into one of raising money to spend collectively on all the other things they couldn't provide themselves.

Within days there had been wide agreement to pay ten per cent of their incomes (though again, I have my suspicions that Paceillo's hand is in their somewhere). This "tithe" as it's quickly become known, is to be collected by the communities themselves. As well as costing next to nothing to gather in, it means of course the collecting is likely to be very thorough (in a community everybody knows everyone else's business).

Aiding this likely thoroughness is that a quarter of the monies raised are for the communities to spend within themselves, the rest going to the area Nonette to spend on their behalf and all its other 80 communities. Of this, a third, a quarter of the total, is to be distributed back to the communities. The richest one gives their surplus above the 81's meridian to the poorest, and so on until the one in the middle gets all of theirs back, though in reality they'll not need to part with it in the first place.

The reason why there has been such wide agreement is the way the surpluses themselves are administered. Each donor community is directly responsible themselves in handing over their money to the recipient one. Both will also be jointly managing how the money is spent. Not that their task will be complicated. It has to be primarily spent on only one thing, the generation of wealth through employment, or put simply, create businesses and jobs. The intention is sensible enough. By enriching poorer communities, the bigger their tithe in time becomes and the less of a subsidy they will need. What is also sensible about the idea is that every donor of every dollar has a say in how it is spent. If there had been something like this in London when I was there, even I might have agreed to paying over something myself.

The quarter the communities raise and retain for themselves is also precisely allocated with so much of a percentage to be saved for contingencies, so much to be spent on this and so much on that. Half of the half actually going to Area Nonette is allocated to the Regional one, half of which is actually redistributed between the Areas, the richer giving to the poorer and again both overseeing how it is spent to create wealth.

Half of each Regional Nonette's remaining half, an eighth of the total Local Nonettes raise, is shared between them and other Regional Nonettes. Though Ceará isn't rich it is better-off than its sister Regional Nonette in Maranhão. So while Maranhão will receive funds, Cearense will collectively have the benefit of investment opportunities.

On those odd moments I had my eyes open, I'd told Roberto that any plan sounding too good to be true usually is. I had not the heart to tell him that he being a student he had yet to experience paying taxes but the moment he did he would soon change his view. So instead I told him that people only ever pay taxes under duress and coercion. I also told him there was nothing in the Nonettes' plans to stop conniving between groups of people to understate their earnings.

To this he asked had I heard that the auditors of elections were to be beefed up to monitor and certify community accounts as well? I said I'd not but told him it would never solve the problem of those who refused to pay. To this he had said, had I heard that those who didn't would be excluded from the seed analysers, soufins, mormics, tunics, teaching machines and everything else the communities handled? I said I'd not heard of this either but added what will happen after the Susem have departed and the things they have provided start breaking down.

He then said had I heard of the planned classes and the programmes for the introduction of manufacturing with the new materials from the new crops? He kept going on and on so enthusiastically I'd again not the heart to dampen his idealism, so I kept reminding him to keep his eyes on the road and slow down. But these cautions had no effect on him either, we were door to door in an hour and a half (I was dripping with trauma by the time we arrived and nigh in need of hospitalisation myself).

James, when I saw him, was still in a terrible sad state. I was with him for an hour and more but in all that time he had not so much as recognised me. His eyes were still looking as though he was far away. On the return to Tabajara I worried about him all the more. It will be indeed a sorrow should he pass away but if he recovers he will not be much better off. He will either end up in the Pelada, or if he is handed back over the border the Brazilian military will probably give him a hard time for he came ashore with nothing but the clothes he was in, no passport or anything.

Roberto, seeing I was concerned, asked could not I ask the Susem to put James to rights as they had him. But I told him what Menpemelo had said, that James not being a Nonette his well-being was of no concern to the Susem. Why should they treat him, she had said, there were a lot more people in need of their assistance, people who were toiling for sufficient achievement points, and James had not a single one.

I also told Roberto of the other worries I had, the shoddy soufins, the besmirching of my reputation, plastics, the fate of the human race, of how I was dreading how Paceillo would rage when she learns of Milophinia's team's discoveries, that she would probably send tocans out to remove the world's chemical refineries forthwith. I also mentioned my further fears of what will happen to us all when the Susem have left and Ceará is invaded by the Brazilian army.

But Roberto was still filled with unbridled optimism, and again I had not the heart to tell him it was all unfounded and he was dooming himself to disappointment. He said there was nothing for the people of Ceará to worry over, they would soon have the new materials to replace plastics. The new industries, he said, which would spring up to make replacement materials would create thousands of jobs. There would be a huge export demand. Even more jobs would be created in removing the plastic. But when I had asked where he thought it was going to be disposed of he was flummoxed, at first. Then he said as plastic came from oil which came from holes in the ground there was no reason why it couldn't go back into other holes.

The prospects of invasion had him laughing as well. Had I not heard, he said, of the plans to create another regional Nonette to the west of Maranhão? Or of the many people from outside, boating down the Amazon in a bid to circumvent the army's cordon? There must be millions of people in Brazil and elsewhere who were sympathetic to the Nonettes, he said.

He was going on enthusing more and more with every breath that I just had to bring him back to Earth, so I reminded him of the grim fate of Conselheiro and his followers at Canudos (the last big anti-government uprising in the Nordeste).

By then we had come to just before the Ibiapaba on the 2-22 where it winds up between some mesas. "Look there!" Roberto had exclaimed and pointed up into the sky.

But I had hurriedly to also shout "Look there!" and point to the bend in the road and the steep drop to the side. When I had calmed down and looked to where Roberto had pointed and saw, flying towards the Ibiapaba, a formation of nine vedas, I told him there had been many such flights these days past.

I also told Roberto of the hundreds more Susem who had arrived in them. There are now so many Susem, I said, that their refectory is always crowded. So many more Susem have now arrived, I had told him, that they had carved out an even bigger, higher ceilinged refectory to accommodate them all. I also told him that though the Susem may be an advanced civilisation, from the way they are currently behaving they are little better than football supporters before a match. They lounge around in groups drinking and smoking, rocking back and forth, then yelling "Pan! pan!" and thrusting clenched fists to the air every time they do. And they are forever doing it except for when they are at dance classes. They are dance mad I told him, there is wall to wall Tamla Motown playing non-stop day and night. What is more, I said, they never seem to tire of it either.

I have no idea what they are up to and each time I have asked, all that I have been told me is "It is nothing." As I said to Roberto, it has always been my experience that whenever a woman says that, apart from when she's demeaning a man's anatomy, it usually means there is something big about to happen. Though I also said to him that I didn't think it could be that ominous because the groups always break up afterwards into fits of laughter.

Another thing I have noticed, I told Roberto, is something that the Susem must have picked up from Rainbow. That they have taken to addressing each other collectively as "Girls". And each time I hear groups of Susem say "Come on girls," they are giggling as though schoolchildren who have just learnt a new rude word.

If I had not worries enough, the moment we arrived back I stepped straight into another. But this one I was able to turn to my advantage.

90: KEN

What a carry on. What a let down. After all that build-up you would have thought they would have had everything sorted out. For days there wouldn't be half an hour pass on SLI without that Rip Thorne coming on drawling "This momentous triumph for justice," and how he was "humbled and privileged to report to the people of the world," and all that sort of old tosh.

Of course, looking back I now realise his lot hadn't actually gone into how it was supposed to happen. Anyway, because of all the coverage I have to have a look. It wasn't just me but everyone else at work as well, we watched on the tele Dave has up in his office.

Ten thirty it starts, "Bosnia, The Trials," and a fanfare of trumpets. Rip Thorne comes on hands to his hips, but Alison and Judy, our two colour retouchers, joke about him having a specially tight pair of jeans for the occasion. He starts off, "Here, nestling in the foothills of these parched, barren mountains, on the western edge of this war-torn land, scene of endless conflicts throughout the centuries for mastery of the fertile plains of the interior, lies this..."

He's then shown from the waist, "...isolated hamlet, known to countless generations of the indigenous people who have dwelt in this pitiless land..." The camera zooms in to just his head and shoulders, Judy sniggers and points out the toupee she reckons he's wearing, "...as, "Carmer Nit Sar May Jesto, the Place of Stones."

He keeps going on about how the Court was specially built, "...so that the wrongs done unto the Bosnian people may be atoned and the cause of justice seen in action and under full glare of television to the entire world..." He is still drawling but the camera now swings around the yard in front of the Court and I see there are indeed stones, they are heaped in piles all round its edge. There are also big crowds milling about, most of whom seem to be women in black and are silent.

"...And waiting reverently outside the Courthouse, in the harsh searing glare and heat of an unforgiving sun, are many of Bosnia's womenfolk. They are gathered here today in an expression of unity and solidarity with their tormented sisters, soon to give testimony of the wretched ordeals they have been subjected to..."

Rip Thorne then interviews some of them. They all jabber back in the local language with somebody interpreting. Alison pokes fun about his suntan make-up starting to streak, but I notice, though no one else appears to, three big trucks coming in the yard. The crowd parts to let them through and each one backs up to what looks like holes in the ground.

Then Rip Thorne at last finds a woman who speaks English, and she is saying "We have come to see justice done to the men who do these terrible things..." But all the same, while she is talking I can still see that from one of the trucks, and over her voice, there are barking and growling sounds coming from the back of it, and I suppose the other two.

Rip Thorne makes no mention of all this barking and growling, neither does another man, off camera, and who takes over from him. Instead this new one goes on about how all the accused are held on this island Incommunicado, without television, radio, newspapers, that this Court is one of seven trying cases, how the "Defendants have been brought to the Courthouse in the dark emptiness of the night...that they all face charges of...assaults against women."

The time comes to nearly eleven and Rip Thorne reappears. Alison and Judy joke about him having his make-up retouched as he says "We have now learned that hearings are about to commence, so it's over to Herbert Finglestein inside the Courthouse. Over to you Herb..."

The picture changes and this "Herb" begins talking, though he also doesn't appear. While he is bantering on describing everything, the camera pans all round the Court and shows that it's packed with women sitting either side of an aisle like in a church with an open doorway at one end and what must be the judge's bench at the other.

The camera then shows another door and this 'Herb' saying it's from where the accused will come out. Then the camera goes to a group of women who he says are the victims. No sooner has he said this, than there is a booming sound. Herb then says it's the front doors closing which means the Court is about to be in session. In a hushed voice he then says "The Court is now standing for the judges." There is a pause and in they walk, three of them.

At first I can't take it in, neither can the others. Though they are wearing gowns and hats, it's obvious that these judges are only kids, or teenagers at most.

However, they don't hang about and I have to say the head judge speaks really good English for a foreigner. He calls out "This court is now in session," and taps his hammer, then, "The first case please. Bring in the accused." With that, this man appears through the door between two big mean looking orientals.

Then we are in for another surprise. Up jumps another young lad, Herb whispers he is the Prosecutor, and he also starts speaking in English. "The accused, Nasar Panic violated this lady," he says pointing to a woman who now gets to her feet.

The judge c alls out to the man "How do you plead, guilty or not guilty?"

He doesn't appear to understand the question but everyone in the Court starts calling "Cako stee sago varatee," as though they're half mocking him. Herb whispers it means, "How do you plead?"

The man then says "Neigh kriv."

But the judge promptly shouts back all sardonically "Only English in this Court, if you please."

The man looks confused but one of the guards whispers something to him and he then says "Nart guil-tee."

"Oh," says the judge and then to the woman, "Is he the man who violated you?"

The Prosecutor whispers in the woman's ear upon which she points her finger at the man and shouts out "Eet was eim, ee do eet."

"What have you to say to that?" says the judge to the man. But the man, still looking confused starts babbling in the local lingo and getting all het up.

"That is enough of that," the judge says and banging down his hammer, "if you still refuse to speak in English in this Court, be quiet and sit down." The two orientals push him onto a bench behind.

The judge mutters to the ones either side of him. Then, and as though looking to the camera, he addresses the Court, "There being no good purpose served in making the details of this shocking case public and having studied thoroughly the victim's testimony, the members of this panel do pass the following majority verdict."

With that all the judges turn to the camera and slowly pick up from in front of them big white cards and hold them aloft. Each has 'Guilty' written on them. I'm reminded of players in a game show, but all the same a roar of approval goes up from the people in Court. As the noise dies down the judge says to the man "You will now step into the well of the Court, sentence will be passed in due course."

That is it, a complete trial all over and done with in the space of a couple of minutes. But even before the guards have taken the man from the dock the judge is calling "And the next case please."

That's just the same, including another woman pointing and shouting "Eet was eim, ee deed it," and the judges holding up 'Guilty' cards. But I do notice that after Herb's "The judge is certainly clear and forthright in his statements..." he didn't say anything more.

I have a load of orders to get out, so I leave the rest watching but as fate has it I'm back in Dave's office just before half past. By then I notice that there are at least a dozen blokes in the well of the Court. Dave says they have all been found guilty though he adds the guards had to smack a couple for being lippy.

I'm then just going back out the door when I notice one of the other judges tapping the head judge's arm and pointing to her watch. He then says "There is just time for one more case." I stop and look. Though it's just the same as the others, at the end the judge turns to the camera and says with a smile and doffing his hat, "Don't go away, we'll be right back after the break," and a load of commercials come on. There's a good few of them. Half are ordinary ones I've seen before but others say "We are proud to be associated with Bosnian people's fight for justice," or things like that. They end and we are back in Court again complete with the judge saying to the camera "Welcome back to The Court at The Place of Stones". Then he's calling "And the next case."

Just before twelve Dave calls me to come and watch what is happening. As I go in his office I see there is now a load of blokes crammed in the well of the Court. The judge is saying "This panel will now pass sentence on the perpetrators of these heinous crimes." There's a pause as the three judges mutter to one another, during which everyone in the office says how many years the guilty should get, Judy and Alison wanting the most.

The judge then looking at the guilty says, "As no good purpose will be served to the community or to the victims by imposing on any of you a custodial sentence, after the break you will therefore be free to leave this Court."

I don't know what to make of it all, it doesn't seem fair to me, the others watching are saying the same but Alison and Judy are really angry. Here are at least two dozen men who've all been found guilty of rape, two of them so Alison says, of young girls, and the judges, including one who is a woman are allowing them to walk free from Court.

Though all the same, as the judge speaks and without a word of protest, and with their arms folded the victims stand up and march down the centre aisle of the Court. The others remaining seated aren't protesting either, but as they are all women I thought they would be bound to.

We are all talking during the commercials. They then end, Herb comes on and banters about the judges' sentences being "Extraordinary...totally unexpected...inexplicable..." During the commercials the Court has emptied, except for the guards and the convicted men.

The judge then says to these men, "You may now leave this Court, but remember you will carry the shame of your terrible deeds for as long as you shall live. This Court is now in recess for thirty minutes."

The guilty begin walking, strolling really, down the aisle talking, and the guards who are behind them aren't hurrying either but stride ahead and open the doors of the Court. The glare of the sun shines in and Herb says "Now over to Rip..."

Rip Thorne appears standing outside the Court. He starts off saying "Thanks Herb. I see the men leaving Court..." But as Thorne speaks he's doing so against a chorus of wails and moans. "The men are now standing in a group," he says. The wails and moans coming from the women change to high pitched shrill whoop whooping, like Indian war cries.

The camera zooms to show the top half of Thorne and he's saying, "The atmosphere is electric...the men have stopped in their tracks.." The whoop whooping gets louder, shriller. Thorne is now in head and shoulders close-up and gasping as though he's been running. The whooping becomes even louder, shriller. The camera then shows the nearest men and Thorne holding his mike to them calling "You sir, what have you to...No good he's...they're turning back...running...no they're trying to...the doors are closing..." Then with a boom, slamming sound Thorne's saying, "They've closed the doors, the Courthouse doors are...was that a rock?...They're throwing..."

Another voice, off camera then screeches "Get down...get dow..." With this Thorne's face promptly disappears but the picture is also suddenly tumbling as though it's falling. The whooping is even louder but also as though it's nearer. Thorne's face reappears but now he is lying on the ground and not really looking to the camera.

Then above the whooping there's shouting and screaming as well as a lot of banging as though thumping on doors. Thorne is then wailing "I'm hit... I'm hit..." Then with him holding his hand to his head and his hair going all over the place, "For Chrissake get me outta here..." There is more screaming and then sounds of hundreds, thousands of something hard hitting something hard, like stones on the doors. The picture skews away from Thorne but as it does it shows actual stones raining all round the camera. Thorne can then be heard groaning.

The screen suddenly goes fizzy white and in almost no time there is a programme about sheep farming in Australia, and Alison is saying to Judy, who both have big smiles and are rubbing their hands, "You were right, he was wearing a toupee."

Billions lost in City 'wipe-out'

By Arthur Todd
City Editor

Another tidal wave of selling swept the City yesterday with the FTSE down 324.7 to a close of 3246, a near 10 per cent loss on the day. Further slides will follow, say City commentators.

The falls follow Tuesday's Wall Street's 12 per cent tumble resulting from the collapse of SouthWest Power. Citi analyst, Cathy Sonting, said: "South-West is only the start. There will be many more to seek Chapter 11 (the US's bankruptcy protection law) before long, some even bigger. For investors its "hold on to your hat's time", it's going to be a bumpy ride for a while yet."

With the Dow slumped to an overnight close of 4882, almost half its level of its high in April, investors have been subjected to one wipe- after another. Whole swathes of industry have been adversely affected by Susem actions.

The only bright light for investors has been US Treasury Bills. The Fed's latest auction Tuesday, for US$50 billion saw a 20 times over-subscription. US government stocks and other premier sovereign government stocks - including the UK - have been racing ahead. Even the UK Treasury' £5.5 billion has already soared to £112 875, yielding a lowly but assured 4.4% and a 27p/e.

How soon these stockmarket slumps will feed into the 'real' economy is anybody's guess, but Bert Bertenheimer of Humbert's School of Economics in Hamburg is currently compiling a report of recommendations and predictions for companies Euro 250 com-

hat the / iselves / Earth / their / claim / planet. / ocated / lost / they / stated / sem's / h / erm / e, / mitte / niun / the / trans / sed / fety o / rest of / ice of / it was / been / an to / Earth / fety of / urther / these / arth's / or the / t, Dr / from / liens / all

News Bulletin

War crimes trial dates announced

RAGUSA: The Prosecutors Office in Ragusa announced yesterday that the first of the trials of those accused of 'Crimes Against Humanity' in the Bosnian War is set for Thursday, August 5th. The first cases will be heard in seven specially built Law Courts throughout Bosnia. No further details were given.

Councils ignore Government's 'energy edict'

COUNCILS throughout Britain are ignoring government instructions not to use the Alien energy units. Many say government cuts have left them with no alternative.

West Essex Council is typical of many defying the government's ban. Council leader Tessa Gorgan is adamant that the council will continue to use the units. She said: been able to avoid layoffs and retain key members of our staff.

"Already we are seeing substantial benefits as a result of the savings. We have been able to renovate the council heads' offices, increase the attendance allowances to council members and retain the head of finance in being able to double his salary and buy him the

Bank lending slumps

- Lending demand at all-time low
- Industry cautious of commitment
- Banks' profits under threat

James Kerr
City Correspondent

Industry's uncertainty over future events has badly affected bank and other lending. The Bank of England's Quarterly Review reveals that the main high street lenders were among the worse hit.

Should this trend - the rate of decline – continue then the outlook for their profits is extremely bleak. With both Westminster and Clayings among others hammered into paying half their last year's profits in Susem 'fines' there are now fears about the soundness of both their capital bases.

Even worse is the further analysis of the lending the banks have made over the past quarter. According to the Bank of England - and many City analysts - much of the banks lending has been crisis loans to companies hit by Susem actions. Another area of lending which must be worrying for banks is the levels of replacement borrowing as opposed to virgin loans.

With so many sectors of business in turmoil - timber, mining, fishing being only the latest - it is perhaps no wonder that caution is the order of the day. Coupled with this is the huge boost to company cashflows brought about by the wide-spread use of soufin power units. City estimates that these are now providing an across the board saving of 28 percent to unit

Shocked Shiekh flee

THE tiny Gulf State Hut has overthrown its rul Shiekh Ob Harabh in apparent bloodless cou The flamboyant Shiek made a hasty getaway his private jet to Londo When the oil was flowin the Shiekh used to boa "All you see belongs me." Hutar is the lat Gulf state to unseat th ruler

In the past month Gulf state after another, suffering from the slump

Medical miracles shown by Susem

By Phelix Verth
Health Correspondent

TEN men and women appeared on last night's telecast claiming to have had lost limbs re-grown by the Susem.

If the claims are true then it would give hope to millions of people throughout the world that they might also benefit from Susem medical technology.

Two of the men, who said they had both lost their lower legs, showed off to the camera where there new limps had grown from, joking with one another over who could wriggle their new toes the most. A woman demonstrated the dexterity of her new fingers by playing with a marionette puppet.

What was perhaps just as astounding was the speed with which the limbs were created - within just a single day; digits took only a matter of hours. One of those watching the telecast was Sir Gerald Adams, Senior Consultant at St Marys Hospital Weybridge and a leading expert in bone grafting and transplants. After the programme he said: "If these claims are true, and their references to the regeneration of reptiles and amphibians limbs, personally has me thinking that they are, then we have been up the wrong road since we began.

"The phenomenon of limb regeneration among lower order vertebrates has always been known of course but in the past it has never been taken into account by the medical profession. It looks as though we have to start from scratch all over again. But personally, I'll give my right arm to know how they do it."

Also shown on the telecast was one of the new community courts which have been set up. It showed members of one community trying the accused of a series of crimes, ranging from the most obscure to

'Wanted' MP goes missing

By Matthew Bride

SIR Hugh Russett Brown, Cheltenham's outspoken MP is reported as missing.

Sir Hugh, who was on an all-party Parliamentary fact finding mission studying sugar production in the Caribbean, disappeared during a tour of Belize.

The head of the delegation, Garry Weston, said: "The entire group had visited the Reddened Whip Plantation at Belomopan in the morning. At about noon as the heat was becoming oppressive, we went off for a spot of lunch at the owner's villa. When we woke up at four there was no Sir Hugh.

"At first we thought he'd gone off on a tour of villa but when, after a couple of hours he hadn't turned up we sent out a search party. When he wasn't to be found in any of the bedrooms or in the gardens of the place we became a little concerned. But by then it was getting dark and we'd a Gala Evening in nearby San Jose laid on by the Belize government to attend, so nothing further could be done.

"When the next morning there was still no sign of Sir Hugh the Belize government sent out a search party. They are still searching for him."

Sir Hugh who is widely known for his outspokenness, has been named by the Bosnian Prosecutor's Office for involvement in supplying military equipment to the former regime in Serbia. Though he has always vehemently denied the charges the evidence presented by the Bosnian Prosecutors has many convinced that the company Sir Hugh was associated with, Zapp plc has a case to answer.

Sir Hugh's Italian born wife, Lady Brigida, said she was sure her husband's disappearance was "unconnected". She said: "Hugh is always going off on little jaunts. He's a very adventurous man, he always has been. I remember our first lo-

Muslems back Pope

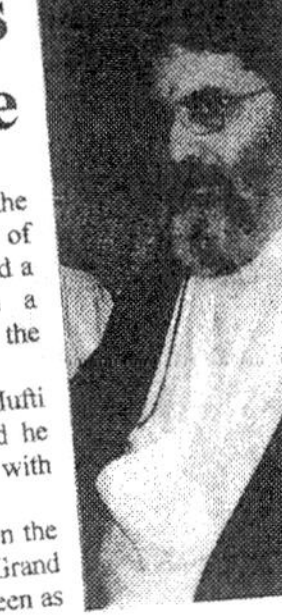

THE Pope's claim that the Susem were messengers of the Antichrist has received a boost of support from a surprising source - the Muslems.

Yesterday the Grand Mufti of West Bromwich said he agreed wholeheartedly with the Pope's stance.

"It is very important in the extreme," says the Grand Mufti, "that truth is seen as

91: H P P

If the shower of stones Rip Thorne and his crew strayed into had not landed them in hospital, Rainbow if she could, would have put them there, single-handed. Her derogations spitting down on them and their short-comings, his especially, were molten. Where she learnt such words I will never know but suddenly, in mid-tirade she became ominously silent.

Fearing for the worst I was all for legging it lest her lava rain down on me. But instead of erupting in rage she burst into tears. And with them came a flow of woe, for her prize project had fizzled fatally on its first day. She had prided herself, she said still sobbing, in it all, from having the idea, negotiating the terms, overseeing its progress at every stage, promoting it in her telecasts, to finally there it was on the TV to be seen by the entire world. And now because of men, Rip Thorne in particular, she had seen the success of her striving snatched from her. She had so wanted, she blubbed, for men to be shown and know what women really felt needs to be done to those who abuse them.

Trying to console her I said there were bound to be others who could take Rip Thorne's place. But she said that everyone from Caught TV (and she stressed the fact that they all were men) had told her that they were refusing to go anywhere near the trials for fear of their lives. As I proffered my hankie her contrariness had me inwardly grin. Here she was, as upset as would be a child losing their pet rabbit, but what she was crying over was the thwarting of her plans to have shown on screens around the world, in real time, the unexpurgated dire doing to death of two dozen wrongdoers.

Taking the hankie and still welling with tears and woe she continued her sad litany of further repercussions resulting from Rip Thorne's crassness. But as she sobbed a small seed of opportunity, of how this particular adversity could be turned to my advantage, began to stir. Soon, after Paceillo had arrived it was ready to put out roots.

Either Paceillo has some way of knowing every action occurring or she has eyes in the back of her head, for Rainbow was still wiping hers when she appeared in the studio. Though she too consoled Rainbow I was soon aware that she wasn't best pleased with the Trials' TV debacle either. Neither, or so she said was Tearo or the Bosnian Nonettes. Great store she added was set by the trials and they could not proceed unless they were seen by everyone and seen to be just, and this meant the televising of them.

My remarking that the trial already taken place wasn't exactly fair received Rainbow's raged "Is rape?" And after her equally adamant "They had the right to defend themselves, which was more than they gave their victims," I deemed it wise not to comment further in that particular direction.

But Paceillo, initially with apparent calmness continued, "If the trials are not shown widely the Bosnian people will lose confidence in their Nonettes.

They have promoted them as a way of eradicating the cause of all conflicts against them." Before I could ask what cause she meant she tartly added "Human males' apparent innate inadequacy made manifest by their unending aggression."

Although abrading I was more than happy to hear her say it. Rainbow's "Televising the trials has to go ahead, the money for each programme is needed by Bosnia's Nonettes," and though I knew this to be not strictly so (there is more currently coming in from fines than can presently be spent) I was happy to hear her say this too. I thought the same but was pleased also with her assertion that advertisers would be wanting their money back.

The soil for my little opportunist seed was being nicely hoed for sowing, though some gentle raking was still required. But a few further questions lightly loaded had the pair of them preparing the ground to a treat. "If televising the trials is that important why not use the wonderful super duper automated television system you have already?" I said

"The trials have to be reported not just relayed, so what is shown has to be directed not merely depicted," replied Rainbow.

"If it's so essential that they are," I said, "then why don't you do them yourself?"

"The programmes I produce here take all my time as it is," she replied and adding, "But even if I did go, it still wouldn't work, a whole team is needed."

The replies were coming just as I wanted. And with my, "If men aren't up to the task why don't you have women do it?" and Rainbow's ireful "And where do you think they will come from? There aren't any women TV production camera crews except for programmes on cooking, knitting and children's programmes," had me all ready for sowing.

I was about to disclose the existence of my little seed and negotiate conditions for its planting out, when Paceillo, to my unanticipated delight, unknowingly brought forth a more than ample supply of fertiliser and loam. They came in the form of further reasons why the trials have to go ahead.

Though her, "Tearo, Anuria, Lathia, Colonel Tambassing, his men, the many young and women of Bosnia, Ragusa and elsewhere who have accomplished the apprehension of those who committed crimes are justified in seeking recognition of their endeavour and achievement," was a tad verbose, it was joyous to hear. As was her (and she barely paused for breath) "If the trials are not shown our (I took this to be Susem) standing will also be compromised."

But I was happier still when she next said "By assisting the correction of some of the imbalances existing on your planet we have established a recognition of our abilities. If it is now shown that even with our resources we are unable to uphold and aid something as elementary as televising these trials our standing will be jeopardised."

Looking first at Rainbow, I launched my offer of solution to their dilemma. "If televising these trials is so important why don't you, in your next telecast ask for capable women television technicians to volunteer?"

"You don't understand," she snapped back (but ooh but I did) "no one outside of Caught TV knows that televising the trials has collapsed, they announced there has been a technical hitch. The moment it's known what has really happened everything will fall into ignominy, we would be seen to have failed."

Again it was more of what I wanted to hear and now I was all nicely ready to open negotiations. "So if you and all these other people are worried over losing face, how do you think I will feel about losing mine?" I said and pausing to let that sink in, then added "If ways were found for televising the trials how much would that be worth?"

Paceillo and Rainbow stared vacantly at me as though what I had asked was academic, so I repeated it but added (and looking at Paceillo), "If I could save your standing would you aid mine in return?"

Both then said "What do you mean?"

I then said "H P P."

After they both exclaimed "What?" I explained, well partly.

As a result I was able to negotiate a most satisfactory arrangement. In return for the Susem re-supplying everyone with new soufins, and this time the long lasting ones they are currently dishing out to the Nonettes, I would arrange for the HPP to take on the televising of the trials.

Of course I didn't, dared not let on, that I had only seen the HPP once and then briefly but I was sure the money and acclaim on offer would entice. Naturally I didn't achieve everything I had wanted and had to be flexible on a couple of points, but I was more than able to turn these minor mutual face-saving concessions to my overall advantage.

Paceillo was insistent that replacement soufins be distributed only to those communities organising themselves into Nonettes. Unless they were, she said, it would be unfair to the existing ones. I did mention to her that societies elsewhere in the world would not, could not form themselves along such lines. There would be chaos if they did and governments would stop anyone anyway from trying. But she said that is the way it has to be, though by then I had realised she was only saying it so as to keep face. So I played along with her and said I would announce it on telecasts as I had for the first soufins. This mollified her and I knew that once the replacement soufins began being made and distributed it would be difficult to stop the process.

And anyway as she had said the Susem would be departing shortly once they had located Pa-tu, it seemed pointless to make an issue of such a trifling procedural detail. But maintaining the charade I played along with her in asking how long the present soufins would last. When she said between 50 and 60 days I turned this to advantage as well, or James's rather.

I said a period of at least thirty days would be needed to provide the necessary promotion of the idea of people forming into Nonettes. Though of course I didn't tell her that I envisaged it as no more than a cosmetic marketing exercise, such as governments do when seeking re-election. I added that I wasn't really the person to put across the necessary information. Someone, I said, whose diction was as clear as Rainbow's was needed, someone also who was knowledgeable of the social and economic affairs of the world. And such a person was to be found in James. Fortunately Rainbow agreed, though her "And he's much more telegenic," did chaff.

All that was needed I said was for the Susem to heal him. But Paceillo said he wasn't a member of a Nonette and to treat him would be unfair to those who were. However, Rainbow, with inspiration said she would see Jorge, who, in Elana's absence is currently the village's community representative, and ask if he would assist James's joining ours. She was back within minutes having Jorge agree to James's temporary nomination pending the village's vote on his inclusion.

While she was away Paceillo probed me more about the HPP. Was I sure they could do as I'd said they would? Why did I know them, but Rainbow not? How did I know them? How did I know they would be resolute enough for the task?

Not daring to lose her confidence I was given little choice than to describe the HPP with perhaps a greater glow than they merited. I said I had personally seen them in action and they had a mightily impressive presence. (Though indeed they do, it had more to do with their physiques than professionalism which was of the over-enthusiastic rank amateur kind).

I told Paceillo that the reason why the HPP were not widely known was because they restricted themselves to working in specialist circles (I could not bring myself to tell her that the actual reason was because they were out and out militant feminists with attitude).

I also felt it necessary to say that I had a direct line of contact to the HPP which I could reach immediately by telephone. The reality of course was slightly different, one of them having a day job working in Princess's office. But I was absolutely truthful to Paceillo when I said I was sure they would put terrible fear into men because they had certainly scared the life out of me when I had met them.

However, when Rainbow returned with the news about Jorge's agreement to include James in out Nonette, Paceillo raised a further reason why the Susem could not help heal him. He has not a single achievement point.

Paceillo said it would be unfair to other Nonettes who were striving for enough points if the Susem treated him ahead of them. Being so close to achieving everything I had no alternative but to trade in all my hard learned points on his behalf. This, though a painful sacrifice, had to be seen I thought in the wider, and dare I say, nobler context.

But before I had time to bask in the warm glow of my achievement and commitment, Paceillo once again asked for my assurance as to the HHP's capabilities. And once again I was given little option but to reply "Of course, of course."

It was at this point however and after Paceillo had said "They had better be," that I realised there was more riding on the successful screening of the trials than I had first been aware. I also learnt why so many more Susem had recently arrived, why they are behaving in the forward manner that they are and why groups of them rocked back and forth in unison. But this was not all, for those already arrived were but the first contingents. Seven and more thousand Susem would soon be on their way.

As Paceillo unfolded the details I grasped further why she had so readily agreed to my proposals. She had told the other Susem, so she said, that the worldwide attention televising the trials would bring will serve in part as a diversionary screen for what is about to also take place. And when she said "I am unable to restrain 'the girls' for much longer," and having already been told what happens, I was inwardly glad to be in the safe sanctuary of the Nonettes.

On my way to Terbel's telephones to make the call to Princess, I couldn't help but notice Rainbow's face as she listened to Paceillo further detailing what is about to occur. Her scowl of sadness was now replaced not just by a smile but a smirk, a big one.

Bear gets his claws caught

By **Charlie Watts**
Media Correspondent

DOUBTS OVER the wisdom of SLI TV's decision to screen live coverage of the Bosnian War Crimes Trials were given substance within hours of the first programme on air. However, SLI bosses are putting on a brave face at the setback. But for how long?

In these days of the battles for ratings, can they hold out?

Transmission of the two hour long programme ended abruptly after little more than an hour. Although SLI said 'technical difficulties' were the reason for the halt, this was has been met with incredulity and derision by viewers and no doubt by advertisers as well.

Media analyst Robert Runcie of Garrod, Olgivy & Dodwell, is in no doubt of the scale of SLI media problems. He said: "There is no doubt about it; Dickie Bear has caught a cold on this one. Not only was the programme material way out of SLI's viewer base but Bear must have lost credibility with advertisers. As I see it, there is no way any of them [the advertisers] will sit back for the remainder of period. They are bound to pull out."

Another group of people who must be having second thoughts over SLI are investors. Over recent weeks SLI share price has soared on the back of fat revenues. Economi...

Rip Thorne cops it in trial fiasco shock

THE long awaited Bosnian War Crimes Trial have collapsed in fiasco and a hail of stones.

TV viewers worldwide saw Kip Thorne, who was billed as a ratings pulling celebrity commentator, was seen to be struck by a volley of stones thrown by an angry crowd of aggrieved onlookers. It was also apparent that Thorne's camera crew also suffered from the attack.

The crowd's anger was fuelled by the trial judges' lenient sentences handed down to 24 men found guilty of rape and other serious assault charges. In a series of speedy no nonsense trials - each lasting no more than five minutes - the panel of judges handed down guilty judgements.

In England anyone guilty of rape can expect nothing less than a five years sentence but often Life if violence is involved.

... that these judges ... down was a slap ... rists and culprits ... to walk free from ... the judges were ... st such liberal at-

BRIEFING

US power companies in shock collapse

SouthWest Power has filed for Chapter 11 protection. It is the latest in a string of United States electricity generators to collapse. SouthWest said yesterday that as both the Federal and State governments have failed to assist in underwriting the company's bank and bond debt, it had no alternative than to cease operations.

Since the universal distribution of Susem energy units in the US, 32 power generators have closed their doors. The fate of the remainder is no less promising. While industry and consumers alike are benefiting from the energy units, as well as cheerfully declining to settle their power bills, few tears are being shed at the power generators' plight.

But in a perverse way these very same consumers may, in the end, be the real losers. While company bosses will walk away from their defunct power plants without too great a personal loss, it is their stockholders and bond owners who will be left empty handed. The biggest losers will be mainly institutional investors, who in turn receive their investment fund from the individual pension payments and savings.

Oil companies running on empty

SCALLOP, hit by the slump in demand for oil issued a profits warning yesterday. With its coffers already heavily depleted by 'Susem fines' it announced last quarter's profits will be substantially down on the same period last year. Oil industry analysts expect Scallop will actually announce an operating loss for the first half of the year.

Though the last of the fabled "Seven Sisters" to report its woes, Scall... is thought to be the hardest hit. It was the only oil major, despite protestations of innocence, to pay the Susem. But it is also, like its "sisters" expected to soon undertake a programme of massive lay-offs.

It is difficult to see where the oil companies can turn next to generate fresh incomes. Having spent the ...

'Computerisation of everything can't be stopped'

By Harold Bone
Industry Correspondent

"THE progressive computerisation of every aspect of industry is inevitable, if we like it or not," says computer expert Ann Norrack.

And humans are stupid if they try to halt this progress, she said. "People must realise labour is based on supply and demand. If computers can take over a task done by humans then they will and must.

"Those people who still think that humans are preferable to dealing with as opposed computers, are living in the past.

"Businesses can only be successful if they are able to progressively reduce their costs. If a machine or computerised system can do it cheaper than a human is currently doing, then that human's will be no longer be needed.

"Of course there are some simple tasks where it is still preferable to use human resources simply because they are cheaper.

"But the moment their ...

they will be als... by non-human... Some ordinar... may not like t... the inevitable progress. Ther... increased unem... but this is unav...

"Ordinary pe... take on board that there ... fewer meaningf...

War trials ha...

By Elana Soam
in Dubrovnik

The trials of those accused of war crimes during the recent Bosnian conflict have received a further setback following the postponement amid confusion on the first day.

The Bosnian Prosecutors Office in Mostar announced yesterday that the planned schedule was being "reappraised" ... television coverage.

A spokesperson said: "We are awaiting a decision from Caught Television as to replacements of more appropriate film crews able to cover the trials and their outcomes professionally."

This is thought to be a reference to the fiasco of Caught's Rip Thorne attempted coup last week to ingratiate himself with ...

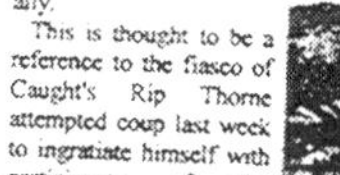

All that Jazz stun Gunners

By **AMY CELESTE**

FINNISH part-timers FC Jazz Turku returned home with a surprise two nil win over Arsenal in the first round of the Eurofa Cup.

While the Finns' win was sweet music to their supporters' ears, it was more the Gunners playing out of tune than a virtuoso performance from the visitors.

After nearly 85 minutes of desultory play, the fiendish Finns scored by a lucky header rebounding off of the head of Arsenal's Steve Jones. The referee's award of an own goal left Arsenal dumbfounded not to mention the 50,000 home side's supporters. Even Jazz's captain Sibe Lius said later it was a fluke.

But three minutes later Jazz's right half, Lind Lampenius in a brilliant solo performance gave the Finns an encore finish by running with the ball from the halfway line and straight into the Gunner's goalmouth before any defender could stop him.

Arsenal's defeat in what was seen before the kick-off as a walkover for them casts serious doubts on their chances in making it to the quarter finals in Italy. Already William Hill has increased Arsenal's odds of making the finals to 100-1. Questions have been asked, however, concerning the circumstances that enabled these so-called 'Finnish no-hopers' beat our so-called 'top-side'.

War Crime inquiry MP named by Bosnian Prosecutors

David Mango
War Crimes reporter

MISSING CHELTENHAM MP Sir Hugh Russet Brown is wanted for questioning by the Bosnian Prosecutor's Office it was disclosed today.

Presenting damming evidence of collaboration with the former Serbian and Croat regimes a spokesperson said she expected the countries concerned to hand over those named for trial without delay.

"As you can see, they are guilty," she said.

Sir Hugh is one of just three Britons named on the list which runs to more than 200 entries. The names, the spokes-person said, were of individuals only. Guilty companies, apart from those named previously, would be issued later she said.

The other Britons named are Peter Radcliffe, of Montenegrin extraction. Mr Radcliffe is liked, prosecutors say, of smuggling ten tons of ...

"Rose, I said I'm not taking calls for the rest of the day."
"He's saying it's critical he talk with you."
"No. Who is he anyway?"
"Linds.. Lindsey or something."
"Don't know him, what does he want, what's he selling? Tell him we're not buying, anything."
"He says it's personal."
"I said no calls."
"Says it's life and death, sounds like he's crying."
"He's selling life insurance? I said no and I mean no. I must complete this report. Take his number, say I'll call him back, tomorrow maybe."
"Says it's not insurance. Says he's calling long distance, Zilla or someplace, still crying."
"Zilla? Where's that?"
"Don't rightly know. Calling you Princess now."
"Princess?...Danny! Put him through, immediately!"
"Yes ma'am."
"Danny! So good to hear you! Where are you? Zilla? Where's..."
"Oh Brazil. This is fantastic! How in the world did..."
"You want what?"
"I don't know if I can do that Danny."
"There's no need to cry. I'll see what I can do, I'll ask.2
"How many! Danny, I think it's way out of their league, can't you think of someone...'
"Oh, so that's what happened, it wasn't a glitch after all."
"Okay, I'll promise not to tell anyone."
"Yes, I know they're all huge and I know they frightened you but I still don't think they'll do that kind of thing."
"Stop crying will you! I'll see what I can do. I'll ask. I'll call you back tomorrow, give me your number."
"Okay, so you'll call me. This time tomorrow?"
"Danny I cannot leave work, I have a report to finish by the..."
"Oh, alright. You'll call me at home this evening?"
"Let me see...that'll be 8pm our time... I don't know if I can, I'll try."
"I promise. Eight o'clock. Bye ..oh you're gone..."
"Rose, could you step in here a moment."

"But Sara you said we had that Transit Costing release to..."
"I know, but for you this is important. It could be your big break."
"You really think? I don't know. Why, the furthest I've ever been is Orlando, never been anyplace abroad before."

"You've...all of you've been selected. My friend from England saw you last year when he was here, remember?"

"England? Oh, that little guy! The one Daisy lifted up over her head!"

"That's the one."

"Oh I remember him now! She sure had him scared there for a moment! His little legs kicking like anything and him yelping "Put me down, put me down!" Oh I remember him! How come he's mixed up with them Aliens?"

"I don't know all. But can you call and ask?"

"I'll try."

"Sara, Nightshade says we've to go to her at the Center."

"What, now?"

"Says she'll only be at Clayton for the next hour, she has a booking over in Belmont at six."

"Okay. Can we make there in time?"

"In your car? You driving?"

"Yes."

"You bet!"

"The Hisogynist Center? And what's that below...Academy of Unarmed Defense Against Men? You never said you changed your name."

"About a month, month and half back. Hisogynist Polyglot Productions became too much in the mouth. And what with the new mayor..."

"You haven't changed though?"

"Nope, same old gang, same multi everything."

"Unarmed defense? That's new."

"Yep. Attendance for shows began falling away. Our videos, DVDs just aren't moving like they once did. And with the City cutting the grant for performances we had to take up self-defense training to still qualify for a grant. Nightshade and Hyacinth are fulltime now, but we all do it."

"But you still do the shows? Is it safe to park here?"

"Safe? You bet, the bums round here know we're just watching for the chance to practice knocking shit out of them! Yep, we still do shows but not as many as we did. Oh, here's Nightshade now."

"You saying we're wanted in Bosnia to televise those trials? You have to be foolin', why Caught TV's the very top people working for them. And if you're not foolin' with us, someone's been foolin' you."

"Rose tell her about that call, was it for real?"

"Sounded pretty real to me. He just wouldn't go away."

"Well, if it's for real...and the money's good, suspect good... Say, what evidence you have anyway it's all for real?"

"I've not any. But he's calling me at eight at home, I'll see what I can get.

What do you want?"

"Hmm.. You online there?"

"Yes, why?"

"Have him send you e-mail confirmation. Now let's see, if it's really for real and we were to go there and take on the televising, what'd we be needin'... Hyacinth, Daisy, Ivy just you step over here a while, we've some talkin' to do, serious talkin'...Myrtle, cancel Belmont for me would you."

"Yes Danny it's me."

"Yes, I've talked with them."

"Most are here now."

"No. They're interested but they've questions."

"Proof Danny, they need proof, can you e-mail me here at home? It's sara at...oh you've got it already. You do it now, and call me back. Bye..."

"Hi."

"Yes, they've read it."

"No, they say they'll agree to do it, in principle."

"No Danny, they've a few conditions..."

"Listen will you."

"All they want you to do is to agree them, they're saying they're not being greedy or anything, they just want recognition. They'll be here for the next hour. You just e-mail me again with agreement..."

"Listen will you! I'll read them over..."

"Yes, I have it, some things are not clear though."

"Okay, but I'll read them through just the same. All forty to be paid $3,000 a day each. Have more of their numbers if they need. Go under their own name. Use their style of close-up camera shots. Free expression in commentary in return for no profanities. Fly to Bosnia in those Alien spaceplane things. But they're not agreeing Oakland."

"No Danny it has to be San Francisco International. You have Caught TV fix that and they can leave by noon tomorrow. Oh, and they want Airport PA of their departure and Caught to arrange TV coverage."

"Good, do that and you've got yourself a deal."

Accused kept on island incommunicado prior to tri

Fresh start for War Trial

From Jessica Gunney
In Dubrovnik

THE BOSNIAN Prosecutors Office announced yester-day that following "full and amicable discussions" with Caught TV's new personnel, the War Trials would recommence and proceed as originally planned

Among those breathing a sigh of relief that the Trials are back on course must be Richard Bear's SLI TV. SLI's share price has suffered badly every since the fiasco of Caught TV's Kip Thorne and other [then] Caught operatives hurriedly leaving their positions in the scene of the first 'Trials' programme.

Missing MP found in Guatemala

GUATEMALA CITY: Missing MP Sir Hugh Russet Brown has been sighted near the small mountain town of Yaloch, 150 miles away in the country's north east.

According to an Interior Ministry statement, Sir Hugh was discovered by plantation workers in a state of exhaustion. Little more is known of Sir Hugh's condition or of how he came to be in such a remote location.

Sir Hugh who was on an all-party Parliamentary fact finding mission to the Caribbean studying sugar production, was reported as missing during the party's visit to neighbouring Belize. An extensive air and land search executed immediately after he was reported as missing, was called off more than a week ago, and Sir Hugh presumed to be dead.

A noted rightwinger, Sir Hugh has been cited by the Bosnian Prosecutor's Office as wanted for questioning over supplying Serbia with stun truncheons. Prior to his departure from Britain Sir Hugh strongly denied the charges. But in the light of revelations released by

Brazilian coup rumours spread

By Nicholas Lobos

RIO DE JANERIO: A claim by Brazil's Chief of Staff that the military and public order situation in the country's northeast was deteriorating has prompted fears of an imminent takeover by the armed forces.

General Vidal da Costa, Commander of the Brazilian armed forces in the northeast region, said recent reconnaissance raids by the Aliens had given his command every reason to believe a major onslaught against his forces was imminent.

He said significant numbers of the army's forward positions were being subjected to "indoctrination assaults" was indication that an attack had to be expected.

Calling for all Brazil's armed forces to be placed on an immediate war footing against Alien attack, General da Costa said it was vital that civilians were removed well away from the army's front line.

This has been interpreted by many as a thinly veiled attack against the Movement Sem Terra ("the Landless Ones") who have been a thorn in the military's side. Although there still exists a State of Emergency throughout Brazil's North East following, recent rioting by the Movement's followers, General da Costa is reported as wanting to smash the organisation once and for all.

In further moves, a seemingly innocuous st... Chiefs of Staff

immediate 50 percent pay rise for the armed forces has sent shivers throughout Brazil. The call has been interpreted by many as a ploy by the Army High Command to bring any waverers in the military on to the High Command's side.

If Brazilian President Rocha agrees to the armed forces' demand for a such a substantial pay rise he will be seen as weak, and thus making a military takeover appear easy. If Rocha refuses the Army's demand they, in turn can say to the rank and file that by supporting them the ordinary soldier will see a substantia... rise in their otherwise meagr... pay.

With an army privat...

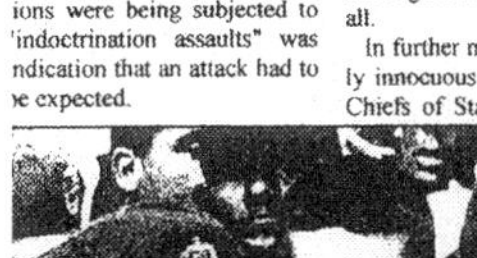

Mixed message on Pelada prisoners' return

By Amber Nightingale

A further 250,000 Serbs and Croats would be returned to their communities within the next few days, as the Susem's telecast said yesterday. However, the outlook for the return of others still held by the Susem is less promising.

Former forestry workers were shown replanting saplings in previously cleared areas of the Amazon forest. Susem telecaster Rainbow Louis said they would only be returned once certain conditions on the part of their former employers had been met.

These included: replacing from with their companies' directors and shareholders and their families; depositing funds with the Bank of Ceará for the replanting and management of 50 trees for 50 years per returned employee.

The return of deep sea fishermen is to be based on a similar financial commitment by their former employers to the replenishment of fish stocks. Meanwhile, Rainbow Louis said all the men would continue the task of reforestation and dam demolition

Mystery surroun... Susem telecaste...

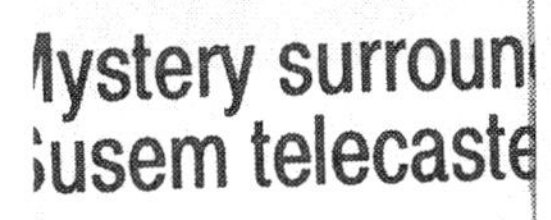

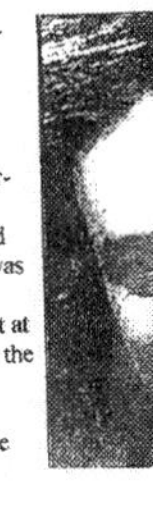

know who the Susem's new teleter is - he is James Powell - but w did he get the job? How did he nage to get to Susem territory? These and many other questions rounded his appearance on yester-'s Susem telecast. It has been vealed that Powell, 24 had worked Morgans Bank in the City and was ade redundant two months ago. fore that he was a student activist at LSE and led the a campaign for the ease of Delano Benson from life prisonment for the murder of lice constable John Whitfield five

The 'Houdini of Irish politics' remains true to form

Chas 'Mahal' O'Higgins - 'at it again'

By Steve O'Hern
In Dublin

CHARLES O'Higgins, the turbulent former Irish taoiseach who quoted Shakespeare upon his retirement seven years ago, yesterday played the part his nation expected of him in the final act of his destruction.

Arriving at Dublin Castle hours before he was due to give evidence to a tribunal that he lied about cash gifts valued above IE10 million (£7 million), O'Higgins deprived the media scrum of the pictures of his humiliation.

But once in the witness stand, the "Houdini of Irish politics," who amassed a personal fortune while on a state salary, was subjected to two hours of brutal questioning about his financial affairs.

The 75 year-old the former boss of Fianna Fail often asked for questions to be repeated but managed to look as relaxed as in his heyday as 'the Boss'.

When asked where the estimated £5.3 million spent on building improvements to his Phoenix Park mansion, nick-named the 'Chas Mahal' came from, O'Higgins said he had no idea hat as such money matters were something too complicated for his understanding he had left those sorts of things to accountants to handle.

Amid laughter, the government prosecutor Mr O' Shaughnessy said: "But you were an accountant and Minister of Finance at the time."

"I was only a presentational accountant and a very quiescent one at that," Mr O'Higgins replied.

He added that when he resigned from office three years ago he hand in-tended to leave public life for good.

But Mr O'Shaughnessy added: "The accountancy practice, O'Higgins, Haughey and Shaft, of which you are a jointly and several liable partner is still in business is it not?"

Mr O'Higgins': "It is."

Mr O'Shaughnessy: "The leaked evidence that this firm is in charge of a IE26 million slush fund to promote the "political process" was not made known to you I suppose?"

"Of that I have no particular recollection," O'Higgins said.

Amid further laughter from the public gallery, O' Shaughnessy said: "You are one of the signatories of payments made by your partnership are you

93: SPHERES

I'm having a terrible run of bad luck. Things I'd planned started off okay but one after another they've all gone awry.

The Susem medical machines fixed James better. Menpemelo said there wasn't much wrong, just a couple of bits here and there inside his skull knocked loose. Though he still had the bruise to his head a couple days' convalescence had him back to his urbane self.

I did my best to impress on him the sacrifices and commitments I had made on his behalf, but like it always is with the young he showed scant appreciation. And Rainbow was all over him, like a mother she was. Though she isn't alone, he had half the women in Tabajara fussing with his recovery. Although it's not really for me to say, it has to be said, James is not a bad looking young man. When he was first walking about and some Susem started eyeing him up, I had to ask Paceillo to tell them to keep their hands off him. A ravaged James is the last thing I needed.

Having kept James from their clutches I set about, during his convalescence, acquainting him to the tenuousness of his stay, what was required to warrant his keep and pay me back my hard earned study points. I stressed to him that he had only to go through the motions but of course to do it with a convincing air of sincerity. Pretend to be a politician I had said to him.

Being a gifted fellow I had also envisaged a speedy repayment of my study points. And it has to be said that for the first couple of days of his recovery James did indeed study hard at his screen. At first I was most encouraged at this, but when I didn't see much in the way of returning points I was moved to ask James why. It was so discouraging him telling me that he had donated half of them to the village in thankful recognition of all they had done for him. "And the other half," I had asked, "what of them?"

"For group use," he had the nerve to reply. And I've still to see a single one repaid. The young can sometimes be so unappreciative. It's been the same with his reporting.

He hit it off with Roberto the moment they met. And no sooner had he recovered than both were off, either in Jorge's truck or in Kubber (and because James and Kubber are forever talking to one another, I have a feeling that they've have hit it off with one another as well). The first day, when he returned enthused with what he had seen I put down to his re-found zest and the exuberance the young so often express for the new. On the second day and with his exhilaration unabated, I had to remind him the purpose of his task. James listened but alas that was all he did.

On the third day James had cast away all caution and became the student, head filled with the idealism I had known when first we met all those years ago. I tried again to impress on him that what was occurring hereabout is an aberration and the world outside is where reality lies. But he would still not take note. I attempted also to persuade him to at least tone down his criticisms of society outside, that change can never be sustained if imposed, 'do gooding' has never done anyone any good. But he still would not take heed.

When James outlined what he had planned to say I was aghast. I told him it will all end in tears if not derision. I repeated to him many times that he has to only go though the motions and nothing more, just so that the Susem supplied replacement soufins before they departed. For when they have gone away everything, including the 'new society', as he is now forever calling the Nonettes, will disappear back into the dust. But he would still not see the sense of what I was saying.

Meanwhile, making matters worse was Rainbow's interventions on James's behalf. She said I was being cynical, that he had every right to be impressed with what the people of Ceará had achieved. Everything he intended to say was fair comment not criticism, she said.

Being older and thinking her a tad worldlier than James I was taken aback at such a stance. I put it to her, that between now and when the Susem depart there would not even be the time, let alone inclination for people in the big wide world outside to change their ways. Everything in Ceará was only because of the Susem. I was again surprised she could be so irritated at such an obvious observation.

For she was of the view, and trenchant too, that the Susem were merely the spark which had at last enabled people to form themselves into an equitable society free from vested interests, free of anyone who wanted to manipulate and dominate them to selfish advantage, free to cohere and conjoin in happiness and harmony, free for individual enterprise to flourish and be for the public good, free to determine individual and collective freedom. She went on and on with free from this, free to do that one after another. All this from somebody who back in London had not the slightest interest in politics let alone political philosophy. And for good measure she berated me for belittling the Nonette movement, saying "We have done nearly all this by ourselves." And noting Rainbow was including herself, I took it she would not be taking my side in the matter.

To cap it all, no sooner had James and Roberto returned with their first filming than she had dropped everything to help edit it for his telecast. She even put his make-up on for him for the close-up shots.

James' idealism is not the only development where I see sadness lurking. Groups of Susem are another. They have taken to what Pheterisco euphemistically terms "nesting." They have set up little fortified redoubts in the mountains and Sertão along the southern borders of Ceará. When she told me what they were doing I didn't know whether to worry that all hell is about to break loose, or just say "those poor defenceless soldiers."

Apart from fawning over James, Rainbow is now well restored to her cool collected self. The arrival of the Hisogynists in Bosnia has pleased her no end. She's says she has struck up a "warm working relationship" with Nightshade, though if their Daisy is anything to go by she should really be prefixed with "Deadly." Though again I have still to receive a single word of thanks from her for getting her out of the hole she was in, nor for that matter from Paceillo in getting her out of hers. Mind you though, she and whole teams of Susem have been more than busy these days past.

They are overseeing the assembling of an armada of machines for the excavation of Pa-tu. Although I'm not sure of the precise location, but from Petruee I have gathered it lies due west up the other end of the Amazon near a place called São Antonio close to the borders with Columbia and Peru. Another stretch of land will no doubt soon be out of bounds.

The only bright spot, if such can be called, has been the chance to talk with Menpemelo about quinths. I had hoped for answers to the bag of questions she left me the last time, but as ever I've gone away with a bigger bag of them.

From what she has told, the four contexts of length, area, volume and time are embedded, are an integral part of the fifth or quinth context, in the same way as the surface of the sea, waves and all, can only exist if there actually is a sea. Similarly, there is much more sea than there is sea surface. Although most of the movement of the sea appears to occur upon (or is it amid?) the surface there is much motion within the sea itself. And this occurs regardless, independently of any movement of the sea's surface but it, however, has an influence on that surface.

But the first thing Menpemelo said was "When two spheres come into contact with one another, what of them is touching?"

I thought about this for a moment and then said "There's nothing touching." Well there isn't. There isn't an 'area' or second context, no line or first context, there's only a nothing context. But something must be touching because one can move the other (I had bar billiards in mind).

"A sphere's point of contact is a point," said Menpemelo, "a point is without context, yet it imparts energy from the context it is of to what it impacts onto. If that should also be a sphere then imparted energy is transferred to its context also by way of a no-context point. In a like manner a curving single context, a line, a linear wave impacting on another will also impart its energy by way of a point or no-context. A point can be interpreted as a catalyst, it effects change to all it comes in contact with, the transference of energy from one entity to another, but leaves no specific imprint of its occurrence."

I grasped this, but I had to concentrate with what she said next.

"Energy can impact as a single linear wave," she said, "or as an unlimited number of waves flowing, oscillating uniformly parallel, such as the undulations observable on the surface of the sea. Should a number of other parallel linear waves cross the path of another, not parallel to them, there will be a collective imparting and impacting of each other's energy at the points of their contacting (whereupon she wove curled fingers of one hand between those of the other). Collectively these points of contact, imparting and impacting, will also form an apparent entity in their own right. This, in one sense will be a secondary context occurrence or, to use other expressions, a plane or field occurrence.

"However, waves, singular and collectively," she continued, "interact with one another not just in a plane but in a multitude of planes. And thus the interactions at these no-context points will form an apparent third, or tertiary, context entity. Something will appear to be, whereas there is, in another sense, nothing there at all."

"Something out of nothing?" I asked.

"Everything which is perceivable is, in one reality, not there. The apparent solidity of a tertiary context entity, or 'thing' is directly relevant to the density of the frothicle clusters of which it is composed and the Secondary waves interacting with them."

I trod with this and tried desperately not to sink.

"The fourth context, that of time is in reality (she gave a tiny smile when she said "reality") the manifestation of the evolution of these point interactions. Time might not appear to have a specific context but in reality (another small smile) it does. In another aspect the waves, Secondary waves, their energy imparted in oscillation without consideration of time, are timeless, their oscillations are always there."

Though sinking slowly I still tried to grasp Menpemelo's logic. But seeing me slithering, she said "Come with me." So I did.

She stood me in front of a window which looked out onto the Sertão below. "See here," she said and rubbing her fingers across the glass. "This pane is a plane, its surface is a secondary context. But on this plane is shown what is beyond it."

As she spoke I could see a truck travelling along the 2-22. "Although you perceive the image as a tertiary context," she said, "there is volume as well as area, what you are observing is an image which has apparent movement. But what you are really observing is a series of fixed images relayed to you from this plane, this pane of glass. These separate images are created from the interaction of waves' no-context points, in this instance those within your visual range. However, each one is travelling, vibrating, oscillating upon your eyes at the rate of two million times faster than your visual neural system, functioning at a slower speed, can register. Because images are arriving on the surface of your eyes faster than can be recorded and processed, all the images are blurred or perceived into one continuous flow."

As she spoke I had thoughts of movie film, how it's made up of separate images but they move faster than the eye can distinguish and so all appear as though they are just one, one continuous flowing movement. And also, if the movie's plot is good, it can be so gripping you no longer think you're merely watching a series of flat fast moving images but are actually watching unfolding events as if they are for real, that you're actually there and the actors aren't acting but they are for real as well.

"But back to this pane," she said, jolting me back.

"Because Secondary waves have a degree of constancy, each are always there, events in which they occur will also always be there. If we were not here to observe the vehicle which is travelling below, we would not know of its existence let alone its journey. Yet both it and its journey would be recorded in subtle changes to the Secondary waves' oscillations. Each 'event' leaves indelible evidence of its occurrence." Seeing me still confused she said "Come with me." So again I did.

"Ah double tubes illustration you vant? No trouble," said Terbal, "soon now it ist coming." And within seconds sherpals along with their "Hados" hurried from their carpet with a vertical glass tube with a handle on its top and which was fitted snugly inside another glass tube. Alongside them was a little glass phial containing a black liquid.

"Between the tubes is a film of viscous liquid," said Menpemelo.

"Glycerine," said Terbal as he floated past.

Menpemelo squeezed a drop of the black liquid into the glycerine and said, as it became a blob, "This is an insoluble carbon based substance."

"Ink," said Terbal as he floated back again.

Menpemelo gave him a glare of a stare whereupon he whizzed away. She then turned the handle of the inner tube. The blob of ink began to stretch and form into a thread. As she continued to turn the tube, the thread went round and round as cotton does a reel, the strands stretching thinner with every turn. She stopped then turned the handle in the opposite direction. The thread began to disappear as though being gathered up. And indeed it was. Soon all the thread was back to being a blob.

"Ooh," I said.

But before I'd time to say more, she gave the inner tube half a turn, squeezed in a second drop and turned the inner tube some more. There were now two sets of threads and soon they were in a criss-crossed tangle. She stopped, then turned the tube backwards once more. And both the threads, disentangling, duly returned to separate blobs.

"Although this phenomenon has been observed here on Earth..."

"Bohm, David, Wholeness and Implicate Order, 1986," interrupted Terbal, then darting back again when Menpemelo him another glare.

"...it aptly illustrates how the interactions of Tertiary and Secondary waves are recordable," she said.

"You mean to say "I said, "that every tiny little thing which has ever happened will have been recorded?"

She gave a nod.

"That means everything is traceable and recallable?"

She gave another nod, then added, “But only in the quinth context.”

I was sinking again.

Seeing that I was, she said, “Think once more of the sea as an analogy. Surface water is continually flowing back into the depths and water from there is continually emerging to the surface.” She paused a moment then changing tack continued, “Think also of the third context being composed of a series of secondary contexts, planes, all compacted so closely that they appear, are perceived as a single entity. Similarly, a plane is made up of a series of first contexts, lines, again all compacted so closely together they appear as one. And a line...”

“Oh no...” I said, “..is no more than a series of points...”

Again she nodded.

“...and points don’t exist.”

And nodding yet again she added “As I have said before, all is energy.”

Then I said “Where does energy come from?”

But before she had a reply Pheterisco appeared. As Menpemelo departed for further directing in the dance, I was left with more than a few questions. But later I had answered some myself.

With Rainbow and Roberto engrossed with James preparing for his next telecast tomorrow, the Pousada empty, and it being a moonless night, I took, for the first time in ages, my telescope to look at the stars. With the lights of the new village now hazing the darkness from the viewing platform, I had to climb high on Mont Macambirá before there was dark enough darkness. I was quite out of breath by the time I had found a good spot. But no sooner had I set up the telescope and looked along the Milky Way, than it dawned on me the significance of what Menpemelo had said.

What I was observing was not just the Milky Way but the spume of a wave upon a cosmic sea and the darkness was the surface of that sea, of space itself. The missing ‘cold dark matter’, the ninety per cent and more of the Universe astronomers calculate is supposed to exist but have never found, was there in the darkness itself. The swirls of all the galaxies, right out to and beyond the Great Wall, were wave crests upon a sea.

The so called ‘matter’ I was observing was no more (and no less of course) than the catalytic interactions of countless ‘no-context' points imparting and impacting energy. Some, such as stars were their concentrations creating brightness, and the black bits in between was where there weren’t so many. But both bright and black were no more than the surface of the Universe. And though I was perched atop Mont Macambirá I was, in a way, sat upon a little bit of wave looking out over that sea.

Then I thought of what Menpemelo said about me registering only one of the every two million images arriving on my eyes. And how it wasn’t necessary to see every one of those either to understand what was going on. One in a hundred would do, say, a billionth of all the ones falling on my eyes, in my ears or all my other senses. That was on just one level, then there were all the other levels and all the combinations of all the levels, and they must come to billions of billions. But I had only to register just the odd one now and then to know what was going on. Like the truck on the 2-22, I had not to look at it every moment to know what it was doing. And high speed photographs of bullets passing through glycerine jelly and leaving marks of their trajectories where it was only necessary to plot the marks of their passing to know where they would have continued to go, or follow their marks back to discover where they had come from.

I looked at the sky again and tried to spot Horologium, the 'Clock Star', but it wasn't yet above the horizon. But as I searched I thought over what Menpemelo said about Secondary waves always being there. If what she says is so, and why should I doubt her, then they must be pre-determined. And if they are, then what determines them? Then I remembered what she had said earlier about carbon, helium, beryllium and oxygen existing in precise ratios down to a third of a billion trillionths to one another throughout the entire Universe. How come they are pre-determined too?

Returning down to Tabajara I still had these musings on my mind. Once there though, all such thoughts rapidly evaporated. Rainbow said, and she had such a smug grin to her face when she told me, that the Hisogynists were already in breach of their contract. Though they were televising the trials they were also participating in meting out the punishments. I feared for the worst.

I'm having a terrible run of bad luck.

All female troupe hospitalize ...

Caught TV's new 'Trials presenters in airport fraca

Janine Lamb
In San Francisco

CAUGHT TELEVISION'S replacement camera and reporting team covering the Bosnian War Trials were involved in serious controversy yesterday. And this was even before they had even left the United States.

The 'Hisogynists', as the 40 strong all-female team insisted on being called, marched in formation to San Francisco International Airport's Press Center yesterday morning and straight into a media conference usually accorded to stars and statesmen. They also caused a media hullabaloo that the organizers were not expecting.

The press conference, organized by Caught Television was meant to restore the channel's flagging confidence to the screening of 'Trials' for first of which abruptly ended in ignominy.

The Hisogynist's, an all-women media troupe based in the Clayton district of San Francisco, are being heavily promoted by Caught as being the right people to handle ...

tunics, black berets and as dark sunglasses, the Hisogynists, at first marched in silent formation past waiting photographers. But, even before they had made it to the airport's Press Center they had attacked four photographers, all of whom later required medical attention.

However, this was not the end of the Hisogynists' altercation with the media

Caught representative Rosemary Halder introduced the Hisogynists' group leader, who in turn announced herself only as 'Nightshade'. In explaining her group's objectives, she said: "We are embarking on an historic mission to see and to show that the wrongs done to our Bosnian sisters will be righted."

However, the rest of what she had to say was drowned out by further scuffles between other members of the Hisogynists and newsmen. To cries of "Male Trash", several reporters were seen being thrown bodily into the

Sperm count down again

MEN'S sperm count is still falling. Today's human male produces less than half of their grandfathers' an international conference on human reproductivity was told yesterday.

The future of mankind's development could be at risk so experts said.

Professor Earnesto Dritto at the Fifth International Annual Reproductivity Symposium at the Barbican said: "Matched against the human sperm counts of four decades ago, today's average is less than half.

"However the rate of decline across the world is accelerating. Since the first Symposium the average decline across the world has been 20 per cent.

"If this rate continues there will come a time when future successful propagation of the human race will be placed in jeopardy," he said.

Another speaker, Professor Helen Radman from the University of Sheppey, said that her researches show that couples now took an average of six months of trying before there was an actual successful conception. This is 50 per cent longer than when the first

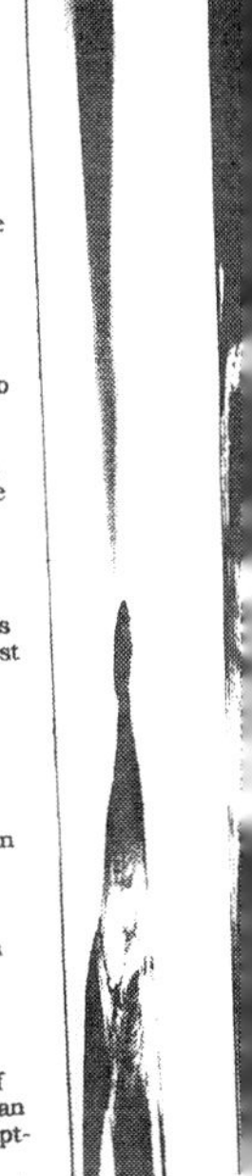

Thugs' terror of thousand pinprick

Erik Senta
In Sarajevo

FORMER Serb-Croat leaders naked and caged like animals in the local zoo yesterday, shook and cowered with terror before crowds wild for revenge.

Beneath 'No throwing' signs in front of the cages, thousands of Bosnians each armed with a length of bamboo tipped with a hatpin confronted the men who once conspired to kill them.

Used to the pomp and perks of high office, 50 one-time bigwigs of the former pariah Croatian and Serbian regimes were being 'temporary' housed in the zoo's cages pending trial for a host of War Crimes against Bosnians and others.

But for the citizens of Sarajevo it was a not-to-be-missed opportunity to ...

from wounds inflicted by successful stabbers these once powerful party bosses, top army and police chiefs stood quaking in tear-filled fright.

The only break in the crowd's silence would be when one of their number managed to plunge a hatpin into the victim, with strikes to the buttocks and genitals attracting the loudest cheers

Once these former rulers had strutted with uniformed ostentation, now they cut pathetic quivering figures begging for mercy from their tormenters.

But mercy was the last thing on the Bosnians' minds. They wanted revenge, and the sweet-...

were neither shouts nor screams of retribution from the people crowding around the cages. There was only silence. The silence of intent and concentration as hundreds jabbed and pointed their hatpin tipped poles as far as was possible through the bars.

The only break in the crowd's silence would be a cheer when one of their number managed to plunge a hatpin into the victim, with strikes to the buttocks and genitals attracting the loudest.

The only respite for the caged former Croat and Serb bosses was the Midday feeding time.

Not that they were hankering for food but at least they received a hose down. Most needed it to wash away the blood and sweat as well as congealed effluent of their vented

Susem say lost spaceship 'found'

THE Susem's lost 'La Ra' spaceship has been located deep in the Amazon jungle it was announced yesterday. Susem telecaster Rainbow Louis said that evidence of wreckage from the lost craft had been located in a remote area of Brazil close to the Peruvian and Columbian borders. Last night experts said the area was the scene of

Former Yugo rulers hatpin zoo ordeal

By Lisa Derventa
In Sarajevo

THE BOSNIAN people yesterday, took revenge on those who once sought to annihilate them. And they did it with hat pins.

Scores of former Serbian and Croatian leaders including Franjo Zlocest and Slobodan Podao, terror-struck and naked were the new 'menagerie' in the cages at the reopened Sarajevo Zoo. However, the crowds of jeering onlookers ...

the bars but bamboo canes spiked with hat pins.

On all sides of every cage packed lines of people, their unsmiling eyes fixed with determined stares bordering on the manic, poked their pin tipped lances between the bars as far as their outstretched arms could reach. All were pointed at the naked body cowering within.

In the cage which once housed the Zoo's jackals was the former Croatian police chief of Mostar, Mate Bob...

and buttocks where onlook... had succeeded stabbing ... with their pins, Boban ... stood stock still with an enci... ling wall of further hundre... of pins just inches away fr... him waiting for his slight... movement.

Boban, who at one ti... boasted at his Mostar forc... efficiency in 'relocati... 100,000 Muslims from th... homes, was in evident distre... Stripped of the authority of h... police chief's uniform he cu...

The Silent Sprung of Amphibians

By **Jay Shaw**

FROGS and toads, newts and salamanders may be 'creepy crawlies' to many of us, but they are 'good' creepy crawlies, for us humans cannot live without them. Or so impassioned scientists claimed yesterday.

At a two day conference at the Natural History Museum animal scientists from around the world voiced their fears of the plummeting populations of the planet's ...

One of the speakers, Professor Pauline Pepper, said: "World populations [of amphibians] have been in decline for the past 30 years or so. However, over the past three years they have completely disappeared from many areas of their natural habitat. "According to field studies conducted by my Department at the University of Sheppey on 120 sites where they were recorded 30 years ago, extensive breeding colonies of both the common toad ...

"This decline has not only been rapid but it is now accelerating. From other, though less extensive records, all of the sites we studied had seemingly healthy breeding colonies of both frogs and toads. Albeit their numbers were reduced, but at the time this was put down to the normal cycles of population variance," she said.

Professor Yuhdo Ham said: "In Japan we have similar problem. Frogs and toads eat many flies and other insects. Their present ...

correspondingly rapid increase in the number of insect pests.

In turn this is forcing our farmers to resort to yet ever higher levels of pesticides to combat these insects," he said.

Other speakers from around the world also voiced their concerns for the recent rapid decline in the numbers of amphibians. Rose Hunter from the Salamander Research Centre at Wood Hole, said: From the rainforests of the tropics to the tundra of the Artic ...

94: KEN

The moment he came on, even before he had gave his name, I said “That looks like that young Jim who Danny had living with him.” A few others in the Greenwood recognised him as well. I couldn’t make it all out, I really couldn’t. And it’s getting so there is more and more Susem stuff on telly. Rainbow nearly every night, there’s the Trials now that they are back on again. This morning’s was a shocker, everyone is talking about it. And now this Jim.

I didn’t take in everything he said, well you can’t. But very interesting and he did have a couple of good points, more than a few when I think about it.

He begins by showing these people crowding round what looks like little allotments. “I am in the village of Santana,” he says, “from these little gardens the villagers produce crops without using chemicals, artificial fertilizers or sprays. Their plants grow so fast from seed to cropping that pests are unable to damage them.” Then he shows piles of potatoes, tomatoes, bags of beans, bags of grain. “Not only are they the very best,” he says, holding a few in his hand, “but productivity is tens of times higher than even the most intensive conventional agriculture.” He reels off loads of facts but of course they don’t mean anything to me.

Then he says “Up to a few months ago, these people were treated as near slaves to labour from dawn to dusk on the plantations of a few rich men who owned all the land and controlled the villagers’ destinies dooming them to life-long misery, ignorance and early death. Now, each of them own their land, are part of the village’s farming cooperative and live in their own small sovereign community. Ignorance is banished, as is illness, poverty and crime.”

Next he is shown walking towards the camera and saying “Up to a few months ago the villagers were condemned to live here...” With that there are all these empty hovels. “...but now they live here.” And there are all these little terraces of houses. Nice they were, like some out-of-the way seaside place in Spain. Next he goes round the corner of one of these houses and there are people sitting down each with what look like little screens on their laps.

“After farming and sending their produce to market,” he says, “there is time to study. Up to a few months ago few could read or write let alone be fluent in English.” He then goes over to some kids and asks them what they are studying. They’ve all got accents of course but I can still make out what they are saying (which is more than can be said for half of those round here) and it’s to do with insects. He next goes over to a group of men who are drinking, some reading papers and others who also have screens on their laps. They don’t talk so clearly but I can still make out what they are saying and the ones with screens say they are studying fish farming.

“All these people,” he says, “including the children, vote in monthly elections to elect their own Nonette representative. They levy their own taxes and decide for themselves how they should be spent.” By now he has walked over to a group of women. “This is Isabella Goma,” he says, picking out one of them and adding, “Isabella is this month’s village representative.” The woman, she’s middle aged and a bit on the wide side, smiles at the camera and Jim asks her “Tell us about the village’s accounts.”

She shows this book and says “This is the money we have received from each person, who are known only by their Nonette number...” and pointing to columns of figures, “These are our achievement points and this is from our Nonette twin...” On she goes listing this and that and finally, “All our accounts are audited monthly and are open to inspection by anyone at any time.”

“So there’s no corruption?” he says.

She gives him a look as though he has upset her and says “How can there be? We all know what happens to our money. We all decide how it is spent.”

Looking to the camera he says “Everyone in Santana, including children pay ten per cent of their earnings to their Nonette, be it from their labour or their learning.” He explains how everyone’s learning earns them what he says are “achievement points” and these could be traded in for money. “They learn to earn,” but he adds “However, I think everyone actually likes studying.” At this the camera swings round and there are all these other groups of people sitting along a terrace with their little screens.

Then he is back to the group of women. “These ladies are Santana’s ward representatives,” he says, and to them “And what is it that you do?”

They are then telling all at once how they’re each responsible for their sections of the village, looking after everyone, making sure they are kept informed of everything going on. One says if they didn’t do their job properly they are voted out. Jim asks who is in charge of this and that and they say they have all these committees. But the one I like the best is the street cleaning committee. When he asks them who is the head of it, one of the women says “Patrico,” and points her finger.

The camera turns to where she is pointing and there is this little kid looking up at the camera. Bold as brass he is, and without a smile he says “No one drops rubbish in Santana.” And as he speaks the camera shows more kids with the same hard, arms folded street-gang look. Another of the women says there is a waiting list among the village kids to join.

After interviewing them Jim next says “Would you like to live like the people of Santana?” And as he speaks the camera is going away from him, then the terrace he is on. “Live like them, no hunger, no poverty, your own home and farm?” The camera now shows all of the village. It’s carved out of this hillside. “Live like them, in a caring community electing representatives of your choosing, ones who are constantly accountable for their actions?”

All of the hill is showing now, it’s a dark curved hump. “Live in a community where you have a say in how every penny, every cent collected from you in taxes is spent, where there isn’t any corruption, crime or cruelty?”

By now there’s not just all the hill showing but loads of others hills all the same and stretching for miles. "Live where there is not only time to study but care for the world about you?"

The camera swoops down between these lines of hills and as it does there are all these little lakes, some with trees round them. "Little by little," he says, "the people of Santana and other Nonette communities are restoring the land to the way it was before Europeans came."

No sooner has he said this than the picture changes to another also sweeping over the ground but this time farmland. "Here, there is no need to use land for agriculture and also, little by little, the plantations are being restored to their natural wilderness." As he speaks there are all these teams of people planting trees. The camera climbs higher and higher and as it does Jim says "Though the Susem have helped the people of Santana, everything the villagers have achieved is as a result of their own endeavour." With that he says goodbye.

On the way home I thought about what Jim had said. I quite fancied the idea of living in that Santana. Bit of farming of a morning, a spot of learning in the afternoon, a few of beers of an evening and some landscaping over the weekend. It would be a nice life that.

But back indoors, writing out the cheque for the next instalment of Council Tax, I thought what say do I have in how this money is spent? It's nigh on two grand a year they're taking off me and a good half must be wasted. And what do I get for it? The bin men calling once a week, big deal. And I have to pay or I'll have the bailiffs come round. For that matter what say do I have in any of it? The only time I hear from a councillor is when they stuff something through the letterbox if there's an election. It would be good if the local councillors, like they do in Santana came round asking me what they should do, well it wouldn't do any harm would it? At least it would keep them up to the mark.

All the same I had a laugh when I opened the letter from the liquidators of London Electricity. It said if I didn't pay them I would be in big trouble. With my little soufin pulsing away in the hall cupboard they can whistle for it!

Guilty rapists face ultimate penalty as men

STONING SLAYINGS PROVOKES UPROAR

By Lisa Brown
War Trials Reporter

TERRIFYING scenes of men being stoned to death were shown on live television for the first time yesterday.

Viewers of SLI TV's Bosnian War Crimes Trials saw more than 20 men, found guilty of charges of rape and other

The men's cries and screams for mercy went unheeded under a hail of stones and other missiles. Although their slayings were over with in matter of minutes, viewers were then shown slow motion replays of some of the more gruesome sequences.

The unseen programme commentator, rather than ... alarm at the

enthusiastically endorsing the women's actions, even encouraging them in the killing of their victims.

Last night many authorities were calling for future progra mmes to be cancelled. The Bishop ... Right ... Latimer ... affront ... justice.

Susem Telecaster mystery

We know who the Susem new television frontman is - he is James Powell - but how did he get the job? How did he manage to get to Susem controlled territory?

These and many other questions surrounded his appearance on yesterday's Susem telecast. It has been revealed that Powell, 24 had worked for Morgans, a prestigious merchant bank in the City but was made redundant two months ago.

Before this Powell was a student activist at the LSE and led the a campaign for the release of Delano Benson from life imprisonment for the murder of police constable John Whi...

THE PENALTY FOR RAPE: DEATH BY STONING

George Lewis
War Trials Correspondent

TWENTY rapists were stoned to death by their victims yesterday. After perfunctory trials before a panel of young judges, 20 men found guilty of rape were escorted from the courthouse just outside the western Bosnian town of Petrovac, and unknowingly to their deaths.

Not one case in the Kamenit sa Mjesto - 'the Place of Stones' - Court lasted more than five minutes. Each man's accuser had only to name him as her attacker for him to be judged guilty as charged.

In the space of an hour and a half guilty verdicts were pronounced on all those men who came before the judges.

The crowded courtroom packed with hundreds of ... ing in stoic silence. After the women had left the court en mass, the judges then cruelly tricked the men into thinking they were free to leave the court and the wrongs of their past misdeeds behind them.

But no sooner had they stepped into the brightness of the midday sun than they were assailed by a hail of stones. Those who were felled by these ...

MP to appeal against deportation to Bosnia

By Polly Portillo
In Guatemala City

SIR Hugh Russet-Brown is to appeal against his deportation to Bosnia. Sir Hugh's lawyer, Pablo Diaz, said that he had been instructed to plead with Guatemala's leader President Hernando Hidawaio for his release or deportation to Britain.

Snr. Diaz said: "Sir Hugh's defence had been that he was visiting our country with the intention of investing many millions of dollars in farmland. He had lost his way and everything has been an unfortunate misunderstanding. It is a great pity the Court decided not to believe him."

Police officials said they were doubtful if the President will ignore the calls of the Bosnian government to act against these proceedings.

Bishop slams SLI's slaughter scenes

The Clergy Watch Team

A TOP Bishop has denounced SLI TV for screening scenes of violence, including the slaying of men in their Bosnia War Trials programme.

On an official visit ... parted from his prepared speech and in forthright terms condemned SLI for showing endless scenes of gratuitous violence.

He said: "By showing the executions of these men in the most bestial manner SLI TV is pandering to the basest tastes of those least able to make mature judge... well have been guilty of acts of violence, such as rape, but it does not mean they should be left to the revenge and brutal justice meted out to them by their victims."

The Bishop, who was opening the River Life Observation Experience at Uppingham, is well known for his strong views against capital ... Reac-

'Trials' bring SLI huge ratings rise

By Amber Nightingale

SLI TV's executives are said to be 'over the moon' with the latest viewing figures. According to JICTAR (the TV ratings monitoring agency) SLI's audience figures since the screening of the Bosnian War Trials programme 'Trials' resumed have risen by a staggering 22 per cent.

SLI's boss Derek Igg said last night: "It just goes to show Dickie Bear was right when he decided to sign up to the Caught deal over the Bosnian War Trials. These figures are proof, if any were needed, that the British viewer wants not only to see justice done but actually seeing it being meted out.

"At SLI we do not give a toss what those lily livered, limp wristed clerics say. The judges of our decisions are the viewing public. And the viewers are saying loud and clear: "We like Trials".

Already dubbed by many as the 'new face' of 'Reality Television', the daily Trials' programme with its mixture of up tempo music, vigorous dance routines and executions of war criminals is proving to be an increasingly popular format with viewers.

SLI also claim that the evening showing of highlights of the programme, including all of the executions is also attracting record viewing figures.

The boost that 'Trials' has given to SLI is further echoed in the rise in the station's advertising rates. According to the advertising agency G.O & D, the price for a 15 second slot in both the daytime and evening 'Trails' programmes has soared by 50 per cent in the past alone.

Head of Media Buying at GOD, Dawn Ammalaya, said: "While the daily Susem news programme shown on SLI has been a money-spinner for Richard Bear, it is as nothing compared to the earnings 'Trials' must be generating for him.

"The station's slogan: 'Get it on the SLI' is also proving to be extremely effective in turning viewers, including those on the other satellite ...

All of Amazon under Alien contro

By Michale Anapolis
In Brazil

AMID rising fears of a possible military coup, Brazilian President Emisto Rocha has been forced to acknowledge that his country's entire Amazon region - a quarter of the country - is now under de facto Susem control.

Addressing the Brazilian Congress President Rocha said both his government and the military were powerless to combat what he described as, "the slow and insidious theft of our country's sovereignty by the Aliens".

The President called on the "people of Brazil to stand steadfast" against the Susem. He also asked for American and EU assistance as well that of as Brazil's South American neighbours for help in "this darkest hour of our country's destiny".

But few, both outside Brazil and within are likely to heed the President's pleas.

For most Brazilians the Amazon region is for all in-

Area under Susem control

tents another country which they know little of and care for even less. Meanwhile, most of the President's fellow countrymen, especially those in urban areas - where the overwhelming majority of Brazilians live - are enjoying the bounty of soufin energy units provided for free care of the Susem.

For most outsiders, the Amazon is synonymous with Brazil's shameful destruction of the region's rainforest and genocidal ...

native peoples. The Susem however, are viewed as protecting and renewing the forest With the Susem telecasts showing almost daily reforestation, dam removal and a host of other environmental regeneration projects - albeit with the forced labour of many of those who caused the Amazon's destruction in the first place - world public opinion is likely to lie with them rather than the Brazilian government

Experts now say that Susem control exists right across much of the north of Brazil from the Ceará in the east to the border with Peru, 2,000 miles away and covering an area of more than 1,500,000 square miles This is bigger area than Western Europe

Although many people who lived and worked in the Amazon region fled the area when the Susem imposed their worldwide bans on min...

number have decided ... remain These, so Suse... telecasts would suggest ha... thrown in their lot with th... Susem backed Nonet... movement.

There have also bee... reports that many peopl... from outside the region hav... circumvented the Brazilia... military's so-called "Ring o... Steel" and entered the region through the remote areas in the west close to the Peruvian border

This is in sharp contrast with the situation in the east Here hundreds of people, mainly poor and landless peasants, have been killed in clashes with the army. The Movement Sem Terra which campaigns on behalf of the rural poor, is urging its followers to avoid the army's eastern barriers and head for the west. However, this is likely to be counterproductive in the long term. Already

95: SIÂN

I was staggered and impressed with what this new fellow James showed. I think Daffyd was as well. Rainbow said he was appearing in a new programme so I made a point of us both watching it.

James began with showing a little hilltop town at night. "Looks attractive doesn't it," he said. And with its little lights it did, and reminded me of somewhere in Italy. "But don't be fooled..." James then said, "...it's the favela of Pirambu, a shantytown. Then the camera showed the place in daylight. It was a terrible slum. As the camera showed the streets and houses, most of which were little more than shacks, he said that the place was once filled with disease, crime and every other nasty thing.

James then said that the Brazilian government had allocated millions of dollars for Pirambu's improvement but all the money had been siphoned off by local officials. Waving a sheaf of papers, which he said were discovered by students in the State Governor's office, they listed the names of these officials.

As he read out their names and the money each of them had taken, the camera climbed further up the hill. Then he said "However, the communities which made up Pirambu have taken destiny into their own hands."

The camera then went over the crest of the hill and down the other side, where there were groups of neat little houses. The camera rose a little higher and showed other clusters of houses and all shining white in the sun. The camera then went back down to eye level and travelled towards one of these groups of new houses.

James then said "This is the Nonette community of Alberto Barreto." The camera wound between the houses and people looking to the camera, all of whom were smiling. The camera then went round a corner to a group of women, then to one of them and James said "This is Maria Bernal, this month's Nonette representative."

This woman described how the community worked, everyone voted, including the children, which surprised me. Another of the women said the community is split into wards, each one electing representatives and they also have to stand for re-election each month.

When James asked, the women one after another, told of the horrific level of violent crime in the old falevas and how the police who had been were just as crooked and thuggish. Because there weren't any jobs, Maria added, many of the people in faleva really did not have any alternative than to turn to crime just to live. But now, she said, that everyone had work there wasn't any crime any more. Another of women said that even Pirambu's street children were now either busily employed within their community or studying. Maria said that now everyone in Alberto Barreto, including the street children had a roof over their heads and food in their stomachs.

James asked how all of this was possible. Emelia, another of the women, said and with a wave of her hand, “Ask them!” The camera then turned and showed a group of boys. Like the women, these boys all talked at once. They told what it was like for them before the Nonette communities existed, hawking sweets, gum, cigarettes every hour of the day, their bodies as well, forced to steal, commit other crimes, of how the policemen and security guards beat, tortured them, even killed some of their friends. When they each gave their ages I was also shocked by how small they were. But when the boys told, then showed what they did now, I was taken aback by just how worldly knowing they were.

These young lads were helping men build a hostel for them. As they showed James round the building site it was also so obvious that they weren't just enjoying themselves but were really proud of what they had achieved. They took him to what must have been the foreman. James asked him where the finance for the building came from. The foreman said “Some from our Nonette twin.”

James explained that all the Nonette communities are linked to one another, each poorer one twinned to a wealthier, the second investing in the first. “Alberto Barreto,” he said, “is twinned with that of Silva Jardim. And this is their liaison representative, Louis Marcos.”

Louis, who said he was a retired accountant, said that he and his committee are responsible to his Nonette for spending their money in Alberto Barreto. The picture then changed to three women, Louis and another man sitting at a table, and James said “Meet Silva Jardim's Liaison Committee.” In no time they had not only told how different things now are, but what a difference it was being in charge of collecting and spending their own money.

“Did they really agree with subsidising their twin Nonette?” James asked them. They responded as if he had upset them. One after another exclaimed they weren't subsidising but investing. Everything going to Alberto Barreto, they said, created jobs, wage earners and wealth. The closer economically their twin became, the less need be invested.

“Or bigger returns!” joked the other man. One of the women changed the subject, saying it was more than just investing. Many people of both Nonettes now knew one another and had become good friends. There was a nodding of heads at this. Another of the women said that the savings in security against crime more than offset whatever they invested in Alberto Barreto. They all nodded again at this and then were talking all at once of how bad the level of crime used to be in Fortaleza and now, with the Nonette communities there was almost no crime at all.

The picture then changed to a man sat under an umbrella reading a paper. “This is Jose Frie, Silva Jardim's policeman,” said James. He explained that Jose was sat where several Nonette community boundaries met. Both he and James then told how the wards and communities policed the area and what little crime there was, was stopped in its tracks. Jose said the Nonettes were grouped into nines and that nine of them made up their local Nonette group and all of them coordinated continuously with each other. He then said "But anyone not wearing these is automatically suspect."

It was then that I realised that everyone shown, including James, were wearing white all-in-one tunics. "And their number!" joked James and pointed to his shoulder.

A woman then appeared and handed Jose a shopping bag and when she had left, James said "This is what actually keeps this post busy, minding people's shopping and parcels." And as he spoke the camera swung beyond him and there was a heap of other bags and boxes!

The picture changed and showed James walking along a tree lined street. He then said "Would you like to live in a community free of crime, no need for police forces or security guards, bars or barbed wire, where the only danger on the streets are motorists?" At that precise moment there was a screeching of a car's brakes followed by a huge bang, and then James saying "Some things, alas, including bad driving have not yet changed!" And as he spoke the camera showed two men standing besides their bumped cars.

The picture changed again, this time showing James with the building site of the street children's hostel in the background, and he saying, "Would you like to live in a society founded on a strong sense of neighbourhood and community, where the well-off willingly help others to become as fortunate?"

The camera next showed the children in earnest discussion with Louis and he writing numbers on a sheet of paper and James saying "Would you like to live in a society where not only do you have the power to say how every penny collected from you in taxes is spent but you are able, even encouraged to take an active part in deciding that spending?" With the camera showing the boys shaking Louis's hand then climbing a ladder into the scaffolding of the building, James added "Live in a society where no one is uncared for?"

The picture changed again, this time showing James standing in front of people queuing by the back of a truck and a man handing out armfuls of what I immediately recognised were soufin energy units. "The Susem have helped the people of Alberto Barreto," he said "but everything this community has achieved is the result of their own and others' endeavour." He then said goodbye.

Seeing those soufins being carried away reminded me of Sam and afterwards while the kettle was boiling I just had to have a look at him. There he was as cold, grey and quiet as ever. Then without really thinking I was stroking him and saying "Thank you Sam, thank you for the heat, thank you for the light and our cups of tea."

'SUSEM STOLE MY GUY' SOBS TV GIRL FRANKIE

another Chron EXCLUSIVE

By LINDA HARTLEY and STEVE MANN
Our Multi-Prize Winning Team

THE BROKEN-HEARTED girlfriend of TV's latest sensation - latest sensation - the new Susem small screen personality, Jim Powell - said last night: "Aliens stole my guy."

Frankie Thorpe, a student researcher at Ardwick Television Academy in Manchester revealed that new the Susem presenter is James Powell, 26 of Islington, north London, who had recently worked at Morgans Bank.

Sobbing, Frankie said: "He just disappeared, it's definitely not like my James. "I blame his disappearance on that man Collins, his old landlord. He always had a Svengali-like hold over him. I just wish I can be with James so I can save him from the clutches of those unworldly beings."

Frankie admitted she and James had argued when they had last met. "But it was only a little tiff, the way that lovers sometimes do. I was all ready to kiss and make up, but now he's been taken from me," she sobbed.

Frankie has just completing her training as a TV researcher under the watchful eye of Ardwick's 'Buck' Rogers, is hoping to work in television when she completes her course of training. She is now "Waiting for the day James will return to my arms.

"Our years together were filled with the bliss of unending romance and the continuous passion of our love-making. During our times abroad, often on remote islands such as the Seychelles we would often walk hand in hand

Pope's War Trials slating questioned

By Maria Carini
in Rome

THE BOSNIAN War Crimes Trials have been denounced as the actions of the Anti-Christ by the Pope.

Issuing a Papal Bull against the Susem, Pope Pius XIII urged Christians throughout the world to unite and join forces to isolate themselves against the Susem. In his most forthright yet condemnation of the Aliens, the Pope said the actions being taken against Croatian Catholics was an abominable wickedness. For there not to have been stronger condemnation against the massacres of defenceless Croats was a stain on all society, he said.

However, the Pope's stand has not been without its critics, even from within Italy. In an editorial the newspaper *La Stampa* accused the Pope of having a selective and muddled memory. "Our noble Pontiff has apparently forgotten his silence towards the thousands of 'devout Catholic Croatians' who went daily to rob and murder those whose only 'crime' was not to be Croatian or Catholic," it said.

Even Rome's *la Repubblica* cast doubt on the Pope's sincerity, under the headline: "What is he trying to say? What is he trying to hide?" it lists a number of Papal questionable involvements with "Croatian thugs" as it terms them, dating back to the 13th century but detailing some of the more recent ones. The most prominent being its backing of the WWII Croatian Fascist leader Ante Pavelic, whos forces massacred 900,000 Serbs, Bosnians, Jews and Gypsies. However, the Pope's attitude towards the recent Bosnian conflict and that of his predecessor's, Pope John Paul towards the '90s conflict also draws the paper's criticism.

Ordinary Italians however, appear to be indifferent to the Pope's views Viewing figures just announced show that Italia 1's, (which carries SLI TV's coverage of the Bosnian War Trials) have reached an all-time high, excluding those for soccer of course.

Polly Portillo from Buenos Aires reports: Argentinean Police claim to have uncovered details of Croatians, once resident in Argentina, receiving Papal funds for the renovation of the Pavlic memorial. Anton Pavlic was the former Croatian fascist leader who escaped after WWII to Argentina disguised as a Catholic priest on a Red Cross passport issued by the Vatican. Ante Pavelic, who died in 1959 was wanted for crimes agains

SLI's ratings see huge r... so does its share price

By Laura Hogg

SLI TV chiefs were over the moon with their latest audience viewer figures. These show that since the re-start of the Bosnian War Trials it has taken a 25 per cent audience share for the live daytime programme and a massive 37 per cent of the repeated highlights during the evening.

Owners of SLI shares have also seen a boost in the value of their holdings. Yesterday SLI's share rose a further 56p closing at an all-time high of 673p.

SLI's boss Derek Igg said: "These figures just go to show how right Dickie [Bear] was in signing up to the Caught deal. The viewers are happy, the shareholders as well and so are the advertisers. And they were the ones we had some worry over.

"We saw some pull out when the first Trials faltered, but oh how they must be ruing doing it. Presently we have hundreds of them queuing up trying to get on. It serves them right.

WORLD NEWS

Hisogynists to advise on 'correctionals'

By Bobby Slant
In Atlanta

Caught TV's Ed Earner announced yesterday that agreement had been reached for the Hisogynists to manage the "post judgement correctional element" of the Bosnian War Trials.

Earner added: "Since the recommencing of the Bosnia Trials programme we have been more than satisfied with their progress. So have, or so it would appear from our ratings data, our viewers and advertisers. However, while the conduct of the trials themselves continue to be conducted on a more than professional basis, we have thought from the outset that their correctional element did not quite match that same high standard. Therefore, and in full agreement with the Bosnian judicial committees, Caught personnel will henceforth assist in this part of the trials.

"Of course it is anticipated that our people in Bosnia will have no more than a minor advisory role in any of the post-trial offender disciplining but we consider they will be able to impute a higher degree of professionalism than hitherto. We at Caught TV are in-

'Aliens attacking... army"- General cl...

...Drew Rosario
...Salvador

...CCUSING the Sus...n of attacking ...rward elements of ...is forces, General ...idal da Costa, call...d for increased ...owers to combat ...hat he calls "this ...lien peril".

Flanked by a coterie of ...llow officers, General da ... 100 of my officers and men being subjected to brutal disorientation at the hands of these alien monsters," the General said. When pressed however, he refused to detail the nature of the attacks against his forces.

However, General da Costa was most insistent that the government could not expect his forces to hold the line against the Aliens without a substantial increase in his command.

Analysts however, question da Costa's reasoning. They point to the absence of casualties at any of the military hospitals as sign that no real military activity against the Susem has actually taken place. Others point to the absence of any aerial activity on the part of da Costa's forces. The conclusion of many is that da Costa is staking his claim to lead in any putsch

SLI Hisogynists in Croat-Serb slayings

By **Jason Kotor**

VIEWERS OF SLI's Bosnian War Crimes Trials programme saw the membrs of its own production team taking an active part in the killing of Serb and Croat men convicted of rape and other charges.

In their distinctive white tunics and wearing yellow crash helmets members of the so called 'Hisogynists' could be clearly seen leading crowds of other women in the stoning to death of the men. With cries of "Kill baby kill", "Get that mother f**ker" and "You male trash you," other Hisogynists were shown throwing stones themselves at the men.

Last night the Bishop of Buckingham was one of a host of Church and other leading figures calling for the screening of the Trials' programme to be ... said: "The showing of such gratuitous violence is an affront to all decent minded people.

continued page 2

- Full blow by blow account on page 3; pictures pages 4, 5

News

Advertisers queuing to get on SLI

SLI TV advertising revenue has rocketed since it began exclusive screening of the Bosnian War Trials.

Station boss Derek Igg said: "When Dickie Bear signed up to Caught deal all the pundits said he was mad. But now SLI has been able to increase is premium on its media rates for both the daytime and evening Bosnian Trials programmes. More people are watching them than any of the soaps both currently and in the past

"We don't know how long the Trials will go on for but while they are SLI is going to continue to increase its earnings and its profits."

Asked if he had any qualms in deriving so much money from so many men being deprived of their lives, Igg said: "On SLI the viewer decides what is shown not over-indulgent moralist toffs

I'm glad Margaret recorded it, we were that busy in the Sallie I had not time to catch all he said. But watching the video of this James this morning I was forever saying "Why can't it be like that over here? Why can't councils and government and all those quango things behave like that?"

Apart from being not a bad looking fellow, James explained everything so that I understood. He began by showing people walking to a building. "These are," he said, "representatives of 81 Nonette communities from the area of Crateus gathering for the thrice weekly meeting of their Area Nonette." Little communities, he said, each of about 700 people, elected a representative and it was those who were going into the building. All told, he said, they spoke for about 60,000 people.

The camera was then inside a large room with a big round table. People began filing in. As they did, James and in a hushed voice, said each community was like a tiny country with all the independence they desired. But, he said, they had each agreed to pool part of their sovereignty to the Area Nonette to manage matters beyond their own abilities such as the roads and, with him chuckling, agreeing the site for the new stadium for the Area's soccer team.

With the camera ranging round the room he next said "All are chosen and elected by their fellow villagers. There is not a single professional politician or rich man's son among them." With people sitting down, he then said "Note that most are women but there are exceptions." With this the camera focused on some men who were old and to my surprise a lad who could have been at school.

The picture changed to a group of people sat around another, smaller table. James explained that the 81 villages were clustered in nine neighbouring groups of nines and that these people, there were nine of them are one such group of representatives. "Sometimes," James said, "there is nothing on the Area Nonette's agenda of relevance to a particular community. So there is no point their representative attending. But should matters relevant arise, one representative of each group of nine is always at the meetings to tell the others.

"And how do people know what is coming up?" he said, and holding out a newspaper, "This is how everyone knows." With this he is flicking open the pages and saying as he did, "This is the local weekly paper, here is the Area's forthcoming business for debate and voting. Here's..." and he turning the page, "...lists of the communities' proposals for future action, and here..." and turning to the front page, "...the results of the Area Nonette's decisions and deeds." With this he read out a list of them, "New cooperative launched, Landscape restoration, first phase begun, Flag design agreed, Auditors office enlargement completed."

James was next shown walking through a door and saying, "This is the Auditors' office and this is Theresa Morno, this month's head auditor." This

Theresa says that there are nine of them, one from each group and they travel the area unannounced continuously inspecting every village's accounts and overseeing elections and so ensuring that they are fair. James added that the auditors' seal of approval is needed before an election was recognised and receive funding from their twinned village as well as from elsewhere.

When James asked this Theresa, she outlined how the money each community raised had to be spent, so much for this so much on that. But a quarter of all the money raised, she said, was set aside for the region as a whole. James then added "More of this later."

With the picture returned to the people sat around the large table, James next said, "The Area Nonette is now in session." And in a hushed tone, "Not everyone will be speaking in English but most will try to." There was a tap of a hammer, silence and a woman stood up. James whispered, "Rosa Tristao, this month's Area representative...she is giving the results of the funding proposals from the Regional Nonette."

On he, she and several others went for five minutes and more. What was shown was abbreviated but the fascinating thing was the absence of any waffle. All of the proceedings were matter-of-fact and straight to the point. A committee head would give their report of what they had done, what was planned, a vote taken and the next head stood to deliver theirs. So different from the windbags I heard the time I attended a council meeting in Upper Street, three hours of nothing and all they had to say to us afterwards was "We take note of your comments but the Council is not bound by them." And when I asked if any of the councillors actually lived in the borough not one of them could say they did.

The picture changed again, this time to outside a larger building, other people walking into it and James saying "These are the representatives of the 81 Area Nonettes from the region of Ceará attending their thrice weekly meeting of the Regional Nonette." Together, he said, they spoke for about five million people. James explained how it is run on similar lines as an Area Nonette except that it is on a larger scale. The Regional dealt with matters the Areas wanted it to handle. He gave a whole list of things but one stood out. This was what was done with money, how each of the wealthier Areas gave part of their taxes directly to poorer ones. But it isn't just the giving. The richer ones are also directly involved in sending teams of their own people to participate in how their money is spent. It was this direct hands-on approach which impressed me.

When I think of the business I have put Sophie's way over repairs not just to our flats but others as well. Every day I'm hearing terrible tales of tenants bounced from office to department trying to get repairs done to their homes. And all they ever receive is "nothing to do with us." It's no wonder Christofides are overflowing with all the work I'm sending them. But it shouldn't be, a little less spent on officials and more on repairs and there would be no need for Sophie forever threatening the council with legal action.

The picture changed again, this time to James sitting by a table with six women and two men. "These are past employees of various former Ministries of Ceará," he said, "and they will tell of what used to happen." Within seconds one after another was detailing all the bribery and corruption which used to go on. A woman who had worked in the Finance Ministry said all the politicians were forever dipping their fingers in the State till but it was the top officials she said who were the worst. They were known as "the Maharajahs" because they took so much. One of the men said that everyone knew it was going on but speaking out against it invited an early death.

But when one of them said all businesses had to pay officials "commission" before they would be awarded a contract, I was inwardly saying, "It's happening right here in London as well." The times I have overheard in the Salutation the money builders pay council officials to get contracts, or dodgy work passed by the inspectors. And that is only the start, the backhanders I hear being given for school catering contracts is shocking.

The picture changed to James standing in front the Regional Nonette building with him walking to the camera. And as he does he says, "Would you like to live in a society where yours and everyone else's voice is not only heard but is actively asked for?"

James is then shown sitting drinking in a bar with three other people. The camera then goes up away from them and to a TV screen showing other people sitting round a table, and it is immediately obvious that this is a Nonette meeting that James and those with him are watching. As the camera comes back to him, he says, "Would you like to live in a society where administration isn't just open, but where interest in it is so great?" With him saying this, the camera swings around the bar and there is a whole crowd more of people looking up at the screen.

The picture changes back to the ex-State employees and James standing in front of them and him saying "Live in a society where corruption and chicanery cannot exist?"

The picture changes yet again, this time to a tiny hall packed with people clapping their hands, a woman on a stage acknowledging them and a man saying"...and Isabella Goma is hereby duly re-elected as Santana's representative." Then James is saying "Live in a society free from distant, establishment controlled organisations foisting powerful men's sons and self-seeking opportunists exploiting the political processes, your vote, your powerlessness for their own personal ends? In fact, live in a society without 'professional' politicians at all?"

James is next shown sitting outside the hall saying that the Susem had helped the Cearánese but really it was the endeavour of people themselves which had achieved such a fair and open society. With this he bids goodbye.

Employer rebut Nonette employm practices

EMPLOYER'S organisations rebutted critical comments made in last night's Susem telecast about employment practices. "It's cloud cuckoo land," according to one source.

CBI spokeswoman, Lucille Bell said: "Unlike the few people living in the area under Susem control, business elsewhere has to live in the real world. The days of a job for life are over. Businesses can only survive if they are able to compete in the global market.

"This means people can only be referenced in terms of inputs as any other commodity. Some people may not like such a state of affairs but there is no altern... alive is business is to survive i... today's world. In this there wi... be losers of course but there wi... also be winners," she said.

Joanna Tardy of Hatche... Tardy, a human resources co... sultancy, was also dismissive ... the Susem's claims that full a... lifetime employment could a... should be available to all. "Ev... if it was possible," she sa... "would it be desirable? T... threat of unemployment, red... dancy concentrates the mi... wonderfully!

"When you are no lon... needed, you are no longer r... vant. Keeping employees ... their toes ensure a diligent, ... working, respectful workfo... Do we seriously want to go b... to the days of full employm... and all those labour troub... No, the Nonette full emp...

SLI's rating to all-time h...

Bolstered by the succes... Bosnian War Crimes pr... SLI TV claims to have ... more than 35 percent of ... television viewers and 45 ... the evenings.

A fortnight ago critics ... Bear were deriding him f... up with Caught TV ... worldwide non-US televis... of the Bosnian War Trial ... At the Trial's outset it see... were right, but the fiasco ... programme was soon ... And now it is Richard Be... laughing.

SLI's shareholders are a... high on the back of Da...

Siobhain O'Hara was one of the first journalists to witness the trials an... sentencing of men charged with assault against women in Bosnia

Swifts and swift justice in Bosnia

THE LITTLE Court house outside the small town of Glamoc in northern Bosnia is identical to six others across the country. Specially built to try those accused of crimes against women during the recent conflict, Glamoc's court house sits halfway up the steep, dry, flinty hill to the east of the town. Its freshly painted exterior glistens white in the sun and like the six other Courts, it is appropriately named "Kamenik sa Mjesto" - the 'Place of Stones'.

In front of the building is a neat, tidy, sand covered courtyard. This morning, long before the sun's rays had dried the night's dampness away, women began gathering here.

As the sun climbs and warms, a further steady stream arrives until several hundred are milling outside the Court's doors.

Though of all ages, most are dressed in black. They stand talking quietly to one another, their voices frequently drowned out by the screeches of countless swifts swooping and swirling through the cloudless sky above in pursuit of their insect prey.

The Hisogynists

At nine o'clock other women arrive. These are dressed in white. They are also head and shoulders taller and are immediately the subject of noisy, animated attention from those in black now crowding round them. These newcomers are the Hisogynists.

One, "Buttercup", her name emblazoned on the front and back of her tunic, addressing the crowding women as "Sisters", continually punches her clenched fist into the air as she coaches them in the things she wants them to do.

With her every instruct ion comes echoing raised fists of endorsement, hesitant at first but as numbers and assuredness grow so does the clamour of the women in black's approval.

As Buttercup speaks, yet more Hisogynists arrive. Their names are also written across their tunics and like hers are those of flowers.

These Hisogynists immediately begin unloading cameras and other television equipment from the big white trucks they have arrived in. Minutes later three black covered trucks climb up the hill and then lumber into the courtyard.

Swifts soar and screech above the Kamenik sa Mjesto Court House in northern Bosnia

These trucks then reverse up to holes in the ground. Their trailers then begin tilting slowly backwards. The crews - all women - and clad in black tunics are also equipped with masks, shields and batons, soon surround the trucks and then open their doors.

With a commotion of snarls and growls, jumbled packs of dogs, large and small, slither and scramble down into the holes.

The Court

At ten o'clock the Court's bell tolls and its large main doors slowly, swing silently open.

With Buttercup's rejoinder: "Now keep it cool in there," many of the women including me, troop inside the Court, the sun's brightness casting our shadows before us.

Either side of a central aisle are rows of wooden benches. All are soon crammed with the women. Some speak but do so in whispers as though in church and with none countenancing a smile.

Those both sides of me give hurried murmured litanies of ordeals, indignities the men facing trial had inflicted on them. Within moments others behind have lent forward, ones in front turned, all pressing details of similar assaults they, their daughters, mothers, sisters have also been subjugated to.

The sunlight is suddenly shut out as the main doors of the Court and with a loud slam close. Their reverberating boom fills the Court. But before the sound dies away, television lights are switched on and instantly illuminate the gloom.

The Judges

A hushed silence now falls. Everyone sits still, backs straight as the three judges, two a step behind the first stride onto the dais.

Nodding acknowledgement, the judges sit behind desks so high that little more than their heads and shoulders show. Or perhaps it is they who were small, for all three are so young they could have been fresh from school. But their young years do not in any way diminish the awe and order of their office.

With the smack of her gavel the chief judge calls for the first case. A door to the side of the Court opens and in marches two large oriental men with a smaller, portly one between them. The Prosecutor, also in his teens reads out the accusation. It is brief, no more than a paragraph. The judge asks of the man: "Guilty or Not guilty?"

The accused

The accused, a Croatian in his late 20's, married and a former policeman, appears confused as the Court's proceedings commence in English. He hurriedly claims not to understand the language. But, harried by the judge, he proclaims his innocence.

A woman is called by the Prosecutor, the accused man's victim he says. Old enough to be this man's mother, she points an

(continued overleaf)

Teachers deride 'dinky' Susem screens

By Daniel Bloom
Education Editor

TEACHERS representatives dismissed the Susem teaching screens as no match for real teaching.

USMWT, the Head Teacher's Union, spokesman, Edmund Cunliffe, said: "These (Susem) screens are perhaps useful for children in backward parts of the world where educational resources are scarce but in no way can and trusted teaching methods in advanced countries such as our own.

"As for the notion of allowing pupils to instruct other pupils is quite frankly, as far as Britain's schools are concerned, a non-starter. If such ersatz teachers were allowed to operate in our schools you would so see standards fall," he said.

Sheena Mc Easton, of the Faculty of Education at the University of Sheppey at machines have been tried in the past but without appreciable results in advancing a child's abilities. The only way to improve on the standards in our schools, irradiating the current 15 percent rate of illiteracy and innumeracy for example, is better, and more resources into schools and teacher training. That of course means more money, something that governments past and present have failed to. It

Alabama Governor in huge loans scam

ALABAMA Governor, George Clint Williams was responsible, it is alleged, of defrauding the Jefferson County Homes and Loans Bank of Birmingham of $60 million.

According to affidavits filed with Alabama's State Attorney's Office, Governor Williams used his State office to secure a series of loans for a string of holiday home developments on Wheeler Lake in the north of Alabama.

Two one-time and apparently now disgruntled employees of Jasper Development Corporation of nearby Chattanooga, Tennessee, claim that Williams and then executives of Jasper Corporation artificially inflated the land value of the sites for development. They say that on three occasions the Governor was handed envelopes which

"Company formations soar...employment for all...skills and labour shortages ...huge surge in growth...business activity and investment at record levels... new region wide banking system is major engine powering dynamic economy..." All very impressive I thought until he said "And now, banking and investment in action..." What he showed was not a bank, well not a proper one, but nothing more than a glorified Christmas savings and loans club.

Five people sat on one side of a table were the "community's banking committee," he said, and the man, whose name apparently is Miguel, sat at the other, was applying for a loan. He went on to say the loan was for a packaging business this Miguel wanted to start. The loan was for less than $200! In a proper bank even an application ten times this sum would not be considered commercially viable.

This young fellow, Powell, the Aliens have for their new programme was all very earnest in his commentary but nonetheless I could not see how lending such small sums could possibly generate the so-called "dynamic economy" over which he endlessly enthused. When he mentioned the amount of supervision and third party guarantees this so-called "bank" attached to the loan it was apparent these villagers were just playing at finance. And to cap it all, if the man's business failed he could repay the loan by studying!

I mentioned the amateurishness of this to June who was watching with me. But she told me to be quiet. Not wishing another upset, I considered it better to abide by her request.

Powell next showed this Miguel stacking pallets of produce upon the back of a truck. He said that the man had secured a contract with a wholesale fruiterer in a nearby town for his family's canes of raspberries. Being a sought after crop in the tropics, so Powell said, there would be a huge demand for raspberries. This Miguel further added that now his community also produced finely cut timber he and his cooperative could supply the raspberries in individual punnets and thus attract premium prices for his produce.

In mid-sentence it seemed, Powell switched from speaking to this would-be market gardener to another man, and saying "This is Augusto Barras, a fruit wholesaler in the town of Sobral." Barras, upon Powell questioning him, explained how his company once had to pay most of its profits in sales, property and turnover taxes, politicians' patronage, police protection and bribes to officials for permits.

Now, he said, he paid just a flat ten per cent of his profits in taxes to his local community. At this I noticed he began waving his arms in an effusive fashion as he related how the savings from increased profitability enabled the company to expand, double its staff and increase their wages. Barras added, because of the increased business the company would actually be paying more money in tax than under the old system. Then he began wagging his

HISOGYNISTS FACING 'MURDE CHARGES IN US

By Adam Peglar
in Bosnia

THE GROUP of US women in charge of televising the Bosnian War Crimes, the self-styled 'Hisogynists' could be facing murder charges according to legal experts.

According to Vincent Gigante, Professor of Law at Cornell University, Ithaca, New York, US nationals committing or participating in acts which are in contravention of US laws will be liable for prosecution should they re-enter US jurisdiction.

Meanwhile, the Hisogynists, apparently unconcerned with such legal considerations were seen on this morning's 'Trials' programme leading one band of local women after another in stoning to death men judged earlier of rape.

Other Hisogynists acting in small groups could also be seen stoning some of the convicted men themselves. In one scene, and filmed in close-up, two of the Hisogynists were clearly shown holding a man down on the ground while a third screamed, "Pay bastard, pay," as she smashed a rock into his face.

One man, apparently surviving a first volley of stones and attempting to flee, was shown being chased by a pair of Hisogynists. One of these Hisogynists, on catching up with the man, was shown striking him on the chin with her fist and with such force that he was physically lifted into the air before falling to the ground. It was not clea from the televised footage i the man was conscious a both Hisogynists next pro ceeded to hurl rocks dow on his face.

But with evident deligh both Hisogynists were ne shown dragging the man apparently lifeless bod towards a large hole in th ground.

Although the inside this hole was not show barks and snarls of do could be heard coming fro within it.

With all the men presu ably now dead, more Hiso nists were shown helpi the local women carry m of the men's bodies similar pits dotted arou the courtyard. Then w triumphal cries of "M trash," they then hurling bodies down into the pits

With other women shown spreading a carpe sand across the courty a voiceover comment said: "Now don't go a we'll be right back after commercial break with live, as it happens co ionals."

Swifts and swift justice in Bosnia
(continued from page 1)

outstretched unwavering arm and in a voice just as assured, denounces him as her attacker.

The judge calls on the man to answer. He stands to reply.

Hundreds of eyes glower to his back. The judge, having to remind him the Court's proceedings are in English, stop him mid-sentence. He jabbers a few further words in Croatian before she sternly admonishes him with: "Sit down and be quiet." The guards either side of him ensure that he immediately does so.

The judgements

In whispers, the three judges confer, nod agreement to one another then each hold up placards with 'Guilty' written on them.

The chief judge's gavel falls. A murmur of approval ripples through the Court. The man is marched into the well in front of the judges' desks. No sooner is he there than the next case is called then the next and the next.

On the cases come. None taking more than five minutes to try. None subjecting the victims as Courts do elsewhere, to a second ordeal - often more humiliating than the first - of being forced to prove and in detail, violation against them in the adversarial atmosphere of male dominated judiciary.

In this Court it is for the perpetrator to prove their innocence. It is also a Court, so I learned where the veracity of the victim's testimony is established in privacy before a case commences.

One after another the accused appear, all no different than a selection of men to be found anywhere; young, not so young, some swagger, others shuffle. All, however are judged guilty. With every fall of the judge's gavel, tension among those sat stoic and silent along the benches grows and grows.

The commercial break

After an hour, though it feels longer, there is a halt in proceedings; the 'commercial break', the women next to me whisper.

There is, however, little break in the silence. One of the now dozen men in the well attempts to protest but a guard hits him. He too then became quiet. The women on the benches continue to heed Buttercup's council of "keep it cool".

A wave of the camerawoman's hand, the tap of the judge's gavel and the Court is in session once more. More men but cases more horrific as if such could be so. Among them of a woman who is old, another blind, a girl not yet in her teens.

At this, the silence along the benches finally breaks. Tears, angry tears well from many of the women. Case by case, with every addition to those awaiting sentence in the well, the atmosphere in the Court becomes tenser and tenser.

By the time two dozen men are crammed in the well, the judges halt for another break. We on the benches, in silence but with the air of tension still taut and with the doors now reopened, troop back outside.

The punishments

The sun is so bright that it takes several seconds to make out the women who have remained in the courtyard. They are in a semi-circle of groups around the edge. Each has assembled small piles of stones. Those who have been in Court now join with them.

So do several Hisogynists who are now wearing yellow crash helmets, visors, gloves and padding added to their tunics. They also carry tiny video cameras.

Though all the women's eyes are on the Court's doors which have now closed again, many stoop to gather up the stones, lining them in the crooks of their arms. No one says a word. The atmosphere is still taut and tense. The screeching of the swifts flying above is the only sound. The minutes slowly pass.

The Court's doors then reopen. The men come out, the sun momentarily blinding them. The women, by now strained taut continue to stand motionless, silent. The doors then click quietly shut.

The stoning

Suddenly, the women began ululating. Their massed blood curdling howls rent the air and all but drown out Buttercup's yelled "Go."

Many of the women step forward letting fly a volley of stones. Most fall short but some hit the men, several of them shouting as if in surprise. Others turn and bang their fists on the Court's closed doors.

Still ululating, the women stride steadfastly forward. They let fly a second volley of stones. More men are hit, all of whom now frantically thump on the closed doors.

Their desperate banging is immediately drowned out by a fusillade of stones hailing down on the doors instead. But many more strike the men who now raise their arms about them in attempts to protect themselves. Many try to flee. But they all do so in vain, for a further fierce flurry of stones beats them back.

Above the men's yelps and women's ululating come the Hisogynists' shouts of "Separate, separate..."

Groups single out their targets. More stones fly. More cries from the men - cries of terror. The women aren't ululating either now but shouting, shouting, roaring the rage of retribution.

Forced from the Court's doors some of the men attempt to run but others are dragged away. Their shrieks and pleas set off the dogs. Barks, howls, snarls, growls now join, mix and meld with the men's cries, screams and screeches of the women. All rising, twisting, churning into a crescendoing cacophony of...

Men, now separated, are surrounded by jeering, baying women. These men beg, plead for their lives. Stones smash into their faces. All of them fall to the ground. From the courtyard walls the remaining women now come, each one is carrying a larger stone; a rock.

Some of the men attempt to escape. Others, are purposely given let to try. One man, his face streaked with pulsing blood runs back and forth trying to evade a dozen women. But he is no more than a mouse caught in the maws of a coven of cats. With stones and shoves he is played and patted between them. Then he too falls. The women hurl their remaining stones down on his now writhing, jerking body. These women now turn to the bringers of the rocks.

The rocks

Each of these women holds hers above her head then hurls it down on his, the third rock cracks open his skull. Bits of brain, like lumps of congealed porridge splat out onto the sand, though his feet still twitch. More rocks dash down on him until they too are stilled. His lifeless body is now dragged away to a pit and its howling hungry dogs.

Another man, blood oozing from where once an eye had been, his hand covered red in attempt to staunch, races for the courtyard's wall. He runs in vain for yet more stones strike him first. The ensuing rain of rocks stoves his skull till bone and brain are as splattered as a dashed dropped egg.

The policeman falls early. He is still screaming for mercy when the first stones smash down on him. The first are aimed not at his head but his genitals. Because he continues to fidget and buck, many strike his stomach instead. One hits there so hard that it causes him to belch a spurt of bile green vomit. Another stone and he regurgitates yet more but this time slicked with blobs of blood. The next stone, having jagged edges, not only tears into his stomach but smashes and exposes part of his rib cage as well. Yet his legs still thrash back and forth. But a rock hurled down on his skull splurging it out as if it is the red of an overripe melon, puts a stop to his frolics.

The dogs

A few minutes more and all the men are downed, stoned and smashed to death, their corpses dragged to the pits and the awaiting dogs. Soon these are all mutely chomping.

Women with birch twig brooms sweep the sand smooth. Others pick up the debris, more collect the stones and rocks putting them back by the walls. None of the women speak. Not then, nor as they file from the yard, walk down the hill.

Only the screeching sounds of the swifts remain.

COUNCIL LEADERS HUGE HOUSING SC

SHEFFIELD Council's Housing Department has been revelations of huge backhanders taken by senior emp crooked selling of leases on Council houses and flats.

Ten senior Housing Department officials have been after the Labour run Council hurriedly met following in *The Star* of alleged corruption.

Acting on information from an ex-employee of Housing Department, who approached this newsp details of their corrupt practices *The Star* is able to re

- **£1,000s changed hands between crooked land Council officials for 242 flats and houses.**
- **These properties had been erased from Dep computer records.**
- **Some of the landlords are not even resident in E**
- **The rents for these properties were paid by u ing tenants to shady 'collector**

United front needed to combat Alien threat,' says General as...

Brazilian Army seizes power

Polly Portillo
in Rio de Janeiro

BRAZILIAN Army strongman, General Videl da Costa has staged the long expected military coup. At 5am local time, armed units of the army and air force took control of key government buildings in Brasilia and in a string of major cities throughout the country.

At a hurriedly arranged press conference General da Costa, justifying the coup, said: "The State is being confronted with both internal and external threats. Law and order both in our cities and the countryside is crumbling before our eyes. The Aliens now occupy a quarter of Brazil and are expanding their domain daily. It is vital in this dark time of threat that all loyal Brazilians unite to confront these two enemies."

Unconfirmed reports say da Costa has 'bought' the military's loyalty with promises of an across the board 50 percent pay rise. The average rank and file soldier, air force cadet is likely to accept the rise to say nothing of the enhanced prestige military rule will provide.

Brazil's provincial police chiefs, as well as the police union have both applauded da Costa's decision to include them in the sweeping pay rises. Observers have taken for granted they will side with the military.

Surprisingly the financial markets have taken the coup in their stride. Most dealers on the Sao Paulo Stock Exchange viewing the military regime as having little or no adverse effect on the financial sector.

If anything, so one market source said, the announcement of the military's control of Brazil's Central Bank meant there would be tighter controls on government spending.

However, military analysts say da Costa is making a cold calculated gamble on his and the army's success. Critics in the media and elsewhere have not been slow to voice their ... to the coup.

News Bulletin

Rio erupts in riots

An estimated 250,000 people took part in a demonstration against Brazil's new military regime. In later clashes with the police many were reported being arrested including the demonstration's organisers. There were a number of similar protests throughout the country.

Huge crowds gathered in Campo de Santana Park in Central Rio, to hear speaker after speaker angrily denounce the new military regime of Vidal da Costa. They then marched on to the Avenida Presidente General Vargas, Rio's main thoroughfare, their numbers growing as they went and bringing traffic to a halt.

By the time the protestors had reached Avenida President General Kubitschek the police attempted to stop the ... but they retreated under a hail of stones and ...

finger in the air exclaiming "And it is fair. Not only does the company have three votes in the community, but a say in how every cent it gives is spent!"

Continuing in the same effusive fashion over the removal of red tape and savings on accountants' fees, Powell also stopped him mid-sentence and asked what assistance he received in financing his company's expansion. Barras said "Why, our Area Bank of course!"

The picture changed to Powell outside a small white building. "This," he said, "is the bank of an Area Nonette. Community banks have upper limits to the amounts they lend but Area banks make bigger loans. However, the lending criteria are the same, no more than eight times what a borrower has in cash and achievement points." Outlining further conditions required of a would-be borrower, Powell was next shown walking to this bank. Though the picture next showed him inside of it, it was much the same as before, people sitting either side a table strewn with papers.

Though at $5,000 the size of this loan was indeed bigger, there was still no possibility of it making any proper commercial sense. In a normal bank such loans are merely assessed on a computer point scoring program. At most it would warrant a clerk aiding the customer to complete the application form. And no ordinary bank could afford to employ such amounts of time with a customer or the supervision of such a small loan.

The picture next showed Powell walking from the bank with a man who had has applied for such a loan. "This is Vincenti Dumont," he says, "and his company used to weave cotton and viscose, but now it weaves 'arach' silk."

The pair of them are next shown against a background of looms and with this Dumont relating a similar litany of past woes as had the fruit wholesaler. He exclaimed the same effusiveness towards what he claimed was the reformed business climate in which his company now thrived is did the fruit wholesaler. Apart from yet further relating how he expanded his workforce as well as their improved working conditions and increased wages, Dumont said his new looms were working non-stop to meet his customers' orders.

Again the picture changed mid-sentence, this time to Powell standing outside a large warehouse-type building and saying "This is Vincenti's biggest customer." As he spoke the camera rose to show the top of this building which had a large illuminated sign reading 'Manuel Cohen - Arach Modes'.

Powell was next shown talking to a man who he said was this Cohen. Although Cohen was as effusive as the weaver, I also noticed that he relied more on his hands and shoulders and reminded me of some of my rag trade customers. Even as Powell asked Cohen about the increased volume of his business and he replying "It's a living," he was also like them in running a tape measure across Powell's arms and shoulders. And as he replied to Powell's further questions he was summoning a bevy of assistants with a range of white tunics in varying styles.

As Powell asked Cohen what benefits his five-fold rise in sales had brought the company, and he holding up a tunic and replying after an intake of breath, "Atrocious margins, but mustn't grumble," two of his assistants were briskly unbuttoning Powell's overall.

With Powell now in a different, closer fitting tunic, and June breaking her silence with "That's nice, it really suits him," he asked Cohen how expansion was financed.

But instead Cohen merely said "I knew you would like it...no, tie the belt to the side sir." But when Powell persisted, Cohen, holding his hands out, replied "Why, the Regional of course." As Cohen replied one of his assistants was tying a large white scarf loosely around Powell's neck.

Powell was next shown standing in front of the first man's packing shed with him and two younger men carrying armfuls of punnets. "Would you," he said, "like to live in a society where endeavour, enterprise even on the smallest scale is actively encouraged, backed, assisted and financed by your fellows?"

Powell was then shown standing in front of Barras's looms and saying "Would you like to live and work in a society with a business climate free of the crippling effects of excessive taxation, extortions of greedy politicians and corrupt grasping officials?"

Powell was next shown walking towards a large white building. And as he did so he said "Would you like to work in a society where the business ethic can only but be open and honest, where everyone has work, has their worth continuously enhanced? Own a business where officialdom and its red tape bureaucracy no longer exists? Run a business where finance from the smallest to the largest company is readily available?" At this point he is shown standing in front of this building, above the doorway of which is written 'The Regional Bank of Ceará'.

The picture then changed to being inside the building and for the first time I am thinking "Now this is what I call a proper bank." There is a banking hall, tellers and later, when the camera travelled to the offices beyond and showed a man in one of them sat behind a good quality desk, I was again thinking "Yes, that's just the kind of office I've always wanted."

Powell then said "This is Edvardo Carvalho, manager of the Regional Bank. This bank coordinates financial flows between Ceará, the other Regional Nonettes, and those in Bosnia and France." This Carvalho then proceeds to give a guided tour of the bank and I was most impressed with everything. The entire building was a humming hive of what are some of the latest facilities. But when he said "This is the International Analysis Unit," I was really impressed.

But then June said "Oh look, they have some of the same toys as your bank." I was inwardly hurt though I considered it best not to say anything.

“But vor you Dommy der var...ist over.”

But I had not time even to ask what he meant before there was a terrible pain to my rear. Hollering, I spun round and saw a line of sherpals speeding to their carpet and collectively holding in their non-running legs a syringe-like object. It was so big and the sherpals so small that they looked like miniature medieval battering rammers. Before I had a swipe at them they had whizzed away. And when I turned round yelling “What have you done... you’ve tricked me, you’ve lured...” Terbal had vanished. The rotter had kept me talking while he had the sherpals creep up on me.

I had been bemoaning to him the haranguing I had just had from some of the Susem. That was an unpleasant experience as well. I still think them unjustified.

I had watched dozens and dozens of Susem, all dolled up in their gossamer party tunics fly south two evenings earlier. They went in flotilla of vedas and had embarked with such an air of euphoria, just like pensioners boarding charabancs for a day out, they were (I had half expected choruses of “’Ere we go, ‘ere we go”). But when they returned this morning sullen and silent, filled with dejection and disgruntlement, some of them, Pheterisco and Petruee in particular, took their ire out on me.

My protests, that I’d nothing to do with it, that I couldn’t be held responsible were in vain. I had told them, as I’d done so many times before, that the actors playing the bishops in the “Autobiography of a Flea” video which they had watched on La-ra were not typical of human males. But they still would not take notice.

I also tried mollifying them by suggesting that perhaps they had come across less than perfect specimens. This didn’t go at all down well either. They all snapped back that they didn’t need any anatomy lessons from me thank you very much, that they knew what a buck male in peak condition looked like when they saw one. And anyway, they had had a weeding out process which threw the weedy ones back.

I then suggested that perhaps the trauma of being so suddenly taken had an unsettling effect on the men’s responses? “No,” they had all replied, that wasn’t the case either. Once the men had been washed and scrubbed they appeared to be more than willing, they said. “You could see they physically were,” Petruee had declared with solemnity as she’d gazed demurely down at her gossamer veiled self.

“And in the first foreplay chases none of them wanted to run very far either,” Pheterisco had declared, and adding assertively, “when I was male I would have to run much faster. It was expected of me as well.”

With images of bacchic events I had naively asked “If the men are willing, what’s the trouble?”

"They do not last!" both they and the other Susem had chorused.

"Don't last?" I'd said.

"Ten of your minutes that is all," Pheterisco had remonstrated, "fifteen at the most. There is no fulfilment in that. As soon as you have had one you want another." At this there was a unison of silent nodding of heads and knowing of looks. "And that is when the trouble starts," she'd said

"Trouble?" I'd asked.

"After their initial climax there is not any vigour remaining," Pheterisco had said.

"Couldn't you rub something on to stimulate and bring them back to life again?"

"We have tried kinna bark, vibrancy therapy, slapping, kicking, everything, but instead they curl up holding themselves as if in pain and then start crying. And as for further chases, either they will not, cannot run or they are running as fast as they can as if trying to elude us."

"But none got away," another of the Susem had muttered darkly.

"Have you tried letting them rest between encounters?"

"What use is that to us?" Pheterisco had snorted.

"Men need rest to recharge themselves," I'd said, "time to get their ardour back."

"But surely that is what the chase is all about," Pheterisco had snapped, adding "when I was male if I did not give my pursuers at least ten minutes of chase I would not have opportunity to replenish my suprarenal glands."

"That is not all," another of the Susem and with seriousness had said, "there is more often that not inadequacy of structure."

"Inadequacy of structure?"

"With many of these males, just as my encounter is commencing and I begin to exert some mild muscular pulsation, they immediately exhibit extreme physical discomfort and I have to release them." At this, no doubt based on like experience, there was another unison nodding of heads.

"And they make such a screeching noise when you do begin to pulse them," another of the Susem had said.

"Which of course," Pheterisco had said, "has an inhibiting effect on the males we have waiting." Then, after a pause, "While your males' shortcomings are disappointing for us older girls, for Petruee they are doubly so." Before I had time to ask why, and she embracing Petruee's shoulder, Pheterisco said "It was to be her first time and she was so looking forward to the experience."

With the images of bacchic events evolving to brutal ones, I had again protested "Why take it out on me? It's not my fault, it wasn't me who made human males the way they are."

But all I received in reply from Pheterisco was, "Humph, you are a male are you not?"

And after my "Well...yes," Pheterisco's, "Therefore you must bear part of the collective responsibility for your fellow males' failings and our disappointment?"

But before I had time to fathom such reasoning let alone rebut it, Pheterisco had said "Our sojourn is but the beginning of what has been anticipated and not just in these parts. Tearo has also made preparations for yet larger parties of our colleagues to arrive in the locality where she is situated. If they, like us," she continued and my jaw dropping, "should meet with the same frustration, and knowing Tearo's temperament, it is likely she will respond more than merely demonstratively."

With dread of an ill-tempered Tearo on the rampage and thoughts of did Big Luis have any brothers, the Susem turned on their heels. But before doing so Pheterisco said "If it was not for a man called Linus we met during our second day there would not have been any satisfaction at all for any of us." Then adding almost as an afterthought, "Fortunately he has decided to stay with us, but of course he can only provide fulfilment to a few." With this, and me thinking what was it this Linus had and did he have any brothers, they strode off.

While the Susem were berating, Terbal had been hovering in the background flitting back and forth, as though eavesdropping. As they departed he glided almost furtively across to me.

"You are not so happy, ya? Problems you haff maybe?" he had asked.

I told him of the Susem dissatisfaction with menkind's shortcomings (and their swift ones as well). I also said, that although I did not consider it to be anything to do with me, I was not looking forward to forever being the butt of Susem sexual angst, especially Tearo's. He listened in silence then he said "You know Dommy, solution I haff vor you maybe."

I asked what he meant.

"To last vor a longer time und increased virmness, dat is vat is vanted, ya?"

"Yes...I suppose so."

"You know Dommy, dese maybe can be done."

"Both? And at the same time?"

"Ya, dere are somedings I am knowing."

Seeing perhaps my look of doubt he flexed his fronds, then said "Ein moment" and sped off. Minutes later he had returned and with a wild waggling exclaimed "I haff it now! I have vormulated chemicals vhich vill do all dese dings, und togedder."

"Oh yeah?" I had said with my doubt continuing

"Oh ya! Vormulation of dese chemicals vill be giving much slowing to your male's comings und more comings going vrom dem also."

"If it's testosterone, forget it. It's been tried, it doesn't work, it wears off and leaves nasty side effects, makes men fat and spotty as well as ratty, and does nothing for the un-firm."

"Nein testosterone dere is."

"If it's sildenafil citrate like Vigora, forget it as well. It's been banned. It made umpteen women go blind. You wouldn't want that to happen to the Susem, especially Tearo."

"Nein citrate is dere also."

"Well, what's in it then? How do you know it won't have side effects?"

"Nein negative side evects is it hafing."

"You mean to tell me your magic formula can keep men physically aroused for a long time? How long anyway?"

"Ya...vor a long, long time."

"But for how long?"

"Dat I am not yet knowing, ve must do experiments. But it vill vork auf dat I am knowing, und mine vormula vill make your males (and in an emphatic tone) much, much virmer. Also I am calculating more girf it vill give as vell."

"So you've something which will keep human males erect for hours, come time after time, make them as hard and firm as can be and increase their girth? It'll make them longer as well I suppose?"

He appeared to think for a moment then said "Nein...not bigger in der lenfs, only bigger in der girfs."

"How much bigger?"

"By how much..I am not knowing, ve must do experiments."

"And how do you expect men to take your magic potion?"

"I am considering it can be given by permeation by vay of der skin perhaps." Then with a waggle of his fronds, "Und if dis can be so den der evect vill be immediate!"

"Immediate?"

"Ya...vell almost. But virst ve must do experiments vor der potency also."

"Potency?"

"Ya, der potency of der vormula must not be too veak or too strong." Then, as I recall, he began backing away from me and saying "But vor you Dommy der var ist..."

No sooner was I rubbing and bewailing the soreness to my backside than I was sensing a swelling to my front one.

99: KEN

"Have you ever appeared in Court," was the first thing Jim said, "be it for the prosecution or for the defence?"

Looking round the pub I had a fair idea which side half of them had.

"Have you ever had to involve yourself in the legal process?" he next asked. "Ever felt it operates against you, exists primarily for the benefit of lawyers, the rich, the powerful and the privileged?"

I noticed a good few round the bar nodding to that, though for most of them "legal process" means the Bill and doing bird. When he next asks "Does your government, council use the law to act unfairly against you, use it to safeguard their interests and arbitrarily changes it to suit themselves?" I was half agreeing with him. But when he said "Have you ever sought protection or redress through the law only to discover it can do nothing for you, or you are too poor to pay its cost?" I was nodding and thinking about when the wife ran off and I tried to get custody of my Chloe.

Then he says "How would you like to live in a society where the rule of law is fair, just and even, open to all and is free? Have a system of justice where lawyers are unneeded? One in which those who are aggrieved have a say in their transgressor's penalty?" I was definitely agreeing to that.

Jim steps back from the camera to show a woman holding a piece of paper. "This is Fellipia Lenoca," he says, "and Fellipia's neighbour's tree is damaging her house. The neighbour refuses to cut its roots back. Fellipia is bringing the matter before the Community Court. To do this she needs signatures of eight others who agree with her."

This Fellipia is next shown walking through a doorway. "This is the Community Court committee's office," Jim says "and Fellipia is registering her complaint." As she comes out again and holding another piece of paper, "This is her receipt," and he adds, "that Fellipia and others like her having to gather such a petition frees the Court from frivolous complaints. But once the Court office has accepted the petition they are obliged to tell the other party to attend the next sitting of the Court."

Jim is then shown standing in front of a group of people. "These nine," he says and pointing to them, "are representatives from each of the community's wards and are today's judging panel. One of them, Amelia," and he pointing her out, "has been appointed by the panel to head them." Jim then said the people in dispute, after putting their case, were bound by the panel's ruling.

If either side didn't abide by it, he said, they stood to lose their community's services. But if either side didn't agree with the Court's decision they could take the matter to the Area Court, though to do this they needed to present a petition with 81 signatures on it. And if they didn't even agree with this Court's judgement they could take it to the Regional's, but they will need an even bigger petition.

“As you can see,” Jim says, “this legal system costs nothing. It is simple, speedy and anyone with a little persistence has full access to it. But what happens,” he said, “when a dispute occurs between persons from different Nonette communities?”

The picture changes and shows more groups. “These men,” he says, pointing to three youths with heads bowed, “are accused of throwing stones and breaking a shop window. This is the shopkeeper,” he says, pointing to a man. “These are nine representatives of his community,” Jim says, “and those over there are from the men’s. Both groups of representatives will hear the case, and the woman sitting between them is from the Area Court and gives her casting vote should there be a deadlock.

“This case,” Jim says, “is the most serious disturbance in Fortaleza for some time, people are quite upset. It has attracted considerable attention.” The camera then pans round beyond these groups and shows a big crowd who had come to watch. As the camera does so, he says “All Court hearings are open and anyone who wants to attend can do so.”

“But,” he next says, “this legal system is not only simple, just and open, it is also unburdened from grappling with matters stemming in the past from failings elsewhere in society. Here, hunger and deprivation no longer exist so there is no need to steal out of desperation. Drug addicts have no need to steal either, they have been rehabilitated. Drug dealers have either fled their communities or are incarcerated refilling the Serra Pelada. So too are loan sharks, pimps and others who once preyed upon the desperate. People suffering mental disorders have either been cured or are being cared for.

“Because everyone wears their Nonette identification number,” at that he points to his, “those who don’t are immediately suspect. Watching community police are always to hand.

“Fraud and evasion no longer exist for there are few regulations or laws to break. Those which do exist are what communities collectively make and agree on. There isn’t a police force to corrupt or officials demanding favours or politicians pressing for backhanders. The administration of order and justice is administered by those who are affected by it, the people themselves. “Would you like to live in a society such as this?” He then said goodbye, but as he did I heard a good few round the pub agreeing with him.

100: PATCHES

Though in the past I've woken with one, I now know it's a physical impossibility to fall asleep in such a state. And this was after nearly a day sitting in a darkened room with applications of cold compresses to numb the throbbing. This morning when it eventually subsided, I was left with a terrible soreness.

Rage usually lasts a little while then wanes away but on this occasion, just as the throbbing, mine was still waxing. During the duration of my indisposition I was seething with what Terbal had done to me. I was still irate afterwards. Not just for the experience he had injected but the embarrassment it brought.

Word went round the village. From my darkened room I could hear the Pousada's patrons asking Rico in a derisive manner as to the current state of my condition. What made it worse was that he kept coming in to enquire. And this morning I have received nothing but knowing looks. Rainbow, when she returned from São Antonio lunchtime was just as bemusedly uncaring.

With rage still with me I sought Terbal to give him a piece of my mind, but he was nowhere to be seen. All the Susem said was that he was where he usually is. Their smirking smiles and "How was it for you?" only added to my ire.

I went back to his erstwhile empty room to wait for him when I half-glanced an albino shadow sliding slowly across the ceiling and down the wall. On giving it my full attention I saw it making for the doorway. As it did I noticed it was forming into fronds. Then I realised it was Terbal in another guise.

"You swine," I shouted, blocking the door and he speeding back to the ceiling.

"No Dommy it ist good," came Terbal's faint, plaintive voice from the film.

"Oh yeah?"

"The vormula is veakened, it vill last vor two hours only I am calculating."

Still irate I accused "Why me? You should have asked? It's unethical."

"You vere der only human male and you vould hafe refused ya?"

"So?"

"But success it has been, it vorks, everyone vill be happy now?"

"You should still have asked," I retorted but grudgingly accepting his logic.

"Und a preparation I hafe made," he said slowly reforming to his usual shape, "vitch can be permeated into der skin und also I hafe a transmission vehicle vor der delivery made as vell."

"What?"

"Patches on der skins," and before I had time to respond, he added "but to know how svift dey vill vork your help I am needing vor more experiments."

"Oh no you're not," I said, eyes instantly peeled and backing against a wall.

"No...no Dommy not on you I am intending, somevun younger."

"What do you mean?" I said with a twinge of hurt.

"Your vriends, Roberto und James, you put der patches on dem, ya?"

"They are my friends, I couldn't do that. And besides, it would be unethical."

"Vell," he said almost with a sigh, "it vill mean Susem are going to be unhappy, und Tearo ven she ist not pleased she vill..."

"I'll do it."

James didn't even begin with a "Good evening," or "Hello," he just gave a smile and then went straight into it. "How good was your education? How much of your time at school was wasted? How much of it was a chore, a bore? How often did you play truant? At school were you ever bullied?"

James took a pause, gave another smile and before I had time to remark to Daffyd on his new tunic, he was firing questions again. "If you enjoyed your education, found it fulfilling, do you on reflection think you could have done better? Your teachers pushed you further? Some could have been better educators?"

He was right, if it hadn't been for Mr Prior giving extra tuition I would never have got into university. James next said "As pupils did you ever conclude that you existed more for the benefit of most of your teachers rather than they for you?" I was agreeing with this as well as thinking of Sam Prior again, how he was the exception.

James then said "If you are a parent are you satisfied with your children's education?" But I didn't have time to even think when he next fired, "Has the advent of computers, Internet and all the other appendages of technology advanced pupils' abilities over and above earlier generations, especially in basic skills of numeracy and literacy?" I was sitting on the edge of the seat and thinking "No." And when he added, "Do you think your children could also do better, that they are not challenged enough, their schools could do better as well?" I was thinking "Yes.2

James then walked towards a group of children. As he did he said "Would you agree with the notion that learning, education pure and simple, is something everyone in society should find interesting, absorbing even? Would you agree that it will be no bad thing if everyone, regardless of who they are, has full and open access to a good education? Agree that any society is better served, becomes richer in every sense if the latent abilities of all people are realised and harnessed to the full? Agree that a person's advancement is best assessed not just against those of others but by their overcoming each personal challenge? Agree that reward is an apt incentive in aiding overcoming each challenge?" I thought "Yes," to all of them.

Just before he had reached the children, James asked "Would you accept that the traditional structure of schools is not the only or even the best way to achieve these aims?" I found myself automatically thinking "Yes," again.

The children, there were nine of them each with little laptop screens, stopped what they were doing and waved to the camera. James held up one of the screens, and pointing his other arm up into the air said "Beyond this screen is each student's tutor. Through the screen are beamed 30 minutes duration real-time teaching modules as well as the tutor's on-line voice. Each module is set at a level just above the student's current ability and the tutor, when necessary, is there to help." Daffyd was now on the edge of his seat.

Handing the screen back, James continued, "At the end of tuition the screen issues a page of questions. The next tuition won't proceed until the page with its answered questions is inserted back into it. The level of reply determines the next level of tuition."

With the children now talking among themselves, he said "Helping to ensure these questions are successfully answered is an assurance of monetary reward to the pupil for doing so. But also helping are the pupil's eight companions." Standing back to show them he said "However, they do not do so solely out of altruism but because it is also to their mutual benefit. The individual modules are interlocked with joint group ones. The levels of these are fixed at the meridian of the group and thus it is in the interest of all nine to ensure that their colleagues also advance individually as fast as possible.

"The especial qualities of this system," James said, now walking away from the children, "is that it impels the more able to assist and liaise with those who aren't, and in their own collective terms. Also it recognises that advancement is based not just on innate cerebral ability but of continual striving. Overcoming difficulties is what advancement is all about, is it not?" Both Daffyd and I were nodding in agreement.

By then James had walked over to another small group but this was a mixture of men, women and children. "The first nine," he said, "was composed of three trios. However, each trio also jointly studies with two further trios from other groups but all at the same level of advancement. Like the first, this group's teaching modules cover a wide range of subjects. But this one's advancement and rewards, individually as well as collectively, depends on passing in all the subjects covered. In a way it is alike to matriculation"

James then walked towards a third group, saying as he did, "Pupils' education and thus their advancement, is not confined to the screens. Entwined with each group teaching module are seminars and field studies. These are given by each pupil taking turns, but with preparation and assistance from their on-line tutor." When he had reached this next group he said, "But those wishing to specialise in specific areas of study also join with like-minded." He asked one of the girls in this group what they were studying.

Barely turning her head she said "Wave resonance interactions in a Tertiary context," and continued writing on her screen.

Giving a smile, James left them and as he walked away said "Some of the teaching modules are related to each community's and individual people's expressed needs. If assistance with growing crops is required, or improving business practice, even repairing shoes, requests through their screens provides tailored modules followed by practical seminars..."

James was next shown sitting at a table, a glass of wine in his hand and continuing, "...such as how to produce an excellent Vinho Verde." He took a sip and then added "The Susem have provided a system of education in which everyone can and willingly participate. It is a system where striving, not intellect, is rewarded. Where no matter what an individual's innate aptitude may be, they are able to participate fully and receive the material rewards of so doing. It is a system where money does not provide an education but where education provides money." With that he held up a number of little cards and said "These are from my studies, each is worth five dollars."

As James spoke a man appeared and laid a knife, fork and napkin in front of him but he continued talking, "The screens, though the result of Susem technology, are not that much more advanced than us humans can produce should we so strive."

A woman then put a plate in front of James and I could see that she was laying out other plates. James continued to talk though, "Here is an educational system where everyone singularly and collectively is continuously and willingly pushed to the full extent of their abilities. A system where schools no longer need exist, where a teacher is not regarded as a special type of person but where everyone is a special type of teacher (Daffyd gave a groan at this but I told him to be quiet, he does annoy me sometimes) and everyone is on 'paid as you learn'," (Daffyd was again just about to say something but thought better of it).

The camera, tilting slightly, then showed people sat with James along the table and others putting dishes of food on it. With a gesture of his hand James said "This is a gastronomy group practical." But as a man topped up his glass, James said "Would you like such a system of education for your children?" then taking another sip, "would you like such an education for yourselves?" He raised his glass to the camera, gave another smile and then said "Goodbye."

"It works! They both came up a treat!"

"Goot, goot. Und how svift vas der evect in coming?"

"Like you said, no sooner than I had slapped the patches on the backs of their necks, than up erect they came."

"Und down?"

"James in two hours six minutes, Roberto ten minutes later."

"Side evects?"

"Furious at first, but calmed down after I had explained it was in the name of science and world harmony. They complained of throbbing and a slight soreness after ten minutes but it didn't worsen"

"Goot..goot. Und now into production ve vill go, ya! Oh, tell me Dommy vat ist dis?"

"The European Summer Cup, First Round and that's...Dynamo Kiev... versus IFK Gothenburg, second leg...looks like it will end being goalless."

"Now tell me Dommy, vere can more of dis be got?"

"What is it...smells like cinnamon?"

"Kinna, trees' bark it ist vrom. It is a vital ingredient in mine vormula."

"Pheterisco mentioned kinna bark. What is it, what does it do?"

"Arousing stimulant, vrom such trees as you haff here, see."

"Oh, bay trees, there's some in Ceará I suppose. But why do you need it, haven't you any?"

"Vat I haff und vat ist on La-ra is not ein kilogramme even. I am calculating vivty times dis ist minimum."

"Fifty kilos of cinnamon?"

"Vell you calculate, ein tenf auf ein gramme vor each patch, ten patches vor each day vor 40 days vor ten thousandt Susem."

"Hang on, that comes to...four million patches. And 20 hours each day for each Susem, surely not?"

"Vell dey haff to rest sometime you know."

"But for 40 days continuously?"

"Oh ya, sometimes dey are more. I haff known dem to be longer, much, much longer. Perhaps dey vill be here vor more dan 40 days. Und den maybe dey vill also vant to give boosters as vell. Perhaps 50 kilogrammes ist not enough, better double it I am now calculating."

"I don't think there'd be enough bay trees in the whole of Ceará for that."

"Vell it has to be vound. Und also dere vill be needed some more chemicals of vhich I haff also not enough.

Errant MP extradi
to stand trial in Bos

y EMMA FELLOW

IR Hugh Russet Brown was extradited to Dubrovnik yesterday to stand trial accused of upplying the previous Serbian nd Croatian regimes with orture equipment.

An ashen faced Sir Hugh was een briefly being escorted rom Dubrovnik airport by a eam of the Kymer Rouge uards. Earlier in the day a Guatemalan military transport lane had flown in with Sir Hugh from base outside of Guatemala City.

Last night a Foreign Office spokesman said "At this present time HM government does not have any representation in Bosnia, therefore we are unable to provide any consular assistance to Sir Hugh, nor any of the other detainees who are British subjects. As there is neither EU nor any Non-Governmental Organisations present there either, there is little we can do.

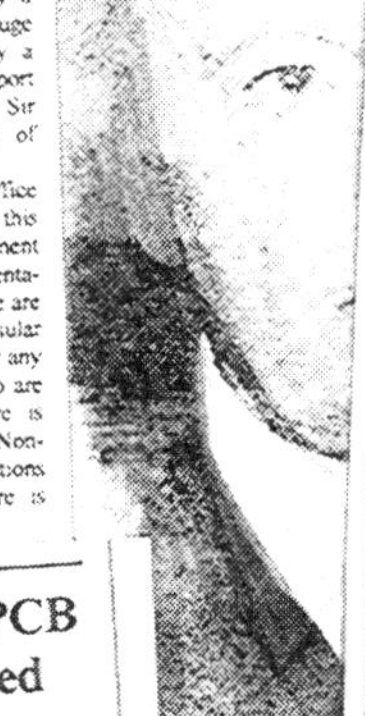

Worldwide PCB ban demanded

Scientists yesterday called for a complete and immediate PCBs. It has now been d that these plastics are l slowly killing off m animals. Some experts a the killer chemicals pose

FOURTH TEST: FURTHER FIASCO RECAST

LAND'S line-up for the h Test against Namib dgebaston on Thursday the same smack of th iocre mixed with desper as the Third.

Lord's yesterday, t d of England's Test Sele 'Tiny' Rambothom, w air of despair said "When gland has its back to the ll it will do what it has vays done, it turns round d fights."

However, the call up of dul O'Mally, from the

WIN FOR LIVERPOOL, ONLY A DRAW FOR ARSENAL

ARSENAL'S goalless draw with Sparta Prague has all but put paid to any hopes of it making it through to the finals of Eurofa Cup. Last night William Hill lengthened Arsenals odds to 250-1. The Gunners lacklustre perfor-

THE Chron

SETTING THE RECORD STRAIGHT

BOSNIA WAR CRIMES TRIAL:
ARE THEY SHOCKING OR ARE THEY NOT?

What do YOU our readers think?

The scenes from the Bosnian War Trials are truly horrific. Bishops and other top people are demanding that TV screenings are banned.

What do YOU our readers think? We are dying to know.

The TV scenes are indeed shocking, so shocking that we dare not print them on our front page. But in order that you the reader are not denied the truth we print, in cooperation with SLI-TV, a special 4 PAGE PULL-OUT PHOTO-PACKED supplement of the Bosnian slayings for you to study, in the comfort of your own home, the real extent of the of evil wicked deeds committed by these heinous Serbo-Croat savages.

Then give us YOUR answers to 2 vital questions:

Should establishment toffs be barred from telling YOU what YOU can see?:

YES/No

Should these murdering Yugo thugs get everything they deserve?:

YES/No

Ring 0800 42 24 38 for 'YES'; 0800 28 28 48 for 'No'

(calls are charged at 49p a minute)

Producers fight Bosnia film rig

By Ian Sayer in Sarajevo

EVEN before the Bosnian War Trials are over film-makers from Hollywood to Japan and Italy are said to be in fierce competition to secure the film rights.

In both Sarajevo and Dubrovnik there are rumours that millions dollars are on offer just to secure a provision agreement with the Bosnian authorities. However, the Governing Councils in both Bosnia and Ragusa have, so far declined to make any announcement regarding any impending deal.

Silvano Magdameni, one of Italy's leading producers, claims he already has backing of a clutch of Nonette communities across Bosnia

Power producers' powerlessness

Don Garcia

Once the cartels of oil, gas, electricity, nuclear fusion, even windpower swaggered the world Once they controlled, dominated our lives. But now these once bold barons' power is gone and they stand bowed before us as broken reeds.

A day does not pass without another of these once mighty titans collapsing in a cloud of dust, debt and dirt. The dust of obsolescence, the debt of ill-considered and unpayable borrowings and the dirt of dubious, not to say illicit, dealings.

Bribery

A day does not pass without yet another revelation of chicanery committed by one or other of the satraps of these once mighty organisations pleading innocence and ignorance of their company's wrong-doing.

Yesterday it was the chairman of Scallop Oil saying he knew nothing of the billions missing from his company's coffers, that it had been spent on bribes to politicians the world over.

Death squads

The day before it was the head of Western Power of California admitting defrauding shareholders as to the costs of environmental compensation liability of its strip mining in Utah. Last week's crop were price fixing, funding death squads in the third world, bribing regulators, blackmailing others. What of tomorrow; who will be paraded before us with admissions of guilt?

And the reason for these dubious dealers' rapid demise? We, the people, have taken (literally) power we need into our own hands. Today there is barely a home or a workplace without a Susem soufin energy unit.

Faustian deal

But the question still has to asked and an answer demanded: why has not such a method of energy generation not been developed, researched, here on Earth? We are told almost nightly by the Susem that the technology behind these energy modules is not so far in advance of our own. Has there been a past Faustian compact between the power cartels and governments to block the necessary research?

Corruption

Perhaps among daily revelations of these unlamented of these powerless power companies all will be revealed.

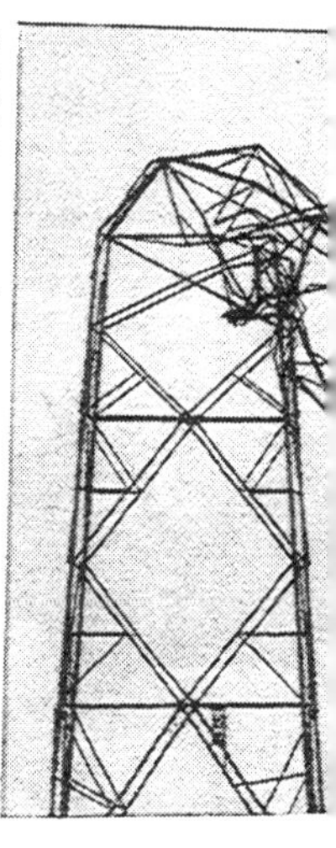

"These give me something ordinary money can't buy..." said James holding up two of the little cards he had shown the other day that he'd got from his learning, "...a session in this and the assurance of my good health." As he spoke I noticed everyone in the Salutation had turned their heads to look.

"This is a mormic," he said, tapping the side of a little booth, "and two study credits are what is needed for it to put my body's cells in perfect working order." He had no sooner spoken than an arm shot out from within the booth. It grabbed a towel lying to the side, disappeared, then a man wrapped in the towel nipped out. He had a surprise on his face to the camera, a piece of paper clutched in his hand but not a word as he darted off.

"And how does the mormic work?" said James, "I will tell you," and he did. "Leukocyte Antigens are the key to perfect health. Every animal has them, including us humans, so ours are called HLA for short. Each of us has four of them. Half of each one we inherit from one parent the other half the other. They are to be found on a chromosome in our every cell and are controllers of its wellbeing. This system protects us from attacks coming from outside of us and also self-attacks from within.

"Sometimes our HLA management is not as adept as it might be in protecting us from the outside. This happens for example when we catch a disease, and as we grow old. Sometimes it overreacts and attacks parts of us instead. Arthritis and ileitis are examples of this occurring.

"With the exception of identical twins nearly all of us have different combinations of HLAs. For some, our HLA combinations manage better protection against particular onslaughts than others. But no matter what our HLA strengths may be they also have their weak spots. The mormic corrects and strengthens a person's HLA into fortifying them fully.

"It does this by checking and cross-referencing all of the body's inter-cellular HLA resonances, those of each cell's components such as proteins and even the resonances of those components' molecules. Any non-beneficial deviance is automatically corrected. This takes about five minutes to complete and its effectiveness lasts for at least six months."

Two boys wrapped in towels and each a ticket in their hands appeared and walked up to this mormic. A woman also appeared and as one of the boys handed her his ticket, James said "She is the keeper of the mormic and under twelve's go half price." One of the boys went inside and no sooner had he chucked out his towel than there was a series of pulsing purple lights.

With the lights flickering to the side of him, James continued talking, everyone in the pub continued watching, and barely a peep out of any of them. "Children, being young are fortunate in having a healthy HLA and because they are still growing, it is vibrant as well. But for us who are older and have had more time to be ill, more opportunity to abuse our bodies, clog arteries with cholesterol, ruin and wrinkle skin with sunlight, tar lungs with smoking and atrophy muscles with indolence, our HLA is weakened. Thus for us the mormic is a godsend. It will right the lot."

"The only difference being," said James continuing, the lights now pulsing blue and the pub still dead quiet, "is that it requires more and frequent sessions before wrongs are righted. But lest it be never forgotten..." and he looking studiously to the camera, "...it is the damage done to our bodies by illness and abuse which eventually ages us all. Thus the further significance of the mormic's workings is that it slows ageing down as well." At this I noticed some of the fellows from Arsenal Sports looking at the screen extra attentively, the older ones especially.

"Here is a system of healthcare," continued James, his earnestness still with him, the second boy taking the first one's place and the pub still agog, "which dispenses with the need for drugs, medicines and other pharmaceuticals. Because it makes humans immune to outside attacks from measles to malarial mosquitoes, there is no longer need for antibiotics to fight-off infection, be it from germs or viruses, for they no longer have any detrimental effect."

Mitchell at the end of the bar shook his glass to me and I knew he was wanting another gin. But as I pushed the optic my eyes were still on the screen, as was everyone else's. With the light now flashing purple behind him, James then said "Though the mormic and what lies behind it are the result of Susem technology, it is not so far in advance of ours. The HLA system has been known to World science for decades, it is still used for instance in matching up organs for transplants."

With the lights behind him turning to blue once more and his earnestness still with him, James continued, "However, HLA's full significance was not realised before it was left languishing, overtaken by the dead end, yet short-term commercially lucrative Human Genome Project. If HLA and Magnetic Resonance Imaging with Phononic Crystallography were combined, medicine would be well on its way to aiding us humans in overcoming our illnesses and ageing."

Like me I don't think anyone in the Salutation knew the slightest what these HLA and other things were really all about. Yet all the same he had everyone's complete attention. I know he had mine.

The second boy came out of the mormic. With him and his friend clutching towels and little pieces of paper they waved to the camera, and as they did James said "Would you like to spend five minutes in a mormic?"

"Sincra it ist known to us," was all I had to go on when Terbal gave me some grey-white powder he said was the main ingredient.

Fortunately, Roberto knew someone in his university's chemistry department who would do an analysis. Being a sensible fellow he appreciated not only the urgency but the need for confidentiality too. Roberto and James were due to film near Fortaleza and soon he had telephoned from there saying the substance was called "Urseenico."

I had never heard of urseenico but Roberto said he had been told to ask for it under the names of 'Realgaro' and 'Orpimenta'. The chemist chap, so he said, had told him, that I could obtain it from vets, tanners and dyers. Though they sounded strange sources for medical supplies and I had no knowing of such places, I felt pressure-bound to pursue, for Terbal had said he had no more than a few day's supply.

When I asked Jorge, still Tabajara's acting Nonette head, if he could help, he said he knew a man who knew a vet in Sobral. Though when we had located him and I said several hundred kilos were required this vet nearly had a fit. A hundred grammes was a lot for him he said and when he mentioned the price I nearly had a fit as well. It would come to thousands and thousands of dollars. I was dispirited to say the least.

But during our return to Tabajara Jorge said the name Realgaro rang a bell and he knew a man in Tianguá who might know where such was to be had. As fate had it this man, a former agricultural chandler, had sacks of the stuff. Though I was mystified when he said that it had been used for dusting crops on the old latifúndios. But I was heartened when he said that to him his Realgaro was now next to worthless and he would thank me to take it off his hands. And what was more he knew other one-time farm suppliers who would be only too pleased to get shot of theirs as well.

Locating the talc which Terbal also said was needed proved easy. Jorge knew another man who had once mined manganese and he had heaps of it lying around old workings and would be more than glad to see the back of it.

Finding someone to make the patches wasn't difficult either. Jorge said he knew yet another man, Manual, who had a factory in Sobral making sticking plasters. This Manual is able to make up the patches in the coarse arach weave Terbal had specified and coated inside with a fine spiked gelatine film. As anything plastic is out, Manual, when I asked, knew another man who could produce paper pouches to put the patches in.

There was of course the small matter of paying for it all, but at the time I had thought this was something I would worry about later for there was still the problem of the cinnamon. How was I to get a hundred kilos of it?

Then Jorge had another stroke of inspiration. He said as cinnamon is used in cooking, it meant that across the whole of Ceará there must be no end of little jars and packets of it languishing in larders. He sent out a message to the Area Nonette which in turn relayed it to the others, and within hours all of Ceará had heard the appeal. It was even broadcast on the radio and the TV. However, there was the small detail of what was to be offered in return.

The only thing to be done was to promise patches. But with the whole project under wraps all that could be said was that every sender of cinnamon would be supplied with a most proficient product especially pleasing to ladies. (After all, if the patches are good enough for the Susem there is the chance they will prove popular with human women as well). From the huge pile of packets, boxes and jars which have arrived these past couple of days it would appear this hunch was spot on. It's also solved the problem of finance.

The size and swiftness of the cinnamon response confirms to me that there is a definite interest for the product. And if the free patches which are sent out are viewed as 'samples', 'tasters' they will generate demand for repeat orders. Word is soon bound to spread and by doing so promotional launch costs can be avoided.

If each patch is priced at half a dollar, the income once sales get going will more than cover costs of the Susem patches and the 'free' samples as well. Keeping the existence of the patches a bit on the quiet side and letting sales climb slowly will also avoid the inevitable teething troubles from upsetting consumer confidence. But with a little marketing skill there is no reason why these patches can't become de rigueur. After all how much is a good evening worth? (Even at twice the price they will be a bargain). In Ceará alone, there must be at least a million couples coupling several times a week. This will mean an annual income of more than $26 million. With the unit production costs, so I have calculated, at less than five cents, there is no reason why it should not become a viable venture.

It's a pity in a way that there has not been time to trial test the patches, but such is the rush to production it's just not been possible. And it would also perhaps have been handy to discover what 'urseenico' actually is. However, it has no side effects, well not on me apart from a slight soreness. But for James and Roberto it was, so they say, barely passing, so therefore it must be alright. I did think of having a list of ingredients printed alongside the instructions on the patches' pouches, but if it's known one of them was used on cattle and crops it could upset people. And anyway, I'm a great believer in never letting trivial truths cast clouds over the making of money.

I watched Powell's programme last night and in many ways I had not inconsiderable pause for thought with what he had to say.

"What is the future of your employment?" was his first question. "How secure is your job, anyone's job?" was the second. Then, "What benefit is there to an individual as well as society, in being without a job, unemployed, unemployable? What sense is there to society in installing machines to replace people if all it offers those people in return is unemployment? What wisdom is there in a society investing resources and time educating, equipping people with skills only to leave them without a job, a chance to enhance those abilities for mutual benefit?"

As he spoke I was reminded of the hundreds of job applications my nephew John has sent off for. And after leaving university more than a year ago and with an honours degree, he has ended up working in a pub in Oxford Street for less pay an hour than the price of two pints of their beer.

Powell was then shown walking through an area strewn with stones and rocks. As he did he said "If you were trained as a skilled worker have you witnessed what you once did reduced to nothing more than a series of unskilled, mechanical processes? And in it doing so have the buyers of this now deskilled service benefited? If you are a recipient of such now deskilled, even de-humanised services, are you better served?"

As he spoke I was thinking not only of those wretched menu voice mails but the Bank's new policy of charging customers for depositing cash at the counter. Compared to the past the Bank's clients barely meet counter assistants these days.

Powell, next shown walking between yet larger rocks, said "What sense is there in demanding an ever higher qualified work-force and then dumbing down an increasing proportion of its members' jobs? In an era when people are active decades longer than were their parents, is it really wise to consign so many to enforced premature retirement, barring them from work, from providing the benefits of their experience to society?"

As he spoke I thought of Jenkins, how he had been advised to take his retirement. Though "advised" is perhaps not strong enough a word, more a case of "or else". And of course it is something I also have to keep an eye on these days. If I had to leave the Bank, even though I am only 46, my age now counts against me, I doubt if I would ever be offered another job again.

Powell, who was now walking between boulders taller than he was, turned to the camera once more and said "Is a society functioning in the best interests of its members if it regards those in work as just another resource, to be installed and disposed of at whim? Where pursuit of short term profit has primacy over the livelihoods of its workers, the quality of service to its purchasers? Where the emphasis of investment is not the creation of employment and harnessing people's abilities but on profit for profit's sake?"

Powell, now walking into what appeared a ravine, and turning to the camera, said "Is society best served when change is determined solely by the impact and requirements of technological development? Where technological change consumes society's resources and is given free reign, regardless of how doubtful the benefits, dire the consequences might be to that society?"

Menu voice mails again came to mind but he, continuing, said "The nightmare of nuclear fission and fusion from which we have been recently relieved, the Human Genome Project from which we have as yet not?" I had heard of that but had never thought it also was dangerous.

The walls of the ravine Powell had walked into became steeper and appeared to be overhanging, but I could see he was coming to the end of it because light was showing beyond his head. Turning once more to the camera, he said "Are such things the inevitable price of so called progress?"

Powell was then shown climbing over a fall of rocks and out of the ravine. As he did he turned and said "Or is there an alterative? A better, human alternative?"

Powell was next shown with the rocks in the background far behind him and he now walking up a grass covered slope. He then said "How would you like to live in a society where everyone not only has a job but one which is worthwhile and secure? Work in a society where, because they are paid to do so, it is in every employer's interest to invest in advancing employees' abilities and skills, and even employ more people? Work in a society where technology is developed to specifically benefit and fulfil the needs of the people and not the other way around?"

As he continued to walk up the slope Powell next said "Would you like to live and work in a society where technology is developed and used not only for the benefit of its people, does not ravage and pollute the world about but is in harmony with it?"

Powell was then shown from the rear but still climbing the grassed slope which now appeared to be a hill. Turning his head, he then said "Would you like to live in a society where investment is directed to generating yet more and ever-skilled employment?" As he continued to walk, the screen showed the top of the hill upon which was a small city glistening white in the sunshine. Just before he waved goodbye he said "would you like to live in a society free from the fear of being without a job?"

Not a word of thanks from anyone. I have had a terrible time with them all. It's always the same, the moment you have something there is a whole horde finding fault, but a blink later there is another lot trying to nick it.

No sooner had Paceillo and the others returned from São Antonio than I had an earful of her ire. I had used Susem substances without consultation, she said. It was wrong of me to introduce something of theirs, she berated, into another's society, and without due consideration to the consequences.

On and on she went but I gathered that I was not alone. While she raged I noticed Terbal, his fronds hanging lank, hovering mute in a corner as though in disgrace. In part though I think Paceillo's mood was due to the machines' days of fruitless drilling and digging. Petruee says that they are still excavating and exploring but she is doubtful if anything is there to be found.

But the village's attitude towards the patches has been mercenarily opposite. Though Jorge didn't say anything himself, in the Pousada it was made most clear to me that if hadn't been for his knowledge and assistance the patches would never have happened.

Seeing what was coming, I promptly proffered part of the potential profits to the village's farm cooperative in exchange for them growing bay tree saplings, the shoots of which would be a future source of cinnamon. They did not exactly reject the offer, they just wanted more. And alas, but knowing never to fight battles which can't be won, I had to settle on their terms rather than mine.

Parting with a quarter was painful enough but I have to supply all of Tabajara's adults with free patches as well (though I did manage to beat them down to one per person every other day).

The villagers are not the only ones who have me over a barrel. Manual has gnawed off five per cent, so have the printer, the retired manganese miner and the ex-agricultural chandler. All this, and as yet, not a single patch produced. The only brightness being is that I have assured supplies at stable prices.

And this Linus the Susem have brought back, he is another confounding thing. The Susem berated me over human beefsteak males' inadequacies but here they are doting over him. I don't know what they see in the man. As he doesn't speak any English I had Roberto have a word with him to find out why he is so special. All he has uncovered is that he is a corporal and his surname's Cunha. There is nothing to the man, he has sloping shoulders and is as skinny as can be. What is worse, he has the disgusting habit of forever licking the sides of his nose.

107: KEN

The first thing Jim said when he came on the box was "If you are living in a democracy, do you know the names of your local councillors, have any of them ever visited you, ever asked what you want them to do?"

"No," and, "never," I thought.

And when he said "Do they take your vote for granted, or dismiss it as not counting for anything?" again it was, "Yeah."

Next he said "If you live in Europe, do you know the name of your MEP?" Before I had time to even shake my head, he had added "Did you know that each one costs taxpayers $3,000,000 a year?" And before I had chance to think anything to that he'd said, "Almost as much as a British MP." Then he said "In other countries politicians cost their taxpayers even more."

And on he went. In once sense I suppose on one level it was all boring but then on the other hand what he said was right, he did have a point, especially when he said "And what has any politician done for you, done for us, we the ordinary people? Each one says they are our representative though in reality what choice do we have? What say do we, the 'ordinary people' have in picking our representatives compared with the influence of unopposed unknowns operating behind closed doors?

"Our only say," he said, "is it not, is to vote for those chosen by others. Perhaps it is no wonder that fewer and fewer of us bother to vote at all for any of our so-called representatives. In the United States, that claimed bastion of democracy, in their last national election, three out of five of the electorate saw no sense in voting for any candidate. The US President was elected to office by less than a quarter of the eligible voters. Is this democracy?

"While ever fewer of us bother to vote," he went on, "the cost of getting elected keeps rising. The last US acknowledged election costs were six billion dollars. Although American taxpayers were charged for a third of this, as they were for those of President Warren's own re-election, he still had to personally raise a further $2,000,000 every single week of the four years of his first term to ensure he would win a second. And this money came not from the ordinary people but the powerful and the rich. How many of them gave without pursuing something in return? Need democracy cost so much, be beholden to the power of vested interests?

"In every European country during the past 30 years, though voters' numbers have barely risen, the costs, even in purchasing terms, of national elections have trebled every decade. Has, during these past 30 years, this thirty-fold increase bought any improvement to Europe's political institutions, the quality of their members?

"In any western democracy, let alone elsewhere's, what chance does an ordinary person, should they believe in the stance of a particular political party, have in running for office? In America anyone who stands for even as a humble Congressman or woman needs to personally raise more than $10 million to fund their election campaign. How many of us, we the ordinary people, have access to such money? Is it no wonder that every Republican member of Congress is a millionaire as are most of the Democrats? Is it any wonder either that most of them are in the pay, beholden to the vested interests of their backers? Is this really representative democracy? Or is it an oligarchy of the rich and privileged?

"Of the politicians you know of, how many can it be said exist for the benefit of their electors, as opposed to their electorate existing for the benefit of them?"

To that I thought "Not a lot."

"Those you consider to be the former," Jim continued, "how many are because they are so-called 'good' constituency MPs, Congressmen, women? Those who give emphasis to dealing with their constituents' woes resulting from mis-governance of the bureaucracies of which they are part? Never the less, in the same way, is this not, as in medieval times, when courtiers deigned audiences to powerless commoners presenting their petitions for the wrongs the king and his court had done unto them?

"But of the latter, the self seekers, who do they hold audience with? Which lobbies, vested interests ply their influence upon them? How much is paid for privileges they bestow? Are these, self-centred individuals pursuing elected office for the perks and patronage it procures, really what democracy should be?

"Or are the democratic societies in which we live democracies in name only? In reality are these supposed democratic societies still akin to those of medieval times where barons with the power of their vested interests jostled with one another for control of the kingdom's wealth, the king's and his courtiers' ears? Societies in which ordinary people are still treated by the powerful as little more than serfs, to be patronised when advantageous, trampled or lulled into indifference when not? Societies in which to the powerful the concept of 'democracy' is little more than a joke. Where to them the ticks and crosses that we the commoners put in ballot boxes are not even worth the paper they're written on?"

"Does it have to be this way, or is there an alternative?" he said. By then I was half torn with still watching or going round the Greenwood for a pint, but then he said "Goodbye."

THE NATION DECIDES

Bosnian executions: 'Cruel or fair, or both?'

By **Bill Tufnell**

THE Bishop of Buckingham and others are leading a crusade to get the Bosnian War Trials banned from television.

Yet SLI TV claims that soaring viewing figures is an indication the public demands justice is seen to be done.

To help with this important moral debate we have asked a number of ordinary people for their views.

Marcie Williams

Marcie Williams of Huyton said: "I am not a regular SLI viewer myself but I always make a point of watching 'Trials'. I think those Hisogynist girls are good fun.

Those two, Buttercup and Daisy are so funny the way they pick the men up and then hold them down underneath that big school-like guillotine.

"And my partner Giles always says that when those other two, Rose and Honeysuckle jump up and pull down on the guillotine arm, the sound it makes when it cuts through the men's spines is the same as when he's cracking open a lobster's claw."

Marcie's friend Mary Dybe, also of Huyton, said: "I like the little dance Nightshade and

Mary Dybe

"And then the way they lift them right up in the air before bringing them down and smashing into the men's faces. And when they have their backs to you so they read "Deadly Poison" I always a little laugh."

Nick MacManus

Nick MacManus, a wrestler from Brixton, said: "What you see on 'Trials' is nothing compared with what I have to put up with.

"When I'm in the ring, if you could hear what the women in the crowd want my opponents to do to me! By comparison the girls on 'Trials' are restrained."

Jaquie Shaw

Jaquie Straw, an accountant, from Blackburn, said: "To my mind

"Well it's cheaper than locking them up isn't it? And it can't be denied that the televising has generated a lot of extra profits for many companies including SLI, of which I and many of my clients are shareholders.

"Also because the daytime 'Trials' is watched by so many of the country's wilfully unemployed youth it keeps them indoors instead of going out and committing crimes."

Harry Harman

Harry Harman, an abattoir owner, from Peckham, has a differing view. He said: "I think that no matter what anyone has done there is no reason to execute them. And showing those bodies lying about, especially all those cut-up ones, is most distressing.

"And as for smashing their faces in with those outsize sledge hammers under the pretext of putting them out of their misery is quite uncalled for.

"If you replay the video of these men in slow motion as I have had cause to do on numerous occasions, you can really see they are in pain.

"What will they be doing with them next? - Stun gunning and hanging them up on hooks I suppose?"

Pam Parker a relationship councillor, from High

Pam Parker

decisions on other people's behalf, I know only too well the difficulties the Bosnian people must have been faced with.

And I must say their approach towards these aberrant males meets with my full approval. After all what use are?

"In this day and age, quite frankly, we are all better off without these sorts of men. The only question I have, is do they want any of ours to deal with?"

Doug Hailsham

Doug Hailsham, a pet food manufacturer from Sleaford, said: "I think what's going on in these trials is an absolute disgrace. The commercial opportunities they are allowing to go to waste. All those prime cuts just being thrown down holes like that is just shocking."

Well dear readers, what do you think of 'Trials'? Do you think that those privileged people living in their ivory towers should used their unelected powerful positions to tell us, the ordinary people

Susem space search – stunning sc

By **Thomas Android**

GIANT Susem machines were shown on last night's telecast, raising countless wedges of rock and earth, hundreds of metres high from the surface of the Amazon rain-forest.

For 20 minutes viewers were shown pairs of giant Susem 'station busters' craft raising oval shaped sections of the ground and hover hundreds of feet in

No sooner had ground risen than hundreds of other, smaller machines were seen crawling down the freshly excavated pits.

A few minutes later, with the smaller machine racing from the excavations, the hovering ovals of rock were shown being 'slotted' back into the same holes they had been raised from. No sooner was each section replaced than others were seen rising from the forest. As the smaller machines left each excavation they too

'Human genes genie can't be put back' says world expert

By **Linda Anker**
Science Correspondent

HAS the human genome research project really fallen into the hands of greedy companies as last night's Susem telecast claimed? "No," say the leading experts engaged in the project.

Professor Sir John Hopkins of the Soane Cancer Research Institute and a leading pioneer in the field said: "It was grossly irresponsible to make such unfounded claims that the HGP is being pursued for solely financial gain by a few powerful vested interests. It is also nothing short of scandalous to suggest that we scientists are pursuing the HGP

As to the Huma Leucocyte Antigens mentioned in the telecas Professor Hopkins wa equally dismissive. He sai "HLAs are so old ha Gene research is muc more exciting, muc more at the cutting edg of the biotechnic revolutio where some of the mo exciting discoveries a being made. My team ha

Brazilian army flees Alien

By **Jason Peel**
In Recife, Brazil

THE Brazilian army is in full retreat, reeling under the thrust of Susem attacks.

Soldiers fleeing the much vaunted 'Wall of Steel' told of thousands of frontline troops retreating in terror from the Alien's onslaughts.

Hospitals overflowing

Medical centres throughout the Northeast of the country are filled with casualties unable to be treated by military field hospitals.

The Northest's regions' two major cities, Natal and Recife, are full of soldiers who have fled their regiments. One nameless soldier said: "Our comrades are taken from us by the Aliens. Then they are returned, their faces filled with fear from their ordeals. Those who saw them fled and we have fled with them.

"We cannot fight them [the Aliens], we have no wish to suffer the ordeals our comrades have."

Doctors in Recife said they were not treating battlefield injuries but what they claimed were psychological attacks on the armed forces.

Traumatic injuries

One paramedic who had ferried many of the wounded, said: "Many [soldiers] are in a state of deep trauma, some have even lost the power of speech. All are in no cond-

Last night Brazil's Military's high command, apparently unaware of the rout in the North-east, in a communiqué mentioned only that the army was being subjected to Susem 'probing attacks'.

The junta's high command spokesman said reports of army's retreat were 'greatly exaggerated'.

The spokesman did acknowledge, however, that some divisions had made tactical withdrawals to previously prepared positions.

A later communiqué stated that reinforcements were being sent to the front to 'repel further attacks'. There are doubts, however, that the Brazilian military will be

Da Costa's plea

The second communiqué also said Colonel Videl da Costa - Brazil's military strong-man - had called on leaders of other South American countries to make common cause and help repel the Aliens. But without pledges of military aid from the US, this is unlikely.

Ronald Lucan in Bahia Salvador reports:

THE Brazilian army has been routed by the Susem. Thousands of troops are in full flight as the Aliens are reported to have attacked over a 700 kilometre-wide front smashing the military's front line.

Major highways southward from both Paraiba and Pernambuco states are clogged with military transports fleeing the Alien blitzkrieg.

Discipline among the retreating soldiers has totally disintegrated with reports of looting and drunkenness in the wake of the Army's retreat.

Refugees streaming into Salvador say order has many provincial cities in the west of Bahia have collapsed into chaos as soldiers go on the rampage. Many deaths are reported to be linked to soldiers robbing and looting as they retreat from

108: SINCERITY

In one sense things are going swimmingly. In another they are not.

Production is flowing smoothly. The Nonettes' distribution network has been a boon, there is now an outlet in every community. The Nonettes' spreading southward means sales can only increase. The Susem are satisfied with their patches and enough cash is coming in to fund a stockpile for Tearo's pals when they arrive. It is so rewarding knowing that I'm bringing happiness and unending fulfilment to so many people.

It has been a struggle though. From the outset I have had to work all hours coordinating production, telephoning, running about ensuring enough of everything was where was needed, overseeing distribution, despatching orders, counting the money. The cinnamon sent by the Cearense went so fast I have had to press Tabajara's farm cooperative three times the past week to lay down yet more groves of bay trees. Apart from sleeping and studying (both late at night) and delivering patches to the Susem, they are the only times I have been in Tabajara let alone the Pousada. I have had to work so hard that there has barely been time for a drink. But then anything worth achieving is always harder than first envisaged.

Manual is busy too. He has had to expand premises, take on more people. It is upsetting though to overhear them calling his place the "Love Patch Factory", so disparaging, demeaning and does nothing to accord the product its due sophistication.

However, there is a real worry brewing, James. He is proving to be a big disappointment to me. If he continues saying the things he is he is going to upset a lot of people and land us all in even bigger trouble once the Susem have flown away. And now that they have found remains of Pa-tu this seems sooner rather than later. In a way it is my own fault I suppose but Rainbow's championing James has now put him beyond any influence I might have had.

But if only he had kept to what I had told him at the outset, go through the motions and nothing more, just go along with Paceillo long enough for the replacement soufins to arrive. But no, he has refused to see sense. And even worse he has become brimming with sincerity. It is so upsetting, I really thought him old enough and he having banking experience, to realise that sincerity is hazardous. No good has ever come from it. It is just another variety of 'do gooding'. And for myself I have always found sincerity, other than the cosmetic kind, bad for business.

Classic Roc[k] promised for 'Trials'

THE BOSNIAN Nonettes and Caught yesterday jointly revealed details o[f a] huge increase in the scale of 'Trials' - popular Bosnian War Crimes Trials spectacular.

The new look 'Trials' is to inc[lude] special set designs and music by legendry French classical rock comp[oser] Jean Charles Chaffonner.

The Kosevo Stadium, Sarajevo, Bos[nia's] premier sports centre, is to be spruce[d up] for the revamped television serie[s]. spokeswoman for Caught said: "It is that the most important part of 'Tr[ials'] those of the punishments of the ringleaders who actually orchestrate[d] atrocities in Bosnia are accorded th[e] prominence they warrant."

The spokeswoman also said that G Brebisdeux, the world famous desig[ner of] the sets for many rock concerts created designs for each program[me] the new TV spectaculars. She sai[d] Brebisdeux's designs had enthusiastically endorsed by all p[arties] including the Hisogynists.

Brehisdeux said: "To me this is a honour. Already I have conferre[d with] Jean Charles who is presently com[posing] his final score for the concerts. T[he] Dipper which is already construc[ted at] the Zoo nearby the stadium [will be] extended into the Kosovo stadiu[m] as will the stadium be extended i[nto the] zoo as well.

"As the actual court cases o[f the] criminals which precede the punis[hments] will take place in the centre of Sa[rajevo]" Brebisdeux said," I am also designi[ng] along the highway along which th[e] will be travelling.

"As for the punishments thems[elves I] am planning for there also be a[n] giant video screens around the sta[dium]

Choreography of Danse Macabre

The Hisogynist's choreography of the Bosnian War Trials' sentencing has won plaudits from many in the world of dance. **Jessica Wynden Hughes**, Senior Reader in Tamala Motown Studies, the University of Sheppey at Leysdown, talks to **Wayne Ignatioff**, dance critic of *Hoofers & Queens* and **Beth Maxton** of Inyerface Dance Company

Jessica: "Would you say that the Hisogynists' increasing use of strong musical rhythms in their punishment routines has added a certain heightened piquancy and zest to their overall performance?

Wayne: *"Oh, definitely yes. It so helps to give a uniformity of movement to their every routine. One cannot but help delight in the coordination in the movement at the prelude to each châtiment.*

The way the first two central performers then hold each arrivée in an érainte aux de luttur posture and with a single sweep up to the dias á madame guillotine."

Beth: "But it's the bit before that what's good as well. About when the blokes first come into the arena and that head Hisogynist, Myrtle reads out the charges, the way she always says: "Lo what have we here...?" And like yesterday, when she said to that fat geezer: "A prison warden...torturing inmates? Oh dear, oh dear.."

And as she said it there were those other Hisogynists dancing in the background in a line like the Temptations used to and they had that music that sounded like the opening bars of 'In the Midnight Hour', great dance number that and..."

Jessica: "You're so right. And I do so like the way that as Myrtle finishes her lines two of her fellow Hisogynists just seem to glide away from the chorus line, take the fellow by the throat and legs and whisk him up to..."

Wayne: *"That was precisely the point I said I thought was so good. And of course Beth is so right about the music, it adds so much to the ethos of the scene. As of course so does the lighting, the illumination of the fumée aux de buée."*

Jessica: "You are so right. The way when the two swing the fellow through the mist as it wafts away to show the guillotine..."

Beth: "Yeah, good innit when the bloke sees what it is and he starts yelling and kicking and that. Did you see that one the other day when they had to really slap him hard before he stopped."

Wayne: *"With rabbit punches like that he'd probably lost consciousness. But with the other fellows the way, as the scene clears each time, the music suddenly changes from andante to fortissimo overlaying any further sounds from them.*

The Tijuana brass was especially good I thought. And I was particularly taken by the way they stop in the middle of the second crescendo to allow the guisto drumbeat to resonate through accompanying tympani as the two further Hisogynists bound to either side of the guillotine's lever.

And the way, with an allegro guisto forte they both spring in unison upwards, snatch the lever and yank it down..."

Beth: "Yeah, but did you see that one the other day, that really fat one, they had to jump up twice before the blade had cut all the way through him."

Jessica: "But afterwards, the way all four Hisogynists step back to make space for the man's to fall to the ground is so good. The way they always seem to get the man to fall so he can actually see he is separated is just so good. The way the musical refrain seems to momentarily fade adds a certain piquancy in the way it allows the man's screams to resonate. And then as the four step back to the chorus line..."

Beth: "And those other ones come forward taking their places, the ones with those big sledge hammers."

Jessica: "And they are such whoppers aren't they..."

Wayne: *"But the way the music after the smorzando takes on appassionato appoggiatura in time with their foot treads and with the raising of the hammers it comes to a sprechgesang as the prima plunges hers down..."*

Beth: "Yeah, when those hammers come down, good innit, I bet those blokes all had eyes in the back of their heads then! Did you see that one the other day, the one they showed in slow motion close-up replay?

You could really see the hammer's head going right in, and you could actually see how it was the same size as the bloke's face, then all that blood and his brain shoots out the sides all over the ground, but did you notice how his ears were still in the same place, funny that."

Jessica: "Yes. But afterwards, the way the Hisogynist's first chorus line make those kicking movements as they sing, "Dash, dash; dash that trash," is just so good..."

Beth: "Kicking movements? They actually were kicking! Did you see their boots? They were steel capped. Did you see that one the other day, Ivy, she kicked the bottom half of that bloke so hard it scooted all the way to the dog pit in one go."

Wayne: *"But didn't you think that as the denouement de rigueur is taking place the next chorus line's refrain is just so appropriate..."*

Beth: "Oh you mean the way they came forward with hosepipes and brooms singing "I'm gonna wash that man right out of this sand."

Jessica: "Oh yes, that was just so good, so Supremish..."

Beth: "Naah, I thought it was more Martha and the Vandellasish myself."

Red Jim slates politicians

POLITICIANS are a bunch of greedy "self seekers" who use their public office solely for their own selfish ends, said new Susem telecaster James Prior yesterday.

Prior claimed that electors votes are worthless because the people in power are never unseated. Prior also maintained that most political parties foisted candidates on the electorate regardless of their wishes.

But last night Britain's political establishment angrily lambasted the allegations made by Prior or 'Red Jim' as many are now calling him.

Replying to the charge that few people know the name of their European Member of Parliament, Quintin Gore, Maidstone's new Lib-Con MP and son of Lord Gore of East Malling, said: "Of course nobody knows their MEP, it's too early for this to happen. What people forget is the European Parliament is a very new institution, it's not even 50 years old."

Alfreda Tosh, Labour MP for Streatham, was just as vehement in condemnation of Red Jim's assertions. Defending her links with the TBWU which sponsors her, she said: "I can definitely

Hisogynists choreograph executions

BY PETER ABLE

VIEWERS of SLI's Bosnia War Trials were treated to a new look presentation yesterday.

The old style massed stone throwing charges of women screaming revenge have been replaced by a more orderly ceremonial.

To chants of: "One, two, three, eight, we will eliminate," a double chorus line of black clad women rained volleys of stones and rocks down on dozens of men judged guilty of rape.

With the men writhing on the ground and to a further refrain of 'Five, eight, seven, nine, kill the swine, kill the swine" the women proceeded to smash the men's skulls with larger rocks until presumably they were dead.

With the women next shown dragging the men's bodies to holes in the ground they further chanted, "Three, eight, seven, six, down the pits, down the pits."

With the last of the men's bodies thrown down the holes and to the awaiting dogs the women then reformed into two lines and chanted "Five, eight, six, seven, we're in heaven, we're in heaven" and clapped their hands above their heads as they did so.

According to telephone survey conducted by SLI immediately after yesterday's 'Trials' programme an overwhelming number of viewers gave the new style punishment routines an enthusiastic thumbs-up.

One such enthusiastic viewer, Joanna Dickens of London, said: "I always derive great satisfaction watching 'Trials'. Seeing those men getting what they deserve is very rewarding. But the new routines do certainly add a sense of style and sophisticat-

109: SIÂN

"If you live in a democracy how much power and influence do the politicians elected from your district have?" was the first thing James said when he came on. "Especially those politicians acting on yours and your district's behalf," was the second. "How independent are they?" was his next. At first I didn't know what to make of it, neither did Daffyd. But James looked relaxed, not at all agitated the way he was the other night. He was still serious though.

"How much control do political parties exert over their members to follow the party line?" he continued. "At least in Spain they are open, if Spanish politicians do not vote for their party's policies they are fined. But in other countries political parties have shot erring supporters for less.

"But politicians, representative or not, powerful or powerless, we can in theory vote for, oust them and governing parties from office. Also we know who they are and what they claim to stand for, apart from getting elected and staying elected that is. What of the governments themselves, their ministries. Who puts them in power? Who ousts them? Who are they?"

The picture changed to showing James walking across a field of grass. After a few steps he said "How much do politicians' powers sprout from the ministries they represent?" He plucked up a toadstool, saying "Politicians and ministers, like toadstools and puffballs, rise, ripen then wither. The average term of a minister in office is 18 months." Then, with him casting the toadstool aside, the picture changed again and showed him walking along the edge of a large cutaway section of the ground below him.

Both of us sat watching not saying anything. The picture promptly changed again, the camera zooming to the top of this cutaway section and showing the earth in detail complete with a fringe of grass and James's boots either side of a tiny toadstool poking out of it. And as the picture changed, James said "Societies, we the people, are like the earth. Just as with fungi, the full power, reach of ministries, bureaucracies are unseen and usually unknown." The camera zoomed to the base of the toadstool then went slowly downwards, showing as it did a network of thin white roots. James continued, "Just as the vast hidden web of a fungus makes and controls toadstools so do ministries their ministers."

The picture changed again, to a big black cube with a green top. It was big because James was stood on it and he was small. He still continued to speak, "Ministries not only make their ministers, but again like fungi..." The picture changed yet again, this time it was as if the camera was zooming, travelling inside the black of this cube. But it was soon cruising between thin white threads, which I suppose were the toadstool's roots, there were masses and masses of them. James continued, "...their immense network of roots spread and spread. And as their roots creep ever further they need to parasitically suck more and more nutriment from the earth to fuel their growth."

The camera still kept travelling but now the roots were so dense it was barely able to move between them. James still continued, "Ministers, like toadstools, exist for only a little time but the fungus creating them lives on. Bureaucracies, like fungi, toadstools or no toadstools, have a life, a power of their own, their roots, tentacles creeping everywhere. And typical of parasitic growths they entwine, often insidiously, their hosts, us, taking from, determining evermore the shapes of our lives. The longer they exist the more extensive they become. And the more they suck from all about them, the more they dominate."

The picture changed back to the grassy field but this time it showed a tall hummock of earth rising from it. As the camera panned down from its top James said "There are other unseen subterranean controllers of lives." The camera was then at the base of the hummock and showed a mass of white ants. But Daffyd said they were termites. All of a sudden the camera was speeding into a tunnel inside the hummock and showing myriads of other termites scurrying along it. James said "Each of these creatures lives for fewer days than we humans live years."

The camera still sped along the tunnel keeping up with the termites. Then all of a sudden it opened into a huge chamber, well it was big compared with the tunnel. No sooner was it there than it panned to the far side. And there was this huge yellow beast. It was as big to the termites crowding around it as a row of terrace houses are to us. It looked horrible, evil. With each of its houses pulsing back and forth, James said "This is their queen and they are her slavish servants. She controls every facet of their lives, which ones shall forage, fight, nurse, who shall live, who shall die, everything. She can live for at least three of our years, that is more than a 1,000 of theirs."

The picture changed yet again. This time it showed buildings. I recognised some of them, the Pentagon, the EU offices in Brussels, Whitehall, Daffyd said another was GCHQ Cheltenham. And James said "What beasts lurk within their bowels?"

The picture changed back to the termite mound with James standing to the side of it and saying "Do our lives have to be controlled in this way, or is there an alternative?" No sooner had he spoken than this big shaggy animal appeared. Daffyd said it was an anteater.

But James said "This is a tamandua." And as he spoke the picture showed it clawing the termite's nest apart.

"What are they?" I said, seeing a big, dark fish-filled tank.

"Don't go near them!" shrieked Rainbow racing across the room and gabbing hold of me, "...even your reflection will have them leaping from the water. They can jump up to a metre from the water, they are that vicious."

"Vicious?"

"They make other piranhas seem like goldfish."

"Oh. But what are they? Why are they here?"

"Indians near the site of Pa-tu's remains told us of them. They are from the upper reaches of the Rio Içá. They are a sub-species of red bellied piranhas. They are new to science."

"Oh yeah?"

"In the past no one including the Indians ever escaped from them. The moment these piranhas see any animal or even just their reflection they will immediately leap from the water and attack them. They are so vicious they can strip a man to the bone in minutes. The Indians regarded them as protectors from outsiders."

"Oh. What are they called?"

"They haven't a name as yet but I've suggested *'Landlordis'*, *'Serrasalmus spilopleura landlordis'*, the 'Landlord'."

"Landlord?"

"Remember when we were at Nell Street? Mr Sullivan?"

"Hard hearted Eamon? Our landlord?"

"And if you were just a day late with the rent, how he would dart round for it and threaten to send in his heavies. Remember what we would call him?"

"...Piranha!"

"Well I thought it time to repay the compliment."

"Very apt. No one rented rent off of mankind as viciously as he did. But why are they here?"

"Because of the drought."

"What's drought got to do with it?"

"As the streams dried up the landlords were trapped in pools. They would have eaten one another if they'd not been rescued."

"Rescued! But why are they here? And how many are there?"

"Ooh, thousands."

"But why are they here?"

"Nightshade said the dogs in Bosnia were becoming glutted and needed to be starved for a week or two, so when I suggested..."

I feared for the worst.

WAR TRIALS: PICTURES THAT WILL SHOCK YOU

FREE! with today's *Chron*: an EIGHT page educational supplement to help you decide on Britain's Number One Controversial Topic:

Should the screening of "Trials" be banned from our screens?

Other newspapers have reprinted a few fuzzy and one-sided pictures snatched from a television screen.

But *The Chron* brings you EIGHT pages of ACTUAL photographs

Eight pages of special extra high quality glazed paper giving enhanced reproduction

Eight photo-packed pages taken by world leading photographers

Eight pages depicting in full detail the horrific scenes of the execution of Bosnian War criminals, their final moments, their ACTUAL DEATHS

Eight action packed pages to help you and your family participate in the topic that's sweeping the country

Eight superb pages only in *The Chron*

Companies co[n] "conniving" ch[...] "contemptable[...]

Bob Monk

A string of top companies dismissed claims made by the Susem's "Red Jim" that they were "conniving" with governments at the expense of the public. Both the CBI and IoD issued statements rebutting the claims made in yesterday's Susem telecast.

The CBI's statement said: "In the comments made on the behalf of Susem visitors are as unfounded as they are unhelpful. In today's fast changing yet uncertain world it is matter of public record that companies both large and small have entered into partnership[s] with all levels of govern[ment].

"But to claim, and with[...] out a shred of evidenc[e] either actual or anti[...] dotal that companies a[re] consorting with gover[n]ments against the pub[lic] interest is little short[...] libellous."

Global Data Servi[ces] which manages So[cial] Security payments fo[r] countries worldwide, [...] of the Red Jim's cla[ims] "Global in providing[...] expertise as well a[s] global reach of skil[...] able to provide a [...] unit cost to state fu[nded] services. Therefore[...] true beneficiary ca[n] only be the taxpa[yer] the longer term. [...] charges against u[s] similar organizati[ons] acting against citiz[...]

Senior civil servants [...] storm at Susem slur[...]

By James Jeller
Parliament Correspondent

WHITEHALL WORKERS hit back yesterday at "Red" Jim Powell, the Susem's new fiery telecaster.

Departmental heads and Under Secretaries said Red Jim's charges that they were scheming manipulators of elected ministers was totally unwarranted.

They said the charge that they were "faceless" was hurtful. All said they had seen many ministers come and go during their years at their ministries but denied they had control of any of them as Red Jim alleged.

Dame Dorothia Fitzherber[t] of the top Civil Servant[s] Union, the Premier League o[f] Mandarins said: "All of us are more than a little discomfited by this young man's unfounded assertions. It is regarded by my members as usually best practice not to comment on unsubstantiated criticism levelled against public servants.

"However, on this occasion it would be against the public interest in failing not to be seen making a robust and full rebuttal of the statements made against our members.

"I can categorically state that at no time whatsoever have any of the members of

News

US Senator scoffs at Susem 'bribery' claims

By Brett Jameson
Political Correspondent

VISITING US Senators dismissed as naive Susem claims of corruption in American political life.

Senator Dick Taft said: "The US public has the best government money can buy. Politics in America has always been

"Business to them is their lifeblood. They accept politics and big business are hand in glove. That is the way they like it. Their Congressman or woman is expected to bring subsidies from Washington to back the corporations in their district. By doing so it also ensures that they safeguard peoples' jobs and livelihoods of their loved ones.

"There may be a little irregularity from time to time but that is the way

Senator Dick Taft

Over here in Europe you have state funding of politicians but do you have any less chicanery? No sir you do not!

"This young man the Aliens now having pumping out crude propaganda, is in my estimation akin to the crude attempts made by the communists of the old Soviet Union.

"You may be sure the US Government will watching for signs of any further moves for terrorist threats to the security of the United States and the rest of the free world. You may be further assured that the government of the United States will not

Mandarins miffed at Red Jim's 'parasites' charge

WHITEHALL Sir Humphries were as red as their tape yesterday at Susem assertions they were scheming parasites.

"Red" Jim Prior, the Susem's new telecaster, accused civil servants of being the real rulers of the country. But this charge has been hotly denied.

Sir William Makespace, Permanent Under Secretary at the Home Office, said: "The man's a burk, he doesn't know a single thing we do, let alone his end from his elbow.

"If he ever shows his face round here he'll get a bunch of fives in the face. As I was saying to the gaffer just they other day, the public just don't understand that we in the

[P]oliticians slam Red [J]im's 'remote' claims

Steven Watt

[SU]SEM telecaster [Re]d Jim' Powell's [ac]cusation that poli[tic]ians do not repre[sen]t the wishes of [th]e electors drew [fie]rce denials from [M]Ps yesterday.

[S]ir Paul Body (LibCon, [...]) said: "It is bad enough that these Alien broadcasts are being shown on satellite television, but for the BBC and ITV to give air time to such libellous trash is little short of scandalous. As I understand it, it's quite outside the terms of both their Charter.

"Already I have put down an Early Day Motion for this question to be addressed as a matter of urgency".

Replying to Red Jim's charge of MPs remoteness from their constituents, Sir Paul said: "As far as I am concerned they are without any foundation. I personally oversee constituency surgeries at least twice a month which is much more than some others.

I was doing the ironing when James came on. At first he had a smile but soon had a look of seriousness about him.

"Though state administrations and officials," he said, "are unelected, anonymous they are, in theory at least, publicly accountable. However, there are other bureaucracies which although they also have increasing control over our lives, are not subject to any public scrutiny whatsoever. And there are many of them." I listened but I hadn't the faintest idea what he was on about. But all the same, as I was doing the sheets, I continued watching.

"Some operate in isolation, others liaise and cooperate with one another. They do so across the world and with each passing year gather ever more information about us. We are rarely informed what is being collected, can never know how accurate it is and this data is never used for our benefit but solely the purposes of the gatherers and their clients." I still hadn't an idea what he was on about.

"We are profiled, categorised by this data. It is packaged, sold from one organisation to another. Once these profiles are gathered they are fixed and regardless how we and our circumstances may change, they are used to assess us. And they dog us for ever. However, these data profiles also determine the circumstances in which we live, what we can do and not do with our lives." I still had no idea what he was on about except it sounded sinister and I didn't like the sound of it.

Then to baffle me even more he seemed to change what he was saying. "The sum of a country's economic activity is referred to as its gross domestic product, or 'GDP' for short. The bigger it's GDP the more powerful a country. Companies like countries also have GDPs, except theirs are called 'sales'. And again like countries the bigger their sales the greater the power and influence they wield. Ranked by the size of GDP or sales, there are in the list of the 100 biggest, thus most powerful, no less than 60 companies. In the next 100 there are 82 companies."

I finished the sheets and was on the pillow cases but at that point, if I was doing something else I would probably have clicked him off. As it was I let him blather on. "These companies now control our lives as much as governments do. In a world driven and determined as it is by credit, a person's data profile determines how they shall live. Poor profile means low or no credit. Restricted credit places restraints upon us, obstructions in our paths." At this he had my attention.

Margaret had her washing machine blow up on her. And with three kids she needed a new one right away. She went to Shellys on the Holloway Road, they had a sale with nought per cent credit. But even though she could easily keep up the payments they turned her down and wouldn't tell her why either. I mentioned it to Sophie. She said they would have run a check on Margaret and soon found she was a single mother and on the Social. And even if she was neither the fact that she lived in a council flat on a "red banded" estate meant she still wouldn't get credit. At the time I didn't know what "red banded" meant. I do now.

"Multinational companies," James continued, "now exert so much power and influence that they effectively control many countries' economies and have a say in all of them. Few of these companies produce what they sell but buy it from small companies in poor countries, over which they wield great power driving down their prices and thus the pay of the workers. Yet because of their enormous power these large companies also control the prices at which goods bearing their name are sold at." James then rolled off a list from jeans and sweat shirts to motor cars and washing machines, half I had heard of but didn't know till then that they weren't made by those companies who said they were. Or that they fixed the shop prices either.

"The people who manage these companies," James went on, "in no way own or control them. Such people come and go but the companies go on. Their administrations are the same. Workers come and go but these companies' bureaucracies still continue exerting control over their suppliers and customers alike.

"Theoretically these companies are owned by their shareholders, but except by selling their shares," he said, "what power do the holders of their shares have? And shares are rarely bought or sold on the basis of a company's morality, usually it is its profit. Most multinational companies' shares are controlled if not owned by other large organisations such as pension funds and insurance companies. In turn, those who manage them are only there for a few years, but these organisations continue for ever.

"It is as if," James said next and with an almost sad sigh, "these huge companies have taken on a life of their own. They flit about the world, playing off government against government, extracting ever bigger tax breaks and subsidies in return for investment in this country or that. They use money for these investments made in the first place from fat, barely taxed profits." By then I was on Becky's duvet cover and my own, and still wondering what he was trying to say. But with the ironing board between me and the TV I couldn't be bothered to click him off.

"With their deep pockets is it any wonder," continued James, now thundering like an Ulsterman, "multinationals find that politicians are easy prey to their blandishments. And as a result, these self-seeking politicians fall over themselves to grant multi-nationals favours in return for personal gain or political prowess in the eyes of their constituencies. How many politicians on leaving or losing office become directors of large companies with no other qualifications than having been in their past public position?

"Senior bureaucrats also succumb to the same susceptibility. In the last twenty years every US Secretary of Defense, average life in office 15 months, has, on leaving that office, joined the board of a major defence contractor to their government." James then began giving out a list of other fellows who had picked up similar perks, but at that point Becky came in the kitchen for a drink so I didn't pay much attention to him. Until that is I heard, "...has joined the board of Securitor." That's the company Sophie said refused Margaret her credit. What is more, she said it's a Belgian one registered in Panama but its head office is in Birmingham and handles the money of a Canadian loan corporation which is owned by a big car company in Detroit. She also said Shellys, which I thought was a local store, is now owned by a Japanese property developer based in Bermuda.

Becky went back to her video and I to the ironing and James. "Most countries have legislation," he said, "to ensure competition between companies. But nowadays with multinationals as powerful as they are, governments in reality are powerless to stop these large companies quietly combining into cosy cartels."

"While we, the ordinary people are the losers from such conniving our loss is exacerbated by our governments being in cahoots with these multinationals. On the micro level they have sold out to these companies, giving them increasing control of our schools, health services and much more of what was once a state's domain. On the macro level all governments, in the name of free trade have been seduced by multinationals into subverting the World Trade Organisation into furthering and safeguarding their interests at the expense of small, poor world producers and all of us, the consumers."

I had never heard of such an organisation, but James sounded so serious that I took it that it must be big and important. But on he thundered, "Government bureaucracies may increasingly control our freedoms but it is multinationals who are ever more controlling our purses and pocket books. However, both governments and these companies are dependent upon us. Dependent on us for one thing which vital to them for their existence, and that is our money. Without tax revenues governments collapse, without sales so would multinational companies..." He was still thumping on when Margaret came round with her washing to use my machine, so in the middle of his, "...is there an alternative to these manmade monsters controlling our lives, can we the..." I clicked him off.

"What do you mean?" she said folding her arms, her eyes narrowing.

I could see it was going to be an uphill task persuading Rainbow to have a quiet word with James about his telecasts.

"All this freedom and democracy stuff that he is on about," I said stepping back just in case I would end up upsetting her, "it turns people off."

"Hmm," was all she said.

"People aren't interested in democracy," I continued. "They might say they are but they are not. Politicians pretend they stand by it and everyone pretends to believe them, but really no one gives a damn. All people want, well those out there in the real world at any rate, is a quiet life and money, the more the better."

As she didn't say anything I pressed on, "The Susem now they have found Pa-tu will be gone within a month, the replacement soufins are set to arrive on schedule, the first ones Terbal says will soon be here, nobody outside of these parts is going to take up being a Nonette and even those round here are bound to fade away once the Susem have gone, we have all had a heck of an experience, leave it at that. Believing James with his telecasts are taken seriously by anyone is the height of wishful thinking and anyway it's just so naive, as if they are going to change anything. Nothing changes and even if it did it would only end it tears. It's okay him bashing politicians, everyone knows they are a bunch of grubby grabbers, not that anyone really cares, but knocking big business is asking for trouble and we are already in enough of it as it is. It'll be alright for you but me, knowing my luck, I'll end up..."

"Have you finished?" she snapped. Then, with her arms still folded she said "For a start only part of Pa-tu has been found. What crashed near São Antonio wasn't even a fifth of what should have been there."

"Well, the rest is bound to be scattered about, all they have to do is look."

"They have. Everywhere from southern Columbia to northern Peru, in fact as far south as Bolivia," she said.

"Well, the rest must still be in space or was burnt up in the atmosphere."

"It wasn't. Paceillo says their calculations from what they have found already indicates not only did Pa-tu crash on Earth but there must have been such a huge explosion that it caused the part they have found to be blasted up into space again only to fall back years later."

"It still means they will be leaving soon though."

"Not until they have found the rest of Pa-tu or what happened to him."

Though heartened that the Susem would be here a while longer I still had concerns. "But it still doesn't mean," I said, returning to the point, "that these telecasts of James will alter anything. You can't force people to change and you can't force change on them either. It won't work, it never has."

"Two," she said quietly, her arms still folded, "if you had not spent so much time with those patches you would have known just how far the Nonettes have now spread."

I had no chance of a word before she had continued, "Did you ever stop to think what was also happening while the search for Pa-tu was going on?" I had not even finished shaking my head before she was adding, "All those vedas going back and forth, to say nothing of the tocans, did you think they would be flying empty?"

"I thought they were helping in the search for..."

"They were ferrying Nonette organisers to the new areas, Colonel Tambassing's men along with hen-gers as well. And just what did you think was being ferried back?"

Seeing I had nothing to say she went on, "With Serbs and Croats going home there is a shortage of men for refilling the Pelada. So those who failed to take notice of the requests I made for non-residents to leave the region..."

"What, all those from the Pa-tu search area?"

"Only the non-natives," she said. "Regrettably many of the others attempted to hide or take no notice. Silly of them really, what with the whole region being ideal Gurkha country, Colonel Tambassing's men have had the time of their lives. They have also had wonderful cooperation from all the native tribes, or so I gather," she said now with a lightness of tone in her voice.

She still had her arms folded as I asked, "How many did they get?"

"I don't know exactly. But I do know it is every drug smuggler, bandit, militias, soldiers, police. All the areas Nonettes have been established are cleared and much else besides. With so many new Nonette communities forming each day the numbers being sent down the Pelada can only grow."

When she saw I was not following her logic, she said "The Truth Trials, they are operating there as well. The last I heard they had picked up more than 10,000 men." Then, almost off-handedly, "Slow at first but when word got out to the coca growers of the prices on offer by the Nonettes for their crops they turned in goodness knows how many traffickers."

She had me confused again and seeing so she stepped across to her desk and picked up a little pile of small sheets of paper. "The first samples," she said, handing them to me and adding, "feel them." And as I did and before I had chance to comment she said "Banknote crisp aren't they?" And they were.

"Made from coca leaf but with added arach and bone tree fibres," she said. "They have been tested in the teaching screens and match up to Susem paper exactly." As I grasped the import of what I had in my hands (teaching screen certificates are now all but bona fide currency) Rainbow continued, "As I understand it, the requirements of the Central Bank for the new banknotes will also more than match the total coca crop of the entire region."

Though of course interesting, I turned the discussion back to James's telecasts. Unfortunately I had only got as far as "But nonetheless...." when Rainbow cut in with "Three. As for the Nonettes fading away, think again. Now communities are spread as far south as Natal and Joao Pessoa the Nonette population is more than 20 million. And that is only here, haven't you heard what is happening in Romania and Bulgaria?"

I shook my head.

"As you know, Serbia like Bosnia and Croatia is now completely Nonetted. Thousands of people in the west of both Romania and Bulgaria are crossing into Serbia. There would be more if their police forces weren't trying to stop them. The Nonettes in Voyvodina alone have received more than 5,000 of their fellow Hungarian minority from Romania. Is this a sign of people not wanting to be part of a Nonette community?"

Stupidly I replied with "Brazil, Bulgaria, the Balkans, they are all poor, out of the way places. It's the rich countries where things matter..."

"There are more poor people in the world than rich ones," she said sternly. "And even in rich countries how many poor people do you think there are? How many are sleeping on the streets just in London? How many did we see in Covent Garden, the Strand?"

I was taken aback by her bashing. And with her eyes narrowing again and her tone still austere she lectured on, "Four. You are saying people aren't interested in democracy? Of course they have not been interested, how could anyone have been? What chance has any ordinary person ever had to be involved in it, in any politics? You know as I do, that the moment they are confronted with conforming to the system they either give it up as being hopeless or they are sucked into it and become corrupted by it like the rest of them?

"Look what has happened to democracy with the advent of the Nonettes. For the first time ever, people, we the ordinary people are able to participate without any need of patronage from anyone. All the people of the Nonettes are able to say how they shall run their lives, not as they are told to. Do you seriously think this is something others don't want, aren't interested in?"

"But I still..." but I was immediately wishing I had not brought up the matter in the first place.

"Don't you 'but' me," she said, her lecturing becoming hectoring. "What James has said about big companies 'Big Brothering' us is fair comment. If he is so wrong they can disprove him can't they? How many other television programmes dare say what he said for fear of these companies' sensitivities?"

As she stormed on part of me was thinking that here was someone, who before she came to Tabajara had not the slightest interest in public causes of any kind and the only paper she read seriously was 'The Stage'. And also was James now having more of an influence on her than she to him. Then, dropping her arms, widening her eyes, softening her tone and initially to my delight said, "I agree with you though about James' last telecast, it wasn't very good."

With my spirits at last brightening, she continued, "And it was rather boring I thought. If I had not been so busy I would most certainly have had him make changes, big changes. It is a pity in a way, I have not had time either to advise him on his next one, that has weaknesses as well. But don't you worry I will find the time to have a word with for his next."

"Soften them a little?" I proffered, "Not quite so critical perhaps?"

"No! More punchy, they need to be much more hard-hitting."

I gave up. Rainbow can be so confounding when she wants.

113: MR MOORE

Young Powell came on the television standing in front of a blackboard and after introducing himself he stood to the side it. Picking up a stick of chalk he said "Here are some facts.

"Last year the governments of the fifteen wealthiest members of the OECD, the rich countries' club, borrowed in the form of bonds, these are IOUs with interest, $120 trillion." Whereupon he began writing this sum, saying as he did, "That is $120 followed by twelve noughts." As he wrote the last of them and with his back still to the camera he added "Or $120,000 for every person in those countries." He wrote this on the board as well but when he had finished said "Or put yet another way, $21,000 for every man, woman and child on this planet. You may wonder," he said turning to the camera and having also written this sum, "what has been done with this money, why was it needed in the first place?"

Knowing the answers, I of course just had to say to June and Raymond who were watching with me, "It's mainly to pay back the money they had borrowed previously plus a bit extra to cover the interest." However, to my disappointment they both asked me to not to interrupt Powell, who, dusting the chalk from his hands then said "Though perhaps the really interesting question is, where did all this money come from?"

I was about to add "From the borrowers lending last year's repayments back to them again," but thought it better to say nothing.

"Large though $120 trillion is," he said next, "it is but a fraction of the amount raised from bonds issued during the same period by the world's biggest companies. If these monies, riches existed waiting to be lent, where were they? What were they? Pots of gold, mines of silver, wells of oil, though they aren't worth much of late, buildings, works of art, government printing presses?

"But there is yet more money that lenders are longing to lend," he said returning to the blackboard, "The exchange of different currencies exists to finance trade between countries. As of now $4 trillion of foreign currencies are needed each day to finance the world's trade." He wrote this number on the board but without putting in the noughts.

Still stood at the board Powell then said "Yet ten times this sum, $40 trillion..." upon which he began writing this, including the noughts, then adding"...is available every day in the world's exchange markets ready and waiting to be instantly invested, exchanged into this currency or that. Though of course..." and turning from the board, "...some people, such as those who lost out and were victims of the Euro's collapse, don't call this investing but speculating, gambling. But again where does all this money come from?"

I bridled somewhat at his use of 'speculating' and 'gambling'. Money markets are highly sophisticated vehicles for managing the requirements and sentiments of the international banking system. Though of course once the Italians had got into trouble everyone knew the Euro was a one way option and sensibly sold it short. Many of the bank's customers and indeed the bank itself did rather nicely out of this. But I also knew the answer to Powell's question, there isn't any. Well not as such. Everyone hedges their funds so if there is a loss it is minimal, but if there's a profit it is maximised because an affected country's central bank always has its reserves to spend in its attempts to shore up its national currency as well as borrowing from all the other countries' banks.

"We are told," Powell continued and changing the subject slightly I noted, "that regardless of the odd hiccup the world's monetary system is basically sound. There is always the IMF to impose its strictures on the wayward in return for baling them out with loans. But where does the IMF get its money from?"

I also knew the answer to this question. I remembered it from my old banking exams. All the countries who are members pledge credits to it. But Powell said and rather gleefully I thought, "There are no pots of gold backing the world's money. All there is are IOUs. And belief, shrouded in hope, that the future IOUs borrowers promise in repayment for their current ones, will still be exchangeable for goods and services in the future."

Powell moved away from the blackboard and walked to a pile of paper. "IOUs," he said picking up a handful and holding some of these sheets closely to the camera (I could indeed see some had "IOU" written, or rather scrawled on them along with the word "Money" but on others I noticed was written 'Betting slip'). "If a convincing enough case was put," he continued, "that these pieces of paper were backed by a solemn enough sounding promise to repay, many people would part with their savings for them, wouldn't they?"

I thought he was joking at this point but without a smile he said, "You may laugh but there are other IOUs which once were valued as valuable but proved to be...", and he screwing up the sheets of paper, "...worthless," upon which he threw them aside adding, "just as the recent collapse of many power companies has shown." Since the Susem arrived," he continued, "share prices of most companies have fallen, risen and gyrated in value across the world's markets and usually all in unison." Then looking straight to the camera he said "Why is this?

"Has the arrival of the Susem," he continued, "changed all companies' worths? Changed the value of their products, that of their employees' skills? And the 'billions' supposedly wiped off of stock markets' prices, where have they gone, who has them now? Or are the values placed on shares merely speculative, priced at what buyers can be induced to pay rather than them representing the actual asset worth of the companies concerned?

"How much are these companies' values based on what is tangible? And how much of them are based on pieces of paper, IOUs in the hands of holders, stock and bond alike?" Whereupon Powell scooped up another handful of paper and cast it in the air, saying as he did so, "Who buys these share certificate IOUs of companies? And where does the money come from to purchase them?

"Some corporate IOUs are bought by individuals but most of the money for shares comes from those who have savings in insurance policies and pensions. And for most of us, we the ordinary people, this indeed means us. And where does the money for our savings come from? It comes, does it not, from our endeavours and labours.

"Comforting isn't it to know," Powell then said and a touch sardonically I thought, "that your hard earned savings are dependent on nothing more than the outcomes of corporate and government IOUs.

"No doubt you keep careful track of your finances but would you know the answers to these five questions?" Powell then walked back to the board, wiped it clean and said "How much money have you paid to insurance and pension companies, including the amounts the government has deducted from your wages for the state pension they eventually give to you?" As he spoke he wrote what he had said. "What percentage of your payments has been invested on your behalf and how much has been siphoned off by those professionals managing your savings for their charges? What are these savings currently worth? What has been their percentage growth? How much of your savings invested by these professionals have later been sold by them at a loss?"

Turning from the board he said "The average return on an individual's institutional and state savings in the major OECD countries, made over the past thirty year period is, once government tax breaks have been excluded, just seven and a half per cent per year. This is little different than the interest most OECD governments pay to purchasers of their own IOUs, which of course are at least backed by the money they collect from us, their taxpayers."

Then with another sardonic smile he said "There are perhaps some supplementary questions you might care to ask those who manage your savings, such as how much time per employee do they spend on deciding per million dollars invested? What is the extent of professional experience of those charged with investing such sums? For the record, in the City of London the market average is one hour and three years respectively. Oh and also, the average time per investment expert working for a particular institution? In London it is less than a year."

I noticed June casting me an unsmiling sideways look. Though she said nothing and her attentions were soon back to Powell who then said "These institutional investing experts, paid the large salaries that they are, and which are derived from our savings, to work on our behalf, snap up shares of risers before they are risen, swiftly sell the failing before they fall, don't they?" He then gave a little laugh and shake of his head as he said "If only this were so.

"Others more expert than I," he said now with a sigh, "have calculated that the odds of someone who gambled their savings at racecourses and dog tracks would produce as great, if not bigger, returns than would the average investing institution from the world's stock markets."

"The surplus of our labours, savings, are taken from us by insurance and pension companies as well as governments, exchanged into IOUs which in turn are wagered as if chips in the casinos of stock markets on the success or otherwise of other IOUs. Is this the safest way of managing our savings?" At this Powell paused and I noticed June gave me another silent glance, so did Raymond.

"Our livelihoods are increasingly dependent on and controlled by financial institutions, corporate and governmental alike," Powell continued, "but institutions which, in turn, are increasingly built upon, constructed with IOUs. Is this really the basis of sound finance? The wellbeing of the world's economies, and thus those of all our lives, are dependent upon ever escalating vagaries of speculation and gambling. Is this wise?"

Powell then reached into his pocket and produced a box. No sooner had he opened it than I could see it was a pack of playing cards. Holding them to the camera he said "I wonder how lucky I will be?" upon which he peeled off the four aces. He gave a nod and a smile then walked past the blackboard, saying as he did so, "Is it safe, sensible for us, we the ordinary people, collectively as well as individually, to give these financial institutions so much control over our livelihoods, our futures?"

As soon as Powell was past the board he was stood in front of more playing cards but now constructed into the shape of a house. He then said "For how long can they go on?" Turning round to the cards he next said "The Joker is in here somewhere..." then, "...ah there it is," whereupon he proceeded to pluck a card from the house. The screen then went blank.

June, without saying anything got up and went into the kitchen but Raymond asked "Dad, what is it you actually do in your bank?"

114: WORRY

James is having me in dread. Bashing governments is bad enough, bad mouthing multinationals is risky at best, but berating the banks really is asking for trouble. And to think he used to work in one. I would have thought he would have known wiser.

Neither he nor Rainbow realise the repercussions of what they are about. This bringing in of the new is all very well for those who have little to lose, the young, the poor, like those round here once were. But out there in the real world people aren't interested in changing things despite their grumbles.

It has always been my experience that the moment someone has a piece of something they are dead set against change. To them change means risk including maybe losing what they already have. The more they have acquired the more they are against it. People who have the most, and thus to them the most to risk, are those in positions of power. Present them with change, no matter how wise, reasoned and well intended it may be they will perceive it as a threat and confront it with everything they can muster to stop it, stay their status.

With the coming of the Susem and then the Nonettes those affected directly, hereabout and in Bosnia, may have benefited from their old orders being swept away. But elsewhere those orders are still very much alive and kicking, their power and influence unaffected, let alone assailed. Usurping them will involve overturning so much of everyone else's lives that theirs will be capsized as well. And that is why there can't be any real change.

The sad thing though is that no one round here, most of all Rainbow and James, appear to have grasped this simple fact of life. And the more they pursue this pursuit of change as they are now doing, the bigger the bucket of tears when everything hereabout all falls down. They have also failed to grasp that those in power defend themselves by attacking at the first opportunity. And this will be the day after the Susem have flown away.

The only bright spot, if such can be called, is that sales of Patches are still going up and up. Demand in Bosnia is rising nicely as well. Another big order from there has just come in.

There is something else I have heard, which if so will give sales a sustained firmness. Women are having their men study extra hard to earn supplementary certificates for further purchases of Patches. The day will come no doubt when "a well educated man" may mean something more than merely learned.

oridwide sightings rise said to be causing authorities grave concern

Massive surge in Susem spaceships sightings seen

Donold Cooke
ien Affairs Editor

NCREASING numbers Susem spacecraft are eing reported from round the world. The eason for the rise is not et known and Alien elecasts have given no ndication for the ncrease. But authorities world-wide are said to be cautiously monitoring events.

The main area of the rise in sightings has been across southern and central to Austria. This is the same region where a month ago a number of other, smaller Alien craft were seen.

But an increase in sightings has been witnessed across North America as well as Australia, New Zealand, southern Africa, and northern India.

Jim Hawkins, a defence analyst who has studied the increased sightings, ... pattern to the spacecrafts' movements.

He said: "All these Alien flights have been over mountainous regions, the Pyrenees, Alps in Europe, the Rockies, Appalachians in the US, the Dividing Range in Australia and so forth. This indicates they are either seeking something from these areas or they are planning something there. So far there have ...

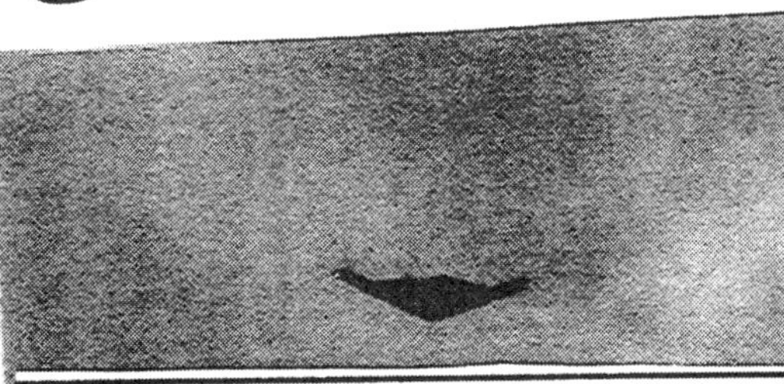

Companies seethe at '... Big Brother' slur acc...

ena Juniper
inary and General Reporter

DUSTRY bosses yesterday nied claims by the Susem's 'Red n' that they are adopting a Big other tactics.

n yesterday's Susem telecast ed Jim' Prior accused busisses across the world of spying d snooping on the lives of dinary people. He also accused em using the information for eir own mercenary purposes.

Mathew Harding, press spokesan for Clayings Bank said: "Yes, e bank does hold information on ... customers.

"This is inevitable, and yes we do use it to market the Bank's products. But it is simply untrue to accuse us of providing that data to other companies. It is something Claying would never do. After all we, like other responsible organizations bind ourselves to all the terms of all the data protection laws."

Prudent Assurance's spokesperson was just as vehement in her denunciations of Red Jim. She said: "At Prudent we make it a positive act of policy never to divulge details of our client base without having obtained their ...

Aliens' forces rush ... fill Brazilian vacu...

By Jon Malcolm
Susem Affairs Editors

FOLLOWING the latest Susem offensive, forces backed by them have rapidly occupied the territories vacated by the fleeing Brazilian army.

In yesterday's Susem telecast, viewers were shown formations of the so called "Nonettes" greeting people of the 'liberated' areas. In one scene, which could have come straight from the film "Zapista", a column of hundreds of men on horseback, in white mili... Movement Sem Terra (The Landless Ones). Over shouts of "Viva liberdade! Terra portodo!" (Freedom, Land for all), the announcer said all newcomers would be given ownership title to land under Nonette control.

Further scenes showed Nonette forces arriving in the coastal city of Natal. The announcer said that earlier there had been extensive arson and looting in the city centre and showed streets of burnt out buildings. She also said ...

Worldwide release campaign yields succes...

Sa. Pelada prisoners to be freed

By Phillip Bangles
Aliens Editor

MANY of the men abducted by the Susem and imprisoned in the Serra Pelada are to be returned it was announced yesterday.

An estimated 100,000 men could be home as early as next week. Their release from captivity follows wide-spread and often bitter campaigns waged by the men's families and supporters against their former employers to agree the Susem's terms.

Woodmen released

Most of those due for return are loggers and other timber workers. The lumber companies have been forced to plant 100 trees and provide each with resources necessary for each man's exchanging a family member or shareholder for each employee held captive.

Trawlermen held

Few trawlermen are expected to be among those being released as most of their former employers have so far failed to decommission their boats.

Miners also held

Also absent from those returning are quarry and opencast mining workers. Again there has been a refusal among their former bosses to turn their quarries over to reclamation.

Although both of these industries are currently subject to fierce campaigns to change their position and speed the imprisoned ...

'I fear the worst' say ... facing arms charges ...

By Jamie Lee
in Racusa

Former Cheltenham MP Sir Hugh Russet-Brown facing charges of supplying arms to the former Croatian regime, spoke of his fears of his forthcoming trial.

Sir Hugh, who professes his innocence, appeared a shadow of his former assertiveness. Speaking in the presence of prison warders, he said he had been treated well during his time in custody ex... electric stun batons he is accused of supplying to the Croatians had been used on him.

Sir Hugh was appearing in the company of other foreign nationals who also face similar charges of arming the Serbs and Croats. Although there are seven other holders of British passports on trial, Sir Hugh and disgraced former businessman, Bernard Ellis, are the only two who are ...

However, Bosnian authorities say their investigations on others are still continuing.

Despite the presence of warders Sir Hugh was able to freely voice his fears of the fairness of his court hearing which is set for two days time. He said: "I have heard rumours that everyone who goes into their (Bosnian) courts is found guilty."

Later, Ragusian legal sources said ...

Alien's spaceship found

By Gertrude Ashcroft
Alien Correspondent

VIEWERS worldwide were last night shown stunning scenes of the Susem recovery of the remains of their missing spacecraft (more pictures pages 6-7).

Susem telecaster Rainbow Louis announced that the lost craft's remains were located more than 500 metres below the surface and spread over an area of 20 square kilometres. The force and speed at which the doomed spaceship crashed to Earth caused it to penetrate deep into the ground pulling the topsoil in after it.

The telecast showed massive columns of rock suspended in midair by the Susem's "veda" space-planes while other mac...

115: KEN

"Time is Tight, Booker T and the MG's, from the movie Uptight," mouthed Dennis. Bleeding know-it-all, didn't need him telling me that.

But I don't say anything, I'm all eyes on the screen. It's like looking out a plane from high up. The music fades, then all a sudden, whoosh, down the picture dives straight though the clouds. It's still going down and down like anything and towards these brown hills. With me thinking that the camera, or whatever, is just about to crash, when, in the nick of time it slows right back and glides down the side of one of these hills. The camera then goes to the bottom of this hill, turns and flies along just above some rocks. The music comes back on and the picture is rising and falling over these rocks as if in time with it.

The camera comes to the end of the hill, then all of a sudden it swings round a corner and with the music still going, the camera shows that halfway up the next hill there's a village of all these white houses.

Then quick as a flash the camera's flying up to this village. There is still the music but in no time the camera is cruising down the main street, people are looking out of their windows, kids outside are waving. The camera still cruises down the street but all of a sudden it veers round a corner, and then, with the music fading, there's young Jim with his arms out half-stretched.

Straight away he says "Welcome to our world of security...yours of tomorrow..." No sooner has he spoken and with the music still faint, the camera passes over him and across to some blokes sitting with their little screen things. The camera then halts and Jim's adding "...a world without unemployment, one where everyone has jobs. A world where everyone's savings are invested in the surest, safest and most speculative-free investment of all, themselves!"

The camera now goes down this next street and with the music still in the background into this square. There are now more people, all sorts, sat studying at their screens, and Jim saying, "Everyone earns from every moment of their study." These people then look up and they are holding handfuls of what looks like money, and all together they shout "Power! Power! We've got the power!" The camera goes forward and Jim is saying "Education pure and simple, not training..." and with more people raising their heads, arms, he adding "...is how the full dynamic of everyone is realised."

The camera flies on, over more people studying at their screens, and Jim next saying "Education is the enabler of invention..." With the camera now whizzing down a tunnel, Jim adds, "...curiosity and questioning are the primers of progress." All of a sudden there is a blue flash of light and the camera is in a cavern which has a greenish glow. It then goes straight across to this clump of weird looking plants, like thin flat trees they are, and from the men stood by them I can see that they are at least twenty feet high. Jim then says "Here forests aren't felled for planks as in your old world. In ours they have been developed to grow as them."

The picture then moves between these trees and Jim says "With accelerated growing, coppices mature from saplings to sawing in seven days." The camera halts in front of two other men. One is holding a soufin, the second a rod pointed at the base of a tree and Jim says "Laser saw, developed here." The tree falls, the camera moves through another wall of flashing blue light and out of the cavern. It then goes along another tunnel, the music is still faint, and into yet another cavern. Here there are more trees, but smaller with glass tubes round them and Jim saying "In your old world trees are felled for furniture, here they are grown, shaped into it. The camera stops at more men and who are carrying wooden squares and Jim saying "Tree window frames grown to size within the week." As the men walk to another tunnel there is a sudden flash of bright white light and Jim saying "Growing time acceleration."

The camera moves on, past the men, through another blue flash of light. With the music fading away to almost nothing, the camera is out in the open again. It next shoots up the side of another hill, over the top and then down the other side and as it does so another, bigger village comes into view. Then it's like before, the music comes on, the camera is cruising down the street and with people looking and waving to it.

The camera goes around a corner, the music fades, and lo and behold there is Jim again. The camera stops and looks down at him. "In our world," he says, looking up, "Everyone is part and participant of their communities." The camera then flies past a queue of people going into a hall. And as they do so they all hold up slips of white paper and shout "Power! Power! We've got the power!" and Jim saying "Monthly community election."

The camera then goes around another corner and there are half a dozen kids lined up at one of those health booth things they have. It hovers by them, they are waving, and Jim says "What does security mean to you, personally? Good health? Continuing good health? In our world every community provides it for all their people all of the time. No heart disease, cancers corrected, ageing slowed."

But no sooner has he spoken, and with the music becoming louder, the camera now cruises along a curved road. It then goes into this market and which has stalls piled with food and people crowded round them. These people then look up all smiling to the camera and with the music fading again, Jim says "Does your security mean freedom from hunger? Here there is food aplenty for everyone." The people then pick up what is in front of them, melons, bananas, tomatoes, and holding them up above their heads, shout, "Power! Power! We've got the power!" and Jim adding "And it's the very best, no chemicals or sprays, organic as can be..." The people put the stuff in their bags and hand over money to the stallholders, and Jim adds"...and everyone has the wherewithal to afford what they want. If they do not have a job all they need do is to study."

The camera flies out of this market, and with the music's coming louder again, past some houses. In no time though it's flying low over what look like allotments but they are all overgrown with weeds and things. The camera then speeds over the edge of what must be a steep hill for it is now flying high up and going towards another hill. But all a sudden the camera turns back and goes along down the side of this hill it has just left. And oh, what a fantastic sight.

All down the side of the hill are lines of little carved terraces, like sets of giant stairs they are. People are standing on them and looking up and waving in time with the music. Behind them are houses, well not ordinary houses but ones built into the hillside itself.

The camera zooms to one of these terraces. With the music fading Jim then says "Does your security mean a home? A safe home, not a landlord's or a moneylender's but your own home, all yours?"

The camera then hovers outside a window of one of the houses and I can see that its frame is made out of one piece of wood. The camera flies through the opened window and into a bedroom, it goes all round, a boy is sitting at a desk with his little screen. Then the camera goes out of the door and down the stairs, along a hallway and into this kitchen, parlour. Nice it is, homely, two women are sitting at a table, one waves to the camera. The camera then goes back down the hall and out of the front door and Jim says "With a little help from our friends these homes have been created, as are theirs, in harmony with the land, not abusing it as so often happens in your old world..." The camera then flies out beyond the terraces and Jim adds,"...in our world all new buildings are in unity with their surroundings."

The camera swoops up and down, back and forth in front of the terraces. People are still swaying and waving in time with the music but now they have soufins in their other hand. Jim then says "Here everyone earns or learns enough money for their homes."

The camera then goes really close to these people. They are still moving in time with the music but now all of them are holding the soufins above their heads. Jim then says "With the soufins, both you and us are experiencing the freedom, boons of portable, personal energy supply." But no sooner had he spoken than the people along the terraces are calling out "Power! Power, we've got the power!" Then, and I still don't understand it, they're next calling out "Power! Power! You've got power! You too can have power!"

The camera then flies up and away from these people and with the music still faint, Jim says "Now is the time for everyone everywhere to grasp this new world, its opportunities, its true security." With the music now coming louder again the camera flies up and up. It is still climbing when all of a sudden it passes back through the clouds. The music then ends and the screen goes fizzy blank.

IF YOU HAVE EVER SAID THAT HANGING IS TOO GOOD FOR THEM

Then "TRIALS" is the show for you!!

By ANGIE SCRAGG

SLI TV's daily programme beamed live from Bosnia is a must if you think criminals are treated too leniently by our Courts.

"Trials" demonstrates just how good Bosnia's progressive system of justice is for victims and perpetrators alike. Victims have the satisfaction of knowing their assailants received what was due to them. Criminals are spared the torture of lingering on Death Row for years or the humiliation of medial and psychiatric reports.

Also, in Bosnia's system of justice there is no wasting of public m[oney] on prisons, which everyone kn[ows] are no more than dens which [turn] petty criminals into professi[onal] ones. It is a system of [...] sentencing and just rapid execu[tion]. Short, sharp and swift, no p[...] footing about.

The Bosnian system also sh[ows] how crime can actually be mad[e to] pay. The TV rights have been g[iven] exclusively to SLI TV afte[r a] ferocious battle between severa[l] TV stations, all desperate to win the rights of a potential gold mine.

Bishop to lead Trials protest march

By Julius le Righteous
Religious Correspondent

The Bishop of Buckingham is to lead a march on SLI TV's Isleworth headquarters in protest against their screening of the Bosnian War Trials.

The Bishop, the Rev Hugh Latimer speaking from his campaign headquarters at [...] said: "It is vital that the many people who are revolted by SLI TV's constant parrying to baser instincts of human nature join with me in saying to SLI TV this must stop."

What response there will be to the Bishop's call to join with him is open to question. SLI has so far declined to comment on

Banks say: 'Codswallop' to Red Jim's 'dodgy financers' swipe

By Ann Imp
City Editor

LAST night's Susem telecast criticising banks and other financial institutions drew swift and angry responses from City and market pundits alike.

Susem telecaster 'Red Jim' Powell claimed the world of global finance was a sham. He accused financial institutions of ripping off ordinary investors in charging enormous hidden fees and giving shoddy service.

But both banks and securities b[ro]kers were [...]tting Red [Jim...]

Head of Hidekitojo Securities' London HQ, Justin Fortin-Green's said: "Powell's ill informed comments do nothing but harm to the whole inter-national financial sector.

"What he and many like him do not grasp is that today's global capital markets are very sophisticated vehicles in the management of cost to yield ratios in maximising positive balance margins in intertransaction trades.

"They are so complex that they are beyond the comprehension of the ordinary layman. But take it from me the most important tool we have in our armoury is confidence. Should that waver then the whole of the worlds financial markets would collapse. And it could also have a knock on effect into the real world."

Darrin Stevens, a senior market maker with May & Day, echoed Fortin-Green's sentiment. He said: "The man's a burk. Just because he's got a toffs voice he thinks he's a bleedin' know all.

"Take it from me when me and the boys are in front of our dealing screens we don't have time to ponce on about the meaning of everything. Where we are ev[ery]thing's deal driven, w[e have] just seconds to buy [or] sell. And when I'm ta[lk]ing dealing I'm talk[ing] millions a throw, you['ve] got to have your marb[les] for that sort of thing. I['m] no wonder everyon[e's] burnt out at 25.

"But if this so-call[ed] Red Jim keeps going [on] the way he is, he's like[ly] to mess everything u[p] for everyone and th[at] means my bonus migh[t] be slashed down to fiv[e] figures. And with the size of the mortgage o[n] my new house out i[n] Billericay I'll be wel[l] screwed," he said.

Riots and rising unrest in Romania

By William Slatina
in Bucharest

THE rising tide of unrest in the northwest Romanian province of Transylvania finally spilled over into full scale violence. Hundreds of people are reported to have been wounded in pitched battles between members of Romanian Hungarian minority and police

The towns of Timisoara, Arad and Deva and many villages close to the border with Serbia saw there worst of the disturbances. The current trouble was sparked off by the deaths of a family of five killed when the car they were in crashed while being pursued by the police

The victims, all from Timisoara, were among the many thousands trying to cross the Romanian frontier into neighbouring Voyvodina region in Serbia An estimated [1]0,000 are reported to have already crossed the border in recent weeks Most are from Romanian oppresssed Hungarian minority

Large numbers of Romanian security forces are deployed along the border in an attempt to stop would-be migrants from joining with fellow Hungarians in Voyvodina and their Nonette communities. Romanian Prime Minister, Ionescu Cervoa, has barred people from crossing the border unless they have paid an "Exit Tax" to cover their cost to the government.

As most of the people who want to leave the country do not have the money - up to $5,000 - [...] undercover [...] those fle[eing ...] border Th[...] fuelled rese[ntment ...] estimated [...] minority

It was this [...] boiled over [...] chase and s[...] were the fi[...]

SLI rating hit[s] all time hig[h]

AUDIENCE VIEWING figures for SLI TV's 'Trials' programme has broken all previous records.

A triumphant Derek Igg said: "It just goes to show how right Dicky Bear was in snapping up the Caught deal. With the exception of the Vatican, "Trials" is now watched in every country in the world.

"It also sends a strong message to our critics. By knocking us they're knocking the people, the ordinary people. So let all these woolly minded, leafy lane living limp-wristed top table toffing so-called 'liberals' shut their holier than thou mouths just this once and let ordinary viewers watch what they like watching which of course is seeing a good topping, the more the merrier."

Aliens Al[ps] abductions

[...] Reynold Grenchen
[...] Zurich

[PO]LICE forces throughout Switzerland and Au[stria iss]ued warnings against walking or climbing in [iso]lated areas of the Alps. Their warnings follo[w a spate]
[...]ing of Alien abductions during yesterday.
[S]cores of climbers across both countries, as w[ell as ...] south-eastern France and southern Germany a[re rep]orted being carried off by the Aliens The [ind]ications are the numbers taken could run into [sev]eral hundreds.
[T]he Bernese Oberland has been the most affect[ed wit]h scores of climbers reported missing, police

Latin defence chiefs meet as Alien invasion spreads

By Craig Penedo
In Rio de Janeiro, Brazil

THE CHIEFS of Staff of a clutch of Latin American countries met in urgent session yesterday in a bid to halt the growing threat posed by the Susem.

Brazil, Colombia, Peru and Bolivia are all suffering incursions by Susem backed forces. Worried Generals and Defence Staff appear to have sunk their differences in the interests of presenting a united front in the face of a common threat

No statement was issued after the gathering and insiders are doubtful if there could have been any substantial progress on a joint plan of action to combat the growing problems posed by the Aliens

Among the difficulties faced by Defence Chiefs are the problems posed by many of their own populations in the affected areas. Rather than fleeing the Susem advances many appear to be welcoming them

Another difficulty, if the Brazilian military is any guide, is unwillingness of frontline soldiers to engage Aliens. The only hope for the four countries' military is that now the Susem claim to have found their missing spacecraft they will depart to whence they came

However, should the Generals then attempt to recover their lost territory and restore the old order they may be doing so against their own people Not that an-

116: EXCITEMENT

James's telecasts have been hit by a whirlwind, Rainbow. She has taken charge. From across the entire region she's enlisted casts of thousands. She has whipped up no end of enthusiasm to assist production, all the Nonettes, even the Susem from Paceillo downwards. The machines and Terbal, too, have joined in. But I'm keeping out of her way.

I see trouble looming, big trouble. James's past telecasts being over-emphatic, and though troublesome, could be dismissed as ineffectual but with Rainbow directing they are bound to be effective. And that is the worry. They run the risk of people actually going along with them. This will create conflict with the majority who won't. As these will include those in positions of power I fear for the worst.

While this is bad enough I can't see the Susem, especially with Paceillo now taking an interest, standing aside from aiding anyone becoming a Nonette. Up to now, apart from the odd grumble of those losing out, the actual impact of the Susem has been benign. The changes they have wrought are those which most people, more so the middle classes in the West, have been in favour of, for no other reason than all have benefited. The Susem, besides dishing out free energy supplies, removing nuclear power, weapons, saving the fishes, forests and all those other faraway green things, have been manna to well-meaning middle class minds. But aside from organising a bit of bashing of the baddies in Bosnia, the Susem haven't actually changed anything. Out there in the big wide world everyone's everyday life continues much as before. And there's the rub.

People, especially the middle classes, while forever advocating change for others are dead against any occurring to themselves. But Paceillo's 'proposals' if applied let alone accepted will transform everything. And that is why, except for a tiny minority there will be vast reaction against. Trouble will come when the Susem intervene on the behalf of would-be Nonettes. It will be against the wishes of everyone else, especially those who are powerful. The Susem will alienate these people and then they really will be viewed as 'Alien Invaders'. What is worse is that the Susem will have no alternative than to wade in. If they don't they will lose face. Should they lose this it will mean that they will be seen as vulnerable and run the risk of being attacked. If they are, it will mean we, I, will be attacked as well. Either way the outlook is grim.

If only James and Rainbow had listened to what I had said none of this needed to have happened. And if they go on the way they are, both of them will end up being reviled. This is another reason why I'm staying away.

The more I think the implications through the more I worry. All the people who don't go along with Paceillo's proposals, or as is more than likely, stopped by governments from doing so, will be fighting over the new soufins from the minority who have them. Because of the inevitable power shortages and a rush to generate all that can be, pollution safeguards will go out of the window. This will mean there will be more muck in the air than before the Susem arrived (so much for their 'good works'). If it wasn't for the Patches I would be laying serious plans for leaving.

It is not that I'm in any way anti-Nonette, far from it. Their network is a wonder for distribution. Outlets for Patches are in every community and at the minimum of cost. Demand for them is growing by the day (to say nothing of the rise of the company's coffers). The Nonettes working in nines is proving a marvel for production too. Working as cells each coordinates with the others. There is no need for any middle management. And senior ones aren't much required either.

Now that production and distribution are running smoothly I have more time to myself. Time to catch up on my studies (I have been nagged of late both by Lucia and my group for missing my practicals). And with the Susem back from researching the remains of Pa-tu, I've also time to have another word with Menpemelo about auras, waves and contexts.

From what she and Terbal have told, everything is composed from three types of waves. There are the spits and spume of Tertiary ones, 'frothicles', which we think of as 'matter'. They evolved from Secondary waves which in turn are what I suppose we call 'energy'. These two types of waves interact and in doing so create differing sorts of resonations. However, both of them are no more than the surface of Primary waves. There are much more of these than the other two, just as there is more sea than its surface. And like the sea, Primary ones are not really waves but currents, like the Gulf Stream is. Though Tertiary and Secondary waves flow over or more usually oscillate on the sea of Primary ones, their interactions are forever going back down into it and becoming part of this sea. As Menpemelo had said, Tertiary waves can revert back into Secondary waves and they, in turn, into Primary waves.

But also, these waves come in three categories, solitons, scalars and vectors. Solitons, apart from being solitary are very big. Menpemelo also says these can travel very fast, faster than the speed of light even, but I'm so not sure of this. Examples of these she says are tidal bores of some rivers such as the Severn's and the whopper on the Amazon. Menpemelo also says the Great Red Eye on Jupiter is soliton produced, though I'm not sure of this either.

Scalars come in walls of waves like those on the sea, and vectors are ones which start from a point then spread out like ripples from a bubble popping up. To complicate things these two categories of waves come in all sizes, speeds and steepness of oscillation.

This is one part, the other is contexts. These are the one, two and three of length, area or plane and volume, as well as the fourth of time. Then there is the fifth context, the quinth. Menpemelo said that in one sense everything, 'matter' or more precisely 'frothicles', and their interactions with Secondary waves are composed of points, zero contexts, and so in another sense they aren't here. It is as if everything has a ghost. Or billions of them rather, for she also said everything which occurs will leave an imprint. And everything which occurs is composed of planes, each a little bit changed (alike in a way, to the airplanes I used to draw in the corners of school exercise books and if the pages were flicked fast enough the airplane would appear as if it was moving). So it is not 'matter' as such which has ghosts but each and every interaction.

Then I remembered Paceillo saying, and Menpemelo too, about the search for Pa-tu, how they could analyse wave signatures left behind by past events. And of her mention of the butterfly migrations from Mexico to Canada, how the grandchildren found their way back to the exact same tree their grand-parents flew from. How it is possible to know which way someone has gone in the snow by their footprints, and if a follower is a Sherlock Holmes it would also be possible to surmise all sorts of things of the walker.

I also remembered Menpemelo's mention of quantums and learnt with Lucia too, that everything is in, made up of, lots of little linked boxes undulating up and down. How there are contents in them at one moment and only the marks of their movement the next. Lucia also mentioned Alice's (Wonderland) Cheshire cat, and how in the end only its smile remained. So as I see it, every-thing all about us is moving, drifting back and forth between the quinth context and just the ordinary ones. And also that we humans aren't aware of this very much but others, animals and the Susem are. And I had also remembered the leaf-cutting ants, how in the quinth context there are relation-ships not just between ants but with one being and another, others.

It was with all these thoughts, especially auras, that I sought out Menpemelo. When I had finally caught up with her, I said "Auras, what exactly are they, what do they consist of?"

"Excitement."

She crestfell me. And to myself I said "What manner of reply is this?"

But being a kindly Job she then elucidated. "As you may recall, every Tertiary, Secondary wave interaction is recorded by subtle changes to the composition of Secondary waves. So too of course are those between Secondary waves themselves."

While this was straight forward, what she said next had me baffled.

"Sentient entities register resonance interactions by way of elevated sensory receptors."

But before I'd time for a "What?" she had said "For example," and taking hold of my hand, "If I blew gently on your skin here you would sense it, but if I blew here," and she doing the same to the back of my head, "you would not. In the same way, some beings' skins such as those of your planet's worms are receptive to Secondary waves in the wavebands of light. However, higher animate orders have evolved specific receptors to such waveband oscillation. Put simply, eyes.

"As I am sure you are already aware," she said, "eyes do not 'see' just as ears do not 'hear'. They, like other sensory organs merely react to, receive the oscillations of Secondary waves and their interaction resonances with Tertiary ones. What is received by them are these oscillations. They do not interpret but merely transmit them onwards to areas within a being's neural networks. Though by so doing they further stimulate within those networks more resonance response interactions.

"A being's neural networks are in a constant state of monitoring and responding to the requirements and functioning of its entity, its body," she continued. "External activated stimuli merely add to and mix with those resonances generated internally. It is the interactions of both these upon which a being interprets and initiates response to external events.

"However, and as I mentioned earlier," she continued, "the data processing functioning, abilities and speed of animate neural cellular structures is extremely limited and slow. All are subject to constant widespread protein renewal and transmission speeds of less than 120 metres a second. Yet, and as again I am sure you are aware, most beings' data analysis and responses function at many, many times this speed, in fact faster than your most advanced digital computing facilities. For example, according to our assessments the computing power required to calculate and calibrate the adjustment of a vertebrates' blood sugar levels due to exposure of five degrees temperature change is greater than your entire planet currently possesses. Yet your body, for example, does it instantly and..." and after she taking a pause, "...throughout its entire existence."

With me inwardly saying "The things she knows," Mempemelo continued. "Incoming stimuli initiating responses within a being's higher neural networks, brain, immediately co-ordinate with their aural falx-cerebri pathways. These are in continual inter-communication between the aura, in higher order vertebrates at least, and the cerebral hemispheres, principally the left frontal lobe. The moment external stimuli initiation occurs discrete packages of data are transmitted from the aura to the cerebral hemispheres."

She took another pause, and probably noticing I was baffled, said "While not a perfect analogy, think of a brain as a computer terminal and the aura as a data bank, hard disk. The aura holds a number of program memory disks. The moment a specific data request is initiated by the brain the relevant disk is on-lined. Of course it is not just a single disk but several, often many. The brain is thus instantly provided with relevant data facilities to enact enabling cerebral and physiological response to incoming stimuli. While aural programs are in situ within the brain they are updated with new stimuli and the consequent response outcomes. This also involves program updating of other disks."

I ventured, "How many?"

But apart from her "Many...many", Menpemelo continued as though I had not interrupted, "At present it is no more than our conjecture, hypothesis of what is occurring within an auralate structure, except that we are aware its data programs are in constant, mutually relative interaction. This is based on observation that it is not merely a passive entity but it is also an initiator and implementer of response and reaction. Thus in a sense a being's aura is a sentient entity in its own right. And as such is capable of communication with other like entities. As I have said, 'excitement'."

By now I was bursting with questions including just what did she mean by 'excitement'. But before I had chance to speak Pheterisco appeared.

"Come and watch," she called with urgency in her voice and a smile to her face, "Rainbow's next telecast is about to be screened." Menpemelo and I were then dragged off to see what she had done.

117: SIÂN

"You will be dancing round your handbag next I suppose? And at your age!" Sometimes Anne can be so cutting.

All the same I felt such a chump. Because I had had the sound turned up I hadn't heard her come in. I was watching James and the people with him. The moment he came on, before he appeared, when the picture showed from high up above the clouds, the same as the last one had started, I knew the music right away. It was "Higher and Higher", about the first record I ever bought. Without a thought I was bopping to it (as you do when nobody is looking). When the people with James sang out "Higher, higher and higher..." I was waving my arms with theirs as well.

Not at first though. The camera zoomed down and flew over rows of factory roofs. It came to the end of these roofs and then swooped over their edges, and with the music fading, there was James. At once he said "Welcome to our world of work...yours of tomorrow...capitalism with a human face."

The camera whizzed down a road between these factories. Outside every one there was a person swaying in time with the music and holding up a big card reading "We have the vote," and James saying "Employing nine people enables a company to participate in their community..." As he said this, more people were coming out of the factories, "...as they tithe a tenth of their profits to their communities," he continued, "it is only equitable that they have as much say...responsibility for their community's management as do the people."

The camera came to the end of the line of factories. It then turned around and went back along them again. By now even more people had streamed out of the buildings and all were holding up soufins. The music came louder. The people were singing "Higher, higher and higher..." (and so was I) and James saying "Every vote also brings free soufins."

Halfway down the road the camera flew inside one of the factories. The music faded and James said "In our world, as studying earns everyone enough to live in comfort...no one need work..." The camera then went over to some people grouped in circles, "...but as in your world," he continued, "everyone likes, wants to work...wants a job to go to, one they like doing..." The people were feeding heaps of white chips into a machine but also were moving and raising arms as in time with the music which was still faint, "...here, just as people study in independent teams so do they work as them," he said.

The camera hovered about these people, they still dancing and waving and James continuing, "Companies assign production to outside teams..." With the camera now going to the other end of the machine, "...of three or nine people all skilled in specific tasks..." The camera then showed lines of little white tubes coming out the machine and onto a conveyor belt and James adding, "...moving from contract after contract." The camera followed the lines of tubes. James then said, "Time isn't frittered on the soullessness of pointless training programmes either...ability is gained through experience...and backed by bespoke screen seminars...hands-on tuitional experience." The camera still followed the lines of tubes. The music came on again, but still faint, and James saying "Operating in this way cuts administration...overheads reduced...operating margins raised..." With the conveyor rolling the tubes out of the building the music came louder. But James still continued, "...as everyone earns from studying, incomes paid to these outside teams have to be higher...old style employee employment has all but faded away." The tubes plopped into boxes. The music came yet louder but James still spoke, "Here earnings are high by your world's standards...but as the leaden hands of taxation, corruption and state bureaucracy of yours do not exist in ours, unit production costs are lower, profitability higher."

The music came even louder. The boxes slid down a chute and onto a lorry. Around it were more people all swaying and singing "Higher, higher and higher..." It was in the middle of this when Anne came in the flat.

I did click the sound down but no sooner was she in the sitting room and being caustic, than she had swept out again. I got up to follow her, worrying that I'd upset her but hearing the bathroom door close I continued watching James. The music was still playing with him now saying"...investment increased...purchasing power higher...sales soaring..." though by then the camera was following the lorry out the factory along a road.

I heard the bathroom door open, then the kitchen's. I went out to see Anne. She had been crying. I asked her what was the matter. When she told me I nearly said "It's your own fault for going out with a married man," but instead I said to her to come and sit down. However, she said she would make some tea. So I went back to watching James.

He was now in the middle of a street market surrounded by hundreds of people swaying in time with the music and he saying "No one in our world is by your standards rich, but neither are any poor...no one need ever be in want, suffer indignities, humiliation of poverty...consumers needing credit have it... all backed by their communities...un-payable debts studied off...purchaser protection irrelevant...producers tied to, part of their communities..." A loud crash came from the kitchen.

Before I even reached the door there were more. I had it open just in time to save the jug I had given Anne for her last birthday, though not the teapot nor half her cups and saucers. The moment I had hold of the jug, Anne was boo-hooing, then cussing this Howard she had been seeing something rotten for going back to his wife.

As I sat back down on the settee, Anne in my arms, I really felt I was her older sister after all. I held her and let her sob on thinking it the best but adding "There, there." It also occurred to me this was the first time in ages someone had dropped her, usually it is she who does the dropping.

Meanwhile on the screen the music still continued and even more people were moving in time with it. But the location had changed to a village square. James's enthusiasm still continued unabated. Over Anne's sobs I listened as best I could,"...Nonette community structures ensure efficient low cost, rapid distribution...everything is now routed though them...mailing lists obsolete ...credit rating data worthless...theft and fraud pointless...eavesdropping, surveillance things of the past..." Yet more people had appeared, and all singing "Higher, higher and higher..."

Anne stopped sobbing. I said "Better now?" She nodded, wiped her eyes, stood up and went to the kitchen mumbling she would make coffee instead. James was still giving forth, "...through the Nonettes people, businesses large and small are completely integrated...no conflict of interest...no old world state interference...no bureaucracies..."

I was about to give Anne a hand when the picture changed to a large square. It was packed with thousands of people. Again all were singing and swaying with the music. James said "Park Municipal, Fortaleza, in front of the old cathedral..." As he spoke the camera panned up and showed many more people who had climbed all over it including the steeple. Above the singing James continued, "...in our world enterprise, invention, endeavour, expertise flourish freely, free from the grasping of state and other of old world vested interests..." The people I noticed, though still raising their arms in time with the music, were holding up soufins and chanting "Power! Power! We've got the power!"

Anne came in with the coffee, handed me mine without saying anything and sat on the floor, resting against me. James still continued, though by now he was almost shouting, "...just as soufins have given both you and us the boon of free personal, portable, clean energy, now is the time for everyone everywhere to grasp our new world of work..."

The people were now chanting "Power! Power! You too can have our power!" By then James actually was shouting, "...a world free from exploitation ...people and commerce in harmony of common interest...everyone a job when they want one, every business is freed from restraints...yet all accountable to all."

Though the crowd were chanting louder and louder the camera began climbing higher and higher. Soon it was back above the clouds again and the screen then went fizzy blank .

The moment people take to beliefs it is always the same, they become just like scientists with theories who demean flaws in their reasoning to irrelevances. None, from Rainbow upwards and downwards, have given a thought to the repercussions of their proposals (or 'imposals' rather).

James with his banking background should know better but he is beyond reasoning with. And Rainbow, filled with the zealotry of the newly converted is all warrior to any suggestion of easing back on her telecasts. She too has slipped into the same self-deluding snare as James, that the cheering of crowds hereabout will have echoes everywhere. When I stated the obvious to Rainbow, that this bit of Brazil is backland, the world outside is where reality lay, she rebutted me with an earful of facts and figures and a fair number of fleas as well.

As for the Susem and Paceillo in particular, she and they are as adamant as before on the terms for replacement soufins. And now that I hear they are closing in on the remaining remains of Pa-tu there is no pressure on them to change their stance. As for the Nonettes, and despite burgeoning numbers and ever expanding domain, they will soon be in Salvador at the rate they are going, and while also now knowledgeable of many things, alas know next to nothing of the complexities and connivings of the big wild world outside.

So when D Day comes there is going to be one heck of a bang. And that is why, with reluctance and though aware the grave risks outside, I have decided on departing before the balloon goes up.

It will be unwise of course do so openly, people would ask questions. Withdrawing the Patches money will take some time as well, changing it to dollars without eyebrows being raised. How I will make my departure is a worry, but an ideal opportunity has arisen. Samples of Patches sent to the Nonettes in Sarajevo have borne serious interest. And it makes commercial sense to pay them a visit. From there it will be simple to locate some safe place.

But with so many questions remaining it also makes sense to use the time remaining to find answers from Terbal and Menpemelo. When last we met she left me hanging on auras and their ever updating disks. Though they are puzzling it is her mention of auras being 'sentient entities' which had me really querulous.

With ever more Susem arriving, it took a while to find Menpemelo with a moment to spare. She is now not just ordinary busy but social busy too. Sometimes there are so many Susem lolling around their refectory smoking, drinking and roistering they are just like 'R'n'Ring' Americans of Vietnam days.

Though unlike those then, the Susem actually are putting the other side's military might to flight. Their "making love not war" and armed with no more than Patches has won them every engagement. And they have no inhibitions in describing to one another what they have been up to either. There have been times when delivering another consignment of Patches and overhearing them practising perfecting their English, I have shuddered at some of the things they have done with those soldiers. Though not out 'pillaging' as such they are doing an awful lot of 'raping' (if their Patch requirement is anything to go by).

Anyway, when at last I had Menpemelo's undivided attention I asked her again about auras and their sentience.

"Sentience," she said, "is the faculty of perception, the antithesis of inanimateness." And then she launched into something entirely different, "Everything is comprised of points. Expressed in a singular content, a line, the movement of one point has effect on the others. Expressed in a bi-context, a plane, field, which as you know is composed of singular contexts, a point's movement will in turn also affect the rest of that field. The same occurs in a tri-context, volume, which, of course is comprised of bi-contexts, horizontal, vertical and multi-hypotenusical.

"Although one point can effect action on others its movement is frequently nullified, resisted, by those of theirs. However, in the quinth context wave oscillation is not as constrained. Auras of sentient entities are composed of interacting yet discrete agglomerations of Secondary waves."

She paused a moment as though formulating what to say next, then she said "Come with me." Taking me by my arm she took me to Terbal. But on the way she continued, "As I mentioned earlier, Secondary waves retain within their individual oscillations prior interactions and resonances with others. Once these resonances have occurred, the resultant reverberations will continue as long as there are further related Secondary wave interactions."

By then I had become confused. Though with Terbal's "Auralate imaging profile you are vanting? Ein moment," my attention was elsewhere. A bevy of sherpals on a carpet and carrying a long white roll flew up. The carpet hovered by a wall, the sherpals ran off of it carrying the roll. Half of them held the top of the roll by the wall, the rest clung to it, their weight unfurling what looked like a screen.

Menpemelo said "Stand behind it." So I did but in no more than a moment she said "You can come out now." And when I did I was amazed.

There was a blank silhouette of my body but all about it were swirls of colour, with most of them around where my head had been. Not a halo though, more alike to long hair straggling up and outwards as if startled by electrostatic shock. "Ooh," I said, "what is that?"

Taking me by the shoulder for a closer look, she said "This is your aura." And before I had time for a word, she added "though what is depicted upon this screen is a simplified image compared to other screens we have on La-ra." And before I had even time for a question she continued, "But all the same, as you can see (and I could) there are concentrations here...and there (and she pointing to bits around my head). These pertain more to your cerebral cortexes...these (and dabbing her fingers to slightly bright streaks along either side of the silhouette) are those such of organs...and these (she pointing to a furze of tiny spikes jutting out all along the outline) cellular resonances."

The moment she paused I was in with "Auras of brains I can perhaps accept, but are you really saying other bits of me have their own bits of it as well?"

"What are you," she said, "an entity composed of cells or a collection of cells combined together?" And before I had a reply, "Both, are you not?" With me nodding to her wisdom she continued, "Would you not agree sentient entities exist as a consequence of harmony of all their constituents?" I nodded again (but thought how sometimes bits of me are in disharmony with other bits). "By the same consideration," she continued, "it is their collective coordination which controls. This paramouncy is best assigned to, exercised from here" (she dabbing her finger at the silhouette of my head).

"But what about all these streaks trailing away from my head? And you said auras only occur in the quinth context and that is why they can't be seen. And now there is this, how is it possible to...?"

Interrupting, Menpemelo answered with "What you observe is not your aura but the effect it has on Secondary wave oscillations with those of your Tertiary waves This is its shadow, its footprint. Your aura exists not just as a single field as depicted here but around you tri-contextually. Its forward facets are obscured by your body's mass and the oscillations of its Secondary waves. Not only are we observing these central fields end-on, they are effectively obscured by the whiteness you can see, but the aural plane shown here is compromised by the aggregate depiction of those in the hemisphere beyond and, of course, you. Aboard La-ra we have multi-context analysis facilities."

"Oh," I said, and though I was listening I was absorbed in seeing a side of me I had not known before. And in the back of my mind I had vague memories of kirlian photographs. Perhaps they weren't merely new-age knick-knacks after all. My mind raced on to Saints in paintings, how had they all come to have halos? Someone must have seen one circling round at least one of their heads? Did some humans have something special which caused them to have visible halos? Did some people have especial enabling eyesight to see them? Was it, is it, something saintly 'do gooders' sport when they are caught by a trick of the light?

Menpemelo's "Attraction and attracting, response and responding resonations," jolted me back. And with her answer to the first question I was all ears again. "As I earlier mentioned, auras attune to those of others but some more so." She then said "Look..." whereupon she too went behind the screen. With the image of me disappearing and hers taking its place, I saw in a moment what Menpemelo meant by 'more so'. She had strands of startled hair stretching far further than had any of mine.

"Oh," I said when she reappeared, "why have you more than me?"

"Hmm," a pause, then, "the best way of explaining these differences is your profile is akin to ours when we are in our juvenile, male form." No doubt sensing the ebb of my esteem, she hastily added, "Not that one is superior to another." But I wasn't assuaged.

Brazilian Junta flees Brasilia

BY OLIVER PICOS
IN RIO DE JANEIRO

GENERAL Vidal de Costa's has hurriedly moved his government from Brasilia back to Rio de Janeiro, Brazil's former capital.

The move is seen as a response to the ever growing threat of Nonette movement which has already spread to Barreiras less than 100 miles to the north of Brasilia.

A spokesman for the Junta admitted that the situation in the Nordeste, the country's northeast, is serious but denied it was out of control.

The spokesman said that the government likened the Nonette movement to the 19th Century Canudos uprising but with Alien support. As soon as the Aliens had departed the Nonette movement would be bound to fade away.

Until the Aliens had departed the government's strategy was to continue to maintain a protective defensive screen at a the Nonettes and the Susem.

Independent reports of the situation in the Nordeste are few due to the Junta's strict clampdown on the media. However, those important few added to those of the Susem telecasts themselves, seem to be at variance to those given out by the military.

According to some unofficial reports circulating in Rio, many thousands of soldiers have suffered at the hands of the Susem and Nonettes.

Others are claiming there have been numerous desertions among the armed forces and morale among those on active service is low.

The Defence Ministry's 'prudent distance' would, if Susem television broadcasts are to be believed, appear to be retreating hundreds of kilometres a week. For how long the Ministry can keep up this pretence of normality is a question being asked by many

Pyreneans panic as Susem swoop

BARCELONA: SCORES of shepherds, dozens of mountaineers have been taken captive by the Aliens. Right across the Pyrenees from San Sebastion to Andorra thousands of people have fled from the mountains and into valley villages and towns.

Police forces and relief agencies are rushing to the aid of those made homeless by

Susem security 'Unsafe' - say experts

By Janis Dingle
Safety Correspondent

LAST NIGHT'S Susem TV programme on Security has been given the thumbs down by string of pension and other experts. Some have even slated it as "dangerously misleading".

Susem presenter, 'Red Jim' Powell, claimed that the Alien-backed Nonette movement had overcome their unemployment and retirement problems. Powell said that in Nonette society no one needed to work just study and they would be given bumper wage packets.

Powell also alluded that there was no ne[...] Nonette pe[...] retirement or ill-health as their communities would look after them "Where have we heard that before?" says pensions expert Peter Lilley, "the flawed post-1945 socialist experiment that is where." Mr Lilley, senior partner of pension brokers Beveridge & Bevin maintains: "Tens of millions were conned into believing their blandishments and were cruelly cheated, these claims are exactly the same."

Steve Dorrell of health insurers Vin Bot was equally dismissive of Red Jim's claims of Nonette medical treatment. He said: "It is the height of [...] is suitable for all illnesses and disabilities. The Alien technology these people out in South America assert they are using to cure their populations could in the long term prove to be dangerous

"They most certainly would not be allowed in this or any other advanced country without being subjected to rigorous evaluation and trials. This could take years. In the real world it is important for people not to be taken in by such gizmos and ensure they are fully insured against their future ill-health."

Meanwhile, others are warning to some of the ideas exp-

Tyrol terror of Susem snatches

By Heidi Lutry
in Salzburg

THOUSANDS of Alpine people have fled in fear of Susem snatch squads. Police forces from France to Austria were on full alert last night and issued urgent warnings against further Alien attacks.

Many fleeing the stricken areas told of Susem craft swooping out of nowhere on unsuspecting

US bankers act against Susem 'crony' charges

By Lucenn Marples
in New York

Wall Street's finest were furious over yesterday's Susem telecast. Because of time differences most Susem telecasts are shown in eastern US during mid-afternoon, close of trading. And time to plan action before markets re-open Also to plan and action there has been.

Even before trading opened today a newly formed action group was not only in being but firing on all guns.

Firing on all guns

Calling themselves the 'Forum for Responsibility in Banking' and headed by the president of the Global Bank Corp, Meridith L Williams III, it issued a no nonsense statement not just rebutting but attacking the Susem claims.

Litmus test

It read: "Finance and banking are the litmus of capitalism's successful management of the world's economies. Today, US banking institutions are at the forefront of not only this success but in bringing success and wellbeing to many millions of people throughout the world.

"It is time, however, that the beacon of US banking success and achievement is taken from under the bushel from where it has been too long and held aloft for all to see. And it's light shine on all people everywhere.

'Unsettling times'

"And in the unsettling times which our extraterrestrial visitors have wrought upon us it is more important than [...]

'STERNIST YET' PROMISED FOR NEXT 'TRAILS'

By NOBBY BAKER

SLI TV said yesterday that the next series of Bosnian War Crimes Trials were for the more senior members of the old Serb and Croatian regimes.

SLI's boss, Derek Igg, said: "Up to now viewers have seen only the monkeys but from next week they can watch the organ grinders getting their just deserts. And because these are the real bigwigs and fat cats behind the war and atrocities in Bosnia they're on trial for more serious [...]

These include a Big Dipper style en-trance for the guilty, the dog pits are to be replaced by fish filled ponds.

There will be live rock concert music by a French group of Jean Charles Chaffonner. Mr Igg also promised that guilty and viewers alike will be in for a big surprise.

Replying to charges made by campaigners against the trials Mr Igg said: "When talking to them make sure they're up front with you and don't go behind your back."

The first part of the new Trials series is scheduled to hit viewers' screens within the next few days.

Dolomites in dread of Alien abductions

TRENTO: ITALIENS and holidaymakers alike fled in their thousands from the Dolomite region of northern Italy as Susem craft captured hundreds of walkers and climbers. Local radio and television stations relayed police warnings to stay away from open areas.

Eye witnesses reported seeing

And seeing so, she just as swiftly diverted attention back to the screen. "See here (and she pointing to concentrations around where her head had been), these are the same as yours and these..." She paused as though still trying to mollify, turned from me and called "Terbal."

"Animate? Bombus, ja? Ein moment."

While he was away Menpemelo continued, "These accentuated nodules here are the same in all beings (she pointing around her head again) but in humans as with us, and as I pointed out in your aura, they are developed to a higher degree than other beings and are indication of a developmental..."

But before she had chance to say more, Terbal, with a line of sherpals sat on a carpet with their legs clasped, came whizzing back. The sherpals then flew behind the screen. With Menpemelo's image disappearing the carpet with the sherpals, legs now unclasped, reappeared the other side leaving behind a line of bumble bees and their auras. Like Menpemelo's and mine they had white bits where they actually were, but lots of little lines darting from them which swooped and meandered from their shapes. What I also noticed was when one bee's lines neared another's they stretched out as though trying to touch but sometimes, though, as the lines neared there was rapid retraction.

Even as I asked "Why are they doing that?" carpet and sherpals were behind the screen gathering them up. Then I was asking "Why don't the sherpals show?"

As bees and carpet swept away, Menpemelo answered by calling "Terbal."

It was the first time I have ever seen him being 'bashful'. But despite his, "I do not vant to," she cajoled him to flit behind the screen. And my "Why don't you come out on it either?" elicited his almost sorrowful, "I am not analogue like you, I am only digital."

Sherpals furled the screen and flew away, Terbal slunk off and Menpemelo said she had to depart as well. But as I walked with her I had more questions. "The white bits of us and the bees', what are they? What makes them?"

"The white you observed was only relative to what else was displayed. In another sense it was not, as such, there at all."

"If bees have auras, what about plants, trees?"

"All animate, cellular structures possess such."

"Every plant and animal, amoebas, all have auras? Souls?"

She stopped, paused, then said "I repeat, all cellular structures possess auras. The only difference being some have developed the auralate nodules I indicated to you. It is these where higher order awareness has developed." Another pause as though for thought, then, "perceived consciousness."

Though Menpemelo then left me I still had questions. If, as she had said earlier, auras have a life of their own, were the white bits I saw our 'ghosts'? She had said her hair-like strands stretched further than mine, so were they the result of extra maturity? What is it they can do that my short ones don't, can't? The bees' entwining ones, what happened when they touched, why did some dart back, was it "friends and foes"? Does each leaf-cutting ant have their

BOYO APPRECIATION DISORDER = BAD!

By **Ted Woodwood**
Welsh Affairs Correspondent

TOM JONES look-a-likes met the Tom Jones Appreciation Society of Pontypridd. The result? Six distressed young men, 50 very disorderly ladies who, in the words of Justice Lloyd, "Were an outrage to public decency and should have known better".

Giving evidence at Cardiff Crown Court, PC David Rees told of the "shocking and most scary experience" of his life. PC Rees was giving evidence against Howard Griffiths, landlord of the Its Not Unusual pub, Bridgend.

PC Rees said he and his fellow officers had found six men wearing nothing but their medallions, surrounded by a crowd of baying women who were, he said, "old enough to be my mother." He added the men were cowering behind tables and were in obvious distress.

Pleading Not Guilty to a charge of running a disorderly house, Mr Griffiths, 38, said he and the compare, Glynn Davies, had done their level best to keep the behaviour of the audience within reasonable bounds.

He said: "But the trouble started as soon as the third Tom Jones finished singing. Glynn had already to tell the ladies to mind their language and to stop throwing items of their clothing at the singers."

When Justice Lloyd asked what the women had been saying, Mr Griffiths said: "Get 'em off" was one, the rest were extremely rude and they were not saying, they were shouting." When asked what they were throwing, Mr Griffiths replied: "Their knickers."

Giving evidence for the prosecution, Garel Rhys, 28, the impersonator at the centre of the disturbances, said: "I had just finished singing 'Tie a Yellow Ribbon' when from the audience there was a call, "Tie this round your old oak tree" and this woman rushed at me waving her a stocking."

Mr Rhys denied he had been performing in a lewd and provocative manner. He agreed his trousers were 'a little on the tight side' but said they were no more so than what the real Tom Jones used to perform in. But Mr Rhys strongly denied that he had stuffed handkerchiefs inside the front of his trousers in order to make him appear more 'manly'.

Asked to describe what happened next, he said: "All of them were shouting, "Show us your oak." I undid another button of my shirt to show willing like but that did not seem to satisfy them.

"They began shouting even louder so I undid another," he said. "But when I refused to go any further the woman with the stocking ripped ... And then there was a mad rush.

"I tried to get off the stage but I tripped, then they were all on me, tearing away at my clothes. Like savages they were."

When asked to describe what happened next, Rhys broke down in tears and the hearing was adjourned for the day. The case continues.

Susem swoop on Swiss soldiers

By Mark Wartau
In Geneva

MORE than 100 Swiss soldiers were abducted by Aliens late yesterday afternoon. Swiss military chiefs are said to be concerned for the men's safety.

The soldiers, mainly reserveists were taking part in annual exercises in Bernese Oberland 30 miles to the east of Geneva. They were waiting for their transport when Susem craft swept down on them.

The men were surrounded by five Susem craft which suddenly appeared out of the sky "as if from nowhere", according to Eva Denvers an eye witness who was on a hillside nearby. She said: "Some of the men appeared to be herded into the craft but others tried running away but they also were soon being taken into the Alien's craft."

In a statement, the Swiss Defence Ministry said that all army manoeuvres had been halted until the situation [of the soldiers' ab...

Hotel book... hit by Suse...

By James Pollard
In Berne

ALPINE TOURISM has been dealt a body blow the Susem. Hotels and pensions are reporting mass cancellations as visitors flee the areas of Susem raids.

The Swiss Hoteliers Association estimates that bookings are down by more than 60 per cent. Their spokesman, Vim Tell said: "This could not have happened at a worst time for our members. After a disastrous start to the summer season we were at least hoping ...

MP found guilty of baton charges faints

By Lawrence Andrews
Political Correspondent

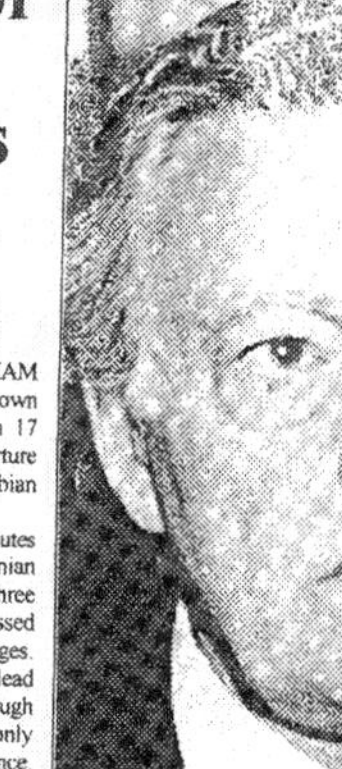

FORMER CHELTENHAM MP Sir Hugh Russett-Brown has been found guilty on 17 charges of selling torture equipment to former Serbian and Croatian regimes.

In the space of a 20 minutes trial - lengthy by Bosnian standards - the panel of three judges unanimously passed guilty verdicts on all charges. Passing sentence the lead judge said that as Sir Hugh was an outsider he would only be given a lenient sentence. But on being told this meant castration Sir Hugh fainted

Trials latest: Fish to replace dogs

THE dogs used in the Bosnian War Trails' punishment routines are to be replaced by piranhas - a breed of carnivorous fish.

A Caught TV official announced yesterday that the packs of dogs used so far in the punishments were due for a rest. She said the placing the dogs are a piranhas which were renewly discovered subspecies of Red Bellied Piranhas and had been named 'Landlords' on account of their ferocity.

Special pools are being made for them in the city's main stadium and are expected to be ready to take the first Landlords. These fish reportedly, can rip flesh

Susem snatch soccer players

By Desmond Dijon
In Lyon

TWO football teams and a referee were seized by the Susem yesterday. Police forces throughout southeastern France have been put on full alert in case of further Alien attacks.

Both teams are amateur sides from Lyon area. According to spectators two Susem craft swooped down ...

Spectators reported seeing several of the Susem's wasp-like flying machines surrounding the players before they were taken into the Alien's craft.

Although many of the spectators initially fled from scene there appears to have been no attempts to abduct any of them. None had chance to run more than a few metres anyway. Several were imme...

Dismal Arsenal limps on

THE Gunners limped to a 0:0 draw with Feyenoord last night. After desultory 90 minutes of play which even had the homeside's fans booing their disgust. However, Arsenal has managed to scrape through to the next round of the Eufora Cup.

What success they will have there up against the Juventus's and Inter-Milan's is not hopeful. With William Ill's odds still standing at 250-1 the Gunner's chances look increasingly forelorn

Woman climber escapes Susem

INNSBRUCK: A woman, one of a group of mountaineers reported abducted by the Susem has been found in a dazed state near the Swiss border.

Oona Grotz 25, from Bonn, was in a party of 12 climbing in Voralberg Mountains when she was taken by the Susem She said: "When they found I ...

SALVADOR FALLS T... NONETTE ADVANC...

By Phillipo Coari
In Sao Paulo

SALVADOR, Brazil's former capital and still one of its biggest cities, has fallen to the Nonette movement without a fight. The last detachments of government forces stole away under cover of darkness.

The loss of Salvador, following on the heels of the government's recent hurried departure from Brasilia is a further major blow to the ruling Junta. General Vidal da Costa's government is now faced with the ... movement spreading into the southern areas of the country where three-quarters of the population live.

The fall of Salvador has al-ready had a dramatic effect on ordinary urban Brazilians' perception of the Susem and the Nonette movement.

Before the city's fall the Nonettes were far away with little or no relevance on their everyday life. As far as the Susem concerned, most Brazilians viewed them with gratitude for the free energy units they had supplied. ...

own aura or do they have a joint, shared one? Do monarch butterflies have a big joint one as well, but stretching all the way from Mexico to Canada, and which goes on for generation after generation?

Once above ground more questions came. If trees have auras, do theirs communicate with each other? Does a forest have a collective one? Do different species have different 'aural languages'? Paceillo said that wave signatures are always there, so if a forest is chopped down does its aura still remain? If it doesn't, how long before it fades away?

Menpemelo said the screen I saw was only a basic one. How much more do their advanced ones show? Do aural strands stretch further than that screen actually showed? The telephone calls I have had, the ones when I've said "I was just about to ring you," and I really was (and they weren't all creditors either) and the times when I have only been thinking of somebody and they have phoned. And when I have mentioned this to other people they all have said they had the same experiences. They couldn't all be coincidences.

And then I thought of all those other people who have had 'near-death experiences'. How they said it was if they were floating above the operating table. Perhaps they hadn't all been imagined after all. And if they hadn't, then it means auras can 'see. And if they can, then can they 'hear'' and everything else as well? And if a person's aura existed after they had been 'dead', how long does it exist afterwards? Forever? But it must be for a long time because Menpemelo said though her body and the other Susem could live for ages, her aura would become tired of her doing so.

Then there's another aspect. How do auras work, work so fast? Though the 120 metres a second speed of nerves Menpemelo mentioned is faster than we can see but, and I have worked it out, by the time my nervous system told me to scratch an itch on my toe a lightwave will be halfway to the moon by then. Waves of electricity, Secondary waves, if unfettered, flow as fast as light but the operating speed of computers and their programs are as nothing to that of auras. And if the nodules she pointed out are where the other form of us humans, Susem and others are supposed to reside, and they didn't look that big, then how can they store, operate, process so much so quickly? And Menpemelo has still not really explained what she meant by 'excitement'. But it's always the same after talking with her, I end up having more questions than I started off with.

And though seeing my aura up on a screen was enlightenment to me, even the moment of this was diminished when I mentioned it to Rainbow and expecting her to be impressed. "Oh that," she said as I sat with her looking at her latest production, "we all had ours done ages ago."

rmy routed   Government flees country   South America severed

Ecuador falls to Aliens

By Maria Salinas
n Lima

Ecuador has finally fallen to the Alien backed Nonette movement. The country, according to Susem communiqués has ceased to exist. Ecuador is now incorporated into the Nonette 'Continental Congress'. Ecuador's occupation by the Nonettes has sent shockwaves throughout Latin America.

With its Andean hinterland and capital Quito lost to Nonette control weeks ago Ecuador's military proved itself further incapable of defending the rest of the country, the central Guayas valley region and coastal cities where most of the population lives.

Every morning for the past two weeks the Ecuadorian army would have retreated to a new 'prepared defensive line'. Yet no matter how much its High Command claimed their forces were being attacked by the Aliens, there were neither sight nor sound of any fighting only headlong flight by frontline forces. There have been no signs either of wounded or injured soldiers being rushed to field or any other hospitals.

Soldiers flee en-masse

There have been many reports however, of units fleeing their positions en-masse. These same reports also tell of groups of soldiers, sometimes in their hundreds being captured by the Aliens without ... erent and exhausted state, barely able to walk. Many, it is said, have even lost the power of speech. The fear among serving soldiers of such fates befalling them has fur-ther sapped morale.

'Nonetteland' welcomed

For the majority of ordinary Ecuadorians, the forthcoming arrival of the Nonettes has been treated with equanimity. Signs of fear and flight among the peasantry have been all but non-existent. Most have appeared swayed by Susem telecasts depicting life in "Nonetteland" and anticipating the supposed benefits they will receive with the Nonettes' arrival.

Most of those among the population fleeing the Nonettes' advance, have been government officials including many police units. Estate owners, members of the business and propertied classes have also fled the affected area in large numbers.

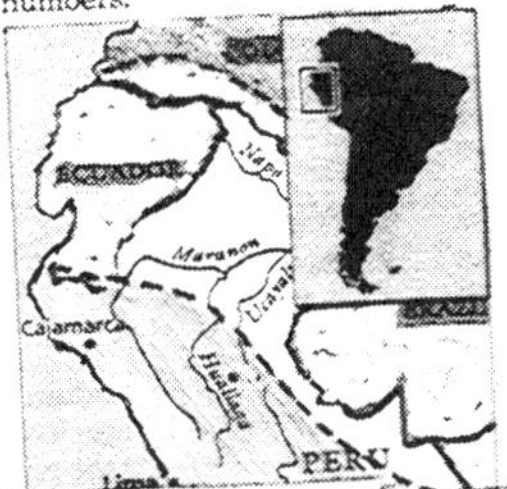

The fire ravaged Ecuadorian port of Guayaquil yesterday as govern...

Following the hurried departure of the government from the country's second city, Guayaquil, to exile in neighbouring Columbia, there have been scenes of near panic at the quayside in a chaotic scramble to board the few boats remaining. The city's airport has been commandeered by the military as have all outward flights. The Ecuadorian airforce has reportedly flown its four squadrons of MiGs to Cali in neighbouring Columbia.

The Pan American highway southward to Peru is also jammed with refugee traffic, including many senior members of the Armed Forces. All of whom now appear to have sunk their differences with Peru ... the US backed OAS in an attempt ... formulate a pan-American respo... to the growing Nonette threat.

The Nonettes now control a swa... of territory stretching from ... Atlantic to Pacific oceans and h... effectively split the continent in t... Moreover, if Nonette broadcasts ... to be believed, it is widening by ... day, up to a 1,000 miles in west... Amazon region.

Are Columbia and Peru nex...

Although much of the area ... Nonettes have overrun is spar... populated they will soon be ... croaching on those in both Peru ... Columbia. Many observers be... that it is only a matter of ... before ...

---

ews

"Don't be fooled by Susem claims" – says MP

BY KELVIN MATINE
POLITICAL EDITOR

A LEADING backbench MP warned last night about being taken in Nonette claims.

In last night's upbeat programme, Susem presenter 'Red Jim' Powell boasted the rapidly spreading populist Nonette movement was the way of the future. At the end of the programme he urged viewers to form similar organisations.

According to Worthing's LibCon MP Sir Paul Blunt, Powell's call was little short against their governments. Sir Paul said: "This was an extremely dangerous thing for the man to do. While sensible and right minded people will not be taken in by such simplistic blandishments there are others who might be gullible to them."

Sir Paul is one of a growing number of MP's and other public figures calling for governments across the EU to mount a campaign to counter the recent spate of what are increasingly being seen as blatant Susem-backed propaganda broadcasts. Sir Paul ... television air-time should be made available to refute the assertions made in the Alien's programmes.

Agreeing with Sir Paul's demand for air time is Hazel Blear, head of Salford Health Action Group which has been set up to curb a spate of teenage pregnancies in her city. Ms Blear said: "A dangerous impression is being given that it will soon be possible to go into one of these Alien health machines and cancel out the chances of conceiving. Young people need to be saved from being led into this deception. There cannot be any reason at all for

---

ALIENS IN SHOCK MONK ATTACK

By BEN SHERMANT

AN ENTIRE monastery of more than 200 hundred Carmelite monks were whisked away in an Alien dawn raid yesterday. Though many of the monks were later found wandering in the nearby hills, as of last night 58 of their Order were still unaccounted for.

When monks at the monastery of St Ambrose, near the small Italian village of ... according to the Abbot, Brother Kevin, who was one of the survivors, all the older monks and those not in good health were ...

Arsenal's hollow win

By DAN "THE MAN" LAVY

ARSENAL beat Dutch champions Feyenoord one nil last night have been the final scoreline but it was shout about let alone celebrate. In what must rate as one of the most desultory matches of the Ufora cup.

The score would have nil-nil had it not been for Feyenoord's fullback Vastlaam's own goal. While bookies William Ill might not be the only ones who see little hope of Arsenal making it beyond the quarter finals, they have at least put their money on the line. Their current odds on a Gunner's cup win is still 250 to 1.

Aliens abduct athletes

From Roberta Maglie
In Milan

FORTY SIX athletes taking part in the Padua to Verona Road Race and three police motorcyclists accompanying them were abducted by Aliens. Dozens of other runners fled and the race was cancelled.

The 46 who were taken in-... isolated and deserted stretch of road near the village of Alonte.

The 46 men were bunched together at the front of the race and had just crested the top of a hill, momentarily passing out of sight of others some 300 metres behind them. When the first of these following runners arrived at the top of the hill they saw two Susem craft had swooped

Come five to eight there was a terrible rush to the bar and we couldn't serve fast enough. But a few moments past, if it wasn't for the TV you could have heard a pin drop. It was this of course which had everyone in the Salutation go quiet. Not that I wasn't myself.

James started as he had the others with "Welcome to..." but this time the picture was different, a little blue-white ball on black. He had no sooner said, than the camera or whatever was dashing to this ball. With me seeing it was the Earth, the camera was whizzing round like one of those satellites but in no time at all it was diving through the clouds.

Down and down it went, going like anything it was, but just when it had me thinking there would be one almighty crash coming, it came to a stop right in front of James, he dressed in white and standing on a road in the middle of nowhere "...our world," he said. Then with his face all but filling the screen, he a smile and me again thinking he really wasn't such a bad looking fellow, he said "Imagine..." And the moment he had, music, a piano came on and it was if he had no need to have said, for the first notes said it again.

From his face the camera went along the road, the piano still played and he then saying "...living in a world like ours." The camera, now flying along the road at a fair pace, turned left and right as it went and showed hillsides as stony as Connaught and with groups of people dressed in black clumped here and there.

The camera then went up over a rise in the road and all of a sudden it was looking down into a valley with a little village all in white at the bottom with a surround of trees and a river flowing by. "Imagine..." James said again, "...a world at peace...free from armies and police forces too."

With the piano still playing, the camera swept down to this village and in no time at all it was gliding along the main street. People, dressed as white as was James, were coming out of the houses and waving, though I noticed none had a smile as such. But James said "Imagine a world free from officials, politicians and tyrannical religion too."

With him again saying "Imagine..," the camera passed into a square and to a whole crowd more of people. As it passed them by and James saying "...a world free of violence, crime and intimidation too," these people also gave a wave but they had not a smile between them either, just looking.

The camera passed out of the square, the village. The piano was still playing and James then said "Imagine living in our world..." And with the camera next flying above the river, "...free from the law of lawyers...but where there is the justice and order of the people and the people's peace as well...accountability and freedom by all, for all...and equality too."

The camera followed the river but as this flowed around a hill there was another village, a bigger one. The camera flew to it and as it did, all along its banks lines of white appeared. But as the camera came closer I saw that they were people and they were all waving as well. Though as the camera flew over them there was the faint sound of them humming in time with the piano.

The camera came to the village, the humming grew louder and James again said "Imagine..." This time the camera was flying above the houses, and he saying"...living in this world of ours..." As the camera looked down I could see the streets were filled with people, all looking up and waving, and he adding "...free from the injustices, indignities of poverty and hunger ...and homelessness too."

The camera flew on over the houses, streets, a square, and still there was the sound of people humming to the music. Then I realised that some of the people in the Sallie had joined in as well. Even when the camera flew away from the village and was following the river again and James was saying "Imagine, a world free from illness and needless suffering too..." there was still the humming. And more of it was coming from those in the Sal as well, it almost drowning out James's "...free too from the tyranny of ignorance and the serfdom of your old world labour..."

The river flowed round another hill, the camera sped fast along above it and the humming faded. The pub's died down as well. But within seconds a big town came into view. Then with the piano playing louder, James again said "Imagine..." and the humming came back. The camera dashed over this town, rising and falling above the houses as it went and with James next saying"...living in our world where those who have plenty have no need to fortify themselves from those who have little...a world where, with enlightened self-interest the wealthy aid those who aren't to be as they." The humming now grew louder.

A few seconds more and the camera had crossed the town to a big hill covered white with people and all of them humming even louder. There were thousands and thousands of them and James, talking louder, again said "Imagine..."

This time he was in the picture, standing right in front of all these people. The camera zoomed in on him as he continued, "...no authorities or officials telling you what to do..." Half turning to the people he waved his arms as though conducting the humming. After a moment he turned back to the camera and said "...but a world where everyone has a say in everything."

People in the Sallie joined in the humming again and James, still facing the camera continued conducting. But now it was as if he was orchestrating the people in the pub as well as those behind him. For when he flattened his hands and patted them downwards everyone in the Sal quietened as well. No sooner than they had, than he said, "Live in a world as ours where there are no countries, no leaden weights of states or governments..."

He now raised his hands again and the humming came louder, but he then lifted one hand above his head and the people behind him began "laa laaing" instead. In no time everyone in the pub was doing the same and when he circled his finger, the people behind him started singing the twiddly bit higher. So did we!

James patted his hands down again and said "A world where all the people, every person, every community is at last, at long last, free from the ways of colonialism and imperialism of your old world's rule..." He raised his hands and we were all "laa laaing" louder again. But a moment later and with him patting them back down James then said, "...a world where every person, every community has self-determination, their own sovereignty...yet interdependence with everyone..."

The "laa laaing" continued though still at a low level. All the same though James raised his voice for "Now the day has come for everyone who yearns to be free...free from those who rule over them...free from those who dictate their lives, to come and join with us...join us so all the world will be as one..." He raised his hands, he kept raising them and in no time we were all singing at the top of our voices. Even when the picture was soaring away from him and the people, we were still singing.

Then the screen went fizzy white and then there was another terrible rush to the bar.

Patches are now turning in real profits. It seems such a pity having to kiss them goodbye but you can't spend money when you are dead.

On the face of it things are going wonderfully. Demand doesn't stop rising but production is keeping nicely apace. Tabajara's growers are planting grove after grove of bay trees. Though Manual's packaging plant operates non-stop, he is expanding it as fast as can be. The Nonette's cellular management has everything working without fuss and their distribution system delivers to everywhere quickly and cheaply. What is more there has not been as much as a murmur from any of those involved wanting a bigger slice of the action. But it can't last.

Demand is driven not from increasing individual use, though there is some of this, but by an expanding market. The Nonettes are spreading so fast they will be in control of all Bahia State by next week (the Brazilian government has already made a rushed return to Rio). The council of regional Nonettes has grown to seven and they have pencilled in a full complement of 81 representatives. As this will mean more than 350 million people, all South America, they are being a trifle heady in their optimism. Just as they are in re-naming it the “Continental Congress” for it will all be snuffed out the moment the Susem leave.

As for them it is an Indian summer of getting all they can before they fly off. And yet another reason why Patch demand has risen. Once the Susem weekly wants could be carried, now a trolley’s worth is needed daily. There are so many Susem who have arrived that there can’t be many left on board La-ra. For fresh arrivals Tabajara has become a cross between an induction and transit centre. Induction for these “new girls” (as the ones who first arrived call them) to “practice” (their word, not mine) on the Latin American military. Transit in that once they have ‘experience’ it’s a departure point for pleasures elsewhere.

But with Latin American armies everywhere falling back (or still fleeing) the new arrivals need to fly ever further afield before there are sufficient concentrations of men on which to practice their “urges” (Tearo’s term). She is in Tabajara just now with Anuria and Lathia to take some more of the “new girls” on a European tour. Though like with the last lot she took across, I don’t think they have sights of its grandeur in mind.

I met her while delivering more patches and to fix up a lift to Sarajevo. She was with Lico and Petruee and the rest of their troupe, all freshly returned from another night’s amouring. They were comparing notes and again practising perfecting their English. Overhearing them as I greeted her I had to remark that weren’t they being rather rough with the men?

But all I received was “Just being friendly...they like it really.”

“Making the men run,” I said, “then knocking them about and whipping them, isn’t that a bit harsh?”

This met with “Just our way...only having a bit of fun...always have to have some play first...not really hurting them, some are being over-sensitive that's all."

"But why do you always have to then hold them down?" I asked.

This met with a bluff "Some of your males are so shy...just helping them get over it..." and a gravelled voiced "Always like it at the start when they are frisky..." With this one adding as she spoke to Tearo, "We had some really rough ones last night, you should have seen..." I thought it best to leave.

Whenever delivering I have tried to meet with Menpemelo. I still want to know what she meant by "excitement" and how auras actually function. But she has been too busy to talk to me. With time running out before I leave it's become pressing, and to have left without knowing would have forever nagged in my mind. I had asked Terbal but he, what with Pa-tu's recovery mission and helping Rainbow, has been too busy to talk with me as well. Or if not, he's watching the football and I can never get him away from that. But today I was in luck, Menpemelo had the time to talk.

She began with "All observation is subject to selective interpretation, is it not?2 I nodded, she continued, "In so doing biased emphasis is accorded by the observer relative to prior perception. However, it is the substance of serious enquiry, is it also not, to obviate such?" I nodded again, though wondered what she was getting at. "However, this can never be achieved in absolute terms simply because there are no absolutes." Seeing me puzzled she said, "On Earth there is a creature you call a unicorn."

I stupidly said "It's mythical, unicorns don't exist."

This met with "That is assertion not verification. You cannot say unicorns do not exist. All you can say is that their probability of so doing is unlikely, and available evidence suggests that there are no such animals. There are no certainties. The only absolute is that there are not any absolutes." She mentioned coelacanths, how Earthly experts once said they could not possibly exist because they had to be extinct and now there are so many found that before sea fishing was stopped, they were regularly shown off to tourists. All the same I still didn't see what it had to do with auras and 'excitement'.

She continued though. "It is perhaps unfortunate so much of human enquiry, the pursuit of perception and understanding, is conducted on the basis that there is certainty, that there are absolutes." Before I could say "So?" she next said "One which has so obscured and stunted enquiry is the assertion that the rate of oscillation of light, electro-magnetic radiation, Secondary waves, is the absolute of speed and time.

"As I mentioned previously the relativity of occurrences exist in terms of their relationship to others. For example, at what speed are we travelling (we were walking)?"

"About four miles, six kilometres an hour," I said.

"Your planet, thus are we, is circling your Sun. In doing so it is travelling at 300,000 kilometres an hour, and in turn our galaxy, as it rotates, is speeding us at a further 200,000 kilometres an hour. Although we may appear, as we walk, to be travelling at six kilometres an hour we are only doing so relative to the immediate environs. In another context we are travelling at

"Nonettes pedd Fools Gold" - say

By Richard Whitey
Political Correspondent

IN AN outspoken attack on recent Nonette television programmes, Prime Minister Edward Campbell said people needed to guard against being taken in by them.

He said: "These [Alien's] programmes have been skilfully crafted to give the impression that a veritable paradise is being created by the people under their control. But this simply cannot be so. I know it and anyone else with a scintilla of commonsense knows it as well.

"It simply is not possible, given the knowledge we have of the region under their control, to have brought about these claimed changes in such a short space of time. I am urging the rest of my cabinet to formulate without delay a package of promotional measures which will show why these Nonette offers are a sham. That they are peddling nothing other than 'Fools Gold' and people should be made aware that it is."

Asked why the government is still allowing the Nonette programmes on the BBC and ITV he said: "The BBC like the ITA is independent of any government or outside control. And as such there is nothing the government can do to alter their current policy. However, we have made perfectly clear to them our disquiet."

Mr Campbell while acknowledging the benefits the Susem have already brought to everyone though the introduction of their soufin energy units and the removal of nuclear power stations said: "It still does not give them the right to bombard the nation's homes with this bogus nonsense."

A spokesman for the BBC said: "We do not really have a 'choice' in transmitting the Alien newscasts. We do not know where

Looming coke price hike fuels crime spree fears

Steven Watts
In Washington

FEDERAL and State Law Enforcement agencies across the US are bracing themselves for a crime surge in the wake of forthcoming falls of cocaine entering the country.

Undercover narcotic officials throughout South and Central America report a dirth of coca base leaving Colombian production centres for onward shipment to Mexican refiners.

The scarcity is seen as direct consequence of the reported Susem control of the major coca producing regions of southern Colombia, Peru and Bolivia.

According to US Drug Czar Kent Walton's office, the price of cocaine is set to soar. An official said: "Street prices of cocaine and cocaine based derivatives (such as crack) are presently stable. Latest forecasts cite Mexican refiners having a maximum of three, four weeks downstream supply.

"There is a consequent high certainty of rapid upward movement in prices reflecting the shortages. It is anticipated supply shortfalls will generate not reduction in usage but rises in robbery and theft offences to fund price rises. It is also likely there will be increases in drug related homicides and associated violence."

Howard Marks in La Paz reports:

TRAVELLERS arriving from the north of Bolivia report the Susem have extended their control to within 200 kilometres of Lake Tititicaca and routes to Cuzco, Peru ... longer open. ... most important ... export - coca leaf - under serious threat.

With the major growing areas in north under S... occupation and the ... routes of the rema... blocked, income already plummeted. ... is thought to have se... economic conseque... for many of the u... social groups in La ... who depend on coca income to fund th... lifestyles.

Experts thumbs down for Nonette workplace

By Helen Boober

"Welcome to the Wacky World of Work - Nonette-style", might well have been the title of "Red Jim's" latest telecast. A world where no one need to work, everyone can lounge about all day - and get paid for doing so! A world where those who do feel like working are paid huge sums for just turning up! Is this really possible in the real world? We asked the experts for there views.

"A recipe for workplace chaos," says Roger Mawkish, head of Human Resources Worldwide. Mr Mawkish said: "If the past 20 years has taught us anything about work and the workplace is that there is no such thing as a free lunch. If a company isn't profitable for its shareholders then it ceases to exist and its employees do no[t] have jobs. I saw no eviden[ce] whatsoever of this significa[nt] aspect as having been addres[s]ed in the programme."

"Pure propaganda of the ... Soviet type," says Profess[or] James Corgill of Sheppey U[ni]versity Sociology Departm[ent]. Prof Corgill, says: "Resea[rch] has found that ordinary peo[ple] left to themselves are poo[r at] giving leadership to others.

"And secondly, other [re]search has shown that ord[inary] people do not like ord[inary] everyday work. Researc[h has] also shown people no[t] with leadership skills o[...] ily need to be told wha[t to do] or they will become co[...] This will leads to an inc[...]

Gleeful geese greet guilty MP

By SHAZZER JONES & TRACE SMITH

AMID a gaggle of eagerly expectant honking geese ex-Cheltenham MP, Sir Hugh Russet-Brown and others found guilty of minor war crimes were led into the local correction centre.

Sir Hugh, who has fallen foul of Ragusa's new no nonsense "three strikes and it's off" rule looked pale and drawn as he was led into the centre. Geese could be heard from all over the

THE BIG DIPPER of DOOM

By Edwin Drood
In Sarajevo, Bosnia

DOZENS OF SENIOR SERB and Croat officials, guilty of abetting war crimes and other atrocities in Bosnia were sawn in half yesterday. Others were eaten alive by ferocious piranha fish.

To continuing roars of approval, a 40,000 capacity crowd at the Kosovo Stadium, Sarajevo were treated to a spectacular two hour long non-stop show of executions.

The big Trials dipper at the Kosovo Stadium Sarajevo yesterday

The circular saw

Spectators at the stadium and billions of televisions viewers worldwide were thrilled not only by the giant circular saw at the end of the big dipper but that the surrounding lake was filled with shoals of 'Landlords' - the most ferocious piranhas known to mankind.

Accompanying the executions was an out-of-this-world light show and the music specially composed and performed by the world famous classical rock composer, Jean Charles Decourseau.

At 15 minute intervals spectators saw group after group of guilty officials boarded onto cars and sent whizzing up and down a 100 metre high big dipper.

The 'Landlords'

The first two dips passed through pools infested with Landlords. Even before the cars became submerged the audience were cheering the spectre of dozens of Landlords leaping from the water and sinking there barbed teeth into the hands

Giant ringside screens provided spectators with close-up pictures of the each 'dipping'.

As the cars made their final descent and with their occupants' attention still distracted by the Landlords clinging to their hands and faces, they failed to notice until almost the last moment the huge circular saw they were bearing down on.

Limbs sawn off

The audience roared with approval at the performances of those in the cars as they tried to but usually only to lose their arms and legs in the process.

Landlords rent flesh

Once the car was through the circular saw, the occupants or rather what was left of them were jettisoned through the air and moments later splashing down into a bigger, Landlord infested pool.

In their attempt to reach the side of the pool any survivors were at instantly covered in Landlords renting flesh from their faces and the stumps of their limbs. However, and to the evident delight of the

half a million kilometres an hour, more if the 1,500 kilometres hourly speed of your planet's daily rotation is included. The velocity, speed of Secondary waves in the frequency spectrum of light is faster or slower relative to the speeds of the rest of Secondary waves' spectrum. Again Earthly enquiry attests the speed of light is finite and in so doing has also equated it to be the meter of time. The first is error, the second the resulting inaccuracies."

Again I was puzzled and perhaps seeing so she said "Come with me," and took me to Anuria, saying as we walked, "As a cosmologist she has a better understanding of galaxy focusing." Confusing me yet more she said "The speed of light as a constant suffices as reliable enough reference for most calibrations in a planetary, even a galactic context but not over greater distances, volumes nor, conversely, within very small ones."

Before I could say "That is a contradiction," she said "Ah there she is."

And Anuria said "Hmm...galaxy focusing? Yes, there is one whose effect can be seen from here..." Fumbling amid her tunic pockets, she produced then flipped open a small pad and added "...and is already known to your astronomers. See here..." and pressing the pad's sides, "...referred by them as 0957+516A and B."

Spots of stars appeared amid the dark of her pad and pointing to two of them she said "A quasi-quasar phenomena, 70,000 of your light years distant ...has a bi-visual image...hence I suppose, your A and B...due to partial refraction through intervening galaxy a quarter of its light emission distance to here..." Although intrigued I still didn't see what she was on about.

Still pressing the pad's sides, its page enlarging to a sheet, the image on it going though umpteen shades of orange, she continued, "Though both emissions present an identical 'red shift'' as I gather you term it, one of course has taken longer to arrive than the other. Therefore..."

"One..." Menpemelo exclaimed, "...is oscillating faster than the other!"

"Or the other travelling slower," said Anuria.

I said "That's just a picture you are showing, how do you know it's not an illusion?" but Menpemelo replied with "Come with us."

Terbal, after he had been pulled away from watching football, said "Ah, split screen you are again vanting?"

And to Menpemelo's "All," his "Ein moment."

After the sherpals delivered, Menpemelo began with "By placing this small yet powerful lamp behind this wall, part of its beam will pass through a gap here..." She lifted up a little shutter and part of the lamp's beam shone through the gap and formed a small semi-circle of bright light on the otherwise black base the other side of the wall.

She then said "If I opened up this next close-by gap..." and she so doing, "...the lamp's light will shine through it as well."

Indeed it did but I was saying "Why is that?" For what I saw wasn't just another small half circle but what was happening in the overlapping segments. There were little ripples as on sand when the wind has blown it.

"Undulating wave interference," Menpemelo said, but before I had time

TIMES

Sawn from crotch to crown in seconds

Trials latest from Sarajevo

From Antony Killigen
Justice Correspondent

HUNDREDS of former top Serb and Croat thugs who committed atrocities and other crimes against humanity have deservedly paid for their evil crimes: After being judged guilty they were sawn in half by a giant circular saw The remains of these wicked wrongdoers' bodies were then eaten by countless thousands of 'Landlords' (the most ferocious and savage piranhas yet known to mankind).

Though the executions of these former top death-camp gauliters might be seen by some liberals and other so called 'do-gooders' as being on the stern side, they were no less than what these Satans in human form deserved and they were at least quick This, sadly, was unlike the painful death these depraved sadists cruelly inflicted on countless innocents who fell into their evil clutches

After 144 separate and thoroughly fair trials, which were all held in public and took the 'no messing' teenage judge the entire afternoon to try, she found all 144 of these once so-called 'high officials' of the former Serb and Croat pariah regimes rightly guilty of the unspeakably vile crimes which they had perpetrated or abetted.

After the last of these murdering bestial brutes had been given the well deserved thumbs-down by the judging panel, the head judge said: "I hereby sentence you all to spend the evening in the National Stadium to reflect on your guilt and then you are free to leave."

When some among these craven thugs - who were all held in a giant dock and were all expecting at least a public whipping and castration, and then to be sent down pits for the remainder of their wicked lives filling them in - heard her judgement some of them openly sniggered at what they arrogantly took as her 'soft touch sentence'

With the Cambodian guards next escorting these once high priests of incarnate wickedness past the silent crowds lining the two miles of their journey to the Stadium, they were ambling and strolling along to what they obviously thought was to be an evening's entertainment But how little did these murdering ex-top dogs of the former pariah regimes know it was they who were going to be the evening's 'entertainment' That once inside the Stadium they would soon be laughing on the other side of their evil faces

Even when each group of these heinously cruel torturers were taken to the Big Dipper's cars and invited to strap themselves in, none of them could see or know what lay in wait. But, from the self-satisfied smirks on their smug evil faces, it was obvious that they still thought they were being taken for a night out at the funfair Nor, as each car whisked them up to the Big Dipper's first peak did any of these perpetrators of unspeakable mutilation and murder know what was coming

Even when they crested the first peak of the Dipper all of them would still have been unknowing of what was about to happen to them But as they were zoomed from the Dipper's crest they soon had the first taste of their rightly deserved fates

The Punishment

AS these cruel craven mutilators of the innocent were hurtled downwards to what they could only have thought was a 'mere unwelcome dip' in the pool lying across the Dipper's first trough, those in the front of each car now well and truly had the smirks wiped off their once smug, evil faces But of course none of them knew they were really just about to get the first proper dose of their long overdue and more than well deserved medicine

Even before the car had touched the water, shoals of Landlords were leaping from it and piercing their needle hard barbed fangs into these twisted, sadistic murderers' evil faces And as these men of unspeakable wickedness tried to tug Landlords from their cheeks and noses, lips and tongues other piranhas leapt out the water and sunk their razor sharp serrated teeth into these heinous ogres' hands. Some of the Landlords had even gone for their throats and necks

One of these ex-top dog murdering bully boys, in a cowardly and , foolhardy attempt to evade his just fate managed to bale out the Dipper's car. But even before he could begin to make his getaway, shoals of Landlords were on him renting at his flesh. He was in such panic that, for a moment, he was virtually running over the surface of the water in his doomed bid to escape Though with his evil face already covered with Landlords chomping into his visage he soon lost his balance toppled backwards.

The pool then erupted into a seething threshing inferno as even more Landlords flashed in for a frenzied feeding on this diabolic sadist's writhing, kicking, jerking body. And the moment the Landlords got him below the water it became red with his blood as they rented and tore the flesh from his limbs In minutes they had stripped his body down to just its skeleton

While this vile diabolic sadist was getting his more than deserved comeuppance, the car carrying the rest of these heinous murdering, torturing bullies shot up to the Dipper's next peak And as it did they could be seen frantically trying to pull the last of the Landlords from their throats and their evil faces, which were increasingly covered in pulsating streams of their blood and twisted in rightly deserved pain and agony -- again, no more than these craven killers deserved to suffer

Even when the car crested over the Dipper's peak these men of unspeakable wickedness were still too distracted by the piranhas to see what lay in the Dipper's next through It was not until these ogres of vileness were at least halfway to it that any of them saw what they were bearing down on: a huge, coarse toothed circular saw going at full tilt

The Highlight

AS these murdering thugs of demonic cruelty shot towards this racing blade and those in the front seats saw what was coming they began to scream and struggle like the craven cowards they were. But it was too late, especially for the ex-top dog thug at the front The saw's blade ripped into him right between the eyes Even before he could have had time to yelp, "Oh no!" it had sawn him in half from his crotch right though to the crown of his evil head As the other bestial bullying ogres behind him tried to duck out of what they rightfully had coming to them their faces were sprayed with spewing blood flecked slivers of this first murdering thug's flesh and bone as well as that of his brain

No matter how much these heinous ex-death camp sadist gauliters twisted and turned none could escape from the more than just fate they deserved. The saw's blade got them all. The second murderous ex-top dog thug only had time to dodge a few inches to one side As a result the blade only sliced off the side of his head but its teeth got him right though an eye

Amid their panicked screams and cries some of the others behind him raised their hands in front of their faces in pathetic bids to protect their heads and faces But of course, as a result, the blade sliced off their arms and hands while simultaneously ripping right though their entire bodies.

Some of these once high and mighty murdering pariah officials who were seated to the rear of the car tried to get out of it but again time had run out for them all None of them got away As a result the blade cut off many of their legs - some getting sliced right up their thighs - as well as ripping right through the rest of their deserving evil bodies

After it had passed the saw's blade the Big Dipper car, now in two halves carried on up to the next peak But in so doing it showered and scattered down bits of these evil murdering ex-top dog thugs' arms and legs as well as their heads and bodies into the Landlord infested waters below Some these craven murderers who had managed to keep their heads and torsos in one piece could be heard making spinelessly pathetic screams as they were tossed hundreds of feet to the water below and the awaiting hordes of ravenous piranhas

Even before these sadistic murdering thugs' remains had splashed and plopped into the water walls of Landlords were leaping out of it and sinking their teeth into the severed bits of their limbs and bodies, which of course, were still warm and lush in blood but also it was now oozing out of them In seconds the entire pool around the Big Dipper was one big heaving, seething cauldron of bobbing bits of human bodies and ferocious fish as the Landlords in their tens of thousands fought in a frantic feeding frenzy to gorge and gobble the chunks of these once craven murdering ogres' corpses. In no time all the water was red with gore from the piranhas' feasting and banqueting on those justly exterminated

A short while later teams of pool cleaners sheathed in padded body armour, carrying hooks on extremely long poles raked the bones from the water

As they were finishing, another party of smug faced heinous craven murderers was boarding the Big Dipper's next car.

Full Report:
Pages 7, 8, 9;
Pictures:
Pages 7, 8, 9, 11-15

for a “What?” she added “By putting this reflective surface here...” And as soon as said, she had a little black shiny strip placed parallel to the wall just in front of the far tips of the lighted semi-circles. She then moved this strip closer so that it stood inside them, a third of the way from their tips.

Again I said “Why is that?” For this time there weren’t sand-like ripples but rings of dark and light in each of the two semi-circles. But even odder were the overlapping segments, they were a curve-sided check pattern of brighter light and darker dark.

“Lightwaves in phase,” she said pointing to the not so dark curves.

“Lightwaves out of phase,” added Anuria pointing to the check’s darker bits, then adding “in-phase lightwaves emphasised,” and pointing to the brighter ones.

“As is observed,” Menpemelo continued, “it is as if all the oscillations’ crests and troughs are informed of the others’ movements, relative positions and speeds.”

This was just the start of what they had to show.

From the flat (‘bi-contextual’ to be precise), Menpemelo and Anuria moved to “lightwaves from a single source expressed tri-contextually.” Menpemelo projected a lamp’s beam onto two mirrors opposite one another, but placed so that the beams reflecting off of them met in mid-air as if those of searchlights. The next sliced through the resulting overlapping vertical half spheres revealing curving rubic cubes of bright and dark. After a pause she said “What is observed are interactions of Secondary waves in the visual facet of their oscillations...a minute fraction of their spectrum.”

And Anuria added “A lower, shallower one as well.”

The next was a “tri-light” stood atop a “bi-light”. Menpemelo and Anuria clicked the lamps for each on and off. The resulting ripples and checks changed as though influenced by one another but with the “bi” having the biggest sway. Menpemelo put a small black shape, it looked like a tree’s, in front of the lamp lighting the “bi”. Ripples and checks where its shape was cast, immediately disappeared. The "tri-light also took on this tree shape but its shadow there didn’t blacken out its waves and checks completely, it just dimmed them down a bit.

She swapped the tree shape for an identical one but made of mesh. Specks of light from the circles where the first shadow had been sparkled through the spheres. “Observe,” she said, "how the light-phases of the bi-context influence those of the ‘tri’ ones.”

Before I could speak she had the next piece in place. Identical to the first, she set it at right angles to and touching, so both formed two sides of a square. Light also shone from its un-shuttered gaps, creating with the first overlapping checks more complex than before, not just in the semi-circles but the sphere sections as well. She put the meshed tree shape in front of the first lamp. Then she stood another, smaller one in front of the lamp of the second. There were two trees amid the spheres and depending where I stood, one was in front of the other as though in 3D.

Mixed response to Nonette economics

Helen Boober
Socio-economics Reporter

YESTERDAY'S Susem telecast - which showed a society happy with its economic lot - has produced mixed views from Business and Academia alike. Their verdict of life in Nonette society was that it was like the curate's egg: good in parts.

Both the CBI and IoD were in favour of the Nonette's low rates of taxation and removal of bureaucratic relation. But both their spokeswomen were dismissive of such possibilities in the 'real world'.

As the CBI's Erika Norman says: "Since time immemorial, business everywhere has always fought against the imposition of tax levels imposed by governments, but its collective success in obtaining any reduction has been minimal.

"In a society starting from scratch and from such a low economic base," she said, "perhaps it is possible but in an advanced one, such as ours there is no chance."

Professor Ian Chance of Snaresbrook University's Department of Criminology, however, was dismissive of 'Red Jim's' claim that because crime no longer existed in Nonette territory, there was no need for any form of surveillance or credit vetting.

Professor Chance said: "You put locks on doors not to keep thieves out but to keep honest people honest. Myself, I think that a lot out there (the Nonettes) are living in cloud cuckoo land.

"Everyone knows that given half a change all of your general public will do all manner of scams," Prof Chance said. "That why everyone has be checked out thoroughly before you lend them a penny. Them Nonettes

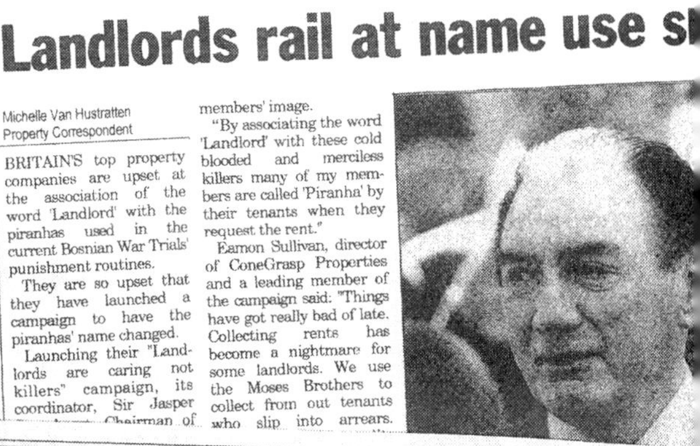

Landlords rail at name use s

Michelle Van Hustratten
Property Correspondent

BRITAIN'S top property companies are upset at the association of the word 'Landlord' with the piranhas used in the current Bosnian War Trials' punishment routines.

They are so upset that they have launched a campaign to have the piranhas' name changed.

Launching their "Landlords are caring not killers" campaign, its coordinator, Sir Jasper ... Chairman of ... members' image.

"By associating the word 'Landlord' with these cold blooded and merciless killers many of my members are called 'Piranha' by their tenants when they request the rent."

Eamon Sullivan, director of ConeGrasp Properties and a leading member of the campaign said: "Things have got really bad of late. Collecting rents has become a nightmare for some landlords. We use the Moses Brothers to collect from out tenants who slip into arrears.

SPECIAL READERS OFFER

VIDEO/DVD OF TRIALS Vol VII:

"The Big Dipper"

See again in the comfort of your own home more than TWO HOURS of highlights of the complete punishment performances of the Big Dipper; comes complete with slow motion close-ups of all the main action:

SEE THEIR FACES AS THEY ARE SAWN IN HALF!
HEAR THEIR SCREAMS AS THE CIRCULAR SAW RIPS INTO THEIR BODIES!
SEE THE LANDLORDS TEARING THE FLESH FROM THEIR BONES!
AND MUCH, MUCH MORE!..

Includes Jean Charles Decoursu's music, specially composed for the Hisogynist's punishment routines: tastefully and caringly edited for you to enjoy and add to your collection:

Call 0800 325 874

Despite the Aliens locating the crash site of their lost spaceship the mass exodus of people from the area continues unabated. Polly Portillo one of the few outsiders in the region from Iruitos, northern Peru

Susem spaceship's search forces further mass exodus

THE SUSEM announcement of a wider search area for further remains of their spacecraft has sent a further flow of refugees fleeing westward to Iquitos, capital of Peru's Loreto province.

Already hopelessly overcrowded from earlier influxes of refugees Iquitos is fast sliding out of police and army control. For several days, river traffic laden with thousands of refugees has arrived at this rundown river port.

Many drowned

New arrivals describe scenes of chaos and panic among those trying to escape the Susem's arrival. Some of the river ferries were so crammed with people that many fell over-board. Three are reported as capsizing with many drowned.

The entire province of Loreto is said by the mayor of Iquitos, Dom Fidel, to now be out of Government control.

Drug traffickers fleeing

He said: "Many are fleeing, including the guerillas, even the narcos (drug traffickers) are quitting.

The Amazon is now the front line between the world and the Alheio (Aliens). Who knows when the Alheio will come here? I am seeking President Leguia's permission to decamp to Chiclayo."

The original Susem search area was centred across the Brazilian border near Sao Antonio. But it now appears to cover an area of three million square kilometres (a million square miles) encompassing southern Colombia and northern Bolivia as well as the whole Brazil's Acre province.

Along the west bank of the Amazon, both north and south of Iquitos, the Peruvian army has hurriedly stations thousands of troops in an attempt to halt any further Susem incursions westward. However, morale among them is said not to be particularly high

Stinging wasps

Recent arrivals like those ... 'vespas' and seeing their delta shaped craft, others claim to have seen columns of men alighting from them.

Among those claiming to have seen these men were a research team from Cornell University. Group leader Walt Shultz, said: "Within minutes of seeing three Alien craft fly over our research station at Letica on the border units of these little guys marched into town Anyone who was not a native was given 15 minutes to get out. Though they weren't armed they came with those wasp things, so we left."

Howard Marks in La Paz reports: Units of the Bolivian armed forces were being rushed north in an effort to quell disturbances in the country's Pando and Bendi provinces as people flee the area which is now under de facto Susem control. Both these border regions are big ... growing areas

Menpemelo moved this second tree and stood it in front of a gap from which the lamp making the spheres, shone. Its meshed image appeared but in only one of the spheres. "Envisage," she said breaking the silence, "the shapes as incoming information, the bi-contexts as templates upon which its encrypting takes place and also as transmitters of such data to the tri-context hologram sphere where it is recorded. As fresh data is received the hologram adjusts what it has already stored. The hologram is capable of responding and changes its profile accordingly to transmissions by any number of bi-context templates. In turn these bi-context templates are receivers of information back from the hologram."

Before I had chance to ask anything we had moved to the next apparatus. Though simpler, it was composed of a circle of sphere-creating sections. Menpemelo clicked on the lamp of the first. Anuria the next, then the next until there was a ring of inter-twinning spheres above the arena. Menpemelo placed a meshed tree in front of one of these lamps. Its speckling shape projected into this lamp's spheres. Then into the pair touching them, though the image was fainter. Then the next pair, then the next and so on. Anuria and Menpemelo stood more meshed tree shapes in front of the other lamps. Soon each sphere set sported a differently arranged thicket of sparkling trees. Then they took the trees away and Anuria, arm and fingers outstretched, held one of them and stuck it into one of the sets of spheres. Immediately its image appeared in all the others.

Putting it back down and with neither she nor Menpemelo saying anything and me struck with awe, we moved on to yet another similar sized circle. But this one was made up of hundreds of much smaller sections. No sooner had the pair of them switched on the lamps than there was a froth of tiny spheres bubbling against one another. "It is possible," Menpemelo then said, "to create smaller and smaller spheres, and more of them, but they would not be visible to our eyes."

Walking over to the split beam apparatus she had first showed me a month ago, Menpemelo said "You will no doubt recall how lightwaves in this went to a particular counter?"

I nodded and she continued, "Also my subsequent mention of Secondary waves recording their interactions with one another and with those of Tertiary waves?"

I nodded again and she again continued, "Within each sphere is embedded such recorded interactions. Now, consider," she said folding her arms across her, "smaller spheres, more compact and containing oscillations at the higher, steeper end of the Secondary wave spectrum." With her seeing me nodding yet again, she added, "And in the quinth context."

Arms still folded she said "A hologram in the visual spectrum and the size of a pea will contain, and this is but a loose analogy, the equivalent processing and storage potential of all of (and she stressing 'all of') your planet's current computer memories."

Even before I could say "Ooh," Anuria added "Visual oscillations are bigger,

In the current controversy over Security raised by the recent Susem broadcast one question needs to be asked:

What is 'security'?

Nora Matthews
Home Affairs Editor

Geraldine Charn, Professor of Sociology at Sheppey University, maintains the nature of people's perception of security is heavily influenced by the nature of the society in which they live. She contends that people view of 'security' stems from their 'fear's.

In her forthcoming book on the subject *The Willing of Want* (HarpCollins) Prof. Charn reveals the extent to which the notion of 'security' has been manipulated by commercial and political interests for their own ends. Prof Charn says: "Rather than addressing genuine concerns people may have about their future well-being. Others, by turning these concerns into 'Fears', exploit them for their selfish ends.

"In many societies the extended family and where there is a close knitting of a community ensures old people continue to have a useful function until their last days if no more than caring for its younger members. At the same time, by living in and being part of such groups they are able to be cared for efficiently and dare I say it, 'cheaply'.

"In the West and other so-called 'advanced societies' we have saddled ourselves not only with the consequences of making old people feel they are redundant but actually making them so. One of which is the high commercial/institutionalised costs of looking after (or 'managed care' to use the commercial jargon). For example, the actual cost of providing an elderly person with a day's adequate nutrition is less than five per cent of providing a single 'Meal on Wheels' plate of indifferent food.

"The charges in providing a week's care for an elderly person in a 'Nursing Home' is more than 20 times that of them being with their own family. Managed care for the elderly nowadays is 'big business' and a very profitable one too. Is it no wonder that some of the world's biggest companies have subsidiaries in this field. The 'knock-on effects of this is that we are all hectored to make increasing financial provision f[or] our old age.

"What is the sense", Prof Charn also said, "of peopl[e] accumulating savings dur[ing] their lifetimes only t[o] leave it (after the 'health carers' have had thei[r] swathe of it) to their chil[dren] who are more ofte[n] than not in their middle 50s. An age group who not only have little need fo[r] their parents' wealth but are already 'entrapped' in the same 'saving for old age treadmill' as them?"

Prof. Charn is advocating an alternative approach to providing for old age. She says money currently being spent for old age would be better spent in encouraging better community relations. This, she says, will be

Fourth test: O'Mally hits Namibians for 6 after 6

ENGLAND'S hopes of a Fourth Test win were boosted yesterday by newcomer Abdul O'Mally. At the close of play he was on 87 including five sixes and four fours.

In a fifth order partnership with Smith then Higgins, O'Mally took England's first day score to 93. Before he strode to the crease at Edgebaston, England's hopes were looking decidedly slim not to say dire. The opening pair Watson and Hillier soon both fell to Bullawao's bowling and van Keipt's wicket keeping.

At the beginning of the second over and the score standing at 3 for 2, the Gods came to England's aid in the form of dark rain bearing clouds. These continued to deluge Birmingham and Edgebaston, in particular with intermittent ...

S. America slashed in tw[o]

Latin's plight falls on deaf US ears

By Roger Ibarra
in Panama City

AT AN emergency meeting of the Organization of American States (OAS), beleaguered leaders of countries affected by the spreading Alien backed Nonette movement called on the US for military help. But they pleaded in vain.

With the loss of Ecuador, increasing swathes of a further four countries falling to Nonette control, Latin American leaders departed with little more than a homely lecture from the US delegates to clean up their domestic policies towards the poor. But as the Peruvian representative, Hernando Voares said: "Even if such action was possible we do not have the time."

Aaron Weiss, head of the US delegation, made it abundantly clear that his country is in no position to help its southern neighbours. With President Warren's administration still reeling from the Tonic-water fiasco, any further military

action in South America would cause a storm of domestic protest.

As one unnamed US delegate commented: "We were castigated by these [S. American] guys back in May for trying to rid the Aliens from their countries. Now they are demanding we wade in there to rescue them!"

This hardening US sentiment against any form of intervention in Latin America was confirmed by Weiss. He s[aid] US public opinion was broa[dly] in favour of the Susem a[nd] against South American [re]gimes. He added succ[ess] against the Alien backed No[nette] movement had as much [to] do with winning the 'hearts an[d] minds' of the affected coun[tries'] populations as com[bating] the Nonettes militarily.

Another of the criticisms lev[ell]ed by US representatives against the South Americans [is] their apparent unwillingness to confront the Nonettes militarily. One US delegate said: "For years they have lavished billions on their armies but when it comes to fighting they run away without so much as firing a shot."

In response to US accusations of military unpreparedness, the South American's retort that the Aliens are waging a 'psycho-war' against which their forces have no defence. So far though, none of the affected soldiers have been shown to be ... from battle injuries con... with a

Bishop in SLI TV's 'Trials' lambaste[d]

'Trials: New heights of cruelty' Bishop alleges

By Lena Gavell
Religious Affairs Editor

A LEADING Bishop slated the media yesterday for their widespread coverage of the Bosnian War Crimes Trials. However, the Bishop, the Rt Rev. Hug Latimer singled out SLI TV for being the worst offender.

With its daily showing of the 'Trials' live televising of the executions of War Criminals, it is proving to be SLI's most popular programme ever and is attracting an all-time record number of viewers.

Attending a gathering at the Uppingham Experience Centre, the Bishop of Buckingham, said: "Those who televise these staged executions are as guilty as those who perpetrate them.

"It is the duty of Christian men and women everywhere to stand up to these purveyors of cruelty and say: 'This must stop,'" he said.

"We are witnessing daily on our television screens and elsewhere new heights of cruelty being meted out to dozens of defenceless men in the name of 'entertainment' and a vehicle for advertising.

"The gratuitous executions of these men, and which are carried out in the most barbarous fashion are serving only to satisfy the basest of human gratification and to swell the pockets of media moguls," the Bishop said.

Bishop Latimer told the conference that he is to spearhead a campaign to get the showing of 'Trials' banned from television and other areas of the media.

Igg's rebuttal

SLI's chief, Derek Igg, in response to the Bishop's allegations said: "Defenceless men my eye. These Balkan ogres were found guilty of committing heinous crimes against women and children.

"When these thugs were committing their outrages against defenceless women and children we never heard even a murmur from these limp wrested bleeding heart bishops."

"When the Orthodox Christian Serbs and Catholic Christian Croats were massacring defenceless Bosnians wholesale we never heard a word of protest coming from the Pope and the Orthodox's head padre either.

"Neither did we hear a single utterance coming out of the mouths our C of E bishops calling on their so-called fellow Christians to stop their wickedness.

"So we at SLI say to these mealy mouthed mitred muftis: 'Stick to your dry sherry and let us get on with our work in ridding the world of sinners in peace,'" he said.

The Bishop of Buckingham was unavailable [for comment] yesterday for comment on Mr Igg's remarks. An aide to the Bishop, however, said that as soon as he returned from inspecting river craft at Uppingham

'Trials': 'Death by the lance' full detail an[d] pics pages 6, 7, 9, 10 Reader's video/DVD offe[r] details page 24

Andean flight of the fearful

FROM POLLY PORTILLO
IN LIMA

THOUSANDS of fear-driven refugees fought one another on Guayaquil's quaysides in desperate bids to board one of the dwindling number of boats prepared to run through the eye of the tightening Nonette noose.

Unscrupulous crews demanded fistfuls of US dollars for barely more than standing space on their skimpy overladen craft to ferry this panic-stuck human cargo along the coast to neighbouring Columbia or Peru.

Portside mayhem was more than matched by events elsewhere in this shell-shocked city. Giant palls of smoked billowed from government offices and barracks as officials hurriedly burnt files of documents. Mobs roamed the streets; buildings in the central business district were sacked and looted. Many were ablaze.

Those unable to flee by sea sought escape southward on the Pan-American Highway. A convoy of vehicles, bumper to bumper, stretched all the way to the Peruvian border 200 miles away. A journey of four hours in normal times today took ten. But a string of crashed and abandoned cars and trucks bore testament that many failed in their desperate drive to the border.

Countless columns were forced to trek in the broiling equatorial sun. At the Peruvian border itself greedy officials were demanding payment from the bewildered refugees for entry into the country and the awaiting tented camps. Red Cross officials expected influx of 100,000 refugees but already this number has been seen as

shallower than those at the higher end of the spectrum."

"Also," Menpemelo said, "in the quinth context there is a lower level of resistance and consequential faster transmission interaction."

Though at last getting a grasp of auras I still had confusion and so asked "What happens when the lights are switched off, the energy is stopped?" But soon half wished I'd not asked for Menpemelo then had me in a tennis match of question and answer.

She began with a pause, as if thinking, then lobbed "To what distance is it possible to see through water?"

"Yards and yards...metres...a long way if clear," I said

"What is mist?"

"Fog, moisture...water."

"Airborne droplets of water to be precise. What is its density relative to actual water?"

"Mist's nothing...a hundredth?"

"More than a thousandth. How far is it possible to see though mist?"

"Inches...centimetres."

"It is possible to see through many metres of failing rain is it not?"

"Yes."

"Then why not mist?"

With me at a loss Menepemelo lobbed her, "What colour is water?"

"Water doesn't have colour, that's why it's clear."

"Frozen water, ice, icicles, what colour are they?"

"They don't have colour either."

"How translucent is ice?"

"Fairly...you can see through it, sometimes for a foot, metre, more."

"What is snow?"

"Frozen water, er.."

"Latticed crystals of ice to be precise. Why is snow white and ice not? Why does snow's white disappear when it melts. Why is the frozen water of snow opaque compared to that of ordinary ice?"

Having finally reduced me to the 'love, nothing' of "Don't know," I had to let her explain. "Entrapped oscillations of full spectrum light," was first. The next, "Light entering a snow flake's lattice of crystals is reflected back and forth by them as would a myriad of mirrors. Snow's entrapment of light is why it appears to be opaque and ice is not. Mist is light entrapped between the reflecting surfaces of water droplets.

"As perhaps previously observed, once lightwaves are within snow or mist and given pertinent conditions, they will remain to reflect from mirror to mirror indefinitely. The energy of this light spectrum's oscillations is never latent, always kinetic, dynamic, always in movement."

Even before she said "Mist and snow are not the only entrappers of Secondary waves," I grasped that the spheres of auras were entrappers of pre-programmed energy, it went in and didn't come out. Then I had another question, "As some of the energy has to come out, how does it come out?"

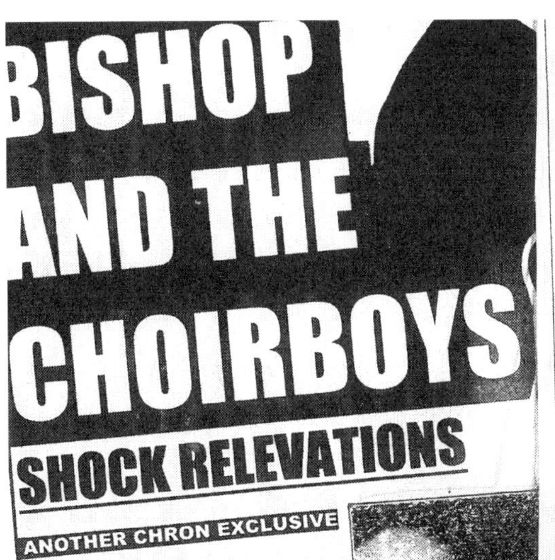

BISHOP AND THE CHOIRBOYS

SHOCK RELEVATIONS

ANOTHER CHRON EXCLUSIVE

By MALCOLM LEAKS

A LEADING leftwing Bishop stood accused yesterday of committing un-Christian acts against a string of innocent young choirboys.

Although this serial molester of the cloth, who cannot be named for legal reasons, we can to reveal the alleged offences were perpetuated when he was a novice priest in a Bury St. Edmonds Church.

Following the shocking disclosures made to this newspaper by one of the Bishop's then juvenile victims - who is now on the stage - we can reveal that this sinning cleric not only has a comfortable home countries diocese but he is a member of the Church of England Synod.

When confronted with the dossier of his wrongdoing not only did the bishop deny the allegations but has had the temerity but to threaten this newspaper with a legal action

SORDID DETAILS OF PERVERT BISHOP: PAGE 3

"Nonettes are Communists" - claim Senators

By Billy Bob
in Washington

The Nonette movement sweeping across South America has been branded by leading Us Senators as: "Nothing less than an Alien-backed 'Communistic' style front whose prime objective is to spread terror."

Testifying before the US Senate Armed Services Subcommittee on the fall Ecuador, a group led by 96 year-old Senators Sam Dich of Iowa and Harold Lonergan, said that the Nonette movement must be seen as a threat to US and Western security and every lawabiding citizen's way of life.

Senator Dich claimed the recent Nonette television programmes clearly showed that the people under Susem control had been 'brain washed' into accepting a Soviet-style dictatorship.

Senator Dich was supported by fellow Senator Harold Lonergan. He said: "The panic Nonette forces caused in Ecuador was the same as with the fall of Phnom Penh. What

Senator Lonergan

enslavement of a once free people back to a Year Zero

"Though this time it is not happening in Asia but right here in America's backyard How long will it be before this Socialism sows its cancerous seeds right here in the US? The time has come for this country to prepare itself for attack against to this threat to our liberty," he said.

"It is essential that the Department of Homeland and Security is as ever watchful and diligent in giving full warning to the American people this Alien creed rearing its ugly head in the United States of America."

However, other voices in the US view events in South America in a less apocalyptic light. Professor David Souter head of IAS a Georgetown University thinktank, is one. He says: "The Nonette phenomenon is more communitarian than communist.

"What we saw down there [in Ecuador] was not mass flight of the population but of the wealthy and privileged along with the government, many of its officials and military personnel.

"The governments in all the Latin countries, democratic or not, have always have always ruled autocratically, perpetuating the power of the 'haves, over the 'have-nots'. It is perhaps no wonder, that given the chance to shake off the grip and nepotism of their rulers the ordinary people have jumped at the chance," he said.

Although Senators Dich and Lonergan are regarded as hawks in US political circles, their views are likely to receive

Cadets snatched in Susem sex swoop

l from nearby ships.

Do the wealthy really get their riches from exploiting the poor?

Is 'Red Jim' right?

By Helena Juniper
Social and Ethics Editor

James Powell, the tabloids' 'Red Jim', one of the Susem's telecasters, has been bombarding us almost weekly with telecasts comparing our contemporary societies unfavourably with the new one taking shape in the Susem controlled northern Brazil.

But are Powell's criticisms justified? And for that matter, are the attacks made against him in the media and elsewhere fair?

Rich getting richer

Powell claims that global capitalism makes the rich richer at the expense of the poor.

Here Powell appears on firm ground. Fewer than 400 individuals ***and not companies*** currently own more than half the world's capital wealth.

Poor getting poorer

The poor South of the world currently pays more each year in interest payments on money owed to the rich North. This sum is more than these developing countries receives in new loans and all other forms of inward investment ***combined.***

In Britain the bottom tenth of the population is now poorer relative to the top tenth than at any time in ***more than a century.***

Twenty years ago in the US ***half*** of the population earned below average incomes, ***today two thirds do.***

Fat cat EU farmers

The EU is financed by a third of VAT paid by member countries' consumers. A third of the EU's expenditure is its Common Agricultural Policy (CAP). Most of the CAP payments go to the EU's farmers, who represent ***less than two per cent*** of the EU's population.

CAP payments guarantee Europe's farmers high minimum prices for their produce. As a result, EU farmers produce ***twice as much*** food as its EU's consumer's can absorb.

This surplus is then dumped at subsidised prices, at a fraction of its cost onto third world markets.

Starving farmers

Farmers in the developing world are unable to compete with such artificially low prices. As a result few of these farmers grow cash crops, especially for export.

But among these farmers who do attempt to grow such crops for export face high first world (such as the EU's) import tariffs. These tariffs are put in place solely to protect rich farmers' artificially and subsidised high prices. And again making it unviable for developing world farmers to grow crops for export.

As a result this they stay poor. But so do people in the first world.

Poor pay to the rich

Poor people pay a higher percentage of their money on food than rich ones. Thus, in both the First and Third World, poor people give money to farmers who - in Britain at least - are rich.

Insult has been added to this injury. Within the EU its rich, highly subsidised farmers are further ***paid yet more money*** - again also out of the CAP - to set aside land ***to grow nothing at all!***

This is but one detailed example of the poor subsidising the rich to become richer. There are many others.

Rich poisoning poor

Powell's claim that people's health is at risk by much of the food sold to them also has substance.

The case of scabies contaminated feed fed to cattle and the resulting 'Mad Cow' disease with its onward transmission of CJD to humans is well documented. But there is another even more insidious example. And like Mad Cow disease it is brought about for the same reason: the unscrupulous exploitation of ignorant people for personal gain by the few.

Two billion of the world's people go hungry, yet more than half the population of the United States have been diagnosed as clinically - thus life expectancy shortened - obese.

It is estimated that just 10 per cent of the sum spent on food by the First World's clinically overweight would feed these hungry two billion.

First World food distributors' spend $75 billion - ***20 per cent of total world advertising expenditure*** - annually on advertising their wares. A sum, which if invested in third world agriculture, would also provide enough food for the hungry.

If First World fatties ate just ten per cent less, the saving of medical costs resulting from their improved health would more than equal that of feeding those two billion hungry.

Rich rob the poor

Powell claims that financial institutions are ripping off the ordinary investors also has substance.

Where does the money come from to pay those huge City salaries? It comes from we the 'little people'. In creaming small amounts from the many - pension and insurance policy holders - ***obscenely huge sums are being creamed-off*** by these so called 'financial advisors'. They claim to direct our savings into better paying investments but in reality, and as we now all know, their number one priority is to make rather more than merely a quick buck or two out of the commission they receive

Abducted climbers found

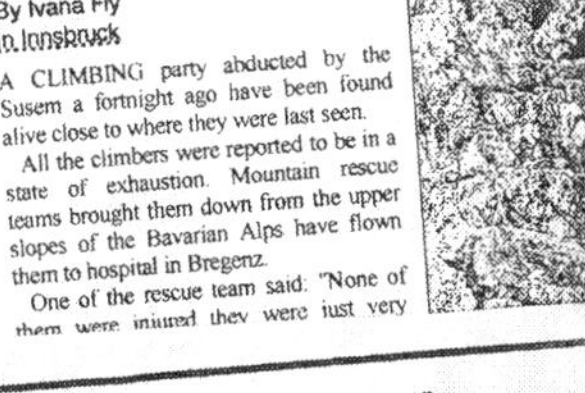

By Ivana Fly
In Innsbruck

A CLIMBING party abducted by the Susem a fortnight ago have been found alive close to where they were last seen.

All the climbers were reported to be in a state of exhaustion. Mountain rescue teams brought them down from the upper slopes of the Bavarian Alps have flown them to hospital in Bregenz.

One of the rescue team said: "None of them were injured they were just very

World leaders for 'Nonette T Crisis Summi

Clive Menace
In Washington

IN a dramatic move to combat the growing threat of the Alien backed Nonette movement, world leaders attended a surprise closed-doors summit meeting.

The first the outside world knew of the meeting was a bland communique issued through the Bloomfield News Service: "At the invitation of the president of the United States of America, fellow leaders of the world community gathered to agree joint policies toward a range of current security concerns."

That such an unprecedented meeting should take place and in such secrecy is indication of t ments worldwi power the None indication has unanimity, if attending.

But events Nonette's glob them must hav president an collective ac officials arou play down broadcasts, many parts is setting a v

But not relishing another forehand of her questions and my net-snared replies, Isaid nothing, just listened.

But instead of Menpemelo continuing Anuria did, "Though visual spectrum Secondary waves oscillate at differing speeds others move faster," she said.

This sparked yet another question. If something moves faster than light then you would see it arrive before it left, how can this be? But all the same I kept mum. Anuria no doubt noticing my frown, said "Light from your sun takes nine of your minutes to oscillate to Earth, while those reflected by way of the moon take one and a half of your seconds more. Such durations are easily measurable and comprehensible but lightwaves oscillating a few millimetres, perhaps not."

As Anuria spoke, she had her pad flipped open, pressed it along the side and said, "In your measurements, a decimal point, eleven noughts and 375 of a second to travel a millimetre."

But Menpemelo said "Or trillionths of one...though across a trillionth of a millimetre...we are not aware of there being devices developed by you (I took this to mean Earthly science) capable of relevantly, accurately measuring such small dimensions and duration. Yet it is within these where variability occurs in the relativity of..."

At this point Terbal floated across (it was half time in the football) and overhearing, interrupted with "I hafe been reading (he had been at the Internet again) der vere at the University of Innsbruck some experiments recently vich hafe transmitted Mozart's 40th symvony encrypted in modules of light at vour und a half times der speed of der light und over ein metre..."

As he spoke, as I looked at his whiteness, his mistiness it dawned on me what he must be composed of, entrapped energy.

With an image of myriad minute mirrors flashing back and forth inside him, I listened on, "...dey vere vright in dere observations but in der understanding of dere mefvords dey vere vrong...but ven (and he giving his fronds a waggle of a shrug) dey not haffing der apparatus to separately measure der oscillations...vat can dey do?"

He glided away (the football had come back on) and Menpemelo continued, "Envisage each aural sphere bounded by a skin. Vibrate, indent it and not only will the rest of its surface be affected but also its contained formations. Envisage, also, this happening so rapidly that relative to animate neural response and perception time, they are faster than instantaneous. This is how, or so we understand, transmission occurs within and between auralate structures as well as they to a being's neural pathways, primarily in you as in us, the falx cerebri."

As Menpemelo spoke she with Anuria went to another piece of kit, a tiny see-saw. Menpemelo next picked up a small packet, then handed Anuria a second, identical one. They placed them either end of the see-saw. It was in balance. They poured the packets' contents, they looked like salt, on to either end of the see-saw. And again it was in balance.

"How many grains are here?" Menpemelo asked.

US President warns Nonettes

By Andy Graham
in Washington

PRESIDENT WARREN, in his first major policy speech since the 'Tonic Water' affair, announced moves by US to combat the growing influence of the Nonette movement.

Speaking at a rally of Army veterans in Pittsburgh, the idly by in the face of the increasingly threat to our national security Day after day the hearts and minds of ordinary Americans are being assailed by the lulling entreaties of this self-styled Nonette movement

"This neo-socialist creed has already destabilised and over-run many of our southern gravely concerned at the deteriorating security situation in our hemisphere, it is presently prudent to stay any course of pro-active response.

"But this does not mean we have for one moment dropped our guard Any foe of the Free World must be seen as a threat to America and all of those basic human rights that she

Outrage at Red Jim's call

By John Tickleby
Social Affairs Correspondent

THE NONETTE'S 'Red Jim' Powell's latest telecast called on viewers worldwide to join up to their style of society. But his 20 minute programme has brought a string of protests from all quarters.

Backed by a chorus of an estimated 10,000 people all dressed in identical white tunics Prior delivered his message to the background of John Lennon's "Imagine".

He claimed the territory under Nonette control was a land of peace and harmony. A land where all deprivation has been banished, the rich work with the poor so they might also be wealth, sickness and disease things of the past.

But what has provoked many politicians' and other professionals' anger ... achieved through the abolition of governments, armies, police forces and any other kind of official authority. He claimed Nonettes lived in interdependent communities managing their own affairs as they saw fit.

One of those outraged at the broadcast is Sir Robert Smythe, the Oxford MP and a fierce critic of the BBC and other channels screening the Nonette programmes in the past. He said: "What was shown last night was the last straw. Pure old-style Socialist propaganda of the most blatant kind.

"Coming as it does on the heels of Prior's earlier programmes, it is already fuel to the flames of a potentially dangerous situation. That the BBC and others should broadcast this un-adulterated mishmash of what is little more than Marxist diatribe are only adding fuel to a potentially damaging

BOSNIAN WAR TRIALS LATEST:

Igg tells carpin clerics to 'Shut i

By ANGIE TUFTS

SLI BOSS Derek Igg gave a blunt message yesterday to criticisms of TV's most popular programme: 'Shut it'.

Derek's tough talk comes in the wake of moves being made to block shock scenes from 'Trials', which is watched worldwide by 100s of millions daily.

The programme's no-holes-barred approach to live showing of Serb and Croat thugs guilty of ... rises in popularity by the day.

It has sent the Hisogynists, a formerly unknown US women's 'performance troupe', to the top of international stardom. With their mixture of dry humour, dance routines and robust workouts on the guilty they have attracted a huge popular following.

"A bunch of bleeding hearts, led my narrow-minded, men-loving clerics is trying to deny millions of ordinary people their chance to see justice being done," said Mr Igg.

Do YOU our readers think it's time that these mealy mouthed mitred humbugs should halt their crusade to stop you from watching shows that you want to see? If YOU think that these clerics must be clamped, then we want to hear from YOU.

As we are also sure the Bishop would want to hear from you, his posh country villa's number is:

01272 874323.

Though reliable sources say he is also to be found hanging outside the gents

Susem's 'Fermic fisheries breakthrou

By Roddy Mackeral
Oceans Editor.

SUSEM BACKED experts are to replenish the world's depleted fish populations. The first regions will be the Adriatic and parts of the western Atlantic.

Explaining the moves, Susem telecaster, Rainbow Louis, said crumb-sized particles of pumice, coated with a film of iron, which she called 'Fermice', had floated on the surface of the sea and encouraged the rapid growth of plant plankton.

These are eaten by animal plankton which in turn are eaten by bigger sea - creatures and so on.

Ms Louis added fur-ther areas of the world's oceans, especially the most over-fished, such as the North Sea, would soon be 'seeded' with the particles.

Ms Louis announced however, that the fish regeneration programme should not be seen as a 'green light' for resumption of deep sea trawling. That she said: "Was a thing of the past."

The programme also showed a series of lakes which were, Ms Louis said, the future of fishing and fish stocks. The lakes she said were created from natural depressions in the ground.

Alien cocaine trade takeover fears rise

By Jonny Brascoe
Narcotics Correspondent

FEARS were expressed yesterday that the real reason for the Alien's presence in the west of Latin America to seize control of the world's cocaine supply and not unearth their lost spacecraft.

Narcotics enforcement agencies and police forces worldwide are said to be anxiously watching for signs of the Alien's infiltration of the drugs trade. The global alarm has been sparked off by a string of reports from the affected regions that supplies to the outside world have slowed to a trickle.

In the US, Perry Noid, an expert on the US drug trade and the barons behind it, said: "It's perfectly obviously what the Aliens are up to. They are after control American's dependen on narcotic drugs. Onc the Aliens have contr of them it means tha they will have control o a significant cohort o our civilian population And once the Aliens have got

Abduction families given hope by climbers find

By Mark Lavello
In Milan

HOPES HAVE risen that the athletes, policemen and others abducted by the Susem will be returned safely.

So far there have been eight reported cases of Alien abductions across southern Europe totalling more than 200 men. The abductions have stretched from Spain to Austria.

The missing men's families and various officials have publicly appealed to the Susem for their safe return but until today it had been to no avail.

However, the reported release of the Austrian climbers has sent hopes soaring among the anxious families of the others who have been taken, that their men will be safely returned.

The parents of one of the 17 years old boy climbers said that they hoping and praying that nothing bad had happened to their sons. One mother said: "My Hans is such a nice boy I hope that the Susem

Castrated MP free to leave Bosnia

By Linda Gruff
in Ragusa

SIR Hugh Russett-Brown looking pale and drawn and in obvious discomfort said he hoped to return to Britain within the next few days.

Sir Hugh said: "As soon as I have arranged for my $500,000 release fee to be delivered to the Bosnian Nonettes I am told I will be free to leave."

Sir Hugh said he had only praise for the new Bosnian regime and

"Thousands, millions, but there must be about the same either end or they would not be in balance," I said.

After her "Correct," she took a pinch from a third packet and said "how many grains do I have in my hand?"

"A hundred, if that?"

"Correct, now watch." No sooner had she sprinkled them on the pile at her end of the see-saw than all the salt grains at Anuria's end slid down and joined Menpemelo's. Brushing her hands she said "A nuance of change can invoke disproportionate emphasis of outcome not just upon the arrangement of particles but the balance of Secondary wave interaction response. A single vibration to the surface of one sphere can incite, excite, its inner structural composition and those of other spheres."

With thoughts of butterflies' beating wings bringing on hurricanes, and relief in at last knowing what Menpemelo meant by "excitement", she called out "We have ended" to Terbal, though I don't think he heard (from the noise, a goal had just been scored) and we walked back down to the refractory with the pair of them talking on and me all attentive.

"Earlier I mentioned as well as showed," Menpemelo said "auras are comprised of discrete yet inter-related parts, nodules. However, their continual collective coordination constitutes what is, as I said then, a 'sentient entity'. In a like manner coordination occurs between one such entity and another, between a nodule of one and those of another, others. The extent to which they do so is relative to their degree of syneresic need."

"What's 'syneresic need'?" I asked.

Anuria said, and as casually as could be, "Syneresic need, synergy, the drawing together of disparate entities for enhanced constituent mutual advantage."

But she had lost me, and seeing so Menpemelo said "I will explain."

She began with "Information is transmitted, inputted to a being's aura via templates. Some templates evolve with the being as it matures but pre-existent ones aid in this maturing..."

I still didn't understand. And again seeing so and giving a slight sigh she said "I will begin at the beginning, right back to the Anthropic Constant, the Anthropic Template."

By now I was all attentiveness of concentration then suddenly all slump of spirit. Pheteriso appeared.

"Anuria! There you are."

With no more than a "Goodbye," from her, a nod and "We will talk on," from Menpemelo, all three went off dancing, and I was left palely loitering yet again. Not just for missing out on what Menpemelo was about to tell but knowing I will never know, for I won't ever see her again.

It's not that I want to go, I have to. I would have happily stayed for it's been good here in Tabajara, to mention nothing of the experience and awareness gained and there is so much more I need to know, but with just two days left it's too late to stop anything.

The future of fishing is fishing with 'fish'

By Roddy Mackeral
Sealife Editor.

ARTIFICAL INLAND lakes carved out of desert depressions and teeming with fish, are they the future of fishing? Are fishing nets a thing of the past? According to the Aliens they are.

In last night's Susem telecast Rainbow Louis took viewers on a flying tour over dozens of lakes, each with their separate micro-climates and eco-systems.

Rainbow said water for the lakes was pumped from rivers as well as from the sea itself. With so much free energy from the Sun solar panels provide not only free pumping and oxygenation of each pond's water but its temperature control as well.

Rainbow said: "Each lake mimics the habitat of certain groups of sea life from the Caribbean to the Arctic." She also said all the fish in the lakes were free from all forms of pollution something which cannot be said of today's oceans.

Viewers were also shown scene that could have been straight out of a marine amusement park - acrobatic dolphins. Each lake has its resident school of them. But apart from doing mid-air back flips they also serve to catch fish.

The programme showed six dolphins herding fish towards a group of people with baskets swimming near the shore. The dolphins, catching the fish in their mouths gave them to the people.

Not long afterwards children were shown sitting astride the

Red Jim: BBC is accused of leftwing bias

By John Tickleby
Media Correspondent

POLITICIANS of all parties have protested at what they consider to be the BBC's and ITV's biased coverage of the latest Nonette broadcast. Government ministers are demanding a mandatory right of reply and rebut the claims made in future broadcasts.

One unnamed government source said: "It is important that a balancing view is given. The government and other bodies are increasingly concerned at the harm these programmes are doing to public confidence."

The BBC and other broadcasters have frequently said that they screen the Nonette programmes on strict comercial considerations. Media analyst George Palmer of G.O.D., said: "The main networks have little choice but to screen the programmes. If they do not their ratings would take a nosedive. The latest viewing figures show audiences have, if anything, shown a rise on all the terrestrial channels for Red Jim's latest programmes.

"These figures also indicate many people who would not normally watch television at this time are making a particular point to see the programmes." This is backed by numerous reports from across Britain where the latest programme ... Here, viewers actually joined in by singing along to the music.

However, such considerations count for little in the eyes of many in political circles. Archie Nicholls the LibCon opposition Home Secretary said: "These [Nonette] programmes are nothing short of Marxist-Communist style propaganda. No political party would be allowed to broadcast such misleading falsehoods as this man Prior is doing. To my mind he is little short of a latterday Lord Haw Haw.

"Unfortunately it appears our broadcasters lack moral fibre and refuse ...

Alien abductions leav[e] authorities guessing

BY SAM ANDRC
ALIEN EDITOR

POLICE forces across southern Europe are to coordinate activities in a bid to combat the string of Alien abductions across their countries.

The task force is to be set up to assess the likelihood of future Susem attacks. Although there have not been any reported disappearances associated with the Susem during the past week, the task force's leader, Commissioner Afredo Fermi, said: "We must all be on our guard, who knows when the Aliens will strike again."

European police forces are not the only ones who have responded to the Alien's abductions. Peter Keeling, the head of a London based group of Susem Watchers, said: "To date all of these Alien abductions have followed a pattern. All those who have been taken are groups of young men of athletic, sporting disposition.

"The first group, the mountaineers, contained a woman, and as soon as the Aliens discovered this, they returned her immediately.

"Therefore, it must follow that the Aliens are using them for experiments of some kind. But on the other hand they could be using them to extract vital fluids which they must be using for building up

US denies massing force for Panama 'invas[ion]'

By Andy Graham
On Capitol Hill

THE PENTAGON dismissed reports that US forces in the western Caribbean were intending to invade Panama. A US Department of Defence spokesman said that the Navy and Army were conducting routine training exercises which were planned "many months in advance" and were in accordance with long term policy objectives which are

News

Bishop in Trials slayings protest vigil

BY DAMIEN TROTTER
RELIGIOUS EDITOR

THE Bishop of Buckingham is to stage an indefinite vigil in protest at the latest round of executions in Bosnian War Trials. In calling the executions 'judicial murders', the Bishop, the Right Reverend Hugh Latimer has nailed his flag firmly to the mast against the conduct of the War Trials punishments.

However, the Bishop is likely to find his week long vigil sparse of supporters even among his fellow clerics. While still denying allegations of molesting choir boys earlier in the week, the parents have

Ex-MP's fine shortfall shock

SIR HUGH Russet Brown, the former Cheltenham MP, has been unable to raise the $500,000 fine to the Bosnian Authorities for War Crimes offences.

Sir Hugh, who has already been castrated after being found guilty of supplying torture equipment to the former Serbian regime, was given 30 days to pay the fine or serve two years hard labour refilling disused quarries.

In an interview Sir Hugh said: "My mother has been willing to raise £50,000 by remortgaging her house, but that is all my family has been willing to find so far. My wife, instead of rushing to help, has now filed papers for divorce and is even refusing to pay a series of parking

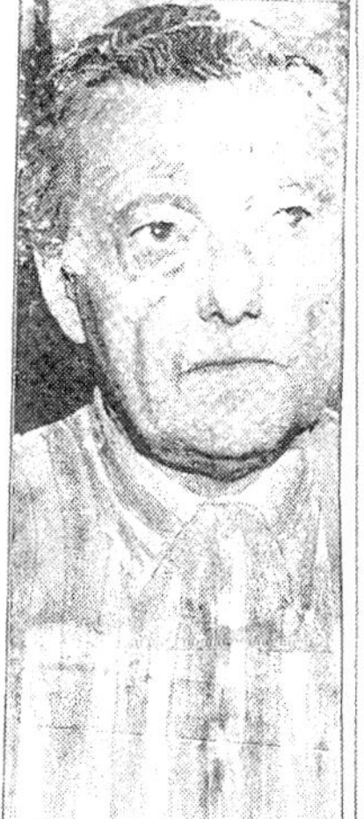

Timber hoarding as prices soar

By John Birch
Our Building Materials Correspondent

FROM LUMBERYARDS to DIY stores, timber prices have shoot through the roof.

Following the Susem block on all non-renewable tree felling, timber merchants have begun hoarding their supplies. Every woodyard is now patrolled by security guards. Some tropical hardwoods are now worth their weight in gold.

Overnight, timber merchants have become rich as the value of their wood has continued to grow. Kevin Latchford, a Croydon timber merchant, said: "I have a knotty problem in that all these extra security costs are shaving away at our margins. But of course we have to take the rough with the smooth and there is no way we would go against the grain by selling any. We are

Susem spaceship fou[nd]

By The Space-Watch Team

THE Susem have located their missing ship, it was claimed yesterday.

In their latest telecast, details were given how the wreckage was found more than 300 metres below the surface near the Peruvian Brazilian border.

The television pictures showed dramatic scenes of the extensive excavations of the crash site. According to the Susem, a cavity more than a kilo-metre square was dug from 50 metres below the surface and descended for more than 250 metres.

It was said the soil and rock of the cavity had been fused to glass which now lines the sides. Also shown were many of the Susem machines involved in the excavation.

David Willetts of Westminster University and an authority on digging deep steep sided pits, said: "The speed, yet finesse of these machines has be marvelled at. But only the privileged few have been able to witness

I could blame James for not heeding my caution but the rot really set in when Rainbow took charge. It's not really her zest of commitment as such which is to blame either, but that it's been so contagious. It's infected every Nonette. And it's grown to such a degree, that for Rainbow's final spectacular, volunteers have been turned away in their tens of thousands.

I have no wish to be churlish about what she has achieved, nor the organisational power of Nonettes. Both are impressive. Through the Nonettes Rainbow has arranged for one from each group of nine to assemble in Diamantina, north of Lençóis down south in Bahia. Millions will be gathered and double, treble this number must be involved in the support groups.

I suppose it could be seen as if I'm decamping but what else can I do? I have tried telling them but they have not listened. Though to be honest I did have a passing pang of conscience in withdrawing so much of the Patch money. But then I am more than justified in taking it, after all it is mine, well most of it is, and what isn't will soon be made up the way sales are going, and I have left enough to cover the day to day costs for a week or so.

Then it's not as if I have not done my bit these months past, and without puffing myself up too much they all , from the Susem to the Nonettes with Rainbow and James in between, have much to thank me for. And I have incurred expenses what with Rainbow's salary and Terbal's Internetting, and James still owes me for all my study points I lent him. So to my way of thinking I have been more than fair with everyone.

All the same it's sad having to go and I'm going to really miss my Lucia teaching screen. If only they had not let themselves get carried away. It's such a pity, such a waste. But then again, it's so typical of human nature, 'do gooding' dooming a good idea.

Though with everyone's attentions distracted by events down south, Rainbow is not back until tonight, Paceillo and her team are still away analysing the remains of Pa-tu, circumstances are just right for a quick flit.

But until this morning though, it looked as if I was going to be stuck. I had planned, in fact arranged, to make it over on Konnet's regular flight to Bosnia. But yesterday every remaining veda at Tabajara, including him, was diverted to help Rainbow. However, Tearo arriving when she did has been a godsend. So when she and the others leave in a few hours' time I will be away with them.

'ope denounces Hisogynis[ts] as "Angels of Satan"

[B]Y IAMA BLASPHEMER
[V]ATICAN CORRESPONDENT

[P]OPE Pius XIII in his weekly [P]apal letter denounced the Hisogynists conducting the Bosnian War Trials punishment routines as being in a "dark compact" with the Susem. He accused the Hiso[gynists of] carrying out their

Calling the Hisogynists "Handmaidens of Satan", the Pope called on all the peoples of the world, not just Christians to denounce them. He said what was happening in the Trials were acts of "incarnate darkness" and added that Christians of all persuasions should pray for the safety and well-being of senior Croats

SLI shares surge as viewing figures soar

By Montgomery Herb

SLI TV's 'Trials' has now taken 35 per cent of daytime viewing and a staggering 42 per cent of the evening TV audience. Derak Igg, SLI's CEO said of the figures: "It just goes to show how wrong those so-called 'media experts' were when they said taking on "Trials" was a big mistake

These figures also show just how misguided these carping clerics and other so-called 'do gooders' are in castigating us for showing the Trials in full. These figures prove we are showing what people want to see a good killing and lots of them."

Later a spokesman for SLI said that Mr Igg was perhaps 'over candid' in his comments.

EXCLUSIVE

ABDUCTED MOUNTAINEERS 'RAPED' BY ALIENS

Fears for missing thousands rise

By NOBBY BAKER

THE SHOCKING truth behind the Alien's 10 day abduction of 12 mountaineers from the Austrian Alps can now be revealed: they were all subjected to enforced non-stop robust lovemaking by the Aliens.

The Chron is able to reveal for the first time, full details what happened to 12 young men in the prime of life during their 10 days and 10 night's ordeal on a bare mountainside.

The terrible story of these helpless victims must heighten fears of the many hundreds of families whose loved ones are still held in the Aliens' clutches

The Chron's Kelvin Higgsy is the first outsider to gain an exclusive interview with three of the climbers the only ones so far who regain their power of speech

In their exhaustive, in-depth interview the three high climbing Alpinists tell what happened to them from the moment they were snatched by the Susem to the day they were set free.

[...] the Alpine party, along with fellow climbers Andre Bumps (24) and Adrie Say (27) were together during their 10 days ordeal. Hans, still weakened and undergoing counselling for post- traumatic shock said: "What happened to us was basically too shocking for me tell but I know I must try if only for the sake of warning others who set out on a moun[...]

RED JIM

Significant or farce?

For several weeks past we have been subjected to a series of Susem backed television programmes. What are to make of them?

Are these programmes of life in 'Nonetteland' to be dismissed as depiction of glorified student agitprop or is there something deeper contained within? What is known is these programmes attract enormous worldwide audiences. From their elaborate no-expense-spared production it can be concluded with certainty they are meant as more than mere 'infotainment'.

All of these programmes have a common theme running through them: life is better for everyone in a Nonette-style society. Maybe. But how are we to know?

How can anyone ascertain the veracity of their presenter's claims of paradise when journalists and others of informed and independent minds are repeatedly denied access to this so-called 'new society'? And because we are not then it is sensible to reserve judgement as to the veracity of their announcer's claims.

This caution notwithstanding it ill behoves the political establishments of both the Developed and Developing Worlds to condemn - as they are - these programmes as propaganda and lies. Many of the criticisms of old world institutions voiced by the Nonette presenter are not without foundation. Politicians' energies would be better spent in putting their own houses in order rather than forever bleating "foul" at the programmes' reproach of them. Therefore the world's leaders would be well advis[ed]

US denies Panama 'invasion'

CLIVE MENACE
IN WASHINGTON

A 20,000 strong US force has reoccupied the former Panama Canal Zone. The Defence Department announced the US had taken up positions across the entire length of the Zone at the invitation of the Panamanian government.

A Department spokesman said: "Premier Alfonson [of Panama] through the auspices of the Organization of American States (OAS) requested the United States to assist his country uphold its national security. Under its OAS treaty obligations the US was duty bound to assist an ally."

However, many defence analysts were sceptical of US moves. According to Edgar Kurtz of the Goldwater Centre for Peace Studies, the Panamanian request for US forces was no more than a fig-leaf to cover US security concerns.

He said: "With the fall of Ecuador to the Nonettes, half of Columbia in their hands, much else of Latin America falling under their control, our government saw taking over the PCZ as an option they dare not refuse in

"Capitalism with a human face" - what do you think?

LAST night 'Red Jim' Powell boasted that he and fellow Alien-backed Nonettes lived in a land flowing with milk and honey. A land where every boss was kind and caring, everyone wanted to work and earned lots of money. A world where no one was ever saddled with debts and all the other miseries of life. But is it all too good to be true?

"Yes it definitely is", say some experts. "No its not", say others. But what do you, our readers think? Here are some of the views we received from random calls to some of you.

Beth Strivers, 35 of Enfield and works for a large call centre said: "Personally I think that the prospect of being able to work as a team is a good idea. Where I work we already do so but the difference is that none of us get to pick the members of our team, they are all appointed by our bosses"

Ray Hudson, 43, a bricklayer from Chatham, said: "As a sub-contractor I have always worked in team so what these Nonettes are doing is nothing new. Myself I would not work in any other away. As far as the idea of everyone getting guaranteed credit, I say why not?"

James Campbell, 51 a retired army officer of Cheltenham said: "Working in teams is a perfectly natural way to operate. The entire British army operates in platoons, it's the same sort of thing isn't it? As for the constant education programmes it was always the policy when I was a serving officer to attend refresher courses, cannot speak too highly of them. To my way of thinking what this young chap Powell is saying makes darned good commonsense."

The Rev Ronald Moran, 63 of Stoke Newington and known to our older readers as "Scarface Moran" said: "In the old days when me and the boys used to do the Banks we always recruit a bespoke team for each job. So what this Nonette's Jim said about working as a team makes per[...]

"Sternest Trials yet" promised (again)

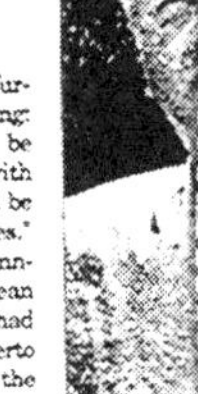

By **Oliver Stonehead**
Media Editor

SLI TV has announced that the final series of the Bosnian War Trials will be the most spectacular yet.

SLI's boss, Derek Igg, said that for the last of the series would be of the all top former leaders of the old Serb and Croat regimes.

Outlining the series Mr Igg said: "The Final Trials will show these heinous b***ards getting their fair and public trial and once they have all been found Guilty they will all be shown being punished."

He declined to give further details except adding: "Viewers of Trials will be more than impressed with the final line up. It will be a 'must be watched series."

A SLI spokesman announced later that Jean Charles Decoursu had composed special concerto "Fin Fatale" for the occasion.

"Will you be quiet!" snapped June scolding Raymond.

Not wishing to cause further upset by mentioning that I also knew the musical refrain was 'Fanfare for the Common Man', I thought it best to say nothing.

I was not particularly keen to watch the programme but it was what June had wanted. Snatches of the music had been on several times since the weekend. The papers had all given details and its "haunting reveille" as the Telegraph described it. They had also mentioned the Susem's newsgirl's accompanying fleeting appearances, or "trailers" as it termed them, and her saying that an "announcement of importance" was to made today at 8pm.

However, with the "haunting reveille" fading away I was hard put to discern any 'announcement' let alone one of "importance". All that the picture showed was near darkness. It was only when their Powell fellow said "From the high sierras of the Andes there are people..." could I make out a group of them waving goodbye to others walking up a hill. The camera then followed these walkers, the hill's crest coming into view and the sky beyond becoming brighter. Suddenly the screen was blasted in sunlight.

It could only have been for an instant but even before I had ceased blinking there was a further trumpet call and Powell's: "...and from the rivers of Amazonia..." Upon which the brightness became misty sunlight and people in canoes were paddling away from a village. With its inhabitants waving the canoeists goodbye and them fading into the mist, there was another trumpet call, another early morning scene of people departing. These were on mules and horses. With others waving handkerchiefs and Powell adding "...from the dry plains of the Seatão..." On it went, reveille after reveille and his, "...shores of the Pacific...the Atlantic...hills...valleys...villages, towns...." to "...cities, there are people travelling."

All very impressive but I could make neither head nor tail of it. Though I considered it best to say nothing and continue to watch.

No sooner had Powell finished with the "cities" than we were back in the "high Andes" once more, though the numbers travelling down from them had increased. The "rivers of Amazonia" had fleets of canoes, the dry plains columns of riders. And in the other locations the numbers on the move had grown as well. There were still the reveilles, though fainter, and Powell continued to repeat "...there are people travelling."

But I was still at a loss to make sense of it all.

Scenes of more groups followed, except such were their numbers that the picture didn't just show but now flew alongside them. From "the Andes" armies descended, canoes gave way to river steamers, trains appeared as did convoys of coaches, cars and lorries. Long columns on foot and horseback rolled across dry plains kicking up clouds of dust and parading flags and banners. The picture sped from group to group with Powell adding "Representatives are on their way..."

RED JIM:

Challenge or sedition?

Mary Siegfeld asks what is the real message of 'Red Jim's broadcasts

"COME and join us so all the world may live as one", were Red Jim Powell's closing words, or rather, a direct plagiarism of John Lennon's. And it was the sentiments of Lennon's "Imagine" which formed the backdrop to last night's Susem 20 minute broadcast.

But was Red Jim's message a plea for us all to live in peace and harmony or was it really an oblique call to us to turn against government and others in authority such as the police and the army? Many leading figures think so.

Professor Howard Neal, head of Sheppey University's Department of Global Affairs, is one who thinks it is. He said: "Each of these [Nonette] programmes would not have been transmitted without a purpose The first ones depicted the claimed idyllic nature of this Nonette society One where no one lost and everyone gained The next programmes focus on the wrongs and shortcomings of our society.

"These last ones are a mixture of how this new style society has rid itself of these shortcomings and for ordinary people across the world to live as the Nonettes do.

"The last programme is the most blatant yet The propaganda effect on ordinary people especially those who are disadvantaged is already enormous It is no surprise many leaders of countries, especially the despotic ones, are worried The question to be asked now is what will be next?"

Prof. Neal's mention of Third World unrest was given substance yesterday in both west and east Africa as people

Scores snared in spreading Susem snatches shock

By BEN SHERMANT

COUNTLESS YOUNG men from the Med to Mexico were abducted by Aliens yesterday. Police forces in the countries concerned were issuing warning to men to take care when travelling alone on in small groups.

Warnings

All the major British travel firms are sending out warnings to holiday makers going to southern Europe to take extra care whilst out in the open such as on the beach

So far no British citizens have been taken by the Aliens, with the victims being confined to foreigners. But curvaceous Tracy Adams (22), a tour guide with Gone Places, gives the warning: "Men, especially young ones, should play it safe and only go out...

Dams burst danger

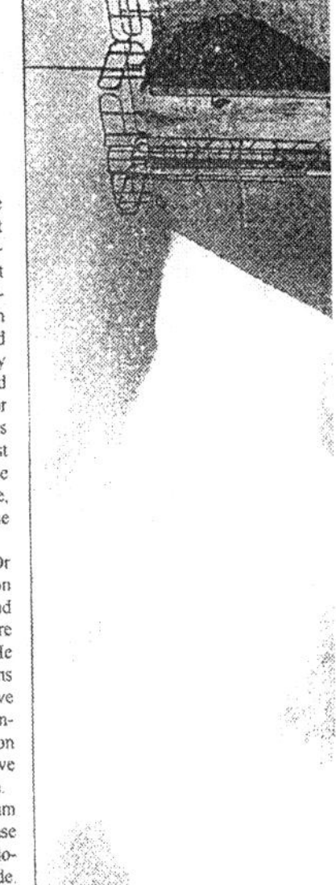

BY MAGNUS BEAVER
ENVIRONMENTAL HAZARDS CORRESPONDENT

SCORES of dams throughout the world are in danger of collapse experts say.

With the global slump for hydro-electric power many of the companies operating and managing many of the world's dams no longer exist. Without regular maintenance and inspections minor faults can quickly turn into potential disasters.

At a conference in London yesterday, called to highlight the dangers posed by many dams. Speaker after speaker voiced their concerns and the dilemmas many countries face. According to many delegates the problem dams cannot be easily drained

Pauline Reeves, a hydrologist at Southend University, said: "In many parts of the world dams serve the duel functions of electricity generation and downstream irrigation. Drain a dam of its stored water and farmland will first be flooded them parched. With the collapse of ... hydroelectric company

Dr Martin Blackman, of the University of Sheppey at Swale, said: "Generating turbines in dams need constant attention. Silt particles if unchecked can build up within the turbines. If one should jam it will not just simply stop it will heat up and explode and this is the major danger facing many dams especially those on east Asian rivers. The Three Gorges dam on the Yangsee, is currently giving me nightmares."

Elsewhere in the world Dr Blackman says the dams on the Zambezi in Africa and Rio Francisco in Brazil are already at danger levels. He said: "Both river systems have, like the Yangsee, have high large silt particle densities. Many of the dams on these rivers have extensive lakes backing up from them.

"The Sobradinho dam should it burst, would release a flood of water 300 kilometres long by 15 wide. Everything to the coast 500 km away would be washed away. The last I heard the dam had been abandoned The local inhabitant's only

TRIALS LATEST:

Once in a lifetime!

SPECIAL READERS OFFER!

THE last and final Bosnian War Trials are about to take place. *The Chron* has been reliably informed as these involve all the top leadership of both the former Serb and Croat regimes that they promise to be the most spectacular Trials and Punishments yet.

In conjunction with SLI TV, *The Chron* is able to offer our readers 100 pairs of ringside seats at the National Stadium in Sarajevo for all the performances of the three day Trail and Punishment event.

The lucky winners of our easy to enter competition (full details below) will be flown directly to Sarajevo, enjoy an all expenses paid 7 nights in the 5 Star Hotel Drina, optional free passes to all the trials and all the Punishment Performances.

How to enter *The Chron's* Easy to Win 'See the Murdering Serbo-Croat Bastards Get Their Just Deserts' Competition.

Just tick ONE of the boxes below which is best:

- **... I think that all those accused of W... should be given a fair trial and if ... cannot be proved they should be free...**
- **... I think that all those accused of W... should be given a fair trial and after ... all been found guilty they should be s...**
- **... I think that a fair trial is a waste of ... these murdering bastards.**

Now complete (IN NO MORE THAN 12 WOR... slogan:

"I think that hanging is too good for these m... bastards, what they should get is ...."

...end your completed form with just £4.99 cheque ...ministrative costs) to *The Chon* at the usual address ...e with credit or debit card at: www.chron@bear.uk

Nonettes - why the worry?

By Helena Juniper

Currently we are witness to a most unseemly scramble of those who rule over us, attempting to shore up their positions in the wake of the onward march of the Nonettes in faraway South America.

In one breath we are told the Nonettes are no more than a quasi-religious cult which will, in time, disappear just as all other such sects have done. Yet in the next breath, we are equally told that this new, Susem backed society is a threat to international security.

But what are mere mortals such as you and I to make of such alternating declarations from our 'rulers'? Indeed, what conclusions are we to draw from the rise of the Nonettes themselves?

It would appear the seemingly unstoppable growth of this movement has come about not by force of arms but because of its popularity. All reports indicate that the numbers of people from outside the region under Nonette control and braving military checkpoints attemptting to join them, far exceeds those who have fled from the area.

That most of those fleeing are landowners, state officials, policemen, politicians and others who once lauded authority and power over the populations from whence they have departed, says more of the ordinary people's wrath against them than any supposed Nonette tyranny. Yet this flight of the unloved sends a loud, clear message to their ilk the world over.

The success of the Nonettes have shown that sustained authority, be it lawfully installed or seized, can be maintained - should it face challenge - only if it has a popular mandate to do so. Those in positions of power across the rest of world will be wise to ensure they have such a mandate lest they too be swept away.

Of course those in such positions in this country and other advanced, democratic societies have no need to worry about such concerns. Or do they?

For more views, opinions and concerns, see pages 9-15

"But to where?" I wondered but still considered it best to say nothing.
The picture next took to the air and looked down at the convoys, columns, and making it evident there were indeed extremely large numbers of people on the move. Having circled numerous groups, with the cameras still swooping and soaring above them, Powell briefly broke the silence with "Trained, prepared...ready..."
"Ready for what?" I nearly said, but with Raymond now as June, head on hands, eyes glued to the screen, I still thought it best to say nothing.
Descending to waist height, the picture then swept along the lines of marchers looking up to their faces. All of which were bereft of expression, their eyes looking fixedly ahead. This, coupled with the arrayed flags fluttering about them added an air of resolute steadfastness. Then, and though it was all but drowned out by the sound of the horses, classical music began playing. It had a similar rhythm as their hooves. I had heard it before but could not place it. With the cameras rising above the marchers again this music became louder.
The music continued, but to my surprise the picture suddenly changed to one quite bereft of people. Now it was of flat topped hills with steep sides, mesas I think they are called. The picture skimmed and sped over them and Powell said "The Bola de Canudos...." Though no sooner had he spoken than the cameras, swinging left and right flew inward from these mesas. And amid Powell's "...in the Chapada Diamantina, the Plateau of Diamonds," it became evident this "Bola" was indeed a bowl and miles across at that.
The cameras sped back towards the mesas and then to the steep sided gaps between. The picture now showed columns of people streaming through these gaps. There was still the music but now it had a booming, echoing quality. With the picture promptly switching back to the tops of the mesas I saw immediately why. As the camera swept over them there were now people beating enormous drums with their hands, all of whom I noticed were clad in white tunics with matching ear muffs.
Just as quickly the picture changed yet again to zooming down around the inside of the Bola and showing a ring of people also all dressed in white with many holding flags. Still more people were marching through the gaps.
Back to the tops of the mesas and showing that the drummers were now being joined by other white-clad people who were lugging huge gongs. Then back to the Bola and a wider ring of people, others marching through the gaps. Back and forth it went, more instruments atop the mesas, more people flowing into the Bola. After several sweeps the drumming gave way to the people clapping their hands in the rhythm of the horses' cantering. Close-up shots of the assembled multitudes followed. I have never seen so many people congregated. But I was still at a loss to make sense of it all.
Then above the clapping Powell suddenly burst in with "Look!"
At this the picture instantly changed to being hundreds of feet up in the air and looking down. Before I could even guess the numbers Powell had added "Three million people!" Then, with the picture then circling downwards,

"These are but the representatives of millions and millions more! Tens of thousands rush to join with us every single day!"

Circling lower, the picture next showed the Bola, a sea of white and flags, with people now crowding up the slopes. With the clapping becoming just audible once more, Powell again exclaimed "Look! A people united...in harmony."

The picture came even lower. Powell, with his voice still raised next said "A people no longer cowed by poverty, illness, ignorance or injustice." The picture came still lower but began circling faster. Powell his voice still raised, exclaimed "Look! A people free from rulers...free from imposed leaders." The picture came even lower. Then Powell, now shouting, cried out "Look! A people who have stood up!"

A thundering boom of drums, bells, chimes, gongs blasted the air, the screen. June and Raymond jolted back. But as the sound of it died down the clapping became faster, louder. In a flash I knew what the music was, it was Tchaikovsky's "1812".

Above the clapping, Powell, voice still raised called out "Now is the time for everyone everywhere to join with us."

There was then another huge crash of bells and chimes. June and Raymond again jolted back. The sound faded. The clapping became louder. The picture zoomed back and forth above the aisles. Powell shouted "You have already the power...now join with us...have everything we have to give."

Yet another loud crash of bells, chimes. This was followed by clapping then Powell again shouting, called out "Time for you to have as us..." The picture swept ever faster over the people, Powell still exclaiming, shouted "...be as we... form as we...come to us...to know as us..."

At the bottom of the screen a small white line of lettering appeared. I leaned forward to read it but June with "Get a pen!" to Raymond, spoke it.

Powell continued, "...we will send one of us to be with you..."

The white line changed to "Details following." June grabbed the pen.

"...all are trained, prepared...ready."

Lines of Internet and e-mail addresses appeared. June wrote furiously.

An even louder blast of chimes, bells. Then, with the sound of them fading, Powell now shouting even louder called out "It is we the people who shall now have the power...and the glory...for ever and..." His voice was then drowned by a deafening roar of "Viva! Viva!" coming from the people. They continued shouting "Viva! Viva! again and again and all of them merging in with their echoes off the mesas.

Though the picture began soaring again, there was still the sound of "Viva!"s echoing around the bowl and only fading as the picture rose yet higher. The screen then went fizzy white.

"Are these your bags?"

Hearing her voice had me startle but its coldness sent a shiver right through. It was as the Dover Customs lady's who fingered me bringing in the tobacco from Belgium, except Rainbow's was a thousand times more terrible. For it wasn't as then, "Open them...please..." Rainbow already had.

This time it wasn't the sardonic "Did you pack these bags yourself sir?" but, as she fingered through the wads, a withering "Yours?" Though with her eyes saying much more, I knew I'd not room for flaffing about 'rights', for this time she had me well and truly banged to them.

Half an hour later and ruing that I had been but minutes from leaving, how Rainbow had returned early, I was nodding to everything she told me to agree. A "spontaneous act of goodwill" in handing over more Patches equity to the villagers as pre-emptive mollification should they query the bank statements and my "temporary" withdrawal of the funds, to donating five per cent of my now much smaller share to Rainbow's good causes. All were painful but she ensured I had no choice and made it clear the consequences, and (with "red-handed...filched..." and much more) humiliatingly so as well.

But Rainbow had further pain and indignity to inflict. I had balked but she had me "offer" to go on TV. Aware, I am sure, that once I had there would be nowhere left for me to go but Tabajara, and she my warder to jangle the keys of "Or shall I tell... (her list was long)?" Giving a deadline of noon today she has had me "in your own words," script everything she dictated.

From the adversity of the occasion there was scant chance of turning anything to advantage. All I could think of was, as politicians do, dressing up unpleasantness as opportunity and the mirage of street traders' something for nothing cries. To my surprise (though I would be the last to ascribe it 'pleasant') things I suggested to aid acceptance, Rainbow agreed without wrangle and readily arranged with Paceillo.

Although what Rainbow wanted I melded into marketing, buyers to buy rather than seller sell, I know inside it's all in vain for imposed change never self-sustains. But I had not choice. No chance either of avoiding terrible ignominy. All my life I have done down 'do gooding', now here I am doomed to be deigned the 'do gooder' of them all. Oh the shame of it.

Suffering such scorn, and on a global scale, is smite enough but the eventual outcome when it all collapses, as sure it must, means curtains for me. And so with heavy heart and thoughts of my hands coming off for souvenirs, I was led lamb-like to the cameras. With Rainbow standing over me it was "Brothers, sisters I have news of great importance..."

3m strong force ready to march World leaders in 'Crisis Summit' Will you join

NONETTE 'HORDES TO INVADE WORLD' THREAT

A 3,000,000 strong force of trained Nonettes is poised to spread their Alien-backed creed across the entire globe.

Last night at the climax of the most spectacular Nonette telecast yet, 'Red' Jim Powell made his dramatic announcement of the coming worldwide invasion.

The amazing television pictures showed that Red Jim's claim to be no empty boast either. All experts are agreed that there must have been at least 3 million people were gathered in front of the cameras.

World leaders have quickly responded to the threat posed by the Nonette challenge. In the US President Warren's spokesman said that a concerted effort on the part of all of the international world community is now urgently needed to combat the Nonette threat head on.

UPROAR AT RED JIM'S 'JOIN US' 'OFFER'

By **Julie Cleasby**

LAST NIGHT'S NONETTE telecast is being hailed as the 'Mother of All Spectaculars'. And the 'Father of All Portents' for world leaders.

Few experts disagreed with Nonette presenter Jim Powell's claim that 3 million people were gathered in the huge natural auditorium in Chapada Diamantina plateau in northern Brazil.

It was not their "come and join us" message which is concerning world leaders, but the three million people who are already members.

'Red' Jim Munroe claimed those assembled were merely the representatives of tens of millions more Nonettes. He further claimed that those assembled were trained to act as

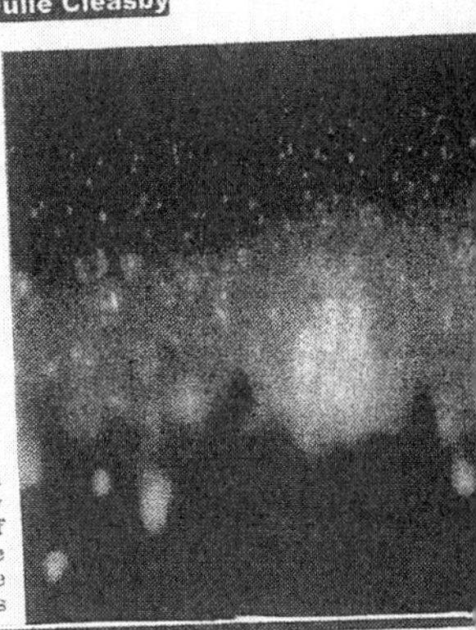

Nonette Evangelical Army threat shock

By **Freida Mongrul**
Chief Editor

YESTERDAY in a dramatic television broadcast, the Susem backed Nonette movement threw down a gauntlet to the rest of the world: "We are coming to convert you." And it is no empty threat.

Viewers worldwide were shown a 3 million strong force of the movement's trained cadres marshalled ready to convert the world to their cause.

The Nonette's TV front- with all the fervour of a southern bible puncher, proclaimed that the New Jerusalem had now arrived.

The programme and its message has already provoked strong reaction both for and against. The official government line has been to dismiss the programme as none so much as "evangelical hot air".

A Home Office spokesman depicted it as little more than an empty American-style religious TV spectacular. Another W... source said: this Powell fellow was preaching, but he will most certainly have no effect on the British public or anyone else in their right mind for that matter."

Unofficially, however, there is said to be increasing government alarm at not just yesterday's programme's influence, but that of the others preceding it. They are seen as being a focus for any potential public dissatisfaction against the Authorities.

One Downing Street insider said: "In a way

123: KEN

You've got to do everything and anything now. People are running about all over the place trying to get round losing their soufins. As Harry said it's as if the Susem have lured us into thinking they were decent, while all the time what they were really doing was getting control over us and now they have got us all held to ransom. Then against all this is that they are saying they have now found their lost spaceship and will be leaving soon.

Of course it's not just in the home where there's going to be trouble but at work. Dave has been saying that if something hasn't been worked out and quickly we are all going to be in deep trouble. He is even talking about having to close the business down if he can't get guaranteed power.

The government says they have alternative emergency supplies but everyone soon saw through all that. Half the power stations don't exist any more and a good lot of the cabling. And because this hasn't been used for ages it's going to have to be replaced and there is no chance of them getting all that done in a month. And this is all the time we've got left. Then there's the oil, there is hardly any of that now all those refineries have closed down.

So when I got home and Melanie from upstairs said there had been this leaflet from the people down at number 21, about forming a street association I didn't laugh as I normally would. But then on the other hand I don't really see how anyone can do anything.

The things Danny Collins read out were so stupid. There is no chance of anyone taking them seriously. As the Express said they are a recipe for chaos. It might be all right out where there are and all those other backward countries where they are poor and have dictators but in this country especially round here there is no chance. All his going on about "communities" is plain stupid. He must know himself they don't really exist anymore, leastways not round here they don't. And all that rubbish he went on about neighbours, I just can't take that seriously either. Everyone knows half the people don't get on with theirs. Round here hardly anyone knows them and if they had mine they wouldn't want to, housing association one side, half of them Indians who I can't make head or tail what they are saying, and on the other a load of blokes in a Buddhist commune and a right strange lot they are, chanting all the time and having lorryloads of health food coming round blocking the road up.

All I do know is that if ever I get my hands on that Danny Collins I'll give him bleeding "Brothers and sisters." Bastard. But then I should have known better. Should have known anything that he got involved with was bound to be iffy.

'THIS DAY OF INFAMY'

EARTH THREATENED WITH ENSLAVEMENT BY ALIENS
MASSIVE WORLDWIDE POWER SHORTAGES LOOMIN
MILLIONS SET TO FREEZE TO DEATH OVER WINTE
GOVERNMENT CALLS FOR CALM AS NATO GOES ON ALE

By Donald Regan and General Staff

THE WORLD IS FACING ITS BIGGEST THREAT SINCE TI BEGAN. The Aliens have demanded that mankind either abides by their order faces widespread power shortages and possibly the end of civilization as we know it.

The Aliens' telecast yesterday, delivered by their human stooge, Daniel Collins, announced that the Aliens' energy units - so called soufins - have no more than a month's power remaining. Collins stated that many of these soufins possessed manufacturing flaws.

Collins said replacement was only available to people abiding by the Aliens' diktat.

Leaders around the world responded angrily and defiantly to Alien's ultimatum.

US President Warren said: "This act of infamy must not and will not go unchallenged. The United States will rise and must rise to this challenge to our nation's sovereignty and the freedom of our people.

"My administration is engaged in urgent discussions with our allies in a bid to coordinate urgent implementation of emergency measures so as to decide what can a

ALIEN FIEN WORLD PO SUPPLY TH

By HOWARD HAWKS
Alien Threats Reporter

THE WORLD'S POWER supply was thrown in j The Aliens' portable energy device, the soufin remaining life in it.

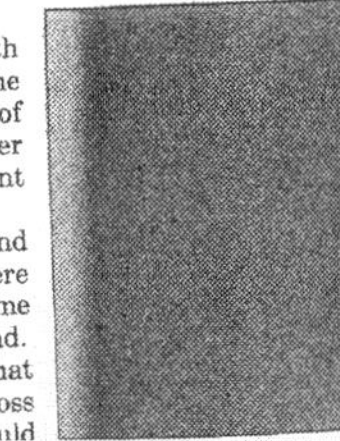

With less than a month remaining to resurrect the defunct traditional means of supply and generation of power remaining panic was evident last night.

Across the world leaders and power authorities alike were said to be rushing to overcome the dire fate awaiting mankind.

There were also fears that millions of people right across the northern hemisphere could

Susem threaten worldwide power shortages

Alien energy units have 'fault'
World leaders plan Energy Summit

By Geraldine Baxter
Economics Editor

The Susem energy units have a manufacturing flaw, it is claimed. In yesterday's Susem telecast, their spokesman, Daniel Collins, announced that the current units have no more than a month's operating life.

He stated that the Aliens will immediately replace faulty units with new ones. But the price demanded by the Aliens for replacement units is such as to be unacceptable to most people.

Collins, who is still facing charges for fraud and embezzlement, said the replacement units would only be available to people belonging to the new 'Nonette' organisations. Consumer analysts however, said that as participation in these groups obliged the members handing over ten per cent of their income, it is doubtful many will join them.

Safety experts were also doubtful over the free rides around Earth in the Aliens' space craft. Ed Kalmer, one of NASA's experts on the former International Space Station, said: "Weightlessness, unless trained for, can be extremeely dangerous. Only

STABBED I THE BAC

By SHAZZER JONES & TRACE SMITH

THE Susem showed their true hand yesterday. We are no grip, AT THEIR MERCY.

"Do as we say or you will live in a world without heat, light or power" is t flung in mankind's face by these Alien invaders.

Leaders around the world have responded angrily to this threat to our energy supplies. A spokesman for the Prime Minister, Edward Campbell, in a terse statement issued last night said: "We treated the Susem as our planetary guests.

"We offered them our every assistance in their search for their missing spacecraft. We accepted their gifts of clean energy in good faith. The entire world community of nations concurred in accepting them as a chance to rid ourselves of their

SHO HOR DOO

By James Mcawber
Crisis reporter

THE WORLD as we know it is about to come to an end

Without power advanced civilizations such as Britain's will collapse into a sea of misery and chaos. Millions of us are se to die in civil war and other types of uprisings as people in desperate scramble for the remaining energy reserves fight each other to the death for them.

As the Aliens' front-man Daniel Collins revealed the earth shattering news yesterd world leader immediately rushed into action in desperate bids to save mankind

"If Megan can then so will I," I thought.

It was seeing her running those sheets off the photocopier which finally stirred me to action. I don't think she would have done it if Mr Griffiths hadn't told her off for phoning and emailing all the council departments trying to drum up support for her "offices community."

"Right, that's it," she said after he had put her back up, "I'll stick to my own street instead."

I had it written in minutes but what to say had been hovering in my mind all morning. I did phone Daffyd because I wanted him to agree but he was in a meeting so I had to go ahead without him. By the time I was back down to the copier two of the others had come to the same conclusion and were running off theirs.

The tenth of our salaries Danny said we have to contribute to our community worried me at first. He saying we should deduct it from what we are already paying in taxes can never happen of course but it's still better to pay on top so as to have the soufins than to be without electricity. And it's not as though we wouldn't be getting any benefit back from the money.

When Danny came on last night and said our soufins wouldn't be lasting much longer I was very worried and extremely cross. I thought we had been terribly let down and cheated as well.

Making it worse was Daffyd. All he could say was it would mean the wind farms being rebuilt. When I said they contribute next to nothing, he said the government would be bound to have emergency supplies running by then. He had also said that there was nothing we could do to change anything. By then I had become so cross with him as well that I went to bed. All the same I was awake most of the night worrying with what we would do.

Because I couldn't sleep I was up at five. I hadn't been in the kitchen long before I was stroking Sam as I do with the cats when they are poorly, and still not really believing he has only a month left. But it was Rowan during breakfast saying "If Sam is going to die, when will we have a new one?" which finally made up my mind. As we drove through Cilgerren on the way to work I outlined what I was thinking. All we needed were another 77 people, twenty families and we would have the 81 people Danny said were needed to start up one of these Nonette communities.

Daffyd said there was no chance of anyone taking it up. Though I didn't say anything then, I just knew he was wrong.

On the way home I had it all worked out. Daffyd and the boys would put my leaflet though every door. But the thing was though, that by the time I arrived home there were others including the WI who had not only come up with the same idea but already had had their leaflet delivered including one put through our door.

ALIEN INFAM

OUBLE WHAMMY

Susem power units shock

"Live by our terms or no energy" say Aliens

By Susan McBeth
Social Affairs Editor

THE WORLD is facing a power meltdown. Soufins, the Susem energy units are faulty.

None have more than 30 days' power remaining - at most. The prospect darkn

...fired stations such as Drax be re-commissioned in time to meet our fuel needs this winter

...s said that the had already re- the fault and had further replace- ...cks ready for ...n well within ...ays of power in th

were more than satisfied with them. One man claimed that each unit has a proven life of more than 100 years.

It was following th inter

likely that they can be met by more than a few isolated groups.

For ordinary consu the out

E HAVE YOU NDER OUR CONTROL"

s' shock treat: "D ce power famine"

...or

SLAPPED the eir power in ...e yesterday.

This day of i Warren acc

ANDERSON HOUSE ...SPONDENT

...S DAY will live on as ...f infamy for the entire ...," President Warren yesterday.

...eaking from the White ...se following an emer...cy meeting with the Joint ...efs of Staff, President ...rren said the American ...ple and the rest of the ...rld were facing one of the ...eatest ever challenges to ...eir freedom.

The President said it was ...tal for the Global Com...unity to face the looming ...nergy crisis in a spirit of ...nity and equanimity.

The President said that the Susem's terms for the supply ...ent soufin energy

the American people, have fought battles throughout our history to ensure that the torch of freedom and liberty was never extinguished

"Many brave American men and women in decades ...t have sacrificed their

Americans ... down this b...

"We ha... selves to ... Susem's s... believing ... true frie... These Al... have com...

Nonette menace in sudden Southern Latin America surge

Latin American leaders in new defence pact

Barney Ica
in São Paulo, Brazil

Armies from Brazil to Peru were in full retreat yester-day as the Susem backed Nonette movement made further huge territorial gains.

States of emergency were issued for the first time in northern Chile and Argentinean provinces bordering Brazil.

Leaders from the six southern Latin American countries in the path of the Nonette's advance met in São Paulo in bid to halt further losses.

After a week's lull in the fighting, Nonette forces and their Susem backers resumed their relentless southward advance. Both Brazil and Bolivia acknowledged losses of territory but Peruvian forces appear to have suffered the biggest setbacks.

Reports from Arequipa, 150 km north of the Chilean border, said Cuzco, Peru's second city has been abandoned without a fight by government forces.

Cuzco's fall would indicate that all the provinces east of the Andes have been lost finally to government control.

However, with the fall a week ago of the port city Chimbote, 500km

Some very worried generals

narrow strip between the Andes and the Pacific coast.

Unconfirmed reports say that the government is planning to relocate to the town of Tacna 10km from Chilean border.

With the loss of Cuzco, the Bolivian capital La Paz is also expected to come under pressure from the Nonettes within days. Already the once steady stream of refugees of the past week has turned into a flood streaming south into neighbouring Chile, Argentina and even Paraguay.

Although the military situation in Bolivia itself

country is now in rebel hands.

The Commander of the Bolivian armed forces, General Pedro Miguel, acknowledged that the area around Lake Titicaca, just 50km north of the capital, was now under Nonette control.

Asked why so few refugees had been seen leaving the area, General Miguel said: "This a matter of deep concern both to the Defence Forces and the government.

"At present we are unable to say why the people are not fleeing from their homes, why they have thrown in their lot with the Aliens."

in the face of Nonette a... vances. He claimed th... Bolivian forces we... often facing weaponry ... against which they h... often little or no defenc...

He also said th... Bolivia was in desper... need of more soph... ticated weaponry to ... fend his country from ... Nonettes. He blamed ... US for not doing more ... help. The General term... them as "their fel... Americans in their t... of great need."

Also giving cause ... increasing concern is ... situation in the M... Grosso area of Brazil.

While the Paalto in ... east of the region is ... firmly under gov... ment control, that of ... west is confused ... some of the unof... reports circulating cl... ing that all of the ... as well as the neigh... ing provinces of Ron... and Acre, have fall... the Nonettes.

If this is the situa... though the Brazilia... fence Forces vehem... deny it - it will be o... concern to the tr... defences of the cou... heartland, its majo... ulation centres of ... Horizonte and São ...

Brazilian dictator ... eral Costa met ... fellow army comm... in São Paulo yeste... discuss the conditi...

I said to all five of them just as I said at the meeting I had arranged in the flats, "Looking after Number One is the only choice each of you have. And the best way of doing that is for everyone to hang together or we'll all freeze separately." I also told them about the flats. If the Council couldn't manage repairs properly, I said, what hope was there of the government organising alternative energy supplies in time for the likes of us, especially with winter no more than a couple of months away.

I had no sooner come on and was behind the bar in the Salutation than I was hearing them all moaning and grieving about the terrible state they had been dumped in over the soufins. Moan, moan, moan, that is all they were doing. Like a clutch of headless chickens they were. I felt like telling them to stop whingeing and get up off their backsides and do something just as we have done in the flats. But of course I have to mind what I say, as Bridie says, it's the customers who pay my wages.

Though when I told her what I thought of them and what I had organised I could see it had set her mind working. When the early evening crowd had drifted off and the later ones arrived, those with their wives, I noticed Bridie was over talking with some of the women. Not long after she had me talking to them as well. I don't know what sort of impression I made but the five of them said they will be over for a visit during the week.

From the start I never saw replacing the soufins as a problem. In many ways the terms for the new ones are just an addition, an extension of what is already happening in the flats. With so many of the tenants coming to me to have Sophie sort out their problems of repairs and everything else, I had more or less an association ready formed. I also knew that the only chance I have for a new soufin myself is organising the others to have them as well.

As I see it there is no point arguing with the government or anyone else about income tax rebates and the like, there isn't the time. A tenth of our earnings might be a bit steep for electricity but it's better than not having any. As I also pointed out at the meeting, if replacement soufins don't arrive or if they are found not to work, we have not lost anything.

And anyway it's not as though we will not benefit from the money. It will be our own and to spend as we think fit. By the end of the meeting I had half the number I needed signed up and more than this again by the time I left for the Sallie this evening.

Alien loonies leftist threat

By **Phillip Brown**
National Security Correspondent

LAST NIGHT'S Susem broadcast showed the Aliens for what they are - evil invaders hell-bent on enslaving the entire world to...

It was this same man, remember, who just a few months ago foisted these infernal energy units on us in the first place.

Collins, in admitting to the world that these...

who remember Dunkirk, a time when this country was faced with just as much a serious threat to its liberty.

For years afterwards...

US Advisors in S America

By Ross Capulyard in Washington

US military advisors are reported to be stationed in both Chile and neighbouring Argentina. Up to 500 US Special Forces are said to have arrived in each country within the past few days.

...active stance, and following the re-occupation of the Panama Canal Zone, the US covertly signaling to its beleaguered Latin American neighbours that it is joining with...

...voracious as those now surfacing against the stationing of US troops in Panama.

Will Stockley, head of the American Veterans Association...

Nonette threat set to spread

By Richard Rankle
World Affairs Editor

THE alien backed Nonette movement is being seen a potential treat to...

Anger at Government energy policy failure

By Richard Rankle
Business Editor

THE SLOWNESS of the government's response to the looming energy crisis is ...widespread alarm...

[our] European partners. These DTI Johnnies don't even know what day of week it is.

"If DTI doesn't get off its backside and sort something out pretty soon, the entire country is going to be in a ...ight mess. We are not talk... ...ills and factories...

"However, while the Department is mindful of Industry's concerns, we are further bounded by our obligations under EU regulation... there is an overall... hensive policy... with our EU partne... very little we can... reference to them... we have no wish... ...but as...

Nonettes overrun more Latin territory

By Paulo Pascales
in Lima

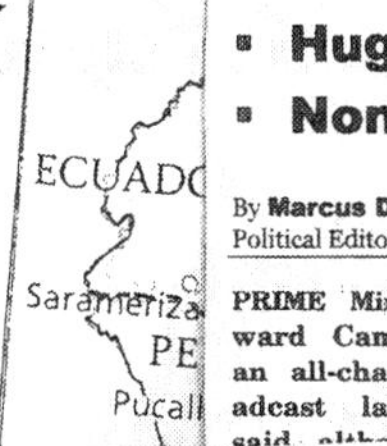

A STATE of Siege covering the whole of Peru was proclaimed by its leader, President Santos today. The proclamation follows the rapidly deteriorating security situation in the country's eastern Amazon region.

Peru's northern Amazonian provinces have already slipped from government control. However...

If these latest sightings of Nonettes are confirmed it is bound to accelerate the flight of the country's wealthy to neighbouring Argentina and Uruguay. Already the face of La Paz is taking on the air of a ghost town. Many banks have closed and up-market restaurants are closing by the day.

The Calacoto district, once home to many of La P... ex-pa...

"We have nothing to fear but fear itself" - PM

- **Campbell's TV address given tepid rati...**
- **Stock markets plummet**
- **Huge energy shortage forecast**
- **Nonette security threat seen**

By **Marcus Dooder**
Political Editor

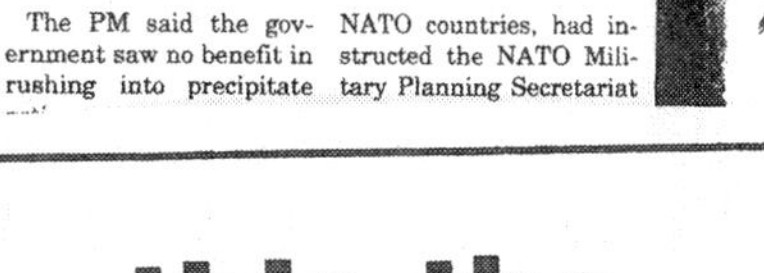

PRIME Minister Ed... ward Campbe... an all-channel... adcast last... said...

The PM said the government saw no benefit in rushing into precipitate...

NATO countries, had instructed the NATO Military Planning Secretariat...

OTSA: Latin leader's desperate pact

Paulo Pascales
Lima

THE face of the ...mbling security situation ...eatening southern Latin ...nerica, leaders of the ...fected countries held an ...ergency summit in a bid to ...lt the seemingly unstoppable advance of the Nonettes.

In a joint declaration the ...aders of the seven countries ...nounced the formation of a ...int military command structure.

General Costa, head of the ...razilian junta said: "Today ...is my country as well as ...ose of Bolivia and Peru ...ho are under attack. It is we ...ree who suffer daily the ...sses of our countries to ...cursions of the Alien in...

seven countri... organisation.

Defence analy... were disparaging... chances in co... onward march... Nonettes. They... alliance as bein... effective than t... joint military ope... ducted by the aff... tries. In the vi... observer, the p... ance was "too litt... "Rearranging the... on the Titanic" b...

Harold Wigge... *Big Tanks Mo...* "With the excep... Falklands War, ... South Americ... have fought ag... nal enemy. It's... for them to beg...

"The only experience the...

Is this the world's most despised man?

By **Phillip Brown**
National Security Correspondent

This is the face of Daniel Collins, the man who told us the Aliens came in peace and wanted to help mankind.

This is the face of the man won worldwide praise for all those free soufins he said he had secured on our behalf.

The face of the man still wanted by the police for criminal damage to the statue of a famous British WWII hero.

The face of the man still wanted for tax evasion and fraud. The face of the fraudster who conned th... entire world into parting inn... cently with our power and petr... stations, and then hooked us a... into becoming addicted to th... highs of Alien energy units.

The face of the uncaring push... who now tells us that our futu... fixes come only by submitting ... living as the Aliens tell us, or el... we go cold turkey and suffer th... agony of life without energy.

This is the face of the man who ... trying to take away the freedo... of you and your children's. Is the... a more despicable act than that?

TEN EASY STEPS TO FORMING YOUR OWN NONETTE GROUP: FULL DETAILS PA...

I could have told everyone months ago it would never last. With Collins involved it just had to be suspect from the start. Now we are all left to live with the consequences.

Thankfully I am safe at the Bank so I do not have the worries as have others as regards job security. It has not been all doom and gloom either. The Bank has never been so busy, energy futures have risen through the roof, and there has been nothing short of a stampede of the bigger clients seeking finance to snap up the defunct power companies. Some of the Middle East sovereign debt has actually risen for the first time in months.

I have also personally been exceptionally busy. This is due to a not insignificant number of my customers contacting me seeking loans for generators and the like. If these potential borrowings requirements and continue as of at present I can at last look forward to a bonus come the end of the year.

Another stroke of good fortune has been successfully negotiating the purchase of a small reconditioned generator from one of my customers. Because of the impending energy shortages and increased demand I have naturally had to pay rather more than the list price as well as to extend his overdraft facilities. But at times such as these one cannot a chooser be.

June however, has, as of yet, to fully appreciate the boon this generator will be during the coming winter months. In fact, and to my alacrity, she has been most dismissive regarding my initiative. She even went so far as to assert that I was "over-reacting."

What is more, and somewhat irritatingly she and some of her friends are filled with forming one of these so-called Nonette communities in the naive belief that their doing so will somehow conjure up replacement soufin units. Needless to add, I have endeavoured on several occasions, and at length to explain to her just how misguided anyone is to place any trust in such a foolhardy scheme. But sadly though, my council, has as yet has fallen on deaf ears.

But nonetheless I am confident that, given time, June and her friends will come to their senses and see through Collins and Powell's schemes. See them for the frauds that they undoubtedly are.

In this vein, and at the end of yesterday's morning conference, Mr Gibbons in a lighthearted mood showed us a report he had asked the people in Research and Analysis to draft on the tax implications of Collins' proposals. We all had a laugh when he read out what their boffins had come up with. According to them, if these so-called proposals were put in place the Bank's profits would more than double. Though the report of course also said the Treasury will never permit such changes.

Mr Gibbons also asked everyone for their views on the report and Collins' television appearances. Not unexpectedly all of those present were of the same view as myself. But I was taken aback somewhat when he addressed Collins as "our illustrious one-time client". But I am sure Mr Gibbons could only have intended this to be a joke as well.

Susem have us nookered" says ludson

Geraldine Baxter
ıstry Analyst

ıe Aliens now have al economic control of our lives," a leading pposition MP claimed esterday. Sir Malcolm ludson, opposition for-ign affairs spokesman, peaking at meeting of ISIS at London's Guild-hall said: "In providing the world with these free soufin units, the Aliens have caused the pre-viously existing energy supply systems to gone into liquidation. The oil industry is greatly diminished. The Aliens have put a stop to open-cast mining including that of coal. They have even kept the most re-mote of communities log-ging their own forests.

"Every nuclear power station has been blasted to the sun. Windpower, thanks to so-called envir-onmental activists top-pling the turbine towers, can be discounted as a source of energy as well. All we are left with is solar power which can provide next to nothing

"Even if Britain and other countries embarked on a rapid reinstatement of those power stations still standing," he said, "it will take months before they can be brought on stream. In short the Susem have us snookered."

Sir Malcolm then outlined a crash pro-gramme of power re-supply which would meet up to 50 percent of Britain's energy needs. He called for an immediate joint govern-ment - industry partner-ship to condu... audit of all re...

More South America cities fall to Nonettes

Venezuela government flees: Columbia collapses

POLLY PORTILLO
IN LA ASUNCION,
ILA MARGARITA

WITH the port La Cruz in Nonette hands remnants of the Venezuelan military still loyal to President Hugo Arias have retreated to the Carib-bean island of Ila Margarita.

Its tiny capital, La As-uncion has been made into Venezuela's de facto seat of government in exile. But few observers expect Arias to remain in office for more than a few weeks.

Such has been the speed and totality of Venezuela's collapse that many thousands of people have sought ref-uge on the country's Carib-bean islands. Although the

Nonettes have not yet invad-ed the capital, the fall of Caracas is seen as imminent.

With news that the port city of Marcaibo had fallen to the Susem backed Nonettes a wave of panic swept Caracas. The government's claim that the army is holding its own against the rebels was seen to be false What had been until then a steady exodus from the capital turned overnight into a panicked flight o... before being surrounded by Nonette insurgents

What the ene... shortages wi... really mean

By Geraldine Baxter
Industry Analyst

Power shortages, black-outs, increased air pollu-tion and petrol rationing are just a few of the obvious things to be ex-pected as the Alien soufin energy units run down. But these, experts are saying, will be just the start. The knock-on eff-ects which will soon kick-in as the energy crisis gathers momentum.

While the government draws up plans to combat the crisis, experts are voicing concerns to the wider consequences of the energy shortages. Dr. Frank Banister of Sheppey University's De-partment of Energy Stud-ies says: "All advanced economies and thus our societies as a whole, depend on the inte-grating effects of all their participating facets.

"Within any dynamic society - such as those of the First World - changes continuously occur. Most do so gradually and pass unnoticed. But yet signif-icant or sudden changes, or both, immediately en-gender corres...

"The losses incurred by advanced economies con-sequent to the collapse of the old power generation and fossil fuel extraction sectors caused by the rapid introduction of soufin energy units, was more than offset by the gain in overall energy costs reducing to almost zero.

"Not only did such gains to these economies outweigh their losses, but in turn those gains, rather than being 'one-offs' - as many observers at the time claimed - they generated further, virt-uous spirals of secondary and tertiary increases in proficiency of production.

"We are now faced with the reverse scenario. With sudden downturns in energy inputs econo-mic activity can only decrease.

"This time though, there are no compen-satory factors offsetting these losses. Therefore, economic activity is set for a significant and rapid contraction. This inevitably will lead to a marked deterioration of returns of...

their value... 'stagflation...

"Employ... will declin... power bo... and indivi... depressed ... ments' 'ta... borrowings... be a drain... market f... which oth... be directe... cial investr...

This al... high levels... a scale uni... decades. M... people's ca... savings - i... retirement ... - will grea... Similarly, ... are bound ... levels not s... 1990s.

"There wi... more, and ... hold dept le... increasing ... families wil... manage. In ... increase p... ures for ce... ment assist... industry a... alike.

'Make-or-Break' sta... for Brazil at Jatai

100,000 strong force to block Nonette advance "They shall not pass," says General Costa

By Linden Sergipe
in Sao Paulo Brazil

The defence forces of OTSA, the military alli-ance of the five southern Latin American coun-tries, have established the largest concentration of military might in the continent's history.

In a move to block the expected Nonette inva-sion, more than 200,000 heavily armed soldiers are entrenched along a 2,000 mile front stretch-ing from the Atlantic to Pacific Oceans.

Augmented by the imp-assable natural barriers of the Andes, the Panat-atal swamplands to the west and Divisos moun-tain range of the centre and east, a "Muro Orgulhoso" - Wall of Might - now straddles Latin America in a bid to defend its southern - most populous - half of the continent from the Nonettes.

Because both Pacific and Atlantic coastal strips are heavily defen-ded - up to a depth of 50 kilometres – Nonette ad-vances along these routes are considered as being blocked. This, military strategists believe, will leave the Nonettes no alternative but to invade the south from the inter-ior of Brazil through gaps in the Divisos's moun-tains.

The main route through the Divisos is the Caiapó Pass in the central state of Goias and just north of the small town of Jatai.

But will they stay and fight or will they fight to go home?

Because Jatai is the gateway from the interior of Brazil to the country's main cities of São Paulo and Rio de Janerio, it is seen as the biggest threat to the south's security. Consequently it is at Jatai that the Brazilian army has concentrated its main forces.

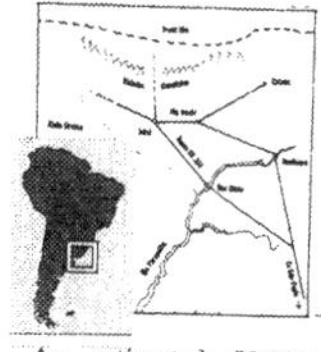

An estimated 30,000 men from Brazil's crack regiments have been de-ployed in what is being described as a "fortified defended position in depth." Though spread over a 40 mile area 'Fort Jatai' also has sensors which will monitor any movement in further out-er perimeter of up to 30 kilometres on the north-ern slopes of the Divisos.

According to Defence Ministry sources, the rat-ionale for Jatai is that the Nonettes have no alternative than to in-vade the south. If they do not, then they will have shown that they are vulnerable and can, consequently be attacked successfully if the forces against them are over-whelming.

When the Nonettes do invade the south, they will have no choice but to advance through the Div-isos at Jatai. Thus they will be channeled in what the military are calling, their "Gauntlet of Wrath."

Many military anal-ysts however, are less sanguine at Brazil's chances of turning back the Nonette tide at Jatai.

"They may well be Brazil's best battalions," says Janes *Big Tanks Monthly's* Harold Wig-gins of Jatai's defenders, "but they are untested in battle against the Non-ettes let al... Susem backers.

"The forces ... may well be ar... teeth with eve... ticated weapo... Brazilian arsen... by every [rumo... advisor, but if... not the will to... alone battle ... experience, t... doomed to de... the start. Or ... wasting their ... money," he said.

General Costa ... the Brazilian ju... ever, is more ... the prospects of ... tary's chances ... "They [the None... come and we w... hilate them. T... not pass," he sa... passing out para... Vargas militar... emy.

At the cerem... General also a... a doubling of ... pay while on ac... vice. This, it h... said, is to ens... troops do just th... active and not de...

US denies S.Am... involvemen...

By Oliver Stoneburgher

127: CANARY

Infamy? Everyone has it in for me. It's so unfair.

Rubbing in the hurt is Roberto. He listens to world news programmes on the radio then sadistically delights in relaying to all and sundry the latest levels of odium sloshing over me, and dire threats awaiting should I ever set foot from here.

Not that I dare. I'd not make a mile before Rainbow broadcast details of my failed flit.

She has me trapped. I've as much manoeuvre as being in the Bastille. And she knows it. Knows as well that she's well and truly 'got' me. Got me just where she wants, how she wants, her talking marionette.

I am dreading going on again this afternoon. Now it's not just her "In your own words," but didactic "Do look to the autocue...do remember to smile... do at least try and sound sincere..."

One small err was all I made and I've forever Rainbow's blade to my back poised for plunging as punishment. It's not fair. And worse, she knows I know that should I ever upset her again, she will as swiftly summon every Nonette to stick and twist their blades between my blades as well.

This isn't all. There are all the galling 'thank yous', dozens and dozens of them. "Thank you for the gift of the shares, thank you for the income you have created for Tabajara, the increased tithe for the whole region," on and on right through to "volunteering to also helping to represent us to the world." There has even been a big bit about me in the local Times. And the resulting fan mail as well.

Although inwardly gnashing, seething and sobbing over my losses I have no choice than to spryly reply "Oh its nothing really...the least I can do...we all need to pull together don't we?...someone has to do it."

I am as a prized canary captive in a gilded cage with admirers stuffing seeds through the bars, tinkling my bell, cooing "Who's a pretty boy then?" but oh so well aware that should I tweet one bum note, make a singe false move, these 'admirers' will have me out of my cage, trussed and taxidermed in a trice. It is all so unfair.

I'm having a terrible time. I fear for the worst.

Caracas - doomed city of the dammed

...an Trugg reports from Caracas of the plight of its not so innocent refugees

...EAR STALKS THIS CITY ...'four million wretched and ...uffering souls. No matter how ...nany times the government of ...Iugo Arias proclaims the ...ilitary's successes the ...Ionettes or the imminent ...rrival of US forces from ...anama, no one in Caracas ...elieves them.

Every day the people of ...his city see the reality of ...enezuela's military prowess: ...housands of deserting sold...ers fleeing the relentless ...dvances of the Nonettes. ...very one of them will ...eadily relate the horror of ...he Susem's assaults.

That military hospitals ...hroughout Caracas are said ...o be overflowing with traum...atized victims of the Aliens' ...attacks adds credence to ...everything these soldiers have to say.

Lawlessness

Deserting soldiers are also held responsible for the surge of lawlessness sweeping Caracas. The frightening increase in shootings, robberies and hijacking deserters have brought now add to the daily misery of soaring prices, food and water shortages as well as all too frequent power cuts.

If these woes were not enough the hard pressed people of this city face the upheaval caused by half a million refugees from the rest of Venezuela. With most of the population now subsisting below the poverty line the p ressure of these outsiders consuming scarce resources is increasingly resented.

Despised refugees

But ordinary peoples' hostility towards these refugees is all the more hostile, because unlike them, most are not from among the poor. In ... are the opposite, the once rich and powerful groups of Venezuela: government officials, mayors, regional politicians, landowners. And all have fled not just in fear of Nonette forces but the retribution of the local populations they once exploited, wielded power over.

Although the government controlled media is widely disbelieved, the daily Nonette newscasts are accepted as being truthful. And every viewer, including Caracas' privileged refugees have all watched the Nonette's 'Truth Committees' in action.

Truth Trials

Each day officials of the old regime who have been left behind by the fleeing armies are show arraigned before these tribunals. Some stand charged with corruption but other are charged with even worse crimes.

Though most of the accused are judged guilty, many, in a bid for leniency, name names and deeds of others guilty of so-called 'Crimes against the People'. As well as officials there are policemen, gangmasters, ranchers and others of the former elites.

But these unfortunates are not the only 'enemies of the people indicted before the 'Truth Committees'. Militias, hoodlums, drug traffickers, pimps, in fact anyone denounced for preying upon the people also face the 'Truth Committees'.

Castration

While viewers cheer at the Committees' verdicts they always roar with approval as the punishments are shown. These range from time in the stocks, public whippings to as public castrations with sheers and attendant gaggles of hungry geese.

Most of the guilty, however, ... in columns and

EU energy ineptitude

By Oliver Stoneburger
Energy reporter

AMID A BARRAGE OF calls for his resignation, Trade Commissioner Henrich Siebe, defended himself and the EU energy policy yesterday. He told a meeting of Europe's business groups that the Commission could play no more than a coordinating role in the crisis.

Siebe, known as the 'Gauliter of Regulation', sought to assure that the Commission was doing everything within its power

Polly Portillo reports from Caçu on the Brazilian frontline

Brazilian forces arme... ready to repulse rebel...

CAÇU IS WITNESS TO THE biggest concentration of military might South America has ever seen.

Caçu is a small scruffy hamlet in the middle of nowhere, 700 kilometres north of São Paulo. It is however, the nearest the Brazilian military are permitting civilians to its front-line with the Nonettes at Jatai 50km away to the northwest.

Caçu straddles Route 364, the main highway from the Third World of Brazil's interior to the north to its First World cities of the south. From the hills above Caçu, Route 364 can be seen snaking kilometre after kilometre up into the Mombuca mountains and northward to Jatai.

Night and day every metre of this twisting highway is covered my armed convoys crawling nonstop, nose to tail all bound for Jatai.

Countless armoured personnel carriers, hundreds of loaded tank transporters, long lines of self propelled artillery, missile batteries and many thousands of trucks laden with material wend their way up through the mountains.

Brazilian soldiers of the 5th Rangers division move up to the Cacu firebase ready ...

Firebases

All are bringing reinforcements to the main Brazilian stronghold just south of the Caiapó Pass, as well as its string of forward Firebases strung out along the cordilleras of the Caiapó and Divisões Mountains, stretching from Mineiros in the west to Montividu 100 km to the east.

Route 364 is not the only means of sending reinforcements to Jatai. The sky overhead is filled with fleets of massive Turnhaus helicopters ferrying in yet more men and supplies.

US Lend Lease

The Turnhaus as well as Blackhawk helicopters are part of the hurried US Lend Lease package to OTSA [the recently formed defence alliance of the seven South American countries]. Both types of helicopters however are reportedly piloted by US advisors who are said to be assisting OTSA.

The same is said of the hundreds of Huey helicopter gunships which have also been seen flying in to Jatai. Although these are under the command of the five newly formed Brazilian Air Cavalry regiments, they are reported to be organised and maintained by US army veterans.

US instructors

Other US military personnel are also said to have been responsible for the deploying the extensive network of remote listening devices north of the Caiapó Pass. These, it is reported, are so sensitive they can detect the specific footfall signatures of different animals as well as those between humans

Apart from the clatter of helicopters there are also the roars of sorties of F15 fighter bombers from both the Brazilian and Argentinean air forces filling these once silent skies. All are armed ready to also attack the Nonettes the moment their presence is reported.

100 battalions

According to OTSA's Supreme Headquarters there are more than 100 battalion strength regiments already in position at Jatai. If this is so, it indicates that there are upwards of 100,000 men already in position all armed to the teeth and poised to repel the anticipated imminent arrival of the Nonette rebel forces.

In addition to these forces however, must be added the extensive reserves stationed with their equipment on the far bank of the Rio Paranà, 50km south of Caçu at São Simão.

São Simão on the southern side of the Rio Paranà has been transformed into a further massive base area for the Jatai Force. Another huge reserve men and material are on standby ready to reinforce those on the frontline.

From Route 364, as it crosses the Rio Paranà it is also possible to see the huge US Airforce 130 Galaxy military cargo planes disgorging further supplies of men and ammunition for the Jatai build-up.

Observers say there will be upward of a further 100,000 men ready to go north to Jatai the moment the Nonettes have been repulsed.

However, and although it has been officially denied, the Rio Paranà is seen as OTSA's second line of defence should there be a retreat from Jatai.

Fight to the finish

Presently though, the idea of any withdrawal has been firmly ruled out ... the head of the Brazil... junta, General Costa. ... has ordered the forces ... Jatai to "Fight to the l... man". If Brazil's mai... conscript army see the... selves as "the last guardi... of their nation's destin... as General Costa ... have it, is yet to be seen.

Meanwhile the Brazili... armed forces sit and w... at 'Fort Jatai' for t... Nonette advance to ... channeled into what OT... calls it's "Gauntlet ... Wrath" of the Caiapó Pass.

How long OTSA's forc... will sit passively waiti... for the enemy to advanc... is still open to questio... Already there are voice... questioning the militar... logic of concentrating ... much of OTSA's availab... manpower and materia... in a single theatre.

Martin Cascaval, a lea... ing analyst of Brazilia... military affairs, speakin... from New York said, "Ther... is one all-weather roa... into Jatai and thus onl... one road out. Should any... thing go wrong there i... no way the military ca... make a retreat.

Dien Bien de ja vu

"It is Dien Bien Phu, Khe Sanh all over again. The only thing [General] Costa and his cronie... have learnt from history is that they have learnt nothing from history."

Sheikh shrieks over oil price prospects

by Oliver Stoneburger
Energy Reporter

SHEIKH OH HARABH, the deposed ruler of the tiny Gulf state of Hutar, was in jubilant mood yesterday. Remarking on the huge rise in oil prices, he said: "The price [of oil] could be more than $100 a barrel this time next month."

The Sheikh was speaking from ... suite in the Dorchest... his home since he was forced from power two months ago. The Sheikh said that he was already in negotiations with his countrymen over his return to Hutar. However, he strongly denied that his resumption of power had anything to do with a reported deal with the British government to sell Hutar's entire oil production for $80 a barrel. The Sheikh said: "Th...

BUSINESS NEWS:

Power shares su...

By Oliver Stoneburger

As one power in the land falls so another rises. We may well be set for a winter of shivers as the soufins' energy ebbs away but come the spring the lights will shine again ... power generation to more than enough to meet our needs will have come on stream. Oil wells will be flowing again as well.

Consortia the world over are being formed daily to meet expected ...

... are knocking on doors to buy ... megawatt they ... generating

Now is the ti... the forward thin... take up the ch... participate in ... the several shar...

128: KEN

Harry stood me a drink. A full pint.

How this unique event came to pass is the result of Beth Prior. She lives down at number 21 and it was her who organised the meeting about getting the new soufins. I had seen her on the street before but hadn't known who she was.

I wasn't going to go at first but Melanie and Susan were intent I went and I didn't want to upset them. But as soon as we arrived and saw these old women pouring out cups of tea I was halfway sure it would be all a waste of time. I felt the same when one of them having taken our names showed us into the back garden. There were a dozen and more already out there, some I knew vaguely and soon saw nothing coming out of them either. I was all set to leave when this Beth Prior strode out.

Half an hour later not only were we agreeing with what she said but all the things she wanted us to do as well. On the way home Melanie said she was a lecturer at a college and that is just how she came across. All self-assured but not bossy, and she spoke well.

She kept everything simple and to the point. No one, she said, could guarantee us a constant supply of electricity. This included the government, and they wouldn't connect up the likes of us unless we paid what was owing to the old London Electricity. If we put our order for replacement soufins in early, at least we would know if they were going to be coming or not and there would also be time to find out if they actually worked. If they didn't work we wouldn't lose anything because we could all have our money back.

No one argued with this but some went on about the rest of the things Danny said had to be done. But she just said "Do you want supplies of power or not?" And after the 'yeses' she said "One step at a time, first things first." No one argued with this either. All we had to do, she went on, was each get four more to join and we would have the 80 minimum Danny said was needed to start. Among our next door neighbours was where we would find the numbers needed, she said. I nearly said something about mine but thought it best not.

However, at this point someone piped up with "What about the money, how will it be collected, how will we know it will be safe?"

Quick as a flash she was back with "If you are so concerned why not stand for election as Treasurer?" Apart from shutting him up, it was at this point another man came out the house. He was carrying a tray of drinks. I warmed to him straight away.

More so with his "There you are boyo," (I don't get called 'boy' much these days). Mrs Prior introduced him as "Sam," then to my surprise added, "my husband" (well he looked a good bit older than her).

...eovers 'temporary measure' says PM Pollution contro...
...ctricity rationing within weeks Emergency powers...

...iovernment in pov... ...tations, refineries g...

...eraldine Baxter
...stry Analyst

...aft of tough, nonon-...se measures to tackle ...tain's looming energy ...is were announced ...terday, in what ...ounts to wholesale ...tionalisation of the ...ntry's remaining pow-... stations and oil refin-...ies. Steps will also be ...ken to takeover the ...pply and distribution of ...maining power and fuel ...ocks.

There is to be a system ...f strict rationing of pow-...r to what Trade and ...ndustry Secretary, Colin ...ike, termed "non-prior-...ty" users. He said the ...overnment's measures ...would mean that in a month's time - when the soufin energy units are set to expire - there would be sufficient energy to meet more than 40 per-cent of the country's needs.

Further measures include:

- **Setting up Super-**visory Boards composed of heads of old electricity and gas companies, the heads of all the major oil companies and a number of senior DTI staff to oversee implementation of the government's measures.
- **A draconian system** of petrol and diesel rationing enforced through cou-...
- **Customs & Excise to** take over the management of the liquidation of the defunct power stations with the specific brief to claw back the amounts outstanding in unpaid bills. The C&E to be granted all the powers necessary to enforce repayment.
- **Setting aside for an** indefinite period all controls on air pollution.
- **Prohibition of all** non-essential use of power, such as advertising displays. The police are to be given increased power to close down offender's businesses as well as giving out on the spot fines.
- **The mass production** of horse liniment embrocation to be used by the very young and pensioners to keep warm this winter.

The PM said: "The government's proposals have been carefully considered and planned in order to make the most of the limited resources available. In no way should they be seen as panic measures."

If these proposals are passed in full, it will mean a drastic reduction of Britain's industrial output. Motoring for pleasure will also become a thing of the past. There will have to be restraints on use of air travel especially for...

Morcombe Bay gas processing platform ...

PM's announcement, leaders across industry were claiming that the proposed measures were not only impractical ... able. Sir Be... head of the ... regulations ... in goodness ... in practice ... reason tha... not functi... this basis...

The world's biggest fraudster

By **Susen McBeth**
Public Life Editor

JUST who is Daniel 'Danny' Collins? How did this man trick all of us so successfully - and so swift and cunningly - into swapping our old power supplies for the Alien's untested energy units?

According to the police, Collins was - and theoretically still is - wanted for a string of small scale frauds, criminal damage in defacing the statue of Arthur 'Bomber' Harris. He is also being sought on the more serious charges of income tax and VAT evasion.

These minor, petty charges apart, there is little in Collins' makeup which marks him out as possessing the attributes necessary to pull off one of the biggest scams of all time. The question: "How did he do it?" is likely, in years to come, to feature in many a University Criminal Sociology Department's curriculum.

One of those who has already attempted to give an answer is Dr. Martin Rees of Snaresbrook University. He said: "Collins obviously used the first tool in every fraudster's book: the innate greed of the 'punter'. Like other crafty conmen Collins spent time in 'softening up the prosect', eg. victim in this case, the public at large.

"It is obvious now to see how he did it. And once again it is a well established move and known to Criminal Sociologists and police forces alike as 'reverse long-term fraud'. This involves, as we now can see in the case of the Alien energy units, of first establishing credit-worthiness among a small group of unsuspecting people.

"These supposed 'lucky few' then extol the 'virtues' of the fraudster to a wider circle of people. In effect they are doing his dirty work for him. In doing so these people generate an alienating gulf of envy between the 'haves' and 'have-nots'.

'We will never s... boasts defiant ...

...ore Colombian cities fall to Nonette reb... ...efugees in mad scramble for the boats

...y Ian Trigg
... Cartagena, Columbia

...ith only the north wes-...ern corner of Columbia ...n government hands, ...eneral Rafael Jani has ...leclared a State of Emergency in a bid to shore up the deteriorating security situation. Few observers however, believe he can succeed.

Most people in the fragment of Columbia still under government control are in state of shock over the speed with which the country fell to the Nonettes. Not even the security forces were able to retreat with much their weaponry and equipment.

With scarcely a tenth of the Colombian armed forces are in combat-ready condition, the ...

Does the General have enough lifeboats?

...ing is not thought to be high. None-the-less, General Jani is upbeat in winning what he sees as the forthcoming decisive campaign.

"We have the Andes to ...

help us,"... said yester... to Genera... forces ca... two 5,00... spurs w... northern ...

Polly Portillo in São Paulo reports on OTSA's victory against the rebels

Brazilians repulse Nonettes

THE NONETTES have been beaten back before the Gates of Jatai by OTSA forces, it was reported yesterday

OTSA Supreme Headquarters, São Paulo, announced that General Augusto de Santos, Commander of OTSA Forces, Jatai had decisively repulsed a heavily armed attack by an estimated 20 Nonette divisions attempting to infiltrate over a wide front across the cordilleras of both the Caiapó and Divisões mountain ranges.

OTSA said that every one of Jatai's forward 15 fire bases from Mineiros in the west to Montividu in the east had reported making contact with Nonette forces and all had engaged the rebels in fierce artillery duels.

At today's briefing, OTSA liaison officer, Major Vicente detailed how Fire Base Claro, due north of Jatai and manned by the Brazilian Special Forces, had detected a Nonette rebel detachment advancing toward it over the cordilleras of Serra do Caiapós 10 km to the north-east of the fire base.

"Within one hour of the rebels' detection," Major Vicente said, "than they were attacking Base Claro Initially with small arms and mortar fire but as soon as Fire Base Claro retaliated against the rebels, the Base came under increasingly heavy mortar attack

"Although Base Claro suffered causalties in the attack, it not only immediately counterattacked with its heavy field artillery and rocket salvos," the Major said. "As soon as Claro signaled for assistance from the other Fire Bases however, it was then that the full scale of the Nonettes' attack was ascertained he said

"Under the cover of darkness," Major Vincente said, "the rebels not only had stealthily infiltrated their forces to within a few kilometres of OTSA's positions but also had done so along the entire length of 120 km front.

"The moment this was known, however, the other 14 forward positions attacked the oncoming rebels with all the firepower at their disposal This was not before time on the part of the Fire Bases," the Major said.

No sooner had they [the fire bases] launched their preemptive strikes," the Major said, "than they were subjected to an immensely fierce rebel bombardment. All the Bases then returned the rebels' fire with a devasta-

All the bases then returned the rebels' fire with a devastating artillery barrage as well as salvos of rockets and heavy mortar These bombardments were later bolstered by long-range artillery attacks from Jatai which shelled the enemy positions until dawn.

"At this time, approximately 0430 hours," the Major said, "the Nonettes, having suffered serious reversals called off their attack against the fire bases and withdrew

"But at 0500 hours, first light, Heuy helicopter gunships from 1st, 2nd and 5th Air Cavalry pursued the retreating rebels forces for many kilometres north of the Serra do Caiapó

"Despite coming under sporadic enemy gunfire all the Cavalry units successfully engaged in mopping up operations By 0700 hours all the Air Cavalry Divisions had successfully annihilated the remaining rebel units and had returned to base."

Major Vicente, acknowledging that some of the Brazilian fire bases had suffered heavy casualties as well as collateral damage He said that all of Jatai's forward positions would be back to operative capacity within the next few days. He also said that the Air Cavalry have suffered the loss of "a number" of their helicopters in the operation but all were due to "technical factors".

The Major said: "The Nonette rebels' attempted invasion has suffered a severe setback at the hands of OTSA forces and they know it

"Our forces at Jatai are now preparing to go over onto the offensive and pursue the rebels until they were completely vanquished. Th... forces of OTSA will ensur... that these rebels will pay ... heavy price for thei... disloyalty to the Brazilia... nation," he said

The victory of the Bra... zilian army against th... Nonettes provides a muc... needed boost to the flaggin... morale of many of OTSA'... senior commanders

Until the success at Jata... the prevailing view amon... the upper echelons o... OTSA's Defence Forces wa... that they could affect litt... more than a slowing the pa... of their forces' retreat unt... the US arrived, or somethir... else turned up to save ther... It would now appear that th... Macawberese approach has last paid off

Although OTSA has repe...ed a Nonette attack it w... have achieved little lasti... success if it does no more

With the drinks there was the chatting. Funny how everyone, although strangers, were all matey. Mrs Prior said in Dare Crescent, our side of Greenwood Road and the bit of Queens Avenue between them, there were 800-odd people, just about the right number to make up a full group. She also said Johnny Patel, who has the newsagents in the parade on the estate the other side of Greenwood Road and who is also getting up a group, had agreed with her that Greenwood Road was a natural boundary between us.

On the way home Melanie joked how we had better get on with "our homework" that Mrs Prior had set us, signing up the neighbours, as we had to have it in by Thursday. And that's another funny thing. I spoke more with those two girls this evening than all the time I've known them.

I left them to try their luck with the ones either side of us, not that I thought they would get much of a result, but I didn't say anything. However, my 'neighbours' were round the corner, in the Greenwood.

I couldn't go in strong of course, I would never get a result if I had and anyway that's not my stamp. But Harry remarking I was late coming in started everything. I had no sooner told him where I had been and what had happened than Dennis, bleeding know-all, sticks his oar in. "What happens," he said all cocky, "if the people from the flats declare war on our side of Greenwood Road and invade us, how are we going to defend ourselves?"

His missus called him a stupid you know what and hit him over the head with her handbag. This shut him up of course but it got a laugh round the pub as well. This then got a bit of a chat going. There were half a dozen actually listening to me, including Harry. I told them the things Beth Prior had said but I could see from the movements on Harry's face it had started him thinking. Then he spoke.

"Can't meet in a back garden if it rains can you?" he said, then, "There is the big room upstairs going spare." But when he said "I won't charge for it," I was naturally suspicious. And when he added that if we agreed to use the room he would also drum up support in the Greenwood, I still didn't catch on why he had become so keen all of a sudden.

I told him it wasn't up to me but to have a word with Beth Prior and gave him her number. He went to phone her but was back within minutes and with a very satisfied smile. He also had a sheet of paper and a felt pen. That's when he said, as he pulled a pint, "This one's on me."

As I sipped it and he wrote out "Get your Free Soufins here, Limited Offer, Join the Greenwood-Dare Nonette, Inaugural Meeting, Sign below," I reckoned I was going to get ten out of ten for my homework.

›vernment ... ›oves slated

ine Baxter
ınalyst

Are the crazy hazy days of pollution all set to return?

ernment's hand- the energy crisis eived a definite -down by industry ıblic alike. Most anded it as inept, ıable and most of s blatantly unfair.

government is d for failing to provisions for such ntingency as the nt crisis. Dr. Iain ams, an energy rt at Sheppey Univ- y, said: "With the s of traditional gy supplies such as and natural gas mmeting, the govern- ıt should have kept at st 90 days worth of pply at the ready.

uring the energy crisis the 1970s and 80s the vernments throughout e world, including our vn, maintained such nounts as strategic eserves.

"But of course the British government, like nany others in the EU, quietly sold off these reserves to in a bid to balance the budgets in the run up to the Euro.

"The same applies to electricity generation. The present government, like those of the past, have been so wedded to privatisation, that they sold such things off.

Now they and we, the ...members of the alike, are suffering the consequences."

Unworkable

The government is claiming more than it can deliver. Even the reduced levels of power generation promised no longer exist. In their dash for cash, the liquidators of the old, defunct power companies sold off all they could of the power and generation networks.

With the price of copper - due to the Susem restrictions on mining - soaring to record levels, thousands of miles of cables have been ripped out and sold or stolen by opportunist thieves. What cabling remains having been left unserviced for so long means it is likely to prove unusable.

Similarly, petrol distribution networks no longer exist or have also fallen into disuse. Not

courts cl the restri the Sus scrap m ing as a tankers been breake and n the N where a ca basis mon ever pro

U

d

and p companies Another s the governi its intenti monies out unpaid ele As Dr. Sociologist Snaresbro

Beware of geeks bearing gi...

By **Albert Searle**
Public Affairs Editor

HOW was it possible the entire world could have been so gullible? How was it we were all taken in by the Susem power units, their so-called 'soufins'? So speedily jettison our traditional modes of energy, their sources of supply?

Much invective may have been heaped on Daniel Collins, the man whom the Susem used so persuasively to convince us - en-masse - to take these untried units.

Collins may well be guilty of 'selling' us something he knew was less than perfect, though to be fair to him, he denies knowingly doing so. But to blame Collins for the imminent shortfall in energy supplies facing the world would be to make him merely a scapegoat.

Others have sought to lay the blame at our own individual doors. That it was our greediness, our partiality to 'somethi... for not...

Howe... such a ... frailty w...

ing it on the wrong persons. After all who can be censured, especially those amongst us who are poor, for wanting to reduce their fuel bills?

No, the blame for our current collective dilemma lies elsewhere.

The roots of our woe lie entwined within the very heart of our modern, supposedly sophisticated global society.

The rogues responsible for our forthcoming world without power are those purveyors of hard nosed, 'no-nonsense', 'can-do' capitalism...

Today we are dictated to - like it or not - by 'Processing'. Every aspect of our lives from cradle to grave and beyond, has become part of a process; everything is 'systemised'. And all done in the name of the great god - 'Efficiency'.

This creed's priests and 'wunderkind' acolyte geeks are accountants, auditors, time-and-motion analysts. They have long decried that 'surplus capacity' to be an abomination of such depravat...

And worse, priestly executiv exalted in their rations by app congregations of t Believers: affluent holders of joint companies. Each ir in dividend, rise in price, cut in taxes Executive-Priests-o ency spirited up fro sell-off of surpluse met by the Devout's uses of "Hallelujah".

But now 'Effici like other gods be has been found to po feet of clay. The mir wrought by its pr merely mirages.

This false god, by moving our 'rainy reserves of energy plunged us into the s of powerlessness portentous poverty which we find oursel now cast.

It is the accountan auditors and analys who have brought us this sorry pass. It is the who are the real culprits

It is they who hav tricked and cheated...

Susem abductions s...

Ivana Fly
Adbuctions Editor

WORLDWIDE WARNINGS of Alien abductions were issued yesterday. They follow the latest spate of Susem raids.

...cks ...ne

all the victims are men. But according to CICAA's chief, Fabio Rigido, there is another, ominous pattern developing in the latest attacks. Sr. Rigido said: "They [the Aliens] are becoming choosy. In the beginning they took all the men they captured. But now they are taking only the young healthy ones, those in good ... The others they return within

General Tucers, CoC of US Southern Command speaks to Andrew Hendr...

The soldiers' General who stands astride the Isthmus

General Armstrong Tucers, CinC of Southern Command

GENERAL ARMSTONG TUCERS, Commander of the ...0,000 strong, US Southern Command, is a patient, careful man He is, in his words: "well aware of the awesome responsibility placed on my shoulders."

The General's task is nothing less than to contain and then repulse the expected invasion of Panama by Nonette insurgents from neighbouring Columbia He also is charged with safeguarding the Panama Canal - vital to US security - from any direct attack.

At 54, General Tucers is just one year from retirement and could have been expected to seek a quieter command with which to end a lifetime's military service than the Southern Command. But to the General, the coming conflict with the Nonettes is one he is eagerly looking forward to

To many in the US Army, including those serving directly under him, General Tucers is looked upon as a 'soldier's General'.

General Tucers also has a reputation for not suffering politicians gladly. The fact, is, suffering Pentagon insiders say, that he only accepted the post of Southern Commander on the understanding

That the General's Command is unencumbered from politicians and the disdain with which he holds them, was evident from his comments as he outlined the task he and his forces face

General Tucers first saw military action in the Vietnam War at siege of Khe Sanh "Vietnam was my first tour of duty," he said, "and Khe Sanh, my baptism of fire.

"We were on course to deliver a knock-out blow to the Vietcong but the politicians in Washington lost their nerve and had us pull out before we had the chance of winning. I saw many men, experienced, battle hardened soldiers, killed at Khe Sanh

General Tucers said that the combination of concentrated fixed military might and airborne firepower were a winning formula for combating insurgent armies such as the Nonettes

"The notion of fighting guerrilla armies with the same mode of tactics as them is wasteful," he said

"How to fight and win low-intensity campaigns is that you make them high-intensity campaigns. As the people down there in Brazil have just shown at Jatai, you take over the routes the enemy have to control if they are to advance

"And the moment the enemy appears, you hit them with everything you've got.

wipe them out or at leas away their will and abi fight.

"If the Nonette gu should attempt to North America the come in only two w land and by sea Nonettes cannot com because one, they do any boats and tw should they get the on some shipping would blow them c water the moment sail.

"This leaves option, which in t the Panamanian Ist this is why we are

"If the Latin ar there in Brazil t that with US assistance these N be beaten back, t of the US's f hardened, exper professional for well placed to decisive knoc They will dri called 'crypto c where they hel in the history b

General Tu forces were c series of o Should any come under a will automati by a circle of positions In

Polly Portillo reports from OTSA's HQ S...

Brazil claim... rebels beaten bac...

Offensive planned but doubts persist

OTSA's commanders, buoyed by intelligence reports of the magnitude of the Nonette' retreat after the Battle of Jatai, are planning to take the war into rebel-controlled territory

OTSAS's aim, it is reported, is to seize back much of the southern Sertão - the semi-desert of central of Brazil Some defence strategists, however, doubt the wisdom of such a campaign Others also question the true size of the OTSA's forces' success.

General Costa, head of the Brazilian junta and his fellow leaders of OTSA countries jointly announced yesterday that it was the "sacred intention" of the Alliance to follow up their victory over the Nonettes at Jatai with full-scale offensive into the ...

have shown that given determination it is possible not only to repulse the enemy but also to crush them

"From now on there will be no more retreat, no more excuses for despondency Now is the moment to grasp the opportunity brought about by the historic victory of our courageous forces Now is the time to pursue these Alien-backed usurpers into their lairs and annihilate them without quarter or mercy"

General Costa's confidence of military success against the Nonettes notwithstanding, there are increasing doubts as to OTAS's ability to carry the war to the rebels There are also reservations as to the actual size of the Brazilian army's victory at Jatai

before being stopp army road-blocks S has also been stepped the huge military base Simão

Martin Casaval, a d analyst and fierce critic Junta, also has his doub said: "If Jatai is such victory how is it that (aren't welcoming the N to see it for themselves?"

Then, more omin Casaval added: "If Nonettes are suppose have been wiped out, has there not been a count of their dead?"

OTSA's spokesman, ponding to Casaval's c ments said that the rea there were not any None dead was that they had ta their causalities with them

129: SIÂN

On Wednesday evening I thought like everyone, that forming a Nonette in Cilgerren was motivated more by the need for new soufins than anything else. And this included Megan Lloyd, vice-chair of the Women's Institute who came round to see me. Now I am not so sure.

There is already talk in the village that our Nonette has been hijacked by extremists, the WI. While they are the very last people I thought of as radicals, I have to agree there is more than a grain of truth to what is being said.

Cilgerren has its Nonette and almost with no more ado than if it was a foregone event. By the time of Friday's meeting 216 of us had already signed up, or so Pat Mealam chair of the WI said. But it's the other things which have set people talking, and worrying. There is nothing wrong with Mrs Mealam or Mrs Lloyd but it is those with them who are odd.

There was nothing wrong either, or so everyone thought, with the WI organising the meeting Friday evening. I had always viewed them as well-meaning but a bit fuddy duddy, and they made jam. I had signed their petitions in the past, we all had, including the ones against the closure of St Dogmaels, Cardigan and its amalgamation with Dyfed General at Fishguard. However, unknown to me until Gwyneth, Geraint the landlord of the Pendre's wife, explained afterwards, it was St Dogmaels closing which had made the women of the WI so strident. Many of them, Gwyneth said, had been helpers there and with it closing down they were no longer needed (or wanted by the Dyfed Health Trust). Not just those from the Cilgerren WI and the one in Cardigan but from as far afield as Aberavon and even Lampeter. Although they all became very organised, the Health Trust refused to change its mind and Huw Howells, our local MP would not support them either, so they became militant, and when the closure went ahead, bitter. Especially towards the Health Trust and Huw Howells.

On the days before the meeting they had run round Cilgerren drumming up support for a Nonette. However, yesterday morning posters appeared announcing that due to increased interest it had been transferred to the Bethlehem Congregational Chapel. It is bigger than the WI's hall but I did wonder if the change hadn't more to do with the WI's 'marketing' than Danny's telecast Thursday evening. He said they had already received more than 15 million Internet 'hits' and might have difficulty keeping up with demand. But either way, come the evening the Bethlehem Chapel was packed.

Things began ordinarily enough including Llwynog Dafis, the deacon, stressing the meeting being held in the Chapel gave it no religious significance whatsoever. Mrs Mealam, who opened the meeting, read out a list of things that had still to be done including demarcating the wards and fixing a date for the elections.

DUCTED CADET
IEN'S SEX HE

SIVE : THE FULL SHOCKNG ST

turned from a four day non-stop forced SEX ORGY ORDEAL with Al

ears for 40 still held - "Many cadets speechless" doctors say

Bovis in San Sebastion reports on the return of the missing Spanish cadets

20 of the 60 ts released from utches, concerns ill held captive t.

spread of the s suffered by these adets, many people ern Spanish naval e worst.

erged of the depths of young men suffered at ls, worried parents and e joined in silent prayer sea port's Buen Pastor cathedral for their sons' and fellow shipmates' safe return and safe recovery from their suffering

Dr Pedro Lopez, one of the doctors at the city's prestigious Hospital Victor Hugo where the cadets are being treated, said: "All the boys are very exhausted from their ordeal. Some are showing signs of rough treatment consistent with kicking and whipping.

All however, are suffering from impairment to their speech with a number unable to speak at all." But these were only some of the details of the terrible injuries and trauma these young men suffered at the hands of the Susem

According to other reports circulating from the hospital as well as the from the rescue party which first found the cadets wandering on the nearby Santa Clara islands, none of the cadets were spared from the Alie frenzied lovemaking

Even the youngest, a mere b reported to have been forced to the Susem's degenerate acts of pe

It has been possible to piece to details of the cadets' ordeal in those who were at the young me they began their recovery.

Because details of these youth so shocking, and as a family ne we know is read by millions of have, in keeping with our strict of barring sex and filth from decided it would be irrespons details of these cadets' **prolon sexual assaults day af** nighttime as well as the tortures including **trampolin**

FREE 4 PAGE SEALED ADULT PULLOUT SUPPLIMENT: F

he Spanish cadets' **shocking sex ordeals** suffered at the

Susem or visit our web site www.chronbear.uk. (parental locking app

Polly Portillo reports from Panama City

Caracas falls to Nonettes

CARACAS, the Venezuelan capital has fallen to the Nonettes. Venezuela has ceased to exist as an independent state. Hugo Arias' government is reported fled the Ila Margarita and sought refuge in the United States.

Hours before the city's fall upwards of 100,000 people were reported besieging the capital's airport in desperate bids to escape before the None

Most of those seeking to escape were supporters of the Arias regime. Their fates are unknown.

With the fall of Caracas, the flight of the Arias government to the US, all northern South America, except for a small enclave in the north of Colombia is now in Nonette hands

In less than three months half a continent has fallen ...

May, the Nonettes as a fighting force, did not exist Within 100 days they have seized control of an area larger than the United States with a population of more than 100 million.

The fall of Caracas also spells the end of any prospect of US intervention coming to the rescue of those trapped behind in the city and the ...

"Nonettes are communists" - US senator claims

BRETT ANDERSON
WASHINGTON CORRESPONDENT

THE Nonette movement is nothing more than a latterday communist front, a leading Senator claimed last night.

Sam Dich, Iowa's outspoken rightwing Republican Senator has long campaigned against the Susem and the Nonette communities they back In a speech to the US Senate, Dich demanded that the Nonettes be recognised as potential threats to the US.

Though the US administration and others had always ignored the Senator's views, attitudes are now charging in Sam Dich's favour.

Though there is widespread concern in the US over the looming energy crisis, the threat of impending of socialism - be it actual or imagined - is an issue which has again taken centre stage in the minds of many Americans and not just those of right.

Senator Sam Dich

The looming fuel shortage however, has been a handy stick with which to beat the drum of 'communist threat'.

Senator Dich, speaking later at a reception in Washington, said: "In the last century the United States faced up to the menace of international communism.

"Though it took the American people many years and at great cost, we finally overcame the evil of its threat to our freedoms and democracy.

"Now this same threat has reared its ugly head once more. And once again the United States must stand firm against this scourge of communism and their fellow traveling liberals.

Sen Dich said: "The American people must be made fully aware of this threat and the sacrifices needed if our great nation is to maintain is power and greatness. There can be no great ...

Is the world under the Susem's sway?

Steven Dunn
Economics Editor

In a flurry of hastily arranged international conferences, forums and summits by world great, good and powerful, there appears to be just two questions which beg answers:

- Just how much power do the Susem have over us?
- How is the world going to live with it?

Many geo-political experts, however, have already answered them. And the sum of their conclusions cannot make happy reading for the world's presidents, prime ministers, secretary-generals, to say nothing of dictators and despots. These experts verdicts can be summed up as: "Either we do as the Susem say or we pay the inevitable collapse of our societies."

One leading US think tank, IoAS in Georgetown, Washington, has gone so far as to predict the collapse of the nation state as we know it. Edward Studgate, one of its senior directors said: "The Aliens have struck everyone's and every society's Achilles heel - energy supply.

"It is not a matter of managing on this or that reduced percentage of power. Modern societies have evolved to generate energy to match demand. In turn their form and functioning is determined by the maximum use of that power.

"Not only are societies 'dedicated energy dependent' but 'multi-faceted layered integrated entities'. Markedly change just one input to such a society - energy supply for example - and the entity will rapidly implode," he said.

Pierre Grenouille, once one of France's leading economic theorists but now at ULCA, is even gloomier. According to his analysis, there will be little or no alternative but to accept the Susem's terms. He said: "Today not only are we dependent on energy but also on the seamlessness of processed data transmission. One or two stoppages every now and then is okay, maybe, but when they become more frequent many other things will begin to falter. In America it will be bad, but in France, which has lost most of its power already, it will be disastrous. That is why I am over here and not there."

What, if anything, can be done to avert the break-up of sovereign states? Dr. John Hansen of Sheppey University sees a glimmer of hope for world leaders. He said: "The Susem have said that once they have located their missing spacecraft they will depart from the Earth. There ... governments shou... until ... have ... have ... sup... ord... the ... the ... are ... ha... al...

...ernment ...o Confidenc... vote threat

...at is en... for Bri... energy LibCon ...rday. ...rth, MP ...n out... ...ngtime ...ment's ...at he ...nace". ...vents ...ght I was day ...ence

Sir Guy Beckworth yesterday

must resign immediately before they are forced to do so and make way for a ...

motion of 'No ...fidence' are seen a... ...mote. He does, how... encapsulate much o... sentiment building amongst many of the ... in the government ... soon as possible.

He added: "Like m... others I have unwav...ingly advocated a po... of extreme caution a... wariness towards t... Aliens' siren overtures.

"But senior members ... this government ...

International scramble for exclusive

Victims to give vital clues on the Aliens

Janine Lewis
in San Sebastion, Spain

Experts fought experts outside the Hospital Victor Hugo in this historic seafaring city today.

University teams from across Europe and the United States were in fierce competition for exclusive access to the cadets abducted by the Susem and who are still recovering.

Many townspeople were taken aback at the sight of supposedl... respected academic... openly fighting with one another. However i... appears that even the prospect of large sums of money offered by the foreign scientists have

Then she said that as more than the required number of people in Cilgerren had already pledged to join and as we needed to get our skates on and not get caught up in the queue for the new soufins, they (the WI) had already emailed the village's Nonette application. I thought this was most high-handed of them but before anyone could say anything she handed over the meeting to Mrs Lloyd.

On Wednesday evening Mrs Lloyd came across as being, well, rather ordinary by but Friday she had all the fervour of Evan Roberts the Divine Movement preacher who had whipped the Bethlehem Chapel's congregation to a frenzy a century ago. She also had taken as gospel what Danny had said in his telecasts and James's as well. "We now have the chance," she said, "to take control of our communities from those who have insidiously filched them from us," (the 'filchers' I gathered later included the Dyfed Health Trust).

When she next said Cilgerren was not alone in sending its application off but those in other places had as well, I had a feeling of uneasiness. When a woman from Aberporth (a "fraternal guest," Mrs Lloyd called her) talked about "solidarity" and us needing to be "united against unrepresentative authority which was bound to attack us," my wariness grew. More so when I noticed many of those applauding her were other women I had not seen before. On they both went, some others too, all from the WI I noted and all were getting more and more carried away with themselves.

I could see some of the audience including Llwynog Dafis himself becoming uncomfortable with the tone of what they were saying, so when Geraint called out what reply had they to the email it came as a bit of light relief.

When Mrs Mealam said they hadn't any as yet, it was evident she was on the defensive. And seeing she was, Geraint gleefully tormented her by saying what was the point of her and "her little friends," as he called them, "ranting" on the way they were when they hadn't sorted this out?

This upset the WI women. Mrs Lloyd lashed back accusing Geraint of being cynical, and when he said he agreed with her they became quite agitated.

Others then joined in, all asking questions and mostly critical of what the WI women had said. It wasn't long before they were raising their voices. And when someone accused Mrs Mealam of packing the meeting with "outsiders", I could see she was upset. So could Llwnnog Dafis.

He was soon on his feet calling for calm. And when he had everyone hushed back down he said it was best if the meeting was called to a close and another held when there had been a reply to the e-mail.

I don't know how many people at the meeting who were thinking of joining now have cold feet, but there is bound to have been a few.

cures us southern ...

Panama safe from Nonette menace" - says General Tucers

n Keele
Clayton, Panama

...tars and Stripes ...lying in triumph ...he entire 51 miles' ... of the Panama

...Panama City on ...acific to Colon on ...aribbean, an estim- ...20,000 US Defence ... have taken up ...ons against possible ...s by the Nonette ... now reported ...acing within 100 ... of the Panamanian ...er.

...neral Armstrong Tu- ... Commander of the ...y re-formed US Sou- ...n Command said: "A ...ective wall of steel as ... as a moat of water ... girds the waist of ... Americas.

...he might of the ...ited States is now ...ayed to protect all the ...tions of Central and ...rth America. May the ...stroyers of Freedom, ... forces of darkness ...tempt to suborn Demo- ...acy and Liberty then ... will hurl them back ...eyond the peaks of Darien."

No sooner had the General Tucers spoken than the air was filled with the deafening roar of a flight of US Marines' British made Harrier jump-jet fighters from the nearby Wright Field air base.

General Tucers added that if the threat to Panama grew, further forces would be stationed in CNZ to defend the region.

One of the problems facing the US and Panamanian forces alike, are the flood of refugees streaming north from neighbouring Columbia and Venezuela. Although most of these arrivals are by sea, a large number are also arriveing by air. It is the latter which is giving both countries' forces the biggest headache.

Few if any of these arrivals are anything but poor. Many are reported to be some of Columbia's drug traffickers and thus automatically on the US Drug Enforcement Agency's "most wanted" list.

However, it is the wealth these new arrivals bring with them which ensures a warm welcome from many of Panama's poorly paid immigration officials. Already there is reported animosity between US and Panamanian officials.

Should this trend continue it could mar the chances of the US carrying out the main purpose of their mission.

There is the question of the US being able actually to stem any anticipated Nonette advance into Panama and the rest of the Americas. Some observers see it as a case of President Warren being pressurised into being seen to be doing something - anything - in the present situation.

With the shadow of Tonicwater still hanging over his administration, the President's area of manoeuvre is extremely limited. If he had been seen to be dithering as he had over the Serb Croat repatriations and the debacle over what is now considered to be a mismanaged policy initiate, President Warren could lose out in any successes

...ndustry set ... ...uffer KO blows

...nter blackouts warning as power ... workers set to be laid off as ind... ...oduction certain to slump to 193...

...a Biggles
...l Correspondent

...TAIN is facing ...ive power cuts ...winter, experts ...cast yesterday.

...less power supplies ...be brought back to ...al, up to 5 million ...ers could be laid off ... output slump to ...s not seen since the ...s and so, bringing yet more misery to an already downhearted and dispirited society.

This is just one of the grim warnings given by top experts at Lemos, Britain's leading think-tank. Project director Gavin Strange said that under present trends, we face no alternative than to make massive, "war-time" rationing of re-sources without the help

...ppies" Okay Yah KO...

...e-retail major collapses ...stors' money lost"

... Stoneburgher

...H.COM is okay ...Once labeled the ...fax for yuppies, ... surviving direct- ...ed last night that ...d to secure fresh ... had no alter- ...ease trading. ...Brenda Dober- ...eally is just so ...We just ...

Fellow director, Martin Lane said: "It's just such a jolly darn rotten shame. Both our families have stood by us throughout this terribly difficult time period but not even they could find the necessary £10,000 to see us through. Now after all our terribly hard work it has all come to absolutely zilch. It just seems that society simply ...

...er rather than with ... was, in its day, on... most highly rated ... merce companies ... terms of prestige ar... capitalisation.

At its IPO it was ... more £1.2billion, ... giddier heights ... within the month a... that four months la... time both Dober...

Alien abductions ebb

By **Phillip Brown**
Abductions Correspondent

AS midnight struck yesterday, the world experienced the first complete Alien abduction-free day for a whole month.

Staff at the Alien Abduction Information Centre, in Milan, were reported left clicking their heel yesterday. Centre chief, Alberto Perelli said: "We do not know what is happening but it has gone very quiet all of a sudden.

"One week ago the Susem were taking as many as 500 people a day, maybe more. But during the past seven days the numbers have been dropping off until yesterday there was no one across the entire globe reported as abducted by the Aliens."

... the past week has been more people have actually been reported released by the Aliens than abducted by them.

Although experts are at a loss to explain this sudden change in Susem activities, all are continuing to counsel extreme caution to members of the public. They still say that we must remain vigilant against the risks of sudden attacks by Susem snatch craft.

Anne Hargrieves of IntraMed, who sends more than 500,000 holidaymakers to the Mediterranean annually, said: "It is vital people do not drop their guard against possible abductions by the Aliens.

"Rule Number One is that in daylight hours it is vital to only travel in mixed sex groups. This is especially important to young men in good to average physical condition.

"Rule Two is make a will just in case you are abducted and don't

US Panama presence resented

By **Paulo Pidde**
In Panama

"GRINGOS IR EMBORA!" - "Americans Go Home" is scrawled on the walls of the former 'School of Americas' ...

...manians, disgruntled at having been peremptorily displaced from their homes and businesses in the former Canal Zone to make way for the American Military

US Forces, in their rush to ... accused

Doubts of Nonette defeat grow

OTSA 'Victory' claims seen as sham

By **Alan Hartley**
In Rio de Janerio

General Costa head of OTSA

THERE HAS not been any Nonette attack against OTSA positions at Jatai or at other point along the front between the two sides.

OTSA's claim to have delivered a defeat against Nonette forces is now seen at best, as little more than misinterpretation of events. At worst, it raises grave doubts of OTAS's ability to take on and win against any battle with the Alien-backed movement.

It has also been revealed that US satellite reconnaissance of all of South America has ceased to exist ever since the Susem detected the satellites spying on them. OTSA forces and presumably those of the US stationed in Panama, are fighting blind

Revelations of the 'Farsa em Jatai' ('Farce at Jatai)', as it is now dubbed by many across much of Brazil, are already sending shockwaves throughout the OTSA Alliance

Already there are reports of dissension between member states as to the future conduct of the campaign against the Nonettes.

The Chilean and Argentinean Defence Ministries, who both consider their armed forces to be better trained and more professional than the Brazilians, are pressing for General Augusto de Santos, the commander of OTSA's forces at Jatai, to be replaced.

As both de Santos and his mentor, General Costa, head of the Brazilian Junta come from the state of Minas Gerais, his replacement is unlikely

It is, however, likely to further deepen the differences between the members of the alliance as to the overall strategy and direction of future campaign policy

US advisors assigned to OTSA are reported attempting to smooth over the differences between the Brazilians and the others

The wider repercussions ... the debacle at Jatai, is amon... the actual OTSA forc... themselves

The morale of the so-calle... 'poor bloody infantry' w... have suffered as news ... Jatai filters down to them

"Callous Conman Collins could kill" - says OAP

By **Nicola Kay**
Social Affairs Editor

THE world's most reviled conman, Daniel Collins, could cause the lingering deaths of ...

Epsom pensioners, Phoebe and Harold Bassant, are among the first OAPs to learn of the terror they will experience this winter without heat and light. Not only do they face freezing to death but almost will also certainly

I tucked Becky in, kissed her goodnight, saw that Patrick was okay then went into the kitchen. I was whacked, I had not stopped all day. I put the kettle on, made some tea, sat down. Then I had a bit of a cry.

I just didn't know what to do. Everything is getting me down but what the Council did this morning is the last straw. It's not as if I can chuck it all in, not now, not without letting everyone down, even if I could my name would be mud in the flats, the Salutation. I have bitten off more than I can chew. If only I had kept my big stupid mouth shut none of this would have happened.

Sophie called it an "NTQ" but as I read it again, "...for repeatedly making to your fellow tenants...racist attacks of a verbal...physically intimidating nature..." it was a terrible hurt. Me? Racist, intimidation? Me who's had more than my own share of that!

There were two of them, "heavies", they had come just before twelve in a big black BMW. That Hayley from the Blackstock office waiting around down outside for them the ten minutes before and forever glancing up at the flats with some man, and he going non-stop on his mobile. Here I am, elected this last week to front the flats' Nonette with 104 votes, only mine and a spoiled one against and the Council is saying I'm reported as being a racist!

The four of them marched into the flats with all the look of a hit squad. But it wasn't till they rang my bell that I realised I was the one they had come for. Me, who had Mrs Nazar downstairs going round promoting myself for the position, even when I had told her not to, she suffering from diabetes the way she is and making herself ill over it, a racist!

Before I could even get to the door they were thumping it and with Hayley hollering "Mrs O'Conner" through the letterbox, that she knew I was "in." Then all of them just barged inside without so much of a "please may we", the bigger one sneering down, the older one parroting my name with Hayley jabbering "She" with my details and he calling her "Ms Thomas" and shoving the papers in my hand. Little five foot nothing me, accused of threatening the neighbours! Here I am, with all the others in the other groups pressing that I organise the Nine we have next to form, threatening the neighbours! I had barely time to read "Notice to Quit" let alone more, than they had made it back to the stairs. I shouted to them but they'd not turned, nor when I ran out the balcony and they roaring off.

I sat sobbing feeling sorry for myself but soon I had such a rage, how dare they! How dare the Council do such a terrible thing, do it to me!

I phoned Sophie the moment they had gone. She calmed me down saying there had to be some mistake, that she would sort it out, that she knew someone in the Council's legal department. But I was panicking half an hour later with her phoning and saying that it wasn't, that it's intentional rubber-stamping the council use for getting rid of tenants who are troublemakers. And when I said, "My complaining over the repairs I suppose?" she said it

Andrew Hendry reports from Por...

Tobago Nonette takeover

Island's UDI sends shockwaves across the Caribbean

Trinidad and Tobago was torn in two yesterday

Tobago, the smaller sister island of this twin island Caribbean country fell to a surprise Nonette takeover As officials of Sir Ramish Patel's Government fled to Trinidad, cheering crowds of Tobagians welcomed the first forces from the nearby Nonette controlled island of Margarita

US Forces on full alert

backed unrest. However, such assistance is not expected to have any direct effect on the current crisis.

The breaking away of Tobago from Trinidad, though taking the authorities by surise comes as no surprise to many in the region. Tobagain citizens have always viewed themselves as not just the

poorer of the two islands but the Cinderella to its Trinidadian ugly sister

Such views are not without reason. Compared with Trinidad, Tobago has been denied most if not all of its share of the development aid, especially from the EU Regional Infrastructure Fund given to the two island state.

At a time when the country as a whole was set to benefit from increased oil revenues, none of it was being spent in Tobago. While this has been a cause of deep resentment among Tobagians there is also a political dimension

British holidaymakers trapped

Up to 600 holiday- makers, including several British, are thought to still be trapped on Tobago The British High Commission in Port of Spain, Trinidad's capital, said, however, that they are not thought to be in any immediate danger

The Foreign Office has issued an Emergency Helpine for concerned relatives It has also issued a travel warnng for entire Caribbean region

A State of Emergency has been issued in Trinidad US Forces are reported to be on full alert and flying 500 Marines to reinforce its Naval facility at Port of Spain. These, it is said, are as a precautionary move to forestall other Nonette backd uprisings elsewhere in the region

A massive EU-US emergency aid package is also said to be being made immeately available to all Caribbean states in a bid to head off other possible Nonette

Huge EU-US aid package rushed to region

The ruling PRP (Popular Right Party) led by Sir Ramish Patel, has maintained total control of all the levers of power including state sector employment and the awarding of government contracts.

Few if any of these contracts have been awarded to members of opposition party's including the tiny Tobago United Party.

Along with government patronage there was widespread corruption within the PRP Nearly all the government officials stationed on Tobago came from Trinidad

So when Tobagians heard the siren voices of the Nonettes in Margarita, they more-or-less collectively saw the chance of throwing of the Trinidadian yoke And they took it.

The wider implications of the Nonette takeover however, are likely to so be felt across the Caribbean as ... whole Tobago is not th... only island where the influ... ence of the Nonettes ha... taken root.

Just 50 miles to the north... the island of Grenada, wh... is still suffering from ... effects of the heavy han... US invasion of more ... two decades ago Bey... Grenada stretch the res... the Windward Islands

Every single one of... island chain has also su... from its bananas ... islands' only export - ... blocked as the result ... trade policies.

With the Nonettes... ising a way out of ... nomic hardships, US... has wrought, it is like...

Nonettism = socialism

Why we should all worry

By **Phillip Brown**
Security Correspondent

FEW of us lamented socialism's demise. Those forced to live under its regime - such as the people of Eastern Europe - still live with the ravages it wrought.

We in the West were fortunate being able to vote socialism from our lives the moment its flaws became apparent and too much damage done. There has been no wish from anyone East or West, for socialism's resurrection let alone its reimposition.

Socialism fell because we as individuals could create a better life for us all than could any of us collectively - no matter how honourable the original intentions - for any individual (the privilegencia excepted). Since socialism's passing, the rise of the individual and individualism has continued from strength to strength. The advent of the internet and E-mail has reinforced both. And both, it could be said, are now unassailable.

Thus the notion - in this day and age - of people, populations openly and willingly adopting any form of collectiveness, socialism - call it what you will - is an affront to commonsense. But this is precisely what the Alien-backed Nonette movement is insistent we embrace. And not just totally either but in all its totalitarianism.

Fortunately, however, it is the potential injustice of the imposition of such a proposed regime, especially towards us as individuals, which will bring about its demise yet once again.

Arguments can be advanced for action to be taken collectively for this measure or that, as and when circumstances dictate. An analysis of successful outcomes of any such actions, however, show it is solely because of individuals acting voluntarily in a common cause. The communal actions which have failed in their objectives are those where individuals have been coerced into participating collectively.

This difference in outcomes is yet another of socialism's inherent inadequacies. And again, why 'Nonettism' can only occur though imposition. And why, in the end it too, like all the other 'ism's' will fail. The only argument which is pertinent to Nonettism is the harm which it - along with its siren calls - will inflict upon us all.

Thus it is in all our mutual interests for us to assist our governments in bringing about the speedy reinstalling of our traditional sources of energy supply. And in the meanwhile, being frugal with what is available. It is afterall, more than just surviving a cold winter which is at stake but our continuing freedom from socialism as well.

Would you place your trust in your neighbour?

By Bob Cannon
Community Correspondent

HOW well do you know your neighbours? And if you know them well, how far would you trust them, a mile? Or would you response be the same as most people in the rest of Britain: "Not an inch".

Yet trust our neighbours - often complete strangers - with everything including our money, is what this new Nonette organisation is pressing on us to accept. It's no wonder many experts have branded this Alien backed movement's rules as a "recipe for chaos."

As leading sociologist, Dr. Martin Rees, of Snaresbrook University, says: "There may well be instances of people being completely trustworthy and look after their neighbours' interests, but they will be very much the exception rather than the ru... was brought up with the Su... school ethos of 'Love thy ne... bour' and while I still subscr... it in theory, in terms of it bei... practical policy in an adult w... being naive

"Unfortunately, as we all k... human nature does not cha... and that nature is essentiall... selfish and self-centred one... no one has succeeded in c... ing it for the better I'm afraid." Dr Rees is also of the view than an...

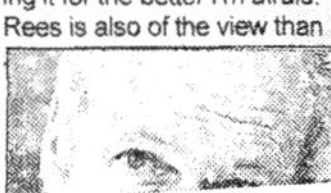

How well do you know your neighbour?

By **Susan McBeth**
Social Affairs Editor

IF you live in the suburbs or a country village you probably know your next door neighbour. You may even be the best of friends with them.

But if like most ... the person living next door to you, let alone formed a bond of friendship and trust with them. Yet this is what the Nonette movement is urging us all to do.

The proponents of this are the new-age cult of happy-clappy 'Love thy Ne...

Nonettes did not attack — Friendly fire slew Brazil troops

Jatai Lie

Polly Portillo reports from São Paulo

THE 527 deaths at Jatai were the result of OTSA forces firing on their own positions There was not any attack by the Nonettes on the Brazilian strongpoint

Thus there bas not been any battles with the Nonettes or any defeat of them.

The position of General Costa and his Junta within the Brazilian armed forces must now be in question.

The repercussions of the debacle at Jatai are however, likely to be felt far beyond the borders of Brazil and the OTSA Alliance.

The truth behind what really took place at Jatai was first revealed by two survivors from one of the firebases at Jatai

One of them, a second lieutenant with a Brazilian artillery detachment and identified only as 'C S' and was stationed at Firebase Claro He said many of the men serving with him at the firebase were conscripts from São Paulo and unused to being in the isolation of Brazil's rural backlands

Most of troops, he said, were in a state of tense battle readiness, all were filled with stories of what happened to those soldiers who had fallen into the hands of the Susem.

"All the men, including me," he said, "were 'trigger happy' and scared shitless of being attacked." He said that the soldiers in the other forward position would have been in same state of tense battle-readiness

At daybreak and after the firing ha... stopped, the lieutenant was charged wit... leading a damage assessment party of th... base. "All the incoming shell and mort... fragments," he said, "were those of o... own munitions as were those shel... which had failed to detonate

"I told my commander of what we h... ascertained. I know he contacted t... CHQ at Jatai but I heard nothing more

The lieutenant said later that day ... suffered a sprained ankle and managed... get invalided out of the upcoming mis...

wasn't that, but my organising the Nonette and with her saying she had also learned that other Council tenants "involved in disruptive activities," were also being served 'NTQ's a terrible cold shudder went through me. I had not needed her telling me either, there is something fishy going on.

Though the Council has me in the dumps there is a heap more getting me down. Between calling Sophie and she calling back, I had the people from Fieldway Road over that I had been watching out for. They came asking for help in setting up a group. They are not the only ones and I don't suppose the last to come round either. Being among the first to hold elections, others were wanting to know how we did it, as well as our working out the Wards, not that there is much to it all. I have tried getting them to talk with the others but because I'm head, well this first month anyway, it's me they are forever asking for, and on the telephone as well, and it doesn't stop there.

With the Fieldway people gone, then Sophie phoning and barely time to take in everything she had said, than Itzal, Mrs Nazel's boy was up with another e-mail from the Nonette HQ about preparing for "Nine times Nine", and here we are still struggling to sort out the first! Itzal is a little angel, I don't know what I would do without him sending and receiving the e-mails the way he does. He has such a serious face, never a smile, and still so worried about his mam that he asked about the mormic health booth thing, when would we be getting one? I had to tell him that I didn't know. Not that he is the only one asking but I was sad for him all the same and his mam.

After he had gone I had just time to get Becky and Patrick ready for the playgroup when Margaret was here to take them. As they were leaving the Ward representatives began arriving. What with sorting the auditors and how the bookkeeping is to be done, picking who is going out to learn from the Nonettes, will they need a passport, how to pick who is to go on the free space flight, where will the Nonette advisor stay? And before I knew it an afternoon was gone. All the while though I had what the Council had done, and what Sophie said, gnawing at me. But I dare not tell any at the meeting in case it would scare them off.

It was the same in the Salutation later. Margaret brought the kids home, I gave them their tea, but at seven I was taking them back to her again then it was off to work. There if anything, it was worse.

Bridie's friends told their friends about what I had first said and it has spread. There has been no end of people coming in and asking how to set up a Nonette. Even the types who would never drink in the Sallie are asking advice, including those from the big houses over Highbury Fields. Bridie is happy with the extra business and of course I would be a liar if I said I minded the attention. But now look where it's got me?

Mexico in Nonette crackdown

Hunt for fifth columnists - Chiapas forces increased

By Ian Trigg
In Mexico City

Mexican armed forces were on the alert yesterday following reports of fresh outbreaks of violence by bands of alleged Nonette backed guerrillas against government security forces throughout the state.

Armed Forces Minister, Raul Martinez said: "Within the past week there have been more than 120 incidents of public disobedience against the police, the army and other security agencies.

"There is abundant evidence that agents of these so-called Nonettes are behind all these disturbances. To ensure that security is immediately reestablished we have strengthened the pacification programme in Chiapas with units of Special Forces."

Martinez's outburst is only the latest government's response to the Nonette movement's growing influence across large swathes of Mexico.

In some states, especially those in the country's impoverished south, Nonettes are reported to be in de facto control of many of the smaller towns and villages.

In turn, this upsurge of the movement's strength has caused many of the government officials and supporters of the ruling PRI party to flee the affected regions.

Fears that they may end up suffering the same fates of their South American counterparts, has obviously been one of the reasons for many of the officials flight.

While Mexico's Defence and Security Ministers talk tough against the Nonettes, others sections of the government are tacitly acknowledging that the only way to combat the movement's growing influence is to tackle the two weaknesses of the current regime: corruption and mismanagement at all levels of the administration.

The impact of the Nonette's television showing of their 'Truth Committees' in the areas falling under the control is meeting with rising chorus of approv... from many people acr... Mexico.

With corruption and cro...ism widespread through... both government and po...cal life, it is doubtful if t... is any way these can ev... eradicated from Me... society.

With the Nonettes ...tem of open, accountab... ministration ordinary p...

"Nonettes will slash liv... standards" - say expe...

10m Britons doomed to Third World pov...

Crime rates will soar - NHS collapse ce...

...y Marcus Dooder
...olitical Editor

...HE Nonette movement, if ... takes hold, could drive ...own Western living stand...ds to Third World levels, ...perts forecast yesterday.

...They also predict that up to ... million Britons could be ...ced below the poverty line if ... country was run on Non...

collapse. These are just a few of a whole raft of facts computed by a leading University's panel of experts.

Dr. Hamish MacCrae, head of Wigtown University's Department of the Future which has investigated the impact of Nonette style regimes, said: "Our research is based on extensive consultation of a wide selection of the members of the public across the whole of Galloway and Dumfies.

"There can be no doubt of the ...

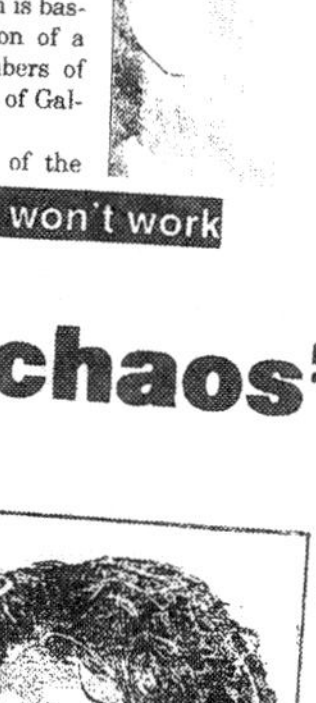

Those nutty Nonette rules in full: Why they can't work, won't work

Nonettes: 'Recipe for chaos'

Geraldine Baxter
Current Affairs Analyst

The Susem's terms for resupply of long lasting soufin energy units have been derided as daft by some experts, dangerous by others. But what do you our readers make of their crazy so-called terms? To help you make up your minds we have printed in full the views of a panel of independent, open-minded experts:

Dr Martin Rees

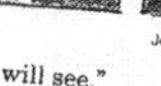

Alan Hardcastle

John Swift

Set upyour own happy clappy community:

Join with 80 of your neighbours to form a group, then expand it up to 730 members; the group will eventually be an independent sovereign state; have elections every month for a leader to represent you.

Dr. Martin Rees, Sociologist, Snarebrook University: "One quarter of all house sales in this country happen because people are unable to get on with their neighbours. Antagonism at these levels preclude any chance of such communities forming urban areas, which is where 90 percent of us happen to live."

Alan Hardcastle, economics specialist and Home Office advisor: "There are already street societies: such as the Neighbourhood Watch. These, like other such attempts have never worked. Their influence in stemming domestic burglary has been close to zero. How on earth could something like these new-fangled communities do any better?"

John Swift a tax consultant to a number of City businesses: "If the head of our Neighbourhood Watch is anything to go by, it's no wonder. He's a right little Hitler. But supposing these independent, sovereign communities are set up, what happens if the State of ... happens then? Does the UN send in Peacekeepers on back garden patrol? To my mind any such communities are a recipe for chaos."

Donate 10 percent of your earnings to your community:

MR: "I can see many things like perpetual motion happen before any government lets its citizens deduct such things from their income tax. And anyway, even if individuals did decide to cough up this 10 percent, who is going to collect it? Who is going to know if people are being honest? As a rule people are less than honest, just ask the Inland Revenue."

JS: "Ten percent of earnings represent 25 percent of the government's current tax take of the GDP. No government could withstand such a huge loss of revenue. Or alternatively, having to hike the overall tax rate to compensate the loss. And this is why they would not let people do it. Also, just who is going to oversee the money collected? Small communities would never be experienced enough to manage the necessary security safeguards. If you but knew the number of postcards I have seen sent by Bank Managers from the Caribbean to their bosses after they ha... sible for collecting their own taxes is fraught with idiocy. In some leafy lane suburb it might be run honestly. But on some of the housing estates I have seen either it would be stolen within minutes or used to finance crime."

Send a member to Nonetteland for 'training' and they in turn, will send an 'advisor to assist your group:

AH: I cannot see how this can happen. Unless they have gone through the proper immigration channels, any so-called Nonette advisors setting foot in this country would be rounded up and deported immediately."

MR: "Anyone from Britain, or any other country going over there, would leave themselves wide open to being brainwashed. Should they try on their return to implement what they have been taught, they will be immediately regarded as Fifth Columnists, 'Enemies Within.'"

JS: "These advisors might be useful in some Third World countries but what on earth can they can they teach anyone from an advanced society such as ours; native crafts? Every day on my way to the City I pass a pair of those Mormons. They are from Utah or somewhere, they have been ... will see."

Teaching screens: once your community has been set up you will receive one:

AH: "Possibly a good idea in theory. Anything which can improve the lamentable educational standards of today's kids is to be welcomed. But unless they are part of a school, I cannot see how any child is going to use them."

MR: "One screen per community? And what are you going to have? A queue, that is what you are going to have. I can just see all the kids waiting patiently for their turn, personally I do not think so! But should it, by rare chance, ever catch on, the teachers' unions would be campaigning to have them banned!"

JS: "As for paying pupils to learn on them, that is plainly stupid. As is the idea of giving children the vote once they have reached a certain educational level."

The Health Scanner; 'earning' enough 'educational points' entitles your community to be scanned by it into perfect health;

AH: "I do not claim to know much about health but this scanning device seems just too good ... hangover let alone ... dicky ticker."

MR: "Unless these sca...ers have been thorough... evaluated and passed ... the MCA, and that w... involve intensive trial... anyone, especially if the... are not a qualified med...ical practitioner, operat...ing them in this country will be committing a criminal - and I mean custodial- offence."

JS: "Just suppose these scanners caught on, do you know the first that would happen? They would have the full wrath of the medical profession, including the entire pharmaceutical industry, down on them like a ton of bricks. And there are not many lobbies more powerful than them."

Councils of communities; your community sends a delegate to represent you on a council of 80 other communities to handle 'area issues'.

AH: "Local town councils are already a joke. This would be the same. However, these new groups would be treading on town councils' turf. There would be chaos not to mention the conflicts with all other already established groups: all ...

131: MR MOORE

Barbados I knew, and Bermuda, but now Barbuda. I had never heard of this particular island until I read about it in today's Telegraph.

Listening to Mr Gibbons reiterating what had been in the papers regarding it being the next Caribbean island going over to a Nonette, I winced as he referred to Collins as "our illustrious ex-client" and glancing at me as he did so. I almost interrupted him to relate what I had heard yesterday from the Neighbourhood Watch, but espying Hilary Saxon who has recently come 'on team' also looking in my direction and June's words, "a crony of failed males with domination complexes" ringing in my ears again, I thought it best not to, just in case she might view me similarly.

Mr Gibbons spoke further of the knock-on effect these Nonette takeovers of islands and other out-of-the-way places are having on international business sentiment as well as the results of the Bank's latest customer opinion survey. He next went around the table soliciting our views and asking how our customers were responding to the current circumstances. After several had given their views including concurring with the survey's findings it was my turn to speak.

I really wanted to say "Wake up! Do not be tricked by these Nonettes. They are peddling fools' gold. Collins is a front duping us just as he did before. We must not sleepwalk into yet another nightmare of their dependency. These offers of free space trips etcetera are Trojan Horses luring us into stampeding to their grip. Believing that Nonettes mean no more than replacement energy units is cloud cuckoo land. I have first hand personal experience as to their true nature. These postage stamp sized countries where they have taken control and already have the new soufins are a smokescreen blinding us to the fact that none of them have actually arrived here. With Collins involved it is highly likely none will ever turn up anyway. And furthermore, I have it on the highest authority that many Nonettes are under investigation by the police for subversion. These Nonettes are a cancer growing in our midst. We must strike out this tumour before it is too late!" But instead I said my customers were much like the others'. The rush of applications for loans had not materialised into actual borrowings. In fact they are at an all time low. As for my customers' fears for the future and of power shortages? They do not, alas, have any.

It is not only my customers who have been taken in by this Nonette fad. Its pernicious effects are appearing everywhere. They are even right here in the Bank. According to Sharon the tearoom is awash with talk of who has joined a Nonette, or thrown in their lot with them to be more precise. But fortunately only the junior grades are affected, so far that is.

On my train of a morning it is the same. I hear no end of tales bemoaning the disruption these Nonettes are causing to people's lives. However, it was Martin Manborn from Harlow and is who Assistant Regional Commander of the Neighbourhood Watch who revealed to me that the Watch Leader, Aldous

Plight of the refugees

Edward Flynn reports from Juque on the Colombian Panamanian bord[er]

An unending human tide of desperate and dispossessed Colombian refugees have overwhelmed the resources of Juquee, this tiny frontier town. Many of those who have fled have brought harrowing accounts of hardships and privation in their headlong flight to escape from the clutches of the Nonettes and horrors of the marauding militias and rogue units of the now defunct Colombian army.

This sudden influx of refugees took local Red Cross and other aid agencies unawares. Until just a few days ago there had been a mere trickle of people fleeing the aftermath the Colombian government's collapse. With the fall of Medellin to the Nonettes a week ago, more than 50,000 people have fled the city in a headlong dash to the Pacific coast and refuge in Panama.

Mass Exodus

Every available boat from pleasure craft to ocean-going freighters as well as frigates of the Colombian navy have made it northward to Panama, each swarming with refugees dreading the consequences of a Nonette takeover. Many of the arrivals have described terrible scenes as headlong scramble for the boats to take them to Panama. Many more however, did not even make their escape this far.

Attacked

Many of the arrivals have told of horrific attacks by militias raiding convoys of fleeing people. "They are no more than highwaymen," said Rodina Marcella, a survivor of one such attack.

"Many people were shot by them in cold blood," she said, "if people did not hand over their money, jewellry quickly enough these bandits executed them straight away. There were many bodies on all the roads."

Rodina also gave chilling accounts of barbarity committed by so called communist FLM guerrillas. Many of the cars, buses and trucks which had left Medellin, she said, had been abandoned on the highway by their owners, the fate of occupants unknown.

Ms Marcella said that many people had first sought to flee with the retreating military northwards to Cartagena on the Caribbean coast but were ambushed by FARC insurgents. "Many people were killed by them, people who had nothing

Panama pleased with US protection

BY CONRAD WILSON IN PANAMA CITY

"AT last the Americans have come to save us!" was the cry of so many Panamanians as they rushed to welcome the arrival of the first of detachments of the Green Berets on their way to their base at nearby Fort Clayton.

An estimated 50,000 flag-waving people lined the main streets of Panama City to give the Americans a rousing welcome. To cheers from the crowds and the strains of a local marching band's rendition of the "Stars and Stripes For Ever", Battalion Commander, Juan Torres yelled: "... be back!" ... ntry is "It's go...

Speaking for many of her fellow Panamanians, Carmen said. "Now they are here we will have stability again, business confidence will be rekindled."

Carman, a 26- year-old estate agent is typical of so ... people in Panama ...

Have Alien abductions ended?

First kidnap-free week for two months
Med resorts breathe sigh of relief

By **Ivana Fly**
Abductions Editor

THE 'All Clear' was given by the Alien Abduction Centre yesterday. But is it too soon for holidaymakers to enjoy the Mediterranean sunshine?

He can come out to play now

Mario Favio of the Alien Abduction Centre, is guardedly optimistic at the prospects of an abduction-free summer. He said: "It is not only in Europe where Alien activity has stopped but in the rest of the world as well.

"Not only has one entire week now passed without an attack," he said, but even before this time the level of them was declining. Therefore this phenomenon can be said to have ended.

"We do not know why the Aliens have ended this activity but the

Others though are more cautious, that the abductions have come to an end.

Harold Jackson, head of H&J Personnel Insurance is one of those who urges caution. He said "Where is the evidence that these Aliens have giving up dragging of

Oil shares gush to new highs

Will Slick
Oil Analyst

Oil shares soared to new highs yesterday Scallop closed at 1428p a 17.5 percent rise on the day and Esso jumped to $9.78, ... esia's Petroha missed the party.

Texan oil prospectors SOR also say its prices rose to $4.55, a new 52-week high. Even GRABLand, the newly formed property to buy up defunct filling stations, was a ... of the sud-

Huge hidden losses uncovered at Okay Yah

By **Steven Dunn**
Economics Editor

FOLLOWING THE crash of Okay Yah, reports were circulating the City yesterday of huge shortfalls in the assets of the collapsed former e-retail giant. There are also further reports that it had greater uncovered liabilities that first thought.

... for the ... to overestimate the value of their cyber assets. Such things as their domain names are usually down in the books as ... lions but ... collapses, ... worth the[m] ... to buy the[m] ... nothing.

"If Oka[y] ... from any ... coms, we ... will be a[n]

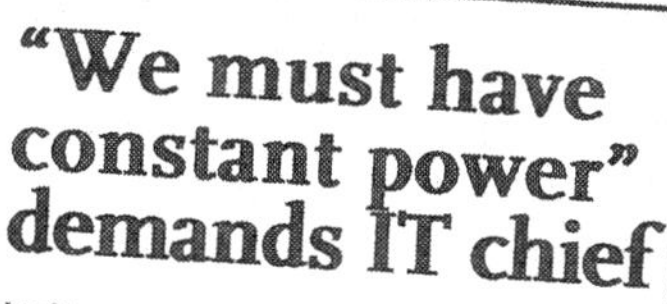

"We must have constant power" demands IT chief

JOY COMBO
IT CORRESPONDENT

INFORMATION technology must be given preference over other power users Britain's IT chief demanded yesterday.

"Though IT is a careful, efficient user of energy," says Sir John Hansen, head of Technofiles, "it is essential that it has a constant uninterrupted supply of power." Sir John, speaking at special one day conference in London on the threats posed by the looming energy crisis said: "Britain had just two choices. It either keeps what it can of its high-tech industries, research centres and the like, or if does not the country will rapidly revert to a Third World country, ravaged by civil war

"I know that some people will suffer, such as those in hospitals," Sir John said, "but I'm afraid it's something we will all have to take in our stride if we are to hold our own in this advanced world. We are talking of millions of jobs ...

OTSA puts brave face of Jatai 'error'

Nonette advance still forecast

Polly Portillo reports from São Paulo

"THE Nonettes are still going to come," is the unwavering dictum of Brazilian strongman, General Ernesto Costa.

The setback at Jatai, he said, was purely the result of untried technology and not because of any weakness on the part of the forces nor their commanders.

The General said that he, personally, had been against the deploying of remote ground listening sensors He only agreed to their installation, he said, at the insistence of US advisors He said, that events had only proved just how right he had been. The devices will now be removed and everyone can get back to "good old-fashioned, tried-and-tested soldiering," he said.

Major Vicente, OTSA's assurer

The Brazilian conviction that the Nonettes must advance southwards is based on the belief that the movement has to either expand or collapse

The only path south for the Nonettes, is though the mountain pass at Jatai

General Costa said that in the light of the situation at Jatai, OTSA forces will now begin making active sweeps of the area immediately to the north of the chain of firebases

How effective these new tactics will be in detecting any advances made by the Nonettes is open to serious question

Leading analyst, Martin Cascava, who is highly critical of the entire Jatai policy, said: "I stand by what I have previously said about Jatai. There is only one all weather road into Jatai and thus there is one such route out. If anything should go wrong there is not adequate means of retreat for ... forces. In terms of tactics, ...

Lither now has definite proof that some Nonettes in the Chelmsford area are "hotbeds of subversive elements", as Martin called them and has handed a complete dossier of their activities to the Police.

But for me the most insidious influence of these Nonettes is occurring in my own home. I dare not mention it at the Bank of course but it is an onerous load I bear. Ever since June took up with these Nonettes it is as if she is a woman possessed. And now that she has been elected to be one of their so-called 'Ward Representatives' I fear that my domestic situation could well deteriorate further.

Once there was an orderly, comforting routine to my life. On my journey home I could relax in the knowledge that June and the boys would be there to greet me, and an evening meal awaiting. Now, more often than not there is an empty house and a note on the microwave, sometimes not even this. Once, our social engagements with friends and acquaintances were arranged well in advance. Now, if June is ever at home she is frequently entertaining a host of people, most of whom I have never met, and often there will still be no supper ready for me either.

I have tried to be as positive as possible including consciously refraining from making adverse comments of Nonettes in June's presence, but sadly my efforts have been quite unappreciated. Even my offer of a helping hand to advise them on their finances was rebuffed. Instead of my banking expertise being welcomed, I was brusquely told I would need to actually join their Nonette, apply for election as Treasurer, be nominated by two members and that already three others were contending for the post. Further disheartening is that both boys have joined her Nonette as well.

But as I have mentioned to Sharon, these Nonettes have an Achilles Heel. People can only have their replacement soufins if they commit themselves to handing over ten per cent of their earnings to them. As soon as the government has the National Grid up and running again they will soon stop paying up. Also, because Collins is involved it is more than probable these replacement soufins will not materialise anyway. And when this happens everyone will soon see this Nonette movement for the sham it has to be.

Nonetheless there is still the everyday reality of the situation. When I return home this evening, what will be there to greet me? A house filled with strangers in 'urgent' discussion? Or, as last night, a Rossmore "heat 'n' eat Spicy Lasagna for One"? Yum, yum!

US beefs up Canal Force

Rising Nonette threat feared as Green Berets, Marines, Seal

Andrew Hendry
Fort Clayton, Panama

In response to the threat posed by the deteriorating security situation in neighbouring Colombia, US forces in Panama have been bolstered by a further influx of 10,000 crack battle hardened troops.

General Armstrong Tucers, Commander of the US Southern Command, welcoming ashore contingents of the US 9th and 25th Logistics Brigades at Colon, said: "May the Beacon of Freedom you bear aloft serve as yet further notice to the forces of darkness that all the peoples of the Americas will never be suborned."

General Tucers said that the deployment of US forces will now be extended beyond the PCZ to as far as the 3,000 feet high San Blas Mountains 50 miles to the east. This, he said, will relieve Panama's own security forces from the area and enabling them to be deployed in strength along the border with Colombia.

This, in part, is acknowledgment of the need to control the increasing numbers of refugees streaming into the country from Colombia and the rest of South America. There are fears that Nonette agents are also entering the country under the guise of refugees.

There are reports that the newly arrived troops are the spearhead of a possible US expeditionary force into neighbouring Colombia and possibly Venezuela as well. The composition of the newly arrived contingents, these reports say, is indicative that this is the case. However, a Southern Command spokesman said: "We are in Panama at the request of this country's government, to defend its sovereignty as well as the rest of Central and North America."

David Souter head of IoS, a Washington think-tank, is also dismissive of further US military involvement. "In all probability," says Souter, "the truth is probably more prosaic, a case of lobbyist infighting between this part of the Army, that part of Air Force, Navy and so forth within the Defense Department to have their interests at least to be seen as part of the action. And just now the PNZ is the only live show in the Pentagon.

"What actual benefit these 30,000 men stationed in Panama are to the defence of the US is any-

Sudden Susem Santorini sex swoop seizes sunning Swedes

Fears rise for 23 men still missing as panic sweeps Med. resort

By **Anthony Theodorou**
Roaming Correspondent

THERE were terrible scenes here yesterday as tourists fled the beaches of this sun drenched Greek island in a desperate bid to escape the latest Susem raid. Last night the island's police reported 23 Swedish holiday makers - all men - were unaccounted for and presumed snatched by the Aliens

As fears rose for the men's safety, Greek ... pressed chief ... tourism ...

Scores more islands at risk Tourists flee Caribbean US on full ale

Caribbean islands fall to Nonettes

Andrew Hendry
In Bridgetown, Barbados

Fear spread the length of the Windward Island chain yesterday as news of island after island falling to Nonette backed insurgents. All talk is of which Caribbean ministate will be the next to suffer a Nonette takeover.

Tobago, Grenada, St. Vincent all have fallen like dominos to the Nonettes. Between Trinidad in the sou... and Porto Rico in the no... there are hundresa of islan... a dozen and more sovere... states, four colonial administrations making up the Windward Island chain. Every one of them a tiny ... paradise in the Carib...

infiltration, there are, however, just too many islands and not enough ships to stop any determined attempts by the Nonettes from landing.

But the Nonette have no ... across the sea

Guatemala slips to Nonettes

Army, police powerless to stop loss

By Paulo Pidde
In Guatemala City

GUATEMALA'S MAYAN regions are now completely outside of Government control. The western and northern provinces of the country are now in Nonette hands.

Every one of government counter-insurgency campaigns against them have failed. All the pacification operations sent ...

have linked up with those in the neighboring Mexican states of Chaipas and Oaxaca.

Unless there is a further influx of US military assistance there is little that government forces can do to halt further losses to the Nonettes. The capital, Guatemala City, is full of ... leaving ...

200,000 pensioners wi... FREEZE to DEATH

"Influenza will wipe out the old in their '000s"

By **Colene Berner**
Health Correspondent

EXPERTS PREDICT up to 50,000 British old-age pensioners could die this winter because of the expected fuel shortages. But experts think this number might increase fourfold if there is a flu outbreak.

"There is no doubt about it elderly people will die this winter," Dr. Michael Fowler, world expert in aging said yesterday.

Dr. Fowler, Head of Gerontology at All Saints, Banstead, a leading centre on aging said: "Without proper heating this winter, older people are bound to die in droves. But if they huddle together with others for warmth, and if there is a flu bug going around they are bound to go down with it and because of their age they are certain to be killed by it.

"Mark my words", Dr. Fowler said, "If old people have to go without their heating there is going to be a lot of crusty brown bread about this winter."

Dr. Fowler was ...

OTSA admits Jatai under attack

Polly Portillo reports from São Paulo

JATAI, the OTSA strongpoint 750km north of São Paulo, is under enemy attack.

After earlier denials of any contact from the Nonettes, Brazil's defence ministry announced yesterday that their 100,000 strong force had fought off a number of strong rebel assaults in recent days.

OTSA liaison officer Major Vicente, said that the Nonette attacks on Jatai were in line with OTSA expectations He ... OTSA has anticipated they would. When the rebels have expended their resources and their forces are sufficiently exposed, then is the moment for OTSA to counterattack."

Although acknowledging there was active fighting taking place at Jatai, Major Vincente was unable to give figures for the number of OTSA causalities.

Replying to the disappearing helicopters from the São Simão airbase, he said they would have been flown to other locations as part of the dispersal policy

Everyone hereabout is jumping up and down thinking they have pulled off a coup, but none has a care for me. None has a care that, as it's my face going out on the TV, it will be my head first off the moment the backlash begins. Not that I have a say in anything, Rainbow marionettes me for the daily newscast then puts me back in my box. Oh, there's celebrity status should I go anywhere and the fan mail is still coming. I even have my own stalkers (though I notice they are pally with Rainbow).

Thirty million and more Internet and email responses and umpteen thousand Nonettes forming around the world may appear impressive, but they are not the success Congress (as everyone hereabout has taken to calling themselves) thinks they are. None have grasped, if outside reports are to go by, the fragility, hostility these fresh forming Nonettes face from much of the world.

But being in no position to comment (Rainbow would tell on me if I did) I keep mum. The same with something else they have not cottoned onto, emails. That these pass between here and the rest the world without hindrance doesn't add up. Or to put it another way, the only sum so doing is that those in authority are storing Nonette enrollers' names for later. And this will be sooner than the Congress realises. Paceillo's team are closing in on Pa-tu.

The Susem are keeping Pa-tu's location quiet just now, though Petruee says it is northern Canada way. As soon as they have finished researching they will be off. Assuming the rest of them have done sating their 'urges' that is.

This is another terrible worry. That the Susem are shameless is bad enough but now their wantoness is run rampant. Once their "R'n'R" was straightforward "S'n'S ("snatch and screw"), soldiers were surrounded, abducted and 'had' (again and again and...) then returned. The unabducted seeing the "violação por anjos depravados" rent upon their fellows and fearing fates similar, fled, often abandoning, such was their fright, their near mute mates where they were slumped. Hard on Susem heels and without so much as a shot needing to be fired, and to cries of "Viva! Viva!" Pedro's forces would then ride into town triumphant. Behind them came the organisers and in no time at all the entire population remaining would be Nonetted.

But the Susem become tired of this and so sought to liven up their outings. With no more 'new girl' inducting experience required they changed tactics. From broad front forward swooping in small squad sorties upon the soldiery they have taken to 'en masse targeting'. Unwittingly, Brazil's military played straight into their hands.

The southern Latin armies swept from the Sertão, and much else, retrenched (retreated) their remaining forces to the pass-ways to the south, the biggest being near the town of Jatai. This to cover the routes down from the interior to Rio and Sáo Paulo. An army, 100,000 strong, with strengthened

'No island safe from...

St. Kitts Nevis in Nonette backed split

Andrew Hendry
Basseterre, St. Kitts

The simmering rancour between the two islands of this tiny Caribbean country have finally surfaced in the long-heralded split of them. But it took the siren overtures of the Nonettes finally to lure little Nevis declare its UDI.

Government officials in the Nevis capital, Charlestown were bundled on broad the hydrofoil between the two islands for the main capital, Basseterre. There are no reports of tourists trapped on Nevis.

The St. Kitts prime minister, Sir Bartholomew Goldings, called for calm and announced his government was offering immediate talks with the Nevis islanders.

Sir Bartholomew said: "It is vital for the people of our two islands to establish a constitutional formula in which both our interests and needs can be met. Where we are able to meet as equals and resolve the ... those on St. Kitts. The people on St. Kitts think those on Nevis backward. The mainlanders have all the government jobs. They even own most of the property on Nevis.

"The two islands, apart from proximity, the English language and colonial history, have little in common.

"Both islands were forced into a union by the British years ago and has mutually disliked each other ever since. Thus for some, the split does not come as a surprise, only the manner of its timing," he said.

On a wider scale the takeover of Nevis by the Nonettes poses grave security considerations not just for St. Kitts but for the rest of the islands in the region.

Already the residue population of nearby island of Montserrat have taken up Nonette offers of assistance for the rehabilitation of their volcano damaged island.

Although the British authorities as yet have not acknowledged any loss of control ...

The economies of all the islands in the region have suffered in recent years from the collapses of both sugar and banana commodity prices as well as the decline in tourist numbers and their dollars.

Coupled with the increaseing restrictions placed on emigration to both Europe and North America, these have combined to bring increasing hardship to growing numbers of the islands' populations.

This deteriorating economic base of most of the eastern Caribbean islands has, in turn, led to social disintegration and rising crime levels, much of it violent. The increasing poverty of these islands has also helped fuel the huge rises in drug-smuggling from Columbia, although Columbia's fall to the Nonettes, has however, markedly reduced this trafficking in recent weeks.

The US Drug Enforcement Agency (DEA) patrols are still conducting their stop and search policy for cocaine and ... While their pat-

Fears for Santorini's shanghaied Swedes rise

By Tommy Marlow in Santorini

IN the aftermath of yesterday's scenes of bedlam and terror following Susem's audacious snatch of sunbathing Swedish soldiers, Santorini's sun drenched beaches were deserted today. Only the island's numerous bars and tavernas were busy though their balconies and outside tables were conspicuously deserted

Fears for the safety of the two dozen abducted blue eyed blond soldiers rose as news of the fates of the Spanish victims of Susem seizures spread among the surviving Swedes.

Hal Stahammer, who is councilling the soldiers who managed to escape the Aliens's clutches said: "When we are hearing of the ordeal suffered by those sea cadets then of ...

"All we can say is that they are young and strong. Every one of them had just completed a tough Tour of Duty in Macedonia and so they are in peak physical condition. We can only hope this helps them withstand whatever the Aliens want them for," he said.

Meanwhile, the Swedish Defence Ministry is arranging ...

Even your washing machine could cause a global c...

IT power worries spre...

...eraldine Baxter
...dustry Analyst

...he developed world is facing a ...reat which, until now, had pass... unnoticed. However, it is a peril ...hich seeps right into the sinews ...d fabric of our way of life: the ...mplete collapse of electronics.

...ccording to a paper submitted ... two Sheppey University Mathematics professors to the leading ...th journal: *'Big Numbers Monthly'*, the world faces immediate ...llapse if as little as 10 percent of ...r electronic systems including ...mputers, stop working properly ... as little as a few hours ...

...puter found in most ... machines will be affe... tions in the voltage ... powering them. Not ... tions caused by p... those due to incons... transmission voltag... start to happen wi... ahead.

"It is all the cons... Chaos Effect," said ... Tiny changes of ... Bunting have di... affect the working ... components in sub... will be so ...

Jatai: Many helicopters and crews 'missing'

OTSA widens Exclusion Zone around troubled strongpo...

THERE is a mood of grim determination at São Simão's sprawling military base Officially all is well but events belie such optimism Unofficially there is a grave crisis in the making

Ostensibly, OTSA's forward base at Jatai is in a state of Red Alert, poised ready to counter and repulse the anticipated advance of the Nonette rebels from Brazil's interior

The pattern of air movements from the São Simão air base however, indicates that something very different is taking place at Jatai.

All of OTAS's helicopters flew out from Sao Simeo but none have returned

Three days ago there was a sudden increase in the number of F15 sorties flying from the São Simão to Jatai, 120km to the north There was also a huge rise in the number of Blackhawk as well as the massive troop carrying Turnhaus helicopters taking off from the air base and flying in the same direction

So numerous were the flights that the cloudless sky to the north of the base was filled with white streaks of the warplanes' vapour trails. Today the same cloudless blue sky north did not have a single [vapour] trail

Many of the people in the nearby town of São Simão not only took to counting the planes flying out of the air base but also counting them back in

On the morning of the first day, outgoing and incoming flights balanced. But in the afternoon, although the same number of F15 returned as flew out, few of the helicopters returned from the one hour return journey

Throughout yesterday morning, not a single helicopter returned. During the afternoon there were not even any outward helicopter flights. Also, during yesterday afternoon, the number of F15s returning to São Simão was less than those which had taken off. The last F15 sortie of yesterday has yet to return.

In the days before the Jatai fiasco became public, São Simão's base commander, General Hugo Rodrigues, allowed the press extensive access to the base facil... and to its personnel inclu... pilots This policy has ... been completely reversed.

Along with extending Jatai Exclusion Zone include the base itself, s... iers are stationed along entire length of Route ... from the bridge over the ... Paraná - which gives a g... vantage point to view the b... - to several kilometres p... the base itself These soldi... ensure vehicles do not s... anywhere along the highw... or people take photographs

To many observers ... missing helicopters a... planes are yet further sign ... the military situation at Ja... is not going well for the Br...ilians and their OTSA pa...ners What must be of as gre...

PM warns against Nonette movement dangers
"100s of UK Nonette groups being formed"

"Nonettes a recipe for chaos and anarchy" - claims Campbell

By Sean Clayton
Political Correspondent

Edward Campbell voiced his anti-Nonette credentials loudly and clearly yesterday. In a no-holds-barred speech to Parliament, the prime minister said that the Nonette ... British way of life," the PM said, "it is a threat to parliamentary democracy as we have known it. The protagonists of this Nonette creed claim it is a true democracy. But it is no such thing. It is nothing more than mob rule - those who shout the loudest will rule the government. And this can only be accomplished by elected representatives working with government and not against it. All of us who sit in this House appreciate only too well the heavy burden of responsibility and duty we bear in upholding the freedoms and liberties all of us have come to take for ...

resolve (or so General Costa said announcing a doubling of the soldiers' pay and armed to the teeth, dug in ready for the Nonette advance. Following the General's soaring rhetoric of "Ela ameaca umpaser" ("they shall not pass") wags nicknamed it "Verdun." Sadly for the military, this strategy assumed the Nonettes are coming. But they aren't.

Everyone across the Congress is busy with the overseas Nonettes. What territorial expansion there is, as the southern Generals must have noticed, is in the north (only the bigger cities in Venezuela and Columbia remain non-Nonetted). And if the generals as well as wags had studied French military history a little closer they would have dubbed Jatai "Dien Bien Phu."

Though of no actual military relevance, Jatai, with its huge number of young men in prime condition promptly drew Susem interest. No sooner were the soldiers in position than the Susem had nesting sites set up in the hills over-looking the base. The same day General Costa edicted "Luta ultimar homen" ("fight to the last man") 'the girls' had the place surrounded. That night they raided it. And the next. By the third the base's outlying positions were abandoned, the remaining soldiery huddled together for mutual protection. Not that it gave them much, Susem 'urges' were only just coming on.

On the fourth night, having studied the hierarchy of the base, the Susem decided on some "extra fun," they raided the officers' quarters and bagged more than a few.

Being defenceless in the face of the hen-ger backed abductions of their fellows, it is possible a soldier's morale will suffer. Hearing, in the quiet of the night and following the latest such raid, coming from the surrounding hills, and between just audible sounds of music, the pained cries of their abducted fellows, it is likely a soldier's morale will decline further. Seeing of an early morning, soundlessly returned in the pre-dawn darkness the thousand and more taken the two nights before, slumped, near naked and speechless, it is probable that a soldier's morale will plummet. But hearing and then seeing their officers returned in the same ungainly states it is an absolute certainty that it will have a like effect on respect and discipline. And so it was. After a week, with relief columns and air attacks aborted (mass driver and pilot abduction), Jatai mutinied. A rabbled rout of retreat and desertion followed.

At first I was surprised that the Susem let this store of prime maledom decamp for I gathered they were having such a 'jolly' time, but another attraction has appeared. Already they have nests in the mountains north of Medellin. From there the Panama Canal is within easy reach. So are the 30,000 crack US Special Forces stationed along it. As Pheterisco says, there are more than enough there to keep 'the girls' going for a week or two. Knowing what is just about to befall these poor defenceless combat hardened soldiers, I did think I could earn brownie points for the future by contacting Princess to warn the Americans to get their men out while they can at least walk. But of course I have not had chance to and anyway it's too late now.

"Aliens 'raped' us"

Sea cadets in sex torture ordeal claim

ALL THE Spanish cadets abducted were sexually molested by the Aliens. The cadets were subjected to one sexual act after another for days on end.

All of the young men were forced into take part in acts of sexual intercourse with the Susem. Some of the cadets were tortured so as to satisfy the Aliens' depraved sexual practices.

As news of the cadets' ordeal spread, fears have grown for the safety of those still in the Aliens' clutches, including the 23 Swedish soldiers snatched from Santorini on Tuesday. Last night the parents and wives of soldiers issued a plea to the Aliens to return them without harm.

Fears rise for missing Swedes

According to a Spanish Navy spokesman, the cadets said they were taken to a remote valley high in the Pyrenees in one of the Aliens' spaceship." He said the cadets were dropped out of the craft into a haze of

hit the ground they were attacked by small flying machines which proceeded to tear off their clothes.

"All men are at risk from Aliens" - experts warn

"Then still in a state of bewilderment they were sprayed with jets of water," the spokesman said. "Still naked and very afraid these young men were prodded by mo[re] of the Aliens' flying weapo[ns] out of the mist into a da[r]kened clearing. But no soo[n]er had the cadets arrived he[re] than it was transformed int[o a] blinding psychedelic li[ght] show and booming w[ith] music.

"The cadets were still [in a] state of fear and confu[sion] when suddenly out of

Trojan' base closure demanded

"Why do the French let Aliens use Villacoublay?" demand MEPs

By Mark Lewis
Political Editor

VILLACOUBLAY must be closed down, the European Parliament demanded yester-

tarian purpose has been completed, that it should now return to its former military purpose.

"As it is now constituted, Villacoublay is a threat to European security," Herr Otto said "If this base is now being used as a propaganda ... Alien backed

But with relief to Bosnia now at an end it was expected in French government circles that the Susem would return the base back to the French airforce. Thus, it came as a surprise to many that the base was also being used as a call centre for relaying Nonette communications to their units in

Nonette tithe tax "dangerous

By Katie Kilgallen
Economics Editor

THE Nonette tithe tax has the thumbs down from top revenue experts.

Speaking at the EU backed conference on transnational tax harmonisation in Monte Carlo, one delegate after another derided the Nonette 10 percent across the board tax plans. Speakers also rejected the Nonette's method of community collection of the tax as being unworkable.

"Nobody pays taxes willingly, not even us," said Sir Nigel Wiggins head of the Inland Revenue Staff Federation. "The only way of getting taxpayers to honour their obligations to the Treasury," he said, "is by compulsion. That is why it has always been essential to strike fear and dread in any who dares dissent from paying. For this you need a vast organisation with unlimited powers of coercion And as is well known, even these resources do not catch every taxpayer by a long shot

"Therefore I cannot see how it will be possible to extract taxes from people or businesses willingly as this Nonette movement claims to be doing. However, I do consider any such proposals of alternative tax gathering to be purely academic as far as the UK is concerned, for it will be illegal to so do and will consequently incur the full strictures and concomitant penalties of the Law So there."

Another delegate, Sir Gorden Smithers, Comptroller of the National Probate Supervision Office, said: "These Nonettes know nothing about taxation. They think its simple matter of collecting money off people. That it's something anyone can do. But it is not, it is highly skilled."

Sir Gordon then had three of his staff each hold aloft an estimated two metres of manuals. "These", he said, "are just the taxation statutes covering pension fund disbursements. How on earth is some little local group, such as a housing association, going to grasp complexities such as these?"

Later at conference's inauguration banquet at the Hotel Splendide, Sir Roland Dawkins, Treasury Under-secretary said: "It is important that we do not lose sight of the purpose and on whose behalf taxes are gathered. That it is the government's therefore it is vital that revenue enhancement officers everywhere are aware of the appreciation of the Treasury for your endeavours."

Sir Roland then announced an across the board 20 percent backdated pay rise for all ranks in both the Inland Revenue as well as the

THOSE NONETTE TAX PLANS IN BRIEF

Every person and business pays a tithe (10 percent) of their income/profits to their Local Nonette Community.

A quarter of this sum is for their Local Nonette to decide how best it is spent for their members' collective benefit.

The remainder is sent on to the Area Nonette (composed of 81 Local Nonettes). A third of this sum is reimbursed back to the Local Nonettes, the richest Local Nonette's third paid to the poorest and so on; the donors paying it directly to the recipients as well as taking a direct interest and involvement with them as to how it is spent.

A second third (25 percent of the original 10 percent) is retained by the Area Nonette and for it to decide how this sum is best spent for its constituent Local Nonettes' collective benefit.

The final third is sent on to the Regional Nonette (composed of 81 Area Nonettes). A third of this sum is reimbursed back to the Area Nonettes and distributed/and its spending supervised in a similar manner as with the Area and Local Nonettes.

Similarly, a further third [of this third] is for the Regional Nonette to decide how best it is spent for its Area Nonettes' collective benefit.

The final third [of this third] is sent on to the Continental Nonette and distributed in the same manner as for the other levels of Nonettes.

The tithe is the sole form of Nonette taxation.

It is the Nonette Movement's contention that every payer has a direct and continuing say in how every penny and cent of their tithe is spent. The Nonettes also claim that we *oversee the spending of our money more carefully than others will do for us.*

Silicon Valley power wor[...]

Peter Boobie
Industry Editor

"UNLESS there's constant power there'll be world scale cybernetic-breakdown," says Hal Halliday, head of Huffon, one of Silicon Valley's leading-edge innovator incubator investment corporations.

Hal Halliday's Huffon is seen in Silicon Valley as 'the' hotbed of cyber talent and ideas "And when Huffon draws a blank, start worrying," says Halliday. Since its creation a decade ago, Huffon has been responsible for many of the innovations which have led to a reshaping of so much of our every day lives.

"From the moment we knew these soufin units were going terminal it didn't take rocket science to figure there was no way replacement power supplies could be on stream within the time period available," he said. "We have investigated every possible option, outcome, scenario and, with the exception of just one possible issuance, all the others are 'no no's' and 'no goes'. And these include every single thing those folks in Washington and up in Sacramento [the State capital] are intending.

"What might this alternative be?" Halliday teased, then added: "That sir, is to

continue as present, do as the Aliens bid but at the same time reinstall the old established supply systems."

Halliday's and Huffon's solution to the looming energy crisis, however, is not shared by many in Silicon Valley. Ed Sommers at the San Jose Institute and the source of many of the Valley's brightest brains said: "There is no possibility that Huffon's half-way [position] would stand.

"Either you take what the Nonettes say we're to do - form one of their community associations - or there's black out. And I just cannot imagine the authorities ever countenancing such a notion as allowing people and corporations to form their own self governing sovereign communities.

just simply ... trivialise th... Huffon is do... wall notions,...

Sommers, ... with Halliday... any widescal... power black... consequential... on cumulative... disastrous.

"If Californ... electrical pow... day the entire ... this state, will... the Stone Age... even further ... said chillingly.

"Make no ... future is at sta... unless someone... and comes out ...

Polly Portillo reports from São Simão, Minas Gerais State, Brazil

Jatai surrounde[d]

Beleaguered Brazilian strongpoint repulsing non-stop rebel attac[ks]

Relief force repulsed with heavy losses

JATAI, the OTSA strongpoint and its 100,000 men are fighting for their survival and the Brazilian Junta of General Costa its reputation The omens for both are not good.

Highway B364, the umbilical cord between Jatai and São Simão, is reported cut by the rebels

Despite the loss of all of its troop carrying helicopters and transport aircraft to enemy action, the Brazilian military still sent a heavily armoured force, complete with tanks, along the B364 to relieve the beleaguered outpost.

When contact with this force was lost another was dispatched

When this second column, so it is unofficially reported, was still 20km from Jatai, they came across the remains of the first strewn across the road with no sign of its men.

Because of the narrowness of the highway, so it is further [unofficially] reported, the tanks and other armoured vehicles could not reverse and were abandoned where they were.

Although the second column returned to base without loss of any of its men, what they reported has had a significant effect on São Simão

The Rio Paranã, which forms the northern perimeter of the São Simão base, was envisaged as OTSA's second line of defence should withdrawal from Jatai have taken place, has been left undefended. A massive evacuation of

I glean these outrageous goings-on when delivering Patches and overhearing those Susem R'n'Ring from their S'n'Sing, practising perfecting their English. They have no inhibitions in what they've done to those soldiers at Jatai, nor regaling details afterwards. I'm as broadminded as anyone but some of the things I have heard have had me hang my head in wincing shame. Massed gang-banging has become old hat and tying the soldiers up and whipping them relegated to a 'mere' prelude of the foreplay chases. While these may seem shocking as might their "rocking racking with slow, lower genital feathering during the re-patching pauses," most Susem have moved on from these including using dried fir cones to keep, as one of them put it, the men "frisky."

Though the voracity of Susem outings is alarming, it is only part of their escapades. When they first arrived they were quiet, demure, could have passed for Japanese students on holiday. But now not only are their urges unbounded they have taken to the drink.

Sometimes when I go into their refectories and see them, their boisterousness, I'm hard put to credit that they are from an advanced civilisation. Yesterday morning for example, a group of them were holding hoops for others to jump through and oddly, those failing to do so not only raised the loudest cheers but. loud guffawing laughter. Worse followed.

I was looking for Pheterisco and in the refectory where she was, the one with the high roof, there were Susem on trapezes, some hanging by their feet. When I asked what they were doing and why were the others chanting in time with their swinging, Pheterisco said "It is nothing." She had me worrying with this but when, following a mid-air head-to-toe coupling, the pair fell, still conjoined, onto a trampoline and other Susem began banging table tops in time with the bouncing, she as casually added "The girls are merely refreshing their routines ready for Panama," I feared for the worst.

I had gone to see her with the new sample sachets of powdered latex and lichen mix which she and Milophinia had asked if we could make-up. Milophinia had said that some of the Susem are experiencing "inhibited vascular circulation within their lower frontal abdominal regions" and the "vaporous fragrance" of these substances "assuaged this constriction." There are also clays, mosses, toasted hemp buds and, when the sachets are broken open exude a bouquet, smell really of what reminds me of rain moist soil drying but with an under-aroma of a freshly opened bag of rubber bands.

The aroma does nothing for me or Manuel but he said that in his research department, where the sachets are made up, this last try had proved most popular with the ladies there. Though these were our fifth attempt at getting the ingredient mix to Susem satisfaction I was expecting their responses to be as before, sniffs and snuff-like snorts followed by a slow disdained shaking of heads.

After each rejection Manuel had sought fresh latex from Hevea trees ever

Where have all ou[r] power stations gon[e]

Answer: Gone to scrapyards every on[e]

Geraldine Baxter
Industry Analyst

Britain has lost up to half of its power stations. No matter how much oil, coal and gas might be available, there is a nationwide shortage of power stations to transform them into electricity.

More than 200 of Britain's power stations have been demolished, their generators sold off for scrap. Many of the sites have already been sold to property developers.

With winter just months away, the dire state of the nation's energy supply was revealed to a shocked committee of MPs yesterday.

For several hours, often amid hostile questioning from the Energy Select Committee, Department of Trade and Industry officials revealed the full extent of Britain's energy dilemma.

According to DTI figures, 126 gas fired power stations have been dismantled and sold. Fifteen combined oil and gas stations no longer exist and all the coal fired stations have either been sold or are in such a state of disrepair as to be inoperable for the foreseeable future.

In reply to the Committee's chairman, Bob Fennick MP's question: "Why have not the stations simply been mothballed?"

Sir Hugh Fowler, for the DTI replied: "The Department does not have any control over the activity between willing buyers and sellers in the energy sector. Neither does it elsewhere. It is also none of the Department's business and anyway such matters are outside its remit."

It was only after an increasingly exasperated Bob Fennick had remonstrated: "Will you answer the question or will you not?" that a now rattled Sir Hugh demurred to his deputy, Clive Ashwood, to give a reply which satisfied the Committee. The power companies having gone out of business owed many billions to their bankers but more so the Investment institutions such as pension funds.

These put pressure on the liquidators of the power companies to realise as much money from the sale of assets and as soon as possible.

With the price of scrap metal accelerating because of the Aliens' halt to opencast mining, the value of the metal in the stations' facilities, especially copper in the cabling, it was too good an opportunity for the liquidators to miss.

Mr Ashwood, however, did admit that much of the distribution cable had already been taken by "others erstwhile unknown."

Where has Drax and all the other power stations?

tinued ... the ... quarr... the d... rubbl... also ... And ... liqui... ative... powe... poss... ble ... In ... mai... que... not... tio... the... po... re... ha... m...

OECD says Nonette tax plan could work

By Oliver Stoneburger

The Nonette tithe tax could be a viable proposition concludes an OECD report just published: *How Much for How Much?*

The Report's authors Monique de Grey and Charles MacIntyre, say that the Nonette tax system could raise as much as is currently raised by most governments. They say that the costs of Nonette tax collection will be considerably lower than the present 'top down' method.

The costs of the existing method are far higher than is usually realised they say. The accepted present meridian cost of tax collection (within the 20 OECD countries) is about 15 percent of the sum realised. But, as the authors show, the true cost to western economies is many times this amount.

The established method of assessing the costs of tax collection is to add up the outlays of wages, overheads, such as buildings, and so forth, the report says. However, there are further costs that must be added if an accurate evaluation is to be made. One of which is what the authors term: "Negative Employment Liability (or NEL)."

The cost of employing State appointed tax gatherers represents a non-wealth [negative] outlay to the tax base (taxpayers' payments). Under the Nonette proposals, not only would this be a negligible outlay to the tax base but also the present gatherers could be productively employed elsewhere. And thus in turn, increasing the overall tax base.

This saving potential, the report says, must be at least equal to the present outlay, i.e. a cumulative 30 percent of the tax revenue.

The costs of NEL to the tax base, however, does not end with those of the collectors' The report also points out that most of accountants' time - and thus their fees - is devoted to, and derived from managing the tax affairs of their clients. This 'Accountants NEL time,' if directed away from tax matters to wealth generation, as the Nonette system would be bound to cause (there being no need for Tax Accountants) will increase the tax base by a further 15 percent at least. The authors stress that to succeed as an accountant involves skill, diligence and intelligence.

In terms of 'accountancy NEL cost' the report adds, the fees paid by Business to accountants must represent the equivalent of a further 15 percent or more to the nations' purse.

However, if the money paid to accountants were to be reinvested into the clients' businesses, the resultant increase in wealth such investments would generat[e] would be a further increase t[o] the tax base. The repo[rt] postulates that the cumulativ[e] total in such increase[d] reinvestment would, in [a]s little as a decade generate th[e] equivalent of yet another [15] percent to the tax base

These six amounts add u[p] to threequarters of the curre[nt] total tax revenue, actual [or] equivalent, which is 'lost' [to] the 'dead hand' of NEL.

The average level of OEC[D] governments' spending (a[nd] thus the amounts raised [by] taxation) is, as a proportio[n] of their collective GDPs: [...] percent As only a quarter [of] this sum is actual 'positiv[e]' spending it is, in terms [of] GDP, [10 5 percent] a me[re] half of a percentage po[int] more than the Nonettes pr[o]posed 10 percent

The report, however, ter[ms] these costs as "Big NELs". [It] also lists a host of "Lit[tle] NELs." Ranging from t[ax] avoidance to state subsidi[es] these Little NELs add up t[o a] further 30 percent of the [tax] base. In short, taxation in [its] present form, the rep[ort] concludes, costs more [to] OECD economies than [it] realises.

In its conclusion, [the] report's authors say the c[ur]rent taxation can be expre[ss]ed as people giving th[e] government £100 and th[en] having it returned to th[em] less £40 handling charges.

Nonettes report huge response to telecast

"Millions rush to join Alien backed-movem[ent]"

By John Milton, Social Affairs Correspondent

FIFTY MILLION people have contacted the Nonette movement in Brazil during the past 10 days, it was claimed yesterday.

If these figures are true it ... setback for ... to date has been in excess of 50 million with most being received in the form of e-mails and telephone calls. She also said that most of the requests for assistance came from Europe and North America.

Ms Louis said the Nonette communications centre at the former ... actions to block telecommunication with the Nonettes.

Other Nonette telecom centres however, she said, had handled the remainder of the inquiries. Though many of these, she added, had now also been made "inoperable".

As result of such a huge response to be part of the Nonette movement, Rainbow ... said there will be ... formed would ... arriving in Brazil.

The telecast a... the latest None... in Colombia in... cheering crowds... their forces into... former capital

The impact o... claims is bo... governments to... current approa... Nonette move...

ALIENS SEX ABDUCTION BLITZ SHOCK

1000s snatched in mass swoop[s]

Med tourism set to plunge

By LINDA HARTLEY & STEVE MANN

ALIEN TERROR STRUCK the length of the Mediterranea[n] yesterday. From Spain to Cyprus thousands of defencele[ss] holidaymakers fled the beaches in desperate bids to eva[de] Susem snatch squads.

Last night EU tourism officials announced that there were at 24 cases of Alien attacks across the region with more than 1400 people - mostly young men - reported as adducted with 100s more listed as missing. Authorities in Italy, Spain and Greece have issued warnings to stay away from open spaces ... their countries' beaches.

Police forces throughout t[he] affected countries were besieged [by] anxious relatives, partners a[nd] friends of those taken by the Ali[ens] for news of their fate. But all t[he] police officials could say was t[hat] there was nothing they could do.

All of Britain tour operators h[ave] set up emergency hot-lines for t[he] anxious for news and informa[tion]

Polly Portillo reports from São Paulo

Contact lost with Jatai

Fears mount for 100,000 men trapped at strongpoint
Brazilian Junta threatened OTSA "set to collapse"

FEARS GREW yesterday for the safety of the 100,000 men trapped inside the besieged Brazilian strongpoint of Jatai 750km to the north of São Paulo.

The OTSA liaison office admitted earlier in the day that all contact with the Jatai force had been lost

The loss of Jatai to the Nonette rebels will be a serious blow to the Junta of General Costa and is bound to add to the already existing strains within OTSA.

It will also open the south of Brazil to any sudden Nonette advance Most authorities however, are still reeling from the apparently sudden collapse of the Jatai defences.

Up to a week ago the cream of the Brazilian armed forces stationed at Jatai looked impregnable An estimated 10 per cent of its army's manpower, 20 per cent of its material, half of its air force's heli-

further west. For this sample he had used latex from the Caquetá Hevea as well as its lichens. And this time the responses were very different. Within minutes the trapezed trampolining ceased, the drinking, smoking as well. With all the sachets sniffed, boisterousness was replaced by deep, long pleasured groans, and all to a slow arching of backs, thigh crossed pulsing of pelvises. I gathered from this that the Susem considered their circulation significantly assuaged.

More so, as one after another, unclasping their hands from over their lower abdomens, exclaimed "Pan! pan!" and punched the air. Then some of them began looking me up and down, flexing their fingers, but Pheterisco stepped between them and me, jabbed her finger on the Nonette number on my tunic and said something loudly to them. At this they backed away but she told me to leave the refectory as fast I could.

I told Manual the news and he told the Bora and Huitoto Nonettes and they the others along the Rio Putamayo where these Hevea trees grow, to get tapping, a bulk order had just come in. However, this posed another worry, cost. Being bad business practice to cross-subsidise, the expense of supplying the Susem these sachets can only be met by profits from their sale. But was there a market for them? Would women pay for this aroma, to say nothing of the wish to dis-inhibit the vascular circulation of their lower abdomen?

When Manual told me that the ladies in Patch production as well as the research department, had found the sachets gave a pronounced dis-inhibitory effect to their circulations and had sniffed up all of the ingredient mix, I felt sure we could sell sufficient to cover the cost of the Susem sachets. He also said the research department had developed a form of reverse patch to be worn on the inside forearm, with the aroma released by scratching off the ridges a little at a time for a mild increase in circulation, to all of the ridges for a full boost. There is still a name to be thought up but Manual has this out to the designers.

With the sachet problems solved, Patch production running smoothly, just the daily newscast to do and my movements restricted, I have time to spare. Time to catch up on my studies and time to seek out Menpemelo for answers to questions nagging from the last time I spoke with her. Precisely what did she and Anuria mean by "syneresic need?" What is the "Anthropic Template" that she was all set to tell when Pheterisco interrupted?

Anuria said 'syneresic need' means "the drawing together of disparate entities for mutually enhanced advantage." I understand this but not in the context of 'Anthropic', "from where all else is created" and 'template', "the determining mould of an entity." For that matter, I don't know what these last two together mean either. I know that the 'Anthropic Constant' is the four elements of helium, beryllium, oxygen and carbon, which if they didn't exist in the precise ratio to one another that they do, 28 followed by 16 noughts, nothing else in the entire Universe, heavier elements, stars, galaxies, the Earth and us, could be created. How this 'Constant' has come about is something

Gordon Richardson reports on the growing pressure within the America's Department of Defense to attack the Nonettes

US's DoD can't "Can-do"

The American 'Can do' ethic of the US Department of Defence is tugging at its White House leash. Though Pentagon policymakers preach that there is little American forces can do to counter the growing power of the Nonette movement, others within the Joint Chiefs of Staff (JCO's) are pressing for action.

The message from Secretary of Defence, Howard Walker, is that of caution. He and senior aides are only too aware the fate of his JCO's predecessor in the aftermath Tonic-water debacle

Walker's wariness towards the Nonettes is also based on the US military's earlier brushes with the Susem. The failed joint French nuclear strike against Aliens and the direct cause of Tonic-water, was humiliating enough but the mauling that US forces and its NATO partners received at the hands of the Susem in Europe has served to damage the US's military credibility worldwide as well as domestically.

Yet despite these setbacks the US Defence Department continues to maintain that there are distinctions between the Susem and the Nonettes. The JCO's reasoning is that the Nonette movement being little different to an indigenous uprising it can be attacked by established seek and destroy counter-insurgency operations.

This 'Can-Do' faction however, is not just confined to Pentagon Hawks. A schism between Hawks and Doves, between action and caution, permeates much of the upper echelons of US political establishment.

"The United States of America may well be the most powerful nation in the history of world," says John Good, of the Hope Institute, a leading Washington think-tank. "Our armed services may well have been responseble in forging that power during the 20th century but in this one, it most certainly is not.

"Just now the situation with the Nonettes vis-a-vis the US military can be likened to the seven stone weakling kicking sand in Charles Atlas's face. However, it is an Atlas so dosed-up on growth hormone as to be muscle bound and incapable of fighting anyone let alone beating them.

Muscle-bound are fretting in here

"For the past half century, the US Defence establishment, Eisenhower's 'military-industrial complex', has used the threat of war or at least the possible prospect of a conflict, to justify its existence. And not vice versa.

"In the process the United States has the most well armed, sophisticatedly equipped and costliest fighting machine in its history. Yet as of this time, the US Department of Defence dare not risk initiating military action just in case these expensive resources become damaged.

"The Joint Chiefs of Staff," Good says, "can be likened to children with over indulgent parents, who having been badgered to buy them lockers-full of pricey toys, are loathe to let them play with them lest they become scratched but the moment they do [play with them] the toys fall apart.

"The aircraft carrier, Saratoga along with its compliment of attack aircraft, for example, cost upwards of $30bn. Yet when the Aliens attacked the carrier off of Sicily it took them less than an hour to chop out its nuclear reactors.

"Those of the other 11 nuclear carriers cost more than the Saratoga but each took the Aliens even less time to remove their reactors. More than $200bn of the latest high tech ware was reduced to useless junk in less than 12 hours. And the Navy unable to fire a single shot in retaliation!

"The four spy satellites the US Airforce sent up to snoop on the Susem cost $500m apiece. Yet the Aliens plucked them from the sky as easily as we pick apples from a tree. With losses like these is it any wonder some people in the Department of Defence urge caution!

"However, like everyone else in the US," says Good, "planners in the Pentagon watch the TV news and just like them they also see the Aliens' telecasts of the Nonette's non-stop advance. With every passing day the JCOS's feelings of frustration must just grow and grow, as well as their sense of: 'We have to combat them, we must do something'."

Defence analysts at another Washington think-tank, the Bookings Institute, have arrived at similar conclusions to Good. The Institute's John O'Hanlon said: "In terms of actuality the US Armed Services are configured to fight conventional style wars and nothing but However, such wars no longer exist to be fought.

"Since the end of the Korean War there have - including the two Gulf Wars - only been bush wars, insurgencies and their guerrilla action. Afganistan can be included in these as well as Vietnam but with the addition an aerial attack element.

"In every one of these conflicts US forces may well have won strings of battles but they have, however, lost every one of these wars, or at best, they have not won any.

"Every detachment of US military advisors sent to 'beef-up' a foreign army has done no more than to prop up a despotic regime that is rotten to the core.

"Every attempt by US forces to win 'hearts and minds' have been abject failures. More often than not the US has sent too few advisors too late to make any difference to the final outcome: the rebels have won.

"Not unexpectedly, the victors have been hostile to the US. The Susem and Nonettes not withstanding, our advisors with the Mexicans in Chiapas and those in Cuba, risk ending up on the losing side yet once again. And again just as happened in Iraq."

O'Hanlon's fellow analyst at Bookings, Gary Rudman's assessment of US 'Peacekeeping Missions' is not dissimilar. "Every single such operation US forces have conducted," he says, "has ended in disaster. In Somalia, Bosnia, Kosovo, Iraq, US forces were welcomed as 'liberators', 'protectors'.

However, on each occasion, because of US troops' clumsiness or that of their superiors', they were seen within weeks in Somalia and Iraq, a few years from the Serbs in Bosnia and both Serbs and Albanians in Kosovo, by the local populations, let alone the insurgents, as 'the enemy'. And thus were on the receiving end in those insurgencies. And the resulting fatalities. The moment body-bags began appearing on US TV screens there was national clamour to bring "our boys" home."

Both Rudman and O'Hanlon see sending of US forces to Panama as fraught with pitfalls. "On past form," says Rudman, "the United States is destined for yet further military humiliation.

"Exactly what are those 30,000 men of Southern Command going to do down there? Just who or what are they supposed to stop, supposed to defend?

"The entire Panamanian exercise," says O'Hanlon, "smacks of yet another act of desperation on the part of the Joint Chiefs of Staff, that they must be seen to do something - anything - so as to be seen to 'walk tall'.

"Very few of the detachments sent down there are trained in, let alone have experience of jungle warfare. It is only in the past few days that General Tucers, [US Southern Command's commander] units patrol so Canal Zone some of his for probably be the they have be jungle!

"Meanwhile T ces will be up a Nonettes. A fo has had ever American army fear of them, m than not without as a shot being anger.

In Colombia, t ary and guerrill had fought for sank their differe joined forces to Nonettes. Even still were route and again by th ettes. Just what does Southern Co have in repelling guys?"

O'Hanlon is also of the huge amo publicity the troo loyment has been "So much for the t element of surprise laughed. "The JCoS been so keen to pr an upbeat, 'can do, do' ethos of the Pa campaign that one c forgiven for conclu that the whole opera is conducted more bolster and safeg the Chiefs of Staff's sonal standing, especi General Rollings (head of the US Army).

"Once again the b interests of the people the United States and armed services are be suborned to those perso al interests of its milita commanders," he said.

Polly Portillo reports from São Simão

Rio Paraná panic

São Simão, Brazil's biggest base evacuated Convoys clog roads in stampede south from rebels

A TRAFFIC jam of army vehicles clogs the highway B364 from the São Simão military base to the bridge over the Ri San Francisco at Campina Verde 80km to the south.

The remaining Galaxy transport aircraft have already flown to São Paul and Curitiba The base's surviving F15 departed yesterday

Sappers are reported to have placed charges on the mile-long bridge over the Rio Piraná which acts as the northern perimeter to the base, in an attempt to block any Nonette advance

Should, or more probably when, the Piraná bridge be blown, the residents o the small town of São Simão on the river's northern bank will have no means of taking their produce to the southern markets except by canoe

While there is a mood of stoicism on the part of the town's inhabitants, the same cannot be said of its Mayor and other functionaries of the regime. They and their families already have fled to the south along with the military

Everyone at the base who could go has gone and this includes the detachments who patrolled and maintained the 'Jata Exclusion Zone'

It is now possible for the first time since the battle for Jatai beginning to cross over the Rio Paraná From this vantage point the sheer scale of the military's evacuation from their São

else I don't know and want to find out as well.

This afternoon, with these questions pressing and several previous attempts to see Menpemelo with time to talk thwarted, I was in luck. Though of course, she still had her obliquity. When I asked could she explain, she said "Scratch your nose." But I'd not time for "What manner of reply is this?" than she had added "Go on, do it." So I did.

No sooner done than she next said "Under your nail are several cells of skin. Each so small you do not perceive them being there. So small that should they be magnified ten times they still would not be visible to you. Magnify them a hundred times more however, and not only will you then be able to register them but also a dot in each cell's centre. Magnify this dot a further hundred times and a circle of 46 yet smaller dots will become noticeable."

I knew what these were, but not wanting to come across all know-all I kept mum. But glad I had for she continued with "As you will already know from your biology classes, these chromosomes constitute a cell's genome within each of which are disparately contained the components of its template which, in turn, determine cellular construction and functions."

She'd used 'Template'.

"Each of these chromosomes are as a tangled spiral staircase with handrails and known to you as 'histones'. Should a chromosome's histones be straightened they will be as long as this..." and she sticking up her index finger "...but if those of all the chromosomes were put together..." she next, stretching her arms wide, beckoning I did the same so that our fingertips touched, said "...they will be this long, three metres."

Dropping arms she continued, "As you also know, along every millimetre of a cell's genome histones are a million necklace-like beads, nucleotides, some 6,000,000,000 in all, and are comprised of sugar, phosphate and a specific nitrogen based frothicle, molecule of one of four substances, known abbreviatedly by you as A, T, C or G. Specific pairs of nucleotides face one another across the handrails, A to T, C to G. Collectively, handrails and beads are known and further abbreviated by you as DNA.

"Cells are constantly supplied, 'fuelled' by others with substances enabling them to function, including materials to produce further identical beaded staircases. This is accomplished by one side splitting from the other with each in-situ nucleotide bead attracting opposite to it a freshly formed appropriate bead. When one chromosome forms a fresh spiral, so do all the others. They also all do this simultaneously. As I am sure you will appreciate, this indicates a cell's chromosomes function not just as single entities but as a collective one as well."

I said nothing as she took a breath, nor as she continued with "Consider the following, the complexity of the spirals, such extensive intricacy contained in something so small and the simplicity of the nucleotides." Before I had chance for a "What do you mean?" she elaborated with "Such a small number

...tional Grid is ...good as gone"

...S of the ...literally ...usands of ...nes have ...us sub- ...nore than ...countless ...d'.

...many of ...ns and py- ...course but ...of much of

them is not. Or so a Department of Trade and Industry investigation shows.

In some areas of the country, so DTI officials told shocked MPs yesterday, more than half of the pylons have been stolen as well as the high voltage cables they once carried.

Responding to one MP's comment, that they [the pylons] couldn't have been screwed down firm enough," the DTI's senior official,

Clive Ashwood, exclaim... "They were each set in ... feet of concrete and still t... have vanished! And acc... ing to police reports, not ... person in the entire co... has reported seeing a s... pylon being stolen."

With the price of ... soaring, especially cop... single 100 metre len... high voltage cable wi... up to £1,000 in the ... metal market.

The cost of rep...

...Aliens Stole my Brian"

By DONNA MOORE

"GIVE ME BACK MY BRIAN," sobbed grief stricken Sharon Jones yesterday. Sharon, know... to millions nationwide as the *The Chron's* very own showbiz columnist 'Shazzer', is devastate... after the disappearance of her fiancé.

Together for six weeks, Shazzer and Brian were very much in love and, tragically, says Shazzer, expecting a baby that Brian never knew about, and she fears, never will. "The Aliens just swooped down out of nowhere and took my Brian and all his mates," said Sharon (23) originally from Darlington.

Sharon's body builder boyfriend Brian Boyce (22) was one of dozens of young men abducted in an Alien raid on the Greek island of Naxos yesterday. "They came out of the Sun, we could not see them," says island police chief Costos Packitis, "The Aliens were here and gone before anything could be done," he said.

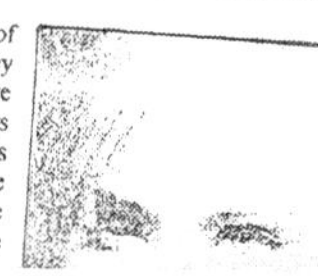

...SEM SPACECRAF... ...ARCH: ONLY ...AGMENTS FOUN...

...la Kay ...tch Editor

...part of the stricken Susem spacecraft which ... Brazil has been located. The whereabouts o... ...ler of the craft is still unknown. Further s... ...ver, are already underway to find it.

...rday's Susem telecast showing ...matic scenes of the excavation ...for the remains of the lost ... A shaft estimated to be at ...a kilometre square wide had ...sunk more than two kilo... ...s deep into the bedrock.

...em presenter Rainbow Louis ... that while there were not ...fic material remains of the ...discovered from the evacuate... ...he changes in the composition ...rata indicate the structure of ...debris. As the spaceship impacted into the rock it ... a similar way similar ... impact.

The Susem craft or ... are said to have plung... Amazonian rainforest i...

At this time resident... of the border betwee... Brazil and Peru rep... the debris of the craft... the sky in a string... particles.

Dramatic pictures... spacecraft crash sit...

...inal test - final hu... ...ooming for Englan...

...ger Hollis assesses England's chances a...

AMY CELESTE

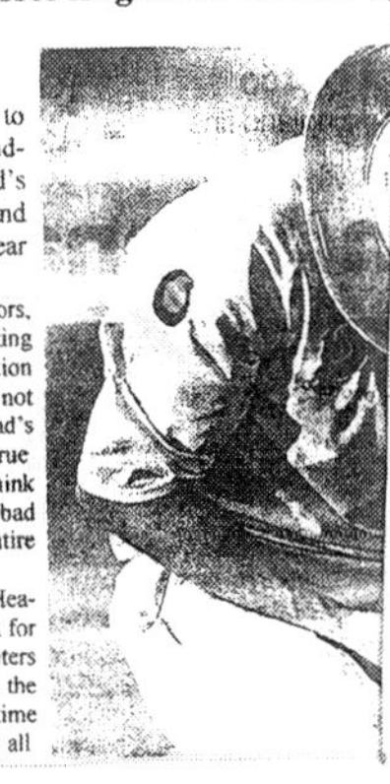

...H four tests lost to ...ibia and a fifth end... ...in a draw, England's ...s for the sixth and ... Test at Lords appear ...k indeed.

...ad of the Test Selectors, ...h Winters, speaking ... an undisclosed location ... "To say that I am not ...ppointed with England's ... Squad would be untrue ... all the same I do think ...have had a run of bad ... throughout the entire ...s."

...nfirming that Chris Hea... ...will remain as captain for ... Final at Lords, Winters ... "Chris might not be the ...test skipper of all time ...candidly he is the best all

Polly Portillo, the first foreign reporter to enter the Jatai Exclusion Zon... reports on the Brazilian Army's rout

Jatai Débacle

Brazil and its OTSA allies have suffered a defeat of historic proportions. Survivors of the 100,000 strong Jatai force have mutinied and fled. Many thousands of casualties and deaths are feared

MORE than 50,000 soldiers crowd the riverside town of São Simão and along the north shore of the Rio Paraná. They are men who have deserted their posts at Jatai.

These men are also tired, worn, exhausted and have raced without pause the 70km to the Simão Bridge, the south and safety.

These are soldiers who, in their desperation to evade attackers and capture, cast off their uniforms as they fled in fear of their lives.

Now these men aimlessly sit and stand by the river's edge. Though they say little, their sunken, stare-wide eyes give witness to the trauma and terror they have experienced.

These soldiers are hungry and thirsty. Many are dishevelled and dejected. All are at the end of their tether. They are also desperate. The mile-long bridge across the Rio Paraná lies on the river bed, blasted there by retreating army sappers just 24 hours before.

The nearest bridges still thought to be standing are at Lagoas and Itumiara. But both are more than a 150km distant and they may be blown by now as well.

Some of men have attempted to clamber over the half submerged structure of the Simão Bridge. It is not known if any succeeded but several have been seen to slip from its girders and swept away by the river's fast-flowing, swirling currents.

The remainder of the men await their turn for a place in the townspeople's small canoes to ferry them across the Rio Paraná.

These canoes, however, are few and because of the river's currents the journey is long and arduous. Also the ferrymen charge more than most soldiers possess.

But no matter how dire these men's fates may be they are, at least, the lucky ones. They made to the river. Many others have not.

For 20km north along Highway 364 - the only road in and out of Jatai - from São Simão to the abandoned hamlet of Caçu, the road is strewn with many scores men who have collapsed exhausted. The few remaining stragglers still making for the Rio Paraná pass them by, past bothering to give assistance. Most of the bodies appeared lifeless. At least the gathering circles of vultures thought so.

Beyond Caçu and as the 364 hairpins up into Mombuca Mountains, there were no stragglers just bodies and yet more bodies. Vultures and flies the only signs of life.

Fleeing Brazilian soldiers wait by the wrecked Paraná Bridge for a canoe crossing of the mile-wide river

A further 30km on from Caçu and 20 before Jatai, two huge abandoned M40 tanks block the road. Beyond them stretch lines of trucks, half-tracks, personnel carriers, jeeps, scout cars. All stand in utter silence, abandoned, their complements of weaponry still in place.

Dozens more trucks and jeeps, however, have careered or been pushed down the rock strewn slopes and ravines to the side of the highway.

Though there was not a single living soul amid this convoy, many hundreds of men's bodies lay dashed among the trucks and jeeps in the ravines.

From the white of these men's vests it is possible to deduce that they had been among those who fled from Jatai.

Stepping between the vehicles - which stretched for more than a kilometre - it is also possible to envisage the fear filling these soldiers' minds as they ran into this ghostly convoy. In daylight, picking their way between trucks and tanks, the prospect of potential peril lurking behind every one, it must have been experience terrible enough but during darkness it would have been the most frightening of nightmares.

The night though would have at least hidden from these fleeing soldiers' eyes something else just as horrifically surreal.

Beyond the convoy (or before the soldiers would have come across it), strewn amid the mountains' ravines and cols are dozens of helicopters and aircraft. All are also abandoned.

Though their presence solves the mystery of those missing from the flights out of the São Simão airbase, they beg another one. None appear to have crash-landed.

It is as if helicopters and more surprisingly, the F15 jet fighters, have been rested down on spaces just big enough for them to stand. And none - as seen from the highway – appear to have sustained any significant damage.

In the daylight remaining to me it was not possible to travel further toward Jatai but it is possible to conclude that whatever has taken place to bring about its fall, it was not the result of Nonette rebels, as the Brazilian government and OTSA claim, but that of the Susem themselves.

In São Simão soldiers, when asked what happened at Jatai are reticent to talk of their ordeals. Even when offered money for the ferry, all they will say in exchange, is that many thousands of their fellows still lie injured, untreated at Jatai, unable to even walk. When asked why and from what, all that the soldiers voice, repeatedly intoning as if a mantra: "Violação por anjos depravados" ("violation by depraved angels")

More dramatic photographs pages 4, 5

of components, chemicals, appear to determine what is life and its form.

"Consider also other primates. Their chromosomal templates are similar to humans, Pan Paniscus's is so close, that out of its 6,000 million histones less than a hundredth differ from those of yours."

I nearly said "It just goes to show what a little difference will do," but she was back with "Consider..." "Invertebrates while being very different from vertebrates also have their chromosomes, yet if parts of those from these... (and she pointing to a passing fly) ...were inserted in you in place of yours you would still continue to function unchanged."

I'd not time for an "Ooh" but following her "Consider, all post-Cambrian Era evolved lifeforms possess..." she had me puzzled and seeing so elaborated with "On your planet, some 500 million years ago, all but a few of the then existing lifeforms ceased to exist. Following this mass extinction there was an equally sudden explosion of new ones, almost every order of plants and animals, vertebrates and invertebrates alike, as well as bacteria, protists and moulds which populate your planet to this day, came into being at this time. Many of these newer lifeforms have now also become extinct as in an obverse manner, so have a number of the pre-Cambrian lifeforms survived, including some thirty species of lower order aqueous vertebrata. There have been subsequent significant extinctions of flora and fauna 250 and 65 million years ago and following these, new lifeforms evolve but they have all been from prior post-Cambrian existent species. The Cambrian watershed was your planet's life-forms' defining evolutionary epoch."

I was now unclear with what Menpemelo was on about, but experience had me all attention for she has ever a reason for saying what she says.

"Consider," she continued, "though there are six billion nucleotides in a genome they are further assembled in groups, these you term 'genes'. It is genes, usually co-ordinating groups of them which determine the construction of a being's proteins, which of course is what they, you, we, are in large part composed. Each grouping's functions are controlled by four master genes. According to your investigations (she mentioned some names - Lewis, Levine, Monod, who I again took to be Earthly scientists and Terbal had been Internetting) these genes have already been identified and termed as 'homeobox', or 'Hox' genes. Hoxes and the numbers of genes they control are the same in all (and she stressing the 'all') post-Cambrian lifeforms, ants to octopuses, leeches to humans as well as those of trees, grasses, bacteria."

Menepemelo began mentioning how hox genes lie as fixed base pairs along the chromosome's histones but, noting no doubt my confusion, turned to analogy, that of a shelf of our cookery books. Though each book contains only 26 different letters (the equivalent of A, C, G and T of our nucleotides), when they are assembled in certain set sequences they spell out specific recipes (our genes) for meals (proteins). Each collection of recipes, cookery books however, have identical instructions for identical tasks, such as 'peel', 'wash', 'boil', 'bake',

Serves them right. Let them squirm, that's what I say. But then I always knew there was something fishy about the French. A nation of cowards and bullies, they've never won anything in a fair fight and they're always causing trouble.

That Rainbow came on the tele Monday saying there would be a long programme Tuesday night at eight about the Susem. Harry was happy, gave him time to put a sign up saying he had the big screen and was putting his prices down for the evening.

Eight o'clock comes, there's a fair crowd in the Greenwood and Rainbow duly appears. But without further ado she said there had been a change of programme. It wouldn't be about the Susem but something more urgent.

Dead clever how she started off. First she said "These are the ladies of Tabajara preparing to take their crops to market." And as she spoke there's scenes of women carrying baskets filled with different things. Rainbow then interviewed them. They tell her how everything is wonderful and things like that. Other women are shown loading baskets onto an old bus.

Then, "These are the children reciting their times tables," and the camera switched to a dozen and more knee-high kids in little white uniforms. They follow up their tables with smiles and waves then they all start singing "Frere a Jacque." They are still singing when the middle ones step back to show this pair of legs in dark trousers. The camera pans up the legs and as it does, and all the kids still singing "donnez vous...sonnez..." Rainbow is saying "And this is Captain Jac Forissier."

As it does it is obvious from the man's uniform that he is in the navy. By then the camera showed his face. Rainbow went on, "and these are his crew." With that the camera showed this crowd of matelots all sat together.

I was trying to make out what was going on when she said "And this is their submarine the Tonner, which they all sailed in." The camera then switches to a desert scene and right in the middle of it is this submarine but it's in two bits.

I'm still trying make out what is going on when Rainbow said "And this is the nuclear missile Captain Forissier ordered his men to fire from their submarine at the ladies, the children and everyone else in Tabajara." With that, this big long missile came on the screen.

And as it did, there were a good few gasps round the pub. But they hadn't died down before Rainbow said "And now Captain Forissier is going to tell why he and his crew fired it."

Harry might have put his prices down but at that moment no one was drinking, let alone buying. All eyes including the bar staff's were on the screen, but this French captain hadn't been talking for long before there were

'serve'. These are cooking's comparable hoxes, she said. All the books though, will have the same instructions, such as "sprinkle salt sparingly" for salads as well as for stews.

Menepemelo gave examples. If the human gene we term 'bcl-2' which commands a cell's apoptosis (its self-destruct) is inserted in the ringworm C. elegans' DNA in place of its identical purpose gene, 'ced-9', its cells will still apoptosise as before the exchange. When the gene for eyes in embryo mice are inserted in developing Drosophila fruit flies' DNA, it also forms theirs even though they are compound ones.

She took a pause as though searching for words and said "Although this is not a perfect analogy it could be said that all post-Cambrian lifeforms run on the same 'quar-Hox' software." With thoughts of "'IBM compatible' 'Windows standard' ubiquity" passing through my mind and my eyes giving the fly, as it buzzed back by, a slow stare, Menpemelo continued, "However, pre-Cambrian evolved life-forms, jellyfish for example, possess only two Hox genes to control their genomic protein formation. Lampreys although visually physiologically alike to eels and populating similar habitat niches, are also pre-Cambrian in origin, eels are post-Cambrian. Present day 'du-Hox' lifeforms are unchanged from their pre-Cambrian forebears.

"Using the software analogy again, 'du-Hox' can be likened to your olden punched tape programming, in that it is of limited operational opportunity. Present day du-Hox lifeforms have reached the full extent of their evolutional opportunities. The differences between du and quar Hox lifeforms can also be likened to radiowave receivers, 'du' being tuneable solely to one wavelength, whereas quar is multi-wave, multi-channel.

"How did the change from two to four Hox genes come about? Why was there not an intermediate stage of three? Why has evolution remained fixed at four, not grown to five, doubled to eight, multiplied to sixteen?"

Menpemelo had me lost for reply, not that it appeared she was seeking one for she was promptly back to "Consider."

"In all lifeforms," she said, "less than a thirtieth of each gene grouping is involved in protein synthesis. Your colleagues (I took these to be Earthly scientists again) being unable to ascertain any of the functions of these remaining twenty-ninths have concluded they therefore have to be superfluous and accordingly deemed them as..." (and she putting on a wry smile) "...'junk DNA'. As I voiced previously, so many of your Earthly conclusions to enquiries are stymied by extrapolated prior-conceptualised assertion."

With me inwardly saying "I wish you'd stop lumping me in with them," Menpemelo continued with "Consider"s but her "Although all lifeforms evolve apparent structural surpluses..." had her see me puzzled, she elaborated with a curt "It is possible for you to exist with one lung, ear, eye," then continued, "...all are used to optimum ambient opportunity, thus in another context evolution does not create surpluses to requirements. Evolution dictates function

rsenal drawn against

AG Munchen in IEFA

unners' chances against German Goliath grim

By JOHN LOUT

RSENAL, having ust scraped a place in he knockout stage of he IEFA Cup in Rome, seem set to suffer a knockout blow from one of Europe's super sides, the German juggernaut, AG Munchen.

After the fixtures had been announced, Gunner's boss, Arno Vanderkort, said: "There is no hiding the fact ... tough fight on its hands. But we have been written off by everyone so many times as having no chance We have still made it to here."

Munchen's manager, Heinz Guderian, however, was cock-a-hoop with the news. He said: "Of this outcome we are already most glad. We shall look upon Arsenal as good training experience for our boys. It will help prepare AG for the real battles which will come after we have beaten the Tommies. For them, the contest is over."

Guderian, known to his ... brought Munich to its astounding success in just three years His fabled 'stormplayers' are feared by most teams across Europe and are seen my many as unbeatable.

Munchen's captain Rohm Mell has, along with Guderian achieved little less than hero status throughout Germany. Speaking yesterday Mell said: "For you Tommy ...

...ment concerned at growing Nonette influence

Nonettes numbers higher than first thought

By James McCarthy
Political Correspondent

THE GROWTH of the Nonette movement in Britain is far greater than was first thought The penetration by the Movement's into all social groups is also deeper than expected

According to an unofficial Home Office report, there are ... groups either already formed or in the process of doing so

The report also shows that the distribution of the groups is evenly spread throughout the UK The report further reveals that membership of the groups is also evenly spread through all social classes.

Not only is the Nonette ... uing rapid expansion is als focusing minds in Whitehall

One such outcome is likel to be in-creased governmen emphasis on the rehabilitat ion of the electricity and gas supply and distribution

Once these are back to normal, it is thought, the standing of the Nonette ...

usem spaceship: ... goes on

...rd of the wreckage ... stricken spaceship ...ll into the Amazonian jungle.

According to the ...elecast, traces of the spaceship's remains unearthed at the Brazilian crash site indi... a collision with the Earth several years earlier.

The announcement of the extension of the search for the rest of the Aliens' spaceship poses further questions as to when and where ...

SUSEM SEX SECRETS BARED

- **Captive soldiers in forced lovemaking with Aliens**
- **Non-stop tortures, beatings and whippings**
- **Kinky love games and group sex for days on end**

CHRON EXCLUSIVE

CHRON reporters Chris Barker and Barbara Jones in Rio reveal what really happened to thousand's of innocent soldiers snatched by sex-crazed Aliens for non-stop lovemaking in the tropical heat and steamy jungles of Brazil; victims of Susem depraved sadism give FULL horrific details of their ordeals

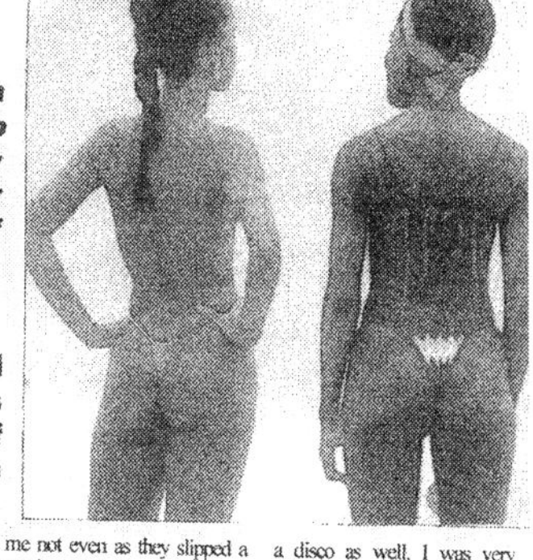

THE GIRLS FROM IPANEMA are still tall and lovely but there are no men on its beaches to see them pass by. In this land of sunshine, samba and skimpy bikinis, even macho men are in hiding.

As news of the Aliens' assaults on soldiers spreads, all the boys from Brazil quake in fear least a Susem sex swoop crush the life out of their manhoods.

Erico Belos, (25) a sergeant with the crack Brazilian Special Forces is one of the 14,000 soldiers snatched by the Susem for no-holes-barred sadio-sex sessions. Speaking from his Rio hospital bed where, because of his injuries he has to lie on his side, Erico gave full details to ***The Chron*** of his forced love-making ordeal by the Aliens

STRIPPED

Sergeant Belos and his entire platoon were 'hoovered up' by the Aliens and driven by their dreaded stinging wasps into one of their craft along with 1,000 others. "We were inside it for just a few minutes when we were pushed out on a misty clearing. The mist was an eerie luminous green. I was very frightened as what would happen to us," he said.

Confused and afraid Erico was instantly set upon by beetle-like machines each the size of his hand. They tore all his clothes off. His naked body was then sprayed with water and more beetles washed and scrubbed him. Stinging wasps next rushed him through the swirling mists.

"These mists began to clear," he said, "and I could make out others of my unit including my friend Carlos. He and the others were also stripped naked. The mists cleared some more and Carlos shouted "Look!" and pointed to the far side of the clearing.

"When I looked I thought I must be in Heaven," he said. "Coming through the swirls of mist were the most beautiful women. There were many of them. They were clad in thin gossamer robes and appeared to float through the air. I thought they were angels.

"Several of these angels clasped me," Erico said, "they were smiling, their hands caressing, stoking my body. They lifted me through the air, I felt so happy. Even as some of them raised my arms above my head

I did not stop them. I did not want them to stop caressing me not even as they slipped a cord round my wrists and tied me to a branch of a tree. I called out 'What are you doing?' but they said nothing," he said.

The Aliens continued to fondle Erico, which he admitted he enjoyed. "What man would not want to have beautiful women pay him such attention? Even when their caresses turned to massaging I still though that perhaps I was in Heaven. Oh how wrong I was," he sobbed.

WHIPPED

While the Aliens continued to feel Erico's naked body he heard music begin to play, the mist fading and in the gathering gloom the space around him became lit. The music then became louder, the lights brighter and at the same time the Susem stopped caressing him.

"Then suddenly," he said, "I felt a terrible pain across my back and I realised I had been whipped. I cried out, then I heard the others crying out as well. I was whipped again and again. The lights become as if at a disco and the music as a disco as well. I was very afraid," he said.

CHASED

"Above the music I heard a roaring sound," he said. "I turned to see. There were now many women gathered the far side of the clearing. I was even more afraid. I began tugging at my cords. To my surprise they became undone.

Then a group of the women began to charge across the clearing. I saw they had canes in their hands," he said.

Petrified, Erico said he ran in fear for his life. "The women chased me and my comrades round the clearing striking us with their canes," he said, "they chased me into the trees. I stumbled and fell."

'THEN THEY TOOK ME - ALL OF THEM'

"I was crying, begging for them to let me go," Erico said, "but they held me down. One of them began to touch my private parts. I was so frightened that I was flaccid. Another stuck something on my shoulder and I found myself immediately in a physically aroused situation

'US must prep... to fight Nonet... before it is too...

Senator Dich demands defence ...

By BRETT ANDERSON
WASHINGTON CORRESPONDENT

Senator Sam Dich

THE United States must rapidly increase defence spending to combat the Nonettes. Calling for an immediate $100bn increase in the US Defence allocation, leading right-wing Senator, Sam Dich, said: "Either the United States crushes the Nonette threat or their cancerous socialist plague will engulf the democratic freedoms of all Americans and cast us down into ... board increase in defence spending is likely to gain fa... wider support than woul...

"All of Britain must be rewired" say experts

Most homes are unsafe

By **Neill Andrill**
Home Safety Editor

HOW SAFE is your wiring? If you have not used your electricity supply for more than three months, then the electrical cables in your home will be suffering from corrosion

If and when you are connected to the mains supply ... erstand about electric... wiring is that it has to hav... power passing through it s... as to keep it free from creep... ing damp.

"In the UK, even in th... summertime there is damp. ... fortnight is about as long ... it's safe to without runnin... electrical power though d...

which in turn determines form and never (and she stressing the 'never') the converse. Such evolutionary precept suggests, does it not, that these 29 thirtieths of a chromosome's structure are not 'evolutionary junk' but purposely existent?"

I'd not had chance to fashion thought of an answer than it was "Consider" again. This time "The size of a primate's egg..." And again seeing me puzzled, she elaborating, "The nucleus of a human egg, just as ours, is little larger than a skin cell's. Yet contained within a fertilised egg's nucleus is encoded a template for prospective progeny. However, this encodement is contained within every one of a being's cells. Within, or so your colleague's reasoning suggests, there is also a further sub-set of genes coding for a progeny's progeny. In a like manner yours were within your parent's parents, and thus by inference within every generation prior to... (and she giving a shrug) ...who is to know 'how long ago' when."

She took a pause and was back to 'Consider'. "Also encoded within the fertilised egg's nucleus, which remember, is many times smaller than you can see, is contained not only instructions for thousands of different proteins but site specific ones." Seeing me puzzled she yet again elaborated, this time with "Look at your thumbs.

"Although both thumbs are composed of the same types of proteins, they are not merely mirror images of one another. If each were transposed onto the hand of the other, the DNA of their cells would still continue to make for their original handedness.

"There are humans who have had their big toes grafted onto their hands to replace lost thumbs. Though these 'toe-thumbs' have continued to thrive, all have stayed as toes including the horniness of their nails. In a toe as in a thumb, let alone the rest of a being's body, there are many types of protein for bones, cartilage, tendons and so on. All of these proteins are site specific. All fold their structures invariably left-handedly into specific bespoke inter-meshing configurations 500 trillion (and she stressing the 'trillion') times every single second.

"Multiply the number of different proteins and their configurations by those of these sites and the resulting figure is millions of trillions. Multiply this figure by the number inter-relating synergies of a being's cells, enzymes and chaperonians, for example, and the number of different proteins will be in their trillions of trillions.

"Encoding instructions for these are, and according to your colleagues' assertions, also supposedly within each genome's progeny DNA sub-set."

With my mind boggled with numbers, Menpemelo dumbfounded me the more with what she said next. "When embryos of higher order vertebrata are first formed they do so by combining parts of two or more fertilised ova, gametes." Seeing me dumbfounded, she elaborated, "Gametes, when first formed, assess selection for optimal proficiency of each others' embryo encoding instructions. Think of this as twins combining their best

IEFA CUP FINAL

Arsenal in non-stop training for Munchen clash

andy Rice in Highbury
nd Felix Gruppen in
unich, Germany

a desperate bid to counter G Munchen's prowess, rsenal have embarked on a hedule of non-stop traing.

With just eight days to go efore the kickoff with the erman soccer colossus at ome's Forum stadium, rsenal's manager Arno anderkort has his work cut ut of he is to get the Gunr's into shape in time

Still reeling from the shock aw in the Octal Finals of e IEFA Cup with the German goliath Arsenal will ive to pull out all the stops it is to avoid an humiliating gh score defeat Gunner's nief coach Brian Seaforth id. "We do not underestimate for a moment the allenge the boys are facing taking on Munchen as our rst team in the knockout."

Vanderkort's and Seaorth's match plan against lunchen is to play a blockg nil-nil game into extra me and win in the suddeneath penalty shoot-out All opes are pinned on Arsenl's Argentinean super-striker, José San Martin.

Bookmakers, usually the ost down-to-earth, no nonense assessors of form, have iven the Gunners' game lan the thumbs down and ave lengthened their odds in Aunchen's favour Last night ... quoting the

That AG Munchen is seen as the all conquering master team of Europe owes much to the genius of their manager Heinz Guderian.

Since Guderian took control of this south German side three seasons ago, he has propelled it to almost instant yet legendary greatness by his simple yet devastating successful strategy.

Known as the 'Lightning Force' this strategy has been as fast as the Munchen squad.

Munchen's last match, against Warsaw Spartek was typical of their style. Within seconds of the off, Munchen's forwards had punched a hole in the Polish defences

Before Warsaw had a chance to encircle Munchen's forwards, the rest of the German side had sped through the gap. Even before Warsaw could regroup for a ounter-attack the Germans d invaded and occupied the tire Polish half and scored eir first goal within the pace of four minutes.

And so it was throughout e entire match. No sooner ad referee given the off each time than within minutes the entire Polish half would be under complete German occupation.

The match against Liege is another example of Guderian's tactical brilliance. In this match Munchen lulled almost the entire French side into their goal area. At which point the Germans took control of the ball and the forwards raced at lightning speed into the Liege's goalmouth. Munchen had already scored their goal before the French forwards had returned to their own half.

After the sixth time the French appeared to give up the will to fight, letting Munchen beat them 10 nil.

Fuel crisis fears soa

Will there be time to rewire the country or generate enough energy deliver supplies to power stations?

By **Nicola Kay**
Business Editor

FUEL fears rose yesterday as the true state of Britain's energy supply situation was made public. With winter approaching the nation is facir... worst ever cri...

The entire dist... system of electric... ply has collapsed. Even if sufficient deliveries of fuel were to be delivered to power stations they could not transmit their electricity to our homes and offices because most of the cabling either has been sold off or stolen.

Many experts are predicting that ... ced. These fears have sent the prices of what supplies do exist sky high.

In London the cost of even an old secondhand generator has risen by a staggering 10 times compared with a month ago. Oil storage tanks have...

Support for movement widespread

Nonette Poll findings shock

By **Jeanette Keeler**

A MORY POLL on the Nonettes shows far more support towards the movement than had been thought. The nationwide survey also reveals that its popularity is spread evenly across the country as well as by social group.

More than a third (35%) of those questioned by Mory said that they were sympathetic towards Nonettes. A similar percentage said they had no opinion for or against the Nonettes. And a surpriseingly less than one in eight (12%) were actually against the movement.

Of the third who said they were pro-Nonette, more than half said they would have no objection to joining a Nonette group if the conditions were advantageous to them.

To find out exactly was this poll would mean for you and your family see page 5 for full details

This would mean, so the pollsters calculate, than more than 1,500,000 families in Britain might consider joining a Nonette group.

If these findings are confirmed by other polling organisations, then it will pose serious questions as to the current government's policy towards the Nonette movement. ...self said: "The Nonette movement has been in existence in the UK for a little more than a fortnight. Already it has had this much impact. May-be the Nonettes are a flash in the pan but then maybe they are not. It most certainly does not make sense to ignore our results."

Professor Ivor Cutt of Wessex University and head of rival pollsters Gamut, said: "I would not be at all surprised if Mory's [findings] are echoed in our far larger poll which will ...

Bishop claims Nonettes are ungodly

Movement are "Fifth columnists"

By Elana Soam
Religious Correspondent

THE Bishop of Buckingham accused the Nonette movement of being no more than agents of the Aliens and are thus a force of darkness

The Bishop, speaking before an invited audience at the Uppingham Observation Centre, said that the Nonettes were the bearers of falsehoods. The entire Nonette movement, he said, was none other than another facet of the forces of Satan which the Susem also personified.

He said that people who were considering joining the Nonette movement should think again Those who choose to join, he warned, could in the end, be condemned to a lifetime of moral imprisonment, regret and remorse for doing such a bad thing.

The Nonette's claim that they are a force for social inclusiveness for all, was no more than a ruse to get people to join them, he contin-... another slur put abo... certain sections of the ... to besmirch his and th... Sl... Television moveme...

The conference at U... ham was part of the ... op's, the Right Rev. Trevor Richards, ca... against the Bosnian ... Crimes Trials and p... ments as well as Sly... continuing screenin... them.

He said he had ... unofficially informed t... next round of trials an... ishments, those of the ... ian and Serbian leade... to be even more besti... the last.

The bishop also denied

Aliens' s... offer w...

Spaceflight could ...

By Bradly Rechon
Science Correspondent

IN a bid to bolster flagging enrollments, the Alien backed Nonette movement is reintroducing its offer of free space flights to new members But their announcement of the trips ran into an immediate storm of criticism from Space experts as being dangerous.

In yesterday's Susem telecast, their front man Daniel Collins tried to tempt viewers to join a Nonette with one of the 1,000 places on 20 flights in the Susem delta winged spaceships

Collins, who is still wanted by police in Britain on fraud charges, said the flights were open to any member of a Nonette formed during the next 10 days. Each flight Collins said, will involve two orbits of the Earth and a fly-by of the Susem's mother-ship, which he called "Sardon"

Junta's Jatai Jitters

Costa regime in coup threat

Polly Portillo reports from Rio de Janeiro

THE BRAZILIAN Junta of General Costa and his OTSA allies were in disarray yesterday as the full impact of their forces' rout and mutiny at Jatai sank in.

Sources within the Brazilian armed forces say that morale in large sections of the army is at an all-time low.

The OTSA Alliance also faces - as the result of the Susem's attacks - the prospect of their forces' refusing to fight. Reports are circulating of widespread dissent within units of both the Argentinean and Chilean armies.

There are also reports, as yet unsubstantiated, that senior ranks in the Brazilian Airforce are pressing for their remaining aircraft be sent to Curita and Pôrto Alegre in the south of the country so as to be beyond the reach of both the Susem and Nonette rebel raids.

The general looked good, till now

Adding to the Junta's woes is the prospect of the US curtailing its military assistance programmes.

Even before the debacle at Jatai relations between the US military and General Costa were said to be strained over deploying US supplied remote sensors. Following the failure of these sensors to prevent the fall of Jatai, relations between the US and OTSA are likely to be even more fraught than now.

It is also unlikely that the outcome of the Susem raids at Jatai will not go unnoticed by US forces stationed in Panama and elsewhere in Latin America such as Chaipas and Cuba

To what extent lessons will be learnt and acted upon is, as a result of OTSA's rout at Jatai is yet another point that the US's

parts to form a singleton. Usually these twins are identical and so there will be no perceptible changes, but when they are non-identical there sometimes are."

This was all new to me and thoughts rushed through my mind. We are all made up from different bits, we're mongrels, chimeras. But more, though the Susem don't give birth to girls we humans do, was this explanation why my friend Sarah, feminine and good-looking though she is, has boy's arms and shoulders, and for my mate Ken's eyes being different, one brown the other hazel?

Menepemelo continued. "One of the outcomes of this gamete selection is varying DNA encoding within the resulting singleton as well as the bases for its trilliard instructions for site specific proteins." Taking a small pause she then added "According to your colleagues' reasoning, there is also within each genome sub-set the faculty for this gamete fusing, and also, of course, one which accomplishes this embryo computation with exacting precision and prior to it evolving into a blastocyst, the embryo's next stage of development which will be no more than 80 hours duration following its first cellular division."

She took another brief pause then continued. "During an embryo's blastocyst development cellular division multiplies to about 100. At this juncture the blastocyst enfolds in on itself to become a mulberry shaped 'morula' and in most vertebrates moves from the fallopian tube to the uterus. Prior to this movement it is possible to remove half of the blastocyst cells but without there being differing effect on the exacting precision required of the embryo's subsequent development. Again, and according to your colleagues, this further compensating faculty is also held within each sub-set."

She stopped for breath but was soon flowing again, though now at Milophiniaesque speed. "That each generation's progeny breeds true to its forebears is indicative of exacting processional precision." Again my puzzlement had her sidetrack, "Some years ago the preserved remains of a man was found amid melting snow in the Ötztal Alps. The body of this man, sobriqueted "Ötzi" was subsequently dated to be more than 5,000 years old. His mitochondrial DNA was found to exactly match with those of people currently dwelling in the Alps' northern valleys. At twenty years per following generation, how many have elapsed since Ötzi died?"

I'd not time for the arithmetic before she was gushing on. "Rodentia have shorter generational sequences than humans, mice 200 days. Desiccated specimens of Mus Muculus discovered in the Tigris valley have been dated at twice the age of Ötzi. Yet they are also chromosomally identical to present day mice. Mosquitoes entrapped in amber three million years ago are identifiable with those flying presently. Breeding at ten generations annually, how many have elapsed between those in the amber and now?"

Me past bothering with arithmetic, she another intake of breath and back to 'processional precision', "Though there is identifiable generational progression

WOR

Susem space flight o 'criminally irrespons says space expert

From Roland Galespie
Aerospace Correspondent

"Flights need to be vetted by experienced professionals" - says expert

THE SUSEM space offer has been given the thumbs down by every leading expert on space flight All say that for ordinary people to travel outside of the Earth's atomsphere let alone its gravitational field was to run grave risks with their safety.

Professor Rodney Jones of Sheppey University's Space Centre, said: "While there is no doubt that the chance of venturing into space is a great attraction to many, it is in their best interests that all aspects of such flights have been checked and evaluated by experienced professionals

Professor Jones said staff at the University's Space Centre were prepared to offer their services and run the risk of venturing into Space in one of the Aliens' space planes and then reporting back with their findings.

Other experts echoed Prof. Jones' commitment and offered to be pathfinders in the space offer in or the exp-

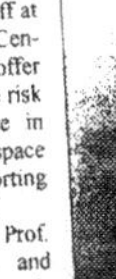

Roma gain strength through Nonette

Seb Estyen reports from Michalovce, Slovakia, on the rapid spread of the Nonette movement among the Roma

Slovakia's ethnic minority are in the forefront in founding Nonette groups across eastern Slovakia.

A weekend meeting of Roma Nonette representatives at Secovce, a village between the regional capital Kosice and Michalovce, saw 130 Nonette groups take part in the formation of a regional umbrella grouping.

A spokeswoman for the regional group claimed that in the province Vchodo alone, there are already more than 8,000 Nonettes, about a quarter of the province's total Roma population

She said that numbers were expected to rise rapidly now that the first delivery of replacement soufin energy units had arrived. However, this is not the only reason for Roma embracing the Nonette movement so fulsomely

The newly elected representative of the group, Natasha Rova said. "For many years Roma people have suffered discrimination and prejudice at the hands of the government, police and

Slovakia's Roma get the strength of the Nonettes around them

"None of them have protected us from violent attacks, rape and murder. The Nonette movement offers the Roma the chance to exist

world network which will give us the protection security we seek. The protection to determine our destiny for ourselves."

Ms Rova, whose family live in the town of Michelovce, is just one of many Roma families who have suffered at the hands of the town's skinhead thugs.

Her father, she said had been beaten senseless by a gang of local thugs, breaking two of his ribs and which had puncture his lung which then had to be removed

"Two of the men who di[d] this," she said, "have bee[n] identified as the sons of th[e] Chief of Police

"Now we Roma have un[it]ed. We are no longer depe[n]dent on the State. No long[er] will we have to suffer [the] indignity of being treated [as] second class citizens in [our] own country

"We have formed our o[wn] security force Also we [are] no longer dependent on [the] State for our energy ne[eds]. Soon we will begin our Nonette based educ[ation] system We can now [look] forward to the time whe[n we] will not need to look [to the] State of Slovakia for [any]thing," Ms Rova said

She added that the[re are] presently two of ou[r]

Energy outlook bleak

EU Power Pact Hope

By Ross Capulyard

Prospects of an orderly share out of Europe's meagre energy supplies collapsed in a welter of recrimination yesterday. Last night energy experts were predicting that countries such as Austria and Denmark stand to be especially badly hit.

At an inter-governmental summit in Lisbon, ministers failed to reach agreement on the allocation of Europe's energy supplies. Energy-producing states such as Britain and Poland refused to cooperate with non-producing members like Austria and Denmark.

The British gov[ernment] spokesman, old Nielson "While the UK [gov]ernment is of co[urse] more than prepare[d to] assist our EU part[ners] in diverting some [of] Britain's North Sea production, there [are] limits as to how far [we] can go.

NONETTE LATEST: More than10,000 UK groups now formed

Nonettes now worldwide

Patricia Palmer
Alien Correspondent

Government's reacted sharply to yesterday's announcement that the millionth Nonette group has now been established. Numbers however, are expected to soar during the coming weeks.

The 1m figure was given by Rainbow Louis during yesterday's Susem telecast She said that this figure was for Nonette groups formed outside the South American and Balkan territories already under their control

Ms Louis also said, that according to the Nonette Coordination Centre at Salvador, groups in process of forming would mean numbers doubling within the next few weeks.

If these claims of Nonette formation are true, they indicate that within less than a month, more than 100 million people have now joined the movement.

If the 100m figure is substantiated it will also represent a serious setback to many governments and other organisations, such as churches in their attempts to downplay the significance of the Alien backed movement.

Rainbow Louis also showed details of the distribution of the Nonette groups These show an even spread throughout most of the world with the exception of the Middle East and Africa. She added however, that the number of Nonettes would have been higher if those wanting to join or form them had not been subjected to intimidation.

Ms Louis said that most of these threats against people wanting to be part of a Nonette came from government and other state-sponsored groups. She also said that the terrorising of such innocent people must stop or there would be appropriate action against the perpetrators.

The announcement of the massive rise in Nonette membership figures brought immediate responses from around the world. A spokesman for the prime minister's office said: "The claims made in the [Susem] broadcast as to the growth of the Nonette movement are of little or no importance to the overwhelming majority of British people They and their so called power units are of little or no consequence in assisting the nation's energ[y] supplies nor in helping t[o] avoid the fuel shortages w[e] will all suffer during the[se] next few months.

"Nevertheless, the [telev]sion] programme is a time[ly] reminder to the people [of] Britain to be aware that [the] Nonette movement is [the] cause of problem we face a[nd] not its solution," the spok[es]man said

Among many of the ne[w]

Andrew Hendry reports from Road To[wn]

Nonettes in 'C[...] banking threa[t]

With the fall of nearby Antigua to the Nonettes, the future of the British Virgin Islands' (BVI) main economic activity is in jeopardy: its highly secretive but extremely lucrative off-shore banking industry.

The Caribbean islands already taken over by Nonettes have either been peopled by indigenous farmers, fishermen ob by employees in the tourist industry. BVI is different. It has a large, non-indigenous international banking and business community.

Whereas the security forces of the islands now under Nonette control were little more than local, lightly armed constabularies, BVI abounds with 'professional secureity'. Security to protect the island's 325 registered banks and the office complexes with their tens of thousands of brass nameplate companies.

Estimates put the number of personnel on the payrolls of private security agencies on the island at between 2,000 and 5,000. Many of these security personnel are foreign nationals and far outnumber the local

policy of total banking secrecy there is the inevitable surveillance surrounding much of its operations. This is expected to also be used thwart any attempted Nonette takeover of the island.

Despite this aura of thoroughgoing security, in the world of offshore international banking even the slightest whiff of uncertainly, could send the 'brass-plates' scurrying with their funds and their secrets elsewhere.

Should any such exodus occur on a sizable scale then the BVI's economy would nosedive and all its secureity and surveillance will count for nothing.

The real guarantor of the BVI's economic security is the nearby American Virgin Islands. A battalion of US Marines supplement contingents of the Florida and Georgian National Guards currently exercising in the territory.

Although unstated, the island chain of the northern Caribbean is increasingly being seen by the US as the front line against the Nonettes. Should either of the

"Aliens held me down" says Priest

Lisa Bassant

Abducted soldiers tell of mass 'rape' by Aliens ordeal

"Many men's manhoods may never recover" - says doctor

By **Lisa Bassant**
in Rio de Janeiro, Brazil

THOUSANDS of innocent young men have been savagely assaulted by packs of sex-crazed Aliens. The cream of the Brazilian army has been subjected to nonstop sadistic sex acts for days on end. Many are mere boys barely out of their teens. All were subjecte[d] to so many perverted tortures they ar[e] unlikely to have a normal love life eve[r] again. Some of the men have still to recove[r] the power of speech.

As the full extent of the horror of these men and boys' ordeal becomes known fear, and panic spreads throughout Brazil. Every man is silently saying: "Will I be next?"

No one was spared from these Alien sex fiends' insatiable lust. Not even men of the cloth. More than a dozen padres were abducted and subjected to forced lovemaking.

One of the padres, speaking from his Rio hospital bed said: "As the Aliens tied me to a tree, whipped my naked body I prayed for the Lord to save me but in vain.

"As the Aliens held me down forcing me to have carnal congress with them, one after another, hour after hour, day after day all I could do no more than lie back and think of Heaven."

This padre, like the thousands of other armed services personnel wh[o] were effectively 'raped' and 'gang banged' by the Susem was als[o] subjected to 48 hours of sex torture and other depraved acts. He wa[s] also forced to take drugs which ke[pt] him in a physically aroused sta[te] throughout his captivity.

Apart from being excruciating[ly] painful, the non-stop lovemaki[ng] made the padre and all the oth[er] men desperate for rest. But the

in mitochondrial DNA it is not proteinaceous. However, should there be the slightest abnormality in any of a progeny's inherited chromosomal protein profile synthesis, let alone genomic sub-set groupings, it is unlikely to survive beyond the onset of such malformation."

Seeing me lost yet again she sidetracked once more with, "The expectant parent will spontaneously discharge such a prospective progeny's embryo. Should a live birth occur it is unlikely to survive into procreational maturity. Humans born with the single malformed gene you term 'CFTR' will suffer cystic fibrosis and succumb, remedial intervention not withstanding, to prior-adult demise."

Though thoughts of Hapsburgs and haemophilia passed through my mind, I had succumbed to just listening. Menpemelo however, still gushed on with corollary, "Sixty or so years ago the population of the Rhine delta experienced an acute and precipitous decline in the availability of food. For more than 100 days in attempting to avert starvation, many consumed plants deleterious to their well-being (the WWII post-Arnhem debacle where the Dutch were reduced to eating tulip bulbs?). Those pregnant during this period bore progeny who, while appearing healthy at birth, subsequently succumbed to many disabling physiologic and psychological malformations.

However, children conceived by these victims matured free from their parents' disabilities, as have the progeny of these children. This suggests confirmation, does it not, according to your colleagues' reasoning that is, of a separate and also separated independent pre-situ DNA progeny sub-set within a lifeform's genome?"

Then she was back to the main path again, "Compounding to this primary cellular chromosomal summation there is the secondary of mitochondrial DNA fidelity. These in turn compound the number to the billions of trillions of trillions. This aggregate, also according to your colleagues, is contained within the microscopic speck which is your cell's nucleus. Is this likely? Is it creditable? Is it possible?" Then giving me a fixed smile, "Or is there another, more plausible explanation?"

But I had no sooner managed "I suppose there must be" and Menpemelo's smile turned to smug nodding, than Pheterisco appeared. I had not even chance for "It's all very interesting but what has this to with the Anthropic Template?" than a group of other Susem appeared and all beckoning Menpemelo join with them.

"I must leave you now," she said, adding as she sped away, "I do not want to miss the First Night."

My "Please don't go," having no effect, I was reduced to "What's the rush? First Night? What First Night, where?"

"Panama."

'Nonettes will not
olve energy shortag
- claims PM

nettes and their backers are cause of short

ADLY RECHON
MICS EDITORS

Nonettes are making
ooming energy crisis
Edward Campbell
ed yesterday.
using the Alien backed
ment of being a
gn influence", the
minister said that they
deluding thousands of
ent people into believ-
... et an assured

"By persuading people to throw in their lot with the Nonettes," the prime minister said, "they have deluded themselves into failing to re-pay their old outstanding gas and electricity bills. By depriving the new power companies of this money it is delaying the timetable for the full domestic re-supply."

The PM, giving the Tony Blair Memorial Lecture, said that he was saddened that some sections of society ... join

with the rest of the na
making the small bu
essary collective co
ment to Great Britain's
being. This was though
a further reference to
who have joined
Nonettes.

In fact, during the le
his lecture, Edward Ca
made several pointe
critical references
Nonettes. The theme
prime minister's
"Personal Giving for
Gain" concerned gi

"Shun this offer, it's another Collins con" claims ex-Home ...

"Susem space trip a scam" says Heywood

By **Marcus Dooder**
Political Editor

FREE space trips are among the latest ploys offered by the Nonette movement in its attempts to drum up membership.

However, within hours of the Aliens' front-man, Daniel Collins giving details of this supposed "offer of a lifetime" many experts were warning the public against it.

Collins, who is still facing arrest on fraud charges, made the offer of free space flights in a telecast yesterday. He said that 1,000 seats were available to the ...

Collins also said that there would be more flights on offer in the coming weeks.

The flights, he said, would be in the Alien's delta space planes and included several orbits of the Earth as well as a flyby of the Aliens' mother ship, Sardon.

Jack Heywood, the ex-Home Secretary and a firm critic of the Nonette movement, said: "Don't touch this offer with a bargepole.

"This is just another of Collins' confidence tricks. We are already reeling from the cruel hoax he played on the entire world over his dud energy units. What is there to say this offer of free ...

into a unified defence

Arsenal: IEFA Cup odds lengthen

THE ODDS of Arsenal winning the IEFA Cup have lengthened to 100-1, the same as the Bulgarian side, Dynamo Sofia. Arsenal striker José San Martin's leg injury has been given by William III as reason.

Nonett
surge
shock

Lisa Biggles
Washington

EWS OF the rapid rise in onette numbers sent shockwaves around the world sterday. In the wake of e huge increase in None power, it means Minis-'s and other top government officials around the be can not now ignore surging strength of this en backed movement.

s yet, nobody knows how many he estimated 100 million people their families who have joined Nonette's have done so for no r reason than to get new re-ement Susem soufin energy s.

st officials are convinced that is the main reason for the ive membership. As soon as y supplies are back to normal

David Souter of the Washington think-tan most people who hav Nonettes have done sincere reasons than energy supplies.

Souter also says th Nonette movement w be a major influence the Third World, it will on those in Developed c

He said: "In the devel most people are low c energy. For them the leading a better quality free from lawlessness a will be the main reason

"The reason for peo First World who join Nonettes will be differen "but the governments of countries in dismissing movement as no mor passing fad risk makin mistake. This Nonette m going to grow a whole lo

overnment warni
ew Alien energy

New units must meet government safety
Users still liable for Power Levy

en Dunn
Editor

N Alien pow-
will still be
safety checks
hey can be
Department of
DoE) spokes-
yesterday
be owners of
lien power
en if they do
ny traditional
ources, will

still be liable to pay the national power levy, he said.

A DoE directive published yesterday, states that under EU regulations, that the UK has no alternative than to ensure that all forms of energy supply carried a Certification of Assured Safety.

The DoE spokesman insisted that the issu-

ing of the directive was in no way aimed at scaring people off of using the new replacement units when they arrive.

He said: "The directive should be seen as nothing other than a timely warning as to the legislation of energy supply use within the EU."

The spokesman was

The crux is in crus - and the glans

Alien abductees' 'penis squeeze' damage may be permanent, doctors' fear

BY HOWARD REMEDE
MEDICAL CORRESPONDENT

AS THE full horror of the Susem's sexual practices becomes known there are fears their victims may never fully recover their manly vigour. More than half the 14,000 soldiers abducted by the Aliens at Jatai could suffer lasting penile disability doctors say.

Dr Maceió Deodor, one of those treating Jatai victims, said: "From the soldiers' debriefings we understand the Susem possess feminine human form and indeed appeared most beautiful to the soldiers. Initially some of the men even thought they were in Heaven and that the Susem were angels. It was only later that they discovered the Susem were actually amorous Amazons with an insatiable sexual appetite."

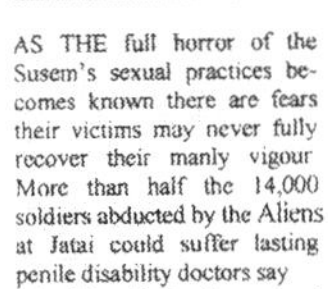

According to the soldiers, not only are the Susem anatomically identical to human women externally but internally as well, with perhaps one exception," he said.

"While it is unusual for the act of penetrative sexual intercourse to last as long as the victims claim, two hours appears to be the minimum," Dr Deodor said, "and equally unusual for the men to maintain an erect penis for this length of time. What is truly exceptional is the strength, force and grip of the Susem's vaginal muscles. It is this phenomenon which has caused the greatest pain and crippling injuries which the soldiers have sustained."

According to Dr Deodor's investigations, the Susem first applied adhesive patches to the victims' backs. These contained a substance causing their penises not only to become immediately erect but also increase in girth.

This instantaneous swelling, Dr Deodor says, would most probably have been because of dilation of blood vessels within the penis rather than any increase in the spongy tissue of the crus (penis shaft). "After two hours of robust intercourse, which was what the Susem continuously subjected the men to," Dr Deodor said, "both crus and the glans (head) of the penis would begin to ache.

"An erect penis, even a sore one would usually be able to tolerate this level of activity without any undue or sustained discomfort. However, continuous acts of intercourse, such as the victims were subjected to for 48 hours and longer, is a very different matter," Dr Deodor said.

"The increased penile girth would also have meant inward swelling effected on the lower urethra within the glans. While the resulting constriction during intercourse would heighten a climax and velocity of spermatic ejaculation, it makes subsequent urination extremely discomforting.

"Another consequence of such prolonged and robust intercourse," Dr Deodor said, "has been acute soreness to the glans itself." Some of the victims Dr Deodor has treated, he said, had almost all the skin of their glans abraded, what he termed, "100 percent red raw."

"During their abduction," Dr Deodor said, "most of the victims suffered further injury by way of the forced insertion - base first - of a dried - thus opened - fir cone into their anuses. The anal sphincter is unable to discharge such a cone and pressure on it from faecal venting widens its wings. Each cone has had to be removed under local anesthetic. During the period of the cone's insertion it would have been extremely discomforting for a victim as would any consequent constipation."

An outcome of the fir cones in the men's anuses, Dr Deodor speculates, is that during boisterous intercourse and with the man in the inferior position he would continuously, almost involuntarily be arching his buttocks upwards. Another consequence of the cones, Dr Deodor surmises, is that the victim would be in a state of full alertness no matter how physically exhausted he might be. "Which after but a few hours," Dr Deoder opines, "I should imagine most men were."

"Towards the end of the second day of the men's abduction," Dr Deodor said, "with their penises swollen and aching from continual erection, sore and abraded by constant intercourse, buttocks and anuses giving chronic as well as acute discomfort, backs and limbs bruised, lacerated from whipping and caning, wrists and ankles also cut and bruised from their being tied up, feet likewise, from being forced to run barefoot, exhausted from so much strenuous exertion but denied, were then subjected to such an excruciatingly painful experience, that it made all these appear as mere irritation.

"From what the victims have related," Dr Deoder continued, "it seems that as the Susem climaxed they pulsed and gripped the men's penises. If this brought the Susem to orgasm or was a consequence of their so doing, it is difficult to say. With each congress, however, not only were the Susems' climaxes more exhilarating to them but their pulsing and gripping became firmer, faster and lasted for longer.

"By the end of the second day such were the heightened levels of Susem orgasms that men had to be held down by other Susem. The final climax was so powerful and sustained, the grip and constriction of the crus of men's penises so strong that they were effectively crushed, compacted to the girth of a pencil for several days afterwards," Dr Deodor said.

133: KEN

I've never had goat before. It wasn't till we had polished it all off that Mrs Ramsheed next door told us what 'baskri gosht' meant. Of course the boys the other side of us stuck to the rice and the rest of her curry, what with them being vegetarians. And that's another thing, I know they are Buddhists but they're not as strange as I had thought they would be.

As Mel said, when we were back in the house, it's funny how once you get talking to people who you don't know, most of them are all right really. And I have to say that since this Nonette has started up, the number of people down our street I have ended up having a chat with is nobody's business.

It's a lot to do with Mrs Prior of course. Since that first meeting there has not been a day without something or other coming from her, how many have joined (we're up to 180 now), our twinning with the town over in the Nonette HQ, when their representative is coming and bringing our new soufins.

Harry letting us have his room upstairs at the Greenwood has given us a place to meet up. While he's happy with all the extra trade of course, so is his missus, Jeanette with, as she puts it, the better class of custom now coming in. Thursday night when we had a meet up with our neighbouring Nonette groups she put on a very nice table of what you would call "proper snacks".

All the same, most of those round here haven't joined, including in the Greenwood, and that's despite all Harry's posters. Myself, I can't see why, after all there is no chance of the government getting their finger out and having the power back on in time, especially round here, not with the cut-off date a fortnight away. But then on the other hand I can see why people are like it, apart from being bone idle and stupid that is.

The stuff on the TV, in the papers. The government's gone mad, I've not seen anything like it. Department of this, Agency of that, their adverts, announcements, and all telling us what they have done to bring things back to normal. There has even been stuff in the post.

The Council is the same. We've had no end of them coming round telling us what they are doing and getting us to meetings so they "can know our needs." But as I said to the lot who came round Tuesday night (four of them there were, "your local councillor Phillip Kenyon-Smith representing you.." and a right toff he was, and they're supposed to be Labour) "Where have you been the last ten years?"

He flaffed on about a "new start, time to get closer to my constituents." And I did have a laugh at the leaflets his "team" handed out, "Your Council... Our Community...an historic rise in Community Charge rebates of up to 20%..." But when I said to him "Can you get my electricity back on?" he went on about how it was outside his 'remit'. And then this morning there is this leaflet from the Housing Department (why we had it I will never know), headed "Important Notice to All Tenants" and then went on about how it's illegal to

"Susem space flights illegal" - warns Law Lord

Minors ineligible - Insurance cover void
Landings trespassing - Boa[...]

By Mark Lewis
Legal Editor

SUSEM Space flights from the Britain taking UK nationals would be breaking a whole raft of laws a leading Law Lord yesterday.

Lord Justice Sir Ken Farquhar warned "Not only would these Alien craft be breaking many laws but so would British subjects who attempted to fly in them."

Sir Kevin said that although anyone in the UK would be risking their lives flying in an Alien spacecraft, his primary concern was for the wellbeing of children who might be induced into taking such a flight.

"Parents of such children would be deemed, in Law," Sir Kevin said, "to be placing them at risk. As a consequence it will be the statuary obligation of Local Authorities to prosecute the parents for cruelty and take their children into care [...] should any of these craft land

Nonettes claim 100m soufin pow[...]

Alien energy huge deman[...]

By Steven Dunn
Economics Editor

THE RESPONSE to the offer of replacement soufin energy units is so strong that there might be difficulty in keeping up with demand it was claimed yesterday.

In less than three weeks deliveries of the new units have passed the 100 million mark.

In a Susem telecast yesterday, Daniel Collins said the demand for the replacement units, which he claimed as nothing short of "miraculous," was straining the Susem's ability to deliver to all who wanted them.

Collins, who is still wanted by the Metropolitan police for suspected fraud, said that the huge demand is also indication of the number of Nonette formations.

Collins also said that people who wanted to have their new replacement soufins in time should join or form a Nonette group as soon as possible.

Also shown in the telecast were the first group of lucky winners of the Susem spaceship flights

Panama Commander shrugs off Nonette [...]

By Paulo Pidde
In Panama

GENERAL ARMSTRONG Tucers, head of US Southern Command, dismissed reported Nonette activity in northern Panama as nothing more than diversionary tactics. General Tucers said it is obvious the rebels are attempting to lure US away from the Canal Zone. He said it is vital that US forces remained stationed along the length of the Canal Zone itself.

Interviewed General Tucers said: "There are no sizable rebel concentrations north of the PCZ. If there were we would, sure as anything, known about them and you can take it from me none have passed this way, either across the Canal or around it by the Pacific or the Caribbean.

"What is being observed are typical diversionary tactics by the Nonette rebels. It's exactly the same as the Vietcong tried at the time of Khe Sanh. We did not fall for it then and I most certainly have no intention in falling for it now," he said.

The General also dismissed reports of the fall of Jatai in

General Armstrong Tucers

"I was a Susem love reject" says porn salesman

Trader witnessed soldiers' two day sex ordeal with Aliens

By MAUREEN COLE

AN ADULT VIDEO SUPPLIER mistakenly snatched in a Susem sex swoop, witnessed the ordeal suffered by 2,000 soldiers forced to take part in non-stop lovemaking frenzy with the Aliens. He is so traumatised by what he has seen that he has given up selling sex products for ever, he says.

Jac Homa's asthma and club foot had kept him from military service. It also saved him from a fate worse than death at the hands of the Aliens. Spurned by the Susem as unsuitable for sex, he laid low in the corner of their love camp and witnessed every sex act and torture to which the soldiers were subjected.

Horna (45) a supplier of porn videos to the army in Sao Paulo, said he had no choice but to follow his clients to Jatai. Bribing his way through the Exclusion Zone checkpoint, he travelled from outpost to outpost selling his wares. But at the last one swarms of the Aliens' feared stinging wasps attacked the troops and they as well as Homa were herded into a Susem craft and flown to their 'love nest'.

While Susem machines stripped and scrubbed the soldiers, they pushed Homa to one side. Although frightened, having learnt from past brushes with authority to keep his head down and stay out of view, he cowered behind a tree. From this vantage point, Horna said he saw much of what took place.

Tied and naked, fondled then whipped

"As the swirls of green mist began to clear I saw hundreds of naked men with their wrists tied above them," he said, "and Susem women fondling their bodies and genitalia. I also saw other Susem appear from the trees the far side of the clearing clutching whips.

"The first Susem glided away from the men. There was music playing but now it became louder, it was like a disco. There were lights but these now became much brighter and were stroboscopic just like in a disco as well. This second group of Susem lashed the soldiers' backs. The men were soon crying out in pain."

Chased and 'had'

After the men had been whipped, Homa said, they were untied from the branches. "Many more Susem now raced from the trees," he said. "They were making 'whooping' sounds as if they were Indians. They also had whips and canes. These Susem forced the men to run across the clearing. Then yet more Susem appeared from the trees on the other side of the clearing.

"Many made flying leaps at the men, wrestling to the ground. There were several Susem to each man. Some men still struggled but when the Susem hit them they stopped. The Susem stuck small patches on the men's backs. The penises of the men near me became erect. Other Susem knelt over the men and engaged in sexual intercourse.

"The clearing was filled with hundreds of Susem making love with the men. This went on without break for at least two hours with the Susem taking turns to have congress with the men. All the while the strobe lighting flashed and loud disco music played.

"Throughout this time I heard, above the music, the men crying out in pain. Afterwards many remained on their backs as if exhausted. But within seconds more Susem emerged and yanked the men to their feet. Those who did not were savagely kicked and beaten by the Susem until they did.

To the woods

"These Susem then chased the men into the trees. The lighting and music faded away. I heard cries of the men coming from the trees. This lasted several minutes then there was silence.

"Two hours later the clearing became lit again. There was also music, Tamla Motown. Many hundreds of Susem then appeared from the trees. They were dancing to the music over by the far side of the clearing where the men had gone. Suddenly these ran out from the trees chased by other Susem.

"Stop in the name of love - before we break you apart"

"The men ran past the first Susem appearing not to notice them and into the clearing. The music changed to 'Stop in the Name of Love'. All the Susem sang this as they proceeded to chase the men with sticks but added, "Before We Break You Apart". One after another of the men were caught by the Susem who then dragged them to edge of the clearing and tied them spread-eagled to the trees.

"Baby, baby where did your love go?"

"When all the men were tied up, more Susem appeared with what looked like feather dusters and as they stroked the men with the dusters especially between their legs they sang "Baby, baby where did your love go?" Other Susem then put patches on the men's backs. Soon all of them had erections.

"You can't hurry love": 2 hours

"More Susem appeared. The music changed to 'You Can't Hurry Love'. The Susem sang this whole dancing in front of the soldiers. Then they leapt upon the men, each Susem gripping as bears do when climbing them.

"The men were soon crying out once more but this did not stop the Susem. For two hours one after another of the Susem were up on the trees upon the men engaged in furious lovemaking which grew in robustness for all of this time," he said.

After this horrific experience the soldiers were, according to Horna, released from the trees. "But no sooner had the men fallen to the ground than they were set upon

conduct political activities on Council owned property, and listed what happens if they caught anyone doing it including evicting them.

The government is the same. No sooner has one lot given their soft soap than there is another shower laying down the law over the consequences if we don't do this or that. This morning in the Express there is half a page on how London Power, the government thing that's taken over the old LEB, is going to offer nought per cent interest loans over five years to pay off the old bills. Then on the next page there is that ex-Home Office git Heywood banging on about the "enemy within" as he called us Nonettes. If this wasn't stupid enough, in the next paragraph he is saying that when all these people from the Nonette HQ come over with the new soufins, they should be rounded up as illegal aliens and "those disloyal 'so-called' citizens abetting them prosecuted."

To me he is right over the top. I can't see what it is that us Nonettes are doing that's so wrong. All we are trying to do is sort out our own electricity and this is only because we have no choice, not a proper one, it's us who are taking the gamble. For all I know these soufins might not work, or even turn up, but it will be our loss, nobody else's. It's our own money we're putting up and what harm is there in that? What gets my goat is all these high-ups who aren't going to suffer from not having power, telling us what to do.

And that's another thing, the papers. They aren't reporting what is actually going on. It's not just all round here that Nonettes have started up either. At work there are five of the others who have, and so has Dave. As he says, nigh all the competition is signing up and so he has no alternative but do the same. And by my reckoning this must be going on all over the place but there is nothing about it in the papers. All there is, apart from "Trials" of course, is stuff about the Poll Tax strikes, all these strange groups, like gays starting up Nonettes and those foreign places going over to them.

The papers aren't reporting any of the things Rainbow is mentioning either. Like the night before last when she showed all those piles of soufins stacked up in some desert place, there were miles and miles of them and all just waiting, she said, to be delivered. There has been nothing about them in the papers. All there has been is bits about Danny and slagging him off for being a shady no-good. This may well be the truth but I still think it's unfair for them to go on about him the way they are, after all I have noticed he's now looking straight to the camera which is something he never used to.

Slovak Security Chiefs on alert against Roma vigilantes

Seb Estyen reports from Michalovce, Slovakia on the reactions of the Security Forces to the burgeoning number of Roma Nonettes

Captain Milan Szabolcs, Michaelovce's burly Chief of Police claims he is under no illusion as to the significance of the local Roma's embrace of the Nonette movement

In the captain's eyes the Roma can only have joined the movement for one reason: to organise against the Slovakian Authorities of which he and his police force are part

Captain Szabolcs denies he has allowed Michalovce to become a centre of racially motivated attacks by neo-Nazi skinheads against the Roma The Captain also denies his force has any part the latest outbreak of violence which has left two Roma dead and 20 injured; four seriously

Though the police are still claiming to be searching for the killers, the Roma accuse them of doing nothing in apprehending the culprits

Michalovce's police are also accused by the Roma as standing by, doing nothing to protect the Roma not just from the local skinheads but many more from elsewhere in the region.

It has been incidents such as these latest killings however, which have caused large numbers of the local Roma population to form themselves into Nonette communities for their own protection against the mayhem in and around Michalovce. Though in forming their own Nonette communities, the Roma are increaseingly opting out of the mainstream life of Michalovce

But it is not just the violence and intimidation which has led so many of the Roma to distance themselves from much of Slovakian society

With the daily assistance of education programmes beamed down from the Nonette controlled communication satellites, the Roma have now equipped themselves with the wherewithal to enable them to function within their increasingly separate society

It is this separateness which is raising Captain Szabolcs' concern and many others of the region's police chiefs According to the Captain: "The gypsies are up to something."

To him that the Roma no longer go cap in hand to the Authorities for housing, medical attention, education, security handouts is most suspicious That the Roma Nonette communities have turned themselves into self-help groups are further grounds for suspicion.

Aggravating the situation, as far as the Captain is concerned, is that the Roma, who endeavour, he believes, to up

Coke price soars to all -time high

Drug dearth drives US crimewave Nonette occupation of Columbia blamed for cocaine cut-off

Howard Jones
In New York

The Nonette's occupation of Columbia has caused the price of cocaine to rise by a staggering eight times in most of the US and elsewhere. By deliberately withholding supplies of the drug to users throughout North America the Nonettes are held directly responsible for the huge upsurge of property crime sweeping many large cities in the US, including many murders and drug induced deaths.

The Cocaine Support Liaison Unit in Greenwich, Connecticut is typical of the care groups who have to live with the effects of the Nonettes blocking the supply to its clients. Unit representative Mary Clarke said: "Coke users are suffering from the price hike.

"Whereas up until just a few weeks ago users would need to rob only one house a day to pay for their fix, they now need to break into at least three homes in a 24 hour time period" she said.

"Many users have been forced, because of the [price] hike, to take to mugging and other street misdemeanours."

Michael O'Rourke, chief of Police in nearby Stamford agrees. He said: "In this town people are really suffering from the short-fall in supply [of cocaine]. Stanford's Police Department is having to cope with a fourfold increase in crime. Yet my officers have received not one cent in extra funding from Hart-ford [the State capital]."

In Connecticut's fashionable New Haven and home to many in the computer and data based industries, the actual shortage of the drug is more a problem than price.

Hank Wangford CEO of new start-up JusDot said: "Because of the current coke irregularities [of supply] the output of our systems engineers, mainframe programmers is being negatively affected. Our guys need to mainline to maintain mainframes."

Because of the cocaine shortage drug demand in the US is said to already be switching to altern-

Nonettes face Crackdown

MPs call for movement to be banned

By Richard Rankie
Polical Editor

NONETTES will be outlawed if six MPs have their way.

Stanley Haines, LibCon MP, has tabled an Early Day Motion for the Alien backed movement to be declared a proscribed org-anisation under the Prevention of Terrorism Act

Mr. Hains, on signing the Motion, said: "This country faces many grave threats posed by this Nonette organisation. It is in league with ... only with Aliens but is ... control

Hains: "Nonettes must be stopped"

that of rogue rebel movement

"It is obvious that this rebel movement is patently working for the overthrow of the elected government of this country and those in other democracies, and is using the Nonette movement to this end

"In being free to function in Britain this foreign backed organisation is privy to sources of information which can be used by them against this country's security interests," he said

Stanley Hayes, MP for Colchester brushed aside reports that his constituency has been particularly hard hit by the Nonette movement. He

Councils issue Nonette tenants eviction threat

By Tony Perry
Social Affairs Correspondent

COUNCILS across England and Wales are to take a tough line against tenants using their homes for political activity. A spokesman for the Local Government Association denied the new policy is aimed against members of the Nonette movement.

The Association's move to evict tenants for holding political meetings in their own homes is without precedent and has brought strong reaction against it from across the political ... liberties

However, the Association's spokesman insisted that its member councils were merely reiterating long established letting practice.

"Councils," he said, "had always prohibited tenants of their residential properties from conducting a whole range of activities from them."

The spokesman said that just as Council and Housing Association tenants could conduct any business from the many business centres, so they could carry out political activities from premises licensed for such

was the veteran Labour MP Tony Stansgate. He said: "It is perfectly obvious what these people are up to. They are trying to nip in the bud council tenants from organising themselves into these Nonette self-help groups. But I am afraid what they have done is to throw the baby of democracy out with the bathwater.

"What these town hal[l] commissars have dem[onstrated]," he said, "an[d] most evidently in m[y] view, is just how remot[e] they are from the peop[le] on whose behalf they a[re] supposedly administra[ting]

Fifty percent energy supply "within weeks"

Progress on distribution faster

By Chang Wong
Power Supply
Correspondent

THE lights will not be going out over Britain this Winter, was the good news from Downing Street yesterday.

Charles Wilson, head of the prime minister's press office said that the levels of North Sea natural gas supplies were being restored back to the former levels at twice the rate than had been thought possible.

Mr Wilson said that the latest figures from the North Sea Office, Great Yarmouth show that the natural gas supply ready to be pumped ashore from the Piper and Auk fields, is almost back to its springtime levels.

This, he said, meant that combined with coal from Britain's remaining deep mines, oil from both the

US troops forced to withdraw from south of Canal Zone

Aliens attack Panama

Andrew Hendry
reports from Fort Clayton

Troops of the US Southern Command have withdrawn patrols from Panama's border region with the former Colombia.

A Southern Command spokesman said the withdrawal was a tactical decision He said: "The presence of US personnel south of the PCZ has been part of our assistance programme with the Panamanian Defence Force. This has been successfully completed. Southern Command is now able to reassign these units back to their duties within the PCZ."

Unofficial sources in Panama City say that the real reason for Southern Command's cancellation of joint patrols with the Panamanians south of the Canal Zone especially in Darien Mountains along the border, has more to do with fears of abduction of US troops by either Nonet[te] rebels or the Susem.

As news of Susem atrociti[es] against OTSA becomes know[n] US soldiers are likely to ha[ve] fears as to their being expose[d] to similar attacks should the[y] also be taken captive by them

134: WEBS

"Consider this spiderling," said Menpemelo.

As the little spider finished shinning up a gossamer strand, it glistening with the rays of the rising sun, I did indeed appraise the tiny fellow. No sooner had it reached the horizontal thread this vertical one was attached to than it was tight-roping along as fast as could be. Then in no time at all it jumped into the air. As it plummeted, jerkedly reeling out fresh thread, Menpemelo said "Before the downward threads can be positioned a horizontal one has first to be in place."

The spider alighted on a leaf of bougainvillaea, stuck the strand down and was running up it again. Then, no doubt caught by the dawn breeze, hurled itself forward into space, spinning out another sheening strand. Before I had time to see where it was headed, Menpemelo, drawing my attention to a few leaves along, said "Consider this spider."

Identical to the first, this spiderling had spun and stuck up a few straight strands more and was swinging from one to the next its spinnerets going full tilt for a web. As I studied, Menpemelo spoke on, "These threads.... (and she pointing to those between some of the straight ones) ...can only be constructed after these... (and she next pointing to some more of the spokes) ...are in place, and only when they are can these secondary radials be put into position." But before I had time to see where this spider was going my gaze was distracted by Menpemelo peering about more of the bougainvillaea growing along the terrace balustrades. With her "Ah yes," she had me looking at a third spider's web.

This was a "here's one I began preparing earlier" of a web. Though the same size as the last it not only had all its spokes but the round bit in the middle half-woven as well. Again Menpemelo said "The central part of the web cannot be constructed until all... (and she pointing) ...these radials are first in place." Though I was all attention to spiders and webs, and just as attentive to her every word, I was at a loss to see what webs had to do with the 'Templates' I had asked her about.

But Menpemelo walked on still looking amid the leaves and I dutifully followed. As she poked and peered and I rubbing the rising sun's warmth into my arms, I glanced out across the undulating expanse of the Sertão, its purple shadows shortening as the new day began. Then with "Ah yes," she had my attention back to the bougainvillaea and webs. This next one was completely completed, its owner sat in the centre waiting for breakfast. "Consider," she continued, "the complexity of all these webs. They are composed step by step from something as simple as lengths of thread. Consider also the spiders themselves. Each has a body no longer than two millimetres, indicating they departed their egg cocoons no earlier than five days ago. Yet not only do they already possess the ability to construct webs but are aware of the reason why they need to do so."

ALIEN ABDUCTIONS - MORE ATTACKS FEARED

"No male is safe" – warns Top Police chief

By WILLIAM WASH

ALIEN ABDUCTIONS are on the rise but there could be even worse to come a leading police chief warned yesterday.

Senior Metropolitan Police Chief Commander Malcolm White said: "Nowhere is safe from the Aliens."

Speaking at a Milan conference on the Aliens' attacks he said: "Now that the beaches of the Mediterranean have been cleared of b...

North Sea Gas figures 'fudged'

By Ross Capulyard

Claims that North Sea natural gas supplies were near their pre-crises levels were thrown into question yesterday

Several City oil analysts said that the government's exuberance is misplaced and based on a misleading interpretation of the Gas Consortium's figures

Rupert Fielding, chief oil analyst at Uber Bank said: "There is no way any of the North Sea gas provid- production facilities in the time it is claimed

"It is not just a matter of turning on the taps. All the rigs, pipelines in the North Sea as well as elsewhere have been on a care and maintenance footing for at least 90 days

"For all or part of the production network - gas head to onshore storage - to be considered safe it has to be thoroughly checked. With most of the previous personnel laid

Slovakia slides to Nonettes

Janos Hanodos
in Snina, Eastern Slovakia

Large areas of Central Europe are now outside government control

Snina's police station is quiet these days. For some, suspiciously quiet Officers report for duty, then, eight hours later, having done little more than click their heels, they clock-off and return to their barracks nearby

It is not that the officers have nothing to police in this eastern Slovakian town but the writ of Snina's finest goes no further than the station and the barracks

The police's peace in Snina is not unique. Forces in towns and villages across large swathes of eastern Slovakia are venturing no further than the security of their stations Not just Slovakia's police forces either but those of the entire western Carpathian Mountain region of neighbouring Hungary, Romania, Ukraine, all have confined themselves to barracks

Across the whole of this remote region the growing power of the Nonette movement has been taken up by entire communities of the region's myriad ethnic groups. Bolstered by the Nonettes of the neighbouring former Yugoslavia, town after village has embraced the movement.

The supply of replacement energy units has undoubtedly spurred many to join the Nonettes but this is only part of the reason for the rapid growth of movement across the region. As important to those who have become Nonettes, is the protection the movement provides to their particular ethnic group

In this European backwater where the idea of nationhood never has been strong, the importance of racial or cultural differences has made many population groups view themselves as minorities in the country they are supposedly citizens. And often they see themselves oppressed minorities

The Nonette movement by dispelling all notion of nationhood or country has removed the need by communities to be protective against outsiders.

With each Nonette group regarding itself as a self-governing community, no one need be part of an unwanted minority anymore With their own power supplies, teaching screens, health booths each Nonette group is increasingly view itself as independent, sovereign 'statelet'.

Though there is, of course, inter-relationships between each Nonette group, none now consider themselves threatened by others Across the entire region a patchwork quilt of different groups now exists. All, however, are

Nonettes to face government clampdown

EU, other governments set to follow Britain's lead

By Mark Lewis
Political Editor

THE Nonette movement could be banned in Britain under government plans announced yesterday. Nonettes will be barred from using government owned buildings including council houses for their meetings.

Schoolchildren will need both their parents' written permission before they can join a Nonette group. Nonettes could be prosecuted for breach of the peace offences in their districts.

Home Office sources said yesterday that the proposed moves by the government are an attempt to forestall the Nonettes from forming themselves into wider, national organisation as has occurred in other countries such as the former Yugoslavia

As one unnamed Whitehall source said: "Can't have them taking over, can we?"

These latest moves against the Nonettes followed demands by many LibCon

Last night the most vocal critic of the Nonettes, right-wing MP Stanley Haines, while welcoming the Home Office's proposals, said that they did not go far enough.

Mr Haines said: "It's another case of too little too late. With every passing day these Nonettes are not only growing in strength but with new recruits handing over 10 per cent of their incomes they are becoming richer as well

"What the government needs to do, and as a matter of urgency, is to round up the

Susem space flights offer: huge response

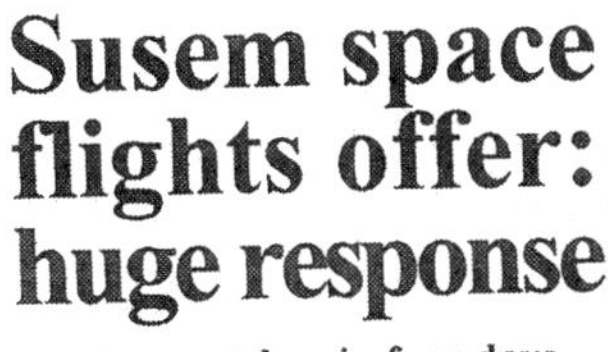

All seats taken in four days
More flight offers planned

From Roland Galespie
Aerospace Correspondent

ALL THE seats on the Susem's Space flight offer have been taken, it was claimed yesterday The response has been so great that further flights will be offered within the next few weeks.

Rainbow Louis, in last night's Susem telecast said that the rapid response to the space flights is also indication of the huge numbers of Nonette groups being formed

Much of her broadcast was of short clips showing chil... which was first screened several months ago Also shown was footage of the Earth and was reputedly taken through a window of another of the Aliens' space plane.

Ms Louis also said t hat 20 of the Susem space craft will be landing at a matching number of locations throughout the world. However, she omitted to give times and places of their arrivals

Rainbow's hour long broadcast also showed more Nonettes receiving their new replacement soufin energy units She claimed that the number of newly formed

Nonettes' Brazil-Argentine 5th column threat

Rebels' growth challenges Juntas

By Paul Pepper
in Rio Janeiro

NUMEROUS NONETTE groups now exist throughout southern Brazil and neighbouring Argentina, Uruguay and Paraguay. The Nonette movement has established itself across all sections of society rich and poor alike. Police and Security forces of all four countries face increasing difficulties in attempting to contain the spread of the movement.

Brazil's and its fellow OTSA members' are reeling from their reverses at the hands of the Susem rebels at Jatai, the Nonette movement is presenting them with an even greater threat. For the Nonettes are quietly, insidiously progressively hollowing out the juntas' authority from within.

Like unseen larvae insidiously gnawing the pith of an erstwhile healthy apple, so the Nonette movement is quietly, yet progressively spreading its influence in towns and villages across the region. And as Nonette influence waxes so that of the government's wanes.

For many who live in the falavas - slums - of Rio de Janeiro, São Paulo and the other large towns of southern Brazil, the government's authority has ceased to exist all together. Nonette self... wildfire in falava after falava Though the movement's influence has grown more on promises than substance, people do at least believe these will be fulfilled

In its bid to counter Nonette influence, General Costa's military government issues daily pledges of reform of its own. But like government promises of the past no one believes them. And worse - for the government - few people see it as 'their' government.

However, absolutely no one views Brazil's police force as 'theirs' To the people of the falavas the police are as despised - and with much justification - as the hoodlums, drug traffickers who once preyed on them. Attempts by the police to stamp out the Nonette movement in the falavas have been thwarted by a wall of silence.

Often police have been confronted with outright attacks from within the falavas Seven days ago, in Rio when police attempted to raid the Nonette centre in Maracanã, a falava in the north of the city, stone throwing youths drove off dozens of police, inflicting injuries on more than a score of them Needless to say, police have not returned to Maracanã.

The news of the solidarity ... Maracanã has emboldened those of other falavas across Brazil as well as Argentina. Police forces, wary of the reception they would receive should they attempt to raid a Nonette have stayed away.

This has played straight into the hands of the Nonettes. Knowing that once organised they can throw off the might of the police the Nonette movement has gained yet further strength The predictions of lawlessness in the falavas, and as predicted by many as the inevitable outcome of police absence has not been borne out by events.

The western São Paulo falava of Santo Amaro has a strong Nonette presence It also has its own home-grown police force. Its Nonette representative, João Percara said: "We had always a big drug problem. But now we don't

"We have told those involved in drug trafficking," he said, "that they will suffer the same fate as those in the regions taken over by the Nonettes This has been sufficient deterrent to make the dealers move on Other crimes have diminished and this has also encouraged more people to join with us."

As government influence and fear of its power wanes daily, the victory over the

As she spoke this fourth spider's breakfast in the form of a tiny fly flew in. With me wondering whether it would stay ensnared, Menpemelo continued, "So alike are all these webs to one another that an arachinologist could determine the spiders' species by merely looking at them."

The fly now had all its legs entangled, wings as well. But Menpemelo's "Envisage..." had my attention again, "...the junction of each strand to another as a co-ordinate, then regard the entire web as a collection of them." With me trying hard to do so and the fly now twanging the web back and forth, she spoke on, "As you will notice, within a narrow degree of proximity each web possesses an identical yet small number of differing, repetitive co-ordinates," (she indicating with her finger each junction of spoke and circle strand). "It is as if the spider, as it plots, positions its web structure, is in receipt of a map set of the sequenced stages of the web's construction."

While the fly, finally failing to free itself, fruitlessly fidgeted forlornly awaiting fate, Menpemelo continued, "Consider further this juncture... (she pointed to where the second outer strand attached to the first) ...as an initiator relay station transmitting these next co-ordinates... (she whizzing her fingers around the web) ...and they in turn, and collectively so, being the combined relay station for these," (she pointing to the woven centre of the web itself).

With the fly's struggling stopped the spider slowly stepped from the web's centre for breakfast. As I watched for what would happen next, Menpemelo still spoke on, "The structure of these webs can be viewed as planes, bi-contexts." But no sooner had she spoken than she was rummaging among the leaves again, this time peering down amid the morning shadows. With the spider upon its prey, knife and fork no doubt at the ready, Menpemelo's "Ah look," drew my attention to another web.

Flanged like a trumpet, a foot and more across, this one was a whopper. And like a trumpet it had a narrowing, curving tunnel of darkness. Worse, stuck high upon the flange as if a "stay away" warning was the dried, sucked-out husk of the occupant's demised male mate. Though fuelled with apprehension, Menpemelo had me kneel with her in front of it (money spiders I'm all right with, it's all the others that I've a dread). "Although this web is more than the bi-context entity of the others," she said, "it is constructed in a similar manner. A small number of initial co-ordinates determine, relay the positions of the next, they the next and so on." As she spoke she touched the web here and there indicating them but with her every prod my foreboding grew.

"This web can be further viewed in terms of volume, a tri-context entity," she said stroking her finger along the side of the flange and me inwardly saying "Don't keep doing that you'll make it come out." But blithely unaware of the danger she kept touching the web as she talked. "Though its form and fabrication is defined by co-ordinates it is further marcated, albeit subsidiarily, by the determining assemblage co-ordinates of these..." (she giving the bougainvillaea's branches a tweak) "...and they by the balustrades, atmospheric

Tom Jones Appreciation Society and the Firemen

A most unusual hen night!

By **Ted Woodward**
Welsh Correspondent

SIX Pontypridd firemen, called to a suspected blaze were seen, by the Tom Jones Appreciation Society. The result? Six distressed young men, 50 very disorderly ladies, who in the words of Justice Lloyd, "Were an outrage to public decency and should have known better."

Giving evidence at Cardiff Crown Court, PC Alan Jenkins said that he and his fellow officers were called to an unattended fire engine in Barry John Street. "But as soon as we stepped out of the patrol car we heard sounds of a disturbance coming from the nearby Green Grass nightclub," he said.

When PC Jenkins and his fellow officers went to investigate the disturbance, they found six firefighters naked with helmets clasped in front of them and stood on tables surrounded by a gang of women.

"All six males were in evident distress," PC Jenkins said. "The women were under the mistaken impression that the firefighters were part of the striptease act booked for that night."

The Court was told by one of the firemen, Glynn Davies (27), that when he and the rest of his crew arrived at the reported blaze they couldn't detect any signs of a fire. But when attempting to gain access to the affected building from the rear, they thought they could do so from the back of the Green Grass nightclub.

Mr Davies, a Leading Firefighter, said: "No sooner had we had set foot in the Green Grass than we were pounced on by all these women. We tried telling them we were firefighters and on duty but it made no difference to them, they still would not let go of us. I personally was very scared, especially when they began shouting, "Get them off."

Assistant Leading Fireman Daffyd Hughes (26) also giving evidence said: "I said to them to let go of us. We had come about a fire. One of the women then shouted to come and light hers. At first I did not grasp what she meant but when the other women holding me burst out with "Come on baby light my fire," the penny dropped I became very frightened. And then a whole crowd of more women started tugging at my uniform."

Fireman Hughes broke down in tears when he was asked by the Prosecution to describe his experience at the hands of the women and the trail was adjourned. The hearing continues.

Kiev issues State of Siege — Countryside out of government control

Army, police in 'anti-delinquency' sweep

Nonette Ukraine threat

By Archum Tambov
in Kiev

The Ukrainian government has declared war on the Nonettes. Yesterday's declaration of a state of siege is acknowledgment of the extent to how Ukrainian President Kurikov feels threatened by the Nonette movement's rising strength.

The growing threat of the Nonettes to the Ukrainian authorities came to a head three days ago when the entire population of western province of Rovno declared they had all now joined the Nonettes, formed their own independent council and no longer recognised the sovereignty of Kiev.

Since then a further four provinces, all in the west of the country, have self-proclaimed their secession from the Ukraine.

The first that central government officials claimed to know of the seriousness of the situation in Rovno was when a truckload of security officials was unceremoniously dumped in the centre of nearby L'vov last Saturday.

Since then more officials from the other affected regions have also been expelled in a similar fashion.

Although a number of top government officials are report-ed to have been summarily dismissed from office over the Rovno debacle, the current deteriorating situation cannot be entirely blamed on incompetence within the administration.

Ukraine, because of its earlier near total dependence on nuclear energy, stands to suffer more than countries from the loss of Susem energy units. Therefore it came as no surprise to many observers that there would be a rapid take-up of replacement Alien energy units from among the Ukrainian population...

But w... ated...

Seven-day shock sentences for Yugo war crimes mass-murderers

Judge's easy terms even stuns guilty

By **Nicola Kay**
in Sarajevo

ONLOOKERS at a Bosnian War Crimes trial gasped in disbelief at the lenient guilty sentences handed down by judges at a major trial of 17 mass murderers. All were given sentences of no more than a week's duration. Even more surprising is that none of the culprits will spend a single day in jail but serve out their sentences in a virtual holiday camp.

In Sarajevo's main Courthouse, a detachment of 17 men, all members of the former Serbian army, stood accused of shelling a crowded apartment complex and nearby school. During a two month period their shelling caused the death... One of the shells fired by them onto a mosque killed 43 worshippers.

The trial, which lasted an entire morning, found all the men guilty as charged, both individually as well as collectively. The senior judge, in her summing up said that all the men were "evil and wicked" deserving nothing other than the sternest punishment.

To those watching the trial, including many of the relatives of the men's victims, this heralded nothing less than immediate public beheading or stronger.

Thus when the judge announced that she was sentencing the guilty men to spend seven days on the same mountainside from where they had fired their shells from, there was perhaps justifiable consternation

NEWS

Nonette increase could be bigger than...

Susem flight success s... rise in Nonette num...

By Mark Humpher
Social Affairs Correspondent

The huge success of the Susem space flight offer is seen as indication that the growth of the Nonette movement is bigger than first thought

In Britain the number of Nonette groups formed was thought to be in 6-8,000 range. But the claim that 500 of the space flight places suggests that the actual number of groups must be considerably higher

However, if those groups in formation were added to this figure then numbers must be approaching the 15,000 level

If the membership of each group is no greater than the Nonette minimum of 81 then upwards of 1,250,000 people in the UK alone, have now joined the movement. If the rate of formation of fresh groups continues at this rate then the size of the movement can be expected to exceed 2,000,000 within the next month.

While there is concern in some quarters of Whitehall at this rapid increase the of Nonette numbers, most government departments are still keeping to their studied indifference to the movement's existence.

A senior Home Office official said: "The purported rapid growth in this Nonette movement's number is due to some people's natural concern for a power supply during the coming winter period. And of course having one of these Alien energy units is a way of overcoming the problem in the interim

"However, as soon as established power supplies are back online, then ordinary people will soon forget these Nonettes And the movement as a whole of course, will soon fade away just as like all these other fringe movements

"The Aliens' space trip will doubtless come... same... have... chanc... free s...

"Bu... they... not g... they... over... In th... after... depar... this N... will b... more... the pa... my w...

Othe... thoug... cerned... of the... ment's... ence w... verse e...

Massive rise in Susem seizures — "Warnings still being igno...

212 men in record Alien Med abductio...

By Richard Rankie
World Affairs Correspondent

THOUSANDS of innocent holiday-makers fled in terror yesterday as Susem snatch craft swept the length of the Mediterranean. From Greece to Spain, beaches emptied as people ran for their lives in desperate bids to avoid the Aliens' flying flotillas of fear Yet a total 212 innocent people - all thought to be males - were abducted by the Aliens.

Last night as hundreds of parents, wives waited anxiously for news of their loved ones, the Alien Abduction Centre in Milan, said that 68 of the Susem's victims had been reported as being released within hours of their abduction. The Centre said this was in line...

Yesterday's raids take the weekly recorded total of Alien abductions to a record 1,324 victims. This is the first time it has exceeded the 1,000 level. The Abduction Centre stressed that these were only those cases reported to it The Centre said it was aware of many other raids and abductions reported as taking place in other, more remote parts of...

more than 15,000 He said that although there were some abductees being returned they were only a trickle compared to those still in Susem hands.

Captain Perscara claimed that earlier reports of the abductees being molested and some sexually assaulted were exaggerated. However, he did admit to there being some substantiated cases of assault but stressed that these ... "few in number."

mainly touris... ed by the A... girlfriends... another as... iously for th... return

Penny S... Swindon, ... with partn... (26), and... ducted by... "All of ou... ing volley... and then... of those...

constituents and so on."

Although my attention was with her and the shaking bush, I also caught from the corner of my eye a darkening within the tunnel's gloom, first one leg then another came round the corner. Big black hairy ones.

Though they then halted I was struggling to my feet. But to my discomfort getaway was thwarted by Menpemelo's restraining hand to my shoulder. With the forefinger of her other hand she continued to point and prod, adding as she did, "The creation of a living entity can be envisaged as being determined, just as are these webs, by a series of step by step semi-self-assembling receptors. Some are tuned to receive limited, concise instruction from a single source, others diverse and from several. In turn they also become transmitters of data, some solely relaying onwards what is received, others a composite of several sources, or from freshly formulated co-ordinates of data from within the station itself. However, all are prior dependent on the database of the first transmission station."

By now I was bursting with questions but also continued giving Menpemelo all the attention I could muster (I was sparing some for the spider in case it came out). She, though, ignoring the menace lurking, continued prodding, saying as she did, "Consider also each message not in the form of a continuous stream of information but as a discrete pulsed package of data, a template." Hearing "Template" had my ears prick up but it was at this moment that the spider finally stomped out of its web and Menpemelo's restraining hand restrained no more.

But the follow-up four minute mile was dashed by her arms clasping my waist and a mocking "Surely you are not afraid of such a small thing!" Alas my frantic protestations that her shaking the web had upset the spider, the reason it was not running off but standing its ground and its legs together meant it was about to attack, spring up at us, sink its poisoned filled fangs in our faces or if it wasn't that sort it would jet hairs in our eyes and blind us, had no effect on her.

Even my plea to at least let go of me so I could get a shoe off and hit it before it got us, made no impression on her either. Instead, still clasping my tunic with one hand she slowly stretched the fingertips of the other towards the spider and despite my "Don't, oh please don't..." she touched, stroked it. Then the spider ran up her arm.

Still stroking the spider, it now nestled in the crook of her elbow relaxed as a bean bag, Menpemelo ambled along the terrace with me to her side, my dread dissipated. As she stroked she spoke, "On an earlier occasion I mentioned the tri-context of an entity is composed of bi-contexts and they in turn, of single ones, lines. And of what are they composed?"

"Er...points."

"And of what context are they?"

"Shun Nonettes or risk excommunication" - Pope threatens

BY ELANA SOAM
RELIGIOUS CORRESPONDENT

POPE Pius XIII in his weekly address, issued his sternest warning yet against joining the Nonette move- ... tion and defilement in their wake".

He said hundreds of churches had been plundered and stripped of many of their sacred possessions, thousands of priests had been forced to flee while others had ...

Many of the Church's confidential archives had been plundered and made public, jeopardizing the safety of many of the Church's senior officials.

While Pope Pius' outburst against the Nonettes is in line ...

Final 'Trials': cruelest yet

- Serb, Croat leaders' punishments promise to be "ACME OF INCLEMENCY"
- Revised routines promise increased bestiality
- Record 2bn viewers expected
- SLI shares rocket as advertising demand soars

By GOLDIE PALMER

THE NEXT 'TRIALS are GUARANTEED to be the cruelest yet. Events will be over three days and contain a host of new routines which are said to have a whole new mix of both quick and slow punishments.

Outlining the three day programme, Dickie Bear, head of SLI Television said, "As soon as we at SLI got the schedule from Caught [the distributors of Trials] we knew we had a TV spectacular on our hands.

"So that our viewers don't miss a single thing we have scrap- ... stop over the three days of the event."

Mr. Bear said that he wasn't at liberty to give precise details of the routines but said that the events would follow that of the past Trials.

He said, "All I can say is that they will start off with the trial of all those murdering bastards and as soon as they are found guilty they will be marched off and get what's ..."

"Show us your choppers" jibe

ABDUCTED FIREFIGHTERS IN HEN-NIGHT HELL

By TED WOODWARD

A gang of women abducted and forcibly stripped an entire crew of firefighters, it was revealed last night. The women then made the men dance on tables in nothing but their helmets and subjected them to a stream of obscenities and threats.

Continuing giving his evidence on the second day of hearing the trial of the 50 women of the Tom Jones Appreciation Society of Pontypridd at Cardiff Crown Court, Assistant Leading Firefighter Daffyd Hughes (26), told the jury what happened when he and his fellow firemen stepped inside 'The Green Grass' nightclub.

"No sooner were we by the door of the club than they were all over us," Firefighter Hughes told the jury.

"Two women grabbed hold of me and were dragging me inside. I said we had come about the fire. But this woman said why didn't I put out hers.

"Then another woman started singing 'Come on baby light my fire.'

"I shouted for them to let go of me and attempted to pull away from ... then appeared from within the club and said: 'Are you being shy big boy?'

"But before I could say anything she said: "What a bit of rough do you?" and then she knocked me to the floor with her forearm.

"Before I could get to my feet even more women were attacking me. From the cries of the rest of the crew I concluded they were under going the same experience as I was," he said.

Firefigher Hughes next gave details of what happened after the women had carried him and the rest of the crew into the club. "From the cries of pain from the rest of crew I concluded it was best not to resist the women and let them remove my uniform as well as put up with the stream of vulgar aspersions as to my private parts.

"When all of us were naked we were manhandled onto tables ..."

PANAMA CANAL ZONE LATEST:

Attacks on base repulsed claims General Tucers

Mass civilian flight from Colon and Panama City

Andrew Hendry
reporting from Colon

GENERAL TUCERS, Commander of US Southern Command, said his forces had successfully beaten off an attack on a forward observation base on Mount Brewster, the 1,000m peak 60km east of the Panama Canal.

General Tucers said the attack took place at 21.00 hours yesterday and lasted for less than 20 minutes.

There were no serious casualties, he said. He declined to give details of the attack other than there had been a brief fire-fight with the rebels who had then immediately retreated.

Remote sensing

General Tucers added, however, that the units at Brewster Base had now been replaced with remote sensing arrays. He said the deployment of his forces within the Canal Zone itself would increase their overall effectiveness.

Replying to questions alleging his forces were at risk from a Jatai-type attack, the General said: "Unlike the OTSA armies, all the men under my command are professionally and combat trained, many have battle experience.

"Unlike the Latin forces, which were composed of poorly trained conscripts, all of my men have voluntarily enlisted. My men know that I and my fellow officers have their safety and security uppermost in our consideration.

"They also know that I will never place them at any unnecessary risk, no matter how small that might be. That is why I have decided to terminate Brewster," he said.

General Tucers

General Tucers stressed that the US presence along the Canal was not primarily to fight but to act as a deterrent against any Nonette rebel advance into Central America as well as keeping the waterway open for shipping.

The general said: "We are here in Panama as peacekeepers but should anyone dare to break the peace then you maybe assured we will as sure as hell break them."

Population fleeing

The population of Panama City and Colon, however, have placed a different interpretation on the attack on Brewster. Whereas a sh... time ago they were welcoming US soldiers as protectors, now they are packing their bags, leaving town and heading for all places north as fast as possible.

The Panama Canal

One Colon resident, Franco Angles, said: "I do not know who attacked at Brewster and I do not really care. It shows however, that whoever they are, they are coming.

"I have read what happened to those guys down in Brazil and if those Space Ladies come to Panama for the Gringos they may well get me as well. I am getting out while I can." This is a prevalent attitude among many Panamanian men.

Nose-to-tail

Traffic on the Pan-American Highway north of Panama City is nose-to-tail as frightened residents flee from what they see as a forthcoming confrontation between US military might ...

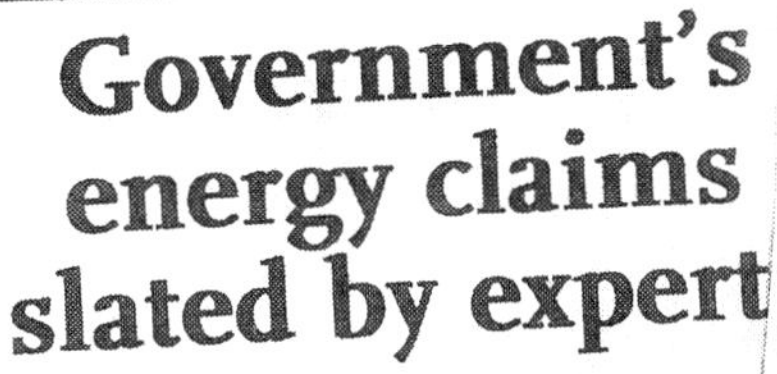

Government's energy claims slated by expert

BY CHANG WONG
POWER SUPPLY CORRESPONDENT

THE government's claims that Britain's energy supplies were turning the corner were dismissed yesterday by a former head of a national power generator as "riddled with holes and irresponsibly misleading."

Sir Hugh Cameron Brown, the former head of NorGen, writing in the current issue of *Big Turbines Monthly*, says: "What none of these government people appear to have grasped is that power supply is a dynamic process. It is also interdependent on all parts of the process operating in perfect coordination with one another. If just one part of the chain should malfunction, the rest of the system will also be adversely affected ..."

"Points don't have any, they are non-contexts. Points don't really exist."

"Except in the..?"

"Quinth context!"

The spider unfurled a leg then another, flopped them either side of Menpemelo's arm and she spoke on, "As you know, the intersection of three bi-contexts determine position within an entity's tri-context. Furthermore, Secondary wave motion encounters resistance from innate Tertiary wave groupings, but in the quinth context resistance within an entity is diminished."

I nodded, she continued, "Though relay station transmission effect occurs in the tri-context, as the spiders' webs indicate, most do so within the quinth context, it being the more proficient context of conduit."

I was struggling hard to take in what she was saying but still thought it best to keep from questioning and continue listening. However, her "Consider also relay transmission stations' fourth-context duration within an entity, some transitory, some preceding its contextual formation, others post-ceding it," had me finally driven to ask "What do you mean?"

But I soon wished I'd not for it drew her rapid "Where are the parameters of an entity? Tri-contextually where are yours? Outer layers of your epidermis? Tips of your hair, particulate bloom of your bodily expiration? Your shadow? The extent at which others can sense you? Your perceived presence by electro-magnetic transmission? Where?"

We had come to the end of the refectory terrace but on turning to walk back she was still firing, "Fourth-contextually from when do you exist? Birth? Conception? Those of you parents? The moment of formulation of components for your assemblage? Theirs back to the supernova eruptions? Their galaxy formation? The Anthropic formation itself? When?"

Without chance to take cover behind "I don't know," Menpemelo's fusillade continued, "At what moment do you cease to exist? Conclusion of cerebral cognitive function? Metabolic cessation, bodily tri-context dis-assembly? Erosion of your presence's influence? Your progeny's? Theirs? And within the quinth where? When? Do not forget also, though the quinth re-evolves out of the other contexts they are transitorily enmeshed in. When discrete auralative entity fades? Total Secondary wave modulation inference erosion? When?"

With Menpemelo now having shot me to silence but realising perhaps she had been a tad strident, stopped shooting and, as though administering balm to my Swiss cheese of bullet holes, assuaged with "Although parameter delineation is ever arbitrary, one for practical purposes in terms of life can be drawn around the possession or not of sentience, but of course even this engenders occasions of contradiction."

Then with a sweep of her arm as though to indicate the Sertão, she said "Consider all of life, its myriad forms animate and plant alike, all in harmony, balance..." (a moment's pause as she'd her hand back to the spider, it swiftly ringing its leg around her stroking finger as if in a "Don't ever stop" plea) "...all

New power supplies ahead of schedule

By Oliver Stoneburger

Half of Britain's energy supplies are expected to be online several weeks earlier than had been thought possible.

North Sea natural gas is coming ashore at near pre-crisis levels. The pipelines from the natural gas storage facilities at Becton, near Great Yarmouth, to power plants in the south of England are being reinstated at a much faster rate than was first thought possible.

Kevin Jaggers MP, Junior DTI Minister said: "The rapid rate of reinstatement of North Sea hydrocarbon distillate is good news for Britain. It is good news for business and domestic consumers alike. It also means that all the essential services can now be maintained.

"If progress continues as is it has, there is no reason why all of Britain cannot expect to have sufficient energy supplies to ensure no one need be without supplies this winter," he said.

Kevin Jaggers also stressed that the success of North Sea gas production was

Yanks to go home

US pull-out could collapse NATO

"Europe: defend yourselves for once" – says Sen. Dich

By Phillip Brown
National Security Correspondent

NATO'S TOP brass were wearing brave faces yesterday as the shock of the US's surprise sudden European cutback sunk in. At the Alliance's Brussels HQ yesterday, senior Commanders were saying there was no need to change their plans for Europe's defense.

But NATO's military planners were soon ready

The planners know that without American control of the Alliance it is doomed to fall apart as their political masters squabble among themselves.

Military analysts were also quick to spot NATO's coming crisis. Arnold Wenger of *Armed Strategy Monthly* said: "Every engagement NATO has been involved in has been bedeviled with infighting between member countries.

"Forget about the Susem attacks on nuclear weapons and power ... which were over ... one could barely blink," he said..

"Focus on the operations before that. Kosovo, Iraq for example, within months every European NATO member had fallen out with each other.

"How long was it before the Serbs and Albanians had their NATO supporters and detractors? And how long after that before there were riots and NATO body-bags?

"How long did it take before the first casualties and NATO countries wanting out? It took US Congress a week to get their forces on th

Government in Nonettes curb move

Alien organisation to face bans

By Jonathan Spender
Political Editor

THE NONETTE movement could face tight restrictions on its activities if new government measures are passed by Parliament.

The fast growing Nonette movement will be stopped from:

- recruiting under 18s without the written consent of both parents
- having foreign Nonette so-called 'advisors' without Passport and Immigration consent
- conducting their activities in central and local government owned premises
- staying away from school.
- engaging in any activity which local police chiefs consider constitutes a breech of the peace

If these and other measures come into law the Nonettes will have been dealt a serious blow to its rapidly growing strength throughout the UK.

In less than a month since its British formation, the Nonette movement is thought to have attracted more than 750,000 members. This rapid growth is undoubtedly due to many people wanting to se... energy units but this not main reason for the government's proposed clampdown.

The main aim of the government moves is to curb the Nonettes' growing influence on the communities where their strength is greatest. The moves are also seen as an attempt to block further growth in other areas.

Police forces across the country have complained of the growing incidences of Nonette vigilantes patrolling their own neighbourhoods without official consent which has brought them into conflict with Neighbourhood Watch groups.

There have been several instances, police say, where Nonette gangs haven taken the law into their own hands.

USURY - the national association moneylenders - say that many of its member have suffered at the hands o Nonette vigilantes.

The major cause of gov ernment concern of th Nonettes however, is thei increasing financial re sources. It is understood tha banking facilities for th movement may be denied t the movement but this wi

US withdrawal: 'Special relationship' sunk

Lights of freedom could go out

NATO infighting blamed for rift

By Marcus Deed
Poltical Editor

THERE is growing bitterness in Whitehall towards the US for its decision to withdraw an estimated 30 per cent of its arm forces from Europe.

The American claim that Europe must look after its own defence is seen by many in the Ministry of Defence as the outcome of EU's campaign for a 'European Dimension' to NATO.

In the words of one MoD official: "The American's tired of European shenanigans over the running of NATO and ... because of

All US forces throughout the world are also being recalled back to America to bolster its defences against the Alien backed Nonette movement.

These force include those stationed in Saudi Arabia as well as Japan and South Korea.

In all, according to *Jane's Military Estimates*, more than a third of US worldwide troop strength is to be re-deployed in America, mainly in the southern states such as Florida and Louisiana. As important are the resources which will also go with the Americans' departure. These ... of the

NATO to be stripped of 50,000 troops 'within weeks'

E U Security Defence Force to take over NATO role

US on Caribbean 'front-line' alert against Nonettes

US forces in worldwide withdrawal

Gordon Richardson
DiplomaticCorrespondent

Up to 200,000 US forces world-wide are to be rushed to the US to strengthen its defence against Nonette attack.

NATO's European Union members are forces are expected to fill the gaps left by the shock US withdrawal.

President Warren said that US forces will return to Europe as soon as the Nonette threat has receded.

Many NATO members are reported as "shocked and alarmed" at the US's unilateral action.

The suddenness of the US's decision to redeploy its NATO forces to America is without precedence.

According to Downing Street sources there was not even prior

Pres. Warren yesterday

consultation with the Ministry of Defence or the prime minister's office.

One MoD insider said: "So much for the Special Relationship. The moment it was inconvenient to the Americans they ditched it."

President Warren, speaking from the White House, said that the decision to order the withdrawal of US forces was taken with "deep regret".

The President said: "As Your Commander in Chief I have to assign the defence of the United States above all other priorities.

"American Defence Forces have always been the defenders of democracy across the world. In the long and noble history of our nation both its men and women have ventured forth throughout the world to defend and uphold the freedoms of all mankind.

"But now it is the turn of these United States of America who are in need of their protection. It is this great country of ours which must once again to defend liberty and all that is right.

Aliens captur youths for 'hare

"Stay indoors" warning to

By Lisa Biggles
Alien Affairs Editor

FEARS rose yesterday for the safety of the men captured by the Aliens. They could be used for sex.

Crime profiling experts at an Alien Abduction conference in Milan warned that the kidnappings bore all the hallmarks of "predatory sex".

Dr. Malcolm Hargrieves of Surrey University speaking at the conference, said: "All the young men who have returned from Alien captivity show the same trauma symptoms and repressed hysteria as do people who have been subjected to serious sexual assaults.

"Every one of the victims who have so far been interviewed have only a partial recollection of what has happened to them during their time in captivity," he said.

Although Dr Hargrieves refused to detail his research reports, other profiling experts at the conference indicated what could be happening.

Dr. Hans Kietal of Vienna, said: "It is obvious that the Aliens have a fetish for the male sexual organ. I think that they must be keeping the men they have taken in some kind of stud farm maybe for breeding purposes. Perhaps they are wanting to create a master race."

evolving from a single source.

"Consider too that life, sentience only establishes within specific pre-determined and pre-determining parameters." Seeing my puzzlement to this, she added "As I said, there are always contradictions with arbitrary delineation. Life is not the only determiner of life. Your planet itself, as ours and others' also determine if life establishes or not, as does the entity and entirety of your planetary system, just as does ours. Warmth of your star, centrifugal and rotational effects of your planet and so on are determinates of the establishment of life. It is not that these demarcate life's form, as many of your colleagues supposit, but whether life can actually begin to form, take root. It is only when they exist within these collective, specific parameters will life sustain. Your term 'Goldilocks' is perhaps an appropriate analogy, though not a 'Goldilocks planet' but one in a 'Goldilocks planetary system'. In a sense Earth, your planetary system, are alive." She took a pause then added "Although not in the specific physiological one."

Though with thoughts of Gaia and bursting with questions, we had walked to where the spider's web was and before I had time to ask any, Menpemelo had knelt, straightened her arm and gently brushed the spider back. It stayed as if bidding goodbye then went back indoors.

Menpemelo rose to her feet and though I had a clutch of "What do you mean"s at the ready, a refectory screen drew back and Pheterisco's head popped out. No sooner had she beckoned, asked if the new patches were ready yet and I had said that I didn't know, that I had been busy with Rainbow's next script, she giving a hurt look in return and making me feel inadequate, than Menpemelo's attention for me was gone. So had the chance for answers.

Though left with nothing more than to tag along ignored, Pheterisco mentioned that Paceillo and her team are returning from researching the remains of Pa-tu. This had me worrying. I tried to glean more but no sooner were we inside than her voice was lost amid the noise. Menpemelo gave a "...'bye, don't follow' wave and both of them made their way to the inner refectory.

Making my way from the outer refectory, wending between the crowds of Susem including those freshly returned from Panama, all drinking with the fervour of soccer supporters celebrating a win, I couldn't help but catch snatches of what had happened up there. Or for that matter, what is still going on for only some of the Susem have come back to Tabajara.

Besides regaling and comparing they were also briefing the next sorties setting off. And just as with Jatai the things I heard had me wincing for those poor men. Not just the ones already 'taken' but those about to be. Myself, if I, and knowing what I know, were in those soldiers' boots I would be prising out every last piece of ironmongery from my person as fast I could. Do so while it can be done painlessly rather than having the sherpals yank them off, especially those in scrotums and places related (there are already a heap of abductees deemed damaged, stunned and stacked to one side).

Nonettes – "passing fad" claims ...

Yet Nonette numbers set to soar say experts

By **Marcus Dooder**
Political Editor

THE Nonette movement was dismissed by the Prime Minister as nothing more than a passing fad.

The PM Edward Campbell, said: "As soon as this Alien backed movement is seen for the shoddy New Age novelty that it is, it will wither away just as Socialism did."

Edward Campbell, ... first speaking ... stage reco... Kingsnort... tion in K... Nonette ... be growi...

But do not be fooled by them. Most people have joined these charlatans for no other reason than to secure their own power supply.

"But the moment the nation's energy supplies have returned to normal they will see the obvious sense in ditching their soufins, leaving the Nonette movement and re-joining the fold. Just you wait and see."

By attempting to downplay the existence of the Nonettes the PM has, in the view of a number of Whitehall insiders, done

First Susem space trips a success

In Earth orbit and no weightlessness - amazing sights
Scientists in scramble to quiz travellers

By Adrian Williams
Space Correspondent

The first Alien space trips received a resounding thumbs up from their passengers yesterday.

All the passengers taking part in the Susem spaceflight from Britain described their trip as the 'Journey of a Lifetime'.

According to all the passengers, leaving Earth's gravity was barely detectable and once in orbit there was no sense of weightlessness. Pat Brookes (45) from Marshfield near Bristol and who was as smooth as the 125 [train] to London

"Even though we must have accelerated away from the ground at an immense speed," said Ms Brookes, who used to be a science teacher, "we felt nothing, just a sense of wonder as we saw the Earth fall away beneath us. We were all glued to the windows. I don't think any of us said a word," she added

Ms Brooke's fellow traveller June Carter, (35) from Bath, said the views from the spaceship's front windows were unforgettable. "Because the interior of the ship was in ... darkness," she ... windows appeared to be bright To see with my own eyes the blue of the Earth against the utter blackness of space is something I will treasure for the rest of my life."

Other passengers spoke of their thrill at seeing the coastline of Britain, then as the spaceship climbed higher, of Europe then of America but it was the sight of the Aliens' mothership, 'Sardon' which impressed many of those on board "It was surrounded by a cocoon of twinkling stars," said Hilary Norman (22), "but as we came closer to these stars, it ... a pathway

"We sailed in the sea of Sardon's stars"

Alien space flight captures travellers' hearts

By Roland Galespie
Aerospace Correspondent

"WE WERE surrounded by a sea of stars," exclaimed Robin Alborn (35), on his return from a Susem spaceflight yesterday.

Mr Alborn's 49 fellow passengers were no less ecstatic as they also described their experiences of the four-hour-long space odyssey orbiting the Earth and a flyby of Sardon, the Susem's mothership.

Robin, a printer from Christchurch, said: "Everything was just amazing but Sardon's stars left me gob-smacked." When the Alien's delta winged spaceship approached the mothership, the space around it was suddenly lighted by twinkling star-like lights.

"There were millions and millions of them," said fellow passenger, Tanya Hawkins (15), "and as we flew towards Sardon the stars moved out of our way as if they were making a path for us Some of the stars which were close to us I could see that they were little tubes with pointed tips. It was these tips which gave ... light," she said.

Tanya, a native of Timaru, was also wowed by Sardon itself said: "He was just so big!" she exclaimed. "He must have been five kilometres long and at least one high. But it was the way he just seemed to hang there motionless There were also hundreds of spacecraft the same as the one we were in and they were tiny compared to him.

Spacewoman Tanya

"As we flew by him, a line and row of lights began shining along his sides ...

Secret Monaco summit signals tough anti-Nonette action

EU-US agree anti-Nonette pact

"These latter-day communists must be crushed," says Shuleman

By Richard Rankie
World Affairs Editor

After a three day undercover summit, US and EU foreign ministers pledged joint moves to combat the Nonettes.

The secrecy of the summit, while taking many observers by surprise, is an indication of the seriousness to which both EU and US government now attach to the growing power of the Nonettes.

A communiqué following the summit said: "Both the US and EU had agreed to establish a joint consultative secretariat to coordinate policies to inform those communities within their respective countries, which are at risk of international Nonette infiltration."

The communiqué also stated that both sides are to exchange information of Nonette activity and assist each other by all means possible.

That the summit has taken place in conditions of such secrecy and on a face-to-face basis is also an indication of the vulnerability, real or imagined, of security of even the most high level encrypted communication.

The meeting is also indication of a change of official attitude towards the presence of the Aliens.

As one senior US State Department official, who asked not to be named, said after the summit: "The name of the game is keep these Nonettes botled up in north Brazil until their Alien backers have departed planet Earth.

"The OTSA forces may well have gotten a bloody nose at the hands of the Aliens at Jatai down there in Brazil but the Nonettes have to venture out to confront OTSA.

"OTSA may well be a Latin outfit but they're in place waiting for a fight with the Nonettes. The moment the Aliens have gone off home then, and now they have been beefed up with outside professional advisors the Nonettes won't stand a chance.

"As for the European theater, there is no way your governments, NATO and other related organisations are going to do anything except surrender.

"With US forces already in position in Panama and the Caribbean, there is also no way," the official said, "these Nonettes are going to advance any further than they have.

"The US-EU and our other major allies are no longer confronted with the threat of external Nonette subversion.

"What we both now face is internal security threat and as far as we in America are concerned it's something we, through the Departmentt of Homeland Security and other related agencies, can handle."

Such an upbeat view of the Nonettes' weakness were expressed by many other American officials, all of whom said the US will be pressing for stronger action by the EU against the growing Nonette presence in the Balkans.

The summit is also being seen as an attempt by the US to mollify its European partners in NATO following Washington's decision to withdraw many of its forces back to America to bolster its southern flank against the Nonettes.

It is now expected that many of these cuts to US forces will not now take place.

The ending of Alien abduction attacks is also seen as further indication that they are in process of departing from Earth.

Now that the remains of their missing space craft has been located, the Susem are expected to return to their to their own planet or wherever they

US Assistant Defence Secretary Shuleman in Monaco

Nonettes are legal rules Attorney General

Decision setback for Haines

By Judith Wigg
Legal Editor

THE NONETTES are legal. And that is the judgment of Britain's top Law Lord the Attorney General, the Right Honorable Lord Chief Justice Sir Crispen Fitzwilliam-Smithers QC

Sir Crispen (75), speaking at the Royal Courts of Justice Disco and Karaoke Nite, said: "I think there's nothing wrong with those Nonettes. In my view, as long as they keep themselves to themselves, keep their noses clean and don't go round upsetting anyone what harm are they doing? After all it's not as though they're breaking the Law or anything, is it?

"And as for that Stan Haines and his lot trying to use the Terrorism Act to stop them," Sir Crispen continued, "you can take it from me, they are talking out their rear ends, they know absolutely zilch, zero about the Law, and that is a fact Take it from me, that Haines lot are nothing but a load of right-wing tosspots who have nothing better to do than go round spouting a load of old tosh."

The Lord Chief Justice, donning his wig and gown, then joined a bench of fellow High Court Judges to dance the Can-Can With the audience clapping and chanting in time with the music, Sir

Sir Crispen and fellow dancers

However, Paceillo's imminent return is the real worry. It means the Susem will soon be off. With every step back to the Pousada my trepidation grew, that there is absolutely nothing I can do to avoid what will happen the moment they have gone. I had such a sense of entrapment and doom but on arriving in the village there was further consternation, the place was deserted.

Thankfully though, I soon heard sounds of applause coming from above and remembering why, raced up the steps. Reaching the top I was in time to see the entire village lined either side of the footpath to the Green welcoming our exchange Nonette. He had just stepped from the Tianguá bus. A gangly, angular young man called Peter from Hamburg. If he had a real smile or not, it was hidden by his spectacles, but all the same he kept clapping his hands in response to the villagers', they in turn enfolding into a jumbled crocodile behind him.

He is one of the first hundred or so to arrive and, like the others, is here for a fortnight to learn as much as possible, and the villagers geared to give him all they know. But for them there is something else attached to Peter's arrival, pride. His arrival, as Jorge says, is tangible recognition from outside of Tabajara's and the entire Nonette movement's achievement.

Peter's arrival and the villagers' welcoming was indeed a stirring sight, admirable even. All the same I saw sadness in the occasion. Not just for the villagers but for every Nonette across Congress, the Balkans, and those freshly forming elsewhere. I joined in the applause of course, for then was not the time to tell, including to Rainbow who was also there, of my foreboding.

Though later and to my alacrity her response to Paceillo returning was most off-putting, a mixture of "You're being thoroughly over-dramatic" and "Don't you worry your little head about such things...us grown-ups will deal with it all in good time." And when I persisted in detailing the peril we faced she retorted with, "Have you finished your script for this afternoon yet?" And when I explained I had been so busy with the new patches that I hadn't had time, she had a cold "You'd better had" look in her eyes and I sensed her knife brushing my back, probing for a plunge.

Rainbow had me beaver with draft after draft to just minutes to going on air before I had her nod and "That'll do."

'That'll do' was twenty minutes' narration of Congress's co-ordination of the consolidating of each of the Nonettes evolving worldwide. Though all are forming as faultless as can be there is not a drop of administration involved, in the old-world bureaucratic sense that is. Thing is though that as I wrote and rewrote it, it dawned on me the similarity between what Rainbow had me relate and Menpemelo's self-forming templates, of how regardless of the differences of incoming data the outgoing formulations are, within narrow parameters, predictable, correlative. From a snippet of information (a name and address) an entire Nonette, stage by stage, comes into being.

Enquires for forming one are first routed through Jacques Forriestier at

Nonettes to face government clampdown

EU, other governments set to follow Britain's lead

By Mark Lewis
Political Editor

THE Nonette movement could be banned in Britain under government plans announced yesterday. Nonettes will be barred from using government owned buildings including council houses for their meetings.

School children will need both their parents' written permission before they can join a Nonette group. Nonettes could be prosecuted if

Home Office sources said yesterday that the proposed moves by the government are an attempt to forestall the Nonettes from forming themselves into wider, national organisation as has occurred in other countries such as those of the former Yugoslavia. As one unnamed Whitehall source said: "Can't have them taking over, can we?"

These latest moves against the Nonettes followed de-... made by many

Haines, while welcoming the Home Office's proposals, said that they did not go far enough.

He said: "It's another case of too little too late. With every passing day these Nonettes are not only growing in strength but with new recruits handing over ten percent of their incomes they are becoming richer as well.

"What the government needs to do, and as a matter of urgency, is to round up the ringleaders and have them detained in order that this ...ab

Alien sex claims scoffed

"It's impossible" say experts

By Laura Jane Jones

CLAIMS THAT the Aliens are forcing the men they have abducted to have sex with them were slammed as "arrant nonsense" by one of the country's leading experts on sexual practices.

The head of Bradford's ... Assault ... Centre, blunt speaking Dr. Edwina Hethlewaite said: "If a man's not willing he'll not get it up, it's as simple as that. All this talk about Aliens' molesting and raping these Spanish lads is just that, all talk.

"It's the ones who put it in who do the raping. And I have not read anything about these cadets being interfered with in that direction, anally or

"If those lads or any of the others have had sex with Aliens it can only have been because they were willing. And it's no use they and the others bleating on about being plied with drink and drugs as it will not wash," she said.

"You know as I do what happens when a man's had too much to drink. He's useless that's what. We've no idea what

Aliens ... lads bu...

EU-US leaders sign Nonette Aggression Pact

Super powers in secret sign-up sets stage for proscribing Nonettes

By Joseph Smith
Political Editor

IN A surprise hush-hush Monaco summit, EU and U.S governments agreed to help each other against the growing Nonette influence.

In a message from the summit both European and US leaders said their aim was to safeguard the democratic freedoms of all our countries against being taken over by "the Forces of Darkness," as American Secretary of State Aaron Osborn, called the Nonette movement.

Officials from both EU and US said that to combat the Nonettes there will have to be a much closer watch kept on all forms of communication.

This they said, while being a small infringement on everybody's right to privacy was a small price to pay for the longer term safety of all our societies as a whole.

They stressed however, that the freedom of the press remains unaltered. While this good news, the statement is similar in tone to the previous curbing of privacy

Govt. admits power delays

'50%' claim back-pedalled

By Steven Dunn
Economics Editor

THE NORTH Sea gas supply figures so triumphantly trumpeted by Downing Street 48 hours ago, are not all they were claimed to be, it seems. Not only were they wildly exaggerated but have brought to the surface the simmering tensions between the PM's press secretary Charles Wilson and Angus Stirling, the Minister for Trade and

..."50 per cent" ...nnounced for ...duction turns ...n based on no ...gle day's pro... just one gas ...g to the DTI ...e of the North ...duction is cur... 25 percent of ...ls and is not ex... for some time.

Founded in 1821. Number 50131

The Sentinel

Social change

Monaco Summit: Superintending deckchairs?

Are the dignitaries gathered in Monaco denouncing the Nonette movement, blind as well as deaf? Are they unable see the changes taking place, hear the clamour for their coming?

Are these high powered plenipotentiaries so utterly unaware that in the space of a few weeks 4,000,000 people in the OECD countries alone - 350,000 of them in Britain - have flocked to the Nonettes? Are they also unaware that the Nonettes promise what our governments have signally failed to assure: electrical energy to power homes, maintain livelihoods?

Do not these men in Monaco [there were no women present] realise that in branding the Nonette movement 'subversive' they stigmatise millions of their fellow citizens as dissidents? Do these men not realise that by extending powers of state surveillance of their contemporaries they widen further the gulf between rulers and ruled or as is likely, propel the latter into indifference for the former?

Rather than eroding our personal privacy and freedoms further on the questionable pretext of combating the Nonettes' supposedly nefarious activities, these men in Monaco would be better advised formulating ways to win society's hearts and minds to the concerns they claim and the status quo they seek to maintain. Or is their condemnation of the Nonettes more a matter of pique than principle?

For decades our leaders preached that State ownership of society's assets and services was 'bad', private possession of them 'good'.

In the name of practicing this 'good' political establishments the world over superintended the transfer of publicly owned and controlled assets - and thus originally paid for by 'we the people' from our taxes - into private hands and exposure to the efficiencies free market which competition, they claimed engenders. But now that these political hierarchies are themselves challenged with practicing what they have persistently preached - be obliged to compete - they are suddenly, steadfastly against it applying to them.

The notion of 'customer loyalty' to a supplier has long been deemed bunkum. A supplier's loyalty to their customers however, is viewed as vital to their staying in business.

With the spread of the Nonette movement, increasing numbers of people have, for the first time a choice of suppliers of governmental administration. To date, and when given the chance, few of them have plumped to keep their custom with the old, long established providers of such services.

Regimes who attempted to insist staying sole purveyors of government rather than competing to retain their 'long established customer-base' have been run out of one country after another by their once supposedly loyal consumers.

Though the countries where such previous suppliers of government are no longer in business may be presently small in number and size, both grow by the day.

Existing governments would be wise, if instead of abiding by their men in Monaco's strictures of employing menace and worse in warding away new - Nonette - suppliers, they competed with them for their citizens' custom.

Rather than brand Nonettes as 'crypto-Socialists' - as some Americans have done - governments would be better advised if they themselves stopped acting like those of the Stalinist tendency.

Instead of cajoling and coercing their citizens to buy administration from the monopoly of their 'company stores' it will be beneficial to them if they learned to live with competition, learned to be nice to their customers. Learned that to stay in business they have to offer a better, or at least a comparative product/package to their Nonette competitors.

Conversely, if governments cannot compete they should follow the further free-market dictum they have long espoused: cease trading, shut up shop, liquidate, distribute assets to creditors and 'stake holders'.

And what is the Nonette package governments must compete with? For First World consumers the Nonettes assured supply of cost-free energy is obviously their main and perhaps sole attraction. Governments, if they are to stay in business must match these terms.

Even as a 'loss leader' governments, need their brand of energy to be delivered free to all. Should they decline to do so then consumers may well be attracted to other components of the Nonettes' package. Components which most governments will have greater difficulty in matching.

The Nonettes' flat ten percent tax rate, free preventative healthcare and an education system which pays those who study, will be hard for existing administrations to equal. But if consumers are also 'buying' these from the Nonettes, they are more than likely to accept much else of what they have to offer.

Things, which while consumers may view as appealing, existing governments will find near impossible to match: no crime, no causes of crime (including depravation), no 'Big Brother' surveillance, individual anonymity. These, if the Nonettes' telecasts are true, are just for starters.

While there are many other aspects of the Nonettes' package which appear appealing to their present purchasers, there is one which governments across the world must have cause to really worry over their citizens clamouring for, something they will never willingly provide despite its apparent present widespread popularity: the abolition of government itself.

These men in Monaco may fulminate over the threat the Nonettes supposedly pose to world order but in reality are they not demanding the preservation of their own exalted positions within as well as the status quo of the state and political establishments which appointed them?

If these men and those who selected them are unable or unwilling to change course and embrace the world of competition, then they will be well advised seeking the more assured employment of rearranging deckchairs on Monaco's beaches rather than on the 'unsinkable' Titanic of State on which they currently embarked.

Police taunted in hen-night club raid

'Is that a truncheon in your trouser or are you just glad to see me?'

By TED WOODWARD

A GANG OF 50 women subjected police to a tirade of obscene taunts during a raid on the Green Grass nightclub Pontypridd, a Court was told yesterday.

Giving evidence against members of the Tom Jones Appreciation Society who are charged with a string of offences including abducting an entire fire crew as well as indecently assaulting them, PC Alun Jenkins said:

"When I and my fellow officers entered the Green Grass club we were shocked at what we saw.

There were six men stood on tables and in a state of evident distress as well as a state of considerable undress. There were also a large number of women chanting to take part in further activities of a lewd nature.

"I called for the women to desist from so doing, whereupon many of them shouted for us to remove our uniforms in the mistaken belief that I and my fellow officers were part of some striptease act. It was the most

Scientists scr... to quiz spacet...

By Roland Browning
Science Editor

SPACE SCIENTISTS are vying to quiz the Susem space-trippers over their experiences.

Several universities are reported to have offered 'significant' sums of money for exclusive rights to some of the space travellers.

Professor Rodney Jones, of Sheppey University's Space Centre, said: "It is very important that the experiences of the people who have gone into space in these Alien craft are thoroughly investigated

Prof. Rodney Jones

been properly debriefe... what they are having to say of little scientific relevan... This is why it is so impor...

Villacoublay (this, I've since gathered, was used to confound outside authorities' anticipated attempts at thwarting Nonette communication) then on to Congress's centre at Salvador. This though does no more than rotationally send them to Regional Nonettes and they then routing them downwards to their local ones. In turn each of these Nonettes twin with enquiring would-be ones and send them step-by-step assistance for formation into actual Nonettes. Because the advice given is based upon collective 'best practice', detail of which is distilled daily from all the Nonettes across Congress, it is the same if for no other reason than the structures of all Nonettes, be they town or country, rich or not, are all the same.

When the evolving twin is 81 members big (ninth full strength) it is next assisted in splitting, expanding to form into a Nonette Nine cluster. In turn the established host twin assigns these Nines to each of its nine wards. The host Nonette also still acts as a single entity aiding the formation and advising the functioning of the new Nonette Nine as a whole. When this is firmly formed it elects a representative to exchange visit with one from their established Nonette twin. In Tabajara's case Lucia has been voted to accompany Peter back to Hamburg. When he and the others who have arrived with him return to their Nonettes they will take more of the ever-lasting soufins. There is the inevitable overlapping between Nonettes, but when this happens either the evolving one has several 'twins' or the overlappers decide between themselves who stays twinned to whom. Once the Nines are established it is intended that they will split and expand into further Nines from which complete Regional Nonettes would have come into being.

Yet impressive though the growth of the Nonettes are, there are 10,000 and more Nines now formed and numbers are rising by the day, it doesn't mean that they are going to last, withstand what is sure to come the moment the Susem have flown off. Even though the Nonettes have taken over umpteen little bits of places throughout the Caribbean and elsewhere, they still cannot withstand onslaughts from the US and all the others.

While this had me filled with worry, Menpemelo's Templates were going around in my head as well. As I understand from what she has said there are packages of 'life-data' or whatever whizzing about the place, and when they come across the right conditions they set up shop and start the business of evolving. One half of me says "It's a load of balony," but the other half says "hang on, there might be something in it after all."

This half has had me thinking how fax machines function. The data they send is actually nothing more than a little package of vibrations. They go all the way up to a satellite, on to another then down to where they are dialled, and transcribe out precisely the same as they were sent. Then I thought of computer programs, how they are sent the same way, little envelopes of them going up and coming down, and when they arrive in the computer they are sent to, they can change its existing programs.

IMPALED TO DEATH!

Packed stadium gives thumbs up police, army chiefs executed for War C

By **Nicola Kay**
in Sarajevo

POLICE AND Army Chiefs of the forn Croat, Serb regimes found guilty of W Crimes were executed by impalement the Kosovo Stadium, Bosnia yesterday

A 60,000 strong audience roared their approval as each of the criminals were dropped onto 4 metre spikes, some taking several minutes before they stopped gyrating their limbs.

Record viewing

Following the real-time screening of the executions, SLI-TV announced that viewing figures were an all-time record.

The trial

On the first day of the final Bosnian War Crimes Trial a total of 54 Croat and Serb senior police and army officers went on trial yesterday morning accused of crimes against humanity and other related offences.

After they had all been found guilty they were marched the three kilometres from the Court in central Sarajevo to the Kosovo Stadium in batches of nine abreast.

Marched naked

Although these former high ranking police and army officers were marched naked to the stadium they were made to wear their helmets signifying their former rank.

Any medals these officers had been awarded by the former regimes were glued on their chests.

Obese beasts

Because most of these officers were no longer in trim physical condition their nudity added, much to the delight and amusement of the thousands of onlookers lining the route.

The lash

That the prisoners marched in good order to the Kosovo Stadium was due to their escort of two metre tall unsmiling, nononsense Kyhmer guards continuously cracking five metre long rhino whips over their heads.

Once in the stadium the guilty were split into threes. The first of them were marched up a flight of steps to the rear of a 15 metre tall stand on which were three small wooden huts.

Cuckoo clocks

Not long after the men were in the huts, th was a roll of drumbe When these ended, do at the front of the h sprung open just as if tl were those of a cuck clocks and revealed t three men.

There was then anoth roll of the drums and tl front of the stand fe away to reveal long, shin metal spikes, their tip two metres below the hut and glinting in the spot lights.

The spikes

With a further roll of the drums the trapdoors of each of the huts opened and all the men dropped straight down on the spikes.

Such was the speed at which the men fell onto the spikes that the tips went completely through

More pictures on pages 5,6,7,8,9

their bodies, penetrating their anuses and exiting through their skulls.

The man in the centre though jolted his head back and his spike as a consequence, came out through his mouth.

At the end of each drum roll the audience in the stadium cheered but after the men had been impaled they broke out into roar of applause which could be heard several kilometres away.

However, there was even greater applause with what happened next

The two men on the outside of the trio were not killed outright and continued to jerk their arms and legs for some minutes before they stopped moving.

The moment they had though, the three spikes tilted forward and the bodies of the men slid off of them and into three holes in the ground immediately in front of the spikes.

The hounds

However, the men's bodies had barely slid from the spikes when packs of dogs which had been in the pits were leaping up and fighting over the corpses.

As soon as the bodies had slid from the spikes these sprang back to the vertical position and another

---

Scores of Serb Croat War Criminals impaled

Death on the spike for top Yugo fiends

By **MERRY MORBIDE**

SCORES of top Serb and Croat War Criminals met their just fates yesterday. All were done to death by being impaled on massive super sharp spikes which went right up through their evil bodies. Their corpses were then torn apart and eaten by huge savage dogs.

In front of a 60,000 capacity crowd at Sarajevo's International Stadium, 54 Serb, Croat top brass and police chiefs each paid the price of their evil deeds.

These once high placed thugs were all found guilty of aiding abetting the worst of the Bosnian War atrocities. Seven of the Serb of the thugs had perpetrated in the massacring 10,000s of innocent people including defenceless women and children.

Following their lengthy yet fair trials, which lasted the entire morning, these mass murderers were marched to the stadium to answer for their unspeakably wicked deeds.

Because of the risk of escape, these ogres of evil were only permitted to wear their helmets and medals.

Record figures for SLI TV's 'Trials

Yugo 'toppings' watched by 45m in UK alon

By Adam Fickle
Media Correspondent

SLI TV'S BOSS Dickie Bear was said to be cock-a-hoop as the ABC Audit Bureau confirmed that the Final Trials had broken all previous British viewing records. According to ABC Final Trials attracted an audience of 45 million people in the UK who watched all or part of the three hour long afternoon programme and a similar figure who watched the 30 minutes of edited highlights in the evening.

SLI's MD Derek Igg said: "These figures just go to show just how sharp Dickie's TV touch is. Just how right he was when he said that people always lil seeing a good topping. Ar as our rising figures for ea series of Trials just go show, people just can't g enough of it, seeing the murdering bastards getti what's been coming to them

"These figures also just to show how wrong the Ivory Tower toffs, such that Bishop of Buckingh were in slagging us off screening the executions these Yugo fiends," he sa

Mr Igg refused to confi or deny rumours that the Caught TV was negotiat the rights for an entir new series of Trials plan for elsewhere in the wo He said: "All I know is if there is one you can

---

Hisogynists surprise new costumes

Titanium chain mail and heat-proof armour

Julia Hawkins
Style Correspondent

The Hisogynists, the world's top Performance Art ensemble could have passed as medieval knights in armour and oxyacetylene welders as they modeled their new costumes for the forthcoming performance of Trials in Sarajevo yesterday.

To the accompaniment the Second Movement of Jean Charles Decoursu's specially composed 'Trials Trilogy', a phalanx of 27 Hisogynists, marched into the arena of Kosovo National Stadium yesterday

Uniformly dressed in loose fitting tunics and trousers of their heads, stretched down to their shoulders and gave the Hisogynists the appearance of industrial welders and medieval knights.

They next formed into three straight lines and began stepping in time to the music - which by then was reminiscent of Wagner's 'Ride of the Valkyries' - up a dune-like rise on the sand covered floor of the arena At the same time, they were circling their arms above their heads as though cracking whips.

No sooner had these Hisogynists started to climb, than above sound of the music a stream of high pitched, shrill whistling could be heard coming from the other side of the were more than two dozen of them and all were clad head to foot, in shining silver chain-mail armour.

As these Hisogynists stood against the skyline their armour glistened and dazzled in the sunlight. All of them were also swirling and cracking whips over their heads. It was these whips which made the screeching sound.

Later in the photo-shoot, when the Hisogynists showed the whips, it was possible to see they had rows of small whistles incorporated within their lengths.

Between the whistles however, were lines of two centemetre toothed wheels, which the representative from Caught TV said were tipped sound they made was like that of a rattlesnake

She also said that the speed at which the end of the whip would be travelling when it was cracked was more than 500km an hour However, the suddenness at which these Hisogynists' showed against the skyline gave them a most awesome arrival

After this second group of Hisogynists had raised the visors of their helmets their leader, Buttercup said her troupe were known as 'Cut' Later the Caught representative said the other Hisogynists were 'Burn'.

The whips Burn will be using in their part of the performance were still under wraps but she added crypt-

Then I thought of radiowaves, how a transmitter beams out specific modulations of them in every direction and radio sets receive them regardless of what they have passed through including brick walls. And the only way they can pass via walls is oscillate through them, there can be umpteen walls on the way, and they do so without distortion either. Yet turn a radio's dial just a smidgen and there is another transmitter's waves coming through the walls and out of the radio. This means there must be thousands and thousands of radio-waves passing through everything, including me, and I have never felt any of them going in or coming out.

It's not just radio stations either but radio everything including even those from stars. Then I thought of mobile telephones, how tapping out just one digit wrong can ring up someone the other side of town to the right number, yet phones send circles and spheres of waves. What is more, all these circles and spheres must be rippling through one another, yet there is barely ever a distortion by one to another. In the quinth context, of course, there will probably be none at all.

Then I thought of what Menpemelo had said about everything originating from a single source. Of how everything which has life in it, us, me, plants are made up of solids, tri-contexts but they are not the source of life itself. It's as if the bits making us up are no more than those of radio receivers and transmitters. Then I realised why there had been all the guffawing by the Susem over the Human Genome and Proteome Projects. All that their researchers will find when they have finally finished are components of our radio sets and not a single thing about the programmes we are receiving and broadcasting. Nor will Earthly scientists discover any of the effects of transmissions between one bit of us and another. All that money those experts have spent has been for nothing, all those Nobel prizes as well.

I had all these things on my mind as I sought solace from the day's tidings but I was not as far as the bar before Jorge told me the news from Sobral. As he related I was worrying all over again. The truck transporting barrels of the new fragrance concentrate from Manual's production department to the patch assembly had been in a crash, some barrels had broken open, the contents spilt, fumes from them blown into town. Though not directly affecting the men, responses by women to the aroma wafting down were very different.

According to Jorge, who had a call from Manual who'd had to barricade himself in his office, it evoked an immediate mood of dis-inhibition. Casting aside propriety, women set about the men (any men, if Manual's scrawny body is anything to go by) with aggressive amorousness. Some, so Jorge said, had taken to going in groups, Love Patches at the ready. Though his "rapto multidão" has to be an exaggeration, it does mean that these new strips need to be handled with care.

It took more than three hours before the effect wore off and men dared come out of hiding, those who had got away that is.

Lancs "no nonsense" policing set to be c

Nonettes fa
of 'zero tol

By **Bill Snatch**
Crime Editor

LANCASTER'S bluff Police Chief, Roy Ardale's response to Nonettes on his "manor" is straight-to-the point: "They are troublemakers. Either get rid of them or lock them up."

Commissioner Ardale's tough, zero tolerance policy towards would-be ... is being applied appointed to run the city's police force.

Ardale's maxim, "Stop it before it begins, stops trouble later" has seen his officers double the numbers of people arrested for suspicion.

increased, t... has been ... main reaso... all drop in ...

It is now ... would-be N... to experie... sioner Ar... methods. ... are produ... complaint... the recei... police's a...

A num... Nonette... complai... police ... one pro... "All of ...

"Put the boot
for Nonette
- says Jack

By **Marcus Dooder**
Political Editor

"Hit them now, hit them hard, hit them before it's too late," says ex-Home Sec.

IN A NO-HOLDS-BARRED attack on the Nonettes, Jack Heywood, the former Home Secretary said: "It is a simple matter of getting them before they get us."

"It is vital every polic... the country is free to ... means at their lawful ... combat this growing ... threat in our midst," he s...

Nonettes kr

Governments in joint Nor

By Tony Perry
World Affairs Editor

GOVERNMENTS across the world are taking a tough line against the Nonettes. Since the Monaco Summit, governments, their security services and police forces have all taken the same decisive actions against the Alien backed Nonette movement, in a determined attempt to block its growth.

In the days following the Summit, hundreds of Nonette centres have been raided by the police and 100s of tons of ...

with many times this num... charged with conspiracy ... other public order offence...

In the US, many states h... taken an equally tough st... against the Nonettes. Figures for the total number of arrests are not yet known but they are thought to be many times more than the EU's. The southern states are said to have seen the greatest number of those taken into custody.

There are also reports that in some parts of the Third World, police action against ...

An unnamed Whitehal... source said: "The Britis... government really has n... choice in the matter. If w... stand back and do nothing w... will be seen as not coopera... ting with our EU and NAT... partners. Also our specia... relationship with the U... would go out of the window.

"Besides, it's better t... attack them now rather tha...

Nuremberg Nonettes clash with police

Police taken by surprise in crackdown

By Ulrich Krougar
in Nuremberg

The centre of Nuremberg was in chaos yesterday. Dozens of cars were ablaze shop windows smashed as hundreds of police fought running battles with Nonette activists throughout the city centre.

A supposedly non-violent protest march turned out to be a cover for a violent confrontation by the Nonettes against the authorities.

Hundreds of people were injured, many seriously. More than 400 Nonette protesters were arrested during the disturbances.

The size of the Nonette protest to an earlier crackdown by the German authorities against the movement's centres took the police by surprise. Official estimates put the number of protesters as 6,000 although Nonette sympathisers claim more than 10,000 took part.

As night fell both sides were accusing each other of starting the violence.

The Bavarian State Prosecutor's Office in Munich said: "The unwarranted Nonette attacks against the security forces is further evidence that this movement does not intend to conform to the proper procedures and respect for the legal processes."

One of the Nonettes who took part in the protest and wished to be unnamed said: "We were deliberately provoked by the police. We were marching on Karolenstrasse ...

PM rebuffs Suser
"insulting threat

"Great Britain will not tolerate 'foreign' interference in its interna

By Mark Lewis
Political Editor

SUSEM claims that the government is harassing Nonettes was angrily rebuffed by PM Edward Campbell last night.

The prime minister, replying to yesterday's Susem telecast telling the government to cease waging its campaign of intimidation against the Nonette movement, said: "These accusations against my government are as uncalled for as they are unfounded I would consider them as an insult to our British sense of fair play, were they not so laughable."

The PM, speaking before an invited audience in the City last night, and departing from his prepared speech on government borrowing, said: "They [the Nonettes] accuse us of putting their adherents under surveillance. This is balderdash. Under the terms of the Anti-Terrorist legislation we put all foreign-funded organisations under routine scrutiny. All governments do."

Speaking at the Worshipful Company of Tax Avoiders' Banquet, the PM said: "The Nonette also claim that my government is actively directing the police forces of this country actively to harass and intimidate them and their movement.

"This is poppycock. I want to say here and now, and what forces of this country are completely independent of and are not subject to government control in their operations any shape or form whatsoever."

The prim... the furthe... that gover... urity serv... Nonettes wo... ed, were li... threat. He s... ment and th... never been ... from anyon... we do not ... now or any t...

"What th... said is tant... ference in th... nal affairs ... thing which... dition wi... countenance."

Response ... telecast was ... many in Wh...

135: SIÂN

A very nice young man called Carlo arrived from Brazil. He came at half eleven and by the time he left this evening everyone in Cilgerren, even those who haven't joined had all taken a shine to him, except of course Mrs Lloyd and her friends from the WI.

They were most put out by the way Carlo put them down. But it was their own fault. The moment the van bringing him from Fishguard arrived they were all over him. He was polite enough but it didn't take him long to see through their fawning and their banners. When he said he had come to speak first with Cilgerren's ward representatives who are currently headed by Gwyneth, and he said the backroom of the Pendre would do nicely, we could all see from the looks on the WI's faces and their banners drooping they were peeved. More so when we later discovered they had done their hall out specially and Mrs Mealam had written a speech of welcome.

Up till a few days ago though, it looked as if Carlo, along with our new soufins he had for us, wasn't coming at all. Everyone thought the government, and goodness knows who else, meant what they said about arresting anyone who came without valid passports as illegal aliens. But at the last moment they backed down saying as long as there wasn't any actual laws broken they wouldn't raise objections. Though this was the day after Rainbow's TV pictures of all those policemen in country after country being rounded up then run and whipped through the streets in their underwear (some not even that) by those big Cambodians who used to be in Bosnia and the stinging wasp things they have. And now I come to think of it, there was one rested on the seat of the van Carlo arrived in.

Carlo wasn't with Gwyneth and the others more than half an hour but she said he was most professional in the way he inspected all the books we have been told to keep, voter registration, accounts, what funds were expected, everything. Then when they had passed muster, he said he could release the new soufins. However, even before Carlo had finished his inspection we had already formed a queue outside the Pendre.

As Gwyneth called our names and numbers we each handed over the tenth of our salaries, including the boys from their pocket money, and Carlo handed over our soufins to Gwyneth, she to our ward representatives who then dished them out to us. They are different from the old ones in that they have a little panel with our Nonette number keyed in. When Gwyneth had to send our numbers, I did wonder why, but now I know.

As soon as she and the others had finished, Carlo then handed her a teaching screen. Everyone's eyes were on it in an instant, even those in the village who aren't yet signed up. Obviously we had seen them before but only on television. He started explaining how to use the screen and how we can earn points from it, as well as extra screens including our own personal

Lancs police taken in sudden Susem snatch

Police forces on full alert as 24 officers abducted

By **Lisa Biggles**
Sudden Shocks Editor

SUSEM ATTACKED and abducted dozens of unarmed off-duty policemen in Lancaster today. Police forces across the UK are on full alert against future Alien raids. The Police Federation is demanding tough action for their members' protection.

The Susem raid was on a block of flats on the Morecombe Road nearby Lancaster's main Rose Street Road Police Station. The dozen flats in the block are understood to be leased to the Lancaster Police Force and outside the flats. Ten or more men were then seen absailing down from it and then racing towards the flats.

According to the eye witness, the spacecraft flew a short distance ahead of him. As it did so, abductors and the flyin objects which were pre sumably the Susem 'stinging wasps'.

The 45 year old ma who witnessed the attac and lives nearby the flat and has asked that hi identity be withheld

Polish police whipped through the streets naked

Susem raid on Warsaw barracks
Dozens of police abducted by Aliens

By Roman Ardov
In Warsaw

More than 90 Polish policemen have been attacked and abducted by Susem backed forces.

The attack on them took place in broad ... of the Polish

Dozens of motorists and pedestrians in the Mokotów district of Warsaw gazed in amazement as two Susem delta winged space planes swooped down "out of nowhere" over Wiejska Street.

Within seconds, groups of men were scaling down from the planes, at least 20 of them, some onlookers said.

ABDUCTED POLIC IN AMAZON GULAG

British officers among 1,000s held in Sierra Pelada he
Prime Minister under pressure to agree Susem de

By Benjamin Gravel
Social Affairs Correspondent

THE BRITISH POLICE officers abducted in the Alien raids on Lancaster and Dudley were shown on yesterday evening's Susem telecast. The men, along with an estimated 3,000 fellow police officers from around the world were shown being forced to work in the Sierra Pelada.

Susem telecaster Rainbow Louis announced that all the police officers abducted were unharmed except for those who had suffered superficial injuries trying to resist their arrest. She said all the men will be released as soon as public undertakings had been given to stop harassing Nonettes.

Within hours of the telecast relatives of the abducted ...

eration were demanding that the government agree the Susem demands. A Federation spokesman said: "All in all what is being asked by Susem in return for these men's release is something which our members can live with."

The Policia et Gendarme Securité (PeGS) in Brussels which represents police trade unions worldwide is also

immediately a terms.

PeGS spok Méchant said authorities an agree immed Susem's requ for our mem all the PeGS sick-leave act

The Sierr big truly ile sc

Susem in worldw police attacks

'Thousands' of police whipped into captiv
Scores of men forced to march naked

By the **Alien Watch Team**

POLICE FORCES around the world were reeling from more than a 1,000 Susem dawn raids on their barracks, section houses and other 'soft targets'. Such was the speed and force of the Susem attacks that 1,000s of police officers were overwhelmed with little or no resistance.

Last night's Susem telecast showed scene after scene of scores of policemen being marched through the streets by the Aliens' Gurkha and ex-Kymer Rouge

countries in Africa and Asia as well as from the US."

Many eye witness accounts confirm both the Abduction Centre's ...

"Ponty 50" bound over with a curfew

By Ted Woodward
Welsh Affairs Editor

THE ENTIRE 50-STRONG membership of Pontypridd's Tom Jones Appreciation Society were sentenced yesterday to spend the nighttime hours at home in the company of their husbands or 'other responsible adult'.

All 50 women were found guilty of committing a string of offences ranging from assaulting a police officer, indecent assault, to committing lewd acts likely to outrage public decency.

After a two-week trial at Cardiff Crown Court, Justice Lloyd passing sentence said to the women: "While it possible to accept it was your hen-night and you became carried away by all those men in uniform, it is, however, not the first time you have appeared before this Court as a result of your committing similar acts of public outrage

"All of you are old enough to be these men's mothers." Justice Lloyd continued "It seems that whenever you are gathered together no decent young man is safe to walk the streets. However, for all your sakes, as well as that of the public's, I trust it will be for the last time.

Dai Young yesterday

"Passing custodial sentences on any of you would be a waste of public money and imposing fines will not serve any useful purpose in curbing your outrageous conduct.

"Therefore," said Justice Lloyd, "in an attempt to protect the public and young men in particular, I sentence all to spend the next months during the hours of darkness in the confines of your own homes, in the company of your family, partners or other responsible adults.

"Should any of you be seen outside of your homes during these hours then you may be sure that you will be immediately sent to prison and for a very long time indeed," he said.

One of those affected by the sentence is Blodwyn Young. Her husband Dai, said: "I don't know what I'm going to do now with Blodwyn round the house all the time.

"Since I've come off the Vigora I've had to have someone else prime the pump first," he said.

Dai, who works in the Shepherds Kilt Factory of

CAMPBELL AGREES TO SUSEM TERMS

Threatened anti-Nonette police action called off
Nonettes jubilant, movement's numbers set to soar

By Anton Jexter
Political Editor

IN A complete reversal of previous policy toward the Nonette movement the government of Robin Brown has ... Susem's terms for

keep to the Laws of this country then they are and always have been entitled to the full protection and freedoms enshrined in those laws. ... it has been

The Prime Minister's change of policy from being anti-Nonette to a neutral position comes less than 48 hours after the abduction of police officers from Dudley and ... government's

ones. But with everyone clamouring to try it out, Gwyneth had to clap her hands and shout "Quiet!" before Carlo could be heard and say everything over again.

The screen wasn't the only thing which had people's attention (though there's still a queue outside the Pendre of those waiting to get on it) but Carlo's tunic as well. So many were trying to touch it that Gwyneth had to tell them to keep their hands off him. Though afterwards Carlo did stand with his arm out so we could all have a feel, so silky white and so soft, yet when we pulled at the fabric it immediately sprung back into shape.

Carlo then asked if we had any questions. Well of course we all had! It wasn't long before Gwyneth with "One at a time, please," had to take over who he had to answer next. As can be imagined the questions ranged over everything, from when will we have our health booth to had he actually seen any of the Susem, and were they really the sex-crazed angels the papers said they are? The questions came non-stop for an hour and I could see by then Carlo was becoming tired, so could Gwyneth. But it was at this point, when she said "This will have to be the last one," that I got mine in.

"Danny," I said, "is a friend of ours, he lived in Cilgerren, have you met him, how is he?" Well, not only did this come as a surprise to Carlo but to most of those present. He said although he hadn't actually met Danny, he was highly thought of throughout the entire Congress not only for his promotional telecasts of the Nonette movement, which Carlo thought were 'noble', but as the person who had developed what he termed "revolutionary drug-free marital aids" which has brought happiness and fulfilment to millions. There was an enormous clamour of more questions at this but Gwyneth shouted out "Enough," and drew the meeting to a close.

Afterwards though, when she took Carlo on a walkabout, it was nice that he asked her if he could pay me a visit. He was here for quite a while asking about Danny. I ended up telling everything I knew but afterwards though, when he said he couldn't wait to tell everyone back home, he had me worried that perhaps I said things I shouldn't have. But when he gave a chuckle and said Danny was an "okay gringo," he put me at ease.

This evening, when Daffyd came home he said Gwyneth had put a sheet of paper up in the Pendre for people to write questions they want Carlo to answer when he comes back on Thursday. He said when he wrote his about the new soufins he couldn't help notice that most of the others were about the "revolutionary marital aids" Carlo had mentioned. As Daffyd said, it just goes to show what is on some people's minds.

n Brief

Galapagos go over to Nonettes

Easter Island and other Pacific islands 'lost'

OLLY PORTILLO IN SANTIAGO

THE last redoubt of the Ecuadorian government fell yesterday as Nonettes took over the Galapagos Archipelago, the Pacific Islands made famous by Charles Darwin. There are also reports of the Chilean controlled Easter Island group has also fallen to the Alien-backed movement

The Susem telecast claim that the Galapagos were in Nonette hands was confirmed by the Ecuadorian government-in-Exile's offices in Santiago. A government spokesman said: "After a valiant campaign against a superior Alien backed opposition of the awful, sovereign government of Eduardo Santos was forced to abandon Ecuador's province of La Galápagos and its people to the rebels."

Other reports, as yet unconfirmed, said government officials had been given the choice of flying from San Cristobel (the islands' main airport) or face investigation by a peoples' tribunal. Most decided to flee to Chile. No more than a handful of the islands' 12,000 population have left with government officials

Police raid 'Nonette der

CEDAR CITY: UTAH: Forty Nonette activists were arrested on conspiracy charges against the Utah legislature and attempting the overthrow the Federal government. Head of Cedar County Police Department, Hank Holloran said: "We could see they were a bunch of no-goods for the start. Out-of-towners fraternizing with known trouble-makers. Caught them red-handed with incriminating documentation," the police chief said.

Did Susem attack snoop on government listening posts?

Home Office denies GCHQ was compromised but rumours persist

Shamus McPaul
Security Correspondent

Following the Susem's worldwide assaults on police stations, the electronic listening posts of many European and other governments were also attacked. Although both the Home Office and the Security Services have denied that Britain's monitoring centres such as GCHQ in Cheltenham and at Rugby as well as the US post at Fylingdales were affected, reports to the contrary persist.

In the latest edition of *Snoops and Spooks Monthly* the magazine's editor Roger Makepiece quotes from a number of MI5 Surveillance Centre sources which claim that Britain's eavesdropping centres along with the US's at Fort Meade, have all been comprised by the Susem raids. Makepiece also claims that the Echelon satellites were also subjected to Susem attacks.

Makepiece says in the article, that this may be as much a reason for the government's about-face over agreeing the Susem terms to cease harassing the Nonettes as it was for the release of the abducted police men. If it transpires that this i the case, then the prospects o future similar attacks of th

Andrew Hendry reports from Alanje on the Panamanian bord

US troops yield Colon for Ft.Clayton

Southern Command suffers Alien attacks 'Colon; tactical withdrawal' - Tucers claims

US forces have been subected to a massive Susem attack. Stationed at Colon, they were reported to have fought off a widespread night raid.

There are said to have been a number of casualties with number of troops missing. General Tucers has announced a tactical withdrawal from the city of Colon itself.

The long awaited assault on the Panama Canal Zone by the Nonettes and their Susem backers took place on US positions at the Caribbean entrance to the canal.

US Southern Command reported that there had ... ties with a number of units reported as 'unaccounted for'.

A Southern spokesman said that communications with individual units had been disrupted as a result of the Susem attack. The spokesman said that the dispersal of units was in accordance with operational strategy and they were expected to make their way to alternative pre-planned positions.

General Tucers has ordered the withdrawal of his forces from Colon city saying that they would be better placed to repulse future attacks free from the confines of ...

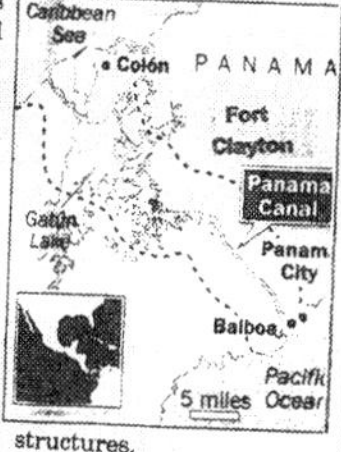

structures.

The General also announced that wounded soldiers had already been airlifted to the US Wilmington stationed in the Caribbean. He made no

Banks deny denying Nonett

Nonette groups claim banks refusing facilities
Government denies telling banks to blacklist Non

By Brian Bunting
Finance Editor

THE MAJOR HIGH street banks denied Nonette claims they are conducting a concerted action to refuse account facilities to the movement. Downing Street also dismissed Nonette assertions that they have told the Banks to blacklist the movement.

The head of the Association of British Clearing Banks, Lord Withington, denying Nonette allegations, said: "There is not a scrap of evidence to back these unfounded claims of any such action, concerted o wise on the part of m ciation's members to d

Heywood warns against Nonette n

Ex-Home Secretary demands Nonettes m

BY MARK LEWIS
POLITICAL EDITOR

THE former Home Secretary, Jack Heywood has demanded that members of the Nonettes breaking the law must be prosecuted just as would other offenders. He said that unless Nonettes are brought to account now it will be impossible to take action against them later.

Addressing the National League of Neighbourhood Watch annual conference, Mr Heywood said: 'This Nonette movement is waging a deliberate and orchestrated campaign against the forces of law and order. It is plain for all to see that the Nonettes are behind the rising tide of public disobedience against the Community Charge. Today 40 councils are suffering from significant numbers of Community Charge payers refusing to honour their obligations."

The ex-Home Secretary also accused the Nonettes of taking the law into their own hands increasingly. He said: "As many of you here today are experiencing the writ of legitimately appointed forces of law and order no longer runs in an increasing number of neighbourhoods. These Nonette groups claim it is they who now patrol the streets where they live. This is errant vigilantism and must be stamped out and stamped out now."

To a chorus of approval from Neighbourhood Watch delegates, Mr Heywood called for the drawing up of a register of those areas suffering from Nonette activity. He said:

SUSEM SNATCH BONDI BUFFS

HUNDREDS OF NUDE GAYS NABBED BY THE ALIENS FOR SEX
BIG WHITES GET THREE AS 1,000S FLEE FOR THEIR LIVES

By **Lisa Biggles**
in Sydney, Australia

MORE than 300 buff bronzing Bruces on Bondi - Australia's premier naturist gay beach - were abducted by the Aliens yesterday.

In desperate bids to escape the Susem's snatch- and-grab robots, thousands of gay sun-seekers fled the packed beach into the sea.

At least three fleeing bathers were carried off by cruising white sharks and presumably eaten.

Last night fears rose for the fate of as many as 300 men snatched by the Susem from Bondi. Sydney police Chief Superintendent Bruce O'Rourke, said: "Naturally we are concerned for the survival and well-being of the abducted bathers.

"All the same," he said, "we have said for years than the lewd goings-on over there [Bondi Beach] were getting utterly out of hand. Maybe after this, things will quieten down and those gays learn to behave themselves and stop doing what ever it is that gays do."

The head of Oz Gay Pride, Bruce Conlan (39), said: The Space Sheilas must have made a mistake. The blokes they have taken do not like women."

Bruce, who is coordinating the emergency centre for the rescue of

More photos: Page 6&7

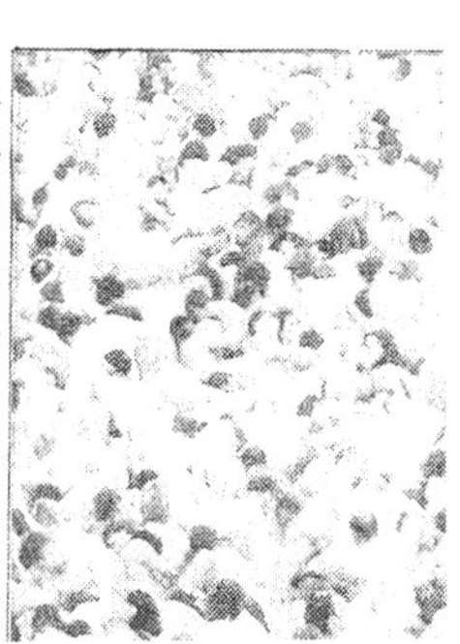

Every night I go to bed, every morning I wake, there is a gnawing "What will Rainbow have me announce next?" If I only knew what she and Congress have up their sleeves, there might be room for manoeuvre but I am in the dark to the last. Pleading is no help, the best I receive is her "Humph..." then "do it" (there is not even a "please" now) and should I ever dare attempt dissent, it's her unsaid "I'll tell them what you did."

That I'm done for when everything falls down is foregone, but it's the not knowing how I'm going to be done which worries me so. The last telecast she had me do, that if anyone messed with the Nonettes we would send the boys round, the Khmer Rouge ones as well as the Gurkhas and hen-gers, still has me in dread. And especially after what happened to those policemen, their brothers of law everywhere must be just waiting to get me.

The new patches are another worry. Production has stalled, money is being lost. I tried humouring Manual that it had been the best offer of company he had had in years but it didn't go down at all well. He's still a scared stare. So have most of Sobral's male population.

Attempting to be positive, I suggested to Manual that he diluted the concentrate with talc before shipping it and only to do so when the wind was in a safe direction, and use a driver who had care. Of the first, in his dash for safety he said he had already done so, of the wind there would be scant chance, but as for the last, such people did not exist in Ceará. Instead, and leaving nothing to chance, Manual has embarked on the opposite, moving the patch assembly lines across town next to the ingredient mixers. I left him amid reconstruction but know it will be ages before he is in proper production. But all the same I did manage to collect enough completed sachets to satisfy the needs of the Susem for the next day or so.

Manual also told me the name his designers have chosen for these new patches, "Vantõn". He said it is from 'vantajoso' or beneficial, and 'tõnica'. I'd not the heart to tell him that there is a shirt-maker with nigh the same name.

But these worries are as nothing when set besides what else I have unearthed. From the first I'd had a nagging suspicion that the Susem were up to something. That their searching for Pa-tu, even sating their 'urges' on men-kind were cloaks for something else. Following what one let slip while bragging over their latest outrages, I now know what it is. Or at least halfway think I do.

Delivering the new sachets to Pheterisco and hearing some Susem comparing notes began the unravelling. Until then I was under the impression that all the Susem had been up in Panama sating on soldiery, but when I heard "Bondi" and "Bruces" in the same sentence I pricked up my ears. Had they really been to Australia I asked?

Attempting 'strine' one of them said "Yeah right sport."

I just had to ask why they had travelled so far when they already had more

Nonette Bank threat dismissed by Clearers

By Oliver Stoneburger

The Brazilian Nonettes' self-styled Bank of Congress announced yesterday that it will step in and offer banking facilities to branches and members of the British Nonette movement

The Brazilian bank's move, however, was dismissed as an empty publicity stunt by the main High Street clearing banks.

"They will need an Operating Licence first," says Withington

"Moreover, because there is no possibility of this so-called bank receiving a Bank of England operating licence, depositors risk having their funds blocked by the DTI."

Chilean natives go over to Nonettes

Mapuche Indians declare UDI from Santiago Army, police refuse to act

Polly Portillo
in Conception, Chile

MAPUCHE Indians of the southern Chilean province of Bio Bio have declared independence as a self-styled Nonette community The government of Edvardo Frei has declared a State of Emergency. In the wake of Jatai both the police and armed forces have de... the rebellion.

The Mapuche, a ... enous minority, have ... side exploitation of ... ades Their protests against the loss of their farmland to multinational agro-business and timber companies have in the past been ruthlessly suppressed by Chilean government Many Mapuche activists have been imprisoned or forced into exile

Government U-turn on fuel bills

Arrears eased for low paid
Rationing still to stay

Prices slashed for prompt payers
"Too little too late" - jibes Haines

By Steven Dunn
Economics Editor

ENERGY PRICES are to be reduced by up to 20 per cent under government plans outlined yesterday. There will also be grants available to people on low incomes towards re-paying arrears to their previous suppliers

The reversal of the government's hardline policy towards power prices comes at a time of the arrival of the first replacement Susem energy units - the so-called 'soufins'- in many parts of Europe A DTI spokesman denied that this was the reason for the policy change.

Giving details of the new policy he said: "Following a review of the overall energy situation and in the light of ... anticipated available ... and gas available this month than there was last month North Sea production is unlikely to attain anything like its previous levels for another two to three months And this is assuming every thing else in the reinstatement of the supply chain goes to plan, which I doubt will be the case."

In giving details of the governments' proposals for the grant scheme to help those on low incomes repay their arrears to the old energy supply companies, the DTI spokesman said: "The scheme's intention is to ensure that no one, no matter their financial circumstances, need be put at a disadvantage when it comes to resupply."

Replying as to why the government did not just sim... government's Sinking Fund but will be funded in the longterm by taxation. The cost to the Treasury in the first year is expected to be in excess of £15bn

The shadow LibCon Minister for Energy, Howard Caine, dismissed both the proposed price cuts and grants as "too little too late" and added: "Yet once again the government has presented us with a mishmash of ill thought proposals which will please no-one but penalises everybody Those consumers who have acted responsibly in paying their debts will be subsidizing those who, irresponsibly, have not Is this fair? I do not think so Those who are low energy users will be financing those who are energy guzzlers. Again this is unfair."

Son of Un-American Activities Committee to be set up

Sen. Dich seen as new MacCarthy

By Billybob Dangger
In Washington

NEVADA SENATOR Sam Dich and other rightwing senators called for the US Senate to reconvene its Un-American Activities Sub-Committee to investigate the extent of Nonette influence in the United States

Senator Dich, a longterm opponent of the Nonettes said: "This organization is ...

... and integrity of our country against the rising red tide of crypto Commies and their fellow travelers

"It is abominable that this Nonette movement is allowed to spread its malign influence throughout our country unchecked

"Therefore I say to its ringleaders: Submit yourselves and your activities to the public scrutiny in front of the democratically elected repre...

First Susem teaching machines arrive

Scramble to earn 'Health Coupons'
"Screens are no substitute for schools" - teachers warn

Alan Carter
Education Correspondent

The first Nonette teaching machines arrived in Britain yesterday

Queues of eager Nonettes ... as they ... did was to ask me to write my name and do a simple sum of addition and I earned one of these coupons.

"If this is all anyone has to do," he said, "then everyone will be able to have a session in a Mormic [the Nonette ... been told, if we have 18 of these coupons we get a session in a Mormic At this rate I will easily have mine by the time ours gets here"

However, not everyone found the teaching machine quite so easy. Mrs Edith ...

BOSNIAN WAR TRIALS: Serb killers soft sentences shock

Seven day 'Walk in the Woods' term outrages victims

By Nicola Kay
In Sarajevo

A GANG of Serb thugs guilty of shelling defenceless civilians murdering 100s of women and children, received nothing more than "Slap on Wrist" sentences yesterday.

Following a lengthy morning-long trial in the central Bosnian city of Vares, 27 Serb soldiers were all found guilty of being part of the Serbian forces which besieged Varies firing more than 250,000 shells and mortars into the city from the surrounding mountains.

More than 850 people were killed during the four months siege.

A further 2,000 people including, many children, were injured and maimed during the 120 day non-stop bombardment of the city.

Spectators in the crowded court - many of them relatives of the victims - as well as the 100s more outside watching the proceedings on close circuit television, cheered as the Judge read out her panel's 'Guilty' verdicts on one Serb after another. There were gasps of disbelief however, at the sentences she and her fellow panel members handed down.

In her summing up the Judge said that all the soldiers were guilty of "unspeakable wickedness" and so deserved the "severest of sentences."

To most of the spectators this implied public beheadings at the very least. Most of those outside the court however, were looking expecting the guilty to appear in the Kosovo Stadium at Sarajevo and to being sawn in half and then eaten by piranhas while they were still alive.

There were cries of disbelief and outrage however, as Judge handed down her actual sentences. Each one of the convicted murderers was sentenced to just seven days of "Contemplative reflection of the evil of your deeds."

When the crowds outside the court learned that the guilty were to spend their sentences on the same hill-sides they had fired their shell from they were quickly dubbed "Holiday Camp Convictions."

This is the second War Crimes Trial to hand down these staggeringly mild guilty sentences and

Forum Stadium blaze: Arsenal Munich clash postponed

Damage minor but match faces 7 day delay

By Alan Piper
In Rome

A BLAZE at Rome's Forum Stadium has delayed Thursday's IEFA Octal final between Arsenal and AG Munchen.

Forum officials say the fire, which occurred in one of the restaurants, has caused minor damage and was soon under control.

An IEFA spokesman said the stadium will re-open after ... completed, which will take no longer than a week.

The delay however, gives Arsenal more time to improve their match fitness. But with the Gunner's star striker, San Martin, still out of action, their chances of defeating AG Munchen do not appear to have improved

William Ill's odds of an Arsenal win are still unchanged at 100-1 against.

Arsenal manager, Arno Vanderkort said: "We see the ... more time to bring the team up to an extra peak of fitness. It is too soon to write off the team's chances."

Munchen's manager, Heinz Guderain, however, is upset by the delay. He said: "As far as we are concerned the contest is over for the Tommies. We know we are going to win, what we do not know is by how many goals.

"The delay means only for us that our players will have less time to prepare for our prepar...

than enough in Panama.

Responses and replies though, were sadly similar, "Strutting about like that they were asking for it."

"But it's a nudist beach."

"So? They were just waiting for it, we could see they were, flexing themselves, prancing, preening one another, running..."

"But Bondi is a gay beach, they're homosexuals."

"So?"

"They only like their fellow males as company, they don't like women."

"So?"

"They are not sexually aroused by females."

"They were by the time we finished with them!"

It was amid their snickering laughter, knowing nudges, rhythmic opening and closing of their hands that my repeated "But why were you in Australia?" had another of them reply with "Day trip to Arnhem Land to see if the rock drawings of us are still there..." dropped the bombshell.

Her "...but when we saw that pack of prime Bruces, their lovely pert round..." was all but lost on me as I took in the significance of what she had said and I pressed her with "Of you?...drawings?...by whom?...when?"

Perhaps it was the wine, the marijuana, the enthused regaling to the others but in the middle of her "...they gave us a bit of a run but it was a definite legs over..." and no more than half turning to me, as an aside, "No, not us but those on the last tour..."

Even before my "Last! You mean..." or interrupt her "...they all had to be whipped and coned before we could..." there was a hush. I was not the only one grasping the gravity of what she had said. So had Petruee.

In an instant she had her hand raised. The talking died and the others, also realising what had been said, trooped under her watching eye from the refectory. As they left and catching her glance at me, I sensed she knew I knew that the cat was out the bag.

In fume and fret I rushed to tell Rainbow what I had learnt, that I had been right all along, the Susem are really up to something, their searching for Pat-tu a guise. But to my alacrity all she could say was that she was too busy overseeing the editing of the new Nonettes' videos to "talk to anyone."

Rainbow's indifference, although dismaying, did not dampen my determination to uncover the real reasons for the Susem being here. I sped back below intent on uncovering the truth.

At first I felt fobbed off. Every Susem I asked also replied that they too were too busy to talk, rushing to somewhere or they knew nothing. But each evasion reinforced my resolve to discover the truth. And so by the time I met Pheterisco, who also claimed to know nothing, I readily accepted her suggestion of asking Paceillo, she just returned from searching for Pa-tu. Knowing that she must know, even the prospect of her abrasiveness did not deter me from

Nonettes in Japan rise

William Sicket reports from Tokyo

In this land 'must have gizmos but no gas, oil or other energy resources, the Nonette movement has seen a massive surge in membership.

From the fish farms of Hokkaido to the sushi bars of Yokohama, Nonette groups have spread with the speed of knotweed.

What began as a wish to secure replacement soufin energy units, has burgeoned into a fully-blown movement with more than five million members and thousands more joining by the day.

Energy shortage fears fuel Nonette surge

It is not just people who are enrolling in the Nonettes but businesses as well. According to the four main Nonette councils, more than 80,000 businesses have already become members of the movement.

With the attraction of secure energy supplies and full voting fights in local affairs these numbers are also set to soar.

Kukkibushi, an Osaka based chip fabricator, along with three other neighbouring companies with a total of 6,000 employees, have even formed their own Nonette, which gives them participating voting rights for the whole Kobe-Osaka region.

The Japanese government, while worried at the Nonettes' rising strength and growing merce, is in fact, powerless to curb it.

In this land of 16,000 registered fringe religions and as many who are many who are not not religious, the government is constitutionally shackled from stopping the activities of any law abiding movement Nonettes included.

Rightwing MPs have voiced fears over the Nonettes' growing numbers. MITI, the Japanese trade ministry, however, has repeatedly said that it is vital business maintains its competetive edge and in effect in encouraging industry to use the new soufins.

The Energy Ministry, concerned for the security of Japan's energy supplies, is also conducting a behind-the-scenes policy encouraging use of the new energy units.

In this land where politicians are widely viewed as "placemen of powerbrokers and shadowy vested interests", the arrival of the Nonettes with their openness and accountability, have been seen as a divine wind of change.

The Nonette movement has also harnessed the long-subdued Japanese desire for the cohesion of communal society.

In this land of 'salaryman' and collective deference to authority, the rise of the Nonette movement has brought security without subservience to the first and power to be revered to the second.

As each day passes, as the Nonette movement moves from being seen as merely a source of

First British Nonettes fly out to South America

Hundred volunteers go for training Heywood warns of brainwashing risk

By LISBET CULPEPPER

SUSEM SPACEPLANES flew more thgan 100 Nonette volunteers from across Britain to South America yesterday. They are expected to be away for at least a wee...

delta-winged craft swept down to nearby Platt Fields. Leslie Saxon, (55) who saw the plane land, said: "There was no noise. The spacecraft swept over from the Oxford Road at tree height.

"No sooner had the plane la... he said, "than all these people ... out from behind the museu... towards the plane. A door slid ... the side...

HISOGYNISTS WHIP UP FRENZY OF CRUELTY

TRIALS 2ND DAY: 60 SERB CROAT BACKERS BURNT BRANDED SLASHED SLICED TO DEATH

By Jessica Gunnery
in Sarajevo

BENT BANKERS, BUSINESSMEN and bureaucrats who backed the former Serb and Croat pariah regimes and found guilty of War Crimes have been burnt and branded by red hot lashes, then slashed and sliced to death by whip-wielding Hisogynists. The men's dismembered bodies were then eaten by huge hounds

The Trial

On the second day of final Bosnian War Crimes Trial a total of 60 Serb and Croat government officials, businessmen and bankers went on trial on charges of being the leading culprits fueling their regimes' war machines, sanction-busting, being accomplices to a string of crimes against humanity as well as a host of other related deviant acts and misdemeanours.

The March

Following a lengthy trial, which lasted the entire afternoon, the judges found all the 60 men guilty as charged.

The men were then marched the two miles from the Court in central Sarajevo to the National Stadium for punishment.

Although these conniving white collar crooks and their equally evilly corrupt bureaucrat cohorts were only stripped to their fancy silk underwear, the early evening crowds lining the roadside could still make out their obese bloated bodies.

Onlookers lining the route cheered each time the unsmiling no-nonsense two metre tall Khymer guards kept these felons in formation with their five metre long bull-whips.

The budgie cages

Inside the stadium, these evil wheeler-dealers were whipped into nine huge three-metre tall metal budgerigar cage-like boxes. These were hoisted onto 10 metre-high gantries and just like budgies, massive cloths were then lowered over the cages.

Lights dimmed

While this was taking place the stadium was filling up with spectators, many of whom had queued for days to get in. With all the seats filled the lights were gradually dimmed to total darkness.

The trampoline

Then to the opening bars of Decoursu's tasteful 'Prelude ... small lights appeared in the darkness and traveling from one end of the arena to the other.

Suddenly a spotlight shone down on to the circle revealing it to be a huge trampoline. Nine Hisogynists dressed in their shiny white tunics were carrying it with one hand, a torch in the other.

The Hisogynists

As the Hisogynists gaily danced away from the trampoline more lights shone on it, lighting up the area around including what was immediately above: one of the cages.

Shaken and stirred

With a fanfare of trumpets the cloth was lifted away and the cage shaken onto its side. To roars of laughter of the 60,000 capacity crowd the cage door opened and the men inside tumbled onto the trampoline, bounced into the air, back down on it again and then onto the sandy ground of the arena.

As these evil embezzlers bounced up and down, further spotlights began illuminating more of the area. As they did the crowd began roaring with delight for they could see what the bouncing criminals could not: groups of more Hisogynists crouched behind the sandy hillocks. These however, were not dressed in white but in dark loose fitting tunics and big helmets with glass visors.

Red hot whips

Suddenly these Hisogynists sprang up from behind the hillocks and wielding big long whips which glowed red in the near darkness.

As the Hisogynists advanced towards the still nonplussed criminals they must have seemed unearthly.

But these white-collar crooks had little time to take in this awesome sight before the Hisogynists were upon them. The crowd roared with approval as these evildoers ... that the reason the whips glowed red was because they actually were red hot.

Lashed and branded

There was roar after approving roar from the crowd as these felons felt the lash of the Hisogynists' whips branding across their backs, sear into their obese bellies, scream in pain they ran from the red hot swishes of justice.

FULL STORY PAGES: 4, 5, 6, 7, 8 & 9
PICS: 2,3,4,5,6,7,9

For a few of these callous crooks it was not fast enough however, and their bodies were whip burnt and branded from their necks to their navels again and again.

As the Hisogynists mercilessly lashed these fleeing fiends further into the arena, their fancy silk vests and pants singed and smouldering, in the darkness, they appeared not to notice they were being chased up another hillock. To their surprise and relief the Hisogynists did not chase them down the other side.

The Stukas

But these racketeers' relief was short-lived. For from behind the next dune came the Stuka-siren sounds of the next Hisogynists' whips.

Though the crowd saw these Hisogynists approaching, the crooks cowering in the sand pit of course could not. Then all of a sudden they did.

Diamond toothed

They saw a line of these Hisogynists standing atop the crest of the dune, saw their head-to-toe chainmail armour glistening silver bright from the spotlights shining on them. Saw the glints of the 1,000s of diamond toothed spinning wheels of their whips. And as Hisogynists marched down the slope swirling them, they heard the rattlesnake-like whir of their wheels, heard the whirs of doom.

Swiss Roll sliced

Though the fiends ran, none escaped the whips. None escaped being sliced as if they were Swiss Rolls. Some tried to protect themselves with their hands and arms but in vain. These were sliced off in an instant.

Banks in massive... accounts loss to... Nonette's shock...

Move seen as boost to Nonette movemen...

By BRIAN BUNTING
FINANCE EDITOR

BRITAIN'S fastest growing Bank, the Nonette Bank of Congress, does not possess a single ATM. Neither does it have any online access. It does not sell insurance, mortgages or any of the other 'financial products' with which the High Street banks besiege the public.

In a matter of days Congress has attracted half a million customers, many

Nonette bank attracts 500,000 customers with old-style banking. 'A branch in every village, in every street' Nonette bank claims

cashiers, queues and no charges - has tapped a demand long dismissed by other banks as outdated: face-to-face contact.

Every local Nonette group has its own ...

to the area ban... which in turn, is ... branch to th... regional bank and s... on all the way t... Congress's Centr... Bank in Brazil.

Ron Nixon (60), t... manager of a Co... gress branch in Har... mersmith, explaine... the workings of the ... system. He said: "W... know our custome... and they know us, ... are all neighbours.

"Nine of our No... ette members ove... see everything," R... said, "so there is ... chance of anythi... going astray. It's th...

seeking her out to discover the truth, have it out with her.

I had to ask again and again for her whereabouts before someone said they knew. With each asking my intent became the more strident. No matter what mood Paceillo might be in I would stand my ground until she had told me.

When at last I found Paceillo she was in a gallery surrounded by other Susem sat in front of screens. As she saw me, and though her face had a gruff 'Not now, I'm busy' frown, to my surprise she simply, almost demurely, said "Yes?"

Though taken off-guard by her quiet tone I sallied forth with "One of the others told me about you Susem being in Australia..."

But I got no further than she as quietly said, but now with a hint of a smile, "Well, girls will be girls, they were merely high spirited that was all."

"No not that. It's the other things they..."

"I agree the fatalities are unfortunate but it was most foolhardy of those men to swim straight into the paths of those passing sharks."

"No not that, it's what the others..."

"Come now, there is no need for alarm, no lasting harm can have been done. In time all of those males' self-induced traumas will dissipate."

"I am not talking about our others," I said still strident, "but your others. One of them said you have been here on Earth before, in the past, that they were going to see the drawings in Australia which had been..."

Her "Oh, did they," cut me short, but with her "Now that is interesting," I had the feeling that she was parrying with me.

Undeterred I pressed on with "Why didn't you say you have been here before, you don't realise the trouble this will mean, I'm in enough of it as it is, you have tricked, deceived me, and anyway what is your real..."

But she coolly defended with "I do not hitherto recall having in any way whatsoever made mention to you or to any other party that our colleagues past or present had or had not previously visited this planet."

Then even more authoritatively, "If however, should you or others have specifically raised this matter then an appropriate response would of course been immediately forthcoming. But as none has been made then there is and has surely been no concomitant obligation or onus on our part to do so. Would you not agree?"

It was touché. Stridency faltered to "All the same you should have..."

She though, as if taking no notice, advanced with "Furthermore, should it have been germane to the purposes of our assignation to do so, then you may be most assured, as would have been others that any information as to our presence hitherto or not would have been readily and freely given."

Stridency spluttered to "Surely you should have..."

She then attacked. "From the accusatory tone of your enquiry am I to conclude anything other than that you are asserting that we, the Susem have been or are being in any way less than totally transparent in the purposes we

'WE WANT OUR MONEY BACK' NONETTES MAKE TAX CUT DEMAND

By Steven Dunn
Economics Editor

THE NONETTE movement has called for the right to deduct the ten per cent they pay to their movement - the so-called 'tithe' - from their income tax.

At a meeting of Nonettes in London yesterday, there were calls for the payments made by members to their branches be deductible from their income and council tax.

'Pigs will fly before any government gives into tax cuts for special interest groups'

One delegate said: "The tithe is spent for the direct benefit of our community. It is money the government and councils do not have to spend.

"Every penny we collect is accounted for as is all expend- our own money it is done more efficiently than either the government or councils could ever do."

A Treasury spokesman said: "HM government's response to any call for special treatment from any one particular interest group is a simple 'No'.

"If any group wishes to press for change, for special treatment then they should go through the proper channels such as lobbying their local MP."

The Nonette call for preferential tax treatment is also seen as naive. One tax consultant said: "Pigs might fly before any government gives into any demands from any group for a cut in tax bill, with the exception of the rich and powerful that is."

The Nonettes' demand for income tax refunds were

Choreography of Danse Macabre

The Hisogynists' choreography of the Bosnian War Trials sentencing has won plaudits from many in the world of dance. **Jessica Wynden Hughes**, now Senior Reader in Contemporary Wagner Studies at Snaresbrook University talks to **Wayne Ignatioff**, dance critic of *Hoofers & Queens* and **Beth Maxton** of Inyerface Dance Company

Jessica: "Would you say that Jean-Charles Decoursu's 'Trials' Symphony, with its eclectic Wagnerian resonances, has added a certain piquancy to the Hisogynist's choreography during their punishment routines in the 'Trials Finale' as well as their overall performance?"

Wayne: *"Oh definitely yes. The second movement Decoursu's 'Trials', 'Sear and Sever' was absolutely packed with Wagner's 'Das Rhiengold' and 'Die Walkure'. The Prelude was most certainly full of 'Waldweben' and 'Siegfried's 'Finzug der Götter in Walhalla', the adagio ma non troppo was just so grazioso sympathetic to the opening dance of the circle of light as it glided across the amphitheatre."*

Beth: **"You mean 'Entry of the Gods in Valhalla'? That was good that wasn't it? And when the spotlights came on and showed it was a trampoline and at the same time that big cover came off that cage and showed all those blokes inside jumping about like distressed budgies."**

Wayne: *"Well I suppose if someone was rattling your cage at such a height you would be a tad agitated as well."*

Jessica: "But when the door of the men's cage swung open and they all tumbled out onto the trampoline wasn't that just so lustig lebhaft umore and the score just so scherzando?

The Hisogynists knelt behind the dune, weren't their costumes just wonderful? Crouched together like that, to me they looked just like a huge brown turtle."

Beth: **"The way they all crept up the dune still all together and when they were on the ridge they all leapt apart and got those big whips out from under their tunics."**

Jessica: "And the way they swirled in the air, those streaks of red made such a wonderful remous de feu against the darkness."

Wayne: *"The score was just perfect as well, so reminiscent of the schnell, allegro of Act One of 'Siegfried's 'Rhein Travail'.*

I did think at first that perhaps the costumes were a tiny bit too heavy but I have to admit they were just perfect in evoking a spectre au affreux."

Beth: **"With those helmets on as well, they must have put the fear up those blokes. And you soon saw why they had to be dressed up like that. Not only were the tips of those whips red hot, they'd have been coming down on those blokes' backs like anything."**

Jessica: "But weren't the men just so umore the way they first ran around in circles, their saltando as the first Hisogynists caught them with the tips of their whips?"

Wayne: *"And wasn't the music just so exquisite?"*

Jessica: "Marvellous, one might add!"

Wayne: *"Indeed one would! Did you notice the way Decoursu slowly built it from adagio to adagiettoi Then as the Hisogynists lashed into those fellows and they began to run, the music broke into lovely rolling courante with those undertones of presto menace then prestissimo, so reminiscent of 'Walkürenritt 'from 'Die Walküre' I thought."*

Beth: **"Oh you mean 'Ride of the Valkyries? Yes it was a bit like that I suppose but that high pitched screeching could've come straight out of the shower scene in 'Psycho'.**

I thought that was really good the way they whipped those blokes in time with the music. Oh, and those Hisogynists really laid into them did they? The way each time one of those blokes got the full welt of the whips across their back, their vests would start smouldering."

Jessica: "Yes, I found that really erotic the way those brand marks came up on those men's backs. It's such a shame they were all so laid obsite un vieillard otherwise I might have found the whole act in its entirety erotic."

Wayne: *"Well, whatever turns you on I suppose. But more to the point the choreography of the chase was, to my mind just superb. Decorsu's underlying accerando agitato of the avanzamento fitted in so well the way the whips fell upon the fellows, burning into their bodies.*

Similarly, the molto lento when the men had been run up the dune and down to the comparative respite of the other side."

Beth; (laughing): **"Didn't last long though did it?"**

Jessica: "You are just so right. And weren't the second Hisogynsts wonderful the way they just stood there on the crest of that dune, their armour glistening silver in the spotlights?"

Wayne: *"Not wishing to appear a killjoy but I did think that the music did have more than a hint of 'Siegfried's 'Funeral March' about it. Not that for one moment did I consider it to be anything other appropriately perfect."*

Beth: **"All the same you've got to agree though that when the music stopp ed so you could hear nothing but the sound of the Hisogynists' whips making those rattling whirring sounds it was really scary. Anyway, it put the fear up those blokes.**

Did you see the way they tried to run back up the side of that hill and because it was so steep they kept sliding back down again!"

Jessica: "When they got back on their feet wasn't that just so superb the way the Hisogynists' whipping movement was in perfect synchronisation with Decoursu's brio vivace."

Wayne: *"It was the way the Hisogynists moved in unison with each other which impressed me; the way they all whipped to the right then whipped to the left, then to the front."*

Beth: **"They would have had to wouldn't they? I know they were in chain-mail armour and visors but they would still have to have watched themselves, especially after you saw what the wheels on those whips did to those blokes, like red hot knives though butter."**

Jessica: "But as the Hisogynists first swirled their whips through the air wasn't the way diamond tips of the wheels' teeth gave a shimmering snake-like lines of light just so awe inspiring?"

Beth: **"Only that first time. Did you see how they once they'd cut through the first of those blokes' bodies they seemed to come that duller? It must've been the blood on them I suppose."**

Wayne: *But I really do think it is important not to lose sight of how jolly difficult it must have been for those girls to have kept in perfect step throughout the whole of their routine as well as keeping in time with the music. Take it from me it must have taken them simply hours and hours of rehearsal."*

Beth: **"All the same you've got to admit that they didn't half make a good show of slicing those blokes up.**

Did you see that one who was down on his knees and he got a whip right round his neck? The way his head came off, did you see how it fell on his legs then rolled off them?"

Jessica: "What I found so visually intriguing was the men's transformation into slabs. There was one I distinctly remember seeing who started to run from the melee being struck by several whips simultaneously and collapsing to one side as though he were a loaf of sliced bread."

Wayne: *"Now that you mention it, were you aware of the score? Not so much Wagner but Strauss, 'Richard, 'Tod und Verkärung' especially the molto agitato as the Hisogynists did the actual transfiguring and again when those packs of black hounds appeared."*

Beth: **"And did you see the size of them? They were enormous."**

Wayne: *"Soon made short work of those men or their slices rather!*

The second cage's release I though

Crashed Susem spaceship foun in high Arcti

Excavation expected to be completed in Could this mean Aliens departure from

By Roland Gallon
Alien Watch Correspondent

THE SUSEM'S lost spaceship has been found. Although the precise location of the massive craft, which crashed into the Earth a century ago, is still to be revealed, it is said to be in the Canadian Arctic.

Excavation of the spaceship's remains is expected to last no more than a week it was said.

Yesterday's Susem telecast announced that remaining sections of the Alien's 40km diameter spaceship had been located in the Queen Elizabeth Islands in Canada's high Arctic.

Hundreds of Alien search craft were shown hovering over the snow-covered wastes. Many more of the Alien machines could be seen rising and falling high into the skies above the Arctic ice floes.

Susem announcer, Rainbow Louis, said that the craft, which crashed into the Earth early in the last century, was destroyed in our upper atmosphere. The research into the spaceship's remains will focus on the reasons for its crashing, she said. It could be thought of as a Space Accident Investigation.

Ms Louis also said that pinpointing the crash site came as the result of the earlier discovery of fragments of the lost craft in the Amazonian region of the former Peru and Brazil

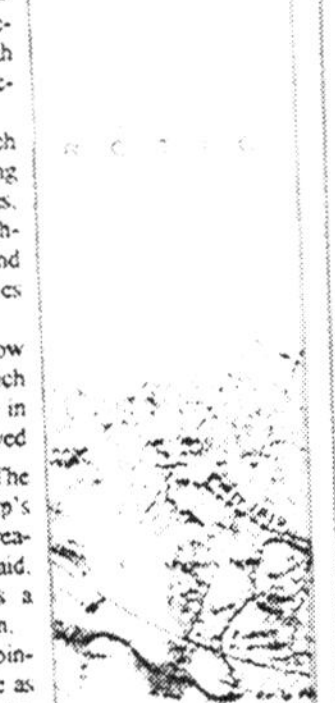

have previously and precisely stated and have continued to do so?"

Stridency slid to a plaintive "No, not really I just sort of..."

And seeing so she rapiered me with "You are accusing me of being a liar, are you not?"

Her words, the cold steely tone she lunged them, had me take a step backwards. The other Susem stared up from their screens. Paceillo stepped to my far side. I turned to face her. In a flash she struck with "Am I to understand you are saying that our presence here is for some malign purpose?"

I fended with "No, it's just that..." but instantly felt a dozen stares stab into my back.

Though Paceillo had still not answered my question she now had the tables turned. Valour vanished, retreat beat. I parried "I'm sorry if..." Alas too late.

She moved between me and the doorway, her glare as cold as her "Sorry? ...you say you are sorry?...then why do you make these assertions?"

Trapped by her "Why?...why?" slashes, knifing stares in my back I proffered a "I didn't mean to..."

To no avail. She slashed again "...You have the temerity to come here, accuse us, me, of possessing some ulterior purpose," and again, "You make unfounded aspersions as to the reasons we have come to your planet and all you can say is 'sorry'?" and yet again, "...That you of all humans should accuse me of such a thing." With me now wishing I had remembered 'Never argue with a woman, they always win', she plunged her "After all I've done for you" right into me.

Defenceless, wounded, escape thwarted, all I could do was seek mercy.

There was none. Instead she struck with merciless swiping blows of "If it was not for me you would...is this how you repay me...after all we have given you..." as I cowered I had thoughts of my mum, schoolmistresses, girlfriends, all the other women in my life, that they are all the same everywhere, the entire Universe, "...you should be ashamed of yourself for...how could you." Then finally the heart stabbing, mortal "If only you knew just how much you have hurt me."

There was silence as I waited for the coup de grace of "You have broken my heart," but it didn't come, nor the sobbed, "Now look what you've done." Instead as I looked up she had her arms folded and a triumphant glower. Paceillo then confounded me the more with "As you have asked, follow me."

I mutely traipsed behind her but convinced as ever that women across the Universe are really as hard as nails, that they just put on a show of hurt so as to extract every last shred of contrition from males to use as barbs for later.

She took me to Terbal. An "Ein moment," and he had rustled up his big hologram globe.

It spun, slowed then stopped. Paceillo pointed to a place in Africa. "Oklo," she said, then "hakken, or known to you as 'Lanthanumic Rare Earth elements'," of which I didn't understand either, though I had heard of 'rare earth metals'.

Hisogynists' chrysalis costumes

nnifer Hughes
ts Correspondent
Sarajevo

HE HISOGYNISTS, the orld's top Performance Art nsemble, were no where to be een as the press gathered to e them model their new ostumes for the forthcoming nd final performance of Trials'.

'Desert mirage of imago butterflies'

Press and photographers, gathered in the arena of the Kosovo National Stadium for the photo-shoot, at first were greeted with nothing more than an undulating sea of sand.

There was still nothing to be seen as just audible sounds of Decoursu's 'Prelude to Trials' drifted across the dunes accompanied by a gusting breeze which sent swirls of sand toward the awaiting photographers.

As the photographers brushed the sand from their lenses, a brilliant, lightning-like flash of light blasted across the stadium, startling everyone.

The knee-high dune immediately in front of the photographers then slowly rose to shoulder height with a pillar of sand in turn rising up from it. Further flashes of lightning followed and with each clap of thunder, another dune rose and from it. Finally, an even brighter flash, the ninth, was followed by a thunderous boom.

With thunder and lightning reverberating around the stadium the pillars suddenly changed to sand-coloured shrouds which began to move and sway in time with the music.

The shrouds then suddenly fell to the ground revealing the Hisogynists in their glistening while tunics.

Each Hisogynist stood motionless as though still pillars then they slowly began swaying their bodies in time with the music. Then all at once they stretched out their arms and revealed bat wings of dazzling butterfly brilliance.

The Hisogynists then slowly glided around, between each other, their wings ever changing kaleidoscopes of yellows, reds, blues, even gold and silver.

Pictures 4, 5, 6 & 7

All nine of the Hisogynists then began to dance faster but as they swirled around and around, dancing faster and faster, the white of their tunics also changed into one set of colours then to another. So did the patterns of their wings. All the costumes however, contrasted with the darkness of their skin and their black flowing hair.

The Hisogynists then abruptly stopped dancing, formed into a line and just as suddenly changed from butterflies to moths: identical black and yellow moths.

The Hisogynists then lent forward as if taking a bow but at the same time each reached from behind their shoulders and pulled a black, skullcap-tight cowl over their heads. Each cap completely enclosed their hair and forehead. The two sides of the front of the cap curved above the eyebbrows and met in a point just over the bridges of their noses.

As the Hisogynists pulled the cowls down over their foreheads each revealed a matching yellow, skull-shaped emblem.

The nine Hisogynists, still in line, then marched from the arena. At the same time the sand humps upon which they had danced and stood slumped back into the dunes as if the shoulders of giants turning in their sleep.

The representative from Caught TV said she was unable to say what the humps were, saying only that all will be revealed on the night. She did say however, she could guarantee that the last night of Trials will be the most spectacular yet.

She also said that because those being punished were the leaders of the former pariah regimes, they warranted the cruelest of punishments. She said: "And mark my words when I say 'cruelest' oh boy do I mean cruel!"

Meanwhile in London th head of SLI TV, Derik Ig

OPEC debt concerns surface

By Oliver Stoneburger
Economics Editor

Oil producing countries rising debt levels have reached c... ...portions, an OECD ...ing states, especially those of the Middle East, were producing insufficient revenue to service their debt interest. The ... loans made to their loans to OPEC countries. The authors say: "Rather than forcing the oil states to grasp the opportunity of higher [oil] prices to reduce their debt ...ls all that the lenders

ABDUCTED BONDI BATHERS FOUND IN RUM JUNGLE

Darwin hospital in urgent medical supplies call

By **Lisa Biggles**
in Darwin, Australia

THE BUFF BONDI BATHERS abducted by the Aliens on Sunday have been found alive just outside the township of Rum Jungle, 20 miles south of Darwin, Northern Territory.

All of the 300-plus victims are reported to have suffered injuries and showed signs of distress and exhaustion.

No fatalities have been reported so far. However, Staff at the Rolf Harris Memorial Hospital in Darwin, where the victims are being treated, issued an urgent call for emergency medical supplies as well as specialists in removing anal implants.

All of the men thought to have been taken by the Susem during their raid on Bondi beach were found wandering in a dazed state by Bruce Cahoon, a Rum Jungle farmer.

He said: "I was out in the paddock at first light as I always am. Usually I catch sight of a few 'roos hopping about and hear the call of the kookaburra in the gum tree but that is all.

"So imagine my surprise," Bruce said, "when I heard this cry of 'Help ...ing fro... the billabong. When I turned in that direction I saw this bunch of blokes crawling up out of it.

"It was the most awesome sight I have ever seen. There were hundreds of them all crawling up the bank. Like a carpet they were and every man jack of them had not a stitch on.

"At first I didn't know what to make of it. But when I caught sight of their private parts and saw the state they were in I knew they must've had

High tech pow... shortage fears f...

Soufin use more widespread than th...

BY THOMAS SPANNER
INDUSTRY CORRESPONDENT

WASHINGTON STATE'S power shortage fears faded further yesterday when the latest influx of soufins energy units arrived in Seattle and neighboring King County.

According to *Big Power Monthly's* latest user survey, more than 150,000 soufin units are already in use throughout the State of Washington alone The new units are set to send this figure past the 500,000 mark.

The major utilities, including Pacific Power and NW Energy, are seeing any expected price hike bonanza disappearing by the day

Art Ransom of Gates University at Auburn said: "As of this moment in time Seattle and all of King County can be considered as operating on soufin power. The chances of the old style power corporations having any market share are zero point zero "

Ransom admitted that he, like many others, is surprised at the extent of continued soufin use He said: "At the time it was first announced the original units were set to fail I was among the first to say: "That is it" But I have to acknowledge that I have been proved so wrong.

"What I and oth... power facilities fail... into account," Rans... "was that in busin... your competitor ha... thing more adva... than you, either yo... have it - or somethin... pdq - or you are out ... iness. The power ... provide is free and y... not get much lower ... costs than that" Ra... added the change the N... movement was causin... cor-porate life was one ... businesses could live wit...

"The typical company... Seattle," Ransom said, "... ally employs no more tha... few dozen people at ... most

"In the past they had ... actual say in the environme... in which they operated. No... with all Nonette business... having voting rights in the... own communities, they ar... empowered to take an active... part in the formulating its... decisions

"In the past, a company to protect itself was obliged to either join trade associations or fund the local politician's re-election campaign

I do not think any of Seattle's Nonette companies will want to go back to those bad old days," he says

Another reason driving the rising use of soufins in Washington is that they are

Panama: "Situation serious but not hopeless" - says Warren

US troops cut-off

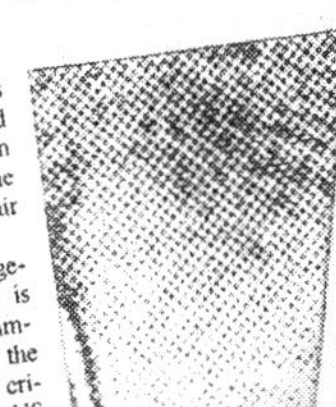

By Paul Ridde
in Washington

THE PANAMA Canal Zone is cut-off from the rest of the country, US President Warren announced yesterday.

The fate of the 30,000 strong force of Southern Command guarding the canal is reported as causing concern to US Defence chiefs

In an all-channel television address, President Warren said that all of Panama south of the Canal Zone was now in Nonette rebel hands The President also acknowledged that much of the north of the country, including those areas adjacent to the Canal Zone itself, were now also under rebel control.

President Warren said that there was no need to be alarmed at the situation. He said: "The rebel force know they must confront the forces of Southern Command before they can move northward into Central America.

"All the while we are in the canal they also know that we are blocking the path of their main forces," the President said. "Be assured that should General Tucers [the C-in-C of Southern Command] require further re-enforcements, the carrier task-forces in both the Caribbean and the Eastern Pac... ...to his immediate

Defence expects said that as there was no possibility of land forces coming to Southern Command's assistance The only way into Panama is by air or by sea.

David Souter of the Georgetown based IoS think-tank is pessimistic at Southern Command's chances of deterring the Nonettes. He is also highly critical of the strategy of US forces being in the Canal Zone at all.

Souter said: "The Canal has been closed to civilian shipping for several weeks. However, commerce has not been measurably affected. Thus the claim that a 30,000 strong force was needed to protect US and world commerce is baloney.

"To place such a strong force in such a restrictive location as the Panama Canal Zone," Souter said, "and without any room to manoeuvre is placing them in the position of sitting ducks.

"The Jatai disaster," he said, "should have sent warning signals to the Department of Defense (DoD) that it was time to admit their mistakes and get out of the Panama

"To what extent," Souter asks, "was such a decision baulked at in order to save face, including that of the DoD and Tucers, in particular. They must be aware of what those ... those guys down

US IRS KOs Nonette Tax

By Ross Capulyard

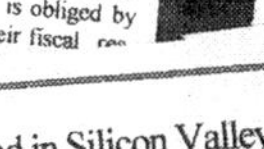

The US Inland Revenue service, America's equivalent to Britain's Inland Revenue has dismissed Nonette pleas for tax concessions.

Revenue Commissioner, John Peracíss, said: "Every individual or entity resident within the United States who is in receipt of income, no matter what its source, is obliged by law to honour their fiscal res...ponsibilities

Soufin use now widespread in Silicon Valley

US tech stocks surge ahead

By Gloria Vaught-Lewis

High-tech companies throughout the western US have shrugged aside government pleas to play safe on energy provision and wait for the resupply of established energy sources.

Countless companies from Seattle to San Diego have stayed with Susem soufins. And now that replacement units are arriving throughout the US, energy supply is set to stay soufin based

John Ventnor, CEO ... HiPoNo, a chip designer, sai... "Not only can we not stop o... process, we must not stop, n... even for a split second. A co... stant, multi-back-up pow... supply - which our soufins p... vide - has been vital Moreo... soufin energy is not only po... tion-free but it is free ene... period. And what is more ... area of operation is cost co... etitive sensitive. Our rivals ... soufins and thus so must we

"Here," she said, jabbing at Oklo, "long ago, amid deposits of uranium ores there were also deposits of the Lanthanum Series of elements..."

"Lutetium, ytterbium und thulium also..." flashed Terbal, zooming comet-like around the globe.

A terse "Thank you Terbal," from Paceillo and she continuing, "Over time reactions which cause these elements' formation occurred as a result of natural decay..."

"Erbium, holmium und dysprosium..." breezed Terbal whizzing round again and showing off.

"...But there are some," continued Paceillo doing her best to ignore him, "in this sequence which can only occur..."

"..Und terbium!" teased Terbal evidently savouring the similarity of his name, following it with "gadolinium, europium" and before Paceillo could get a swipe at him, zoom off into an elliptical orbit.

"...As a result of nuclear fission," continued Paceillo, teeth gritted, "the element..."

Terbal's "Ja it ist samarium!" was the most he managed as he sped by and Paceillo's shout had him change to a non-orbital trajectory of his TV screens and back to the football.

"The next element in the series," continued Paceillo, calm returned, "is promethium. This has an important and unique property. It does not exist outside of the process of nuclear fission reactions of stars. On your planet at Oklo the uranium ore deposits there transmuted into a number of stellar-like isotopes. This singular out-of-star chain reaction also brought about on Earth, albeit transiently, promethium.

"That such reactions should have taken place uniquely on your planet has been of interest. That they have continued, though now rarely, the out-of-planet radiation from these reactions, low level letum-like waves, has cautioned a watch be kept lest this progressive diminution vary.

"It was the registering of such subsequent variations, abrupt and markedly upward ones, which apparently occasioned Pa-tu to divert from his pre-arranged destination to investigate. Regrettably he did so with unfortunate consequences."

Though I had questions I also had difficulty grasping the moment of what Paceillo had said, so thought it best to answer questions with care. As at this point she had paused, I asked "Do you mean when the reaction became critical there was a meltdown, a nuclear explosion?"

"There have been several," Paceillo replied, "Most causing no more than localised destruction but some appear to have affected your entire planet."

Becoming bolder I ventured "How, in what way?"

She had another pause as if searching for words, then, "You have an expression, 'Nuclear Winter'. The bigger ones would be similar."

Though this triggered more questions about 'natural' nuclear explosions I still wanted to know why they had caused the Susem to visit Earth. I asked

BAILIFFS' TARRED AND FEATHERED SHOCK

Lambeth Poll tax protest riot Police blame Nonette

By BILLY MARTIN
Express Special Report

TWO BAILIFFS, seized by a gang of protesters were tied to lampposts and tarred and feathered. For more than an hour police were prevented from rescuing them but later made a number of arrests. GBA - the bailiffs' association - is demanding fuller protection for its members.

Atherford Road, a usually peaceful cul-de-sac off Clapham Common, was the scene of a ferocious attack on four County Court bailiffs yesterday by a 300-strong mob.

The bailiffs' removal truck was used by rioters to block the entrance to the street, preventing police from entering the street. The truck was later set on fire.

The four man team of bailiffs had gone to Atherford Road to evict a family which had refused to pay their Community Taxes

One of the bailiffs who managed to escape from the protesters said that within minutes of their arrival a crowd gathered shouting at them to leave.

The bailiff who escaped, Bruce Fors (25) speaking from his hospital bed, said: "We were on perfectly legit business. We had a perfect legal right of entry to the premises We had previously seized all the salable goods from the property but as their val-

Naturally we told them to mind their own business," he said.

The protesters, according to Mr Fors, then attacked him and his colleagues. Many of them, he claims, were armed with baseball bats and other such weapons.

While Mr Fors and a fellow bailiff managed to evade their attackers, both the head bailiff and his number two were beaten to the ground then tied to lamp-posts and coated in industrial adhesive and feathers. They remained there for several hours before police could free them.

Last night, however, those living on Atherford Road, gave a different account of what happened.

One said: "We gave them the bloody good hiding they had been asking for. They are scum. If they come here again they will get more of the same and worse."

According to another of the residents the bailiffs were in the process of kicking the front door of the house in as

Pope condemns Trials as 'bestial'

'An abomination of evil' - Pontiff says

BY HILARY HOWELLS
RELIGIOUS CORRESPONDENT

POPE PIUS XIII has branded the forthcoming 'Final Trials' as an even greater evil than the previous Trials. He said that his pleas for clemency

be given the right to their lives in order they might atone for their misdeeds."

His Holiness said that he had been told that the forthcoming Trials are expected to be the most bestial yet.

Many areas being 'hollowed out' by Nonettes

EU frets over Nonette growth

By Timothy Ryans

European Foreign ministers were given a gloomy assessment of the growth of Nonette influence at their Brussels conference yesterday.

An increasing number of regions, especially in Poland, the Baltic States, both EU and state administrations are either ignored or bypassed.

The problem is reported as growing. In the southern Polish provinces bordering the Carpathian mountain

tent they are running separate administrations and economies. With arrival of numerous replacement energy units into the region the situation is likely to deteriorate further, EU officials fear.

A similar pattern of socio-economic separateness is occurring in the Baltic states, especially among the Russian minorities in the border regions of Belarus and Pskov

The whole of the southern Carpathian region is said to be under

are also concern for its future within the EU.

Much of the rapid growth of Nonettes in these areas has been laid at the widespread disillusionment with the EU's failure to improve their socio-economic well-being as well as the political accountability of their ruling elites. The Nonette movement, however, is viewed by many as the complete antithesis of EU's remoteness and indifference.

Every Nonette community appoints, as well

areas of Nonette activit are also under eac community's direct con trol. This includes the own gathering of the own taxes. In shor members of Nonett are in direct control every aspect of the own lives. This is som thing that the EU unlikely to be ever ab to compete with.

If the rising influen of the Nonettes w confined to the east fringes of the EU, mi sters would have wo enough but the grow of the Nonette mo

PM slams Nonette tax dema

'There are no special ca – Campbell tells Nonet

BY MARK LEWIS
POLITICAL CORRESPONDENT

THE Nonettes will not be given any tax concessions. The prime minister, Edward Campbell, has, turned down the Nonettes' demand for the 10 per cent they donate to their movement to be deducted from their income tax.

Speaking at a City engagement, the PM said: "Paying taxes is a duty all of us have to

ular sources of government revenue and expenditure, let alone is being desirable.

"Ever since income tax was introduced two centuries ago," the PM said, "the Treasury has received innumerable requests for special treatment from one interest group after another. All of them have received the same reply: 'No, no, no'. The Nonette movement is no exception and there can never be one."

The PM, who was attending

Nonettes thrive on Indonesian break-u

By Pranu Parekh
in Jakarta

As Jakarta's power wanes so the influence of the Nonettes waxes From Batu in the west of this island archipelago to Papua in the east, more than a dozen Nonette communities have unilaterally declared their independence from the Indonesian state.

The military, their forces stretched to breaking point quelling the disturbances across Sumatra and Java, appear unable or unwilling to bring any of these Nonettes back under government control.

But with each passing day the chances of General Teungku Wiranto's government doing so in the future becomes ever fewer.

In the past week alone, Nonette groups in Kalimantan (Borneo) and Celebes have declared they are no longer part of Indonesia. They join other Nonette groups in the

Sumatra, Amron and in much of Papua who already have established de-facto control of their islands and communities.

General Wiranto accuses the Nonettes of conspiring with outsiders to break-up of Indonesia and thus weaken the country. But an increasing number of observers have concluded that the country was already fragmenting. The rise of the Nonettes being no more than local communities taking control of their own affairs.

Jan van der Post, an expert on Indonesia, said: From east to west, Indonesia stretches over 5,000 km, consists of an

from strict Muslim to a ism. Since independence years ago the country has held together by mili force, one which is increasingly steeped in ruption. It is a wonder I nesia has existed as a un state for as long as it has."

According to van der Po the first outsider to visit W Kalimantan after the upris there - the Nonettes are in control of not just of the m towns of Anjungan and P ianak, which bore the brun the fighting, but through the Dayak settlements, fur inland. "Already," he s

Communications blocked
Scores of Alien craft seen

Re-enforcements missing
Rescue bids 'Jatai stymie

Panama fears grow

Andrew Hendry
In San José, Costa Rica

Fears rose yesterday for the safety of the 30.000 US troops of Southern Command.

Department of Defence officials admitted that communications to the Canal base at Fort Clayton were not receiving responses.

Unofficial sources claim that all levels of transmission with Clayton were being compromised by the Susem.

It was also revealed that a force of 200 marines sent into

Colon from the US Navy's fleet off-shore in Carribbean to the beleaguered garrison, had also ceased to make contact with the fleet once they had landed north of the city.

If this force is also lost to the Susem it represents a further setback to US attempts to rescue forces of Southern Command.

Of as much concern to any relief of Southern Command's forces, are numerous sightings of Alien delta winged planes over the Canal Zone There are also claimed sightings of the Aliens' larger

cigar shaped craft in th vicinity of Colon.

Defence chiefs are mindf of OTSA's experiences i sending relief and rescu missions to its besieged bas at Jatai. Each force sent int rescue those forces at Jata were promptly overwhelme by the Susem. Not only wer these units also taken in t captivity they were subjecte to extensive torture and phys ical humiliation.

It is doubtful if the Dep artment of Defence would ris repeating the same action.. U

"What would these upward changes have to do with Pa-tu coming here."

But it was as if I had not asked for Paceillo continued, "That such eruptions would have had deleterious consequences on a planet-wide basis is evident in the ubiquitous yet layered deposition of these Lanthanide elements resulting from their fall-out." Another pause as though searching for words, then "Terbal!"

"Ja der ist similar Lanthanide levels in chordate und basalt assays but der depositions auf der post-Phanaeozoic rock vormations are much, much more..." Terbal had lost me, more so when he broke into figures.

Paceillo interrupted with "The levels of Lanthanide elements found in meteorites and from within your planet's interior are similar and accord with those found throughout the Universe. But in rock strata laid down on your planet long after its subsequent, initial formation their levels are significantly higher..."

"Und der post-promethium deterioration elements are much higher, neodymium by six times und cerium it ist by ten times!"

"Because these geologically recent depositions are found throughout the surface layers of your planet's post-Phanaeozonic rock stratas, it indicates they would have been laid down at the same time."

"Ja, dere were vour, der last would haff been as recent as...70 million years ago, less maybe..."

I did ask about 'Nuclear Winter', mass extinctions and again why the Susem and Pa-tu had come here. And why had he crashed. But both continued with the outcome of the Oklo eruptions. From Paceillo, "Though your planet is far from the main routes of our travel, the effect of its letumic pollution has been of constant concern to all those who have passed."

From Terbal, "Ja but it is dese uramiumic pollutionings, der malformations vich haff come, dey are der explanations maybe auf der gender separational diverences between the livevorms?"

Despite being told that planet Earth was deigned a nuclear polluter in the Galactic backwaters inhabited by radioactively deformed mutants, I again asked "Why did Pa-tu need to come here, why did he crash?"

Eventually I had answers, though they prompted more questions. "Planetary Crust Displacement" was the first, "Beta Taurid Showers" the second.

In the early 1900s in response to monitors earlier recording upward changes radiating from Earth, Pa-tu diverted from a voyage to Alpha Centuri and rushed to investigate. Not having travelled to our planetary system before, Pa-tu used pre-set navigation programs compiled from earlier Susem visits. Since the last, about 10,000 years ago, there had been changes in the orbit of Venus. It was no longer between Earth and Mars.

Complicating matters for Pa-tu was that in the process of moving to its present orbit, Venus caused Earth's axis to suddenly tilt from Hudson Bay way and the southern Indian Ocean to where it is now. In attempting to compensate for this oversight Pa-tu veered straight into the tail of Comet Encke, the Beta Taurid Shower, which when Pa-tu arrived in 1908 was particularly strong.

Police, bailiffs injured, cars, trucks torched
1,000 strong mob force police retreat Scores of causalities, arrests

LAMBETH POLL TAX RIOT

By Tony Perry
Civil Disorder Correspondent

LONDON'S most violent riot in a decade broke out in Clapham yesterday. A 1,000 strong rampaging mob of Community Charge protesters fought police in pitched battles. Dozen of vehicles were set on fire. Scores of people, including 12 police officers, were injured by rioters. Police made more than 50 arrests.

In the early hours of yesterday morning 20 police officers escorted a team of seven County Court bailiffs to repossess a house in Atherford Road, a cul-de-sac off Clapham Common.

No sooner had the police and bailiffs arrived at the property than they were subjected to a hail of bricks, bottles and petrol bombs by hundreds of protesters lying in wait.

Bailiffs clubbed

Many of the mob wielded clubs or lengths of scaffold poles which they used to attack the police and the bailiffs. Others rioters were armed with canisters of red paint which they sprayed the bailiffs.

The bailiffs being singled out by the mob were subjected to savage assaults by the crowd. All seven bailiffs required hospital treatment.

"Utterly reprehensible"

Metropolitan Police Commissioner, Sir Paul Harrier said last night: "The actions of the protesters are utterly reprehensible. This was a deli-

The Home Secretary, Claire Long, has demanded an immediate investigation into the incident.

More pictures pages 4,5,6 & 7

The Met claimed the disturbance had been deliberately planned Police sources said that officers were accompanying County Court bailiffs following an earlier attack against them during which two bailiffs were tied to lampposts and tarred and feathered.

Police attacked

Within minutes of the bailiffs' and their police escort arriving at the house, the entrance to Atherford Road was blocked by one of the bailiffs' trucks which was seized by the crowd.

When officers called for assistance they found that both their phones and radios were jammed.

Police sources said that the officers were powerless to stop the mob attacking the bailiffs.

BAD lands multi-million Hutar orde
2,000 vital defence jobs saved on

Defence expor Mid East boo

By Oliver Stoneburger
Economics Editor

The oil-rich state of Hutar has placed a £500m order with British Air Defence for a squadron of 20 new jet fighters

The order for the super fast NE 109s was hailed throughout Mersyside and has safeguarded the future of 2,000 skilled defence jobs at BAD's threatened Huyton plant

A jubilant Sir Harold Roberts, BAD's CEO said:

"This order could not have come at a better time With other countries' defence contractors being unfairly subsidised to the hilt we were not even getting a look in

"It was only when we could get our own government to provide a £100m research grant for a new camel sanctuary in Hutar that we were able to swing the order

Export course Sir planned cutback go ahe did not those o we will complai importa

---

New soufin energy units arrive
500,000 homes, businesses safeguarded

By Gareth Marshall
Economics Correspondent

BRITAIN'S first replacement soufin units arrived yesterday. Half million homes and businesses can rest assured of warmth of power this winter.

The Department of Energy has warned that the units must be tested by safety experts before they can be certified as safe for use. The new owners of the units - all members of the Nonette movement - are unlikely to take much notice

The energy units' arrival however, is likely to drive a further increase in Nonette membership.

People across Britain were

down from the skies. To a small number of watchers, however, the carpets' arrivals were not only known but the precise locations of their landings as well.

Throughout Britain more than 1,000 Nonette communities waited in pre-designated parks, fields and other open spaces for their units' to arrive.

Within a few hours of the soufins' arrival not only had they all been delivered to every local Nonette community but to their individual Nonette members themselves. These replacement soufins' are only the first of many more expected to arrive during the coming weeks.

Dow, Nasdaq, FTSE share in stoc surge as power shortage scares fa

Markets nudg pre-soufin slump highs

By Arthur Todd
City Editor

With yesterday's 258 point rise the Dow Jones Index to 12,482 it is within a whisper of the 12,623 high it enjoyed before the Susem dud soufin scare.

The high-tech Nasdaq has shown an even bigger per centage rise. At yesterday's close it

stood at 2876 massive 42 per cent rise from soufin dud slump.

Citi's market analy Kathy Sontag, sa "The rise has primar been driven by increa ing confidence that power dearth predic at the time will not n take place. Data energy generation icates however, there is like

---

Governments flee to US - Canal Zone cut-off

Panama, Costa Ric slide to Nonettes

Andrew Hendry
In San Jose and
John Hopkins
In Washington

WITH THE exodus of the Panamanian and Costa Rican governments to the United States, both countries are set to fall under Nonette control.

Though Costa Rica has not experienced the widespread panic flight of refugees seen in Panama and other Latin American countries, both San Jose International airport and the Caribbean port city of Limon are crowded with many thousands of people desperate to leave the country.

In the wake of the collapse of the US Southern Command in the Panama Canal Zone there is widespread concern across the United States. Families of the soldiers stationed in the Zone are pressing for their immediate return.

To date, however, both the White House and the Pentagon insist that there that there will not any

south-spine of Costa Rica, is now under complete Nonette control. So is the Pan-American Highway which runs between the mountains and the Pacific coast.

Travellers who sought to leave the country for Nicaragua on other roads, also report that even the bridges across the Rio San Juan - which forms the border - are in Nonette hands. Only the east of the country currently remains free of the rebels.

Most Costa Ricans however, including many of those in San Jose, are resigned to a Nonette takeover of their country. For them the arrival of the movement's forces is viewed with indifference by some but with enthusiasm by the majority.

Even the prospect of being isolated from the outside world appears to be of little concern to the majority of the population. Most of whom see the arriving Nonettes as bringing them an improvement to their standard and quality of life.

There is, however,

mand in Panama.

Carlos Mendez, a journalist with Panama's *Confidencial* newspaper and who is remaining in Costa Rica, said: "Who in Panama were the Americans to protect from the Nonettes? The US forces went there not to protect the people of Panama,

Costa Rica or the rest of Central America but the interests of the United States. We were not even notified of their decision to re-occupy Panama, they [the US] just said they coming and that was that.

"What has Tucers [the US C-in-C in Panama] achieved? His forces have

---

Major banks dema Congress's closu
Nonette bank is operating without BoE Lic

By Oliver Stoneburger

AS THE Nonette's Congress Bank announced its millionth account holder, High Street clearing banks are demanding that the Bank of England step in and stop its operations and the immediate confiscation of its assets.

Clavings' Chairman Sir Roger Foscoe, who is leading the campaign for Congress's closures, said: "This so-called Nonette bank is breaking every rule in the book.

Ordinary members of the public including those of this Nonette organisation, stand to lose every penny they have deposited with it," Sir Roger

"Public must be protected" demands Bank Chief

"People must realise," he said, "that deposit takers are licenced and policed for their benefit as well as the financial industry as a whole."

Sir Roger, like the heads of other major banks, international as well as British, are concerned that if Congress is not stopped now the effects of its collapse could lead to a loss of confidence to all banks

Sir Roger denied tha and the other main b against Congress b was a taking their c He said: "Neither Cl the other banks Congress as a bank le competitor.

"When all is said an this 'so called' Congres is little more than a g pub Christmas saving loan club. It has nothing with professional bankin far as we are concerned the main source of concerns.

"To the ordinary layman Congress may well appe be a bank. However, shou

The huge numbers of these meteorites were more than he could deflect. In his attempts to avoid them he came perilously close to Earth, skimming through its outer atmosphere at too steep a trajectory. These sudden course changes coupled with the atmosphere's friction caused Pa-tu to disintegrate. Part of him was blasted back into space, falling to Earth a quarter of a century later. The rest just simply exploded, vapourising with a very large bang high above Siberia.

The link between the Taurid Beta Shower and Tunguska I had heard before. So had Paceillo and Terbal. They made short shrift of Earthly experts' theories.

"The effects," said Paceillo, "were recorded by you (Earthly experts again) as far away as the eastern Pacific. Your Northern hemisphere's night-time skies were illuminated for two days by the atmospheric disturbances caused by the explosion, which you have acknowledged being the equivalent of 200 kilotonnes of your trinitrotoluene explosive, and its shockwave reverberated round your planet twice. Yet you maintain that this was caused by what is no more than a shower of granules partially compacted into fist sized nodules? Your retro-calculations of the kinematic dynamics of the event, while underestimating the magnitude of Pa-tu's size and speed, acknowledge that the collider with your planet weighed a million tonnes and was travelling at more than 100,000 kilometres an hour."

Next I tried them on Venus and its altered orbit. In an instant I was given a quick course on the laws of multiple heavenly bodies' dynamics in associated trajectories from Paceillo, as well as she saying that Venus is a proto-planet, it having previously been a Jovian moon. From Terbal a list of "your astro-physicists" from Velikovsky and Bass to Ransom and Hoffe whose mathematics concurred with those of the Susem, as well as their acknowledging the impossibility of precisely plotting planets' paths beyond 300 years. Terbal also gave a long list, ranging from before the Medes to the Mayans, all of whom reported and recorded Venus's wanderings about the heavens.

I asked how they could be so sure of so many of the details of Pa-tu's demise. Paceillo reiterated what she had told me on La-ra but soon progressed to 'points', the quinth context and the stored record within Secondary wave configurations. She also said that the Susem had the material findings from Pa-tu's remains here in westernmost Brazil to help them.

Next was 'Planetary Crust Displacement'. I was given another quick course. This one on "A planet's core's mantle dynamo distortion consequent on anomalous retrograde rotational effects (in this case Venus's) destabilising centrifugal pressures generating upon lithospheric stability" (most of which went over my head). It was not long though before the names Hapgood and Einstein (Albert) were bounded about along with details of how their conclusions and mathematics of such sudden shifts accorded with the Susem. Wegner's name followed, of how his contemporaries had deemed his concept of 'Continental Drift' as daft.

Taxes must rise or Govt. spending cut - economists predict

Concerns over government borrowing grow

By Ross Capulyard
Economics Correspondent

EITHER TAXES rise or government spending must be drastically cut. This is the stark conclusion of economists of Uber Bank.

The level of government debt, the Bank says, is already at crisis levels. Each new loan the Treasury receives is doing little more than cover interest payments on existing debt.

Writing in *'Big Loans Monthly'*, Uber Bank economists, Nicholas Brenner and Margaret Holt say that all OECD governments could face massive shortfalls in their expected tax revenues because of the widespread introduction of replacement soufin energy units.

In their report, *'How Safe is State Debt?'* the economists say that the extensive revenue losses all governments have suffered because of the introduction of the original soufins could be made much worse.

In Britain, they say, the losses from petrol and diesel duty alone represents more than five per cent - £20bn - of the government's expected tax income. Further revenue losses from the collapse of power companies and other business sectors adversely affected by the soufins - such as the oil industry - will add up to a further £40bn - 10 per cent - revenue shortfall.

The report points out that this shortfall has been met by the five-fold increase in the Public Sector Borrowing Requirement (PSBR). That such a huge increase in government borrowing have been more than matched by the willingness of banks and other money market sectors to lend to the government.

This willingness, however, has in large part, been due to the excess liquidity of the lenders themselves. Prior to the Susem's arrival, there had an excess money market liquidity but the worldwide decline in corporate sector borrowing requirement had exacerbated the situation as far as lenders were concerned.

In this situation - a surfeit of lenders and a shortage of borrowers - governments, including that of the UK, have had little difficulty in raising funds to cover their revenue shortfalls. The British government, for example, has had little difficulty in borrowing the necessary finance to cover the needs of resurrecting the power supply network. Neither have the new power generators and supply companies found any obstacles in finding the funds they needed to set up operations.

However, the report says, this fresh wave of government borrowing like all past loans is based on the premise that the lenders would be paid interest on their loans, as well as the principal being nominally secured against assets. These, so the reports say, are now both in question.

Brenner and Holt dryly observe that business inevitably interprets other people's difficulties as commercial opportunities. Following the failings of the first soufins, the projected demands for re-establishing traditional power generation and supply was viewed as an assured source of income.

It was against this projected income flow that much of much of the bank and institutional lending was advanced. But with the arrival of the replacement soufins, the amount of this income, significantly, will be below these original projections.

If the numbers of new soufins grow - as the report predicts they will - then the power companies are going to experience difficulties in servicing their loens let alone the capital repayments. The government's position is little better.

The report points out that there are already increasing as well as unplanned-for demands on the government's taxation revenue, containing the growing influence of the Nonettes being but one of them. Another is the need for extra debt interest repayment on its borrowing.

These further demands on government spending can only be met by increasing income or by raising taxes, or by reducing out-goings, cuts in services.

If the government fails to do one or the other of these - or both - it with need either to increase its own borrowings, or renegotiate its existing loans.

Should it do this, then lenders, no matter how 'flush' they may be, will need either to demand a higher rate of interest or decline to take on the risk. Such a case is currently facing Italy and Portugal's governments.

If the scenario facing both governments and banks is not grim enough, Brenner and Holt say, take the Nonettes' demand for income tax rebates into the equation.

If the government were to give in to the Nonettes' demands, its tax base would be under even greater pressure. One of the conclusions of the report is for the banking sector to impress upon governments that even if they decided to give into the Nonettes, they are not in a position to do so.

Brenner and Holt also add that it is in the banks' interest to support governments in standing up to the Nonettes. If the banks fail and governments do give in then the funds they have lent may not be repaid.

Should this occur, the report remarks ominously, depositors with the banks then might withdraw their funds from them. In turn, if there is a run on the banks and government guarantees are seen as worthless, then the entire financial fabric of the country could be thrown into jeopardy.

The report cautions both banks and governments to take steps to head-off any such eventuality. For Britain it proposes the immediate setting up of a joint Treasury-bank task-force to establish plans against such a possible future eventuality.

In their conclusions Brenner and Holt give a gloomy

Soufin energy units arrival coul see Nonette surge

By Irene Palmer
Economics Editor

THE ARRIVAL of soufin power units has dealt a major blow to the government's energy policies. The new units' arrival is also set to see a massive rise in Nonette numbers.

Confidence in the government energy plans is also set to slump as the consequences of the scale of soufin replacement power units sinks in.

The Cabinet knows that failure to provide full power to consumers will result in yet more people joining the Nonette movement. Even before the units' arrival concerns were raised in both Whitehall and Downing Street over the growth of the Nonettes as well as the movement's growing influence.

Ministers are also aware that there are now more members in the Nonette...

Movement's growth raises government concerns

Though the government has rebuffed Nonette calls for reductions in income taxes, ministers see growing financial resources accruing to the movement could pose a potential threat to government authority.

Some sources estimate that nationally, the Nonette movement's income is now more than £50m a week. If the Nonettes continue their phenomenal rate of growth, this sum will also bound to soar.

Should Nonette numbers no more than double, their combined income will be...

While much of this income will be spent - so the Nonettes claim - on their own communities, ministers are aware the Nonettes' structure enables them to direct this income stream to a unified national purpose should they so decide.

Another dashed plank of the government's energy polices was the belief that consumers would not pay up to £80 a week - 10 per cent of their incomes - for their electricity and gas supplies.

For the million and more people who now have a replacement soufin units - and their cost-free energy - this is evidently not been the case.

Yet, contradictorily, the government has been berated that the charges it has announced for the supply of established gas and electricity supply - an estimated £8 a week - are too high.

Some experts, however,

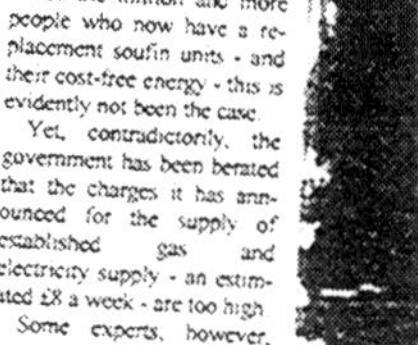

EU says 'No' to Nonettes on tax

By Brian Bunting
Finance Editor

'There can be no concessions'- say finance ministers

NONETTE DEMANDS for tax concessions were given the ...

... of their incomes members pay over to the movement.

The ministers firm and united stand against the Nonette demands has surprised many tax experts. Hans ...

More governments veto Nonettes tax cut call

By Jade Witherspoon
Diplomatic Editor

OECD survey shows "unseemly unanimity" against any tax concessions

FROM AUSTRIA to Zambia, governments around the world have shunned Nonette calls for tax concession, an OECD survey shows.

The Paris based think-tank ...

... taxation levels for members of the Alien back-ed movement.

The head of OECD's monitoring division, Lynne Pollock, said that the survey was the first in the organisation's history where all the governments had given an identical ...

Panama Crisis:

Southern Command concerns grow

Contact with beleaguered garrison lost

By John Roscoe
in Washington

FURTHER REPORTED sightings of Susem delta space craft over the Panama Canal Zone (PNZ) have heightened fears for the safety of the 30,000 soldiers of the US Southern Command.

In Washington the Department of Defence (DoD) has denied that further rescue attempts to relieve the beleaguered force have been called off.

A DoD spokesman said: "The situation of Southern Command's PCZ defence is currently in the process of re-evaluation. The Department of the Navy is standing by to provide every assistance to General Tucers [C in C

"While the overall situation is serious it can by no means be considered as critical."

An increasing number of families of the soldiers serving with Southern Command are petitioning the Pentagon for the immediate withdrawal from Panama. The fears of many of the families are that their men might suffer the same fate as the Brazilian forces.

Lauren Watkins, from Cleveland Ohio and who's husband Ryan is serving with Southern Command, said: "I have read what happened to those men down there in Latin America and I do not want that to happen to my Ryan."

Mrs Watkins is not alone in voicing concern for the ...

England gears up for Sixth Test

Final Test seen as England's last chance to save standing

By Bobby Benerd
Cricket Correspondent

TEST SELECTORS were putting on a brave face yesterday as they named the squad for the forthcoming Test against Namibia at Lords next week.

Head of the selectors, Alan Barraclough, announcing the English side, said "We have picked a number of newcomers as well as recalling some of those who we still consider to show potential in fielding, ...

As Paceillo had Terbal re-configure his globe back to the way the Earth was 10,000 years ago, her "We have no more than the records of the past travellers to go by," sounded innocuous enough and up to then what they had related fitted within the realms of the possible, plausible even. However, what followed had me amazed. But not at first though.

The globe showed Hudson Bay near the top complete with icecap stretching across Canada and another one in the southern Indian Ocean.

Paceillo, pointing to a string of islands which appeared where Antarctica now is, said "According to the records of our last visit this was the centre of an association of communities which stretched to here..." (and she brushing her right hand up the west coast of South America, and with her left, stretching across to southern India, Indochina, then north to Japan) "...and to here, as well as here..." (she rippling her fingers into the Caribbean then across to the Mediterranean). Though as her fingers arrived at Gibraltar there was not a strait and not much Mediterranean, only lakes each side of Sicily. As she dabbed her finger by the Lebanon I saw there was not a Black Sea either, only a puddle in the middle.

Before I could ask why, Terbal said "Ocean levels vere lower at dis time by 200 metres approximately, der polar ice cover vas more extensive although der Earth vas again varming up."

Paceillo continued, "Most of the vestiges of the communities, being coastal settlements are now submerged. Our records show there was council given by us to people during our last visit regarding Venus's then orbital instability and the likelihood of some degree of planetary crust displacement. However, the record also indicates our forecast at the time was that any change would be less than has actually occurred.

"Our prognosis of the outcomes, but based on the geological record of the displacement, indicate that within 200 days the climate of these islands...(she pointing back to Antarctica) would have changed from the current climate of this...(South Island, New Zealand) to that...(Kerguelen) or this...(Iceland) and in another 200 days this...(Greenland). Further cooling would have rapidly followed. This ice cover...(Hudson Bay) though thawing rapidly would have had most of its melt-water retained here...(the Great Lakes, a huge swathe to the east, west and south of them) though some would have drained through this river system here...(the Mississippi).

Paceillo outlined what the Susem thought happened to the islands' survivors, their exodus to the adjacent regions, the worldwide trading network collapsing, tensions between refugees and host populations being as disruptive as that to local agriculture caused by the abrupt change to the climate.

"Though this disturbance," she continued, "would have likely to have continued for some time, the pressure caused by the rising level, increased mass of this melt-water would have remorselessly increased..." As she pointed to it I noticed that Terbal had changed things so there now was huge inland sea stretching from Hudson Bay south to St Louis. "Also," continued Paceillo,

Snatched videos and sound data give damning evidence of police provocation and harsh beatings

Clapham Riot: Police 'lies' exposed

David Mango
Social Affairs Editor

Damning evidence that the Clapham Riot was started by the police and bailiffs was revealed publicly yesterday - from the police's own video and audio tapes.

The tapes were snatched from the police's observation vehicle during the Atherford Road Poll Tax protest. The tapes contain derogatory and racist remarks made by the police observation team even before they arrived at the scene.

Clips from the video show that the bailiffs were armed with baseball bats and lengths of scaffold poles. They also show the bailiffs waving them at the protesters as well as making obscene gestures to them.

Both audio and video tape show people crowded in front of the house with others arriving joining them carrying placards and banners. Police

Later clips show yet more protesters fighting with both police and bailiffs as well as burning vehicles.

The tapes, it is claimed, were taken from the police car after it,too had been set alight.

Last night the Metropolitan Police Commissioner, Sir Paul Harrier, said he was deeply disturbed by the accusations of police misconduct and called for the tapes to be handed to the police so that they might be studied.

Claire Long the Home Secretary has demanded an immediate investigation into the claims against the police.

If the tapes are genuine then they will be a damning indictment against the Metropolitan Police.

The tapes do, however, give weight to the Atherford Road resident's claim that their Nonette association had protested peacefully. That they had been provoked into responding against both police and bailiffs.

One of Atherford's representatives said: "We have

News

Bailiffs demand protection

Outbreaks of violence frighten bailiffs

By Tony Perry
Social Affairs Editor

BRITAIN'S bailiffs are demanding personal protection. Following a spate of attacks against their members, GBA, the national bailiffs' association is demanding protection before they undertake any further debt recovery.

The knock-on effect, their leaders say, could

attacks on bailiffs in Hinckley, Leics, where three bailiffs were chased though the streets by an angry mob, the GBA is calling its members out on a nationwide day of protest.

GBA spokesman, Barry Ives said: "The situation is definitely getting right out of order. Not a day goes by without some of the boys coming up against one of those street pro-

Banks deny blacklisting governments

"We are just being careful" they claim

By Brian Billing
Finance Editor

INTERNATIONAL BANKS and other leading financial institutions denied allegations that they are refusing to lend to governments and other state-backed organisations.

All the leading banks claimed yesterday that they will lend to anyone including governments providing it is viable for them to do so.

Otto Schacht, head of giant Uber Bank said: "Uber is

anyone else's. Therefore it is for us to decide what is in the best interests of our shareholders and not any government diktat.

"All banks are restricted in what they can and cannot do by a web of government, EU, US, WTO regulations, one of which is making provisions for doubtful debts.

"When these are made what we have left is what we can lend and nothing more. Just now, as far as sovereign or government loans are concerned, Uber's coffers are bare."

Herr Schacht also said that Uber, like other banks, had been forced to make provision for billions of dollars against loans to South American countries which are

currently in the hands of the Nonette rebels.

He said that there are many other countries on Uber's critical list and that the resources from the bank's other sectors have to be transferred to cover the shortfalls in sovereign debt repayment.

John Mason, London head of BancLeviathan which has also suffered from massive South American debt defaults, said: "Most of the major banks including BancLev can only currently lend against a borrower's income flow.

"In the case of sovereign-country loans, it is important that there be adequate revenues coming into that country's Treasury which

"Just now as far as the UK is concerned," Mr Mason said, "we are seeing precipitate declines not only in central government taxation flows but also as importantly the deterioration of the prospects for future taxation revenues."

Mr Mason stressed that Britain is not the only leading country experiencing 'sovereign loan famine' but added that the situation was not being helped by the continual Nonette demands for reductions in their income tax deductions.

The view in the City is that the government has to demonstrate to the markets a clear intention to increase its tax revenues in order for it to

'Nonette vigilantes must stop'- Police Chief says

Youth's parents sue police for negligence

By Tony Perry
Social Affairs Editor

COMMANDER Nigel Roland, Head of Hertfordshire Police, reacted angrily to the latest outbreak of Nonette vigilantism.

Commander Roland said that as a result of Nonettes' taking the law into their own hands against a 17 year old Harlow youth, accused by them of bag snatching, his force faces legal proceedings for negligence from the youth's family.

The youth - who cannot be named for legal reasons - was caught by members of a Nonette group in Bishopbury, Harlow, after it was alleged he had snatched the handbag of a pensioner who was waiting at a bus stop.

Cdr. Roland said: "If this young man did, indeed, commit the offence his attackers accused him of then of course, they had their rights as ordinary members of the public to apprehend him and make a 'citizen's arrest'.

Though, of course we, like police forces everywhere strongly advise against so-called 'public spirited' 'have-a-goism' and always remind the public that their proper

report all suspected criminal activity to the police in order that we might deal with the matter in a proper and professional manner.

"But a citizen's arrest," he said, "is as far as members of the public are permitted by law to go.

Consequently there most certainly is no excuse whatsoever for parading that young man naked through the streets with a placard round his neck bearing his name and address, as well as details of his alleged offences. This is not only going beyond what the law permits but is, in fact, breaking it.

"It was not until three hours after the young man said he was first attacked," Cdr. Roland said, "that he was dumped - still in a state of complete undress - on the main Harlow Road in a traumatised and distressed state. During his time of enforced restraint he also said that he was repeatedly assaulted by a number of other people.

"Hertfordshire's Serious Crime Squad are currently investigating this latest case of Nonette vigilantism. Police are calling for witnesses to help with their inquiries. Anyone who witnessed the

George in surprise Arsenal shake-up

Vanderkort ousted

By GRAHAM BOOTH

IN A bid to boost the Gunners' current lacklustre performance, Arsenal's directors have sacked team manager Arno Vanderkort and given the job to Graham George.

Vanderkort is said to have accepted a seven figure sum in settlement.

Graham George

There was an air of grim determination at Highbury yesterday as news of George's comeback became known.

While many supporters were

Fears grow for Panama troops

Warren facing calls for rescue action

By Brett Anderson
in Washington

US PRESIDENT Warren is facing increasing pressure from across the United States for the immediate withdrawal of the 30,000 strong Southern Command force from the Panama Canal Zone.

Both the White House and the Pentagon, however, appear unwilling or unable to give into these growing demands.

Many thousands of families of the soldiers serving in Panama are clamouring for a rescue mission to be mounted to save them from further attacks by the Aliens.

Many Congressmen and Senators say that they are being deluged with demands from anxious relatives of men to press US military to take immediate action.

There are reports however, that the reason why no such relief has been mounted already is that it is regarded by the Department of Defence (DoD) as 'Mission Too Impossible'.

DoD officials fear that should such a rescue operation fail and further soldiers become trapped in Panama or worse, fall into the hands of the Aliens there will be an even louder public outcry.

David Souter of IoS, a Georgetown think-tank said: "The Brazilian military refused to go into Jatai and get their men out. And that was after the Susem had left. The attacks on Panama are still going on.

"The reason why the Brazilians would not take the necessary action to bring their men out was because they could not. No one would go there [Jatai] lest they suffered the same fate.

"Do you really think," Souter queried, "the DoD would dare risk ordering any of our forces to go in there [Panama]?"

Souter also mentioned that the one relief force which did land in Panama disappeared without trace moments after they had landed.

The Pentagon has already acknowledged that

"during this period there were marked increases in tectonic upheaval, earthquakes, volcanic eruptions brought about by the displacement, especially here... (she ran her finger along the Andes to what is now the Aleutians) the abrupt darkening by ash deposition from volcanic eruptions falling on adjacent remaining ice cols would have caused sudden inflows of fresh melt-water and just as sudden breach through here...(the St Lawrence) or here...(the Hudson Strait) perhaps both. The outcome would have been Atlantic-wide tidal waves, rapid rises of world ocean levels. Agri-pisciculture would have ceased due to the sudden submerging of fertile soils and their adjacent littorals. Ambient air temperatures brought about by the immediate influx of so much cold water would have rapidly declined. Organised societies would have ceased, population levels plummeted, survivors soon becoming 'de-civilised'."

In a lighter mood Paceillo related more of the record of the last Susem visit, their meetings with the Australian aborigines, the Ituri tribesmen in the forests east of Oklo and the Dogan tribes further to the west.

As she spoke I thought "That's Atlantis and the Deluge done, what next?" Still nagging though was the original question, "Why had the Susem come here now?" Being an advanced civilisation, with sensors across the heavens, they would have no need to come here. This Oklo couldn't be that dangerous because if it was, we would have known about it ages ago. For that matter what danger was there in the early 1900s, especially of the nuclear variety? Atomic reactors didn't exist until the 1930s. If what Paceillo had said is so, then all her talk about when the Susem first came here, of 'discovering' Earth's so-called 'letum waves', just did not add up.

Neither did what the Susem had originally said about our men. They must have known there were separate sexes from their last visit. Or did they make mayhem with men then, just as they're doing now? All the same I stuck to listening. It was what Paceillo had to say next which confounded me the more.

"Records of our last visit," she said, "further show that we suggested precautions be taken for such eventuality. Advice and instruction was also given as to how these could be brought about. When we arrived on this visit we were first of the view that this advice would have indeed been heeded. Unfortunately, just as in previous times it is evident that such has not been the case. Furthermore, it appears that technical assistance we provided was used for other, inappropriate purposes."

Her "previous times", "inappropriate purposes" had me confused. I had a heap of questions but I kept to listening. With the globe back to the present, Paceillo pointed to southern Peru, the western Andes, adding, "This is the only site we have established evidence of our advice being heeded but even this has been long abandoned. However, the fuller extant of our record of your planet shows this continuing pattern of evolving societal groups followed by their collapse before sustainable progress is re-established."

By now she had almost the tired tone of a schoolteacher reflecting the

Teachers' lea
voice fears ov
Nonette scree
spread

"No substitute for teachers" claims Union head

BY SIEGFRED OLMANN
EDUCATION CORRESPONDENT

Iain MacTaggart

WITH THE upsurge of Nonette teaching screens spreading in the Nonette movement, many of Britain's teachers are voicing concern about their impact on traditional education.

The National Association of Teachers (NAT) is demanding that the screens' use be curbed.

Head of NAT, Iain MacTaggart, said: "All members of the teaching "that parents do not lose sight of the importance of the National Curriculum. If their children do not attain the

Mr MacTaggart's co cerns come on top of rep that the coupons earned fr passing the Teach Screens' tests are be accepted as payment by so

---

TRIALS LATEST : IN FULL - IN DETAIL - 8 PAGES OF PICS

EATEN ALIVE!
MONSTER MANTISES GOBBLE UP DESPOTS

Giant robot insects yank dictators' arms and legs off Baskerville hounds gorge on tyrants' intestines

By MAUREEN GROVE

HUGE PRAYING MANTISES tore arms, legs and heads from former Serb and Croat leaders and their henchmen and then ate them.

For two hours a 60,000 capacity crowd at the National Stadium, Sarajevo, was treated to an action-packed performance of unparalleled cruelty and brutality as both former Serb and Croat dictators, along with their closest cronies, were ripped apart and eaten by 10 metre-tall praying mantis-like robots.

SNATCHED AND EATEN

Directed by Hisogynists standing astride their backs - each one dressed as if giant shimmering butterflies - the mantises snatched and ate one ringleader after another.

SPRAYED OUT AS MINCE SLURRY

Within moments of the mantises munching the last of each murderer's torso, the audience was treated to the further spectacle of each entire digested corpse sprayed as a slurry of mince from the insects' rear ends and then being gobbled up by packs of big black dogs.

From beginning to end the audience - including an estimated 2bn TV viewers world-wide - were treated to a non-stop spectacular of never-before-seen acts of bestiality and savagery as the tyrants were held like candy bars by the monster mantises.

HEADS CHOMPED OFF

With their legs kicking and jerking these men of evil had their heads champed off. Yet other once top-dogs were having their limbs yanked from their bodies - just as some humans do to insects - then eat-en by the mantises as if they were drumsticks.

FIENDS' EVIL FACES

The audience was also able to watch close-ups of the action on ringside screens - relayed from cameras inside the man two metre-wide eyes - inc these once powerful fiends' as they were eaten.

LAST LAUGH DICKIE'S

The head of SLI TV, Derek Igg, talking of the overall success of 'Trials' and last night's record viewing figures, said: "They all laughed at Dickie [Bear] when he took on 'Trials' but now these high-up know-alls have egg over their smug faces.

It just goes to show how right Dickie was when he said people like nothing more than to see a good topping and that they can't get enough of seeing those evil murdering bastards getting it.

"And take it from me," Derek added, "last night's toppings, 62 in space of two hours, is going to take some beating."

Media analysts are already saying that SLI's earnings from 'Trials' will mean bumper dividends for shareholders.

Siobhain O'Hara in Sarajevo reports:

FOLLOWING the lengthy, afternoon-long trial on charges of being the perpetrators of Bosnian War Crimes, of crime and atrocities against humanity, the former Croatian dictator, Franjo Prost, his Serbian counterpart, Milo Gadan and the coteries of their closest co-conspirators, all 62 of them were found guilty.

They were then marched the two kilometres to the National Stadium dressed in nothing more than their vests and pants. Once in the arena they were whipped into nine big cages which were then covered with cloths.

With a fanfare of trumpets heralding the opening bars of Decousu's melodious 'Prelude to Trial's Overture' the stadium lights dimmed to total darkness.

As strains of the first movement of Trials next gently drifted across the arena and reminiscent as it was of Van Gelis's 'Chariots of Fire', one overhead spotlight after another beamed down. These lights gradually illuminated the arena and a pack of large black dogs slowly padding around its otherwise deserted, sand-covered, undulating surface.

A further beam of light then shone down onto one of the cages and the dogs now sat in front of it.

With the music now fading away the cloth slid off of the cage as its door slowly swung open. The dogs then padded inside of it and the men ran out.

Chased by the dogs the men ran to the centre of the arena. One man - the former Croatian Police Chief, Mate Josip - ran faster than the others. He ran towards a small sand hill.

No sooner was he on this

Before Josip could even change direction the mantis snatched him in its claw.

Still holding Josip, the mantis rose higher out of the sand. With the police chief now held several metres in the air the mantis then opened its eyes and look down at him.

At the same time a Hisogynist, who had been crouched unnoticed on the mantis's back, sprang to her feet.

Shaking off her sand-coloured cloak she revealed a glittering costume which, with its bat-wings gave her the appearance of a butterfly.

The other men fled from the mantis but several of them ran into the paths of further mantises which, as they rose from the sand dunes also grabbed them in their claws. The remaining men, now no longer chased by the dogs, ran farther into the arena.

But [of course] unknown to them other mantises were lurking beneath the sand. As a consequence these murderers were also unaware of these mantises as they rose up from the sand and began stealthily creeping up on them.

Some of the dramatic effect was lost however, by sections of the audience shouting: "It's behind you."

This, though, did not lessen the look of terror in the men's faces as the mantises bore down on them snatched them up in their claws and held them in the air. Nor, as the mantises begin pulling the men's arms and legs off.

The screams of these men, as they bucked and writhed and were shown in close-up from large screens positioned around the terraces. There were roars of approval as the mantises began eating the men's arms and legs. But

---

Councils plead
for more money

Poll Tax strike beginning to bite

Barry Davies
Home Affairs
Correspondent

COUNCILS throughout the country are making urgent pleas to the Treasury for immediate injections of cash. Their calls are seen as yet further evidence that the "Poll Tax Strike" is beginning to bite.

There is however, another and perhaps more worrying reason for many councils' current cash crisis, a collapse of confidence.

Many councils are reporting a reluctance on the part of money markets and City institutions to hold Local Government bonds.

A clutch of metropolitan councils, including several in London are also faced with City and other lenders' demands for accelerated repayment of their existing short-term loans.

Faced with this crisis of confidence in their financial situation, Local Government leaders are to seek Treasury assistance in covering the shortfalls many of them are experiencing.

Manchester Councillor Brian Heatlewaite, who is leading the delegation to the Treasury, said: "All local authorities were suffering cash-flow shortages before this non-payment of Council Tax broke out but it's been the last straw for many of them including us in Manchester.

"It's a case of either we get substantial Treasury assistance or we are given no alternative than to cut services," Cllr Heatlewaite said, "No one wants to go down that road but with the current sentiment of the financial markets turning against local government, then either the

---

'Red tide' th
- warns Di

Senator call for purge of Nonettes and 'f

BY BRETT ANDERSON
IN WASHINGTON

"THE red tide which has swept through the Americas is set to engulf the United States of America itself unless urgent measures are taken," warned US Senator Sam Dich yesterday.

Addressing the Senate Foreign Affairs sub-committee on the Mexican crisis, Senator Dich, said: "We are witnessing one country after another subsumed into an ever deepening ocean of red darkness. Government after government have been forced to flee their own countries.

"A day does not pass when

Senator Sam Dich

we forced to watch these Aliens deluging our television screens with gloating scenes of their kangaroo courts, their

sions' sentencing statesmen, politicians, administrators, businessmen even men of the Church who have been caught in their net, to unjust and inhuman punishments including hard labour and public castration.

"Day after day the minds of the people of the United States are being brainwashed by these scenes of brutality. How long will it be before ordinary people begin to see us, their democratically elected representatives in the same, evilly warped light?"

Sam Dich, the right-wing Utah Senator, called on the government to take control of

---

President in Panama families scuffle

By Paulo Ridde
In New York

ANGRY ANTI-PANAMA PROTESTERS shouted and jostled President Warren in Pittsburgh yesterday.

Although the President was unharmed by the incident he appeared visibly shaken by the protesters.

Last night White House spokesman Larry Waters said: "While President Warren was surprised at the unscheduled meeting with servicemen's families during his visit to the

"The President is thankful in being able to take the opportunity in of saying that he too shares the concerns of the families of Southern Command's forces stationed in Panama. At no time was the President's security placed in jeopardy."

The 'Pittsburgh Outburst' - as the incident has been dubbed - is yet another sign of the growing wave of protest across the United States against the stationing of its forces in the Panama Canal

fecklessness of her pupils, and I still thought it best not to ask questions especially as she continued in the same vexed vein. "The society which was established here," she said, and pointing to an island in Lake Huron, "is another typical example. It had all the indications of progress but according to the visit before last's record, its people had disappeared without trace."

I now ventured "When was this?"

Her reply had me most astounded. "Ooh about 85,000 years ago," she said.

Following my "What!" and in her pause, I rushed in with "There can't be. Humans weren't in North America until 12,000 years ago, mankind wasn't in anything more than tribes of hunters, there wasn't even Homo Sapiens then."

With a shrug she said "If you say so," then "Terbal"

In an instant it was "Sheguiandah, Manitoullin Island...1951-5, Thomas Lee, archaeologist National Museum Canada...team's excavations convirmed human societal artefacts...vrom 120-80,000 years...date perimeter convirmation by geologists Vayne State University..."

Paceillo interrupted with "This is just from your colleagues' investigations."

"...Artivacts convirm extensive trading viff metvorking..."

"Also here" interrupted Paceillo again and pointing to the Jordan valley.

Immediately Terbal had switched to "Extensive voodvorking...evidence of metal tools...date 500,000 years, convirmed 1989, Naama Goren-Inbar, University of Jerusalem...more artivacts."

"And here," said Paceillo and pointing to northern Italy.

Terbal continued, "Castenedolo...vosselised Homo Sapiens skeletons unearved 1860-80...carbon dating British Museum 1969 established age auf 3.5 million years...remains auf boat-like craft also vound suggesting..."

"This was," said Paceillo pointing to northern Italy, "then a lake shore."

"...Drowning," continued Terbal.

"But," continued Paceillo, "they were contemporaneous with these Homo Sapiens," (and pointing to Lake Victoria, the Rift Valley).

I could hold back no more and rushed in with, "This simply isn't so, humans, modern ones didn't exist then, you're just saying all this, where's your..."

But from behind me came "Evidence enough?" I turned and there was Menpemelo folding out her pocket screen. It had a picture of a grey flat rock with lines of little dents but the moment she said "These fossilised footprints..." I had recognised that they were just that.

And Terbal was immediately elaborating, "Olduvai Gorge...recorded 1978 Leakey expedition...50 vootprints crossing 23 metres auf recently deposited volcanic ash...made by dree hominoids valking...verified Russell Tuttle, anatomist University auf Chicago.."

I had no sooner said "They would have been apemen," than wished I had not for Paceillo just as quickly said "As your Professor Tuttle observed, all apes have divergent big toes, only hominoids have non-divergent toes... (and with Menpemelo's screen now showing enlargements) ...these footprints are most

Treasury rebuffs Councils' cash pl

Town halls in services cut dilemma

Andrea Hardy
Local Government Correspondent

Local Government leaders came away empty-handed from their meeting with Treasury officeials yesterday.

The Treasury has turned down requests for extra funds to cover shortfalls in council revenues caused by the bailiffs' "Poll Tax" strike.

Admitting defeat, Manchester councillor, Brian Heathlewaite, who led the Local Authorities' delegation said: "Treasury officials turned us down without so much as listening to our arguments.

"In not so many words they [Treasury officials] told us that we were on our own. They said we must redouble our efforts to collect the Community Charge owed to us and in the meantime reduce our costs.

"What this means," Councilor Heathlewaite said, "is that ordinary people are going to suffer a loss of services which not only have they

the bailiffs to force peop to pay their Communi Charge there is nothi else councils can do make them pay up."

Councillor Heathlewaite

Non-payment of the Community Charge is only part of the financial problem Councils face. Fellow delegation member, Valerie Martin, of Lambeth Council, said: "What is just as worrying for many councils, especially here in London, is the massive increase in the withdrawal of funds placed with councils.

"It is not just City institutions who are encashing council paper but ordinary people as well. All are worried that we might run out of money and be unable to pay.

"The Treasury in refusing us assistance," she said, "is doing little more than sending out the message that the government is not going to stand by us."

Councillor Martin said

CHRON SPECIAL VIDEO/DVD OFFER

THE LAST TRIALS The Finale: The MANTISES!

SHOWS SCORES OF TOP MURDERING YUGO THUGS BEING EATEN ALIVE BY MONSTER MANTISES

SEE the Serb, Croat dictators as they are let out their cages
SEE these once top thugs as they're chased by huge Baskerville hounds
SEE the Monster Mantises snatch these callous killers in their claws
SEE the Hisogynists in their glittering butterfly costumes
SEE these star studded stunners astride the Mighty Mantises' backs
SEE the Balkan butchers writhe and squirm as they are lifted to mouths of mantises
SEE their evil faces in close-up as Mantises' teeth and talons tug at their limbs
SEE these butchering Balkan bastards as the Mantises twist and tug at their limbs
HEAR their screams as the Mantises pull their arms and legs off and eat them
SEE these fiends' faces as the blood pumps out of their stumps
SEE the Hisogynists as their costumes change to Death's Head Hawk moths
SEE these 'Moths of Doom' direct the Mantises to dispatch the Balkan despots
SEE the Mantises as they bite these murdering Balkan bullies' heads off
SEE these odious ogres' heads in close-up as the Mantises munch them
SEE the blood and bits of brain as they dribble down their bodies
SEE these murdering Balkan bastards' bodies as the Mantises gobble them up
SEE the Baskerville hounds sitting round the Mantises' rear ends
SEE the Mantises as they squirt slurries of the murderers' minced remains
SEE the dogs as they lap it up

SEE in the comfort of your own home more than two hours of tastefully and caringly edited highlights of all the Praying Mantises' and Hisogynists' performances; also includes Jean Charles Decoursu's musical score 'Mantis' which was specially composed for the event.

For a copy of this Limited Collector's Edition call: 0800 154 154 154 with your credit/debit card details at the ready

Kirk ban lifte

George brings back 'Glaswegian from Hell' for IFEA Munich clash

By Don Jonsen

THE BAN ON Don Kirk has been lifted. In a specially convened Premiership Association meeting Arsenal boss Graham George, charmed them into reversing the year-long ban on the wayward Scot.

Arsenal sources say that Graham was able to show that video evidence which appeared to show Kirk head-butting the three Tottenham players in end-of-season Derby was inconclusive. George also persuaded the Premiership bosses that Kirk had only assaulted the other three Spurs players in self defence.

With Kirk back in the frame for the

POLL TAX RIOTS SHOC

'Scab' bailiffs pelted with stones
'Official' bailiffs to blacklist Burnley

By Susam McBeth

A POSSE of Spanish bailiffs were pelted with a barrage of bricks and bottles as they sought to repossess council houses and flats of non-payers of Burnley's Community Charge.

Last night angry residents of Trawden Estate were calling for a council-wide rent strike by all the council's tenants.

GBH, the national bailiffs association has deplored Burnley's actions and said that even when the present strike was over its members would still black the council.

A Burnley council spokesman said: "The council deeply regrets the actions that have taken part on the Trawden Estate.

"The use of foreign bailiffs was not authorised by the council but were engaged by Grasp-alot plc, the company contracted to manage the administration of Burnley's Community Charge collection.

"We have already informed the Estate's councillors of this unfortunate incident and have asked them to accept and convey our deepest of apologises to the residents.

"Although both of the councillors are presently away on business we have already sent members of the Burnley's

Warren announces Panama rescue bid

By Brett Anderson
in Washington

THE 30,000 STRONG force of the US's Southern Command is to be rescued from the Panama Canal Zone.

A specially formed task force is undertake the mission which is expected to begin within the next few days

In the President's address to the nation, President Warren, said that he was determined that every man serving with Southern Command will be brought out of the Canal Zone

While the President did not mention specific details of the rescue mission, he did say that it was fraught with risk but that he was sure that the American people would be behind him in wish it

Special Forces thought to be in Canal rescue bid

Last night political commentators were saying that President Warren, stung by the strength of public outcry at the soldiers' plight and what they saw as the Pentagon's indifference or at best inaction, was forced into taking action to free the soldiers.

But the President's decision is not without its critics. Howard Stone of CVN said: "Yet once again we have a President formulating policy on the hoof rather than thinking

certainly made by non-divergent toes are they not?" As ever, Paceillo was right.

Almost defensively I blurted, "It doesn't mean they were anything more than primitive..." but met with Menpemelo clicking the side of her screen.

As she nonchalantly said "What about these?" the screen showed a black and white picture of a pestle and mortar.

Terbal broke into fresh commentary, "Smifsonian Institution..." and as Paceillo pointed to California, "...Table Mountain, vestern Yosemite...numerous artivacts unearved 1850-77 in alluvial gravel deposits...in excess of 500 metres below ground surface...duration auf deposition 33-50 million years...human skeletal bones including skulls present....many artivacts manuvactured vrom andesite...nearest deposits auf dis 150 kilometres distant... necklaces auf drilled mastodon ivory..."

This was just the start. For the next hour, as Menpemelo's screen flashed up image after image and as Paceillo pointed around the globe, Terbal narrated. With their continued reiterated "These are just from your own investigations," I was shown not just those of bones and stone things but cubes of milled nickel carbon steel, gold bracelets, necklaces and scores of other 'manufactured' objects, and not just tens but hundreds of millions of years old. Paceillo, as she pointed to each place, America, Germany, Russia, Scotland, on and on, added how over time the world changes, sites become buried, if not underground then under water. She also said that, although the Susem record was more extensive than ours, it shows that nearly everything ever created disintegrated long ago.

As they progressed and though stunned to silence, forming in my mind was "Why haven't I, 'we' been told about all this? Why have we been 'fed' this 'Out of Africa' guff, how we are 'recent', come down from the apes, modern man no more than 30,000 years old."

And as Menpemelo's screen flipped up another bed of rock, this thought grew. With Paceillo pointing to Texas, Terbal said, "Paluxy River, 1969...14 human vootprints each 285 millimetres complete viff all vive toes in vossilised mud-flats...more van 110 million years old...line auf 134 prints auf dree toed dinosaur also...crossing human steps und impressing on dem..."

More images, dates and places of footprints followed from America, Africa, Turkey, Turkmenistan, all of humans' alongside those of dinosaurs.

The screen image changed from footprints to that of just a single foot, a shoeprint. As Terbal intoned "Nevada 1922...age 213 million years, verified by Rockeveller Institute..." I saw not only was it complete with sole and heel but detail of stitching attaching them to the shoe's welt as well. Another shoeprint and Terbal's, "Antelope Springs, Utah 1968...oil shale deposition 250 million years duration...250 by 90 millimetres..."

"Notice," interrupted Paceillo, "the indentation of the toes. It has been caused by the wearer stepping onto what is clearly a trilobite shellfish, a genus which, as you know (but of course I didn't) became extinct 200 million years ago, the indentation in the heel of another trilobite which crawled over the shoe's imprint only after it had been made."

School truancy shock surge f[...]

Teaching Screen ban demanded

By Chris Stimson
Education Correspondent

SCHOOLS across Britain are experiencing massive rises in truancy, teaching professionals claimed yesterday.

At the Conference of the National Association of School Attendance Enforcement Officers, speaker after speaker told of their increased workload since the Nonette teaching screens arrived.

Ealing's Head of Enforcement, David Hall said: "In the space of just one month my department's workload has doubled.

"Yet we have not received a single extra penny from the Department of Education and Employment," he said.

"Previously we were able to put pressure on the truant's parents. But now truants' parents, especially of one of these Nonette groups, tell us to mind our own business.

Iain MacTaggart

"We have had more than one parent go as far as to tell my officers that their children are learning more from these screens than they ever did at their schools."

Another speaker, Eric Simpson of Bradford's Enforcement Department, said: "Ever since shops started accepting the coupons these screens give out in exchange for things such as sweets and [...] has given children every incentive to study at them rather than at school."

The National Association of Teachers representative, Iain MacTaggart, said: "My members initially welcomed the smaller class sizes because of extensive truancy.

"However, if truancy remains at their present high levels and heaven forbid that they should grow any higher," he said "it will lead inevitably to many of my members losing their jobs, especially those on fixed term contracts.

"With all national and local government expenditure under pressure it will be only a matter of time before classes are consolidated with fewer teaching jobs available."

Mr MacTaggart was not alone in demanding extra resources be made available to combat the growing trend of school [...]

Government in pa[...] spending cuts dr[...]

Taxes set to soar and services slashed as revenues [...]

By Irene Palmer
Economics Editor

THE CABINET is expected to agree unprecedented cuts in government spending. The Departments of Health, Social Security and Education are said to at the forefront of the cuts.

The sudden cut in spending is in response to the government being faced with pressures drastically reduce borrowing while at the same time being suffering a rapid decline in its anticipated tax revenues.

A senior Treasury official said that the government was given little choice but to act. "Hard times call for hard measures," he said. "Think of the government as a family which spends and borrows against its anticipated income," he said, "but as the same time as this family discovers its expected income is suddenly reduced by 20 per cent the Bank Manager calls in the overdraft and puts up the cost of future borrowing.

"Something has to give, including cuts in the household budgets. This is the situation currently facing, not just our government, but also those across the entire OECD."

Although Whitehall refuses to comment officially on the planned cuts, there are many insiders prepared to speak off-the-record, itself a surprising new departure and leading to suspicions that they are 'officially leaking' the bad news drip by drip.

Several of these unofficial reports said a massive on tax evasion, is planned With it there are also planned increases in the powers to the Inland Revenue and Customs and Excise, as well as extra personnel in a bid to crackdown.

Other off-the-record reports blame the money markets for the government's problems.

Another Treasury official said: "The Financial Markets are twitchy. All the major banks have lost a packet from the Nonettes taking over one country after another that they have lent money to.

"Elsewhere the [money] markets see the Nonettes increasing in numbers and power. They also see that governments, particularly in the West, suffering from falling tax revenues. It's no wonder they are wary of taking on more lending until [...]

Northern Argentina goes over to Nonette[...]

Jujuy and Salta Provinces oust Governo[...]

Polly Portillo
from Buenos Aires

ARGENTINA'S northernmost, poorest and most corrupt provinces of Jujuy and Salata have gone over to the Nonettes.

More disaffected provinces in the region are expected to follow suit. Many thousands of refugees are reported to have fled the area.

The central government in Buenos Aires has declared a national state of emergency. The army has rushed forces to the region and detachments of paramilitary police are said to be massing in nearby Tucumán. So far no casualties have been reported.

Last night Argentinean President Carlos la Rua called the two provinces' breakaway a 'national tragedy of historic proportions'. The President said that it was important that at "this difficult time" the entire Argentinean nation unites in "helping our fellow countrymen" in Jujuy and Salta to reflect on their "ill-judged" actions and return to "the welcoming arms of us, their brothers."

The President's guarded response to the Nonette rebels was matched by both members of Congress and the armed forces.

Argentina's leaders need no reminding that the main Nonette forces and their Susem backers are less than 200km away. That they could come swiftly to the breakaway provinces' defence and inflict heavy losses to the Argentinean forces.

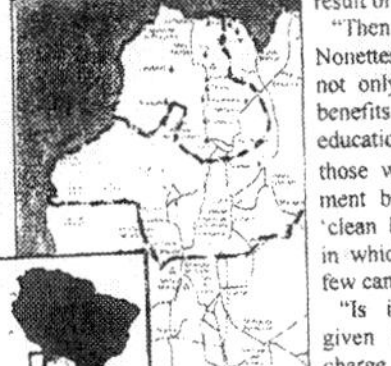

For many observers in Buenos Aires and the country's second city, Córdoba, there is little surprise at the uprising. Several of them are already predicting that more provinces in Argentina's economically depressed northwest will breakaway in the coming weeks.

Fernando Alvarez, of the Alfa think-tank, said: "The region is plagued with corruption and cronyism. In the northwest the gap between the few rich and the many poor is shocking even by Argentinean standards.

"Because of extensive and engrained corruption within the ruling elite of the region - politicians, the bureaucracy, landowners, even the church hierarchy - there has been a complete absence of inward investment.

"Consequently, unemployment in the Northwest is three times the national average. It is the only region in the country where the population is actually falling as a result of economic migra[...]

"Then along come [...] Nonettes. They have bro[...] not only the direct ma[...] benefits of free ene[...] education and healthcar[...] those who join their m[...]ment but also they offe[...] 'clean hands' administra[...] in which all rather than [...] few can participate activel[...]

"Is it any wonder, [...] given the chance to [...] charge of their own fut[...] the population has grabbe[...] with both hands?" he said.

Another commenta[...] Rene Faveloro of [...] *Assunsion*, Argentina's le[...]ing newspaper, said: [...] comes as no surprise that [...] ruling establishment of [...] Northwest have fled [...] region.

"These elites on see[...] their power usurped by [...] Nonettes and mindful of [...] consequences of bei[...] arraigned before a Nonet[...] 'Truth Commission' [...] charges of corruption a[...] then found guilty got o[...] while they could.

"It is no wonder either th[...] the police and army, havi[...] seen what happened to th[...] Brazilians at Jatai, are reluc[...]ant to enter Jujuy or Salata."

With the growth [...] numerous Nonette grou[...] throughout the rest of Argen[...]tina many people also a[...] asking: "Which province wi[...] be next?" but "What [...] anything can be done to sto[...] the Nonettes?"

Others however, are no[...] stopping to ask. Every sea[...] on Aerolineas Argentina's flights to the US and Europe are fully booked.

International news

Surprise mission of mercy by unarmed non-combatants save soldi[...] 20,000 casualties, many tortured; medics on standby, hospitals clear

Girl scouts and nuns in dramatic Panama Force rescu[...]

Ian Trigg
In Washington

In an act of supreme bravery and daring, 2,000 girl scouts and nuns in a top secret mission have successfully rescued thousands of trapped, injured soldiers of the US Southern Command from Panama.

The scouts and nuns were secretly recruited by the Pentagon from across the southern United States. They were flown to the US Navy's Sixth Fleet stationed 15 miles off-shore of Panama's Caribbean coast.

At first light yesterday morning, navy launches of the Sixth Fleet, piloted by the scouts landed their troops as well as nuns at the port of Colon.

During the day First Aid teams of both the scouts and nuns worked non-stop transporting wounded soldiers to the waiting launches. These then ferried the men back to waiting US Navy hospital ships. By yesterday evening, more than 8,000 wounded and traumatised troops had been brought to safety.

It is understood that during the coming days further troops of both scouts and nuns will risk travelling along the length of Panama Canal itself. There are plans, it is reported, for the scouts to make for the western end of the Canal and where the main Southern Command force is reported to be situated.

Other reports, however, say that Susem attacks against these troops are still taking place.

Neither the US Army nor the Department of Defense have given details of the soldiers' extent of the injuries except to state that although severe, none are considered life-threatening.

Further, and as yet unconfirmed reports say that all the men evacuated are in need of immediate surgery.

Late yesterday casualties were arriving at the US air base at Pensacola, Florida.

From Pensacola the wounded are being dispersed for treatment to hospitals and other medical facilities across southern US.

Although the precise nature of the injuries suffered by US forces, have not, as yet been officially disclosed, it has been reported that they are similar to those suffered by the OTSA forces at Jatai.

Should the injuries suffered by Southern Command's forces indeed be the same as the Brazilians, then there is the likelihood the victims can expect to suffer lasting damage to their penises.

If these unofficial reports are confirmed it is likely that US Army will be facing, huge multi-million dollar claims for compensation from the injured soldiers as well as from their families

In Brief

Nonette coupon use spreads

Even pubs take them now

THE WASHINGTON Pub, Hampstead, is credited with being the first to offer pints at half price in exchange for a Nonette teaching screen coupon.

Other nearby pubs, not wishing to lose the Nonette trade, were soon following suit. Ma[...] non-Nonette pub-goers soon saw advantage joining the Nonettes.

As the number of participating pubs has swelled and coupons in landlords' hands grown, the breweries soon saw its sense of accepting them in exchange for supplies of beer, wine and spirits. So did other supplier[...] Then one thing, it seems, has led to another.

Not only are pubs filled with people studying for drink but also amusement machines and televisions are, often as not, switched off!

Many shops now also accept the coupons instead of cash. One of the advantages for traders in accepting the coupons are the tax advantages: no tax! However, it is only a

I spluttered, "Humans, dinosaurs existing at the same time? Surely not?"

But straight back Paceillo said, "They still are." And just as swiftly she had Menpemelo's screen show shots of dozens of dinosaurs, apparently all alive and well and living in Likouala, a swamp twice the size of Ireland up the side of the River Congo. The bigger ones, like elephants with long necks, Paceillo said we would call Diplodocus and some of the smaller species, she added, the Pharaohs once had as pets. To prove this point she not only had Menpemelo's screen show 5,000 year old Egyptian vases with carved images of these beasts complete with halters but also stressed the anatomical accurateness of the other animals, lions and buffaloes which were depicted on the vases as well. Not content with this, Paceillo next had the screen show cave drawings from France and Spain of dinosaurs alongside precisely portrayed bison, deer and horses, adding that there had once been many of them about.

Though thoughts of serpents, dragons and St George passed through my mind, other, angrier ones were hardening in there as well. I had accepted, if Susem knowledge and notions are anything to go by, that Earthly scientists have a heck of a lot wrong, that there is ignorance and prejudice along with woolly thinking and unfounded assertions throughout their professions.

In a way I had come to terms with this but for them to knowingly withhold, deny so many truths, facts, evidence at complete variance to their so-called 'theories' that they have been pumping out, amounts to nothing less than one gigantic con. Generation after generation of them had been brainwashing us with lies, yet at the same time they have had this information hidden away in their museums, institutes and other fancy places. And all the money they have had off of us, us 'ordinary' people. Why, they are no more, the whole stinking lot of them, than a bunch of lying conniving charlatans who should be run out of town or at least stripped of their high faluting ways.

But I was stopped mid-thought by Paceillo's "It is our understanding that Homo Sapiens, or close companions, have existed on Earth for many millions of years. Populations and societal groupings have risen and declined numerous times. By some criterion your current society has developed further than those of the past, but by other considerations it is still immature."

I had nothing to say to this for I didn't really know what to make of what she had said. Though I still didn't have a real answer to why the Susem had come here, it was now almost beside the point. Anyway, then was not the time to ask.

Giving a knowing schoolteacher smile, Paceillo said "I hope that this information has been of assistance," then, "I must now depart," and promptly did so.

But Menpemelo, as if sensing the ire in my mind towards Earthly scientists said, almost wistfully, "A theory which needs to reject evidence in order to survive is not a theory but a theogony, the perpetuation of a myth. And proponents of theogonies are theologues, priests." Upon which she too gave a smile (a wry one) and then also departed.

And Terbal having closed down his globe was back watching the football.

Movement's closed economic system set to cause market instability

Nonette bloc poses threat to world trade - say economists

By Ross Capulyard and Matt Henderson

The disruption the Nonettes have caused to the world's 'Global Economy' is little more than an irritation compared to the threat they now pose.

Unless the world's leading trading blocks, the European Union (EU), North American Free Trade Association (NAFTA), Association of South East Asian Nations (ASEAN), unite in a concerted action to protect themselves, then both advanced and developing economics alike could face economic meltdown.

In a recent paper, ***'Nonette economics?:"You ain't seen nothing yet"*** published in the latest issue of the prestigious ***'Big Worries Monthly'*** the authors, Charles Marle and David Wilkins both economic professors at MIT, first list the economic gains and losses to the world caused the Nonettes.

To date, the costs, they say, are - in global terms -- minimal. Losses to governments and banks which have lent to countries - mainly in Latin America - which have been taken over by the Nonettes, amount to some $100 billion.

Such an amount, the authors say, is less than one per cent of US Treasury bonds, less than 10 per cent of what passes through the London money markets ***every single day***.

Current effects

The sum total of world trade lost because of the Nonettes overrunning these countries, as well as the northern half of Brazil, is less than two per cent-age points. The authors point out that as far as Brazil is concerned, the tax revenue rais-ed by the city of São Paulo alone, is five times that of the area currently under Nonette control.

None of the territories under Nonette rule, Marle and Wilkins say, possess or control resources or commodities vital to the rest of the world. The only exception being is the cessation of cocaine from the former Columbia.

They add, however, that as cocaine was never part of the formal world economy, it has little detrimental effect upon it. Similarly, the once international importance of the Caribbean island states taken over by the Nonettes had been as tax havens and money launderers. Their closures make actually benefited the world's formal economy.

The potential disruption to world energy supplies and distribution caused by the failure of the first soufin power units appears not to have been realised.

Effects of soufins

The take-up of replacement soufin units, Marle and Wilkins say, has surprised most forecasters including themselves. However, it is in the size and scale of this uptake, they claim, that the seed of a potential worldwide crises lies.

Although official figures do not currently exist for the number of replacement units in use outside Nonette controlled areas, they must be, Marle and Wilkins say, already in excess of 100 million, with their numbers rising rapidly.

They also say that the main areas of the units' distribution is not in the developing world but in the advanced economies. While many units are for domestic purposes, increasing numbers are being used by business including in vehicles.

While business's have been obliged to use these cost-free energy units - or lose custom to competitors who already do [use them] - they also have no choice other than to join the Nonette movement as part of the bargain.

The authors mention, however, that to date, there has been little reported resistance to joining the Nonette movement from business soufin users.

Closed economies

The regions under Nonette control: the former Yugoslavia, areas of eastern central Europe, assorted islands as well as others in Latin America are 'closed' to non-Nonettes; closed commercially as well as socio-politically.

The economies o f these Nonette regions, the authors say, not only function increasingly independently of the rest of the world but are rapidly developing along quite different lines - and apparently more successfully so - than those of the outside world.

The Nonette's so-called 'Continental Congress' of South America is, for instance not only actively trading with other Nonette controlled territories but it is also enmeshing them both economically as well as politically, into a single economic bloc. The Congress is also welding them into a single socio-political entity as well.

Not even the old Soviet Union managed this degree of separation from the rest of the world, Marle and Wilkins say.

Capital formation

One of the major differences powering this economic separateness is the method of its financing. In the outside world, the control of capital - wealth - has congregated into ever fewer hands but in the Nonette economy, not only does the complete opposite apply - capital is in the hands of all - it is funded differently.

Whereas the outside world generates increases in capital (cash supply) by central banks issuing extra bonds (IOUs backed solely by 'confidence') the Nonettes generate their increases in capital by individuals earning bonds - income - through study, thus tangibly increasing the collective educational ability - and subsequent wealth - of their citizens.

It is this difference in capital creation, Marle and Wilkins say, which poses the biggest threat to the outside world's economic and political stability.

As more and more people and businesses in the developed world change over to the Nonette system - direct, new wealth-generation through education - then not only will two separate, yet intertwined economies be operating and competing for allegiance in the same physical space (including taxation) but also within their populations.

If no more than a small number of those opting for the 'Nonette economy' and who also hold central bank IOUs - no matter how far removed from direct ownership they might be - decide to cash them in, then the old world's capital base - along with its 'confidence' - could disappear within a frighteningly short time, they say.

Economies threatened

Marle and Wilkins add that even a gold ingot is worthless if nobody wants to buy it. The same applies not only to stocks and bonds but also to currencies as well. They say that economies where the currencies became worthless - such as the Weimar Republic's - they are eventually replaced by those which was not.

Should confidence in the developed world's currencies falter, they say, then the stronger one which people may well turn to - the Nonettes' - will also entail taking on an entirely new socio-political way of life as well.

DMA warns on 'unseen dangers'

Doctors doubt Nonette 'booths'

BY DAVID MCKEILTY
MEDICAL EDITOR

WHILE welcoming the arrival of the first of so-called 'Mormic' Health Booths in Britain, the DMA, the leading doctors' association, said that they can never be a substitute for professional medical care.

The first of 27 booths to arrive in Britain were delivered to Nonette groups around country yesterday. No sooner had each of the booths and their instructors arrived at their destinations than long queues of Nonette members had formed waiting for their supposed 'miracle cures'.

The Mormics, which look like instant-photo booths, gave each 'patient' less than 15 minutes of treatment.

At a Nonette centre in Swindon which had one of the booths those waiting their turn were made to queue in nothing but their bath robes or dressing gowns and probably risked hypothermia into the bargain. However, none of those queuing seemed to really mind this discomfort.

Flashing lights

Having paid their 'admission' of 18 Nonette teaching coupons, each person then had to suffer the further ignominy of taking off their robes and dropping them outside the booth while it 'treated' them.

Pins-and-needles

And what a bizarre treatment it appeared to give. People waiting outside for their turn were given a show of

Last night both doctors and electronic experts alike were casting doubts on the booths' effectiveness in curing people.

One GP, Dr Howard Jones, said: "Human bodies not only are complex things but also each one is so different from another. Therefore, I cannot see how it is possible that a single uniform type of treatment, be it from one of these booths or any other mode of treatment, can apply to everyone. It just is not possible.

'Psychosomatic'

"This only 'one size fits all' medical treatment is 'psychosomatic', the so-called 'doctor's coloured water syndrome': if your GP says its good for you then it must be good. But this will only work in a tiny percentage of cases. If this is the case of these health booths, then people will soon see them for the hoaxes they most probably are."

Dr Jones' colleague, Dr William Johns also warned against the dangers of the booths. He said: "If these booths work by way of electromagnetic waves similar to radiotherapy then one part of sof[t] body tissue is going to be damaged at the expense of others.

'Could be harmful'

"Over the long-term," he said, "this is mor[e] than likely to harm th[e] body overall. One o[f the] things we in the medica[l] profession are constantl[y] bombarded with by ou[r] patients is to give th[e] latest treatment: th[e]

Refugee resentment grows in US

"They are fugitives from justice not refugees" - claims Senator

Gordon Richardson
in New York

There is growing resentment of the huge influx of refugees entering the United States from Mexico and elsewhere in Latin America

In the eyes of many ordinary Americans these new arrivals are not genuine refugees but crooks, corrupt bureaucrats and politicians fleeing the justice and punishment due to them.

An estimated 2,000 refugees from Latin American countries are arriving in the US each day Many of the arrivals are originally from countries - such as Peru and northern Brazil - which have already been overrun by the Nonettes.

While some land with little more than the clothes they are

Each day's Susem telecast gives a list of names of 10 or so of those wanted for trial. Alongside each person's name and reputed crimes is their present whereabouts. It is the repeated: 'thought to be in the United States' which caused widespread resentment against the Latin American arrivals.

It is the recent change in the telecasts from 'thought to be ' to specific addresses of the wanted people however, which has sparked calls for the accused to either be deported or face trail in the US.

It is believed that much of the detail of addresses has been fed to the Latin Nonettes by other such groups in the United State.

Several of those accused in the telecasts have been on the receiving end of protests and

"They were the only groups who could go in - and come out," says Waters

Warren reveals Panama 'miracle' rescue

Gordon Richardson
in Washington

Girl scouts and nuns have boldly ventured where heavily armed, battle trained soldiers fear to tread.

These young women, without a single weapon of war let alone defence between them, have pulled off what the most powerful army on Earth has failed to do.

Two 'low tech' organisations have effortless accomplished what the most sophisticatedly equipped military force has failed to achieve Why?

The answer to this question - which is on the tongues on millions throughout America and rest of the world - was answered yesterday by White House spokesman Larry Waters

He said: "A joint Joint Chiefs of Staff and National Security option paper on the rescue of Southern Command listed the hazards a rescue operation would face

"One, the Alien attacks on the men would be, in all probability would be similar to those suffered by OTSA forces at Jatai This ruled out sending any males into the Canal Zone, especially those of US forces.

"Two, although this meant we had to send in a completely female force, we could not risk exposing any female military units in case they, too, were mistaken for males. Yet we had to deploy a force which was disciplined and organised. It also had to possess a multi-task facility, crew boats, have reconnoitring and navigation skills, medical expertise and just as importantly the stamina of lifting and transporting the wounded men to safety

"By process of elimination this left only two organisations: the Girl Scouts of America and female religious orders. The scouts also possessed another vital capability: semaphore

The Panama Canal

With all electro-magnetic communication degraded – especially radiophonic and microwave - semaphore was the only safe method of distance communication.

"The option paper took account of the sexual dimension of the situation but concluded that sex would probably be the last thing on the men's minds

"The paper also took on board the notion that these young ladies could be shocked and scared by what they saw but on conferring with both girl scouts and nuns they assured us it was something they could handle. And so it has proved to be "

Mr Waters acknowledged that the decision to send in scouts and nuns to rescue the soldiers was a difficult one but said: "What other choice did we have? To critics of the operation: Who would they have sent in? Take it from me both these organisations were professionals especially in negotiating fees. We had to pay every one of them $500 a day each but a further $100 bounty on every man

"Requested by the legitimate security concerns of local communities," my foot! The Neighbourhood Watch? Since when have they had any sense of neighbourliness? If anyone is watching over the community it is us Nonettes. And since when in all the years that these Neighbourhood Watches have existed, not that I have seen much sign of them round here, has the Council shown the slightest interest in them? Never. Not until now that is.

What the Council is setting up with these Watch people might make some sense if there was a rise in crime. But with the inter-Nonette 'Note and Help' posts now in place, anything suspicious is stopped before it's begun. The only trouble there has been locally was the beginnings of a fight outside the Crown the other Saturday but three Nonette patrols were there within minutes of the landlord calling. They had the two groups separated, walked in opposite directions and put on buses by the time the actual police turned up. And not a word of thanks from them did they get. Instead the police bad mouthed our patrols, calling them "have-a-go vigilantes," "kangaroos." If this wasn't bad enough, one policeman even said if they "took the law into their own hands" again they would be arrested instead.

But this is exactly what the Council by paying the Watch for security firms to patrol the streets are doing. And the ones they are hiring aren't proper 'security firms' but a bunch of thugs. What the Council is really paying them for though is to keep a watch on us 'Nonette neighbours'.

It didn't take long though before most of us saw through the Council and Watch's little game. Not just ours either, half the others are up to the same tricks. Of course it can't be them acting on their own, the government's behind them, that is if the papers and TV are anything to go by. They are filled with one government puff after another. In one breath it will be what they have done to bring "things back to normal" then in the next it will be knocking us Nonettes and advising people against joining. These past days it has been one smear after another about the so-called "upsurge in Poll Tax Riots" and how we Nonettes are behind them.

Some individual ones may have been at the beginning but now these 'riots', or protests to be more precise, have taken on a life all of their own. Heaps of people have stopped paying. The only actual 'riot' there has been was in Clapham and that was the bailiffs' own fault for being so heavy-handed. But the outcome has been that bailiffs everywhere are refusing to collect for Councils unless they have police protection! What happens next including my NTQ (of which I've heard not a thing) I shudder to think.

That the government and councils alike are anti-Nonette is one thing but accusing us of things we haven't done is bordering on the criminal. When all is said and done all we are doing is looking after ourselves. And where is the harm in that I would like to know?

Emergency cuts not as bad as feared

Five per cent off government spendin
Defence and Police to get more

Phillip Mayhew
Economic Correspondent

In a tough no-nonsense speech the Chancellor, Peter Handel, said it was important not only to rein in government overspending but also to be seen to be reining it in.

The Chancellor said that it was vital that the government showed clearly it was serious in what it said.

The Chancellor, in announcing a range of across-the-board cuts said that they were not cuts as such but more a correction to bring government spending back into line and reflect the new realities that we, as a nation and our European partners face at this time.

The main changes announced in the Chancellor's 'mini-Budget' speech are:

- Spending ministries - including Social Security, Health, Education – are to immediately repay five per cent of their existing budget allocations for the current financial year back to the Treasury;
- UK contributions to the EU to be held n escrow while they are re-negotiated;
- All overseas aid to be subject to a six nonths' rescheduling;
- Defence spending to increase by an mmediate 10 per cent - £2.5bn - and is earmarked for rises in salaries as well as a bid to increase the service's ranks; a arget of 10,000 new recruits to serve with the Army in the next two months has been set;
- The Home Office to receive a further ncrease similar to that of defence and earmarked for the police in a the lower ranks' - such as c salaries in line with those security forces as well a recruitment; Special Constab paid for the first time.

"Difficult times c difficult measures" – say

City welcome Chancellor's "F hand mini-budg

- There will be NO increase in a or duties; remaining taxes an duty on share and securities deal be scrapped from the first of next
- The Inland Revenue and Cust Excise to increase the num Revenue Investigation Officers further 25,000 in a bid to cracke none and under-payment All f Officers to be awarded bonuses b the tax payments realised;
- Tax repayments by the Treasu be reduced to two years down f present seven; the changes t immediate effect.

The Chancellors' budget was g strong thumbs-up in the City No were Peter Handel's measures a ced than the pound surged in rising a full three cents against the to $1.15. Last night, ForEx traders

Uprising in Mexico

Andrew Hendrey
from Mexico City

Mexico's southern provinces have fallen to the Nonettes Only the north of the Yucatan is thought to be still in government hands

A reported 20,000 troops have fled in face of Nonette forces and are said to be falling back on Caribbean port of Veracruz and the capital, Mexico City The commander of Mexico's southern forces is thought to be in rebel hands

Rebels overrun South

The swiftness and size of the Mexican army's defeat has taken everyone, including the government of Amado Fluentes, completely by surprise General Jesus Rebollo, commander of government forces in the south of the country and most of his high command are thought to be among the many thousands of soldiers captured by the rebels and is an indication of the swiftness of his army's collapse

There are further, as yet unconfirmed, reports that many of the government forces actually went over to the Nonettes and may yet be another reason why the rebels' success has been so rapid

The Nonette-backed uprising follows within days of the withdrawal of US military advisors from the state of Chiapas.

It is from Chiapas that the uprising is said to have originated

Chiapas, the scene of several earlier clashes between the indigenous Mayan population and the Mexican - and latterly US - military.

The former presence of US peacekeepers is seen as a further reason for the sudden collapse of government forces

Although the US Army conducted extensive 'hearts and minds' pacification programmes in Chiapas it was largely

The corruption, endemic within both the Mexican armed forces and civil administration, more often than not nullified the US's 'good works'

Govt. forces flee Nonette takeover

US advisors were also viewed by the Mayans being on the side of the Mexican forces and by association against them. The earlier actions by US forces when they to first arrived to crush the earlier Zapatist rebellion also alienated the Mayans against them.

Although Mexico is a single state it is, in reality two very separate countries - a north and a south - with the Madre dei Sur Mountains and Riŏ Balbas forming the border between them

The peoples of each Mexico, including the languages they speak, are very different. So are their economies. The north has benefited from Mexico's NAFTA membership The south has suffered from it.

The administration of the north is corrupt. The administration of the south is controlled by northerners and is ultra-corrupt

It is the south which has rebelled against the north.

The states of Guerrero, Oaxaca, Chiapas, Veracruz, Tabasco, Campeche, Quintana and Yucatan have long histories of administrative corruption and ruthless exploitation by outsiders.

It comes of little surprise that many of those joining the military's flight north are members of the administration as well as politicians, landowners, businessmen and others who have lined their pockets at the expense of the

Nonette protestors in Mexico City yesterday

indigenous southerners

These refugees are probably also mindful of the consequences of appearing before a Nonette 'Truth Committee'

Following the military collapse in the south, the Mexican High Command in a bid to stem further rebel advances, have rushed forces to defend a line at Puebla 100km south of the capital

State of Emergency declared

Many heavily armed convoys has been seen passing through the city on their way to the front.

Meanwhile much of Mexico City has been thrown in a state of panic and confusion as a result of the crisis

There is also talk that the government of Amado Fluenties' has ordered a crackdown on the Nonette movement within the rest of the country That such a move is effective or counter-productive - as it has been in other Latin American countries which eventually fell to the Nonettes - remains to be seen.

Already the 1.2m people of Chimalhuacan, a slum on the eastern edge of the capital, are under effective Nonette control. There are many Chimalhuacans throughout Mexico

In many respects Mexico has already been [illegible] out by the Nonettes

The movement is reported to be operating throughout the country It difficult to see how the government or the army and police can do little more than temporarily and superficially stop the movement's growth and influence

US on Red alert

It is already too late, however, to eradicate one of the main reasons for the Nonettes' rise in the first place corruption

Every level of Mexican public administration - even that of the Church - is not only corrupt but also is viewed by the public as being so.

In turn such administrators - even the few honest ones - are thought of as crooked Until the coming of the Nonettes most Mexicans saw corruption as little more than inevitable fact of life.

Peso slumps

The Nonettes, practicing a policy of openness and public accountability and thus honesty, has provided people no only with an alternative administration but also one by which the government can be judged against.

That the Nonette derive their power from the ordinary people themselves has also

SCROUNGERS KNOCKED

- Dole seekers pay-outs slashed
- Child benefits means-tested
- Single mothers told: "Live with p

By Susan McBeth
Political Editor

NO LONGER will the nation's scroungers be able to rely on state hand-outs to subsidise their life-style of idleness.

In a major crackdown on abusers of hard-working taxpayers' largesse, the DSS at long last has decided to wield the whip against the nation's freeloaders.

From tomorrow claimants of the so-called 'job-seekers allowance' will have to prove they are genuinely actively seeking proper jobs.

A DSS spokesman said that unless dole scroungers can independently verify they have been to at least three interviews in the past week, they will not receive a penny of taxpayers' hard earned money.

Also, these spongers will be required to sign a

Should any of them be caught attempting to defraud the taxpayer they will not only be automatically subjected to the loss of their benefits permanently but also will be open to an automatic criminal prosecution, which could include a custodial sentence: ie, they will go prison.

Single mothers – another category rife with benefit abuse - also face a tougher regime.

From tomorrow any under-age mother who attempts to claim money off the taxpayer will either have to live with her parents or those of her child's father's.

Only under exceptional circumstances, DSS officials say, will these child mothers be eligible to receive state handouts.

The DSS's new tough, no-nonsense policy is in response to the government's cutting back on its easy going spenddrift

"None of the men could walk, sit or stand," say saviours

Girl scouts tell of Panama mercy mission

Gordon Richardson
in Lafayette Louisiana

Naomi Smith and Lauren Jones, two pretty 15 year olds attending Lafayette High School in Lafayette, LA were absent from school this past week. And they were not playing hooky They were in Colon, Panama bringing injured and wounded soldiers of Southern Command to safety.

Naomi and Lauren from the 17th Lafeyette Troop, were among the 2,000 Girl Scouts and 500 nuns who took part in the top-secret "Operation Oberon", the mercy rescue mission of the beleaguered forces of Southern Command in the Panama Canal Zone

Both young ladies spent three busy days as stretcher-bearers carrying the wounded and injured from the Teddy Roosevelt Military Hospital in Colon and other locations in the deserted port city to waiting rescue ships.

confidentiality agreement to keep details of the logistics of the mission secret, both girls were free to give details of their duties.

"We spent three entire days," said Naomi, "carrying the men to the launches. As I have a Proficiency in First Aid, I was also able to apply cold compresses to the men's wounded parts.

"During all my time in Colon I did not find one man who was not in need of such welcome comfort," she said

When asked if they were afraid of what they might find, Lauren said: "No Girls who had Proficiencies in pathfinding and aqua swimming went ashore and reconnoitred the area the night before we landed."

Lauren also confirmed other reports that the all the men had suffered injures consistent to their being subjected to various tortures while in the hands of the Aliens

Lauren said: "While all the

Naomi Smith and Lauren Jones in Lafayette yesterday

men were unable to sit or stand, or even lie on their backs, none of the several hundred we carried showed signs of battle wounds such as fractures. Except for one man, that is."

When asked to explain Lauren said: "When two of the other girls with us asked one of the men they were carrying what the Space Ladies had done and he told them, they laughed so much they dropped the stretcher and he tumbled right down the stairs and broke both legs."

When asked what did she think of the wounds and torture inflicted by Susem's on the soldiers, Naomi said: "Those Space Ladies had our men lovemaking for two entire days. Now isn't that something. Just how did they do that? As for what they did to our guys," she said, "I've seen better."

Our own Area Nonette is now set up and is working a treat. It stretches from Highbury Corner to Stroud Green. With me re-elected to represent our own one, and despite delegating everything, I still have my work cut out with all the things I have been sent to the Area Nonette to do.

Our Area meetings are held in an old factory just off Fonthill Road that one of the other delegates owns. What still surprises me is how quickly everything on the agendas is settled. No argy bargy, no speechifying and definitely no party politics. Apart from divvying out the contributions and fixing the twinnings, auditors and a few things more, the big issues have been electing our delegate to the Regional Nonette, London North and telling her, Anne Gibbons from Fieldway Road, what we want done. Top of the list is a call to the government for a thirty per cent cut in our income tax to cover our tithe. Not for a moment will it happen of course but with Nonettes nationally set to demand the same, people everywhere are sure to sit up and take notice.

Next is our weekly newspaper, 'The Barn' (the name is a compromise). So many business Nonettes have already placed adverts in it that it's gone to double the pages planned and is already in profit and this is without a single page yet printed! The Highbury Nonette which won the draw to handle the first edition has had heaps of contributions and some from professional journalists. Of course when London North is set up we will have our very own daily paper and some balanced reporting at last.

One thing I am sure they will be running stories on is the effect of teaching screens. It's not just Becky and her chums but all the kids who are in front of them studying away for hours and as quiet as mice, not just children either but grown-ups as well. And I have to say, little Itzal downstairs is a most enterprising young man. He had every member in our block studying like mad so we will have enough points for our own screen. But no sooner had our screen arrived than he had everyone studying even harder for more points towards our health booth!

With so many children studying so hard I would have thought teachers would be overjoyed. But there is not a jot of it. Their unions are campaigning for the screens to be banned claiming that they are behind the rise in truancy. That if it gets any worse their members will be out of a job. As more and more Nonette owned shops are accepting points as part payment, kids round here are joining up in droves, with their parents following suit. What doctors will say when the health booths arrive I dread to think!

Chancellor's Faustian pac
with bankers gives Britain
breathing space

t is the markets who rule Britannia now

hillip Mayhew
Economics Correspondent

n return for a financier friendly budget the global money markets have delivered on their half of the Chancellor's Faustian bargain: assuring Sterling's value.

In bowing to the baying of bankers, the Chancellor, Peter Handel, has obliged our pockets and purses as well, is sure to leave a certain bitterness in the mouths of many.

For the less fortunate among us and who are - more by misfortune than fecklessness - dependent on the state for financial assistance, there will be an increasing hardship. For it is they who are the sacrificial victims in ... may well prove to be unpalatable to everyone.

The raison d'être of hiring the extra tax inspectors can, at a pinch perhaps be justified. But the recruitment of 10,000 soldiers and the same number of police there is no apparent justification.

What war is there looming which justifies the hurried enlistment of so ... soldiers refuse to w... against them.

Similarly, what re... behind the reason for ... den need to recruit ... extra police?

Rather than there b... upsurge in lawlessne... is an actual fall in th... figures. And the... NACRO say, includ...

lleries, libraries to close - OAP services are halved – street cleaning cut

Manchester to slash services

ore Councils expected to follow suit as Poll Tax bailiffs' strike bi...

icholas Janis
ome Affairs
orrespondent

Manchester Council is cutting a wide range of services in a desperate bid to reduce spending. The cuts are expected to hit many of the facilities Manchester provides. The Council claimed that after ... ment the cuts as a matter of urgency.

All of Manchester Council owned and run art galleries and libraries are to close by the end of the month. Funding for the other 'cultural activitie... the Council is involve... with will also come to a... end. This expected to h... they are. The Council's street cleaning and refuse budgets are to be cut by a third. Only the sewerage and the public health budgets remain unscathed.

every one who has len... money wanting it b... and all nigh at the s... time, something had... give. And that was us,... people of this great cit...

Manchester is unl...

Waves of Mexicans
wave Mexico goodby

Wealthy in massed flight to US and Euro

Ian Trigg
in Mexico

Half a million Mexicans are attempting to flee the country so reports claim.

Airport and coach stations are crammed with would-be refugees seeking to leave for the US, Canada, Europe, in fact anywhere, in a desperate bid to escape the Nonettes.

Any hopes that the Amado Fluentics government had that by proclaiming a State of Emergency it would calm the country's jittery nerves has backfired.

Instead it has the opposite effect in heightening the sense of panic and doom among many Mexicans, particularly the wealthier.

To the west of Mexico City where the biggest exodus is taking place, is thronged with removal trucks and 'For Sale' signs.

In the plush suburb of Jurarez property prices have halved in just a matter of days. Real estate realtor, Gustavo Diaz, said: "We have many sellers but not one single buyer. Many of those ...

"Fiscal firmness the only wa...

Money mar
thumbs-up
boosts sterlin

By Arthur Todd
City Editor

The Chancellor was the toast of the City yesterday. The Square Mile showed its appreciation Peter Handel's scrapping of the remaining taxes and stamp duty on share dealing by sending the Footsie up by an impressive 135 points to close at 7283.

The international money markets also gave the Chancellor their seal of approval by boosting Sterling to a six month high against the US dollar to $1.22 - a hearty 5 cents gain on the day. Some leading Forex traders are saying that not only be good for the markets but for Britain as a whole. Head markets trader at stockbrokers Ramp & Punt, Derek Boyd said: "These taxes were more a nuisance than anything. Now they have gone it means that a lot of people who did not have a tax record can come out and play the market." Derek - or 'Del Boy' as he is known by fellow traders - said: "There's a lot of money, serious money come into this county since those tax havens have been taken over. And these over-...

PM rebukes 'Cut taxes or e...

"We will not be told what to do by a petty crook"

By Mark Lewis
Political Editor

"WE cannot and we will not be told by this man, this petty crook how we should manage the running of this country" - was the Prime Minister's angry rebuff to the Nonettes' latest call for a reduction in income tax.

In a telecast yesterday, Susem spokesman Daniel Collins - who is still wanted by the police in Britain for fraud - repeated the Nonettes' demand for the right to deduct the 10 per cent of their income, which they give to the movement, to be deductible from their income tax.

Collins said that now the Nonettes numbered in their millions it was grossly unfair for them not be compensated for the savings they were bringing to government spending.

This argument, however, cut little ice with the PM.

Speaking after a meeting in the City, Edward Campbell said: "Just how many times must it be spelt out that the answer to any unilateral tax reduction, deduction is "No?"

"Britain cannot make changes to its fiscal policy even if it wants to," the PM said. "Should we do so, then under EU rules, we would be liable immediately for punitive penalties.

"The United Kingdom economy is not an island," he said. "It is enmeshed with ...

Nonettes ...
tax cut de...

Government's respons...

By Irene Palmer
Economic Editor

SUSEM front-man, Daniel Collins called, yesterday on world governments to allow members of the Nonette movement to deduct ten per cent of their incomes from their tax bills.

Although there has not been as yet, any government response to his demands, it is likely to be studiously ignored, especially by the Treasury.

Collins - who is still wanted by the police for fraud, tax evasion and criminal damage ... quick to point out the impossibility of any government meeting the Nonettes' tax demands.

Until a few months ago nearly all of the government's tax haul was spent on providing goods and services to the country. A small amount, however, was set aside to pay interest on its loans as well as make capital repayment of those loans.

The amount required to service and repay these loans has not changed but the sentiment of the lenders has.

Hans Sharpening, chief economist at the giant Uber ...

Troops in big top trapeze tortures

Soldiers subjected to 'frightful' sex ordeals with 'swinging Susem sirens'

By Brett Anderson
in Dallas

MORE than 1,000 US marines serving with Southern Command in the Panama Canal Zone and captured by the Susem were subjected to 48 hours of non-stop sex tortures, many involving trapezes.

According to unconfirmed reports, not one single soldier serving with Southern Command and captured by the Susem was spared from unending sessions of bondage and whippings as well as an entire range of other kinky sex ordeals and depravity including torture.

According to these reports, all the men who fell into the Aliens' clutches were taken to their hideaways. Once there, captive and helpless, the Marines were subjected to one degenerate sexual ...

Marine Sgt. Rolf Howard, who was one of those abducted by the Aliens and is recovering from his ordeal at the US Navy Hospital, Corpus Christi, Texas, said: "We all knew from the Brazilians what to expect that Aliens were going to do to us.

"We knew we would be tied up and whipped, that they would submit us to torture, abuse our naked bodies with lust and sate their uncontrolled sexual desires upon us. But none of us were prepared for what these Alien females had me and my men do.

"While other prisoners were being tied up to trees and carnally abused by packs of these Susem, we had our feet tied to trapezes and patches put on our backs which immediately, physic...

minutes of being hauled aloft not only could I see many of other men similarly suspended but also there were dozens more Susem swinging from trapezes as well.

"These Alien women began swinging back and forth. Then one after another of them let go, sailed through the air with the greatest of ease, and with their arms and legs wide apart. Within seconds all of them had landed on many of the men. The men cried out in pain.

"I thought it was because of the increase in weight upon their ankles. But when one of these Alien women landed onto me I then knew why the men were crying out in pain.

"In all my days I have never experienced such forcefully aggressive inter...

PM, Chancellor give cold shoulder to Nonette tax demands

"There can be no special cases" - says Handel

By Rebecca Simons
Political Correspondent

NONETTE DEMANDS for tax rebates has received its sternest rebuff yet.

Rather than giving in to the movement's campaign, both the Prime Minister, Edward Campbell and the Chancellor, Peter Handel, in a joint 'Meet the Press' gathering yesterday turned down all ...

The Prime Minister said: "These Nonettes claim they are spending for the benefit and betterment of their members. Good for them. But in Britain there are many other organisations, such as charities which collect money from the public and in turn use it on good works for the less fortunate in our society. They are not asking for tax ... why not the charities? Why not every other Tom, Dick and Harry who can rustle some reason for a rebate? My answer is, yet again and I sincerely hope for the last time: No."

The Chancellor said rather than now being the time for tax giveaways it was one to tighten the tax net. "The reason we are appointing ...

I've been wanting to get at them for years.

I needed neither prompt nor prod from Rainbow either. The script was in my head from the first, typed as fast as my fingers could go.

They were forever badgering with begging letters. I gave something the once to quieten them but they had the nerve to carp for more. If they were hard up it would have been different and I would have willingly lent them a bob or two to tide them over. But they're rolling in it. For myself I saw no sense handing over more of my hard-earned dough just so they could continue the life of Riley. Their phone calls, visits became so bad I had pay others to keep them off my back, leave me in peace to get on with eking a living.

Of course with just some their offices, records gone it won't change much. They will soon find further ways of filching from the likes of us ordinary, decent hardworking folk. But all the same, ooh what satisfaction announcing it. And doing so just the night before!

With Paceillo back in Tabajara her presence has soon been felt, especially with Rainbow and through her, Elana, and through her, Congress (where most representatives are women just now). All exhibit a mode of reasoning which while logical enough has a certain naïveté. The tax attacks are a case in point. Congress said the new Nonettes' tithes should be deductible from taxes levied on them by governments. As these tithes come from the Nonettes' own purses, spent exclusively for the benefit of their communities, are completely accountable, because intervening interests between payers and beneficiaries aren't involved, the moneys are spent efficiently. As the tithes, so Congress reasoned, represent funds governments would supposedly be spending on these people's behalf, it was only fair. I saw the flaws straight away.

At the time I said nothing, I wrote and telecast what I was told, but all the same thought nothing would come of it. Then officialdom's folly broke out. Instead of discussing, negotiating the 'proposal' away to nothing, Taxmen every-where derided, decried it. Silly of them really. Especially as their spokesmen rebutting it were just that, men. Congress, and Paceillo were most upset.

Another such 'suggestion' came from Rainbow. The wider promotion of Love Patches she said would help boost, strengthen the new Nonettes. To me, being at the sharp end, it's a no-hoper but despite my playing it down, she also mentioned it to Elana and in turn, she to Tabajara's growers' cooperative and they to the others they are linked to. So enthusiastic was the response all agreed a go-ahead. Manual in supporting them was just as bad.

No thought did any of them give to the pitfalls awaiting. They may know about crops and products but nothing of the markets out there in the big wide world. The whole idea smacks of delusion and worse, 'do gooding'. It is sure to flop and there will be losses. This will mean a drop in profits, earnings, mine included. But not daring to upset Rainbow I had said nothing.

SUSEM BLAST BUILDINGS INTO SPACE W

ALIENS ATTA TAX & CUST

Roger Dangermoss
General Correspondent

In a series of early morning raids, Susem spaceships blasted five of Britain's Inland Revenue and Custom and Excise Offices into space.

Staff were given just 10 hours warning of the impending attacks. Offices in London, Southend, Prest- on and Glasgow were attacked and buildings blasted out of the ground and rocketed to the sun.

At just after 6am this morning four massive Susem spacecraft broke through the clouds above west London and circled the Inland Revenue Offices at Kew.

Within minutes of their arrival, these craft - the same as those that had eliminated the nuclear power stations in May - hovered over the Tax Offices and were beaming down walls of brilliant blue light around the office complex.

Seconds later the eight-storey buildings were rising up into the air.

Staff given just hours to flee

Hundreds of smaller Susem delta-winged craft, in close formation and approaching at very fast speeds, converged under the building. With a further huge flash of

Huge crowds cheer

The whole operation lasted only a matter of minutes but not before huge crowds of onlookers had broken out into spontaneous applause.

Several accidents were reported caused by motorists crashing into others who had stopped on nearby roads to watch the event.

At the same time that the Susem were attacking Kew, more of their craft were attacking Tax and Excise offices across the rest of the country. All followed the same pattern and were over within minutes.

Head of the Inland Revenue, Sir Norman Slater, said: "Because of the vague nature of the warning we did not know which of our offices were going to be attacked we had to put them all on an 'at risk' alert.

"Furthermore, because of the short time of notice period, senior staff members across the UK were obliged to work through the night retrieving as much of their essential data as has been possible.

rescued in the few ho A that the police allo us to enter our premise

"Just as unfortu has been the disrupt caused to those off which were not attac The overall situatio currently unclear ex ing to say that invari there will be delays i operations.

"Presently we ar questing that all em ers operating regis PAYE schemes on of their employees s not remit such pay to us until we i them to so do."

"We will not cowed" -says

A Downing Street sman said: "The attacks on Inland ue and Excise of quite unjustified. of revenue to the ment will obviou rupt our s ab supply services public. However there may be d in the short-term not be bowed actions or be di as how to ma governing of Britain includi as we see fit."

Elsewhere in ry including Pr sgow and South Inland Revenu

That Susem 'Tax threat'

The following is the full text of the Susem/Nonette ultimatum made yesterday by the Aliens' front-man Daniel Collins:

"HERE IN THE Congress we contribute a tenth of our income for the mutual benefit of us all. This amount is quite adequate to finance our collective needs.

"An increasing number of people across the rest of the world have also formed into Nonettes. The latest figure indicates that more than 500 million people have now done so. Including those of us in the Congress, our worldwide strength will soon be more than a billion.

"The tenth of their income which individual Nonettes contribute is spent exclusively for the collective benefit of not just their own community but those who are less financially fortunate as well.

The collection and disbursements of this 10 per cent is without any administrative cost. Every penny, cent, or peso received and spent is fully accountable. Records of every transaction are freely available for all to inspect.

"Such spending and its cost-free transference by and between Nonettes, is of considerable fiscal saving to those who currently exercise administrative control - such as governments - over the wider population including those who are Nonettes. It is only equitable therefore, that the 10 per cent a Nonette gives to his or her community should be deductible from what they currently pay to these governmental administrations by way of taxes.

"The Nonette movement has repeatedly asked all governments to acknowledge this saving accruing to them by reimbursing individual Nonettes for their 10 per cent contribution in a matching reduction in what is currently taken from them by these governments.

"Unfortunately not one such government has acceded to the righteousness of this request. Moreover, many of them have vehemently repudiated to acknowledge the iniquity of their refusal. Instead governments have denied the righteousness of the Nonettes with the brute and unreasoning might of their entrenched positions.

"It is irrational that this unreasonableness and selfishness on the part of governments should continue unchallenged. Therefore, the Nonettes have and most regrettably so, been forced by these governments to match the might of their unreasonableness with the might of our reasonableness in return.

"In 10 hours time 63 government tax collecting centres with be removed in the same manner and to the same location as were all the nuclear power stations. It is sincerely hoped on the part of Nonettes everywhere that in the days ahead, governments do at least enter into meaningful discussion in order that our reasoned and not unreasonable request be acceded."

SUSEM BLAST TAX OFFICES TO THE SUN!

- Aliens in worldwide tax attacks
- Scant notice given claim Inland Rev
- London, Glasgow, Preston hit
- Campbell vows resistance

By ROLAND GALLEY

FIVE MAJOR UK tax offices have been shot to the sun by Susem spaceships. The nation's top taxman, Sir Norman Slater said the Inland Revenue was taken by complete surprise by the Aliens' attacks and their swiftness.

Dawn attack

Other senior tax officials said that Britain's tax collection could be disrupted for weeks to come as a result of the raids

At just after 6am this morning the massive spaceships - each more than a kilometre in length – descended out the clouds and hovered over the doomed tax offices Within seconds the spacecraft were beaming down a wall of blue purple lights around the stricken buildings. No sooner were the buildings surrounded by the beams than they were rising up from the ground

Rocketed in air

When the office blocks had risen to about 300 metres fleets of hundreds of the Susems' smaller delta winged craft, flying in close formation fly beneath the buildings. These then emitted an explosion of brilliant white light and a thunderous boom. The buildings then zoomed up through the clouds and headed for a fiery end in the sun.

The entire operation lasted no more than a few minutes. The spaceships then flew off to their next target. By 7am London time the Aliens had blasted more than 60 tax offices around the world into space and the white heat of the sun.

At Kew in London as well as Glasgow and Preston, motorists and others on their way to work stopped to watch the spaceships.

Crowds cheer

There were loud cheers from the crowds as they watch the tax offices be-ing blasted into space

The drama of today's events unfolded at 8.15pm yesterday evening during the Susem telecast with Daniel Collins announcing that as governments had not given to Nonette demands selected tax offices throughout OECD countries would be sent to the sun in 10 hours time.

Because Collins did not give details of which tax offices were going to be attacked it had meant that thousands of taxmen and women worked feverishly throughout the night in a bid to retrieve as much essential data as they could. All of Inland Revenue's more than 3,000 tax offices were affected.

Police caught

Britain's police forces were also caught unprepared to handle the situation. An officer from Kent police said: "We did not even know where all the tax and Customs and Excise offices were. We did not know either what the scale of the attacks would be. All we could do was hope for the best but plan for the worst. This mean putting cordons round all the tax offices we knew about and evacuating as many people as we could."

Many of the people affected by the police cordons from entering their homes and businesses or forced to leave them were angry at the disruption the raids caused A Maidstone resident who lives close by the town's tax office and was forced to leave her home said: "I blame the tax people for all this. If they had done what that Danny had said there would not have been all this mularky."

The PM defiant

The Prime Minister, in a live broadcast, late last night from Downing Street, said: "This is completely unjustified. Targeting undefended civilian buildings for attack is reprehensible.

Mystery punter puts £50,000 on IFEA Arsenal win

BOOKMAKERS, WM ILL announced yesterday that an unnamed overseas punter has placed a £50,000 bet on an Arsenal win in the IFEA Championship.

A spokesman for Ills said: "While we welcome such mammoth ment of Arsenal's IFEA chances."

Even the return of soccer's bad boy Don Kirk to Highbury has left Ills unmoved.

Last night their odds for Arsenal's bringing home the IFEA Cup were unchanged

Not that keeping quiet did me any good. Word has got round, I know not from where, Rainbow denies it is her, that I have experience in advertising promotion. Now that so many new Nonette newspapers have started I have been lumbered with seeing the project through. Though not before everyone concerned had gone over my head and put the brief to Manual's designers.

These designers promptly demonstrated that they had not an ounce of flair. Even the cooperatives saw that these fellows' "Erectile dysfunction diminished with Love Patch" was rubbish. As was their next attempt at snappy slogans and being witty, "Something for the weak end Sir?"

No understanding had they that Love Patches are not a male's but a woman's product. I have done my best but see only failure. And when this happens and losses mount, who will get the blame? Why, me of course. But with Rainbow backing it as well as insisting on giving her 'suggestions', what can I do? Nothing. To my mind they are not playing fair with me.

The good news though is that Manual is back in full production of 'Vantona'. I am still not sure of the name but keeping the Susem supplied is blessing enough. The pilot sales of the 'scratch 'n' sniff' strips are also most encouraging. For myself, I'm surprised at just how widespread lower abdominal vascular inhibition is among women. Not needing to pay anything out of the Vantona sales to the cooperatives, as I have for the Love Patches, it means I will also make more than the necessary margin on them.

Though Rainbow and the cooperatives' misguided 'do gooding' is set to fail, I've had opportunity to actually do some genuine good. It is something which, while providing passing and anonymous altruistic pleasure, is sure to bring happiness to millions, especially supporters of Arsenal FC.

Its seed sprang from the Susem sating on soldiery in Panama. They are rather impressed with the quality of this catch, "good goers" is a phrase bandied about the refectories. So much so, that all, including Tearo and 'her girls' are currently up there. Like a frenzy of gannets to a shoal of fish they are. But as with all good things this particular 'happy time' is drawing to a close. Only the American high command, embedded in their bunkers remain to be 'had' but they can't be counted on as being buck, let alone 'goers'.

But with the Susem showing scant sign of departing just yet, their urges unabated, the supply of buck males in Panama nigh exhausted, it is merely a matter of time before they seek happy times elsewhere. Therefore, 10,000 plus Susem, multiplied by the number of their satings per day (at least half a dozen each), times, say, a month, equals a very large number of non-Nonette males set to be severely seen-to anytime soon. As this number is certain, it is only sensible if some Susem attention is pointed in a mutually beneficial direction, especially when Tearo and her troupe return to Europe, one of which is assisting Arsenal winning the European Cup.

By the Susem paying a visit to the team Arsenal are next set to play against a couple of days before the match, they will, apart from securing top quality

onette tax challeng...

Campbell: 'We will not give in'

PM defiant against Alien threats

By MARK LEWIS
POLITICAL EDITOR

THE administration of Britain is for the benefit of all the people of this country, rich and poor, young and old, traditional and new British alike," the Prime Minister said yesterday.

"There are not and neither will there ever be, special cases or groups who have preference at the expense of the rest of us," he said.

In a rousing and defiant speech to the Commons, ... Minister pled- ... Susem raids on Tax and Excise offices had been a terrible blow it was by no means mortal.

He said: "Many times throughout Britain's long and noble history, the sovereignty of our nation and the freedom of its people have been threatened by outsiders.

"But none have ever succeeded. Britain has never been cowed, the patriotism of the British people has never been in doubt. And so it is now.

"We said 'No' the Spanish, we said the same ... in our darkest hour we said 'No' to the Germans. And we say 'No' to the Susem and their Nonette followers now.

"No matter how often and where these forces attack us we will never surrender our inalienable right to tax the income and expenditures of our people as we see fit.

"If these so-called Nonettes want to change this long established practice then let them stand as a properly reconoised political party in the next election and let the people, the ordinary people vote

The most dread return address is no more!

Stephen Young
Social Affairs Editor

We have all had one delivered through our door, those of us in the South East at any rate.

All have the same manilla brown colour. All are unwanted. All carry an air of menace and threat. All have the same message printed on them: 'If undelivered please return to the Inland Revenue Sorting Office, Ruskin Avenue,

The Aliens had it yesterday. Just now the entire block along with 62 other of such unloved redoubts are speeding towards the sun at 100,000 mph with an e.t.a of Thursday, next week.

Bystanders in their thousands clapped and cheered as the Inland Revenue's west London fortress was propelled skywards by the Aliens' spaceships.

Countless thousands more throughout London and the home counties were doubtless celebrating along with them. But how many tens of thousands more will be silently saying and perhaps not so silently: "That's got them off my back for a bit."

How many of us will be thinking: "If the government backs down, gives in to the Nonettes I'll join them and then I won't have to pay so much tax either."

How many of us are also

Peso and shares slump to record lov...

Funds flee north of the borde...

By Matthew Colotian
South American Economic Correspondent

The Mexican Peso was in freefall yesterday closing at 19.75 to the dollar, a halving of its value in three days

There are indications that the currency will fall further before it stabilises. ForEx brokers report a complete absence of buyers and only further heavy selling of the peso.

Nydia Iglesais, head of Bancamex's ForEx, said that the peso could fall to 50-60 to the dollar. Other brokers are more bearish over the currency saying that until the military situation is clarified the peso is valueless.

The Mexican MCit stockmarket has also seen steep falls with a further 642 point loss on the day and bring a 2463 fall to 3547 in the past three days

Citi analyst, K... Sontag said the MC... set to fall yet furth... the days ahead ... said: "Do not be ... prised if MCit ... slides right on ... past the 2,000 m... without even pausi... for breath."

One area unaffec... by the peso turbule... is the *maquiladoras* ... the north of ...

US prepares to defend borders from Nonettes - and Mexicans

Pentagon switches forces to border

Andrew Hendry
from Brownsville, Texas

The forces stationed along the southern coast line of the US to guard against the chance of a Nonette sea-borne invasion are to be switched to bolster the defence of the US-Mexican border.

Already one of the most heavily protected and patrolled borders in the world, defence of the 2,000 mile-long line between Brownsville, Texas and Imperial Beach, California is to be strengthened by an estimated further 200,000 troops.

Both the National Guard of the four border states, as well as the Pentagon, are to coordinate in defending the frontier.

National Guard contingents from another five southern states are also to be stationed in the border region. The Department of Defence announced that there will be an in-depth defence up to 200 miles

Although both the DoD and National Guards say that the deployment along the borders is against the Nonettes, it is open knowledge that their true purpose is to stop the expected wave of refugees already fleeing Mexico.

That this is so, is evidenced here in Brownsville and other towns along the Texan border of the increased police activity.

Vehicles are not just subject to spotchecks at the border crossings as happened in the past but at all points many miles north of the frontier as well.

Scores of illegal immigrants have been caught by such action it has, so police say, resulted in many other wanted criminal being apprehended.

However these checks have caused numerous mile-long traffic hold-ups and resentment from many motorists.

It is difficult to see what

The Barn Nonette

The weekly newspaper of and for Nonettes from Highbury Fields to Highbury Vale

Welcome!

WELCOME TO THE BARN our Nine Nonettes' brand-new, very own weekly newspaper.

We hope that in the weeks to come we can report on the many matters which concern our group of Nine Nonettes. We also intend to report on many of the local matters which other media so far have declined for one reason or another to report. Our editorial policy is that of Nonette newspapers elsewhere, in that each edition is edited by our individual Nonettes in rotation. In this way we will not become stale or - we hope - boring.

While this first edition contains some 'interesting' stories we are sure that you will have some even more revealing tales of your own that we will be only too ready to print!

This week's news in brief..

HOUSING REPAIR SCAM: we name the guilty council officials taking backhanders
THE MORMIC IS COMING!: details of when the health scan booth will arrive
CRIME LEVELS: how crime in Nonette-patrolled streets compares with before we began
OUR BANK: the loans we have made; the new jobs they have brought
WHO TAKES TEACHING VOUCHERS?: a list of every shop, store, business which accepts them
AREA NONETTE MEETING: this week's agenda in full
FOOTBALL: what are Highbury's Nine chances against Highgate's?
HOW WE HAVE GROWN!: all the facts and figures of each of our Nonettes

The lowdown on a council's greasy palms

A COUNCIL BUILDING SURVEYOR employed in overseeing contracts for repairs on council-owned properties was a director of three of the building companies he regularly gave work to. But instead of criminal charges being brought against him, or at least being summarily dismissed, he has been merely 'asked' to take early retirement!

While council tenants suffered from a funds-shortage and delays to the repair their dilapidated, leaking, damp homes, certain individuals waxed fat on their misery. Why was it allowed to happen?

Although all the facts of the case were known to the head of the Housing Department, Howard Dawkins, as long ago as last December, he has sat on the case. Not even Councillors with direct responsibility for housing have been told. Here is hoping they are now. But was the guilty man acting alone? Has he the finger on others in his department such as Mr Dawkins himself?

The guilty surveyor who had for worked for the council for 12 years is Stephen Watson of 10 King George's Avenue, Harlow. While number 10 is a modest enough residence we can reveal that it is not

Trooper tells of two hour bouncing sex torture terror ordeal

"I was forced to make love with an Alien on a trampoline"

By Lisa Biggles
Big Shocks Correspondent

With his eyes still filled wide with terror, Trooper Vance G. Spens, of Trenton, New Jersey told of his two day ordeal at the hands of the Aliens.

Speaking from his hospital bed at the US Air Force's recuperation facility in Fort Worth, Texas, Trooper Spens told what happened when he and his fellow soldiers were forced to take part in non-stop sex acts of the utmost depravity.

Still showing signs of pain from the injuries inflicted on him by the Susem, Trooper Spens detailed a long list of the acts of gross indecency he and his fellow soldiers were subjected to.

These included being whipped and caned, made to run naked and being tied to trees. They were also forced to take part in one act of vigorous sexual intercourse after another. None of which lasted for less than two hours.

But then came the ...

Trooper Spens said: "It was a terrifying experience having one of those space ladies gripping you - and I mean gripping you, not just with her arms and legs, but gripping your penis as well - and then been hurtled more than 20 feet onto that trampoline. As we bounced up and down, my back was in agony.

males who can 'go' the couple of hours of a single Susem sating, it will ensure the rival side will be fielding their B teams.

Terbal, the avid football fan he is, located all the pre-match practice pitches and the colours of each teams' shirts. It took time fixing the details but my catalyst of delight, following a few quiet words with Tearo, has been discreetly put in place and without so much as arousing attention. Naturally I have had a little flutter on the outcome but I am sure the Love Patches' petty cash account will not miss such minor borrowings.

Another of Rainbow's suggestions and accepted throughout Congress has more sense. With the new Nonette newspapers coming into their own and to dissipate the continuing anti-Nonette bias of mainstream papers, a thousand of them are to be invited to freely visit anywhere across Congress, the established ones to fund the costs of those of the Nonettes'. As no other media such as TV will be made the offer, it is one the papers cannot refuse. The rub is if the established papers' reporting doesn't accord with the Nonette ones they will have some explaining to do to their readers. Though there is more behind Rainbow's reasoning on this and Congress's agreeing to it.

That the Susem haven't left, now that Pa-tu's remains have been found, has benefits. The longer they stay the more chance there will be of the new Nonettes consolidating, which in turn means I have more of a chance surviving once they have gone. Time enough anyway for Arsenal to win me sufficient to pay my way from trouble. But there is the other side to the Susem staying, that they are here for more than just the locating of Pa-tu.

However, as yet, I have to admit that I've not been entirely successful in unearthing the real reason why they are still here on Earth. Even when I have enquired in the most oblique manner, I still meet with nothing but evasiveness. Menpemelo, when I met up with her and she had time to talk, was typical of the other Susem. All she would say on the subject was a Sphinx-like "There is no reason other than we have not yet departed," but later she let slip something which, while innocuous in itself, forebodes what is afoot. Also, and I do not know if it was in part to deflect my enquiring, she instead told me more about the Anthropic Template.

I was all attention as she explained, but as ever she began with questions.

"For how many of your years has life existed on your planet?"

"A couple of billion?" I said.

"Four billion actually, though it took half of this time to evolve the first single-celled lifeforms such as amoebae. For how many millions of years have humans existed on Earth?"

"Two, three hundred, if what you and Pacillo say is so."

"How many cells are you composed of?"

"Ooh billions."

"More than 100,000 billions actually, though whales have more. Each cell

NYPD nets record numbe[r] of narcotic ba[r]

"They are just turning themselves in" - says Police Commissioner

Gordon Richardson in New York

With the arrest Hernando 'Blowtorch' Gonzalez, the former boss of the feared Tijuana drug cartel and his top henchmen, New York's Police Department have added yet another to their record haul of big name arrests

Police Commissioner, Patrick O'Reilly, said: "We don't even have to look for these guys, they are just turning themselves in. They get off the plane, walk up to the first [police] officer they see and say 'I am a fugitive from justice, arrest me'. We have had others turn up in precincts in limos to be so much info that we are going to be busy for weeks," he said "We have had men turning themselves who we did not even know existed and testify to crimes and misdemeanors we were unaware of

"All have been extremely nervous I think it can be said that all these felons have an element of their seeking protective custody, in as much that they prefer to be behind our bars than those of Nonettes."

While other major US cities' Police Departments have notched up their own hauls of major criminals fleeing Latin America and now Mexico, New York's haul of traffickers is by far the big-

Girl Scout patrols report General Tucers

Aliens still attacking Pa

By Paulo Ridde in Belize

FORCES OF US Southern Command are still suffering Susem attacks against their positions in the western part of the Panama Canal

Survivors of earlier Susem abduction raids say that the the Southern's Commander is preparing to fight rather than attempt to organise a break-out from the encircling Alien forces.

Pathfinder patrols of Girl Scouts who have sailed across the two central lakes of the Panama Canal, reported seeing numerous Susem delta winged craft attacking the area which has been identified as Fort Clayton, Southern Command's HQ

Latest casualty reports from the US Navy's 6th Fleet, stationed off the Panamanian coast indicate that more than 20,000 soldiers have been abducted by the Aliens.

All are said to have suffered extensive injuries and psychological damage by

"We were made to run Aliens' gauntlet of feather dusters"

Officer tells of terrible tickling ordeal

BY BRETT ANDERSON IN HOUSTON, TEXAS

SECOND Lieutenant Paul Davenport of Cleveland, Ohio, serving with 7th Air Cav in the Panama Canal Zone and who was abducted by the Aliens, told how he and the others were subjected to endless sexual perversions at the hands of their abductors. One of which was the humiliation of the feather duster-like canes.

Speaking from his hospital bed in the US Army Hospital in Houston, Texas, where he is recovering from his ordeal, Lt Davenport gave details of how he and the other men were forced by the Aliens to run naked through a line of many more Aliens wielding canes which were identical to feather dusters.

"We had already been subjected to several hours of forced sexual intercourse with the Alien women," Lt Davenport said, "then, and although we were all physically exhausted, we were chased by an entire horde of these Alien women wielding whips.

"They chased us down between an avenue of trees." he said: "Being made to run barefoot and naked over open ground was painful enough but being forced to be physically and sexually aroused at the same time was excruciating.

No sooner were we running down this avenue when hundreds more Aliens sprang out from behind the trees and began brushing and stroking us between our legs with these feather dusters.

"Then they surrounded us. We were so tired that we were soon over-powered and then I received a

The Nonette

THE DAILY NEWSPAPER OF AND FOR NONETTES OF NORTH LONDON

WELCOME!

Welcome to the North London edition of ***THE NONETTE*** - the Nonettes' daily newspaper.

Our editorial policy:

Each week's edition of *The North London Nonette* is edited by representatives from each of our Regional Nonettes in rotation. It is they and no others who decide the content and make-up of each day's edition.

The North London edition of *The Nonette* is linked with our sister papers, which are also constituted on identical lines as our own. Many of the reports in this edition are syndicated from these other editions. In this way we are also able to publish firsthand reports of events from around the world. In many respects The Nonette is the first World Newspaper.

The Nonette's will publish what it concludes to be truthful and considers to be in the interests of the truth. Should anyone or entity consider The Nonette has untruthfully represented them and can establish as such, this paper will, as a matter of policy, invite them to publish their own correction. The Nonette will also, should such an occasion arise summit itself for judgment before any Nonette appointed Court - but no other.

TODAY'S MAIN NEWS STORIES IN BRIEF:

London Council officials skimmed off millions - *and got away with it!*

Carmen council's rent review officer Benjamin Roach, has just taken early retirement. He has also taken residence of a very large house on the outskirts of Kingston Jamaica. Mr Roach was the only person Carmen-rent review office.

He was responsible for liaison with all of the borough's private landlords many of whom are large privately owned property companies such as the Rigby School Estate and Bucks Estates.

It was part of Mr Roach's remit to fix a 'fair rent' Compared with other neighbouring boroughs these recent increases in Carmen are four times as high. It is also known that Mr Roach and his wife received private

Nonettes blamed for truancy rise

"Some schools could close" says Education Head

BY SIEGFRED OLIMANN EDUCATION CORRESPONDENT

TRUANCY in many schools is now as high as 30 per cent In some areas the entire educational system could soon collapse, Attendance Enforcement Officers say.

The Department of Education and Employment (DEoE) said that they were fully aware of rising truancy levels. The DEoE also acknowledged that the worst hit schools are in the inner city areas of London, Birmingham and Liverpool

A DEoE spokesman said, however, that school attendance was very much a matter for LEAs and the schools themselves to resolve.

Though there was little the Department could do and it was not possible for it to intervene directly, the DEoE was keeping a close eye on the situation

As to providing extra funds to LEAs to help combat truancy, the official said that ... truancy.

Camden's head of Education, Kenneth Weight said: "Camden parents can rest assured that my Department takes the matter of school non-attendance very seriously. Currently my department is taking every measure in its power to resolve the situation immediately as a matter of utmost urgency.

"While truancy is a matter for individual schools," Mr Weight said, "and though my Department is not really in a position to intervene in their day-to-day affairs, we have already had a number of in-depth discussions with school heads on the subject."

Mr Weight also said that his Department was pressing the DEoE for further funds to appoint more Attendance Enforcement Officers but they were still awaiting a reply from the Department

"Until then," he said there is nothing more we can do. Though if the non-attendance situation continues, we may have to consider consolidate- ... at any one time is said to be the worst affected school in the borough.

School Head, Patrick Reagan, blames the high level of truancy on the Nonettes. He said: "The situation is grossly unfair to schools such as St Ambrose whose catchment area is also one which has a high level of Nonette activity, especially among children

"Until we are in a position to pay children to learn, then schools are not going to be able to compete with these Nonette teaching screens

"My main concern," Mr Reagan said, "is the effect the screens and high truancy levels will have on St Ambrose itself

"Already we are in fierce competition with other schools in the area

"If the parents who were planning on sending their children to St Ambrose see its school rolls drop any further then they are going to send their children to a school where they are not

"Already staff morale is at

may well catch the children, threaten to prosecute their parents but neither are going to have any immediate effect on truancy levels.

"What is worse for teachers' morale is that these screens are indoctrinating our pupils' minds with facts and figures which are the different from the school curriculum

"Every time this happens there is usually disruption in the classroom This inevit-

is specific to function, yet all do so as a collective entity. On your planet, in less than 2,000 million years, something as simple as amoebae evolved into multi-cellular, seemingly self-replicating entities, conscious of self."

With me puzzling with 'seemingly', she changed tack, and recapping from a talk ago, said "A being's form is determined by function. The efficiency of which is defined by the context it is situate or amid, which in turn is demarcated by the context it is itself inhere, and so on all the way back to the Anthropic Constant itself.

"The notion that evolution is determined within a lifeform by its response to external tri-contextual criteria," she continued, "is a doctrine widely held (I took this as by Earthly scientists). Scrutiny however, evidences this as an insupportable theogony. Two billion years is insufficient for internally, random chance generated modification to effect the evolutionary progression occasioning beings such as humans. Random assembly of your alphabet's 26 letters at the rate of one every second into it's A to Z sequence would take more than 10 billion years. The human genome has six billion specific sequenced characters."

Menpemelo said that change to 'within' originates from 'without', 'withins' being the manifestation of converging 'withouts'. However, it was what were these 'without's' which had me hanging on her every word. But she had me suspended from them a while yet, for next came the doings of DNA.

"From the smallest virus to the biggest blue whale, tallest tree," she said, "all life is defined, determined by the universality of DNA and its evolutionary forebear RNA. That this is so is testimony of their efficiency, durability.

"In a viable, sustainable lifeform, efficiency dictates excess is neither created nor sustained, there will not be 'junk' (she'd a smile at this). In humans as with us Susem no more than a thirtieth of the DNA helix appears to transcribe function within and between cells. What of the other 29 thirtieths, what is their function?"

Seeing I'd not an answer, she then said "They are where receptors for post-Anthropic transmission are situated." This had me most puzzled but I thought it best to keep to listening.

Menpemelo said, as she had previously, such transmission came as pulsed packets. Each DNA 'receptor' and also groupings of them are 'receptive' to specific packets and why some animals, though possessing near similar DNA, such as us humans and bonobos, are receptive to different ones and so produce differing results. In the same way some animals and plants, while disparate from one another, have some receptors the same and so have identical features, though not always for the same purposes. Butterflies and beetles which have wings like leaves was one example she gave, another is how the eyes of an octopus are nigh the same as ours.

She still had me puzzled. More so when she said most transmission into cells' DNA as well as within the cells themselves occurred in the quinth context.

Susem: spare our men... PLEASE!

'Panama Wives' in dramatic love plea to Aliens

By **Mary Jones**
in New York

A DRAMATIC plea to the Susem to spare the remaining soldiers trapped in Panama was made by their wives yesterday.

Bravely fighting back tears, Mrs Susan Pelham, who's husband Jonathan is one of the estimated 10,000 soldiers still trapped in Panama by the Aliens, said: "Our message to those Susem ladies is: 'Please don't harm our men. Have your fill of them if you must but please be gentle with them. We love them so much and we want them to be able to love us as much when they return. Thank you."

"We have only just been married," sobs Sue

Mrs. Pelham who is a leading member of SCFF - the nationwide support of families of soldiers serving with Southern Command in Panama - is also leading SCFF's demand for an immediate upgrading of facilities in the treatment of men who have already suffered at the hands of the Aliens.

Susan Pelham

Mrs Pelham is pressing for the Department of Defence to provide immediate funds for a programme of silicon implants for the men whose penises have been compacted irreparably by the Susem.

Susan is also pressing for urgent research to be conducted into the possibility of inserting handheld air-pump catheters into the men's penises in order that they might function as normally as possible.

Should there be a chance of this of this new form of experimental therapy working it means that it would bring hope of a normal, full married life for tens of thousands of victims of the

Warren calls on Tucers to negotiate truce with Susem

"Let this needless suffering now end" says President. But will Aliens listen?

Gordon Richardson
in Washington

President Warren has called on General Tucers, C-in-C of the Southern Command, to surrender and withdraw his remaining forces to Panama City where a naval task force is waiting to carry them to safety.

The President also called

President Warren

General Tucers

juries inflicted on the soldiers of Southern Command. He said: "Already 20,000 soldiers in the prime of their lives may well have been permanently deprived of what it is to be a complete man.

"No useful purpose will be served both to those forces still remaining in Panama Canal Zone as well as the people of the United States as a

munication with Panama was being blocked he sincerely hoped General Tucers could hear his call for a cessation of action. He added however, that he had given the Girl Scouts a personally signed letter in the hope that one of their patrols could manage somehow to deliver it to the General.

One question which the President did not address

But before I had chance for "Then why is there need of the DNA we with microscopes can see?" she had added that there are some parts of the transmitting which is done tri-contextually. She said it is more efficient but also that these were for the simpler parts, and why earlier, lower order fauna and flora have more of these than us higher ones. Water lilies, ferns and grasses were examples she gave. They have sixty times more tri-context DNA than us humans, so have frogs and newts. Land crabs, carp and fruit flies however, and though I would not have thought it, are all quite advanced. Like us they have done away with most of their tri-context DNA. Mice and E. coli are also more evolved than I would have guessed.

With me still puzzled, Menpemelo moved on to the action of 'withouts' in the quinth context. The first thing she said was that much of the data going into cells was formulated not just outside of them, but outside the being they compose. In a flash I saw what she was depicting, auras. At last I had explanation of what they actually are, where the 'what' of us is formulated. I wanted to shout "Eureka!" but instead kept to listening.

Once auras, have completed the data packets defining how the various bits of us are to be, they are sent on into the DNA of our relevant cells. DNA can be thought of, Menpemelo said, as hardware, auras where our soft-ware programs are stored. And written.

What gets written is a summation of inputs received from our bodies' interactions as well as from outside, beyond our auras. Should faults occur in our DNA as a result of, say, imperfect apoptosis, then our aural software won't download into it properly. Similarly, if the input to the software changes, be it a result of altered data arriving from our bodies or 'extra-aurally', it will have difficulty transcribing on into our DNA. When either of these changes become too distorted, degraded, our bodies die. Menpemelo also said there are further programs for adjusting our DNA to changing software. This she termed 'evolution', and when it doesn't, 'extinction'.

But this is not all what happens in these transcriptions. The aura of a "sentient entity", as Menpemelo termed it, can communicate with those of other 'entities'. No sooner had she said it than I had a little twinge of sadness as I remembered poor Henrietta, how I had only to think of a bath and she would be out from snoozing and heading for a soak and a scrub. When Menpemelo added the higher the 'sentience' the greater the communication, I had another little twinge as I thought of Anne, how she always knew what I was thinking, then gave me an earful of bashing.

Faith healers laying on hands, pets knowing their owner's illnesses passed through my mind, questions too, but I still listened on, for Menpemelo next explained where and how data to auras comes from. And of the formulation of the Anthropic Template itself.

It is all to do with points, which the quinth context is, and their configurations. Points which form Secondary waves, energy, so Menpemelo reminded, are the

JS urged to clamp do[wn] on corrupt refugees

BRETT ANDERSON
WASHINGTON

[TH]E head of the US General [A]ccounting Office (GAO) has [ca]lled for corrupt foreign [bu]reaucrats fleeing to the US [to] be refused entry into [A]merica.

Egbert Down, director of [th]e GAO, claimed that the [a]uthorities' toleration of so [m]any crooked foreign officials already in the US was [g]iving its own public servants [a] bad name.

"Whether we like it or not millions of people across the United States watch the Nonettes' telecasts. Every day these viewers are shown lists of corrupt officials of the former government of the countries taken over by the Nonettes. Alongside the names of these officials are listed not only their misdemeanors but also their present whereabouts.

"And nine out of every ten are in the US. Not infrequently even their current street addresses are given.

"Many ordinary people, convicted of minor offences - even in their distant past - are automatically refused entry into the United States," Mr ...

GAO's Egbert Down yesterday

...rendous crimes ranging from civil rights abuses to the theft of millions of dollars, free entry and movement into our country.

"The American people are not blind to this blatant abuse of our hospitality," Mr Down said, "and increasing numbers are saying 'If these fleeing foreign bureaucrats are all corrupt and our public officials are letting them in - no questions asked - then it means they do not regard them as crooked.

"'Therefore', these people are saying, 'our public ...

And once ot... icans begin ha... tons, then we ... slippery slope ...

"It is matter ... importance," ... ially during ... times, that w... American peo... nation's publ... not only abso... also their pro... unblemished...

"Therefore ... foreigners m... back to face ... own countr... to account ...

DON KIRK MIRACLE!

ARSENAL IN 8-2 WIN OVER MUNCHEN

German juggernaut's blitzkrieg repulsed by plucky British attacker

By JONATHON CHESHIRE

ARSENAL has won a spectacular victory against AG Munchen. Not only did the plucky British side win, they beat the Germans by a massive 8-2 margin.

While new Arsenal centre forward, Don Kirk scored four of the goals his skilful tactics gav[e] openings for Pankorsk[i] and Zedena to head an[d] kick another four ball[s] into the back of the German net. Last nigh[t] jubilant Arsenal's fan[s] were calling Kirk's playing skills not short o[f] miraculous.

The Germans, so confident were they of a walkover, foolishly did not play their star players but sent on many of their B-list reserves.

Only when it was too late did Munchen's manager, Heinz Guderian realise that by not playing his 'A Team' he had thrown away the chances ...

More councils slash services

117 cities, towns in emergency cost-cutting drives
Depositors queue to withdraw savings despite rate hike

By Lawrence Coy
Local Government Correspondent

"THERE ARE NO sacred cows, only Statutory Services," said Rotherham's mayor, Edward Brown, announcing a raft of emergency spending cuts.

Rotherham is just one of more than a hundred towns and cities across Britain who have been forced to follow Manchester's lead in cutting council-run services to the bone.

Rotherham's Head of Finance, Kevin White, spelt out his and other councils' dilemmas. "Basically we are in a no win situation," he said. "We have a legal obligation to maintain a number of vital services such as roads, education and the police. These we have to pay for if we want to or not.

"We receive a certain amount of money from central government and the rest from the people of Rotherham by way of the Community Charge.

"Once people see that others around them are getting away with not paying," he continued," they stop doing so as well. And what with the bailiffs still refusing to act unless they have police protection and they refusing act against the Nonettes - who are the main culprits behind the Community Tax strike - the numbers of people who are not paying grows by the day.

Bradford's Kevin White

"It does not take too many to stop paying theirs before depositors with the council, both large and small start to fret about the safety of the funds and they withdraw their money from us.

"This past week alone, our Treasurer's office has had a constant queue of people and organisations withdrawing their investments. The big boys down in London are no better.

"Currently Rotherham has more than £100 million in loan debt to financial institutions. In the past we, like all the other councils were able to keep these debts serviced by a combination of interest repayments and new loans to pay off the old ones.

These financial institutions were happy to go along with this. They earned commissions on the business and always knew that should the worst come to the worst, central government would always copper-bottom their loans.

"But when the Treasury refused to fund our Community Tax strike losses, the whole caboodle started to unravel. We cannot raise any more money from City institutions.

"In turn none of them are willing to lend us any new money. Should we default on any of our current loans and the government does not bail us out, then all the loans fall due for immediate payment.

"Rotherham is not in a position to pay any of these. Should we sell off the few remaining assets we have not already sold, there would still be insufficient funds to pay everyone we owe. Technically speaking, Rotherham council is trading while knowingly insolvent but then so are all councils.

"In the meanwhile the council's bankers would call in our overdraft and we would have to shut up shop.

"In short, unless Rotherham's non-payers of the Community Charge pay up what they owe and pay up quickly and we cut our non-statutory services by 50 per cent, your council, ladies and gentlemen, will be well and truly shafted."

"Handel: recruiting serge[ant] for Nonettes" - claims Ha[ins]

Movement's membership figures see sudden post-Budget ...

BY TONY PERRY
POLITICAL EDITOR

MORE than 100,000 people are reported to have joined the Nonette movement since the Chancellor's mini-budget a week ago.

This sudden surge in Nonette numbers must take some of the shine from Peter Handel's much vaunted monetary masterstroke.

The Chancellor may have received a thumbs-up from the international markets but a significant number of the UK public have given it the thumbs-down.

Many of those joining the Nonettes are thought be those who will suffer directly from the cuts in government spending, including the unemployed and others dependent on state benefits.

There are however, so Nonette sources say, many others who have enrolled in the ...

Although there are no verifiable figures for Nonette UK membership, this latest surge in numbers is thought to have sent the size of the Nonette movement beyond three million.

Experts say that if the movement continues to grow at the present rate it is likely to reach what market researchers term 'critical mass'.

When this point is reached, experts say, not only will the Nonettes become a 'mass movement' but also other people will consider it is in their own interests to join it (the old trade union movement is such an example). They will have little choice but to become a member.

Leading opposition LibCon MP, Stan Hains, voiced these fears yesterday when he accused the government of causing the huge rise in Nonette numbers.

He said: "The government ...

Stanley Haines

our nation's history Messrs Campbell and Handel have allowed this country to slip into the clutches of international bankers but at the same time they are driving increasing numbers of our people into the arms of an Alien controlled organisation ...

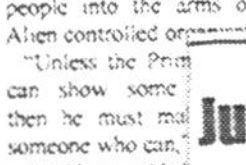

"Unless the Prim[e] ... can show some ... then he must ma... someone who can," ... Mr Hains added ... should be an ...

Pet...

He said ... were elec... everything ... suade peo... governme... includes ... all."

A Dow... man ...

Just when you thought it was safe to go outside . . .

THEY'RE BACK!

Surprise Susem sex swoop scatters Sardinian swimmers
Hundreds snatched for forced lovemaking with Aliens

By MORAGG BULL

AFTER A THREE WEEK LULL Susem snatch and grab robots returned to Europe' holiday spots yesterday. Bathers on Sardinian beaches ran for their lives as swarms of the feared Susem stinging 'vespas' herded scores of unsuspecting holidaymakers into the Aliens' delta-winged space-planes.

Last night the Alien Abduction Centre in Milan said that 327 men were taken by the Aliens, but of these 43 were returned within a few hours. Although dazed they were said to have been unharmed.

Centre spokesman Argento Palma said: "Those who have ... healthy. Those who were sent back were either old, unhealthy or both."

Last night anxious relatives and friends waited for news of the abducted men. At the holiday resort of Cala Sisine, near where the abductions took place, many of the victim's partners were said to be in a state of shock.

Rebecca Harris's (23) partner, Timothy, who was one of the three British men taken by the Aliens said: "I fear the worst. I have read what happened to those men in Brazil and those soldiers in ...

Final Test, First day
Namibia 321 for 0...

Butterfingered fielders benefit batsmen

BY WAYNE YATES

Namibia opening duo Rusniak and le Grange hit ball after ball into the hands England's fielders. It is a pity for England that none of them managed to say in their side's hands long enough to count as a catch.

Having won the toss Namibia opted to bat first. Facing England's new spin bowlers Hurst and Eddington, for the first time, both Rusniak and le Grange showed just how much ...

crests of primary waves' ripples. Primary waves she hastened to add were soliton waves. It's only when Secondary waves, energy, become concentratedly concertinaed that they pack punch. It's from the crests of Secondary waves when they are like this that the froth of Tertiary waves, or frothicles, form.

But the high points of Primary waves have to be at precisely positioned intervals before Secondary waves can form their power-packed concertinas. In the same way these also have to be precisely peaked for Tertiary waves to form. Each point though is only propitiously placed for a fleeting moment.

Points are as quantums, Menpemelo said, and when they are not part of a wave they are participating in putting together 'withouts'. Not every point is involved in waves or compiling, and from what she said, it's only one in a very few.

As she explained, I had thoughts of my quantum matchboxes. Inside each one is energy and 'matter'. Or alternatively there is 'life'. In one sense they are the same, undulating waves of boxes, but in another they're not. Energy and 'matter' (contrary to what we have always been told) do not make 'life'. Although life comes from the same source as energy and matter, it is formed from the quinth context of points, and is separate, different from them. In turn all points for energy, matter, life, stem from the Anthropic Constant. And they are what constitute the Anthropic Template.

But even before I had time to dwell upon the moment of this awareness Menpemelo had me plunged into 'complexity'. First she mentioned computer software and data disks. Their encoding no more than dots and blanks, binary 'ons' and 'offs', the configuration in which they're assembled creating programs. Hardware followed. The fabrication of a computer chip is the focused tele-scoping down from a master matrix many times larger.

'Withouts' are similar assemblies, their dots being the incoming packets of data referred to by Menpemelo when she spoke about spider webs. These packets however, are 'maxi-dots', for each, in turn is made up of layered combinations of the interactions of the components of the Anthropic Constant itself.

As she explained I had still to keep hold of the notion that all this is going on in the quinth context. Also, of the concept of being surrounded by an aura, which at the same time, is made up of billions of little 'auralettes'. Again it's another quantum, just as the 'us' of us is. We are the sum of our cells yet at the same time the singularity of self. I did think things were becoming too complex but then thought how the interaction of our cells is no less. And they all get on with one another without trouble (well, most of the time).

Menpemelo pressed home this point, how it is harmony making the Universe and everything within it go round. Then she pressed on with the workings of 'withouts'. As she did it struck me how alike it was to the balls of light experiments she and Anuria showed me and, for that matter, how Terbal functions. Data goes in then it's bounced around from one surface receptor to another. What is reflected, transmitted back, is an amalgam of the

Gunners could win Cup-win-odds shorten

Arsenal to face Barcelona

By AMY CELESTE

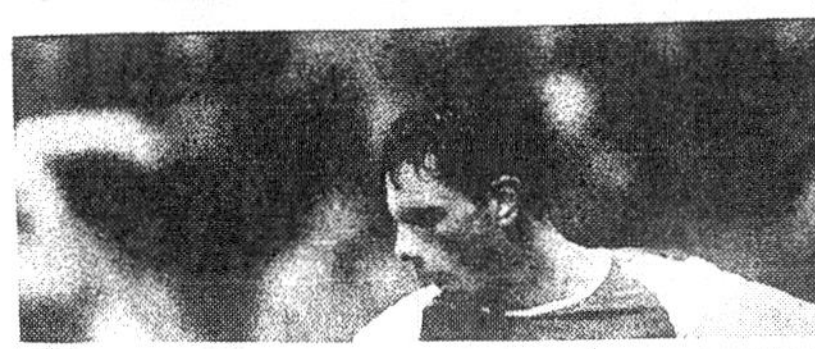

BOUYED BY Arsenal's shock victory against the Germans, Gunner's come-back supremo, Graham George is ensuring his squad knuckle-down to non-stop, no-nonsense dawn-to-dusk work-outs for their forthcoming Quarter Final clash against as-yet-unbeaten Barcelona.

With their fiery wayward "wunder-kind", soccer's bad-boy, Don Kirk all set to lead the charge against the Spanish superstar side, Arsenal claims that, after beating the Germans, Barcelona will be a walkover.

Although William Ill's have shortened the odds of Arsenal's bringing back the IFEA Cup to Highbury to 50-1 and the entire nation rooting for their win over the Catalan king-pins, soccer punters still view the Gunner's high-goal score win against Munchen as a fluke.

George maybe putting his faith in more miracles from Don Kirk but Barcelona have one of their own: their swarthy giant Galician goalkeeper, Enrico Motril. At two-metres-plus tall, Montil is known through-out Spain, both on and off the pitch as El Gordo - 'The Big One'.

This mighty man-mountain has proved more than a match for many sharp-footed centre forwards. His powerful ball punch and kick has landed endless opposing players in hospital.

While Spanish senoritas swoon at his sight, especially the several score he is said to have sired sons to, this idol of the Iberians poses problems to an attacker

Nonette newspa[per] to be censured

By **Joy Frampton**
Media Correspondent

New papers 'libelous' say leading QC

THE new Nonette newspapers could be facing massive claims for damages a leading libel QC said yesterday.

Officials in a total of 58 UK local councils were named in a num[ber of news]paper-style tracts put out by Nonette groups.

Many of those councils named are threatening legal actions against the Nonettes.

Councils in turmoil over bribery allegations

William Butler-Clarke QC, said that all the Nonette papers he had seen so far had been libelous and could face claims not only

He said: "I... these public[ations]... they will st[and]... in their o[wn]... courts. They... Britain and... ject to its... other.

"I also no[te]... them are... the Post O[ffice]... paper and... further offi[ces]...

"If I wer[e]... the editor... of these r[...]... Clarke s[aid]... indeed be...

At the...

ASA condemns Nonette 'vu[lgar]' sex aid ad

"Breaks guidelines but we are power[less]"

By **Andre Capplewood**
Media Correspondent

Mathew Alder

THE Advertising Standard Agency considers that the Nonettes' sex aid advertisement to be in blatant breach of the Agency's code of practice, if it had appeared in a mainstream paper.

Head of the ASA, Mathew Alder said that as the Nonette newspapers were not members of the NPA (Newspaper Publishers' Association) there was nothing the ASA could do directly.

"However," Mr Alder

Family Planners slam Nonette sex aid ad

By Tony Perry
Social Affairs Correspondent

"Totally irresponsible" says FPA head

ADVERTISEMENTS in yesterday's Nonette newspapers for the 'Love Patch' sex aid were condemned as irresponsible and potentially dangerous by Family Planning professionals.

The Patches' unsupervised use could lead to a rash of underage pregnancies and the spread of sexually transmitted diseases among young people it was claimed.

The full page advertisements which appeared in Nonette newspapers claimed that the Patches would give

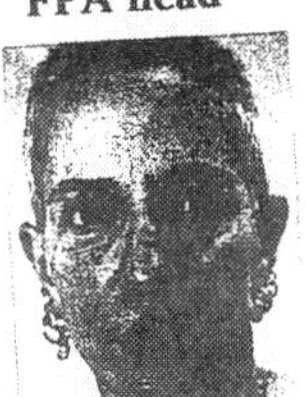

Dame Stella Willis

Head of the South East's

diately withdrawn.

Dame Stella said: "Family planning must always be left to the professionals not to amateurs, no matter how well meaning they might be, though I very much doubt if any of these Nonettes are.

"But what is totally irresponsible on the part of these Nonettes," Dame Stella said, "is that many members of their movement, so I am reliably informed, are teenagers and other children.

"Should these patches fall into their hands," she said, "goodness knows what will happen. The mention that users of these patches need extra large size condoms has only made the matter worse,

"Nowhere is safe now" - say experts

ALIEN ATTACKS WIDEN

By **Phillip Brown**
Abductions Correspondent

"ALL men everywhere are at risk of Alien abduction and serious sexual assault," the Alien Abduction Centre cautioned yesterday.

The warning came after a day which saw the highest number of Susem raids yet. Meanwhile, survivors of earlier abductions have been returned from their ordeals. All tell same horrific stories of assault and abuse during their captivity.

A total of 83 Alien abductions were reported during the 24 hour period to midnight CET yesterday. The Alien Abduction Centre in Milan said that a reported 2,452 men had fallen into Susem hands although a further 731, originally taken ... Aliens were released unharmed within a few hours after being abducted. All of these, the Centre reported, were either old or in less than perfect health.

Although yesterday's Susem raids ranged from California to Thailand, the north of Europe, from Finland to France, suffered the brunt of abductions. One of resorts affected was Jersey in the Channel Islands. Here, a

Fizer protests at Nonette sex aid claim

"Vigra is not harmful" - says company

By Burt Bunson
Legal Editor

FIZER, the troubled pharmaceucal company and makers of the infamous sex aid drug, Vigra, hit out yesterday at Nonette claims that the drug was harmful.

The company said that they were taking legal action to stop the Nonettes making further "unsubstantiated statements" against Vigra.

A Fizer spokesman said: "Vigra is not harmful. ... the main

as well as our creditors.

"Therefore, Fizer plc along with our US parent company Fizer Inc., are taking immediate action against all the Nonette groups which publish and distribute the advertisement."

The Fizer spokesman said that while Vigra and all the other similar drugs had been banned both in America and Europe, the new Nonette Love Patches were not.

He said that the cases of Vigra turning people blind had to be seen against the

Government revenue shortfalls to receive standby back[ing]

Banks back Campbe[ll] over Alien's Tax attac[k]

By Ross Capulyard
Economics Correspondant

Major banks pledged their support for the government over Nonette demands yesterday.

In a joint statement both sides of the inter-government-banking liaison committee said: "The UK government's prudent financial polices must not be allowed to be jeopardised by events outside its control.

"It is one of the pillars of the committee's liaison to assist in the implementation of the Chancellor's pragmatic financial and taxation initiatives. The banking side of the committee has undertaken to en-sure that the anticipated taxation revenue temporally delayed as a consequence of the recent attacks upon IR facilities, is covered by further funding by the banking consortium. In return the UK government will ensure that they will use every means possible to re-coup these taxation shortfalls. The committee will review the [sit]uation at the next meeti[ng in] two weeks time."

Many City commen[tators] are of the view that as government and banks [are in] the same boat they have [no] choice other than to [pull] together and agree [a] common direction.

Whether they are pa[ddling] to or from a waterfall re[mains] to be seen. The conseq[uences] of a tax crack-down co[uld be] a major revolt by taxpay[ers]

"No surrender" says Tuce[rs]

'Maverick' Commander on his own says Pentagon

By Paulo Ridd
Reporting from Belize

GENERAL ARMSTRONG TUCERS, C-in-C of Southern Command, has vowed to ignore President Warren's order to withdraw his remaining forces from the Panama Canal Zone.

The Pentagon said that the General would face a court-marshal unless he presented himself and his forces immediately to the US Navy already anchored off Panama City.

According to messages relayed along the Panama Canal by Girl Scout Pathfinder Patrols, General Tucers and a group of fellow senior officers are preparing to fight what is reported as their 'last stand' against the Susem.

According to the Scout Pathfinders - who had penetrated as far west as within five miles from Fort Clayton - six of their Patrol were initially taken prisoner by a Rangers' Detachment who thought they were Susem in disguise.

It was while they were trying to convince the soldiers who they really were, that they came into contact with two senior officers who told them that there would be "no surrender".

Military analysts have identified them as Generals Barry Paisley and Ian McCaffrey, both of whom served with General Tucers at Khe Sanh during the height of the Vietnam War.

The Girl Scouts' Patrols also said they thought that between 500 and 1,000 troops were preparing to stand with General Tucers and were busy constructing a series of underground bunkers in which to deploy roughly one third of

receptor's and several previous sources' transmissions.

Then Menpemelo was on to quantums again. How we are the solidity we see, touch and feel, yet at the same time an aura buzzing with pulsed packets of data zipping back and forth. But there is more to it than just this (quantums again). It is the zipping and buzzing which is also what we are. And more yet, the seemingly solid part of us is merely the resulting by-product of all this zipping and buzzing. It's this zipping and buzzing which is the really relevant part of us living things.

As she unfolded this, Menpemelo again used the analogy of computers. What is seen on screens isn't the data keyed or spoken in, but this data after it has been relayed through the hard and software interacting with one another. It is they who are the actual determiners of outcome. The image on screen is a 'mere' by-product of their interplay. If their interaction becomes "dyslexic" as she put it, neither the 'inputter' or 'receiver' can directly control or amend the result.

At this point I was about to say "Oh yeah, what about reproduction and growth then?" but she beat me to the point by reminding that though it is the quinth context from which the other contexts evolve, it's from them which the quinth re-evolves. She then added 'efficiency' to the equation. Some things are better done in one context than another. But added I had to remember all were involved in 'sentience' including the fourth of time. She also reminded me that the tri-context was for simpler, humbler tasks including, as she put it, "the transmutation of non-sentience into sentience."

Menpemelo elaborated. "Sustenance, food is derived from the effects of Secondary waves, those from your sun for example, upon Tertiary ones such as soil and water, but it is the aura of a plant's seed, then of the plant itself which directs transmutation of sun, soil and water into growth," she said. "It is the aura of the consumer of the plant which directs absorption. A plant when consumed is no longer alive, it is 'non-sentient', aura-less."

This had me pondering about plants' auras and those of everything else which gets eaten, what happens to them? Again Menpemelo gave the answer before I could ask. Some aural programs last longer than others, she said, adding "Though the higher the level and complexity the more post tri-context sentience aural formation will exist." I took this to mean that when something physically dies its aura hangs about for a bit.

Detail followed. Maxi-dots of defunct programs recycle to those freshly forming, or alternatively atrophy back to points, fading away on a wave. But every now and then they don't. They linger on. Though 'without' programs such as these are bereft of hardware of their own to download into, they still try their level best to do so into whatever is around, including other "sentient entities". As she said this I had thoughts of ghosts, reincarnations, children who claim to have lived past lives.

Before I had time ask about these Menpemelo moved onto to interrelation-

OECD, G9, EU, NAFTA, WTO, Banks' 'Unity Summit' shuns Nonette tax demands

"We must hang together or we will be hanged separately" – says Bank chief

Ronald Haggler and Joanna Watkins report from Davos

In an unprecedented show of strength and unity, heads and representatives of the world's economic institutions, governments and major banks rejected Nonette demands for tax concessions

Although the Davos Summit was called to strengthen world financing of sovereign debt, the Nonettes cast their shadow over the entire proceedings

Spectre

At workshop groups and Plenary Sessions alike, Nonettes and their tax demands peppered discussions Even the first day's briefing communiqué contained a passage reaffirming resistance to any concessions to the Nonettes.

It was not just their demands for tax reductions with which the Nonettes coloured meetings during the first of this weekend's Davos Summit meetings

Dominoes

In many ways it is the Nonette movement and to a lesser extent their Susem backers which precipitated the need for this global gathering.

The domino-like fall of Latin American countries has left both developed countries and the banking community alike nursing huge - and for some, painful – losses

Who is next?

As one banker, who wished to remain anonymous said: "It is not just those countries who have fallen but who will be ... especially in South East Asia and Central Europe are also giving rise to anxiety

Hollowing Out

Many conversations were filled with the socio-economic 'Hollowing Out' by the Nonettes of an increasing number of countries

All but a few of the government delegates at this Swiss spa resort admitted to suffering from the phenolmenon.

Although the imminent arrival of the new Nonette currency was dismissed by some, the consensus is it will have a yet further adverse impact on governments' control of the micro aspects of their countries' economies.

Sovereign Debt

The main focus of the Summit, however, was on sovereign debt within developed countries and the need to reduce non-commercial debt levels

Several government delegates said they were facing rising resistance and unpopularity from their electorates by the tightening of state spending and increases in taxation needed to reduce their government's borrowing

Representatives of most of the major banks, responsible for coordinating much of the sovereign loans, were generally unsympathetic to such difficulties.

Otto Schacht, head of Uber Bank, addressing the Summit, said: "Nobody likes paying taxes, including me ... we have lent them, then we too will go kaput

Bogeymen Banks

"For some people banks are big bad bogeymen," Herr Schacht said, "and maybe we are but it must be remembered just who the banks' actual owners are.

They are their shareholders And these, for the most part are insurance companies and pension funds. And who's money are they using to buy shares in our banks? Many of the very same people who are grumbling over paying their taxes that is who!

"If people do not pay their taxes, their governments cannot pay us and we will not have any money to pay dividends to our shareholders, such as the pension funds. In turn these will provide smaller payments to their pensioners. And probably by a larger amount than the taxes these people should have paid in the first place Like it or not," he told the Summit, "we are all in this together."

Period of correction

Max Boon of BancLeviathan said: "This period of correction in sovereign lending sentiment cannot be completely blamed on the Nonettes.

It would have had to happen whether they existed or not. For too long banks have lent too much and on too easy terms Banks and the financial markets in general have been competing over too ... have allowed ourselves, wrongly in my view, to be cajoled by governments and others to write off too many of our loans

Sentiment Pendulum

Now that the sentiment pendulum is swinging in the opposite direction it is no wonder both we and our sovereign clients have been obliged to respond it, in knuckling down and putting our financing on a sounder, firmer footing

Like it or not, it is something we all have to submit ourselves to in order that in the longer term both banks and governments working in harmony, restore a sounder financial basis for all of our clients and citizens respectively."

Crying wolf

Such views were not shared by everyone In the eyes of several delegates, the bankers are crying wolf over the need for earlier repayment of their sovereign loans.

Either this or they're totally unaware of the delicate and often fraught position of many governments. One said: "These bankers have not had their offices blasted to the sun as our tax people have. They have not been subjected to thousands of people cheering and singing 'Oh Happy Day' as their offices zoomed up through the clouds.

"These bankers have not had to confront their clients as we have our electorates who ...

Otto Schacht: Uber's um...

By Oliver Sroneburger

"When it rains on your friend you do not fold up your umbrella, you lend it to him," said Otto Schacht, head of the giant Uber Bank yesterday.

Herr Schacht was commenting on the worldwide Alien attacks on tax offices across all the countries of OECD

"Your Chancellor Handel is a wise man," Herr Schacht said, "he is also a courageous one. He alone only knew what had to be done to restore confidence in the sovereign loans market He also had the strength of conviction to seize the bull by the horns and do it.

"Although in the short-term," Herr Schacht said, "there will be unpleasantness for some, in the longer term all will benefit everyone

"Your Chancellor Handels's bold initiatives have led to others across the EU and else- ... Your Mr Handel has single-handedly saved the day for both countries and international banking. Therefore, it is in the best interests of the banking community that we give every assistance and support to your government and others with the same determination to see their plans for taxation through

"As for the [Susem] attacks themselves, they will not succeed They will be counterproductive just as it was when, in the 1940s, my country attacked your cities

"Our bombing did not make you give up but instead made you more resolute and we lost

"You bombed us and again what was achieved? As with your country it was the opposite of what was hoped by your leaders and we Germans fought you all the harder And so it will be this time Your

Nonette papers c... face D Notice ...

Voluntary code break could risk nation...

BY DAVID GAUNLETT
HOME SECURITY EDITOR

THE 'D Notice' system which ensures the confidentiality of Britain's national security has been breached by the new Nonette newspapers.

As a result of the Nonettes' revelations, the safety of the nation could have been seriously jeopardised.

The head of the D Notice ... Deal, said that the Notice's voluntary code had been disregarded by the Nonette newspapers

By naming active members of Britain's security services they had threatened not only the safety of these men but also possibly that of their colleagues.

The D Notice Committee - the joint press and government watchdog - to which newspap... automati... security ... - has be... WWI

Past b... have be... mum b... regulati...

Altho... Notice ... icised i... out-of-d...

Banks dismiss new currency

By Steven Dunn
Economics Editor

THE NEW Nonette currency set to circulate among UK Nonette groups soon, was described as worthless by the head of Clayings, Britain's biggest banks. At best the so-called Nonette could be of as little value as other 'soft' third world currencies.

Nonette currency 'valueless', - claims Bank Chief

According to Sir Roger Foscoe, Clayings' chairman, the value of each of the world's major currencies such as the pound, US dollar or German mark is set against its exchange rate of a basket of other like currencies. Each of these currencies, Sir Roger, said are 'freely convertible' Should there be excess in demand in one currency then all the central banks of the respective countries sell their holdings of this particular currency so that there are no shortages of the particular currency Conversely if more people sell a particular currency than buy it the surplus resulting is brought up by the central banks and so its value is maintained

Sir Roger Foscoe

As the Nonette currency is not held by the central banks - something Sir Roger said will not happen - it does not have any independently verifiable valuation. "For example," Sir Roger asks, "what happens if all these Nonette people start changing their pounds, marks and whatever into this new so-called currency? What are their banks going to do with all this hard currency? They are going to be able to do nothing except change it into another hard currency. After all, none of the main banks are going to touch this Nonette with a barge pole!" Sir Roger also said that the areas where the Nonette is

Bulgarians in surprise 1-0 win over French

By Andrew Keilty

SOFIA DYNAMO'S last minute penalty kick scored the winning goal against Lille and so brings them a place in the semi-finals of the IEFA Cup.

Dynamo was awarded the disputed penalty against the Lille's striker, Le Crouieu's foul on the Bulgarian's centre half Inoff Thered in the 89th minute of a desultory game.

Italian referee, Grasso Palma, in giving the penalty drew the anger of the thousands of French fans. The Lille players had no choice but to go along with the ref's decision even though both player's were well apart at the time of the supposed foul.

The actual goal itself owed more to luck than skill on the part of Dynamo's scorer Demetri Burgas's

LOVE PATCHES ALL SOLD!

5m snapped up on first day

"No more a for week" - say Nonettes

By ALAN SMITH

LONG QUEUES formed outside Nonette centres yesterday as the first batches of 'Love Patches' went on sale. Supplies in many centres were exhausted by lunchtime.

The demand for the patches took many people by surprise - including the Nonettes themselves.

Nonette centres across Britain have seen nothing like it, many weary helpers said yesterday. At one centre in Esher, Surrey people queued nonstop until its supply of patches were all gone Even when they were, there was still a queue of yet more people placing orders for next week's delivery

Last night the Nonette newspapers said that an estimated five million patches had been sold

ships between the programs. While most, most the time, she said, are focused on the "entity" they have created, they do not do so in isolation. There is an awareness, association between those of one being's programs and those of others. Some go so far, she said, as to frequently function as a collective whole. Ant colonies is one example. Birds when swirling in flocks, fish swishing in shoals, locusts set on swarming, are others.

Next came synergy. Plants and their particular pollinators, ants and aphids, microflora on man and every living else were examples she gave of programs of one lifeform harmonising with those of another. Similar synergy, she said, exists collectively between whole groups of beings, such as a forest, though not as intensively.

Threading through all she told, a theme almost, was that most living things existed, responded not just tri-contextually but matter-of-factly within 'withouts' as well, it being merely part of life and living. Another recurring theme was that harmony always asserts over disharmony. Discord is instability, she said, and so will not sustain, it eventually dissipating back to points then waves.

Evolution came up again with Menpemelo debunking Darwinism with bats and birds. An animal born distinct from its fellows is most unlikely to survive long enough to produce progeny with its differences. "It takes more than one of a kind to procreate," she'd said. Adding it is not just feathers and fluttering wings needed for flight. Hollow bones, specialised muscles, beaks and big hearts and all had to evolve near simultaneously. Should just one attribute be absent there would not be 'lift off'. And a flightless flight-like form would be most terrestrially challenged and prompt prey to a predator. She had a little laugh at Earthly scientists' latest theory of animals developing wings for gliding down from heights in pursuit of food. "How much energy would be spent climbing up again and with only two feet?" she joked.

For flight to evolve, Menpemelo said, changes needed to affect a group of animals collectively, to the same degrees and in short order. "How will such changes happen?" she had asked rhetorically.

With me not knowing of course, Menpemelo unfolded the 'how'. It didn't just apply to birds either but to every other living thing, we humans included. "In the very beginning," she began, "the incoming program of the Anthropic Template is only able to initiate upon the interactions of Secondary waves and the Tertiary ones of rudimentary aggregates such as gases, water, isotopes, of carbon. Simple secondary programs result.

"From these programs, however, continuously complex ones develop. In the processes of so doing tri-context entities transmute ever multitudinous components within them. The rate at which this occurs is relative, however, to the ambient environment pertaining. It took more than two billion years before nucleated cellular lifeforms, such as amoebae, evolved on Earth."

She momentarily mentioned how Tertiary waves, frothicles, form elements

SUSEM II WORLDWIDE SEX RAIDS

Fears rise for thousands taken Aliens for forced lovemaking sessions

By LINDA HARTLEY

FEARS ROSE YESTERDAY for the fate of several thousand young men snatched in a series of worldwide lightning Susem raids. Though Europe and America bore the brunt of the abductions, countries as far apart as Australia and Canada also were subjected to Alien attacks.

It is the first time that the so-called 'sex raids' have occurred over such a wide area at the same time. The Aliens also attacked further north than usual with resort of Deauville, on France's Channel coast experiencing a Susem attack yesterday afternoon where an estimated 50 young men bathing on the beaches were taken.

In the United States both Santa Cr and nearby Monterey saw a whole ser of raids when more than 200 bathers a even dinghy sailors were report abducted. Further north in Oregon the were further raids at along the entir shoreline of Lincoln County. Althoug the full number of those abducted is a yet unknown, beaches to the south o Newport had 60 young men taken in a single Susem abduction raid

CHRON EXCLUSIVE

"MY NON-STOP SEX ROMP HELL WITH THE ALIENS"

BRITISH SURVIVOR OF SUSEM SEX RAIDS TELLS HOW HE WAS:

FORCED into24 hours of non-stop 'robust' lovemaking
FORCED to undergo torture by sex-crazed Susem she-devils
FORCED to be an Alien sex toy for their kinky love games

By Tracy Howard and Wayne Flynn

DAVE STRACHEN, a 26-year old architect was holidaying in Sardinia with his wife Trudy when he was abducted by the Aliens. Dave said that he and hundreds of other young men, also taken captive by the Susem, were forced to take part in non-stop sex sessions with his abductors.

Recovering from his 24-hour ordeal, Dave, who is in Carliari hospital, said: "As a result of my ordeal, doctors have told me I will be unable to perform my marital duties for some weeks to come.

"The doctors say that the Aliens have given me 'molto completamente attenzione' which I think translates as: 'a very thorough seeing to'. And presently that is precisely how I feel, well and truly f**ked."

Herded

Dave, who hails from Haywards Heath, Sussex, told how he and the others were stripped and scrubbed by the Aliens' robots and then herded into a swirling green mist.

"At the time," he said, "I was scared witless. I could make out some of the other men through the mist but as it started to clear I began to make out the shapes of what I reasoned were the Susem

"The mist cleared some more and not only could I see we were in a wooded clearing but just how many other men were with me, there must have hundreds of us.

Good lookers

"I could also make out the Susem women. I have to admit that they were all good lookers.

"There must have been 40-50 of these Susem and [they] were all dressed in the same thin, gossamer-like one piece trouser tunics

"They also seemed to walk towards us as if in slow motion, like they were gliding ... surprise. As I turned round I saw these other Susem darting away through the trees

'Nice sensation'

"I also saw that the other men had had the same thing happen to them. Then I felt this 'nice' sensation and when I glanced down, I saw my manliness was not only erect but there was more of him.

"By now the first Susem women were just a few feet away and were rubbing their hands up and down their fronts and swaying their bodies from side to side. It was obvious what was coming next.

"Although I'm a married man it was hard to refuse, especially as my manliness was just that - very. When one of them reached out to me I found myself going towards her I said: "Hello, my name's Dave what's yours?" but she said nothing just smiled

"Well, one thing led to another as it does and there we were, with her on top of me I kept saying: "This is nice," because to be absolutely frank it was. At the time that is

She said nothing

"All the same, she still said nothing just sort of kept smiling down at me I did my best to please her, as you do But being on my back I was somewhat limited.

Heaving bodies

"While we were making love I was also aware there were hundreds of others couplings I have been to a few way-out parties in my ... but I have never seen ... rising and falling all over the place. Thing was though I noticed that all the men were like me - in the inferior position.

"Because I'd had my watch taken off, I no idea of the time or its passing. But I did remember thinking: "She's taking her time." I did try to change position but her grip of my shoulders was so strong there was little I could do but continue to lie there and let her continue to have her way with me

She gripped me

"It was not long after this than she was gripping me somewhere else. At first it was a gentle pulsing rhythm and I again thought "this is nice" but them she was gripping me firmer and for longer.

"It was also starting to hurt. I said to her: "Careful, easy now, no need to grip me that hard," but she took no notice and kept on doing it Then she was really hurting me.

"I was then calling out for her to stop, that it was not fun any more. But instead of stopping she gripped all the firmer and pulsed me faster.

"I tried to get her off me Then to my surprise there were these other Susem holding my arms legs I was then pleading for them to let me go

Yelling and crying

"I was also aware of other men yelling and crying out in pain. I was very frightened Then all of sudden the Susem I was having love with stopped and knelt back off of me I was so relieved. But ...

Davos Disarray

Nonette issue splits 'Unity Summit'

RONALD HAGGLER AND JOANNA WATKINS
REPORT FROM DAVOS

France's de Bray: pro

US's Housings: anti

THE Unity Summit of the world's major trading groups, nations and financial institutions, ended in disarray yesterday over contact with the Nonettes

A minority, led by the French, proposed that a dialogue be opened with the Alien backed movement Their proposals, however, were vehemently opposed by the US and a majority of the other delegates

Although, the French and others are in a minority in calling for contact with the Nonettes, they have caused splits within both the European Union and World Trade Organisation, a trail of events reminiscent of the heated dispute during these same factions in the lead up to the war and Iraq.

Unless the differences between the two positions can be resolved quickly, observers say, they will stymie and thus weaken the chances of a unified front against the Nonettes.

The French representative, Minister of Finance, Raymond de Bray, said: "We have to face reality The Nonettes' exist. It is idiocy to ignore them They grow stronger by the day The longer the rest of the world delays in working out some form of co-existence with them the more difficult it will be to do so at a later time"

Arnold Housings, US Secretary of Finance who Nonettes, strongly condemned the French position He said: "It is rich coming from de Bray. The French appear to have forgotten it was they who, in May, fired a nuclear missile at the Aliens in an attempt to wipe them out Only somebody who has not been directly affected by the depredations of the Nonettes could utter something so simple-minded.

"We did not remove the communist threat, by accommodating ourselves with the Soviets but by containing them," Mr Housings said "For democracies to parlay with the Nonettes will be nothing other than stabbing in the back those nations of Latin America and elsewhere who are daily battling to contain them

"Now is not the time for talking but devising ways of combating and rolling back these crypto-socialists"

Housings, whose officer son served in Panama and was captured by the Susem, is a noted hardliner towards the Nonettes He is also reputed having lost his father in the Normandy landings and regards them as an ungrateful nation.

The final Summit declaration, however, kept to the main purpose of the Davos meeting All those attending the Summit reaffirmed to act in unison in reducing their national budgets and accelerate their debt repayments. In return the banks pledged to continue their financial support to all countries keeping to these reforms. There was also mention of the worldwide Susem attacks on tax offices.

The banks said they would consider any shortfalls in government revenue income brought about by Susem actions as 'temporary' and would not adversely affect their sovereign lending commitments

The Nonettes, as if a spectre at the feast, were also present in the final communiqué It said that although all those present were affected by the Nonettes growing influence they were a matter be left to ...

Kirk bevies up for Arsenal-Barcelona clash

By STEVEN FOX

ARSENAL'S wayward wundekind, Don Kirk, was sticking to his strict training regime in preparation for Thursday's battle against the Spanish titans, Barcelona.

Part of Kirk's regime is than he never gets out of bed before 10 o'clock.

So dependent are the Gunners on Kirk's winning skills that they have also to accept his large in-take of what George euphemistically terms 'Don Kirk's spirit' - a 15 year old single malt. While this regime may have stunned the Germans it still ... against. The 50-1 odds against Arsenal actually bringing back the cup to Highbury still stand unchanged. A William IIIs spokesman said: "Even should Arsenal pull off a win against Barcelona, IC Milan are still in the frame.

"All the serious ...

step by identically progressive step, so that the structure of them including all the complexities of their interactions is the same throughout the entire Universe. That this is so is evidenced, she said, by spectrography. Then she continued.

"As complexity advances, the pace of subsidiary program formation accelerates, again albeit irregularly. Change is slowed by consolidation, speeded by springing from this merging and combining. The advent of RNA is such an example, Hox genes another. Each advance facilitates divergence enabling subsequent optimising of the ambient environment.

"Program progression is also subject to retrogressive mutation. A situation where incremental levels of data inhere within the Anthropic Template are unable to forward into the subordinate ones. When this occurs there is program retrenchment and discontinuance of degenerative formation usually resulting in extensive extinction among such lifeforms. Newer, more progressive entities evolve from program coordinates prior to such regress."

"Do you mean it was this," I said getting in a quick question, "not cataclysms which caused all those mass extinctions?" but wished I had not, for her face had forbearance as she answered.

"On your planet catastrophes have undoubtedly occurred but as evidence illustrates, life here has not expired. A cataclysm might speed extinction of vulnerable species but would not by itself occasion it. If such had been then all life would have expired, would it have not?"

Then, as though I had not interrupted, Menpemelo continued. Programs retrench to where they have gone wrong and begin anew, she said. With each fresh start progress is not only rapid but parts of the old programs are often reincorporated. She reminded me not to forget that 'life' effects the environment just as it in turn influences life.

I had also to remember, she said, that all living things including us have lots of smaller ones, "entozoa" Menpemelo called them, not just on our backs to bite but within as well. I winced when she said that more than a twentieth of us is entozoa living in us. These though are also programmed into shaping the way we are. Each one of us is as a vast city for them, billions walking and working in our every nook and cranny. Which, in turn, must mean that not only are there our auras surrounding us but those of our entozoa as well.

When the programs of a being (and those of all within) reach a critical combination there is 'lift off', or "inhere progression," as Menpemelo put it. She also stressed that just as a creature hosts a community of others it has to be part of one as well, a herd, a shoal, for such changes to occur, the programs of every last one coordinated to the advancement. Eggs were an example of this she said. The first of a clutch is laid long before the last but all the chicks are programmed to complete their development and hatch at the same time. Cuckoos in nests are another. Their chicks, though very different

HUNDREDS OF SOUTHEAST MEN ABDUCTED BY ALIENS - BUT MANY ARE RETURNED

SUSEM SEX CRAFT STRIKE BRITAIN

By MAGNUS PEPPER

BRITAIN SUFFERED its first major Susem sex raids yesterday Last night police sources said than more than 600 men were thought to have been abducted by the Aliens. More than 100 men - mainly elderly were returned unharmed within hours of their capture.

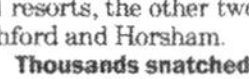

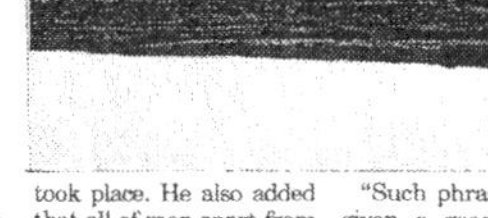

The South East was subjected to a total of 12 separate raids ranging from Thanet in the east to Southsea in the west. Although 10 of the raids took place at various coastal resorts, the other two occurred as far inland as Ashford and Horsham.

According to police reports the attacks took place between 12.10 at Broadstairs and 12.30 at Southsea.

Each attack was over within a matter of a few minutes.

Hove attacked

At Hove, East Sussex, one eye witness, Edith Chambers (54) said that two Susem craft zoomed in from the Channel and within seconds their snatch and grab robots were chasing groups of men along the beach.

"No sooner had I heard their cries than two more of these spaceships were right in front of them. Ramps on them came down and the men where chased up inside.

"No sooner were they in than the ramp came up and the spaceships flew off. It was all over in seconds."

The Alien attacks on the South East were only part of more than 80 other raids across Europe ranging from Hamburg to the south of Spain.

Thousands snatched

Italy, however, bore the brunt of the raids. According to the Alien Abduction Centre in Milan a total of 2,420 men were abducted. Of these, according to the Centre more 800 were returned, physically unharmed within a few hours.

Abduction Centre spokesman, Alfredo Rossi, said: "The pattern of today's Aliens' attacks is the same as those on previous days. However, we are observing an increasing higher 'rejection rate' by the Susem. It is as if they are becoming really picky.

Weedy thrown back

"Up to a week or so ago it was older men and those in poor health. But now it is also those men who, how shall I say, 'weedy' who are also, and again shall I say, are 'thrown back'."

Snr. Rossi also said that those men taken during earlier raids were being returned at about the same rate which fresh abductions took place. He also added that all of men apart from suffering from severe sexual assault only a smal minority were now requireing medical treatment.

Violence down

He said: "We are not seeing the levels of gratuitous violence inflicted on the current victims as was observed when the first raids took place. This is not to say that all the victims have not suffered traumatic experiences.

"It is no understatement to say," he said, "that all the victims have been subjected to the male equivalent of being not just raped but of multiply raped and thus, like women say it is with them they will be traumatised for many years to come."

Harold Paste, a psychiatrist writes: There has been much ribald comment on the fate suffered by the young men abducted by the Susem and then subjected to prolonged sexual assault.

"Such phrases as: 'b given a good seeing 'screwed speechle although doubtless lig hearted, give rise to a gr lack of understanding the trauma experienc by the victims, most whom are young men.

"It is often not unde stood - and especially most women - that me more so youths are vul erable, are very sensiti creatures.

Men: the gentler sex

"Men's air of strengt boldness is in reality facade to cover their senses c inner vulnerability. Men ar also forced by their peer to keep up this 'macho image lest they be branded as 'weak'.

"But the moment a man's manly facade is taken away - such as the Susem have done to their victims - he has revealed to himself and probably for the first time, just what a delicate sensitive creature he is."

SUSEM SEX RAIDS RANGE EVEN WIDER

- ***Denmark, Germany, Holland attacked by Aliens***
- ***Aliens abduct 4,000 worldwide***
- ***Returned victims were all 'tortured' but will recover from sex ordeals - doctors say***

By CINDY BRUTEMAN

DUTCH, DANISH AND GERMAN SUNSEEKERS fled in th thousands yesterday as scores of Susem snatch-and-gr robots drove hordes of hapless bathers into the Aliens' 's craft'.

In less than an hour yesterday afternoon the Frisian Islands from Denmark to Holland were the scene of a reported 42 separate surprise raids by the Aliens.

No group of bathers large or small was safe from the Susem's swan-size flying robots or their fearsome, stinging 'vespas'. Eye witnesses who escaped the raiding parties said that the abductions were all over in a matter of just a few minutes.

Camilla Andarsen who with her boyfriend Hans, was sunbathing on the Danish island of Fano when the Aliens swooped, said: "Both of us were almost asleep when I heard all this shouting.

"When I looked to where it came from I saw this line of men running towards us. But eve n before I could work out what was happening, flying robots appeared and from the air and attacked Hans.

"I tried to hold Hans but it was no good, these machines were jabbing and pecking at him. I felt a jab to my arm and when I looked I saw a big hornet.

"It was such a surprise that I let go of Hans. The last I saw of Hans was of him and the other men being pushed up into this plane like-thing."

Camilla is still waiting for Hans to return but said: "I have read what happened to those men in Brazil and Panama. If this happens to Hans it means he is not going to be any good and I will have to find a ..."

Arsenal BEATS Barcelona 5-1!

Don Kirk 'miracle' hat-trick

By JAMIE REDDIE

A TRIUMPHANT DON KIRK was carried shoulder-high by his teammates as Arsenal celebrated their stupendous 5-1 win over Barcelona in the IEFA quarter finals at the Forum Stadium, Rome.

To thousands of ecstatic English fans, Don Kirk's hat-trick was nothing short of a miracle.

Though questions no doubt will be asked of the Spanish side's lack-lustre performance, it does not detract in the slightest from Arsenal's fantastic achievement.

Kirk, celebrating his three goals in 12 minutes, said: "Before the match I dreaded facing the Barcelona keeper, Motril. They did not

IEFA Cup – Arsen al's playing wa indifferent, Barce lona's was abysmal.

Mystery still sur rounds why the Spaniards did not play their star strikers such as centre forward, Calella, and left winger, Bisbal, and the rest of their front-line. The major surprise is, of course, the absence of their famed - and

Final Test: 2nd Day: Namibia declare 622-1

Bee swarm and bad light stops play

By JOSEPH IMPITT
CRICKET CORRESPONDEN

ENGLAND'S bowlers fielders failed to di Namibia's batsmen. It swarm of bees, seve which stung opening b le Grange mid-run and up their first wicket.

In his controversial d awarding England a ru and which dismayed n the spectators - refe masuta interpreted the the game strictly to the

Next into bat was D He had hardly reac crease when the skies and the match was b a halt because of t These conditions throughout the after by tea all play was a for the day

Rather than rese orrow, Namibia dec

Cunga Jim a.k.a. Love Patch Man!

By BRITTA RUFF

WHAT DOES A GAL want from her guy? Cunilingus four times a week and he always wipes the worktops down after doing the washing up? Am I right or am I right?

Every time my young man James comes round for supper he gets my kitchen so spick and span afterwards it was as if he had licked it clean. Then afterwards ...? Let's just say I call his tongue 'Heineken'.

But now I have my young man on Love Patch. Or should I say I have it on him! Girls, take it from me, Love Patch makes James a fuller man and a longer one. Not in the length sense but the time one, two blissful, heavenly mind blowing, gripping hours of climax after orgasm after orgasm.

Nowadays (or should I say nowa-nights!) after I have had my fill of Heineken its "Hello Love Patch Man!" And it's so quick. No sooner have I put a Patch on James's back than up he comes

I have to admit though that the first time I put a Patch on James it did make his eyes water a little. I do not know if it was out of surprise or pain but I do remember thinking "That's a girth a gal can really get to grips with!"

And another thing I can tell you about these Love Patches applies to those of us gals who have an older fella in our lives I gave a pack of Patches to my gran for her to try out on grandad She is over the moon with them

Do you remember how it was with the older fellas in those days of Vigra? How they used go in the bathroom for half an hour waiting for their Vigra to take effec then come out and say: "Drop your kaks and cop this," by which time of course all your yearning had worn away? But not any more, not with Love Patch

Not only does my gran say that once she's a Patch on grandad he is up in a trice but what had become as scraggy as his neck now looks like a young man's And performs like one as well, all two hours' worth.

So gals no matter how good you guy may be he's not a patch on what Love Patch can make him do!

from their put-upon proxy parents, are not perceived as different from them by them. Once a herd had taken to flight and flourished, divergence programs for hawks, humming birds, flocking flamingos, lonesome albatrosses could be written.

Menpemelo detailed yet more about divergent programs, progression, integratives, all the way to us and why we humans are so special, different from apes. It is to do with long-term memory. We are not alone in this. Whales, dolphins possess it as well but we are best shaped to make the most of it.

She stressed there is a difference between the programs enabling us do things where intellect is not required, 'cerebrate', such as driving a car, going for a drink, and the ones where it is, 'cerebral'. This she said, as far as us humans are concerned, has been, according to Susem records, another case of backwards and forward progression.

This had me more puzzled yet, and seeing so, Menpemelo retraced a little. I had to remember, she said, that although secondary aural programs were being continually modified and thus ever higher levels of complexity and sophistication were coming about, they are all prior dependent, influenced by the Anthropic Template itself. The more advanced aura-late programs become so more of its data could in turn 'download' into them.

I'd also to remember aura-late advancement is not constant. Most of the time programs freshly formed in one generation are not passed to the next. To develop and be sustained, programs had to do so in the context of the being's fellow flock as a whole. If the untoward occurs, such as a famine, and the group becomes weakened or there is disruption between them, there will be a slip back. This slipping can go on for generations before there is advancement again.

Cerebral long-term memory among us humans, she said, is most tentative. The 'programs' for it are not in our auras when we are born but develop like speech in association with fellow humans (and their auras). A confirmation of this, she said, were human infants who having been nurtured by monkeys and wolves were then 'rescued'. With me thinking of Mowglie, she detailed how these children, besides being bereft of the power of speech, showed not the slightest sign of the intellectual retentiveness which comes with long-term memory.

Amid stressing yet again how harmony, accord makes for progress, discord backwardness, she unveiled more of the study the Susem have made of our cerebral long-term memory. However, it was in doing so that she let slip what else the Susem have sought on Earth. And now found.

Oh, and it is bad news for us blokes.

Love Patch sales soar

.....and so does Nonette membership!

RODDY BARKER
Special Correspondent

SALES OF LOVE PATCHES in Britain are now more than a million packs a week. There are still shortages in some areas but these are because of distribution hiccups rather than supply.

The patches have also brought a fresh surge in Nonette membership. The past week alone has seen a rise of 280,000 joining the movement.

Britain is not alone in its demand for the patches nor its increase in Nonette membership Europe, North America and many other places around the world have also seen similar rises.

ories Ceará say that the demand was greater than originally expected but now that further supplies of the vital plant extracts which go into the patches are now on-stream, Love Patch production is now sufficient to meet current demands.

The income generated by the sales of the patches to Nonette communities will of course be a fillip to funding their activities The rise in membership has also brought a boost to communities' incomes In some areas including here in north London, Nonette membership now makes up 100 per cent of a community's catchment area

With the arrival next week of our Nonette currency it means that all Nonette communities can change over to dealing into new-style money. The ex-

BRITAIN COMES UNDER FURTHER SUSEM ATTACK

SUSEM SNATCH BRIGHTON MEN

Forced sex with Aliens fears rise

By TRACEY SMITH

BRITAIN HAS SUFFERED another devastating Susem sex raid. Brighton bathers and ordinary pedestrians alike fled in terror as Alien snatch and grab delta spaceships swept the south coast re sort's beaches.

At least 50 men are known to have been abducted in the raid which lasted no more than a few minutes.

Last night fears rose for the missing men. Six men snatched by the Aliens however, were found, two hours later outside the nearby town of Lewis. All were said to be in a dazed state but otherwise unharmed by their ordeal.

A Brighton police spokesman said: "At 12.06 hours this morning two space craft were observed proceeding in an easterly direction from Hove along the sea front of Brighton at approximately five metres height. At 12.08 a further said vehicle was observed travelling in a westerly direction towards the first two aforementioned craft.

"At 12.12 all three craft were observed flying in a straight line in the direction of Dieppe. Between 12.08 and 12.12 a number of men, clad only in swimming apparel were seen running, as if being chased from the first vehicles towards the second where-upon they were embarked into the aforementioned vehicles.

"But wit-nesses have reported that several of the men were shouting as they ran, as though they were suffering from pain of some kind.

"At approximately 15.17 hours six men in swimming costumes were observed in the Lewis area in a confused state. As to the whereabouts of those males reported

Arsenal's winning ways worries bookies' investors

By Grahame Tulbut

The FTSE's recent moderate rises continued uninterrupted yesterday with even a 27 5 gain on the day to 8052.

Even some of the high tech stocks experienced modest gains for the first time in weeks

However, there were laggards to this cheery scene. Among the downs were all the usual suspects, energy, oil and mining. A surprise guest to this gloomy corner was William Ill, who was off 15p at 287p Market gossip said Arsenal's current run of amazing form (or is it just luck as Spurs fans claim?) is set to depress the betting chain's profits

If Arsenal should bring back the IEFA Cup to Highbury then a certain big punter who placed a £50,000 1000-1 bet on an Arsenal win would walk away with all of Ill's expected profits for the year

Ill's have denied any suggestion for their share price's slump and said the big money was on Milan winning the IEFA champion-

UK Nonettes rise to 5m

Numbers set to soar further Nonettes claim

BY TONY PERRY
HOME AFFAIRS EDITOR

THE Nonette movement has grown to more than 5m members it was claimed yesterday.

Although this figure includes as many as 2m school-age children as well as companies who have also joined the movement, they represent a phenomenal rate of growth in less than three months. While these figures, which appeared in Nonette

independently verified, they are viewed by many outside the Nonette movement as broadly accurate.

Part of the reason for the Nonettes' rapid growth is undoubtedly because of people wanting to secure replacement energy units. However, the fallback in membership predicted once ordinary energy supplies were restored has not occurred. The now widespread use of Nonette teaching screens and has

rsenal Barcelona wi velcomed by Milan

ayne Strettan

MILAN, IEFA favourites are sed with Arsen- 5-1 win over elona.

"It makes our task of winning much easier," said Milan boss, Benito Carosso.

Semi-final, 'walkover' – says AC's boss

According to Carosso, next week's IEFA semi-final between Milan and Arsenal does not pose any threat to Italians. Few will doubt Carosso's confidence.

On past form there is no comparison between the two teams. In terms of both scoring and possession Milan is leagues ahead of the Gunners.

Although Don Kirk may have woven miracles for Arsenal, is he really on the same level as the likes of Milan's Begamo and Ozukini?

It is not only strikers where Milan has strength over Arsenal but in defence. It is here that Arsenal's major weakness compared not just with Milan's but the Spanish as well.

Although Arsenal's win over Barcelona is not be demeaned they should never have conceded the one goal they did. The slipshod defence by both

Susem said to be closing in on C-in-C's HQ

General Tucers' last stand expected soon

By Gordon Howe
in Washington

HOW BIG will General Tucers' last stand against the Susem be? While wags in Washington smirk: "Five inches, five and a half max", more sober assessments are being made.

Department of Defense (DoD) insiders say there are already campaigns waging within its upper echelons of the DoD on whom to pin the blame for the entire Panama debacle.

One faction, it is said, hope General Tucers comes out of Panama alive so that he carry the can for what is being viewed as the Pentagon's biggest blunder of all time Others are casting their accusations elsewhere.

But whoever is burdened with the blame, one thing has already changed: that of the military itself.

No longer will the US taxpayer put up with generals' spending limitless sums of their money on ever fancier - and ever expensive toys - for a very big bill will soon be wending its way to the DoD's door, one likely to leave its coffers bare for a very long time to come.

Lawyers across the US are sharpening their litigation knives in anticipation of the vast sums that 30,000 soldiers and their partners will sue the DoD for over the Panama

General Armstrong Tucers

fiasco.

One law firm, Temple Pattern Baldness said, "Not only were the soldiers severely screwed by the Susem but also by the DoD as well."

Susan Pelham, head of Southern Command Family and Friends (SCFF), the victims support group said: "The Pentagon must have had full details of what happened to those soldiers in Brazil.

"They must have realised the same thing would happen to our men in the [Panama Canal Zone] PCZ and got them out in time.

"Yet the DoD did nothing They have screwed up and we are going to screw them for every last cent so that our loved ones can fully recover and screw us.

Life is so trying. Tuesday evenings had always been set aside for June and the boys to accompany me to our athletic club. It was an opportunity for all the family to spend time together sharing a common interest. But of late I have been the only one prepared to make the effort.

Once, upon my arrival from work on the Tuesday, I would be met by all three, their kit packed ready to depart. Now, if any of them are at home, I am greeted no matter my exhortations, with a chorus from both boys of "Boring, boring." June is as bad, not only in declining to join with me at our club meetings but in taking their side. Either she is busy with her "Nonette work," as she calls it, or is sitting in front of their wretched screen studying with them.

Needless to say relations at home are not at their rosiest. But this is just the start of the woes I am faced with daily. Once there was an orderly routine to my working day. Now there is chaos. Once there were rules, regulations, codes of conduct upon which one could rely on others to abide by. Not any longer. Once there were sanctions which could be imposed on wayward customers, foreclose on their mortgages, withdraw overdrafts. Alas these are gone. Nowadays a bank manager's lot is not a happy one.

The government said that only a tiny minority had joined these Nonette groups. It asked us and the other banks to decline them account facilities. We went along with this. And where did it get us? We and the other banks have lost half a million customers, that is where. Within the week the Nonettes' bank over in Brazil had set up branches in every group across the country, their members closing accounts with us in protest.

Though this was blow enough, most left owing us money which, until the bailiffs return to their duties, we have no way of recouping. It is all very well the Bank of England claiming they are "infinitesimal" but it has affected all of our other accounts. Repayment delinquency is rampant.

It is one thing for Mr Gibbons to tell us we must ask the customers nicely to keep up their repayments, but it is quite another getting even half of them to pay a penny. And the rest only do so if we undertake to increase their overdrafts to cover the repayments. With the situation the way it is I can say goodbye to my year-end bonus. If it was not for the increase in the money supply and the government borrowing knowing no limits, I just do not know how we and the other banks would manage.

According to Hilary Saxon every local government council which banks with us, and because of the Community Charge strikes, has increased their borrowing requirements. And this is another thing. Anyone would have thought, considering the crisis we are in, that Mr Gibbons' day-to-day hands-on-management was vital. But following Ms Saxon's recent promotion to Chief of Corporate Client Liaison, he is away half of the time introducing her to them. Sharon tells me there has already been talk in the tearoom.

FINAL TEST DECLARED A DRAW

ALIENS ATTACK LORDS CRICKET

Thousands flee as Aliens abduct Namibian Eleven
England's batsmen rejected by Susem and thrown back

By **PHIL CARPE**
at Lords Cricket Ground

IT IS A TOSS UP over which is more humiliating for the English Test Squad: to be 18 for 6 after 12 overs or have their batsmen rejected by Aliens as being physically inadequate for sex. Yesterday morning England suffered both.

After 12 overs and 90 minutes of desultory batting, easy catches and five "Howzat's", two Susem spacecraft swept over Lords' hallowed ground and then landed.

While thousands of spectators fled for their lives, the 14 men on the pitch were abducted and flown off before anyone in the Long Room could mutter: "Another gin and tonic if you will," to the bartender.

While the entire Namibian eleven and Indian umpire, Rajah Patel, were flown off to goodness knows where, the two English batsmen, Hargrieves and Scott, were unceremoniously dumped on Primrose Hill three miles away.

The police were still at Lords when the two batsmen arrived at the players' entrance. Scott was

Nonette firms to pay staff in Nonette money

Tax dilemma for Inland Revenue

By Ross Capulyard

Nonette owned businesses could pay some of their employee's wages and salaries in the new Nonette currency it was revealed yesterday.

Notes of the new currency - also called Nonette - come in 5, 10, 20,50 and 100 unit denominations and are expected to go into circulation within days.

The exchange rate, so a Nonette bank repressentative said, will be on a par with the US$, or £0.83p. This is the same rate as in areas already under Nonette control.

Companies using the Nonette will not be making PAYE deductions from the proportion of wages paid in Nonettes.

One Nonette company boss in Newbury said: "Paying our employees in Nonettes will be entirely up to them.

"As you know it is against the law to pay employees in kind so what they are paid in Nonettes will not count for official emolument purposes.

"In effect those taking Nonettes will, for tax purposes, be taking a cut in wages," he said.

The Newbury boss, who did not want to be named, said that his company had no intention of getting into a confrontation with the Inland Revenue.

He said: "Like other firms in the Newbury area, skilled employees are thin on the ground. It is they who determine their wages more than we employers.

"If they want to be paid partly in Nonettes then that is what we will do. Even firms who are not in the Nonettes will have little choice but to do likewise," he said.

An Inland Revenue spokesman said: "Tax is payable on income received. If an employee elects to be paid in full or in part in kind then its value will be deemed as taxable income and they will be assessed for tax liability accordingly."

The spokesman, however, declined to say if Nonette currency notes were worth what the Nonettes say they are worth or just the value of the note's paper.

This is the bind in which the Inland Revenue could find itself. If the taxman says the Nonette currency is worth what the Nonettes say it is, and levies tax according, it - and government - will, in effect be recognising the legitimacy of the new currency.

If it does not then Britain's tax base could see a drastic shrinkage

"Nowhere is safe from these flying fiends" - Met Head warns

SUSEM IN LONDON SEX SWOOP SNATCH

By ALAN SMITH

THE SUSEM mounted scores of daylight snatch and grab raids across the South East of England yesterday. Most than 800 men were abducted but many were found unharmed later during the day.

In the space of 30 minutes between noon and 12.30 yesterday afternoon, Alien craft attacked and abducted their victims across an area ranging from Sevenoaks in the east to Newbury in the west, as well as several in London area.

By late afternoon however, more than 200 of those taken were returned. Although badly shaken by their ordeal no casualties have been reported.

Last night, as fears rose for those taken by the Aliens, Metropolitan Police Commissioner, Sir Paul Harrier said: "In the light of today's and other recent attacks by the Aliens we strongly advise that males, especially younger men should stay away from all open spaces during daylight hours."

Sir Paul said that the attacks were in or near such spaces, not just parks and sports grounds but even such places as paved pedestrian precincts.

All the eye witnesses to the Aliens' raids said that they were all over in a matter of minutes. The attack in Tooting, south London, was typical of many others. People walking on Tooting Bec Common said the abduction raid lasted no more than two minutes.

One of those on the Common and witnessed the raid was Camilla Harding (23). She said: "I was walking

down and flying things shot out of it and began buzzing about the boys.

"In no time the boys were shouting out as if in pain and began running away from the flying things, like small swans they were. Both Margery and myself immediately ducked down behind a tree. I was petrified and I think everyone else who were also hiding behind the other trees were as well.

"All the same, me and Marge could see these flying swans chasing the boys to the far side of park. No sooner were they halfway across than this other space plane swooped down and a running board come out.

"I also noticed that two of the boys tried running to the sides but these other, wasp-like things seemed to drive them back in the direction of the second space ship.

"No sooner was the last of the boys up the running board

‘Nonettes a b[...] to world tra[...]

"New Iron Curtain threat facing Free World"-

By Irene Palmer
Economics Editor

WORLD trade is facing one of its biggest threats yet, the head of the World Trade Organisation (WTO) warned yesterday.

Bhara Chidambaram, President of the WTO, addressing the annual meeting of the world trade body in Madrid, said that as more regions fall under Nonette control they become closed to world trade.

Many international companies had been forced out of an increasing number of their traditional markets.

Scores of major companies are likely to experience significant downturns in both revenue and prospects of future growth as a result of the Nonette takeovers.

Mr Chidambaram said there is increasing evidence that the Nonette regions are now trading on a significant scale between themselves.

He said: "The regions under Nonette control are purposely excluding the rest of the world from their markets. As soon as an area comes under Nonette control and once the previous government's administration has been extinguished, it is as if curtain comes down between them and the rest of the free world."

The President said that repeated offers of investment and financial assistance from the outside world had been ignored. "All [our] attempts to

Bhara Chidambaram, WTO President

form trading relationships with these Nonette entities have met with nothing other than a wall of silence," he said.

"These Nonette groupings," he added, "appear intent on denying the people under their control the benefits of access to the free world markets. I shudder to think what deprivation these poor people must be undergoing."

During his opening address Mr Chidambaram also pointed to a number of vacant seats around the conference hall. "These," he said, "are the seats on which delegates of independent, sovereign countries once sat. Countries which presently, are under Nonette occupation. How many more seats will become vacant in the coming months?"

The President said, that although WTO's overtures had been rebuffed its representatives would still continue

Susem survi[...] lucky esca[...]

"It was on account of my asthma"

By **Julia Corsby**
Social Correspondent

EIGHTEEN YEAR OLD Jack Brown was one of those lucky enough to avoid the ordeals facing his friends and many thousands of other men at the hands of the Susem.

Jack was originally snatched along with eight of his friends by a Susem abduction robot squad. But within minutes of being rushed abroad the Aliens' spacecraft, he was pushed out of the craft and fell to the ground dazed but otherwise unharmed.

Jack, from Streatham, south London, is a fresher at the Greenwich University. He said he had just finished attending a pre-semester lecture at the university and was walking with some of his fellow students across Greenwich Park up to the Observatory.

Jack said: "We had a few hours to kill before the afternoon lecture so we went for a bit of a walk. I did not really want to go but at the same time I wanted to be with the rest of my group."

Jack and his friends had just entered the park when two Susem spacecraft swooped down and abducted them. Once they had been herded aboard the spaceship by the Susem robots and it had taken off, they were subjected to inspection by other robots.

Jack said: "We were bundled together with our heads down. I was extremely frightened, I think the others were as well.

"I sensed the craft take off. I did not really have a chance to look around before these other robots, like large beetles they were, started prodding us.

"Within minutes I saw the door of the spaceship

[...] the Susem are only interested in young men at the peak condition. And so, ironically, it is perhaps best for young men to pretend that they are unwell.

This is not all Sharon tells me. She says many of the lower grades are up in arms over the new staffing procedures. There is even talk of the Staff Association planning a 'rolling sick leave' action. I have done my best to explain to Sharon that due to the loss of so much business we are 'overbanked' yet again, but I do not suppose this will have any effect on her or the others.

There is something else Sharon has mentioned several times and which I consider to be much more disturbing than mere staff dissatisfaction. This is the growing number of Nonette members among them.

While obviously keeping quiet regarding my own domestic situation, I have warned Mr Gibbons and the others of this growing menace within our ranks and that it must stamped out before it is too late. Regrettably my concerns have been dismissed as an 'over-reaction'. But I have seen at first hand from customers' businesses what happens once these Nonettes get a grip. It only takes a few to join and within the week they are all members, with the owner pressurised into refunding ten per cent of their wages once taken as income tax.

Not that they are any better. I have had three so far who have gone the whole hog and joined the Nonettes themselves. None accord me the respect they used to. On my visits they treat me as if I am just another supplier touting for business. It is so demeaning.

I am not alone in suffering from this cavalier attitude either. The two accountant colleagues who I had previously placed to handle these customers' tax affairs have received the same short shift, that their services are no longer required. When one of them insisted on a termination fee for the return of the company's books he was told to use them as lavatory paper. Needless to say, there goes another source of commission earnings.

The only encouraging spot has been what Martin Manborn has said. When I met him the other day he told me he has it on good authority that certain top echelons within the Home Office and MoD now have plans drawn up to combat the Nonette menace head on. It is all hush-hush at the moment, he said, but he did add that members of the Watch are to be drafted in en-masse to assist its implementation. The Authorities, he said, are just waiting for the right moment and then they will spring into action and crush these "fifth columnists" as he called them, once and for all.

I have not mentioned this to June but when the government does act I am sure, like everyone else, she and the boys will see it is all to their good and that respect for order and authority is the proper path to advancement.

Libel Lawyers slate Nonette 'newspapers'

By Phillip Piles
Legal Editor

NONETTE newspapers are little more than new age religious tracts peddling unbridled libels a top Law Lord said yesterday

Mainstream newspapers' reputation for probity is being harmed by those of the Nonettes, the head of the Newspapers Publishers Society (NPS) said

By adopting layouts identical to real newspapers the Nonettes are confusing members of the public into thinking they were legitimate

They are also using underhand methods to rob genuine newspapers of their rightful readership. As a result of their unfair practices, Nonette papers were harming the circulation of all legitimate daily newspapers.

Sir Kevin Smith QC, guest speaker at yesterday's Law and Media Conference, said that many solicitors and barristers were being frustrated daily in bringing legal action against the Nonette publications

government action was needed to resolve the current bailiffs and warrant officers strike Sir Kevin said: "Presently these [Nonette] tracts are getting away with blue murder The stream of unfounded accusations coming off of their presses, is in itself, nothing short of scandalous

"Their scandal-mongering brings mainstream papers into disrepute" - says QC

"Because writs cannot be served on these publications, many members of the legal profession are losing potentially very large sums of money, not just for their clients but for themselves as well," he said.

Holding aloft a Nonette publication, Sir Kevin said: "I found this in the hands of one of my servants"

Sir Kevin then proceeded to show how article after article would have resulted in a libel

are at least a £1m in legal fees just going to waste because of this pointless bailiffs' strike"

Sir Kevin's views were echoed by the Head of the NPS, Michael Simmonds He said that it was in the interests of all legitimate newspapers to do everything in their power to block the Nonette papers as soon as possible before they did any further harm to the newspaper industry

"The good name of our profession for honesty, fairness and decency is vital," he said. "The Nonette's so-called papers continually publishing allegations of corruption in high places and their purported detailing of malpractice in this country's multinational companies, could lead the general public into thinking that our Society's member newspapers' well researched reporting is equally suspect and irresponsible."

Other NPS members also voiced their disquiet over the Nonette papers Times marketing manager, Timothy Bullins, said that his paper's sales were being badly hit by the Nonettes.

tried everything to keep up sales, including even bigger page three pictures but still our sales are slipping What people want is scandal and exposure of people in high places.

Because of the NPS code of decency and right of legal pre-publication vetting we are handicapped It is not fair," he said

Marketing managers from other national newspapers also complained the Nonette papers unfair practices. Andrew Martin, circulation manager for the Chronicle said: "The 'Love Patch' offers these Nonette newspapers are running we could not get away with claims like that, the ASA would be down on us like a ton of bricks. And what is more, the fact that you have to buy their papers to get the coupon to get these Patches means that all of u legitimate papers are losin millions of copies a week. is not fair," he said.

Sales managers for many the papers said that adve tising revenue was also bei hit by the Nonette papers. T Graphic's head of display sa

Banks, businesses back Government

By Natalie Pearle

The big guns of British businesses and banks have joined forces with the government yesterday in warning against the danger the Nonettes pose to industry and the wider UK economy

'Don't damage economy' - Nonettes warned

The heads of the Association of British Industry (ABI), the Confederation of Directors (CoD) and the Joint Government-Banks Liaison Committee met at Downing Street yesterday to hammer out a common strategy to combat the growing economic threat of Nonettes.

CoD Director General, Sir Hartley Collins, said many of his members were being adversely affected by their smaller competitors taking business from them

"All we ask for," Sir Hartley said, "and we are determined to get it, is a level playing field. Most of these small businesses are Nonettes and are buying from others which are also Nonette-controlled

"Because most of them are trading in this new Nonette money they are not charging the tax that legitimate business, such as our members are obliged to do. This tax evasion by these smaller businesses must be stamped out."

Sir Harley's opposite number at the ABI, Lord Mycroft, was more forthright in his denunciation of Nonette controlled companies and the threat they pose to legitimate businesses

He said: "We have agreed with the PM that urgent action has to be taken without any delay to stop these dodgy Nonette firms in their tracks.

"The ABI has undertaken to provide the PM with a complete list of all the firms we catch involve-ed in this tax dodging in order the Inland Revenue and VAT can come down hard on these nefarious under-cutters and stop them from damaging my members' interests any further."

A spokesman for the Government-Banks Liaison Committee said: "In areas of the country where the Nonette movement's presence is strong, prices in the local retail sector are significantly lower than those places where the movement is thin on the ground.

National retail chains, such as larger supermarkets, have seen their sales volumes decline in localities where the Nonette presence is strong.

"Taxpayers are being cheated by this Nonette backed activity.

"It is in their interests as well as the wider UK economy as a whole, that the government is eager to galvanise the assistance of the major organisations in the business sector in helping to bring these tax evaders to book

Put simply, we consider these Nonette controlled businesses as cheats and as such they deserve nothing less than public condemnation. We have, therefore, agreed on a joint approach in bringing to an end these blatant abuses which are not just badly affecting legitimate businesses but denying law abiding taxpayers

US in deep disarray over Nonettes

Washington in 'befriend or fight them' dilemma

Jackson Goffer
International Policy Editor

WITH THE FALL of the Yucatan peninsula to the Nonettes, all Central America is now under their control. Large parts of Argentina, Brazil and Chile appear set to follow suit. Thousands of refugees from these and other countries stream into the United States every day.

Across Canada and the US itself, an estimated 35m of their own citizens have now joined the Nonette movement. In some states, especially those of the US northwest, entire communities are solidly Nonette.

Nonettes on the rise

Europe is also faced with a similar situation. An area stretching from the Baltic to the Balkans has passed into Nonette control.

With the Nonettes taking control of Kiev, the western half of the Ukraine has all but separated from the rest of the country. Across the EU itself more than 80m people are now thought to be members of the movement.

It is against this gloomy scenario that US foreign policy specialists are drawing up new guidelines to tackle what they view as a dramatically changed security situation.

'The French position'

At present, White House insiders say, the administration is torn between two schools. One, dubbed the 'French Position', is acknowledging the Nonettes as a force, that they are here to stay and it is best to come to peacefully coexist with it sooner rather than later.

'The Dich position'

The other is that the Nonettes, more so the Latin American Continental Congress, are a threat to America's world dominance and a foe to be fought and eliminated. This position is dubbed the 'Dich Position' after the rightwing Senator

Further complicating US policy makers' difficulties is that of the United States itself. For almost a century America has been viewed across the world as the major player in its affairs.

Within the US itself, however, most native born Americans have yet to set foot outside the country. To this majority, events outside of the United States are of little or no relevance.

Until recently this dichotomy was something the administration in Washington did not need to take into account regarding US foreign policy. Now, however, an increasing number of Americans are members of the Nonette movement.

Any attack against the Nonettes overseas would be viewed by US Nonettes as an attack against them as well. Alternatively, should the administration attack its own Nonettes as being 'fifth columnists' it may well run the risk of alienating many more people in the US than merely members of the Nonette movement.

US patriotism

Although the sense of patriotism in the United States is far higher than elsewhere - the Stars and Stripes are flown on a scale not seen of national flags in Europe - it is for the country not the government.

Though a smaller percentage of the US population are Nonettes than in Europe, sentiment towards the movement by the population as a whole is generally sympathetic to rather than against it.

Even the rout of United States forces in Panama has not led to anti-Nonette sentiment. Indeed, what public anger there has been over the Panama debacle is against the administration and the Department of Defense in particular for embarking on the episode in the first place

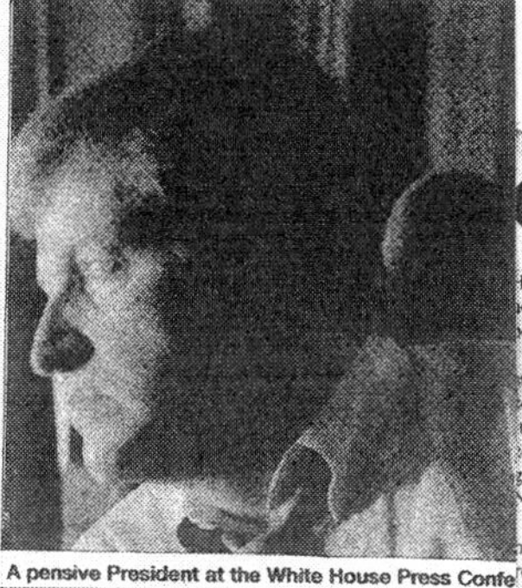

A pensive President at the White House Press Confe

Panama debacle

Unlike previous forays abroad by US forces, no one was killed in Panama except General Tucers and his was the result of a heart attack.

The Panama fiasco has however, shackled US policy makers with another constraint. Even if its forces were willing to fight against the Nonettes, the public would be vehemently against it, more so the families of those are serving with US forces. Stories of what happened to the 30,000 soldiers stationed in Panama are still making news. As are the numerous multi-million dollar lawsuits against the DoD by the affected soldiers and their families.

Tonic Water fiasco

The daily Nonette telecast is yet another constraint on the US policy. The half hour programme is widely watched throughout America, so much so, that all the major networks have now adjusted their schedules to take account of its screening. The two attempts by the administration to mount similar counter program-

Ever since the First World War, America has been the most powerful country on earth. This status has been achieved not just because of its overwhelming force of arms and economic prowess but by the 'American Way' as well. People and societies everywhere adapted their style of doing things to that of America. This global consensus of 'Americanisation' is now faltering.

Americana's end

Although not yet articulated into American foreign policy itself, this changing world perception is surely shaping it. Global 'Americana' which the US took for granted and for so long synonymous with the 'American Way', is increasingly being discarded in favour of the 'Nonette Way' of doing things.

Unless the US is able to formulate policy to successfully counter the Nonettes, then its superpower status is set not only to wane but to do so faster than even the gloomiest White House forecasters predict.

© *Jackson Goffer*

OUR GOOD NAME

e who robs us of our good name is one the richer but leaves us all the oorer.

The Nonette movement has accused us nd other reputable newspapers of being onniving appeasers. In their so-called 'newspapers' they assert we and our olleagues in the media buckled to overnment pressure in adopting an anti-Nonette stance in our reporting.

Furthermore, these parvenu papers ave gone so far as claiming that at the recent Downing Street economic summit - to which we along with other leading companies were naturally invited - we signed up to a supposedly "hidden agenda" to back not only the government but also "big business" as well

In the normal course of things, such unfounded and libelous slurs would evoke no more a response from this newspaper than would a lion whisking away a fly In this instance, however, we dare not - for the sake of our good name if nothing else - let such slanderous assertions pass unanswered

The government did not threaten to withdraw their advertising spend with us unless we undertook to take an anti Nonette line. Even should such a preposterous proposal have been made by the government we would immediately have rejected it out of hand

What we are in agreement with the government over is that in these troubled times is that it is vital the beacon of stability is not jeopardised

We have not agreed to a "hidden agenda", signed a "compact" with anyone over anything let alone "big business and the banks" to "go easy on them" in return for their increased advertising spend in this paper. The truth is quite the opposite; we report the truth, nothing more and nothing less

We are, however, ever mindful never to fall foul of Stanley Baldwin's acerbic dictum of the press: "Power without responsibility, the morals of a harlot." It has thus been an abiding principal of thi newspaper to wield our power carefully never irresponsibly.

As such it is in the interests of all an the nation's economic wellbeing i particular, to help ensure that our majo companies are not unfairly harmed b needlessly reporting scurrilous tittle tattle about them every time they make minor error of judgment. After all wh does not make a mistake every now an then?

While we are rebutting these baseles slurs to our good name it is perhaps pertinent moment to castigate two othe unfounded rumours This newspaper' staff journalists write exclusively for and no other. None of them, so we hav ascertained, have ever supplied any these Nonette papers with news iten they have written for us and which w have refused to publish because the reports were critical of our maj advertisers

Secondly, we have not sought govern ment assistance or that of business an banks, to stop these new Nonette pape because they were harming our circula tion

In the long history of this newspap we had had many who endeavoured compete us out of the industry All hav failed We do not view these upsta Nonette here today-gone-tomorrow p squeaks as any different from those times past who have assailed our unriv led position as Britain's leading new paper.

And the reason for this newspaper continued century of success? Why it our unblemished reputation for honest integrity and, above all, fearlessne Courage to search for and publish th truth without fear or favour from a quarter This is what lies behind o good name And something we will fig to the end to stop others - no matter w they may be - from ever stealing it fro us.

The heyday of men is over.

Us men will not be done down as such, it's just that we will not be up to it, shaping the future that is. Ours will be as mere sex objects, playthings, one night stands and stood-ups. Then as soon as we are past our 'stud by' date it's either a sex change, should we pass muster, or a one way ticket to the renderers for recycling on the basis we are a waste of space. With such a future no woman is going to knowingly give birth to boys. Males will be bred out. Having one will be an aberration, a freak.

Menpemelo didn't say as such, but what she showed, did. These were life-sized holograms of brains, human male and female, and similar Susem ones. Parts of all four were lit blue. "Cerebrate regions," she said, and pointing to the males' right fronts, "supplementary motor areas, more extensive than in females."

The blue went. Pink appeared. There was a little in the left hemisphere of the male Susem brain. More pink in the human male's but also mostly in the left side. But both female brains had piles of pink, and in both halves.

"Superior temporal regions, cerebral processing," Menpemelo said, "and (and she stressing the 'and' as she pointed to the right hemispheres) long-term memory reception and transmission. As you can see, human females are no less developed than are we. That your males possess more than ours indicates that a degree of cerebral 'gender hybridisation' has evolved in them."

The differences between the brains of human males and theirs had puzzled the Susem. But this hybridising, they realised was created by the abnormality (to them) of our, and as Menpemelo put it, "perpetuated male phase." Because of men's "inability to mature" into women, she said, the 'hardware' in human male brains had evolved to receive long-term memory 'software' programs which everywhere else the Susem knew to be an exclusive female preserve.

She also said, and almost as if in passing, that the uniqueness of cerebral long-term memory in us human males illustrated just how flexible the Anthropic Template is in establishing diverse ways of downloading programs into our auras. With me thinking, "Well that's all right then," she added, "However, this hybridisation is of finite progression." Before I had time for a "What do you mean?" she pointed me back to the brains and explained.

"Evolution does not create surpluses," she said. "The higher density of cerebral and long-term memory receptors in females is indicative, is it not, of their heightened aura-late capability and intellectual potential relative to those of your males?

"That such evident capability and potential have not been realised singularly and collectively within your recent historical societal record cannot but be, if in no other than objective considerations, judged as abnormal." Then giving a shrug as if in sorrow, added "And to the continuing detriment of all humans as well as your entire planet."

"Nonettes are threat to NGOs" – claims Camfa

Overseas charities suffer worldwide ousting by Nonett

By Anton Drexter
Charities Editor

AS MORE REGIONS OF the world are taken over by the Nonettes, aid agencies are being denied access to in-creasing numbers of people in need of their assistance.

Many of the aid agencies or Non-Governmental Organisations (NGOs) as they prefer to be known, expressed their fears for the wellbeing of those now under Nonette control.

At a conference 'NGOs Under Treat', held in the Royal Albert Hall, London yesterday, many of the 15,000 delegates from the leading NGOs from Europe and the US voiced their fears for the future of their operations.

"People are being denied our aid" - says top NGO chief

Lady Eloigne Richie, president of Camfam, said: "The poor people of the world need not just our help but the expertise of our field officers as well.

"Camfam," Lady Richie said, "has many dedicated and skilled people who are committed to helping the populations of undeveloped countries. However, and sadly, our offers of assistance are increasingly being spurned by those communities falling under Nonette control.

"It is a tragedy," she said, "that so many of our officers who are absolutely committed to helping the poor of the world, are being blocked by this rebel movement."

Lady Richie's comments on the Nonettes' were echoed by Howard Kingston, Catholic Aid's director of operations in Eastern Europe. He told the conference that more than 100 of his field officers had been forced out of the western Ukraine by the Nonettes.

He said: "As soon as a region falls under Nonette control, we and the other NGO's are given the ultimatum of either joining [the Nonettes] or leaving. This would mean that my officers handing over 10 per cent of their UK-based salary to them.

"Not only have many of my officers rightly refused to do so," Mr Kingston said, "but also those who initially agreed to cooperate found that when they revealed how much they were actually being paid, they were on the receiving end of abuse and threats from the very people they were trying to help.

"Fearing for their safety my officers have also been forced to leave the area."

Mr Kingston received applause from the delegates when he said: "What many of these people fail to realise, and others elsewhere in Third World, is that if NGOs are to help them we need expert staff. To do this we have to pay the appropriate salary levels and expenses, which means those current in the UK and other such advanced countries."

Mr Kingston received further applause when he said: "I just know that the people of the Ukraine just like those in the rest of the Third World, need our help. And we in turn are determined to give them our help. It is criminal that the Nonette movement should consistently deny NGOs access to so many people whom we want to help."

The under-secretary for Overseas Development, Dame Edith Cutler, said that the government would support all NGOs in their vital work. Although the government had reduced the amount of over-

Rising arrears shies lenders from new loans

Banks, Building Societies blame Nonettes for loan rationing

By Oliver Stoneburger

Mortgage arrears have become so serious that they are forcing many building societies, banks and other lenders to restrict mortgages to only a fortunate few The Nonette movement is blamed for the rising level of unpaid debt

With the traditional method of ensuring regular repayments in abeyance because of the bailiffs' strike many lenders have been forced to take the "softly, softly" approach to recovering their arrears

Debt recovery departments of banks and building societies are desperately trying to cope with the rapidly increasing workload. Harold Broad. Head of Credit Control at the Bradford Building Society, said: "The current arrears situation is spiraling out of control.

"In the beginning it was those homeowners

Now it's spread to previously good, reliable payers

"The situation for us is similar to that faced by many Councils over the Poll Tax strike," Mr Webb said. "As soon as some people are seen to be getting away with not paying others follow suit.

"These are followed, he said, "by the next group who not only have the money to pay but also by not doing so, spend it on something else. And so it

at of it) I see the situation deteriorating yet further."

The head of Clayings mortgage department, Kevin Hawks, is even gloomier about the prospects of recovering arrears once the bailiffs' strike is over.

In Hawks' view the cause of the rising debt mountain he and other mortgage providers are facing is solely because of the Nonettes.

He said: "The worst arrears problems are in those areas where the

send out a demand for the arrears to be paid to one of our customers, they, more likely than is not, go and join their local Nonette

"But they know as well as we do," he said, "there is nothing we can do except ask nicely, appeal to their better nature. And a fat lot of good that does us

"What is worse, the counseling companies we use report that when they do visit someone who is in arrears, they, more often than not are made aware of a Nonette 'solidarity delegation' waiting outside the house This can be very intimidating

"The police decline to do anything, saying that mortgage arrears are a 'civil matter'. The County Courts have ceased to offer any form of enforcement proceedings. No matter what judgments we

Why we must resist the new socialist tyranny - by the Rt. Honourable Sir William Hutchins MP

Why the Nonettes are EVIL

DURING THE LAST CENTURY many millions of people paid with their lives fighting to protect the democratic freedoms we all take for granted today.

Many of our parents' generation, however, paid with their lives resisting tyranny. Those who survived shouldered the horrendous material price of resistance.

We paid in the loss of our cities to Nazi bombing, the enormous financial costs in winning the World War and then maintaining a strong, vigilant defence against the Soviet Union during the long years of the Cold War which followed.

Sir William Hutchins MP, scourge of the left

During this long night of the Soviet threat the people of the democratic West gazed, often sadly, towards the Iron Curtain.

They feared for the fate of their fellow freedom loving brethren trapped in the darkness of the so-called 'socialist' authoritarian regimes of the East.

The democracies of the West, however, not only had to guard against this continuing menace of socialist authoritarianism from the East but also its insidious fellow-travellers in their very midst: so-called 'democratic socialism'.

For decades the freedom loving peoples of the West were plagued by the clasp of socialism's cancerous tentacles. These 'lefties' insidiously crept and wove their way into very fabric of our society, in education, government administration, organised labour.

Fortunately for the fate of Western civilisation, the desire for freedom and individual liberty, for which so many had fought and died for, overcame 'democratic' socialism's perverting influence.

Little by little, courage-unpicked socialism's tentacle threads from the fabric of democracy.

As each stand was unplucked out, everyone, from the highest to the humblest began to benefit from its eradication. Even our present government's historically long rule is due in no small part because of its ridding itself of all notions of socialism.

With the demise of socialism, along with the benefits its eradication brought to ordinary individual people, the strength of the Western democracies grew.

With this regained power they were at last able to help their brethren still held captive in the East to challenge and then overthrow the tyrannical regimes which enslaved them in the long dark night of authoritarian socialism.

As one socialist dictatorship after another fell to the fury of the people yearning to be free, the beacons of freedom and liberty began to burn brightly once more. As each flame illuminated socialism's darkness, so it became a pathfinder for yet more.

Within just a few years the whole world was lit by freedom's flame and the demons of socialism, with scant place to hide, began, at last to wither and shrivel, to be blown as chaff by the wind of progress into the domain of the past.

Sadly, even before there was time for the benefits of socialism's eradication to filter down to all the people, the socialist devil has reincarnated itself in a new guise: the Nonette movement.

Already a new Iron Curtain has come down between the peoples of free world and the Nonette collectivist dictatorships of Eastern Europe and South America.

Once again the world is treated to the sight of opponents to the Nonettes' one party rule forced to flee their homelands. Once again we in the West are faced with the spectre of our own "homegrown" socialists re-emerging to start up their insidious practices once more.

In the days of the Cold War, the authoritarian socialist regimes sheltered behind the skirts of the military power. But once the Western democracies had developed the means to disable this military might - through finance and technological advances - the socialist regimes it upheld, quickly collapsed.

But both this finance and technology did not come from the socialist infiltrated countries of western Europe but from the United States, a society where socialism was prevented ever from taking root.

Today, these latter-day socialist Nonettes shelter behind the skirts of the Aliens' power and use it to place their fellow travellers not just throughout Western Europe but in the United States as well.

Today the threat to our democratic freedoms being subsumed by socialist tyranny is even greater than was ever threatened by the Nazis or Communists of the past. Therefore it is more important for the long established democracies of the West to unite in containing this new socialist threat to our hard fought freedoms.

Nonettes make 'Come over and see us' offer

1,000 papers offered freedom to inspect Latin American territory under Nonette control

THE Nonettes have challenged the world's media to visit the countries they have overrun and report on conditions of the people ruled by their Alien-backed regime.

In yesterday's Susem telecast, their presenter Rainbow Louis, announced that 1,000 places were available to the Press to visit anywhere they wished in Nonette-controlled Latin America.

Ms Louis said that journalists from the outside world will be free to travel wherever they wished. She also claimed that journalists could see what wanted to, that their reporting will not be censored by the

I almost interrupted with "What on Earth are you on about?" but knowing Menpemelo has ever a reason for all she says, I stayed mum. She reiterated that evolution comes from within a group, never individuals. Progress evolved from harmony within such a group and with the environment it was part of. Discord within it and with its environment brought regression.

Every aspect of evolution from the downloading of programs into our auras to the determination of our physical form, she said, is done by females, never males. At this I did exclaim, "How can this be. It is obvious we inherit half of us from our fathers?"

But soon wished I had not, for it promptly drew her "Tri-contextually spermatozoon initiated programs provide for an embryo's placental envelope, nothing else. The prime function of males, although it may take several generations to effect, is as a conduit for the exchange of genetic material between females. Programs for the cellular symbiotic mitochondrion within the embryo, for which there is no requirement of genetic interchange, are exclusively matriarchal in initiation."

Menpemelo also said how earlier, more lowly lifeforms reproduced asexually, but progress determined these proto-Eves freed themselves from the 'encumbrance' of their internal Adams so as to concentrate on the more important things of life such as evolution and having a good time. With their sisters' other halves floating free it also provided a bigger pick'n'mix of each others' genetic programs, thus accelerating growth and change.

Then with "As I was saying," she continued, "To advance evolutionarily, females require harmony within their circle, and males of the group are also in a like state especially with their surroundings. Apart from Earth, with everywhere else we know this is not a problem, males become female before they mature and so are easily kept quiescent while in this juvenile phase.

"That your males of many species live on into maturity does not appear to pose insurmountable evolutionary difficulties, except perhaps of slowing the development of program receptors. All the while there is continuing harmony within and without each group, evolution progresses. The formation of cerebral, long-term memory receptors in human males does not appear to slow this progress. However, advances observed during our colleagues' earlier visits appeared on this visit to have regressed."

It was after my "What do you mean?" that Menpemelo unfolded just what had been 'observed' before and is set to occur again, but this time with a difference. Many earlier humans, she said, possessed the ability to project their auras at will, beyond their beings. Indians in their teepees did it, Amazonian ones lolling on hammocks could do it, even Australian Aborigines on walkabouts did it. All could leave their bodies behind and soar with the eagles, stalk with jaguars, hover with their ancestors atop Ayres Rock.

A time when women and some men, more so their auras, mingled merrily not only with their kin but others dwelling far away, as well as with their forbears. In this Eden, Menpemelo said, there had been unbridled happiness

Accountants warning to Nonette businesses

Proper accounts must be kept says consultant

By Ross Capulyard

Nonette owned businesses must still maintain proper accounting records, one of Britain's leading accountants warned yesterday

Maurice Philips, senior tax consultant at Friers, Dickson & Hawks, said: "All businesses have a legal obligation to pay taxes on their profits

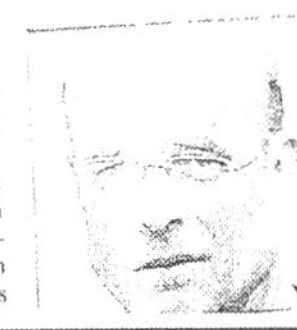

dispensing with their services.

In his view, the Nonette movement was little more than a passing fashion, while the Inland Revenue will last for ever.

Mr Philips, a former tax inspector before he took early retirement, added that i companies did not keep prop er tax accounts, they could

Doctors warn on Nonette health booth dangers

"Health depends on more than machines" - say BDA

By Janis Culner
Health Correspondent

THE NONETTE HEALTH booths, which are now installed in Nonette centres across Britain could pose long term health problems doctors warned yesterday.

The Doctors' Medical Association [DMA] issued a warning that the booths, of which several thousands are thought to be in operation throughout the country, could be failing to spot the vital signs of many illnesses. They said that the booths have not been properly tested by medical experts and could in themselves have long term effects on people's health in the same way that mobile phones were.

A DMA spokesman said that although the medical profession had no real idea

A doctor speaks about H booths

how the booths operated it is suspected that there must be some form of radiation involved which operated at a cellular level. The Association has requested details of these booths' workings from the Nonettes but so far no response has been received from any of them

The DMA also said that the booths were having one positive effect In many areas of the country patients no longer needed to make an appointment to see their GPs The spokesman said that in many group medical centres there were doctors waiting for patients

Hospital waiting lists are also becoming shorter as many patients waiting for minor surgery, such as varicose veins and hernias, canceled their appointments and were treated by the booths instead

"If this continues," the spokesman joked, "doctors will be all to take their full leave entitlement." However, many in the profession as a

We will challenge the Nonettes on their record

We take up the Nonette gauntlet

By **Phillip Brown**
Ethics and Integrity Correspondent

THE ALIEN backed Nonette regime has challenged this newspaper and other leading publications to inspect and report on the consequence of their rule.

The Nonettes through their spokeswoman, have said our reporters shall have a completely free and unfettered access to all aspects of the "new" society they claim to have created.

After previously denying us and the rest of the world's media the right to investigate their territory, this precipitate volte-face on the part of the Nonettes must naturally be viewed with caution.

Nonetheless, on behalf of you, our readers and the wider public in general, this paper would be failing in its duty if we declined to respond to the ... happening behind their Iron Curtain.

There are strings attached to the Nonettes offer: journalists must first travel to the city of Natal; fly there from the Susem occupied air base of Villacoublay near Paris in one of their space 'planes; apply for a seat on a 'plane' with a branch of their movement here in London, and lastly, spon...

Villacoublay near Paris

accompany our reporter.

Although the last two conditions are onerous and we state clearly that this paper neither endorses or recognises the Nonette movement, in the interests of investigative reporting, we have reluctantly decided to abide by all these conditions.

Our reporter, Malcolm Fallow, has bravely volunteered to undertake the assignment to Nonette

Savers hit B. Societies, Ba

"Deposits safe" says Bank of England

By Brian Boating
Finance Editor

QUEUES FORMED outside hundreds of building societies' branches yesterday as savers rushed to withdraw their money.

Many banks also saw steady streams of anxious customers withdrawing cash from their accounts.

In a bid to calm savers' fears the Bank of England was forced to issue a statement assuring that all deposits with the financial institutions not only were safe but also were secured by its own guarantees.

Most depositors, however, remained unconvinced by the Bank's guarantee.

With mortgage arrears snowballing and other financial institutions including credit card companies also rumoured to be suffering increasing mountains of debt, savers' fears of bank collapses appear set to grow

Those withdrawing their money from building societies and banks are individuals and the amounts in question are small compared to the total sums invested by the major city institutions. But the crises of confidence, however, could have serious consequences on the country's financial well-being.

Once leading City expert said it would "only need one building society branch to close it doors and the situation could quickly grow to crisis proportions".

John Davidson MP, the Shadow Cabinets finance spokesman, said it was "vital that the government made an

10 tips to save your fella from the Aliens' clutches

By BRITTA RUFF

GALS we all know what happens to fellas once our Susem sisters have had their way with them. They can't do what we want fellas to do for a long time. Am I right or am I right? So as save the hassle of getting a replacement fella in, here's some helpful hints to keep your Lotherio out of the clutches of those feisty Susem gals:

1. **Don't let him out during the daylight hours:** Our Susem sisters only send their press gangs out during the day. But if you have to send him out during daylight hours, then here is what to do:
2. **Dress him up as lady:** No slacks and jumpers mind you. And remember it has to be the full feminine thing: either one of your dresses or in a skirt and blouse, high heels and handbag. To be on the safe side a wig and make-up should also be part of your fella's wardrobe.
3. **Make sure he walks properly**: Dressing him in your clothes is not enough, he has stand and walk like us gals to be convincing. Train him to walk as we do.
4. **If he refuses to wear your clothes at least get him in a kilt:** Scottish kilts can be expensive and the different clans cause problems but there is a good value range from Welsh Shepherds Supply Company; they come three shades: Valley Green, Brecon Brown and Snowden White.
5. **If he has a beard or other facial hair, have him shave it off:** Either this or have him pretend to be a circus lady. Personally I advise against this as being too risky.
6. **If he refuses to dress up in women's clothes get him to wear his grandfather's:** Our Susem sisters' taste in men appears to be just ours: they throw our clapped-out oldies back.
7. **Have him use a walking stick or a zimmer frame:** The Susem are very selective, they only take top quality fellas.
8. **Ground him from playing any outdoor game and pursuits:** It's those open spaces where the Susem strike the most often, remember.
9. **Keep him off the beach:** Another risky place; and even in the garden skimpy trunks are a definite no-no, he will still be a tempting morsel to our Susem sisters. And lastly:
10. **Have him join the Nonettes:** There may be nothing to it but a little bird tells me that no Nonette men have been taken by the Susem.

Have your fella: do as I tip and it will help him keep his Lotherio intact all just for you! Byee!

Nonettes blamed f County Court cris

CCJs pointless

Repossessions unenforceable, say Clerks

Debt collection slumps

Credit controls tighten

By Ursula Banks
Courts Correspondent

CREDITORS suing debtors through the Courts now do so in vain, senior County Court officials claim

Since the bailiffs' strike only a handful of Court judgments have been enforceed Debt collection agencies also a report a significant downturn in the amount of debt recovery

At the County Court Clerks Association's annual meeting in Leeds yesterday, the Association's president, Earnest Webb, said: "There are cases in the courts that plaintiffs are not even bothering to turn up to plead

"It appears that each time a County Court summons is issued it's as if it's an invitation card to join the Nonettes

"The Community Charge strike and that of the bailiffs', have had such an effect than an increasing number of debtors are ceasing to pay what they owe," Mr Webb said "This is beginning to affect the workings of many courts

Earnest Webb, a

"Most are ex serious downtu If the decline c present rate th of sittings in th obviously dec this will me about growing allow many p unfilled"

Building S other mortgag now stopped i ing for reposs

and harmony. And program after layered Anthropic program progressively downloaded in the auras and thus minds. But now, she said, it has all but gone by. We humans had regressed "Yet again," she had added, almost as if in reproach.

Following my "Ooh," and subdued "how? why?" she looked at me fixedly and said "Your males."

Menpemelo elaborated. All the while men busied themselves logging trees, lugging home the occasional bison for tea and being available for the girls' stud nights, the world was well for women. They could get on with the really important things, cultivating crops, baking bread, bearing girls with bettered brains. The thing was though that bits of this betterment hybridised into those of boys. And that is when all the trouble started.

"We can only surmise what happened," Menpemelo said turning to the holograms again. "However, as your males lack faculties to evolve cerebral receptors to the same degree as women, it is inevitable many cerebral programs will have distorted as they downloaded into male auras.

"This distortion would not have disrupted human harmony with Nature. At first that is, but the degradation this malformation made," she said, pointing to the patches of pink amid the blue in the human male hologram, "would have inexorably increased."

Though I looked I still did not understand what Menpemelo meant. And no doubt seeing so, she changed tack and said "You have a saying, "a little knowledge in the wrong hands is a dangerous thing." This is as it is with most of your males' cerebral programs. What little they do possess has not been used to enhance cerebral progress but has embellished the cerebrate. While your males were quiescent this malformation would not have been of consequence."

Seeing that I still did not understand she curtly said "Using another of your sayings, it was "a disaster waiting to happen". And when 12,000 years ago much of your world was engulfed by suddenly rising sea levels, this latent aberration skulking in many male brains compounded that catastrophe."

Noting no doubt that I still didn't understand, she as brusquely said "At that time the human population compared with today's was minuscule. It was also widely scattered, though just as today, it was concentrated on fertile littorals and lower river valleys. Up to that time there were abundant resources with no need for anyone to compete for them. All would have prospered. Societal groupings could only sustain by consensus rather than coercion. In such surroundings the cerebral prowess of women would not have been suborned by the cerebrate power of men.

"Following the sudden 200 metre rise in sea levels consequent to your planet's crust displacement and elimination of Atlanticean cultures, survivors would have been left with scant resources. It is thus probable that these would have been contested. The conflict and subsequent coercion involved in such contests would undoubtedly have been cerebrate, not cerebral in initiation."

Ills still have Milan down for victory over Gunners

By Jim Broke
Soccer Correspondent

DESPITE ARSENAL'S current run of IEFA wins, the odds are still against its continuing. Although William Ill admitted they had made a loss on the Gunners-Barcelona quarter finals they still place Arsenal at 10-1 against

The manager of Ill's Highbury betting shop said he was a Gunners' fan and had no part in setting the odds for next week's semi final.

He said the odds are calculated by experts and on the numbers and size of the bets taken "Until such times as these change from what they are now and head office tells me differently, that is the situation," he said Elsewhere in Highbury, Arsenal support-

Bank of England to increase money supply

Inflation fears dismissed as BoE printing presses roa

By Steven Scotford
Economics Correspondent

In a bid to overcome the current run on banks and building societies, the Bank of England is to temporarily increase the UK money supply.

In response to what the Chancellor, Peter Handel, claimed is a 'transient irrationality' the Bank's printing presses are to work overtime to produce the necessary supplies of notes to meet the current rise in demand for cash.

Bank chiefs are hoping that this latest action will restore confidence in the country's financial institutions

But the Bank of England's move to increase the money supply is not without its critics

Richard Wiggens, of the influential finance magazine, *Big Worries Monthly*, said: "This is the very last thing the Bank or the government should have done. The amount of money already withdrawn from banks and building societies is unlikely to be used to reduce personal debt

"Those withdrawing the funds are likely to be the least indebted members of society This increase however is likely to be used for the purchase of goods and services rather than acquiring further long-term financial assets

"Pumping yet more cash into the system is like adding petrol to the flames. There w be a boom in the hi street which will followed by inflati bursting out all ov again

"It must also borne in mind that t increase in the mor supply is not backed any government l issue. It is truly pa money," he said

Last night a Treas spokesman dismis fears of inflation 'unfounded and mi formed' He said: "

Nonettes set to cause 'massive' property slump

"UK house prices could fall by up to 20 per cent" – says Estate Agent

By Bruce Ipper
Property Editor

House prices are set to fall by up to 20 per cent because of the Nonettes leading estate agents claim This could see the price of the average home slump by a massive £30,000

North London estate agents, Basand Thieves, said that if the current mortgage famine continues house prices must fall if vendors are to attract cash buyers. "These are the only people able to buy property at the moment," said the head of Thieves, Harry Courbe.

Mr Courbe said that the number of houses coming onto the market had also fallen dramatically in the past few weeks "At this time of the year, we would be expecting a pick-up compared with the summer but compared with last month the number of new properties than halved," he said

The cause of this sudden change has been the result of lenders' declining to advance mortgages This, said Mr Courbe, is a direct cause of the huge rise in arrears and the inability of both building societies and banks to do anything to restore the situation. Until lenders have some means of assur-

'Nonettes are behind crisis' - claims Heywood

Ex-Home Sec in 'Told you so' speech

By Joseph Spin
Political Editor

Ex Home Sec.Heywood: "I told you the Nonettes would cause trouble"

THE NONETTES are behind the cash confidence crisis sweeping Britain and other leading countries, Jack Heywood, the ex-Home Secretary, claimed yesterday.

Mr Heywood said that he had long warned that the Nonettes would cause Britain and other countries' downfall "My worst predictions are coming true," Mr Heywood told a conference of senior police officers yesterday.

Mr Heywood said evidence that the Nonettes are behind the cash crisis is there for all to see "It is the Nonettes who sparked off the Community Charge non-payments movement. It is they who are behind the bailiffs' strike.

By appealing to the minority of our population who live by the 'If you can get away with it do so' credo, the Nonettes have become a movement which has nothing but contempt for the institutions of law and order, which the rest of us law abiding citizens live by

"By blatantly ignoring the law of the land," Mr Heywood said, "this Alien backed movement is fast becoming a law unto themselves properly constituted forces of law and order, the judiciary and the police must be given all the necessary powers and resources to combat and root out this growing lawlessness within society "

The ex-Home Secretary, to loud applause from the audience, called on the government to provide the police with military assistance to backup their presence on the streets

He said: "If we can do it in Northern Ireland to bring the rule of law and protection of citizens then we can do it other parts of the United Kingdom as well."

Mr Heywood said that it was vital that the County Court judgments were not only enforced but were seen to be so "There are an increasing number of areas in Britain," Mr Heywood said "where the Sovereign's wri no longer runs. This is a intolerable situation whic cannot be allowed to cont inue, no matter what the ci cumstances, no matter w the cost to eradicate it."

FRESH SUSEM SEX RAIDING SORTIES STRIKE ACROSS ENGLAND, FRANCE

ALIENS SNATCH 200 LONDON MEN

Youths in Susem clutches could be force into sex and bondage torture sessions

By JENNA JAMESON

FEARS ROSE last night for the fate of hundreds of young men, including many Londoners who have fallen into the Aliens' clutches and forced to take part in non-stop 'robust' sex sessions.

These, experts say, could involve not only forced lovemaking with the lust-crazed Susem, but also torture including bondage. Past captives of the Aliens have all reported being tied up to trees and whipped by these extra-terrestrial she-devil sex fiends and then tickled.

The Alien raids which took place across the Southeast follow a lull ... until yesterday

Malcolm Fallow reports from Natal in Nonette held terri

Paris to Brazil by Veda 55 minutes

Amazing flight in Alien space plane

THE VIEWS from the Susem Veda 'space plane were marvelous, its vertical take-off and landing was as smooth cream. And we flew at 5,000 miles an hour.

There were neither attendants or flight crew on board. Nor were there any visible controls, just the Veda itself. Or rather himself. No sooner were the first passengers inside the Veda's cabin than "he" announced his name was that he was "Kershaw". He also sounded very 'butch'.

With all the 50 plus journalists on board and Kershaw's: "Right boys and girls we are all ready to go," his doors then closed and "go" we most certainly did. The ground fell away at such

Seeing me still confused she brusquely said "Brawn not brain."

In their bid to survive, she said, the victors would have perceived that might, more so theirs, was righteous. What couldn't be controlled, dominated were viewed as threats which must be conquered, coerced into submission. The cerebral superiority of women would have been viewed by men as intimidating.

With brawn power men put women in their place, under maledom's thumb. Women no longer lived to Nature's free order but under that of men's. Women were robbed of the birthright intellect of their mothers' pre-eminent minds. Menkind gained nothing from this theft but humanity became the poorer for its passing.

In the smash, grab dash for dominance of all they surveyed men mindlessly raised regimes to re-enforce their power. These not only subjugated women but grew so strong that their omnipotence enslaved their creators' sons as well. Mankind may have been washed out of Eden by the Flood, but men and the regressive forces they thoughtlessly unleashed finally wrecked, ravished and destroyed it.

Not everywhere though. Eden still existed in much of the Americas, Australia, as well as a few other 'undiscovered' places. Here humans, and until recently, still lived in harmony with their surroundings, still sent their auras heavenward. But the coming of our civilization soon doomed even these last havens.

As Menpemelo unfolded this sorry tale, I slowly filled with disbelief. It was so far fetched I thought it daft. Though I said nothing while she spoke, the moment she paused I was overflowing. "I accept what you say about females being responsible for evolution," I said, conceding a point to soften her, "I'll even go along with women being cleverer in some areas, but it is simply not true that men, us men, have been as you say."

I should have noted that Menpemelo said nothing to this but I was still all of a flow, "I know enough about our world's history to tell you there is not a scrap of evidence to support what you say of women anywhere ever being in a superior position to men." She still said nothing, just folded her arms and looked fixedly at me. I should have noted this as well and stopped but stupidly flowed on. "Even the tribes of America and elsewhere were always ruled by chiefs who were all men and their warriors were always men as well. Their women were subservient to them. They all were..."

"Who provides your planet's histories?" she said, stopping me mid-flow.

"Well, historians, explorers, officials..."

"Men," she snapped most coldly, "all are men."

I had not chance to respond before her "Men, men, always men recording the actions of other men. Men subjectively interpreting events through the perceptions of other men, men incapable of countenancing anything occurring without the exclusive hand of yet more men. Men reporting on the activities of a race dominated by males, one from which women have been purposely excluded." She went on like this for quite a while, and it got worse as well.

Soon I had my back to the wall in more ways than one. When she moved on to menkind wrecking the planet, and though I wish I'd kept my mouth shut, I fought back with, "It's all very well you coming here with your superior past and saying everything with hindsight, but if it wasn't for our present civilization we humans wouldn't have made the progress we have."

I got no further than before her near-shouted "Progress! You call continual suppression of cerebral advancement, progress? Is the deliberate structuring of your societies to purposely exclude the very forces which advance your species, progress? A society where those serving no evolutionary purpose regressively dominate those who do, you call this progress? Is it progress that the cerebrally endowed are suppressed by the cerebrally stymied?"

Her last words hurt as did her "Human males, as with all other species, exist evolutionarily for no other purpose than as a mere conduit of generational codices between females and furnishing some passing pleasure, while they retain the vigor to so do, that is (her slow sneer as she looked me up and down hurt as well).

"The innovations of your so-called civilizations, when set against the potential advances wasted through cerebrate males suppressing cerebrally superior females, are little more than technological trinkets. Your purported philosophies are nothing other than the ephemeral introspections of theologues. Any society perpetuating continual suppression of cerebral evolution is nothing other than effete. Your human male dominated groupings have assembled one successive empty ended edifice after another. All founded on the inherent, unstable coercive maleo-centric precept of cerebrateness.

"As your species has experienced for these many thousands of years past, and to its continuing cost, such endemic instability assures inevitable implosion of every one of them. The only sustainable societal form is based on the stability brought by cerebral predominating cerebrate. And to so do the latter has to be expunged from its matrix."

Then, as though running out of steam, Menpemelo unfolded her arms and with "As I was saying," continued as if I had not interrupted. Despite repression of cerebral evolution, she said, embers of our golden past still flicker in some people's auras. What is more the Susem had been intentionally looking for signs of them. She gave a whole list of names (Terbal's Internetting), Ingo Swann was one I caught, Gerald Croiset another. She called them 'Remote Viewers'. All can project themselves to places far away, and are able to tell people standing next to them what they are seeing in the place they have projected themselves to. Thing was though, all on her list were men.

Before I had remarked on this, Menpemelo, her eye on me, said "Though only men exhibiting these innate abilities have been studied (by Earthly scientists I supposed), there will be many others as yet unacknowledged with like attributes." She also mentioned dowsers, diviners, how they have similar aptitudes. All are examples, she said, of aura-late programs managing to manifest themselves. With thoughtful 'group therapy', she added, we would all recoup as much and more.

Recovery, from what Menpemelo said, could be likened to dumb-struck stroke sufferers, simultaneously stirring from sleep-walking comas, helping one another regain their power of speech. I had to remember, she said, that during our eons of cerebral trance, the Anthropic Template's waves had not stopped flowing by. A little patience in surroundings of harmony, she said, and aura-late programs long dormant, would be down in our minds in no time at all. From what she also said, 'remote viewing' is child's talk compared to the scholarly conversations awaiting us once our cerebra are in their strides. This isn't flight of fancy either, it has started to happen right here and right now.

As Menpemelo said, across Congress harmony now reigns supreme. More to the point, women are its cursorers. The surge in academic advancement by women, and of all ages, I was already aware of, as well as the older ones' renown as whippers-in of their families' educationally indolent to study. Though this boosts household income their innate perseverance has propelled most ahead of men in achievement as well as earnings. Women are also to the fore in organising their Nonettes, being a majority of those elected, and at all levels. Males everywhere have little choice other than to be 'quiescent' (not that Love Patches haven't helped to tire them into tranquility). In this new world of harmony, women, Menpemelo said, now have their heads together in other ways as well.

Many, she said, know the thinking of others, and a commonality of view on what to do is often arrived at without need of actual discussion. After she had told this I ventured "How do you know?"

But cryptic as ever she said "We just do."

All the same I pressed her on this. The Susem are conscious, she said, of 'aura-late communication' between the minds of women and that it is increasing. The Susem can 'hear' what is being thought. Obviously it is something I want to be in on as well and my spirits rose when she said the Susem are also aware that some of us men can also 'talk and hear' thought. All anyone need do, she said, is to be in a state of harmony with everyone and everything, and in no time they will be 'thinking in' along with the rest. But Menpemelo dashed me down with what she had to say next.

'Thought talk' is dependent on software in our auras being receptive to relevant Anthropic programs, as well as being capable of downloading them to the hardware in our heads. The thing is though, that while with women this all comes as standard, for males it doesn't.

During the suppression (by maledom, as Menpemelo insistently kept adding) of women's inherent aura-late programming, its absence in men wasn't something much noticed (especially by males). Now that suppression has ceased (at least across Congress) it's little more than, as far as women are concerned, dusting down these dormant programs, brushing up on using them and 'thought talk' processes perfectly.

But for us blokes it's different. If we are ever to 'thought talk' let alone 'listen in' we have to make do with an amalgam of a bits of this and that program. As Menpemelo kept rubbing in (and a tad gleefully I thought), men's prime (she used "sole") purpose is procreation, "It is all males are evolved for," she said. Men's auras might, with difficulty, chance, cobble together some Heath Robinson of a program but it's just the start of our cerebral shortcomings.

Menpemelo outlined what else is awaiting womenkind. I had to remember, she first said, that our physical form is but a facet of ourselves. More significant is our aura, the zipping and buzzing between its programs and those of our cells' 'auralettes'. Just as important as these interactions are those between our auras and others. Not only among humans, she said, but with "sentience" in general. Reaching out for these though, is beyond the cerebral grasp of most men.

"Progression begets further progression but for males, cerebrally, alas not," she said dabbing her finger about the right hemisphere of the hologram of ours. "As you can see," she added, "a complete absence of relevant tri-context cerebral receptors, let alone those of the quinth."

I ventured another "What do you mean?" Sentience, she replied is a two way affair. The more minds harmonise with others the more each evolves access to ever advanced Anthropic programs, they in turn also fashioning password entry to the next and so on. After unison of thought auras advance, she said, to travelling beyond our bodies, 'remote viewing'.

The next, she said, is communicating at will with auras of other lifeforms. Advancing from this is the ability of leaving not just our bodies but being as one with all of life on Earth, what Menpemelo called 'Gaia planeing' This though, or so she said, is beyond the minds of most of us men.

I asked why. Jabbing her finger at our male hologram once more, and with a tone of finality she reiterated "Your males just do not have the relevant receptors," and adding that "Anyone possessing four limbs and perseverance can ascend the highest peak, but no matter how informed of mountains a paraplegic may be, they will have difficulty climbing even the lowest. However, anyone who is born limbless, such as your males cerebrally are..." (she didn't bother finishing the sentence).

"The sole route your males can progress to 'Gaia planeing' and beyond, is that they become female. However, changing gender can cerebrally benefit no more than a few, the young, those with an innate ability of creativity, but this will be all. For the remainder," she said shrugging her shoulders, "such as those who are (and looking me up and down again) no longer young, there is not species benefit in so doing. Attempting to modify any of these will be as pointless as it is unnecessary, after all (and she smiling smugly) there is not a shortage of your females."

Downhearted and half wanting to ask "What do think will happen to us blokes then?" the other half pressed her for what is in store for women. She duly obliged, stressing again how our aura is the more important part of being. For women, singularly but more so collectively, she said, auras will evolve to interact with ever advanced Anthropic programs. The insights conferred on existence, how women relate themselves to it will increase, auras journeying further from their beings and for longer.

Rubbing in yet more 'inferiority', Menepemelo teased how, because most men's minds are 'linear', they are restricted to focusing on only one thing at a time, whereas women with their more developed, 'multi-planed' minds can concentrate on many, and all at once. She also used it as analogy for women's auras being in more than one place and level of awareness all at the same time. A bit like quantums I suppose, except there will be more than just two things in each aura-late matchbox, four, then five, then more.

The more auralate programs evolve, she said, the more they interact, enfold into the Anthropic Template itself. As this increases, auras become so freely 'detachable' from bodies they are no longer dependent on their physical existence. They become separate sentient entities in their own right. Even when a person physically dies, her aura being freed, lives on. And for a long time, thousands of years she said, before fading away to waves.

It is the Susem understanding, Menpemelo said, that auras are not just enfolded into the Anthropic Template but inevitably influence the make-up of its programs, enriching them with yet more wisdom, awareness. Which in time eventually download into the auras of others. And on it goes, each generation aiding the imparting of insights to future ones. It's not just with humans either but all cerebral life throughout the Universe in its entirety.

In one sense, she said, as a result of so much 'sentience' flowing amid the Universe, it could itself also be thought of as aware, conscious, alive. Just as Tertiary waves, frothicles, 'matter' revert to Secondary ones of energy, and they back to Primary waves, then all the way back again to energy, so too does cerebral-ness. To auras, then to the Anthropic Template and then all the way back into life again.

Men's future came again to mind. I asked her how many generations it will take for these higher levels of being to evolve in women.

"Potentially, none," she said.

She elaborated. "The numbers of women Nonettes are already sufficient to ensure rapid evolution. Within two to three years most will be Gaia planeing. Men will be slower of course. For those with the right faculties it could be a decade, though perhaps longer."

Because transference of genetic material is not involved, Menpemelo added, time is not a constraint. "It is the numbers of like minds which determine the speed of progress," she said, adding that as the human 'herd' of Nonettes is already large, rapidly increasing (and with men's cerebrateness 'quiescent') the numbers alone will ensure it will soon flock to auralate flight.

I asked again about what she thought will happen to blokes. Her reply was not heartening. "The ratio of one fecund male to a hundred women is more than adequate to provide for human procreation," she said. "Such a ratio

Poverty is a thing of the past in Salvador

Hunger eliminated, homelessness eradicated under the Nonettes

By Ian Trigg
In Salvador

Young orphans no longer hawk cigarettes or shine shoes in Salvador None need seek shelter or sleep in the city's sewers either.

All of these youngsters are now to be seen seated in front of screens studying and earning from them as well. These children, however, are not alone in their study

Across Salvador, many tens of thousands of others who were once condemned to a life of grinding poverty are to be seen in earnest study

An hour in front of a Susem teaching screen earns sufficient to pay for food and lodging for several days

As studying beats begging and hawking, and even theft, this once most violent and crime-ridden of South American cities is now a centre of mass learning and study.

With study providing greater returns than stealing, Salvador is also crime-free - ... its 500 year-old history.

With everyone part of a Nonette there is also a palpable sense of community, which is quite absent elsewhere in the outside world.

Every person not only belongs to a community but also they are an integral part of it, directly involved in shaping its functioning and activities

This mass involvement is not out of any sense of 'civic pride' either - though there is much of this in evidence - but because it is in an individual's own vested interest to be immersed in their Nonette

It is this new found sense of "belonging" which itself, has become such a massive driving force for social change in Salvador

With education and the income it generates, there has been a huge increase in spending power from a large section of the population which in the past was condemned to poverty in squalour in the notorious slums of

Natal - crime free city

It's free of police as well

By Grace Rapallo
In Natal

Natal's central police station is perched on the top of a hill and commands splendid views of the old city and Atlantic Ocean. Behind the station stands the local prison. Both are also busy places.

Of policemen and prisoners, however, there are none An army of workmen are converting the station into a hotel. The prison behind it is experiencing a similar makeover and is being transformed into restaurants and a leisure complex.

Not only are police absent in the old town of Natal but in the rest of the city as well. In fact in the entire state Natal is police-free. After all, there is no crime.

With the arrival of the Nonettes in Natal, police officers of the former regime either fled or stopped being policemen

Each Nonette group – consisting of no more than 800 people – have set up their own neighbourhood security force and court, which in turn administers its own justice

Maria Parati, head of the Nonettes of the street on which the old police station stands, said: "The two major causes of crime: poverty and corruption, have been eradicated.

"If people want more money," she said, "all they need do is study From this not only do they earn money but acquire abilities which in turn generate earning capacity.

"Because every detail of each Nonette transaction is known to all, and our spending of every cent subject to public scrutiny, there is not any corruption," Ms Parati said.

"Should anyone in our Nonette harm someone in another Nonette then both groups together decide what is an appropriate course of action to resolve the matter

"If neither can agree it is sent to the Area Nonette for them to adjudicate. But so far we have not had any disagreements," she added

Night time is usually a dangerous time in third world cities but Natal again lived up to its crime-free claim. I had

No Rules No Regulations No Laws NO CHAOS

In Nonetteland anything goes - just don't upset anyone

BY ROGER PAYNE
REPORTS FROM RECIFE

IF LAWS DO NOT EXIST there are none to break. If there are not rules or regulations there is no need for administration, bureaucracy or red tape. Or need to bribe an official. The result? Everything runs smoothly, in Recife, at least.

Law and policing, such as they are, are handled within each small Nonette group. In turn each Nonette group coordinates, where needs be, with other groups.

Every ninth person within the group is on call in case of civil emergencies. In turn these can quickly summon larger numbers of volunteers.

There were some people directing and regulating traffic at the beginning of Nonette rule but with drivers' car registration also the same as their own personal identity number it is easy for anyone quickly to trace them back to their own Nonette call on their own Nonette for support.

"Should anything of this nature arise," said Margarita Veado, head of a local Nonette, "information of the transgressor is sent immediately to their Nonette, a court panel is convened, usually the same day and a judgment made.

It is quick, cheap and effective. Details of the transgressor are usually published in the relevant newspapers

"This naming and shaming, she says, also acts as a strong deterrent against anyone committing anything they should not have done."

Bumper crops which never see the light of day

Alice Johnson sees
Nonette agriculture in action

Speed not spraying is the Susem secret to stopping pests

FIVE MINUTES equals an earth day in Nonette farming techniques. Maize is cropped within 16 hours of being sown Ripened oranges are picked within 10 hours of blossoms blooming These and every other crop are grown and harvested within the same incredible short spaces of time. All, however, are grown underground

Should this method of cultivation prove as successful as the Nonettes claim, then a truly agricultural revolution awaits the rest of the world But the science behind Nonette farming is even more revolutionary and must ultimately change the way we view the world in which we live.

With unlimited cost-free energy, the Nonettes are using Susem technology to carve huge glass walled caverns both underground and into cliff faces It is in these caverns that the Nonettes grow their crops

Seeds for each crop are treated in a small cabinet and then sown onto two metre diameter waist-high tables of some obviously nutrient-rich substance

I was unable to discover the workings of the cabinet nor what the substance in which ... nutrient were subjected to pulses of intense light which swung from one side of the table to the other and lasted for no longer than two or three minutes.

The lighting, however, was interspersed with as few minutes of near darkness, during which a mist of water was sprayed over the table.

As the lights came on again green shoots were appearing out of the nutrient. The pulsing lights then went through a series of colour changes. Also as the shoots grew to seedlings fans gently blew air across the table's surface

I returned to the table two hours later and saw it was by then covered in fully grown plants half a metre high. When, at the end of the day I returned again, people were harvesting the fully ripened maize.

Between my visits I was given indication - and no more - of what occurred in the seed cabinet. The out-side world sees the manipulation of plants' genes along with herbicides and eliminating pests as the path to increased crop yields The Nonettes, however, exploit something of a plant's make-up which appears to be as yet unused by us.

From what I was told, plants and all other living things posses structures which control the functioning of genes and the formation of proteins. It is the understand-

Edward Sheldron probes the very nerve centre of rebels' realm

Fortaleza - heart of the revolution

FORTALEZA was the first major Brazilian city taken by the Nonette rebels.

It is from this Atlantic port, the former capital of the once backward state of Ceara, which the Nonette uprising against the ruling regimes of the entire South American continent was first begun And it is this city which is still the controlling nerve centre of the entire worldwide Nonette movement

It is Fortaleza which was also witness to the founding of the Congress of the Americas

Here in Fortaleza that the founders of the Nonettes declared the tenets of their revolutionary principles which have been the guiding light of the movement's takeover of even more territories around the world.

Although the Congress is the all powerful hub of the Nonette movement, it does not hold its meetings in the marble pillared palace of the former Ceara Assembly - this has been converted to nightclub and dance hall - or the massive banqueting hall of the equally sumptuous former Governor's residence - this is being converted to a housing complex No, the Nonettes convene in a run-down disused clothing factory in the once equally rundown western bairro - district - of Fatima.

... delegates from Nonette groups near and far, assemble in near constant session to deliberate on the workings of their new-found realm

One delegate, Maria de Nonato, from the western city of Teresina, told how, like all her fellow delegates, she is elected for just one month, after which she must seek re-election.

Ms de Nonato said: "I am here as a representative of the Nonettes of my city, to abide by their wishes, achieve what they have sent me here to do.

... is deciding and then to do as my Nonette tells me. It does not matter who represents Teresina, the outcome will always what my city decides not the delegate," she said

Ms de Nonato also said that details of every level of Nonette meetings from local associations up to Congress itself are also listed in newspapers and on television and radio "As result," she said, "everyone knows what is being proposed, everything is open Not only are there not any secrets there is no sense ...

... be so? Can an organisation which just a few months ago did not exist and has grown so powerful, really have achieved so much without needing to resort to subterfuge and under-cover deals? Unlikely.

To discover the real truth behind the extraordinary rise of Nonette power it is necessary to travel beyond Fortaleza and into the interior of Ceara, to the heart of Nonette power.

Just south of the Equator, in the middle of a sun scorched desert lies the fabled mountain oasis of the

will also ensure these males remain forever quiescent. Evolution dictates that surpluses will not be sustained. The numbers of males in excess of this ratio are unnecessary for your species' progress. Indeed their very existence entails the needless consumption of your planet's resources, and for no species benefit, and so they will inevitably become extinct."

"You mean ninety-nine per cent of us blokes have got to go?"

Her smug smile as she nodded was also disheartening. So was her "Throughout your current recent human history your males have copiously demonstrated that collectively their prolonged and pointless post-fecund presence has impaired the cerebral elevation of your species. As this advancement has now recommenced, it appears at last to be sustainable. In order this progress be safeguarded it is essential that these superfluous males, more so the overtly cerebrate ones, be quickly removed."

"Removed? Quickly? What do you mean? Where to?"

"Does it matter?" she said giving a nonchalant shrug. "There is extensive environment damage caused by your males in need of rehabilitation, but your women will doubtless find uses for these needless males, such as..."

"Such as what?"

But Menpemelo's attention was not now with me. Her "I must leave you," had me turning my head.

Pheterisco and some of the other Susem were beckoning to her.

"Please don't go. I want to know..."

"I must go," she said insistently, "I do not want to miss the last night."

"Last night? What last night?"

"Panama."

Everyone is a student - and a teacher

No one plays truant either

Alan Carter
In Belem

Everywhere everyone is studying. Young and old alike are either sat in front of their teaching screens or in earnest tutorial groups

All the old schools are now closed down and many former teachers are to be seen studying alongside their former pupils.

The Nonettes' claim to have stamped out illiteracy appears to be fully creditable. Achieving such a feat and in such a short time - a matter of months - must rate as one of the astounding triumphs of the Nonette rule.

The Nonettes' system of 'earn as you learn' education has been a powerful motive in encouraging everyone to study so hard but it is not the only reason for the Nonettes' success.

Another and perhaps more compelling reason is studying for the simple enjoyable sake of it.

While the method of Nonette education in the outside world is spreading, here in northern Brazil and other places of Nonettes rule, it is in full swing.

Because education is so comprehensive, with everyone linked to several different study groups, it is all but impossible to opt out of attending "classes" To do so would be seen as letting fellow students down

There is also a marked difference in objectives between the aims of Nonette education and the outside world's.

Ours is geared to achieving high grades and examination successes: a system which favours the academically gifted.

The Nonette system, however, aspires to achievement one, no matter how 'remedial' they may be, is encouraged, cajoled as well as rewarded, for their own personal accomplishments.

Even the academically gifted only obtain advancement - and payment - if they progress beyond their current levels of ability.

But no matter how brilliant or able a student may be, their individual advancement and thus income, is also dependent on their coaching their fellows to advance their levels of ability. Indeed the gap between teacher and student itself has become blurred To teach in many respects is an integral part of studying.

There are many slogans bandied about but one which is heard most is: "Advancement entails struggle" It is this constant air of challenge and overcoming it which pervades much of Nonette education

Another is that the students themselves are party to determining what they are taught

With the exception of beginners, all students - everyone else that is - receive the image of 'Lucia' on their screens In [illegible] Lucia who is reportedly beginning to appear on increasing numbers of British Nonettes' screens And like their Lucia, the Brazilian one is viewed as each student's personal friend as well as the fount of universal knowledge and wisdom to all who speak (interact) with her.

Although Lucia is doubtless a creation of Susem technology, everyone assures me that she actually exists.

While this may well be akin to believing in Santa Claus, Lucia is held by everyone with an affection bordering on saintliness. It is this Lucia, however, who informs each student what she has received from others elsewhere and which she considers pertinent to them.

It must be stressed that as I am not a Nonette I have yet to see Lucia's image on any Nonette screen. Each time I have approached someone studying at their screen they say I am not to look. When I have asked why, I am told: "Because Lucia says you are not to."

In a way the sight of tiny children closing their screens as I approach them is un- [illegible] no way did I

In Santana everyone is wearing white

Alex Ball reports from
Fiera de Santana, Bahia

WEARING WHITE in Salvador is optional but here in Santana, 30km to the west, it is de rigeur.

Everyone, young and old alike wears an all in one white boiler-suit Some of Santana's citizen's don them with indifference but most wear theirs with style.

The suit I was given to wear came in a carton little bigger than a matchbox The box was opened and the tunic shaken out. Though it appeared to be little bigger than a toddler's romper suit, my guide stretched it a little and then had me step into it.

To my utter surprise the suit continued to stretch until it fitted me Not only did it stretch to comfortably encompass my frame, it kept me cool in the tropical heat and in the afternoon when it rained its hood along with the rest of the suit kept me dry

This super spotless suit also has other attributes including pockets, lots of them. A series of small ones down the front and several more around my waist and hips with yet more on my legs So many in fact, that I had no need of my shoulder carrying case.

On the breast and shoulders was space for - should I have been one - my Nonette identity number This suit I am told, has other impressive qualities. Not only does it allow my bodily expiration to pass through its fibres, it does not allow moisture to pass the other way. In many ways it is like a second skin

Now for the really amazing part: the suit is derived from spider webs! The actual substance is called 'Arach' This is grown and harvested as cotton and is another of the many advances brought about by the Susem

While it is at first uncanny to see a bustling street of people all clad in white there is another equally odd sight No one appears to be overweight This, so my guide tells me, is the result of regular treatment issued by the

Nonette farming could mean the end of agri-business

Alice Johnson unearths the secrets of the Nonette agricultural miracle

THE NONETTE agricultural miracle does not involve genetic modification, nor the use of pesticides or herbicides. Instead it relies on time or rather a phenomenal acceleration in the speed of plant growth to produce the Nonettes' huge increases in production.

The Nonettes grow crops from sowing to harvesting in as short a time as 10 to 12 hours. All the crops, from corn and pulses to vegetables and fruit are full of flavour and texture as any I have tasted. And an added bonus is they do not possess intro- [illegible] how provided by the Susem in producing their amazing high levels of agricultural productivity

The farmers I have asked for details of the Aliens' technology have been cagey in divulging how the massive increases of plant productivity are achieved. However, from what has been intimated there is more to plants' DNA than their genes.

There is, apparently, something which determines the make-up of genes themselves. It is this which the Susem and now the Nonettes have used to bring about their stunning advances in plant growth

What is yet more intriguing is that whatever this phenomenon is, it lies even beyond any molecular structure of genes or proteins.

Yet confusingly the Nonette as if they were meaning in an extra dimension

Genes and proteins, so one farmer said, can be likened to a table of plates of cooked food Plant scientists in the outside world, she said, are doing no more than replacing one plate with another. All they are accomplishing is rearranging the menu.

Susem agriculture however, has not only identified a plate's separate ingredients but what they were like when raw as well as how they are actually cooked Whereas plants in their natural state grow at slow-cooker speed, Susem agriculture has accelerated to that of a microwave oven

Yet there is more to mystery to the Nonettes' farming technique. Another farmer said that the entity of a plant does

Nonettes: a land of earning by learning

Everyone is a hardworking student

By Tony Perry
in Salvador

PEOPLE MAY have a job but at evenings and weekends everyone, it seems, is set on studying hard Yet there are no schools or colleges Neither are there teachers as such - let alone lecturers

The teaching screens supplied by Susem, while common enough in the outside world, exist in abundance in Nonette controlled territory.

Individuals as well as groups of people, young and old alike, are to be seen either sitting in front of their screens or giving lectures and presentations to their fellows

Yet more students can be seen on field courses carrying out the practical side of their studies

One obvious incentive to such studiousness in front of the screens is the prospect of earning from them Many people are to be seen studying in bars earning their money for their drink. But there is another reason why people study so much: they have no choice in the matter

With everyone part of several classes and group progress dependent on collective participation and advancement - and thus further earnings - the stick of coercion matches the carrot of money

While families in the rest of the world work hard in order their children have a better education, here it is often the reverse: study is seen as a way of boosting family income

Grandmothers have a new role within the family Many have the fearsome reputation of 'whippers in' for their both their grandchildren and their

Edward Sheldron the first outside journalist to ever reach the nerve centre of Aliens

Serra da Ibiapaba - citadel of the Susem

THE Susem citadel of the Serra da Ibiapaba can be seen from many miles away across the sun baked plain of the Sertao.

By day its forbidding, sheer sided, kilometre-high cliff-faces appear blue but towards evening it glows like a beacon from the reflect-ed rays of the setting sun.

The Ibiapaba Mountains deep in desolate backlands of Brazil's interior are a near impenetrable natural fortress. They are also the Susem base here on Earth.

During daylight the barren, backland plain surrounding the Ibiapaba blisters under the remitting heat of the equatorial sun. But by night temperatures plummet so rapidly that even rocks crack with the cold.

It is from across this lifeless land that Susem spacecraft can be seen arriving and departing from the Ibiapaba.

There is but a single highway across this stretch of the Sertao. By day it is filled halt as motorists stop to look at the Susem spaceships flying overhead. There have been many accidents.

Close by the cliff-face of the Ibiapaba itself, yet more crowds of onlookers gaze upwards at Susem craft flying from hangers carved deep into the rock-face.

At night the upper levels of the cliffs are lit with the lights of the communities of the Ibiapaba who, with Susem [illegible] cloud forest fringed crest that the seeds of the Nonette movement were first sown.

It was in the town of Tiangua at the foot of the mountains, where the forces of the former regime first fled the Nonette rebels as they surged down from the mountains of the Ibiapaba

The only route up onto the Ibiapaba is along the edge of a torturous rock strewn precipice where just one slip brings instant death But once upon [illegible] evening mists.

Although the Ibiapaba is isolated, near impenetrable, many thousands of Nonettes travel to this cradle of the revolution every single day.

The original townships and villages along the entire length of the Ibiapaba are now deserted, many even demolished. Fields lie untended, bereft of crops, many overgrown Farming for the Nonettes on the Ibiapaba is conducted now like the homes, entirely below

As summer progressed there was criticism at the sentences passed on men guilty of besieging, bombarding the defenceless inhabitants of towns and cities of Bosnia. Why, people asked, had the judgments been so lenient of those who had fired a million shells into Sarajevo from the overlooking Trebevic and Igman mountains, killing thousands, maiming more?

Why, it was also asked, had those guilty of mortaring Goražde, Tuzla, Zenica to bloody submission been sentenced to nothing more than to spend seven days upon the hillsides where they had aimed their murdering fire?

Why had, many asked, including the guilty themselves, the judgment of every one of these crimes repeatedly contained nothing more than the mild admonishment, "...in contemplative atonement of your evil deeds"?

Others demanded that these guilty men, as well as those who had systematically torched orchards the length of the Neretva Valley, murdering their owners, at least be subjected to the severity of punishment of those they had viewed on 'Trials'. The same was said of the men who had massacred Bosnians in Mostar, firing field guns at pointblank range into apartment blocks, burning worshippers alive in the mosque at Jajce and many more of the atrocities committed against innocent, defenceless people.

The Hisogynists said 'contemplation' did not make for good TV action. But as the weeks progressed and growing numbers of sentences were served, another question came to be asked, "Where are the returnees?"

Many people across Bosnia had seen the tall, stocky, inscrutable Khmer guards marching groups of the guilty in parties of twenty and more, yoked three abreast, outstretched arms lashed to staves, up onto the forested slopes from whence they had rained their murderous fire. Watchers had also seen these guards walk back down again, staves sloped over shoulders.

Residents of Miljevici, a suburb of Sarajevo at the foot of the mountainous slopes of the Trebevic Wildlife Park and from where most of the shelling of the city had come, saw such groups pass almost daily. They also saw the dawn arrival of flocks of birds and, with the dusk, their departing swirls.

But the guilty, taken to the slopes of the Trebevic for their week's 'Contemplative Atonement', saw neither the birds' arrival nor departure. Nor did they see the men who had arrived before them, for each group was taken to a lower level than the last. By late August when the final groups arrived they climbed no higher than 200 metres.

Nonetheless, these men began their 'First Day' just as the others had, breakfasting at sunrise on sausage, cheese and yogurt, then marched along the same route past scattered shell casings, rusting artillery pieces, copious heaps of emptied rakija bottles (the local home-made brandy which had so inebriately fired-up the firers), and then into a quiet woodland glade.

Children renew forests

Alan Brown watches children tending their trees

THE COACH had taken three hours to make the 100km journey from Sao Luis to a patch of scrub and overgrown field just outside the hamlet of Pigui.

But no sooner had the coach lumbered to a halt than dozens of school-age children were streaming out of its doors.

Without even as much as hesitating, the children were rushing to inspect the progress of their newly planted trees. Soon there were whoops of pleasure at the saplings' growth.

The trees are part of a forest renewal programme. Many thousands of hectares around Pigui are under active reforestation.

Each 20 hectare section of the new forest has been

Across the lands of the Nonettes..

Women are in charge

On Nonette councils it is men who are in the minority

John Robinson reports from Manaus

The Nonettes' Amazonian Regional Council, based in Manaus comprises 81 delegates, 55 of them women. Manaus is not an exception. In other Nonette Councils, large and small, women are usually in the majority.

At political and administrative levels men have found themselves pushed into second place. The reasons for this state of affairs stems from the formation of the Nonette communities themselves.

..and no arguing

Elections to all Nonette Community Councils, representing no more than 800 people - a village, a street - are held each month. Apart from coordinating their communities' affairs the person elected also represents them in an assembly of another 80 similar communities. Collectively, these represent some 60,000 people, a town.

This town council coordinates the activities local Nonettes delegates to it. This larger Nonette also elects one of their number - again only for a month at a time - to represent them at the Regional Nonette which comprises of a further 80 towns made up of about 5 million people.

In turn, this Nonette sends one of their number to represent them at the Congress itself.

Each local community is also divided into nine wards. These smaller groups are usually comprised of neighbouring families. Because women, more often than not, manage family and home, it usually they who vote for one of their own. Children, who also have the right to vote, either plump for one of their in their life: their mothers or her friends and neighbours.

It is from among these 'ward sisters' who are usually elected to their communities' posts of tax gathering (or 'tythe' as it is known), allocation of funds and spending, and so on. In turn, it is from among these, more often than not, that a communities' delegate is elected.

The local Nonettes decide which powers to retain and those to delegate to their town Nonette.

Each local Nonette spends half of their income on their own requirements, the rest is given to their town Nonette to spend on the collective behalf of all the local Nonettes.

It is this sum and how it is spent, which local delegates are also mandated by their communities to oversee. Delegates are also answerable to their local communities on the town's expenditure. As one delegate said: "It is our own money, we are very careful how it is spent."

A third of what is given over to the town by the 40 Wealthiest Nonette is ear-[marked to be spent on the] poorest 40. The richest one gives to the poorest and so until the 41st neither gives or receives. Not only does each donor Nonette give their money directly to the recipient community they also have a direct say and hands-on involvement in how it is spent.

As businesses are also enfranchised into the Nonette movement (they have the vote) and are still, for the most part owned and managed by men, it is they who are to the fore in the commercial side of the joint Nonette investment committees.

Nonetheless it the family-to-family aspect of the liaison which has the greatest impact. And it is women who have the greatest involvement. As one delegate said: "Families are the bedrock from which all communities spring. Once the aspirations of our families are seen by us as realisable then we have every reason to ensure these ambitions are not jeopardised.

"A strong sense of community with one's neighbours is one of the ways of realising and safeguarding family aspirations. Every assistance to this end is likely to be welcomed than rebuffed. Women, be they rich or poor, have more things in common than do men."

One outcome of such extensive inter-community contact is a unified sense of purpose of the town as a whole.

Another is the large number of football and basketball leagues based on the town's local Nonette. In Maues, a town to the east of Manaus there is even a Nonettes over-50s basketball league.

While there is a strong sense of community at local and town level the same is true of the region as a whole. For just as the richer and poorer parts of a town are integrated with one another, so do the 81 towns of the regional Nonette.

A further third of the funds that towns receive from their local communities is sent on - plus delegate - to the regional Nonette to spend on the towns' collective behalf. Part of the 40 wealthiest towns' funds are spent on 40 poorest, and again on a direct town twinning basis.

As the proceedings of the Regional Nonettes are televised live, just as are those of the Congress itself, everyone can be informed of proceedings as well as the performance of their own delegates.

The activities of all the Nonettes are also reported in the numerous newspapers which are published.

Whereas in the rest of the world, politics is often regarded with indifference, in Nonetteland it is followed with lively interest by everyone.

In part this is because of the belief that an individual's vote really does count: a person, their friends and neighbours can really change things. If

No Leaders No Politicians No Officials NO NEED

ROGER HANSON

Reports from Quito

PEOPLE DEPENDENT ON their neighbours' re-election are in no position to be leaders, let alone be dictatorial. The best anyone can do and many willingly aspire, is to be none other than a delegate, an emissary.

In many parts of this city there are Nonette delegates who have been pressurised into representing their communities.

With every Nonette delegate being a fellow neighbour of those who elect him - though in Quito it's more often a 'her' - any idea of political parties is far from everyone's minds.

One resident of San Sebastian, a Quito suburb said: "In the old days of politicians we the people existed for their benefit, nowadays our Nonette representatives exist for ours. The likes of them [politicians] will never come here again, they would not dare [to]"

Local Nonette communities manage their own day-to-day affairs and finances. They also have their own rules and regulations but if San Sebastion is a guide, there are not many and what few there are can be changed on a residents' show of hands.

With officialdom absent from their daily lives, people and communities can go about their business as they please.

As a San Sebastion shopkeeper commented: "Because there are no rules or laws there are none to break. Because there are no officials there are none to demand payment for permits. Nor is there the need to bribe them."

There is, however, a powerful incentive for everyone to be a lawabiding, model citizen. That of their community itself.

To offend the community means ostracism, ignominy. And not just within a transgressor's own local Nonette but every other one as well.

Should anyone persist in causing complaint they face a community court to plead their case. However, the judge

Nonettes: the land of plent

Hugo Gurney reports from Pessoa

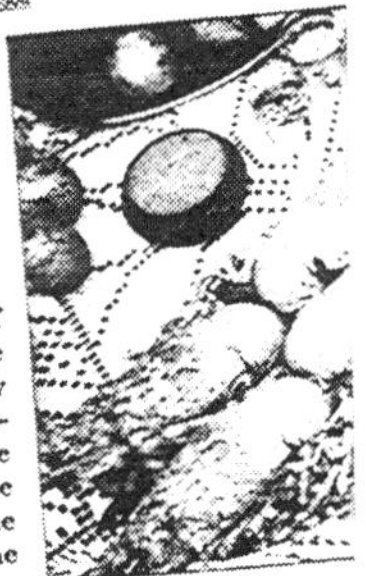

FOOD GLORIOUS FOOD and lots of it. Fine wines flowing like water, beers and bacardi as well.

Feasts fit for kings are available for all in this seaside city.

But the people of Pessoa are not alone in their culinary heaven. Such gastronomic delights are available to all the people across the lands of the Nonettes.

Where once people were forced to subsist on meagre fare now there are prepared feasts awaiting them every day and no washing-up either.

Such has been the huge increase in food production across the territory under Nonette control that there is plenty for everyone. There has also been a surge in culinary master-classes.

So much so than community restaurants have opened up in countless Nonette communities.

Just one hour's study in front of a teaching screen earns enough for a slap-up night out.

Classes in wine making have also seen a similar surge of membership in the vintner's arts. Though it is still early days, some rather fine Vinho Verde's are already quenching the

It was here, amid the dappling of morning sunlight that the men's 'Contemplative Atonement' began. One by one they were loosened from their staves, grasped by four of the guards while a fifth, taking hold of the long arms of lawn-edging shears, administered the mandatory castration.

Each 'snip' and screech was followed by a 'plop' as parted members were tossed atop a bluebottle-black, now knee high pulsating pile of similarly severed scrotums. As each one landed it caused a momentary ripple and the flies briefly to buzz up. But as the castrates, now wincing, were herded further into the forest the scrotum pile still moved. For in that late summer warmth, hatching maggots in their wriggling millions, progressing to pupation, greedily gorged upon the putrefying penises and testicles.

As the men, these callous killers of women and children, hobbling and snivelling, were cajoled along the woodland path, and because of their perceived discomfort, they were doubtless unaware of myriad watching eyes. Eyes which followed their every stumbling step all the way to the individual trees they would rest against during their 'stay of contemplation'.

Many of the watchers also heard the men's next screams as thick, wide-headed nails, hammered through hands secured outstretched arms around the trees' trunks. Previous arrivals may have heard these cries for release but none called back. Such wails were soon stifled however when the guards sprayed all the men's faces and mouths with sustenance for their stay, honey. These murderers of the innocent were then left to their 'contemplation'. But they were not alone for long for the first visitors soon arrived, the flies.

Within minutes the men's faces swarmed black with them, sickening several into regurgitating their half-digested breakfasts. But even as vomit dribbled from their mouths, dripped from chins or dried on beards, flies fed on its yogurt-creamed slivers of sausage and cheese.

Wasps followed to devour the flies. But they also feasted on the vomit and in doing so stung many men's faces. At the same time, descending from the foliage above and the leaf litter below, came the ants. In twos and threes at first, but within the hour foraging columns were on all the men. No matter how they tugged, twitched, none could shake the ants away. And like the flies, the ants were not just content with the honey and vomit. They also sought the salinity of mucus in noses, moistness under eyelids.

By keeping their eyes tightly closed the men found some respite from the flies, but no matter how closely they crossed their legs the ants still crawled into each man's bloodied, urine, sweat-wet castration gash, as well as up into their anuses, which like their bladders were now incontinently venting.

Sparrows, starlings and other insect-eating birds soon arrived. They brought the men some respite from the flies but it was short-lived. For in feeding on them, the birds also pecked the men's faces. However, by continually shaking their heads it provided some protection from these birds' beaks. But not from those of the now arriving rooks, ravens and crows.

Hugo Gurney reports on a long-term benefit

Nonette Brazil: land of beautiful people

In Nonette Brazil obesity has been banished and anorexia ousted.

On every street, open spaces – anywhere under Nonette rule - there is the pleasing sight of beautiful bodies both young and old. Some are chubby, some are slender and others somewhere in between but all in rude good health.

This healthy state of affairs, say its Nonette proponents, is another outcome of the long-term benefits of their 'Mormic' health booths.

If what they say is true, users of these booths around the world can expect the same good fortune from visiting them.

In the seaside resort of Arraial, 200km south of Salvador, Gloria Jacobina, who is in charge of her Nonette community's Mormic, explained some of the mysteries surrounding its workings.

She said: "A Mormic works by first establishes signatures and then corrects any existent divergence within them back to the norm.

"With each session in the Mormic it progressively refines the signatures and as an outcome ensures cells are formed and function to the optimum of their efficiency."

Gloria also added that between each monthly session in the Mormic not only did a person's body as a whole have time to adjust to the correcting changes but so did all the microscopic beasties living on and in us.

These, so she said, make up 10 per cent of our body weight and we cannot live without them.

Another effect of the Mormics is that facelifts are things of the past. For not only has every Nonette a perfect body but also skin as well. Folds and wrinkles are banished. Once the Mormics have established themselves as the a person's

No Mobiles No E mail No Internet NO NEED

ROGER HANSON

from Guayaquil on Nonette communication

FOR THE NONETTES OF GUAYAQUIL cyber-space as we know it is a thing of the past. In this Pacific port city of the former state of Ecuador, people do not appear to require phones or any other apparatus to contact one another. It is all done in their heads.

Call it extra-sensory perception if you will but it is happening here and on a wide scale. Not just in this city either but all across the entire territory of the Nonettes.

When hands-free mobile phones first became commonplace, passersby often mistook phone users for disturbed people talking to them-

Explaining how this unique method communication works, Maria Ambato, head of a Nonette in the central suburb of Roca, said: "It is a case of a person's mind knowing what another is thinking.

"Everyone," she says, "who has [frequent] use of a telephone has experienced some-

Greg Weston reports on the Nonette civil engineering achievements

Roads of glass, bridges of bone

CATCH the light right and a Nonette-made road glistens as a silver thread snaking across the landscape.

Step a few feet to one side and much of it disappears. But travel on the road and it is a dark grey. It is also covered with small studs.

Welcome to Nonette road building. Though the crowns of the studs cause the road to glisten when seen from afar they also give it a durable non-skid surface on which to drive. The grey colour of the road's surface however, is the more amazing: it is that of glass.

The Nonettes, obvious-ly using Susem technology, have developed a system of instant road building. Following the minimum of preparation a machine slowly hovers above the surface heating the ground to more than 1,000 degrees and melting it, be it sand, clay, rock into film of glass. As the film cools the tail-end of the machine makes the studded surface.

As the machine travels at some 5 kph, once rutted tracks to isolated villages become all-weather highways in a matter of hours.

Tens of thousands of kilometres of roads have already been constructed across the backlands of the Brazilian Sertao.

Because glass is so elastic the road is able to expand and contract at the same rate as the surface it passes over and so never cracks or buckles. It also never needs to be resurfaced.

Another feat of Nonette civil engineering is their bridge-building. Bridges are also made of sand melted into glass but they are re-enforced with bone. The Nonettes have genetically modified a species of willow to grow bone instead of wood.

Bone, so the Nonettes claim, has a greater tensile strength that steel. Bundles of coppiced branches of 'bone willow' are placed either end of the bridge's planned span covered in sand which is then fused to glass but before it has solidified more bundles of bone are added which in turn are covered with sand and fused to glass. This continues until the two sides meet.

The resulting bridges are slender, graceful, glistening strands of light streaking across rivers and ravines. They are also quick to build and like the roads virtually maintenance-free.

As one Nonette engineer said, both bridges and roads

Edward Sheldron reports from the Nonettes prison

Serra Pelada - the Amazon gulag run by its inmates

THE world's biggest man-made hole, deep in the heart of the Amazon jungle is being refilled by convicts of the Nonettes. Yet it is run and controlled by its own inmates.

From the air the convicts in the Serra Pelada look like a huge army of ants. But this 1,000 feet deep, mile wide, hand-dug pit is the prison of 100,000 and more convicts of the Nonette regime.

Where once 200,000 graimpeiros - prospectors - dug relentlessly deeper in their search for gold and rubies, almost as many men are now refilling it.

From the length and breadth of Latin America under Nonette control men judged guilty by their communities for crimes against them, labour from dawn to dusk refilling the Pelada.

Under the unremitting glare of the tropical sun, former politicians, mayors, police chiefs and bureaucrats, toil alongside pimps, murderers, death squads and wife beaters, hauling sack after sack of former mine debris down onto the ever rising pit floor.

Men used to the good life, living off of the backs of the poor, now experience the hard life of forced labour.

No one is excused the harsh regime. Divided into work gangs each must fulfill a daily quota of lugging 50 kilo sacks of spoil down into the Pelada. No matter how elevated a man's former status in the Pelada he is no more than just another 'formiga' - an ant.

There is no chance of escape from the Pelada either. As one inmate said: "We can walk from here but where would we walk to? Who would give us shelter?"

Every prisoner also knows the consequences of being caught. Not only do they face a mandatory castration but the wrath of their fellow work gang members who, in their absence, would have to make good his quota.

There are only two ways out of the Pelada. One is death - and there have a number - the other is to take charge of a work gang. Once a convict has fulfilled a ninth of his quota (sentence) he rises to gang master of nine men

However, if he were to leave the Pelada itself, he must next have to rise to senior gang master. This is determined by his gang completing their joint quota.

The sooner the requisite number of sacks are filled the sooner he receives promotion. Thus not only does every convict work hard they are also worked hard.

There are several more levels of promotion to work for before a prisoner earns his release from the Pelada. The outcome however, is a regime with the minimum of administration and one which is run by the inmates themselves.

It is thought that the Pelada will take many years before it is completely refilled. There may not be enough mining

Tiny Tots and their cuddly bambi friends

By PAULA GRADY

ALL THE LITTLE CHILDREN looked so sweet as they squealed with delight and wonderment when they said hello to their new friends: six tiny baby deer.

Delicately the little fawns stepped from the carrier, fluttering their big bambi eyes as they walked unsteadily on young legs into their new home.

At first these baby deer from the forest were filled with shyness but soon they were cuddled up nice and safe in the boys and girls' loving arms, glugging hungrily from their feeding bottles.

For the six and seven year-old children the little fawns were their big treat. They are also their next big challenge. For during the coming year they are to be the baby deer's mummies and daddies.

The baby deer are part of the children's big plan to bring back all the birds and animals which once roamed the forests a long time ago

In the same way as these birds attack lambs, they clasped their claws either side of a man's scalp. No matter how much a man shook his head, from such a perch these birds' powerful, probing beaks easily pecked right through the man's eyelids. And then, with a single wrench and twist, the birds would pluck an entire eye from its socket. By early afternoon all the men were sightless.

Though shrieking at being blinded the men soon had their lips pursed to silence. For having devoured their eyes, ravens and rooks cawed and jostled for further facial tidbits. Lips, noses, and should a man still cry out, his tongue. Though the men tugged frantically against their clamping nails in desperate bids to escape these avian attacks, all any of them achieved was fresh bleeding from the holes in their hands.

As the blood trickled down their palms, wrists, glistening before congealing, it attracted the rasping, tugging beaks of magpies, jackdaws and jays. So did the steady pulsing rivulets from their eyeless sockets, as they melded with the honey and vomit into wrinkling films of sheening coagulation.

The commotion of these birds' frenzied feeding attracted opportunist raptors, buzzards, hawks, then waddling down the hillside as they now had no need to fly, metre-tall griffin vultures, their swaying crops and bloated bellies smeared with the human detritus littering the levels above.

The men, now in dread terror kicked, bucked, twisted, tugged. But none stopped the flocking birds' ceaseless cawing, jostling cacophony of pecking, clawing, nibbling, gobbling at their blood-fresh flesh.

Though silent, the insects were more voracious. In their thousands they sucked, masticated upon the men's bodies. Especially rapacious were the ants. Armies of them now scurried into men's every orifice, ears to anuses, eye sockets to exposed urethras, ceaselessly carving off flesh for their larders.

With the coolness of dusk birds flew to roost, insects ceased their sucking. For the men, snivelling, fearful, sweat cold, pecked, stung, clothes ripped, torn and like their bodies, streaked in saliva and blood, smeared and smelling of sick, excrement, and sodden in urine, this provided some respite. But it was short-lived. For in the gathering gloom there now came the creatures of the night.

Voles, shrews to feed on the insects trapped in the honey vomit gore. Hordes of mice also fed upon its globules of sausage and cheese. But these were soon scampering inside men's clothes, gnawing, nibbling at their bodies, their detritus. Once again the men were bucking, tugging as they attempted to shake them away. And once again their efforts were in vain. The mice only decamped with the arrival of more aggressive rodents, the rats.

Such had been the summer's surfeit of human fare that rats had bred so numerous they came not in ones or twos but as packs. Hundreds, then a flowing carpet of thousands ran up the men's legs, bodies, surged, scurried

My visit to paradise

By **Hugo Gurney**
reports from Arraial, Bahia

If eating good food and never becoming fat (let alone ill), drinking fine wine and never suffering a hangover, making love all day - and night - with beautiful people with perfectly formed bodies and libidos which never flag is your idea of Paradise, then Arraial is the place for you

If a simple life, one with few possessions, no need to work except when the mood takes you, where a few hours of enjoyable study yields sufficient income to meet material needs is also your idea of Paradise then Arraial and the towns and villages along this sun blessed Atlantic coast is the place for you.

If Paradise is living in a society where there are no rules, regulations or authorities ordering you what to do, one where everyone is free do whatever they want, yet at same time there is no crime or lawlessness, then Arraial and entire surrounding Recôncavo region is the place for you

If Paradise is a place where some people are rich but no one is poor, where illness and disease is eliminated, as are illiteracy and ignorance, then you. Should widespread repair of blighted cities, rehabilitation of ravaged countryside and forests alike be on your list for paradise then Bahia is also the place for you

However, if a society where armies are absent, police forces, politicians and bureaucrats are as well, is also a requirement for Paradise along with a world where old men and their organisations no longer wield any power or influence, then all of Latin America where the Nonettes are in charge is the place for you.

Sitting by the beach, sipping sangrias and calpirinhas, dining on the finest lobster and guavas, the soft evening breezes filled with scent of borganvilla one moment, marijuana the next and an unending parade of beautiful women and equally handsome men ambling by, it is difficult not to be envious of the inhabitants of Arraial.

It is also difficult not be amazed at the speed with which the Nonettes have brought such changes to not just Arraial but to all of Latin America where they have

Cocaine is in the money now

John Richards reports on the fate of 'Big White'

WHEN THE drug barons fled from the Nonette advance what happened to the cocaine they left behind? What fates awaited coca farmers, their crops, and their livelihoods?

Life under the Nonettes appears to be good for both the farmers and their coca bushes.

For the first time they are able to grow them on the hillsides besides their villages rather than clear stretches of virgin forest many kilometres away as they did under the old regime.

Neither have farmers to fear any government forces destroying their crops.

According to one Nonette community head there is now more coca under cultivation than at any time in the past. The bushes are grown, she said to meet a growing demand.

This 'demand' however, is not for the cocaine the bushes' leaves produce but paper from their fibre.

Coca leaves along with arach silk are what all Nonette bank notes are made from So too are the study vouchers of Nonette teaching screen.

Scores of Nonette communities along the Andean foothills have been contracted by the Central Bank of Congress to produce fixed quotas of leaves.

The money the farmers receive for their crops is, so sources in Quito claim, more than they were ever paid by the old drug barons.

Some of the Nonettes have even taken the process several stages further. Not only are they growing arach alongside their coca crop but have

No laws no lawlessness

Roger Hanson
reports from Maceio, Alagoas

THERE IS AN old man who sits in a booth at the intersection of Rue Prie and Rue Concertos. He is there day and night, or at least other men like him are.

There is another old man in another booth at the next major intersection. And the next and so on throughout this Atlantic coast city Every Nonette city is the same. At intervals along this region's beautiful unspoilt beaches are yet other - although younger - men. All do the same thing: they watch over everyone. Anything untoward is relayed to the next man and so on. Should there be emergencies each one can summon a host of volunteers.

In a society where the underlying causes of crime: hunger, poverty, need and ignorance have been eliminated, these watchers provide a yet further layer of reassureance to Maceio's citizens With the strength of Nonette security around them, everyone is freed to do as they wish. Adding to this air of freedom is the awareness that as laws, rules and regulations no longer exist there are none to break.

Though everyone can indulge and imbibe in anything they want, Maceio is a most law abiding city Marijuana is widely smoked. Corner kiosks sell ready-made reefers in packs of 20, each one claiming to be '20 per cent tdc' which - so I am told - is 'good stuff'. Cocaine is easily available but if price - the equivalent of $5 a gram - is a guide, few people partake. Heroin is also obtainable and sells at a similar sum. Both these drugs just as others are viewed as socially 'naff' Regular sessions in a Mormic cancels any craving for them. Addicts, actual and would-be also have the opprobrium of their local Nonette to contend with.

The same aura of community disapproval has also influenced standards of driving. While the roads are as busy as usual, no reports of so-called 'road-rage' have been reported since the Nonettes have

A host of little children and their butterfly friends

By **PAULA GRADY**

A MYRIAD of bright blue butterflies fluttered on the party of tiny boys and girls. As all the children shrieked and giggled with delight, the butterflies settled on their little crisp white tunics.

The children, having looked after the butterflies since they were caterpillars, think of them as their very own special friends Although they are no more than seven and eight years old, the boys and girls are already experts in the world of butterflies. And of course these children are already familiar with the grown ups' word of 'lepidoptery' for butterflies One little boy, looking everso studiously earnest referred to blue butterflies as "morpho cantira". But

The most watched lady talks

Alice Johnson talks to Rainbow Louis

THE FACE of Rainbow Louis is known the world over So are her perfectly enunciated vowels

Governments and authorities have protested and denounced what Ms Louis has had to say in her daily newscasts. Many have demanded her newscasts be banned from their countries' screens Others have attempted to produce programmes refuting what she has to say. None have yet to succeed in denting the worldwide popularity of her newscasts Nor match Rainbow's viewing figures of billions.

But what of Rainbow herself? Just who *is* this attractive young woman and most English sounding of ladies? How in heavens did she find herself in one of the most isolated of places on earth?

"I trained as an actress but because of the colour of my skin I was never offered any work," she said "I became tired of being labelled 'an out of work actress' so when I was offered this opportunity I just had to take it."

However, when asked if, as an actress that her job was a human face for the Susem and just that, a job, it drew Rainbow's impassioned: "I have been part of the Nonette movement from the moment of its creation. It is now my life.

"When I first arrived here I had absolutely no idea of just how wretched conditions in Brazil were for so many people

"Having witnessed the changes brought by the Nonettes, the empowerment they have given to ordinary people, their elimination of poverty, illness and illiteracy it is impossible for any person not to be totally committed," she said

Rainbow was equally forthright in her views of the Susem themselves She said: "I met the Susem within hours of my arrival In many ways 'the girls' [as she calls the Susem] are just like you and me I cannot for a moment see why anyone should be scared of their presence

"They came to Earth to find their lost spaceship While they were searching for it they have given us the benefit of their assistance It would have been silly to have refused it."

Tackled on the Susem assaults on men brought peels of laughter from Rainbow, and: "Well girls will be girls! The Susem, had been travelling for many years. It is perfectly natural they would be seeking a period of rest and recreation If it is acceptable for men, soldiers to go on so-called 'R'n'R' leave' why shouldn't women be free to do the same?"

Rainbow said the Susem had a different approach towards men than to us

"They do not regard men as their equals," she said "For the Susem the word 'men' is usually prefixed by 'only'."

Rainbow also revealed what been long suspected that there are not any Susem men. "Of course they exist," she said, "but there are none on this voyage In Susem society men are looked on as little more than children "

Asked about her former boss and co-presenter, Danny Collins, Rainbow said: "Danny is the reason I'm here, it was he who told me the job was on offer but that is all."

Rainbow laughed when I told her that Collins was seen not only as a Spengali figure who had lured her to Brazil but also as fraudster who had tricked everyone into using the soufin energy units and so caused the worldwide energy crisis. "Nobody manipulates me! If anything I tell Danny what to do! Whatever his shortcomings Danny is well regarded in the Congress for introducing Love Patches and Vanton."

Asked if she had been scared by the attempted the French nuclear missile attack, Rainbow said although she was at first but only for a moment

"But as soon as Sardon [one of the Susem spaceships] has demonstrated his authority as supreme master of the skies, a missile from any direction was simply a mere nuisance, rather than any considerable threat," she said

Greg Weston reports on the Nonettes amazing method of irrigation

Water without the dams

HUNDREDS of dams across tributaries of the Amazon have been smashed open. Countless work gangs from the Nonette Serra Pelada labour camp are restoring the rivers and the surrounding once drowned land. Other work gangs from the Pelada are busily installing further sections of the Nonettes' unique irrigation system.

Ends of pipes are put in rivers at kilometre intervals. The other ends are connected to yet more pipes, all of which are sunk beneath the ground. Water from the rivers is pumped through a labyrinth of thousands of yet more ... delivered to towns, villages as well as being used for agriculture. Should a river's flow become low, then extraction is switched to rivers where it is not.

Being buried beneath the ground, the pipe-lines are kept at a constant temperature. Because the water is pumped the length of the system, there is the minimum of earthwork disturbance to install the pipelines

Evaporation is also eliminated Although Nonette agriculture is conducted underground in specially constructed caverns and so evaporation is further kept to a minimum, part of their farming methods actually depends on

Out on the Sertao – the semi-desert scrub-land which covers much of Brazil's interior - plants are grown to extract iron ore and other minerals. Tubes from the irrigation system pump a fine spray of water two metres into the air above these plants The micro-cloud cover formed by the spray keeps the plants cool as well as the ground around them. The precipitation from the clouds as well as the density of the clouds themselves is adjusted to the plants' requirements.

The iron ore, which passes from the plants' roots to its leaves, is collected then they are cropped

across arms, faces, throats. In their terror men who still had tongues screamed in panicked pain as rats bit, tore, defecated into their flesh. The tongueless coughed, spurted globules of blood as they too frantically bucked and writhed in attempting to shake the rats from them. None succeeded.

Only the scent and snapping of arriving foxes, and later the snarls of the Park's wolves, drove the rats away. But not all. For some had already bitten their way through men's castration cuts, anal sphincters, clawing up inside their body cavities. As foxes and wolves in snarling skirmishes tugged, pulled at the men's legs, rats silently gorged on their intestines. But as the night wore on they also fed on the more succulent kidneys, livers, lungs.

Being bigger, the wolves edged foxes aside from the choicest flesh, loins, buttocks. However, being able to spring into the air for roosting birds, foxes feasted from where the wolves could not reach, fingers, hands, arms. For some of the men this brought release, of sorts.

When foxes had bitten away sufficient of a man's last hand for him to finally wrench the remainder through the nail, he would inevitably plunge forwards onto the ground. Because of the honey, vomit and gore on his face it was quickly covered in a thick mask of leaves, twigs, earth. Crawling, scrabbling in sightlessness, leaf litter also stuck to the blood, excrement and sick still smearing his body and clothes. Soon such men no longer possessed human form but became as if dread, scuffling forest incubuses.

But those who still had awareness (and limbs) and attempted escape, did not get far. It was not just wolves and foxes' attentions these shuffling humps attracted, but the Park's bears. These came not for the flesh on limbs but the softer tissue of abdomens. With their long rasping claws they had already ripped the more obese men's bellies open, gorging on their raked out intestines. But these were still slip slopping from stomachs, along with gore smeared rats making their escapes, when the bears became distracted by snarling wolves dancing around the first would-be absconder.

Once aware of these circling wolves' snapping snarls, the now dirt matted shuffling hump abruptly stopped its scuffling. But not for long.

With one wolf's darting bite, this heap of leaves and twigs rapidly reverted back to a man, a frantically kicking, arms flaying, squealing, writhing, groping man fighting for his very life. But as the wolves, now as a pack, had hold of his legs, arms, tugging, biting, tearing into them, his fight was set to cease.

No sooner had he succumbed to the wolves, than bears were upon him. If there were screams they would have been lost amid roars and snarls as beasts in a frenzied scrum tore, clawed for their choice parts of his body.

On it went. Hump after shuffling hump, first squirming, wriggling, shrieking, next frantically writhing, kicking as wolves tugged off, bit away limbs, and bears tore faces from skulls for their honey, ripped out innards for organs until each would-be escaper was left a bloody disemboweled pile of

Soccer in a sea of flags - and an unusual anthem

MICHAEL HAWKS
REPORTS FROM SALVADOR

THE match between Recife and Salvador drew 80,000 fans to the giant Tororo stadium. The fixture was eagerly awaited. So was the outcome, both teams were evenly matched.

Import-ant though the game was, the pre-match build-up was the more spectacular.

Although the game was an evening kick-off, supporters from both sides began gathering in the park in front of the stadium from first light.

Groups of them arrived with all the paraphernalia soccer fans the world over bring to matches: scarves, team shirts and so on. But each group also brought something extra: their Nonette community's flag.

Every Nonette community it seems, has their own flag. These flags fly from masts in most communities. Their emblems are frequently emblazoned on street signs, letters and even the masthead of the numerous Nonette newspapers. Nonette flags are also brought to sporting fixtures

By noon with yet more groups arriving, each with their flag, the park resembled more of a medieval tourna-ment gathering than fans waiting for a match. ... opposite sides of the park, festivities had commenced.

These began with the Recife supporters humming. This was then taken up by Salvador's. It was a slow melodic hum to begin then be-came louder and louder. Although not an opera buff the tune was reminiscent of the Verdi's 'March of the Hebrew Slaves'.

After several minutes however, both sides burst into song. A few at first, then more and more joined in, not just heartily, but as if from the heart as well. The song was indeed about how they had been enslaved and now they were free, that soon all people would also live in freedom.

Later it was revealed the fans were singing what is in effect the Nonettes anthem.

The singing continued for several minutes then died away but only to begin again moments later. The humming however, as if a counter melody still continued.

In fact it never stopped. The volume rose and fell but after a while it was as though the tune was inside of one's head as well.

The humming continued both inside and out of heads as the fans from each side formed up into columns. As all of the fans were clad in their white tunics, the colours of flags appeared all the more vivid

'Democracy' is dead - long live democracy!

ROGER PAYNE reports from Bogata of Nonette democracy in action

"DEMOCRACY IS A TERRIBLE FORM OF GOVERNMENT," Sir Winston Churchill once said, then added, "however, all the other forms are worse." But now there is a form of government which is wonderful, it really does work, it is truly fair and equitable. It is called 'democracy'.

Democracy: 'Of the people, for the people, by the people', the one to which Churchill claimed he was referring has never actually existed before.

The Western 'democracies' are in reality nothing more than oligarchies: 'Of the parties, for the parties by the parties'. Though for many so-called democratic countries, 'parties' is interchangeable with 'privileged'.

But here in the lands of the Nonettes true democracy reigns supreme: a system of representation where every person's vote effects an election's outcome.

In the west we are given little or no choice in who is to represent us except this or that ambitious outsider parachuted in by their political cliques

complete with an agenda for his own personal aggrandize-ment.

But for the Nonettes every person elected actually is a peoples' representative, they are one of their own community.

In Nonette society power really is in the hands of the people And this includes the right of each community to manage their own affairs as they see fit

It is a society where each community has achieved self-determination, their political and economic independence

The wider Nonette society can be likened to a confederation of small independent states, voluntarily banded together for the mutual benefit of all their peoples And in the process of so doing have become united in a single commonwealth of not nations or states but of communities, of the people.

The people of the Nonettes, freed from the rule of oligarchs and their institutions which enslaved them, have demonstrated their grat-

All the little children pick their posies of pretty flowers

By PAULA GRADY

THE LITTLE CHILDREN looked everso sweet as they picked armfuls of absolutely gorgeous flowers to take home to their mummies and daddies.

As soon as the gates of flower garden were opened two dozen and more tiny tots, all dressed in their smart, snow white little tunics were running into the garden to see all the pretty flowers.

There were shrieks of delight and wonderment as they first looked on all the sumptuous blooms: red ones, yellow, blue, white and lots of other lovely colours and filled with such heavenly scents.

There were little flowers and big ones, some so huge they had grown even taller than the children.

After the little boys and girls had looked at all the flowers, they asked the grown-ups with them lots of questions

Nonettes: A World where women are in total control

Carole Edge reports on how women are now in charge

"Nowadays we never have to compromise," said Sonia Mendiha speaking of her husband, "I don't allow it any more." And so say all women in the land of the Nonettes.

In a few short months not only have women taken charge of their lives from men but are in control of everything else as well. And this includes men.

As the armies of the old regime fled from the Susem and the advancing Nonettes, the institutions of the old order either left with the departing soldiers or just simply ceased to exist.

The vacuum these defunct - and exclusively male - organisations created was immediately filled by those of the Nonettes.

Power in Nonette society, unlike that in the outside world, comes from the bottom up, not the top down.

With the Nonettes it is families and the communities they create, where power now lies. It is women who hold sway in both families and neighbourhoods.

Not only are sensible husbands and children aware of what is good for them, they also know which way to vote in the monthly community elections.

The result? Women are elected on to and run everything in their communities. They also represent them on all higher levels of Nonette councils.

Indeed this month's head of the Congress itself is a woman: Gorina Campos. Six of her seven deputies are also women.

Men, in this once most machismo of societies, might complain about women now being in charge but there is precious little they can do to change it.

Not only have men seen political power pass from their hands but also economic leverage as well.

With the Nonettes' system of 'earn as you learn' comprehensive education, no women need be financially dependent on her husband. Many women with children now comm.- and household incomes bigger than their husbands can earn.

With the economic power and the household 'authority' it brought to men usurped, many husbands have discovered - often to their cost - they are no longer needed or required. A mother and her children can now be quite self-sufficient economically.

Businesses employing women are also obliged to do so on their terms

Gorina Campos, head of Congress and fellow delegate Vivian de Sousa

rather than the boss's.

Women's new found political and economic independence has also brought striking social changes in its wake.

The widespread use of Love Patches has found women increasingly taking the lead in relationships. The sweeping away of old regime's institute-ions, including the authority of the Church, has led to the repressive sexual taboos to which they gave rise, been swept a way as well

One result of so many changes and new found freedoms in women's lives is that their former society enforced inhibitions, have also been cast aside.

For the first time women are free to do as they please. And have what they want as well.

Aiding this change has been the introduction of a powdered substance called 'Vanton'. Its manufacturers, Laboratories Ceara - the same people who produce Love Patches - claim Vanton "relieves inhibited vascular circulation within the lower frontal abdominal regions" but it is heavily promoted as: "The Aroma created by women for women" and, "As used by the Susem."

Vanton is also marketed in the form of an adhesive strip of cachets which are worn on the forearm. Many women can be seen, especially of an evening while socialising, sniffing Van-ton. The effects are immediate.

Any sexual inhibition a woman might have had instantly vanishes. Often so do any men who happen to be present.

Parts of many towns - so some men claim - are no longer safe for them to walk at night. Women have taken over the streets so many men also

bone, sinew and skin, as bears and wolves alike raced, tussled for the next feast heap of rustling leaves.

Foxes, their smaller size excluding them from this ferocious snarling, roaring orgy, turned on men remaining nailed to the trees, the obese ones, their ripped out distended intestines dangling like tangled strings of sausages. Foxes grabbed these between their teeth and as if dogs thieving from butchers' shops ran away with them. As the men's intestines reeled out of their bodies, other foxes chased each other in challenge. Fatty white strips soon criss-crossed the clearing, wound around trees with entrapped rats racing their slithery lengths desperately seeking escape.

With no more heaps to savage, wolves and bears also returned to the men on the trees, some of whom jerked, jolted as the animals' claws and fangs tore into them, but not many. A few men still groaned, squealed but as the night wore on they also became ever less. Between feeding bouts animals played, more so the cubs, with the littering of bones, feet, heads.

The last attracted the Park's lynxes. Though not normally eaters of carrion these lynxes had by summer's end become most partial to human brain. Unseen by the other animals they quietly waited until a skull was sufficiently cracked, then quickly darted out to snatch it and speed into the undergrowth, and paw, chew, lick the skull until it was clean as a milk saucer.

With the arriving dawn the animals, as glutted as on nights before, languorously padded about the men's carcasses as if diners at the close of yet another buffet disinterestedly picking at plates. But with bellies filled they eventually wandered off to their dens and lairs.

As the last revellers were leaving, the Park's boars arrived. These late-comers having already sampled on the fresh scrotums, grunted and rummaged amid the debris for leftovers, bits of rib cage here, an ear, a nose there, some shreds of scalp, a part-gnawed shin. After an hour or so they too had moved on.

Daylight revealed the clearing from end to end to be a strewn charnel of human detritus. Most men on the trees hung lopsidedly from one nail rather than by two. None had both their legs. Some of the bodies twitched, wriggled but this was due more to the rats still inside them than any spark of life.

With the sunrise the men's second day of 'Contemplation' commenced.

A woman's ideal world

Alice Johnson reports from Praia do Araçaji, Maranhão

THE BEACH stretched for miles, the sand glistened white with the sun, the sea warm, blue and inviting Except for three companions, the beach was deserted

For we four women to be on such a beach unescorted but unworried, is indication of how much the Nonette movement has changed society

Before the Nonettes it would have been unthinkable - or insane - for women to have sat unaccompanied on such an isolated beach without the risk of men pestering or worse

But now men know that should there be just a single incident, the entire beach is automatically closed to them The power of the Nonettes is such that any ban would be also ruthlessly enforced.

There have been beach closures because of men but they are few. The Nonette policy on beaches however, is just one indication of the changing roles and balances developing between the sexes

Where once men exclusively commanded the heights of society from religion and law to education and health, the new Nonette society is predominantly female.

Moreover, whereas the power men once wielded stemmed from position and privilege, the new found authority of women has arisen by way of the ballot box and the popular vote

The structure of Nonette society is such that it is unlikely, if not impossible, for this state of affairs to change

For to do so, especially by men, would mean jettisoning every other benefit the Nonettes have brought to men of all walks of life.

The upshot of this change of roles is to be seen everywhere

Women now have higher incomes than their male counterparts In part this has come from their ability to learn faster from their teaching screens.

Women are also in the lead of new business start-ups Many of these are the new industries which use Susem-backed technology.

It is the capital women have generated from study, however, which has been responsible for much of their business success.

With their new found economic independence, women have also begun not only to assert themselves in an increasing number of other areas of society but to also dominate it. And in the process of so doing have skewed society to women's advantage, which is not necessarily mutually to that of men's

One of my companions expressed the changes thus: "Before the Nonettes it was as if women were left-handers in a right-handed society

"We could manage, get by, but we were always at a disadvantage, aware we lived in a right man's world. But now the glove is on the other hand and men have to become used to living in a woman's world."

It is not as though there are any anti-male sentiments among woman as such but more a case of women increasingly regarding men as less than their equals.

As another companion put it: "For men it is: 'We love you guys, but in a patronising sort of way' "

With the increasing use by women of 'Vanton' - a de-inhibitory stimulant - there is also a marked change in women's amorous approach

The little children's Teddy Bears' Picnic

By PAULA GRADY

WITH THE AFTERNOON SUNSHINE sparkling through the trees above, the little children looked everso sweet as they sat with their teddy bears having their picnic in a really lovely woodland glade.

Like the children, each teddy bear had his napkin neatly tied over his front so he would not have any crumbs caught in his fur. Some of the teddy bears were as tiny as little babies but there were also big bears.

But all of the teddy bears were on their very best behaviour. And along with the children the teddy bears sat round a big blue and white checkered cloth as good as gold as they waited for their afternoon's picnic

And like all the little boys and girls, each teddy bear had a little plate in front of them as well as a cup and saucer for their tea

Then when all the children and their teddy bears were ready, one of the big girls served them with cucumber sandwiches while another big girl played the part of mother and poured the tea from a big

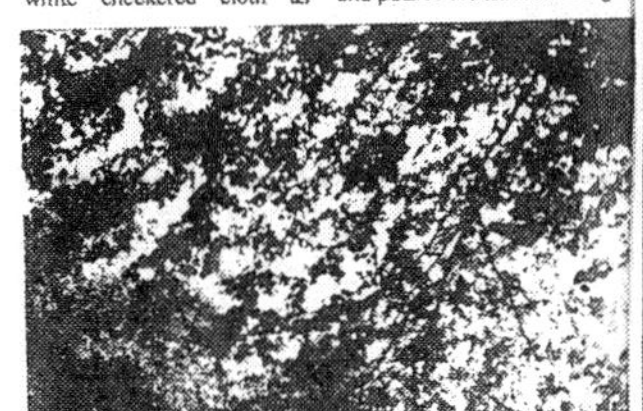

Roger Sheldon interviews the head of the Congress's Central Bank

Springtime for Nonettes and their currency

but Winter for dollars and pounds

THE WORLD'S currencies have no future Global capital markets are set to collapse. These and other ominous forecasts for the world's financial system were made by Earnesto Cavallho, Head of the Nonettes' Central Bank of the Congress

Earnesto Cavallho is a mild mannered man and at 54, chubby, balding and bespectacled. He does not smoke and rarely sips anything stronger than mineral water. In short, he looks the epitome of the small town bank manager he once was.

But such appearances are deceptive. Earnesto Cavallho is one of the masterminds who, in a matter of a few short months has overseen the staggering growth of the Nonette currency - the 'nonette' - from little more than a local credit union to one which is sending shivers through the world's financial markets and governments alike

Ernesto Cavallho head of Congress's Central Bank

Knock-out blow

But Sr Cavallho say that the Nonettes are now set to deliver a knock-out blow to the world's economic system

As the Nonette movement has spread, its currency has followed in its wake.

Within days of the Nonettes taking control of a new region the 'nonette' becomes its sole currency. Even the US dollar has been discarded.

With Nonette communities appearing across the world, the nonette has, in many respects, now become an alternative international currency.

As Sr Cavallho unfolded the secrets behind the nonette's success he likened money to love and marriage. "When a man proposes to a woman and says he will love and cherish her for ever," he said, "where will the substance of that statement be?

Will it be in any material or other commitment on the part of the man to the woman? Or is it in the belief by her that what he says is true?"

Before there was time to reply, SrCavallho elaborated: "The capital - money supply - which backs the Nonette currency comes from the study and learning of each person and collectively that of their communities.

Universal learning

This continuous universal study creates an educated and skilled workforce as well as society in general. It also stimulates advance, innovation and entrepreneurship. All generate increased, sustained wealth for both people and peoples alike

"Exchanging credits earned from studying into money also stimulates demand for goods and services.

"In turn this increases overall wealth for both communities and individuals. And onwards this virtuous, upward circle progresses: education engendering enterprise, this wealth and this into investment.

Copper-bottomed

"It is from this continuous deepening and widening pool of wealth that the 100 per cent capital backing of our currency is based.

"Put simply: one unit of study equals one unit of wealth and albeit indirectly, one unit of capital. Our 'Nonette man' as it were, has made good on his promises to our woman.

"But under your old system of money and capital creation," Sr Cavellho said, "there is only the promise. A promise which, when called upon, cannot be fulfilled

"However, the ordinary people of your society are not only as the woman who chooses to believe in the man's promises of love and who also does not ask for proof but she is in no position other than to do so.

"It is as if she was forced to believe the man, obliged to marry him."

Again Sr Cavallho elaborated: "Your governments and Central Banks issue bonds - IOUs - to which they attach certain values.

Worthless bonds

"Because other financial institutions give money to governments for these bonds, they are presumed to possess a monetary, asset worth "But these bonds are just that, a presumption. In reality the only asset of monetary value the lenders receive for their loans is the paper the bonds are printed on

"Anything else are the borrowers' promises Promises to pay interest, promises to repay their debts at some future date.

"Governments may be sincere in their promises, that they will have the ability to repay. But in truth they do not. If they did they would not need to borrow, to issue IOUs in the first place.

"With these bonds, these pieces of paper, the lender - usually financial institutions such as banks - produce currency notes equivalent to the sums of the bonds.

"This doubling of non-existent asset value is called: 'increasing the money supply'

Paper money

"This 'new money' eventually filters down to ordinary people, which they are given in return for their goods and labour

"Though there are many layers of transaction between the issuers of the bonds and the ordinary people, those involved are few in number and in cahoots with borrowing governments. These few have thus a very strong interest in perpetuating such a state of affairs, if for no other reason it makes them exceedingly rich. Have you ever heard of a 'poor banker'?" said Sr Cavallho smiling

"Though these few wax rich, it is the poor suffering majority who pay the price of this inequity.

"It is they who pay for the cost of these bonds out of the taxes taken from them For some it is more than half of their taxes.

"But there has been nothing your people can do. It is as if our woman, believing the man's promises, having married him, borne children, discovers not only are his promises empty lies but he abuses and batters her.

"Yet like so many women in loveless marriages and with brutal husbands, she has nowhere to go, no refuge. And so it is with your unfortunate people who live under the thumb of this financial regime"

Sr Cavallho said it was spurious that the notion of our 'old' world's financial system functioning in the way it does and for so long, was proof of its efficiently and durability.

"It was once 'normal' for a man to beat his wife," he said, "but it does not mean it was any more justifiable then than it is now, especially from the viewpoint of the woman.

"In a like manner because governments and bankers have always short-changed ordinary people over money, it does not justify their abuses or that they should continue.

"But now ever increasing numbers of people do have an alternative. Not just here in the Congress but everywhere there is a Nonette.

"Ordinary people for the first time have access to a 100 per cent, copperbottomed currency, one which is under the control of the people themselves Governments and bankers have no part to play. There is nothing they can filch from the people

"However, as more people switch their monetary transactions to the nonette and away from your old worth-less money then fatal flaws, inherent within your financial systems will become apparent

"As soon as enough people remove their wealth from your old money its value will waver. More people will then seek to exchange their old money for some other form of wealth, such as goods. This, inevitably, will be followed by widespread refusal to trade in your old money.

Chilling prediction

"It will be as if our woman has finally got herself together and says to her lying, bullying husband: 'I am independent now, I don't need you anymore, I want out of this marriage, goodbye' And as she slams the door the whole of his house comes crashing down on his head.

"And so it will be for the palaces of your old financial institutions and governments alike."

Sr Cavallho's chilling prediction might not be fulfilled but neither should it be dismissed.

This is paradise

Hugo Gurney reports from Igarassu, Recife

THE SUN ALWAYS SHINES, the beaches are golden and stretch for miles. The sea, for those wish to swim, is wonderfully warm.

But for those who have no wish for such exertion there are alternatives: sitting under the shade of palm trees sipping ice-cold caipirnha (a thirst quenching drink of cachaça and limes); picking at large charcoal grilled lobsters; watching bevies of beautiful young girls in next-to-nothing swimsuits gambol

And when the day is done, partying. Everyone, it seems, parties in Igarassu.

Should such hedonist pursuits begin to jade there is always the alternative of a job, of which there are plenty to be had and the going rate in Recife is not bad.

But if this does not work anymore - a few extra hours of [enjoyable] study generates sufficient income to cover any material needs.

With the elimination of poverty and ill health (including obesity, hangovers and embarrassing infections) along with crime and corruption, it could be said that life here it is Paradise.

Not only is it paradise but a miracle. Within the space of a few short months the Nonette movement has changed what was one of the most unequal and squalid of societies into the fairest.

People are now pleased to talk to their neighbours, even enjoy meals

She's my very own 'Lucy in the sky with diamonds', she really is.

I get home from work, have a bit of tea then I'm clicking on my screen and it's her "Hello Ken how are you today?" Oh I don't half look forward to seeing her face, a little charmer she is. The way speaks is lovely as well, English with just that touch of foreign. When after we've had a bit of a chat and she says "Okay Ken, we're going to do some good physics tonight, eh?" she has me ready to study till I drop.

In a way you could say Lucy's voice is sexy, that she is sexy, but it's not like that. It's as if she's the 'girl next door', the perfect teacher I never had at school or the sister I never had either. Not all rolled into one but all of them separate. I have come to look upon her as one of the best pals I have ever had, and to be honest I've only known her a month.

It's not just with me either but the girls upstairs, Mel and Susan as well. Apart from studying on my own account I do a bit with them. And I have to say since we have had our screens I really get on with the pair of them. Of course, when we are all sat round studying, Lucy never misses making a comment to them about how my physics is coming along, nor Susan's art history or Mel's astronomy.

That's another thing about this studying, the practicals. The number of art galleries Susan has taken us round is nobody's business. And though you can't see many stars from round here I do know that the one which can actually be seen is Venus, though of course it's not really star but a planet. It's been good fun as well taking the girls down the Science Museum, and last week when we went all the way out to Kew to see the water pumping station which has just been restored.

It's the same with my group in the Greenwood. I do have some good times with the lads. The subjects we are studying, one night it's chemistry, another about food, then local history. The things I've learnt and still am learning.

The mixed study groups we have with the other ones are good as well, especially the kids. And I have to say they do have sharp minds, all of them. Last week's chess practical they gave had us old 'uns banged to rights in minutes. All three of them and still not twelve years old, but they were playing two of us at the same time and they had us all checkmated before we knew it, again and again. Dead shaming it was, not just the way they shouted "Timber!" every time they took our pieces, but it was their non-stop "Timber!"

Another thing about the kids round here that impresses me, now that nigh on all the schools have closed down, is there's none of them hanging about the streets or thieving. They are all into non-stop learning. Not just in front of their screens either but in giving their own classes, and all by themselves. Except of course when they're running the street-cleaning.

Just what threat are the Nonettes?

And who should feel threatened by them, asks Roger Sheldon

IF THE NONETTES have anything to hide I have yet to discover what it might be.

Having travelled wherever I wanted, seen all I have sought and much more besides, had answers to every question asked, it has to be acknowledged that the Nonettes are the most open society in the world.

So open in fact that it could almost be termed 'perfect'.

As has been said to me many times: "If everything is in the open there will nothing to hide nor mistakes made."

What threat?

If the Nonette movement is a threat, then it is difficult to see - in terms of ordinary people - to whom they pose it.

Though many individual Nonettes are actively dedicated to furthering the movement's aims and advancing its cause, it does not appear to possess armed forces of any kind.

Not only are armies absent but police forces as well. In fact authority of any kind has been abolished.

Yet Nonette society is the most law abiding - crime no longer exists - as well as the most organised.

Welfare

Nonette communities are such that the welfare and well-being of all is assured. No one need want under the Nonettes and thus no one has a motive to steal.

Everyone, young and old alike it seems, is engaged in something be it work, study, representing their Nonette. Or they are otherwise enjoying the equally important matters of life: eating, drinking and making love.

Nonette society is so structured that while nobody need work economic activity is at such a pitch that there are surpluses of everything.

Businesses large and small are freed from the bugbears which plague businesses the world over: officialdom, corruption and taxes..

These and much more have also been abolished. Yet at the same time - by having 'the vote' – businesses are enmeshed into the Nonette community they are part of and thus in turn, are bound by what it decides.

Harmony

The outcome being a harmony of interest between industry and people (as opposed to acrimony which so frequently exists between them in much of the outside world).

Another outcome of such harmony has been the near elimination of industrial and agricultural pollution.

The clean energy resulting from universal use of soufin power units has obviously contributed to the success of the former, just as changes in farming practice - most crops are grown underground - has assisted the latter.

Renewal

Both however, have led to a massive surge in the renewal of the urban environment as well as the countryside.

Many thousands of hectares of once agricultural land already have been restored to their pristine state. Reforestation is also taking place but on such a massive scale it would make a green campaigner green with envy.

Openness

Although political parties no longer exist, democracy is very much alive and well.

Nonette community elections take place monthly. The record of delegates already elected is scrutinised in such detail it would cause our politicians to quake. Voting turnout would amaze former political pundits. It is, including children - who like businesses also have the vote - virtually total.

Aiding voters in their deliberations are myriad newspapers. Every town Nonette has a weekly paper, each area and region daily journals.

Meetings of town Nonettes and upward to Congress itself are also reported live on television and radio. All attract large audiences.

Integration

Politics however, is but part of people's involvement in their Nonette.

While communities on a town level are intertwined with one another, each Nonette is also twinned with other Nonettes in other regions.

Whereas twinned cities in the outside world means little more than a few exchange visits between each others' schoolchildren and mayoral junkets, here in the Congress community exchanges take place almost continuously and on a massive scale.

One result of such activity are large numbers of people travelling across the country to visit one another.

Another is the integration and strengthening of the wider Nonette society with a deepening sense of unity.

As this sense of unity grows the chances of the Nonette movement disintegrating, as many outsiders have hoped, fades by the day.

Privacy

A further outcome of community liaisons has been a huge increase in postal services.

While in the outside world letter-writing has died, here in the Congress it is booming. But with differences.

For postal purposes people are known only by their Nonette number not their name. As a consequence junk mail does not exist but privacy does.

In the rest of the world the fight for individual privacy has long been given up as lost. But here in Congress it is supreme.

With the absence of out-side authority there is no one with the intent - let alone facilities - to conduct surveillance on anyone.

Similarly, distance selling is conducted on a business-to-Nonette community basis, not to individuals. The savings and benefits to businesses, communities and individuals alike is palpable

Another area where privacy and individual freedom has long been lost in the West does not exist in the Congress: the Internet.

This, along with mobile phones would have little relevance in people's lives even if they did exist.

With relevant information and interactivity available from the Nonette teaching screens and the universally adored 'Lucia' all questions asked of her are answered.

The person-to-person contact of the 'chat room', in the light of such extensive face-to-face inter-Nonette contact would be looked on with askance.

With such extensive inter-community business networks between Nonette the commercial prospects for the Internet would also be zero.

Communication

People do communicate with each other and not merely by letter and telephone.

The Nonettes have developed an ability to communicate between themselves by thinking.

How this has been accomplished remains a mystery [to me] but it happens and on a wide scale especially among women.

Women in power

Women in Nonette society in many respects have gained more from the changes than men.

Such has been the rise in their status that the concept of women's 'equality' with men is considered outdated by many of both sexes.

Here in Congress women are superior. And that, as they say, is that, no arguments.

All Nonettes, however, acknowledge that the amazing success of their movement could not have taken place without the arrival and continuing presence of the Susem.

The Susem

But many argue and with some cause, that the Susem have been no more than a catalyst in the Nonettes movement formation in cohering what was already latent among people in the first place.

If it was not, so it is argued, no matter what the Susem's endeavours were, they would have failed.

As to the Susem themselves and though few have actually seen them, they are viewed in many respects as the ancient Greeks viewed their Gods on Mount Olympus.

The people know the Susem are on Ibiapaba Mountains in Ceara and all have seen their spacecraft flying back and forth but like the Greeks they are not part of their day-to-day lives.

As for the Susem's exploits, especially the amorous ones - all of which are reported in detail - they are viewed with a smile.

Confidence

Threats of invasion by forces of the old regime however, are usually met with a shrug and a: "What does anyone have to invade with?"

There is also the knowledge that increasing numbers of people in the outside world are forming Nonettes with each passing day. Adding to this air of indifference (or confidence) is the widely held view "that we Nonettes are the future."

The threatened

Perhaps it is to those whose power stems from the institutions of past to whom the Nonettes are a threat.

And I have to say that ever since Mrs Prior got the kids involved in this, when the council stopped doing it, Dare Crescent has never been so clean. Not only that but should anyone drop as much as a crisp packet there will be one of the kids shouting out "Pick that up." It's more than anyone's life is worth not to either, they can summon back-up in no time.

It's the same with the rubbish collection, ever since the council gave up doing that as well. The kids insist everything has to be sorted and put in the bags they provide. As they charge by the sack it means everyone keeps refuse to a minimum. Of course being the enterprising lot they are they're making money the other end as well by selling on the recyclables. No wonder there's a waiting list of other kids to get on the team.

Most people down Dare Crescent have joined our Nonette now. The few who haven't usually turn out to work for the government, the council. But even some of those have joined. Again, it's the kids who are behind much of the rise in numbers. Once they have joined it's not long before their parents see sense and sign up as well, "pester power" I think it's called.

The prospect of earning money from the screens is a big reason why the kids joined the Nonettes but as so often happens one thing leads to another. In joining, it gives the kids voting rights and their say carries as much as anyone else's. As a result, some of our Nonette money has been spent in their direction including new sports kits for all of them.

That's not to belittle them though. At the meetings the questions they ask are as probing as anyone's. Though, of course, Mrs Prior has them all organised in doing her 'little tasks', delivering leaflets, dishing out voting forms. However, they are not the only group Beth Prior has organised. Another is her band of biddies a.k.a. the street's tithe inspectors. And nobody but nobody messes with them, as Dave Brown will testify.

He came in the Greenwood a couple of days ago shaking like anything, his clothes all over the place and a big red bruise right across his face. We all thought he'd been mugged. But when blurted out "They were waiting in the shadows for me to come home...as soon as I opened the gate it was "Mr Brown we want a word with you"...I tried making it to the front door but one of them jumped me and got me with her umbrella...the Inland Revenue's nothing compared to them...they knew all about me, everything, including the gold scrap..."

He wittered on about how he tried to reason with them, how two of them overturned a table on top of him shouting "Now will you pay" as they banged it up and down, while the others took his soufin until he paid up. All the same, if he was expecting sympathy for 'under-declaring' he got scant little from the Greenwood, especially from Harry. He withdrew Dave's Nonette drinks discount until the cheque he had paid over to 'Beth's biddies' had cleared.

MILAN COCKSURE OF IFEA WIN

Arsenal seen as mere sparring partners

By Phil Martin

IC MILAN, still odds-on favourites for Friday's IFEA semi-final with Arsenal, view the match as little more than practice for their final cup win.

In an exclusive interview with the Chron, Milan manager, Benito Carosso, said: "Although we have the finest players that money can buy, as a team they perform as a single, powerful unbeatable unit. That this is evident is shown by our unbroken record of victories not only in every round of the IFEA contest but also in the whole of the last Italian season.

"Compared with some of the sides we have played against, Arsenal are many leagues below us. While the outcome of any match cannot be assured until the final whistle, we do ... losing against your Gunners. In my country the bets are not on our chances of beating Arsenal but by how many goals we shall win."

With strikers such as Begamo, Ozukini and Potere, Snr Carosso's claims are no idle boast. Milan's defence is also second to none. Goalkeeper Agilita has an impressive record of saves.

In response to Arsenal's victories against Munich and Barcelona, Snr. Carrosso said: "Although they won against these two teams their success has been no more than luck and chance. Milan however, does not depend on such things.

"While Arsenal's wins have made our task in getting to the IFEA final all the easier, I have to confess I still puzzled as to why both the ...

Soufin take-up set to cause capacity surplu...

Government facing energy supply glut

By Oliver Stoneburger

The rapid increase in the use of the Aliens' soufin energy units is threatening to throw the government's power supply plans into disarray. The Treasury is urging an urgent review of Britain's energy renewal programme in a bid to cut costs.

Whereas as little as a few months ago there were fears of a UK wide energy shortage, the country is on course for a surplus of generating capacity. Many of the power supply contracts the government has entered into with the generators are set to leave the Energy Corporation nursing huge debts.

As for the generators themselves, their future and longer term profitability are equally grim. City investors have already drastically downgraded the energy sector's share prices.

Should the increase in soufin use continue to ... then the knock-on effects of generating surpluses is seen as adversely affecting a whole range of secondary suppliers such as cable manufacturers and installers. Primary energy suppliers such coal, oil and gas will also be adversely affected. Share prices in all three sectors fell to new lows yesterday.

The one crumb of comfort for both suppliers and generators are the contracts they have ...

More states fall into rebel hands as army is routed   Capital under t...

Mexico collapse fears rise

Andrew Hendry reports from Mexico City

MUCH OF CENTRAL MEXICO has fallen into Nonette hands.

A 50,000 strong force of Mexico's crack regiments fled in disarray from rebel forces. Large numbers of soldiers are said to be trapped behind rebel lines or taken prisoner. Many desertions from the Mexican army have also been reported. Huge quantities of weaponry and supplies are also said to have fallen into rebel hands.

Stock market, peso plummet

After several weeks of comparative calm the suddeness of the government forces' collapse is all the more traumatic. Details of the army's defeat in the face of the Nonette advance are sketchy. However, reports indicate that the first attacks occurred in the early hours of this morning in the eastern state of Tabasco.

Government forces stationed on the western side of Lake ... Nonette ... reinforcements being sent to relieve them, the opposite is reported to have happened. Units stationed along the entire length of Mexico's Caribbean coastal region retreated inland.

US rushes forces to border

Further troops joined in the withdrawal. It took the elite forces of the Presidential Guard, who were dispatched to the front to stem the army's rout. At noon an area south of a line stretching from Alvarada in the east to Coalcomin in the west was reported to be under Nonette control. However, it is also reported that the rebels still have to cross the strategic Rio Balsas. Government forces deployed along the northern bank of the river are reported as being heavily reinforced.

With the Nonette no more than 50km from the capital, Mexico City, there are fears it could be the scene of further fighting been them and ...

Tax take fall leaves hole in government revenues

By Lawrence Bowen

THE latest treasury figures show that last month saw a five per-cent like-for-like drop in all forms of taxation receipts with the same period last year.

Shortfall could herald tax hike or spending cuts

This across-the-board shortfall is all the more staggering as it comes after the latest round of tax increases as well as both the Inland Revenue and Customs & Excise's crackdown on late taxpayers.

Indeed the figures indicate that both departments failed to even meet their pre mini-Budget targets. These shortfalls will come as a severe blow to the Chancellor's debt reduction hopes.

Many City analysts are predicting that the government will have no alternative other than to embark on a further round of spending cuts. Justin Patel, chief economist at Grenfells said: As the Treasury's latest revenue enhancement programmes have proved ineffective, the Chancellor's only course of action is to reduce the PSBR (public sector borrowing requirement)

"Nonette effect" to blame says Handel

"Unless the PSBR is rapidly brought into line with revenue, there will be strong downward pressures on the pound. There are already several worrying inflationary trends within the UK economy. Should the pound deteriorate further against the dollar it will only make matters worse. This is bound to hurt the economy as a whole," he said.

In the Commons Peter Handel said: "While the latest Revenue's and Excise figures are disappointing we will not shirk from our responsibilities of maintaining a tight and balanced budget. The lower than expected returns are in no small way due to the dilatory behaviour of an increasing number of taxpayers in honouring their responsibilities in paying what is legally due from them.

"Much of the blame for this increased fiscal delinquency must be laid at the door of the Nonette movement. Whatever steps are needed to collect the current imbalance, it will fall not on non-payers but will affect the pockets of those of us who have already fulfilled their fiscal responsibilities and paid what is due. This is patently unfair, thus I challenge the Nonettes to justify why they have cause in ...

SUSEM IN NEW WA... OF SEX SNATCHES

Both Europe and N. America suff...

By Shelia Kiddler

BEACHES ACROSS the Mediterranean came under Susem snatch and grab attacks yesterday.

More than 500 men were reported abducted by the Aliens. Both the east and west coasts of America also suffered similar numbers of Alien kidnappings.

The European abductions, the first for a fortnight, ranged from the island of Rhodes in the east to Malaga in the west. Last night the Alien Abduction Centre in Milan said a total of 493 males, mostly young, were reported as snatched by the Susem.

The attacks followed a similar pattern of previous Alien raids. Groups of men were surrounded then chased by Aliens' 'flying geese' and their stinging wasp robots into one of their smaller spacecraft and whisked away. Each attack lasting no more than minutes.

A spokesman for the Abduction Centre said: "While we continually warn young men not to venture outside of ...

That's another reason why others have joined the Nonettes, Harry's ten per cent discount. It's not just in the Greenwood either but a good number of other pubs round here as well. Shops are the same.

I was a bit apprehensive at first wearing the lapel badges that have been made up with our Nonette numbers on. All the same, seeing how the shops which are also in the Nonettes treated customers who are wearing them soon had me pinning mine on. As for the white tunics, and even though most of the kids wear them, I don't think they will catch on.

As far as shops are concerned, again it's a case of once one of them became a Nonette and started attracting Nonette customers, others have joined up as well. That and the Nonette money of course. It wasn't long either before the shops, and the cash and carries they go to, were trading in Nonette money as well. Because there is no tax everything is cheaper in Nonette money than in pounds. And that is another reason why so many other people have joined the Nonettes.

Again it's the kids who started it all. Once one shop took the teaching screen coupons in exchange for sweets and cigarettes, the others had no choice but to follow suit. Then one thing led to another and other shops joined in. Except for the big supermarkets and chain stores there is hardly a shop round here now that hasn't their Nonette number in the window.

Another reason adding to Nonette numbers is security. We all take it in turn to go out in threes for a few hours, just walking up and down keeping an eye on things. Obvious it's hard to say how much crime has been stopped, excepting that since we have been doing it no one in Dare Crescent has had their house or car broken into. But more to the point it is the knowing that there is someone out there which gives that feeling of security. Anyway it's more than we ever had from the police.

Of course the replacement soufins caused most people to join the Nonettes in the first place. With mains electricity coming back on there must be some people switching back to it, although I've not actually heard of anyone who has. However, there has been many more that have just joined Nonettes because they decided to. On one level it's easy to see why.

A month ago even I gave the idea of 'community' no chance but now I have to admit I was wrong. Not only that, but it's the number of people who actually want to be part of one, a community, which has surprised me. Here in Dare Crescent it can be said that we are 'all one' now. I've even heard some of the old people say it's back to how it was during the 1940's.

It's not just round here either but with the other groups in our Area Nonette as well. Although in terms of income, our Nonette is about in the middle of the range and so the amount of money we hand over to the one we're paired to is no more that a couple of hundred quid a week, we also get to meet up with all other groups, including the better off ones up in Highbury and the poorer ones off the Holloway Road.

Aliens to bla[...] for Tax ris[...] says Hand[...]

More spending cuts on the

By Stephen Sacker

FURTHER GOVERNMENT spending could be on the way unless more taxes are collected.

The Chancellor, Peter Mandel, blamed the Alien attacks on Inland Revenue's offices and the chaos this caused for last month's massive shortfall in income tax and VAT.

The Chancellor also singled out the Alien backed Nonette movement for the slump in the nation's tax take. He said that if there is not an immediate increase in taxpayers coughing up what they owe then there will have to be further reductions in government spending.

Addressing the Co[...] Chancellor said th[...] that keep a balance[...] central plank of th[...] mic policies is f[...] Having made this[...] not waver from it.

"To do so would[...] hard-won interna[...] financial reliability[...] the world's money[...] the value of the p[...] hours This would[...] servicing our loans[...] yet greater burden[...] ate level of interest[...]

Mexico 'hollowed out' by Nonettes

US fears its southern neighbour could implode

By Joyce Allenby-Smith

A member of the Atlixca Nonette calls on soldiers to join with them

THE LASTEST ADVANCES of Nonette forces in Mexico and the inability of the forces of Amado Fuentes' government to contain them, has sent alarm though the US administration However, the Nonettes' latest success comes as no surprise to many in the US, as well as those in Mexico itself

Hernando Arizpe of *La Journalista* said: "The army's defeat by the Nonettes comes as little surprise Despite its size, it is poorly trained and composed mainly of conscripts Neither should anyone be surprised at the speed of their retreat. There will have been few serving soldiers who have not heard of the fate which befell the Americans in Panama as well as the Brazilians at Jatai These will have also led to the troops' low morale. Desertions from the army are said to be running at an all-time high

"The low numbers of fatalities in the army's retreat is also indication of the troops' unwillingness to fight The majority of the army's casualties appear to be come from the 'friendly fire' of their own forces The army's own vehicles caused more injuries than in any actual fighting," Arizpe said.

Adding to Amado Fuentes' and his army commanders' difficulties is the rapid growth of the Nonette movement within the rest of the country still under government control. It is among the poorer sections of Mexican society where the Nonettes have grown the fastest It is also from among these groups however, where most of the army's conscripts are drawn.

In the towns and villages where troops are stationed and where Nonette groups have formed, ordinary soldiers have been confronted with banners bearing: "Who are you fighting for? For us or for the rich and powerful? Attempts by the police and even the Catholic Church to crackdown on the Nonettes and remove these banners have proved counter-productive. All they have done is to alienate yet more people from the government and state alike, as well as the church.

Adding to the slump in army morale are the social and cultural changes the Nonettes have brought. One of which is the rapid improvement in their living standards. When serving soldiers see it is possible to earn a far higher income being a Nonette than the army p[...] them, they have a furt[...] reason to side with - and many cases join - the Nonett[...]

So widespread are Non[...] groups across the country [...] many of the soldiers will co[...] from areas where these gro[...] already exist. Thus to f[...] against the Nonettes is, a[...] where, to be attacking t[...] own communities, indeed o[...] their own families Adding[...] the conflicts of loyalty [...] those towards their superi[...] most of whom come a diffe[...] class to the regular soldiers.

Nonette revaluation

"Dollar overvalued" - say Nonettes US Federal Reserve says: "So what"

By Patricia Young in New York

THE NONETTE has been revalued. The new exchange rate is set at $1.05, a five percent rise in value. The pound is now valued at £1.26p to the Nonette.

In the City the news of the Nonette's revaluation was met with a mixture of indifference and derision. Wall Street's reactions were similar.

Arthur Rubin head of the US Federal Reserve, on hearing this supposed threat to the US currency, said: "So what?"

Elaborating his views, Mr Rubins added: "That this supposed Nonette currency has been revalued has no more significance than saying I need more tokens to get gifts from a catalogue. Very interesting maybe but of no relevance to the real world.

"Lets just suppose for a moment this Nonette coupon thing is thought by some people to be worth something, then look what its up against? Here in New York something like $3 trillion of stocks and bonds are traded every single day. By comparison, this Nonette currency is a puny as Fiji's.

"Just now I have a whole list of problems on my plate but I can definitely tell you than this Nonette thing is not one of them," he said.

Hans Friegal, of the giant Uber bank said: "And just how is this Nonette to be valued? What is it to be set again-

ARSENAL REBUTS EASY WINS SLURS

By GEORGE DALEY

"We won fair and square," says Gunner's George

ARSENAL MANAGER, Graham George, angrily dismissed suggestions that the Gunner's unexpected victories over Munchen and Barcelona were because of a fluke and good luck. George said: "If there was any luck involved in our winning form, it was of our own making.

"But more than just luck is involved in winning. Skill, tactics and stamina are far [...]portant. So is the sheer determ-[...] been behind the high level of morale of all the members of the Arsenal squad," George said.

"Arsenal never underestimates the challenge of any opposition but neither do we lose sight of the fact that every game we play, we play to win and nothing - I and repeat, nothing - less," he said.

But despite George's claims of Arsenal's hard fought success, questions are still being asked as to why both Munchen and Barcelona failed to field their star players. Both the boss of the German side, Hans Guiderin and his Spanish counterpart, Leon Rampas, have been tightlipped over their sides' shock defeats. Rampas has given the investigation by the Spanish Football Authorities as the reason for his silence.

Barcelona and Munchen have not been [...] only sides to suffer surprise defeats in

Sheik's shriek at oil slump

Gulf producers' debts set to grow as oil price falls

By Brian Telford

With the latest fall in oil prices to $15.50 a barrel many producers' hoped-for riches are proving to be a mirage.

The slump in prices has also brought disappointment to many banks and businesses who advanced credits and loans to the oil producers

The sheiks and emirs of the Gulf States are among those, who having borrowed and spent more than most are suffering the biggest crisis. The ruler of the tiny Gulf State of Hutur, Sheik ob Harabh is one of those reeling from the recent fall in prices.

Speaking from the Royal Palace, the Sheik said: "With oil at this low price how can I be expected to pay for the new jet fighters, tanks, guided missile systems? I do not have money left to pay my armed forces wages beyond the end of the month.

More European regions slip into Nonette control

EU chiefs voice 'hollowing out' fear as budget cuts loom

By Marcia Lutenburg
European Correspondent

AT A CRISES MEETING in Brussels yesterday, the EU Commission expressed fears at the rising number of areas sliding out of EU control, into the hands of the Nonettes

Adding to Commissioners' woes are the EU's rapidly depleting coffers as other member states in the wake of their budgetary difficulties, follow Britain's lead in withholding their contributions to Brussels.

According to the Commission large swathes of eastern and central Europe including in the Ukraine, Belarus and the Balkans are now outside the control of those countries' governments. EU officials fear that both the Ukraine and Belarus could soon cease to exist as sovereign nations. Many of the autonomous Russian republics are also thought to be under similar threat

However, it is the growth of Nonette-controlled areas within the EU itself which are alarming the Commission While many officials in Brussels have privately written off much of the east of Hungary and Poland, Slovakia and the Baltic states to the Nonettes, it is the rising number of Nonette-controlled areas within 'core EU' States" which are causing their greatest concern

In both northern Italy and the length of Apennines, groups of villages, one after another have gone over to the Nonettes and ignoring both state and central government laws and administration. With their own Nonette administrations installed, both state and government officials have been ignored. There have also been instances, such as in the small Apennine town of Fabrino, where the mayor and other officials were marched out of town by the townspeople.

However, Italy, so the Commission says, is by no means the worst affected. The north west of Spain and northern Portugal are increasingly coming under the sway of separate Nonette administrations. In both these regions the Nonette currency is increasingly used in place of the national one

The Commission said that Nonette controlled areas are depriving both governments and the EU itself of much needed taxation and other revenues What

As Sam Prior says we are now handling serious money. Dare Crescent's income alone is twenty grand a week and our area Nonette has £5 million a month to spend. It's not just a case of lots of people wanting a say in how it's spent either, but that all of us are more-or-less obliged to decide how it is spent. As Sam also says "It's 'our' money."

In a way Sam Prior is another reason why our Nonette has grown, or at least why so many people have stayed. When, at the beginning we elected him to represent us at the Area Nonette, he said he would do it for a month. But he did such a good job that we elected him unopposed the next month then again for this one. Not only does he let everyone know what's going on over at the Area HQ, but his missus and 'her' kids are forever delivering leaflets asking what we should do about each thing that comes up at the Area Nonette including what the money should be spent on.

Mr Prior isn't just well-liked by us grown-ups but the kids as well. He's a retired schoolteacher, but the thing is that in a way he still is a schoolmaster, again the one I wished I had had when I was at school but never did. Not only does he know the kids and talks with them but every week he finds the time to take a dozen of them down the Old Vic or the Globe to see Shakespeare and he's always a waiting list.

But my actual teacher of course, is Lucy. And tonight ooh did she beam me down some diamonds of thought. Not only do I now know there's no such thing as a 'solid', but why there can't be.

Having taken me through the idea that everything is best expressed in 'contexts' and not 'dimensions', lines only exist in the context of planes, they in context of volumes and they only exist in the context of time, she then showed how lines, single contexts are actually made up of points. Lucy next showed a deck of playing cards and how it appeared to be a three context object. Then she dealt the cards and as she did she said to think of them as planes, two contexts.

Lucy next showed a reel of cotton, how it was thick as her thumb. Then she reeled out the thread and said to think of it as a line, a single context. After this Lucy was stood by a billiard table. As she potted the green she asked "When one sphere touches another, what is touching what?"

I said "Points."

Quick as a flash she was back with "What context is a point?"

When I replied it doesn't have one she nodded in agreement and said "If a point has nothing (and she potting another ball) then what is happening here?" I was lost for an answer.

Lucy then explained all about points, how on one level they are nothing but on another everything is made up of them. Dead interesting it was. She gave me cause for a lot of thought especially when she showed how points are really part of waves.

Government spending to be slashed

By Launa Sutherland
Economics Correspondent

Savage all round cuts expected

GOVERNMENT SPENDING is to be slashed by further five per cent These cuts come on top of those made a month ago. All spending departments, including education and health are expected to see their budgets cut by as much as 10 per cent It is local government, however, which will suffer the worst of the cutbacks

Announcing the cuts, the Chancellor, Peter Handel said because of the massive shortfall in tax revenues there was no alternative other than to reduce government spending immediately

The Chancellor said the prospect of increasing government borrowing no longer existed and so the only course open in the present circumstances, was to match spending against income.

The Chancellor said: "Either Britain demonstrates to the international [financial] community we intend to stand by our obligations in keeping a sound financial regime, or the value of the pound will plummet within a matter of hours.

"There is no alternative" - Handel claims

"Should the government fail and the pound does indeed fall, then we will all face the spectre of massive and dreadful inflation. This is a prospect I refuse to countenance under any circumstance."

The Chancellor, while acknowledging the cuts will cause widespread layoffs among many public sector workers as well as the loss of local government services, said: "Presently a team from the Treasury, in conjunction with the Bank of England, are negotiating with the international community a massive rephrasing of maturing short term government stock into longer dated bonds

"Thus it is vital for the Treasury team to negotiate from a position of strength. If it is seen we have failed to deliver on our commitments and obligations then we will not achieve our objectives and the pound will suffer as a consequence.

"Yes, there will be some sectors which will experience some short-term difficulties but as I have said, there is no alternative [to the cuts]"

Councils to bear brunt of cuts

With local government budgets set to shrink, many Councils last night were drawing up their own list of emergency spending cuts Harold Slipwaite, chairman of the Association of Borough Councils (ABC) said: "Our members are devastated at these latest reduction of central government grant. How on earth can we be expected to carry out statuary obligation to our towns and cities?

"The ABC will present our members' case to the relevant ministers as a matter of urgency but we are adamant that our

---

Julia Hodges reports from Washington & Andrew Hendrey from San Diego, California

'American forces will not cross Rio Grande' - says Warren

US not to intervene in Mexico crisis but National Guard to be put on full alert to thwart 'illegals' and Nonettes

US PRESIDENT JOHN WARREN ruled out any military intervention in Mexico. Speaking at the weekly White House press conference, the President said that the present crisis in Mexico was a matter for the government of Amado Fluntes to resolve.

While saying the US had every sympathy with Mexicans it would be in the best interests of both countries if they refrained from becoming involved in each others' internal affairs.

However, the President also announced that a further 5,000 members of the National Guard will reinforce those already stationed along the US-Mexico border as a precautionary measure

Following America's re-cent debacle in Panama, US public opinion is in no mood for any further foreign military involvement of any kind.

Should there be any such intervention it would also be widely seen as an attack against the Nonettes. This is one organisation President Warren would be loathe to antagonise. While the size of the Nonette movement in the US is proportionally smaller than in other western countries, its numbers are still in excess of 30m and growing rapidly The Nonettes have become one of the largest organisations in the US.

Despite the President's reluctance to become involved in Mexico there are rising concerns across the border regions. A major concern is the fate of the *maquiladoras* These are factories and assembly plants located along the Mexican side of the border. Many of them are owned in full or part by US companies. What would happen should they fall into rebel hands?

Another border concern is the shortage of migrants to work on farms in the US. California's Imperial Valley where some 20,000 of them are required at any one time, is one such region facing labour shortages. Already the Valley's farmers have been forced to pay higher wages and improve working conditions in order to attract the required numbers of these seasonal workers.

While the rise of so many Nonette groups throughout Mexico has caused a sharp reduction in those seeking work in the US, many who have returned to work, have done so as Nonettes.

Many more, once they are in US, have also formed into Nonette groups and are dictating their terms of employment. The same is true of many of those working in the *maquiladoras.*

Although economic migrants from Mexico are a thing of the past, along the border there is still no shortage of those seeking to cross its both legally and illegally.

Most of these migrants, however are neither poor or seeking work Nearly all are either members of Mexico's political classes or alleged criminals.

Arsenal's shock secret Susem pact sham win

By Phil Martin

THE ALIENS HAVE robbed Barcelona of surefire victory over Arsenal in the IFEA quarter-final, Spanish soccer authorities accused yesterday.

The Susem, so the Spanish claim, abducted the entire Barcelona side several days before the match and subjected them to 48 hours ordeal of non-stop sexual assault.

Aliens accused of match fixing

The team was so savagely attacked that players were in no condition to play So serious were many of their injuries that it is doubtful that they will ever play professionally again, Spanish authorities said.

Barcelona's manager, Leon Rampas, said: "I have been barred from speaking until today but I knew that from the moment all of my team were taken something terrible was happening to them That all were taken including the coach just five days before the match [with Arsenal] I knew that there must have been dirty work going on.

Barcelona demands replay

"When our men returned and we saw what the Aliens had done to them I was filled with tears Many years of my life's work have been ruined. I was utterly gutted Most of the team will never play again. Players who cost us millions of dollars are now not worth a cent."

Nonette Revaluation:

The first pebbles of an avalanche?

The change in the exchange rate should not be dismissed warns **Edmund Faith**

IF YOU ARE PAYING in Nonettes only 19 are needed instead of the 20 required yesterday. If you are paid in Nonettes you have just received a five per cent pay rise. However, if you are a trader and you sell in both Nonettes and sterling what are you to do?

As a shopkeeper do you accept a reduction in profit on your Nonette sales or do you increase the pounds and pence price of your goods? What of your suppliers? Will you buy from them in pounds if they also increase their sterling prices or will you seek a reduction in their Nonette price?

If you are one of those larger shopkeepers who, so far have refused to accept payment in Nonettes, what do you do in response to those of your suppliers who also trade in Nonettes and have raised their sterling prices? Do you pass the sterling price rise on, or do you accept lower profit margins?

The outcome, as far as retail prices are concerned, is likely to be somewhere between the two: a rise and a slimming of margins. Whatever the mixture, the result, however, will be an increase in sterling retail prices The increases may be minor and only be apparent on 'small ticket' items where absolute margins are already wafer thin. Nevertheless, such increases are more than likely to persuade consumers to buy more in Nonettes than in pounds.

The Nonette Central Bank gave inflationary trends in the US and other leading economies as the reason for their upping the value of the Nonette currency How valid is this?

Before any serious assessment of this can be made it is essential that the total value - and thus significance - of the Nonettes in circulation are viewed in terms of 'so-called' hard currencies such as the dollar, Euromark and pound.

By such comparisons the Nonette is indeed small. However, most of the hard currency in circulation is not in the hands of 'ordinary' people such as you and me.

In the high flying world of financiers and bankers there have indeed been some inflationary trends

One such is the increases to the world's money supply. Governments, Central Banks of every major economy have, over the past months, increased the amounts of their currencies in circulation at faster rates than at any time in the past decade Although increases in Japan are negligible, those of the US and Britain have been significantly above the average. Put simply, the Bank of England's and the US Federal Reserve's printing presses have been busier than elsewhere

This rapid increase, so we are told by the BofE and the Fed, is to ensure liquidity in the money markets. More than 70 percent of world's inter-market transactions take place in London and New York. It is in the interests of both markets to keep matters this way.

Another reason for this rapid increase - especially as far as Britain is concerned - is ensuring the High Street banks and building societies do not run out of cash money (notes and coins) should there be a further panic by customers as happened last month. "Should just one bank close its doors", so a bankers' maxim goes, "then the rest will be following suit within the hour". It is this fear which also has the BofE keep its printing presses working overtime.

Which brings us back to the "inflationary trends" which so exercises the Nonette Bank. With so many more 'pound notes' in circulation there is every likelihood that significant amounts will seep into the everyday financial lives of we ordinary people. Or put another way, the value of the pounds in our pockets will be diluted.

It would be churlish to accuse the Nonette Bank of being Machiavellian in upgrading the Nonette; that it is intent on purposely precipitating a destabilisation of the major currencies. But nonetheless this has been - no matter how minute it may be – precisely what they have accomplished.

The question now to asked is how long will it be before there is yet another revaluation?

The journalists, photographers came and saw. But from arrival to departure they were conquered, romanced, seduced, lured and 'loved' without pause except for meal breaks and drink, though the reporter from the Mormon paper in Utah took a little longer before her lower abdominal inhibitions were overcome. Though once they were, her rapacity, so I am told, knew no bounds.

Being so busy indulging delight, the journalists had scant time for the trivialities of writing and reporting but each one's dedicated bevy of aides, drivers, escorts, guides and companions helped out by filing copy for them. As a goodwill gesture Love Patches and Vantona scratch'n'sniff strips were provided free-of-charge. But such were the demands of free love, that the journalists' junket has cost Laboratories Ceará dear.

This is not to demean for a moment the dedication and noble sacrifice made by so many young men and women across Congress to ensure the journalists, especially the grotesque ones, delivered what was wanted of them, in Congress's and Rainbow's eyes that is. Not for an instant has the actuality been distorted by this assisted reportage, Rainbow merely ensured that the young people recruited to look after the journalists guaranteed that their reportage was objective, factual, truthful.

In the ordinary course of things the cost of donating patches and strips could have been met from trade margins, but those of the strips have recently taken a pounding from the suppliers of the Heava latex and lichens, the Bora and Huitoto indians. Terrible hard bargainers they are.

The fourfold price increase was bad enough but their delegation arrived in Tabajara armed to the teeth with data, production schedules, market analysis and proposals for worldwide distribution. They also insisted on, and got, profit sharing, equity participation and seats on the board. All this from people who, until they joined the Nonettes a few months ago, had scarce contact with the outside world. Sometimes I'm of the mind education can be troublesome.

I tried parrying with them, that they were suppliers of just two ingredients. Not only did they 'remind' me that these were the vital ones, the remainder widely available, they also showed photographs of groves upon groves of Heava saplings they already have under cultivation. Knowing I need to keep the Susem satisfied at all costs and competition always bad for business, I had no alternative than to agree everything else they 'proposed'.

This included Anglicising the strips' name. The Love Patch promotion being so successful, both the Bora and Huitoto also 'suggested' the new one be on the same lines. I have done my best but all the same have a terrible dread it might fail. If it does I could be ousted from control.

That margins have taken a knock is worry enough but there has been another worry, 'Rampenho'. Rainbow told Pheterisco that many men, under-

Cuts are Nonette recruiting sergeant -Haines claims

By Silvester Cleeve
Parliamentary Reporter

"We will fight tooth and claw to stop cuts" say LibCons

ACCUSING THE government of being in hock to International Bankers, LibCon leader, Stanley Haines said the latest spending cuts will drive yet more people into the hands of the Nonettes He said that the LibCons will do everything in their power to stop the government from "committing this act of extreme folly."

Speaking at West Wickham in the forthcoming by-election campaign, Mr Hayes said "Just because the governmen presently has a large Westminster majority it does not mea they should be allowed to rid roughshod over the electorat Make no mistake, these late cuts are going to hurt ever ordinary man and woman this country

"By its actions Downi Street appears to be total oblivious to what is happeni in Britain. Do they not reali why so many people are paying their taxes? Why th latest cuts will drive yet mor

Captured US Special Forces shown on television

President Warren demands urgent investigation as anger rises nationwide at Pentagon denial of Mexican involvement

By Brett Anderson
in Washington

THERE WAS ANGER AND disbelief across America yesterday as US servicemen, captured along with 50,000 Mexican troops, were shown on the latest Susem telecast.

The Pentagon's denial of any involvement in Mexico was met with disbelief by many commentators. President Warren has ordered an immediate investigation into the affair.

Some of the 54 US Special Forces captured in Mexico in American army uniforms

A total of 54 US military personnel were paraded by the Nonettes on television yesterday. Although all the men appeared to be of Latin American appearance and were dressed in Mexican army uniforms as each appeared on screen they were shown along with their identification discs or 'dog tags'.

All the men said they had not been mistreated and none appeared to show signs of physical assault

the men were free to return to America and invited the Pentagon to send a boat to the Nonette-controlled port of Campeche to ship them back to the US. The announcer added that five of the men had opted to remain with the Nonettes.

with relatives of the captured servicemen pleading for their immediate return. Anger rose however, when a Pentagon spokesman denied any military involvement in Mexico, claiming that the captured men were not serving with US forces

gon's denial has been viewed as adding fuel the flames of increasing public disquiet at the Department of Defense's actions.

David Souter of the Washington based IoAS think-tank said: "It is almost

Markets give Handel thu

Sterling rises against US$

By Oliver Stoneburger

The world's money markets showed their approval of the Chancellors latest spending plans by marking up the pound against the dollar and other major currencies At yesterday's close the Sterling Index rose 2 points to 97.3.

In Frankfurt, an Uber Bank spokesman said that the Chancellor's latest moves were a "timely corrective measure and thus demonstrated to the financial community, Britain's willingness to respond to any further budgetary imbalances."

The same positive sentiments were expressed by all the other world's leading financial institutions. Some went as far as saying that Britain was setting an example of pragmatic realism for other countries to follow

John Mason, European head of BancLeviathan speaking in London yesterday said: "Chancellor Handel has earned for Britain alpha plus status.

"Your Chancellor's firm policies ensure that banks such as BancLev will be more than willing to stand by your country through these current trying times."

Replying to the effects on the consequences of the latest cuts, Mr Mason said: "Throughout history each generation has had to pick up the tab for the mistakes of the one before. It was not this Bank's present management who lent its money carelessly and neither was your current legislators who pursued irresponsibly wasteful and costly polices.

"But it agement who m past err are lef ponsibi the boo there i time to medic but th treatm strong to be.

"Th munit tain leadin faced reveni ackno is litt time short why and your may long has and

'Nonettes in Northwest takeover' - Senator claims

Joanne Miller reports on the rapid growth of Nonettes in Washington and Oregon

THE STATE of Washington is a long way from Washington DC, yet events in the first are jangling Senatorial nerves in the second. Senator Sam Dich and other rightwing senators are demanding a full investigation into the rising power of the Nonette movement across America's north-west states.

Both Oregon and Washington State, with their abundant supplies of hydroelectric power would, on the face of it, appear to be among the very last parts of America to embrace the use of soufin energy units. But embrace them they have. Out of a combined population of 10 million an estimated 3 million of the energy units are thought to be already in operation throughout both states with their numbers rising 30-40,000 a week

One of the main reasons for this prolific growth in soufin use is in Seattle, the computer capital of America. With the exception and perhaps also because of Microsoft most of the companies in the area are small, staffed by young people and fiercely competitive. Their employees are also highly

Systems said: "Once the competition has an edge, either you match them or close down before you're closed down. Then before you know it, what was once cutting edge becomes standard. And that is why everyone, every business has to have a free, clean energy soufin."

Senator Sam Dich

Of course soufins come with Nonette collectivist strings attached. Yet even the community based structures of the movement

been embraced fulsomely by both company bosses and worker alike.

According Kathleen Druker, head of Bremerton Resource: "Belonging to our Nonette means not only are we are to relate directly to our immediate community but also so are they with us It is left to us both to decide our modus vivendi rather impersonal, unelected, official state and Federal authorities. With the Nonettes there is no imposed bureaucracy What rules and regulation there are, are those we have drawn up between ourselves and our Nonette and so we happily abide by them. All in all, the Nonettes are more business-friendly than state and Federal government."

The Nonette groups in both Oregon and Washington claim that more than 15 per cent of employees in both states now work for Nonette controlled companies. The number of yet more businesses joining the Nonettes is also reported to be accelerating. The Nonette movement is also gaining a reputation for new business

ment's collectivist nature i proving to be more efficient i providing finance than estab lished mainstream institution such as banks and venture capitalists As the movement's siz increases, the tenth of thei wages its members pay to it, i now representing considerabl capital sums. According to th Nonettes more than a annualised $150m is available for new businesses

In the same way Nonette members give preference t buying from Nonette-owne shops. As more and more customers switch their purchases to them many mainstream companies, the bigger corporations are beginning t see a substantial drop in their sales

Many in the Northwest (and not just Nonettes), say that Senator Dich's outburst against movement is on behalf of the big national corporations who are losing so much business to Nonettes. Should the Nonette movement growth in Oregon and Washington be repeated across the rest of America then

IFEA bosses says better security is neede

Our hands are clea - claims George

y Georgia Manson

ARSENAL BOSS, Graham George, angrily deni allegations that his team are in league with t Aliens over the abduction and sexual assault he entire Barcelona side. Meanwhile the IFEA o step up security on the four teams remaining he competition.

Speaking during a training session for the forthcoming Arsenal-IC Milan semi-final, George said: "In the past we have been accused of being in league with the devil but to say we have linked up with the Aliens is as preposterous as it is laughable. We hav

tely no contact with t Susem whatsoever.

"As I have said repeated Arsenal's IFEA's success down to nothing other th the skill of the players a our determination to win. Arsenal our players' welf including their security

There's more to love than making it

Why can't women make that 'First Move'?

By **Britta Ruff**

LOVE PATCHES have been a boon in making men more the way we women want them. Also as it is we who hold the Patches, it is we who decide whether our men will be making love to us or not. But as we women know all too well, there's more to love than making it.

One of those ways is not merely finding our Mr Right but getting our hands on him We women are still tied to all those social mores it is men who have to do the wooing

Oh we women have our wiles and our ways of bringing ourselves to a would-be beau's attention but we must never make that 'first move'. Should we ever make it then we run the risk of being branded 'brazen', 'too forward', 'a man-eater' or just plain 'common', 'cheap'.

Even if we've not a care of what others think, we women are still (and because of our 'lady-like' upbringing) inhibited from making that first move. Inhibited not just psychologically but physiologically as well.

It's time we women overcame and shook off this repression society has forced on us

If men can make that first move then why can't we? Our inner desires are no less and often probably more than theirs

If you should meet your Adonis at a party, at work or even on the street why can't you be free to ask him for that date? If men can wolf whistle at us then why shouldn't we be free to do the same to them? It's time we women had this equality with men Why shouldn't we have the same freedoms as they have? It's me who have repressed us with 'lady-like inhibition but it's us women will have to

neath their veneer of macho manliness, are shy, timid creatures and easily frightened, and thus a gentler approach might yield better results. Pheterisco duly relayed this to the Susem, all of whom, especially Milophinia took note. She then formulated a mixture which, as she put it, "Will induce your males to be conducive to meeting with us."

The formula itself, much the same as Love Patches but finer particulate, less talc with added lemon and one or two other things, presented no difficulties in making up. Manual's research department not only had the first batches ready within the day, trying it out on unsuspecting males with immediate success, but had given it its name. 'Ram' from 'ramalhete, 'bouquet' and 'penho' 'of arousal'. This sounds innocent enough, conjuring up as it does images of a delicate dab of scent on a woman's wrists, neck, or the contained fragrance of a nose-gay. But for the Susem, while abiding the letter of Rainbow's council, their collectivist spirit dies hard. They have ordered it up in crop-dusting quantities. I fear for the worst.

The sheer volume of Susem requirement, however, presented the real problem. Not of supply but cost. Their demands could cripple company coffers. But with necessity ever the mother of invention, a solution, or rather a potential market for Rampenho soon sprang to the fore, Vanton users.

Such has been the success of Vanton in repressing lower abdominal inhibition that increasing numbers of its users have overcome all of their other, amorous inhibitions as well. This has led to a dearth of young men venturing out after dark lest they be 'got' and 'had'. In turn this has caused a pent-up demand from demanding Vanton takers needing to assuage away this wave of shyness in their would-be beaus. Thus Rampenho was a remedy whose time had come.

It's taken some running about but the first of the discreet, palm-size canisters of Rampenho spray will be rolling off the production lines ready for Congress-wide distribution within the week. Market testing was conducted on the visiting journalists by their guides and couriers. All, including those journalists intent on actually reporting, immediately succumbed to its arousing effects. With luck, profits from the sales of Rampenho canisters will cover the cost of supplying the barrels of it to the Susem.

How soon supplies of Rampenho will be with Tearo and her troupe over in Europe is as yet unknown but meanwhile they are doing grand job on Arsenal's behalf. And the chances of my little wager affording a modest return are looking brighter by the day. For now my adept juggling of the petty cash's accounts keeps this minor borrowing from inquiring eyes.

The wager was in hope, that once the Susem departed and the Nonette movement crushed, the winnings would pay my way from trouble. But now, with events in the outside world going the Nonettes' way, I have a feeling that even when the Susem have flown-off they are set to last a while. Time enough and strength enough anyway, for me to negotiate 'settlements' with all

00s snatched for forced lovemaking with Alien

Susem in big Med sex raid

By JENNIFER PRATT

EARS ROSE LAST NIGHT for the safety of more than 750 men abducted in Susem 'swoop'n'snatch' raids across both Italy and southern France. Some of the young men taken by the Aliens are thought to be British soccer fans in Italy for the Milan Arsenal IEFA semi-final.

The Alien Abduction Centre in Milan said the numbers of men taken was largest for more than a month. The Centre said that the raids were concentrated on western Italian resorts including Salerno and Capri in the south and long the Ligurian coast in the north. In France the attacks were concentrated between St Tropez and Monte Carlo.

Roger Wardle who has had 15 of his mates snatched by the Suse

According to eye witnesses the raids took a similar pattern to earlier abductions, the sudden appearance of Susem low 'flying geese' robots chasing groups of men towards an Alien craft which has suddenly swooped down from high above. The men were then driven up the ramp of the waiting craft. Within seconds the ramp is raised and the craft has zoomed out of sight.

According to Roger Wardle who is leading a party of 4 Arsenal supporters for the IEFA championships, 15 of his party are thought to have bee abducted by the Susem. M Wardle said, "Although at th moment in time we are n absolutely certain who ha been taken by the Aliens a who hasn't, we do know th

Joanne Miller reports from Washington & David Howth from Burlingto

Nonettes in Vermont UDI

President Warren in emergency talks
Wall Street slumps Dollar plunges
Dich demands military occupation of New England State

SHOCKWAVES SHOOK THE US yesterday as the part of the state of Vermont unilaterally declared independence from both the state and the United States itself. Three counties, in the extreme north of the state, announced they will now run their own affairs under a Nonette aegis.

President Warren held in emergency talks with senior White House aides, Congressional leaders and top Senators in a bid to resolve the crisis.

Rightwingers, including Sen. Dich, are urging tough, even military action to stamp out what they see as a threat to US integrity. Moderates, however, including Defense Secretary Wilmington, are urging caution and restraint fearful of sparking a public backlash against any over-hasty action.

Wall Street reacted with alarm on the news and to the likelihood of further US regions following Vermont's lead. The Dow fell 256 at one point but recovered to close at 8725, a fall of 72 on the day. The dollar's index fell to 115.6, wiping out all its recent gains against European currencies.

The three counties declaring independence: Orleans, Lamoille and Caledonia, cover 1,000 square miles and are mainly rural. The biggest town, Newport (population 5,000) is little more than a village. Most people work on small farms which dot the area or commute to nearby Burlington, Vermont's biggest city. There are also many retirement and weekend homes throughout the area.

Yesterday, on the few roads leading into the affected region, there were highway police patrols parked on one side of the county line and groups of residents on the other. Both however, were outnumbered by crowds of onlookers, many of whom held placards expressing support for the area's UDI, though there were others proclaiming the counties' inhabitants as traitors and rebels.

In the counties themselves there appeared little sign of the national hubris caused by the inhabitants' Nonette movement's declaration of secession. In Lamboille County's main town, Hyde Park (population 1,623), apart from the increase in tourist traffic, life appeared to be carrying on as normally as in any other small American town.

Carol Montgomary, head of the local Nonette, said: "With everyone in Lamboille [county] a member and those over in Orleans and Caledonia [counties] the same, we all agreed to take the next logical step. With the cutback of [Federal] farming subsidiaries most of the farmers stood to lose their livelihoods and left

Joint VAT & Tax hit squads to blitz businesses

Slack taxpayers to face penal fines a
Chancellor cracks down on shirkers

By Harvey Daniels

BRITAIN'S TAXMEN ARE TO COMBINE FORCES in a bid to collect more t £30bn owed to the government in overtaxes and duties. The combined force been granted special emergency powers to raid the homes of businessmen who withholding tax debts.

Announcing the new moves, the Chancellor, Peter Handel, said: "What the new force will be doing is no more than collecting what has already been agreed is owed to the Inland Revenue and the Customs and Excise.

"For far too long a delinquent minority of taxpayers in this country have hung on to money which rightfully belongs to the Crown.

"We have been patient with these laggards for far too long but now the gloves are off. And be assured, we will take what is rightfully ours and with all due force if necessary, if not in cash then in the seizure of the offender's assets. Those who have already paid their taxes and duty have no cause to fear by these new regulations," he said.

The Chancellor's new tough tax moves came under a barrage of fierce criticism from both the opposition benches and small business organisations.

Opposition leader, Stanley Hains, called the Chancellor's tax move as "a desperate act of a desperate man". Mr Hains said: "By his actions Chancellor has, at a stroke, this country down the ro slope to a totalitarian po state. And in so doing the p ent government has becom recruiting sergeant to Nonettes."

To loud opposition cheers Hains said in the forthcom West Wickham by-elect voters will show at the b box just how disgusted they with the government of R Brown.

"Do not be at all be surpris voters give their thumbs-dow

IEFA-Susem scandal latest:

MUNCHEN, LILLE, HEYEN SUFFERED ALIEN ATTAC

By Phil Martin

Contest must be called off soccer officials demand

A STRING OF TOP IEFA soccer sides have been abducted and assaulted by the Susem. Bosses of the affected clubs are calling for the entire contest to be cancelled.

As well as Barcelona, the French side, Lille, the German champions Munchen and the Dutch team, Heyenoord all revealed that they had been victims of Alien abductions.

Many players it is said, are in hospital as a result of the injuries suffered at the hands of the Susem.

Heyenoord's manager Wim van der Vot said: "During a training session four days before our match with Dynamo Sofia our entire side was taken by the Susem.

"They also took away our team's coach and some of the ground staff. When we were told of the situation we did not know what we could do except to hope for our boys' safe return.

"Meanwhile we had to do to the best we could with our reserve players. But after what happened to the others it was very hard for us to persuade them to even leave their hotel rooms let alone train

Meeting those Mr Rights but only for the night

By Britta Ruff

GIRLS, IF YOU HEARD THIS FROM A BLOKE: "I went non-stop all night. I gave all seven of them a good seeing-to...by the time I'd finished with them they were lying there gasping for breath and speechless," what would you think?

That it was physically impossible for him or any man to do? That he was lying and bragging out of his rear end? If you did you'd be right once and right twice.

But if you heard it from one of us girls, not only you would know it is physically possible but also well within what we can do. And some of us may well have done so time and again. The thing is, though, we have to keep quiet about our conquests.

It's all right for blokes to have their one night stands, boast about scoring and the 'birds they've pulled". But we're not supposed to pull blokes let alone tell anyone that we did in case we're thought of as common or cheap. Why can't we have the same freedom as blokes to tell it like is? Why are we forced to be demure and discrete? Why can't we show our real feelings towards blokes. Why can't we act like them and 'pull' blokes?

Having Love Patches to slap on them is one thing but actually getting hold of them is another matter entirely. It's time we girls overcame our inhibitions about being 'lady-like' and really act on our true feelings. It's time we had the same freedoms as blokes to go out and get what we want. When we see our hunk of Mr Right we should have the freedom and the right to pull him. And just like with blokes

concerned for a quieter life. This at least has been a comforting thought during the Vantona and Rampenho travails these days past.

There have been a few other thoughts as well though. One of which has been what Milophinia told me about planets, ours in particular. When I met with her regarding the Rampenho formula, she and her fellow pisciculturists had recently returned from their latest sea seeding trip. She told how sprinkling iron on certain sections of the sea caused plankton to grow. These to attract bigger beings to feed on them, then yet bigger ones and so on until there were shoals of thriving fish.

Naively I said "It's already been done. It didn't work. After a brief plankton bloom the iron filings fell to the bottom."

"We know," she had replied and then explained that as far as she was concerned iron is but part of what is involved. She said that her team coated iron dust and glucose on granules of pumice. Also adhered were desiccated plankton and bacteria. However, Milophinia and her team are not using any old pumice, or glucose, plankton and bacteria either.

Lava, she said, comes in various densities. Some forms of it float, while others submerge to differing degrees. Upon each type were plankton and bacteria which thrived at particular levels. There is mostly plant plankton at the top, zoo plankton at the lower levels with glucose spinning out in strips. Not only do these strips string the iron and pumice together in wide, semi-submerged webs but provide start-up sustenance for plankton and bacteria alike.

Plankton, Milophinia said, are level specific. So too are the bacteria, or rather the mix of them. And this is where what she said really became interesting.

The bacterial mix, Milophinia said, is of what we call cyanobacteria (these not only photo-synthesize but take carbon dioxide from the air and give oxygen in return) and proteobacteria which do not do either of these. There are a lot of the first bacteria near the surface but increasingly more of the second the lower down in the water they are. At thirty metres below there are only proteos. Though zoo plankton consume both types of bacteria as well as the plant plankton, different species were also particular to how much of each bacteria they ate.

I then asked Milophinia "Why are there the different types of bacteria? What is the significance of their difference?"

"Proteobacteria," she said, "are what you term 'Precambrian' in origin. Their evolved habitat is the environs of your planet's underwater tectonic vents such as those of the mid-Atlantic. Cyanobacteria though possessing similarities to them evolved in surface waters subsequent to the Earth's satellitic orbit around your planet Jupiter changing to a stellar and closer one around your Sun.

With me instantly recalling what Menpemelo had told me about planets some months ago, my attention to what Milophinia had to say grew the more.

'Ponty 50' curfew lifted

BY TED WOODWARD
WELSH AFFAIRS REPORTER

THE dusk to dawn curfew sentence on the 50 strong Tom Jones Appreciation Society of Pontypridd was lifted and their sentences overturned yesterday.

The curfew imposed after Cardiff Crown Court found the 50 women, all from the Rhonda area guilty of affray and unlawful imprisonment of firemen at a Pontypridd nightclub.

Mary Williams QC representing the women at the Appeal Hearing, said, that the original sentence was out all proportion to what actually took place.

Ms Williams said: "What occurred during these ladies' hen-night was nothing more than over-enthusiastic horseplay and mistaken identity. To claim that they terrorised those firemen is laughable.

"These are grown men remember? If they are strong and robust enough to be firefighters then surely they are capable of looking after themselves in the company of mere women?" she said.

Rejecting the Crown prosecution's case that the women had a long history of molesting men and needed to remain under curfew in the name of the public good, Judge Hilary Norman, said she did not find it creditable that women the of same years as herself, could possibly behave in the manner alleged. She said: "What is wrong with these men? Are they sissies or something?"

Blodwyn Hard

After the appeal hearing, Blodwyn Hard, speaking for the rest of her 50 middle-aged friends, said: "We are very grateful to Judge Norman for removing the dark cloud which hung over all our heads.

"We are also extremely thankful for all the financial and other support we have received from every Tom Jones Appreciation Society Chapters across the whole of Britain and Ireland as well as those of the Jerry Dorsy Appreciation Society. It is our intention to have a big celebration up in London in a few weeks time to show how grateful we are."

Asked if she and her friends will be seeking compensation for being wrongly convicted, Mrs Hard said: "This is a matter for our solicitors but there are strong feelings against Judge Lloyd whom

NONETTE READERS OFFER

Ladies

Do you suffer from lower frontal abdominal inhibition?

BANISH IT TODAY WITH

WANTON!

a fragrance formulated by women exclusively for women
eliminates inhibitions and shyness
arouses your inner yearnings - instantly!
once you have experienced the magical wonder of this bouquet
you will always want to be a

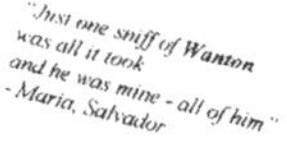

*"For me the effects of **Wanton** were instant - I saw, I sniffed, I had him"*
- Fifi, Lencois

*Since I've been taking **Wanton** I want for men no more - I go out and get them"*
- Dorlores, Quito

*"Since we have been using **Wanton** our nights out are filled with action and men"*
- Women's All in Wrestling Team of Sao Luis

*"All my life I was so shy with men but with **Wanton** I've made up for lost time"*
- Ms J S (87), Natal

Wanton Woman!

- ♥ **Wanton** contains a specially formulated fragrance used for countless eons by women everywhere across the Galaxy and beyond, **for freedom from inhibition.**
- ♥ **Wanton** is already used by **millions** of women across the lands of Nonettes to counter all physiological feelings and every psychological sense of shyness.
- ♥ **Wanton** is created from **completely natural compounds** which only occur on Earth in the hidden depths of the Amazon rainforest.
- ♥ **Wanton** comes in six scratch'n'sniff sachets arranged on an adhesive strip discreetly worn on the under forearm - a single sachet's bouquet to overcome mild inhibition; but scratch all six and **all sense of shyness vanishes - instantly!**
- ♥ **Wanton** does not give adverse reaction to any known allergies.
- ♥ **Wanton** six sachet strip can be yours for as little as an hour's tuition credit - one hour's study for **endless hours of inhibition-free indulgence!**

Supplies of **Wanton** sachet strips are now available from your nearest Nonette Centre. Each six sachet strip set is priced for Nonette members at **only** N2 (or the equivalent in your local currency) N4 for non-Nonettes (another good reason for enrolling today!)

Wanton – "bringing lasting freedom from inhibition for all women – everywhere"

Made under license by **Laboratories Ceará** Tabajara - Ceará - Continental Congress of America

Joanne Miller reports on the rapid grow...

UK Nonettes surge to 9m

PM dismisses Alien backed groups' rise as 'Not significant'

Nonette groups claimed their UK membership has now passed the nine million mark. New members are also joining at the rate of more than 5,000 a day, the organisation claimed.

Announcing the figures, Nonette news-sheets gave a national breakdown of their membership. These show there has been a uniform growth across the country. Also that there is little difference in membership between social classes.

A spokesperson for the London West Regional Nonette said: "There latest [membership] figures also include businesses and other similar organisations as well as individual Nonettes. While a breakdown between individual and corporate membership is not available, we do know that both are growing at the same healthy rate"

If the Nonette figures prove to be accurate then they represent a staggering rise in an organisation which has been in existence for no more than a few months. If this rate of growth continues there is every likelihood that a majority of the UK population will have joined by the end of the year.

However, a Downing Street spokesman, speaking in response to the figures, said: It is important to remember that as yet 85 per cent of the British public have declined to associate with this Nonette movement. It is also important to be aware that the United Kingdom is a parliamentary democracy. It is the will of the majority and their elected representatives who decide how the country is governed."

However, there is said to be growing alarm within Whitehall

"Although periodic abrupt upwellings of globules of tectonic vent heated water and containing their ambient lifeforms," she had said, "propel through the colder, denser waters between the ocean floor and the solar heated near surface, they remain physiologically and genetically disparate from cyano-bacteria and their subsequent evolved lifeforms. Following Earth's change to stellar orbit, Antrophic determinates will still inevitably effect upon these Precambrian lifeforms. Even in solar orbit, their optimal evolutionary progression will still be within the pre-existing constrictions determined by coordinates effecting on them during Jovian orbit."

As she gushed on I was bursting with questions, and the moment she'd stopped for breath I got in "You mean life of the deep sea vents and seeps weren't where all of today's comes from?"

"That is so," she had said.

But with my, "What about shrimps, sponges, sea anemones and things like them which have been seen down there? They must be where today's surface one's are from?" I noted, as she shook her head, a tired schoolteacher tone to her voice as she said "In the beginning..."

Milophinia then explained, again just as Menpemelo had said earlier, that things in space, especially planetary systems, are not static but dynamic. Change one bit and much more besides will be affected.

Gas clouds, Milophinia said, swirl through space. Should such a cloud alight upon a star, its centrifugal force will cause some of the cloud to circle it. If the star is such as our sun when it was younger than today, the denser billows of gas pick up speed, start spinning and candy floss-wrap more of the cloud around them and become giant gas balls such as Saturn and Jupiter.

Such spinning giants orbit their star sometimes closer, sometimes further away, Milophinia aid. Circle too close or into the path of solar flares, she added and they will be burnt to nothing. However if such a planet gyrates to too far away, spins too fast, it will whizz back out into space.

What is more, those settling into a Goldilocks orbit and are also of a Goldilocks size, such as Saturn and Jupiter, not only will they stay around to keep going round, Milophinia said, but will do something else. Because of their distance from the sun, and the power of its attraction less, the stronger is the effect of theirs to passing lumps of rock, ice and other debris of exploding star systems. Even to this day, Milophinia said, Saturn and Jupiter and their moons act as our solar system's vacuum cleaners sucking up most of whatever is passing. The Asteroid and Kuyper Belt's, she added, are its flypapers.

Most of the passing rocks sink into these planets but some start circling them. Over time these orbiting rocks attract others to them and water-ice as well. Milophinia said there is more ice in space than Earthly scientists realise. The bigger a circling lump, moon, becomes, the more the rocks in its centre compact. Compacting converts the rocks' latent energy into heat and event-

Inflation fears groundless says Bank of England

Money supply surges

By Julia Noble
Financial Editor

Last month saw the biggest increase in the UK money supply for more than a decade. Bank of England figures show that the increase in M1 - the notes and coins in our pockets - rose to an annual 12 4 percent.

The Bank said the increase was more because of technical factors rather than any intentional devaluation of monetary worth

Although the Bank did not specify what the factors were which lead to the rise but it thought by many in the City to because of restructuring of government medium term gilts (loan stock).

While most city commentators were bullish on the supply increases' inflationary effects, Howard Johnson, an economist with the investment house, Jayson Arga, was critical of the Bank of England's moves He said: In normal times - and we are not living in normal times remember - if M1 money supply increases much beyond the increase in value of goods and services the result is inflation

"The 12 month growth of the UK economy has been no more than 3-4 percent What now must be taken into account, however, is the growing amount of economic activity within the UK which is taking place not in sterling but in Nonettes.

"The trouble with most conventional economists is that they only see the future through their rearview mirror. Although the effects of the Nonette currency is currently small there is every sign that it will grow over the next year

Should this rise be no more than 5 per cent then the amount of sterling already in circulation will, by itself, represent a growth in the money supply Increasing it by yet more - as the Bank of England has done is the equivalent of adding fuel to the inflationary fire to an already overheated econ-

'Vermont UDI a joke' - neighbours jibe

David Howth
from Burlington, Vermont

WHILE RURAL VERMONT'S declaration of secession from the US is causing palpations in the White House and the rest of the US, it was greeted with derision in nearby Burlington.

Burlington, tiny Vermont's capital and where half of the state's 600,000 population live, townspeople view their country cousins as both back-woodmen and backward think that the three affected counties' UDI is little more than a publicity stunt in a bid to bring much needed tourist revenue to an economically depressed area.

The south of Vermont is little more than a commuter belt for Boston and Springfield but the north of the state still remains wedded to its historic rural roots of farming and forestry.

Tucked away in the far corner of New England, Vermont has a long history has returned Independents to Congress and the Senate more years than not.

In keeping with this independent tradition, the Nonette movement in Vermont has spread widely throughout the State. According to the Nonettes a reason for their growth is the movement's appeal to the many scattered rural communities who have suffered from declining farm incomes.

IFEA Abduction Crisis latest:

"It could have been us" - says Arsenal's George

By Jan Coleman

ARSENAL'S ENTIRE IEFA SQUAD narrowly missed being victims to the Susem, Arsenal's boss, Graham George, claimed yesterday. He said that the Aliens struck less than a mile away from where the Gunners were on a regular training session.

"I hope that our narrow miss lays to rest once and for all that in some way Arsenal's run of success has anything to do with the nonsense that these Aliens are fixing matches in our favour

"Naturally everyone in squad is sorry for what has happened to the other players and we all have had a whip round to send those in hospital some flowers and get-well cards."

Meanwhile, George said, Arsenal is training hard for their forthcoming semi-final match with Milan. Security for the team has been stepped up with every member of the squad given around-the-clock

Council worker 'Day of action' str

Lay-off threat sparks union fury

By **Neill Pollard**
Social Affairs Editor

MANY Council-run services are set to grind to a halt next Tuesday as public sector workers stage a nationwide "Day of Action".

The strike is in response to massive layoffs threatened by councils in a bid to conform to the latest round of government public sector spending cuts.

Brian Bunting, head of UPSW, the main council workers' union said: "While my members have no wish whatsoever to cause any inconvenience to members of the public, the County Halls of Britain have given us no alternative other than to respond in most forceful way possible to this savage threat to my members livelihoods."

According to figures released by the Association of Borough Councils (ABC) an estimated 100,000 council workers could face immediate compulsory redundancy as a result of cuts of local government funding.

Harold Slipwaite, chairman of the ABC said the threatened strike was a "pointless act of folly which would achieve

Mr Slipwai earlier after a Jonathan Wi minister for ment, said: help at this di those us in ment fight b selves. It is vit pull together a united front w face the Treasu

"Coming on previous cuts a munity Char ments, Counci country are problems in even their statu to their citizens.

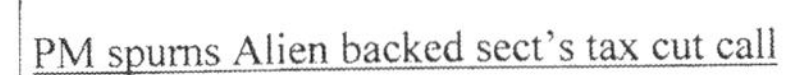

PM spurns Alien backed sect's tax cut call

"I am sick and tired of Nonette - storms Campbe

Handel hints taxes may rise to cover shortfall

By William Carlisle
Political Editor

THE PRIME MINISTER, Edward Campbell, angrily rebuffed the latest Nonette demand for cuts in their income tax.

Instead both the PM and Peter Handel, the Chancellor, hinted that rather than any taxes being cut they may actually have to rise to meet the shortfall in government revenues

The PM, speaking at a City engagement said: "I am sick and tired of hearing these incessant pleas from this so-called peoples' movement for

Edward Campbell yesterday

preferential treatment As I have said repeatedly, there are not and neither will there ever be any 'special cases' as far as taxation is concerned.

"We all must pay fair share of the tax the PM said.

Peter Handel, also the Off-shore In Forum with the PM, unless more taxes are p may well have to rise.

The Chancellor sa blame for the tax shor solely with the Nonet the Susem. Their atta Inland Revenue offic month, he said, had ca much disruption tha collection of taxes ha seriously delayed. He "We were on target for our repayment schedule

Much of Russia now 'socialist'

Rapid growth of Nonettes worries Kremlin

By **Henrietta Yang**

MUCH TO THE DISMAY of the Vladic Shavall, the Russian president, socialism is not only flourishing in his country but is spreading at an ever increasing rate.

The Nonette movement is now firmly established from Murmansk in the far north to Asrakhan on the Caspian; Smolensk in the west to Sakhalin in the east. According to Nonette publications there are now a total of 12,842 local Nonette groups that have been formed.

Some of Russia's autonomous regions, Nonettes claim, such as Tarterstan and Udmurt are now wholly under the movement's effective control. While acknowledging that the original regimes still exist, the Nonettes say that these are no longer in control of anything meaningful.

Economic activity in these and an increasing number of other regions is entirely in the hands of various Nonette groups.

The reason Nonettes give for the rapid growth of their movement in Russia, is much the same as in other parts of the world: a clean-hands, open administration in the hands of the people themselves.

The reports from Russia also mention the continual attempts of the official state administration to harass the movement's activeties as well as attacks from the Russian mafia.

However, given the rapid growth of the Nonette movement throughout Russia there is the likelihood of both central government as well as the country's criminal groups - often interlinked with one another – being forced on the defensive.

Indeed this appears to be already happening. According to Nonettes, the town of Kolemina, 100 kiometres to the southeast of Moscow, a group of 20 men found guilty in Nonette court of being members of a protection racket and were summarily castrated. The Nonettes say than further 40 and more men also belonging to the gang have fled the area.

Another example of what the Nonettes call; "Peoples'

ually they become molten. Milophinia said I had to bear in mind that all but a wafer thin crust of Earth itself is still molten, more of it than even an orange to its skin.

As the rocks melt, the iron within them, it being the heaviest, densest, sinks to the core. However, if there is sufficient iron near the centre but not yet molten, its inherent magnetism will act as a dynamo and cause the moon to spin. Any water, it being lighter, will, because of the moon's spinning, centrifuge towards the surface. Once there it freezes. Water-ice, it being a bad conductor of heat, keeps heat made by the molten rocks locked within. This locked-in heat keeps much of the remaining water liquid. The ice-covered moons around Jupiter, such as Ganymede and Europa, Milophinia said, are examples of this occurring. So is that of Titan around Saturn.

Further rocks raining down on the moon will be slowed by the density of the ice and water and only indent into the surface, mantle. Bigger rocks, however, will penetrate through it. The turbulence these bring causes molten rock, lava, to burst through thin bits of the mantle including out of the holes made by the falling rocks in the first place. Convection generated by the molten centre also causes lava to ooze out of the cracks.

Superheated water bubbling along the thin bits causes minerals within the rocks, especially sulphur, sodium and potassium to precipitate. These last two Milophinia said, cause Secondary waves, electricity, to be released. As water is an efficient conductor of electricity there will be strong localised charged energy fields. When all these constituents, heat, water, minerals and charged fields are present it is possible for the Anthropic Template to effect upon them and life, or 'self-replicating entities' as Milophinia called them, come into being.

I had asked if it was possible for such 'entities', albeit in suspended animation, to be already present on the rocks which rained down on these moons. With her "It is possible but unlikely," Milophinia had a smile, the first I have seen since I have known her.

"Whatever event propels and accelerates rock through space," she said, "will be 'cataclysmic' such as a star exploding. The velocity, energy, heat, intensity of Secondary wave radiation would have disseminated sentience to its non-auralate constituents. While sentience suspends animation at low temperatures, it cannot withstand high ones. At the onset of their trajectory such rocks would be baked to more than 1,000 degrees. During their journey, they will be exposed to constant cosmic ray bombardment. Even a rock travelling at 1,000,000 kilometres an hour from Sirius, one of your nearest stars, will take 3,000 years to reach the environs of Jupiter."

Then, as though I had not uttered, Milophinia continued. With rocks still raining down on the moon, she said, not only does its mass increase but so does its own centrifugal force. This attracts yet more rocks to land upon it. The moon's greater pulling power attracts something else, another moon.

All Wanton strips sold!

"No more for a week" - say Nonettes

By Olivia Bowman
Family Planning Affairs Correspondent

AFTER A SLOW START every single Wanton strip has been snapped up, new supplies will not be available for a week

The strips, which claim to suppress feelings of inhibition, are now proving to be a hit with the nation's women. A Nonette spokeswoman said: "We knew that Wanton is a big hit in the Congress but we had no idea the demand for the strips would be as strong over here."

Users of Wanton say the sachets have had a powerful effect in not only suppressing feelings of inhibition but in banishing them altogether. One Wanton user, Tamara Jones (32) said: "Before I started taking Wanton all my friends used to laugh at my shyness, especially in male company but not anymore.

"Now than I am taking Wanton all my feelings of shyness are in the past. Now if I see a man that I fancy I just go up to him and say: "Come with me big boy."

Other Wanton users have also found that the sachets have made big changes to their

Sinkiang seccession Beijing blames Nonettes

China's 'Wild West' slides out of government control

Siobhain O'Hara
reports from Urumchi

DURING the lull since the Susem abduction of police forces six weeks ago and this past weekend the Nonette movement has expanded at lightning speed among the indigenous population of this remote northwest province.

The past few days have witnessed the inevitable consequences of Nonette empowerment - a unilateral declaration of independence

Sinkiang - or Uygur as the Beijing authorities renamed it - is the size of Germany but with a small and widely scattered native population of Turkish Ughurs. For the past half century the Ughurs have suffered a massive influx of Han Chinese who have tipped the population balance in their favour.

While the Ughurs have suffered at the hands of the communist authorities in Beijing there has been little actual racial tension between them and the Chinese immigrants.

The incomers' sheer numbers however, has sparked many sporadic protests by the Ughurs. All of which, in the past have been savagely suppressed by the communist authorities.

The advent of the Nonettes in Sinkiang and their distribution of Alien energy units spurred a rapid expansion of the movement throughout Ughur communities.

The initial communist crackdown on the Urghurs was muted by the fact that so many of the Han Chinese - across China as a whole - also embraced the use the soutin energy units The arrival of the Susem police abduction raids stopped any further harassment in its steps

The Chinese authorities have accused the Nonette movement as being a hotbed of Ughur 'splitists'. As the weekend's events have shown, their claims were justified. The only way Beijing can assert its cont-

Nonettes speeding Indonesia break up

Many islands now out of bounds to Government forc

By Adam Littlejohn
East Asia Correspondent

THE future of Indonesia is looking bleaker by the day. Yesterday brought news of a further clutch of islands passing under Nonette control and government forces being ignominiously bundled on boats and dispatched back to Djakarta.

The island of Kalimantan (Borneo) is now fully under Nonette control. So is much of Celebes and all of the islands east to Irian.

While this is news bad enough for the government of Susilo Yudhuyono, it is loss of huge swathes in the island of Sumatra which are of even more concern.

The north of Sumatra, the troubled province of Aceh has already declared itself for the Nonettes

That the Nonettes have been successful in organising in Aceh raises concerns to governments beyond Indonesia. Although suffering for decades from separatist, pro-independence movements, Aech has abundant supplies of natural gas, and thus

As great, if not deeper concern to many Islamic regimes is that Aceh is the most militantly Islamic region in the whole of South east Asia

That even the rigid and enforced authority of the male centred - and sometimes brutish - Islamic power in Aceh have been unable to stem the growing power of the Nonettes must be sending shudders though theocratic regimes elsewhere.

No matter how vehemently Islamic clerics condemn the Nonettes they appear unable to counter the influence of the daily Susem television newscasts and the wonders and freedoms they show Nonettes enjoying.

Islamic leaders in Aceh, just as religious leaders elsewhere, have also been unable to bridge and identify with younger age groups. And as elsewhere in the world it is, more often than not, children who are the bringers of Nonette revolution. Once they have joined, their parents, more so their mothers, are soon following suit.

As in male dominated societies elsewhere, Aceh's religious leaders have tried to

IFEA Abduction Crisis latest:

IEFA-SLI IN CRISIS TALKS OVER CUP HALT

Contest could be cancelled IFEA say

By Nick Peters

IEFA OFFICIALS and top SLI-TV and RAT-TV executives were in urgent crisis talks over the IFEA contest.

The outcome could effect the forthcoming Arsenal-Milan semi-final. Derek Igg, head of SLI, who is attending the meeting in Rome said: "These abductions have been bad news for all concerned especially the affected clubs. Everyone at SLI feels for players who have been subjected to what must have been a truly traumatic experience.

"None-the-less these attacks have been the result of inadequate security. When a jeweller as much as most of soccer sides have cost - he guards his shop as if it were Fort Knox. But what security have these clubs got to guard their players? Usually nothing more than a couple of old blokes standing outside the training ground. To my way of thinking this is bordering on the criminally negligence."

The head of RAT-TV, SLI's partner in the TV consortium for the IEFA Cup, Silvio Collionni said that it was in everyone's interest that the contest had to continue as planned. He said: "We have a contract with the IFEA Either they keep to it or we will sue them for billions."

Snr. Collionni said that if

Nonettes devalue dollar – yet again

New rate: £1.26 = N1 $1.10 = N1

By Julia Noble
Finance Editor

Within the space of little more than a week the Nonette Central Bank has revalued its currency - the nonette - by a further 5 per cent The pound is now worth N0.74

According to Nonette publications, the Nonette Central Bank gave inflationary trends in the US and other leading economies. Retail outlets accepting the nonette are reported as already having adjusted their prices in response to the revaluation

For the increasing number of people in Britain who take their salaries in nonettes it will mean an effective 10 per cent pay rise for them compared with the rest of us who are pa in 'ordinary' mone Whether or not the ri ing value of the nonett leads to yet more peopl electing to be paid in Nonettes remains to be seen

Shopkeepers who buy in nonettes but sell in pounds as well as nonettes, have seen the value of their sterling sales rise by 5 per cent.

Their advantage over 'straight' retailers, especially the bigger ones such as the supermarkets, is like to encourage more outlets also to accept the nonette

City response to the revaluation was, at best, indifferent As one money marketmaker said: "Big deal Here, we don't play in

Grants, subsidies, CAP slashed as Brussels runs out of money

EU in emergency crisis panic cutbacks

By Oliver Stoneburger

The European Commission has run out of money. The Commission said that because member states have not paid their dues it has nothing to pay the Union's farmers their subsidies. Neither does it have any money to pay anyone else

The President of the Commission, Erhardt Kleist, said that unless the situation improves, the EU itself could cease to exist.

Herr Kleist, speaking after a meeting with EU fiscal department heads, said: "The financial problem currently facing my administration is that a certain number of member states of the EU have not paid their statuary contributions to the Commission. Therefore we will have no alternative other than to hold in abeyance all future payments to every eligible recipient."

Asked how many EU members were withholding their contributions, Herr Kleist said: "All of them."

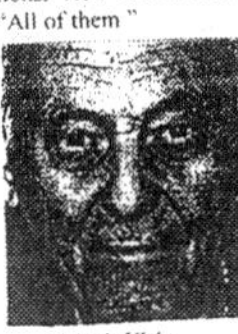

Erhadt Kleist

The President also said that the Commission was at the very limit of its borrowing facilities. "In the past," Herr Keist said, "we would have had no trouble with finding the extra money to tide us over but our bankers have refused to extend our overdraft What is also aggravating the situation is that even the VAT money which is supposed to be handed over has been withheld from us

"It is important t the Commission h bands its remain funds so that we c continue paying employees and co their expenses," H Kleist said.

The Commissio staff, the most lavis paid public servants the whole of Europe, reported to resisting cuts in both their n bers and salary lev There is also much in the EU's corridors

There are moons which spin swiftly, she said, and those which spin slowly or not at all. Swift spinners are high in iron and so have magnetospheres, whereas slow and non-spinners are low in iron and do not have such a sphere. Like swift spinners repel, opposite ones attract, but a slow or non-spinner, should it come close to one which is swift, merely circles it. Such circling steadies its host's swift spinning to a regular rotation. Milophinia gave distance and size equations for little moons circling bigger ones, but put simply Earth's moon has a strong stabilising influence, those of Mars' next to nothing.

Meanwhile, stabilised or not, life on the hot wet surface of the moon has a hard time. Rocks still rain down smashing and churning. What survives bombardment from above is as often as not obliterated by lava welling from below. With every rocky deluge not only does the moon become bigger but so does the strength of its centrifugal power, which in turn attracts yet more rocks to crash into it. This continues for a long time, in Earth's case, Milophinia said, more than three billion years. Then after a turbulence too many, the moon is knocked from its orbit and becomes a solar circling planet.

If the new planet should sail towards the sun, as did the Earth, its icy surface melts. Slowly to begin with, but once sufficient rock strewn slush exposes to the Sun's rays it accelerates. Much of the meltwater evaporates into space exposing parts of the mantle. Turbulent convection within the planet's core still continues with lava erupting through cracks and holes in its mantle. Gas and fumes from these mix with the evaporating water and an atmosphere forms. This traps warmth and moisture as well as shielding the surface from many of space's rocks and rays.

Although planetary Earth thrived, Mars, so Milophinia said, had no such luck. It was knocked into solar orbit too soon. Mars had neither sufficient size nor locked-in heat to keep its molten magna moving and so it seized up. But even before Mars had became a cold solid lump, nigh on all of its water had gone and what life there was died out.

On Earth, life, though now living in conditions of comparative calm, also had a hard time. Milophinia said once the Earth had started circling the Sun more changes occurred to it than first meets the eye. She mentioned a long list of things from water salinity to magnetic polarity, but the upshot of them all was that only those species acclimatising quickly enough to the new world survived.

However, even ones which went as far as adapting to life on the surface, such as the jelly fishes and lampreys as well as proteobacteria, were all eventually locked in an evolutionary dead-end. Milophinia said this was not just because of the constrictions caused by the then conditions on Earth but also the narrowness of the Anthropic Template effecting on them. I didn't fully understand what she meant by this, but because she was talking so fast I'd not chance to get a word in, let alone a question. She did say, however, it had something to do with the low levels of electrical charge with which the then

Nonettes:

Flocking Filipinos threat frets Concla

Islands, cities fall under the sway of Nonettes

Siobhain O'Hara
reports from Quezon City

QUEZON CITY is, for all intents and purposes, no longer under central government control.

The mayor, Hernando Lucayo still resides in his ornate mansion on the Square of the Republic but this is as far as his writ now runs. The chief of police is still in his headquarters on General MacArthur Street but his forces no longer police the city.

Within the space of a few months one district of this sprawling city of two million, after another has passed into the control of the Nonettes

The children joined the movement first, then their parents, then quickly followed by the local businesses both large and small.

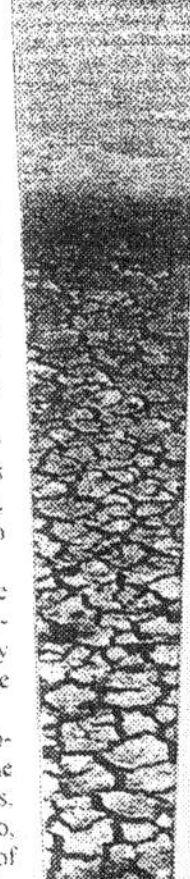

With much of the city's economic activity now in the hands of Nonette business's, the national currency, the peso, has been ditched in favour of the nonette. As soon as the takeover became effective, governments, both local and national stopped receiving taxes, officials and police their bribes

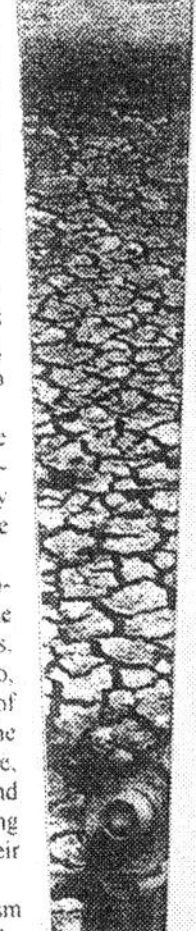

Quezon City is a microcosm of what is taking place the length and breath of the Philippines.

From Luzon in the north to Mindanao in the south an estimated 30 million people now are thought to be members of the Nonette movement.

Both the Catholic Church and Islamic clerics have inveighed, often vehemently against the Nonettes, as have the government of Maria Conclaves but without any apparent effect

As the Nonettes has demonstrated elsewhere in the world, no matter how powerful religious authoritarianism may be, if its leaders are unable to deliver material progress they will lose out to those who do.

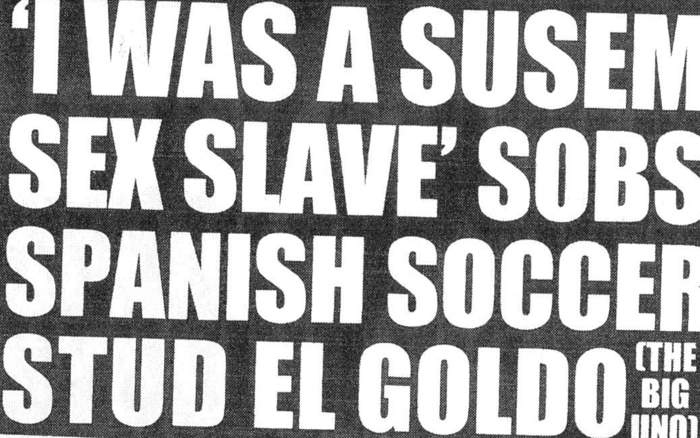

Chron Exclusive

'I WAS A SUSEM SEX SLAVE' SOBS SPANISH SOCCER STUD EL GOLDO (THE BIG UNO)

By TRISH McDIGG

SPANISH SOCCER STAR, Enrico Motril, speaking exclusively to the *Chron*, told, for the first time his ordeal in the clutches of the sex-craved Susem.

Speaking from his hospital bed, Enrico, Barcelona's champion goalkeeper spoke frankly of his 24 hours, non-stop, no-holes-barred, kinky sado-sex hell he and his fellow team members were subjected to by the Aliens.

Iberian idol

This idol of the Iberians also claimed that he was on the receiving end of 'extra special' treatment at the hands of one of the Aliens in particular.

Enrico Motril, a swarthy two-metres-plus tall bearded giant of a man, is known throughout Spain as El Goldo' (the 'Big One') for his prowess on the pitch and off of it.

It is said Motril has made so many senoritas swoon that he has sired several scores of sons during his legendary marathon lovemaking sessions

Lovemaking over

But as Enrico unfolded details of his injuries he suffered at the hands of the Susem it appears that his lovemaking days are no more There are also doubts if he will be able to play professionally again either

Barcelona's Motril recovering in hospital yesterday

Perverted sex acts

Still in obvious pain and distress from his ordeals Enrico said: "From morning to evening the Susem women forced me and my fellow team mates to take part in one degrading perverted sex act with them after another.

Non-stop ordeals

"We were begging them to let us go, to stop doing such terrible things to our bodies but they refused to listen to our entreaties.

"As soon as one group of Aliens had sated their lusts on us another group would appear and have their way with us I was terrified. My hands did not stop shaking

Terror of 'Tearo'

"Then as the sun began to set, out of the shadows there came yet another group of Susem

"As they appeared the others began chorusing "Tearo, Tearo" or something like this. And then I saw this Tearo and my heart was filled with yet greater fear."

"Because I am bigger than my team mates it was not possible for me to make myself inconspicuous from this Tearo

They held me down

'During the hours of my earlier ordeals and because of my strength of Alien women to hold me down as they took it in turns satisfy themselves from me But with this Tearo it was different

I was her plaything

"From then until the morning I was her plaything Such was the size and power of this Alien woman and although I tried to resist her she had no need for the others And her demands on my masculinity were more onerous than any of the other Aliens' had been.

Lengthy congress

"After each of this Tearo's lengthy congress with me and though I was filled with pain and weariness she would return within minutes as though refreshed and force me to make love with her yet again

She hit me

"Each time I attempted to refuse her advances she would strike me with her forearm or kick me in the shin. My career could now be over if

IEFA Chiefs SLI-TV set to hammer restart deal page 64

Arsenal-Milan semi final set for go ahead page 63

further shock Susem sex outrages details pages 6,7,8, 9,10,11,12

Californian Nonettes on the rise

Silicon Valley and Farmers unite

Joanne Miller
reports from San Jose

SAN JOSE, the capital of Silicon Valley has two competing administrations and economies: the official ones and their Nonette counterpart

The mayor of San Jose, Van Wagner, his fellow Councillors and the rest of City Hall who run the official one, worry over the rise of their rival

Mayor Wagner worries that his administration and its fast declining income from City sales tax receipts - which have already plummeted by 30 per cent in the past month alone - will grind to halt Aides to the mayor are currently involved in an increasingly desperate programme of spending cuts in a bid to match their falling income

Meanwhile the influence of San Jose's Nonette administration grows and grows. In a matter of months half the town's population have joined the movement

So have many of its businesses A reason for this astounding growth has been the free energy which joining the Nonettes brings

To Californians, who have for years suffered from power shortages and erratic supply, the Susem soufin energy were effectively "manna from heaven"

As Wagner ruefully laments, energy supply has always been outside his remit and there nothing he or his administration could do to ... attractions.

He said, "Once one business has access to a constant and limitless supply of cost-free energy their competitors have no choice but to follow suit

"No matter what the long term outcomes of these units may be," says Wagner, "business is concerned only with the now, two months, maybe three at most

"Meanwhile, one corporation after another gets hooked up with this Nonette thing and before you know it they're paying and trading in this Nonette currency It's the same with the population as well and nobody is paying taxes anymore "

What is happening in San Jose is being reflected, says Mayor Wagner, in the rest of California. In the agricultural parts of the State such as the Imperial and Napa Valleys, the impact of the Nonette movement is doing more than increasing productivity, it is changing the very face of farming itself

Not only is there a shortage of Mexican contract workers but those who do cross the border command huge rises in pay and improved working conditions

Farmers across the State have also been hit by a further "double whammy" of lower cost competition from Nonette agricultural produce and the trading preference of Nonette consumers to buy from their fellow member producers

Not wanting to be blocked out of this fast growing Nonette market, farmers are increasingly obliged to join the movement as well Although reliable figures are scarce, there is abundant collaborative evidence to suggest that a quarter of California gross output is now channelled though Nonette businesses There is also evidence that the rate of switchover from mainstream to Nonette controlled commerce is accelerating

While Mayor Wagner and his counterparts across California are increasingly marginalised, the rest of the state's political establishment, both Democrat and Republican, is also experiencing a growing loss of influence Both parties, it is said, are experiencing a fall in contributions from ordinary people

Several Congressmen, from both parties, have declared against the Nonettes but most are adopting a cautious wait-and-see approach towards the movement lest they be caught the wrong side of voter sentiment in next year's mid-term elections.

One right-wing Congressman, Richard Gephardt, who has denounced the Nonettes, likens them to the socialist movement founded by Upton Sinclair in the 1930s

While Sinclair came to prominence in the Depression and the Hovervilles of that era, his teachings have little or no relevance to the thrust of the Nonette movement of today In fact, rather the reverse is true

Instead of demanding greater government involvement

life had been first infused.

Meanwhile, up on the sunlit surface the atmosphere was on an electrical high, zapping lightning down to Earth in non-stop storms. With warmth, water also in abundance, the Anthropic Template effected the formation of life all over again. But this time the Template's effects were not just confined to a few strips of deep sea vents. Now it had the planet's entire surface upon which to play. And this second time around the life the Template invoked did not just exist, it exploded, everywhere. Within a few million years 'new' life surpassed the levels the 'old' had taken billions to reach.

The rest is history but as Milophinia outlined what occurred, thoughts formed in my mind, that there is, here on Earth, existing side by side, two comp-letely separate lifeforms. The later one, in effect, 'us' interloped on the first. These first ones are feeble forms compared to the robust ones of 'us'. Was this robustness the result, the reason why we post-Cambrians have four Hox genes and the 'Pre's' only two? Or was it the other way round? Will we be superseded by more vigorous lifeforms, ones with eight Hoxes? Do these already exist and we don't know about them yet? Is there life else-where which works on sixteen and evolves super beings in a flash?

I managed to get a question in about this but Milophinia said that though it was possible, the Susem did not know of any. She also reminded that determinates of all of us 'sentient entities' are within our auras not our beings. So if such forms of eight and sixteen Hox beings do exist, our auras, or women's auras rather, would, over the eons, eventually download back into them. However, she also said the Susem are not aware of this happening either.

At this point Milophinia, having spoken more to me since I have known her, bid goodbye and I was left with a bag of questions begging answers. By the end of the evening I had more.

When it became dark I took my telescope up onto the Mount Macambirá. Though it has been a while since I stargazed last, Jupiter and Saturn, their moons were on my mind. As things turned out I had no luck locating let alone seeing either planet. But as I waited for them to appear over the horizon I thought of the Earth, of how it would have been those years ago when first it sailed away from Jupiter towards the Sun, how instead of being the blue and white of now it would have been a shining silver ball with the sunlight glistening off of it. Then I thought of the moons around Jupiter, Ganymede, Europa, Io. Have they life on them yet? Is it like the life we have down in our deep sea vents, big worms and anemones? How many of these moons are ready to start anew as planets?

Still waiting for Jupiter to appear I swung my telescope from the horizon to the Milky Way and peered at black bits darkening out patches of stars. I know these are gas, dust clouds, but wondered how much more is swirling around individual stars, spinning new Jupiters and Saturns?

Then I thought of what Milophinia said, and Menpemelo for that matter,

lovement's rapid spread threatens state

Japanese Nonette r worries governme

Anna Chelmsford
st Asia Correspondent

A COUNTRY dependent imported energy supplies, Nonette soufin energy units e proved to be a godsend to Japanese people and Indus- alike. But the rapid growth the Nonette movement ched with the units is itself rying the Japanese horities

he spread of the Nonette vement into all parts of ntry and sections of society ow such of a size than it is fast becoming an administrative, socio-economic and constitutional entity in its own right.

Masaru Aigisawa, of the *Nikkei Post*, who has followed the growth of the Nonette movement said: "Latest figures indicate that 18-20 million people are now Nonettes.

"With the cell structure and hierarchy of the movement it has now become a separate nation within the same territory as the state itself.

"All number of state institutions have been affected adversely by Nonette system is on collapse in many represents a sym in Japanese societ

"Historically children have reverential of institutions but n students of all age Nonette system is and has also show old system.

"Also, Nonette pays money for think this will b more popular in th

SUSEM SOCCER SNATCHES - LATEST:

'She picked me up, slapped me down and 'had' me' -SOBS MAN-MOUNTAIN

By Michelle Young

ENRICO MOTRIL, the mighty man-mountain of Spanish soccer has met his lovematch with one of his Alien abductors - she is even bigger than he is. And from all accounts stronger as well.

Montril and the rest of the Barcelona squad are recovering from their Alien abduction ordeal in a Rome hospital.

Such are their injuries suffered at the hands of the Susem there are doubts if any of the Spanish side will be fit enough to play for many months. ed to the most severe and serious assaults.

Motril, speaking from his hospital bed and still emotionally distressed after his day-and-night-long enforced love-in with the Susem, said: "While we all suffered at the hands of these Alien women I was singled out for special

"Because I tried to resist the Susem advances I was subjected to horrifically bestial treatment." Montril then showed the Chinese burns the Susem gave him.

As he told how one of the Susem picked him up by his legs and slapped him down on the ground and eagerly jumped astride him "Even though I ple-

Spanish growers gr to the Nonettes

y Thomas Drake
Valencia, Spain

NOT JOINING the Nonettes not an option," said Manuel omes, a farmer in Engura, alencia "Either we farmers in and adopt their methods of rowing our crops or we will e forced out of business."

"If you can't beat them join them" - say Spain's farmers

A growing number of farmers in this lush farming district of southern Spain have come to he same conclusion as Snr. Gomes. Within the past week more than 200 farmers are reported joining their local Nonette groups

For the growers of Valenc it not merely a case of pr ducing better crops and lower costs but of not bei shut out of the increasing powerful Nonette tradi network

It is the rapidly growing si of the Nonette trading syste which is increasing worryi the Spanish authorities

As Nonettes give tra preference to other Nonet groups and transact th business in nonettes. bo provincial and national gover ments are losing considerab taxation revenue Although a ministration throughout south

Panama families sue Pentagon for $300bn

By Harry Wilmot
In New York

The US Department of Defence is facing a massive $100 billion Class Action lawsuit

Lawyers acting for the 30,000 Southern Command servicemen and their families have filed a claim for compensation and damages for injuries and trauma suffer-ed during the men's abduction and captivity by the Susem

"They screwed us up; we're going to screw them"

The lawsuit alleges that the DoD by stationing the men in the Panama Canal Zone acted in an irresponsible manner and needlessly jeopardized their safety and well-being

The DoD, the lawsuit claims, knew from the Brazilian military's experience what would happen to US servicemen if they fell into the hands of the Susem and so should have evacuated them while there was ample time and opportunity to do so

'Southern Command Families in Fear' (SCFF), the umbrella group of the servicemen's families who have filed the lawsuit, are demanding that resources be made available for research into ways of restoring the affected men to full and active life

Mrs Susan Pelham

SCFF spokesperson, Susan Pelham, whose husband Jonathan is one of the Panama victims, said: "There are 30,000 families across America who are condemned to live with and cope daily with the tragedy of their husbands unable to live their lives as full men

"While our marriage is strong, there are many which have collapsed as a direct result of the husband's inability to fulfill his martial duties

"We are demanding that there be urgent medical research into the rehabilitation of our menfolk's damaged members We are also calling for a nationwide campaign on behalf of our loved ones over-

Anti-Nonette League demands action before it's too late

"Curb Nonettes" Warren urged

BY BRETT ANDERSON
IN NEW YORK

THE security of the United States is now under threat both at home and abroad not only from anti-American Islamic fundamentalist terror groups. It is the Nonettes who now pose the greatest threat to the US the newly founded Anti-Nonette League claimed yesterday.

'Crypto-socialists'

Branding the Nonettes as 'Crypto-socialists', the President of the League, Howard Winnaker, Dean of Williamsburg University, said the values that make America strong are under threat from the Alien backed movement.

Speaking in Washington at the League's inauguration, Dean Winnaker said: "The United States of America and its institutions, all of which have made our nation strong and the bastion of democratic freedoms, are under threat as never before.

"This threat comes from one source and one source only," Dean Winnaker said, "the Nonette movement. This cryto-socialist organization is spreading insidiously through the entire fabric of this great nation and the rest of the world alike as a cancerous growth.

Malign tumor

"Unless this malign Alien tumor is exorcized from the body of American society and exorcized now, it will surely take control us. Today, not tomorrow, is the time for action."

The League says it has attracted backing and funding from a wide range of national organizations and major corporations.

Faiths threatened

The League also claims to have the support of many professional and institutional bodies as well as Churches and other faith-based groups.

All the delegates addressing the League's inaugural meeting decried the growing threat the Nonettes pose to their own professions.

One delegate, Dr Ronald Duke, said that as a surgeon, he has personally witnessed the consequences of the growing influence of the Nonettes in his own hospital. He said: "In the past month alone the number of patients presenting for heart surgery has halved. And the reason? Why these darn Nonette health booth contraptions that's why. My hospital, George Bush Memorial, is losing vital income streams to this new-age movement.

Patient income slump

"The George Bush Hospital is not alone in suffering a serious downturn in patient-care income. The entire medical profession along with HMOs, drug companies and a whole range of other health-care providers are all suffering from these Nonettes meddling in matters which they have no right.

"Unless these 'new-agers' are stopped from hijacking our patients, established medical care procedures right across the entire US will be in grave danger of collapse."

Another delegate, Ralph Toolson who is also President of the Association of American Teachers, said his Association's members were suffering increased unemployment from falling rolls and reduced classes caused by the Nonettes' subverting of children's minds from attending school.

Warping young minds

"What is worse," Mr Toolson said, "are the falsehoods these Aliens are indoctrinating our children's minds with through their so-called teaching screens.

"What they are imparting is in total contradiction to what is taught in school. As an instance, a physics teacher in Illinois last week, explaining atomic theory to a Seventh Grade class, was told by his pupils that the Nonette screens said there are no such things as atoms.

Mental breakdown

"When he reaffirmed that atoms do indeed exist, he was then subjected by the entire class to a continuous barrage of: "Prove it!" When he was unable to do so to their satisfaction they walked out on him. He is now suffering from a mental breakdown."

A corporate member of the League, Norman Framek, CFO of the Burger Prince, said: "My organization has long synergergized with all America's universities. We provide the means by which countless thousands of students traditionally earn money by working for us to pay their way through college.

Ungrateful youngsters

"But now so many students, these once potential employees, are failing to uptake the opportunities we provide of paid work in favor of these Alien teaching screens and this funny money they pay out. Even our offers of fast-track payment enhancement programs are being spurned by these ungrateful youngsters."

A number of faith-based organizations were also represented at the League's inauguration. Many of their delegates said Nonettes propaganda actively turning people away from their churches.

Several claimed the Nonettes were deliberately targeting children who in turn, were disaffecting their parents away from worshipping in their churches.

Other delegates, including American Families, said it was vital for the League to focus on combating the growing influence of the Nonettes.

Forging links

All agreed it was important to forge anew the importance between the ordinary citizens and their leaders both political and spiritual.

The League called on President Warren and governors of all 50 States to make Federal and State funds available so that the League could bring home to the ordinary people of America how vital it was for them to believe in traditional American values of respect and reverence towards those in authority.

about our auras, or women's rather, downloading into later generations. What happens while they are waiting? Are there big clouds of their aruas whizzing about the heavens and all 'mind talking' umpteen to the dozen? Of course, with me being only a bloke I have no chance of ever joining them. The best I can ever hope for is to come back as a tree and that is only if I behave myself from now on. But knowing my luck I will come back as a clump of clover, be munched up by a passing cow and that would be my lot.

I turned to the horizon once more. As I waited for sight of Jupiter and Saturn I peered at the Large Magellanic Cloud, my favourite galaxy. After I had picked it out I looked for the Small Magellanic Cloud. I couldn't find it but as I searched and half wondered if it had flown off, I had another thought. If Earthly astronomers say they see the Universe expanding, how can there be such a thing as the Anthropic Constant? It's not possible for there to be both a constant and an expansion at the same time. One of them must be wrong or at least misinterpreting what is being observed.

Though I then gave up on looking for Jupiter and Saturn, folded the telescope, walked back down to the village, I still had this thought in my mind. But once I had set foot in the Pousada such thoughts were abruptly brushed to the back burner by Rainbow and her "Where have you been?"

I had no chance to tell before she began berating harder. I should not have gone off without telling her. I had left her no time to fully brief me on the script for an emergency telecast. There was barely an hour remaining for me to write it. And present as well. As she outlined what was wanted I unthinkingly blurted "Oh no, why me? I'll be slaughtered for this."

It met with her cold "Do as you're told or I'll..." Though her eyes said the rest, Rainbow as curtly added "Your hair needs washing. And do shave properly." In between doing both I drafted what she wanted. I had to rewrite five times before she said, and with barely minutes to go, "That'll do."

But amid the rush oh was I fretting and inwardly muttering "Please don't let it be Citibank and what remains of my money in their branch in Miami." And later, "Why won't these world leaders just do as they are told, it will save so much trouble. When will these men learn never to argue with a woman, not only will she always win but arguing with women upsets them and that is even worse, especially when she's Paceillo."

5,000 men snatched in Alien sex swoops

Hospitals overflowing with Susem lovemaking victims

By **Lisa Biggles**
Alien watch Editor

MORE THAN 5,000 MEN were abducted by the Aliens yesterday. The Susem snatch and grab raids were the biggest yet and ranged from Australia, the US to Europe. Many hospitals in the affected countries were reported as already overflowing with the victims of previous Alien abductions.

All Europe's coastal resorts witnessed unprecedented numbers of young men snatched by Susem raiders. The Alien Abduction Centre in Milan reported that 432 men were taken in Greece, more than 350 in Italy and a similar number from Spanish beaches.

The Centre also said that the Susem had struck Swedish and Finish resorts for the first time.

According to a Centre spokesman the abductions followed the same pattern of previous raids: the sudden appearance of Aliens' low flying robot 'geese' chasing and herding groups of young men into just as suddenly appearing Susem craft, which then zoom away at high speed. Just as devastating is the panic by other holiday-makers on the

IEFA to go ahead

TV Networks withdraw legal action

By Celia Hemmingway
Media Correspondent

THE IEFA COMMITTEE have hammered out a last minute deal with all the major sports TV networks to go ahead with the final rounds of the competition.

Speaking after the meeting IFEA President, Franco Gramaldi said: "In view of football supporters and enthusiasts' overwhelming demand that the IEFA competition should continue and mindful of our legal obligations to our sponsors, we can confirm that the remaining rounds will take place as planned."

Snr Gramaldi also announced that security for the players of the remaining four teams will be stepped up. The President also said that fresh training grounds for the four teams will and will be kept secret.

IEFA's President also announced that a full investigations into some of the earlier fixtures will be conducted as a matter of urgency but will not begin until after the Final had been played.

Despite Snr Gramaldi's upbeat statement on the IEFA competition continuing, it comes as the result of heavy pressure and arm twisting from the TV networks covering the matches. Not only are the networks the competition's main sponsors but they stood to lose sizable advertising revenues if the remaining matches were cancelled.

SLI TV's boss, Dickie Bear, is reported to have used the threat of legal action against IEFA if the competition was called off.

IEFA, it knowing that Bear would sue them for hundreds

Med hospitals "bursting at seams" with Susem victims

Huge backlog of men requiring organ transplants

BY RICHARD RANKIE
MEDICAL EDITOR

MANY of Europe's hospitals are overflowing with Alien abductees recovering from their ordeals.

As fast as victims of Susem attacks are discharged they are replaced by further influxes of fresh casualties.

So many victims of Alien abductions are recovering in Athina Nosokomion, Athens' main hospital, that routine operations have had to be cancelled.

Dr Kypros Hexioka, Head of Athina's Accident and Emergency Department, said: "My hos-pital is presently treating more than 200 patients who are victims of Alien abduction assault or 'Triple A'.

"All but a small minority of Triple A patients are non-Greek and my staff often have great difficulty in communicating with them. Our resources are at breaking point.

"As fast as we can discharge them or repatriate them to their own countries, the beds are taken by yet another influx of victims.

"It is perhaps fortunate for us that the injuries exhibited by Triple A victims follow a similar pattern and so we have been able to standardise remedial procedures.

"In many respects my hospital's treatment of these Triple A cases is fast resembling a conveyor belt operation.

"At the beginning we had difficulties with the nursing staff in their treatment of Tripe A cases. Now that nurses are more experienced in treating these patients they know it is inappropriate to express emotion in front of them such as laughing and sniggering."

However, Dr Hexioka stressed that while hospitals across Europe such as his, can provide remedial care to alleviate the victims' pain, they do not have the facilities or expertise to bring victims full recovery.

Some of the Tripe A patients who have not been badly assaulted by the Susem will stage a full recovery, Dr Hexioka said, and need no more that counselling, but there will be others who will require transplants.

"Penis transplantation, like hand transplants," Dr Hexioka said, "is still in its infancy. There are only a few centres of expertise worldwide, and of course, there is bound to be a donor shortage."

Support for SCFF action firm

'Complete quickly' DoD urged

By Anna Trempleton
In Washington

AS US PUBLIC support for Panama victims grows, the Pentagon is being urged to quickly settle their multi billion damages claim before public and Congressional support against the Department of Defense hardens.

The Panama victims and their families' support group, SCFF claimed yesterday to have backing from a majority in both Congress and the Senate for their case.

Senator John Andrew, who is a member of the Senate's Armed Services Committee, said: "Just now the DoD needs bad publicity like a hole in the head.

"I am urging the Department to settle this legitimate and deserving case as soon as possible before any further damage is done to the standing of our national defence agencies."

David Souter, of the Washington based IoS think tank said: "The DOD is in a hole of its own making. If they settle the SCFF's claim on its terms there will be nothing left for them to buy new defence equipment. If DoD holds out from settling and still lose then they will have to go to Congress for more money which will be hostile toward them.

"It is unlikely that any Congressman or Senator, should they wish to be re-elected, will do anything but support families - and do so openly - the SCFF.

"Just now, because of the Panama fiasco, morale in all branches of the US Armed Services is at an all time low. It's is extremely doubtful if any serving soldier is willing to go into action knowing

Susan Pelham head of SCFF

they too will meet up with those Susem women."

Souter also thinks that if the DoD fights the Panama claim they run a further risk, that of a shortage of new recruits.

He said: "Until recently, for America youngsters without high school education or skills, the military was for many of them the only paid job open to them. But with the spread of these Nonette groups and the fact that youngsters can earn money by studying at these teaching screens the incentive to enlist is falling away by the day.

Should the DoD enmesh themselves in another bout of negative publicity, showing they have little care for their personnel's safety then enlistment will decline. The DoD

Bookie still betting on Milan, Moscow IFEA final

By **Phil Martin**

ARSENAL'S IEFA odds may have shortened but William III still give the Gunner's no more than one in 10 chance of bringing the cup back to Highbury.

An III's spokesman said that the smart money is on Milan to be the IEFA champions. He said: "On present form it's Milan to win against Arsenal and Moscow Sparta to beat Sofia Dynamo. Of those two the odds are unquestionably in the Italian's favour."

III's Arsenal brush-off has not dented thousands of Gunner's fans from having a flutter on their team's pulling-off a win in Rome in two days time.

Roger King, of Drayton Park, an ardent Arsenal supporter and who has placed a sizable bet on an Arsenal win, said: "Our team are on a winning streak.

"Ten to one is good as far as I'm concerned," says Roger, "but not as good as that punter who put on that 50 grand at a 1,000 to one. When William III pays that out it's going to really hit them. Mind you it's no more

144: SIÂN

At work I'm rushed off my feet. We all are. Not just here but when I was up in London at the Association, everyone there said they are as well. I have never known anything like it. Ever since I started all those years ago, I had become resigned to continual decline, with branches closing every time there were spending cuts.

In London, although everyone said Lending and membership have both risen, it is Reference which is bearing the brunt. In a way I suppose I should be glad, heartened even, that so many people are using libraries again, especially the children, but after so many years of cutbacks there are just not the resources to run things properly.

Mr Griffiths put in for extra funding so we could stay open for longer but the finance department turned him down flat. They told him that the Library's funding stays as it is. If we want more to cover our overtime he will have to take it out of our new book allocation. Well, as the purpose of libraries is books, what are we to do? But we can't very well turn people away either.

I had thought the Internet would be sufficient for all the information people wanted. But there's not a bit of it. Oh I grant that our own terminals, like everyone else's, help out but they are booked up ages in advance. All the same I still would have thought those who have Internet at home would have been sufficient. But no, people still come into the Library asking for all the things that aren't on the Net. Marilyn, who handles the local history archives is so busy she doesn't know if she's coming or going.

It is obvious what is behind this sudden surge of enthusiasm, the Nonette teaching screens. Now that so many people have their own individual screens and are studying from them, as well as in groups, the demand on us in the Library is bound to keep on growing and growing.

Though the screens have increased our workload no end, I will be among the first to sing their praises. I have never seen Rowan and Glynn work so hard! Since both boys had a screen of their own, they are either sat in front of them or busy preparing for the practical lessons Lucia sets them.

And she is lovely. It didn't take long before I was looking on her, well we all were, not just as a wonderful teacher but as a friend. Lucia has such a lovely face, lovely eyes. And when the other day she said "No Siân, like this," and shook her head, she had such a lovely smile as she laughed that I wanted to reach out right there and then and give her a great big hug.

In a way, I am sure half the reason both boys study so hard is just to please her as well. The other half of course is the money. It's probably the reason why the Library is inundated with requests, especially from the children. I don't think there is a single child in the whole of Cilgerren who doesn't have their own screen. Not that there hasn't been worries over them.

When we first received the letter from Glynn's school saying he had been

Susem Bank Threat

Huge queues at b

"No cause for panic" says Clayings head as AT

By **Steven Dunn**
Economics Editor

MILLIONS OF PEOPLE queued at banks across Britain yesterday. All came to withdraw their savings before the Aliens carried out their threat to strip the banks of their money tomorrow evening.

So great was the demand of customers to withdraw their savings, several smaller branch banks temporarily ran out of cash.

Throughout the day bank chiefs repeatedly assured customers there was no need for alarm, that there were adequate funds to meet demand.

So great was the demand of customers to withdraw their funds that many city centre banks stayed open for several hours beyond their normal closing hours.

Sir Roger Phillips, chairman of Clayings said: "Demand for cash withdrawal from every one of the Bank's branches has been at unprecedented levels ... ensure all the Bank's customers' requests are met in full and on demand. However, customers should be aware that there may well be penalties in withdrawing from certain high interest bearing accounts."

Sir Roger also said the Bank of England and clearing banks will ensure temporary cash shortages in one bank will be made good by reserves from another.

The Bank of England also confirmed that adequate supplies of currency - notes and coins - are on hand to meet all foreseeable demand.

A BoE spokesman said: "People are over-reacting to the current situation. There really is no cause to panic. While there may be a temporary cessation of certain modes of withdrawal, such as from ATMs and other cash dispensers, everyone who wishes to withdraw their funds from their banks will continue to be able to so."

With most ATMs emptied

"Slash taxes or Big banks get it" – threatens Collins

MAJOR BANKS FACING SUSEM HEIST THREAT

Markets turmoil and slump expected

By **Tony McDooffer**
Banking Editor

Banks worldwide were thrown into turmoil yesterday by the Susem threatening to remove all the money held by them and redistribute it to ordinary people.

The ultimatum against banks, given by the Susem front man, Danny Collins, in a telecast yesterday, gave governments five days to concede Nonette tax rebate demands.

"There will be no surrender" says PM

Within minutes of the telecast ending, Downing Street issued a statement which said there will be no change in government policy on taxation.

Collins did not, however, specify which of the major banks have been targeted nor how many are likely to be affected.

The broadcast, made at 9pm BST and with all the world's major markets closed, meant there could be no immediate effect on share values ... government stocks.

In early trading in Tokyo the Nikki index was down ... more 500 points. When Eu...

Susem threat crisis:

'There will be no surrender' - says Campbell

Finance ministers, banks in urgent talks

By **Phillip Brown**
General Correspondent

BRITAIN WILL NOT GIVE in to the Nonette demands for tax concessions, Edward Campbell said yesterday.

The Prime Minister said: "The current system of taxation in Britain was one that was agreed by a democratically elected government and could not ... changed by fiat to suit the interests ... any particular group. It is for Brita... elected representatives to decide how ... nation is taxed and not by anyone else."

The Chancellor, Peter Handel, appearing with the PM, said: "Even if we wanted to change Britain's levels and method of taxation we are not in a position to do so. Neither is any other government anywhere else.

"To make substantial changes to any country's tax regime, such as is being...

Arsenal thrash Milan 8-2!

Don Kirk's miracle hat trick

Milan-Gunners fans in running street clashes

By AMY CELESTE

WHAT A MATCH! WHAT AN OUTCOME - AN 8-2 WIN FOR ARSENAL!

IC Milan, the odds-on favourite for the IFEA Cup, went down to a staggeringly historic massive defeat at the hands of Arsenal at Rome's Forum Stadium last night. Arsenal, playing at their very best since the IFEA Cup competition began, ran rings around Milan's lacklustre defenders time and again.

Don Kirk, Gunner's 'Wild Child' centre forward, who scored within minutes of the off, set the whole tone of the match.

By the half-time whistle Kirk had kicked his second ball into the back of the Milan and bringing Arsenal's tally to 4-0. Ten minutes into the second half the wile-some Scot had scored his hat-trick. He would have had a fourth to his tally had it not been for the blatant one-sidedness of the Hungarian referee, Janos Begam.

Although Arsenal were on the top of their form the same could not be said of Milan. None of their forwards could

That Bank threat in full

By **Barry Russell**
Aliens activities reporter

The following is the full text of Collins' broadcast:

"HERE IN CONGRESS WE contribute a tenth of our incomes for the mutual benefit of us all. This amount is quite adequate to finance our collective needs.

"More than a billion people across the rest of the world have also become part of the Nonette movement.

"Each of these Nonette groups also contribute a tenth of their incomes to their community. This sum is spent for the collective benefit not just of their community but for those who are less financially fortunate as well.

"Collection and disbursement of this 10 per cent is without administrative cost. Every penny, cent, peso received and spent is fully accountable. Records of every transaction are also freely available for all to inspect.

"Such spending and its cost-free transference by and between Nonettes is of considerable fiscal saving to those who currently exercise administrative control - such as governments - over the wider population including those who are Nonettes.

"As was expressed on an earlier occasion, it is only equitable that the 10 per cent a Nonette gives to his or her community be deductible from what is currently taken from them by these governmental administrations by way of taxes.

"Unfortunately this most reasonable request has not, as yet, been acceded to by a single government. Indeed every one of them has used the right of their might to vindicate their continuing intransigence.

"Among the justifications given by governments for their refusal to reimburse Nonettes, is that they are not in a position to do so. They, cite that the taxes they levy are needed to repay money owed by them to their lenders.

"As the money unfairly taken from Nonettes by governments, has been given over to these lenders - such as banks - it is only reasonable that it is they who return it to the Nonettes.

"Unless governments themselves have not already undertaken to return to the Nonettes their money, all the money held by an already selected number of these lenders, will, in precisely five days from now, be removed and handed over to the Nonettes.

"This will include all of these institutions' overnight money market and inter-bank transactions. Any sum in excess of that due to Nonettes will of course be returned to these affected lenders.

"By cracking all of the real-time RSA ciphers and other encryption systems Banks and other lending institutions use to make and record monetary transfers, other currency bearing assets and securities, the Susem are able, effortlessly, to effect instantaneous redirection of them into Nonette custody.

"As every computer operating and retrieval system is and will continue to be monitored in real-time, any changes will of course, be monitored and simultaneously responded to."

playing truant and unless we made him attend we faced a Parenting Order and that he could be taken into care, I was very cross with him. I was even more worried when Rowan owned up to playing truant as well. I told Daffyd to give them both a good telling-off.

At the outset though, Daffyd said there was no point, we couldn't really do anything not with both of us out at work. It was pointless stopping their pocket money with them earning so much from their screens and we couldn't very well confiscate these. This would be tantamount to telling the boys education was bad, he said.

All the same I insisted he had a word with them, tell them their futures were at stake, and should this fail to get through to them, they should go to school for my sake. He took the boys for a walk but when they came back I could sense an atmosphere. I put up with their incessant humming the Nonette anthem, the one which sounds like the March of the Hebrew Slaves, for a few days, but in the end, especially when I discovered half their pals weren't going to school either, I couldn't take it any more and gave in.

But I don't know why I bothered though. A week later there was another letter from Glynn's school, this time from the teachers. They asked us to see he attended school for their sakes. If Glynn and the others didn't turn up, they said, the school would be amalgamated with another and half of them would lose their jobs. When Glynn saw the letter he said to write back telling them to study at screens of their own and earn a living that way.

Teachers aren't alone in being considerate all of a sudden, doctors are as well. In Llanelli, so Brenda at work said, her local health-centre has taken to knocking on doors inquiring if anyone is ill and can they treat them. Brenda says she has been told that even the drug companies are paying for the doctors to go round.

Of course they, just as the teachers and a few others, have been complaining like anything at the government's moves to cut back their hours, to say nothing of pay. They also know and I'm sure the government does as well, that they will be on a hiding to nothing if they go out on strike. All this will achieve is yet more people joining the Nonettes so as to use the Mormic health booths and then doctors will be needed even less.

Another group complaining at the loss of business are supermarkets. For once many of the local shops are undercutting them. Those in the village most certainly are and they, unlike the big stores, also take our Nonette money. Gwyneth in the Pendre says it's not just shops, or the Pendre either for that matter, which now rely on Nonette money for much of their turnover but their suppliers as well. Refuse to take the nonette, she said, means they lose the business, permanently. Do that, she said, and they will soon be out of business.

It is obvious why the prices are so low in Nonette shops, they are not charging for taxes. Mr Evans on the corner has gone so far as to put a big board in his window listing just how much is being saved if people pay in nonettes, the difference being what the government takes out of our 'old

Susem bank threat crisis:

Cash crash coming - claims expert

Gertrude Monbrow
Financial Editor

There were many instances of people's patience having snapped, as across Britain millions of people spent another frustrating day queuing at banks to withdraw a further tranche of £400 from their accounts.

Queues biggest yet

"Banks will soon have to close their doors," a top finance analyst claimed last night, as they will have run out of money. The former UK head of Morgans Bank, Robert Glendenning, speaking on *Money News* said that at the present rate of withdrawals, banks worldwide will soon run out of ready cash. Mr Glendenning said: "Regulatory authorities across the OECD and many other jurisdictions ensure banks keep a minimum of 20 per cent of their deposits in cash and realisable assets such as government bonds.

"Under normal circumstances banks will keep no more than 2-3 per cent of their deposits in cash form.

"At the current rate of withdrawals, this lower level will already have been passed banks," he said. "They will now be realising - cashing in - government bonds they hold. Central banks will provide cash against these but even here there are limits. Just now, I should imagine Central Bank printing facilities are working non-stop.

Fights break out

"When these Central Banks cannot supply with demand you have trouble, big trouble.

"Right now crunch-time must be just about on us. I would not be at all surprised if several banks are getting ready to close their doors to [their] customers and then things will really hit the fan."

Robert Glendenning

Mr Glendenning's comments, however, were dismissed by both the Association of Clearing Banks (ACB) and the Bank of ... said Mr Glendenning's comments were 'unhelpful' and would cause undue concern among ordinary bank customers. The spokesman said: "It is vital at this time not to inject any cause for panic in the current fluid situation."

Union threatens strike action

"The ACB assures customers, both large and small, that their money is absolutely safe. It must never be forgotten that all British banks operate under the strictest financial regulatory regime of any country in the w...

"It is not for noth... City of London's ... reputation for prob... envy of every oth... and has made L... world's premier ... foreign exchange...

"The only diffic... have currently ... logistics, of get... massive increases ... demanded by cust... where it is needed."

There were ... reports of scuffle... out. Police again w... to several incidents ... angry customers d... to withdraw the... ...ary chec...

Outrage at banks' cash lim...

'It's our money we want it back' - customers fume

By **Nicola Kay**
Home Affairs Correspondent

OUTRAGE WAS WIDESPREAD yesterday as millions of bank customers were told they could only withdraw limited sums of money from their accounts.

Fights and scuffles broke out at many banks as customers, having queued for hours, were told they faced a £400 daily limit.

Police were called at one Glasgow branch of the Royal Bank as more than two dozen building workers, wanting to cash their weekly pay cheques, were told of the £400 limit.

When they attempted to snatch the money bags of a security delivery which had ... its members had been subjected to threatening behaviour and insult language from aggrieved customers.

Queuing for hours to take even a limited sum of money from their accounts was frustrating enough for ordinary people for many businesses that depend on cash transactions, the £400 limited as ...

World chaos threat as bank cuts bite

Money markets panic as major banks cease Forex trading

By Steven Dunn
City Editor

INTERNATIONAL FINANCIAL markets were thrown into disarray yesterday as major banks withdrew from the foreign exchange markets.

Several of the major banking groups cited that ...

In the City there were many reports, although unconfirmed, that inter-bank and overnight lending have also been put on hold. Simon Rees of CSSB said: "All the major banks have gone short. They are all desperate to shore up their own market positions. They are all frightened of ...ing monetary flows," Rees said, "the banks dare not even divert any of their M1 or M2 position into secondary or third party domiciles other than their client base. But with the current heightened cash demand on the banks from that same retail client base they are also forced to ...

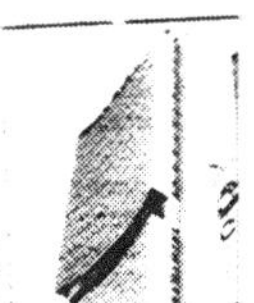

Banks cash clampdown

£400 daily limit "Come back tomorrow for more" – customers told

By Gary Marshell
Financial Correspondent

BRITAIN'S high street banks have imposed a £400 daily limit on all cash withdrawals.

This limit will continue, banks say, until the deadline of the Susem ultimatum has passed.

The cash limits are the consequence of yesterday's ... has access to a reasonable amount of it.

"It is important to bear in mind that the increased demand for cash is more than most bank branches usually have. But rest assured the banks are doing all in their power to get money to their branches.

"After all," the spokesman said, "it is not a case that banks do not have the funds ...

Susem threat crisis

Panicking banks urge 'urgent action' on tax

"Doors could close" – warns Clayings chief

By **Phillip Brown**
Financial Editor

INTERNATIONAL BANKS are reported to be in urgent crisis talks with governments in desperate bids to end the current worldwide cash panic. Banks such as Leviathan and Uber are said to be urging governments to agree Nonette tax demands before the international financial markets suffer irreparable damage. Most governments, including the UK and US, are reported to be resisting bank demands.

Financial analysts say that unless governments back down, banks will come under increasing pressure from shareholders to take unilateral action and cease making on demand cash payments to account holders.

Should banks be forced to take such moves, confidence in the banking system would be irreparably dashed, analysts say.

According to Dr Alan Carter, Head of Banking Studies, the University of Sheppey at Leysdown, banks are in a worse situation than they let on.

Dr Carter said: "From the banks' standpoint there is more riding on the money we deposit with them than merely its denominated worth.

"When you deposit £1,000 say, with your bank, it is obliged by the Bank of England, to keep £200 of this in cash and government- then free to lend the remaining £800.

"This it most certainly does and with interest. In return for the loan, the bank levies a charge over the borrower's assets. In banking jargon the bank has 'securitised' the loan.

"The bank then sells this securitised loan to a financial institution such as a pension fund.

"Your £1,000 has now, in the bank's eyes grown to £1,800. The bank now lends 80 per cent of this extra £800 and again sells on this securitised loan thus making the sum grow to £2,440.

"This 'new' money is then loaned yet again and so on, until eventually your £1,000 has grown to nearly £5,000.

"On every loan of this new money or nonexistent money rather, the bank charges arrangement fees as well as levying interest on it, which, of course is paid by the borrowers of these loans to the bank in 'real money'.

"In the course of a year a bank will earn more than £500 by way of fees and interest on your original £1,000 of which it will pay you £50, if that. In short, banks make all their money from having unfettered control of yours and other people's money.

"In one sense they are also making money out of money which, in actuality does not exist.

"Until recently banks have relied on the premise that only a tiny percentage of the original cash deposits will ever be withdrawn at any one time. When you withdraw £1 from your account you are, from the bank's point of view, also making off with a further £4 of theirs. Just as librarians regard the library's books as 'theirs' rather its members', banks also regard deposits as really 'theirs' rather than the customers.

"Thus the recent increased numbers of account holders withdrawing their money threatens to strip banks of all their money as well. In addition, because banks regard the money they receive as theirs there is little more than a few percentage points of deposits available for payment on demand.

"In short, banks have spent, been living off of their customers' money. And this is why they are in urgent talks with governments everywhere in urging them to agree Nonette terms for tax cuts without further delay lest they have to shut up shop or their doors."

According to many in the City no matter what deal is hammered out between government and banks, confidence in the banking system has been dealt a mortal blow from which it might not recover.

Wm Ill share slump... Arsenal win prosp...

Big bet set to slash bookie's pro...

By Anne-Marie Farthy

With Arsenal's surprise IFEA semi-final win over AC Milan, shares in Wm Ill nose-dived. By yesterday's close they had slumped to 124p a fall of 47p.

Although most City analysts think Ill's will have lost heavily on Milan's defeat, there are worries about the size of the payout they will have to make, should Arsenal bring the IFEA cup back to Highbury.

One wager in particular stands to wipe out the group's entire profits. At the time the £50,000 1,000-1 bet on an Arsenal IFEA ... sion the bookie now regrets, the stockmarket is punishing them for it.

Ill's however, is putting a brave face on the prospect of paying out the biggest win in history. A spokesman for Ill's said: "While Arsenal's win over AC Milan is good news for many English soccer lovers it was only the semi-final. The other half of this leg, the match between Dynamo Sofia and Moscow Spartek has not yet been played. On present form Moscow are odds on favourites to win and to win easily at that.

"Although we have shorten...

money', as his poster puts it.

However, now we Nonettes have the chance to deduct, or "elect to" in the government's jargon, our tithe from income tax, it might mean ordinary money will stage a comeback. But with the shops taking the nonette being cheaper than those which do not, it will still be widely accepted.

Another reason the nonette will be used is the government themselves. They are so stupid in not recognising the nonette as legal tender. In the Inland Revenue's eyes, so they say, a nonette is only worth the paper it is printed on. But all they are doing is driving goodness knows how many people to take their pay in nonettes with no tax deducted. How long this will go on for I shudder to think, but I do know that both the electronics factories at the end of the village are now paying most of their staff in nonettes.

And another thing. While they are saying the nonette is worth no more than paper, over in Llandrissant at the Royal Mint, so a friend of Daffyd at work told him, who has a brother working there, says everyone is on unlimited overtime printing up banknotes day and night. And where's the value for these I would like to know? Leastways we all know where the value of our nonettes come from. Our hard work studying, that is where.

While our Cilgerren Nonette deals in both moneys, the prices in nonettes for the Mormic and Love Patches are less than half that in ordinary money. And I have to say, the Patches are selling like hot cakes! As soon as new supplies arrive they are gone the same day. Of course with Gwyneth giving priority to Nonette members, the Patches have been a driving force in drumming up new members. (Gwyneth said, and though I promised not to tell anyone, even Mrs Mealam and some of her friends in WI have been buying them!).

There are still some people in Cilgerren who have yet to join our Nonette but their numbers are dwindling. The prospect of income tax rebates is bound to swing many of them to joining us. As Gwyneth says, "Who wants to pay money to the government?" All the same our Nonette has already grown to such a size it effectively shapes village life. Not that it's without challenges. It's quite a responsibility handling our money.

At the last meeting, Brian Jones, he's on the Finance Committee, said our monthly sales from Patches, our newspaper and the Mormic as well as the tithe money we keep back for ourselves, are now more than £50,000 a month. I was surprised at this, well, we only started our Nonette a month and a half ago! Gwyneth has asked what we should spend it on and she's put up a sheet in the Pendre for ideas. Of course there's been complete agreement to continue funding Llangoedmor Almshouses up at Penraldt Fach.

With the Council cuts the place was in a terrible state. There were so few staff that the old people had to fend for themselves half of the time. And with the latest cuts it meant there would be just two staff to look after more than a hundred. But Cilgerren's Nonette has taken Llangoedmor under its wing.

Susem threat crisis: First cracks appear

Luxembourg agrees Nonette terms

Germans could follow

Freida Mersch
In Luxembourg

WITH JUST THREE days to go before the Susem bank threat takes effect, the tax haven Principality of Luxembourg has agreed with international banks to accept Nonette terms for tax cuts

From midnight all Luxembourgers who are members of the Nonette movement will be able to cut their tax payments by 10 per cent of their incomes

In return for Nonette tax concessions, banks have agreed a one year loan repayment "holiday" of Luxembourg's sovereign debt The Principality's Prime Minister, Henri Etrange, speaking after the day long negotiations said: "We hope the agreement [on tax concessions] will satisfy the aspirations of all concerned

"My government will have to legislate some major changes on how we are to spend our money but we have at least been given some breathing time in which to do it."

The Head of Banc Luxembourg, Eduard Du Bious who led the consortium of banks negotiating with the government, said: 'Today both sides have struck a noble agreement.

"While we have both make painful concessions, the outcome will be to the greater benefit of all citizens' businesses We have now shown the way for other countries to follow."

Even as M Du Bious spoke, there were reports of several of the German Lander (states) also entering negotiations with a number of leading German and other banks for a package of tax concessions

Both North Rhine Westphalia and Palatinate as well as Hesse which contains the major financial centre of Frankfurt, are said to be among the Lander taking part in the talks

Although not responsible for Germany's tax regime, the Landar play an important part in its collection

If a sizable number of Lander do agree these Nonette tax demands, it will be a major blow to the Federal government.

Most of the major international banks have indicated that time is running out for the necessary negotiations between them and other governments including the US and UK's.

Henri Etrange, Luxembourg's PM announcing capitulation

Susem threat crisis

California in tax talks with bank

Bank majors poised for Golden State domicile

Joanne Miller
from Sacramento

With the threat of Susem action against banks looming closer, the legislature of California, America's richest, most populous state is reported to be on standby to rubber stamp emergency laws giving tax concessions to Nonettes

California Governor, John Richmond, revealed yesterday that he and his staff have been in secret negotiations with all the major banking corporations operating in the state. Governor Richmond said he was optimistic agreement will be reached between his administration and banks to overcome California's public banking crisis

The Governor was hopeful that an agreement will be ready for signing later today or early tomorrow

There are indications, however, that the deal with the banks will involve their

San Francisco, banking city of California and its most Nonetted

to claw back 10 per cent of the incomes they currently pay in both income and sales taxes.

Republican rightwingers, such as Vaughn Hollis and Ralph Chetwyne, who have been campaigning against the Nonette movement, are reported to be against tax concessions which will benefit the Alien backed movement.

But faced with the prospect ...lapse ... well ...e

major banks relocating their operations to the state, they are unlikely to vote against any deal the Governor strikes with banks

Although the US Inland Revenue Service (IRS) is the nation's tax collecting authority, it is unlikely they could ever be in a position to enforce payment or collection in California if the state itself has contrary legislation

Should such a 10 per cent

tax deducti... between C... banks, then... have w... immediate... throughout... states acros... pressed by... public to fo... tax conc... Nonettes.

It has b... during the... the crisis,... has not bee...

Susem crisis threat

Governments in "follow my neighbour" as Banks threaten: "Agree tax cuts or we leave"

Falling like ninepins

London, Washington still holding out

By Albert Wishbone
Financial Editor

European governments were queuing up to announce cave-ins to bank brokered Nonette tax concessions

Following Luxembourg's deal with leading banks to sanction tax cuts in return for rescheduling sovereign debt, a slew of others states followed suit As of this morning only Britain, among European countries, was holding out against agreeing tax cuts to Nonettes

Within hours of Luxembourg's announcement, neighbouring Belgium had followed suit Thirty minutes later both the Netherlands and German governments said they had signed similar deals with a consortium of banks

With announcements following one another in such quick succession it soon became evident governments of many, if not all countries, have been in secret negotiations with their opposite banking numbers on tax reductions

Because of the similarity of the agreements it also became evident that banks worldwide had been conducting negotiations in concert with one another

Following the Italian government's announcement, a Banca Scaltro official, speaking off the record, said: "We made governments an offer they couldn't refuse. Either they agreed our financial packages in return for tax concessions, or we closed the banking system down in their country and left them to answer to their public "

The picture across east and south Asia was the same Once one government publicly announced they had struck a deal with the banks, others quickly

The Japanese, one of the last Asian governments to announce agreement, was greeted with widespread cheers and relief: most of the country's banks had already closed their doors But in being the world's second biggest economy, Japan's agreement on tax cuts is also the most significant It is bound to increase pressure on both the US and the UK to also agree similar reductions.

With just two days remaining before the Susem deadline kicks in, financial analysts in New York and London are factoring in that both US and UK governments along with their Canadian counterparts will agree terms in line with other leading economies

With California set to announce agreement with banks and a slew of other western US States set to follow suit, both the White House and the IRS are set to come under heavy Wall Street pressure to agree immediate Nonette tax concessions

Such is the degree of certainty [of agreement] on Wall Street that it has already factored in the effects of such on deal on bank and finance house stocks, all of which have come up off the floor.

Citi analyst, Kathy Sontag, said: "With the rebound of stocks in both sectors it means that at least for the corporations concerned, they are now worth more than their break-up values "

However, Sontag, like other bank watchers think the financial institutions have received such a mauling at the hands of their account holders, it will be some time yet before their public standing and stock values return to pre-crisis levels.

Public confidence in bank and the

Susem threat crisis

Campbell throws in towel

"Britain's sovereignty compromised" - says bitter PM

By **Phillip Brown**
Westminster Correspondent

THE GOVERNMENT HAS AGREED WITH A consortium of the world's leading banks to give tax concessions to members of the Nonette movement in return for a year-long repayment holiday of government debt and percentage interest reduction.

Under the terms of the agreement, members of the Nonette movement will receive tax refunds equivalent to 10 per cent of their salaries In return Nonettes have to provide proof they have paid this refund to their local Nonette group

The cost to the Inland Revenue of the concessions has been calculated at an annual £4-6bn, though this figure could rise if more people joined the Nonettes However, if the tax deductions of Nonette owned businesses are taken into account as well VAT losses, the Treasury could be looking at a year-on-year revenue shortfall in excess of £10bn

Balanced against this figure however, is the saving of lower interest on Britain's sovereign debt as well as savings on the rescheduling of the actual repayments Some City analysts have gone as far as to predict that the overall effects to the Treasury will be broadly neutral.

Edward Campbell, announcing the agreement with the banks to Parliament, said: "Today is a sad one Britain has been given no choice other than to surrender a degree of its sovereignty.

However, given the urgency of stabilising dangerously unsettled conditions within both the financial markets and banking sectors, the government has had no alternative other than agree a revision of Britain's system of taxation

"Should we have failed to assent to this, then international support for the pound would have been in jeopardy.

"However, in so agreeing we have been able to win for Britain advantageous terms

...d with

Not only has the place seen a lick of paint for the first time in years, but all its plumbing is now working properly as well. Although we are paying for extra staff, the almshouses themselves are producing an extra "income stream", as Brian Jones put it. With everyone at Llangoedmor enrolled in our Nonette it didn't take long for some of them to 'graduate' to their individual screens. A few are a bit on the slow side but as Gwyneth says, none of them are watching daytime TV any longer. They haven't the time or inclination she said.

What is more, now they have all had several sessions in the Mormic, some are getting a bit of life back. Megan Davies, 'Our lady of the Mormic', who has been on a course in using it, says for older people, once they have had a few goes in it, their hearts and other parts of their bodies start showing signs of renewal. So when Gwyneth said (after I promised not to tell anyone) she had orders for Love Patches from Llangoedmor I wasn't really as surprised as I said I was. All the same though, I dread to think of the goings on up there, well most of them are even older than my parents.

It is not just old people who are benefiting from the Mormic, we all are. As Megan Davies says, the main point of the Mormic is to keep healthy people healthy. Regular attendance she says nips anything nasty in the bud. And since we have been using it I have to say none of us have had as much as a cold. Mrs Evans next door says her little boy has not had one single asthma attack since using the Mormic, and looking at him you can see he's got colour back in his cheeks for the first time in ages. Another thing I have noticed is Daffyd. He's lost a bit of tummy since using the Mormic, well it can't be the food because I haven't had him on a diet for months.

Anyway, getting back to the Library. The present crisis is worrying but it's what is coming that I'm really dreading. When I was up in London I got talking with Roger White of the Westminster Business Library and he said he had been told in confidence by a senior government economist that because of the income tax rebates, Whitehall has drawn up secret emergency plans for sweeping cuts to the Local Government Support Grant. It will mean, he said, Councils everywhere forced to cut back to providing little more than essential services and obviously these won't include libraries. From what Roger White said he was also told, it will mean thousands of compulsory redundancies and early retirement all round.

I had wanted to mention this at our next branch meeting as a matter of urgency, but as I have promised him not to tell anyone, I can't say anything. All the same though, it's very worrying. Well, I'm too young to retire and if we are all to lose our jobs what will I do? But it will be so sad if the Library has to close, especially now everyone is using us again.

PRESIDENT'S POLICY POSER

To act or not to act on the Nonettes is President Warren's dilemma

Gordon Richardson
In Washington

Following the enforced tax concessions to the Nonette movement, US government has suffered a yet further blow to its authority

The tax concessions coming as they do against the backdrop of the continuing deteriorating security situation, places President Warren between a rock and a hard place

Should the President act to curb the Nonettes' growing power, he will automatically alienate the estimated 50m people in the US who have now joined the movement But even should he attempt to use military force against them he then also risks alienating the many more Americans who – following the Panamanian and Mexican fiascos - are against further US military action of any kind both at home as well as abroad

Not that the President has much room of manoeuvre to enforce any authority With the continuing presence of the Susem, it is extremely doubtful (to put it mildly) if any military or law enforcement agency could muster a single soldier or policeman to act against the Nonettes

However, if the President does not curb the Nonettes and their power and influence continues to grow, he risks seeing one area of the country after another slipping out of both State and Federal control

The present furore over three counties in the New Vermont will be as nothing if the states of Washington and Oregon break away

If California or any part of it does likewise, then the US security situation will rapidly unwind

It is against this background that many of those to the right of the political spectrum are urging the President to take action to protect the integrity of the US

As they see it, it is vital to act now or it will be too late It is known that many in the Department of Defense as well as in many states' National Guard are eager to take on the Nonette movement

Big business across the US is also calling for action against the Nonettes. The oil and energy lobbies are demanding an end of what that claim as unfair competition from the Nonettes

Adding to this is that as the influence of the Nonettes grows, many more 'mainstream' businesses are claiming that they are losing out to Nonette companies

However, as more and more districts of the US become 'Nonetted' it is impossible for businesses to operate unless they too join the movement

In doing so, of course, these businesses are not only disregarding all forms of national legislation but also begin trading in the Nonette currency as well as paying their staff in it

In turn this is exerting pressure from 'straight' businesses for preferential treatment on taxation. Should there be any tax concessions given to

Susem crisis threat: aftermath

Banks count the cost

By Bruce Cuneff
In New York

"OH SURE WE'VE taken a hit," says Ed Rutters, New York Head of Morgans. "But leastways, we're still open for business, which is better than being closed," he adds ruefully.

According to Rutters, major banks, in settling the 'Banks and Tax' crisis, have foregone the equivalent of a year's profits

"But what alternative did we or governments have?" he asks "Either we wrapped up deals with enough of them and quickly, or we'd be out of business, governments out of its mind with the mother of all financial crisis

"And you can take it from me," he said, "it was we banks who had to twist governmental arms not the other way round It is also we banks who're funding these tax cuts not they "

However, what is now worrying Rutter and other senior bankers are the longer term consequences of the crisis

One of the casualties is confidence in the banking system itself. "Once people lose trust in banks they place faith in the underside of their mattresses instead", says Joel

"Another casualty" says Earl, "is the wider financial market The past few days has blown the frailty of the international financial system wide open Already they are calls for a full overhaul of the way money markets operate including the removal of the opacity surrounding so much of their operations

"These demands come not only from ordinary bank customers but from leading members of the investment industry", he says

Mark Withers, Head of Fidelity Trust, a leading US mutual fund (unit trust), said: "The gambling simply has to stop From now on in there

Susem threat crisis: The Winners

Nonette numbers set to surge

By Albert Wishbone
Social Affairs Editor

As the full impact of Nonette tax cuts sinks in, governments around the world are counting the cost of their concessions to the Alien backed movement International banks are also counting the losses to their bottom lines.

Both governments and banks have to come to terms with a new and fast growing rival for peoples' attentions and allegiances: the Nonettes

There is now a real risk that should governments, especially those in the developed world, alienate their populations, there will be a flow of people in the Nonettes' direction

Tax cuts offer means millions could join Alien movement

Pressure is now on government's to match, if not better, the tax and other advantages of belonging to the Nonette movement. Should they fail in this and other 'hearts and minds' initiatives, the remorseless rise in Nonette numbers will accelerate

As soon as more than 20 per cent of a population group ... join a mass movement, then the influence they wield over the rest of society effectively shapes its functioning The rise and influence of trade union movements on the rest of working populations is an example of this

The Nonette movement though, is more than just a mass organisation. Whereas the likes of trade unions function within the confines of the society they evolve from, keep to its laws and regulations, Nonettes are increasingly functioning as a totally separate society altogether. And on all levels into the bargain.

High Streets expect mini boom

Although critics of the Nonettes have levelled that it is only able to exist under the protection of the Susem umbrella and benefits from their soufin energy units, the movement itself has now become an independent force in its own right. And an increasingly powerful one as well

According to the UK Nonette movement twice the number of people joined the movement during the week of the crisis than the week before One of the reasons given for joining, so the Nonettes claim, are their community banks

The whereabouts of every pound deposited with a Nonette bank is known to and has the agreement of its account holder, whether it be held on call access, loaned or invested and where.

This level of reassurance is something 'straight' banks are going to be hard put to match It may well also be to their cost

The inability of high street banks to pay customers their money during the crisis has dented confidence in the banking system to a far greater degree than financial institutions have so far acknowledged, in public at least

Should there be any significant shift of account holders of high street banks to Nonette ones, then the financial system will be hit in more ways than just the loss of bank customers.

Nonettes also trade in their own currency, the Nonette It is entirely separate from the rest of the world's currencies

The Nonette's valuation is also formulated on an entirely different basis from 'straight' currencies as well Every Nonette in circulation is backed by a unit increase of their members' abilities through either study or labour

The strength of this basis of currency valuation over the weakness of 'straight'

MILAN FANS CLA... 'ALIENS 'HAD' OU...

By Edward McSw...

AC MILAN'S ENTIRE first squad, including star strikers, Begamo, Ozukini and Potere are feared kidnapped by Susem for forced sex.

Following IC Milan's shock 2-8 semi-final defeat against Arsenal, both police and Italian Football authorities, in cooperation with IC's management to unearth details of the team's abduction. According to Milan's management the entire team were staying in a top secret location which was also heavily guarded.

"We were robbed of sure victory" - IC boss claims

Uppermost in the minds of the inquiry teams mind is the possibility of spies in league with the Aliens who betrayed IC's whereabouts to them.

IC Milan's boss, Benito Carosso, said that no more than a handful of people knew where his team was staying.

Speaking yesterday, Snr Carosso said: "My players were staying in a remote location, they did not travel anywhere in the open air, even the coach that transported them to practice did so in the hotel's underground car-park.

"The stadium where they played was overseen by a helicopter hovering above the grounds.

"We had more than a 100 security guards both surrounding the stadium and inside it as well. And still our boys were taken.

"It now appears they were not the only ones either but all the ground staff as well were taken by these Alien sex fiends."

Has con-man Collins struck again?

"Susem bank threat a scam" ... code guru

By Tony Perry
Security Correspondent

SUSEM FRONTMAN, Danny Collins, conned the world's governments, banks and public alike into believing the Aliens had cracked the financial markets' computer codes, a top cipher expert claimed yesterday.

Leonard Merkle, whose organisation, Anorak De-crypts, advises scores of leading companies in the financial sector on data security, said there has not been any evidence that security of any of the major banks' computer systems have been tampered with

Mr Merkle said: "Apart from our own scrutiny of client codifications, every single [data security] industry source we have contacted confirms there has not been one encryption compromise incident

"At Anorak we were mystified as to how it could be possible to hijack real-time RSA ciphers for the simple reason that the encryption base as well as the encryption itself is always changing

"What you have had is this guy Collins coming on the television, saying these Susem have cracked the banks' encryptions, everyone believes him even though he provides not one iota of proof

"He chooses a time when every bank across the world is closed and by the time they do open there's an around the block queue outside wanting their money out

"From then on, no matter what we or anyone might say, no one is interested in listening, let alone in believing us," he said

Further doubts over the validity of Collins' Susem threat are also being voiced by others in the computer code encryption profession.

Collins, who is still wanted by the police for fraud and false accounting and criminal

COLLINS' CASH IMPOUNDED

Conman's $500,000 external Miami account found

By Richard Rankie
In Miami

AN account in a Miami bank containing over US$500,000 and thought to belong to wanted fraudster, Daniel Collins, has been unearthed and impounded by US banking authorities.

Picked up in a swoop of dormant external accounts by the bank during the recent bank and tax crisis, the $500,000 is believed to be part of the proceeds of Collins' murky business deals.

An official for the bank said: "Most of the dormant externals [accounts] escrowed probably belong to drug trade Latinos but the account name of this one not being [Latino] along with its coinciden-

That Paceillo didn't really mean it, it was all just pretend, is as far as I am concerned beside the point. That she has achieved what she wanted by feint, front and pretense is all well and good but the outcome means that for all intents and purposes, I can kiss the remainder of my money in Miami goodbye.

If it wasn't for what I am making from Patches, strips and sprays I might be forced to take a day job. Though the income from all three is handy, I still have to work hard for it. Because sales overseas have seriously exceeded expectations I have to labour from early morning right round to noon, and even sometimes after then. Though I have delegated as much of management as possible to the cooperatives I still need a hands-on approach to the really important matters such as counting and accounting the money.

Even here there are difficulties. Hevea latex's fourfold price rise eroding margins is bad enough, but the new Boro and Huitoto directors are more of a worry. Still filled with the novelty of their new found role they keenly scrutinise every area of activity. I have my work cut out shuffling funds from one ledger to another. I just hope I can keep signs of the minor petty cash imbalances from their inquisitive eyes long enough for my wager to pay out.

I had another worry for a while when the doings of Tearo and troupe became public, but thankfully the commonsense of Mammon ensured the final still takes place. With only the Bulgarians to beat it will be a walkover for Arsenal, especially after Tearo's troupe have paid the young men from Sofia a pre-match get-together. With my winnings, not only will the losses in Miami be made good, and petty cash borrowings balanced, but enough remaining to afford lasting comfort. The only worry I will have with this is the enjoyable one of stashing the winnings somewhere secretively safe, like Liechtenstein (one place at least which will never be Nonetted).

I had another worry gnawing. Though academic, it had been dogging since I spoke with Milophenia about planets and my continuing attempts to see Saturn, Jupiter, their moons. During the night-time hours searching the heavens, given up and stared at the stars instead, it was there nagging me the more. How can the Universe be constant, the Anthropic one, yet at the same time be expanding as Earthly astronomers say they are seeing and the furthest moving away the fastest? However, since talking to Terbal (I caught him in front of his TVs waiting for the Sofia Dynamo, Moscow Spartak semi-final kick off) I have not only the answer but understanding, explanation, to much more besides. Though, and as ever, I have been left with yet more questions begging answers.

That the Sun circles the Earth, Terbal said, is based on observation of the seemingly obvious and as a concept serves most of our planetary pursuits well enough. In the same manner, using the speed of light (it no more than a segment of Secondary wave modulation, he reminded) as a constant is also

Argentina reneges on IMF debts – again

But fears others will follow grow

By Rita Pynya
In Buenos Aires

Pleading special case status, Argentina has defaulted on its sovereign debt to the International Monetary Fund.

The Fund has confirmed that the $100m payment due against the troubled Latin American country's $250bn debt to the IMF has not been paid.

Argentinean finance minister, Hernado Mendoza, said that because his country had been forced to substantially increase defence spending in combating the Nonette threat in neighbouring Brazil and Chile, there was nothing left to pay creditors.

Medoza also said that his government is having difficulty in cutting Argentina's public sector debt. Sr Mendosa said: "Because of the Nonette takeover of our northern provinces, we are not in any position to alienate any sectors of working population including public employees.

"Should we do so, not only will they go out on strike," Mendoza said, "but also we will end up driving yet more of them and other people into the hands of the Nonettes.

"Then it will not just be Argentina but the entire region that will have even bigger security troubles than it has presently."

Many bankers however, were dismissive of Argentina's claims, many consider that it is, once again, crying wolf as well as attempting to blackmail the IMF into withholding sanctions against their overseas holdings.

Susem bank threat: the losers

Banks lose 500,000 accounts to Nonettes

Simple and safe wins over sophistication and uncertainty

By Albert Wishbone
Economics Editor

Since the banking and tax crises, High Street banks have lost more than 500,000 accounts to Nonette banks.

Big banks' setback

The huge scale of the move away from mainstream banks represents a major setback to wider banking system as a whole.

Though Nonettes form the majority of those leaving the formal banking system they are by no means the only ones.

What is worse for High Street banks, is that the move to Nonette banks while showing no signs of slowing may in fact be set to accelerate.

Safe havens

Nonette community banks are seen by their account holders not only as safe havens for their money but also readily accessible institutions as well. They also provide the alternative currency of the 'nonette' – the movements' own currency - which is now viewed by increasing numbers of people as safer than sterling.

'Old time' banking is back

As a result of the banking crisis, increasing numbers of people are switching to what they see as the simpler yet more reliable system of 'old-time' banking offered by Nonette community banks. Not for them the complexity of e-banking, direct debits, ATMs and the other plethora of modern banking 'products' but instead what they see as small, simple local banks, where those one side of the counter know everyone on the other. As most Nonette banks are housed above a pub, in local meeting halls and the like, there is, apart from evening opening hours, a feeling of homeliness and familiarity.

'Keep banking simple'

Paul Hammond, manager of a Nonette bank in Stroud said: "Nonette banks are based on the 'keep it simple' principle.

"For too long," he says, "people have suffered a banking system tailored for the benefit of banks rather than their customers.

Big banks' hidden charges

"The services and products provided by these banks are not only more complicated than they need be but customers are charged for them whether they like it or not. Even the services that these banks claim are free have hidden charges behind them.

"And of course, as the recent banking crisis has shown, these banks make huge profits from customers' money which they never pass back to them.

10 per cent interest paid

"In contrast, our customers have a straight forward paying-in-cum-account book and 10 per cent annual interest on current accounts plus a share of whatever they agree to invest their savings in."

Total anonymity

Although simple in operation, Nonette banks offer a sophistication which High Street banks will be hard put to match. One is anonymity.

Account holders are known by the Nonette number and not by name. Another is the opportunity for customers to participate in the running of their bank including overseeing where their funds are invested and lent.

Pound/nonette conversion

Another, is opportunity to exchange pounds for nonettes. As increasing numbers of people's salaries are paid in nonettes, the number of accounts in the currency are also set to increase and is again something ordinary banks are unable to offer.

As the Nonette movement itself generates increases, the number of nonette currency notes - principally through their study credits – increasing amounts are available for use as ordinary cash

Nonette's value rising

With the upward revaluation of the nonette against sterling, the transfer of pounds into nonettes is also increasing.

There is of course, the funding available to local Nonette banks from the Nonette movement itself. Such is the size of its collective income that it is now, in financial term and apart from the government, Britain's biggest organisation.

The Nonette movement by paying for the goods and services it buys from the mainstream companies in sterling, ensures that its Nonette banks are able to get rid of the pounds they receive in exchange for nonettes.

Nonette sources say it is anticipated the increase of Nonette currency notes in circulation will march step in step with value of sterling use by the movement's members.

Sterling set to fall

Should the nonette continue its upward rise against sterling and ever more people use the nonette in place of it, then the value of pound will fall. And should the pound's fall not be checked then High Street banks could be faced with a glut of

Pontiff accuses Susem of 'soccer skullduggery'

Pope denounces Aliens as evil abomination

By **Holly Heath**
In Rome

POPE PIUS XIII roundly castigated the Aliens for their attacks against Europe's leading soccer clubs.

The Pope said that the latest Susem abductions were yet further evidence of their evil intentions towards all mankind

As fears for the missing Milan players rise, the Pope, using his strongest words of condemnation against the Susem yet, said: "Our hearts go out to all those young men who are held in the clutches of these evil Aliens.

"Christians across the world must pray for the safe deliverance of this flower of youth. We must pray that they are spared the subjection and defilement other have suffered at the hands of these daughters of the devil incarnate."

Roger Fry also reports from Rome: Vatican sources denied yesterday that the Pope's outburst against the Susem has anything to with reports that he had bet heavily on a Milan IFEA semi-final win.

Cardinal Petro Connalggi said: "His Holiness does not do this sort of thing, although he, like many of us may have prayed for Milian's success in

INFLATION FEARS RISE

Massive rise in money supply

By Ross Capulyard

In the wake of the banking and tax crisis, the Bank of England has increased Britain's money supply to its highest level in recent years

According to the latest monthly figures released by the Bank yesterday, the rise in the value of money in circulation is set to increase by 10 per cent This comes on top last month's record rise

The Bank said the increase was a precautionary measure and will not mean the new notes will necessarily go into immediate circulation Fears were voiced however, that the rise in the supply will cause inflationary pressures

Roy Bellamy, economics editor of *Big Worries Monthly* said: "Increasing the [money] supply at this time is about the worst thing the Bank could sanction. They appear not to realise they're adding high octane to an economy already smouldering with inflation

"Last month's money supply rise was as dangerous as it was unwarranted but since then there's been a whole lot more cash pumped into the economy

Most of the cash withdrawn from banks during the banking tax crisis is still out there By now it will be burning holes in people's pocket books and purses

"There has not been, however, any increase in retailers' inventories Thus, you have all the ingredients for runaway inflation."

The massive rise in the money supply has another dimension Until recently the Bank of England had been charged witht maintaining a tight rein on inflation

But this is now a role or concern at least from which it has quietly disengaged itself The Bank appears to be, or has bee

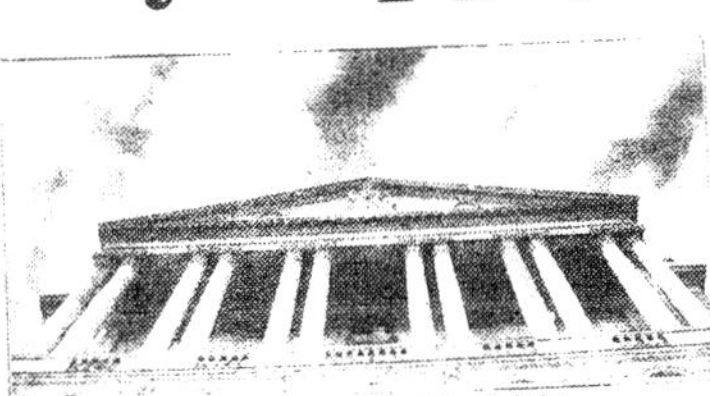

The Bank of England is no longer concerned about inflation

Nonettes' penis replacement offer

Regrow chance for assault victims - but there are drawbacks

By Alan Bodings
Medical Correspondent

THE Nonettes have offered the hope of new penises to more 100,000 victims of Susem sexual encounters The offer, however, comes with a big drawback: join the Nonettes first, then study hard

In yesterday's Susem telecast, Nonette front-man Danny Collins, said the Aliens had given the Nonettes the medical technology to regrow limbs and other body parts.

Showing 'before and after' clips of people who, he claimed, have had their legs, arms, noses and pertinently, penises regrown, Collins said, that just as reptiles and other animals regrew lost limbs, so could humans.

Collins said, that although it is perfectly possible to live an ordinary life without a pen-is, he knew, speaking as a man himself, just how important to male esteem it was possessing one.

Collins said that while it is best not to lose one's penis in the first place and that being a member of the Nonettes is one way of ensuring this, every man who has lost theirs can now have another re-grown courtesy of the Nonettes

Collins then spelt out the Nonettes' terms for replacement penises: join the Nonettes, provide 1,000 study credits However, Collins also said that for a fortnight only there is a 'Buy two get one free' special offer, to all Nonette groups

Once replacement hopefuls have sufficient study credits and the endorsement of their Nonette, they are free to visit the body parts replacement centre in the Nonette Congress

Collins said that their technology is so advanced it takes less than a day to regrow even

useful as a workaday guide. But none the less the notion of it being universally uniform is as proven as the Sun's circling once was.

Terbal said our Milky Way galaxy is, in relative terms, close to a cluster of other galaxies and collectively called by us the 'Local Group', and light from one side of it currently takes 5 million years to reach the other. Distance enough, he said, to observe if there is any pulling apart. But, he said, even observations of our own astronomers evidence the opposite, all our 'Local Group's galaxies are coming closer together. There are, he said, even grander groups of galaxies. One, known to us as the Great Wall, is a hundred times the size of ours. But no matter how huge, every single one is doing the same, gathering in, not spreading out.

Terbal reminded me yet again that Earthly astronomers' theory of a 'big bang' universe beginning and ensuing expansion is just that, a theory, nothing more. He added that rather than it being formulated from fact, facts had interpreted to fit and flaws ignored, no matter how telling these may be, such as 'their' universe's missing nigh 99 per cent of its substance.

When Earthly astronomers peer through their telescopes, what they are actually seeing, Terbal said, are Tertiary and Secondary waves, such as stars, being carried within an undulating Primary wave, the tops of which appear to travel faster than the troughs, such as the one we are currently in. This is evidenced, he said, by galaxies, as seen from Earth, appearing increas-ingly laterally ovate the nearer the waves' crests they were.

Our Universe, Terbal said, is as a rolling, joined-up figure-of-eight shaped soliton wave akin to the single sidedness of a mobius strip. According to Susem observations, he said, there is an entwined necklace of such strips.

"Does this mean," I asked, "there are other universes?"

Terbal said this could be a definition but added that our universe's Primary wave wasn't a single sheet as such but a myriad of intermeshing minor ones just as a rope is composed of strands and strings of strands. He also said some objects observed in one 'universe' were within strands originating in others. As he mentioned this I wondered was this why (our astronomers' convoluted calculations aside) some stars we see are older than our universe is understood to be?

Terbal likened what's occurring to blooming and fruiting. The soliton mobius strands of Primary waves go smoothly round and round but after a while imperfection, Secondary waves, appear. This imperfection spreads and eventually contages the rest of the strand. In turn, some of this sea-like surface of Secondary waves, energy, spumes into Tertiary ones. Those of hydrogen at first but from these fuse those of helium, from them berylium, they oxygen and carbon. It is only when these last four have honed to the ratio of 28 with 16 noughts, can their mobius strand be said to come into Anthropic bloom, their subsequent fruitings are galaxies.

NONETTE REVALUED BY 10%

New rate now N1 = £1.39, $1.21

By Oliver Stoneburger

Within the space of a fortnight the Nonette Central Bank has revalued its currency - the nonette - by a further 10 per cent The pound is now worth N0.66.

According to Nonette publications, the Nonette Central Bank gave the rapid inflationary rises in both North American and European economies as the reason for downgrading their currencies.

Retailers trading mainly in nonettes are their stocks rise as well as profits.

For the estimated 2m people in the UK who now take all or part of their salaries in nonettes, it means that in the space of little more than a month they have had an effective 20 per cent pay rise relative to the rest of us who are still paid in sterling

This growing disparity however, is bound to see an increase of people opting to be paid in the Nonette currency.

Shopkeepers who

What effect the change will have on larger retailers such as supermarkets remains to be seen There will increasing pressure, however, for some of them at least, also to begin trading in nonetties

Response in the City to the rise in the nonette's value is that it is a shot across the bows of the Bank of England and other central banks

Missing Milan players found in mountains

Entire team brought down strapped across backs of pack mules

By **Lisa Biggles** in Rome and **John Wiggens** in Ascoli

THE AC MILAN SOCCER TEAM, abducted by the Susem has been found in a remote region of the Appenine Mountains.

An AC Milan spokesman said that the entire team, along with all the support staff kidnapped with them were found alive but extremely exhausted and dehydrated.

They all are now reported recovering in hospital at Ascoli, 60 miles north of Rome.

The entire AC Milan side, including their multi-million dollar strikers Begamo, Ozukini and Potere were brought down the mountains strapped over the backs of pack mules

The entire AC Milan squad, including their support staff were discovered by shepherds visiting isolated summer pastures on the upper slopes of the 8,000 feet high Mont Vettore.

The players were first seen by Davido Lurgio the young son of one of the shepherds from the small village of Astorara

Davido said: "I heard bleatings coming from the woodland by the side of my father's pasture. I thought they were from some of our flock caught in the trees maybe

"But when I ran to where they came from I saw these men crawling through the undergrowth. At first I thought them to be evil spirits and I was very afraid

"However, when one of the men said he was Eric Begamo, I saw that it was indeed him.

"I called to my father. Soon he had telephoned to our village for assistance. Because Mont Vettore is so steep there are not roads, only

"Even helicopters cannot come so high Because there were so many men there was not even enough mules in Astorara and so those in Castro and even Balzo were also required to bring the men down to where helicopters could come"

Davido and his father gave the Milan players sheep's milk during the hours it took for the mule train to arrive He also described how, because the players were so exhausted from their ordeal and were no condition to sit on the mules, they had to be laid and tied across their backs.

After the Milan players had been brought down from the mountains, a fleet of helicopters whisked the men to hospital in Ascoli

Dr Francisco Ogami of Ospedale Generale in Ascoli, said that all the men were suffering from extreme exhaustion and had suffered serious and prolonged assaults during their period of abduction.

Dr Ogami said: "We are hopeful that some of the men will make a full recovery, but we are not altogether confident due to the seriousness of injuries sustained while held captive."

For some of the players, Dr Ogami said. "Their playing

HUGE HIGH ST BOOM TAKES O

By Doug Addick
Consumer Reporter

HIGH STREET SALES are booming and shopkeepers are smiling Britain's sudden spending spree has caught many retailers by surprise and already there are signs of shortages of many items.

"Its like Christmas" say retailers

Having withdrawn all their money from their accounts during the banking tax crisis, many people are in no hurry to put it back

With confidence in everything financial at an all-time low, the British public is embarking with a vengeance on their favourite pastime: shopping.

One electrical retailer in Reading said demand has been so strong and products from his suppliers so delayed, that he has had to introduce a form of rationing

He said: "I just keep putting my prices up, just like everyone else" He also said that prices on the high street had to rise anyway because suppliers are putting their prices up as well

Coinciding with this sudden sales bonanza are the banks' lending to retailers Eager, though some say 'desperate' to claw back some of their lost account business, especially credit cards, banks are

Inflation lets rip

"And it's too late to stop now" - says think-tank

By Gary Marshell
Economics Correspondent

BRITAIN'S INFLATION is rising at the fastest in more than a decade and is set to accelerate. If High Street prices continue to rise at the present rate, experts predict that the RPI is set to show a year-on-year increase of a staggering 25 per cent

A survey released yesterday by Consumer Watch, a leading retail think-tank, shows that since the end of the banking tax crisis, sales in every retail sector have witnessed unprecedented rises in demand

The survey says the surge in High Street sales was initially per cent rise in the money supply but now other factors were at work as well

John Wilkenson, one of the compilers of the survey, said: "It's a classic inflation scenario of too much money chasing too few goods But this time the increases of money in people's pockets is coming from several sources and all at the same time

"Because trust in banks has slumped as a result of the recent crisis, people are spending their money instead.

"Banks, losing so much of their retail customer base, yet at same time now awash with funds, are lending it to retailers at giveaway rates of interest

this cheap money to provide extended finance to customers for the purchase of their goods. In this 'buy now, pay very much later' situation, not only are retailers able to inflate prices of their goods but also tell consumers it is better they buy now before prices go up even more," he said

Pauline Pepper, another compiler of the survey, said that she saw no signs of current inflationary trends abating but rather the reverse, that they are all set to accelerate

Ms Pepper said: "There are two factors that are novel to this latest bout of inflation. The Court Bailiffs' strike is still continuing, the country is

Scratch'n'sniff strips a soaraway success

Women want Wanton!

By **Susan McBeth**
Social Affairs Reporter

WANTON STRIPS HAVE been such a success in alleviating inhibition that as soon as fresh stocks arrive they are immediately snapped up. In some parts of the country demand has been so strong that there are even waiting lists for them.

As news of *Wanton's* effectiveness banishing inhibition spread, women of all ages have taken to its easy-to-take sachet strips in a big way

For most women the arousing aroma of a single sachet is sufficient to banish all feelings of shyness. But inhaling the aroma of two sachets, all sense of repression is banished for hours on end

"With just two sniffs of *Wanton* I feel no need to wait to be asked anymore, I do the asking instead," said one more than satisfied user

She however, appears not to be the only person experiencing the dis-inhibitory powers of the aroma If the Nonettes' - the sole distributors of *Wanton* - sales figures for the new aroma are to be believed British sales are a massive 2.5m strips being sold every week

At one local Nonette centre in St Albans the lady in charge of *Wanton* and *Love Patch* sales, said: "Strips are outstripping Patches We are in a permanent sold-out situation with them

"Even before new supplies of strips have arrived there's a queue and most of those are already on the waiting list"

There are reports however, of some young women and some not so young, snorting all of the strip's six sachets at once then socialising in groups

With *Love Patches* at the ready, they then go looking for men Within the past week many St Albans men claim to have been on the receiving end of such attentions. Some men are scared to go out alone

Terbal gave his fronds a waggle as though in mirth as he said that if the universe was as our astronomers surmise, ever evenly expanding from a dot, there would be a just as even disbursement of galaxies. But, he said, and as Earthly astronomers also observe, galaxies are not only congregated into strips, there are vast areas of the heavens bereft of as much as a single star. What is actually in these all black bits, he said, are young mobius strands, some in bloom, some still to bud. Matured mobius strands are those with the glowing groves of ripening and ripened galaxies.

Minor mobius strings, Terbal said, often evolve into strips in their own right. But at the same time some of the existing ones become so shredded of their strands that they become combined with adjoining ones. This merging, he added, just as with strings stripping away, is usually gradual but sometimes it is sudden. When this happens there is, he said, an enormous discharge of energy as the Secondary waves within the strings' Primary one adjust to the change, just as energy built up in a tectonic shift suddenly releases as an earthquake. As he spoke I thought, could these be what cosmic rays are?

Terbal said although the mobiuses of universes were, overall, slow in their swirling, the strings of strands they are composed of move, oscillate at differing speeds to one another. Sometimes these strips separate, other times their edges brush one another. When this happens the speeding energy of the collider boosts acceleration of the other, just as a multistage rocket does. Some strands of these mobiuses, he said, can end up going really fast. Evidence of this, he said, is to be found in galaxies within the outer strands, again as seen from Earth, appearing increasingly obliquely ovate the further they are from us, as well as moving faster of course. But eventually, he added, this acceleration is imparted to other colliding strands and they slow down. And so it goes on, ripening and rotting with fresh strips forming into new universes. As Terbal spoke, I grasped that Earthly astronomers are seeing two sets of seemingly speeding 'expansion' and not the singular one they say they are.

He waggled his fronds again and again, as if in mirth, when he mused that 'gravity waves' our astronomers say they have detected signs of are no such thing. What is observed, he said, are the differing speeds between mobius strands. Indeed the concept of gravity itself, Terbal said, just as had Menpemelo earlier, is, in our scientists' terms, much misunderstood.

What we call 'gravity', Terbal said, is none other than the effects of Secondary waves, 'energy', compacting their froth of Tertiary waves, 'matter' into one another. As far as Earth is concerned, it being our biggest (and nearest) enmeshment of 'Tertiary froth', incoming matter carried on the crests of Secondary waves, be it those of a meteor or merely an apple from a tree, will, in the ordinary course of things, be 'attracted' to it.

This attraction, Terbal said, once the velocity of Secondary waves bringing matter Earthwards had flowed on, is not as forceful as we are led to believe and

CHRON EXCLUSIVE

MILAN VICTIMS TELL OF 48 HOURS NONSTOP SEX HELL WITH ALIENS

THE TERRIBLE TERROR OF TITANIC TEARO

Is she the most savage Susem of them all?

JOHN TRAVERS & FLORINA PALAZZIO in Rome

MEET TEARO: she who is two metres plus tall, weighs 100 kilos and more. She's also all muscle and she likes men, lots of them. And one after another as well!

It's no wonder either that this Tearo is known as the Susem she-devil of then all. Not only did Tearo make love to entire Milan squad but also the entire Milan squad are now suffering from crushed, compacted penises as a result.

Speaking from his hospital bed, Milan striker, Luigi Begamo, told how he was filled with terror as he first caught sight of Tearo

Having already been forced to indulge in many hours of forced lovemaking with one Susem after another, subjected to bondage, whipping and a host of other kinky sex acts, Bergamo, Milan's once champion striker then came face to face with the titanic Tearo

"Many of us were held captive in a woodland glade," Luigi said, "and everyone of us was yet once again on our backs, forcibly engaged in a prolonged session of robust lovemaking with the Susem women

"There were many more of these women around the edges of the clearing waiting their turn to sate their lust on us. Then these began chanting Tearo's name, just as my fans chant mine

"The women who were holding me down also began chanting her name So did the one who was astride me Then this titan of a woman they called Tearo strode out from the trees and I was filled with terror and foreboding"

The other Susem women, Luigi said, then freed the men from their grip But this was only so they could be 'presented' to Tearo

Luigi said "Her eyes fell on Carlo [Agilita, Milan's goalkeeper] She made a grab at him At first he tried to run from her but because he was still in an aroused condition he was unable to run very fast and she soon had him in her grasp What happened next to poor Carlo was terrible

"No sooner had this Tearo hold of Carlo by his legs, than she lifted him high in the air, then swung him around above her head Then she slammed Carlo down onto the ground and was immediately in robust congress with him I could see that his legs were scuffling in an agitated manner and he was crying out in pain

"I was then taken by more of the Susem and also soon engaged in yet more lovemaking as were the rest of my reluctant team-mates

"Some time passed in this activity Carlo then let out a most terrible scream I looked to where he was and saw this Tearo climbing to her feet and that Carlo had his hands clutched between legs which were now frantically thrashing and scuffling

"Within minutes the rest of us were hauled onto our feet again The Susem began chanting Tearo's name once again She began casting her eyes about us men once more They then alighted on me

"I tried to run from her but I was unsuccessful in evading

Fleet Street suffers Nonette success

Circulation slump sees ad income slashed

By Ben Collins
Media Editor

BROADSHEETS AND red tops alike are suffering their sharpest slump in circulation and advertising revenue for a decade Meanwhile sales and income of Nonette newspapers continue to rise and rise

The editor of a Docklands-based national newspaper, blamed the unfair competition his and other dailies papers face from their Nonette counterparts

He said that the Nonettes with their lower overheads, including labour costs, assured circulation of all of their papers as well as co-operative advertisers, have products mainstream newspapers cannot hope to match

There are other reasons for the Nonette papers' success One of which is that they carry more actual news than ordinary papers

Nonette news reports are also hard hitting With no large advertisers to please and free from any concern of Britain's libel laws, the Nonettes can print anything want

While both sides deny it, Nonette papers are also an assured outlet of stories Fleet Street papers refuse to print

Barely a day passes without at least one Nonette paper running a corruption story And tales of corruption in high places is, apart from sex scandals, what people like to read about

Massive response to Nonettes' penis replacement offer

First British victims set to fly out for member re-growth

BY KRISTINA DOROW
HEALTH EDITOR

A staggering 200,000 victims of Susem sex attacks have signed up for replacement penises the Nonettes announced yesterday

Some 950 British men are among the first of 10,000 cases worldwide who are set to travel to the Nonette Tissue Regrowth Centre in Brazil within the next few days

The speed and size of the response of the victims to the Nonette offer has come to many in the movement as a big surprise

A Nonette spokeswoman in communities had raised the required number study points in record time

"It would appear that this issue is something these men and their partners miss and is viewed as very important to them," the smiling spokeswoman said

According to details released by the Nonette Tissue Regrowth Centre that the new penises will be exact copies of the patients' original ones

However, those whose original penis had been circumcised will need to have this procedure done by their own surgeons as it is not included in the replacement and who fell victim to the Susem are said to have joined the Nonette movement

According to Susan Pelham, who speaks for SCFF, the victims' support group said that even she was surprised at the speed at which so many of the soldiers and their families had joined the Nonette movement

Ms Pelham, whose husband was one of the victims, and has, along with the rest of her family also joined the Nonettes said "I think it fair to say that all of us in the SCFF are deeply appreciative of the support and hard work of the Nonette communities we are

Wolf whistling women were on 'Wanton'

New Nonette drug claimed to be behind men's molesting

By **Susan McBeth**
West London Correspondent

HAMMERSMITH HAS BEEN hit by hordes of over-amorous women high on Wanton, Brook Green Magistrates Court was told yesterday.

Basil Easton JP, sentencing six Fulham women to be bound over for breach of the peace, said "Lately it seems that as soon as it gets dark women such as you come out, all high on this *Wanton* drug and cause no end of trouble, especially molesting men and of all ages"

The six women who are aged between 18 and 25 were arrested outside their place of work for indecently assaulting two building workers

According to PC Hawkins, who called to the scene of the offences "Both men were in state of obvious distress They were also partly undressed as well

Shocking scenes at London singles club

"Wanton women were totally out of order"
- says battered bouncer

By TRACE SMITH

"WOMEN ARE ALWAYS LET in the club, no questions asked, and of course no frisking," said Wayne Bettons, chief bouncer at the Sands singles club, Putney. Speaking from his hospital bed Mr Sands said: "There was at least a dozen of them and they came in quiet enough.

"For the first hour or so they were well behaved, a bit high spirited but nothing as you'd be worried about. Then they all went in the ladies Well, when they came out it was a totally different situation altogether

"There was no end of blokes complaining about these women's goings on, that they were being touched up by them and that sort of thing

"At first we told them they had to be joking but when two of the lads on the bar came out and said they said they were being molested by these women as well, I went into the club itself to investigate

"When I saw what some of these women were doing to two of the male patrons I told them it was well outside what is permitted They told me to mind my own business, even though one of men was in an obvious state of distress.

can be countered more easily than thought. I had to bear in mind, he said, that what we humans have come to consider 'solid' is no such thing. There is only 'solidity' relative to another, less or more, just as a hammer is to a thumb, and it to a blob of blancmange. But no matter how seemingly solid something appears it still has much, much more space than substance. From what he said the actual froth of the entire Earth is little more than a mouse is to the church of nothingness, or Primary wave to be precise, in which it is situate. As he spoke I thought of vests, a string one. It hangs like a vest, feels like one and flattens blancmanges just like a vest, but all the same it has more hole than vest.

To demonstrate the feeble force of 'gravity' Terbal showed me to a tiny bar magnet an inch long and said to pick up pins with it, which I duly did. He had me raise it above my head and note how the pins still stuck. As I held the magnet he said to also note how slight its power was.

To counteract the force of the Earth's 'pull', Terbal said, all that is needed is the focusing of an opposing force. Most humans, just as the Susem, he said, possess this ability, it needing just practice to accomplish. No doubt noting my askance he used an analogy of bicycles (how he knew of these I know not). He said to the unknowing a bicycle with its thin wheels and just two small spots touching the ground appears an improbable mode of transport, anyone attempting to ride it would fall off. And those first so doing usually do just that, fall off. But once would-be cyclists master concentrating their innate ability of balance, they not only became adept at bicycling but can accomplish amazing things with its two thin wheels.

Terbal said a cyclist's ability to concentrate their balance is already within them before they stepped astride a bike, it just needing focusing. In a like manner, he said, so is our ability to levitate. It being little more than concentrating, focusing similarly innate, what he termed 'kinesis', power underfoot. He used another analogy, wooden floors, elephants and stiletto high heels (how he knew of the last I know not either). Herds of heavy elephants leave little more than dust smudges treading across such a floor, but a single seven stone lady in stiletto heels will indent her every step.

Terbal said that according to Susem investigations there are already recorded Earthly instances of this occurring spontaneously and others, albeit it unknowingly, happening as an outcome of kinesis concentration.

I then said, changing the subject somewhat, "What about the Moon and the tides it causes? Are they not proof of gravity and its power?"

Terbal soon had me back down in my place. The Moon, he said, does not cause seas to tide. If it did, those of the Caspian, Black and Mediterranean would as well, and a big bore many times the Amazon's would roar down the Dardanelles four times a day. But spring or neap, these and other landlocked (or near as) seas stay nigh non-tidal.

What is actually happening, Terbal said, is the half of the Earth's mantle

almost unnoticed, have seen massive rises in their Nonette movements. First, Naina Tajani in Madras, reports on India.

The coalesce of the castes

TO A PEOPLE WHO HISTORICALLY have been united by their sense of 'Indianess' yet at same time disunited by their insularity of caste, something very unusual is taking place the length and breadth of India: the castes are uniting. And on a massive scale, all thanks to the Nonettes.

The origins of India's Nonette movement lie with the widespread take-up of original soufin energy units which arrived across the sub-continent during early summer.

With the units' subsequent failure and their replacement conditional on forming Nonette groups, it was thought by many to signal the reversion back to traditional low energy use especially by the India's rural poor.

The pundits, however, have been proved wrong. Much to their and other observers surprise and the alacrity of politicians in particular, the Indian Nonette movement has been revitalised by replacement soufin units.

Having experienced the benefits of the first units, millions of people across the country were receptive to the terms involved in acquiring the second ones.

Fueling this willingness was and still is, are the daily Susem television newscasts beamed into millions of Indian homes and villages.

It was not lost on many India viewers, that economically, the northeast of Brazil – where the initial Nonette movement began – was akin to much of India itself.

With the daily showing of widespread and rapid improvements to the lives of Brazil's rural poor brought by the Nonettes, many of India's similarly rural poor and lower in castes, quickly organised themselves into Nonette groups.

It was not long however, before many higher caste Indians, seeing the benefits Nonettes brought to their lower caste brethren, were wanting the same. And so India's Nonette movement while growing rapidly, formed along caste lines.

India's Nonettes have harnessed the new to unite the country's castes

"We are all separate," he said, "yet at the same time all together in matters which are of common interest to us. In the past there were always shocking things going on between different castes with people, villages and so forth, all at daggers drawn fighting one another over every this and that, but now this has all stopped.

"Nowadays no caste is at the throats of another. We are able to sort everything out including our differences at regional Nonette assembly which of course is fully multi-caste."

Another strong impetus to the growth of the India's Nonette movement has come from the high tech end of its economy. India's computer industry, centered on Bangalore in neighbouring state of Karnataka, is now mostly run as Nonettes

the state's 50m population are fully paid up members of the movement. And this despite incessant strictures from the state's politicians.

However, following the recent overnight takeover of Mysore in the south of Kanataka, by the Nonettes, the state's politicians have been noticeable by their absence.

The subsequent appearance of many politicians and officials at publicly held Truth Commissions on charges of corruption followed by the just as public castrations of many of them is thought to have persuaded those politicians 'who got away' to reside in Delhi for the time being.

Computer software is not the only area of Indian commerce responding to overseas Nonettes. Agriculture, is another

CITY CENTRES 'NOT SAFE FOR SINGLE MEN'

Nonette love drug blamed for attacks outbreak

By Tony Perry
Ordinary Reporter

WANTON, the Nonette 'love drug' is behind sudden surge of city centre attacks on men by women, the Police Federation (NAPO) said yesterday.

Britain's town and cities are increasingly becoming no-go areas for young unaccompanied men, a NAPO spokesman warned.

Even CCTV often fails to give protection from attacks. The operators monitoring the systems have difficulty in identifying immediately the differences between 'ordinary' high spiritedness and actual assault.

The NAPO spokesman said: "Because of the shortage in police numbers of many forces, officers cannot be expected to attend every such incident. And very often when officers do arrive they

Judge condemns Wanton dru

Man 'ravished' by "drug crazed pack of women"

SPIRITED HORSEPLAY IS one thing but what happened to a Hinckley man went beyond the bounds of reasonable behaviour, Leicester Magistrates Court was told yesterday.

Andrew Fox (24) was abducted by the six women from a pub car park and then indecently assaulted by them in the back of his delivery van.

Mr Fox only escaped a serious sexual attack when fellow drinkers left

Beijing's 'Interesting times'

By Helen Moi in Hong Kong

If Mao Zedong were alive today he would probably say: "Power comes from the screen of a TV"

Day in, day out, Susem telecasts beam news of the life under the Nonettes. The people of China are among the most avid of viewers. Though the Beijing authorities rage and wage a war of words against the programmes, they have failed to stop their message getting through.

Neither has the Chinese government managed to stop the rapid spread of the Nonette movement itself.

The sudden Nonette 'police action' of three months ago and its summary deportation of hundreds of government officials and police has not been lost on Beijing. Nor has the humiliation of having these officials marched naked past massed crowds of jeering onlookers.

With Beijing unwilling to take any direct action against the Nonettes, or just as likely the fear and reluctance of their officials to so act, the movement has spread like wildfire across the whole of China.

Rural poor and city dwellers alike have seized upon the material benefits of belonging to the Nonettes such as soufin energy units and teaching screens in such numbers that

Shanghai, China's largest city and now almost totally under Nonette control

it has more than 200m members.

However, it more than these material benefits which make the Nonettes such an attractive option. And it is this that is exercising the minds of the government in Beijing.

In what officials call 'splitism', the Nonettes are accused of threatening the national unity and thus, by association, the security of China.

Already, so Beijing claims, by not cracking down on the Ughur separatists in Sinkiang province, the entire region is slipping out of Chinese control. This supposedly 'autonomous republic' the size of France, is also, though Beijing is loath to admit it,

now fully Nonetted and has lready claim its self-determination.

Beijing's power is also on the wane in a number of other 'autonomous' regions such as Quinhai and eastern Inner Mongolia, while that of their Nonettes is very much on the rise.

What Beijing has lost sight of and perhaps has failed to grasp from the start, is that the peoples of China are as varied and culturally different as those of Europe.

Zhu Feng, one this month's members in Nonette assembly said: "The people of China are very different from one another. Those in the south speak as different a tongue

from the people of the north as do Spaniards and Swedes. Between those in Taiwan and Tibet the difference is even greater.

"Throughout the history of China one group has always enforced their hegemony over the others in the name of China and the dynasty of which they were part. Now, for the very first time, all the different peoples of China have the right of self-determination yet at the same time are united as one people on a basis of mutual cooperation rather than the coercion of the past."

One area of China where the Nonettes have taken complete control is Hong Kong.

Women to face pub ban threat

By TREVOR MURPHY

GROUPS OF SIX or more single women are to be barred from a major Midlands pub chain. The move comes after a series of upsetting incidents.

Nigel Williams, marketing director of the Happy Drinker Group, which has more than 200 pubs and restaurants in the Birmingham and Wolverhampton area, said: "Our traditional young male customers are suffering from a serious rise in molesting and groping, as well as other unwarranted interference by groups of unaccompanied women.

"Night after night," Mr Williams said, "these females steam into our pubs mob-handed and before you know it they're forcing themselves onto the men, breaking up their conversations, chatting them up, buying them drinks and generally making a general nuisance of themselves. And heaven help any man who is on his own.

"Staff of many of our Happy Drinker pubs have not been immune from these females' attentions either," he said.

"Over the past week alone we have logged more than 30 incidents in which bar and security staff have been on these insatiable

Nigel Williams

nearest the Moon rises, relative to the core, towards it. More in the middle thanthe edges but the average across the hemisphere, he said, is about 20 centimetres. The opposite hemisphere compresses a little in response as well. It is this continuing Earth-wide rise and fall which causes the movable, ocean water, to move, to slosh back and forth.

With me thinking, "If the Moon moves the mantle, mountains and all rather than just the lighter weighing water, then this is yet further demonstrable proof of gravity is it not?"

But no. And as if knowing my thoughts, Terbal said the Moon pulls nothing, but rather the reverse. The larger Earth, as it were, is forever trying to stretch out and make a grab at it. The Moon, however, stays just out of its grasp (thank goodness). Because the Earth's rotation is slowing, the power of its reach becomes the less and the Moon, as a result, circles ever further from us, by two centimetres a year he said.

Terbal said I had to ever remember that the Earth is much bigger that its Tertiary wave, matter, component. Secondary waves, energy, constitute a far greater one. While 'Tertiary wave Earth' has a diameter of 12,000 kilometres, 'Secondary wave Earth's' is more than 600,000 km.

Terbal said to envisage Secondary waves flowing through space as a river current and washing against a semi-submerged vortex, the Earth. While most of the current flows on, some is deflected by the vortex and because of Earth's rotation, Secondary waves whirl around it as if multiple lighthouse beams. It is this continuous swirl of energy of 'Secondary wave- size Earth' which deflects, 'attracts', entraps the froth of Tertiary waves into the orbit of its maw, be they meteors or apples, and thence 'Tertiary Earth'-wards. He said the attracting effects of Secondary wave swirling has already been established by Earthly astronomers Lense and Thirring. His fronds waggled a little however as he remarked it was a pity that they and others had not grasped the significance of their observations.

It is also this effect of Secondary wave Earth, he continued, which in trying to snatch the Moon, tugs our planetary Tertiary waves with it and hence causes oceans to rise and tide. 'Secondary wave-Sun', he said, is not as big as might first be thought. This is because it rotates at a slower speed than the Earth, taking 30 days to do a complete turn. When the Moon is closer to the Sun than is the Earth it is tugged a little towards it. The Earth in response grasps out for the Moon the more, not much but enough to raise Tertiary terra not-so-firma a centimetre or so more and spring higher tides. This extra upward tugging, he said, also causes the Earth itself to quake and volcanoes puff bigger plumes.

Terbal said everything Tertiary which whirls in space including our own galaxy has its bigger Secondary wave sister. The Milky Way's, he said, had in times past snaffled up several smaller, slower swirling galaxies which had come too close. The Magellanic Clouds, he said, are next on the Milky Way's

Police chief warns hitchhikers

'MEN, DON'T ACCEPT LIFTS FROM WOMEN DRIVERS'

By STEVEN WILSON South Coast Correspondent

HITCHHIKERS ACROSS THE SOUTH WERE WARNED by West Sussex police yesterday, not to accept lifts from women drivers. The police's warning comes after a string of serious sexual assaults against young male hitchhikers across the county.

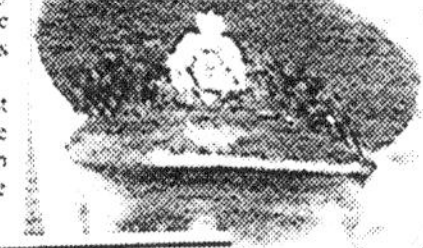

Chichester police revealed yesterday that in the past week alone there have been seven incidents reported of attacks on young men seeking lifts.

Chief Inspector Walters of West Sussex said: "These attacks have followed a similar pattern. A young man accepts the offer of a lift from a vehicle driven by a woman motorist.

SOLDIERS' 'PASSION WAGON' ORDEAL

Grappling grannies in sex-nap spree

By DONNA MARKS

MORE THAN A DOZEN WELSH SOLDIERS were abducted by a coach-load of sex-mad grannies it was claimed yesterday.

As night fell, hundreds of police across south Wales sought the coach and its women passengers. Men were warned by police to be on their guard against further such attacks

The attacks on the men ranged across the Principality from Haverford West in Dyfed to Crickhowell in Gwent.

According to Welsh police, only one coach party carried out the attacks but they admit others could be involved.

Head of Gwent police, Glynn Howells said: "We are

distressed state as a result of their ordeal.

"Until this coach is located and those responsible for carrying out these attacks are apprehended, no man is safe," he said.

Gwent police said, however, that they lack resources to stop and search all the coaches on the county's roads.

Jocks' cabers Tossed

Strapping Taff troupe gets kilt secret straight

By JOHN HACKNEY

THE WELSH AND SCOTTISH women's national hockey teams' thoughts of the sticks and balls of their game soon turned to those of another sport when they attended an after-match Scottish dancing evening in Inverness.

After strong snorts of Wanton - the new Nonette sex drug - the strapping and now amourous Amazons of the valleys, wanting to know what Scotsmen wore under kilts, surreptitiously sidled up to a bunch of Jocks and stuck Love Patches on their necks.

On seeing the Scots' rapidly rising arousal and realising they wore nothing under their kilts, both teams of buxom belles soon sent sporrans flying and kilts akimbo as they tore the tartan and tackled the terrified Tams of the Shanter.

An evening of Strip the Willow and Highland Fling was soon one of Highlanders flung from one group of jolly hockey-stickers to another. The girls even gave gay Gordon a comeuppance or two.

Not only did both teams achieve a high score but they also committed umpteen red-card fouls against stunned Jocks, leaving them in a distressed state and a near undressed one as well.

Wanton blamed for men's pub stayaway

Even barmen are scarce

By Susan McBeth
Drinks Correspondent

"ONCE WOMEN WERE women but now they act like blokes," said Harold Mince, barman at the newly renamed Queens Head, Islington.

"What is more," he added, casting a watchful eye over the pub's near all-female clientele, "the women treat blokes the same way as blokes used to treat women and most blokes can't handle that."

No sooner had Harold spoken, than two men entered the pub and I was aware of an immediate hushing of conversation and many eyes turning in their direction.

As the men made for the bar I also saw some of the women sniffing at *Wanton* sachets on their sleeves.

No sooner were the men at the bar than two of these women had joined them and were attempting to pay for their drinks.

The men, taken aback by this, tried to refuse the women's offer but both were insistent that they paid.

The men eventually agreed but from the speed with which they drunk their pint, one wo-

Men - do you feel threatened by new woman?

asks James Bugle

Will *Wanton* make us men the fairer sex?

THERE WILL BE FEW of us men who have been spared an encounter with *Wanton Woman*. Her telephone calls, emails asking for a date. The unsolicited gifts of after-shave, body rub and so on.

And more pertinently her blatant, no nonsense telling what she wants, and worse what she wants to do to us once she gets the chance.

I do not know about you but I find it all rather scary.

Ever since the use of this Wanton drug, fragrance, or whatever it is became widespread, social mores have gone haywire.

The pleasures of conducting relationships with the opposite sex have, as far as Wanton Woman is concerned, have gone out of the window.

Now it's more a case of them saying "Hello" and sticking one of those Love Patches on the back of neck, dragging you off to their boudoirs and having

'Passion Wagon' panic hits North Wales coast

SEX-NAP COACH GRANNIES STRIKE SEASIDE RESORTS

By DAVID REES-WILLIAMS

NORTH WALES POLICE ARE HUNTING A coach party of women who carried out a series of abductions and sexual assaults against men across north Wales yesterday.

Last night, as roadblocks were mounted on main roads out of the region, there were fears that the women could strike again.

The coach party struck at a string of north Wales' resorts including Colwyn Bay, Llandudno and Bangor.

According to the police the attacks followed a similar pattern. The coach would stop just in front of the intended victim. A woman would descend from the front door of the coach and ask for directions. While the unsuspecting victim would be giving them information, a group of other

behind them and the coach driving off.

The victims are then subjected to a series of non-stop assaults by the women.

Police say that several of the victims reported that several of the coach's seats had been removed so as to allow for the assaults to take place.

They also say not only were the victims assaulted with 'Love Patches' (the Nonette love drug) but those who attempted to

TV viewing figures soar as men stay home

By STEVE MANN

AFTER YEARS OF falling audiences, major television networks report a sudden massive surge in viewing figures with sports channels showing the biggest rises. Video and DVD rental outlets also report bumper rises in customer numbers.

And the reason for this return to the small screen? In a word: **Wanton.**

Such has been the success of the new Nonette inhibition relieving drug, that men are shying away from evenings out.

Pubs, clubs, discos and other places where sexes once socialised are being viewed by many men as definite no go areas.

With the widespread use of Wanton many men say

menu, in a few billion years that is.

As if in conclusion, he said I had to bear in mind that although on the grand scale of things the strength of Secondary wave Earth has a far reaching and powerful effect, on the smaller one it isn't much. Pointing me back to the magnet again, Terbal said it takes little to counter the strength of Secondary waves, adding that the Susem had been doing so for ages.

I asked him just how this is done, but by the noise coming from his TV screens I gathered the match was about to begin. Almost as if off-hand, disinterested, he said, "Kisnesis...it ist used vor all...vedas, sherpals...La ra... soufins." And finally, with the referee about to blow his whistle for the off, "How do you vink I move also?"

With the Bulgarians scoring within seconds, Terbal, his fronds all a waggle with glee, attention for me or anything else now gone, I wandered off mulling what he had said. But on stepping up to the outside I was confronted with another worry. A very big worry indeed, or so they said.

Monks make B line for A pl

Monastery empties as Susem spray love scent

By HOLLY HEVEL
Religious Correspondent

AN UNGODLY EXPERIENCE befell Greek Orthodox monks as a spraying Susem space craft swept over their monastery on the island of Crete.

Every monk, young and old, abandoned their devotions and rushed lemming-like to awaiting Susem space ships which whisked them away.

Though many of the older monks were later found on the mainland and in a confused state, none showed any sign of distress at their ordeal or of their fortunate escape from the clutches of the Susem.

The monastery's abbot Father

THOUSANDS RUSH FOR LOVEMAKING WITH ALIENS!

SUSEM SHOCK PIED PIPER SEX PLOY LURE

By PHIL SMITH

SUSEM SNATCH'N'GRAB SEX RAIDS TOOK A surprise turn yesterday: no snatch, no grab.

In their place, long lines of men queued eager to board the Aliens' craft whisking them away to an unknown lovemaking rendezvous with the Susem.

Beaches the length of the Mediterranean were subjected to the sudden appearance of low, slow flying Susem craft spraying a lemon scented substance.

All the Alien attacks were almost identical to the one reported at Pelekas, a Corfu resort.

Pied Piper scent

Within moments of the men inhaling the spray they were running zombie-like behind the craft, oblivious to the cries of women and children for them to come back.

The men, however, still ran after the Susem craft even when a second suddenly dived from the skies and landed right in front of them and opened its doors.

They went willingly

Without slowing, the men then ran inside this second space plane. As soon as it was full its doors slammed closed and flew off just as suddenly as it arrived.

The many men left behind showed signs of great distress of not being allowed on board.

Rejection distress

Although the older and less athletic men taken by the craft were later found a few miles away, none showed any relief at their release.

Instead, all of these men appeared to be extremely upset and distressed at their rejection. It took several hours before these they and those left behind were able to return to normal and grasp just what a narrow escape they had had.

Thousands taken

According to the Alien Abduction Centre in Milan a record 3,401 men across Europe were abducted during the course of yesterday.

Similar attacks however, took place in Australia, the US and Canada. On the

Coach snatch now nationwi

'Not us,' claim T J Societ abduction outrages soar

By SUSAN McBETH
Abductions Reporter

SOLDIERS across the country confined them selves to barracks yesterday following a nationwide spate of coach assisted sex attacks by women, some of whom are said to be old enough to be the victims' mothers.

Meanwhile as police mounted road blocks in attempts to catch the perpetrators, scores of coach operators protested before the alarm was raised.

The victims, mainly off-duty soldiers, each reported similar experiences as the first abductees in Wales, of first being asked for directions by a middle aged woman, then being seized from behind by a group of yet more women and bundled into the coach.

Once the coach had driven off, the victims were then stripped nearly naked and forced to engage in lovemaking with the women.

After several hours of

Safety scare as Patch death toll rises

The bank manager the actress and a Love Patch

By Ursula Trust
Court Correspondent

THE MANAGER OF CLAYINGS, Fulham Road branch, John Johnson (47) died suddenly from wearing a Love Patch, a coroner's court was told yesterday.

Although the actual cause of the middle aged manager's death was a heart attack, he is the 12th UK bank manager reported in the past week alone to have suddenly died while using a Love Patch.

In her evidence, Ms Fleur Hartley-Rogers, (22), an actress, acknowledged she was present in the bank manager's office at the time of his collapse.

Ms Hartley-Rogers said that she had an appointment with Mr Johnson to discuss an extension of her overdraft.

The actress who is presently 'resting' said that during their discussions she noticed that Mr Johnson showed signs of being unwell and so she thought it best to leave him alone so that he might have time for a "little rest".

Replying as to why she did not report the manager's condition to a member of the bank's staff, Ms Hartley-Rogers said: "It was lunchtime and everybody seemed so busy I just didn't think it was my place to interrupt them."

Asked if she thought it unusual for the manager to be in a state of near undress, she said that she had no wish to pass judgment on other peoples' dress style.

Ms Sharon Warren (19), an office support staff member, said she found Mr Johnson lying on the floor in front of is desk as though having fallen backwards and with his trousers and underpants down around his ankles.

Ms Warren said she also saw that he had a "sticky patch" on his hip.

Ms Warren added that Mr Johnson's visitor's records showed that Ms Hartley-Rogers had had an interview with the manager every month and always at the same time.

Ms Warren further added that records also showed th the manager had many lunch-time appointments with cus omers who were in the theatrical professions.

Home Office pathologis Dr Howard Johnson, said th the manager's heart atta was caused by a major failu of the upper left ventricle.

Dr Johnson said that wh this was the most freque cause of a heart attack, it h in this incidence, been brou about by an acute slowing the blood to the heart its which in turn was caused the slowing of the circulat

Fleur Hartley-Rogers attending Court yesterday

Men-only carriages for Tube and trains

'Men must be given protection from groping' says LT

By Tony Perry
Men's Editor

TO COMBAT THE RISE of rush-hour groping on the London's Underground men-only carriages are to be introduced as a matter of urgency LT announced yesterday.

The recent upsurge of incidents of men being molested on both the tube and the national rail network has become so widespread that it is planned that the restricted men-only carriages could be in service as soon as next month.

London Transport, announcing the new service, said it is introducing it as a matter of urgency.

LT is also stepping up its late night patrols to give protection to men, especially those travelling alone. LT's moves come after a spate of late night assaults on lone male passengers on both its trains as well as throughout the stations themselves.

Announcing the new security patrols, an Underground spokesman said: "For many of our male customers being a victim of an unwanted physical molesting by gangs of females is a traumatic and frightening experience.

"Many of these male victims have been left in such a distressed state that they have become frightened from ever travelling on the Underground ever again.

"As it is not possible to police all of trains effectively - especially during the rush hour – men-only carriages are the only means we have at our disposal to give protection to our male customers who feel threatened by this upsurge in assaults against them as well combating this growing

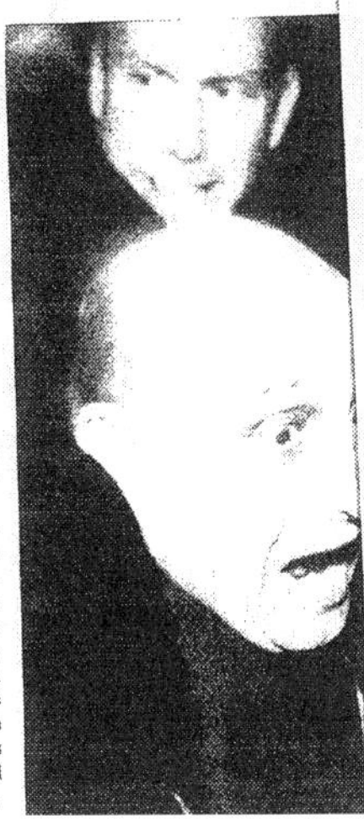

Little me. They elected me delegate for the Regional Nonette. Little five foot nothing me to represent our Area Nonette. Me, who just a few months ago was no more than a mum and worked behind a bar, picked to speak for all those thousands of people.

I had not asked, put my name forward but had been chosen. Not just by the other 80 round the table but backed by almost everyone in each of their Nonettes. Oh I had option to refuse but how could I? How could I let down so many who have said for me? What could I do but stand up, say I was honoured, moved, do my best?

I was quivering as I got to my feet and a tear or two to wipe away but when I came home oh how I cried. Though it is for only for a month I cried for what I have let myself in for. Cried that I'm in enough trouble as it is. Cried for not keeping my big stupid mouth shut. But then I couldn't really, not after what happened.

I had to speak out. It's so wrong. These MI5 people have no right, no need to spy on us. We have nothing to hide. All they, anyone, need do is ask and they will be told. Told everything, anything they want to know about us. Heavens above every tiny thing we do is in the papers for all to see to the point where people are probably bored numb with it. Though they have been caught red-handed not a single word of apology have they made, let alone owned up for what they have done.

Until that evening when it happened, right in front of my own eyes I didn't think possible, in Ulster perhaps but not here in London. What those so-called 'security agents' did to that poor boy was shocking. If I had not been there goodness knows what they would have done to him. And they were lucky to get away with their own lives. If I had not shouted out, acted as I did, I'm sure they would have been lynched.

The disks, what's on them beggars belief. At first, when little Kemel from downstairs told me what he and the others uncovered it didn't sink in. But later when he showed me, I was stunned and disgusted. I also saw why those men came after Tony, the young boy who rang my door that evening. The police are still demanding we hand him over. They've a fat chance of that and anyway it will be a while yet before he recovers.

Tony called the one evening I was in. I could see he had been running and his eyes wide scared. He said he knew me from the Sallie, those there told him where I was. I'd not even time to ask what he wanted before he gasped "Take it, it's all there," thrust a big envelope in my hand and made back down the stairs.

Kemel, who had been checking the new memberships with me, shouted from the balcony, "Look, look!"

But I'd not the chance for this either, before I heard, then saw men running

Women to face strict work harassment code

Top bosses in desperate plea to stem male workplace stayaway

By PHIL SMITH

ALARMED AT THE RECENT SUDDEN SURGE OF sexual harassment in the workplace and soaring compensation claims, the Confederation of Directors (CoD) Britain's top bosses' club has drawn up a strict code of conduct in a bid to stamp it out.

According to CoD's head, Howard Pearce, male workplace absenteeism is running at record levels.

In some companies, Mr Pearce said, more than half of the male employee are regularly reporting sick rather than face the trauma of constant sexual harassment from their female colleagues.

Introducing the new code, Mr Pearce said: "It is important to remember that improper conduct in the workplace is not only demeaning and humiliating to the victims but it also has a negative effect on a company's productivity."

Singling out female managers and supervisors for special attention, he said: "Those in positions of authority bear a special responsibility towards all employees who suffer sexual harassment in the workplace.

"It is no longer good enough," he said, "for them to dismiss complaints as 'just horseplay' or shrugging them off with "girls will be girls" and other such unthinking remarks.

"Indeed there has been several reported instances of female managers rather setting a positive example of propriety, have themselves blatantly indulged in harassing their hapless junior male employees. All this must stop and stop immediately" he said.

The main points of the new code are:

- **NO touching**: Keep your hands to yourself, bottom pinching and groping your male colleagues are definitely out
- **NO staring**: Avert your gaze from men's bodies and no 'knowing looks' into their eyes either
- **NO sidling**: Keep your distance; coming too close to men can upset and intimidate them
- **NO smut**: Suggestive language of a sexual nature is out and so are double entendres
- **NO flaunting**: Suggestive body language is out as well
- **NO following lone men into the photocopying room or store cupboards**
- **NO use of Wanton during working hours**: (or Love Patches either)

SUSEM'S SEX SPRAY SHOCK

'There is NO defence against Alien's weapon of mass seduction' say experts

By PHIL SMITH

AS CONCERNS ROSE for the safety of more than 8,000 men overcome by the new Susem sex spray, experts in biological and chemical warfare voiced fears of its devastating effects.

People around the world yesterday helplessly reeled under non-stop attacks from the new Susem weapon. More than 8,000 people worldwide were reported as succumbing to its power and fell into the Aliens' clutches.

"There is no antidote to the new Susem sex weapon"

A single sniff of this Alien's new chemical seduction weapon, experts say, turns people into unthinking automatons, mindlessly transfixed by its aroma for hours on end and complying with Susem whims.

No one, experts say, except women and children have immunity from the Aliens' chemical cocktails' horrendous mind-bending powers.

According to women who witnessed first-hand, the Susem attacks on their husbands, partners, other loved ones, all the men instantly succumbed to the chemicals' effects and mindlessly ran after the craft spraying it.

"There is no protection from it either" experts say

"Daddy couldn't get enough of it," said one little girl of her father who was one of those who fell victim to the spray. Though fortunately for her daddy, he was denied a place on the Alien's abduction space plane.

Graham Mansfield, Head of the Department of Biological and Chemical Warfare at Snaresbrook University, said: "The scope, size and range of these new forms of Susem attack, as well as its potency to overwhelm their human prey, strongly suggests that it is unlikely to be a one-off exercise.

"While theoretically it is possible to devise an antidote to counteract this chemical agent," Dr Mansfield said, "it has not been researched as yet, let alone developed.

"What we do know," he said, "is that it is a most powerful mind controlling agent of all time."

"Hiding behind closed doors is no protection from this chemical and its effects"

Dr Mansfield also said that because of the strong likelihood of the Susem using the chemical spray again, it will be necessary for everyone to wear protective clothing - including gas masks.

Professor Angela Clark, head of Urban Terrorist Studies at Sheppey University, said: "If this chemical is used in a crowded urban situation the consequences will be horrendous.

"Men mindlessly being lured into running after women without thought of

Safety scares rise as Patch death toll soars

Love Patch deaths soar

Coroner calls for Nonette sex aid ban

By PHIL SMITH

WITH THE SUDDEN death from a heart attack by Pudsey councillor, Harold Jefferies while using a Love Patch, a Leeds coroner has called for a ban on the Patchs' use.

The 43 year old councillor's death brings the number of confirmed UK Patch fatalities to 82 within the past 10 days

But for the estimated 10 million British users of the Nonette sex aid, any call to outlaw them is set to face stiff resistance from satisfied users.

Leeds Coroners Court heard how Councillor Jefferies had suffered a fatal heart attack while visiting a Pudsey single mother of two, to

WARNING TO ALL MEN

If a coach stops near you - RUN FOR YOUR LIFE!

By *The Chron's* PUBLIC CONCERN TEAM

EVEN PARKED COACHES POSE A PERIL: especially those with smoked glass windows. For lurking unseen behind the panes could well be a preying pack of willful women waiting, poised to pounce upon you and mercilessly sate their uncontrolled carnal desires on your body.

And before you smirk "Chance would be fine thing", be aware of the no-holds-barred, lust hell awaiting any man unfortunate enough to fall into the clutches of these cruising coteries of sex-craved shameless she-devils.

Read what happened to Corporal Tommy Hughes (23) of the Welsh Fusiliers, the day he stepped out of his camp at Sennybridge, Powys.

Coach glided to a halt

As Cpl. Hughes walked along the road he thought nothing of a coach gliding silently to a halt a few yards ahead of him.

Cpl Hughes thought nothing unusual about the smartly dressed middle aged woman who stepped coach and asked for directions.

She asked for 'help'

Being the gentleman that he is, Cpl. Hughes was only too willing to assist the woman. But as he gave directions the corporal was unaware that the woman had lured him into a trap.

For as Cpl. Hughes gave directions a clutch of other women crept stealthily from the rear door and then in a sudden rush threw a net over him.

Overpowered

Overpowered and helpless Cpl Hughes was man handled towards the coach's rear door.

"I tried to resist them," Cpl. Hughes said, speaking from his sickbed, "but one of the ladies gave me such a smack round the head that for a moment I didn't know what was happening."

Woman struck him

And in that moment, still stunned and surprise-ed, Cpl. Hughes was dragged on board the coach which then drove off.

Once inside the coach, the corporal was traumatised with terror at what he saw: the coach had had much of its seating removed and converted for lovemaking.

Resistance futile

Any resistance, Cpl Hughes said, was in vain. The more he struggled the more the women hit him. "I tried telling the ladies to stop tugging at my clothes," he said, "but that didn't stop them."

No inhibition

The women, Cp[l] Hughes said, showed n[o] sense of inhibition o[r] restraint. They showed n[o] sense of mercy either.

Tommy Hughes th[e] experienced first hand th[e] consequences of *Wanto[n]* the Nonette sex-drug.

"As soon as one of the[m] had slapped a *Love Pat[ch]* on me," Tommy sa[id] "they were like animals [I] kept telling them I ha[d] bad back but it made [no] difference. One after [an]other, they were on [me] having their way.

Trauma

"I don't think I'll e[ver] forget the experience. [I] more than two ho[urs] although it felt longe[r] was held down subjected to one sexual

IEFA Semi final

Sofia beats Moscow 9-3

Shock win raises Arsenal's cup chances

By AMY CELESTE

SOFIA DYNAMO have scored a surprise and resounding 9-3 win over Moscow Spartek in the IFEA semi-final at Rome's Forum Stad-

The Russians were no match for the plucky Sofia side, most of whom are part-timers. Apart from Polvdiv, Dynamo's forwards Gabrova and Kotel were also responsible for their side's goal-fest. All three were responsible for seven of Sofia's score, the remaining tw

up the stairs. I thought them to be police. Tony, halfway down, ran back up and to the landing above. The men, five of them, chased after him, with no notice of me. The next floor is to the roof but the door was locked. The men had him cornered. They shouted "Where are they? Come on..."

Tony managed no more than "Don't..." and they had hit him.

One kept shouting "Where?...come on...you know..." and effing and blinding something terrible. Tony cried out again and again, and I could hear they were hitting and kicking him. I was petrified.

Then it was though there was another me in me and I ran to the stairs, shouted up "Stop that, you stop that!" It was if I had caught them freeze-frame for they stopped as they were.

All stared down. Then one shouted "Get inside, close your door."

There was fear through me, I was shaking with it but I still yelled "You stop that, you leave him alone!"

Then as if in slow motion, the one who shouted, came step by step, down the stairs his eyes fixed on me the while. On my landing, his eyes still on me, he said "I know who you are. Mrs Aileen O'Conner isn't it?" He had such a terrible menace to him. Before I knew it I'd backed to my door

With his "You've got them haven't you?" it was if everything was fast forward. Before I knew it he had me backed right into the flat. He filled the door. I opened my mouth, nothing came out. He began shouting "You've got them haven't you? Haven't you? Where are they? Come on, give."

The envelope was in my mind. I looked but saw it gone. He was then into the flat. I backed across the hall to the sitting room. Then he was across the hall into the room. I kept stepping back. Then it was his quieter "Come on, come on, give them to me Aileen, that's a good girl." He still kept coming towards me. Then I was against the table. He looked at the papers piled on it, fingered through them knocking some on the floor. I was so frightened that still no words came. I kept thinking of the envelope and Kemel but there was no sign of him either.

He flick glanced about the room, picking up more papers, throwing them down. Then, as though mocking, he said "Quite a little lair you've got here haven't you?" Still no words came to me. Then half looking at the papers, then to me, he shouted "Come on tell me...tell me bitch or do I..."

He'd no further and I'd my voice and was screaming "Don't you call me that...don't you dare call me..." but the bleeper on his tunic went off.

Another man was at the door shouting "Kev, trouble...come quick... now!" and he dashed out. I heard them all running down the stairs.

I'd not time to collect myself, cry, do anything when there was a terrible commotion coming from the courtyard. I ran to see. There was a crowd, with more streaming in from the street, two silver cars, the first already moving to go out of the yard. The men on the stairs ran out of the flats and to the second, its doors open and revving up like anything.

It was only later did I learn from Kemel that he had clambered over the balcony to his flat below, taking the envelope with him. He had also run to Ron Edwards in the booth on the corner and who had raised the alarm including in the Kings Head, where everyone there piled out to the rescue. Within minutes there were hundreds of people making into the courtyard.

The first car screeched to go out of the yard but people coming in blocked its way. The car reversed. Then drove straight at the crowd, drove right into them. Some jumped out of its way but others were sent flying.

The car didn't get far though. Bricks were through its windscreen and it careered into the courtyard gatepost. The car was still revving as the crowd had it heaved on its side, pulling at the doors, smashing the windows.

The men in the second car had already jumped out and two managed to make it through the crowd, back to the flats. Bricks downed one, the other ran in the entrance the far side but people coming down the stairs booted him back out.

People were shouting and hitting the men, ripping at their clothes. When more people ran out of my entrance, they had seen the state Tony was in, shouting what the men had done the crowd's rage grew the more. Then above the shouting there were screams. Those of the men.

All the while I watched I'd not a word but was shock shaking. Shaking with what I had just been through, shaking with what I was witnessing. But hearing those screams had me see in an instant what was set to happen. Then it was though this other me in me took over again and I shouted the top of my voice "Stop that! Stop it!"

I could not have been the only one looking from the flats who shouted but because I was high up, my voice echoing off the walls must have made it the louder. But whatever, it stopped everyone as they were. Then, and I just don't know what came over me, I was shouting "Hold them, search them. Don't harm them."

I was down those stairs as fast as anything. In the yard I was brushing people aside and shouting again. Shouting to bring the men together and once they had been dragged to where their cars were I was shouting, "Why are you here? What is it you want?" and when they said nothing, shouting, "Stop kicking them."

I still do not know why I did what I did except of my time in the pub calming people down. Nor for that matter do I know why people did as I told them. All I can think was that enough of them knew I was the head of our Nonette.

Though it was dark in the yard I could see the men had been badly beaten about the head and face, most were bloodied and bruised. But with people shouting to lynch, castrate them, I knew they were not out of danger or people from keeping their heads either. Again it must have been from my time in the pub in calming things down by distracting attention and so I was shouting "Search their cars, search them, the ground for what they've dropped. Quickly!"

Dozens were then doing as I said but I was still shouting. This time help for Tony, those hit by the car. People on the ground floor carried them inside. Others ran up to Doctor Almed for help. Joan Wilkinson from upstairs, an ex-nurse, was with those who had been hurt doing what she could.

Not only were all twelve of the men searched but stripped to their vests and pants then forced face down in a line. All of them were trembling, groaning, most had dirtied their pants. Soon people were coming to me with ID cards, radios. Others brought papers, palm-holds found in the cars.

Though the atmosphere calmed it was still tense. When wives of those hit by the car began baying for the men's blood, making to kick at them, others trying to join in, I had to shout again. This time to form a cordon round the men. All the same I knew the situation might still boil over, that if the men weren't soon out of the yard, there could be no telling what would happen. Yet at the same time I felt I had to know who the men were, why they had come after Tony, why had one thought I was connected with him.

In the situation I did only what I saw was open to me. But now wished I had not or at least done it differently. Their IDs showed them working for a security company in Watford but what was in the cars indicated they were not ordinary heavies. Having called for people to get cameras, their mobile phones, recorders I shouted to turn the men on their backs. When they were I told them they had better talk if they wanted to get away from the flats in one piece.

With cameras flashing, people recording all that the men said, the crowd listening to their every word, it also had the effect of calming everyone down again. When some of the men said their company was sub-contracted to MI5 there were gasps all round. More when "Kev" said Tony was wanted for hacking into its computer system and they had orders to silence him. Then another said Tony had actually stolen an agent's laptop. It was only afterwards did I discover the 'agent' was his own father!

With the men telling everything, forming in my mind was awareness that there was no chance of them just leaving the yard, they had to go in a way the crowd could accept. They had to at least be humiliated. I thought of the men in "Trials". I shouted again, this time for poles and rope. At first this frightened the men but when they saw they were not going to be hanged but yoked together I think it came as a relief. Then three abreast, each with a letter of 'Secret Police' lipsticked on their vests they were run up the Blackstock Road to Finsbury Park, jeered and pelted with fruit all the way.

The police came the next day but found no one who said they had seen or heard a thing, let alone being able to help them with their inquiries.

Doctors warn on passion poison ...

Love Patches contain arsenic

By Harriat Curlon
Health Correspondent

LOVE PATCHES CONTAIN ARSENIC IT WAS revealed yesterday. The potential lethal poison has been positively identified in the patches by Hartlepool Public Health Laboratory following an analysis of the ingredients of their claimed 'magic formula

The exposure of the patches' poison led to calls for their immediate ban.

Laboratory head, Dr Tony Mead, said arsenic is one of the chemicals his team has identified in Love Patches make-up.

While admitting that much of their other ingredients

Dr Mead said "While at last we have learned of the link between Love Patches and the longlasting arousal they give, we also now know why they are causing a rising toll of heart attacks in their mature male users

"Arsenic slows blood's circulation," he said, "and in do-

Captured 'spies' paraded through streets naked

Jeering crowds pelt and spit on suspected spooks

By RONALD SCARMAN in North London

EIGHT MEN, ALLEGED BY NONETTES TO BE working for the Security Services, were paraded, near-naked, through north London streets last night.

The men, accused by the Nonettes of attacking their members, were yoked together and made to run a gauntlet of angry crowds pelting them with rotten fruit and other street rubbish.

The alleged agents, who had also been badly beaten during the disturbances, were later rescued by a police helicopter from a nearby park. They were flown to hospital where their condition was said to be serious though not life threatening.

Police investigating the incident, which took place in Blackstock Road, Finsbury Park and adjoining streets have as yet to make any arrests.

According to people in ...

Park, North London. Residents of a nearby housing estate were angered at seeing eight men attack a youth who lived on the estate.

There are unconfirmed re-ports that the men, attempting to escape residents coming to the youth's aid and had purposely driven their cars into them.

A Scotland Yard spokesman said: "Such outbreaks of mob violence will not be tolerated under

ARSENAL FAVOURITES FOR IEFA CUP

Sofia seen as walkover by cock-a-hoop Gunners

By JOANNA JONES

THERE WAS A broad smile on the Arsenal boss, Graham George's face yesterday. While congratulating Sofia Dynamo on their amazing 9-3 win against Moscow Spartek, he is confid-...

George said: "A game is never over until the final whistle but Arsenal's maxim is that we always play to win.

"As we have shown in recent form, this determination to win has brought Arsenal nothing but success.

George said although Arsenal are confident of victory, the entire squad is training non-stop at heavily guarded secret location. "Make no mistake," he said, "we are taking no chances, not at this late stage in the day."

Although there have not ...

Ill's shares crash

By Ross Capulyard

Shares on Britain's leading bookie, Wm Ill crashed through the floor yesterday

In the space of a few hours Ill's shares fell from 136p to just 26p and wiping £500m off

favourites to win the IFEA cup, Ill's will have to pay out up to £200m on bets placed with them

Greg Howland of Grenfell's said "By sticking to a policy that

placed £50,000 at 1000-1 is set to walk away with £50m Even when they reduced their odds down to 10-1 there were still tens of thousands piling in and placing serious ...

As Home Office denies spying cla...

NONETTES NAM... 'M15 AGENTS'

By Mark Lewis
Political Editor

THE eight men attacked by a mob in north London were working for M15, the Nonettes claimed yesterday.

The Nonette movement also released details that led up to the attacks. The Home Office denied all knowledge of the attack victims or Nonette spying claims.

According to the Nonettes, the eight men were employed by TWD Services, a security company based in Watford, Herts.

Giving the names of four of the men, as well as showing documents purported to have been found on them, the Nonette spokeswoman said that half of the men had chased one of their movement's members into a block of flats and savagely attacked him.

The victim, a 20-year-old student, still recovering from his injuries at hidden location, was delivering computer disks that had come into his possession to another Nonette member.

Claiming that the disks contained evidence of the security services' surveillance of the Nonettes, their spokeswoman said that the men were attempting to recover them from the student and when they failed to find them on him, attacked him instead.

Again, according to the spokeswoman, she said that when residents of the flats and others, rushed to the student's aid, the men panicked and attempted to escape the crowd.

In doing so they purposely drove their cars into a crowd of yet more people who were blocking their escape and injuring several of them. The crowd enraged by the men's actions then dragged them from their cars.

The spokeswoman said: "It is fortunate ... men that the ... Nonette repre... was able to ... everyone, for the... knowing what wo... happened to the... they had not."

The Nonettes s... the two cars the m... in are awaiting c... by their owners ... people hurt in th... have received com... ion for their inju... damage to ... caused by the... actions.

The Nonette ... woman said that ... material on the di... been transcribe... disks will also b... available to their ... The Nonettes al... that the data on t... will be made pu... soon as possible.

The Scotland Ya... that it was the ... duty to report... breaches of law... the residents of th... find any evidence wh...

Ian Lansdale reports on North London disturbance

FINSBURY PARK RIOT: NOBODY SAW ANYTHING

THERE WAS A HEAVY POLICE PRESENCE on the Blackstock Road, Finsbury Park, this morning but no signs of anything else out of the ordinary. Nothing to indicate that one of London's most serious outbreaks of mob violence in years broke out on this nondescript north London street last night.

According to the police, eight men, stripped to their underwear, badly beaten and yoked together, were forced to run from one end of Blackstock Road to the other. They were also forced to run a gauntlet of angry crowds pelting them with rotten fruit and street rubbish.

To the police's frustration, none of those living or working on the street say they saw anything. There are not any residents who admit even hearing anything out of the ordinary either.

There are no witnesses in the block of flats where the actual savage beatings of the eight supposed agent took place either. To the police's evident frustration nobody in the flats is able or willing to assist them with their enquiries.

There are signs however, that something did recently take place here. In the courtyard of the flats: a freshly broken section of wall, the yard's gate freshly ripped off of its hinges. But again there are no witnesses. Or in the words of one policeman: ...

Finsbury Park tube station and Arsenal's former stadium.

Blackstock Road is, however, like much of the area: a Nonette stronghold.

According to some of the police investigating the riot, it is the Nonettes who orchestrated the attacks on the eight men as well as being behind the riot itself.

It is also the Nonettes, so some police again claim, who have stopped local residents from cooperating with them in identifying the ringleaders.

The local Nonettes, however, are sticking to their policy of not speaking to the Press let alone to the police, who they increasingly regard as 'the enemy'.

Nonettes, so police also believe, were responsible for blocking off adjoining streets, denying them the chance of rescuing the eight men.

According to Scotland Yard's central surveillance centre, CCTV cameras on Seven Sisters and Holloway Roads - both passing Blackstock Road - as well as at the Finsbury Park intersection, showed traffic congestion and alerted

There is only one thing to do with adversity. Turn it to advantage and if possible a business opportunity.

It is also important to keep a cool head and a steady hand on the tiller. When a company is doing well, know-all lower management seek senior say in its every aspect. However, the moment matters go awry they are busy not in righting wrong but unloading responsibility and opining blame on their seniors. They panic. And panic along with negative immaturity was what the cooperatives' representatives presented to me.

Half were filled with acrimony and angst claiming they had been kept in the dark about Love Patches' formula, others with woe that they and their blessed bay trees were done for. But some tough, no nonsense talking on my part rammed a hard dose of realism into their inexperienced heads.

As I said to them, how was I to know 'ursênico' was Brazilian for 'arsenic'? How was I to know that the regular Congress-wide use of mormics, in keeping men's hearts healthy, hid its effects and was also the reason why the balding ones had their hair come back? And further, it was a matter of record, I told them, that from the very outset I voiced reservations as to the wisdom of overseas sales especially to non-Nonettes.

But be that as it may, I told them, they had to grasp the fact there is nothing wrong with Love Patches, they are perfectly safe, a little bit of arsenic never did anyone any harm. It was the men wearing them who were to blame. If these men, I said, had joined the Nonettes, used a mormic, then none of them would have had a heart attack let alone died.

All their talk, I told the representatives, of 'corporate duty of care', 'moral responsibility' and the like, was management mumbo jumbo they had picked up from reading too many "How to do it" business books. As I pointed out, these are written by those who can't do it. In a properly run business, I said, 'remorse', 'regret' are PR speak seeking sympathy and to keep custom coming. "Never forget," I told them, "consumers exist for the benefit of providers and never the other way round. Lose sight of this and a business is doomed."

As for paying 'compensation' to 'victims' families, I reminded them, it will have to be paid for in higher prices or thinner margins for the Nonettes who sell the Patches. As they derive much of their income from Patch sales it will hit them hard. "Do you want to hurt our fellow Nonettes?" I asked.

I also told them that should there be any chancers who dare sue, then let them try. We will insist on having every claim heard in local courts and full details of their sex lives spread over the newspapers. When some said this was not being ethical I told them, "In professionally run businesses 'ethics' is nothing other than a place east of London."

When others insisted on a 'product recall', reduce Patch strength so as to make them 'safe' from causing further fatalities, it is important to protect

Entire Moscow Spartek squad ...

Russians come clean on Susem sex abductions

Every player 'finished off' by Alien's titanic Tear...

By John Carter in Rome, Ivan Grigoff in Moscow

MOSCOW SPARTEK'S IEFA SEMI FINAL 9-3 defeat by Sofia was due solely to their entire first division squad being abducted by the Susem, it was revealed yesterday.

Apart from all the Russian ... subjected to 48 ...

According to Russian sources none of the team are ... of play-

Nonettes accuse government of "Big Browser" snooping

'WHY ARE YOU SPYING ON US?

Nonettes demand government comes clean on spying allegations

By Phillip Brown
Security Correspondent

NONETTES DEMANDED yesterday to know why the government is spying on them.

Presenting print-outs and copies of computer disks which have come into their possession, Nonettes accused the security services of conducting surveillance operations on the movement as well as 'targeting' many of their members.

If Nonette claims are ... likely to ... intercepted and linked with visual recognition systems such as CCTV.

This level of surveillance, Nonettes say, indicates that the government is actively and intentionally spying on them.

A Nonette spokesman, Brian White, said: "We would like to know why the government feels it needs to snoop on us. While the Nonette movement is fully accountable to its members, every facet of our activities is open to public scrutiny and this includes govern-

They also called on the government to give a public undertaking not to conduct any further surveillance on the movement without their knowledge and consent.

The Nonettes said documents found in the cars of the eight men who attacked the student at Finsbury Park, showed they were employed by a Watford based security company which has been sub-contracted by M15 to locate the missing tapes.

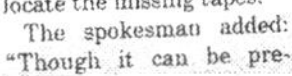

The spokesman added: "Though it can be pre-

WIFE ACCUSED OF L PATCH MURDER

By CAROLE SMITH Courts Correspondent

DID SHE OR DID SHE NOT? That was the question Worcester magistrates faced yesterday in the case of a 42-year-old married woman accused of murdering her husband by luring him into a 24 hour non-stop marathon lovemaking bout with the aid of Love Patches.

The prosecution allege that Mrs Margaret Robbins, a hair stylist of Fulborough Road, Ruchwick purposely made love with her husband John, an unemployed abattoir operative for an entire night in the full knowledge that because of his weak heart it would kill him.

Robbins, in denying the charge against her said that her husband's death was nothing other than a tragic accident.

Prosecuting QC, Martin Fotherson, said Robbins stood to benefit from a £200,000 insurance policy taken out on her husband's life six months earlier.

The prosecuting QC said to Robbins: "I put it to you that at the same time as you took out this policy, you had already intended to do away with your husband, had you not?"

In reply Robbins said that she had not taken the out the policy but had been sold it by a financial advisor. And that both she and her husband were joint signatories to the policy.

Fotherson QC then said to Robbins: "This financial advisor was more that just a advisor was he not? I put it to you that you were and still are having an affair with this man?"

Robbins denied that she was having extra-marital relations with anyone. She said that she and the financial advisor ...

Martin Fotherson QC

Home Office pathologist, Dr Peter Gibbs, giving evidence for the prosecution, said that he found marks on John Robbins' body indicating that he had had at least 14 separate Love Patches adhered to his back and neck.

Dr Gibbs said that the police had handed to him a similar number of Love Patch wrappers they had retrieved from a waste bin in the kitchen of Robbins' house.

Fotherson QC then said to Robbins: I put it to you that, to put it quite bluntly, you literary f**ked your husband to death, yes or no?"

The judge, Justice Wilkens then intervened, saying he would not countenance such vulgar language in his court.

The hearing was then adjourned while Justice Wilkens summoned Fotherson QC to his chambers for a reprimand.

The trial continues.

Government denies spying on Nonettes

MI5 saying nothing

By Mark Lewis
Political Editor

THE government has not been spying on the Nonettes, Whitehall stated yesterday.

Both the Home Office and the Downing Press Office issued statements refuting Nonette claims that the security services are conducting surveillance operations on the movement and its activities.

The Home Office spokesman said: "The security of the United Kingdom and all of its peoples is of paramount importance to Her Majesty's Government

"To facilitate this objective and under terms of successive legislation enacted to this end, the security services of this country are charged with monitoring the activities of ...

Downing Street spokesman denying allegations of spying on Nonettes

ment agencies with intelligence support, enabling them to ensure the protection of the general population from terrorist and other related criminal activity.

"The security services of the UK at no time conduct surveillance operations, neither ...

they have been subjected to unwarranted investigation by the security services, complaint to this effect should be made immediately to the appropriate law enforcement agency.

"Failure to do so, however, will in itself, constit-

A Downing Street spokesman said: "Anyone working for the government, regardless of their position or capacity, must act lawfully at all times.

"The government does not spy on the law abiding. The security services do conduct surveillance operations on people and organisations but only those considered to be acting unlawfully.

"There are those who are critical of this government and its policies, just as there always have been and doubtless will be in the future. However, Britain is a democracy and it is people's right to criticise the government of the day.

"It does not mean however, that the government, including the present administration, has anything to gain, let alone havis the right, legally and morally, to spy on and harass their opponents.

"While accepting that ...

Britta Ruff bemoans men's sudden shyness

Where have all the geezers gone?

WANTON IS WONDERFUL in getting over all our feminin... inhibitions but there's one drawback with it: availabi... blokes. Have you noticed how lately there are none about?

Unattached, single ones out on their own that this. And when I do spot one, the moment I get anywhere near them they're running off.

I'm not alone in this either. All my mates say the same: "NO FELLAS!" let alone ones with looks and a bit of go in them.

It's not for want of looking either, or hunting to be honest. There's not a single one in the clubs or the gyms. Those that are there are under the eye of their other half's so you can't do anything

As for blokes out on the street o... anywhere like that there's no chanc... with them either. I've tried.

As soon as you say anything to the... make a move they're all a blubber a... running back to their offices o... building sites.

One of my mates who meets u... with blokes in a café up on the A... says the same. As soon as she goe... up to any of them they're makin... for the cabs of their trucks, lockin... themselves in and driving off as fa... as they can.

STOLEN SNOOPING DISKS SCANDEL:

Government snooping on Nonettes confirmed

Nonettes enraged at scale of government surveillance

By Andrew Witting
Security Reporter

M15 KEEPS TABS ON MORE than 10,000 Nonettes it was revealed yesterday.

Nonettes, angry at the revelations, are demanding government apologises for what they call "unauthorised intrusion into their personal lives".

The Nonettes are also threatening the release of further details of state sponsored snooping contained on computer disks that are now in their possession.

The disks, Nonettes claim, show that the prime minister is directly involved in the setting up a nationwide surveillance network on the Nonettes.

part of a unified network of monitoring Nonette activity including CCTV.

The disks also show that other monitoring centres, not operated by the police, such as those run by councils and private organisations are also integrated into the national police network.

The Nonettes revealed that face and voice recognition software, integrated into CCTV monitoring systems, have been programmed to pick out and keep tabs on the movement and whereabouts of "many thousands" of its members.

The disks also reveal, Nonettes say, that car registration numbers of those Nonettes on MI5's 'hit list' also have been integrated into

Nonette spokesman, Brian White, said: "The disks also reveal that the surveillance system which has been set up is so sophisticated that CCTV cameras can identify a person from as little as the pattern of their ear.

"There is also indication," Mr White said, "that not only is the programs' data coordinated by GCHQ, Cheltenham but that it is also passed on as part of the Echelon programme, to the American National Security Agency in Fort Langly, Virginia."

CCTV surveillance, the disks reveal, is not the only area of government snooping. Phone calls and text messages are also monitored as are e-mails. Even ordinary mail has been subjected to routine wide-

'brand quality', I all but blew my top. "Not one woman who purchased Patches," I said, "has been harmed by them. It's the men they stuck them on who keeled over. Most of these will have been old or clapped out and because of their weak hearts, even if they hadn't had Patches on them, they wouldn't have lasted much longer.

"Reduce Patch strength and its effectiveness will be likewise," I told them, "and then you really will have complainers, millions of them, all women, and all bitter." As far as I was concerned, I said, they were welcome to deal with them, and with the Susem for that matter.

Not only did this shut them up but I told them there was no alternative than to keep Patch strength unchanged. "Weaken it," I said, "and not only will the Susem find alternative producers, but these will take over the market and we will all lose a fortune let alone the growers their bay trees." (Naturally I didn't think it politic to mention that if the cooperatives didn't see sense, I'd the Huitoto lined up to grow replacement trees).

There were others who wittered that we must at least be seen doing something in response to the deaths. "The men who died from using Love Patches," I told them, "are just that, dead. However, their widows present an ideal marketing opportunity to promote new products. By announcing that we will award them a year's supply of Patches and Wanton strips plus seven days free holiday with their replacement partners, we can use them as a focus for a worldwide campaign promoting Rampenho by also giving them a month's supply of it in return for their endorsements."

When I told them increased sales of Rampenho, which will have its name Anglicised, means greater demand for bay leaf extract, there were smiles from all the growers. As for adding health warnings on Patches, I reminded them that when women put them on men they weren't interested in their health but in them doing what they put the Patches on them for in the first place, namely two solid hours of hard lovemaking.

However, in order to reduce risks of women's weak-hearted partners dying on them, I said, and just as importantly, save them the bother of redressing and dragging their dead bodies to less embarrassing spots, we will introduce a milder Patch to be sold in single sachets so as to also reduce the risk of women unintentionally slapping on booster ones mid-passion. This will mean, I added, we will be able to specifically cater for those who know their partners are past their best. It will also mean a yet further increase in demand for bay leaves.

With now smiles all round I almost said "Class, dismiss! And get on with your work." But instead reminded them we are running a business not a charity. Also that our prime intent is making money, and in future to leave 'customer care' and 'do-gooding' for others to nanny over.

Though the cooperatives were put back down in their place I was left wondering why I bothered with such an ungrateful lot. If it wasn't for my

Aphrodisiac's amour agent

"Love Patches have no more arsenic than oysters" – says expert

By **Harriet Curren**
Health Correspondent

LIFE MAY BE A BOWL OF cherries but love is in a dish of oysters. The age-old claim that slipping down mouthfuls of these silvery scallops really does make a man's sagging ardour, well harder, is confirmed by recently published scientific research.

In the latest edition of *Molluscs Monthly*, Professor Howard Knight, head of the Department of Marine Pharmacology, the University of Sheppey at Harty, found that in field trials between two groups of male students, the first who ate oysters, the second not, that the eaters performed better than non-eaters.

From questionnaire replies given by the males' partners, both groups were able to be assessed on a 1-10 rating. The oyster eaters achieved a significantly higher score than non-eaters.

The reason for the oyster groups' higher rating Professor Knight, said was most probably because of the mol-

Professor Knight said: "Despite popular belief, arsenic is not poisonous as such, only too much of it is but then that's the same for everything, including water.

"Our bodies," he said, "have at least 7mg of endogenous arsenic and can easily absorb as much again without any ill-effects, in a person in good health, that is. As this research has shown, an actual increase of arsenic has done these young people a power of good.

"Indeed the menfolk of Styria, in Austria, were arsenic ores are abundant, actually eat mouthfuls of the stuff for the good of their health and to the satisfaction of their womenfolk," he said.

Professor Knight said that as far as he was concerned the amounts of arsenic found in Love Patches, while in terms of bodily absorption was on the "high side", was nothing for a healthy person to worry about.

He said: "Taking arsenic is like alcohol, you have to pace yourself. However, those with cirrhosis know they have go easy on the booze, similarly those with weak hearts, have to go easy on the lovemaking."

Nonettes name 'Big Brother' snoopers

MPs call for inquiry as civil servants are reported spying on their neighbours

By **Phillip Brown**
National Security Correspondent

NONETTES REVEALED yesterday the names of dozens of security service personnel listed on the computer disks that have come into their possession.

The disks also show that many civil servants are reporting on Nonettes and their activities in the areas where they live to the security services.

Downing Street issued a statement denouncing the disclosure of the names, saying that the safety of many innocent people could have been put at risk.

The leader of the opposition, Stanley Haines, and other LibCon MP's, have called for ...

The Nonettes showed a list of 53 names and contact numbers of those whom they claim are members of M15 and GIS.

The Nonettes also gave a further list of names, contact numbers and e-mail addresses of 127 people, who they say are senior civil servants.

Nonette spokesman, Brian White, said: "In the light of the information contained on these disks, it is little wonder the Secret Services were desperate to get them back."

Mr White said that since the revelations of the first disks, the Nonettes have received further information from many people in the movement confirming what the disks said and yet more evidence that government organisations

ively involved in surveillance of them.

Demanding a public apology from the government and as public an undertaking not to do so in the future, Mr White also said that there is a rising tide of anger among many Nonettes against the government over their spying activities.

The Nonettes also wanted to know, he said, why the government have gone to such lengths to find out about the Nonettes when every facet of their activeities is open to public scrutiny.

"Or does the government have a totally different agenda?" he asked "Are we Nonettes seen as a threat by them? Are there plans for dirty tricks campaign against us? The

RAGING MOBS SMASH CCTVS

- Thousands of spy cameras out of action
- Police forces 'blinded' by loss

By **JOHN WITHERS**
Security Correspondent

THOUSANDS OF CCTV cameras were attacked and put out of action last night as rampaging mobs in scores of towns and cities across Britain fought running battles with the police. Many hundreds of arrests were made.

The outbreak of violence, police say, was coordinated and they blame the Nonettes for being behind it.

The damage to CCTV security systems is said to run into millions of pounds.

In London, crowds chanting: "Blind Big Brother" surged along the Euston and Marylebone Roads and had, police say, damaged most of the CCTV cameras along both roads before they were apprehended

... these attacks, other

POUND IN DUMP SLUMP JUMP

Nonette up 10 per cen

By Ross Capulyard

Because of rising sterling inflation, the nonette has been revalued by 10 per cent. The pound is now worth N0 59 5

According to Nonette newspapers, the Central Bank of Congress has downgraded their currencies because of the rapid increase in inflation in both North America and European non-Nonette economies. Retailers trading mainly in nonettes are said to have already adjusted their sterling prices upwards in res-

their salaries in nonettes, it means that in the space of little more than a month they have seen their pay rise by 30 per cent relative to those who are still paid in sterling

As with the previous revaluation, the growing disparity between the two currencies is bound to see yet more people opting to be paid in the Non-ette currency.

The effect of this revaluation on the wider UK economy is hard to predict. Uber Bank economist Harold Smithers, thinks that the equivalent of 10 per

the face of it, seem large but in growth terms it is little short of staggering

"Admittedly part of this growth is a result of the recent tax changes and the bank crisis preceding them but the rate of increase, if anything, is, as a consequence, set to accelerate

"In turn, this is more than likely to see yet more people opting to use the nonette instead of pounds sterling," he said.

With the boom in high street sales showing little signs of slowing consumers could

Susem threat to bank may have been a empty one, ordinary account holders appear to be in no mood to trust them with the money

Coupled with the desperation of banks maintain lending at a price, usually at no co to retailers, it is perhaps not surprising the Nonettes' Central Bank is revaluing currency

It is also comes as surprise either the ordinary consumer although they may yet have articulated as such, are al showing their lack

Nonettes to launch own post services

Security concerns also affect faxes, phones, e-mails: Post Office set to suffer major losses

By Jess Patman
Security Correspondent

CONCERNED AT MAIL interception, Nonettes have launched their own postal system

The new service, run on the same lines as those in areas already under Nonette control, guarantees absolute security as well as same-day local delivery and a next-day national service.

The Nonettes also say the new postal service will be considerably cheaper than the Royal Mail.

Outlining the new service, the Nonette spokeswoman said that all anyone need do was write the recipient's Nonette number on the envelope and it will be delivered to them.

Nobody but they and their local Nonette will know who they are. She said that a sequence of just ten numbers and letters will locate every person on earth.

Post handed in at a local Nonette office can be delivered quickly to addresses in the same and neighbouring Nonettes. Mail for Nonettes further a field is sent to the area Nonette which, in turn, sends mail onto adjoining area Nonettes or to the regional one or on to other regional centres.

The spokeswoman said that many ex and retired Royal Mail employees will be operating the system.

She also said that while Nonette system will be junk-mail free, it offers direct mail companies a much more cost-effective method of reaching potential customers.

By needing only to deliver to a Nonette group it would promote their products directly on their behalf

If this method of mail order proves successful it could deal a body blow to the Post Office which currently derives the majority of its revenues from delivering junk mail.

This new service will also put pressure on direct mail companies to join the Nonettes rather than see their competitors steal much of their business.

Last night the Post Office said they were studying the implications but said that in running a rival service the Nonettes would be operating illegally.

Because of the Nonettes' wider security concerns, they also said that the movement would cease using telephones, faxes and e-mails in the conduct of its business. The Nonettes also recommended that until such times as the government gives verifiable undertakings that they have stopped spying on the movement that individual Nonettes should also cease using telephone for their own personal safety and security

The Nonettes also announced that a number of their members will be travelling to the Nonettes headquarters in Brazil to study and learn the method of auto communication which thought and messages can be transmitted directly from one person to another.

This new method of transmission, coupled with the Nonettes ceasing to use telephones could well deal a body blow to most of the embattled telecom companies still reeling from the collapse of mobile telephone use.

initiative and enterprise as well as connections with the Susem, none of them would be reaping the riches they are. For that matter, neither would the Boro and Huitoto be making money from Wanton strips either. And if they and the cooperatives continue to poke their noses into everything, especially the accounts, I might well chuck it all in and leave them to it.

Forming in the back of my mind is the thought I could do just that. Lull both groups to boost their production then sell them my shares. With both believing sales and profits are higher than they actually are I can ramp the share price. With both falling over themselves to buy, I can command a higher price for mine. With the proceeds plus my wager from Arsenal's IEFA win, not only will I be able to bribe myself out of Tabajara, and from Rainbow's leash, but use it to finance another project taking shape, which, when it comes to fruition will really make some serious money.

Again it's my connections with the Susem which led to the idea. I found out about it by asking more of what Terbal called 'kinesis'. This is the power source the Susem use including that of their spacecraft. Although the principle is simple, it's replicating Susem technology, harnessing it, where the real prize lies. This is what I sought and think I have uncovered. Needless to say, just as previously, I have been left with yet more questions begging answers. However, I also found out about the 'Time Tunnels' the Susem use and how universes come into being.

When Menpemelo, months ago, first explained Tertiary waves, 'wavicles', 'frothicles' (or what Earthly scientists term 'particles', 'matter'), she said they evolve from Secondary waves, energy, similar to spume forming from cresting waves of water. She had also said that frothicles usually form into two interlocking groups of three wavicles and can be likened to our physicists' positive and negative halves of atoms' nuclei, the wavicles, quarks.

However, Terbal, when I spoke with him, gave deeper detail. He said although, like spume, Tertiary frothicles have been nominally 'looped off' from Secondary waves, they retain these waves' inherent energy, albeit in a locked in, latent, state. But over time frothicles unlock, reverting, releasing their energy back into Secondary waves. Terbal used burning coal as analogy of this. He later used that of elephants and stiletto heels in explaining more efficient ways of returning Tertiary wave energy to Secondary waves as well as using it to counter their 'attracting' power.

He mentioned shadows. Of the illusion they give when falling on a surface, in being bi-conexts, planes. How a shadow falling on to a transparent surface appears to possess both a top and underside. Should the shadow further fall upon another, separated, yet parallel clear surface, there will be two almost identical double-sided shadows. He then said add a third such surface and there will be three identical shadows. These 'entities', Terbal said, though possessing 'form' are without apparent 'mass'. He said envisage this shadowy trio being alike to wavicles in each half of a frothicle.

Compensation offer for Patch victims' partners

Milder patches promised

Tracy Barnett
Medical Editor

Laboratories Ceará, makers of Love Patches, are offering a full compensation package to the partners of victims of Patch users.

In a statement released yesterday Laboratories Ceará said: "Here in Tabajara our eyes are filled with tears of sadness and our hearts heavy with sorrow for the recent losses of *Love Patch* customers' partners while wearing our patches.

"Although we are conscious that these men who have died represent a minuscule fraction of the many hundreds of millions of more than satisfied users of *Love Patches* and their partners worldwide and also that none of them were actually members of any Nonette, we at **Laboratories Ceará** nevertheless are filled with remorse at the loss of any *Love Patch* customers' partner's due to untimely demise.

"**Laboratories Ceará** also wishes to emphasise that we do not shirk for a single moment our blame in failing to stress firmly enough how important it is for *Love Patch* users to refrain from engaging partners with less than healthy hearts in prolonged and/or robust congress.

"Neither do we wish to avoid acknowledging our irresponsibility in failing to stress how important it is for *Love Patch* users whose partners' hearts are less than fully healthy, to join the Nonettes immediately so they might avail themselves of the benefits of mormic health booths which restore the complete body to virile healthiness and well able to withstand the prolonged rigours *Love Patch* application often occasions.

"In order that we might effect some small redress to every *Love Patch* customer who has lost a partner while wearing one of our patches, we at **Laboratories Ceará**, in our commitment to strive for nothing less than fully satisfied customers, are giving a **year's free supply of *Love Patches*** plus a seven days, all reasonable expenses paid holiday of their choice for both themselves and a replacement partner.

"**Laboratories Ceará** will also donate immediately to them, **absolutely free of charge**, a generous supply of our latest product: **'RAMPANT'**, which we know they will find very handy.

"Because **Laboratories Ceará** is deeply committed to avoiding further fatalities from users' partners' whose hearts are not as healthy as they might, we are **immediately introducing a milder Love Patch.**

"At **Laboratories Ceará** we are fully devoted to nothing less than the complete satisfaction of all our customers.

"Should any customer require our assistance, or if we can in some small way be of help, we beg you, please do not hesitate for a moment to contact us.

"You may be most sincerely assured that the sole purpose of our existence is to be of service in bringing you full and lasting satisfaction."

Civil servants facing Nonette eviction threat

Government employees suffer 'You're Big Brother's children' taunt

David Mango

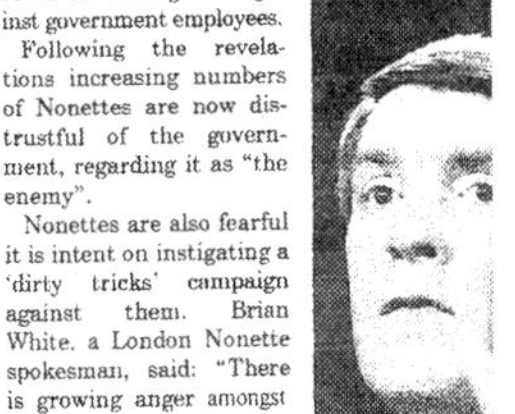

Spy fever has swept through the Nonettes and civil servants are in their sights.

Shaken by revelations of security services' snooping on their movement and evidence of some civil servants telling MI5 of their local Nonette groups' activities, the movement has launched a "Know your neighbour" campaign. Watch is to be kept on government employees in Nonette areas.

Even those employees who are Nonette members are expected to come under scrutiny.

Nonettes say they have no intention of intimidating civil servants. But, they also say, that evidence revealed by the security services' computer disks which came into their possession, give ... to be on their guard against government employees.

Following the revelations increasing numbers of Nonettes are now distrustful of the government, regarding it as "the enemy".

Nonettes are also fearful it is intent on instigating a 'dirty tricks' campaign against them. Brian White, a London Nonette spokesman, said: "There is growing anger amongst

Chile set to fall to Nonettes

Santiago surrounded by rebels

POLLY PORTILLO
IN SANTIAGO

THE CHILIAN government declared a state of siege yesterday. However, apart from the capital Santiago and the nearby port city of Valparaiso, the government's edict is unlikely to have any significant effect.

With the exception of a few pockets to the north of Santiago, such as La Serina and Caldara, the rest of the country has now elected to join the Nonette Contin-

Chile's northern provinces had been overrun by the Nonettes several months ago but the rest of the country, apart from the indigenous Indian province of Mapuche, was thought to be securely under government control.

Although the Nonettes have been active throughout Chile it was not thought that the major cities would become vulnerable to the advances of the Congress so quickly.

As the Nonette force's grip tightens there has already been a huge backlog of those Chilians attempting to flee the country, mainly to the

Nonette protesters stymie police with new weapon: Sex

'Blind the snoopers' rage attacks grow

1,000's of CCTV's smashed nationwide

BY TONY PERRY
DISTURBANCES REPORTER

IN a second night of nationwide disturbances many thousands more CCTVs were vandalised and put out of action.

In some city centres damage to cameras was so extensive that police were 'blinded' to yet further outbreaks of violence.

The night-time attacks against CCTVs followed a day of numerous random acts of violence on the cameras in shopping centres, rail and Underground stations.

Both Euston and King's Cross, London and Piccadilly stations, Manchester, were the scenes of particularly violent actions against the cameras.

Pleas by several police forces, that CCTV cameras were solely installed to protect the public from criminals, went unheeded.

There were several incidents of police themselves coming under attack by mobs of protesters as they attempted to stop them more sinister weapon against hard pressed police forces. A rapid response team had to call reinforcements to free them from a group of women attempting to assault and ravish them.

A similar outbreak occurred in Wilmslow, Manchester. Four policeman in a patrol car attempting to stop a mob smashing cameras in the town centre, were pounced on by a 20-strong group of women and dragged off into a nearby park.

One of the officers who managed to escape raised the alarm but not before he, too, had tunic and shirt ripped open and was, so Wilmsow police say, "pawed and groped" by the women. The three assaulted police officers are said to recovering from their ordeal.

Blaming the Nonette drug, Wanton, for the assaults, Head of Manchester Police, Commander, Brian Clutterbuck, called

NONETTE READERS OFFER

"I might not be young at heart anymore but since Love Patch I am young again where it matters" - Pascal Lopez (87), Quito

Ladies

Inner pleasure from Outer Space

LOVE PATCH!

"What was once a joy ... a pleasure, since Love ... has become whopper ... - Ms R T Lowe

"Since Love Patch, I have my Carlos work hard all day, study hard all evening so that he is hard all night" - Mrs B F Naval

"Since I have put Love Patches on my men my love life has come to grips with something entirely ... - S R Lencous

"Since I put my Hernando on Love Patch he's been like a rod of iron sleeved in silk night after night" - Mrs M K Salvador

For the young at heart whose hearts are not so young

NEW! LOVE PATCH LITE!

Comes in single sealed 'one at a time' safety sachets

Gives one whole hour of firm pleasure

... to MILLIONS of ..., daytime after daytime too! ... on Earth! ... this day on, no man's manhood need ever disappoint you ... potion ensures, regardless of the age of your man his manhood will give you GUARANTEED TWO WHOLE HOURS of **continuous climactic satisfaction***

- ***Love Patch's*** potion is made from entirely natural ingredients and is thus **absolutely safe**
- ***Love Patch's*** only side effect is possible tiredness after use!
- ***Love Patch*** is free of harmful sildenafil citrate nitrates and other man-made substances
- ***Love Patch*** is easy to apply: stick it on your man - he'll be ready in seconds and go for hours!
- ***Love Patch's*** pack of three patches can be yours for as little as an hour's tuition credit – just one hour's hard study by your man and he will yield you **six hours of hard pleasure!**

Supplies of **Love Patch** are now available from your nearest Nonette Centre. Packs priced at just 2Nonettes (or the equivalent in your local currency) for Nonette members, or 4Nonettes for non-members.

Because stocks of **Love Patch** are presently limited only four packs are available per customer, *preference will be given to Nonette members (another good reason for joining the Nonettes!)*

* *Family planning note: if using condoms in conjunction with Love Patch you will need the extra large size - not because of any increase in manhood length but that of girth!*

If any Love Patch fails to keep your man's manhood rock solid hard for one single second less than **TWO ENTIRE HOURS**, *Laboratories Ceará will refund your purchase price in full!*

Love Patch - **"bringing inner pleasure to all women – everywhere"**

Made under license by **Laboratories Ceará** Tabajara - Ceará - Continental Congress of America
Love Patches measure 2x3cm and come in handy peel'n'seal packs and have a pre-use life of 100 days at room/handbag temperature

He next said to visualise the top shadow, wavicle, being smaller than the bottom one and the one in between, between them in size as well. The three wavicles in the other half of the frothicle are the same except in reverse, the smallest at the bottom, and together all six wavicles approximating to a lemon-like ovoid sphere. Terbal then said to envisage the trio of each half moving, wave-like, oscillating at the same speed, though not in unison with one another, in response to the flow of Secondary waves brushing past the end tips of them.

This oscillating effects a charge to the surfaces of the wavicles, positive on one side, negative on the other. The charge is more pronounced at the crests than in the troughs. Crests on one side of a wavicle are troughs on the other and (being troughs) possess a weak charge. As the wavicles are buffeted to and fro by Secondary waves, the polarities between each wavicle are alternately attracting and 'non-attracting' one another and thus, albeit it weakly and perpetually fleetingly, holding wavicles in position relative to one another. The charge of the wavicles in one half of the frothicle will, however, be more positive than negative, with the other half being the opposite.

Terbal next said there are frothicles and frothicles, with some being bigger than others. Different ones, but not always in size, have different numbers of ripples to their wavicles. Usually the more ripples the more compressed the wavicles become.

This compression occurs, Terbal said, when there is a concentration of Secondary waves, and also when these are oscillating very fast such as in a star, more so should it be about to explode. When this occurs some of the Secondary waves' energy is imparted, stored, into the frothicles. This can happen to them again and again with each time more energy being pushed into the wavicles and causing not only their ripples to increase but become increasingly compressed. Sometimes, however, Secondary waves oscillate so fast (thus powerfully) they collide frothicles together and fuse them into one another. But Terbal said this fusion only happens to the frothicles with wavicles having a few (and thus uncompressed) ripples.

Over time a frothicle's wavicle latent energy is leached away by Secondary waves' buffeting past them in a similar way that sea waves erode shingle to sand. Each time a frothicle loses ripples from its wavicles it 'decays' into a less vibrant one and so on down until, with the last of its wavicles' vibrancy gone, it completely dissipates back to Secondary wave energy.

Though decay is gradual, usually billions of years, and the dissipation of wavicle energy causing barely a ripple as it is integrated into the current of Secondary waves, there are times, Terbal said, when frothicles, more so those whose wavicles have many ripples will, as it were, burst open, their wavicles' compressed energy springing, radiating out in a sudden surge. This surge energises passing Secondary waves to ripple, oscillate much faster. This suddenly increased Secondary wave energy radiates against other,

Banks los
to Nonett

Millions in acco
switch to N bank

By Lucy Danker

BRITAIN'S BANKS hav lost more than five millio accounts to Nonette bank it was claimed yesterday.

According to a poll take by Mory's Market Re search, one in five Hig Street bank account holder have switched over t Nonette banking.

If Mory's findings ar confirmed it will be major blow to some o Britain's biggest banks. Th account losses also ar affecting bank share adversely.

Yesterday saw major fall in all the leading clearers share prices. Clayings sav

Scientist scoff at 'Big Bro super-compute

'Nonette claims nonsense' – says Home Office

By Thomas Deerie
Science Correspondent

NONETTE claims that the US government has a massive supercomputer facility storing personal details of everyone in the world, were dismissed as "complete and utter bilge" by leading scientists and computer experts yesterday.

Nonette sources however, claimed to have irrefutable evidence of the facility's existence. According to the organisation, an array of Stone Washed super-computers is installed at the US's National Security Agency's headquarters at Langley, Virginia.

According to Nonettes, details held by British government departments are routinely sent to the US.

Under the Echelon satellite surveillance system every telephone, e-mail even Internet usage is logged, recorded and analysed in 'real time'

The Home Office maintains that this surveillance is no more than routine and is part of an ongoing international effort to combat the treat of global terrorism.

The Nonettes, however, dismiss such claims as a smokescreen for the real purpose behind this state eavesdropping. Brian White, the Nonettes' London spokesman said, "There is not an iota of evidence that Echelon or any of the other state spying on individual citizens have caught a single terrorist."

Mr White claims that the

NONETTE READERS' OFFER

Ladies

Do you suffer from beau bashfulness?

BANISH IT TODAY WITH

RAMPANT!

a fragrance formulated by women for women
for use on men
HARDENS ARDOUR IN AN INSTANT!

once your intended has sniffed just one pulse of this bouquet
he will rapidly become a

Rampant Man!

- ***Rampant*** contains a specially formulated fragrance used for countless eons by women everywhere across the Galaxy and beyond **to banish male inhibition and shyness.**
- ***Rampant*** is already used by **MILLIONS** of women across the lands of the Nonettes to induce instant physical and psychological amatory arousal of their men.
- ***Rampant*** is formulated from fully **natural compounds** which only occur on Earth in the remote Sertão
- ***Rampant*** comes in a discreet palm-size spray - a single pulse of ***Rampant*** aimed at your intended is sufficient to **instantly repress his every reluctance** and just as rapidly, **arouse his amorous urges both physically and psychologically** - each spray gives up to 50 pulses-worth of potential pleasure!
- ***Rampant*** does not cause adverse reaction to any known allergies and can be safely used in conjunction with both **Wanton** and **Love Patches**.
- ***Rampant*** three-spray-pack can be yours for as little as an hour's tuition credit - just one hour's study **for endless hours free for you to do as you desire with any man you desire to desire**!

Supplies of **Rampant** three-spray-packs are now available from your nearest Nonette Centre. Each pack is priced for Nonette members at **only** N2 (or the equivalent in your local currency) N4 for non-Nonettes (another good reason for enrolling with us today!)

***Rampant* – "enabling women to help men overcome reluctance and inhibition"**

Made under licence by **Laboratories Ceará** Tabajara - Ceará - Continental Congress of America

Joanne Miller reports on the continuing rapid growth of Nonettes

UK Nonettes surge to 11m

PM dismisses Alien backed groups' rise as 'Not significant'

MORE THAN 11 million people and many businesses across the UK are now members of the Nonette movement With this latest rise in numbers, the Nonettes are now Britain's biggest mass organisation ever

Announcing the sudden surge in membership, Nonette spokeswoman. Diane Moor, said: "Growth has occurred evenly across the country as well as among social classes and age groups

"We attribute this latest increase in our rate of growth partly to the rising value of the nonette as well as its increasing use as the currency of choice But a more important factor behind the rise, however, is the now established advantages and benefits of being part of the movement "

Commenting on the latest figures, the prime minister, Edward Campbell said: "It is important to keep them in proportion to the population as a whole There are 49 million people who have declined to associate with this terrorist extra-terrestrial

less vibrant frothicles as if in a rush. This causes wavicles in these frothicles to oscillate more than they are conditioned to do. These then cause Secondary waves passing them to also oscillate faster, hitting and upsetting other frothicles.

The radiation of this sudden release of energy causes widespread disturbance and continues for a long time before its effects are dissipated. All strengths of frothicles are affected, Terbal said, but those whose wavicles have only a small number of ripples are affected the most. What is more, should different frothicles be clumped together, moleculed, once one is oscillating faster, the entire molecule will be automatically 'irradiated'.

Terbal said both the slow and sudden release of wavicle radiation is going on all the time wherever there are frothicles. However, there is also a universal natural upper limit to wavicle oscillation within a frothicle. Once this has been reached further Secondary wave energy, under natural circumstances, is either 'rebuffed' by frothicles or in turn, they decay. As Terbal spoke he stressed "natural circumstances". Later I understood why.

Up to this point Terbal had explained everything in terms of our Earthly dimensions, 'contexts'. He next explained Tertiary waves within the quinth context. He said, just as had Menpemelo earlier, that everything is composed of points, yet at the same time they are 'non-contexts'. He also said, as Menpemelo had, that within the quinth context there is a lower level of resistance to the transmission of the effects of all forms of [wave] motion.

From the honing of a universe's Anthropic Constant to its maturity, orderliness is established within precise limits. The reason for this, Terbal said, is that there is an upper level to a universe's creation, transmutation of frothicle wavicle intensity, or elements, this being uranium.

The universe's naturally occurring 'imbalances', Terbal said, eventually dissipate, disruption being confined to what he termed "calculable parameters". Unnatural ones are not. And with little to check or counter them, their effects are extensive, deep and wide ranging.

Even though long ago, Earth's 'natural' nuclear explosions at Oklo had, Terbal said, 'unnatural' repercussions far beyond our solar system. He said it took millions of years before their destabilising effects faded away. I asked "What were these, what did they do?"

Terbal explained. He again said that waves are composed of non-context points. It is these which form waves, no matter how big, how steep or fast they are, into smooth parabolic curves. In what he termed "contra-dynamic equilibrium", positioning points of wavicles are influenced by those of Secondary waves and these by Primary ones. In reverse, wavicles' points also influence those of Secondary waves, and they Primary ones.

Unnatural frothicles are those with an enforced excess of ripples to their wavicles. In containing them some wavicle positioning points are pushed out of parabolic alignment, the ripples get a dent in them. Uranium frothicles, at the upper limit of natural wavicle concentration, can however be evolved into forms, isotopes, which exceed this limit. Though the wavicles of these isotopes bend out of line, they are little more than wobbles compared to the massive dents in neptunium wavicles. Though the other 'unnaturals', plutonium, americium and upwards, have dents in their wavicles all eventually decay down to neptunium.

But no matter how short or long these unnaturals take to decay, plutonium 30 years, neptunium 30,000 years, they are contaging passing Secondary waves with their dented deformity. These waves go on to infect dents in wavicles of other, natural frothicles. Those close to unnaturals will of course be more irradiated than those further away, but nonetheless the contagion spreads and spreads.

In time this contagion of the unnaturals dies down and is no longer discernible, here on Earth that is. But out in space it still ripples ever outward infecting all in its path. These ripples, waves, are those Paceillo had earlier referred to as "letum waves".

Eventually, these letum waves, Terbal said, ripple to the very edges of the strand of the primary wave within which we, along with umpteen million other stars, are set. He reminded that the mobius strip of the universe is composed of intermeshing sheets and strands of Primary waves, along the edges of which, he said, are dense concentrations of Secondary waves all oscillating at extremely fast speeds. There are also concentrations of freshly forming frothicles (they have only a positive half). Should letum waves effect on these embryo frothicles, they being the simplest ones of them all, they will become very distorted and very quickly so.

Terbal said the edges of sheets, strands, of Primary waves usually mesh into one another but sometimes one overlays another and yet others have strips of gap between them. It is these gaps which are the 'Time Tunnels' the Susem use to travel from one part of the universe to another.

He said Earthly scientists in expressing 'time' in terms of light's speed, had the constant the wrong way round. While light's speed is in fact not constant, that of time is. Time is the same throughout the universe, being neither faster nor slower. It is time which is the universe's constant. It is by this only that the relativity of everything in the universe is to be measured. He then said "But if dere is no universe dere ist not time."

With one end of a gap being the same moment as the other, the Susem are able to 'momentarily' leave one part of the universe and instantly be at another many 'light years' away. They manage this by cocooning their spacecraft in dense, thick layers of the embryonic frothicles forming along the strip's edge, then bouncing, skimming, as it were, along a side of the gap. Terbal said there are many such voids and the Susem use them to travel all over the place.

Terbal also said these voids are not that difficult to spot. The gap nearest to us and the one the Susem use to travel to our part of the universe has already been spotted by our astronomers, Vallerga and Welsh being two names he mentioned. It's more than 500 'light years' long and stretches from near the star we call Adhara all the way to Sirius. The Susem 'home' star, Saldes, is about five light years from the gap and about halfway along it.

It was fear of our sheet's edges gap's frothicles being mutated by letum wave radiation, and thus ruining one of the Susem travel routes, which had Paceillo order the prompt removal of everything 'unnaturally nuclear' from the face of the Earth. I asked about the voids. What exactly were they, was anything in them? Terbal said "Non-aligned un-compounded non-contexts," but seeing I didn't understand, he explained.

He reminded that everything is composed of points, non-contexts, 'nothings'. Should a nothing knock into another nothing it still results in a nothing (or "2 x 0 = 0", as he put it). Even a squillion billion times nought is still a nought. However, while agglomerations of nothings add up to a nothing, they are, none the less, he said, still compacted agglomerations.

Should such a string of compacted clustered points of nothing align then they will unravel as it were and form a wave. Once such a wave of unravelling compacted points forms, it attracts more and more of them until there is a universe of unravelling points. This 'something out of nothing' doesn't come about suddenly, like a "big bang", but imperceptibly evolves. Terbal added that the reverse also occurs. Compacted points, once utterly unravelled, revert to 'singular (1 x 0 = 0) nothings'.

Such singular nothings, Terbal's "un-compounded non-contexts", within the rolling strip of a mobius Primary wave and amid those points still unravelling, will pass unnoticed and without untoward influence. Eventually though, with the majority of points unravelled, the Primary wave strand of which they are part, dissipates back into a timeless void of singular nothings. Sometimes this entropy is reversed and the strip re-energised by colliding, merging into another which has most of its points yet to unravel.

Terbal also said sometimes these points unravel mid-strand, making a hole as it were. And just like ones in a pullover, it can keep unravelling and unravelling, pulling strands into an emptiness of singular nothings until, he said, like with jumpers, there is more hole than fabric strand. The more mature strings and strands of a mobius strip become, such as those with galaxies, the greater the likelihood of their unravelling mid-strand.

In passing almost, he added that our scientists not only had the concept of time confused but of how elements begin as well. He said the first fully fledged ones form along the edges of Primary wave strands by Secondary waves fusing pairs of embryo frothicles. It is within condensing clusters of these that the next, beryllium, oxygen, carbon, are further fused and formed.

But it was pluses and minuses of wavicles which I really found interesting, or rather their strong and weak charges. Terbal said envisage a frothicles' wavicles ceasing sliding back and forth and stopping with their stronger charged crests nuzzled into the weaker charged troughs. Terbal next said to think of such a stoppage lasting for no more than an instant. However, in this minute moment he said, there will be sufficient release of energy to overcome the 'attracting' force of 'Secondary wave Earth' ('gravity').

As far as the Susem are concerned, Terbal said, and humans for that matter (but not pigs apparently), achieving this release is a case of mind over matter. Just as refining the ability of balance comes with focusing the mind, so too (and with practice) does that of neutralising 'gravity'.

By consistently momentarily concentrating all one's mind and bodily energy (about a tenth of a horsepower) to frothicles of the underfoot, Terbal said, it is possible to levitate a metre and more. With him adding that less effort is required for a centimetre or so, I asked how I could master just this much but he wasn't encouraging. He said it's essential to be young, it being difficult for those older to learn new physical skills.

With me musing "No change there then," Terbal next said wavicle stopping occasionally occurs by chance and not just to frothicles of the feet. The resulting release of 'kinesis' energy haphazardly zipping out of other bits of the body, he said, can cause all manner of upsets. Should this kinesis knock against things it can send them flying all over the place. He did mention poltergeists but before I had chance to ask him more about this he moved on to something even more interesting, 'artificial kinesis'.

This kinesis has millions of times more power than the flesh and blood variety. It is the means the Susem use to power everything and in essence it is simple. The Susem are able to control the positioning of wavicles. Any frothicles can generate kinesis but embryo frothicles, hydrogen, are the ones the Susem usually use, their single set of wavicles being simpler to control, and of course, it is universally available. What is more, it's easy to store, they use the hydrogen in water.

One drop apparently works wonders. It has enough hydrogen to keep a soufin going for ever. Part of the skill is the coordinated discharging of the wavicle energy from frothicles. Another is recharging wavicles. And this is where the oxygen of water comes in handy. There is a lot of energy in oxygen frothicles. The Susem have mastered the controlled transference of energy from these to those of hydrogen.

I did ask what happens when energy in wavicles had been used up, but soon wished not. With a disdainful waggle of his fronds, Terbal said frothicles were constantly recharged by Secondary waves flowing past wavicle tips. He said to remember that the sum of Tertiary waves, frothicles, is minute compared to Secondary ones. He then described how the Susem tap kinesis energy from frothicles and I became very interested indeed.

Of late, a day does not pass without my being subjected to some sniggered jibe or another. Yesterday evening at the club meeting, no sooner had I stepped on to the track than it was "Serviced any good debts lately Graham?... what's your rate on overdrafts?..." and other innuendo. Moreover, telling these supposed 'clubmates' that I have nothing to do with retail banking had no effect whatso- ever in curbing these demeaning remarks.

Just because a few erstwhile colleagues have been caught with their trousers down during office hours and with unfortunate consequences, it in no way warrants the aspersion that all us bank managers behave in such an unprofessional manner.

Obviously I am man enough to take this crass ribaldry in my stride but it is the effects of them which are so disheartening. During my weekly club meetings I would frequently be asked for advice by my fellow athletes regarding their financial affairs, assistance of which I was more than willing to give. But now such requests for help, the respect this accorded, have been replaced by this smirking derision.

This diminishing of respect is not just manifest within my social circles, it is also apparent even in the Bank itself. Hitherto, apart from my seniors and immediate colleagues, I was addressed by both my title and surname. But this is now not the case. I have lost count of the occasions I have asked Sharon not to address me by my first name. What is worse however are those of yet junior rank referring to me as "Gray" or even "Gram".

I have raised the matter of this breakdown in discipline at the morning conference on several occasions. Sadly, my concerns regarding this pernicious and undue familiarity by juniors towards us managers have been totally disregarded. While in no way wishing to appear critical of Mr Gibbons' judgment, I can safely say that the rot set in when he and those at head office condoned these Nonette people to operate within the Bank.

It is one thing for him to say that there is no alternative other than to recognise them, but quite another having to work with the consequences. Of course now that these Nonettes command undue tax advantages, increasing numbers of staff have gone over to them. Nevertheless, while it may be all very well for the likes of Mr Gibbons to say that if we do not give the lower grades greater responsibility and freedom to make decisions we will lose them, but he does nothing to address the demoralising effect this is having on us senior managers.

While I am among the first to concur with his assertion that recent upheavals in the markets as well as the new tax climate have given us all an extra workload, it does not follow, however, that those at junior levels should be allowed to take over responsibilities which hitherto have been the preserve of senior management. If matters continue as they are I could well find myself

Govt. anti-Nonette press move thwarted

Crowds beat back police

By John Miller-Jones
East Midlands Correspondent

GOVERNMENT ATTEMPTS to clamp down on Nonette newspapers suffered a serious setback yesterday.

Angry crowds beat back Leicester police attempts to seize printing presses on which the movement's newspapers are printed.

Last night, Nonette printing plants and newspaper offices across Britain, were surrounded by many thousands of the movement's members in a bid to stop further police action against them.

According to Nonette claims more than 200 police raided the movement's Leicester offices early yesterday morning.

Within minutes of the police's arrival local Nonette branches had summoned fellow members to confront

Pulling apart?

As UK Nonettes claim that their membership has grown to more than 11million, Hilary Norman reports on the rise of Britain's newest nation

SCOTS, WELSH and Ulstermen have home rule but keep allegiance to the Crown.

The Nonettes, however, and now with more members than all three countries' populations combined, are creating a self-governing nation with allegiance to nobody but themselves.

Although sharing the same territory as all four countries of the UK, the Nonette movement is nevertheless, evolving into an increasingly independent and very foreign country.

Real democracy

With their system of participatory 'bottom up' democracy the Nonettes are not only diverging from the rest of Britain politically but administratively as well.

As a direct outcome of the Nonettes' novel form of democracy, the movement's system of administration, in also being participatory, is alien to Britain as well.

Although Nonette administration, unlike the established ones, functions without need of bureaucratic hierarchy, it is, so individual Nonettes say, all the more efficient for it.

The Nonette administration also operates with total indifference to that of Whitehall's. And now that the Nonettes have secured their own tax regime it is free of the grip of the Treasury's bureaucracy as well.

The 'nonette', at first dismissed by bankers as 'funny money' is now the currency of choice of the more than 4 million people in the UK who have opted to have their wages paid in it.

The nonette

The nonette is also the currency funding an estimated 10 per cent of British economic actively. Its almost weekly rise in value against sterling may well mean that this percentage is set to grow. And with it will come the likelihood of further economic separation between that of the Nonettes' and that of the rest of the UK.

Increasing this comercial divergence is the Nonettes' banking system and now postal service as well.

While the Post Office is expected to immediately suffer serious loss of business to the latter, High Street banks are set to suffer even more over the longer term from the former.

However, they are not the only mainstream businesses adversely affected by those of the Nonettes.

There are now few areas of economic activity which are not suffering from the loss of trade to their Nonette rivals.

As more and more businesses see little alternative to joining the Nonettes in order to survive, so the strength and separateness of their combined economic power grows.

Markets suffering

Already there are reports in the City that major supermarkets are starting to suffer. The recent falls in their share prices suggests this may well be the case. Should just one of these go over to the Nonettes, there will a thundering stampede of others following in their wake.

There is yet a further area where the Nonettes are fast establishing their independence: that of law and order.

Nonette Law

In the many areas where the Nonettes are strong, it is they who police their own neighbourhoods. And of course these areas being crime and incident free, the 'official' police forces are free to concentrate their resources elsewhere.

The same, so Nonette sources say, will soon apply to the Crown's judiciary: the Nonettes are now setting up their own courts as well.

These courts, so Nonettes say, will operate along the same lines as those in regions already under the movement's control.

However, under the Nonette system, justice, is dispensed without need of lawyers and barristers, or judges for that matter. It is a system of justice, so Nonettes claim, which is fast, free and fair.

If indeed the Nonette system of settling disputes is as they say, it is likely prove very popular. It will also be yet another degree of separateness between Nonette and the rest of the UK.

Soufins

What started as no more than desire to secure assured energy supplies – soufins - the Nonettes have grown into a movement which has changed the lives of millions of people.

The Nonettes are also posing a challenge to the rest of the country, more so to the powers-that-be at Westminster and in Whitehall.

Even should the soufin power units cease tomorrow, it is doubtful if the Nonette movement itself will follow suit. Too many people having experienced running their own affairs are unlikely to go back, as they see it, to the "bad old ways".

Cynics say Westminster, in giving home rule to Scotland, Wales and Ulster, gave them nothing more than the empty trappings of power. That the real thing: control of tax revenues and the dispensing of the allocation of their spending is still firmly in the grip of Whitehall.

Nonette wealth

By this measure the Nonette movement of the UK, with their estimated current £25bn annual income (but rapidly rising), have not only acquired real power for themselves but also are increasingly threatening Westminster and Whitehall for more of theirs.

Although the government by turn has ignored the Nonettes' existence or attempted blocking their onward march, they have failed at every attempt.

Moreover, each government reverse has been handled so ineptly by them that it has propelled the Nonettes towards yet further independence from the UK state.

Indeed, professed government indifference and then reaction to the Nonettes, has strengthened them in encouraging yet more people to join the movement.

Government spying

The revelations of government spying on the Nonettes has not only increased the movement's animosity towards Westminster and Whitehall but also, following this latest incident, that, as opinion polls show, public sympathy towards the movement has actually risen.

This exposé of state snooping has also reduced chances of it and the Nonettes establishing any form of cohabitation, let alone cooperation with central government.

But if both Westminster and the Nonettes are to co-exist, there has to be an accommodation between them. However, if events of Nonette growth over-seas are any guide, it is in more of the government's interest to make the first conciliatory moves rather than the Nonettes'.

Cohabitation

The longer the government leaves making any such moves, the smaller the chance there is of a 'peaceable cohabitation' of the two in the same house that is Great Britain.

Should there not be such an accommodation then, eventually, one of them will have to go. As things stand it would be less than wise to place bets on the outcome.

Nonette mobs force civil servants to flee home

Government to offer emergency accommodation to staff affected by Nonette 'spy outing'

By Roger Granite
Security Editor

SCORES OF SENIOR civil servants have been forced to flee their homes in fear of Nonette mobs.

Government concern at the growing crisis faced by increasing numbers of its key staff, is providing emergency alternative temporary accommodation to those made homeless.

Meanwhile, Downing Street ... tions into the leaking of names and addresses of officials listed as conducting surveillance operations on Nonette activities.

It is thought, however, that government personnel, sympathetic to the Nonette movement, have passed on names and addresses of the civil servants involved.

Hackers are also believed to have penetrated government data systems.

Although civil servants across the UK have been the targets of the Nonettes, those in the London area have borne the brunt of the attacks.

However there has not been any reports of any physical assaults on those named in the leaked files. Most of those who were have been subjected to threats and other intimidation by Nonettes.

While police have attempted to halt the attacks, a Metropolitan police spokesman said: "While we are doing our utmost to curtail these instances of harassment, it is difficult to apprehend any of the culprits.

"It must also be appreciated that, currently, we are facing an extreme manpower shortage. We simply do not have the officers to deal with the number of such outbreaks."

It is understood that the Home Office has commandeered a number of vacant office buildings across the city of London with the intention of setting up a comprehensive

without any meaningful management role whatsoever.

Furthermore, the existence of these Nonette groups within the Bank has brought about a most disturbing working atmosphere especially in the general office areas where the majority of the junior grades work. Most of these of course are female and mainly young, indeed some barely out of school. In the past, whenever I had occasion to visit these clerical areas, I was aware of how timid and unsure of themselves most of these younger girls were. Indeed, many of them would rather shy away behind their terminals than acknowledge me, leaving their line supervisors to take my instructions. But nevertheless, being a senior manager I was always accorded a certain degree of deference. Unfortunately this is now no longer so.

It is not that I am unaccustomed to female attention, quite the contrary. Being a man, even though married, I quite welcome it. But that said, there are nonetheless, limits. To say that these young office girls are being unduly forward is to put it mildly and there is certainly no sign of shyness anymore. Some of the older women, and who I would have thought should know better, have become just as over familiar as well. The manner in which they have started looking at me, especially to my eyes every time I endeavour to explain my requirements is most unsettling. Also it is the way they have taken to standing so close to me. On more than one occasion I found myself walking backwards from them. I have now ceased venturing into any of the general clerical areas, leaving it to Sharon to liaise my instructions with them.

Several colleagues with whom I travel in with of a morning, and while acknowledging a similar state of affairs in their own departments, have also informed me that all these young girls are becoming hooked on this new Nonette drug Wanton. If this is so, then indeed it has made them just that. What is more, I have also been told that many other women are taking this drug as well and losing all sense of propriety. Another colleague told me that some of the streets in Harlow, let alone London, are no longer safe for a man to walk at night. Obviously this drug should be banned immediately but alas nowadays, what with the police being powerless against these Nonettes, I do not suppose there is anything that can be done to combat it.

A further worrying aspect of these young women's new found assertiveness has manifested itself in another and more insidious manner. Although I now leave it to Sharon to communicate my orders to the clerical grades, they are frequently disobeyed or "amended" as she diplomatically puts it.

Just as galling is that more often as not Sharon concurs with their judgments. It is no use my pointing out that it is for me, as a manager, to decide what approach to take vis-a-vis this customer or that, because Sharon merely says "Your group decided this will be a more productive approach."

This is not merely a matter of changing an odd word here or there, or even the whole thrust of the letter, but in how I should actually be handling a customer's account. And what is worse it has not stopped there either.

Kent town in Nonette takeover

Cranbrook UDI shocks Council, Gov

By Lucile Sewers

CRANBROOK Nonettes have declared UDI from Britain.

The Kent town's 6,000 residents have either to agree to Nonette rule or suffer the consequences of staying. Last night several of Cranbrook's residents were preparing to leave.

Cranbrook's UDI decision is no *'Passport to Pimlico'* farce The tiny Kent town is only the latest of more than 200 communities across Britain which have declared for "self determination", as Nonettes term it.

As yet, none of them have had their 'independence' recognised by the authorities. However, the rapid growth in the number of further 'Cranbrooks' could soon be more than a mere thorn in the authorities' side.

Presently, Kent County Council officials in Maidstone are adopting a 'softly, softly' approach to Cranbook's action as well as to four other areas elsewhere in the county which also have declared UDI

Privately, however, some of the County Council's top brass are alarmed at events As one official, who declined to be named, said: "The situation is slipping out of control. Yet what action is there that we take?

Police refuse to act against 'rebels'

"The police have refused to act against disaffected areas ... that it's a civil matt...

A tax collector's lot is not a happy one

WENDY GILES reports on the Inland Revenue's burgeoning therapy centres

THE TAXMAN is not collecting enough of our taxes, the chancellor, Peter Handel, claimed yesterday.

Businesses are also at fault. The chancellor stated that a rising number of companies are not collecting their employees' PAYE and not paying their corporation tax, or VAT either.

> *"Those at Westminster have no idea what is happening in the real world"*

Nonettes, of course, also came in for a tongue-lashing from the chancellor. They are, he said, guilty of spreading confusion among ordinary taxpayers; misleading us into withholding all the other taxes we have to pay.

It was, however, Britain's taxmen and women themselves who were singled out for the chancellor's fiercest chastisement.

Peter Handel said that even allowing for the Nonettes' 10 per cent tax allowance, the latest Treasury figures show that both the Inland Revenue and the Customs and Excise tax-take is the lowest in decades. And worse, so the chancellor said, the costs of collection have rocketed. In some sections of the Inland Revenue, overheads have more than doubled.

The chancellor said he was taking urgent steps to slash the tax men's spending. He added: "At a time when Britain is fighting for its financial life, it is deeply disappointing to learn that instead of net Treasury income rising it has, in fact, fallen. This cannot and will not be allowed to continue."

But what of the tax officeials themselves? Why has there been such a shortfall in tax collection?

According to John Higgens, head of the Inland Revenue's Staff Association, morale among the tax collectors is at an all-time low. Mr Biggens said: "People, including those at Westminster, have no idea of what is happening out there in the real world.

"From the Inland Revenue's standpoint," Mr Biggins said, "90 per cent of UK tax collection used to a simple matter of PAYT - pay as you're told - or else.

"But now, with millions of taxpayers unilaterally switching to PAYP - pay as you please - my members are unable to handle the situation.

> *"Now we have to ask for the money nicely; this is utterly alien to a tax inspector"*

"As far as we were concerned PAYP was only for the rich and powerful: the people who employed us as tax advisors once we had taken retirement.

"Now, if we want ordinary taxpayers to pay up what they owe, we not only have be nice to them but also have to ask for the money nicely as well. And this is something which is utterly alien to any tax collector. It has completely thrown us," he said.

In a bid to come to terms with the new situation, both Inland Revenue and Customs and Excise have sent many of their collectors on crash courses in politeness and civil behaviour.

But, as one senior tax official, who wished to be nameless, admitted, the dropout rate from these courses has been high. He said: "Less than 43 per cent of our personnel stay the course and of those who do, the pass rate is averaging 46 per cent."

The same official added that the days when the Inland Revenue was above the law also appear to be over.

> *"What is worse, we tax inspectors have lost all our power and authority"*

He said: "It is all very well the Treasury having all embracing extra-legal powers but it is quite another matter enforcing them.

"The moment our officials attempt to enforce collection, such as the seizure of goods, they are confronted by an army of these Nonettes.

"Some Inland Revenue personnel have been physically manhandled off of a defaulter's premises. Moreover, the delinquent nonpayer has, in all probability, joined the Nonettes into the bargain."

In a further attempt to stem the tax men's plummeting morale, the Inland Revenue has set up numerous therapy clinics and self-help discussion groups.

The head of one such clinic in north London, Dr Lizbet Schrumpfen, said: "All of my patients are in extreme states of depression. With the power and authority they once wielded over their fellow human beings swept from under them, many of my patients feel as if their entire reason for living has ceased to exist."

One of Dr Schrumpfen's patients, who is being treated for severe trauma, told of the experiences to which he and many of his colleagues have been subjected.

Introducing himself only as "Eric" he said: "It used to be good, we were all on a roll. Being on commission it was easy-pleasy. Everyone was earning loads of money.

"All we ever had to do was send a heavy letter to the punters and most of them would pay up without as much as a dickybird.

"But now all we get back, if we get anything," Eric said, "are our letters returned with "Up yours" written on them and some have actually been used as toilet paper.

"It's not as though we can 'go in heavy' either. The last time any of the lads tried, they were set upon by all these women high on that *Wanton*. The men never stood a chance. The things those women did to them were diabolical, two of them are still missing.

"Of course, none of us are earning either, leastways not like we used to," Eric said.

"But what is worse," he said, "is that we tax collectors have lost all our authority and respect. All our power and dignity is gone, we're nobody anymore, I don't know how I can carry on." At this point Eric burst into tears and he began shaking violently. Two men in white coats led him away.

> *"These men are not suffering from inferiority complexes; they actually are inferior"*
> **Dr Liz Schrumpfen**

Dr Schrupfen, who is preparing a paper on the phenomenon of 'Tcts' (Tax Collector Trauma Syndrome), said: "Some authorities have diagnosed these men as suffering from inferiority complexes.

"It is my observation, however, that they do not have any such complex, they actually are inferior human males.

"My researches have ascertained that all of these affected males are unable to sustain friendships outside of their environment.

"Women only mated with these males because of the large sums of money they earned, which of course is no longer the case.

"With these males' ability to threaten their fellow humans with impunity now gone, they are experiencing perceptions of powerlessness and inadequacy, which is having a detrimental effect on their mental health."

Arsenal's boss toss loss to Sofi

Gunners to go in red, Dynamo to go in go

By AMY CELESTE in ROME

ARSENAL BOSS Graham George came out of pre-match purdah yesterday to meet with his Sofia Dynamo opposite number, Dragan Pernik, to settle a serious strip poser: who was going to go in the gold?

Not only are Arsenal and Dynamo's league strips both red but also their international strips are of similar hues, Gunner's gold, Dynamo's dark yellow.

TV chiefs covering tomorrow's IEFA Final, demanded one of the finalists played in their league strip so as to give viewers colour contrast and prevent commentator confusion.

Arsenal argued as they were ahead in alphabetical order they had the right to choose but Dynamo disagreed.

With neither side showing sign of budging, SLI TV head, Dicky Bear, ordered a toss-up decider.

IEFA's Swedish president Walter Blekinge met with both sides' managers in the centre of the pitch at Rome's Forum stadium, the site of tomorrow's clash.

Both bosses drew straws to decide who would call. Dragan got the short straw and George called for heads. Blekinge tossed his gold korona coin but to George's dismay and Dragan's delight it came down head first.

As Dragan held aloft Dynamo's gold yellow shirt for photographers and all to see, George glumly looked on.

But aware Arsenal are bookies' odds-on final favourite's, he shrugged off his toss-up loss. George said his side would still win regardless of what they played in, he just felt sorry for fans who always

Drug crazed women behind rise in forced l

Gang bang pa sex threat wa

By Michael Roberts
Men's Matters Editor

SEX ATTACKS ON MEN are on the rise police warned yesterday. Packs of sex crazed women, high on the Nonette *Wanton* love drug, are cruising the streets in unmarked transit vans hunting down lone males to sate uncontrolled lusts on their bodies.

In the past week alone, Scotland Yard says, across the Metropolitan area, there have been more than 200 such reported attacks on men.

Most of these attacks, they say, follow a similar pattern. A van stops alongside the intended victim, women spring from its back doors and immediately spray him with Rampant the Nonettes' newest love drug

Sexually aroused and made helpless by its effects, the man, unable to fend off the women's advances, is then dragged in the back of the van which then drives off.

Even before the van reaches its destination - usually an isolated spot - the women have their victim pinned down, ripping off his clothes, slapping Love Patches on him, pawing and groping his body

But once the women have arrived at their chosen location, the man's real ordeal begins. For hour after terrifying hour he is subjected to one frenzied sex assault after another.

Although the victim is fully awake while these attacks are committed, he is, because of the effects of the drugs, putty in these female fiends' hands

For hour after hour he is degraded to being no more than their sex toy upon which they

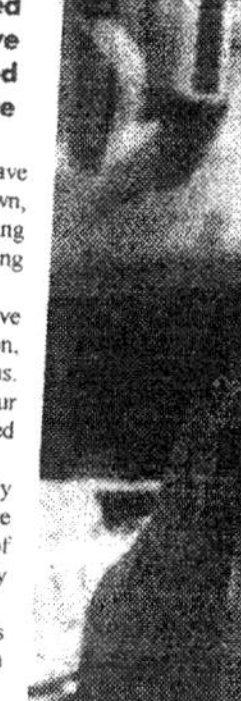

Should any of my customers have one of these Nonette groups operating in their business, then automatically it seems 'my' group in the Bank deals directly with theirs. While this is most annoying, there is nothing either I or anyone can do to stop them. Naturally, I have remonstrated with Mr Gibbons regarding this breakdown in procedure but he obliquely said "Have any of your customers complained?"

While I have had to reply that as yet, none had, but what Mr Gibbons and others fail to grasp is just where all this blatant disregard of proper procedures will lead. For all I know customers could be getting away with blue murder, just as Collins did. And then where will everyone be? Blaming me again, that is where, just as they also did over the entire Water Filters fiasco. But again there is nothing that can be done. It is not as though I can resign in protest either, for what else at my age can I do?

All that can be hoped for is that the government comes to its senses and stops this Nonette movement in its tracks and bans it. But even I have to admit this is looking more remote by the day. I have asked Martin Manborn of the Watch several times when the Home Office and MoD are going to act against them. He though merely repeats that they are still awaiting orders for the 'right moment' to strike. I just hope this 'right moment' arrives soon or it will be too late.

There is another area of my life however where all semblance of order and discipline have long since disappeared. This of course is my own personal domestic situation. For all intents and purposes I am little more than a stranger in my own home. A home, which more often than not, is empty when I return of an evening. I no longer know where the boys are except that they are no longer attending their schools, both of which I gather have now closed their doors.

June, on the rare occasions I see her, has barely a word to say. Naturally I have made attempts to rekindle our marriage but alas she has been most unresponsive. She was most off-handed when I told her that as I was the one who kept the roof over the family's head, I have at least the right to be shown some appreciation. She replied that neither she nor the boys needed anything from me, they earned quite enough from study and working with their Nonette group "thank you very much."

When I then pointed out to her that it is me who pays the mortgage, she was just as dismissive, saying why bother paying it, no one else pays theirs. When I explained ours is with the Bank, that I have no choice other than pay it, and anyway it is automatically deducted from my salary, she merely shrugged her shoulders, saying this was my problem, not hers.

Another time, when I broached the matter of the boys' whereabouts and reminded her that as their father I have both rights and responsibilities over them, she was just as dismissive. She said it was neither up to me nor her, but the boys themselves, to decide what they wanted to do.

IEFA Final

Wm III's staff told to pray for for Sofia win

'Our only hope' says bookie's boss

By STEVEN POOTER
City Editor

IF ARSENAL BRING BACK the IEFA Cup to Highbury, Wm III, one of Britain's biggest bookies has had it.

So huge are the value and high the odds of bets placed with III's on an Arsenal win tomorrow night, that the company faces a profits wipe-out.

One bet alone, placed when odds on an Arsenal IEFA win were a 1,000 to 1, could force III's to pay out £50m.

Harold Goldberg, head of Wm III, in a message to all the firm's managers, said: "Should Sofia fail to win in tomorrow night's IEFA Final, your company will be faced with little alternative than significantly to reduce the size of its operations.

"While the company has endeavoured to disengage it-self from the insidious situation it has unwittingly found itself in, it has, as yet, met with less than complete success.

"All that remains to us all is the power of positive thought.

"Therefore on the behalf of your company and the well-being of all employees I ask most sincerely that all of us spend a few minutes in quiet contemplation wishing for Sofia's success.

"If any employee considers this can best be done as a prayer then I will personally say amen to this."

Perhaps III's employees might also pray for the company's share price as well.

With Arsenal looking a surefire IEFA winner the City has already marked down the bookie's share price to an all-ti

ALIENS IN ROME SEX-FEST ORGY

As Vatican slates sudden Susem 'Pied Piper' swoop IEFA finalists spirited to ultra-safe secret hidaway

By Clive Woodward
in Rome

FEARS ROSE LAST night for the fate of more than 600 men still held captive by Susem in a Rome city-centre park.

Italian police warned all men to stay under cover until further notice

Pope condemns raid

Pope Pius condemned the Alien attack on Rome and called for prayers to be said in all of the city's churches for the men's safety.

Thousands of men, Italians and tourists alike, fled Rome's streets in fear as swarms of Alien 'Pied Piper' scent spraying and snatch craft made sudden surprise raids across the city's central Pantheon district.

'Love aroma'

Police sources said that more than 600 men fell victim of the Susem 'love aroma'. Police also say that many times this number were lured into Alien craft but appear to have been rejected by them.

Sex in the park

Doria Pamphill, a park, just half a mile from the Vatican, was reported to have been taken over by Aliens. Last night carabinieri - paramilitary police had cordoned off the park and surrounding streets.

Spanish Steps

The first Susem attacks began at noon. Eye witnesses said that an Alien craft appeared over Rome's famous Spanish Steps. It flew at no more than 10 metres above the Steps. Many of the men on them began to run after the craft.

Pied Piper

Sara Fell, (35) who was on the Steps at the time of the attack, said: "It was like the Pied Piper of Hamlyn. Every single man was

UK Nonettes rise to record 12m

By Phillip Motor
Political Correspondent

MORE THAN 12 million people, businesses and other groups, now belong to the Nonette movement it was announced yesterday.

From a standing start just months ago the Nonettes are now by far Britain's biggest organisation. With its members donating one tenth of their income to movement, it is also the country's richest.

Spurred on by income tax rebates as well as free energy supplies and Alien backed healthcare, Nonette numbers have continued to soar.

The sales of Susem sex aids not only have boosted the movement's membership but also their coffers.

Nonette spokeswoman, Joanne Willows said: "The growth in our membership has been spread evenly both by region and social class.

"In terms of people we now represent nearly a quarter of the British population as a whole. This is in line with our movement's growth across the rest of Europe."

The Prime Minister, Edward Campbell, in response to the latest surge in Nonette numbers, said: "What these figures actually show is that four out of five people in Britain have declined to have anything to do with this extra-terrestrial-backed organisation. However, what these figures do not show is that an extremely high percentage of those claiming to belong to this association are children and teenagers.

"While these young people may well be sincere in their beliefs, they are still, nonetheless, those of youthful naiveté. More mature minds however, are viewing this Nonette movement with a greater sense of objectivity. It will soon be plain to see these claims for

Hain demands reoccupation as non-Nonettes ouste

Nonette town takeovers spread

By Shimon Allenby

ANOTHER CLUTCH of villages and suburbs across Britain came under Nonette control yesterday. From Daliburgh in the Hebrides, to Salcombe and Roborough in Devon a further seven communities declared UDI from the United Kingdom

What was once viewed in Whitehall, until a few days ago as mixture of pointless local protest and crass high jinks, is now giving cause for serious concern among senior civil servants.

Adding to their anxiety are the growing numbers of people being forced to flee their homes in the affected areas.

In a number of instances family members have become separated from one another.

As of last night a total 215 places, varying in size from the 10,000 inhabitants of Chapel-en-Frith, Debryshire to the 60 people of the hamlet Maesmynis, Powys, in all totalling a population of 250,000, have declared independence from the UK.

Parts of two London suburbs, Claygate and West Mosley have also declared 'Home Rule' from the rest of the country.

Should Whitehall, in a bid to curb and

Of course I have tried on numerous occasions to see things from June's point of view. I have even gone as far as telling her that as far as I was concerned I had no objections to her involvement with these Nonettes, I just didn't want them to come between us. But she has consistently refused to see reason. Indeed yesterday evening when I once again offered her this accommodation, she retorted that because of my refusal to join these Nonettes, I had come between her and them. She further said that my refusal to join them was blocking her chances of advancing within her group.

During this altercation and after saying she was having difficulty in accommodating me, June issued what amounted to an ultimatum, either join her Nonette group or find somewhere else to live. Even before I had chance to tell her that even if I wanted to join with her, I was in no position to do so, she had flounced out of the house.

Obviously I am sure she said this in the heat of the moment and could not have meant it, but all the same it was very upsetting and made me most agitated. So much so that I found myself unconsciously shaking in time with the washing machine as it spin dried my running kit.

In the club car park after the meeting and away from the ribaldry I fell into conversation with John Cook, a fellow member. Apparently he is experiencing a similar non-conjugal situation to my own. However, he also said that as a civil servant, and following the revelations of the security services' surveillance of the Nonette movement, people such as him were being forced either to move from a Nonette dominated area or give up working for the government. What is more, he also said that even government employees who are Nonettes are being forced to choose between working for them or leave the movement altogether.

While it is not anything like this where I live, it is what John said next which gave me a jolt. Although stressing it was purely hypothetical, he said that if things go on as they are, then anyone who hasn't joined the Nonettes will be automatically seen as suspect by them. This immediately rang with what June had said earlier in the evening.

John said, when I asked, that he didn't know what he will do next, except that he is definitely not resigning his position. In many respects he is of a like mind to myself regarding these Nonettes. John said that if things continue as they are, there will be a complete breakdown in the functioning of society. He said that if these Nonettes and their activities are allowed to continue unchecked there will be a civil war in this country.

But as I said to him, with the Aliens protecting these Nonettes, just what is there apart from a miracle that anyone can do to stop them?

ARSENAL IN 9-0 DEFEAT S

Did Susem get to Gunners first?

By AMY CELESTE

EVEN THE LOWER DEPTHS of the Diadora League would have walked over Arsenal last night. Fans booed in disbelief as the odds-on IFEA favourites were thrashed to a shock 9-0 defeat by Sofia Dynamo.

With Dynamo's centre forward, Zagora, scoring within two minutes of the off, it was obvious to everyone something had happened to Arsenal.

As Gunner's goalkeeper, Tarson let an easy save slip from his fingers giving Zagora his second goal, fears rose that Arsenal may well been pre-match scored by the Susem.

Even Graham George's wunderkind, scorer Kirk, failed to find a way though the Dynamo defence, not that he was in the Bulgarian's half for much of the match.

As for Kirk's fellow forwards, Henri and Bergan, they barely crossed into Dynamo's half the entire match.

But even with the Arsenal squad confined to their own half most of the game, they were still unable to halt Dynamo driving one ball after another in the back of their net.

By half time the ...

Thousands mourn missing pay-out millions

ILL'S SHARES SOAR ON IEFA ARSENAL KO

"Our prayers have been answered" - beams bookie's boss

By Jade Read

SHARES IN WM ILL SHOT FROM 27p TO 128p in minutes of the Stock Exchange opening yesterday.

With Arsenal's shock 9-0 defeat at the hands of Sofia Dynamo in last night's IEFA Cup saving the bookmaker from a mega pay-out to the estimated 100,000 punters who bet heavily on an Arsenal win. Profits are expected to be even higher than original City forecasts.

As Ill's boss, Harold Goldberg, celebrated with fellow directors and senior staff at Sofia's win, he said: "It would appear that our prayers have been answered."

Mr Goldberg, said while both his sons are Tottenham supporters, he is more interested in tennis than soccer and had no feelings for Arsenal either way.

He said: "Of course I am sorry for Arsenal supporters including those who placed ... Arsenal fans at their team's defeat either but for all the money they lost betting on them to win, to say nothing of what punters would have had if they had won.

Gunner's supporter, Bria[n] O'Rourke, was typical o[f] most fans. He said: "O[f] course I'm gutted ove[r] Arsenal performance, wh[ich] wouldn't be?

"But it's the money I p[ut] £200 on them when they we[re] at 10-1. It came out of what was putting away for Chris...

POPE HELD BY ALIENS!

Vatican under Susem occupation Fear for Pontiff's safety rise

By MARK CLINTON in ROME

THE VATICAN has been invaded by the Susem and the Pope taken prisoner. Italian armed forces have been placed on full alert.

The Vatican - a sovereign state in the heart of Rome - is ringed by paramilitary police. Prayers for the Pope's safety were said in churches throughout Rome and across the world.

At just before 11 o'clock yesterday morning Susem spacecraft were seen to surround the 40 hectare Holy See enclave. Moments later most of the Vatican's 1,000 staff including the famous Swiss Guards, as well as several hundreds of worshippers, were fleeing across the Piazza San Pietro in front of St Peter's basilica.

Minutes later two larger Alien craft were seen to land on the square and an unknown number of Susem then marched into the Vatican.

According to an unnamed ... weekly audience in the Papal Audience Hall when the attacks took place.

"His Holiness," the source said, "was in the corridor between the hall and his private apartments in the Stanze di Rafaello.

"The Alien's infernal flying beasts surrounded his Holiness and his advisors were forced to retreat back towards the Vatican's Borgia Apartments."

"Those of us who rushed to protect him were beaten back by these beasts. They then forced us to flee for the relevant safety of the ...

Taxmen to form new police force

Redundant tax collectors offered police special status

By Andrew Hendrey
Social Affairs Editor

Demoralised and redundant tax men have been offered a new role: that of policemen.

Under an agreement with the Home Office, the Treasury has agreed to second surplus tax inspectors to assist police forces across the country in a variety of security duties.

Announcing the move, the Home Secretary, Clare Long, said: "At this time the move to make use of the Treasury's current underused revenue personnel to help re-enforce the nation's over stretched police forces makes perfect sense.

"Moreover, it ties in perfectly with the Home Office's 'Secure Britain' strategy in tackling the country's deteriorating security situation."

Treasury revenue under-secretary, Sir Nigel Barton, speaking with the Home Secretary said: "In excess of 20,000 Inland Revenue personnel have already signaled their willing-ness to serve in this new force.

"It has been agreed with the Home Office that they will function in the same capacity as special constables. However, as they will act as a separate command from ordinary special constables this new force will be known as 'B Specials'".

The Taxman's staff association, IRSA, is backing the new police force. IRSA secretary, John Higgens said: "My members are over the moon with the chance of being in this new police force. For many of them, being restored to a position of authority has boosted their morale end.

"Mark my words, as s[oon] as we in the Revenue h[ave] our new uniforms [and] truncheons we will be [out] there apprehending wro[ng]doers. Not unnatura[lly] many of these are alrea[dy] known to the Inland Reve[nue]

149: DOOM

I'm done for. Lost everything. Oh what am I going to do. All that money gone, gone for ever. I had it in my grasp, it was mine, all mine. To have it snatched away like that is so unfair. And at the last moment. If only they had kept to the same shirts.

Losing all that money is heartbreaking enough but it's only the start of the terrible things befallen me. Life is so unfair. I always knew giving those young Huitoto lads education would lead to trouble. Their nosing about the accounts, misconstruing everything as they did, making all those unfounded accusations against me was a mean thing to do. They didn't even have the decency to confront, let alone give me a chance to explain to them what "directors' drawings" means. No, they just went straight to the cooperatives with their groundless accusations. I tried explaining I was keeping it as a surprise and they would have all benefited. But even they refused to listen. They had no sense of pity let alone compassion for what I have been through. When I think of all the things I have done for them and this is how they repay me. It's so hard to take. And there was no need for them to call me all those names. It wasn't as though it was that much money. All I really did was just borrow it. I would have paid it all back. I tried telling them this as well but again they refused to listen. Oh if only Arsenal had kept to the same shirts none of this would have happened.

It was a most terrible harrowing experience they put me through, quite uncalled for. Most of the village turned out. It was so humiliating. If it hadn't been for Rainbow telling the court that should I disappear off of the TV, questions would be asked. This thankfully stopped me from being packed off to the Pelada and a life of hard labour as some of them demanded.

Rainbow also told the cooperatives that it was in their interests if what had happened went no further than Tabajara. Should it do so, she said, they would lose creditability with fellow cooperatives for letting it happen. Instead of the Pelada I have been confined to my room in the Pousada until further notice and told to get on with my studies.

But denouement didn't end there. In return for this 'leniency' Rainbow brokered a deal with the cooperatives, Huitoto and Boro, stripping me of all my shares in the Patches and Strips, divvying them out between themselves, with Rainbow and her 'charitable trust' bagging the most.

And now I am left with nothing, not my even freedom. I don't know what I'm going to do. The only time I'm allowed out of the Pousada is to make another TV appearance. Even then it's under close escort. And it goes without saying that any contact with the Susem has ended. Anyway Rainbow's probably told them about everything.

One small error of judgment was all I made and this is how I'm treated. It's not fair.

IEFA Final

JUST WHAT DID HAPPEN TO ARSENAL?

BRIAN SLEET in Rome investigates Gunners' shock defeat

AS ROME'S FORUM stadium packs away the last of the flags, bunting and other vestiges of the IEFA Cup Final ready for the weekend's Italia Athletic championships, questions are still being asked of Arsenal's abysmal performance.

One theory puts Arsenal's 9-0 defeat down to the predications of the Susem.

Should this be so then it would be a marked departure from the Aliens' normal mode of operation.

Although the entire team, including substitutes, played as though they were "abanzed out", as one fan put it, they were, unlike other Alien adbuctees, still able to walk.

Indeed none of them showed any sign of being in actual pain or discomfort. Neither was the squad abducted, to be found days later in a remote mountain valley as have other IEFA sides.

Although Arsenal's boss, Graham George, is still tight-lipped about what happened, he has let it be known there was nothing wrong with the team when he left them at their then secret practice pitch location at Reiti, north-east of Rome, for the meeting with Dynamo Sofia to resolve the dispute over both sides' strip for the Final.

It was when George returned to Reiti that evening, that he found the entire squad including support staff, lying about the pitch in a semi-conscious

SUSEM VATICAN OCCUPATION: SECOND DAY

FEARS FOR POPE RISE

Thousands pray for Pontiff
Italian park sex ordeal over

By MARK CLINTON in ROME

FEARS FOR POPE PIUS XIII's safety grew yesterday. More than 24 hours have passed since the Alien attack on the Vatican and their abduction of the 76-year-old Austrian born Pontiff.

Pope Pius, who, in the past, has been highly critical of Susem, is thought to be held captive in the Vatican's Borgia Apartments. This sumptuous suite of rooms, installed in 1501 by the then Pope, Alexander VI's daughter, Lucrezaia, are next to the Sistine Chapel.

2,000 Alien orgy victims in hospital overflow

There are fears that the Aliens - all of whom are thought to be female - may be subjecting the 76 year old Pontiff to sexual harassment and possibly also physical and indecent assault.

As the victims of the earlier Susem sex outrages were ferried to hospitals throughout Rome, concerns that the Pope might well be subjected to the same degrading experience grew.

The Pontiff is reported to be suffering from a weak heart and if he is forced to indulge in the same physically strenuous it could seriously affect his health.

Papal officials throughout

B Columbia set to fall to Nonettes

Canadian $ collapse as N fears grow

By Oliver Stoneburger

The Canadian dollar was in free fall yesterday as fears of Nonette groups taking control of British Columbia, grew.

During a day of frantic trading, the Canadian currency closed at C$2.37, a massive US$0.57 fall on the day. Shares around the world also suffered huge slides with the Dow losing 453.72 and the FTSE 372.

With Nonette groups on Vancouver Island and the province's capital Victoria declareing their own, separate administration, concerns rose as to the future of British Columbia Canada's westernmost and

Security companies to bolster police

Watch, T A also to be on Home Office standby list

By **Madeline Polster**
Home Affairs Correspondent

SECURITY COMPANies and organisations are set take over many of the nation's policing operations if Home Office proposals receive cabinet approval.

Under plans drawn-up by a Home Office working party, police forces across Britain can call on approved security companies and organisations to assist in routine activities such as patrolling streets.

The Home Secretary, Clare Long, said that the aim of the proposals: 'A Secure Britain', is to free-up greater police numbers to combat Britain's worsening security situation.

The Home Secretary said: "With police forces across the United Kingdom facing greater difficulties of overstretch than ever before, it is vital that as many officers as is humanly possible are available to focus on protecting the nation's vital security needs and which, moreover, they have been professionally trained to undertake.

"Therefore it makes commonsense," she said, "to utilise the skills of other experienced security professionals to assist the police in those areas which are of a non-frontline nature, such as over-seeing children's playgrounds."

Ms Long said that only a select number of topnotch companies and organisations will be on the Home Office's approved list for police security assistance.

She added that each company will be closely vetted before it is approved and will subject to stringent safeguards and constant monitoring.

Among those likely to be on the Home Office's list are companies such as Group 40 and Securifore, both of whom already number of Britain's pri

Also to be include such organisations as Watch (the former N bourhood Watch) and T orial Army.

Although 'A Secure ain' does not specif mention the Nonette name, there is no mist that it is they who a the Home Secretary's s

Up to a couple of weeks ago it was all peace and light round here. Not now though. And as a result I have made a decision.

Our Nonette up Dare Crescent is getting along nicely. Only a handful of flats haven't signed up. It's much the same in most of the other Nonettes round here. Every shop and pub from Highbury to Stroud Green is in a Nonette and, what with the government's tax pay-back, all the rag trade places up Fonthill Road way have signed up as well.

The tax cuts for us Nonettes has brought a big surge in membership especially among those who don't have kids (those who have, had no choice from the start). The money coming into the Dare Nonette and what we have to spend now tops thirty grand a week, though a growing part of this is in nonettes. But as Sam Prior says, "It's all our own money boyo."

Working out what we spend it on, our bit that is, is always a subject of lively debate, not that the remainder we send on to the Area Nonette receives any less scrutiny. All the same, there are no real disagreements, leastways should there be, they can always be put to a vote and you can't argue with that.

Our Nonette bank is doing well, especially during the run on High Street ones. It was during this that nonettes really came in handy. Anyone short of cash needed do no more than study at their screens for a couple of hours and they had enough for the housekeeping. After the crisis was over though, there were a good few people up Dare Crescent, including me, who not only moved their savings out of the building society and put them with our bank but have converted them to nonettes as well. And what with the pound going down we have all been quids in.

Love Patches and Wanton have turned out to be nice little earners for our Nonette as well, as has this new Rampant. Wanton caused a bit of a stir and kept young lads in at night but it was no worry for me, I'm past the age where I'm going get pounced on by a women.

I don't know if it was Wanton or our street patrols and note and help booths, but the whole area has become crime-free, no thieving, no shoplifting. In fact it's became so law-abiding there aren't even drunks outside Finsbury Park, including during the day. And that is saying something.

Of course another reason, perhaps the main one, why so much crime had been knocked on the head, is the teaching screens. Most villains can make more studying from them than thieving, and with a lot less bother.

And I have learnt such a lot from that Lucia. Every night, weekends, she has me studying away and enjoying every minute of it. And it isn't just at home either, she has had me studying at work as well.

I don't know where it started but all the firms that are Nonettes, such as ours, have staff studying during the periods they have nothing to do, with earnings of course going to the company. During the week of the banking

Currencies in turmoil

£ and $ in major devaluation against Nonette

By Walter Mathers

FOLLOWING Friday's the massive fall of the Canadian currency, it was the turn of other major currencies to take a tumble, including the US dollar itself

The Nonette central bank has revalued the nonette against the US$ but this time by a massive 15 per cent.

The nonette is now worth US$1.53. Sterling not only ended the day lower against the nonette at just N0.52c but fell against the US currency as well.

Adding to sterling's woes, as well as those of other European currencies, is the uncertainty of the region's security situation.

The Nonette central bank cited rising inflationary pressures within the US and leading economies, as well as general uncertainty for the nonette's revaluation.

The Nonette Central Bank also stated it has doubts regarding OECD countries in general being able to maintain continued confidence in their currencies. The bank singled out both Japan and Belgium as giving it particular cause for concern. Both countries' currencies fell massively as a consequence.

While as a little as a month ago the Nonette currency was regarded as no more than a joke, it is now being taken seriously by an increaseing number of major banks.

So are the pronouncements of the Nonette central bank itself.

With each revaluation of the nonette, increasing numbers of the movement's members have ditched their national currencies in favour of it. The cumulative effect of such switching is now being felt by banks and retailers alike.

Howard Watkins, senior retail analyst at stockbrokers Howett Gilken, said: "As the number of stores accepting the nonette increases, many of them are also seeing an increasing volume of their business being transacted in this alter-native currency. In large part of course, this has been brought about by the rising value of the nonette

"While these businesses have also joined the Nonette movement itself, thus changing emphasis from the formal economy to theirs," Watkins said, "a further outcome is a decline in their demand for sterling.

"In turn this has left High Street banks with an excess of cash - notes and coins

"Whereas up to a short while ago these banks were all but lending money to retailers at zero interest, it now appears they can't even give it away.

"How long will it be before lenders are actually paying borrowers to borrow?"

With a surfeit of money, including cash sloshing about the financial system and its declining value against the nonette, it is likely an increasing number of both consumers and savers will switch to the Nonette currency

---

SUSEM VATICAN OCCUPATION: THIRD DAY

POPE 'RAPED' BY ALIENS

Aide claims Pontiff endured 24 hour sex session with Susem

By MARK CLINTON in ROME

THE ALIEN INVASION OF THE VATICAN IS OVER.

The Pope, Pious XIII is reported unharmed by his ordeal at the hands of his Susem captors.

Two Alien craft were seen hovering above St Peter's basilica yesterday evening by police surrounding the Vatican and then accelerating to the west.

Moments later one of the aides, who was also taken prisoner with the Pope, contacted the Italian authorities informing them of the Alien's departure.

A team of doctors and other medical experts were seen entering the Vatican then, less than an hour later, leaving it.

Papal authorities have yet to release details of any injuries suffered by the Pope during his period of captivity.

Unofficial Vatican sources, however, claim that His Holiness was sexually assaulted by the Susem, as were those held captive with him.

According to one of the papal aides, they were all forced to continually participate in one intimate act after another with the Aliens.

The same source said that both the Pope and those trapped with him, including several cardinals were forced to romp throughout the Borgas suite of rooms includ-

---

Brussels beleaguered

Flanders falling to Nonettes

By Harriett Togart in Brussels

FROM ANTWERP in the east, to Ostend in the west, scores of Belgian towns, cities and villages are now outside government control and under that of Nonettes.

Even in Brussels, the country's capital and that of European Union, many of its suburbs are also effectively run by Nonettes.

In an emergency session of the Belgian parliament, yesterday, deputies of all parties demanded immediate government action to rectify the loss of state authority across the Flanders region.

Several right-wing MPs tabled motions that a state of emergency be declared and official control be reestab-

interior minister, Luc van Harn said "How and who is going to enforce such a move?"

Pieter Straaten of Antwerp's *Das Morgan*, said: "In many respects the only real surprise of the Nonette takeovers is not that they happened but they came about so quickly.

"Here in Antwerp everyday life carries on much as normal, except there are no longer taxes to pay such as VAT which means everything is now much cheaper

"Most businesses and shops have welcomed the changeover if for no other reason than to be rid of regulations and form filling.

"There was some initial trouble with the city's trams and bus services but the managers eventually saw there was no sense their objecting

"Enough of their drivers were Nonettes and had threatened to commandeer the trams, so what could managers do but agree?

"Some of the car assembly plants and other multinational companies in Antwerp's Industrial area have still to accept the changeover but even they are happily dealing with their local sub-contractors, most of whom are now Nonettes.

"The port of Antwerp has still to change over to the Nonettes but then it was always rather separate from the city itself.

"As for the city's old administration and its employees, many still turn up for work but there is nothing for them to do. As for the politicians, they have either left town or are remaining in their holiday villas I think that they, like

rest of us, will have seen t
Truth Trials which have tak
place in other places where t
Nonettes have taken over.

"As for the city employe
who worked in our museu
and art galleries, they are n
employed by our city Nonett

"There was some troul
with the police when th
attempted to impound t
collections of the Natio
Gallery and other places but
did not last long. Once some
Antwerp's ladies sprayed the
with the 'Rampant' drug, th
soon gave up.

"As for the police the
selves, what remains of t
numbers that is, they have
alternative than to accept t
new order.

"Should they attempt to
against the wishes of Nonet
they know that they can

crisis, when we were dead quiet, Dave had us studying like nobody's business, or rather he and Lucia did. To me it's amazing the way she's able to tailor lessons, our ones at work anyway, to fit in with the particular business. We had a whole week brushing up on this skill, that presentation technique, and on and on. And no let up either.

It might have been the results of our studying or just things in general but as soon as the government gave in over the tax we were stacked out with work. Ad agencies, design studios, rang non-stop and our two reps were bringing it in by the armful. All the other processing houses were the same.

It wasn't long before we were charging rush premiums and giving preferences, with other Nonette businesses coming first, as well as anyone paying in nonettes. I was surprised at the number of those big agencies who were more than willing to pay us in them.

It's the same with suppliers. Dealing with those who are also Nonettes and paying them in nonettes means we have preference as well. As Dave said, because paying in nonettes means no taxes, prices can be cut yet margins kept. Because of this, let alone all the things like free power, a good few businesses must have joined the Nonettes these past weeks.

As Dave said, dealing with other Nonette businesses also means safer business. If any of them have cash-flow problems, all the staff have to do is no more than study and generate the money to pay their bills that way. Another safeguard is Nonette courts for settling disputes. They are quick, free and produce a definite result, none of which can be said of ordinary ones. The only people who get any money out of them are the legal trade.

Another lot who have lost out from Nonette business are accountants. As Dave said, tax accounting and avoidance are only relevant if you are paying taxes. If you are not, then they aren't either, and neither is there need for accountants. Our one who used to charge £500 a day just to come in is having a very hard time, not that there's much sympathy for the man.

That was the way it was up to a fortnight ago. Everything and everyone was getting along nicely, with the Nonette numbers growing by the day. And Nonettes were, as Sam Prior put it, "enabling people to run more of their own lives for themselves." Then all this spying stuff comes out.

It's changed everything. It's made a lot of people very angry. Not just over what those thugs did to that young lad who fingered those computer disks, or what was on them, but all the other snooping that's been going on.

The smashing of those CCTVs I was against, however, and though it was criminal, given the circumstances it's understandable. But what these revelations about government spying have actually done is put ordinary people in a position where they have either to be for the Nonettes or against us.

The government spying on Nonettes has definitely poisoned the atmosphere. People have been set against one another, made them suspicious. In our Nonette and I suppose others as well, anyone working for the government,

Pope says sex is 'vital religious experien

Vatican lifts nuns, priest chastity vow

By MARK CLINTON in ROME

CATHOLIC CLERICS are now free to ha sex, the Pope ruled yesterday. Nuns are al to be freed from their chastity vows. The ne freedoms are expected to cause dramat change to the Catholic Church's relationsh between clergy and parishioners.

The Vatican is also to introduce a mass internship for apprentice priests and novice nuns.

Welcoming the first 50 strong intake of interns from south-east Asia, the Pope said: "These young people will soon become used to the new ways of spreading the word of God."

The new Vatican Head of Corporate Affairs, Cardinal Luigi Cohen, said: "His Holiness has realised that the papal edicts on clerical celibacy have been based on a total misconception. Celibacy only applies to marriage and not sex.

"In the old days," Cardinal Cohen said, "when marriage was tied-in with chastity, celibacy had some sort of rationale but nowadays when such things as virgin brides are a thing of the past it no longer makes sense.

"Because of his Holiness's recent congress with the Susem ladies, he has come to realise just what a spiritually uplifting experience sex is."

According to Cardinal Cohen, the Pope has also decided that the Catholic Church has to bring itself more in line with modern times.

The Cardinal said that

POPE PIUS LAUDS 'ANGELIC' SUSEM

'I had Heavenly experiences' - proclaims Pontiff

By MARK CLINTON in Rome

"I WAS IN THE PRESENCE OF ANGLES," THE POPE said yesterday. Speaking for the first time since his captivity at the hands of the Susem, the Pope, Pius XIII said he had been wrong in his earlier condemnation of the Aliens.

The 76-year-old pontiff, looking fresh and invigorated despite his 24 hours captivity said: "These angels have bestowed into me the unique gift of their communion with their deeper, fuller meaning of heaven that lies beyond our own small earthly confines.

"They have bequeathed," the Pope said, "this priceless gift to me so that I might endow it to all of humankind."

The Pope also said that as a result of his revelations much of the Catholic Church's teaching and doctrines were 'backward' and 'cruel'.

Many of the clergy hierarchy, he said will have to change their ways of thinking and behavour and to do so will a minute's delay. Pop Pius said: "The Church and all those within it must adopt these new teachings these new revelations have brought or depart fothwith."

Nuns deny sex abduction charge

By Richard Trough
Courts Correspondent

"We were just bringing them back for religious instruction," Mother Superior claims

TWEVE NUNS from a Harlesden nunnery, forced three Kilburn men into a mini-bus where they sprayed them with the Nonette sex drug, *Wanton* with the intent of sexually assaulting them, a cou was told yesterday.

All 12, from the Litt Sisters of Mercy orde denied the charges.

Speaking for the pros cution, Brian Whittike QC, said: "The thre victims were subjected to truly traumatic experience

"At 10.30pm they wer walking on Kilburn High Road when they came clos to a parked mini-bus whe they were suddenly sur rounded by a number of the accused.

"The women didn't eve pretend to have

PAPACY LAUNCHES MAJOR MODERNISING THRUST

Vatican to 'get with it'

from Joyce Grandique in Rome

THE ROMAN CATHOLIC Church is set to zap itself up-to-date with a vengeance.

In a bid to bring the Catholic Church into the modern day and halt falling attendances, the old-style religion is to make way to a new, more vibrant style of churchgoing.

Cathedrals to be converted to shopping malls

Under Vatican proposals announced today, traditional church services will be scrapped in favour of *"top-of-the-pops"* musical experiences including laser-light shows.

Arrangers from leading record labels are to be recruited to transform church services.

Churches to be discos

Top designers from the fashion world have also been appointed to redesign the centuries' old monastic wear.

Announcing the new proposals, *'Get the Vatican Habit'*, Papal spokesman Cardinal Cohen said: "Following His Holiness's revelatory experiences with the Susem ladies, he has realised it is vital that the Catholic Church gets more in touch with the younger generation.

Monasteries to be motels

"The Church has a massive portfolio of under-utilised prime real estate including a clutch of city centre churches and cathedrals. Currently these are not generating enough income to cover overheads, whereas they could be earning huge sums of money.

Nunneries to offer b'n'b and saunas

"To enhance the Church's full revenue potential his Holiness is to bring in modern management skills and all senior members of the

Cardinal Cohen, the Pope's manager of corporate affairs

church, cardinals, bishops and so on, are to be offered retraining or early retirement. There will also be a mass induction of young business graduates who, after a crash theology course, will be fast-tracked to senior positions within the Church such as archbishops.

"The Church, also in ... will be an equal opportunity employer. This means that senior positions within the Church will be open to young women as well as men. And as far as his Holiness is concerned, the more the better," the Cardinal said.

The new moves are likely to meet with resistance from traditional quarters within the church. But the

or even the council and the like, has been automatically looked upon as potential spies no matter how much they say they aren't. And some public sector workers who are Nonettes are saying they are now also being discriminated against by their bosses at work because they are in the Nonettes.

There has even been talk of forcing them to either stop working in the public sector or leave the Nonettes. Personally, I'm against this, I think people should be trusted. Just as bad in my view, is the demand for those people in Dare Crescent who aren't Nonettes to either join us or clear out.

There are some including Sam Prior doing their best to calm things down before it all gets out of hand. Like he says, either we hang together or "dark forces" will hang us all separately. Naturally I'm with him on this and I've done my bit to get people to see sense, that it's a free country (well, sort of) and people can do as they please. They don't have to be part of anything including us. But it's hard going especially round the Greenwood.

As Roger, who I sometime drink with, says, the disks show MI5 or whatever used exactly the same information gathering techniques as the law does when they mount a surveillance operation against someone, or "fitting them up" as he puts it. Therefore, he says, they have to be planning to take action against us Nonettes. And the fact that the government is offering alternative accommodation to 'key personnel' who want to move out of Nonette areas, also shows, he says, that they are just waiting to strike. To me, talk like that is over the top but it's nigh on impossible to change attitudes like Roger's.

And that's another thing these disks have done. The government and everything associated with them, including the police, are being seen by Nonettes as enemies. Again I think this is wrong. I've no more time for the police than the next man, but all the same most of them are probably halfway decent and they should at least be given the benefit of the doubt.

As I see it, if things aren't handled properly the entire movement can end up pulling itself apart because of suspicion and this would be a great pity. All the same, it's one thing going on about it and quite another doing something to stop it happening. Therefore, I've decided to put my money where my mouth is and take a more active part in our Nonette.

As it happens this fitted in with something else I have been thinking about, taking part-early retirement from work, cutting down to two and a half days a week. Dave agreed to it, for as I said to him, it will give Jason, the young lad who helps me, a chance to ease himself into my studio manager's job without any disruption to the firm. Another benefit is being able to take a lump sum out of my pension. Naturally I have converted it into nonettes. I've already seen a ten per cent rise which is not bad going.

Richard Byron and **Carla Pancia** in **Barcelona** report from on yesterday's

EU 'Security though unity' summit

AMID TIGHT SECURITY, EU leaders gathered in Barcelona for an emergency one-day summit on future European security.

With the fall of Flanders to the Nonettes fresh in their minds, presidents, prime-ministers, their security chiefs and counter-terrorist experts came to this Spanish city to agree a coordinated plan of action to reverse the threat facing them by the growing power of the Nonettes. Nothing much has been agreed.

Police teargas protestors at the EU summit in Barcelona yesterday: more pictures page 7

No common ground

Split between hawks, such as Edward Campbell and Helmut Gebogen, the German chancellor and doves like the French President, Charles Coubré and Silvio Prega, the new Italian prime minister, there was little common ground between the two sides.

Apart from the loss of Flanders, several EU leaders are concerned that similar situations could occur in their own countries. Large areas of Portugal and north-west Spain as well as much of central Italy, could be the next to declare for the Nonettes.

Speaking after the close of morning session, summit host, Spanish prime minister, Fernando Caloteiro, said that democracy in Europe is under threat from the Nonettes.

Snr Caloteiro also said that the speed with which the summit had been arranged was an indication of the urgency he and the other leaders attach to the situation of Europe's internal security.

As the Spanish PM spoke, hundreds of police sharp-shooters stood watch on the rooftops surrounding the conference chamber

While ministers held a working lunch, thousands of armed, baton-wielding police fought back several hundred demonstrators protesting against the summit and stopped them from breaching the 2km wide ring of tanks and armoured personnel carriers circling the conference hall.

Many in the crowd claimed they lived in the area surrounding the conference hall and were protesting at being forced to leave their homes. During the disturbances police fired several volleys of plastic bullets at the demonstrators.

Speaking after the lunch, the British Prime Minister, Edward Campbell said: "We are gathered here today as the democratically elected heads of our respective countries. The task we all face is one of how are we to safeguard our democratic way of life for the well-being of those who have elected us."

Much else of what Mr Campbell had to say was drowned out by the roar of helicopter gunships protecting the conference. The rest of his prepared text concerned protecting Europe's parliamentary democracies.

The PM, whose antipathy towards the Nonettes is stronger that most of his EU counterparts, said that the Nonette movement posed the greatest threat to the freedoms of ordinary men and women of Europe since World War Two.

Adding that it was his and his fellow leaders' united concern to protect these freedoms from the dark forces of anarchy which, Mr Campbell claimed, the Nonette movement represented.

Speaking before the start of the afternoon session of the conference, the German chancellor, Herr Gebogen said: "In many parts of our country this Nonette movement has grown strong, more so in the eastern provinces.

"It is of great concern to us," the German Chancellor said. "If the security situation continues to deteriorate we will be forced to take strong action to repress this civil delinquency by Nonettes.

"We also have information that they are receiving support from across the River Oder. We have called upon the authorities in Warsaw for this infiltration to stop but to no effect.

"This is a situation which cannot continue. While we Germans have no wish to invade Poland, the deteriorating security situation cannot continue as it is. However, should it regress any further, we may have to consider a police action in force, just as we are contemplating for Belgium should the situation there also get out of hand."

Many observers, however, see Chancellor Gebogen's strong line against the Nonettes, as mainly for domestic German consumption.

Helmut Gebogen is under heavy pressure in Germany to reveal details of his involvement in loans by directors - to the fugitive tycoon Gunter Kirsch.

The afternoon's session of the conference was considerably delayed because of the overrunning of the working lunch.

This session was further disrupted, as were the protests, by a flight of F15 fighters of the Spanish air force - which was also protecting the meeting – strafing a passing pelican which was mistaken for a terrorist flying a microlight aircraft. The pelican later died of its injuries.

Nothing agreed

At the end of the afternoon session, the French president, Charles Courbé, explaining his administration's position said: "I speak not only for the people of France but on the behalf of all my fellow Europeans, including those who are aligned with the Nonette movement.

"There is no need for conflict," the President said, "between our differing persuasions. Now is the moment, for the sake of all the peoples of Europe, is the time to build bridges between us not dig ditches.

"Now is the moment for cohabitation between our democracy and that of the Nonettes'. And we must all seize this moment now."

While President Coubré's conciliatory position towards the Nonette is unlikely to be shared by many of the other leaders present, he has little choice other than to take a moderate line.

With the Villacoublay airbase, outside Paris, still under nominal Susem control, the French government is loathe to appear anti-Nonette.

With France's presidential election barely two months away, Coubré also knows any sense of French public unease could dash his chances of re-election.

It is an election the President is desperate to win, for should his centre-right rival, Paul Javlin do so instead, Coubré would automatically lose political immunity and be forced to face answering charges of corruption and gerrymandering while mayor of Bordeaux.

As the President spoke he, along with those present, was obliged to wipe away tears from his eyes caused by the wind blowing fumes of tear gas discharged by the police beating back demonstrators attempting to break through their cordon.

Although the protesters were more than a kilometre away their chants of: *"De presa, correm que commença d'intre de mitja houra"* could be clearly heard. Much of their anger apparently was because they would miss seeing *'Encorvada'* a popular TV soap.

The new Italian Prime Minister, Silvio Plega, also adopted a moderate line towards the Nonettes similar to the French.

The Italian PM said: "Today the very integrity of our democratic way of life is under challenge from the Nonettes.

As leader of the Italian nation," he said, "it has fallen to me to make the voice of my people heard in the conference chambers of Europe. And that voice is calling for moderation and caution towards this new and dynamic movement.

"Today, I have called for all of Europe's leaders join with me in an honest and frank discussion of the shortcomings of our systems of representative government, and why it has been unable to withstand the growing power of the Nonettes.

"I have also urged my colleagues to join with me in approaching our historic task with an air of humility. That we should seek agreement, a union with the Nonettes and utilise their dynamism so that together, all Europeans, once again, can be a strong and powerful force in the world."

The occasion of Barcelona summit, marked the first time in three years that Silvio Plega's had returned to Spain.

The Italian PM is still facing a warrant here for his arrest, having been found guilty in absentia on charges of bribery and corruption during his ownership of a Spanish TV station. But as a foreign head of state he now has international diplomatic immunity.

The formal summit meeting having ended, the EU leaders departed to a working banquet at the Catalonian President's palace.

Because of the late running of the conference, however, a "Meet the People" walkabout with local mayors and other civic leaders as well as selected passersby in the city's historic Ramblas district had to be cancelled

Protestors clubbed

As the leaders' cavalcade of armourplated limousines with their bullet-proof glass and escort of police motorcycle outriders sped away at top speed, baton-wielding paramilitary police beat back demonstrators either side of the ministers' route. The falling rain had rendered the polices' tear gas ineffective against the protesters.

As with previous EU summits, this one day meeting produced little of relevance let alone substance.

With all but two EU members currently withholding their contributions from Brussels, the EU is all but collapsing into bankruptcy as a consequence. It was doubtful even before this summit took place, that anything meaningful could emerge from it.

As for the future of European security, the prospects of any radical change to the current drift are slight.

Moreover, as those at the summit and every-one else, knows, Europe's security forces are unable to take any action against the Nonettes. Should they do so they run the risk of the Susem attacking them. And there is not a single policeman or soldier willing to risk the consequences of falling into the Aliens' clutches.

As for the EU leaders themselves, the Barcelona summit was yet again more a cosmetic exercise in appearing to be concerned about a problem rather than actually doing anything to solve it. Possibly the best that can be said is that they had a nice junketing day out.

Carla Pancia writes: Many of the Barcelona residents evacuated from their homes because of the summit, accused police of burgling them during their absence. Spanish police have declined to comment on the accusations.

Siste sex threa both brot

Monks rail ag Pope's new d

By ALAN DAVI

"PERHAPS THEY come again tonight," Friar Ambrose, a nervously looked a gatehouse of his mona

Friar Ambrose p across the mist shr Tuscan valley that ates his monastery Georgio from St. Isal kilometres away.

As he spoke, b monks were busily ricading his monas gateway in anticipati yet another visit fro Isabel's nuns.

"Yesterday evening' rages were more te than the night's be Friar Ambrose said. " of my brother monk still in a state of shoc had grown used to sisters from St. Isabel gentle, angelic fellow b but now it as if the she-devils filled crazed, lustful desire."

Friar Ambrose, a showed the monas refectory, said: "It was where many of the bro were subjected to vile de

It's all very well Tearo smirking that when in Rome do Romans, but having finished off footballers they were at a loose end, it was just too good an opportunity to pass up, they were "gentle" with him. But now look what's happened. I always knew those naughty videos the Susem saw when they first arrived would lead to trouble, especially the one about the Borgias and the things they did to the Pope atop the banqueting table. And now nuns are freed from their vows I fear for the worst.

The cooperatives, Bora and Huitoto, realising there is more to running a business than owning it, discovered I wasn't as dispensable as they first thought. In giving them the benefit of my management expertise in overcoming their difficulties of supply, demand, costs and income (the first three are rising, the fourth not), I have gained a measure of rehabilitation, some freedom of movement.

Being exercised in accounting irregularities I soon established there are none. I also found that receipts of finished Patches, strips and sprays leaving Manual's assembly lines matched those of ingredients delivered to them. Yet even allowing for supplies to the Susem and natural wastage it still meant mountains of the stuff is missing.

I did wonder whether Susem urges had risen to a frenzy of wantonness, but on inquiring down below, Pheterisco said "No." If anything, she added, their demands are down. I soon saw why. Not only had Tearo and troupe returned but so had, it seemed, those from everywhere else as well. Susem refectories were packed cacophonies of mirthful regaling.

On presenting my puzzlement at the missing amounts to the cooperatives, several sheepishly acknowledged diverting production to supplying the Susem. Though knowing but not telling that such was not so, I asked at who's behest they had. All replied "Rainbow's."

Though still obliged to broadcast to her dictates, Rainbow's sternness has softened. Instead of directives she's taken to talking to me again. Not that I am not suspicious of what could belie her change of mood, but it at least allowed me to ask if she, or her charity rather, being a major shareholder of both Wanton and Rampant, knew where these surplus stocks might lie. I added, so as to narrow her response, that several cooperatives had told me she asked for their production to be delivered to destinations she designated.

Rainbow's sphinx-like "Ooh did they now?" reply said more than she was saying. But being aware she's aware that I'm aware I need her more than she needs me, I deemed it best not to press. I did however add that the missing amounts amounted to several tonnes, the cost of which could cripple the companies and cost shareholders dear. To this she said nothing.

When I asked did she know why so many Susem were suddenly here in Tabajara, she just as smilingly said "Ooh, are there now?"

AUGHTY NUNS NAB MEN FOR STEAMY CLOISTER LOVE-INS

Oh Sisters! How shocking!

By Robert Kilmer

CONTINENTAL NUNNERIES are witnessing waves of freshly feisty sisters in intense passion plays with lay men, it was claimed yesterday.

Freed from their former vows of chastity, nuns from Norway to Naples have taken up the Pope's new edict - that sex is good for the soul - with the dedication of true believers.

Many a town has witnessed a mass of nuns enticing would-be converts back to their cloisters for the new-style religious communion.

Police and city authorities across Europe have been rebuffed in their attempts to curb nuns' evangelising fervour.

As one Italian police chief said: There is nothing my men can do to stop these them. Flocks of these nuns come into town waving thuribles (hand held incense burners) filled with *Rampant*.

"Should any of my men try to stop them," the police chief said, "they are swiftly under the drug's spell and are boarding the nuns' motor buses. A dozen of my men are still missing, presumed still undergoing conversion

Many nuns, however, view the new Papal ruling as helping them to get closer to lay people.

The abbess of a nunnery near Nice, Mother Dominux, said: "We were novices to start with but all the sisters are now well versed in the ways of this vibrant expression of our faith which they have found to be superior to the old ways."

Mother Dominux along with her sisters have also given up the abbey habit in favour of fetching little numbers specially designed by Abirachi, the leading Italian fashion house. The new range of cloister-wear: 'Nun Shall See' certainly shows a lot of nun.

Mother Dominux's off-the-shoulder bolero blouse left little to the imagination. Neither did her transparent net-mini skirt and fish-net stockings.

Asked whether this dramatic change of dress may provoke unwanted attention from unsavory characters, Mother Dominux replied: "Oh the contrary, any attention, I repeat, any attention, is most welcome.

"God does not discriminate," the abbess added, "from those whom wish

SUSEM LOVE RAIDS LULL

No Alien abductions for days

By Grace Pontins in Milan

WHERE HAVE SUSEM GONE? What are they planning next?

Officials at the Alien Abduction Centre in Milan are puzzled at the sudden end of Alien sex raids. Centre spokesman, Benito Avanchi, said: "In the past whenever there has been a cessation of Susem raids it has been because of some event elsewhere, such as the Panama episode.

"But having checked, we can say that there is nothing such as this occurring anywhere."

While the Centre is still cautioning against any relaxation of its guidelines

Newfoundlan Nonettes declare UDI

Province's fisheries set to gain from

By John Howard in Halifax, Nova Scotia

THE CANADIAN province of Newfoundland announced its independence from Canada yesterday.

The province's Nonette council said that they intended to revert back to their pre-1948 independent status.

Both Ottawa and Washington were reported to have placed security forces on high alert.

Announcing the move in the provincial capital of St Johns, Nonette representative Len Mac Dermid said: "Today the people of Newfoundland and not politicians or bureaucrats in Ottawa who will be in charge of their own destiny."

Newfoundland, Canada's most eastern province has always considered itself to be separate from the rest of the country. The Province only joined with the rest of Canada as the result of dire economic necessity some 60 years ago.

However, since the collapse of the fishing industry which the Province's was hugely dependent, it has

POPE IN KARAOKE NIGHT COLLAPSE

Pontiff in emergency hospital dash

By MARK CLINTON in ROME

POPE PIUS XIII COLLAPSED WITH A suspected heart attack late yesterday evening. Doctors at Rome's Trento Ospitailita clinic said that the 76-year-old Pontiff is in intensive care and receiving round the clock medication for his condition.

The clinic refused to deny or confirm if the Pope has suffered a heart attack.

The Pope is reported to have collapee while singing the last words of 'Unchained Melody'.

An aide to Pope Pius, Sister Lucretia, said: "His Holiness sang the ballad full of zest but unfortunately he held onto the last words for a little too long and the strain appears to have been too much for him."

The Vatican's Saturday evening Karaoke night - another of the innovations introduced by Pius XIII - was attended by the Roman Catholic Church's hierarchy as well as the latest Vatican interns, 50 of whom had arrived earlier in the day.

Sister Lucretia said: "His Holiness, having spent the day with the new interns in his private apartments, was looking forward to the evening. He had been practicing his rendition of "Unchained Melody all afternoon.

"While everyone in the Vatican is concerned for His Holiness's health," Sister Lucretia said, "and we are all praying for his speedy recovery his sudden collapse has also been a deep disappointment to many of us.

"We had spent many hours preparing a surprise banquet for the Pope in the Borgia Apartments. As you know this where His Holiness spent many spiritually uplifting hours with the Susem ladies."

It's 3 o'clock, Anne's finally asleep. I don't want a day like that again.

From the moment I stepped off the train at Paddington it's been one upset after another. The Association meeting was a complete waste of time. I left it wondering why I bothered to come. Though goodness only knows what would have happened to Anne if I had not been in London.

The meeting had barely begun and I was cross. Half were already resigned to the closures, saying we should accept the severance terms as the best offer we are likely to get. The rest of us though were set on campaigning not just against the closures of our libraries but to fight them, take direct action, sit-ins even. With no common ground, neither side giving any, nothing was decided, or agreed to anyway. So rather than being united we are each left to fend for our own, or as the delegate from Brighton, Gerald Fitzmaurice put it, "Be picked off one by one."

I had thought Anne, as she worked for the DTI, would be more sympathetic than she was. But as I tried explaining what happened at the meeting, how my job and my livelihood along with all the libraries were about to disappear, she replied that because of the tax cuts it was inevitable. When I said as a civil servant, her job was as much on the line as mine, she was just as off-hand. "If I lost my job," she said, "I will know who thank for it, the Nonettes." Even when I protested that I'm a Nonette, she retorted "You have only yourself to blame for supporting them, haven't you?"

I tried changing the subject but Anne was still just as caustic towards the Nonettes. As I had not stayed at her flat for some time, I asked what it was like living in Islington these days. Apart from her "What do you mean by that?" and my "Nothing" reply, she said "Even if I wanted to sell the flat I couldn't." Before I'd time for a "Why?" she said "The Nonettes are now so strong round here that property prices have collapsed. No person in their right mind would want to buy in Islington, let alone be able to get a mortgage. I have lost thousands on mine."

I did say that houses were selling well enough where we lived but Anne snapped "It may be alright for people like you out in the sticks but here in London it's completely different."

I said if so many people had joined the Nonettes, then by themselves they would create a market for houses. I mentioned that as I walked up from the Underground, along the Liverpool Road, I had noticed in nearly every window posters saying "Nonette" in big letters, and surely some of these flats came up for sale. But Anne dismissed this, saying they would bound to be what she called "public sector housing."

"And anyway," she said, "who would want to buy in Islington with all these Nonette gangs hanging round every street corner?"

I ribbed Anne at this. I said I had seen these "gangs" as I walked along

Government set for savage cuts

500,000 face job loss threat as tax take plummets

By Rob Mortimer
Economics Editor

FEARS ROSE YESTERDAY among public sector workers of yet another savage round of job cuts.

More than 500,000 government employees could be facing compulsory redundancy.

As the Nonette tax cuts take effect government income is set to fall by as much as £30bn.

With major institutions, such as pension funds, shunning gilt edged stock as well as selling much of what they already hold, City analysts predict that there will be an added shortfall of a further £40bn.

Combined, these two amounts alone represent a quarter of all central government income.

The scale of the financial dilemma facing the Chancellor, Peter Handel, is not what to cut but which services can be retained.

While it is thought that the security services and the police will largely escape the cuts, everything reduction in their budgets.

Some services, such education and health, are likely to have their spending cut by as much as 50 per cent.

Whitehall sources are saying that the government is already steeling itself for a wave of protest not only from the trade unions but also from many of their own backbenchers.

Newcastle MP, Kevin Routh, said: "If the proposed cutbacks are anything as severe as these leaked reports say they are, then I for one am going to be unable to support them.

"Both the National Health Service and the education system in this country," Mr Routh said, "will be effectively destroyed.

"In saying that demand for both has suffered as a result of the Nonettes is beside the point.

"Effectively what the government is saying is, "Join the Nonettes". What those ivory tower boffins in Whitehall must realise that

EMERGENCY BUDGET

"There is no alternativ claims Campbell

Millions to lose jobs as services cut to the

By Harry Bernd
in Westminster

Against the backdrop of a fall in tax revenue, the Chancellor Peter Handel unveiled to a packed yet sombre House of Parliament an emergency budget packed with a raft of sweeping and savage cut in government spending.

The Chancellor said that the effect of the Nonette income tax dispensation is currently exceeding original Treasury projections.

The Chancellor added that on the newly revised projections there is likely to be a shortfall in excess of £80 billion between current central government spending and resources to pay for them.

Mr Handel said: "In normal times any shortfall between government income and expenditure. But these are not normal times.

"Presently should the United Kingdom seek to borrow on the international money markets we could do so only by paying high rates of interest. The domestic market has for all intents and purposes dried up completely.

Social Security, Education, NHS slashed Police, Defence spared

"However, should be seen to be borrowing and at the same time not reducing our expenditure then will be the certainty that the value of Sterling will plummet on the world's exchanges

"Therefore," the Chancellor said, "the government is faced with no alternative that to reduce expenditure to match present income levels. This will mean that all but essential services, such as those vital to national security will have to pared accordingly."

Among those facing cuts are:

SOCIAL SECURITY Claimants of all benefits ranging from unemployment to pensions will have a 50 per cent cut in their entitlements. The cuts are to take immediate effect

EDUCATION, NHS will both suffer a 30 per cent

Education and Health are also will also face further cuts should they fail to make further efficiencies in their services.

DEFENCE, POLICE are the only areas to escape unscathed from Chancellor's axe. They are, however, expected to both make substantial cuts in their expenditure and divert the saving to strengthening national security.

CAPITAL SPENDING QUASHED. Except for nation security spending on all capital projects are to be put on hold until the government's financial situation improves. Such projects as new hospitals will be mothballed indefinitely.

With previous budget cuts already reducing government spending to the minimum, the only option open to the services, such as schools, hospitals is a massive laying off of personnel. This is set to amount to upwards of one million government employees

The chancellor, blaming

Govt. emergency spending cuts:

Teachers facing long holidays

By **Julia Trillow**
Education Correspondent

BRITAIN'S HARD PRESSED teaching profession is set to receive a further massive body blow: accept pay cuts or take redundancy.

As education authorities across the country

David Harper, head of Surrey's Education Authority, said: "These latest cut could be the last straw for education in this county.

"We have already seen our budget cut as a result of falling school rolls and now we have to make do

PLASTIC BULLETS FIRED CARSOVERTURNED HUNDREDS INJU

POLICE, NONETTES IN CLAPHAM CLASH

"We were provoked" - claims Met

By **Roger Granite**
in South London

THE SOUTH LONDON suburb of Clapham was the scene of a series of vicious running battles between police and Nonette protesters last night.

Police vehicles were overturned and set alight as several hundred demonstrators fought with police.

Officers were forced to fire repeated rounds of plastic bullets in an effort to quell the protesters.

Scores of police and an unknown number of Nonettes were injured in the disturbance which took more than four hours in being brought under police control.

A Scotland Yard spokesman said: "While officers were investigating an attempted attack on surveillance cameras at Clapham Underground station they were attacked by more than 50 youths.

Although police reinforcements were immediately on the scene, they were confronted on arrival at the scene by a number of violent protestors. Within minutes

Liverpool Road to her flat and they were anything but. They were just ordinary young boys and girls. The moment they saw my Nonette lapel badge, I said, they had smiled, said "Hello" and I chatted with some of them. "As for intimid-ating anyone," I said, "you should see the police checkpoints in the West End, or the security guards at the Underground for that matter." She hurrmphed at this saying I could not possibly know what these "youths" were really like.

Even when I changed the subject and asked how she and her new man were getting on, Anne was as dismissive about him as the Nonettes. With her snapping back "You mean Philip?" after I had called him "Phil," and she adding "oh him," I gathered then that things weren't going too well there either, so I decided to stop talking altogether and watch television instead.

By then it was almost 8 o'clock and time for the Nonette Hour. No sooner had its drumbeat signature tune come on, than Anne said "Do we have to watch this?" adding she had booked a table at my favourite restaurant in Camden Passage and didn't want us to be late. Though I said I always watched it, I had to compromise on seeing just the first half hour.

Even then I had to put up with Anne's caustic remarks of what was shown, or Rainbow rather, then Danny when he came on. When I said to be quiet and listen she glowered and sat with her arms folded.

Though Anne didn't say anything she still 'tsked' and kept looking at her watch. Then at half eight she was on her feet and with "Lets go or we will be late," switched off with Danny in mid-sentence and disdainfully added "Become quite a little bossy boots, hasn't he?"

In the restaurant it was just as bad. On my remarking how much cheaper the dishes were in nonettes than pounds I casually said it was another good reason for the Nonettes and why hadn't she joined? But Anne icily replied "I do not join anything."

Stupidly I said, just as I had to her before, how there were so many advantages in being a Nonette. But she replied, and loudly, that she was sick and tired of being told by goodness knows who to join and the last thing she wanted was to hear it coming from me as well.

At this outburst I almost brought myself to ask her why she was in such a ratty mood, what had happened to put her all on edge? But concluding it was probably due to this Philip, and after such a heavy day I was by then in no mood to put up with any more argument, so I talked about mum and dad, how their move to Cilgerren was progressing.

Walking home along Upper Street, past the bars and pubs packed with young people and some not so young but all smooching with one another, Anne said "That's another reason for not joining the Nonettes. Look at them, they are either high on Wanton or Rampant, they have no sense of self-control. You will never catch me behaving like that."

I did say they seemed to be quite happy and enjoying themselves, nobody

Security services to work with police

By Kyle Regan
Security Affairs Editor

BECAUSE OF THE DETERiorating security situation nation-ally, both MI5 and MI6 are to assist police forces throughout the United Kingdom, the Home Office announced yesterday.

Both services are to make available intelligence details on suspected and potential troublemakers.

News of the move was warmly welcomed by many police forces, including the Metropolitan Police.

A Scotland Yard spokesman said: "What with the current manpower shortage worsening, the extra resources will mean that many more officers can be freed to perform the actual task of policing London's streets."

While the prospect of the security tie-up is likely to raise a number of civil liberty concerns, it is widely

Govt. emergency spending cuts:

Only core NHS services to stay

By Janet Harper
Health Editor

WITH BUDGET CUTS expected to begin immediately, hospitals, clinics and surgeries across Britain are drawing up emergency plans to cope with this latest cash crisis.

In their dash to slim down services many health authorities are anticipating laying off many thousands of key staff.

At Whitton Hey Hospital in Manchester, chief registrar, Dr John Watkins said: "With these latest cuts we are putting the Whitton on an effective wartime footing.

"As of tomorrow we will only be able to provide accident and emergency facilities. All other services will be put on hold

The dilemma facing Whitton Hey is being echoed by every NHS hospital across the country. Figures released by the British Doctors Association (BDA) indicate that as many as a third of NHS staff from consultants to trainee nurses could be facing compulsory redundancy by the end of the month.

The BDA, however, said that it is fighting to stop the worst of the proposed cuts being borne by its members.

A BDA spokesman said: "While it is possible that many of those in the profession who are presently employed by the NHS will move over to the private sector or relocate abroad, there are many who are not in a position to do so."

is in urgent talks with the Ministry of Health is the safeguarding doctors' NHS pensions. The spokesman said: "we are demanding not only are our members' pension entitlements ring fenced but so are their annual increments as well."

Asked about the outlook for NHS patients and waiting lists, the BDA spokesman said: Of course the BDA is most concerned for the wellbeing and treatment of patients in the light of these cutbacks. What is more waiting lists are bound to lengthen. Though as you can see, however, there is not much the BDA can do patients and waiting lists."

While the medical profession concerns itself for the welfare of ...

Govt. emergency spending cuts

Mass strike thr against layoffs th

By Harry Bernd
Industrial Relations Reporter

PUBLIC SECTOR UNIONS are to stage a series of nationwide "Days of Action" strikes in protest against government cutbacks, the TUC announced yesterday.

With an expected 500,000 compulsory redundancies to announced within a matter of days, public sector unions, Convivia and Fraturnis are to strike.

Leaders of both Conviva – repressenting non-medical hospital employees - and Fraturnis - the municipal workers union - said that they had been given no alternative but to "convene the day-long withdrawal of labour so as to send a clear and unequivocal warning to the government that their willful destruction of ordinary working men and women's livelihoods cannot be allowed to take

Lord Cluff, head of Convivia, said that all public sector employees are expected to take part in the first day of action on Thursday week. He said: "Every member of my union those of other unions are very angry with the government's latest moves. They are totally unnecessary."

A spokesman for the Department of Employment said: "The unions' threatened action is to be deeply regretted. It is going to help no-one. On the contrary, many millions of the general public will suffer as a consequence of the unions' actions.

"Britain is facing its worst ever economic crisis," the spokesman said. "We must all make sacrifices, some of which, of course, sadly will be painful for some.

"However, now is the time," he said, "for the whole nation to pull together and not apart. We must devise ways to safeguard the lively-

Nonette revalued

£ cut to N0.45

As sterling slips, exchange curbs hinted

By Bob Godoy

STERLING WAS DEvalued by a massive 13 per cent against the nonette yesterday.

In the space of a month, sterling has more than halved in value against the Nonette currency.

This latest fall is expected to put further pressure on the Camp-bell government to recognise the nonette as legal tender.

The Nonette Central Bank (NCB), citing excessive money supply in all the world's major currencies as reason for the nonette's revaluation, said that further rises in its value cannot be ruled out.

The NCB also hinted that it has put a number of currencies "on watch" as to their future exchangeability with the nonette.

The NCB said that there are limits as to how much of other currencies Nonette economies can absorb.

In an article in Nonette newspapers, the head of the NCB in Britain, outlining its position said: "Wherever possible Nonette groups obtain goods and services from Nonette businesses and naturally they trade in nonettes.

"As more and more businesses join the Nonettes," he said, "the need to trade with non-Nonette companies declines. So does the need for non-nonette currencies. Some Nonette groups even in Britain are now trading exclusively in nonettes.

"As the volume of nonettes in circulation increases, the number of Nonette retailers continues to grow, the need to use other currencies is bound to decline.

"Thus, as far as individual Nonettes are concerned as well as Nonette councils, other currencies become increasingly irrelevant, superfluous.

"Futhermore, with the value of the nonette continuing to appreciate against these other currencies, the price comparisons between an ever increasing range of goods and services are being priced solely in nonettes."

'Police started Clapham riot' claim Nonettes

By Rodney Harrison in Clapham

POLICE FOMENTED Tuesday's night's disturbances in Clapham, south London, it was alleged yesterday.

Many of those involved in the disturbances claimed that police deliberately attacked them.

As Nonette groups and residents cleared debris-strewn streets, many of those involved in the disturbances said police deliberately lured Nonette groups into resisting them.

Eye witnesses at the Olive Grove pub on the edge of Clapham Common - where the disturbance began - said five policemen entered the pub and grabbed a newly arrived customer who they 'accused of driving a stolen car.

The man, who is well known locally as a Nonette activist, was dragged out side by the police, witnesses said.

When other Nonettes went outside with him all were attacked by yet more police, who they claim, were in waiting for them

"They [the police] came mob-handed looking for a fight with us Nonettes," said one of those involved in the braw, "and they got a bloody good hiding."

The man, who refused to give

fighting or being drunk. Anne though, was still scornful of all the amorous activity, adding that the police were frightened of stopping it in case girls sprayed Rampant on them. Though I had a little laugh at this, Anne didn't seem to think it funny.

As we walked along, and though I had stopped saying anything, I thought, as I had so many times before, that while I'm two years older than Anne, she is for ever treating me as though I am the younger sister. But the moment we walked through to Liverpool Road and away from the bright lights, this all changed.

Outside some of the houses were groups of people. I asked Anne what was going on. She said they were probably Nonettes holding silent protests outside homes of those they thought were government people denounced for spying on them, and adding "They have degenerated into the threatening louts I always said they would."

I was a bit put out by this and said the people picketing appeared peaceable enough, that with the library closures I would probably be doing the same in the coming weeks. I also said I would be cross with anyone spying on me and wouldn't like them as neighbours either. She hurrmphed at this but as we reached Liverpool Road and were about to cross it, she groaned "Oh no."

From where we were I could see another group of people and these were outside Anne's house. I also noticed she had become very apprehensive.

"Come on," I said, putting my arm in hers, "let's see what they want." Then, having half tugged her across the road and being all older sister, "No point running away, face them." But it was as if Anne had been struck dumb.

There were eight of them. As we came to the gate one of the men said "Oh hello again."

I asked "Can I help you?" and stared hard in their faces. I don't know if it was the librarian authoritarian tone of my voice or Nonette badge which did the trick but they backed away and let us pass.

We stepped up to the door but as I turned to look back at them, one of the women, looking past me to Anne, asked "When can we have a word?"

With Anne still saying nothing, I said, and as firmly as I could, "I am her older sister. Anything you have to say you can address to me."

As Anne fumbled for her keys one of the men said "Is she going?" and before I had a reply, he added "We don't want spies living round here."

Anne had the key turning in the lock and before I had barely time to say "I will deal with everything," she had the door open and we were inside. No sooner was the door closed than I had her up those stairs as fast as her legs could go. Once inside her flat, oh was I her older sister, a very annoyed and anxious older sister!

I was so cross with her. Before I knew it my voice was raised, demanding to know what was going on, what had she been doing? At first Anne stood there

BRITTANY SECEDES

Coubré declares State of Siege

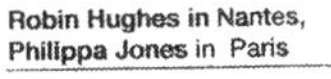

Robin Hughes in Nantes, Philippa Jones in Paris

MUCH OF BRITTANY proclaimed their independence from Paris yesterday.

French President Charles Coubré declared an immediate State of Siege throughout the northwest of the country.

Police and security forces are reported being sent to the region.

Nonette representatives in Finisterre, Côtes-du-Nord and Morbihan, France's three westernmost departments, comprising of some two million population, declared in the city of Loudéac yesterday, that they no longer recognised the authority of the French state.

The three departments join Corsica in declaring their independence from Paris.

The historic province of Brittany was removed from France's maps more than three decades ago and replaced by three new 'departments'.

Although done in the name of administrative efficiency by Paris, the loss of Brittany's name disaffected many of the province's population. It also increased their sense of alienation and insularity from the rest of the country.

Although Paris has in recent years, in an effort to group to ridicule (though not before they had killed a waitress in a botched bomb attack) the government in Paris concluded that they had overcome the province's sense of 'separateness'

What the administrators in Paris failed to account for, however, was something more important to Breton than blue striped jumpers and berets: the region's economy.

With the cut-backs in aid both from central government and the EU in Brussels, the two mainstays of Brittany's economy – agriculture and fishing – have all but collapsed.

Although the Susem attacks on Bretons' trawler fleets and confining them to port, the economic boost to those who joined the Nonettes and used their teaching screen more than made up for fishing communities' losses.

Although there has been a phenomenal growth of the Nonette movement throughout the rural regions of France as a whole it has been none stronger than in Brittany.

Breton trawlermen, however also cast their eyes at their trans-Atlantic fishermen cousins on the [once] French held islands of St Pierre and Miquelon as well as those in Newfoundland.

Dow Jones 250 company sends Wall Street shockw

Mydere joins Nonett

By Nathan Yedot

MYDERE INC, the Minnesota tool company has opted to walk away from the world of corporate America.

The company's CEO, David Mydere Junior, son of the founder Carl Mydere, said that all the employees and managers of companies' plants and subsidiaries worldwide had unanimously agreed the changeover.

He said: "Missing last quarter's profit forecast had a devastating affect on Mydere's share price.

"We were, as a consequence, under enormous pressure from Morgans, our bankers along with Wall Street carpetbagger stockholders, to accept a takeover from the Alverston Corporation.

"Mydere missed the last quarter [profit] forecast because of falling market share to smaller competitors who," he said, "being Nonette run companies, were sup-plying our clientele who had also joined the movement.

Therefore, as we saw it, our company would be far better off within the Nonette movement than outside of it."

When asked about Mydere's legal obligations to its stockholders, Mydere said: "Genuine, long-term holders of company stock will continue to own their proportion of the company assets but as for the carpetbaggers, quite frankly, Mydere doesn't give a damn.

"And this applies to our bankers, the IRS

Market turmoil prompts bank to act

Nonette Central Bank halts convertibility

By Oliver Stoneburger

The Nonette Central Bank has halted all future foreign currency transactions.

World currency markets were thrown into turmoil on the news.

Government paper and other loan stocks suffered their biggest one-day falls in living memory.

The Nonette Central Bank (NCB), while calling the block on nonette convertibility "temporary", contends that it is likely, following yesterday's collapses, to become permanent.

The NCB announcement added that the volume and rate of nonette currency currently being generated is sufficient for the Nonette organisation's needs for of nonettes in worldwide circulation is nominally puny compared to that of 'ordinary' currencies, it is nevertheless the confidence denting effect that the NCB move apparently has had on international markets which caused yesterday's falls.

With the demand for Sterling M1 - notes and coins - continuing to fall, ever greater numbers of consumers (such as you and I) are switching out of Sterling to using nonettes.

With each nonette upward revaluation against sterling, goods sold in pounds appear ever more expensive and so the rate of consumer switchover accelerates even more. With it comes a slump of consumer confidence in sterling.

currencies - which is now causing bankers the world over, sleepless nights and market speculators their jitters.

To both bankers and speculators money means more than paper, it is also government stocks and bonds. If sterling is losing value in the mind of consumers, the bonds which back it also fall in value.

But if stockholders sell their holdings of Treasury paper what can they use the cash for? For one thing they cannot buy nonettes.

However, with increasing numbers of retailers only accepting nonettes - and thus to them it is sterling which is now the 'funny money' - the increasing fear is that the pound could become valueless.

Hebrides UDI shock

State of Emergency could be declared MoD in moves to re-occupy Benbecula base

THE 30,000 strong population of the Outer Hebrides declared their independence from the United Kingdom yesterday

The remote islands' 12 strong police force were evacuated during the day on various inter-island ferries.

Other government employees and their families also left with the police officers The takeover appears to be peaceful and there were no reports of violence or any casualties.

The remote Scottish islands' UDI came as a shock to both governments in London and Edinburgh

"Totally unexpected" was Whitehall's tightlipped response to the news of the Hebrides' breakaway.

Privately however, officials in London are saying it is a Scottish matter and for the Scots alone to settle

According to reports from Stornaway, the main Hebridian town, the islands affected are Lewis and Harris, North and South Uist, Benbecula and Barra

Although the Outer Hebrides stretch for more than 120 miles off of the northwest coast of Scotland they are, apart from their small population, of little economic or strategic importance to the rest of Britain.

A London Nonette spokesman speaking on the islanders' council, which represented almost everyone living in Western Isles, will now be able to run their own affairs for their own benefit and not that of outsiders.

Reports from Hebrides say that one of the islanders' main grievances, is that of land ownership and of their crofts.

Unlike most of Britain, the islanders have traditionally lived a communal way of life. And this, it is said led easily to the speedy formation of many Nonette groups throughout the Western Isles.

With the boost given to the islands' economy from Nonette teaching machines it has also brought about a marked improvment to their standard of living

Although previously the recipients of extensive EU subsidies these have markedly decline in recent years. One of the islanders' longstanding gripes of this aid, however, what that none of this supposed largess from Brussels actually went to, and into their pockets and purses.

Instead it went into over elaborate and state rune infrastructure projects. What jobs these generated went mainly to outsiders and not to the islanders.

Nonette teaching machines, however, have acted in the

Stayrosy to take nonette

Other big store chains could soon follow

By Barabara Nielson
Economic Correspondent

STAYROSY Supermarkets chain is to take the nonette. Other major retailers such as Setco and Safebury are likely also to be forced into taking the Nonettes' currency.

A spokesman for Stayrosy's parent company, the John Barnes Partnership said: "With Group sales increasingly adversely affected by competitors there was no alternative other than to accommodate the wishes of increasing numbers of our customers who want to make their purchases with partnership has voted unanimously to be run on Nonette lines.

He also said the move to take nonettes will also enable the Group to deal with suppliers who are also Nonettes.

As part of Stayrosy's new pro-Nonette policy, products made by Nonette companies will be labelled accordingly so that Nonette customers can support their fellow members.

As part of the partnership's changeover to a Nonette-run business there will be an immediate changeover to Nonette taxation soon as their computer system will allow. The spokesman said that the changeover will saves the company "many millions" during the coming year.

Stayrosy's changeover to accepting the nonette is a major blow to the Chancellor, Peter Handel's, economic forecasts.

Although it will be difficult for major competitors to follow Stayrosy's move immediately, pressure is bound to grow for the convertibility of the nonette.

While this is something the government is loathe to

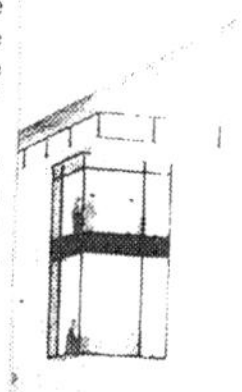

sullen, head bowed. It was only when I grabbed hold of her, and all but shouted "Look at me, I need to know," did I see in her face just how distressed she was. As I held, cuddled, felt her trembling, heard her sobbing, I realised how frightened she was as well.

I had out of her just what had been going on and it was half as to be expected. Man trouble, or rather another married one. She had met this Philip at some inter-department security meeting, one thing led to another, including him staying at the flat and telling her he was going to leave his wife. Like a fool she believed him. It was only later did she realise his real motives for their 'liaison' but by then it was too late.

Anne has not been alone of course. From what I have read in our papers, hundreds of Nonettes who are or were working for the government provided no end of information to the movement of one ministry after another prying on them. With it came lists of names. This Philip's was on one of them and apparently so was Anne's.

She said he had asked for information on her neighbourhood Nonette groups. Not being a Nonette, Anne didn't really know anything about them but pretended to him she knew more than she did so as to impress him. Believing that he was romantically interested in her, Anne had tried to find out what she could about the Nonettes. However, when he found what she told him wasn't really much use, she then realised his attachment for her wasn't even physical let alone romantic.

Amid tears and her fist-clenched "He used me" tantrums, I also got from her that this evening's Nonette visit was not the first. Although the earlier ones amounted to no more than people standing by her front gate and sticking notes through the letterbox, Anne had, stupidly, done nothing. Neither had this Philip. The last thing he had told her was, or so she said, "As you know nothing you have nothing to worry about." Since then, or so she again said, he has been "unobtainable".

I didn't know whether to believe her or not but all the same I was very upset. My own sister spying on us Nonettes. Even if it was all pretend make-believe she knows full well I am one of them, my whole family are. But there was nothing to be achieved in chastising her. What damage Anne has done is done, what is left is to try and put it right.

Also, as she was in no fit state to make any decisions on what to do to get herself out of the trouble she's in, I have made them for her. The first of which is get her out of harm's way. She is coming home with me to Cilgerren. At least I can keep an eye on her there.

Why Anne has to keep getting involved with married men I shall never know. I have told her again and again that they bring nothing but trouble and heartache.

POLLY PORTILLO REPORTS FROM TRELEW, CHU

Patagonia goe over to Nonette

Argentina declares state of sie

Argentina's Patagonian provinces have elected to secede from the country and join the Nonette Continental Congress.

The Argentinean government has declared a state of siege. Police and military forces have been rushed to the region.

Coming just few weeks after the collapse of most of neighbouring Chile to the Nonettes, Patagonia's secession has thrown the government of General Augusto Rosaio off balance.

Rather than threatening to clamp down on the Nonette rebels in north of country, it is his own regime which is now under threat.

While the Nonette movement is active throughout Argentina, the Patagonian provinces' breakaway has come as a complete surprise to most observers.

Although the region comprises a third of the country, it is sparsely populated. With few towns of major importance and most of land in the hands of a few large estates holders it was thought that the Nonette movement would have little attraction.

However, along with many in Argentina, Patagonians both rich and poor, have suffered for decades from the country's chronic economic mismanagement. As such most of southern Argentina was susceptible to the blandishments of the Nonettes.

It was, however, in this former Welsh stronghold of Chubut than the Nonette movement gained its first

NUNS DENY SEX ROMP RAMPAGE

'Just being friendly' claims Mother Superior

By Robert Kilmer

Nuns from the Little Sisters of Mercy before their Court appearance yesterday

A FLOCK OF NUNS abducted youths and forced them to take part in orgies it was claimed yesterday.

The nuns, all from the Order of Sisters of Little Mercy, Harlesden, north-west London, denied the allegations.

Sister Cynthia, speaking for the Order said: "All that the sisters were doing was being friendly. They did no more that invite some young people back to the nunnery for a "Getting to know you evening".

"While some of the Sisters, in the light of his Holiness, Pope Pius's edict, might have appeared a little boisterous, it amounted to no more than girlish high spirits.

"Those young men who claimed they were molested are just being over sensitive. "As for these men's claims that they were bound and tortured, they are totally unfounded. I have received assurances from the particular Sisters who were involved in the incident, that all the men concerned willingly let themselves be tied up and whipped.

However, I have laid down that in future if visitors are under 18, they must have parental consent before the Sisters indulge that sort of thing."

Sister Cynthia said that since the nunnery had begun their "Getting to know you evenings" her Order had numerous new recruits and halted the decline in their numbers.

She said: "However, to attract and keep this new blood we have to move with the times and go easy on the religious side of things. But all we are doing really is keeping to the spirit of his Holiness's edict.

"We now have a business manager and the karate lessons are proving most popular as is the drama class. Next week we are putting on a new play: "The Spanish Inquisition", its going to be very realistic," Sister Cynthia said.

Nonettes slash Italy in two

'Stab in the back' cries Plega as Rome seeks NATO aid

By Antonio Ruskin
in Rome

ITALY was in turmoil yesterday as Nonettes took control of three of country's key central provinces and effectively splitting it in two.

The government of Silvio Plega called for NATO assistance in quelling what he said was a "stab in the back".

Nonettes across southern Tuscany and Marche, as well as the central province of Umbria, declared in Perugia, the provincial capital, yesterday that they no longer recognised the government of Rome and

Although the Nonette movement has been active throughout much of central and northern Italy, establishing de-facto control in many areas, the link-up between so many of their groups has caught Silvio Plega's government off balance.

The fear now for Plega's administration is that the central provinces' UDI may well not be the last.

Marco Menta, speaking for the Nonettes in Perugia said: "There are many factors involved in the success of movement.

"Undoubtedly the Nonettes policy of 'clean hands, no

Long to seek love drugs curb

Wanton, Rampant to be classed as offensive weapons

By Michael Roberts
Social Affairs Correspondent

NONETTE love drugs, *Wanton* and *Rampant* could be banned. The Home Secretary, Clare Long, said that she is determined to stamp out the use of the drugs.

The Home Secretary said: "These drugs are being used increasingly against unsuspecting third parties including the police.

Nonettes numbers surge to 14m

Movement's amazing growth now boosted by big businesses signing u

By Phillip Motor
General Stuff Correspondent

DESPITE THE GOVERNMENT's daily castigation of the Nonettes, their numbers have grown to a new record high.

According to the Nonette

14.3 million people and businesses across the UK are now members of the movement.

If these latest figures for the movement's growth are accurate - and past ones have been – then they also represent a major blow to the government's anti-Nonette policies.

bell's policies, it appears, have made the slightest impact in slowing the Nonette's rate of growth either. At present the movement is growing at the rate of more than 2 million a month. But more worryingly for the government are the increasing numbers of businesses and

ing up to movement.

Announcing the latest figure, Nonette spokesperson, Joanne Green, said that while the growth of the movement had been uniform across the country as well in terms of social class, there has been a significant rise in the number of medium and larger sized companies joining

them.

Ms Green also said that a number of organizations were also encouraging their members to join the Nonettes.

"These range," Ms Green said, from branches of the Women's Institute on one hand, to fan clubs such as those of the mature sex-idols Jerry Dorsey and Tom

153: GOING, GOING

While in business double-dealing comes as standard it is hard to take from the supposedly trustworthy, such as Rainbow. Not only has she charge of the missing Wanton and Rampant concentrate but she has also snaffled all the unused Susem stocks as well. That these are not now needed is another worry, a terrible one. The Susem are leaving.

Though Rainbow has known for some time they are departing she didn't bother telling me. Neither does she appear to grasp the dire fate awaiting us all the moment the Susem have flown off. I asked why she didn't at least try to persuade Paceillo to stay a while longer, time enough for Nonettes to grow stronger, gain the upper edge, but she nonchalantly said, "There is nothing to be done."

With Pa-tu's remains recovered, she said, his crash inquiry completed, and causes of letum waves obliterated, the prime reasons why the Susem came to Earth are completed. With a long journey ahead of them, Paceillo was, she added, adamant there is not a moment to spare.

Knowing I had no chance of changing Paceillo's mind, I tried with Pheterisco to see if she would persuade her to postpone departure but with scant success. She said that as the Susem rutting season is over and amorous urges waned, there is no sense in their staying. Both Menpemelo and Milophinia said it is not a matter of wanting to leave, but wanting to go. The others said much the same, adding that they liked travelling. The only exception is Tearo and she is right down in the dumps with having to go. She spent some time telling how she wanted to stay, that she would really miss being here.

With each Susem blank I drew, my worries grew the more. Despite governments having nothing nuclear remaining, their reaction, the moment it's known the Susem umbrella has gone, will be to rain down their arsenals of other nasties on us Nonettes here in the Congress and elsewhere as well. And what has Congress to defend itself with? Nothing.

And what have I? Nothing either. No money, no freedom and no chance of escaping. Whichever way I turn, I am snookered. If only the Susem had stayed for just a little while longer we might have been alright.

It was during my desperate quest to persuade the Susem to stay that I stumbled on another jigsaw piece of the missing concentrate. In some of the chambers where Paceillo and her teams once worked, and now cleared of their screens, I came across teams of masked, bio-suited people busily scooping veritable mountains and drums of it into small paper bags, of which there were many, many thousands. They were also putting it into what I took to be fire extinguishers. Not wishing to interfere or ask what they were doing, I quietly stole away.

But on mentioning what I had seen to Rainbow and hoping for her explanation, all she said was "Oh did you now?"

TOM AND JERRY TO HIT LONDON

Will this be the hen party from hell?

By Michael Roberts
Police and Security Reporter

AN EXPECTED 5,000 strong throng of mature women are heading for London. Yes, the Tom Jones Appreciation Society is coming to town.

These diehard fans of the Rhonda Wonder are coming to celebrate the quashing of their fellow fans' - the "Ponty 40" - jail terms for molesting firemen.

Joining in the celebrations are many hundreds of Jerry Dorsy devotees and whose fan club has also actively campaigned for the "Ponty 40's" freedom.

The celebrations, already dubbed the "Tom & Jerry", had been threatened with a police ban. However, after organisers' assurances of good behaviour, Scotland Yard put it on hold. Metropolitan Police commissioner, Sir Malcolm Flannery, said: "We have no wish to deprive these ladies (whom I gather are old enough to be some of my men's mothers) of their little weekend knees-up."

When asked about the risk of a repeat of incidents which led to the "Ponty 40's" original convictions and imprisonment, Sir Malcolm said: "To be absolutely frank, we in the Met think that the South Wales Force over-reacted to what happened down there. They went in heavyhanded.

"But of course Welsh police will not have had the experience we in the Met have in handling crowds and mass gatherings.

"If our lads can handle 50,000 West Ham supporters when they lose a home game without any trouble," the commissioner said, "then you can take it from me, that this little girlie get-together will be a piece of cake.

"Don't you worry, us boys in blue will have no trouble in handling a bunch of blue-rinsed grannies."

Gwyn Davies

Also brushing aside fears that the gathering would be a repeat of the South Wales mayhem, the London end of the Tom & Jerry weekend, feisty blond, Gwyn Davies, (45) said: "All we will be doing is celebrating the freeing from wrongful imprisonment of 40 of our members who were found entirely innocent of all charges against them and have suffered the terrible trauma of being wrongfully locked up in the first place.

"Although there are more of us coming up to London than we first thought, everything will be very low key.

"There will be a meeting at the old Hammersmith Odeon," said Gwyn, "more a homage really, for we have all seen Tom perform there in the past.

"After Hammersmith there will be combined coach tours of London and maybe a brief walkabout."

Margaret Williams

Gwyn's number two, pouting grandmother of five, Margaret Williams, (49), said: "It is planned we will visit the other places where Tom performed, such as the London Palladium in the West End.

"We have also arranged to visit some of the hotels where he used to stay, such as the ones up in Marble Arch and Park Lane.

"Part of our arrang... ments has been the bloc... booking of some of the... hotels so we can all st... close together and look ... the rooms where he slep... We have managed ... negotiate some ve... reasonable rates.

"But essentially," Marg... ret said, "everything ... going to be very quiet." S... added that hairdressi... salons are "very busy eve... where"

CAMPBELL FO... NATIONAL UNI... COALITION GO...

Lib Cons join to face 'National crisis'

...TERRY BRAMBLE
... Westminster

...RITAIN IS to have a ...oalition government. ...A government of national unity has been ...formed.

The surprise move comes ...in the wake of the worsening ...security situation and the ...worst economic crisis in ...years, the prime minister, Edward Campbell said.

Announcing the move, the prime minister said that the Lib Cons and a number of other smaller parties had accepted his offer to enter into a coalition.

Several Lib Con shadow ministers have been given senior cabinet posts, including opposition leader, ... Hayes who will

'Together we stand, divided we fall' says Hayes

minister. Among other top ministers effected by the reshuffle is Home Secretary Clare Long. She will be replaced my LibCon right-wing Woking MP Christopher Thrasher

The PM said that Britain is facing such serious threats to stability and order that it is vital to present a united front to the problems confronting the nation and the entire international community.

The PM said: "The time for inter-party bickering is over. From now on it is important that all politicians work together in the ...

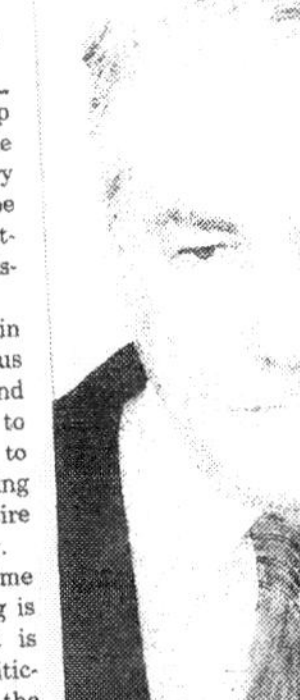

'Nonette love drugs must be banned' - Police chief de...

WPCs IN SE... ATTACK SHOC...

By ALAN DAVIES

FOUR WOMEN POLICE officers were accused of behaving like wild animals, indulged in a two hours non-stop frenzy of wantonly ferocious sex attacks on a group of Lincoln youths, it was claimed yesterday.

Angry parents of the six teenage boys, who they claim, were the policewomen's victims, said their sons were subjected to such traumatic experiences that they could scarred for the rest of their lives.

Through the parents' solicitor, Howard Levy, they intend to press for an urgent inquiry into the officers' conduct as well as bring civil proceedings against the police.

All the boys, three of whom are still of school age were, they claim, handcuffed and molested by the officers. They also allege that the policewomen forcibly removed articles of their clothing before and during the time that the offences were being committed.

A statement issued by Lincolnshire Police Authority, while acknowledging the incident took place, claims that the officers concerned were lured into a trap by the youths and a number of young women who were with them.

A police spokesman said: "The officers concerned, all of whom have been suspended from duty while an investigation of the incident takes place, offer their sympathies and full apologises to the parents and families of these young men for their conduct, which did take place in fact.

"Furthermore, the officers, all of whom have exemplary records of service, have asked that it be made known that are deeply sorry for what has taken place and for bringing the police force into disrepute.

The officers claim, however, that they acted as a result of the Nonette drug Wanton being surreptitiously administered to them by a number of young women who were present with the youths at time of

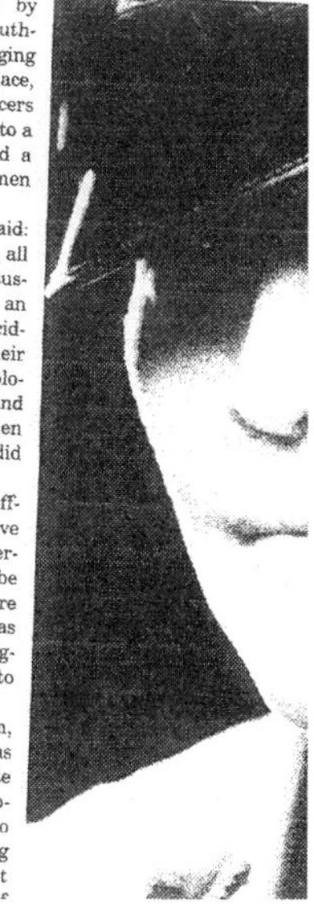

Sterling slump in bond dump panic

Huge FTSE boost as asset spree search spreads

By Harold Jones
City Editor

Government stocks slumped to new lows yesterday as investors large and small dumped bonds and upped their asset-buying sprees.

The FTSE rose a massive 352 points on the day to close at 5646.2.

Gold, other precious metals were again in heavy demand and notched up yet further record gains.

"We are buying everything and anything bar [government] paper," said one major fund manager, adding, "currently it is nigh on impossible to place meaningful monetary values on our buys but no one dares be ... asset worth."

Fund managers' "Get out of money" thumbs-down threat warning to Govt.

Darlings of the day were highly-geared small caps. Investors' sensed that for many of these companies' sterling debts will tumble yet further relative to their net asset worth. Some market watchers are even speculating that such indebtedness will soon be next to worthless.

Along with the winners however, there were some big losers: financial stocks. The entire banking sector was bombed out as a result of the flight from anything to do ... week all the banking majors have suffered a more than halving of their market value.

The BoE's "irrational panic" which had gripped markets has again pile-driven gilt edged and other government issues further into the ground. Even their now eye-watering P/Es had no effect on their holders' hell bent on ditching them and at any price.

Older City hands while worrying over the consequences of market illiquidity, are also concerned for the safety of long-term valuation of shares. Already there is talk in the Square Mile of pricing stocks in nonettes.

I'd a tear or two as I packed Becky and Patrick's things but m'mam and dad are here in the morning to take them back to Wexford. I don't know what I will do without them but I do know I have not the choice. I couldn't live should anything happen to either Becky or Patrick.

And through my sobs I found myself mumbling, as I have so many times before, "I'm no more than a single mum, I've not qualifications, experience, I did nothing more than work in a pub. What in heaven's name am I doing in this murky dirty world of spying and 'security'?" Then another voice in me said, as it always does, "It's too late now."

And I know in my heart of hearts, even if I wanted to stop I couldn't. It's not a matter of not wanting to let everyone down, or of not being able to look them in the face if I did, but because of this Kothra I have no choice other than to stay. There is nowhere I can go. Kothra would find me no matter where I went.

I had never heard of Kothra before the District Nonette re-elected me to the Regional, and because of what happened in the flats, how I handled it, had me plunged in the thick of "security matters." Reading through the reports, files slipped to us by Nonettes working in government and other places, it's obvious those snooping on us have not heard of this Kothra either. Neither, from what they say, have most government ministers.

Before I became involved I had no idea just how extensive surveillance on us Nonettes has been, still is. And it is only after I did, that it was made very plain to me just what happens to these "intelligence reports", who reads them, who they are really for.

Every report about us is eventually sent to a huge computer at the GCHQ in Cheltenham. From there they are sent to a massive computer system in America called Echelon. It is not just information about Nonettes which is sent across but on everyone else as well. Everything we say, send, our phone calls, emails, Internet are all listened into then fed into this Echelon. Details of everyone's bank accounts, tapes from security cameras and much, much more go into it as well.

Some of the disk files even go so far as to show close-ups of peoples' ear patterns taken from CCTV cameras. It's not only MI5 who have been snooping on us. The police, big companies, hospitals, schools, and on and on are now all linked up with this GCHQ computer. We are not alone though, all the other 'advanced' countries also send the same information on their people across to this Echelon as well.

But it doesn't end there. After Echelon has processed all this data it's passed to an even more powerful computer. This is Kothra.

When we were first told about Kothra, everyone wondered why he and Echelon for that matter, wanted all this information on everyone. It couldn't be

Gilt slump:

'GOVERNMENT MUST ACT' BANKS DEMAND

Financial markets 'could collapse in days' – Clayings head

By Oliver Stoneburger

MAJOR BANKS, along with leading City financial institutions, met with a Bank of England director for urgent talks in a desperate bid to stem the growing crisis gripping the world's financial markets.

With the panic selling of both gilts and bank sector shares there are fears that the entire world financial system could soon be on the brink of collapse.

While the first wave of panic selling was confined to the markets, it has now begun to ripple down to ordinary, individual share and bond holders.

The National Savings centre in Bootle was reported to be snowed under with demands for redemptions of government loan stock.

There are fears that if National Savings...

NONETTES WARN GOVERNMENT WORKERS:

'JOIN US OR ELSE'

Collins urges wives to tell 'wrongdoing' husbands to jump ship

By Michael Roberts
Media Correspondent

"COME OVER TO THE Nonettes and bring your secrets of official wrongdoing with you and we will spare you," civil servants and other government workers were told yesterday.

Whitehall, however, dismissed the Nonette move as typical of their empty scare tactics.

In the latest Nonette newscast, the movement's spokesman, Danny Collins, said that as the days of governments and nation states were numbered it will be in the interests of all those working for them to join the Nonettes now, rather than face the movement's 'truth trials' later.

Collins said: "Now that we Nonettes are worldwide there will be nowhere for the guilty to run to.

"There will be no-one who can escape the wrath and the judgment of we the people."

As Collins said: "This will film clips of the Sierra Pelada, the Nonettes' Amazonian gulag and its prisoners lifting bags of spoil down into the vast pit were shown.

Collins claimed that all the men shown were former senior government officials and others who Nonette truth trials had found guilty of corruption and other 'crimes against the people'.

Collins next said: "If you are a wife of a government official, or their daughter, mother, sister, mistress and you know they have been up to no good, then tell them to come over to the Nonettes with their secrets. If they fail to do so then this is the fate awaiting them."

There was then shown a clip of men yoked together, three abreast being run across a field by a whip wielding gang-master in what Collins claimed was a

No sooner had he spoken that there was a muffled explosion and shouts and screams.

Collins then said: "No matter what the penalty may be, this is mandatory."

A further clip then showed a man with his arms held outstretched and trousers down around his ankles.

There was also a horse standing either side of him. The chants and cheers of an audience could also be heard. As the camera came closer to the man and the horses, it became apparent that either end of a length of wire was attached to slip collars on the horses.

The wire also appeared to be looped around the man's scrotum.

To the approving roars of the crowd, the horses' hind quarters were slapped by two women. As the horses sped off in opposite directions the wire around the

VATman Bat Ma

Customs & Excise to beef up B spec

By Jed Catt

REDUNDANT VAT INSPECTORS and Customs Officers are to join the B specials, the Tax man's new police force.

Announcing the move, the Treasury and Home Office said that a further 20,000 Customs & Excise men and women are to help Britain's beleaguered police forces combat the war against growing lawlessness.

A Customs spokesman said: "This move comes as a god-send. Morale was rock bottom among

Thrasher's Auxiliaries

50,000 strong Law and Order force to be formed

By Madeline Polster
Law and Order Correspondent

ARE YOU A MEMBER OF A hunt and at loose-end now that fox hunting is banned?

Are you ex-army and can't find work; a night club bouncer with time to spare, or just simply big and strong and like throwing you weight about?

If the answer is 'yes' to all or any of the above, then the Home Secretary has a job for you in the Auxiliaries.

Announcing the launch of the campaign for the no-nonsense force, the new Home Secretary Christopher Thrasher, said that he was alarmed at the deteriorating security situation Britain is facing.

The Home Secretary said: "A day does not pass without my receiving news of yet another further outrage against police forces up and down the country.

"Britain's police forces are being willfully prevented from carrying out their lawful duties by orchestrated mobs of Nonette and other law-breakers. This has to stop and I am

Nonette world government meets

'Independence and self-determination for all' call

By Morris McDonald
Nonette Watch Correspondent

IN A LOW-KEY ceremony, 81 delegates representing Nonettes from across the world, met in Fortaleza, northeast Brazil yesterday.

In their opening addresses many delegates claimed that it is now Nonettes and not nation states who truly represent the peoples of the world.

The representatives also called on governments to acknowledge that they are now outdated and to relinquish power to the people.

The congress claimed that the total number of Nonettes world-wide is now more than 1.5bn and growing by more than 10 million people every

as the government says, that it's vital in combating international terrorists. This Echelon hasn't caught any terrorists let alone 'international' ones. Neither could they be for fighting crime and fraud. There is as much of both as before Echelon and Kothra were set up. Only in Nonette areas has crime gone down and it has nothing to do with computers or "information gathering." Either Echelon and Kothra were duff we said, or there was another explanation. Then the penny dropped.

I don't know about the others but it has had me worrying. When the Susem first arrived there were fears that they would enslave us. But the reality is we already had an Alien set on doing it, our very own man-made one, Kothra.

The information governments gather on people, especially us Nonettes isn't really for them, nor MI5, the CIA or whatever, but for this Kothra. And the more info they feed him the more powerful he becomes. And the more he does the greater his appetite for more info on us grows. If things go on as they are, this Kothra will know everything about everyone. This will make him extremely powerful, and he will control us, all of us.

This is why it is pointless my going anywhere but here, why Becky and Patrick have to go with m'mam and dad. Being "one of the Nonette ring-leaders" as the file on me has it, heaven knows what could happen except of course Kothra will have me tracked down wherever I went.

Because of what happened and my name in the papers, the Regional insist I have an escort and be driven everywhere. Something could still happen to me but if I went back to Wexford I would have no protection at all.

Some of the other Regional representatives pooh poohed our worries about Kothra, saying we were being paranoid. Even when we pointed out how all files on us Nonettes followed an identical format, used the same wording, jargon, abbreviations, they still wouldn't take Kothra seriously. In their eyes he is nothing more than an info-bound moron. They argue that the government, security services, police are our real enemies, that we should concentrate combating them, not fretting about Kothra.

These same Nonettes also say that because most of the info in the files is so inaccurate it's worse than useless to anyone who wanted to use it. Though I agree those making these reports know next to nothing about the movement, but belittling them misses their real relevance.

To Kothra, no matter how many levels and layers these reports pass through, they will, as far as he is concerned, be the actual truth. If a file on us says black is white, then in his mind white can only be black. It is the repercussions of this which has me and others worrying. Should Kothra, because of his duff data, direct action against Nonettes, it won't be a simple case of the security forces making flat-footed blunders that is the danger but of them doing things in which people get hurt.

I had all but finished the packing by the time Rainbow came on the TV. She showed a huge crowd, mostly women the Congress have trained in telepathy and who are on their way home to train yet more of us Nonettes. Rainbow mentioned telepathy enabled people to communicate mind-to-mind as well as creating a unity of thought and purpose. As she said "Unity," it was as if a bell buzzed in my head and I was mired back in thoughts of security and spying, the other troubles they have caused.

Many Nonettes demand we take on the government, force it to stop snooping on us. But what these 'activists' are doing is straining the unity of the movement to near breaking point. So much time and effort is spent damping down their hot heads, driving home that nothing is gained but much lost by confrontation, especially with the government.

What they fail to grasp is that even should the authorities want to stop snooping, Kothra will not let them. They have lost sight that it's the movement's sense of unity, unity of purpose, which is one of our strengths. They also fail to see that another of our strengths, is that we are still viewed by most people as moderates.

While the authorities, with the threat of the Susem acting against them, won't risk outright attacks on Nonettes, it's not stopped the police and others provoking some activists into clashing with them. Neither has it stopped the government branding the entire movement 'extremist'.

If only these activists could see that if we Nonettes just continue as we are then everything will go our way. With our numbers and influence growing by the day all we have to do is wait and governments everywhere will weaken away to irrelevance. And with luck so will this Kothra.

A while later Danny came on. He said Nonette numbers worldwide now top the billion mark. As I listened on to his "We are the future...tomorrow belongs to us.." it was if he was echoing my thoughts. More so as he said "There are those who seek to sow dissent within our ranks, destroy us...do not let them! Never forget, united we stand, divided we will fall."

But with his "The old world is a-changing..." Becky ran in the room, her swimsuit in her hand. I told her "Yes, the sea back home would still be warm enough to swim in," then I carried her upstairs, telling her she had a long day tomorrow.

After I had her tucked in, taken a peep at Patrick, I was back down and without knowing almost, straight in the kitchen, rooting in the table drawer for the photos I had brought back the last time I was home. The photo of me in my swimsuit, the same age as Becky, the photo I had brought specially to show Danny and he not here to see it.

Then I was back in front of the TV, Becky's swimsuit in my other hand. It was as if I was showing him both. Silly really.

Danny said goodbye, the programme ended, I clicked off the TV but I was still holding, looking at the photo, the swimsuit. I had another little sob tear as I half-wished I could be back then, back, free from this dirty murky world of snooping. And of Kothra.

155: GONE

By last night Paceillo and the rest of her crew were all who remained, the last of the other Susem having departed during the days before.

At first light Colonel Tambassing's Gurkhas were lining up one side of the green in front of the old village. Matching massed ranks of Pedro's men took up formation on the other. The entire village also assembled to watch and hurrah their goodbyes.

At minutes to noon, the appointed hour, Paceillo and the others appeared. There was much shaking of hands, posies from children and salutes of farewell from the soldiers, as all nine passed along their ranks, Pedro's first then the Gurkhas'. All was orderly, emotions restrained. Until, that is, it came to Tearo's turn to return Colonel Tambassing's salute.

It was if parting was too much for her, for she broke ranks and clasped the Colonel to her bosom. He, in turn, flung his arms up around her. Though but brief their embrace was noted by many, as was Tearo's evident and tearful distress. But with composure briskly regained, she as hurriedly rejoined the others departing back below.

While I noted this with the same dispassion as the rest of the morning's ceremony, I was also filling up with fraught. With my pleas to at least keep the Susem departure quiet having met with over-confident "Nonettes do not have secrets," what are we to do now? What am I to do?

As I quick marched with the villagers and soldiers to the viewing platform on Monte Macambirá, fears for our fates filled me the more. The moment the Susem departure is known, Nonettes everywhere will be done down. And while nowhere will be safe, Tabajara, being symbolically significant is sure to be singled out for assault.

As soldiers and villagers clamoured to the edge, as they waved to Kubber flying away, their hurrahs melded with those below. As I looked down at the ant-size figures packing the plain to the horizon and as I thought of the future awaiting them all, awaiting me, my mind flooded with foreboding.

This afternoon, attempting to divert my thoughts from our looming demise, I again visited the disused Susem chambers to check on the twenty tonnes and more of Wanton and Rampant concentrate Rainbow had appropriated. But no sooner was I there, though, than panic swept over me. Not one gramme remained.

Asking Rainbow for explanation, adding that I saw it was still there the day before the 500 telepathy trainees visited us, she replied "Oh did you now?" Then just as curtly she said "Here is your script. You're on in two hours."

I read it through with increasing alacrity but my "I can't...oh please not me..." pleas met with Rainbow's cold, silently said look of "Do it or I'll..."

This evening, with despair and hopelessness lapping ever higher, it was once again "Brothers, sisters, I have news of great importance..."

Market crisis: Why?

Are the world's financial markets on the brink of collapse? Why has catastrophe struck so suddenly? Can market confidence be restored?

Greg Drew of *Big Worries Monthly* explains the background of the present crisis and what must be done

FOR KNEE-JERKING politicians, financiers and their ilk, blame for our current 'Crisis of Capitalism' is to be laid, fair and squarely at the door of the Nonettes. But should these leaders of government and business so do, they will be venting their spleen at the wrong address.

While the Nonettes undoubtedly have an influence on capitalism's current woes, the cause for the crisis lies within capitalism itself. Or rather capitalism as it has come to be

Once upon a time

Once upon a time investors brought a company's shares as just that: an investment. With the proceeds raised in the sale offering of its shares, the company invested it in its future growth and subsequent prosperity. Its shareholders derived dividend income from the profits earned by this wealth generating capital investment. Investors in the company would also, of course, benefit from this increased wealth in the form of the company's consequential rising share price.

In this long ago, companies also funded their expansion - and thus wealth - by borrowing money from banks and other financial institutions. In turn banks benefited out of the interest they charged on such borrowing.

Bankers taking the trouble to know their borrowers, the validity of their intended investment outcomes and the quality of management to achieve them, produced better results than bankers who did not. The same was true of investors.

But as capital and financial markets grew bigger the world became too complicated for ordinary bankers and investors alike.

Investment Banks

And so step forward the investment banks. Step forward too business schools, accountants, auditors and a whole host of other business and financial experts and advisors.

Also step forward the senior management of companies awarded 'stock options'. Shareholders eagerly sanctioned these as an incentive to produce higher profits and thus higher dividends. And just as importantly: a higher market price for their shares.

With this unholy trinity at a company's helm its reason d'etre - the production and supply of competitive and innovative goods and services - changed emphasis to making profits pure and simple. And the sooner the better.

The benefits of R&D and other long-term investment were jettisoned in the name of short-term profitability. Assets were "sweated" in pursuit of the same aim. For that matter and for the same reason, employees were similarly 'sweated' as well.

As successive accounting quarters passed, what a company actually produced or did mattered less and less. What mattered more to a company's shareholders and its bankers (and its chief executive as well) were higher and higher profits.

But should a company's single quarter's profits falter its shares slumped and bankers charged more for borrowing. And worse, existing loans could and were called in and assets fire-sale sold. Or even yet worse for the company (more so for its management) it would be snapped up by a rival.

Driven by investors' sticks for forever increasing earnings, companies were forced - in endeavouring to maintain share price - to offer their clairvoyanced carrots of 'profit forecasts'. But in doing so they made, alas for them, rods for their own backs: the actual [profits] now had to meet the forecast.

Sweated assets

In their attempts to meet these self-imposed prophecies, executives 'sweated' assets and employees with ever increased ferocity.

And when there was no more 'sweat' from which to produce profits, the former were sold and the latter 'let go'. In their place, companies - in their unending quest for yet higher quarters' profits - brought up other companies and in turn, sweated and stripped their assets.

Amid this sweating and stripping, teams of management consultants massaged and creatively embellished bottom lines. They also pronounced authoritatively their endorsement of the next quarter's 'profit forecast'.

Banks buy businesses

But worse was to follow. These consultants were as often as not, also 'advising for' the companies' major shareholders and bankers (who increasingly became either sides of the same coin) as well as the companies themselves.

The inevitable then occurred: [investment] bankers began buying up businesses. One such bank, for example, owned the biggest pub chain in Britain, another half the cement factories in SE Asia.

As time passed, ownership - or control - of ever more companies passed into the ever fewer hands of bankers.

Businesses buy banks

Banks themselves were not immune, bigger got bigger by buying up smaller [banks]. The next inevitability then occurred: the biggest businesses became bankers. In the US for example, GM and GE made more money from 'financial products' than their manufactured ones.

Adding into this swirling, melding medley came 'sophisticated financial products': derivatives, futures, puts, options and on and on. So complicated were these 'financial vehicles' that not only were rocket scientists and Nobel prize-winning mathematicians required to create them but also only the likes of such academe could figure out how they actually worked.

Though these 'financial tools' were beyond the abilities and brainpower of bankers to comprehend, all the while 'their whizz-kids' used them to conjurer up a dazzle of instant billions or just as quickly bezzle them into smoky 'off-balance sheet' darkness, they were happy.

There were watchdogs appointed to halt this agglomeration of corporate power as well as those to clean up the smoky mirror shenanigans of high finance but they were soon toothless.

Carpet-bagging politicians

Politicians, their campaign finance provided by corporate backers, pulled out every last one these watchdogs' fangs. Indeed it is said of the US Congress and Senate, that they are the very best government [corporate] money could buy.

Although this ever-speeding swirl of financial hubris was there for all to see, most of us chose not to look. Who reads the financial pages of even the broadsheet newspapers? What journalists, who write on them, are there long enough to grasp what's really going on? What media is not owned by a corporation directly involved in this monetary maddened-go-round? What publication or TV station is not dependent on the advertising revenue of these corporate agglomerates?

Short termism

There were, however, some who sagely shook their heads at this milking of companies dry for short-term profit.

There have been others who muttered that this swirling financial turmoil was turning into a tornado of stupidity; a whirlwind which would wreck all in its path. Among the shakers and mutterers, were (surprise, surprise) increasing numbers of company managers.

However, all acknowledged there was nothing that could be done to extract contemporary capitalism from the vortex it had spun for itself. That soon - rather than later - it would inevitably suck us all down one almighty financial plug-hole of complete corporate collapse. Then along came the Nonettes.

The Nonettes arrive

With the Nonettes offering businesses enfranchisement into their movement, companies joined them: small in size and number to begin with but as the movement grew, so did the number and size of the businesses.

Although cohering group-like, Nonette companies are more than just another business trade association. With the use of their own - nonette - currency, freed from taxation, regulation and the bureaucracy, companies could afford to free themselves from another shackle: the banks.

The managers of some stock exchange-listed companies soon saw that not only were they losing 'market share' to Nonette businesses but also in joining with them they could afford to shake off yet other shackles: speculating shareholders and the need for short-term profitability.

Once one publicly listed company had taken the plunge - Mydere Inc, in the US - and having survived their [now ex]investment bankers' wrat and threats, others have dived in.

Although a clutch of companies in the Dow Jones 250 and five in the FTSE 250 - most notably Hithern Direct - have now joined the Nonettes, others are rumoured planning to follow suit. It is, in part, fear of this which has led to panic-buying of asset rich companies' shares.

With the ending of nonette convertibility, so these investors reason, once a company has gone over to the Nonettes, the chance of their ever holding its [hard asset backed] shares will be lost. These investors, no doubt also know the need of the newly Nonetted companies to service, let alone repay their existing bank loans, is next to zero.

It has been this fear of the banks' loans going bad and on a massive scale, which has led to their share prices being hammered. This, in turn, has led to the complete curtailment of bank lending. Which, again in turn, has led to the entire banking system being awash with money. Money which, of course, is losing its value - against the nonette - by the day.

Because banks have been returning (in desperation, some say) this 'unwanted' cash to the Bank of England (government) and redeeming (cancelling) their loan stock (gilts), the price of these has also plummeted.

This fall has led to yet the second wave of panicked selling, this time of gilts. Even our grannies are cashing in their National Savings certificates.

The [old] establishment of world corporate finance is being shaken to its narrow - and always wobbly – foundations. That of the Nonettes, however, grows stronger, wider. On paper the financial 'establishment' is still many times the size of the Nonettes but it is just that: 'on paper'.

Once, in times of turmoil, central banks (controllers of money supply), such as the Bank of England, more so the US Federal Reserve, would step in and effectively dictate terms of resolving the crisis.

Banks lose control

But there is no longer this small coterie of bankers in sole (dictatorial) control of the world's money. Every day around the world hundreds of millions of Nonettes, studying at their teaching screens generate a rival money supply: more and more nonettes.

The value of nonette currency is backed by the rising collective and educative ability of the Nonettes and the enterprise, wealth-generating activities this stimulates.

Nonette - more than paper

Arguably, this is what should back a currency. However, the old establishment's [hard] currencies are backed by nothing more than 'confidence' [in them]. Should this confidence wane yet further, a point will be reached where [ordinary] people view it for what it actually is: paper; and worthless paper at that.

Whole rotten edifice

Communism collapsed not from without but from within because its foundations were shaky: it failed to come up with - along with liberty - the economic goods. The moment its subjects could heave against them with impunity, the "whole rotten edifice" (to quote a certain German) "came crashing down". The foundations upon which the edifice of corporate capitalism is built are not much more robust. Moreover, increasing numbers of people are increasingly heaving against it; and with impunity.

To shore up, safeguard the future of corporate capitalism, it has to be reformed from the top [radically] to the very base of its foundations.

Commerce must be separated from politicians; finance taken out of the control of bankers; management out of the hands of stock option owning executives and shareholders.

Reforms urgently needed

But who is to carry out these - now pressing - reforms? Businessmen, bankers, politicians, lawyers, who? Who has the p ower - in the limited time left - to reform corporate capitalism before it, like communism, collapses into the oblivion of history?

Should corporate capitalism collapse, however, much else of the established order's authority will fall with it. Should confidence in hard [paper] currencies plummet, the power of nation state authority will sink with them. (With what for instance, would a government pay its police and security forces?)

It is evident for all to see that these Nonette people are carrying on with the same total disregard of the law as before the Aliens departed. The police may well be arresting some but these are small fry, their ringleaders are still at large.

This is not all. They are taking over one place after another. Entire villages, suburbs, are now no-go areas, including I might add, my own of Bishopbury. Needless to say I am now completely estranged from both June and the boys. Fortunately, Martin Manborn has kindly found me alternative accommodation in the former office block he has moved into at Harlow.

Though my room is rudimentary and the dining facilities limited, the building and its perimeter fences are at least fully patrolled and guarded by professional security personnel. This apparently, so Martin says, is more than can be said for other buildings sequestered by his department, several of which have been attacked by Nonettes spraying their odious slogans.

It is all very well the Government saying NATO is preparing to roll back Nonettes in Europe, South America and goodness knows elsewhere, but they appear to be totally incapable of rolling them back in Harlow. Before the Bank placed me on temporary leave, the journey to and from the station was a nightmare. Driving in the morning convoy through Nonette picket lines was extremely intimidating. And where were the police in all this? Not a single officer was to be seen. Their excuse of 'overstretch' is simply not good enough. What has happened to the 50,000 increase in their ranks? This is something we would all very much like to know.

Being asked to step down from my position as a senior manager, even though it is temporarily, came as a blow. It is so wrong to be told that despite all my years of loyal service to the Bank, I have been brushed aside in order to appease the dictates of junior staff. Yet again it has all been the cause of the insidious influence of these Nonettes.

All the same I had thought I would have received fuller backing from Mr Gibbons than I did for the position I took, that it is a manager's role to manage and junior staff to do as they are told. In my view Mr Gibbons has been unduly influenced by Hilary Saxon who always sides with female members of staff and as I have since learned, is also reputed to be in the Nonette movement.

Nonetheless, being on leave, I have been able to productively use my time assisting Martin and his colleagues in the Watch. In turn this, as well as my banking experience and expertise of course, has led to me providing financial and management advice to his Watch commander Brian Mellow and his company, Strategic Deliveries.

Obviously I keep in regular contact with the Bank not only with regard to my return from leave but that of my salary as well. The Bank, while still deducting my mortgage repayments, has still to amend the direct debit transfer

Collins lays down No nonsense Nonette gau

'The times they have a-changed

By Wendy Gilbert
General reporter

WORLD LEADERS were warned yesterday that if they attempted to stop the Nonettes they will be hastening their own demise.

In forthright and blunt Nonette telecast, their frontman, Daniel Collins, said the onward march of the Nonettes was unstoppable and that anyone getting in the movement's way will be trampled by it.

will be viewed as an attack on all.

Collins, who faces drugs and embezzlement charges in Britain, claimed that even though the Aliens had left Earth, the Nonette movement is still growing

SUSEM LEAVE!

ALIENS LOW KEY ADIE

By CLARE MIDDLETON

OUR ALIEN VISITORS, the Susem, have departed Earth and are returning on their journey into space.

The Susem departure was announced on yesterday's Nonette telecast.

Programme presenter, Rainbow Louis, said that having completed their acident investigation of their crashed spacecraft, a 'mothership', Sara, the Susem ar continuing their pr arranged ... planet several hundred light years distant.

News of the Alien's departure caught most

Auxiliary uniform row settled

Fabio Martinez
Security Correspondent

THE ROW OVER the uniform for the planned Police support militia force, the Auxiliaries, has been settled.

The Home office had wanted the proposed force's new uniform to be the same as that of the regular police: black.

Territorial Army's: khaki.

But after a Home Office/Scotland Yard working party had met seven times before the compromise agreed upon: the top half of the uniform will be the police's - a black tunic - and the bottom will be the army's - khaki trousers and in the case of horse mounted officers, fawn

'UK markets on kni - claims bank ch

'Money could soon be worthle

By Oliver Stoneburger

Stocks, shares, bonds, even money could soon be worthless, a top banker warned yesterday.

Confidence in the world's currencies' including sterling, is now so low that they could easily be worth less than the paper they are printed on.

Sir Hugh Cushion, director of the

cial markets is poised on a knife edge. One wrong move and that confidence could disappear in an instant."

Sir Hugh, addressing a meeting of City analysts, said: "Like them or hate then, we, in financial community have all to come to terms with the Nonette movement and the nonette

the nonette is great, that w no alternative negotiate an modation wit movement a currency."

While declin confirm if C and other ba in talks wi Nonette mo Sir Hugh a ledged that i

'FREE AT LAST' SAYS WARREN

White House call for 'restoration of democracy and commonsense'

By FELICITY BRIANT
in Washington

US PRESIDENT WARREN yesterday called for a renewal of democracy and return to traditional American values of order, respect and decency.

The President said that the departure of the Aliens was the lifting of a dark cloud which had cloaked the entire world in a dark night of anarchy and chaos.

President Warren, giving his first weekly nationwide radio talk in more than three months, said: "The United States of America has suffered greatly from Susem attacks.

President Warren

"The pernicious influence of their malign neo-communist creed has permeated deep into the fabric of our great nation.

"But all this is past and faces to the future for we have much work to do.

"Our nation's defence capabilities, destroyed by the Aliens, must be rebuilt. And this must be accomplished with all due speed for time is not on our side.

President to immediately enforce wide ranging law and order powers

"It is vital to re-establish America as the pre-eminent nation and spearhead of a global defensive coalition to safeguard the world's freedom from future extra-terrestrial attacks.

"As leader of the world," President Warren said, "it is the destined duty of the American peoples to shoulder, along with our allies the rolling back of those forces of anarchy and tyranny who have subsume

NATIONAL SECURITY CRISIS:

PM UNITES MPs

'Either we hang together or the Nonettes will surely hang us separately' - Campbell warns Parliament

By Madeline Polster
Home Affairs Correspondent

PARLIAMENT GAVE the government a free hand yesterday to implement vital security legislation to halt Britain's sliding into civil disorder and chaos.

In a forthright, no-nonsense speech to parliament yesterday, the Prime Minister, Edward Campbell, said: "Great Britain, its democratic freedoms and parliamentary traditions, is faced with the gravest threat since the Battle of Britain.

column intent on nothing less than the insidious usurping of our democratic way of life."

To a standing ovation from all MPs, he said: "It is not this so-called Nonette assembly which is the democratic forum of this country but this House and nowhere else.

"It is you, the elected members of parliament who are the rightful representative of your constituencies and you only."

The Prime Minister said that because of the urgency of the situation MPs should

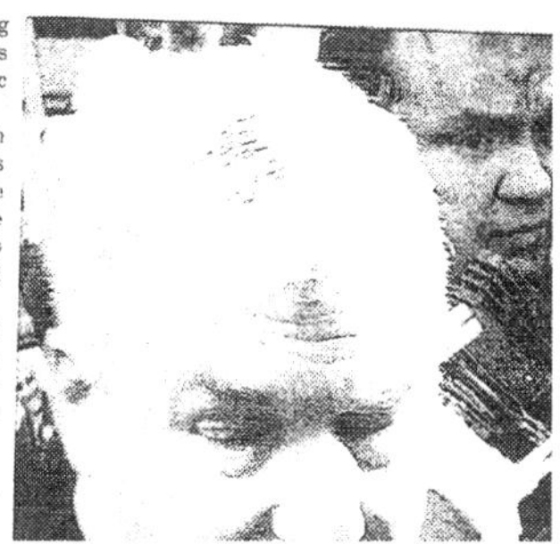

to the joint account I have with June. It is most frustrating to be told by a girl at the Bank's customer call centre in Gateshead that both of our signatures are required before the computer can activate my request. Yet, as I found to my dismay, this same computer has quite happily allowed June to have the entire amount of what is paid into our account whisked straight into her own personal one the moment it arrives.

While it is all very well for Martin and the others chortling that this a case of a bank manager getting a dose of his own medicine, it means that after paying for my room little is left for day-to-day living expenses. If it wasn't for my remuneration from Strategic Deliveries I would be facing significant financial restraint. This is not to say what I receive goes very far.

I am stunned by just how much prices in the shops have risen, for ordinary people such as myself that is. Of course, this is yet another example of the Nonettes' malign influence. Retailers in Harlow, so I have learnt, are obliged to accept this nonette coupon money or suffer serious loss of business. What is worse is that its constant upward rate of exchange value has dragged up the sterling price of goods with it.

A further and annoying consequence of these nonette coupons is at supermarkets. While service is quicker at the sterling checkout than nonette ones, more often than not I am the only such customer. It is most unnerving having so many people staring at me, both in-store and out in the car park.

Petrol supply or its non-availability rather, is yet another problem brought about by Nonettes. If it wasn't for the government filling station out by the motorway, Harlow would be without a single retail petrol outlet whatsoever. Running out of petrol is also a hazard I continually face on my visits to Strategic Deliveries' customers.

Although I act for Brian Mellow in an advisory capacity, he has also suggested that by my meeting Strategic Deliveries' customers face-to-face I will get to know more of the running of his business. To further reduce overheads Brian has sensibly suggested combining my visits with the company's deliveries to these customers. Not only is this a task I am more than happy to expedite but the extra income is extremely helpful.

Most customers are in the medical supplies trades, or so the labelling on the boxes which I deliver indicates. I would, however, have expected their premises to be considerably cleaner than they generally are.

Most of those I visit, so I have learned, are also members of the Watch, and naturally my having known Collins always helps in my conversations with them. One, a large jovial fellow, 'Big Mal' as Brian calls him, said "We have to knuckle down to this," as he helped me with a particularly heavy box marked 'Dusters'. He then mentioned that the go-ahead for a big government push against the Nonettes is expected any day now and the Watch will be playing a big part in it. When I remarked the box made jangling sounds he began laughing. I still do not know why though.

REVAMPED ALLIANCE TO ASSIST MEMBER STATES

NATO given new powers

Anita Frank
reports from Mons, Belgium

NATO is to be given sweeping new powers to assist member states' national security it was announced yesterday.

The Alliance's extended role is to begin with immediate effect.

The hastily convened meeting of the Alliance's Defence Ministers and military chiefs, took place less than 30km from the border with the Belgian breakaway province of Flanders and which must be top of NATO's list of intended targets.

Both the United States and United Kingdom's are reported to be the driving force in pushing the new measures.

Although there was no specific mention of the Nonettes and the threat

Nonettes facing stiff curbs

Campbell demands government's right to rule enforce

By Morris McDonald
In Westminster

BRITAIN'S NONETTE movement is to face curbs, Edward Campbell said yesterday.

Police and the security services are to be given to extra powers to combat the movement's activities.

In a no-holes-bared uncompromising speech to parliament yesterday, the prime minister said that nobody or organisation is above the law.

And as such, everyone must obey the laws of the land or face the full consequences of transgressing them.

The PM told the House that the government will be seeking to pass a range of tough emergency measures which will bring the "nightmare of the past few months to an end".

"It is time," the PM said, "for us all to wake up and face the cold hard reality that this country is facing."

He said that while he personally regretted some of restrictions on personal freedoms the new legislation will entail but if Britain was to maintain any stability, there was no alternative to them.

"And anyway," he said, "they are nowhere as draconian as other countries are enacting."

Although Edward Campbell did not give details of the new measures they are expected to

COLLINS CALLS ON SOLDIERS TO DESERT

Wanted conman's: 'Make Love not War' plea rebuffed

By Charles Roberts
Security Affairs Editor

POLICE AND ARMED FORCES worldwide, were urged to lay down their arms and join the Nonettes. Movement frontman Collins, called on police, soldiers to desert their posts and side with the movement.

In a Nonette newscast yesterday, Collins said: "Policemen, members of the armed services, you are ordinary people like us.

"We the Nonettes are the future. We are progress. The old established order you are charged to uphold is of reaction, controlled by those

"Join with us and you too will share in our golden future of health, wealth and happiness."

Along with his Nonette enticements to defect, Collins all issued a warning to police and soldiers should they not do so.

Showing footage of Sierra Pelada, the Nonettes' Amazonian

ers refilling it, he said: "To those who attack any Nonette, this is one of the futures awaiting you."

A Home Office spokesman said: "What this man [Collins] has said is tantamount to disaffection and is as such treason, which of is a serious offence and should he be judged guilty could be

NEW GOVERNMENT SECURITY MEASURES

Too much too late

Why Campbell's anti-Nonette laws will fail

By TERRY BRAMBLE
Political Analyst

WHILE THE WORD 'Nonette' never once passed Edward Campbell's lips in parliament yesterday, everyone who listened to him was aware that every single emergency measure the government intends to introduce is tailored specifically to crush the Nonette movement.

However, it is one thing for governments to bring in tough new laws but it is quite another to enforce them.

The prime minister runs the risk that a too heavy handed application of his get-tough approach may unwittingly be throwing out the baby with the bath water.

He, or rather those who are given leave to apply his proposed measures may well alienate many more people than just Nonettes.

The effectiveness of any policy is not how many people sympathise with it but how many it antagonises. It is they who organise against and galvanise support from the wider public.

Currently there are in excess of 14 million Nonettes in Britain and they are very organised. Not only will they be able to further count on their fellow Nonettes worldwide but also they have the tacit sympathies of many of those who are not [yet] members of the movement.

The effectiveness of any law also depends on who is to enforce it.

The resources of law enforcement in Britain - the police, armed services - are not nearly sufficient to take on the Nonettes.

Neither are the Home Secretary's newly formed B Specials and Auxiliaries. These, or 'Thrashers' Bashers' as they are already being derisory dubbed (or more ominously, the 'Black and Tans' by others) may well be capable of meting out some rough 'no nonsense' policing but they are unlikely to have the brainpower to match that of their brawn's

Moreover, it will be difficult, if not impossible, to lock up 14 million people. Even, if all the Nonette movement's 'ringleaders' (and Nonettes do not have leaders, remember?) were rounded up where they be kept? In Britain's already overcrowded prisons?

'Desperate times, desperate measures' says Campbe

NONETTES TO FACE HARSH CLAMPDOWN

Terrorist laws to curb movement's power

By William Marshall
In Westminster

THE GOVERNMENT'S 'Anti-terrorism, Crime and Security Act' is to be strengthened by the addition of a raft of provisions from Northern Ireland's anti-terrorist laws. These new provisions will apply to the entire United Kingdom for the first time.

The new laws are expected to be rushed through parliament and be in force as soon as next week.

Unveiling the government's new draconian law and order proposals to parliament yesterday, the Prime Minister, Edward Campbell said: "Tough times require tough measures to combat them."

The new laws will give UK police forces the power to detain suspects for up to 28 days without charge

Special jury-free courts will be able to pass sentences on people charged with a range of offences from theft to affray and physical violence as well as a new ranges of 'Anti-National acts'.

'Anti-National acts' echo the provisions of the US's 'Homeland' and 'Patriot' laws. These are reported to include any individual who is considered to be engaged in any activity which is deemed to be against the interests of the state.

The intended legislation will also give police and security services powers to wiretap and eavesdrop on private communications without the need for a judicial consent.

Public gatherings of more than 10 people will require police permission. Failure to inform the police will

There will also be a new offence of 'Aggravated dissent'. Anyone found guilty of publicly inciting others to disobey or break any law will face a mandatory custodial sentence.

The press and other media are also to face further curbs on both what they publish as well as the terms under which they can publish.

Contravention of these and other new Press laws will automatically attract confiscation of printing plant and heavy fines and possible prison sentences for the publishers.

The prime minister also said the government was drawing up further measures to safeguard banking and other financial institutions.

Mr Campbell said it was essential that the practice

157: DONE FOR

Every morning Rainbow wheels another bunch of ten year-old toughies into the Pousada. Also wheeled in is her "And now boys and girls you are going to help Danny rehearse his programme."

As she speaks they are crowding around, smiling trustingly up at me. Even though I am not properly awake I am very aware that behind Rainbow's 'nice lady' tone is her unsaid 'nasty' one of "And if he doesn't do exactly as he's told, I'll tell you what he did." Then grabbing hold of my hands these children, walking behind her, take me to the TV studios.

Once I worried how to compose what Rainbow told me to say, but now she has the scripts written for me by another bunch of kids. Once I worried over the consequences of what she had me say, especially those pertinent to my chances of longevity, but now such concerns are pointless. Though everyone across Congress still refuses to acknowledge it, we're all done for.

In the studio these ten year-olds, initially deferential, swiftly transmute to terrifying taskmasters forever pulling apart how I deliver my script. A script so artful that it not only has my idiom of phraseology to a tee, but comes complete with casting instruction including when to smile. All the same, and although outrageous and pugnacious, the substance of these scripts is academic, irrelevant, childish even. Congress and Nonettes everywhere are utterly defenceless against the terrors which are all set ready to come.

Though the scripts are inane, pointless, filled with empty threats, the children take them with utmost seriousness including my delivery. I try my best to humour them but by the seventh, eighth read-through my exasperation begins to rise. There are times when they all but have me cry, cry out "Get real...do you really think all this means anything to anyone out there in the real world...don't you realise all the governments are still in power...can't you see no matter what you have me say it will have no effect on them...not only are they in power they have got armies, mountains of weapons...can't you see that not only is this all a stupid waste of time, it's only making matters worse...there is nothing we can do to stop them from coming and getting us...as soon as the Americans have their satellites back in place they are going to rain missiles down on us, they are going blow and blast us all to bits...there is no escape...we are all going to die..," but instead and knowing what would happen the moment Rainbow should hear of such an outburst, I usually once again begin, "Brothers, sisters..

COLLINS RALLIES NONETTES

'The future belongs to us' fugitive war

By **Ryan Reagan**
Nonette Affairs Correspondent

"DO NOT LET THEM TAKE AWAY WHAT IS yours" was the Nonette rallying call yesterday.

Nonette spokesman Daniel Collins, in the movement's latest telecast said: "The future belongs to we the people. Do not allow the forces of authoritarianism and reaction stand in your way."

Sounding almost Churchillian, Collins, who still faces charges in Britain for fraud and other offences, said that anyone opposing the Nonettes will face the consequences once they take power.

Showing prisoners in the Nonette's Serra Pelada Amazonian gulag, he said: "This is the fate awaiting those who harm us."

opposing the Nonettes to join the movement. He said: "We Nonettes are the future, do not fight battles which cannot be won. The days of nation states are over. Do not be on the losing side."

Collins then added ominously: "If you are against us for no other reason than to protect the privilege of your position at the expense of we the ordinary people, then do not expect mercy."

The mayor of Chilean city of Valdiva who had been found guilty by a Nonette truth commission of fraud was then paraded before the cameras. The man had his trousers around his ankles and it was evident that he did not enjoy the length of cheese wire being looped around his both his

Walmar dumps Dow, joins Nonettes

More corporations set to follow store's lead
Record 1,023 one day Wall Street fall

By Oliver Stoneburger

WALMAR, one of America's biggest discount chains, delisted itself from the Dow Jones Index yesterday.

Walmar, one of the US biggest corporations will also be restructuring itself

a staggering 1,023 on t[he] day to 3,456, a new 50 y[ear] low.

Although not the first delist from the Dow, Wal[mar] is by far the largest corporation to quit

Paras poised to retake Outer Hebrides

Islanders given "surrender or be invaded" ultima[tum]

By Hannah Ginnet

The outer Hebrides' UDI is set to end.

A brigade of 5th Paras is on standby ready to reclaim the military base on the Hebridean island of Benbecula as soon as they receive the go-

Along with other Nonette overrun areas, the remote Outer Hebrides, 50 miles off the northwest Scottish coast has been given a last chance to stop their unlawful sit-in Colonel Mike Basford said that the paras had no wish to

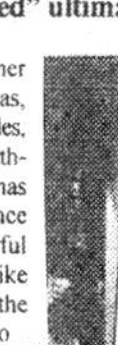

Pentagon denies invasion task force plans

'We do not have any plans to attack Nonettes' DoD chief claims

By Wayne Sebson
in Washington & Charleston

REPORTS THAT the United States is assembling a naval task force to invade Nonette territory in South and Central America were denied by the Department of Defense yesterday.

US Defense Secretary, Howard Shutz, said: "The United States has no intentions let alone plans to invade anyone, least of all anywhere in South America.

"The United States will not, I repeat, will not, attack any country unless we are attacked first.

"As of this moment in time the DoD's primary focus is the rebuilding our nation's defenses in order that we may defend ourselves against future extra-terrestrial attacks."

Yet despite official denials there are persistent reports of US forces preparing for a major military operation.

Naval facilities at San Diego, California and Norfolk, Virginia are said to be working nonstop refitting the once nuclear powered aircraft carriers with conventional turbines.

There are also reports of large numbers of landing craft being assembled at ports all along the Florida and Gulf coasts.

Defense analysts are split between hawks and doves in their predictions of future moves by US military.

The Jackson Center for Defense Studies, Charleston, headed by retired rear-admiral Howard "Hard Jack" Jackson is urging the Pentagon to take immediate action against the Nonettes.

Admiral Jackson said: "You hit your opponent hard, you hit them first, you hit them before th...

The aircraft carrier US Harry Truman leaving Norfolk, Virginia on sea trials after being fitted

"The United States has to meet the Nonette threat head on," the admiral said. "Although the Aliens have deteriorated much of US defensive strike capability, sufficient has survived to mount an operation against and destroy the Nonette command and control center down there in Latin America with minimal risk to our own forces.

"Presently there is a proactive window of operational opportunity for the US to take-out any potential Nonette offensive capability.

"Unless these Nonettes are eliminated now, not only will they grow yet more powerful but inevitably will develop a military

David Souter, of the IoAS think-tank, Washington, however, is dismissive of any American military action against the Nonettes. He said: "Two things: who are the Pentagon going to hit and what have they got to hit them with? How do you bomb, burn and missile three million square miles of territory into submission?

"The history of warfare," Souter says, shows that attacking civilians only results in that population turning against the attackers.

"But more fundamental," Souter says, "is the US's ability to wage any military campaign. And just now the

"Apart from facing hu[ge] legal suit from the Panam[a] victims, Washington's coffe[rs] are empty and the financi[al] markets are teetering o[n] the edge of collapse.

"Should the DoD even s[o] much as attempt an[y] military action against th[e] Nonettes," Souter says "there will be such a backlash right across the US that'll make all previous anti-war protests look like a picnic.

"The trouble for the folk in the Pentagon is that they have grown accustomed to there always being unlimited funds available to them. But those days are now over."

Peter Holden, also of IoAS said that despite

Government rebuffs Banks' 'help' plea

By **Paul Hemmingday**
Political Correspondent

THE CHANCELLOR, Peter Handel, has turned down demands from leading banks to recognise the nonette.

With the world's money markets in turmoil there are fears among many in City and elsewhere, that confidence in leading currencies such as sterling and the dollar could collapse.

Sir Hugh Cushion, chairman of Clayings Bank and who led the delegation, speaking after the meeting with the chancellor, said:

"We had hoped that once we had explained our grave market concerns.

"We endeavoured to press upon the Chancellor the accelerating rate at which businesses across the country as well as broad are shunning the use of hard currencies in favour of the nonette.

"We had hoped that there would have been a favourable response from the Chancellor for our proposals for convertibility between Sterling and the nonette.

"Unfortunately, we have failed to receive the positive outcome fo...

'Recognise nonette or we will all go under' - pleads Clayings head

with Mr Handel that we had been seeking."

Sir Hugh and many in the financial community are lobbying hard for the nonette to be recognised officially as legal tender.

Sir Hugh said that there are growing fears throughout the Banking sector that unless a deal is done on full convertibility between the two monetary systems there could be a

Sir Hugh outlined after the meeting the sector's concerns: "Just now all the banks have more money - notes and the like - than we know what to do with.

"Even if we should return it back to the Bank of England and other issuing banks, all we would get in return are government IOUs and quite frankly we are up to the gunnels with these and we can't even give these away either, nobody wants them."

Sir Hugh then said: "No matter how many candles a candle maker ...

electric lights, his candles weren't even worth the wax they were made of.

"With ever increasing numbers of people and businesses small and large dealing solely in nonettes we bankers and hard currencies run the risk of going the same way as candle-makers and their candles.

"The only chance for hard currencies to retain value and bankers to remain in business is to come to some arrangement with the Nonette Central Bank for an orderly transition

"Thus it is essential for this government and others to do a deal with the Nonettes before it is too late."

A Treasury spokesman said: "Government policy towards the Nonettes and other extra-parliamentary organisations is unchanged.

"Under the terms of the current emergency legislation they are proscribed. Thus HM Government, by entering into any negotiateion with any such entity would be contrary to its continuing determin[a]tion of maintaining the...

"Serious disturbances broke out earlier this evening in London's West End as supporters of the Tom and Jerry Convention clashed with police in the Marble Arch, Hyde Park area. Surrounding streets have been cordoned off and traffic diverted as police battle with more than 5,000 fans.

"We now go over live to our reporter, Martin Willis in Park Lane. Martin can you tell us what is happening?"

"Terrible scenes here, Laurie. As night falls as many as 500 police could be held in Hyde Park itself by Tom and Jerry fans. Fleets of ambulances are ferrying wounded officers to nearby hospitals, many of whom are reported to be in a traumatised condition. Further police reinforcements, many in riot gear and gas masks and carrying riot shields are on standby ready - as soon as conditions allow - to enter the park and rescue fellow officers including two detachments of mounted police."

"Martin, briefly, can you tell us how the trouble started, what caused it?"

"Hard to say exactly, Laurie. According to remaining staff in the Park Lane hotels I've spoken to - female staff that is - late this afternoon Tom and Jerry fans staying in one of the nearby hotels accosted male members of staff and hotel customers alike, and led them across Park Lane into Hyde Park itself."

"Well what is so exceptional about that?"

"We're talking dozens of men here, Laurie. And these Tom and Jerry fans - all of whom you must be remember are mature women - were taking the men to a farewell rally of several thousand other fans

"Why didn't the hotel call the police?"

"They did, Laurie, but according to Scotland Yard all available police were dealing with a yet worse outbreak of Tom and Jerry trouble in nearby Marble Arch and the Edgware Road. Where, so police say, the women were also accosting men and taking them to Hyde Park."

"And this counted as a serious disturbance?"

"We're talking entire bus queues here, Laurie, passing male pedestrians, motorists, hundreds of innocent men, many of whom at the time were with their wives or partners."

"But Martin, how is it possible for these mature women to get so many men - absolute strangers - to follow them?"

"*Rampant* Laurie, *Rampant*, the Nonette love drug. Tom and Jerry fans sprayed it on all the men including the police trying to stop them."

"But why has it been necessary to close off the whole of Park Lane and surrounding streets?"

"Abandoned cars, Laurie. Marble Arch is littered with them. Male drivers, once they'd caught a whiff of *Rampant*, so police say, stopped their cars where they were and followed the ladies."

"Oh come on Martin, you're not telling us Rampant *is that powerful?"*

"Apparently so, Laurie, as the police later found to their cost."

"Why? What happened?"

"With the abducted men including police now in Hyde Park, yet more police went into the park to rescue their fellow officers as well as the other men. But Laurie, it was like dousing flames with petrol. Wave after wave went in, including as I said, two detachments of mounted police. The police went in but none came out, well not until just minutes ago that is, when some officers made it back to the police lines and then

Nonettes overrun Mexico

US closes borders as thousands of officials, politicians, police flee

By Jose Dominquez
in Brownsville, Texas

NONETTES have gained complete control of Mexico.

In a surprise move both the President and prime minister fled the capital Mexico City and sought political asylum in the US.

Yesterday there were reported to be only small pockets of resistance against the new regime.

Following news of the government's fall, many tens of thousands of refugees are reported as heading for the Texan border.

The authorities in Austin, Texas' state capital, have ordered that its border with Mexico be closed.

That Mexico was under severe pressure from the Nonettes has been there for all to see.

What has surprised observers, however, is the speed and suddenness of the government's collapse.

Pentagon denies SDI attacks on Nonette satellites

Star Wars missiles threaten world communication

By Wayne Sebson
in Los Angles

THE US AIR FORCE has launched missile attacks against Nonette satellites, it was claimed yesterday.

According to three former workers at the Vandenberg rocket base, California, four SDI satellite busting missiles were fired during the past week at Susem-installed communications satellites.

None, of the missiles, so the former employees state, hit their intended targets.

Two exploded before they reached their targets, one hit a weather satellite and the fourth exploded close to an Indian communication

Senate blames Nonette for US economic turndow

House passes tough anti-Nonette cur

By Mathew Walberg
in Washington

IN THE WAKE OF THE deepening market slump affecting the United States' both the Senate and Congress yesterday, laid the blame at the Nonette movement for nation's current economic woes.

Both houses passed into

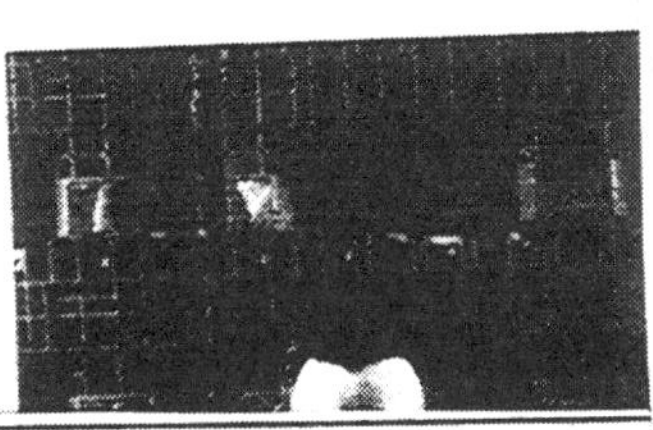

'The gloves are off' Home Secretary warns None

'Who rules Britain' Thrasher throws down gauntlet

By TERRY BRAMBLE
Political Analyst

IN A TOUGH, no-nonsense speech, the new National Government Home Secretary, Chris Thrasher, warned Nonettes to tow the line or face the consequences.

The Home Secretary said: "In this the United Kingdom no one is above the law and this includes any of those self-styled self-styled, self-governing Non-

"If these Nonettes refuse to be law abiding and this includes paying their taxes, it will be they, not the government who pay the price.

This country has had to tolerate their nonsense for long enough but now those days are over, and for ever."

Chris Thrasher, the former Lib Con shadow Home ... and noted right-

S American juntas ready for 'Revanche'

BY TOM YORK
IN SAO PAULO

WITH THE US TASK FORCE widely reported to be on the verge of invading northern South America, the surviving leaders of the southern half of the continent are gearing up to take advantage of the situation.

In Sao Paulo, headquarters of Brazil's military, leaders are reported to have drawn up plans for an immediate attack against the Nonettes once the American action is under way.

A spokesman for the Brazilian high command said: "Now is our chance to reclaim our country from these rebels.

"They have nothing to defend themselves with. For us it will be a walkover. Once they have tasted the might of our armed forces and the

Spouse splits soar say AATW

By Howard Wholks
in Denver, Colorado

WITH THEIR WEALTH waning America's top executives are being dumped and divorced at record rates, it was claimed yesterday.

At the annual convention of the American Association of Trophy Wives (AATW) in Colorado Springs, speaker after speaker gave accounts of how their former spouses had fallen down on their marriage contracts and so had to be let go.

President of the AATW, Trish Stanton (25) and former fourth wife of Hubert Darnsfledt III, CEO of Dulruth Oil, said: "With the worth of Hubert's stock tanking to near zero, he was patently unable to facilitate [the] terms of our prenuptial contract.

"Because he breached [his contract]," Ms Stanton said, "I had to divorce and [put a] lien [on] his material [assets] including the 17 residences.

"I am not alone in being obliged to this situation," said Trish, daughter of Senator Mike Stanton, "right now a full 40 per cent of AATW members are being forced to terminat prenuptials because of breach"

Among those troph wives whose husband ha also 'breached' is Rose marie Nutskalz. She said "Just now, because of my former spouse's declining revenue stream I am having to mine new seams of opportunity.

"Maybe," Rosemarie said, "I'll go with other AATW members and join this new Nonette thing that is taking

only on hands and knees, minus uniforms and much else. All, so I'm told, are in a distressed, physically and emotionally exhausted condition."

"Are any of them injured?"

"No actual injuries reported so far, Laurie, just distressed and exhausted, although I am told some of the officers have lost the power of coherent speech.

"Oh, I am now able to talk to the head of the Metropolitan Police, Sir Malcolm Flannery.

"Sir Malcolm, can you tell us what is the situation at the moment?"

"Well, Martin, as of this moment in time I am able to confirm that although the security situation is still fluid, it is basically confined to the northeast Hyde Park area. However, as a further precautionary measure, we have had no alternative than to close off a somewhat wider area to the general public."

"How big an area are we talking?"

"All of Hyde Park, parts of the West End, Knightsbridge, Bayswater."

"You're talking most of central London? Aren't you overreacting?"

"Look, the Met's responsible for law and order in London. There's 5,000 Tom and Jerry women in there, all in a highly sex drug-crazed state. They could break out at any moment, anything could happen. Although we've thrown every available officer in London into surrounding the park and now have another helicopter hovering overhead..."

"What happened to the first?"

"The crew opened its door to give a loud hailer warning to the women and, so I'm told, they received a shot of this *Rampant* drug lobbed into the chopper, and except from knowing it landed safely, we've not heard from them since."

"Sir Malcolm, admit it, for all intents and purposes you've a full scale riot on your hands. Why haven't you used CS gas, sent in women police officers, firemen to hose the women down, dampen their ardour?"

"We've already sent in WPCs, bevies of them, but these Tom and Jerry women got them high on that *Wanton* and they promptly joined in assaulting their male colleagues, and who you must remember have also lost all sense of self-control as well

"And CS, when we did manage to use it only made matters worse. When CS, apparently, mixes with Wanton, it heightens women's sex drives to hitherto unknown levels of ferocity, or so my officers who've made it back have said. As for firemen, forget it. They won't go near the place, not after what happened to those other firemen in south Wales.

"As I said there is nothing we can do except wait until these women have sated their lusts on my men and fall asleep. Then we'll apprehend them or perhaps just escort them out of London.

"Now if you'll excuse me, I must visit the officers who have managed to escape from these Tom and Jerry women...oh look what they've done to...that's diabolical, look at the state of his body... there's no call for them to have done that to him...it's those Nonettes who're behind this...look at them, look what they've done...well, that's half the Met's rugby team gone for a burton...these Nonette sex drugs must be banned... and that man, look at that...he won't be having much of a love life...oh my poor boys, look what those women have done to them, they're cruel sex-crazed fiends, that's what ...there's another 500 of my lads in there, all ruined...the compensation will cripple us...they were all good boys, none on them would ever hurt a fly...oh look at him, there was no call to put his handcuffs on..

"Martin? Martin, are you still there? We appear to have lost Martin Willis. We now go over to the radio car and for an interview with the Home Secretary, Christopher Thrasher."

Drug crazed grannies sate lust o

500 POLIC IN HYDE PA TOM & JERI PASSION HE

By ALAN DAVIES

HUNDREDS OF POLICEMEN were lured into a passion trap laid by a 5,000 strong horde of lust sated Tom & Jerry fans in London's Hyde Park yesterday.

No sooner had the boys in blue - many barely out of their teens - fallen prey to these blue rinsed grannies than they were forced to take part in night-long hell of frenzied love-making.

Even police reinforcements, in a desperate bid to rescue their fellow officers, fell victim to the Tom & Jerry she-devils' sex drug sprays.

Wave after wave of policemen went to the rescue but none came out until hours later and then on their hands and knees, their uniforms ripped from their bodies and all needing hospital treatment for their injuries.

By nightfall much of Hyde Park was a sea of writhing near-naked pulsat-

vigorous, non-stop love-making.

With each police officer up against a pack of *Wanton* drug-crazed women, he never stood a chance.

While many officers cried for help, pleaded for mercy, their uniforms were ripped from them and their young rippling muscular bodies were pawed and clawed by the women as they sated their unbridled lusts and desires on the helpless officers.

With so many determined granny-like women hunting

HYDE PARK OUTRAGE SHOCK

Tom & Jerry 'gang-bang' 500 police

'They're still at large' – warns Met

By Michael Roberts
in Central London

FIVE THOUSAND TOM & JERRY FANS subjected 500 policemen and scores of other men into all-night non-stop, no-holes-barred lewd sex-sessions in London's Hyde Park yesterday.

Hospitals across the capital have been inundated with wounded and traumatised officers.

Met fails in bids to rescue PCs from fans' sex hell

policemen are still unaccounted for and thought to still be held captive by the fans.

Two thousand police reinforcements, rushed to Hyde Park, were forced to stand by powerless to rescue fellow officers from the clutches of sex crazed Tom & J

Hospitals overflowing with injured officers

Even repeated charges of mounted police failed to break up the mayhem and in turn were also overwhelmed and became victim

'This is the last straw' Home Sec says

TOM & JERRY SEX THREAT

Missing police: Wives' fears grow

Hundreds of police set to quit fo

By Robert Kilmer

FEARS GREW YESTERDAY for the safety of more than a dozen police officers still missing following the Tom & Jerry riots. Last night Metropolitan Police Commissioner, Sir Malcolm Flannery, appealed publicly for the return of his men.

The Commissioner said: "As far as the missing officers are concerned, I have this to say to Tom and Jerry fans: "If you still have our men, please can we have them back?

"The Met has no intention in pressing charges against you. In return for my officers' release the Met will guarantee you a safe conduct out of London."

Sir Malcolm admitted that the Met was powerless to act against the fans. He said: "Unfortunately the Met does not have the means to act against these Tom and Jerry women.

"As a consequence we

Met facing massive PTSD compensation claims

"Not only do I have more than 500 of my men out of action as a result of what happened to them in Hyde Park but the Met is not in a position to risk losing any more officers in coming to close quarters these Tom and Jerry women.

Nonette 'love drugs' blamed for T&J outrage

Blaming Nonette love

TOM & JERRY SEX THREAT

'We lost control' - Met admit

By Robert Kilmer

THE ANTI-RIOT GAS - C S - has no effect on *Wanton* drug users, the head of the Metropolitan Police, Sir Malcolm Flannery admitted yesterday.

What is worse, Scotland Yard fears that not only is CS ineffective in deterring *Wanton* users, the chemical composition of CS has the reverse effect: **it actually heightens the drug user's libido to hitherto unknown levels of ferocity.**

Professor John Snowcroft, a Scotland Yard advisor said: "Using CS against people already high on *Wanton* can be likened to dousing flames with petrol."

Prof. Snowcroft also acknowledged that without CS gas, UK police forces will have difficulty finding adequate replacements in the near future. Prof.

'Riot gas 'useless' against women' on Wanton - says Yard

Snowcroft is that **supplies of CS gas may already have fallen into the hands of *Wanton* users.**

The professor said: "If they [*Wanton* users] snort CS as well, it may well be not a case of police forces being unable to repulse them but the officers themselves could be in danger of finding themselves in difficulties. Just you try running from a pack of sex-crazed women in full riot gear."

Meanwhile with so many officers hospitalised as a result of their injuries, there are fears that London will be at the mercy of Tom and Jerry fans who are still occupying hotels in the Park Lane region of London's

Tom & Jerry women threat to National security and decency' - says Campbell

Thrasher: 'Nonettes behind Hyde Park outr

As Met morale slumps and resignations grow, Police Chiefs demand ban on Nonette se

From Joyce Grandique

THE NONETTES WERE definitely behind the Tom & Jerry Hyde Park outrage, the Home Secretary, Christopher Thrasher, alleged yesterday.

that he had firm evidence that the Nonette movement intentionally supplied the 5,000 strong Tom & Jerry convention with excessive amounts of their sex drugs with the deliberate aim of provoking lawlessness in the heart of London.

Addressing parliament, the Home Secretary said:

"These so-called Nonettes are intent on nothing less than the destabilising the security forces of Great Britain.

"That they deliberately

159: KEN

There were a good few hundred in Clissold Park, kids holding a protest gig against the ban on Nonettes. They held up the traffic, made me walk from Newington Green, but apart from that they weren't doing any harm.

I stopped to listen. Others walking up Green Lanes did the same. Then all of a sudden, through the trees came these mounted auxiliaries, the first time I had seen any. They looked half naff, half horrible in their riding hats and ninja hoods. There were a dozen, then more of them.

I thought there would at least be a bit of argy bargy, but no, they charged straight into the kids, beating, clubbing, driving them right onto the railings. The poor little sods never stood a chance.

Being close to the railings I saw everything including one auxiliary deliberately charge his horse at a young girl. Tiny she was, like my little Chloe, screaming out really loud as she ran from him. He whacked her with his stave, knocking her to the ground. Everyone with me yelled, shouted for him, them, to leave the kids alone. All the cars beeped their horns, but the bastards kept on beating, clubbing the kids.

We were still yelling when two auxiliaries rode over near where I was. I saw the rifles holstered to their saddles. One waved his stave in the air, shouted for us to "move on." He got mouthfuls back. Then the second one reached for his rifle, shotgun, double-barrelled.

Before he had it raised though, let alone cocked, a brick hit him in the head. He jolted back, howled out, his hat came off, the gun fell out of his hands. At this the first auxiliary had his gun out, cocked, then pointing at us. He was also hit by bricks, stones, and actually came off of his horse. The second dismounted, grabbed hold of his gun. The first did the same.

A lot more bricks and stones were thrown. Then it was "bang, bang, bang," people screaming, hitting the deck and a load more, like me, haring through the flats the other side of Green Lanes. I think I heard more shooting but didn't stop till I was all the way up to Dare Crescent.

I was gasping, shaking like anything. Oh was I in a state. I didn't go home but to the Greenwood to tell Harry and the others what happened. And did I need a drink. I wasn't the only one in the pub who had seen and been through what I had and, like me, they were all shook-up as well.

By the second pint I'd calmed down. But I'd also become angry. Steaming angry. Steaming at what those bastards did to those poor kids, steaming at their firing on ordinary people, no rubber bullets, no warnings, nothing. Harry's dad said they were just like the Black and Tans in Ireland.

And oh was I narked at some of the people in the pub. Their spineless, pathetic "it's all over now for Nonettes...nothing we can do..."

I was all set to give them a piece of my mind when Beth Prior rushed in sob-shrieking "Come quickly! Come quickly! They're taking Sam."

NONETTES BANNED

NONETTES THREAT TO NATION'
ECURITY' - SAYS THRASHER
JSE OF NONETTE PROHIBITEI
'EACHING SCREENS ILLEGAI

By Michael Roberts
t Westminster

BRITAIN'S 14M STRONG NONETTE MOVE nent was declared illegal yesterday. Bot he Prime Minister, Edward Campbell an Home Secretary, Christopher Thrashe accused the movement of being the bigge threat to national security Britain has ev had to face.

The Home Secretary said: "The question has to asked: Who rules Britain?

Our democratically elected government or this foreign backed creed? A creed which has overthrown one democratic government after another across the world and denied ordinary people their democratic freedoms.

"For too long," Home Secretary said, "the Nonette movement in this country

others like it, to know th underneath the gover ment's velvet glove of reaso ableness and fair play is t iron fist of resolute det mination to protect t security of Great Britain.

"From this moment t government's gloves off.

"And should these N ettes want a bare knuc fight, I for one shall m sure they get one. Brit

STATE OF EMERGENCY DECLARED

MARSHALL LAW IN FORCE - HABEAS CORPUS, HUMAN RIGHTS DROPPED - INTERNMENT WITHOUT TRIAL - GATHERINGS IN PUBLIC BANNED - NONETTES BANNED - LEADERS TAKEN INTO PROTECTIVE CUSTODY - GOVT. TAKEOVER AIRWAVES - PRESS RESTRICTIONS - MOTORWAYS CLOSED - EU GOVTS. FOLLOW UK LEAD - MOBILE PHONES, E-MAILS, INTERNET BLOCKED

By Michael Roberts
In Westminster

A STATE OF EMERGENCY covering the whole of Great Britain and Northern Ireland was declared at midnight. It is the most draconian legislation ever.

During a special sitting of parliament yesterday evening, the government forced through the "Special Powers Enabling Act, Emergency Regulations" bill which was then passed into law with immediate effect.

MAIN POINTS OF THE ENABLING ACT ARE:

- **Habeas Corpus suspended: police can hold suspects indefinitely without charge**
- **European Human Rights Act and other related human rights legislation suspended**
- **... illegal: protesters face mandatory imprisonm**

TOP NONET ARRESTED

Dawn raids net key ring

By Ryan Reagan
In Westminster

IN A SERIES OF DAWN RAIDS, NATIO wide, police and auxiliary forces arrest many hundreds of leading Nonettes and taken them into what police termed as "protective custody". The Home Secretary Christopher Thrasher, said he was "ove the moon" with the success of the raids.

A Home Office spokesman, while declining to give specific details of the arrests said that "several hundred" prominent Nonettes had been detained as a result of police action.

The spokesman also said that because of the emergency regulations, he was unable to give further details except that all Nonettes who have been

arrested are in secure det tion centres and were well looked after accordance in accor with regulations.

The Home Secretary statement, said: "A po ially insurrectionary ation has been nipp the bud. We have m the Nonette ring-le safely under lock an It is just a matter of t

NONETTE THREAT:

'It will soon be all over' - says PM

By John Hodgeson
In Westminster

THE STATE OF EMERGENCY could be lifted in a matter of weeks, Prime Minister, Edward Campbell hinted yesterday.

In an upbeat speech to parliament, the PM said that with all prominent Nonette leaders in custody it was now only a matter of time before th...

EU Enabling Laws get off to patchy start

'Must try harder' – says Campbell

By Uri Freidlander

While the enforcement of Enabling Laws in Britain was seen as a series of successes for the country's police and security organisations, the same cannot be said for several of our fellow EU partners.

There is mounting Whitehall concern that the coordinated introduction of the Europe-wide ban on the Nonette movement is faltering.

In a statement from Downing Street yesterday, the Prime Minister, Edward Campbell, said that he ha already expressed hi concern to a numbe of fellow EU leaders a their lack of progres in containing th security threats i their countries. H said: "They must t harder in counteri the Nonette threat.

Nonettes responsi for Mway ban - says Minister

Nonettes to blame for Mobile, e-mail, Internet blocks

'SEX DRUGS WERE A THREAT TO POLICE' SAYS MET CHIEF

Massive Nonette drug hoard seized

By **David Roach**
Crime Reporter

B SPECIAL POLICE seized an estimated kilogram stockpile of the Nonette drug '*Rampant*' yesterday.

In dawn raids on a number of flats in north

custody for questioning as a result of the find.

Metropolitan Police Commissioner, Sir Malcolm Flannerly said: "*Rampant*' is one of the drugs used against my officers in the Hyde Park outage.

"There is not a shadow of

Scotland Yard's forensic experts calculate, is more than enough to disable every police officer in London.

"The seizure of this highly dangerous drug means not only has it been taken out of circulation but Nonettes across the capital

Nonette satellites survive attack attempt

Pentagon denies SDI missile miss

By Brett Murphy
In Los Angles

THE US AIRFORCE fired a number of ballistic missiles at Nonette satellites, all

One series of missiles was fired from the US Air Force's Vandenburg missile site in California and the second series from Johnson Island in the Pacific.

scientists who work Vandenburg, were uously denied by Pentagon.

It said that there h been any launches a

So the government has declared a 'State of Emergency'? A fat lot of good that has done them! Within the hour of the broadcast announcing it and all the things we are not supposed to do, our Nonette flags were fluttering from one end of Cilgerren to the other. "Government-free Zone" signs were put up either end of the village just as quickly.

Within the day all of west Wales, if it wasn't "government free" was "government-irrelevant". According to Gwyneth in the Pendre, although everywhere else has their flags flying as well, Aberystwyth and Barmouth, so she said, have actually gone the whole hog and declared UDI.

I never wanted it to come to an "us and them" situation but what choice has the government given everyone? What choice have they given us Nonettes, other than to stop them stopping us? As Daffyd said, they started it.

By yesterday what with the M4 motorway being blocked with cars and lorries crashed on to it, most of the other main roads were also free of police. They and their auxiliaries did attempt to mount some checkpoints, but once Mrs Mealam and the rest of her WI friends paid a visit to the ones around Llanelli and word spread of what they did to the men they got their hands on, most of the other checkpoints were soon deserted as well.

It wasn't just the police who confined themselves to their stations but the army and air force as well. However, no sooner had Mrs Mealam and company done with the police than they were post haste to Haverfordwest and the barracks of the Royal Welsh Fusiliers.

When I heard what the WI did to those young soldiers I was shocked. Then impressed that 200 mature women, without so much as a shot being fired, could bring the entire garrison to its knees. Only the Haverfordwest Nonette's intervention saved the day, for the soldiers that is.

The Welsh WI are not alone in putting police and soldiers to flight. From the news coming into the Pendre, the WI nationwide has, to a woman, dropped their jam-making spoons and gone young men hunting. But it's not just the WI either. Other groups have jumped at the chance of bagging some. With sales of Wanton and Rampant now restricted to Nonettes there has been a surge in signing-ups. I did think husbands might complain but Mr Mealam said he is glad he can get back to gardening. But what I do know is the mass conversion of so many young soldiers (and some not so) to the Nonettes is better than there being fighting and shooting.

Having brought rural Wales and much of elsewhere under Nonette sway, Mrs Mealam and her WI friends took today off for a "little rest" to recharge their batteries. This evening though, they set off in a fleet of coaches all loaded to the gunnels with fire extinguishers charged with Rampant and armfuls of Wanton. According to Gwyneth they are going up to London, but stopping off here and there "to help out" as she put it.

POLICE IN NATIONWID
NONETTE SEX DRUGS HU

'CS has fallen into Nonette hands' - Police Chief cla

By DEAN RADCLIFFE
CRIME REPORTER

POLICE AND security forces across Britain are conducting a desperate nationwide search to uncover stocks of Nonette sex-drugs *Rampant* and *Wanton*.

Although several raids on suspected targets have already been made, police admit that they have yet to locate any significant quantities of the drugs.

A Scotland Yard spokesman, announcing the current lack of police success, said: "The searches police officers that it instantly distracts and disables them from their duties.

Police forces through-out the UK are appealing to members of the public for leads in helping the security forces to locate the whereabouts of these highly dangerous drugs."

Fears over the power of the Nonette sex-drugs have been mounting ever since they were first introduced into Britain.

However, it has been the recent dramatic rise in their use against police and other places. The north England has been the wo affected.

A string of police st tions across North Yor shire and County Durha have been targeted syste atically and overrun those, who police clai were Nonette women.

As worrying to the poli is that during these raid sticks of the anti-riot gas spray have been stol by the attackers.

It is known that wh this gas is inhaled in c junction with the Non drug *Wanton* it produce

---

We must win international fight against Non

NONETTES GI
GLOBAL THRAS

Worldwide Nonette crackdown ga

By **Shelia Barker-Mann**
Defence & Security Editor

BRITAIN, THE U.S. AND OUR NATO ALLIES are in the final countdown to roll back the worldwide Nonette threat.

Within the next few days many of the people ... expect to be pipelines.

Documents found durin the police action, prove Beijing authorities say, th the Chinese Nonette we

---

US moves to war f

Mexico loss jitters White House in frenzy of a

By Brett Murphy
In Washington

PRESIDENT WARREN placed US alert it was announced yesterday.

Following the fall of Mexico to t the continuing deterioration of situation within the US all Americ to provide assistance to the enforcement agencies in maintain throughout the United States.

The President's move means that actions outside the country have

---

US Regl Banks in Nonette collapse shock

'They're falling like ten pins" - says bank chief

By Mathew Walberg

A string of U.S regional banks closed their doors yesterday. Hundreds more are could follow during the coming days.

The collapses follow the stalling of talks with US other financial and the bankin over nonette con

With confiden dollar plummeti day and flight

SCORES INJURED IN 'MISTAKEN' NONETTE RAID

UPROAR AS AUXILIARIES ATTACK OAPs

By **Ryan Reagan**
Nonette Affairs Correspondent

RESIDENTS OF A BLOCK OF FLATS FLED IN terror as detachments of armed and masked Auxiliary Police attacked them with baseball bats, rifle butts and clubs in their hunt for a fugitive Nonette.

It was only after the Auxiliaries' raid on the flats in Monica Court, Enfield, north London, did they discover that they had gone to the wrong block of flats.

During the raid, numerous cars were damaged, doors were kicked in and scores of innocent people attacked by the Auxiliaries in their own homes.

Last night more than two dozen people were still detained in hospital as a result of injuries they received at the hands of the masked police. Two elderly residents suffered heart

Last night angry residents were demanding the arrest of the Auxiliaries who carried out the raid. One resident said: "These Auxiliaries were more than thugs. are supposed to be ing democracy then going a funny way it."

An Enfield police man said: "We ar concerned at the A Police presence at Court. While we carrying out a full igation as a mat urgency, I can assu residents that we

---

'Everyone must pay up or else' - threaten Tax Polic

B Specials in huge tax raid successes

By Timothy Hunter

THE B SPECIALS marked their first week of active duty with a string of successful nationwide raids on known tax fraudsters.

Motorists shot by checkpoint police

Wives accuse Auxiliaries of 'shoot to kill' attack

By Jude Cannings

TWO MOTORISTS WERE SHO Auxiliary police in Bedford last ni

One of the motorists is in h suffering from serious head i The shootings took place as t cars took a wrong turning at the

---

Campbell 'resignatio rumour rebuffed

By Paul Hemmingday
Political Corespondent

REPORTS that the prime minister, Edward Campbell, ... to resign on health my government in putting the 'Great' back in Britain that I do not have time to be ill."

Along with the reports of the PM's health there is

It is understoo cabinet hardliners the Home Secretar Thrasher, are pres a tougher line ag Nonettes.

Others hawks,

FEARS RISE FOR SCORES OF OFFICERS SNATCHED FOR 'LOVEM

Lancs police lose doz

Wives' fears rise for missing men held by Non

BY ROBIN LOGG & EDWARD DEWER

MARAUDING BANDS OF MATURE WOMEN are prowling the country hunting down young men for sex, particularly those in uniform: policemen, soldiers.

Once men in uniform have fallen into the clutches of these sex-hungry she-devils, they are subjected to hours and hours of one perverted sexual ordeal after another.

And when these women have done with them these poor men's worn, torn, exhausted, spent bodies are cast uncaringly aside for fresher victims.

On the M6 motorway, every police checkpoint from Preston to Carlisle fell victim to a coach convoy of Cumberland women that

Hundreds of sex-drug crazed women pounced upon the unsuspecting officers. Two hours later with the mist lifting, rescuers were greeted by trail of near as naked, spent bodies strewn along the hard shoulder.

As many as 200 officers, some of them married, could be off active duty for an indefinite period while they recover from the injuries and trauma they have received at the hands of the Cumberland she-devils.

Lancaster police sources say that a further 27

Only one officer ma aged to escape the atta and then only because had lost his sense of sme However, he was forced flee across open countr side and it was sever hours before he kne where he was.

Last night, as anxio wives of the missir officers appealed for the men's safe return, the were fears that the mis ing officers could be he captive in a Cumberlar love camp and being forc to take part in sex acts.

There were also deman from the missing officer relatives for greater pr tection in the future f

---

Tom & Jerry still in town

And their 'friends' are coming to join them!

By Andrea Baxter
in the West End

DESPITE THE emergency there is one area of London where police and other security forces are noticeable by their absence: Park Lane and the surrounding streets. The Tom & Jerry Convention are still in residence.

With the slump in hotel bookings because of the emergency situation, along with sympathetic hotel - now all female - staff, the mature Tom & Jerry women are enjoying a free-of- charge stay at the area's posh hotels.

One of the convention's organisers, feisty blond, Gwyn Davies, (45), said: "With everyone having such a lovely time it seemed a shame not to go on for a bit longer.

"Most of us you see," said Gwyn, "have never set foot in let alone stayed in such posh places as Park Lane and it's all free.

"What is more, now that some of us have been offered work in the newspapers there is no knowing how long we might be staying up in London."

Gwyn's number two, pouting grandmother of five, Margaret Williams, (49), said: "The hotels are so lovely and what with them being free and all. We couldn't afford to come originally. So it's seems silly not to take advantag of such a one in a lifetim opportunity, doesn't it?"

Apart from the luxury o London's finest hotel Tom & Jerry ladies are als enjoying those of sever Metropolitan police office who are still being held in

161: AILEEN

I'm so cold. And I hurt. Hurt from the auxiliaries hitting me. Hurt from the things they have done, say, call me.

I'm so very cold. I have nothing but this damp, grubby blanket. When they brought me here they made me take off my clothes and won't give me them back till I tell them what they say I know. But I don't know what they say I do. And when I first said I didn't, they hit me. Hit and slapped me again and again, then one stubbed his cigarette out on my shoulder. And they kept on calling me things, filthy, dirty, terrible things.

From the moment the auxiliaries smashed into the flat, held me as they searched, pulled through everything, they were calling me filthy things. As they dragged, shoved me down the stairs, threw me in their transit, they never stopped their swearing. Once in the van they kept threatening to do terrible things to me. A hundred, more, auxiliaries raided the flats, shooting, clubbing at people trying to stop them taking me off. It was horrible.

I'm so cold. There is no heating. I can't get myself dry. The floor, walls are filthy damp. A tiny broken window high up is the only fresh air but I have to perch on the boxes I have as a bed to reach it. I am so hungry but what was given me to eat made me ill. The one chance to wash is when I rinse the bucket I have for a toilet. I am so tired but I'm not able to sleep. They forever shake me awake for another bout of questioning, shouting, hitting, slapping and all the other horrible things. Knowing Patrick and Becky are safe with m'mam and dad is all that keeps me from cracking up.

I'm so frightened, scared not knowing what will happen. I keep saying to myself that I'm nothing more than a single mother, and all I have done is speak up for the people in my flats and only because they elected me to. I keep telling the same to these auxiliaries but they continue accusing me of being a "ringleader" and know Nonette plans against the government.

But this morning, when without thinking, I said "There are no plans," it was terrible what they did. No sooner had one of the men shouted that if I knew there's none then I must know something, than a second man threw a bucket of water over me. Even though I cried out that I didn't know anything, slipped to the floor, another chucked more water on me. Then, before I could get to my feet, a third tipped a bucket of sand over my head.

The first man kept shouting "Tell me, tell me," the others laughing, jeering. Only when I said I had my period starting, I needed a bathroom urgently, I was bleeding, did they stop. Even then they had no feelings. Though I was crying, pleading, it took the man shouting to see blood coming from me before he told the others to get me out of the room.

The toilet they took me to was filthy. I'd not chance to wash myself properly, and with a man by the door watching, no privacy. I felt so humiliated.

I'm so very cold. I try to keep from shivering, crying, but it's so hard.

The Sentinel

Government censorship

We will not be muzzled

THE government's Enabling Laws place severe restrictions on press freedom. This draconian legislation lays down that the press may only publish what accords with government officials' approval.

Moreover, should publications disobey, they face immediate government sanctions: printing facilities confiscated, publishers fined, editors and journalists imprisoned.

While we in the British media have been - though after considerable protest - law abiding, our erstwhile overseas competitors have not. Satellite television channels continue to beam programmes, including Nonette newscasts, into the world's homes - including British households - unimpeded.

These broadcasters claim - and with some justification - that they are unable to block Nonette transmissions. The government maintains that TV viewers face the threat of prosecution for watching Nonette programmes.

However, it is a threat - if those companies advertising on these channels is a guide - that is being cheerfully ignored by a very large section of the population.

Yet worse faces the law abiding British media. A reason why Nonette newscasts are so universally popular, besides being eminently watchable, is that they have proved to be both creditable and truthful (and perhaps why so many governments detested them).

Viewers currently tuning into these newscasts, are unlikely to be unworldly. Nor will it be stretching creditability in concluding that these viewers compare what they see in Nonette newscasts with what they currently read in British newspapers. The former is seen as creditable, the latter most certainly not.

Not only have newspaper sales slumped to crisis levels but advertisers have departed the print media in droves and in the direction of satellite TV. Compounding these losses is, of course, another: that of revenue.

In a bid to staunch this fiscal haemorrhage suffered in being law abiding, we have, along with others in the print media, sought recompense from the government to remedy this injurious loss. All of our entreaties to them have been rebuffed. Not only is this manifestly unfair, it is unconscionable.

Because of government mistreatment of us in the media, we are, in turn, given no alternative than to "heal ourselves", to nurse our circulations, advertising and revenues back to health. The only remedy for our recovery is to stop taking the government's medicine and take the tonic which kept us alive and healthy in the first place: giving our readers the truth.

So, and as of today, along with others in the media, we are on this road to recovery. Furthermore, to ensure this recovery is pushed back into remission and stop government 'orderlies' forcibly injecting their unhealthy medication into us, we have engaged the services of 'nursing staff' from a rival agency: the Nonettes, including those of the Tom & Jerry convention who are still in London.

We are assured that these Nonettes will provide intensive round-the-clock care for all our facilities and staff. However, to ensure our male employees are not mistaken as outsiders, they, along with many other members of staff, have been enrolled - on a strictly temporary basis - into Nonettes and the safe-conduct identity tag membership provides.

The Nonette movement has also offered to speed our recovery by providing - again on a strictly trial basis - the nationwide distribution of all of our publications. In this same vein - yet again on a strictly trial basis - and because of our staff numbers, we will run our organisation on Nonette lines.

We have taken this course so that we may reliably report and at first hand, what it is like to be a Nonette-run business; to experience for example what it is like to free from government red tape and taxes.

Thus, and though favouring or disfavouring no one, government policies and actions, those of the Nonettes or anyone else, we will report the truth and nothing but the truth.

And finally: today's copy of your paper is priced in both pounds and nonettes.

Thrasher PM

ampbell resigns on medical grounds

By KELVIN REDNAP

ISTOPHER THRASHER, the former ie Secretary is Britain' new Prime ister. He succeeds Edward nbell who has been forced to

olice to get new gas-m

ubber 'over-uniforms' to be issued a

Police beatings - concern grows

'Auxiliaries out of control' claim MPs

usiness support for movement still rising

Govt. anti-Nonette business plan failing

By Oliver Stoneburger

Government attempts o woo business away from the Nonettes appears to be Even thoug movement, ur State of En reg-ulations is organisation, Nonette mem iness has left it More galling government is ... are jo ment's The

Thousands injured as mounted B Specials ch

Auxiliaries quell 'Peterloo' riot

Hundreds of arrests made at Nonette back

By Michael Rees
In Manchester

In the resulting chaos caused by the auxiliaries, many of ... agair man

Auxiliaries, B Specials to be given increased powers

Police morale plummet

Officers' wives' Nonette sex assaults fears r

All Security forces to be armed and could shoot on sig

POLICE TO GET ANTI SEX SPRAY WEAPONS

Full Riot Act to back Emergency regulatio

By Ryan Reagan
Security Correspondent

BRITIAN'S POLICE AND SECURITY FORCES are to be equipped of new weapons to help them combat increasing lawless announced yesterday.

The Ministry of Defence has successfully converted a fleet tanks into high powered cannons. More than 50,000 of the n tective rubber uniforms and gas masks are being issued to sec

The tanks are designed to send jets of water hundreds of metres and so deter rioters at a safe distance. The effect of the water cannonade will also 'wash' particulate of Nonette sex sprays from the air. The new-style all-in-one protective uniforms and gas masks have successfully completed their field trials and are already in mass production.

Announcing the new public-order weapons, the Prime Minister, Christopher Thrasher, said that they will help police and other law enforcement agencies ... what he termed

"At last members of the police and security forces who have valiantly been defending democracy on our behalf now have the tools to give them the upper hand in combating wanton disrespect of the laws of this country."

Although the PM's announcement of the new weapons was fully endorsed by MPs, there was apprehension on Mr Thrasher's further measures that all members of the security forces are to be armed. He said it was essential that police officers had the authority automatically to

Brushing a cerns on p unarmed m public, the F times call fo There are number of r house who return to th cies for fea the hands o How many members a same or si many mor and wome deprived of services of ically electe "Parliam

By ... Secu ... FEA ... and ... ass ... epar ... d I ... anti ... s h ... to w ... ack ... nd n ... fficial ... ite is ... easin ... the ... repo ... men ... quit

Warren's Nonette crackdown crumbles

'Banning only made us stronge... says movement

US military resolve falters

Latin America invasion put on hold

By Mathew Walberg in Washington

THE "ON-OFF" U.S. invasion of Latin America was definitely on 'off' yesterday.

A leaked Department of Defense (DoD) report points to alarmingly low levels of battle readiness.

With US forces assembling in many Gulf and Atlantic bases, the report suggests that all branches of the armed services

hood, the of the m ing to re civil powe Another the report of the leve with-in t services. It have been reading for top brass. In the m the bases sa report says,

Idaho 'seced in Nonette ta

Washington loses last western s

With Idaho's other major population centres already declared for the Nonettes, a huge swathe of the US is now under the movement's control.

From the Dakotas in the east, to Washington and California in the west both state and federal administrations go little further than their offices and police officers' motor vehicles

The military, including the air force and navy

Congress alarm at 'internal refugees'

Fugitive flight reaching crisis level

By Michael Rees
In Washington

THE FLIGHT of refugees from Nonette controlled areas within the US to Washington, New York and other major cities has now grown to crisis proportions.

So great are the numbers of those fleeing the Nonettes that some resid-

It was a very swanky banquet. In their endeavour to impress, Tabajara's cordon bleu master class excelled themselves. From presentation of the first platefuls to the last, the guests, vintners and vine growers up from Valparaisco oohed and aahed admiration. They "yum yummed" with each course as well. The local wine also came in for their accolades and with production now prodigious, it flowed like water the evening through.

Being among the first to arrive I was also able to admire the crisp white linen-topped tables set out the length of the terrace, the cutlery, glassware. Adding to this sparkling show was the sight and scents of lilac and hibiscus blooms laid along the tables. However, as the other diners gathered, sipped ice-cold calpirinha aperitifs, we were, to my mind, as the condemned sitting down to the last supper.

As such I consumed each course as if indeed it was the last. Though our demise when it comes is bound to be so sudden that the victims, us, me, will never know. For days I have been dreading the moment. That it hasn't happened yet is little short of a miracle. With the American's missiles missing our Susem satellites, it stands to reason it is merely a matter of time before they switch to easier terrestrial targets instead. And Tabajara being the main centre of communications has to be number one on the US hit list.

As the repast progressed and though there was much detailed discussion among the diners of the finer arts of viniculture, there was also talk of southern Chile's slipping from government control. There was mention too of all Argentina's Patagonian provinces applying to be part of Congress as well. While I listened, attentively so when addressed, my mind was still filled with our impending oblivion and just how lucky they, the guests, were in maybe making it out of here alive. Myself having no such luck or chance.

The evening mellowed as did the diners, while aromas of coffee, cigars replaced those of the flowers. Guests and hosts sauntered along the terrace, the younger ones dancing in the disco below. But I still had this foreboding that the missiles are all set ready to rain down on us, down on me.

Recognised by some of the visitors from my television appearances, they pressed for autographs. As I signed, several even congratulated me on my, as one put it, "heroic stirring tone". But none appeared aware that with our broadcasts being blocked and banned by governments the world over, there is now next to no one to see them, let alone be stirred by what I say.

Neither did I dare inform these 'fans' of the terrible tortures Rainbow's pre-teen toughies subject me to every day, that I am no more than her glove puppet coerced into parroting their pointless scripts. Nor how, with the Susem umbrella gone, and no matter about Nonette gains in Chile or elsewhere, once the Americans start firing their missiles we are all done for. No dared mention either that they should all run for their lives while they may.

Wales falls to Nonette - and the WI

Shock rout sends government reeling

By Ted Woodward
Welsh Correspondent

AN ARMY OF NONETTE women several thousand strong, armed only with sex-drugs, have overrun every police station, army

cing Nonette forces

The loss of Wales to the Nonettes comes as a serious setback for the government. Last night the cabinet was reported planning moves to reverse the deteriorating security situation.

remained in governm
Though both strong
surrounded and were n
ed to hold out the nigh
ing to Nonette sourc
less than 72 hours for th
many of them from

Nonettes step passive resista

By Ryan Reagan
In Chelsea

ed within a stone's throw of Westminster in nearby Chelsea.

Meeting in the warehouse of a

The assembly the more tha detained by sec

Hundreds of police, soldiers snatched for 'Love Camp duties'

Lake District, Lancs. all lost to Nonettes

Cornwall, Cotswolds set go over as well

By Liz Parry
General Reporter

THERE WAS PANIC in Whitehall and Westminster yesterday as news of the dramatic countrywide rout of se

Nonette WI women conquer all before them

Nonettes after it was also made known that male membership gives guaranteed protection from movement's shock troops of amourous

no defence again women.

"They are like mals. The moment snorted that *War* sprayed everywhe *Rampant* that's it men run out an

Nonettes capture tanks and troops - Govt. security policy in disarray

M.way 'scuffle' scuttles Challenger challenge

Wendy Jones reports on the 'Second Battle of Edgehill'

A military operation mounted against Nonette positions on the M40 motorway north of Banbury, has been routed and completely annihilated by members of Women's Institute.

Even though backed by new water cannon equipped

country still under their control.

Although initially heavily outnumbered and armed only with fire extinguishers charged with the *Rampant* - the Nonette sex drug - and cheese wire, the WI women, stopped all six tanks

had finished speaking, his men were opening their tanks' hatch covers and leaping into the embraces of yet more women who had also been lying in wait down the embankments.

While this incident was taking place, yet more

'Most pension funds now worthless' - says ban

MORE MAJORS COULD FOLLOW - BORROWING DEARTH H
MAMMOTH BAD LOANS WRITE-OFF BLOW - SAVERS

Clayings qui investment ban

By Oliver Stoneburger

However in so doing

Tom & Jerry offer to 'help out'

More newspapers defy news gag

By Robert Kilmer

THE GOVERNMENT'S emergency regulations received dramatic setback yesterday yet more newspapers revol against news censorship.

During the day a further national and a string of reg newspapers have fallen in be

Nonettes demand rel of 'political prisone

Movement claims 40,000 interned by security

By Andrew Baxter
Nonette Affairs Editor

MORE than 40,000 Nonettes are being held in internment by the security forces, it was

A Nonette spokesperson said: "Having checked every prison and remand centre, we know that those Nonettes who have been arrested are not held in any of them. So where are they? What conditions are they

under the em tions, said in a provisions of t order does n relevant autho to the general details of thos

Judi Jones reports from Aspen, Colorado, *Howard Williams* in

More US states secede to None

Colorado, Minnesota UDIs shake Warren - Can Am

ASPEN, AMERICA'S PREMier ski resort and second home to many of the US's once mega rich, was the scene of the latest Nonette triumph.

Almost entire state of

Colorado's declaration was followed within hours by Minnesota's UDI. In the state's twin cities of St Paul and Minneapolis, record crowds cheered their joint Nonette council's declarat-

NATO COLLECTIVE SECURITY PLANS

Much of Europe to Nonette contr

By Barbara Lee
In Paris

WITH THE remnants of the Polish government seeking refuge in Paris, there are growing fears among western European governments that their countries could be the next to fall to the Nonette.

Italy and Luxembourg

rol, the country is effectively cut in two. In the eyes of many Italians, especially those in the north, the country has already ceased to exist as a sovereign state.

Many politicians from parties are pressing Silv Plega, the Italian prime minister, to launch counter attacks against the Nonettes

GREEN LIGHT FOR RED LIGHT ON AMBER- BY KELLY

Soho No Go, so-so

THE OLDEST PROFESSION is taking up a new one: education, education, education. With the Tom & Jerry ladies still prowling London's West End, non-Nonette men are noticeably thin on the ground, pimps and police especially.

With the mass signing-up of the area's 'ladies' into the Nonettes and opportunity to earn oodles studying at their personal teaching machines, the need to earn in 'other ways' is all in the past. But the bordellos of old are not all empty or used as schoolrooms, some are being used for something else.

In certain Soho streets, fresh batches of Nonette 'love camp' inmates arrive daily to cope with the growing demands o

THE GAS MASK

INCORPORATING WOMENS'S RUBBERWEAR DAILY

YOUNG POLICEMEN GO IN RUBBER AND MASKS

Britta Ruff reports on the British bobby's new unifor

GALS, CAN THIS BE A DREAM COME TRUE!!??: Young policemen dressed from h to toe in spanking new, all-in-one uniforms made out of rubber!

Lots of them! Everywhere! And if the boys in blue in their rubberwear doesn't w you enough, there's more: they all are wearing gas masks as well!

Not only this but these young rubber rozzers are out in the open, on duty, patrolling in their **sheen shine sexy rubberwear.**

What is more, and though I am told they are in city centres all over the country, down here in old London town, these **young, rubber-clad officers** are also going about in groups; **bevies and bevies of them.**

I have been goggle-eyed watching these **young constables, standing, parading, strutting in their midnight blue rubber.**

I have also have a good close-up butchers of them as well. Studied the way these new uniforms **cling** and **stretch** all **sexy taut** against their **lithe young muscular bodies.**

Every time I've watched these young policemen move, **bend, arch their bodies, flex themselves,** seen how their rubber apparel is **padded in all right places,** it is all I can do to hold myself back from rushing out clasping them, **running my hands over their all-in-ones,** feeling, sensing the texture, the firmness of their bodies.

And when these young law enforcers **don their gas masks** I have found myself **coming over all orgasmic at the sight of them!**

I just know that should you too, dear readers, see, study these young rubber clad policemen as much as I have, **you will** also **be filled** with the same **desires and longing.**

Longing to be with at least one of these young enforcers, **your hand and his in his handcuffs,** your **bodies clasped, entwined, rubber to rubber, gas mask to gas mask, visor to visor, hear his passion panted breathing through his respirator as you writhe together in bonded passion.**

And with your ardour rising to unbounded heights of ecstatic desire, **ripping his uniform wide open** and **sating your yearning** on **his lithe young naked throbbing, muscular body.**

But now, dear readers you too can have the opportunity of seeing for yourselves these nice young policemen in their all-in-one rubberwear........

From the outset of the emergency I had been more than prepared to assist Mellows and his Watch associates fulfil their contracts with the security services. Indeed I did so as much out of a sense of duty as the remuneration it afforded. However, I have become increasingly disgruntled that my extensive banking experience is not utilised and instead of being denigrated to little more than a glorified van driver. Moreover, if it had not been for my acute need to generate sufficient funds to cover my living expenses I would have ceased giving the Watch my support some time ago.

Thus it was with a sense of duress and increasing irritation that I undertook the job of replacement driver for Malcolm Mullens' security custody company, even though it was late in the afternoon and away from my regular routes. The brief was to pick up catering supplies from Broxbourne and deliver them to one of Mullens' 'Internee Custody Centres' near Hatfield. When I caught the foul smell of the containers loaded into the van at the less than hygienic premises I collected from, my sense of annoyance grew yet more.

Because of the security situation I was restricted to motorways and A roads, and thus the journey to Hatfield, what with the police checkpoints, took twice as long as it normally would have done. Not only did I find this bothersome but for more than an hour I was assailed by the noxious fumes given off from these containers. It was not long either before they had me thinking "pig swill."

When I arrived at the supposed 'Internee Custody Centre' I was further aghast by what I found. Not only was it situated on a run-down factory estate but it most certainly did not have the appearance of being such a 'Centre'. There were no security fences, nor sign of guards. It was, so I discovered and to my astonishment, no more than a collection of shabby warehouses. What is more, I was obliged to repeatedly bang on the gates before a man opened them.

Because I was not the regular driver, I was treated by the gatekeeper and the rest of the staff in a most suspicious and surly manner. Not that I was much impressed with them. From the way they conducted themselves, and addressed me, I was soon thinking "louts in uniforms."

Having parked my van in the yard I requested assistance in unloading the containers. However, none was offered and when I inquired where they should be put, my annoyance grew in being off-handedly told by one these young louts to "take them through there Pops." Only the intimidating nature of his fellow thugs stopped me from remonstrating with him over his rudeness in addressing me as "Pops." Instead I said nothing and wheeled the containers along a corridor as he had directed.

No sooner had I entered it, than, not only was I glad that I had said nothing to him but I was further perturbed by what I saw and heard. Though the reddish smears along one of the walls might not have been blood, there was no mistaking that the sounds I heard were those of a person screaming.

Hundreds injured, many 'missing in action'

Welsh women overrun SAS bas

Wives, mothers' 'Love camp' torture fears

By Ted Woodward
in Worcester

THE SAS military base at Hereford was stormed and sacked in matter of hours by wave after wave of Welsh WI women.

Local hospitals are reported overflowing with hundreds of wounded trauma-

Britain's toughest troops, feared by soldiers and terrorists the world over, were defenceless in the face of the crack battalions of the Nonette-backed Welsh WI.

In a matter of hours and without their firing a shot in anger let alone self-defence, an estimated 2,000

Nonettes demand prisoner release

Where are the 'lost Nonettes'? Who's got them?

By Dean Radcliffe
in Manchester

DEMANDS for the release of the 40,000 Nonettes held under the emergency regulations grew yesterday. Concerns were also voiced for the safety and well-being of those he

A No
which p
appallin

Nonette prisoners rescued

60 detainees found in 'appalling conditions'

By Roger Talburt
East Midlands correspondent

SIXTY NONETTE DETAINEES held in disused farm buildings near Nottingham were rescued yesterday.

They were being held, so Nonettes said, in "appallingly filthy and wretched conditions". Many of the prisoners are undergoing medical attention for injuries received during their captivity.

The prisoners were located

Auxiliaries' Derby break out thwarted

Many hurt as crowd fired on crowd

By John Watkins
East Midlands Correspondent

A FAILED BREAKOUT ATTEMPT through Nonette lines by Auxiliaries in Derby to the M1 motorway resulted in scores of wounded.

With their southbound convoy blocked by Nonettes, Auxiliaries fired into a crowd blocking roads

100S OF TANKS FALL INTO NONETTE HANDS

WI TAKE DONNINGTON BASE

By Ryan Reagan
Nonette Correspondent

DONNINGTON, Britain's main military maintenance base fell to the Woman's Institute yesterday.

Many hundreds of

As many as 2,000 soldiers and other personnel have also been taken prisoner. Their fate is unknown but it thought that many will be held in Welsh WI 'Love Camps'.

The loss of the

With hundreds of tanks now at their command, Nonettes are expected to launch further assaults on the remaining military positions in the north as well as those further south.

The attack on Don-

in with fire extinguishers also loaded with the sex drug.

Yesterday's ground assaults were led by the WI's Newtown and Welshpool brigades who are reputed to be ferocious in their attacks.

Their use of cheese

Police, Auxiliaries, security forces trapped in city ce

Preston poised to fall to Nonettes

AMY RICHARDS reports from the frontline

MORE than 2,000 police and security forces were thought trapped in Preston city centre last night.

The similar numbers are reported injured or taken prisoner in a failed an attempted escape from Nonette columns reported closing in on the town from

police, territorial army units and other security forces based in Preston, attempted a breakout to east of the town to the M6 motorway and the safety of Manchester, 30km to the south.

By noon however, remnants of the estimated 4,000 strong force, many on

Barricades at either e of Preston's Fishergate hurriedly erected in a hold back the approa Nonettes. The city's Stanley prison has been commandeered security forces.

As night fell local ho als were reported fille overflowing with the inj

Thrasher rebuffs Nonette demands

'We do not have truck with criminals' – says PM

By Paul Hemmingday
in Westminster

will not at any time having dealings with criminal or

then it is certain that the security situation facing

Thrasher 'outraged' a Preston prisoners plig

Security guards paraded through streets naked, placa

By Michael Johnson
Political Correspondent

SECURITY GUARDS accused of maltreating internees were paraded

and addresses as well as the offences it is claimed they committed.

The guards were made to walk past jeering crowds, many of whom hurled not

ettes said they had all appeared before one of the movement's 'truth commissions' and were adjudged guilty by it.

The Prime Minister, on hearing of their fate, is

Nonettes accuse security forces of 'war crimes'

Outrage at Preston internees' plight

'What has happened to the other 40,000?' Nonettes demand

By Amy Richards
in Preston

Widespread outrage rose last night as details of Nonettes interned under emergency regulations became known.

All the prisoners were subjected to appalling treatment and are in need of urgent attention resulting from injuries sustained at the hands of prison officers during their period of detention at an internment camp in Preston, Lancs.

According to Preston Nonettes, all the victims

at the hands of security guards who are nothing more than thugs.

"We demand the immediate and unconditional release of all those held without trial under the so-called emergency regulations. We also demand an immediate public inquiry into the conduct of all aspects of the application of these regulations and the conduct of those

The p
light a
control
position

Cost-cutting leads to prisoner sub-contracting to thug

Securifore accountan spills internee beans

By Oliver Stoneburger

FEARS grew yesterday for the safety of Nonettes interned under emergency regulations.

A senior official of Securifore, one of the government's registered custody providers, has revealed for the first time what has actually happened to the 40,000 'missing' internees.

Instead of prisoners being in the safe care of approved custody providers such as Securifore, they are - in a bid to boost profits - subcontracted out to a string of cheaper, unregulated security companies.

Senior Secuifore accountant, Eric Douteux, who fell into WI hands when their forces took Derby, gave

and others from the Belgian registered security company, were working with Home Office officials in a desperate attempt to bring internees placed with a security contractor, BKS, based in the near-by town of Belper, back into Securifore's custody.

BKS and many other such subcontractors, Douteaux said, are refusing to hand back prisoners under their control to his and the Home Office team, until they are paid 'blood money'.

Under questioning, the accountant admitted that both Securifore and other custody providers as well as the Home Office knew of the terrible conditions many

Douteaux also admitted that the exact whereabouts of many of these prisoners is currently unknown.

Douteux's added that knowledge of the internees' plight was the reason both custody providers and the government had not revealed details on their conditions let alone released any of them. "They [the government and providers] wouldn't dare," he said.

Douteux said that because of the rapid advance of the Nonettes, many of the subcontractors had fled to the south of the country to escape falling into their hands and face truth trials.

He said that these subcontractors were also tak

Nonettes in Argentina takeov

Rest of S America set to fall

POLLY PORTILLO
FROM BUENOS AIRES

BUENOS AIRES, the last remaining stronghold of the military junta, fell to

of his military jun being sought by groups. It is though ever, that they hav neighbouring Urugu

The fall of the A

Italian govt. MPs flee to US

Spain, Portugal set to fall to Nonettes

By Roberto Plato
Foreign Desk

ITALIAN PRIME MINISTER, Silvio Plega and many members of his cabinet, along with several hundred MPs, are reported as having flown to the US and are seeking political asylum in the US.

Plega's departure comes as the first truth trials commence in Milan

I was alarmed by the screams. Then horrified by what I saw as I pushed the trolley past the partly opened door of the room they came from. Though no more than a glimpse, I saw a man who appeared naked and face down along a bench with uniformed men holding him and others striking him.

To my further alacrity I was noticed by another man in the room, a warder, upon which he rushed to the door shouting "Who the fuck are you?"

His outburst unnerved me. With more screams, then groans, coming from within the room, and almost without knowing, I mumbled "Delivering food for..."

But before I could say more, this warder, swearing at me yet again, pointed to where the kitchens were. Then having told me to depart as quickly as possible, added most menacingly, "And remember, my friend, you've seen nothing, if you know what's good for you. Know what I mean yeah?"

The kitchens were squalid and stank. There was also no one there. The corridor was similarly deserted of people. I wheeled the trolley back along it as fast as possible. Passing the door which had been ajar but was now closed, I could still hear the cries of the man being beaten. Though hearing him was most disconcerting, I became further aware of my hands shaking, which in turn caused the trolley to rattle most noisily.

I have to say that I was most concerned for my safety and wanted to be out of the corridor and the building as quickly as possible. My attention, however, was then distracted by tapping on the small windows of other doors along the corridor. Though barely lit, I could make out fuzzy pink shapes moving behind their wired frosted glass panes. I then realised these were faces of people pressed against the glass. Seeing them alarmed me yet more. I did not know whether to attend to them or to leave the trolley and flee.

However, the decision was then instantly taken from me. The corridor's erstwhile silence was suddenly shattered by warders charging through the outer door. Pushing past me, the lout who had called me 'Pops', shouted "You. Get that fucking trolley out of here."

I did as he bid without further delay, though not before being aware of doors being hastily unlocked and guards entering, shouting at those inside. As I went through the outer buildings I noticed the yard was absent of the louts who had been there, they doubtlessly attending to the unfortunate inmates. There was no one manning the outer gates either.

I had no difficulty unlocking these gates but could only keep them from automatically shutting again by yanking back the left one's powered closure arm. It was only when I came to close this gate as I departed, did I discover my actions had also disabled its locking mechanism. Hitherto, I would not normally have committed such wanton vandalism but such was my desperation to be away from the place that I no longer cared.

All the North, Scotland set to fall into Nonette hand

Catterick overrun by Nonettes

Rampant filled 'shells' force base's surrend

Fears for soldiers' safety rise

By **Ryan Reagan**
Nonette Affairs Correspondent

CATTERICK CAMP, one of Britain's major

The Ministry of Defence (MoD) is reported to be rushing reinforcements to Yorkshire in a bid to retake the camp

base began in th hours of yesterday m when six Challenge in WI hands, fro positions in the

12 DEAD AS B SPECIALS OPEN FIRE ON CROWD

100's wounded in Manchester protes

BY GEORGE SENNER
IN MANCHESTER

TWELVE PEOPLE WERE KILLED and more than 200 injured when police opened fire on an estimated 5,000 protesters marching on Manchester town hall yesterday. Many of the injuries were caused by protesters fleeing from the shooting

Last night the

Nonettes res guards from lynching

Mob storms Preston prison in out

By **Amy Richards**
in Preston

FORMER PRISON GUARDS guilty of mistreating Nonette internees were rescued from almost certain death at the hands of an outraged mob by other Nonettes.

As news of the horrendous treatment meted out by the guilty men to their helpless captives became known, the rage of the people of Preston boiled over.

Nonettes reope more Motorway

MOTORWAYS THOUGHOUT THE NO and west of England as well as all of Wale now reopened to normal traffic.

Closed under the government's emer regulations but now under Nonette contr entire length of the M6 as well as the M now open to the public.

Many other stretched of the Mot network are also open for public use.

Thousands feared captured for 'Love camp dut

Nonettes overrun Aldershot, S'hurs

Welsh women in mass soldier snatch shock

WI sex tanks ring top brass trainee academy

By **Ryan Reagan**
Nonette Affairs Correspondent

ALDERSHOT, the south of England's premier military base has fallen t the Nonettes. The entire base fell to a WI led attack in a matter of hour yesterday evening.

Many thousands of soldiers fled in disarray in the face of the Nonett onslaught, which is reported to have been merciless. Many thousand more men have been taken prisoner for Nonette 'Love camp duties'.

A few hours after the surrender of Aldershot, near-

shown they are powerless to stop, let alone reverse, Nonette advances

assault was taking place further WI-led forces base

'LOST' PRISONERS FOUN BOUND AND GAGGED

Hunt for other 'lost' Nonettes stepped up

By **Ryan Reagan**

MORE THAN A HUNDRED Nonette internees were freed from an abandoned truck on the M1 motorway outside Northampton. According to the prisoners, they had been marooned on the motorway for several hours before being rescued.

When found, all the victims were handcuffed hand and foot to the truck's frame-work. The prisoners' mouths were also gagged with adhesive tape.

The truck itself had run out of fuel and is thought to be the reason for being

location they had been originally held, several of the internees thought it was in the Sheffield, Rotherham area. They also said they had left in a convoy of many other vehicles.

During their captivity all the victims say they were verbally and physically

London Auxiliaries beat back protester

More than a 100 people w taken to hospital yesterday B Specials attacked protes in Hammersmith's K Street.

After the street had b cleared of protesters, the l of the B Specials said: "T

Police condemn Nonette 'firesticks

Low tech terror weapon thwarts Tans

By Philipa Stewart
Security Correspondent

SECURITY FORCES in Northampton were sent reeling yesterday in the face of the new Nonette terror weapon: the firestick.

Last night, Northants police chief, Commander Kevin Jones, threatened that anyone found in possess-

The firestick, a single use weapon, is simple in design but lethal in effect. Similar to the German WWII Panzervurst hand-held anti-tank mortar, a firestick consists of ball of inflammable jellied oil mixed with industrial glue stuck on the tip of a stick, such as a hammer. At the base of the ball is a disposable lighter.

On throwing the stick the lighter ignites the ball. The glue ensures that the ball sticks to whatever surface it lands on. If it is a vehicle, such as a car and the fireball sticks near its petrol tank, the heat will

and the car to be engulfe in flames.

If it sticks to an arm oured car it will heat th armour and in turn forc the occupants to escap before the heat overcome them.

However, should a fire ball stick to a person an because of the strength o its stickiness it will caus severe burns to tha person.

According to Commande Jones, the only defenc against firesticks is to 'tak out' inter fires

As clashes between Nonette and security forces rise, the World Congress sa

'Stop the violenc

But passive resistance call set to be ignored

By Janet Rothberg
Security Correspondent

The World Nonette Congress issued its strongest condemnation yet against what it sees as the growing tide of violence sweeping the world.

Both pro and anti-Nonet-

said: "The future belongs to we the people. Patience and passive resistance will bring about the inevitable downfall of those who resist the will of ordinary humankind. Violence will not achieve this outcome any quicker."

However, in the eyes of the many who are meting ence Congress plores, its call fall on deaf

urity forces despera fighting rearguard acti against Nonettes and ot protesters, there are the signs that violence both sides is set to escal in Britain.

With the Thrasher g ernment giving the nod the B Specials in the us live fire against protest the scene is set for more civilian deaths their hands. Nonettes, h

Hamburg rocked as police attack Nonette women's peace march

German police fire on demo - many killed

By Geraldine Richt
in Hamburg

MORE THAN 50 p shot dead by Ham firing into Nonette marching to the yesterday. Hundred reported wounde seriously.

The deaths later sp serious rioting thro city. There were run battles with police fought to regain Hamburg's city centr

In a statement m media yesterday even burg police chief, Wurtenburg, said demonstration ha unauthorized and

Clayings denies difficultie

Bank panic sweeps Cit

By Oliver Stoneburger

IN THE WAKE of a string of US bank collapses, major high street clearer, Clayings Bank denied it was also about to close its doors.

The Bank of England, however, is reported to be monitor-

those of other m banks and buil societies.

In a prepared s ment, Clayings "Although we, with financial in tions, are facing cult trading co ions, Clayings reassure both d account holder

Nonette heroine thought shot dead by police

Lucia 'murdered'

LUCIA the woman wh cyber persona appear several billion None on their teaching scre is reported to have d from wounds recei when Hamburg po fired into an unarm protest march.

Lucia, who is from t north-eastern Brazil, w working as an advisor Nonettes in northe Germany.

Last night as man thousands of Nonett and ordinary people alik kept silent vigil outsid Hamburg's Felder hosp tal were openly distraugh at the news that Lucia

THRASHER IN NONETTE U-TURN

Govt. offers talks with movement's moderates

By **Paul Hemmingday**
Political Correspondent

Christopher Thrasher, the Prime Minister, has offered the Nonette movement face to face exploratory talks last night.

Following a Downing Street meeting with senior defence staff, the Prime Minister said: "In the inter-

prepared to meet with responsible members of the Nonette organisation to see if it is possible to address their concerns.

"It is in the interests of all that both sides make a serious and sincere endeavour to establish a common ground between our mutual positions in such areas as national security and the

mentary democratic trad ions. My government's do is open to the Nonettes, await their call."

The PM's about tu comes in face of a string police and military securi reverses at the hands Nonette groups across th country, mainly in th north and west. With t

However, no sooner had I opened my van door, than in the silence of the yard I heard a voice, a woman's, calling for help. I looked to whence it came. She called again and I saw it was from a broken cellar window.

I could have ignored her but instead and though I couldn't see inside the window, found myself kneeling down to it. When this woman called out once more I found myself, again without knowing why, replying "I will get help." As I went to the van, and on hearing her further plaintive "Please," I, yet again instinctively, called out "Hold on." I then heard her cell door being unlocked.

I drove out of the yard then ran back to close the opened gate. It was as I pulled it to that I discovered its lock was jammed in the open position. Not wanting to risk drawing attention to myself and to what I had done, I departed as quietly as possible, but the moment I was on the main road I drove as fast as I could all the way to the motorway junction.

I had by then also taken another road, the one to Damascus. The worm had turned. Though traumatised by what I had been witness to, I was incensed that I and doubtless all other right-thinking people were being deliberately misled by the government. We had been deceived into not supporting the rule of law, but that of thuggery.

By the time I reached the motorway roundabout, I had, in my mind, unalterably resolved as to what I had to do. As I can never countenance the abetting of thuggery, I therefore had to be against the government. There could be no middle ground. Thus, though I stopped at the checkpoint, I did not tell the police there what I knew. Neither did I return to the motorway. Instead I drove all the way round and turned off onto the road to Hatfield.

To my initial surprise it did not take long to locate a Nonette group. Once I had allayed their suspicions and then apprised them of the Custody Centre's existence and situation pertaining there, it was all action.

In no time, or so it seemed, I was accompanying a column of several hundred Nonettes back to the camp. Other groups were already creating disturbances on the other side of Hatfield so as to draw all the police away from where we were headed. My knowing the gates were unlocked was our trump card. I was also able to provide information as to the camp's layout.

I drove my van straight at the unlocked gate. Nonettes leapt out of the van's rear doors, others charged in behind us. We took those thugs completely by surprise. Some attempted to fight but were soon overpowered. Others, however, fled into the main building and in a foolhardy attempt to evade capture, started a fire which in turn caused the power supply to fail.

Because I knew the whereabouts of the prisoners it was me who led the rescue party. With smoke billowing from doorways and windows and with an air of increasing desperation, we smashed down door after cell door. However, I was seeking one person in particular. I kept calling until I found her. And when at last I heard her voice, it was me who carried her in my arms out of that burning building.

BERLIN FALLS TO NONETTES

Angry crowds storm Reichstag as Lucia shooting rage flare

y Lydia Gunney
/orld Affairs Correspondent

HE GERMAN CHANCELLOR Ielmut Gebogen and the rest of is government fled Berlin esterday and sought asylum in ;witzerland.

Stunned and enraged at the hooting by Hamburg police of Vonette icon Lucia million of Germans stormed government building across the country ncluding the Reichstag itself.

While many other of

NONETTES SNUB THRASHER OFFER

'Meet our demands first' Nonettes say

By Paul Hemmingday
Political Corespondent

DOWNING STREET'S 'Peace talks' offer received a resounding Nonette thumbs down yesterday.

A statement in the movement's ... demanded the immediate ... detention centres before they will hold talks with the government.

In the statement, titled: 'The future belongs to we the people', the movement also demanded that paramilitary forces, such as the Auxiliaries and B Specials be immediately disbanded

GCHQ burn to the groun

Government electronic eavesdropping e

By Andrew Hendry
Security Affairs Editor

GCHQ, the government's Cheltenham based spy station and which listened into everyone's telephone conversations, was a burnt-out shell last night.

Nonette and WI forces who had besieged the base for more than a week said that the building was deliberately set on fire by remaining staff before they surrendered.

Wrongdoers beware!

Hisogynists to make new mega series

By TIM JEFFRIES

THEY WERE HARD, THEY WERE MEAN, THEY WERE cruel and now they are back on our screens with a vengeance! Yes, the Hisogynists have signed up for a second series of their stunning punishment routines.

Promising to be crueler and bestial than ever before, lead Hisogynist, Hyacinth said: "There is a whole heap of no good male trash out there and oh man are we going to cut them down to size, and then cut them some more."

According to Caught TV, who signed the mega deal with the Hisogynists, there will be 20 televised shows which will be performed

Derek Igg, head of SLI-TV, which has again acquired the non-North America world-wide distribution of the Hisogynist shows, said: "The first shows will feature US politicians and others who, after they have been found guilty of their crimes, will be getting the chop.

"After the girls have finished in America they are coming over to Europe to do at least six two-hour

Rio, Sao Pa fall to Non

Brazilian junta flees to Po

POLLY PORTILLO
REPORTS FROM SAO PAULO.

AMID SCENES OF WILD jubilation the citizens of Sao Paulo, Brazil's largest city welcomed the forces of the Continental Congress.

Although in many ways

Top Brass 'mutiny'

'Unable to support civil power' - says Field Marshall

By Oren Pollard
Military Affairs Editor

ALL Britain's armed forces have been ordered to stand down from helping the ... cerned at the ease with which the Nonettes are inflicting one reverse after another against the armed services, more so the army itself.

There are also reports that the JCS is negotiating with the Nonettes for the return of their tanks as well as soldiers.

Ministry of Defence (MoD) officials at first

THRASHER UPS NONETTE OFFER

PM makes 'Co-habitation' power sharing offer

By Paul Hemmingday
Political Corespondent

THE GOVERNMENT is preparing to offer Nonettes a powersharing role.

Downing Street said that it is ready for face-to-face talks with the movement without any pre-conditions. "It is vital that talks begin without a moment's delay," Mr Thrasher said yesterday.

The further softening of ... wards the Nonettes is thought to be as a direct outcome of the Army's Joint Chiefs of Staff (JCS) decision to adopt a position of neutrality between the

One source the Pr ier ref JCS's terms

Britta Ruff visits Catterick, the Nonettes' newest 'Love Camp'

A soldier a day helps you work, rest and play

"ATTENTION!" bellowed Sgt. Major Dodds and 250 soldiers smartly stamp their feet together. Even before the sound of her command has faded, Elaine Dodds is next shouting: "Ready for inspection, Ma'am."

'Ma'am' is Catterick's new Nonette commanding officer, ex-Royal Marine captain, Audry Henderson, who then conducts her inspection. As Audry walks between the lines of men, all standing smartly to attention in their full dress uniforms, a group of us women walk behind her carrying out our 'inspections'.

What absolute bliss! Lines and lines of nice young men in their nice smart uniforms. And every one of them available for a day's DIY and UNW (*know what I mean? Nudge, nudge!!*). As we give these young soldiers the once-over, I'm sure of one thing, it certainly beats hanging around lorry parks scouting for a pick up.

With inspection completed and selections made, Elaine then calls out the numbers of soldiers who have been picked and instructs them to take two paces forward.

These selected young men then step smartly behind their mistresses to their cars and chauffeur them home and for a hard day's work (*nudge, nudge!!*)

The remaining soldiers, on Elaine's: "Fall out" and "left, right, left right..." are marched to their 'tasks' for the day.

This parade and selection is but one of dozens taking place throughout the length and breadth of Catterick camp each morning. And every day thousands of women from across Yorkshire and the North East, paying as little as 5 nonettes, call at this windswept Yorkshire camp for a nice young man in uniform.

The ladies are also assured that every soldier is freshly washed and scrubbed, ready for work and play the whole day through. There is however, a discount on a weekly rate and "pic'n'mix" block bookings are gaining increasing popularity with many women's groups.

I am visiting Catterick in the company of a number of dominatrix colleagues up from London who are giving a week's master-class to the Yorkshire WI. (In Soho, so my friend Arabella Coutt, or Ms Whiplash as she professionally known, says, business there is taking a severe beating).

Fortunately for Arabella and her friends, these master classes are turning out to be most popular with the N Yorks WI. Not only are attendance figures rising by the day, she says, but so enthusiastic are some of the women to wield the whip and the cane, that they have to be restrained and told to "go gently" with soldiers.

Arabella also says many of the local ladies have taken the classes so much to heart that they are even turning already dressed in the correct costume-wear complete with mask, cane, handcuffs, whips and chains.

Clayings Bank bank

Depositors, shareholders stand to lose everything

By Mark Humphries

CLAYINGS BANK one of the UK's premier financial institutions, has gone into voluntary liquidation.

The bank's collapse followed an unprecedented spate of withdrawals funds by deposit account holders.

Claying's sudden collapse puts a question mark over the future of the banking system as a whole.

Throughout crowds of depositors with Clayings crowded around many of its

news were clearly

Pound rich are new poo

Even $ wealth now "worthless"

By John Murry
Economics Editor

IN A MATTER OF days millionaires and even billionaires the world over have seen their fortunes turn to dust and valueless piles paper.

With the collapsing of banks like houses of cards, there is now nowhere and no one prepared to accept these once opulent peoples' cash.

Only those canny or lucky enough to turn their cash into material assets and then back into nonettes will live with their wealth for another day.

For those unlucky enough or foolishly beguiled by government 'assurances' that the Nonette movement would soon collapse, they are now paying a truly heavy price.

For many of the world's plutocrats their wealth also brought them power and influence. This has now also departed.

165: AILEEN

Gray is such a lovely man. He's my knight in shining armour who came to my rescue. I might not be up to an Aoife for him but Gray is most certainly my Strongbow.

At the end of each day when he returns from leading Nonettes rounding up those terrible men of the Watch, he's by my bedside. I've never known a man so kind and gentle as Gray. Nor show me so much care and affection.

When I think of the risks he must have taken rescuing me, oh and the others, the things he saved us from, I'll be in his debt to my dying day. When Gray told me it was my calling for help which moved him to rescue us. How he searched and searched, kept calling out till he heard my voice again, he had me blubbing my eyes out.

Gray had no idea what I looked like and those last moments, what with him and the others breaking down the doors, the darkness, smoke everywhere and me lying on the floor from the guards' thumping, how he recognised my little whimpers, is nothing short of a miracle. I remember Gray lifting me up but because of the darkness I couldn't see him, it was just his voice that had me know it was him.

In the darkness of course he couldn't see that I'd not a stitch on! And when he carried me outside and did catch sight of me I couldn't have been a pretty sight, not with my face all puffed-up the way it was.

Gray must have had me in his arms for several minutes before we set eyes on one another. Of course until then I'd no knowing what he looked like either. If ever there was a blind date, ours most certainly was that!

And Gray's such a gentleman. The moment he saw I was in the all-together he had his coat off and around me as fast as could be. Though now I know him a little more, I think Gray was the more embarrassed at he seeing me in nothing than I was! But I do remember his eyes. At the time I was hurting so and could sense there was something wrong with my legs. Though he wears glasses and it was dark, I could still see I'd him crying.

I don't remember more of the evening. Gray says a doctor there with them gave me a jab of something to stop the pain and I passed out. All I know is that the next morning when I awoke, there was Gray. It was only later that I learned he'd been by my bedside the night through. He was there the mornings after as well, and the evenings too. I kept telling him to get some rest himself but he would not hear of it.

While it will be some time yet before I can walk again, the base of my back is still badly bashed, I am, now the bruises have gone down, back to looking more my old self. And it's nice each evening having Gray telling me how much better I'm getting. He bringing me flowers is nice as well.

Talking with Gray is also nice. It took time though before I had him tell about himself. At first he was so held back, straight-laced almost. But once

Paris about to fall to Nonettes

'Le state' set to fold as capital is encircled

By Hannan Ammar
in Paris

PARIS is expected to fall into the Nonettes within a matter of days.

With much of the France already under the control of

MANY FEARED DEAD AS B SPECIALS HAMMERED
RIOTS ROCK MANCHESTER

By Liam Packard-Ball
Northern Correspondent

MANCHESTER centre was a b[...] ground last nigh[...] Nonettes took [...] revenge on B Spe[...] and Auxiliaries.

With regular polic[...] sent, B Specials we[...] to fend for them[...] against tens of [...] sands of Nonette[...] their supporters.

In Piccadilly, [...] city centre, angr[...] armed with fi[...] attacked more [...] hundred Special[...]

Although the [...] fired into the [...] they were force[...] as many office[...] set alight by fir[...]

The fate [...] attacked by fir[...] unknown but [...] are feared for[...]

Florida UDI

Most US now under Nonette control

By Dan Klutz
in Miami

THE people of Miami and surrounding counties of Broward and Palm Beach voted overwhelmingly yesterday to join with the rest of Florida in becoming members of the Congress of North America.

With the last of the Sunshine State's population seceding from the US, it leaves, only Atlantic City and parts of New York along the eastern

THRASHER OFFER[S] NONETTES TALK[S] ON POWER SHARIN[G]

'There will be no pre-conditions except that of urgency' says

By Kevin Burton-Parker
in Westminster

WITH MUCH OF BRITAIN outside of the major conurbations now in Nonette hands, the prime minister, Chris Thrasher, called on the Nonette Congress to enter into powersharing talks.

The PM said [...]

talks would be without any pre-conditions and would also concern security issues.

In a statement issued by Downing Street, he said: "In the interests of all the United Kingdom citizens, it is vital that the present security situation is brought

Bank manager hero in prisoner fire rescue dram[a]

Internees saved from certain deat[h] as fleeing guards burn down ga[...]

By Madeline Polster
in Hatfield, Herts.

MORE THAN EIGHTY Nonette prisoners were rescued from a burning Hatfield warehouse yesterday. These lucky internees owe their lives to the singlehanded heroism of retired Harlow bank manager, Graham Moore (45).

If it had not been for Graham's courage and fearlessness it is almost certain that all the victims would have perished in the flames or fallen to their deaths from the crumbling building.

It is was Graham, who, having discovered by chance the terrible conditions Nonette internees were being held in at a secret internment centre on the outskirts of Hatfield, raised the alarm.

Having gathered a band of Hatfield Nonettes to help with the rescue, Graham then led them to the disused Nyde industrial estate just off of the A1 on the outskirts of this Hertford town.

When Nonettes finally gained entry into the make-shift prison they were [...]

NONETTES GIVE GOVERNMENT ULTIMATUM
'FREE OUR IMPRISONED MEMBERS OR WE WILL'

'Check every building for missing Nonettes' call

By Ryan Reagan
Nonette Correspondent

NONETTES ARE demanding the immediate and unconditional release of all internees.

The movement also demanded that the government gives details of the [...]

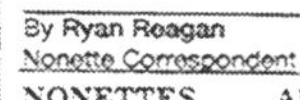

Anger at rescued captives ordeal

ions under which they are being held.

The demands come in the wake of the latest internment camp scandal at Hatfield, Herts. There, guards deliberately set fire to camp buildings before

KOTHRA 'killed off'

Giant brain blown up

By Nicholas Rendall
in Baltimore, Maryland

KOTHRA, the US's Department of Homeland Security's giant computer was blown to smithereens yesterday.

Following two days of fight-ing against marines and NSA personnel fiercely defending Fort Wace, Maryland, where Kothra was situated, Nonettes finally managed to destroy the tennis court-sized computer.

A Nonette spokesperson said: "KOTHRA stood for "Controller of The Human Race" and it was scheduled to do just that and within a very short time period.

"If we had not intervened when we did it would have been unstoppable and all of humanity would have enslaved by this evil computer."

The existence of KOTHRA was long denied by US authorities. Its development was conducted under the guise of genome research conducted by the computer giant BIM under its 'Stone Wash' program

Ploughshears pl[...]

Armed forces to recycle weaponry

By William Gybb
Military Correspondent

THE ARMY is to go into business. The Joint Chiefs of Staff, in a bid to boost morale and finances have, in association with a number of Nonette groups, formed a company to sell off all the military's tanks, personal carriers and so forth for recycling.

Field Marshal, Sir Victor Hammond, speaking for the Joint Chiefs said: "With the money from the government have gone AWOL, we in the services have been left little choice other than to turn stock in to cash so to speak.

"What is more we have established a good working relationship with these Nonettes.

"One of the reasons we in the military get along with Nonettes is that in many ways they are formed along similar lines to ourselves.

"Therefore, not only are they able to understand us, which is more than those MoD wallahs ever did, not only does it makes darned good sense but also to work together."

Sir Victor, outlining the joint ventures the army and Nonettes have signed to, added: "Quite frankly, what with the price of scrap metal these days, the money we are getting for some of our equipment is more than that they cost in the first place.

"Moreover, if we didn't find the money to pay the men we could have a mutiny on our hands. And nobody wants that sort of thing do they?

"The agricultural side of the coin has of course been to and we all had a jolly good

I'd begun teasing those laces loose he was like those men in the Sallie who would pour their hearts out to me over the bar. Not that I minded for a moment, in fact, the more Gray told, the more I wanted him to tell and the more I wanted to hug him and say "There, there, it's alright now."

Though when Gray told how he had lost everything he had worked for, that it was too late for him to start again, I found myself working hard to buck his spirits up. I don't know how much of a PR job I did persuading Gray that the Nonettes is where his future lies but once he had joined with us he became a changed man. It wasn't long either before he was giving the local Nonettes the low-down on the men he had worked for.

Gray's spirits rose all the higher when the Nonettes asked for his help locating members of the Watch and the whereabouts of more of the missing Nonettes. Not only did Gray rise to the task but he's been a great success. Also he secretly rather likes the nicknames Nonette have given him, "Hammer of the Watch," though the one Gray likes best is, "Watch Finder General."

Because Gray knows who is who in the Watch and where many of them are, we have rounded up scores and scores of them. What is more, Gray says, being an experienced bank manager and having interviewed countless customers about their overdrafts, he can instinctively tell when the Watch people are lying. Gray also says it gives him the same bank manager's pleasure having them throw themselves on his mercy in owning up to what they have done and undertaking to do everything he tells them in the hope of leniency, just as his bank customers did.

Another thing which has made Gray come out of himself is his teaching screen. At first he was chary of it and Lucia, but now Gray's become used to it and her, he is often giving them as much attention as he does me! Again not that I mind for a moment. With Gray sitting the side of me, we both at our screens concentrating on the sociology course I've us both on, we are as happy and contented as can be.

Another of the things we do together is watch the TV, especially Rainbow. Then the night before last the most amazing thing happened.

Rainbow had been giving the news for half an hour or so, and with both Gray and me watching in silence. She then said "And now over to..." and on came Danny.

Maybe it was me showing off but when I said to Gray I knew Danny from old, that I used to serve him when I worked in the Salutation, Gray then said, and he could have knocked me down with a feather, "He used to be one of my customers too."

Now how's about that for a coincidence! What is more, when I said I had always found Danny to be a wonderful man and that all those things said about him being a con man and trickster just weren't true, Gray was nodding his head in full agreement.

Thrasher does a 'Maxwell' on pensions

Unions claim Govt. sold £50bn pension assets to bankers

By Oliver Stoneburger

Millions of pensioners are facing financial ruin. The government, it was claimed yesterday, has secretly sold off more than £50bn of public sector workers' pension fund assets in a bid to shore up its plummeting tax take.

Upwards of seven million public sector workers are ... pounds of their pension savings completely.

News of the government's raid on public sector pension funds was revealed by Cardiff-based Nonette group yesterday.

Nonette spokesperson, Glyn Morgan, said: "From documents and other evidence now in our possession, it is patently clear that every public employee from caretakers to to[p] manager, stand to lose ever[y] penny of their pensions."

The documents i[n] Nonette hands show tha[t] the Treasury has diverte[d] assets held by both loca[l] and central governmen[t] employers to a string o[f] international banks an[d] other financial organisations.

The government throug[h] the Treasury working in ...

PROTESTERS MOWN DOWN BY AUTOMATIC GUN FIRE

30 DEAD TANS FIRE ON KINGS X MARCHERS

HUNDREDS WOUNDED IN FIRING

'NO WARNING GIVEN' SAY PROTESTERS

By Samuel Veron
in Central London

THIRTY UNARMED PROTEST MARCHERS WERE SHOT DEAD BY B Specials outside Kings Cross station yesterday.

Hundreds more marchers were wounded as security forces on either side of the Euston Road opened fire on them with automatic weapons including, reportedly, a machine gun.

Last night, as grieving relatives protest against the new curfew on ...

THRASHER TALKS OFFER SPURNED

'Release all detainees first' Nonettes demand

By Paula Rump
in Central London

THE PRIME MINISTER'S offer to the Nonettes of talks on powersharing received the movement's thumbs down yesterday.

... government while the detainees were still imprisoned would be tantamount to acknowledging that they were being held hostage by the government as bargaining chips.

The Nonette also demand ... said: "These so-called 'Special Police' are no more than government ap... thugs.

"Across Britain ... have shot and kille[d] ... than 2,000 innocent ... and wounded many ...

Abandoned Nonet[te] detainees rescue[d]

Hundreds left chained and manacled for two days

By Paula Rump
in Peterborough

A HUNDRED AND SIXTY Nonette detainees were rescued yesterday after being abandoned by their gaolers for two days without food ... depot near Peterborough, were discovered shackled to their beds in makeshift cells.

All of those imprisoned had been left by their Watch gaolers for more than 48 hours without food or water. All the victims were ...

TAN'S PERRY BARR SHOOTING HA[...]

Birmingham[...] erupt in fury

Many Auxiliaries, Specials killed as protesters' r[...]

By Liam Packard-Ball
in Central Birmingham

SECURITY FORCES IN Birmingham's New Street fled for their lives last night as a 50,000 strong force of protesters attacked them with volleys of firesticks. An unknown number of the security forces are thought to have been killed in the disturbances.

Both Auxiliaries and B Specials suffered scores of casualties, many seriously burned from firestick attacks.

The fury of protesters was sparked off by B Specials earlier in the day shooting dead two youths in the Perry Barr district of the city.

This sparked of a series of incidents against security forces across the city culminating in last night's attacks in the centre of Birmingham.

Many of the B Specials and Auxiliaries, or 'Black and Tans' as the protesters call them, were reportedly fleeing Birmingham by rail when angry crowds caught them in front of the train station.

MISSING NONETTES:

50 BODIES FOUN[D] IN MASS GRAV[E]

ALL VICTIMS SHOT IN THE HEAD AT POINT BLANK R[ANGE]

By JOANNE WILLIAMS

THE REMAINS OF SOME 50 NONETTES WERE UNEARTHED FROM A HASTILY DUG MASS GRAVE IN ESSEX YESTERDAY.

First indications are that all of the victims had also been shot in the head from point blank range.

The Nonette Congress has issued an urgent appeal for the whereabouts of the more 30,000 Nonettes who are still known to be missing.

The site of the murdered Nonettes' grave was ...

It's funny how things unravelled the way they did, though at the time it was very worrying. There was a fire in the council offices in Llanelli. By all accounts it wasn't a very big one and was soon put out. But when the firemen checked through the rest of the building they found the head of finance had attempted to commit suicide in his office by hanging himself. After they cut him down and revived him, he confessed to starting the fire. He also told them why he had done it. He had been party in abetting the government, he said, to swipe all the money the council's employees had paid into their pension fund "to help pay off international bankers," as he put it.

Well, people soon put two and two together. "If it's happened in Llanelli," they said, "what about our council?" With the police and judiciary running off along with the security forces, the only people who could do anything were us Nonettes. And that is what happened. Nonettes took over, occupied every council office, town hall, even government offices. In hours of the takeover youngsters were searching through the computers. By the end of their first day they had uncovered no end of goings on.

We had all heard stories about the "Taffia," south Wales politicians, councillors dipping their hands in Town Hall tills, but I always dismissed them as just that, stories. However, what these young computer whiz kids unearthed showed not only were the stories all true but they are only the tip of the iceberg, the fiddling has been large scale and endemic.

As for the Welsh Assembly, well, those young lads found there had been kickback after kickback. No wonder the place cost a fortune. But these revelations were as nothing compared to those of our pension funds.

When those youngsters discovered every council employee's contributions, including mine, had been cybered off to the Treasury up in London, there was uproar. It wasn't just us here in Wales who were affected either but every other council employee across the UK as well. It is all very well the government then saying their taking our money was "only a temporary expedient" and all their other weasel words, but the fact remains that they have had our money and without so much as a by our leave either.

Well, anyone who had still been supporting the government had the rug pulled from under them. When our Regional Nonette voted to seize all government and council property in Wales, sell it and give the proceeds to those of us who had lost out, there was a stampede of council employees and pensioners to join their local Nonette.

However, as soon as the Nonette in Merthyr announced they were to hold a Truth Trial there was another stampede, this time of councillors and officials making a beeline for the Severn Bridge and England. Gwyneth in the Pendre said that when she met Pam Mealham, who with the other WI women, is back for a few days' rest, told her that on their coach's way back from

Government denies pension 'theft'

'Temporary refinancing expedient' – Minister claims

By Timothy Gordon
Political Editor

IN THE FACE of a rising storm of protest from ... allegations of any financial skullduggery.

Treasury under secretary, Timothy Whyte, said that all public employee pension number of financial institutions" concerning pensions denied that there had been any underhand dealing with them.

'PROTESTERS FIRED FIRST' - B SPECIALS CHIEF CLAIMS

'We were defending ourselves from an armed m...'

By Samuel Veron
in Central London

THE DETACHMENT OF B SPECIALS WHO FIRED ON PROTESTERS, KILLIN... 40 and wounding hundreds more, were unrepentant yesterday.

According to the Specials not only were the protesters made aware th... were breaking the law by marching, but also they were "armed to tee... and had already fired some of their weapons at the security forces.

Commander Aubury Andrews, head of the Specials said: "My men had been forced to return fire on these Nonette people.

"These people knew from the start that by marching they were contravening the emergency regulations.

"They must also have known that we are empowered by the government to use any means at our dis... weapons including dozens of automatic rifles, machine pistols as well as sticks and clubs."

Andrews was unable to explain the absence of any firesticks, (the Nonettes' usual weapon of choice) left behind as the marchers fled. He also denied that the weapons Specials claim to have found, had been planted.

number two, James Sm... said: "As customs offic... we do not have conce... about people only with... law we are empowere... execute.

"If the law states we... shoot people in the ex... ion of our duties, the... will shoot them. That... there is to it. We are s... of these Nonette peopl... complaining about the... ent but as customs o...

PENSIONS SCANDAL

UBER BANK IN GOVT HOODWINK SWAP

Valuable assets hawked for worthless sterling

By Dennis Droner
Corruption Editor

THE GOVERNMENT... desperate need for re... sold off public employee... funds' assets for £20... from the giant inter...

Bradford Truth Trials sentences shock

Hard labour for bent councillors, officials

By Philipa Stewart
Northern Correspondent

FIVE FORMER COUNCILLORS and 15 top town hall officials found guilty at Bradford Nonette truth trial of fraud, were sentenced to three years hard labour yesterday.

PENSIONS SCANDAL

TOP POLITICIANS BEHIND SELL-OFF

Secret documents names guilty ministe...

By Dennis Droner
Corruption Editor

SENIOR POLITICAL figures ... main parties

As anger among public sector employees and pensioners grew, there were demands from the unions for an immediate government clarification into the affair.

... dubbed "Maxwell 2", the ...

Truth Trials threat sends MPs scurrying southwards

Top officials also flee to London

By Kevin Burton-Parker
Political Editor

POLITICIANS OF ALL HU... government officials and support... across Britain are reported to...

PENSIONS SCANDAL

'MAXWELL 2' CORRUPTION WEB SPREADS

Politicians, officials flee protestors

By Dennis Droner
Corruption Editor

FURTHER REVELATIONS of the "Maxwell 2" pensions sell-off scandal made public yesterday, show that ... officials in both ...

The new evidence, gleaned ... computer records, now in the h... of Nonettes, also shows wides... corruption of many local g... ment councillors.

There are also rep orts that ... of those named in the reve...

NONETTES GIVE TANS, SPECIALS ULTIMATUM:

'SURRENDER OR BE HUNTED DOWN WITHOUT MERCY'

By Samuel Veron
Nonette Affairs Correspondent

THE SECURITY FORCES ARE GIVEN 24 HOURS to surrender to the Nonettes or face being ruthlessly hunted down without mercy.

The Nonette Congress's demand for all the security services, including B Specials, Auxiliaries and Watch to be captured, comes in the wake of Husden atrocities.

Calling on members of the security forces to turn themselves in, a Nonette spokesperson said: "If you are a member of any of these [security] organisations and you have nothing to ... then you ... fear from a...

"If you d...

As Husden massacre victims rise to 62, fears for Nonettes still missing ...

AS MORE OF BRITAIN FALLS TO NONETTES, GOVT TO MAK...

M25 to be defe...

By TIM JEFFRIES

IN A BID TO HALT any surprise Nonette advance on London, the government has stationed its remaining forces in an outer ring around the capital it was revealed yesterday.

Running along a line corresponding to the M25 motorway, the area covered is reported to include Heathrow, which, along with the Northolt airbase was closed to civilian use yesterday.

There are doubts among defence analysts, however, if such a position is really defensible.

With large amounts of unaccounted routes into the

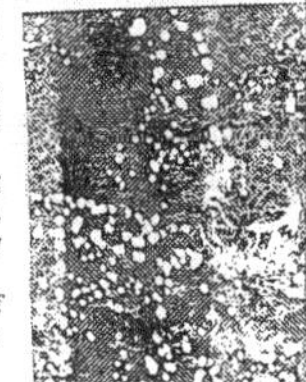

Nonettes publish Truth Trials "Wanted" list

50,000 MPs, councillors, officials flee to London

By Kevin Burton-Parker
Political Editor

UPWARDS OF 50,000 politicians, from MPs to local councillors from across Britain are thought to have upped sticks and moved to London.

Thousands of top government officials from the regions are also reported to have moved to the capital.

... from areas which are either currently under the control of Nonettes or set to become so.

Certain areas of central London, such Westminster and Chelsea, are reported to be inundated with out-of-town councillors and government officials seeking accommodation. The government is thought to have made empty offices available to house the

With the number of Nonette Truth Trials increasing, many of the politicians and officials accused of anti-Nonette activities as well as corruption, are reported by Nonettes to have fled their homes. Nonettes also say that such was the speed of many of the officials departure that even the missing men's wives were unaware of their departure

Aldershot, they gave a lift to some Tom Jones ladies who were going to Pontypridd and they had told her that up in London it's packed with Welsh MPs and councillors. Good riddance to them that's what I say.

Anyway, the first valuations of the council property our Nonettes have taken over look like being more than enough to cover the missing money. Already there have been offers for many of the buildings, though none for the Welsh Assembly. There is talk of demolition, grassing it over.

With all the councils out of business and any money from London out of the question, we in the library had another worry, how we were going to get paid? Who was going to pay us? Well, in the end there was only one thing the library could do and that was to join the Nonettes as well.

We had to make concessions but everything has turned out for the best. One thing we had to give in on was the books themselves. In the past we always saw them as 'our books', we were their guardians and they only left the library under sufferance. But now, in exchange for funding, each Nonette member is the guardian of ten books. There was a rush in the beginning for the best books, but one thing which came out of the change is that the library has never had so many people browsing and borrowing.

What is more, with the guardians' names on the covers, there is no end of them keeping an eye on 'their books' making sure they do not go missing. Also, should any of those borrowed become overdue, we need to do no more than tell their guardians and they go round to bring them back for free. Another innovation proving popular is that for the price of just one nonette people can become guardians of the new books as well as being consulted on those we like to buy. It's so popular that there is a waiting list.

Now that nearly everyone in Wales is a Nonette and we are in charge of our own affairs, one of the things which has struck me most is the enthusiasm young people are showing towards the movement. Exposing council corruption and the pension scandal has had them praised the length and breadth of Wales, but their work on our newspapers has won them plaudits too. From reporting to production and distribution, there is barely a paper which does not depend on them. Some are staffed entirely by teenagers.

Where children do reign supreme is street cleaning. Cilgerren has never been so clean and tidy. Woe betide anyone dropping so much as a sweet wrapper. In an instant there will be a gang of children demanding it be picked up, and administering mandatory shaming into the bargain. Now that my two have places on the cleaning team it wasn't long before they had us grown-ups under their strict recycling regime as well.

And another thing, Anne, she's changed, well towards Danny anyway. In the past when he came on we had to tell her to be quiet, stop hissing at him. Now we don't have to. No sooner is there his "Brothers, sisters.." than she's all eyes for him, listening intently to all he says. Yesterday she even paid him a compliment, said his voice is better now that he has intonation.

Everyones' 'old' debts wiped out as

BIG BANKS COLLAPSE

£,$ worthless

By TERRY KIPPERT

A string of major banks closed their doors for the last time yesterday.

As soon as the US dollar was deemed worthless, other currencies soon followed suit including sterling.

Even those banks still technically in existence are expected to follow the majors today and declare themselves bankrupt.

While those people still holding current accounts in the old money in these banks will be losers, their numbers are dwarfed by those who will benefit from having their 'old money' debts, including mortgages and credit card completely wiped out.

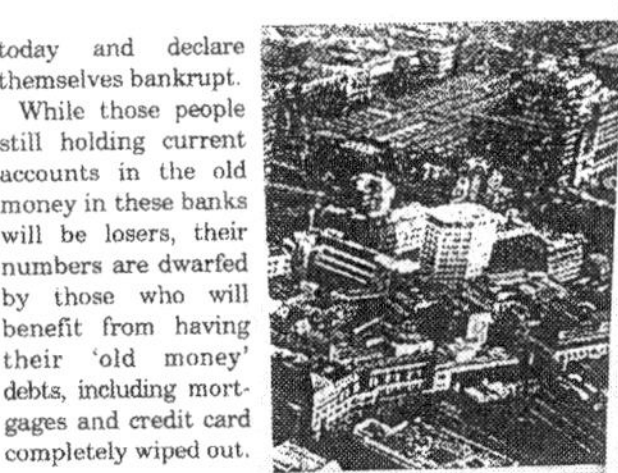

TANS LYNCH

Town Hall gutted in Nonette revenge a

By TIM JEFFRIES

SCORES OF B SPECIALS were lynched yesterday in a Nonette revenge attack for Wednesday's Kings Cross shooting.

Though most of the security police were rescued by other Nonettes, a number of them, including Specials' Commander Andrews, were found to be dead by the time they were cut down from the nearby trees.

Both the Camden Town Hall (Specials' strongpoint) and the St Pancreas Hotel on the opposite side of the Euston Road were attacked in the early morning by an estimated 2,000-strong Nonette force armed with firesticks.

The St Pancreas Hotel suffered only minor damage during the attack but Camden Town Hall was completely gutted.

For 20 minutes the B Specials, or 'Tans' as they are more commonly called, fired on the protestors in desperate attempts to defend themselves. However, they were unable to withstand the onslaught of firesticks fired against and then into the Town Hall's windows.

With the building soon ablaze, the Tans were forced to flee from the Town Hall or succumb to the flames.

As the Tans emerged from the rear of the blazing building many in the crowd laying in wait, attacked them with further volleys of firesticks, their tunics soon also catching fire.

Other protesters, already angered by the Tans firing on them, as well as for their earlier killing of Nonettes on Wednesday, dragged a number of the them to trees lining the Euston Road.

Among the victims were the head of Tans, Aubury Andrews and his assistant commander, James Smith, both former Customs officers from Dover.

Andrews and Smith along with other former Customs officers were dragged by the enraged protestors to nearby trees and lynched.

Stockmarkets' global collapse

Stocks, shares, bonds all worthless

By Oliver Stoneburger

LIKE A COLLAPSING HOUSE OF CARDS, THE WORLD'S stockmarkets, one after another, finally fell into inglorious oblivion. Although long seen by many as inevitable, th speed of the final collapse took most observers by surpris

In a single day trillions of dollars of paper wealth w rendered worthless as first Tokyo's Nikki Index fell its la 127 points to zero, then Shanghai and Hong Kong index

Nonettes ring the southeast

Checkpoint searches for fleeing fugitives stepped up

By **Madeline Polster** with the Nonettes

AS THE FIRST MAJOR Nonette Truth Trials take place in Preston and York, up to half a million government officials, politicians, security personnel are thought to have fled to the southeast of the country already.

Others have sought refuge in cities still under government control such as Manchester and Birmingham.

However, many thousands of officials are still at large in the regions under Nonette control, a spoke-

Road blocks have been set up on all roads leading out of these areas in a bid to catch those on the Nonettes wanted lists.

The checkpoints in place are another attempt to rescue any more Nonette internees being transported to the south.

Top of the Nonettes 'wanted list' are Auxiliaries and B Specials. Both, so Nonettes say, are directly responsible for many vicious attacks against the movement as well as the public in general. According to the Nonette spokesperson

Plutocrats plead poverty

Former billionaires forced to beg

William Houghton reports from Washington

MANY OF AMERICA'S once rich and powerful are nowadays to be seen on streets of Washington begging for their next meal and shelter for the night.

If they are lucky they may find a space in the makeshift tented camp which is springing up on the White House Lawn.

With their dollar fortunes now worthless and having fled their homes for the safety of Washington, these men have lost everything they once owned.

Without the wherewithal to afford food or to pay for accommodation, these once financiers, speculators, defense industry CEOs and others who backed the admin-

Red bracers hit paid dirt

Wall Street meets its Skid Ro

By Mathew Walberg

For the once mighty moguls at Merrells and Morgans their top-dog reign of capitalism is over. The cowboys at Salomons and Smith Barneys are past corporate America's last chance saloon and the Bear Stearns are all abaft. The buccaneers at Goldman are sacked and the remaining men at Leh lean.

Yes, for Wall Street's red braced finest the days of billion dollar deals and fort-

big dick dealers of yesterday are down and out and out of time.

Once these high paid hucksters strode Wall Street as the towering titans of stocks and bonds. Their every day was spent wheeler-dealer churning and skimming the savings of the many for the ever increasing enrichment of the plutocratic few.

But now f...

them, their uppence has well and truly come. They are all reduced to sticking "For Sale" signs on their autos just as their great-granddaddies did in the crash of '29.

The greenback goddess of avarice that these high priests of capitalism extolled inestors slavishly to worship, has now not only shown she's fe...

Even the Dow ... domain these amoral ... ragers once held in ... manipulated sway is ... more than a sagged, ... punched-drunk bag.

First it was the sma... listed corporations ... arting the DJ Industri... slipping the Street's ... but bigger ones and at ... ever faster rate ...

THRASHER STILL PINNIN HOPES ON US RESCUE

PM in negotiations with Presiden

By William Gybb Military Correspondent

WITH MOST EUROPEAN countries slipping out of control of their governments, the Ministry of Defence has given backing to a new cabinet plan for an immediate security alliance with the US.

The plan is for the use of the remaining American forces still stationed in the UK, to assist the police and other security services in maintaining law and order.

Presently it is thought that there are more than 10,000 US military personnel stationed in Britain. It

The steward blew his whistle and it was our turn to march forward out of Penton Street. I had never been on a demo before, protesting and that is not really my stamp, and I did feel awkward wearing a Nonette tunic. But the moment we turned into the Pentonville Road and I saw all of those other men marching down the hill towards King's Cross, that all went. There were thousands, thousands of them, and all in white. And there were the flags, hundreds, Nonette ones.

I strapped on the holster I had, unfurled our flag, stuck it in the holder and down we marched as well. No smiles, no chatting, just the sound of feet, flags. And if the others were like me, every man Jack of us was filled with cold hard anger. We were going to get those Black and Tan bastards once and for all. And all those others they fronted for as well. Make them pay for what they've done. Make them suffer.

As we marched there were also the thoughts. Sam Prior, what those Tans did to him. They had no call knocking him about like that. It was only when a woman up Canning Road, whose window overlooked the yard at the back of Highbury Vale police station, told us about seeing him and the others, did we know where the Tans had taken him.

Down we marched, flags flying. Then, as the Caledonian Road came in view, there were blasts of stewards' whistles coming up the hill and we all stood to. Before the whistles behind us faded there were sounds of more whistling coming up from the bottom of the hill but this time from the marchers themselves and their cheering. I soon saw why. A convoy of laden tank transporters and their crews passed out of the Caledonian and down the Gray's Inn Road. I had counted 20 of them when Pete Jones, to the side of me, said "We all know where those girls are going, down Whitehall."

Another blast of the stewards' whistles and it was left right, left right once more. No smiling or talking, I was still holding our flag and still thoughts about Sam Prior, of that night at Highbury Vale we got him and the others out. How, from first spotting them though that woman's window, it took two days before we could spring them. Two whole days, in which those Black and Tan bastards knocked the living daylights out of the poor sod.

Down we marched, still no smiles or talking, still thoughts of Sam, of working out how we were to free him, all the things we had to do, putting up with the no-hopers saying we hadn't a chance, with Beth Prior, the state she was in, crying and everything. It wasn't easy persuading Murat in the garage to use his heavy towing truck, nor finding enough others willing to go in with us, getting tooled up, fixing with neighbouring Nonettes to stage an Arsenal v Spurs fans-style fight on the Blackstock Road just down from the station so as to draw the police's and Tans' attention away, to the hour before getting the people in Canning Road to move their cars so Murat could get a clear run up the street for

Nonettes, WI move on Londo

Bristol now in Nonette hands

By Philipa Stewart
in the Midlands

WITH BRISTOL'S LAST remaining pockets of resistance surrendering to Nonette, WI forces, London and cities across the Midlands and South Coast form Malvern to Brighton have also fallen into Nonette hands and there are dangers of remaining ...

Adding to the g... ment's security woes ... fate of those force... loyal to them in other ... such as Manchester, ...

WASHINGTON SET TO FALL TO NONETTES

ANDREWS AIRBASE IN THE HANDS OF NOW

By Janet Rothberg
in New York

THE DISTRICT OF COLUMBIA was in a state of turmoil yesterday as news of Andrews airforce base falling into the hands of the National Organisation for Women (NOW).

With all other escape routes from the capital now closed to non-Nonettes, panic has broken out among those people on the movement's "Wanted List".

According to Nonettes there are thought to be upward of 40,000 such 'fugitives' in the Washington area.

President Warren, every Congressman and Senator are reported as being on the Wanted List.

With the White House lawn now a packed refugee camp of shacks and tents, there are new fears of outbreaks of disease, including dysentery.

There are also health fears due to the smoke from the many fires lit by the refugees in an attempt to keep warm as well as to cook by, Adding to their smoke-borne woes is the further smoke rising from the many fires started by officials desperately burning documents lest they fall into Nonette hands.

While all of the administration's shredders are also reported to be working overtime there are fears that the shredded paper could be recomposed as happened during the 1980 Tehran hostage crisis.

There is ... amounting ... refugees th... not been n... the Nonett...

Many of ... their futur... hands of th... prospects ... Trial' is a ... foreboding...

Althoug... attempts ... ton to n... Most hav... of NOW ... back befo...

The fa... has brou...

Uzbekistan offers asylu

...but at a price

By Devlan Randes

THE BELEAGURED MINisters including the prime minister were thrown an asylum lifeline yesterday by the president of Uzbekistan.

If the prime minister and the Cabinet take up ... offer of life in central Asia or not is, however, another matter for it comes with strings attached.

In a speech in the Uzbekistan capital of Tashkent, President for Life, Imomali Rahmonov, said that Uzbeki... citizenship is offered ... world leaders and busin... men.

All that is required ... them is that they con... to the state brand of Musl... ism and donate two ... grams of gold to Uz...

Secret Police HQ gutted by fire

Ferocious fireball arrow storm s...

By Kieron Blackwell
Security Editor

CAMELFORD HOUSE, the grim, fortress-like building by Vauxhall Bridge and the London headquarters of Britain's secret services, was left a smouldering ruin last night.

Although heavily defended, the spies' HQ was no match for the all out Nonette attack.

Responding to Nonette Congress's call for the apprehension of all members of the security services, more than 5,000 London Nonettes marched and then surrounded the secret police HQ.

Calls by the Nonettes for the spies' to surrender was met with a burst of automatic fire, believed to be from on the roof of Came... House. The Nonettes ... attacked the building..

Within minutes the ... emplacements were ... out by Nonette ar... shooting fireball ... arrows on to the build... roof. At the same ... volley after volley of fu... fireball tipped arrows ... fired at the windows. A... Nonette remarked: "It... like Agincourt".

With the building shea... in a wall of flame, the ... of the fireballs that ... stuck to windows ... shattered the glass.

As further fireball-ti... volleys penetrated the ... broken windows the ... building was soon ablaz...

As the agents fled ... the building the Non...

WI, Nonette advance o... London

M25 breached - Northolt in WI h...

By Philipa Stewart
in London

NONETTE AND WI forces now surround London. The government's outer defence perimeter has been breached at several points to the north-west of the capital.

The Northolt air force base was overrun by the WI within a matter of hours yesterday morning.

Fears for the base's 200 personnel grew when it became know they had been taken prisoner by the Welsh WI.

With much of Bri... under Nonette control, ... the government that is ... on the defensive. It is ... Nonettes who are de... mining events. It is t... strategy of progres... encirclement which has ... Thrasher government t... ped in London and ... creaseingly narrowing ... option of manouvre.

Not only is the Thras... administration becom... ever-more beleaguered ... also its support is fal... across those parts of Brit... which has still to c... under Nonette control.

Judi Jones reports from Fayetteville, North Carolina

Ride of the Valkyries

"I LIKE THE SMELL OF BENZAL in the morning," said Colonel Kilgore sniffing at the canister CS gas while at the same time taking a snort of *Wanton*. "It gets my mojo going the entire day through," she adds in her deep Texan drawl.

It is early morning, the sun is breaking over the tops of trees surrounding a clearing on the eastern slopes of the Blue Ridge Mountains. Colonel Kilgore, donning sunshades, Stetson and strapping more strips of *Wanton* to her tunic, strides across the clearing to a fleet of six Huey helicopter gunships. Each one is emblazoned with slogans: 'Base Buster, 'Game Hunter', 'Male Taker', another, intriguingly: 'Chopper Lips Cowl'.

All, however, have rows of little white matchstick men painted on their sides under yet another, bigger 'Valkyrie' logo. This also adorns the backs of the crew's white tunics and of the other Nonettes and NOW (the National Organization for Women) 'combatants' mustered with them.

With helicopter rotors starting to turn, Colonel Kilgore, who once served with the US 7th Air Cavalry, makes swooping moves with her hands to the pilots. They, all Air Cav veterans to a woman, nod heads in agreement. Today's target destination is Pine Air-force Base, to the west of Fort Bragg.

Above the noise of the 'copters Colonel Kilgore shouts: "Happy hunting guys!" and with everyone punching fists into the air in unison response, she steps up aboard her Huey. I clamber in after her.

As we climb above the trees and above the noise of the chopper, Billie Kilgore explains the mission: "Bragg is now cleared of 'game' (the word the women use for serving men). Remnants of Green Berets, Special Forces retreated to Pine. NOW Abrams [tanks] rampanted Bragg but [they are] unable to penetrate Pine's foam [water spray] shield. We're called in to staunch [it]."

Twenty minutes later, 30 miles to the east and having swept down the hillsides, barely above the treetops (to "minimize [radar] signature," says Billie), three of the Hueys, including ours skirt to the north of Pine Airforce base and the bigger, sprawling one of Fort Bragg. The other choppers veer to the south.

As we fly over roads leading to the base itself, Billie points to long lines of waiting *Rampant* firing tanks, personnel carriers, their white uniformed crews and the other NOW forces' alongside them.

"Most ex-military," says Billie and chuckling, adds, "If only the [US]AAF [had] known where combat training women would lead!"

During the flight Billie also tells how hers and other groups of Air Cav vets are called in by Nonette forces 'neutralizing' resisting bases across the US. She then adds: "And we all like men, strong, virile, young men. Plenty and often."

Once past Fort Bragg a stretch of water comes into view. "Spring Lake," points out Billie.

We turn southward and at the same time begin to climb higher above the lake. At 1,000 feet three specks, the other gunships, fly towards us. Rendezvous made, each group makes a V formation, ours in front of the other. With the sun now directly behind us, we head due west. And at full speed.

Pine Airforce base comes into view. There is a bustle of crew strapping-on fire extinguishers, stowing lengths of cheese wire, taking yet further sniffs at the *Wanton* strips on their arms.

All six Hueys go into a steep dive. At 400 feet our co-pilot slips a disk into a cassette player. Some of the crew don ear mufflers. Suddenly there is a near deafening sound of Wagner's 'Ride of the Valkyries'.

At 300 feet our Huey fires its missiles. They slam into buildings, men run out from them. The two other gunships veer to the left and right of us. They fire their missiles at water tenders on the base's perimeter.

At 200 feet the tell-tale brown plumes of *Rampant* from exploding missiles rises into the air. At a hundred our Hueys are circling looking to land. The other three swoop over past us.

We land. Shouts of: "Go, go, go..." Everyone leaps from the Huey. The music through the now open doors is deafening.

The second trio of gunships circle, then hover back and forth over buildings. They spray down yet more *Rampant* as if crop dusting.

The women from the first Hueys race to the nearby buildings. The air is thick with the cinnamon scent of *Rampant*. Men run out of its brown haze towards the women as if in "glad to see you" greeting. The women brush past them and into the buildings, their extinguishers and cheese wires at the ready.

The other three gunships land by the base's underground hangers. Their crews run towards the hanger air intakes then pump *Rampant* from their extinguishers into the vents.

More men emerge from the buildings and hangers while others run from the direction of the water tenders. Behind these is now a... army of white clad NOW wome... disembarking from tanks, personne... carriers, trucks. Yet more men from al... directions run towards the women.

As sheets of white 'surrender' clot... appear from more and mor... windows, the ground for hundreds o... yards in all directions is covered in ... writhing mass of men and wome... engaged in robust congress.

Groups of other men also sti... induced by *Rampant's* arousal effec... follow behind a lone women as if Pie... Piper's children and into the backs ... cavernous trucks whose doors a... then slammed shut behind them. ... these trucks are driven away ... Nonette 'Love Camps' others ta... their place.

Several hours later and with th... now thoroughly 'congressed' m... bodily lugged on to yet more truck... Pine Airforce base is, like Fort Brag... also completely cleared of 'game'.

maximum impact.

Just before our group got to King's Cross there came from those up ahead of us a low, gentle humming of "We, the people." Then we were joining in. Like waves it was. Hum the tune for few bars then stop, hear it carrying on behind us and as it rippled away another wave coming from the front. As we marched onto the Euston Road on it went again and again.

Though I joined in with them I still had thoughts of that night. Of Murat reversing his truck full tilt up Canning Road at those 12 foot high police gates, the almighty bang as he smacked into them, how they had still held, we thinking it wasn't going to work, Murat going right up on the pavement the other side and reversing into the gates again, this time straight on. Oh did they go then. Came right off their hinges they did.

On we marched past St Pancras, then the blackened remains of Camden Town Hall which the Tans had used as a vantage point for firing on protesters. As I looked up at the bits of rope still hanging from the trees outside of it, I had thoughts of what happened to those Tans at Highbury Vale.

We had rushed through the yard, into the station, Mike Williams, who had been in the army, leading, shouting "Go, go, go" as he had half the lads charge into the front of the station for the cell door keys and they all tooled-up with fireballs, wrenches, clubs. Then the fighting with the Tans, who hadn't been expected to be there, their shooting Mike's kid brother Adrian, Mike losing his rag and with his monkey wrench nigh on braining all those Tans single-handed including the three already on the floor ablaze with fireball. Then of the desk sergeant, the two police with him leading us down the cells, unlocking them, we seeing the state the prisoners were in, the sergeant pleading it was none of the police's doing, me and Pete Jones holding the others off from smacking them by saying they were worth more alive as hostages than dead, getting the prisoners out across the yard, Canning Road. Some including Sam and Adrian had to be carried, then passed through the houses, gardens to Wyatt Road and away.

On we marched, still the waves of everyone humming. Though as we passed Euston station those ahead of us began singing the actual words, not loud or anything, almost a murmur. Those with me also began singing "We, the people. United, no chains can bind us. No rulers divide or despots destroy," a pause, a long one, more humming, then, "We are the people. Tomorrow is ours." I didn't know any more so I la la-ed along instead except for the "We are the people" at the start of each verse.

But as I la la-ed I'd still thoughts of that night. In many ways, getting the prisoners out of the cells was the easy part, getting ourselves away was the harder one. Mike, being military minded had the foresight to have the lads pick up the Tans' guns. If he hadn't I hate to think what would have happened, or if we hadn't had the three police as hostages either.

At the time it was all "Go, go, go." It was only later did it have an effect on

Ministers' 'Arab' getawa bid foiled

Gold ingots seized at checkpoint

By Kevin Burton-Parker
Political Editor

GOVERNMENT MINISTERS dressed in Arab costumes were seized in west London last night.

Seven ministers, including Treasury under-secretary, Timothy Whyte, were stopped by Nonettes who had unexpectedly taken control of the west London suburb of Brentford.

According to the Nonettes the seven ministers were traveling in a minibus and were attempting to go to

All seven were said to be in possession of a number of gold bars as well as false passports and false beards.

When stopped at a road-block manned by local Nonettes, the ministers' ruse was soon uncovered when they were shown to be unable to speak any Arabic.

The head of Brentford Nonette said that travel documents found on the ministers indicated that they were intending to travel to Uzbekistan in

France falls to Nonettes

National Assembly surrenders as 'Armistice offer' rebuffe

HOWARD WILLIMS reports from BORDEAUX

FRANCE HAS CEASED TO EXIST AS A SOVEREIGN STATE, NONETTES HAVE TAKEN OVER

Following yesterday's surrender of the French Assembly and the total dénouement of senators by thousands of Association de Femes, power in France has now passed to the Nonettes.

After the National Assembly's retreat from Paris to Bordeaux, President Coubre and his government had hoped to establish a degree of 'co-habitation' with Nonette movement

assured an ever increasingly jittery Assembly and Senate that his negotiators were on the verge of agreeing with the Nonettes for a duel sovereignty of France.

The plan, as outlined by the President was for the Nonettes to have control of the north and west of the country and his government to continue in power over the rest of the country.

Langres and the Swiss border with the seat of government at Clermont Ferrand, 10 kilometres north of the earlier capital of Vichy.

However, Coubre had neglected to take account of the Association de Femes (AdeF). While his negotiators were meeting with Nonette representatives at Tours the AdeF struck.

Swiftly overcoming the security surrounding the government's provisional headquarters at Bordeaux's Hotel du Parc, the women of

of senators and hotel s with *Rampant*.

Within in minutes of AdeF's attack the en building and its surrounc gardens were a sea of wr ing copulating bodies.

Soon further waves of AdeF descended on the h and also sated themselve the hapless senators. senators now powerless resist the women who w now attacking them organised groups.

While the attack on Hotel du Park in progr Nonette representatives

Tans in fight for their lives

'Capture or eliminate' ca

By **Samuel Veron**
Security Correspondent

REMNENTS OF THE GOVernment's once all powerful security forces were fighting for their lives yesterday.

Having earlier retreated into the centre of London and other major cities, B Specials and Auxiliaries alike are now restricted to a few isolated pockets.

Because of these security forces' atrocities, Nonettes and the public at large are

the B Specials – former Inland Revenue and Custom & Excise inspectors – an Auxiliaries – known a 'Tans' – to surrender o face the consequences.

Ms Cameron said: " have this to say to thes men: "Give yourself u now as many thousands your fellows have done an we will guarantee you safety.

"Should you refuse th offer then we cannot he responsible for what mig happen to you." She add

More 'missing' found

Many Watch rounded up

By Harry Williams
in London

With most of Britain now under Nonette control increasing numbers of the missing internees are being released. According to the Nonettes' information centre in London, the number of its members still

concerned for the safety o those still missing. We ar still continuing wit utmost urgency to locat those still unaccounted fo We are still urging ever one to search for them."

The success in locati

Truth Court hands down confiscati

Anti-Nonettes could lose everything

By Brian Walters
in Chelmsford

A judgment given by a Truth Trial Court in Chelmsford yesterday will have sent shivers though many anti-Nonettes: they stand to lose all of their assets.

Five members of the

a string of assaults an other acts against Nonette internees in their car Although the five men wer not present at their trai the three judges ordere the immediate confiscatio of all their assets as well a their mandatory castration and 10 years hard labo

THEY'RE BACK!

SUSEM RETURN TO EARTH

By TIM JEFFRIES

THE ALIENS HAVE ARRIVED BACK ON Earth it was announced yesterday.

In a special telecast, Nonette announcer, Rainbow Louis, said the Susem return had come as much as a surprise to her as anyone.

Showing live footage of the Susem spacecraft descending to their original base on Earth, Rainbow said that the Aliens planned to stay on Earth for at least six months.

Rainbow did not give any reasons for the Susem return. However, she stressed that the Susem have told her that they will not be looking for any amorous encountera with any males

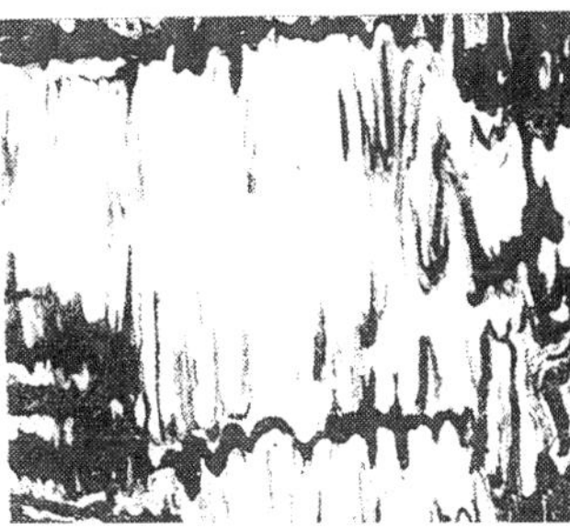

'Nowhere to run, no place to hide'

Nonettes give Thrasher surrender ultimatum

By Paula Rump
Nonette Correspondent

IN THEIR STRONGEST challenge yet, the Nonette Congress called on the government to surrender to them.

With the area of the government's writ shrinking by the day, there are thought to be more than 100,000 people in central London area, mainly in Whitehall and Westminster, who have sought refuge from the Nonettes.

In turn, the Nonettes are in no mood to compromise with the Thrasher government. Their spokesperson,

TUBE CHAOS LOOMS

Security 'impossible' says LT

Adding to the chaos of London's public transport mayhem, LT chiefs say that most of the Underground in the Westminster, Whitehall and Victoria are 'no-go' areas for ordinary tube users.

The cause, so LT says, is due to the over-rigourous ... checks being

affected stations by Security guards patrolling the area.

As a consequence, the District and Circle Lines services will stop at South Kensington in the west and Temple in the East. The Victoria Line will terminate at Oxford Circus and at Vauxhall. The Jubilee and ... will also be

me and the others. I still shudder to think what would have happened if those Tans had got us. They and police were blocking both ends of Canning Road, loud-hailing that they were armed, Mike shouting back that we had hostages, marching the sergeant and the other two out, showing them off, the lads letting off shots to keep the Tans at bay while us others got the sergeant strapped up on the front of Murat's cab, the two police tied on the back, we then climbing, clinging onto the truck, Murat roaring out of that yard, lights blazing, siren blaring, going like a bat out of hell down Canning Road, smashing through police cars, the lads firing left and right and I did see some Tans get hit, across Mountgrove, how that sergeant never got hurt is a miracle, up Wilberforce, straight through the one-way barriers, dumping the truck in the flats off Somerfield Road, us legging it back to the Greenwood as an alibi, taking the sergeant and the other two with us just in case of trouble, they in too much of a state to resist. Harry had them hid in his cellar for three days. In the end they saw sense and joined us Nonettes.

Still marching, holding our flag, still the quiet singing. But as we turned into Gower Street, another nigh identical column was marching down from Camden Town but they were going down the Tottenham Court Road. As we passed UCH we could see them through the street the side of the hospital. I could also hear that they were humming, singing the same as us. By the time we passed the university itself though, the singing on both streets became louder and louder, as if one was trying to outdo the other. Also, like myself, most of those with me only knew the first verse and "We the people" at the start of the other ones. As a result they were sung loudest.

Another thing about the singing getting louder, it got more body, feeling, as if the words came from inside, they were actually meant. Anyway the more I sung them the more I meant them. Before I knew it I was all wet in the eyes. But I wasn't the only one. Those Tans, those behind them who had lorded it over us, might have tried to crush us Nonettes but none of them was going to take away what was ours. We asked for nothing from them and we took nothing either. If we had broken the law it was only because they forced us to, and then only to defend ourselves against them and their bovver boys. The more I sang and thought about what they have done to us, those poor kids in Clissold Park, to Sam, at least he's safely away in Wales now, all the other diabolical things those Tans have done to thousands of us other Nonettes, the more worked up I got.

With Centre Point coming into view the singing became a roar. We were nearing our target, the MoD buildings round the back of it and the Tans holed up in them. Now it was pay-back time. All across the centre of London we had those Tans caught like rats in a trap. Along with the other flag carriers I lowered ours, removed it so there was just the sharpened steel pike-head. Those Tans were going to be begging for mercy by the time we finished with them. Not that they were ever going to be getting any.

HEATHROW CUT OF

Government's last escape route blocked

By Philipa Stewart
In Central London

THE EASTERN END OF the M4 motorway was firmly in Nonette WI hands yesterday.

Heathrow airport is now cut off from the rest of London.

With the Nonettes surprise breakthrough of the government's defences along the western M25 security forces retreated eastward to Hammersmith.

By the end of the day all of western London north of the Thames was outside of government control and under that of the Nonettes.

The loss to the government of this vital central London/Heathrow corridor, means that its last lifeline with the rest of world and escape route is now

While it is possible the government to ma tain a helicopter li between Westminster a Heathrow, it is doubtful there are pilots prepar to risk flying between t two.

With reports of WI tan moving into the area su rounding Heathrow, the is every chance that t airport itself could soon closed in

Susem to make World tour

Space ladies in meet the people visits

By Paula Kemp
Nonette Correspondent

THE SUSEM ARE TO make a world tour it was announced yesterday.

Rainbow Louis, in her daily telecast said that all the estimated 10,000 Susem will be taking part in the tour.

While details of the tour are yet to be announced, they will include several appearances across Europe including the Moselle river valley, the Mediterranean and possibly Scandinavia.

There will also be visits to both North and South America, across Asia and the Far East and Australia.

Ms Louis said that the it is their wish to meet as many people as possible.

As soon as details of the Susem plans are known, she added, ticket allocations will be given to first to children from as many Nonette groups as possible.

Ms Louis also said that the visits by the Susem

Husden Atrocity:

MASS MURDERE CAUGHT IN DAW

'All have pleaded guilty' say Nonettes

By William Howe in London

THE MEN WHO COMMITTED THE mass murders 62 Nonettes at Husden, Essex, have been caught.

Seventeen members of the Watch were rounded up in dawn raids across Essex and North London. All of the men are now

The killing of Nonettes is the worst atrocity committed against Nonettes although others yet to be unearthed have not been ruled out. According to the Nonette information centre there are still more than a 1,000 Nonettes still listed as 'missing'.

Politicians in last ditch stand to hold back WI, Nonettes

MPs, civil servants to man Westminster barricades

By Kevin Burton-Parker
Political Editor

MPS, TOP CIVIL servants and others sheltering in Whitehall and Westminster are to be pressed into aiding the security services defend the enclave against advance of the Nonettes and the WI.

This last ditch stand is being made while Chris Thrasher hammers out a settlement deal with the Nonette Congress.

The PM is thought to pinning his hopes that the newly installed barrier of high power pressured water hoses will hold back the Nonette forces massing around the central area. It is intended that their foamed water spray of Nonette *Rampant* attacks.

Shoring up Westminster's defences are a further 30,0000 Auxiliaries and B Specials, or 'Tans' as they are more commonly known.

Like the MPs, and civil servants they will fighting alongside, many of the Tans are also on the Nonettes' 'Wanted' list

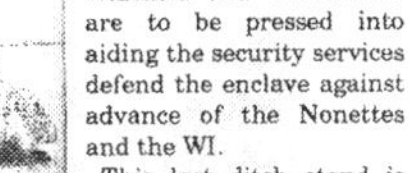

Big game makes way for MPs

Safari parks to house politicians and 'other miscreants'

By Kevin Burton-Parker
Political Editor

BRITAIN'S SAFARI PARKS are being cleared of their big game to make way for smaller one.

Lions, tigers and monkeys alike are vacating their 12-feet-high wire mesh enclosures to make way for an estimated 100,000 politicians, top civil servants and others who collaborated with the government against Nonettes. They will be held there until their trials

Regent's Park and othe zoos also are going to b used but will house th more senior members the Thrasher regime.

The Monkey House Regents Park is reporte to be set aside for th prime minister and h Cabinet.

All parks and zoos w be open to the public usual and under the sam conditions: Don't feed th animals or put hands in the cage.

HISOGYNISTS LISTS OPEN

Tax and VAT men are tops the for chop

By Marilyn Hodges
Entertainment Correspondent

Lists opened yesterday for British entries in the new Hisogynist TV spectaculars.

Announcing the lists SLI TV's Derek Igg said: "We have negotiated a good deal with Caught TV for the British quota to the new series. The British contribution will be for up to 500 evil bastards to participate in the Hisogynist routines."

Mr Igg said that those found guilty by the courts would be eligible to have their names put forward. He said: "Although there is likely to be some politicians on the list but according to our initial soundings it is mainly the Auxiliaries and B Specials who most people definitely want to see get the chop."

Mr Igg said that although SLI had been given outline of Hisogynists' new it from me they are set to be the cruelest and most bestial yet. And when I say cruel and bestial oh do I mean cruel and bestial."

Tans to be hel in the Tower

'It's for their own safety' - say Nonettes

By Philipa Stewart
Social Affairs Correspondent

THE TOWER OF LONDON is to receive its first prisoners since World War I. The Tower, along with other former high security prisons such as Dartmoor and Parkhurst, are set to house upwards of 30,000 men of the former Auxiliaries, B Specials and other security forces pending their trials for the crimes they have committed.

A Nonette spokesperson said: "At the moment we do not know precisely what crimes these men is running so high that f their own safety, it is be that they are held protective custody un their trials and sentencing.

There is widesprea public clamour, howeve for trials to take place as soon as possible. Th follows reports, yet to b confirmed, that th sentencing of the Specials - former Tax an Customs inspectors – wi be of the traditional Towe of London kind.

There has already, so i is also reported no end o volunteers to wield th axe. Other reports say tha both sides of Londo Bridge and other bridge across the Thames ar already being lined wit spikes in anticipation

PENSIONS SCANDEL

More Govt. property seiz

By Adam Holroyd
Nonette Affairs Editor

A STRING OF GOVERNment properties across Britain were taken over Nonette councils yesterday.

Like those properties seized during the past few days they will be sold off, actually amount to more than the amount stolen by the government.

Meanwhile the list of those one-time ministers and officials who were party to the pension funds

Guilty to be guaranteed a fair trial

Mass hearings could start as soon as next week

By Kieron Blackwell
Court Correspondent

ALL POLITICIANS, top civil servants and other miscreants already in Nonette hands could be tried as soon as next week.

Only the availability of shipping to take them to Angola and other places for mine clearing is holding up the final trial times.

Emma Watkins (13), one of the three judges appointed to preside over the London trials, said: "The trial date is provisionally set for next Thursday. Because those on trial number is like likely to be more than

100,000 the only available venue is Hyde Park.

"Nonetheless, because I and my fellow judges wish to see all of the accused get a fair hearing, if needs be, we are prepared to spend the entire day on sentencing them.

"Obviously we will all bend over backwards order to see that they get a fair trial," Watkins said, add "Which, by the way more than they gave fellow Nonettes."

One of Emma's fel judges, Alan Thomp (12), said than althoug

"We now return to Whitehall where a 10,000 strong security force defending members of the Thrasher government are battling with Nonette-backed women's groups in a desperate bid not to fall into their hands. A further 20,000 MPs, councillors, top civil servants, and other government supporters are also thought to have sought refuge inside various government buildings.

"We go first to our reporter John Howard in a helicopter above Whitehall. John, what is happening?"

"In the hour since the water screen surrounding Whitehall was broken and WI tanks in the Strand began firing their *Rampant* shells, Laurie, Nonette women have surged into Whitehall from all directions. As I speak, fighting, if it can be called that, is at its fiercest at the Trafalgar Square end of Whitehall itself and over at Horse Guards Parade.

"Another thing, Laurie. In the past hour convoys of huge trucks moving slowly along roads leading to both the Westminster and Lambeth bridges have appeared. Stretching bumper to bumper all the way to the Elephant, they are..."

"Thank you John, we now go over to Georgina Carter overlooking the front-line at Trafalgar Square. Georgina what is happening? What can you see?"

"From where I'm standing, Laurie, in front of the National Gallery, I can look straight down Whitehall and where an hour ago there was a wall of water from high pressure fire hoses, there is now a sea of white-clad Nonettes, mainly WI women, still surging into Whitehall. To the side of me I can see yet further contingents of women strapping on fire extinguishers charged with *Rampant* as well as *Wanton* strips on their forearms. Some are sniffing at CS gas canisters... ooh a blast of a whistle and they're off. Groups of a 100 and more are racing..."

"Georgina, what is that we can hear being called out?"

"Oh that. It's what the Susem shouted as they had all those men. To the women it's become their war cry."

"But what actually is it, Georgina?"

"Oh, the actual words, *(laughing)* "Come on girls, don't want to get an ugly one!"

"Thank you Georgina. We are getting reports of major events in St James's Park. We go over to Martin Willis. Martin, what are these developments?"

"Terrible scenes here, Laurie. From where I'm standing on the balcony of Carlton House Terrace, I can see more than 5,000 Tom & Jerry women who have marched down Lower Regent Street, now going into St James's Park.

"The Tom & Jerry, Laurie, are regarded as the real bruisers of the Nonette movement. The fates of security forces and MPs trapped in Whitehall, should the Tom & Jerry's get their hands on them, is too terrible to contemplate..."

"Going to have to stop you there Martin, we are getting reports of developments in Victoria. We'll go over to Jackie Woods outside St James's Park station. Jackie what's happening?"

"Laurie, the most fantastic sight. The station is supposed to be closed yet hundreds of Nonettes are marching out of the main exit. How they got here is a complete mystery...there are hundreds of them... they are still coming out of the station and all heading for Parliament Square... some are now slipping out of their white tunics...oh my!.."

"What Jackie, what?"

"They're all dressed in black rubberwear ...some are putting gas masks..."

"Sorry Jackie but we've breaking news from Trafalgar Square. Georgina."

"Yes Laurie, amazing scenes...listen to the cheers...a 1,000 strong force of North Yorks WI women has arrived down from the Charing Cross Road..."

"Yes, so?"

"It's what's on the back of their tunics, Laurie..."The Dominatrix"...oh and they are disrobing...wow! Nothing left to the imagination there!...I hope they won't feel the cold...they're picking up their whips, canes, clubs....strapping *Wanton* strips on their arms, sniffing CS...they're off to Whitehall...and here come the first men, they're being..."

"Sorry Georgina but we're received news Heathrow has surrendered to WI Nonettes without further resistance...what is more, detachments of the Welsh WI have already left the area and heading for London. John, do you see anything?"

"Yes, Laurie. I don't know if it is actually them but a column of what looks like scout cars, personnel carriers are moving along Knightsbridge...Hyde Park Corner...into Constitution Hill. It must be them!...the Welsh women have arrived Laurie...those poor security men, MPs...rugby scrums will be nothing.."

"Thank you John, over to Martin now actually in St James's Park. Martin can you see the Welsh WI yet?"

"Not a sign, Laurie. The park though is packed with groups of Nonette women subjecting men to forced sexual acts ...screams and cries as they've their..."

"Thank you Martin, now back to John Howard. Developments, John?"

"Amazing Laurie. security forces defending Parliament Square are being pushed back into the Houses of Parliament by hundreds of black-clad women ...others are retreating into Whitehall... the entire length of which is jam-packed, shoulder to shoulder, with guards...and those the other end of the street are reeling back in the face of yet more women in black, scantily clad ones...oh look, those in the middle are being forced into the arch under the Banqueting House and straight into Horse Guards Parade.. oh no!...Nonette women are.."

"Thanks John, now back to Martin."

"Terrible scenes here, Laurie. Welsh WI arrived...headed straight for Horse Guards Parade, joining Tom & Jerry women ...snatching men, carrying them off...the women, no sense of shame, pity...acres, acres of writhing near-naked men...terrified, helpless...cruelly hurtled from one sex drug-crazed coven after another... held down, beaten...forced to submit to frenzied non-stop fornicat.."

"Thanks Martin. Georgina what's..."

"Its the same here Laurie, except there's not the grass!... and it's going to be more than knees which are sore tomorrow morning!...the Square's packed tight with women and their males engaged in continuous group lovemaking...men are being dunked in the fountains, washed and scrubbed by the women for more lovemaking...oh, Dominatrix snatch squads are dragging back men who aren't guards ...they must be MPs...they are being lashed to Nelson's Column...oh look at the size of those whips...the force.."

"Thanks Georgina. John, can you confirm if Nonettes have breached the Houses of Parliament's security?"

"Yes, Laurie they appear to have done so...as I speak dozens of MPs, like rats jumping a sinking ship, are throwing themselves off of the balconies into the Thames in desperate bids to escape falling into Nonette hands...oh, several are being swept away by the current.."

"Martin! What on earth's the matt.."

"Help, Laurie, help!...Welsh women have spotted me...they're coming to get...help! ...oh no, oh no...oh please don't, I've a bad bac..."

169: "AAH!"

Talk about the cavalry arriving after the fighting is fought and won. Talk about having brusquely left us beleaguered in the lurch to stand David-like alone against the Goliaths and Philistines bent on our annihilation, and when we have finally won and licking wounds, they return as if nothing has happened. Talk about being oh-so-sure there wasn't a second to spare, they were late as it was and then, weeks later, just as perfunctorily deciding not only is there time after all but so much so that they are going on a six month world tour, venues and dates to be announced. The gall of it all.

And why have the Susem returned? Why have 10,000 plus superior beings from an advanced civilization, speeding away in a spaceship miles wide at next to the speed of light en route to Sirius and beyond, suddenly turned about and come back to this backward planet of ours? Why, so I've now gathered, were the advanced collective computing power of Terbal and the other Sinteens compiled to plot, re-calibrate their route, several light months shaved off here, a short cut between Sirius A and B there, so that Pa-tu's return to earth would mean they could still arrive in time for their conference Alpha Centauri way? Had they forgotten something, left a task undone perhaps? Oh no. Tearo is the reason why. She had been moping.

Word of the Susem arrival in Tabajara soon spread and a large crowd gathered in greeting. And when the reason for their return, the compassion towards Tearo known, and Colonel Tambassing sought, the crowd grew the more. By the time the Colonel arrived, he had been down in Tianguá arranging transport home for him and his men, those assembled around the old village side of the green were numbered in their thousands.

No sooner had he stepped through the parting hurrahing lines of assembled well-wishers with them promptly changing to deferential clapping, than Tearo, with all the bashfulness of a shy bride, appeared from down below. Both she and the Colonel first stood gazing at one another as if in disbelief, then each took a step closer, closer. Then, oblivious to all those present, and with arms outstretched, both broke into a headlong race to embrace. With Tearo's tearful cry, "My baby, oh my baby," she stooped a little and the Colonel in mid-step upward, passionately clasped their arms around one another. And with the Colonel's diminutive feet brushing Tearo's knees, everyone, inwardly, outwardly, all went "Aah!"

Smothering each other in a lather of kisses and still seemingly oblivious to all those present, Tearo, with the Colonel firmly in her arms, speedily stepped into the trees behind them. They were last seen headed towards the slopes of Monte Macambirá, doubtless to cross the threshold of some leafy glade in which to confirm their relationship.

There has not been sight or sign of them these two days past. There is talk of sending out search parties but no one really thinks it wise to intrude.

"While the trials in Hyde Park continue, the first contingents of those found guilty are now nearing Westminster Pier and the barges waiting to ferry them to Tilbury for transportation to the former Angola to carry out their sentences. We now go over to Jennie James in Victoria Street."

"Hello Laurie. As the column of the convicted trudge towards Parliament Square what a sorry sight they are. And in the first group, which has the former prime minister, Christopher Thrasher, still at its head and most of his one-time cabinet, I can see that several of them, apparently having collapsed, are being carried on the backs of the others."

"Well Jennie, I imagine it must have been a quite a trek for them all the way from their holding pens in Regent's Park. But from what we can hear, Jennie, it sounds as if the column is getting as noisy a reception as they received in Baker Street and Park Lane."

"That's right Laurie, from what I've also gathered, most of those lining Victoria Street think that the four year sentences of mine-clearing is too lenient. There is also widespread disbelief that none of those found guilty of the more serious crimes were not served with mandatory castration orders as well."

"I think, Jennie, the reason for this is that the judges thought this would take up too much time and lead to delays in the ships leaving Tilbury. I am also told the guilty would face such an order for any transgressions while in Angola."

"And another matter which has angered many of those here is that the guilty have been given leave to appeal against their sentences."

"But Jennie, they can only appeal from Angola and they could run the risk of having their sentences increased. Thank you, Jenny. We now go over to Adam Smith at Westminster Bridge."

"The first contingent has now arrived at the bridge, Laurie. Ex-regimental sergeant major Elaine Wright is calling out for them to halt...she's ordering the first hundred or so, including the former prime minister, to step forward and down onto Westminster Pier...she's now ordering others, junior ministers...MPs... in groups of 50 to march onto the bridge itself ...the prime minister's party is now stepping down into the hold of a waiting barge...those now on the bridge are being ordered to stand on meshed rope squares the width of the road itself.."

"What are these meshes for, Adam?"

"Not sure Laurie, but they must be connected with the mobile cranes stationed along the bridge and the line of barges moored below it...oh, I now see why...corners, sides of the first mesh are rising...forming into a net...oh it's being lifted into the air... swung over the bridge...lowered into one of the barges' holds...there goes another...oh, I gather from the cheering of the crowds lining both sides of the Thames, that this is meeting with their approval.."

"Have to stop you there Adam...news is coming in that missing reporter Martin Willis has been found ...Martin was among a contingent of guilty marched to Hyde Park from Whipsnade. Now back to you Adam... what is the cheering we hear for?"

"It's "Bon voyage" and "Good riddance" Laurie, and is coming from crowds both sides of the river as the prime minister's barge slips its moorings...makes its way downstream...more cheering as other barges join it...the crowds are now singing "You are sailing..."

171: THE ELVES

No sooner had the first well-wishers' letters arrived than Rainbow's "little elves," as she calls her gang of pre-teen toughies, were rifling through them for the money. And when I, and in no uncertain terms, told these young hoodlums that the letters were addressed to me and so they were mine, I received a chorus of "Rainbow says..."

However, remonstrating with Rainbow at their blatant intrusion into my privacy was met with her diffident "The gifts are more theirs, ours, than yours." Even when I pointed out to her that it was me, me alone who had stirred the uncommitted in their millions to join with Nonettes overthrowing the forces of oppression, she still refused to call off her elves. And when I told her it was my face viewers identified with and had had so many send so much, and thus their donations were mine by right to dispense, Rainbow brusquely rebuffed me with "That's all you were, a face."

Worse has followed. The only way I have been able to retrieve any crumbs from this manifest unfairness is agreeing to welcome the groups of Nonettes who arrive from all over to bestow their gratitude and awards for my sterling performances. After I have received their thanks, I have to say "Oh it was nothing...humbled yet proud to have done my duty...it was really a team effort on the part of so many."

When visitors ask, as they invariably do, "Can we meet the rest of the team?" out scamper the elves. They then gaze 'sweetly' (sickeningly so) up at the visitors and taking me by my hands, proceed to chorus "Uncle Danny has given all his money to us and Rainbow's good causes." The visitors then go "Aah!" and hand over even more.

It's the same with reporters who come to interview. Having first sung my praises they then unknowingly broadcast the charade of the elves. The resulting news reports have moved, and still are moving, yet more people to send letters of thanks accompanied with their donations, sackloads of them.

The 'thank you' letter every donor receives and is led to believe is hand-written by me is yet another facet of this fiction. I shudder to think what will happen when it gets out that it's the elves sitting at benches in their grotto who actually pen the replies. The rascals have my handwriting off to a tee. Neither does anyone know that should I make one wrong move, say one word out of place, the little hoodlums will turn on me and duff me up.

All Rainbow allows me is a meagre few per cent of what comes in. Just as tardy are the villagers. Though they're effusive with thanks for bringing them so many customers for their craftwork, Patches, and the Pousada is forever packed with diners, not a nonette have any of them proffered me.

Still, I've been able to put enough by to launch kinesis. All the same, Tabajara isn't the opportune place to do it. But now, with my popularity riding high as well as regaining freedom of movement, it's time to go home.

Last night we watched the most spectacular three hours of television I have ever seen. Making it all the more of a visual feast was the absence of sound let alone commentary. Aileen was most moved by it all, poor girl, she wept through half a box of tissues before the evening was all over!

It wasn't just the evening either but the build-up during the days prior to the event which also had people glued to their television screens. These were filled with pictures of the millions of young people from across the length and breadth of Europe, all clad in their white tunics and all converging on the river Mosel. I was further most impressed with how well the travel and accommodation arrangements worked out. While the Rhineland Nonettes organise d their end with the Teutonic efficiency to be expected of them, our side acquitted themselves with no less aplomb. From start to finish everybody pitched in and the concerns voiced for the younger children's wellbeing have proved to be quite unfounded.

The evening itself was nothing short of a tour de force of production and direction. Though with the Susem behind it, it could not have been anything less than total perfection! There were cameras sited everywhere, and it was doubtless the Susem who arranged for the street lighting for miles around be switched off. I would not put it past them either to have controlled the weather. The evening, like the day, was warm and cloudless.

Throughout the afternoon our television was filled with pictures of children, exuberant with anticipation and headed to their allocated positions upon the 200 metre high steep hillsides either side of the Mosel. The evening, however, began with images of the sunset. This went on for several minutes. Then the cameras suddenly swung to the east.

Stretching to the horizon was a line of approaching Susem spaceships, sunlight glistening off of them. From the camera angles below the top of the river's hillsides, it seemed as if they had suddenly appeared from nowhere. Cameras then zoomed in on the ships and from the graininess of the picture it was evident they were many thousands of feet above.

No sooner were they hovering directly over the curves and bends of Mosel than what at first appeared to be confetti began spiralling down from them. However, it soon became clear they were the smaller Susem spacecraft. As these flew ever lower and now luminously glowing against the darkening sky, their numerous spirals flowed into one another. Soon these craft were zooming back and forth between the river's hillsides, our screens filled with rising and falling speeding streaks of white light.

These craft then began showering clouds of golden flakes which sparkled in the darkness. In no time our screen was filled with a swirling, shimmering blizzard of them. It was through this haze of gold that the white-clad forms of the Susem now appeared.

173: AILEEN

The Susem are like us except that they're beautiful, so beautiful. As the first ones stepped through the gold, brushing flakes of it from their tunics and their hair, they'd a slow stride of a stroll. Ooh and their hair was gorgeous dark, long. But the gold wasn't gold, it was little bee, butterfly things which flew off, then danced, fluttered about the Susem. And the children as the Susem came towards them were all jigging up and down, their eyes near popping out their heads they were that excited. Then the Susem had their arms held out and the children were running to them. As they bent down, lifted up, clasped the children giving them all a hug and a hold, they'd such lovely smiles. And the children, their faces, their eyes, some were crying with happiness. As the Susem lifted up the boys and girls, with others holding round their legs, bees and butterflies were flitting about them, flying in little halos around the children's heads. Other bees skip-marched single file up children's arms, over their heads, down the other arm and hopped across to the next one's. And as they did they'd the children laughing, giggling like anything. There was a butterfly all by itself in the palm of a little girl's hand, her eyes wide with delight at it fluttering its wings as if a ballerina dancing. And when it closed its wings as if taking a bow, the smile on the little girl's face was lovely as she watched it fly away upwards. The picture, following the butterfly, was soon filled with hundreds and hundreds of spacecraft hovering up the hill like upside down staircases, all glowing in the dark and dozens and dozens of Susem stepping from them. These Susem were soon going from one terrace up to another. The way they moved was so graceful, as though floating though the air. As soon as they'd glided to each group of children there was a mad rush for their hugs and holds. Other children though were clambering aboard the spacecraft which, when full, promptly whizzed off with them. Then pictures from inside the craft, of the children, noses pressed to windows viewing the stars, the Moselle winding silver in the dark below, oh and of other spacecraft cruising by, the children all waving to one another. Back to the Susem, more children clamouring round them for a hug and hold. Bees and butterflies were everywhere, flying in amazing formations, running up and down the children. Everyone filled with smiles, laughter. But as one group of children ran to the Susem there was a little girl left behind in the rush. As she sat there all alone I then saw she was like me, she wasn't able to walk. The way her little face looked up to the picture, her eyes wide filled with almost crying had me feeling for her. But in an instant a Susem was by the little girl, taking her in her arms, rocking, hugging her. As she stroked the little girl's hair, kissed away tears, coaxed a smile to her little face, ooh I was wanting her Nonette to be as ours, studying to send her to where Danny is, so she can walk again as well.

174: KEN

The look on that little girl's face had the entire pub in tears. Even Harry was dabbing his eyes. The thing was though it didn't stop with the little girl, the crying that is. Because there wasn't commentary or music there was nothing to drown out people sobbing, and so made it come over all the louder. This started others off.

I can quite understand why so many people became emotional. The entire three hours was that moving it was hard not to keep watching. By the end, and because it aroused so many people's inner passions towards their partners, some of whom had been complete strangers to one another before they came in the Greenwood, Harry had to tell more than a few to go home and do it there.

Another thing about this Susem programme is the repeats. It's been on all the channels and every night since. Or if it's not that, it's interviews with kids who were actually there. And if they aren't interviewing or showing the repeat, there are experts blabbering on about it. But whatever, one thing it has done is to knock the football right on the head, especially in the Greenwood. As Harry says, either he keeps showing the repeats or he has a half empty pub. Of course every time it is on there's all the sobbing and luvvy duvvy.

Speaking of football though, I had a bit of a surprise the other day. There was a knock on the door first thing, and there, bold as brass, was Danny. Taken right back I was seeing him, but he hadn't been in the house five minutes before he was saying now that there wasn't anybody looking for him, he was moving back. I soon put him right about that.

He might well have gone up in the world, I told him, but round here, especially with Arsenal fans, his name is mud. I don't think he realised just how much people hold him personally responsible for what those Susem women did to the team, nor for all the money lost betting on a win. I told him the best thing he could do was to shoot off before anyone saw him.

He was a bit down about this but brightened up when he told me of this new house he was buying down in Wales near where his old place was in Cilgerren. Naturally I told him about Sam Prior, how our Nonette arranged with the one down there for him to convalesce, and to look him up, pass on our regards. Danny did start to go on about what happened to him in Brazil but I told him to save the details for when I came down for a visit. I did ask him though why he had left, what he had come back for, but when he started telling me something about a new type of energy, I soon saw he was up to another of his "take a little from a lot" schemes.

Anyway, with the next Susem show on Table Mountain due the weekend, they are already showing kids travelling down there, it means, what with the repeats, there will be no football all next week either.

175: SIÂN

When Gwyneth said that her friend Judith Rees, who works at Evens & Evens, told her that Danny had bought Neuadd Trefawr, she could have knocked me down with a feather. What is more, Judith told her, not only has Danny also bought the 92 acres offered with it, but he paid cash.

Even before I could say "I thought he was still in Brazil, what does he want a great big place like that for, what is he doing over here, he must be loaded, did you see that he gave away all the money people sent him to those children?" Gwyneth said Judith had also told her that Danny is onto something really big. And this, she added, is why he is here and not there.

When I asked her what it was though, she said she didn't really know but Judith had told her it's to do with energy. Danny, she'd said, has all the know-how on the type the Susem use, the same as powers our soufins. Gwyneth also said Judith had told her that the surveyor, when he returned the keys, told her that Danny had told him that he is going to cut out big business and offer all Nonette groups the chance to take part in the development of this new energy and so share in the profits. Gwyneth said that Danny had also told the surveyor that because demand will be massive, investment will be limited to a mere twenty nonettes per Nonette.

Gwyneth, however, then said that she had been told everything she told me in strictest confidence by Judith and I had to promise not to tell a soul. If it got out, Gwyneth said, she would get it in the neck from Judith and so would she from Mr Evans for breach of trust. Well, this put me in a terrible dilemma. How could I not tell my own sister that Danny is living just five miles away? If I didn't, and Anne found out I knew about Danny and hadn't told her, it would be me who got it in the neck from her.

When I arrived home Anne was still out shopping with Beth in Cardigan. Although telling Daffyd doesn't count, asking him what to do was no help either. With Sam and Beth staying here, he said, as well as Anne, the house was crowded enough, but with mum and dad also about to stay while waiting to move into their new house, one less would be more than welcome.

I nearly hit him at this, but when he said that ever since Anne had watched those children with the Susem she'd become broody, I did clump him. Though I have to say Anne has become very quiet since then. All the same, the moment she came home and I'd given her and Beth a cup of tea, I told her, but only after she had also promised not to tell anyone else.

Well, before I knew it she had her hat and coat back on and was out of the door. Later, when I looked, I noticed she had also taken Glynn's motorbike. Thing was though, I still got in the neck, from Gwyneth.

Anne, so Gwyneth said, stopped off at the Pendre and bought some of those Patch things. Well, she soon put two and two together. Daffyd had to buy her Bicardi Breezers all evening before she was placated.

"Oh, hello Anne. What a surprise! Didn't ever expect see you. How did you know I was here?"

"I'm staying with Siân and Daffyd. Heard you were back in the area. I was passing, thought I'd say hello. Well go on then, invite me in."

"...Once this would have been such a beautiful garden...but now so overgrown...this terrace really catches the afternoon sun but look, see the balustrades are falling away...this wall also needs repairing, there's..."

"I like you hair. You look so much better with it short. Pity you wouldn't ever let me cut it like that. What made you see sense and change?"

"When I began the television thing, I had to have it cut or Rainbow..."

"They are really lovely windows. What are they like from the inside?"

"...Welcome to Neuadd Trefawr! Or, in English, the 'Big House' This would have been the dining room...the previous owner used..."

"Welcome home my hero! Let me give you a great big hug and a...You really are very courageous you know, those television broadcasts gave so many people the resolve to resist, fight. I am so proud of you."

"Oh it wasn't such as a big deal as it looked. The truth is, Rainbow..."

"You are so right, it is a big house and such lovely windows. Which way to the kitchen? Along here? Come on, make me some tea."

"Sorry about the mug. I've not had chance to..."

"Oh don't mind that. Any Earl Grey? Oh never mind that either! Tell me, as you're so famous why ever did you leave Taba or whatever it's called?"

"Tabajara. I left to launch kinesis. I didn't ever want to be famous or anything, it's just that I didn't have any choice. Of course with Rainbow..."

"Oh for goodness sake! Will you stop mentioning that woman's name."

"Oh you're not still going on about all that are you? If it upsets you I'm sorry, but the world has moved on, we're no longer together, remember? Remember as well it was you who ended it. And what is more, it's all a long time ago."

"You did sleep with her, didn't you? Didn't you? Go on, admit it."

"I told you I did'n...huh. Oh alright, I did."

"Bastard, bastard, you bastard. I knew all along you did. Why did you lie? You humiliated me. You, you..."

"Oh! Ouh! That hurt. Ouh! There's no need to...Ooh now, sorry, I..."

"You hurt me, hurt me. Oh, ooh, now look what you've..."

"Oh don't cry Anne. Don't cry. Come here...there, there..."

"Hold me closer. Closer...kiss me again. Oh Danny I've missed you, missed you so much. Remember how you used to call me "Grace"? Said it's what my name means. Ooh, kiss me again...again...and again."

"There, that's my girl. Want to see the rest of the house?"

"Oh, yes please mister!"

"...This is the main staircase...on this landing there's six bedrooms...this front one I'm using just now as..."

"You've not made your bed."

"Well, I wasn't expecting anyone, and anyway I've only just..."

"At least the sheets are clean I suppose. Well come on then, take hold of your side...there, that's better...go on, puff the pillows up."

"What are you doing?"

"You can see perfectly well what I'm doing."

"Ooh, you have lost weight."

"It's all the anxiety and worry you've put me through. Now get this on.."

"Oh...ooh!"

"..and get 'em off!"

THE END

All views, opinions, observations and comments of this book are welcomed. Please send them to:

Mammas Press
41 Brownswood Road
LONDON
N4 2HP

Or:

www.mammaspress.com

All responses will be gratefully received, acknowledged and if relevant, replied to.

Further copies of "**Brothers, sisters..** are also available from Mammas Press at the address above.

Mammas Press seeks distributors and co-publishers of all of our publications.